Argot and Slang

Argot and Slang

By
A. Barrére

Ross & Perry Inc.
Washington, D.C.

© Ross & Perry, Inc. 2001 All rights reserved.

Protected under the Berne Convention. Published 2001

Printed in The United States of America
Ross & Perry, Inc. Publishers
717 Second St., N.E., Suite 200
Washington, D.C. 20002
Telephone (202) 675-8300
Facsimile (202) 675-8400
info@RossPerry.com

SAN 253-8555

Library of Congress Control Number: 2001092411

ISBN 1-931641-21-8

♾ The paper used in this publication meets the requirements for permanence established by
the American National Standard for Information Sciences "Permanence of Paper for Printed
Library Materials" (ANSI Z39.48-1984).

PREFACE.

HE publication of a dictionary of French
cant and slang demands some explanation
from the author. During a long course of
philological studies, extending over many
years, I have been in the habit of putting
on record, for my own edification, a large
number of those cant and slang terms and quaint expressions of
which the English and French tongues furnish an abundant harvest. Whatever of this nature I heard from the lips of persons
to whom they are familiar, or gleaned from the perusal of
modern works and newspapers, I carefully noted down, until my
note-book had assumed such dimensions that the idea of completing a collection already considerable was suggested. It
was pointed out to me, as an inducement to venture on so
arduous an undertaking, that it must prove, from its very nature,
not only an object of curiosity and interest to the lover of
philological studies and the public at large, but also one of
utility to the English reader of modern French works of fiction.
The fact is not to be ignored that the chief works of the so-
called Naturalistic School do certainly find their way to this
country, where they command a large number of readers.

These productions of modern French fiction dwell with complaisance on the vices of society, dissect them patiently, often
with power and talent, and too often exaggerate them. It is not
within my province to pass a judgment upon their analytical
study of all that is gross in human nature.   But, from a
philological point of view, the men and women whom they
place as actors on the stage of their human comedy are
interesting, whatever they may be in other respects. Some of
them belong to the very dregs of society, possessing a language
of their own, forcible, picturesque, and graphic. This language
sometimes embodies in a single word a whole train of philosophical ideas, and is dashed with a grim humour, with a species
of wit which not often misses the mark. Moreover, these
labourers, roughs, street arabs, thieves, and worse than thieves
—these Coupeaus, Bec-Salés, Mes-Bottes, Lantiers—are not the
sole possessors of a vernacular which, to a certain extent, is the
exponent of their idiosyncrasies. Slang has invaded all classes
of society, and is often used for want of terms sufficiently strong
or pointed to convey the speaker's real feelings. It seems to
be resorted to in order to make up for the shortcomings of
a well-balanced and polished tongue, which will not lend itself
to exaggeration and violence of utterance.   Journalists, artists,
politicians, men of fashion, soldiers, even women talk *argot*,
sometimes unawares, and these as well as the lower classes are
depicted in the Naturalistic novel. Now, although the study of
French is daily acquiring more and more importance in England, the professors of that language do not as a rule initiate
their pupils—and very naturally so—into the mysteries of the
vernacular of the highest and lowest strata of society, into the
cynical but pithy and humorous jargon of the *voyou* from the
heights of Montmartre or Ménilmontant, nor even into the lisp-

ing twaddle of the languid *gommeux* who lolls on the Boulevard des Italiens. Hence English readers of *L'Assommoir* and other similar works find themselves puzzled at every line, and turn in vain for assistance to their dictionaries. The present volume aims at filling the vacant space on the shelves of all who read for something besides the passing of an idle hour. An *English slang equivalent* of the *English rendering* has been inserted whenever that was possible, and because the meaning of a term is better conveyed by examples, as many quotations as the limits of the *Dictionary* would admit have been reproduced from different authors.

A few words on the manner in which the work has been compiled are due to the reader. In order to complete my own private information, specially with reference to old cant, I have drawn as freely as seemed to me legitimate on works of a similar character—Michel's, Delvau's, Rigaud's, Lorédan Larchey's excellent *Dictionnaire Historique d'Argot*, Vilatte's *Parisismen*, a very complete work on French *argot* rendered into German. But by far the most important portion of my collection has been gathered from Vidocq's productions, Balzac's works, *The Memoirs of Monsieur Claude*, formerly superintendent of the detective department in Paris, and from other works to be mentioned hereafter. To an inspector of the detective force in Paris, Monsieur Lagaillarde, I am indebted for many of the terms of the phraseology used by the worthies with whom his functions have brought him in contact.

Again, newspapers of both countries have also brought in their contingent, but the most interesting sources of information, as being the most original, have been workpeople, soldiers, pickpockets, and other malefactors having done their " time," or likely to be " wanted " at a short notice. The members of the light-fingered gentry were not easily to be got at, as their natural suspicions precluded their realizing at once my object, and it required some diplomacy and pains to succeed in enlisting their services. In one particular instance I was deprived of my informants in a rather summary manner. Two brothers, members of a family which strongly reminded one of E. Sue's Martials, inasmuch as the father had mounted the scaffold, the mother was in prison, and other members had met with similar accidents, had volunteered to become my collaborators, and were willing to furnish information the more valuable, it seemed to me, as coming from such distinguished individuals. Unfortunately for the *Dictionary* the brothers were apprehended when coming to my rendez-vous, and are now, I believe, far on their way to the penal settlement of New Caledonia.

I have to thank numerous correspondents, French and English officers, journalists, and artists, for coming to my assistance and furnishing me with valuable information. My best thanks are due also to M. Godefroy Durand for his admirable etching.

As regards the English part, I am considerably indebted to the *Slang Dictionary* published by Messrs. Chatto and Windus, to the *History and Curious Adventures of Bampfylde-Moore Carew, King of the Mendicants,* as well as to the various journals of the day, and to verbal inquiries among all classes of people.

I have not attempted, except in a few cases, to trace the origin of words, as an etymological history of cant would be the work of a lifetime.

It is somewhat difficult to know exactly where to draw the line, and to decide whether a word belongs to slang or should be rejected. I have been guided on this point by Littré, and any terms mentioned by him as having passed into the language

I have discarded. I have introduced a small number of what might be termed eccentricities of language, which, though not strictly slang, deserve recording on account of their quaintness. To the English reader I need not, I trust, apologize for not having recoiled, in my desire for completeness, before certain unsavoury terms, and for having thus acted upon Victor Hugo's recommendation, " Quand la chose est, dites le mot."

AUTHORITIES
CONSULTED AND QUOTED.

About (Edmond). Trente et Quarante. Paris.

Almanach Chantant, 1869.

Amusemens à la Grecque ou les Soirées de la Halle par un ami de feu Vadé. Paris, 1764.

Amusemens rapsodi-poétiques. 1773.

Apothicaire (*l'*) *empoisonné*, dans les Maistres d'Hostel aux Halles. 1671.

Audebrand (Philibert). Petits Mémoires d'une Stalle d'Orchestre. Paris, 1885.

Balzac (Honoré de). La Cousine Bette.—La dernière Incarnation de Vautrin.—La Physiologie du Mariage. — Les Chouans. — Le Père Goriot. Paris, 1884.

Banville (Théodore de). La Cuisinière poétique.

Bonnetain (Paul). L'Opium. Paris, 1886.—Au Tonkin. Paris, 1885.

Boutmy (Eugène). Dictionnaire de l'Argot des Typographes. Paris, 1883.

Brantome (Pierre de). Vie des Dames galantes. Paris, 1822.

Canler. Mémoires. Paris.

Caylus (Comte de). Les Ecosseuses ou les Œufs de Pâques. 1739.

Champfleury. La Mascarade de la Vie parisienne.

Chatillon (Auguste de). Poésies. Paris, 1866.

Cim (Albert). Institution de Demoiselles. Paris, 1887.

Citrons (les) de Javotte. Histoire de Carnaval. Amsterdam, 1756.

Claude. Mémoires. Paris.

Courteline (Georges). Les Gaîtés de l'Escadron. Paris, N. D.

Daudet (Alphonse). Les Rois en Exil. Paris, 1886.

Debans (Camille). Histoire de tous les Diables. Paris, 1882.

Delcourt (Pierre). Paris Voleur. Paris, 1887.

Delvau. La Langue Verte. Paris.

Drapeau (*le*) *de la mère Duchesne* contre les fâcheux et les intrigants. Paris, 1792.

Dubut de Laforest. Le Gaga. Paris, 1886.

France (Hector). Le Roman du Curé. Bruxelles, 1877.—L'Homme qui tue. Bruxelles, 1878.—*Préface* de Par devant Notaire. Bruxelles, 1880.—L'Amour au Pays Bleu. Londres, 1885.—Le

Péché de Sœur Cunégonde. Paris, N. D. — Marie - Queue - de - Vache. Paris, N. D. — Les Va-nu-pieds de Londres. Paris, 1885.—La Pudique Albion. Paris, 1885.— Les Nuits de Londres. Paris, 1885. —Sous le Burnous. Paris, 1886. —*Préface* du Pays des Brouillards. Paris, 1886.—Londres illustré. Paris, 1886. — La Pucelle de Tebessa. Paris, 1887.—L'Armée de John Bull. Paris, 1887.—A Travers l'Espagne. Paris, 1887.

Frébault (Elie). La Vie de Paris : guide pittoresque et pratique du visiteur. Paris, 1878.

Frison (Gustave). Aventures du Colonel Ronchonot. Paris, 1886.

Gaboriau (Emile). Monsieur Lecoq. Paris, 1885.

Gautier (Théophile). Les Jeune-France. Paris, 1885.

Gavarni. Les Gens de Paris. Paris.

Génin (F.). Récréations philologiques. Paris, 1858.

Gennes (Charles Dubois de). Le Troupier tel qu'il est à cheval. Paris, 1862.

Gill (André). La Muse à Bibi. Paris, N. D.

Goncourt (E. de). La Fille Elisa. Paris.

Grandval. Le Vice puni ou Cartouche.

Gyp. Le plus heureux de tous. Paris, 1886.

Hugo (Victor). Le dernier Jour d'un Condamné.—Les Misérables. —Claude Gueux.

Humbert (A.). Mon Bagne.

Huysmans. Les Sœurs Vatard. Marthe. Paris.

Kapp (E.). La Joie des Pauvres. Paris, 1887.

Larchey (Lorédan). Dictionnaire Historique d'Argot. Paris, 1881.

Laurin (A.). Le Million de l'Ouvrière. Paris, 1887.

Le Jargon ou Langage de l'Argot réformé. Epinal, N. D.

Le Roux (Philibert Joseph). Dictionnaire comique, satyrique, critique, burlesque et proverbial. Lyon, 1735.

Leroy (Charles). Guibollard et Ramollot. Paris, N. D.

Les Premières Œuvres Poétiques du Capitaine Lasphrise. 1599.

Macé (G.). Mon premier Crime. Paris, 1886.

Mahalin (Paul). Mesdames de Cœur-Volant. Paris, 1886.

Malot (Hector). Baccara. Paris, 1886.

Merlin (Léon). La Langue Verte du Troupier. Paris, 1886.

Michel (Francisque). Dict. d'Argot ou Etudes de Philologie comparée sur l'Argot. Paris, 1856.

Michel (Louise). Les Microbes humains. Paris, 1886.

Molière (Jean Baptiste Poquelin). Œuvres. Paris.

Monnier (Henri). L'Exécution.

Montaigne (Michel de). Œuvres. 1825.

Monteil (Edgar). Cornebois. Paris, 1884.

Montluc (Adrien de). La Comédie des proverbes. 1633.

Mouillon (F.). Déclaration d'amour d'un imprimeur typographe à une jeune brocheuse. Paris, 1886.

Nadaud (Gustave). Chansons populaires. Paris, 1876.

Nisard (Charles). De quelques
Parisianismes populaires et autres
Locutions. Paris, 1876.—Curio-
sités de l'Etymologie française.
Paris, 1863.

Nodier (Charles). Œuvres.

Poissardiana (*le*). 1756.

Poulot (Denis). Le Sublime.

Quellien (N.). L'argot des Nomades
de la Basse - Bretagne. Paris,
1886.

Rabelais (François). Œuvres. Paris.

Raccoleurs (*les*). Paris, 1756.

Riche-en-gueule ou le nouveau Vadé.
Paris, 1821.

Richepin (Jean). La Chanson des
Gueux. Paris, N. D.—Le Pavé.
Paris, 1886.—La Glu. Paris, N.D.
—La Mer. Paris, 1886.—Les
Morts bizarres. Paris, N. D.—
Braves Gens. Paris.

Rigaud (Lucien). Dictionnaire
d'Argot moderne. Paris, 1881.

Rigolboche. Mémoires.

Scarron (Paul). Gigantomachie.
Paris, 1737.

Scholl (Aurélien). L'Esprit du
Boulevard. Paris, 1887.

Sermet (Julien). Une Cabotine.
Paris, 1886.

Sirven (Alfred). Au Pays des
Roublards. Paris, 1886.

Sue (Eugène). Les Mystères de
Paris. Paris, N. D.

Tallemant des Réaux. Historiettes.
Paris, 1835.

Tardieu. Etude médico-légale sur
les attentats aux mœurs.

Taxil (Léo). Histoire de la Prostitution. Paris, N. D.

Theo-Critt. Nos Farces à Saumur.
Paris, 1884.

Vidocq. Mémoires. Paris, 1829.—
Les Voleurs.—Les vrais Mystères
de Paris.

Villon (François). Œuvres com-
plètes. Paris, N. D.

Zola (Emile). Nana.—L'Assommoir.
—Au Bonheur des Dames. Paris,
1885.—La Terre. Paris, 1887.

Addison. The Spectator.

Ainsworth (W. Harrison). Rookwood.

Bampfylde-Moore Carew (The History and Curious Adventures of).
London, N. D.

Brome (Richard). Joviall Crew; or,
The Merry Beggars. 1652.

Chatto and Windus. The Slang
Dictionary. London, 1885.

Davies (T. Lewis O.). A Supple-

mentary English Glossary. London, 1881.

Dickens (Charles). Works.

Fielding (Henry). Amelia.—The
History of the Life of the late Mr.
Jonathan Wild the Great. 1886.

Greenwood (James). The Seven
Curses of London. N. D.

Harman (Thomas). Caveat or
Warening for Common Cursetors.
London, 1568.

Horsley (Rev. J. W.). Autobiography of a Thief, *Macmillan's Magazine*, 1879.—Prison Notes. 1887.

Kingsley. Westward Ho. Ravenshoe. Two Years Ago.

Lytton (Henry Bulwer). Paul Clifford.

Pascoe (C. E.). Every-day Life in our Public Schools. London, N. D.

Shakespeare (William). Works.

La Marotte.
La Nation.
La Vie Parisienne.
La Vie Populaire.
Le Clairon.
Le Cri du Peuple.
L'Echo de Paris.
L'Evénement.
Le Figaro.
Le Gaulois.
Le Gil Blas.

L'Intermédiaire des Chercheurs et Curieux.
Le Journal Amusant.
Le Père Duchêne. 1793.
Le Petit Journal.
Le Petit Journal pour rire.
Le Radical.
Le Tam-Tam.
Le Voltaire.
Paris.
Paris Journal.

Punch.
The Globe.

The Graphic.
The Pink 'Un.

POPULAR SONGS AND PIECES OF POETRY.

Barrère (Pierre). Le Bœuf rouge et le Bœuf blanc.

Baumaine et Blondelet. Les Locutions vicieuses.

Ben et d'Herville. Ou's qu'est ma Pip'lette.

Bois (E. du). C'est Pitanchard. —De la Bastille à Montparnasse.

Burani et Buquet. La Chanson du Gavroche.

Carré. J'ai mon Coup d'feu.

Clément. Chanson.

Dans la chambre de nos abbés.

Denneville. Une Tournée de Lurons.

Garnier (L.). Y a plus moyen d'rigoler.

Jouy (Jules). Le Pochard et les Saints.—La Neige.

La Chanson du Bataillon d'Afrique.

Lamentations du portier d'en face.

Le Mirliton.

Maginn (Dr.). The Death of Socrates. Vidocq's Song.

Ouvrard. J'suis Fantassin.

Queyriaux. Va donc, eh, Fourneau !

The Leary Man.

The Sandman's Wedding.

INTRODUCTION.

RGOT pervades the whole of French society. It may be heard everywhere, and it is now difficult to peruse a newspaper or open a new novel without meeting with a sprinkling of some of the jargon dialects of the day. These take their rise in the slums, on the boulevards, in workshops, barracks, and studios, and even in the lobbies of the Houses of Legislature. From the beggar to the diplomatist, every class possesses its own vernacular, borrowed more or less from its special avocations. The language of the dangerous classes, which so often savours of evil or bloody deeds, of human suffering, and also of the anguish and fears of the ever-tracked and ever-watchful criminal, though often disguised under a would-be humorous garb, cannot but be interesting to the philosopher. "Everybody," says Charles Nodier, "must feel that there is more ingenuity in argot than in algebra itself, and that this quality is due to the power it possesses of making language figurative and graphic. With algebra, only calculations can be achieved ; with argot, however ignoble and impure its source, a nation and society might be renovated. . . . Argot is generally formed with ability because it is the outcome of the urgent necessities of a class of men not lacking in brains. . . . The jargon of the lower classes, which is due to the inventive genius of thieves, is redundant with sparkling wit, and gives evidence of wonderfully imaginative powers."

If criminals are odious, they are not always vulgar, and a study of their mode of expression possesses certain features of interest. The ordinary slang of the higher strata of French society, as compared with that of the lower classes, being based often on mere distortion of words or misappropriation of meaning, is in many cases vulgar and silly; it casts a stain over a language which has already suffered so much at the hands of the lesser stars of the Naturalistic School. A coarse sentiment, a craving for more violent sensations, will find expression in the jargon of the day. People are no longer content with being astonished, they must be crushed or flattened (épatés), or knocked over (renversés), and so forth; and the silly "on dirait du veau," repeated *ad nauseam*, seldom fails to raise a laugh. Our English neighbours do not seem to be better off. "So universal," says a writer in *Household Words*, September 24, 1853, "has the use of slang terms become, that in all societies they are substituted for, and have almost usurped the place of wit. An audience will sit in a theatre and listen to a string of brilliant witticisms with perfect immobility, but let some fellow rush forward and roar out 'It's all serene,' or 'catch 'em alive, oh!' (this last is sure to take), pit, boxes, and gallery roar with laughter." It must be said, however, on the other hand, that the slang term is often much more expressive than its corresponding synonym in the ordinary language. Moreover, it is often witty, and capable of suggesting a humorous idea with singular felicity.

Argot is but a bastard tongue grafted on the mother stem, and though it is no easy matter to coin a word that shall remain and take rank among those of any language, yet the field of argot, already so extensive, is ever pushing back its boundaries, the additions surging in together with new ideas, novel fashions, but especially through the necessities of that class of people whose primary interest it is to make themselves unintelligible to their victims, the public, and their enemies, the police. "Argot," again quoting Nodier's words, "is an artificial, unsettled tongue, without a syntax properly so called, of which the only object is to disguise under conventional metaphors ideas which are intended to be conveyed to adepts. Consequently its vocabulary must needs change whenever it has become familiar to outsiders, and we find in *Le Jargon de l'Argot Réformé* curious traces of a like revolution. In every country the men who speak a cant language belong to the lowest, most contemptible stratum of society, but its study, if looked upon as an outcome of the intellect, presents important features, and synoptic tables of its synonyms might prove interesting to the linguist."

The use of argot in works of any literary pretensions is of modern introduction. However, Villon, the famous poet of the fifteenth century, a *vaurien* whose misdeeds had wellnigh brought him to the gallows, as he informs us :—

> Je suis François, dont ce me poise,
> Né de Paris emprès Ponthoise,
> Or, d'une corde d'une toise,
> Saura mon col que mon cul poise—

Villon himself has given, under the title of *Jargon ou Jobelin de Maistre François Villon*, a series of short poems worded in the jargon of the vagabonds and thieves his boon companions, now almost unintelligible.

In our days Eugène Sue, Balzac, and Victor Hugo have introduced argot in some of their works, taking, no doubt, Vidocq as an authority on the subject ; while more recently M. Jean Richepin, in his *Chanson des Gueux*, rhymes in the lingo of roughs, bullies, vagabonds, and thieves ; and many others have followed suit. Balzac thus expresses his admiration for argot : " People will perhaps be astonished if we venture to assert that no tongue is more energetic, more picturesque than the tongue of that subterranean world which since the birth of capitals grovels in cellars, in sinks of vice, in the lowest stage floors of societies. For is not the world a theatre ? The lowest stage floor is the ground basement under the stage of the opera house where the machinery, the phantoms, the devils, when not in use, are stowed away. Each word of the language recalls a brutal image, either ingenious or terrible. In the jargon one does not sleep, ' on pionce.' Notice with what energy that word expresses the uneasy slumbers of the tracked, tired, suspicious animal called thief, which, as soon as it is in safety, sinks down and rolls into the abysses of deep and necessary sleep, with the powerful wings of suspicion constantly spread over it— an awful repose, comparable to that of the wild beast, which sleeps and snores, but whose ears nevertheless remain ever watchful.

b

Everything is fierce in this idiom. The initial or final syllables of words, the words themselves, are harsh and astounding. A woman is a *largue.* And what poetry! Straw is ' *la plume de Beauce.*' The word midnight is rendered by *douze plombes crossent.* Does not that make one shudder?"

Victor Hugo, after Balzac, has devoted a whole chapter to argot in his *Misérables,* and both these great authors have left little to be said on the subject. Victor Hugo, dealing with its Protean character, writes : "Argot being the idiom of corruption, is quickly corrupted. Besides, as it always seeks secrecy, so soon as it feels itself understood it transforms itself. . . . For this reason argot is subject to perpetual transformation—a secret and rapid work which ever goes on. It makes more progress in ten years than the regular language in ten centuries."

In spite of the successive revolutions referred to, a number of old cant words are still used in their original form. Some have been, besides, more or less distorted by different processes, the results of these alterations being subjected in their turn to fresh disguises. As for slang proper, it is mostly metaphoric.

A large proportion of the vocabulary of argot is to be traced to the early Romance idiom, or to some of our country patois, the offsprings of the ancient Langue d'oc and Langue d'oil. Some of the terms draw their origin from the Italian language and jargon, and were imported by Italian quacks and sharpers. Such are lime (*shirt*), fourline (*thief*), macaronner (*to inform against*), rabouin (*devil*), rif (*fire*), escarpe (*thief, murderer*), respectively from lima, forlano, macaronare, rabuino, ruffo, scarpa, some of which belong to the Romany, as lima. The German schlafen has given schloffer, and the Latin fur has provided us with the verb affurer. Several are of Greek parentage : arton (*bread*), from the accusative αρτον ; ornie (*fowl*), from ορνις ; pier (*to drink*), piolle (*tavern*), pion (*drunk*), from πιεῖν.

The word argot itself, formerly a cant word, but which has now gained admittance into the *Dictionnaire de l'Académie,* is but the corruption of jargon, called by the Italians "lingua gerga," abbreviated into "gergo," from which the French word sprang,—gergo itself being derived, according to Salvini, from the Greek ιερός (*sacred*). Hence lingua gerga, *sacred language,* only known to the initiated.   M. Génin thus traces the origin of argot : lingua hiera, then lingua gerga, il gergo ; hence jergon or jargon, finally argot.

Grandval makes Cartouche, the famous cutpurse and highway-man, and one of his comrades show much erudition in their remarks on the origin of the word :—

> Mais à propos d'argot, dit alors Limosin,
> Ne m'apprendrez-vous pas, vous qui parlez latin,
> D'où cette belle langue a pris son origine ?
> — De la ville d'Argos, et je l'ai lu dans Pline,
> Répondit Balagny. Le grand Agamemnon
> Fit fleurir dans Argos cet éloquent jargon.
> Comme sa cour alors étoit des plus brillantes,
> Les dames de son tems s'y rendirent savantes :
> Electre le parloit, dit-on, divinement ;
> Iphigénie aussi l'*entravoit gourdement.*
> Jusqu'aux champs phrygiens les Grecs le transportèrent :
> Tous les chefs en argot leurs soldats haranguèrent,
> Connoissant quelle étoit sa force et sa vertu
> A pouvoir relever un courage abattu.
> J'ai vu, s'il m'en souvient, dans Ovide ou Virgile,
> Que lorsqu'on disputa pour les armes d'Achille,
> L'éloquent roi d'Ithaque en eût été le sot
> S'il n'eût pas su charmer ses juges en argot.
> — Tu dis vrai, Balagny, reprit alors Cartouche ;
> Mais cette langue sort d'une plus vieille souche,
> Et j'ai lu quelque part, dans un certain bouquin
> D'argot traduit en grec, de grec mis en latin,
> Et depuis en françois, que Jason et Thésée,
> Hercule, Philoctète, Admète, Hylas, Lyncée,
> Castor, Pollux, Orphée et tant d'autres héros
> Qui *trimèrent* pincer la toison à Colchos,
> Dans le navire *Argo*, pendant leur long voyage,
> Inventèrent entre eux ce sublime langage
> Afin de mieux tromper le roi Colchidien
> Et que de leur projet il ne soupçonnât rien.
> Après que la toison fut par eux embandée,
> Jason, à son retour, l'apprit à sa Médée,
> Qui depuis s'en servit dans ses enchantements,
> Hercule en ses travaux l'employa fort longtems ;
> Thésée en ses exploits, Orphée en sa musique
> Avec utilité le mirent en pratique.
> Enfin tous les doubleurs de la riche toison,
> De leur navire Argo lui donnèrent le nom.
> Amis, voici quelle est son étymologie.

A certain number of slang terms proceed from uniform and systematic alterations in the body of the French word, but these methods do not seem to have produced many expressions holding a permanent place in the dialect. Such is the " langage en lem," much used by butchers some forty years ago, but now only known to a few. But a very small number of words thus coined have passed into the main body of the lingo, as being too lengthy, and because argot has a general tendency to brevity.

The more usual suffixes used are mar, anche, inche, in, ingue, o, orgue, aille, ière, muche, mon, mont, oque, ègue, igue, which give such terms as—

épicemar	for épicier,
boutanche	— boutique,
aminceminche	— ami,
burlin } burlingue }	— bureau,
camaro	— camarade,
bonorgue	— bon,
vouzaille	— vous,
mézière	— me,
petmuche	— pet,
cabermon	— cabaret,
gilmont	— gilet,
loufoque	— fou,
chamègue	— chameau,
mézigue	— me.

The army has furnished a large contingent to slang, and has provided us with such words as colon (*colonel*) ; petit colon (*lieutenant-colonel*) ; la femme du régiment (*big drum*) ; la malle (*prison*) ; un bleu (*recruit*) ; poulet d'Inde (*steed*), and the humorous expression, sortir sur les jambes d'un autre (*to be confined to barracks, or to the guard-room*).

Much-maligned animals have been put into requisition, the fish tribe serving to denominate the Paris bully, that plague of certain quarters.

With the parts of the body might be formed a complete orchestra. Thus "guitare" stands for the head; "flûtes" for legs; "grosse caisse" for the body; "trompette" does duty for the face, "mirliton" for the nose, and "sifflet" for the throat.

The study of the slang jargon of a nation—a language which is not the expression of conventional ideas, but the unvarnished and rude expression of life in its true aspects—may give us an insight into the foibles and predominant vices of those who use it.

Now though the French as a nation are not hard drinkers, yet we must come to the conclusion—in the face of the many synonyms of the single word drunk, whilst there is not one for the word sober—that Parisian workmen have either a lively imagination, or that they would scarcely prove eligible for recruits in the Blue Ribbon Army. Intoxication—from a state of gentle inebriation, when one is "allumé," or "elevated," to the helpless state when the "poivrot," or "lushington," is "asphyxié," or "regularly scammered," when he can't "see a hole in a ladder," or when he "laps the gutter"—has no less than eighty synonyms.

The French possess comparatively few terms for the word money ; but, in spite of the well-worn saying, "l'or est une chimère," or the insincere exclamation, "l'or, ce vil métal !" the argot vocabulary shows as many as fifty-four synonyms for the " needful." The English are still richer, for Her Majesty's coin is known by more than one hundred and thirty slang words, from the humble " brown " (halfpenny) to the " long-tailed one " (bank-note).

Though there is no evidence that the social evil has a greater hold on Paris than on London or Berlin, yet the Parisians have no less than one hundred and fifty distinct slang synonyms to indicate the different varieties of " unfortunates," many being borrowed from the names of animals, such as " vache," " chameau," " biche," &c. Some of the other terms are highly suggestive and appropriate. So we have " omnibus," " fleur de macadam," " demoiselle du bitume," " autel de besoin," the dismal " pompe funèbre," the ignoble " paillasse de corps de garde," and the " grenier à coups de sabre," which reflects on the brutality of soldiers towards the fallen ones.

For the *head* the French jargon can boast of about fifty representative slang terms, some of which have been borrowed from the vegetable kingdom. Homage is rendered to its superior or governing powers by such epithets as " boussole " and " Sorbonne," and a compliment is paid to its inventive genius by the term, " la boîte à surprises," which is, however, degraded into " la tronche " when it has rolled into the executioner's basket. But it is treated with still more irreverence when deprived of its natural ornament,—so that a man with a bald pate is described as having no more " pail-lasson à la porte," or " mouron sur la cage." He is also said some-times to sport a " tête de veau."

Grim humour is displayed in the long list of metaphors to describe death, the promoters of the slang expressions having borrowed from the technical vocabulary of their craft. Thus soldiers describe it as " défiler la parade," for which English military men have the equivalent, " to lose the number of one's mess ; " " passer l'arme à gauche;" " descendre la garde," after which the soldier will never be called again on sentry duty ; "recevoir son décompte," or deferred pay. People who are habitual sufferers from toothache have no doubt contributed the expression, " n'avoir plus mal aux dents;" sailors, " casser son câble " and " déralinguer;" coachmen, " casser son fouet ; " drummers, " avaler ses baguettes," their sticks being henceforth useless to them ; billiard-players are responsible for " dévisser son billard ; " servants for " déchirer son tablier." Then what horrible philosophy in the expression, " mettre la table pour les asticots ! "

A person of sound mind finds no place in the argot vocabulary ; but madness, from the mild state which scarcely goes beyond eccentricity to the confirmed lunatic, has found many definitions, the single expression " to be cracked" being represented by a number of comical synonyms, many of them referring to the presence of some troublesome animal in the brain, such as " un moustique dans la boîte au sel " or " un hanneton dans le plafond."

Courage has but one or two equivalents, but the act of the coward who vanishes, or the thief who seeks to escape the clutches of the police, has received due attention from the promoters of argot. Thus we have the highly picturesque expressions, " faire patatrot," which gives an impression of the patter of the runaway's feet ; " se faire une paire de mains courantes," literally to make for oneself a pair of running hands ; " se déguiser en cerf," to imitate that swift animal the deer ; " fusiller le plancher," which reminds one of the quick rat-tat of feet on the boards.

To show kindness to one, as far as I have been able to notice, is not represented, but the act of doing bodily injury, or fighting, has furnished the slang vocabulary with a rich contingent, the least forcible of which is certainly not the amiable invitation expressed

in the words of the Paris rough, "viens que j'te mange le nez !" or
"numérote tes abattis que j'te démolisse !"

What ingenuity and precision of simile some of these vagaries of
language offer ! The man who is annoyed, badgered, is compared
to an elephant with a small tormentor in a part of his body by which
he can be effectually driven to despair, whilst deprived of all means
of retaliation—he is then said to have "un rat dans la trompe !"
He who gets drunk carves out for himself a wooden face, and "se
sculpter une gueule de bois" certainly evokes the sight of the stolid,
stupid features of the "lushington," with half-open mouth and lack-
lustre eyes.

The career of an unlucky criminal may thus be described in his
own picturesque but awful language. The "pègre" (*thief*), or "escarpe" (*murderer*), who has been imprudent enough to allow himself to be "paumé marron" (*caught in the act*) whilst busy effecting
a "choppin" (*theft*), or committing the more serious offence of
"faire un gas à la dure" (*to rob with violence*), using the knife
when "lavant son linge dans la saignante" (*murdering*), or yet the
summary process of breaking into a house and killing all the inmates, "faire une maison entière," will probably be taken by "la
rousse" (*police*), first of all before the "quart d'œil" (*police magistrate*), from whose office he will be conveyed to the dépôt in the
"panier à salade" (*prison van*), having perhaps in the meanwhile
spent a night in the "violon" (*cells at the police station*). In due
time he will be brought into the presence of a very inquisitive person,
the "curieux," who will do his utmost to pump him, "entraver dans
ses flanches," or make him reveal his accomplices, "manger le
morceau," or, again, to say all he knows about the affair, "débiner le
truc." From two to six months after this preliminary examination,
he will be brought into the awful presence of the "léon" (*president
of assize court*), at the "carré des gerbes," where he sits in his red
robes, administering justice. Now, suffering from a violent attack
of "fièvre" (*charge*), the prisoner puts all his hopes in his "parrains d'altèque" (*witnesses for the defence*), and in his "médecin"
(*counsel*), who will try whether a "purgation" (*speech for the defence*)
will not cure him of his ailment, especially should he have an attack
of "redoublement de fièvre" (*new charge*). Should the medicine
be ineffectual, and the "hésiteurs opinants" (*jurymen*) have pro-

nounced against him, he leaves the " planche au pain " (*bar*) to return whence he came, to the " hôpital " (*prison*), which he will only
leave when " guéri " (*free*).   But should he be " un cheval de retour " (*old offender*), he will probably be given a free passage to go
" se laver les pieds dans le grand pré " (*be transported*) to " La
Nouvelle " (*New Caledonia*), or " Cayenne les Eaux ; " or, worse
still, he may be left for some time in the " boîte au sel " (*condemned
cell*) at La Roquette, attired in a " ligotante de rifle " (*strait waistcoat*), attended by a " mouton " (*spy*), who tries to get at his secrets,
and now and then receiving the exhortations of the " ratichon "
(*priest*).   At an early hour one morning he is apprised by the
" maugrée " (*director*) that he is to suffer the penalty of the law.
After " la toilette " by " Charlot " (*cutting off the hair by the executioner*), he is assisted to the " Abbaye de Monte-à-regret " (*guillotine*),
where, after the " sanglier " (*priest*) has given him a final embrace,
the " soubrettes de Charlot " (*executioner's assistants*) seize him, and
make him play " à la main chaude " (*hot cockles*).   Charlot pulls
a string, when the criminal is turned into " un bœuf " (*is executed*)
by being made to " éternuer dans le son " (*guillotined*).   His
" machabée " (*remains*) is then taken to the " champ de navets "
(*cemetery*).

For the following I am indebted to the courtesy of the Rev. J. W.
Horsley, Chaplain to H. M. Prison, Clerkenwell, who, in his highly
interesting *Prison Notes* makes the following remarks on thieves'
slang : " It has its antiquity, as well as its vitality and power of
growth and development by constant accretion ; in it are preserved
many words interesting to the student of language, and from it have
passed not a few words into the ordinary stock of the Queen's
English.   Of multifold origin, it is yet mainly derived from Romany
or gipsy talk, and thereby contains a large Eastern element, in which
old Sanscrit roots may readily be traced.   Many of these words
would be unintelligible to ordinary folk, but some have passed into
common speech.   For instance, the words bamboozle, daddy, pal
(companion or friend), mull (to make a mull or mess of a thing),
bosh (from the Persian), are pure gipsy words, but have found some
lodging, if not a home, in our vernacular.   Then there are survivals
(not always of the fittest) from the tongue of our Teutonic ancestors,
so that Dr. Latham, the philologist, says : ' The thieves of London '

(and he might still more have said the professional tramps) 'are the conservators of Anglo-Saxonisms.' Next, there are the cosmopolitan absorptions from many a tongue. From the French *bouilli* we probably get the prison slang term 'bull' for a ration of meat. Chat, thieves' slang for house, is obviously *château*. Steel, the familiar name for Coldbath Fields Prison, is an appropriation and abbreviation of Bastille ; and he who 'does a tray' (serves three months' imprisonment) therein, borrows his word from our Gallican neighbours. So from the Italian we get *casa* for house, filly (*figlia*) for daughter, donny (*donna*) for woman, and omee (*uomo*) for man. The Spanish gives us *don*, which the Universities have not despised as a useful term. From the German we get durrynacker, for a female hawker, from *dorf*, 'a village,' and *nachgehen*, 'to run after.' From Scotland we borrow *duds*, for clothes, and from the Hebrew *shoful*, for base coin.

" Purely of native manufacture, however, and entirely artificial, are the two classes of rhyming and back-slang which mingle with cant to make a whole. By the former any word that rhymes with the one you mean to use is put in its place, and gradually becomes accepted. This has the merit of unintelligibility when it is desired not to let chance passers-by know of what we are speaking, which naturally occurs not seldom in the days of detectives and plain-clothes constables. Suppose I have 'touched' (*i.e.*, been successful in some robbery), and feel inclined for some relaxation in company with my sweetheart (or one of them), I might address her thus : ' Come, cows and kisses, put the battle of the Nile on your Barnet Fair, and a rogue and villain in your sky-rocket ; call a flounder and dab with a tidy Charing Cross, and we'll go for a Bushey Park along the frog and toad into the live eels.' This would apparently be but a pendant to the celebrated bit of nonsense extemporized by Foote, but, as a matter of fact, to a master or mistress of rhyming slang it would at once be understood as : ' Come, missus, put a tile (hat) on your hair, and a shilling in your pocket ; call a cab with a tidy horse, and we'll go for a lark along the road into the fields.'

"And the second class of manufactured slang is that largely patronized by costermongers. It is called back-slang, and simply consists of spelling (more or less accurately) words backwards.

Thus, ' Hi, yob ! kool that enif elrig with the nael ekom.   Sap her
a top o' reeb and a tib of occabot,' is only, ' Hi, boy ! look at that
fine girl with the lean moke (donkey).   Pass her a pot of beer and
a bit of tobacco.'   The art or merit of this form of slang consists in
the rapidity, often most remarkable, with which such words can be
reversed.   Thus a gentleman, wishing to test the skill of a professor
of the art with a word not in common use in the market, asked his
coster friend what was the back-slang for hippopotamus.   At
once he answered, ' Sumatopoppy,' the *y* being euphoniously put
for *ih*.

  " Considering that in the manufacture of the domestic and social
slang of nicknames or pet names not a little humour or wit is com-
monly found, it might be imagined that thieves' slang would be
a great treasure-house of humorous expression.   That this is not
the case arises from the fact that there is very little glitter even in
what they take for gold, and that their life is mainly one of
miserable anxiety, suspicion, and fear ; forced and gin-inspired is
their merriment, and dismal, for the most part, are their faces when
not assuming an air of bravado, which deceives not even their companions.   Some traces of humour are to be found in certain euphe-
misms, such as the delicate expression ' fingersmith ' as descriptive
of a trade which a blunt world might call that of a pickpocket.   Or,
again, to get three months' hard labour is more pleasantly described
as getting thirteen clean shirts, one being served out in prison each
week.   The tread-wheel, again, is more politely called the everlasting staircase, or the wheel of life, or the vertical case-grinder.
Penal servitude is dignified with the appellation of serving Her
Majesty for nothing ; and even an attempt is made to lighten the
horror of the climax of a criminal career by speaking of dying in a
horse's nightcap, *i.e.*, a halter."

  The English public schools, but especially the military establishments, seem to be not unimportant manufacturing centres for slang.
Only a small proportion, however, of the expressions coined there
appear to have been adopted by the general slang-talking public, as
most are local terms, and can only be used at their own birthplace.
The same expressions in some cases have a totally different signification according to the places where they are in vogue.   Thus
gentlemen cadets at the " Shop," *i.e.*, the Royal Military Academy,

will talk of the doctor as being the " skipper " or " boss," whereas elsewhere " boss " refers to one who excels in any game or work, and is synonymous of " swagger man." The expression " tosh," meaning bath, seems to have been imported by students from Eton, Harrow, and Charterhouse, to the " Shop," where " to tosh " means to bathe, to wash, but also to toss an obnoxious individual into a cold bath, advantage being taken of his being in full uniform. Another expression connected with the forced application of cold water at the above establishment is termed " chamber singing " at Eton, a penalty enforced on the new boys of singing a song in public, with the alternative (according to the *Everyday Life in our Public Schools* of C. E. Pascoe) of drinking a nauseous mixture of salt and beer ; the corresponding penalty on the occasion of the arrival of unfortunate " snookers " at the R. M. Academy used to consist some few years ago of splashing them with cold water and throwing wet sponges at their heads, when they could not or would not contribute some ditty or other to the musical entertainment.

" Extra " at Harrow is a punishment which consists of writing out grammar for two and a half hours under the supervision of a master. The word extra at the " Shop " already mentioned is corrupted into " hoxter." The hoxter consists in the painful ordeal of being compelled to turn out of bed at an early hour, and march up and down with full equipment under the watchful eye of a corporal. Again, we have here the suggestive terms : " greasers," for fried potatoes ; " squish," for marmalade ; " whales," for sardines ; " vaseline," for honey ; " grass," for vegetables ; and to be " roosted " is to be placed under arrest ; whilst " to q." means to qualify at the term examination. Here a man who is vexed or angry " loses his shirt " or his " hair ; " at Shrewsbury he is " in a swot ; " and at Winchester " front." At the latter school a clique or party they term a " pitch up ; " the word " Johnnies " (newly joined at Sandhurst, termed also " Johns,") being sometimes used with a like signification by young officers, and the inquiry may occasionally be heard, " I say, old fellow, any more Johnnies coming ? "

LE JARGON OU JOBELIN DE MAISTRE FRANÇOIS VILLON.

BALLADE III.

PÉLICANS,
  Qui, en tous temps,
  Avancez dedans le pogois
   Gourde piarde,
   Et sur la tarde,
  Desboursez les povres nyois,
  Et pour soustenir vostre pois,
  Les duppes sont privez de caire,
  Sans faire haire,
  Ne hault braiere,
Mais plantez ils sont comme joncz,
Pour les sires qui sont si longs.

  Souvent aux arques
  A leurs marques,
Se laissent tous desbouser
  Pour ruer,
  Et enterver
Pour leur contre, que lors faisons
La fée aux arques respons.
Vous ruez deux coups, ou bien troys,
  Aux gallois.
  Deux, ou troys

Mineront trestout aux frontz,
Pour les sires qui sont si longs.

Et psource, benars
Coquillars,
Rebecquez vous de la Montjoye
Qui desvoye
Votre proye,
Et vous fera de tout brouer,
Pour joncher et enterver,
Qui est aux pigeons bien cher ;
Pour rifler
Et placquer
Les angels, de mal tous rondz
Pour les sires qui sont si longs.

ENVOI.

De paour des hurmes
Et des grumes,
Rassurez vous en droguerie
Et faerie,
Et ne soyez plus sur les joncz,
Pour les sires qui sont si longs.

TRANSLATION.

Police spies, who at all times drink good wine at the tavern, and at night empty poor simpletons' purses, and to provide for your extortions silly thieves have to part with their money, without complaining or clamouring, yet they are planted in jail, like so many reeds, to be plucked by the gaunt hangmen.

Oftentimes at the cashboxes, at places marked out for plunder, they allow themselves to be despoiled, when fighting and resisting to save their confederate, while we are practising our arts on the hidden coffers. You make two or three onsets on the boon companions. Two or three will mark them all for the gallows.

Hence, ye simple-minded vagabonds, turn away from the gallows, which gives you the colic and will deprive you of all, that you may deceive and steal what is of so much value to the dupes, that you may outwit and thrash the police, so eager to bring you to the scaffold.

For fear of the gibbet and the beam, exert more cunning and be more wily, and be no longer in prison, thence to be brought to the scaffold.

SONNET EN AUTHENTIQUE LANGAGE SOUDARDANT.[1]

(*Extrait des Premières Œuvres Poétiques du Capitaine Lasphrise.*)

ACCIPANT [2] du marpaut [3] la galiere [4] pourrie,
Grivolant [5] porte-flambe [6] enfile le trimart.[7]
Mais en despit de Gille,[8] ô geux, ton Girouart,[9]
A la mette [10] on lura [11] ta biotte [12] conie.[13]

Tu peux gourd pioller [14] me credant [15] et morfie [16]
De l'ornion,[17] du morne : [18] et de l'oygnan [19] criart,
De l'artois blanchemin.[20] Que ton riflant chouart [21]
Ne rive [22] du Courrier l'andrumelle gaudie.[23]

Ne ronce point du sabre [24] au mion [25] du taudis,

---

1 Langage soudardant, *soldiers' lingo.*
2 Accipant, *for* recevant.
3 Marpaut, *host.*
4 Galiere, *mare.*
5 Grivolant, *name for a soldier.*
6 Flambe, *sword.*
7 Trimart, *road.*
8 Gille, *name for a runaway.*
9 Girouart, *patron.*
10 Mette, *wine-shop ; morning ; thieves' meeting-place.*
11 Lura, *will see.*
12 Biotte, *steed.*
13 Conie, *dead.*

14 Gourd pioller, *drink heavily.*
15 Me credant, *for* me croyant.
16 Morfie, *eat.*
17 Ornion, *capon.*
18 Morne, *mutton.*
19 Oygnan, *for* oignon.
20 Artois blanchemin, *white bread.*
21 Riflant chouart, *fiery penis.*
22 Rive, *refers to coition.*
23 Andrumelle gaudie, *jolly girl.*
24 Ne ronce point du sabre, *do not lay the stick on.*
25 Mion, *boy, waiter.*

Qui n'aille au Gaulfarault,[1] gergonant de tesis,[2]
Que son journal[3] o flus[4] n'empoupe ta fouillouse.[5]

N'embiant[6] on rouillarde,[7] et de noir roupillant,[8]
Sur la gourde fretille,[9] et sur le gourd volant,[10]
Ainsi tu ne luras l'accolante tortouse.[11]

SIXTEENTH CENTURY.

DIALOGUE BETWEEN A HEADMAN IN THE CANTING CREW AND A VAGABOND.

(From Thomas Harman's Caveat or Warening for Common Cursetors, vulgarly called Vagabones, 1568.)

Upright Man.

 ENE Lightmans[12] to thy quarromes,[13] in what lipken[14] hast thou lypped[15] in this darkemans,[16] whether in a lybbege[17] or in the strummel?[18]

Roge. I couched a hogshead[19] in a Skypper[20] this darkemans.

Man. I towre[21] the strummel trine[22] upon thy nachbet[23] and Togman.[24]

Roge. I saye by the Salomon[25] I will lage it of[26] with a gage of bene bouse;[27] then cut to my nose watch.[28]

Man. Why, hast thou any lowre[29] in thy bonge[30] to bouse?[31]

1 Gaulfarault, *master of a bawdy house.*
2 Gergonant de tesis, *complaining of thee.*
3 Journal, *pocket-book.*
4 O flus, *or pack of cards.*
5 N'empoupe ta fouillouse, *fill thy pocket.*
6 N'embiant, *not travelling.*
7 Rouillarde, *drinks.*
8 De noir roupillant, *sleeping at night.*
9 Gourde fretille, *thick straw.*
10 Volant, *cloak.*
11 Tortouse, *rope.*
12 Bene Lightmans, *good day.*
13 Quarromes, *body.*
14 Lipken, *house.*
15 Lypped, *slept.*
16 Darkemans, *night.*
17 Lybbege, *bed.*
18 Strummel, *straw.*
19 Couched a hogshead, *lay down to sleep.*
20 Skypper, *barn.*
21 I towre, *I see.*
22 Trine, *hang.*
23 Nachbet, *cap.*
24 Togman, *coat.*
25 Salomon, *mass.*
26 Lage it of, *wipe it off.*
27 Gage of bene bouse, *quart of good drink.*
28 Cut to my nose watch, *say what you will to me.*
29 Lowre, *money.*
30 Bonge, *purse.*
31 To bouse, *to drink.*

Roge.   But a flagge,[1] a wyn,[2] and a make.[3]

Man.   Why, where is the kene[4] that hath the ben bouse?

Roge.   A bene mort[5] hereby at the signe of the prauncer.[6]

Man.   I cutt it is quyer[7] bouse, I bousd a flagge the last darkmans.

Roge.   But bouse there a bord,[8] and thou shalt haue beneship.[9]   Tower ye yander is the kene, dup the gygger,[10] and maund[11] that is bene shyp.

Man.   This bouse is as benship as rome bouse.[12]   Now I tower that ben bouse makes nase nabes.[13]   Maunde of this morte what ben pecke[14] is in her ken.

Roge.   She has a Cacling chete,[15] a grunting chete,[16] ruff Pecke,[17] Cassan,[18] and poplarr of yarum.[19]

Man.   That is benship to our watche.[20]   Now we haue well bousd, let vs strike some chete.[21]   Yonder dwelleth a quyer cuffen,[22] it were benship to myll[23] hym.

Roge.   Now bynge we a waste[24] to the hygh pad,[25] the ruffmanes[26] is by.

Man.   So may we happen on the Harmanes,[27] and cly the Tarke,[28] or to the quyerken[29] and skower quyaer crampings,[30] and so to tryning on the chates.[31]   Gerry gan,[32] the ruffian[33] clye the.[34]

Roge.   What, stowe your bene,[35] cofe,[36] and sut benat wydds,[37] and byng we to rome vyle,[38] to nyp a bonge;[39] so shall we haue lowre for the bousing ken,[40] and when we byng back to the deuseauyel,[41] we wyll fylche some duddes[42] of the Ruffemans,[43] or myll the ken for a lagge of dudes.[44]

1 Flagge, *groat.*
2 Wyn, *penny.*
3 Make, *halfpenny.*
4 Kene, *house.*
5 Bene mort, *good woman.*
6 Prauncer, *horse.*
7 Quyer, *bad.*
8 Bord, *shilling.*
9 Beneship, *excellent.*
10 Dup the gygger, *open the door.*
11 Maund, *ask.*
12 Rome bouse, *wine.*
13 Nase nabes, *drunken head.*
14 Pecke, *meat.*
15 Cacling chete, *fowl.*
16 Grunting chete, *pig.*
17 Ruff pecke, *bacon.*
18 Cassan, *cheese.*
19 Poplarr of yarum, *milk porridge.*
20 To our watche, *for us.*
21 Strike some chete, *steal something.*
22 Quyer cuffen, *magistrate.*
23 Myll, *rob.*

24 Bynge we a waste, *let us away.*
25 Pad, *road.*
26 Ruffmanes, *wood.*
27 Harmanes, *stocks.*
28 Cly the Tarke, *be whipped.*
29 Quyerken, *prison.*
30 Skower quyaer crampings, *be shackled with bolts and fetters.*
31 Chates, *gallows.*
32 Gerry gan, *hold your tongue.*
33 Ruffian, *devil.*
34 Clye the, *take thee.*
35 Stowe your bene, *hold your peace.*
36 Cofe, *good fellow.*
37 Sut benat wydds, *speak better words.*
38 Rome vyle, *London.*
39 Nyp a bonge, *cut a purse.*
40 Bousing ken, *alehouse.*
41 Deuseauyel, *country.*
42 Duddes, *linen clothes.*
43 Ruffemans, *hedges.*
44 Lagge of dudes, *parcel of clothes.*

DIALOGUE DE DEUX ARGOTIERS,[1]

L'UN POLISSON[2] ET L'AUTRE MALINGREUX,[3] QUI SE RENCONTRENT
JUSTE À LA LOURDE[4] D'UNE VERGNE.[5]

(*Extrait du Jargon de l'Argot.*)

Le Malingreux.

L A haute[6] t'aquige[7] en chenastre[8] santé.

Le Polisson. Et tézière[9] aussi, fanandel;[10] où trimardes[11]-tu ?

Le Malingreux. En ce pasquelin[12] de Berry, on m'a rouscaillé[13] que trucher[14] était chenastre; et en cette vergne fiche-t-on la thune[15] gourdement?[16]

Le Polisson. Quelque peu, pas guère.

Le Malingreux. La rousse[17] y est-elle chenastre ?

Le Polisson. Nenni; c'est ce qui me fait ambier[18] hors de cette vergne; car si je n'eusse eu du michon,[19] je fusse cosni[20] de faim.

[1] Argotiers, *members of the "canting crew."*
[2] Polisson, *half-naked beggar.*
[3] Malingreux, *maimed or sick beggar.*
[4] Lourde, *gate.*
[5] Vergne, *town.*
[6] La haute, *the Almighty.*
[7] Aquige, *keep.*
[8] Chenastre, *good.*
[9] Tézière, *thee.*
[10] Fanandel, *comrade.*
[11] Trimardes, *going.*
[12] Pasquelin, *country.*
[13] Rouscaillé, *told.*
[14] Trucher, *to beg.*
[15] Fiche-t-on la thune, *do they give alms.*
[16] Gourdement, *much.*
[17] La rousse, *the police.*
[18] Ambier, *go.*
[19] Michon, *money.*
[20] Cosni, *died.*

Le Malingreux. Y a-t-il un castu [1] dans cette vergne.

Le Polisson. Jaspin. [2]

Le Malingreux. Est-il chenu ? [3]

Le Polisson. Pas guère ; les pioles [4] ne sont que de fretille. [5] . . .

Le Malingreux. Veux-tu venir prendre de la morfe [6] et piausser [7] avec mézière [8] en une des pioles que tu m'as rouscaillées ?

Le Polisson. Il n'y a ni ronds, [9] ni herplis, [10] en ma felouse ; [11] je vais piausser en quelque grenasse. [12]

Le Malingreux. Encore que n'y ayez du michon, ne laissez pas de venir, car il y a deux menées [13] de ronds en ma henne, [14] et deux ornies [15] en mon gueulard, [16] que j'ai égraillées [17] sur le trimar ; [18] bions [19] les faire riffoder, [20] veux-tu ?

Le Polisson. Girole, [21] et béni soit le grand havre, [22] qui m'a fait rencontrer si chenastre occasion ; je vais me réjouir et chanter une petite chanson. . . .

Le Malingreux. Si tu veux trimer [23] de compagnie avec mézière, nous aquigerons grande chère, [24] je sais bien aquiger les luques, [25] engrailler l'ornie, casser la hane aux frémions, [26] pour épouser la fourcandière, [27] si quelques rovaux [28] me mouchaillent. [29]

Le Polisson. Ah ! le havre garde mézière, je ne fus jamais ni fourgue [30] ni doubleux. [31]

Le Malingreux. Ni mézière non plus, je rouscaille [32] tous les luisans [33] au grand havre de l'oraison.

---

1 Castu, *hospital.*

2 Jaspin, *yes.*

3 Chenu, *good.*

4 Pioles, *rooms.*

5 Fretille, *straw.*

6 Morfe, *food.*

7 Piausser, *to sleep.*

8 Mézière, *me.*

9 Ronds, *halfpence.*

10 Herplis, *farthings.*

11 Felouse, *pocket.*

12 Grenasse, *barn.*

13 Menées, *dozen.*

14 Henne, *purse.*

15 Ornies, *hens.*

16 Gueulard, *wallet.*

17 Egraillées, *hooked.*

18 Trimar, *road.*

19 Bions, *let us go.*

20 Riffoder, *cook.*

21 Girole, *so be it.*

22 Havre, *God.*

23 Trimer, *to walk.*

24 Aquigerons grande chère, *will live well.*

25 Aquiger les luques, *prepare pictures.*

26 Casser la hane aux frémions, *steal purses at fairs.*

27 Epouser la fourcandière, *to throw away the stolen property.*

28 Rovaux, *police.*

29 Mouchaillent, *see.*

30 Fourgue, *receiver of stolen property.*

31 Doubleux, *thief.*

32 Je rouscaille, *I pray.*

33 Tous les luisans, *every day.*

SEVENTEENTH CENTURY.

OATH OF FRENCH MENDICANTS AND TRAMPS.

(Extrait du Jargon de l'Argot.)

POUR affermir l'état de cette monarchie argotique, les argotiers ordonnèrent de tenir par chaque an les états généraux, pour aviser aux affaires de l'état, qui étaient tenus anciennement jouste la vergne [1] de Fontaine-le-Comte, et à présent translolés [2] en Languedoc ; parceque ce chenastre pharaut [3] du Languedoc, Anne de Montmorency, a fiché une grande somme de michons, [4] pour être employée tous les ans, la Semaine Sainte, pour fouquer à morphe toutime [5] les argotiers qui se confesseront et communieront le Jeudi-Saint, et prieront le grand-Havre [6] pour sézière. [7] . . . .

Auxdits états généraux on procède, premièrement, à l'élection du grand-coëre, [8] ou bien on continue celui d'auparavant ; . . . . après l'élection, le grand-coëre commande à tous les argotiers [9] nouveaux venus, de se mettre à quatre pieds contre la dure, [10] puis s'assied sur l'un d'eux ; . . . . après que les anciens argotiers ont rendu compte de leurs vocations, les nouveaux venus s'approchent et fichent ronds en la saliverne, [11] puis on leur fait faire les sermens en cette sorte.

Premièrement, ils mettent le bout de leur sabre dans la dure, puis on leur fait lever la louche [12] gauche et non la droite, parcequ'ils disent que c'est une erreur de cour, puis rouscaillent [13] en cette manière : J'attrime en trèpeligour ; [14] puis de rechef, trèpeligour du tour.

[1] Jouste la vergne, *close to the town.*
[2] Translolés, *transferred.*
[3] Chenastre pharaut, *good gentleman.*
[4] Michons, *money.*
[5] Fouquer à morphe toutime, *to nourish all.*
[6] Grand-Havre, *God.*
[7] Sézière, *him.*
[8] Grand-coëre, *king of rogues.*
[9] Argotiers, *members of the fraternity.*
[10] Dure, *ground.*
[11] Fichent ronds en la saliverne, *throw pence in the plate.*
[12] Louche, *hand.*
[13] Rouscaillent, *speak.*
[14] J'attrime en trèpeligour, *I take it as a vagabond.*

Après on leur fait promettre et jurer de rendre obéissance au cagou [1] de leur province, auquel ils sont laissés en charge, pour leur apprendre les tours du métier ; . . . . après que les états sont finis, chacun se départ, et les cagous bient [2] en la province qui leur a été ordonnée, et emmènent avec sézières leurs apprentis, pour leur apprendre et exercer l'argot.

Seventeenth Century.

ENGLISH GIPSIES' OATH.

(Extract from Bampfylde-Moore Carew, King of the Mendicants.)

WHEN a fresh recruit is admitted into this fraternity, he is to take the following oath, administered by the principal maunder,[3] after going through the annexed form :—

First a new name is given him, by which he is ever after to be called ; then, standing up in the middle of the assembly, and directing his face to the dimber damber, or principal man of the gang, he repeats the following oath, which is dictated to him by some experienced member of the fraternity :—

"I, Crank Cuffin, do swear to be a true brother, and that I will in all things obey the commands of the great tawny prince,[4] keep his counsel, and not divulge the secrets of my brethren.

"I will never leave or forsake the company, but observe and keep all the times of appointment, either by day or by night, in every place whatever.

"I will not teach anyone to cant ; nor will I disclose any of our mysteries to them.

"I will take my prince's part against all that shall oppose him, or any of us, according to the utmost of my ability ; nor will I suffer him, or anyone

---

1 Cagou, *chief.*
2 Bient, *go.*
3 Maunder, *beggar.*

4 Tawny prince, *Prince Prig, the head of the gipsies.*

belonging to us, to be abased by any strange abrams,[1] ruffies,[2] hookers,[3] palliardes,[4] swaddlers,[5] Irish toyles,[6] swigmen,[7] whip Jacks,[8] Jarkmen,[9] bawdy baskets,[10] dommerars,[11] clapper dogeons,[12] patricoes,[13] or curtails ;[14] but I will defend him, or them, as much as I can, against all other outliers whatever. I will not conceal aught I win out of libkins,[15] or from the ruffmans,[16] but will preserve it for the use of the company. Lastly, I will cleave to my doxy,[17] wap[18] stiffly, and will bring her duds,[19] margery praters,[20] gobblers,[21] grunting cheats,[22] or tibs of the buttery,[23] or anything else I can come at, as winnings for her wappings."[24]

THE SAME OATH IN VERSE.

" I, Crank Cuffin, swear to be
True to this fraternity ;

*   *   *   *

Serve them truly and no other,
And be faithful to my brother ;
Suffer none, from far or near,
With their rights to interfere ;
No strange Abram, ruffler[25] crack,
Hooker of another pack,
Rogue,[26] or rascal, frater,[27] maunderer,[28]
Irish toyle, or other wanderer ;

[1] Abrams, *half-naked beggars.*
[2] Ruffies, *beggars who sham the old soldier.*
[3] Hookers, *thieves who beg in the daytime and steal at night from shops with a hook.*
[4] Palliardes, *ragged beggars.*
[5] Swaddlers, *Irish Roman Catholics who pretend conversion.*
[6] Toyles, *beggars with pedlar's pack.*
[7] Swigmen, *beggars.*
[8] Whip Jacks, *beggars who sham the shipwrecked sailor.*
[9] Jarkmen, *learned beggars, begging-letter impostors.*
[10] Bawdy baskets, *prostitutes.*
[11] Dommerars, *dumb beggars.*
[12] Clapper dogeons, *beggars by birth.*
[13] Patricoes, *those who perform the marriage ceremony.*

[14] Curtails, *second in command, with short cloak.*
[15] Libkins, *lodgings.*
[16] Ruffmans, *bushes or woods.*
[17] Doxy, *mistress.*
[18] Wap, *to lie with a woman.*
[19] Duds, *clothes.*
[20] Margery praters, *hens.*
[21] Gobblers, *ducks.*
[22] Grunting cheats, *pigs.*
[23] Tibs of the buttery, *geese.*
[24] Wappings, *coition.*
[25] Ruffler, *mendicant who shams the wounded soldier.*
[26] Rogue, *beggar who shams lameness.*
[27] Frater, *one with a licence, who begs for an hospital.*
[28] Maunderer, *tramp.*

No dimber-damber,[1] angler,[2] dancer,[3]
Prig of cackler,[4] prig of prancer,[5]
No swigman, swaddler, clapper dudgeon,
Cadge-cloak,[6] curtal, or curmudgeon,
No whip-Jack, palliard, patrico,
No jarkman, be he high or low,
No dummerar, or Romany,
No member of the family,
No ballad-basket, bouncing buffer,
Nor any other will I suffer,
But stall-off[7] now and for ever
All outliers whatsoever ;
And as I keep to the fore-gone
So may help me Salamon."[8]

[1] Dimber-damber, *head of gang.*
[2] Angler, see Hooker.
[3] Dancer, *thief who effects an entrance by the attic window.*
[4] Prig of cackler, *one who steals poultry.*

[5] Prig of prancer, *horse-stealer.*
[6] Cadge-cloak, *beggar.*
[7] Stall-off, *avoid.*
[8] Salamon, *the oath, mass.*

JERRY JUNIPER'S CHANT.

(From Ainsworth's Rookwood.)

IN a box[1] of the stone jug[2] I was born,
Of a hempen widow[3] the kid[4] forlorn,
    Fake away!
And my father, as I've heard say,
    Fake away!
Was a merchant of capers gay,
Who cut his last fling with great applause,
Nix my doll pals, fake away![5]
To the tune of hearty choke with caper sauce.
    Fake away!
The knucks[6] in quod[7] did my schoolmen[8] play,
    Fake away!
And put me up to the time of day,[9]
Until at last there was none so knowing,
No such sneaksman[10] or buzgloak[11] going,
    Fake away!

[1] Box, *cell.*
[2] Stone jug, *Newgate.*
[3] Hempen widow, *woman whose husband has been hanged.*
[4] Kid, *child.*
[5] Nix my doll pals, fake away! *never mind, friends, on! on!*

[6] Knucks, *thieves.*
[7] Quod, *prison.*
[8] Schoolmen, *fellows of the gang.*
[9] Put me up to the time of day, *made a knowing one of me, taught me thieving.*
[10] Sneaksman, *shoplifter.*
[11] Buzgloak, *pickpocket.*

Fogles [1] and fawnies [2] soon went their way,
 Fake away !
To the spout [3] with the sneezers [4] in grand array,
No dummy hunter [5] had forks so fly, [6]
No knuckler so deftly could fake a cly, [7]
 Fake away !
No slourd hoxter [8] my snipes [9] could stay,
 Fake away !
None knap a reader [10] like me in the lay. [11]
Soon then I mounted in swell street-high,
Nix my doll pals, fake away !
Soon then I mounted in swell street-high,
And sported my flashest toggery, [12]
 Fake away !
Fainly resolved I would make my hay,
 Fake away !
While Mercury's star shed a single ray ;
And ne'er was there seen such a dashing prig, [13]
Nix my doll pals, fake away !
And ne'er was there seen such a dashing prig,
With my strummel faked [14] in the newest twig, [15]
 Fake away !
With my fawnied famms [16] and my onions gay, [17]
 Fake away !
My thimble of ridge, [18] and my driz kemesa, [19]
All my togs [20] were so niblike [21] and plash. [22]
Readily the queer screens [23] I then could smash. [24]
 Fake away !
But my nuttiest blowen, [25] one fine day,
 Fake away !

1 Fogles, *silk handkerchiefs.*
2 Fawnies, *rings.*
3 Spout, *pawnbroker's.*
4 Sneezers, *snuff-boxes.*
5 Dummy hunter, *stealer of pocket books.*
6 Forks so fly, *such nimble fingers.*
7 No knuckler so deftly could fake a cly, *no pickpocket so skilfully could pick a pocket.*
8 Slourd hoxter, *inside pocket buttoned up.*
9 Snipes, *scissors.*
10 Knap a reader, *steal a pocket book.*
11 Lay, *robbery, dodge.*

12 Flashest toggery, *best made clothes.*
13 Prig, *thief.*
14 Strummel faked, *hair dressed.*
15 Twig, *fashion.*
16 Fawnied famms, *hands bejewelled.*
17 Onions, *seals.*
18 Thimble of ridge, *gold watch.*
19 Driz kemesa, *shirt with lace frill.*
20 Togs, *clothes.*
21 Niblike, *fashionable.*
22 Plash, *fine.*
23 Queer screens, *forged notes.*
24 Smash, *pass.*
25 Nuttiest blowen, *favourite girl.*

To the beaks [1] did her fancy man betray,
And thus was I bowled at last,
And into the jug for a lay was cast,
    Fake away !
But I slipped my darbies [2] one morn in May,
And gave to the dubsman [3] a holiday.
And here I am, pals, merry and free,
A regular rollicking romany. [4]

EIGHTEENTH CENTURY.

THE GAME OF HIGH TOBY.

SUNG BY DICK TURPIN.

(*From Ainsworth's Rookwood.*)

OW Oliver [5] puts his black nightcap on,
    And every star its glim [6] is hiding,
    And forth to the heath is the Sampsman [7] gone,
    His matchless cherry-black [8] prancer riding ;
Merrily over the common he flies,
Fast and free as the rush of rocket,
His crape-covered vizard drawn over his eyes,
His tol [9] by his side, and his pops [10] in his pocket.

Chorus.

So who can name
So merry a game
As the game of all games—High Toby ? [11]

The traveller hears him, away ! away !
Over the wide wide heath he scurries ;

---

[1] Beaks, *magistrates.*
[2] Darbies, *handcuffs.*
[3] Dubsman, *turnkey.*
[4] Romany, *gipsy.*
[5] Oliver, *the moon.*
[6] Glim, *light.*

[7] Sampsman, *highwayman.*
[8] Cherry-black, *cherry coloured—black.*
[9] Tol, *sword.*
[10] Pops, *pistols.*
[11] High Toby, *highway robbery.*

He heeds not the thunderbolt summons to stay,
But ever the faster and faster he hurries.
But what daisy-cutter can match that black tit?
He is caught—he must " stand and deliver ; "
Then out with the dummy,[1] and off with the bit,[2]
Oh, the game of High Toby for ever !
Chorus.

Believe me there is not a game, my brave boys,
To compare with the game of High Toby ;
No rapture can equal the Tobyman's joys,
To blue devils blue plumbs [3] give the go-by ;
And what if at length, boys, he come to the Crap,[4]
Even rack-punch has some bitter in it,
For the Mare with three legs,[5] boys, I care not a rap,
'Twill be over in less than a minute !
Chorus.

EIGHTEENTH CENTURY.

CHANSON.

(*Extrait du Vice Puni ou Cartouche,* 1725.)

ANANDELS [6] en cette Piolle [7]
On vit chenument ; [8]
Arton, Pivois et Criolle [9]
On a gourdement.[10]
Pitanchons, faisons riolle [11]
Jusqu'au Jugement.

Icicaille [12] est le Théâtre
Du Petit Dardant ; [13]

[1] Dummy, *pocket-book.*
[2] Bit, *money.*
[3] Blue plumbs, *bullets.*
[4] Crap, *gallows.*
[5] Mare with three legs, *ibid.*
[6] Fanandels, *comrades.*
[7] Piolle, *house, tavern.*
[8] Chenument, *well.*

[9] Arton, pivois et criolle, *bread, wine, and meat.*
[10] Gourdement, *in plenty.*
[11] Pitanchons, faisons riolle, *let us drink, amuse ourselves.*
[12] Icicaille, *here.*
[13] Petit Dardant, *Cupid.*

Fonçons à ce Mion[1] folâtre
Notre Palpitant.[2]
Pitanchons Pivois chenâtre[3]
Jusques au Luisant.[4]

[1] Fonçons à ce Mion, *let us give this boy.*
[2] Palpitant, *heart.*
[3] Chenâtre, *good.*
[4] Luisant, *day.*

VIDOCQ'S SLANG SONG.

N roulant de vergne en vergne [1]
Pour apprendre à goupiner, [2]
J'ai rencontré la mercandière, [3]
Lonfa malura dondaine,
Qui du pivois solisait, [4]
Lonfa malura dondé.

    J'ai rencontré la mercandière
    Qui du pivois solisait ;
Je lui jaspine en bigorne ; [5]
Lonfa malura dondaine,
Qu'as tu donc à morfiller ? [6]
Lonfa malura dondé.

    Je lui jaspine en bigorne ;
    Qu'as tu donc à morfiller ?
J'ai du chenu [7] pivois sans lance. [8]
Lonfa malura dondaine,
Et du larton savonné [9]
Lonfa malura dondé.

[1] Vergne, *town.*
[2] Goupiner, *to steal.*
[3] Mercandière, *tradeswoman.*
[4] Du pivois solisait, *sold wine.*
[5] Jaspine en bigorne, *say in cant.*

[6] Morfiller, *to eat and drink.*
[7] Chenu, *good.*
[8] Lance, *water.*
[9] Larton savonné, *white bread.*

J'ai du chenu pivois sans lance
Et du larton savonné,
Une lourde [1] et une tournante,[2]
Lonfa malura dondaine,
Et un pieu [3] pour roupiller [4]
Lonfa malura dondé.

Une lourde, une tournante
Et un pieu pour roupiller.
J'enquille [5] dans sa cambriole,[6]
Lonfa malura dondaine,
Espérant de l'entifler,[7]
Lonfa malura dondé.

J'enquille dans sa cambriole
Espérant de l'entifler ;
Je rembroque [8] au coin du rifle,[9]
Lonfa malura dondaine,
Un messière [10] qui pionçait,[11]
Lonfa malura dondé.

Je rembroque au coin du rifle
Un messière qui pionçait ;
J'ai sondé dans ses vallades,[12]
Lonfa malura dondaine,
Son carle [13] j'ai pessigué,[14]
Lonfa malura dondé.

J'ai sondé dans ses vallades,
Son carle j'ai pessigué,
Son carle et sa tocquante,[15]
Lonfa malura dondaine,
Et ses attaches de cé,[16]
Lonfa malura dondé.

Son carle et sa tocquante,
Et ses attaches de cé,

[1] Lourde, *door.*	[9] Rifle, *fire.*
[2] Tournante, *key.*	[10] Messière, *man.*
[3] Pieu, *bed.*	[11] Pionçait, *was sleeping.*
[4] Roupiller, *to sleep.*	[12] Vallades, *pockets.*
[5] J'enquille, *I enter.*	[13] Carle, *money.*
[6] Cambriole, *room.*	[14] Pessigué, *taken.*
[7] Entifler, *to marry.*	[15] Tocquante, *watch.*
[8] Rembroque, *see.*	[16] Attaches de cé, *silver buckles.*

Son coulant [1] et sa montante,[2]
Lonfa malura dondaine,
Et son combre galuché [3]
Lonfa malura dondé.

Son coulant et sa montante
Et son combre galuché,
Son frusque,[4] aussi sa lisette,[5]
Lonfa malura dondaine,
Et ses tirants brodanchés,[6]
Lonfa malura dondé.

Son frusque, aussi sa lisette
Et ses tirants brodanchés.
Crompe,[7] crompe, mercandière,
Lonfa malura dondaine,
Car nous serions béquillés,[8]
Lonfa malura dondé.

Crompe, crompe, mercandière,
Car nous serions béquillés.
Sur la placarde de vergne,[9]
Lonfa malura dondaine,
Il nous faudrait gambiller,[10]
Lonfa malura dondé.

Sur la placarde de vergne
Il nous faudrait gambiller,
Allumés [11] de toutes ces largues,[12]
Lonfa malura dondaine,
Et du trèpe [13] rassemblé,
Lonfa malura dondé.

Allumés de toutes ces largues
Et du trèpe rassemblé ;
Et de ces charlots bons drilles,[14]

[1] Coulant, *chain.*
[2] Montante, *breeches.*
[3] Combre galuché, *laced hat.*
[4] Frusque, *coat.*
[5] Lisette, *waistcoat.*
[6] Tirants brodanchés, *embroidered stockings.*
[7] Crompe, *run away.*

[8] Béquillés, *hanged.*
[9] Placarde de vergne, *public place.*
[10] Gambiller, *to dance.*
[11] Allumés, *looked at.*
[12] Largues, *women.*
[13] Trèpe, *crowd.*
[14] Charlots bons drilles, *jolly thieves.*

Lonfa malura dondaine,
Tous aboulant [1] goupiner.
Lonfa malura dondé.

BEGINNING OF NINETEENTH CENTURY.

THE SAME SONG VERSIFIED BY WILLIAM MAGINN.

S from ken [2] to ken I was going,
   Doing a bit on the prigging lay, [3]
Who should I meet but a jolly blowen, [4]
    Tol lol, lol lol, tol derol ay ;
Who should I meet but a jolly blowen,
Who was fly [5] to the time o' day ? [6]

Who should I meet but a jolly blowen,
   Who was fly to the time of day.
I pattered in flash, [7] like a covey [8] knowing,
    Tol lol, &c.,
" Ay, bub or grubby, [9] I say."

I pattered in flash like a covey knowing,
" Ay, bub or grubby, I say."
" Lots of gatter," [10] quo' she, " are flowing,
    Tol lol, &c.,
Lend me a lift in the family way. [11]

" Lots of gatter," quo' she, " are flowing,
Lend me a lift in the family way.
You may have a crib [12] to stow in,
    Tol lol, &c.,
Welcome, my pal, [13] as the flowers in May."

1 Aboulant, *coming.*
2 Ken, *shop, house.*
3 Prigging lay, *thieving business.*
4 Blowen, *girl, strumpet, sweetheart.*
5 Fly (contraction of flash), *awake, up to, practised in.*
6 Time o' day, *knowledge of business, thieving.*

7 Pattered in flash, *spoke in slang.*
8 Covey, *man.*
9 Bub and grub, *drink and food.*
10 Gatter, *porter.*
11 Family, *the thieves in general;* the family way, *the thieving line.*
12 Crib, *bed.*
13 Pal, *friend, companion, paramour.*

" You may have a crib to stow in,
Welcome, my pal, as the flowers in May."
To her ken at once I go in,
    Tol lol, &c.,
Where in a corner out of the way ;

To her ken at once I go in,
Where in a corner out of the way,
With his smeller [1] a trumpet blowing,
    Tol lol, &c.,
A regular swell cove [2] lushy [3] lay.

With his smeller a trumpet blowing,
A regular swell cove lushy lay.
To his clies [4] my hooks [5] I throw in,
    Tol lol, &c.,
And collar his dragons [6] clear away.

To his clies my hooks I throw in,
And collar his dragons clear away.
Then his ticker [7] I set a-going,
    Tol lol, &c.,
And his onions, [8] chain and key.

Then his ticker I set a-going,
With his onions, chain and key ;
Next slipt off his bottom clo'ing,
    Tol lol, &c.,
And his ginger head topper gay.

Next slipt off his bottom clo'ing,
And his ginger head topper gay.
Then his other toggery [9] stowing,
    Tol lol, &c.,
All with the swag [10] I sneak away.

Then his other toggery stowing,
All with the swag I sneak away.

1 Smeller, *nose.*
2 Swell cove, *gentleman, dandy.*
3 Lushy, *drunk.*
4 Clies, *pockets.*
5 Hooks, *fingers.*

6 Collar his dragons, *take his sovereigns.*
7 Ticker, *watch.*
8 Onions, *seals.*
9 Toggery, *clothes.*
10 Swag, *plunder.*

Tramp it, tramp it, my jolly blowen,
　　Tol lol, &c.,
Or be grabbed[1] by the beaks[2] we may.

Tramp it, tramp it, my jolly blowen,
Or be grabbed by the beaks we may.
And we shall caper a-heel-and-toeing,
　　Tol lol, &c.,
A Newgate hornpipe some fine day.

And we shall caper a-heel-and-toeing,
A Newgate hornpipe some fine day,
With the mots[3] their ogles[4] throwing,
　　Tol lol, &c.,
And old Cotton[5] humming his pray.[6]

With the mots their ogles throwing,
And old Cotton humming his pray,
And the fogle-hunters[7] doing,
　　Tol lol, &c.,
Their morning fake[8] in the prigging lay.

[1] Grabbed, *taken.*
[2] Beaks, *police officers.*
[3] Mots, *girls.*
[4] Ogles, *eyes.*

[5] Old Cotton, *the ordinary of Newgate.*
[6] Humming his pray, *saying prayers.*
[7] Fogle-hunters, *pickpockets.*
[8] Morning fake, *morning thieving.*

Beginning of Nineteenth Century.

COMMANDEMENTS.

UN seul sentiment t'animera
Celui de grinchir gourdement.[1]
Jorne et sorgue[2] tu poisseras[3]
Boucart et baïte[4] chenument.[5]
Le morceau tu ne mangeras[6]
De crainte de tomber au plan.[7]
Chenâtre fourgat[8] litreras[9]
Afin de solir[10] sûrement.
Du grand pré[11] tu te cramperas[12]
Pour rabattre à Pantin[13] lestement.
Cambriolle[14] tu maquilleras[15]
Par carouble[16] et esquintement.[17]
La raille,[18] maron,[19] te servira[20]
Pour un deuxième gerbement.[21]
Dans le nez toujours tu auras[22]
Macarons[23] et cabestans.[24]
Pour grinchir tu préféreras
Les fêtes aux turbinements.[25]
Jamais tu ne rengracieras[26]
Plutôt caner[27] en goupinant.[28]

1 Grinchir gourdement, *to steal well.*
2 Jorne et sorgue, *day and night.*
3 Tu poisseras, *shalt thou steal.*
4 Boucart et baïte, *shop and room.*
5 Chenument, *well.*
6 Le morceau tu ne mangeras, *thou shalt reveal nothing.*
7 Plan, *prison.*
8 Chenâtre fourgat, *good receiver.*
9 Litreras, *shalt thou have.*
10 Solir, *sell.*
11 Grand pré, *hulks.*
12 Tu te cramperas, *shalt thou escape.*
13 Pour rabattre à Pantin, *to return to Paris.*
14 Cambriolle, *room.*
15 Tu maquilleras, *thou shalt "do."*
16 Carouble, *false key.*
17 Esquintement, *breaking open.*
18 Raille, *police.*
19 Maron, *in the act.*
20 Servira, *will catch.*
21 Gerbement, *trial.*
22 Dans le nez . . . , *thou shalt always abhor.*
23 Macarons, *informers.*
24 Cabestans, *police.*
25 Turbinements, *work-days.*
26 Rengracieras, *repent, lead an honest life.*
27 Caner, *to die.*
28 Goupinant, *stealing.*

BEGINNING OF NINETEENTH CENTURY.

CHANSON EN ARGOT.

*Attribuée par Vidocq à un nommé Winter, forçat au bagne de
Toulon en* 1829.

RAVAILLANT d'ordinaire,
La sorgue[1] dans Pantin,[2]
Dans mainte et mainte affaire
Faisant très bon choppin ;[3]
Ma gente cambriote,[4]
Rendoublée de camelote,[5]
De la dalle[6] au flaquet ;[7]
Je vivais sans disgrâce,
Sans regoût ni morace,[8]
Sans taff[9] et sans regret.

J'ai fait par comblance[10]
Gironde larguecapé,[11]
Soiffant picton sans lance,[12]
Pivois non maquillé,[13]
Tirants, passes à la rousse,[14]
Attaches de gratousse,[15]
Combriot galuché.
Cheminant en bon drille,
Un jour à la Courtille,
J'm'en étais enganté.[16]

1 Sorgue, *night.*
2 Pantin *Paris.*
3 Choppin, *theft.*
4 Cambriote, *room.*
5 Rendoublée de camelote, *full of stolen
property.*
6 Dalle, *money.*
7 Flaquet, *waistcoat pocket.*
8 Sans regoût ni morace, *free from care,
quietly and carelessly.*

9 Taff, *fear.*
10 Par comblance, *into the bargain.*
11 Gironde larguecapé, *pretty mistress.*
12 Soiffant . . . , *drinking wine without
water.*
13 Pivois non maquillé, *pure wine.*
14 Passes à la rousse, *elegant shoes.*
15 Attaches de gratousse, *lace frill.*
16 Enganté, *in love with.*

En faisant nos gambades,
Un grand messière franc [1]
Voulant faire parade,
Serre un bogue d'orient. [2]
Après la gambriade, [3]
Le filant sus l'estrade, [4]
D'esbrouf je l'estourbis, [5]
J'enflaque [6] sa limace, [7]
Son bogue, ses frusques, ses passes. [8]
J'm'en fus au fouraillis. [9]

Par contretemps, ma largue, [10]
Voulant s'piquer d'honneur,
Craignant que je la nargue,
Moi qui n'suis pas taffeur, [11]
Pour gonfler ses valades,
Encasque [12] dans un rade, [13]
Sert des sigues [14] à foison ;
On la crible à la grive, [15]
Je m'la donne [16] et m'esquive,
Elle est pommée maron. [17]

Le quart d'œil [18] lui jabotte, [19]
Mange sur tes nonneurs [20]
Lui tire une carotte, [21]
Lui montant la couleur. [22]
L'on vient, on me ligotte, [23]
Adieu, ma cambriote,
Mon beau pieu, mes dardants, [24]
Je monte à la cigogne, [25]

1 Messière franc, *citizen.*
2 Bogue d'orient, *gold watch.*
3 Gambriade, *dance.*
4 Le filant sus l'estrade, *following him on the boulevard.*
5 D'esbrouf je l'estourbis, *I stun him.*
6 J'enflaque, *I seize.*
7 Limace, *shirt.*
8 Passes, *shoes.*
9 Fouraillis, *receiver's place.*
10 Largue, *girl.*
11 Taffeur, *poltroon.*
12 Encasque, *enters.*
13 Rade, *shop.*
14 Sert des sigues, *steals gold pieces.*
15 Crible à la grive, *cry out thieves.*
16 Je m'la donne, *I make off.*
17 Pommée maron, *caught in the act.*
18 Quart d'œil, *commissaire de police.*
19 Jabotte, *says.*
20 Mange sur tes nonneurs, *inform against your accomplices.*
21 Tire une carotte, *lays a trap for her.*
22 Montant la couleur, *deceiving her.*
23 Ligotte, *bind.*
24 Dardants, *loves.*
25 Cigogne, *tribunal.*

On me gerbe à la grotte,[1]
Au tap [2] et pour douze ans.

Ma largue n'sera plus gironde,
Je serai vioc [3] aussi ;
Faudra pour plaire au monde,
Clinquant, frusque, maquis.[4]
Tout passe dans la tigne,[5]
Et quoiqu'on en jaspine,
C'est un foutu flanchet.[6]
Douze longes de tirade,[7]
Pour une rigolade,[8]
Pour un moment d'attrait.

[1] Gerbe à la grotte, *sentenced to the hulks.*
[2] Tap, *pillory.*
[3] Vioc, *old.*
[4] Maquis, *rouge.*

[5] Tigne, *world.*
[6] Foutu flanchet, *bad job.*
[7] Longes de tirade, *years in the hulks.*
[8] Rigolade, *amusement*

THE DEATH OF SOCRATES.

BY THE REV. ROBERT BURROWES, DEAN OF ST. FINBAR'S
CATHEDRAL, CORK.

From the Reliques of Father Prout, collected and arranged by Oliver Yorke
(Rev. Francis Mahony).

HE night before Larry was stretched,
  The boys they all paid him a visit ;
A bit in their sacks too they fetched—
  They sweated their duds [1] till they riz it ;
For Larry was always the lad,
  When a friend was condemned to the squeezer, [2]
But he'd pawn all the togs that he had,
  Just to help the poor boy to a sneezer, [3]
And moisten his gob 'fore he died.

"'Pon my conscience, dear Larry," says I,
  "I'm sorry to see you in trouble,
And your life's cheerful noggin run dry,
  And yourself going off like its bubble ! "
"Hould your tongue in that matter," says he ;

---

1 Sweated their duds, *pawned their*
clothes.

2 Squeezer, *rope.*
3 Sneezer, *pocket handkerchief.*

" For the neckcloth [1] I don't care a button,
And by this time to-morrow you'll see
Your Larry will be dead as mutton ;
All for what ? 'Kase his courage was good ! "

The boys they came crowding in fast ;
They drew their stools close round about him,
Six glims [2] round his coffin they placed—
He couldn't be well waked without 'em.
I axed if he was fit to die
Without having duly repented ?
Says Larry, " That's all in my eye,
And all by the clargy invented,
To make a fat bit for themselves."

Then the cards being called for, they played,
Till Larry found one of them cheated ;
Quick he made a hard rap at his head,
The lad being easily heated.
" So ye chate me because I'm in grief !
Oh ! is that, by the Holy, the rason ?
Soon I'll give you to know, you d—d thief,
That you're cracking your jokes out of sason,
And scuttle your nob [3] with my fist."

Then in came the priest with his book,
He spoke him so smooth and so civil ;
Larry tipped him a Kilmainham look,
And pitched his big wig to the divil.
Then raising a little his head
To get a sweet drop of the bottle,
And pitiful sighing he said,
" Oh, the hemp will be soon round my throttle,[4]
And choke my poor windpipe to death ! "

So mournful these last words he spoke
We all vented our tears in a shower ;
For my part I thought my heart broke
To see him cut down like a flower !
On his travels we watched him next day,
Oh, the hangman I thought I could kill him !

---

1 Neckcloth, *rope.*
2 Glims, *candles.*

3 Scuttle your nob, *break your head.*
4 Throttle, *neck.*

Not one word did our poor Larry say,
Nor changed till he came to " King William ; "
Och, my dear ! then his colour turned white !

When he came to the nubbling chit,[1]
He was tucked up so neat and so pretty ;
The rumbler[2] jugged off from his feet,
And he died with his face to the city.
He kicked, too, but that was all pride,
For soon you might see 'twas all over ;
And as soon as the noose was untied,
Then at darkey we waked him in clover,
And sent him to take a ground sweat.

NINETEENTH CENTURY.

LETTER FROM A THIEF AT THE HULKS.

Written in 1876 (*quoted by Lorédan Larchey, Dict. Hist. d'Argot*).

E la traverse[3] de Lontou.[4]—Mon cher camerluche,[5] me voilà enfin démarré de ce maudit ponton d'amar-rage, par la grâce du meke[6] ou du barbé,[7] et sans être aquigé, qui nous a trimballé[8] igo[9] après nous avoir secoué pendant quinze reluis[10] au milieu des prés salés.[11]

Tu m'as bonni[12] avant de décarrer[13] que je te raccorde[14] par une lazagen[15] du truc[16] dont les artoupans[17] de cette traverse nous ont pessignés.[18] Je bonnirai qu'ils nous

1 Nubbling chit, *gallows.*	10 Reluis, *days.*
2 Rumbler, *cart.*	11 Prés salés, *sea.*
3 Traverse, *hulks.*	12 Bonni, *said.*
4 Lontou, *Toulon.*	13 Décarrer, *going.*
5 Camerluche, *comrade.*	14 Raccorde, *relate.*
6 Meke, *god.*	15 Lazagen, *letter.*
7 Barbé, *devil.*	16 Truc, *manner.*
8 Trimballé, *brought.*	17 Artoupans, *warders.*
9 Igo, *here.*	18 Pessignés, *received.*

ont embroqués [1] d'une chasse [2] moustique [3] attendu que le quart d'œil [4] de Rochefort nous a rafilé la manquesse [5] auprès de son camerluche de cette traverse.

Les gaffiers [6] sont plus mouchiques [7] que lago ; [8] il faut igo avoir le loubion en poigne [9] pour leur jacter ; [10] ou ils vous bousculent en véritables artoupans. La cavale [11] est plus difficile que lago ; cependant les messiers de cambrouse [12] n'ont pas la même chaleur à pessigner [13] les fagots en campe. [14]

La tortillade [15] est la même pour la quantité, mais le pivois [16] est plus chenu, le larton [17] un peu plus savonné [18] que lago et la batouse à limace [19] plus chenue aussi.

La satonnade [20] roule à balouf. [21] Le toc [22] est un bridon de gaye [23] qui a une poigne esquintante. [24]

Rien de plus à te bonnir sinon que la Fouine, Classique, Escarpe et Crève-Cœur te refilent [25] leurs bécots de chouettes, [26] et pour mon arga, [27] que je serai jusqu'au moment de canner [28] ton dévoué.

LA HYÈNE.

[1] Embroqués, *looked at.*

[2] Chasse, *eye.*

[3] Moustique, *bad.*

[4] Quart d'œil, *commissaire de police.*

[5] Rafilé la manquesse, *given a bad character.*

[6] Gaffiers, *warders, guards.*

[7] Mouchiques, *bad.*

[8] Lago, *over there.*

[9] Loubion en poigne, *hat in hand.*

[10] Jacter, *to speak.*

[11] Cavale, *flight.*

[12] Messiers de cambrouse, *country folk.*

[13] Pessigner, *to molest.*

[14] Fagots en campe, *runaway convicts.*

[15] Tortillade, *food.*

[16] Pivois, *wine.*

[17] Larton, *bread.*

[18] Savonné, *white.*

[19] Batouse à limace, *linen.*

[20] Satonnade, *bastinade.*

[21] A balouf, *terribly.*

[22] Toc, *executioner.*

[23] Bridon de gaye, *horse-bridle.*

[24] Poigne esquintante, *terribly strong hand.*

[25] Refilent, *send.*

[26] Bécots de chouettes, *fondest kisses.*

[27] Pour mon arga, *on my part, as for me.*

[28] Canner, *to die.*

NINETEENTH CENTURY.

AUTOBIOGRAPHY OF A THIEF IN THIEVES' LANGUAGE.

By J. W. HORSLEY,
*Chaplain of H. M. Prison,
Clerkenwell.*

TRANSLATED
INTO THE LANGUAGE OF
FRENCH THIEVES.

 WAS born in 1853 at Stamford Hill, Middlesex. My parents removed from there to Stoke Newington, when I was sent to an infant school. Some time afterwards I was taken by two pals (companions) to an orchard to cop (steal) some fruit, me being a mug (inexperienced) at the game. This got to my father's ears. When I went home he set about me with a strap until he was tired. He thought that was not enough, but tied me to a bedstead. You may be sure what followed. I got loose, tied a blanket and a counterpane together, fastened it to the bedstead, and let myself out of the window, and did not go home that

 E suis né en 1853 à Stamford Hill, Middlesex. Mes parents, de *lago*, allèrent *se pioler* à Stoke Newington, et l'on m'envoya à une école maternelle. Peu de temps après, deux de mes *fanandels* me menèrent à un verger pour *grinchir* des fruits, mais je n'étais qu'un *sinve* à ce *flanche*. Mon *dab* apprit la chose, et quand je *rentolai à la caginotte* il me *refila une purge* avec une courroie *jusqu'à plus soif*. Pensant que ce n'était pas assez, il me *ligota* au *pieu*. Vous vous doutez de ce qui arriva. Je me débarassai des *ligotes*, attachai un *embarras* à une couverture que je fixai au *pieu*, et je me laissai glisser par la *vanterne*. Je ne *rappli-*

night, but met my two pals and dossed (slept) in a haystack. Early next morning my pals said they knew where we could get some toke (food), and took me to a terrace. We went down the dancers (steps) to a safe, and cleared it out. Two or three days after I met my mother, who in tears begged of me to go home; so I went home. My parents moved to Clapton, when they sent me to school. My pals used to send stiffs (notes) to the schoolmaster, saying that I was wanted at home; but instead of that we used to go and smug snowy (steal linen) that was hung out to dry, or rob the bakers' barrows. Things went from bad to worse, so I was obliged to leave home again. This time I palled in with some older hands at the game, who used to take me a parlour-jumping (robbing rooms), putting me in where the windows was open. I used to take anything there was to steal, and at last they told me all about wedge (silver-plate), how I should know it by the ramp (hall-mark—rampant lion?); we used to break it up in small pieces and sell it to watchmakers, and afterwards to a fence down the Lane (Petticoat Lane). Two or three times a week I used to go to the Brit. (Britannia Theatre) in Hoxton, or the gaff (penny music-room) in Shoreditch. I used to steal anything to make money to go to these places. Some nights I used to sleep at my pals' houses, sometimes in a shed where there was a fire kept burning night and day. All this time I had

quai pas à la niche cette *nogue-là*, mais j'allai retrouver mes deux *fanandes* et je *pioncai* dans une meule de foin. Au *matois* mes *fanandels* me *bonnirent* qu'ils *conobraient* où nous pouvions *acquiger* de la *tortillade* et me menèrent à une rangée de *pioles*. Nous dégringolons les *grimpants*. Nous *embardons* dans un garde-manger et nous le *rinçons*. Deux ou trois *reluis* après, je me *casse le mufle* sur ma *dabuche*, qui, en *chialant*, me supplie de *rappliquer à la niche*, ce que j'ai fait. Mes parents alors ont déménagé et sont allés à Clapton. Alors on m'a envoyé à l'école. Mes *camerluches balançaient* des *lazagnes* au maître d'école disant qu'on me demandait à la *niche*, mais au lieu de cela nous allions *déflorer la pictouse* ou *rincer* les *bagnoles* des *lartonniers*. Les choses allèrent de mal en pis et je fus obligé de *redécarrer de la niche*. Cette fois je me mis avec des *fanandes* plus *affranchis*, qui me menaient avec eux *rincer les cambriolles*, me faisant *enquiller* par les *vanternes* ouvertes. Je *mettais la pogne* sur toute la *camelote* bonne à *grinchir*, et enfin ils me firent *entraver* tout le *truc* de la *blanquette*, et comment je la *reconobrerais* par la marque; nous la *frangissions* en petits morceaux et nous la *fourgattions* chez des *boguistes* et ensuite chez un *fourgue* qui demeurait dans la Lane. Deux ou trois fois par semaine je suis allé au Brit. de Hoxton ou au *beuglant* de Shoreditch. Je *grinchissais* n'importe quelle *camelote* pour *affurer de la thune* afin d'aller à ces endroits.

escaped the hands of the reelers (police), but one day I was taken for robbing a baker's cart, and got twenty-one days. While there I made pals with another one who came from Shoreditch, and promised to meet him when we got out, which I did, and we used to go together, and left the other pals at Clapton.

At last one day we was at St. John's Wood. I went in after some wedge. While picking some up off the table I frightened a cat, which upset a lot of plates when jumping out of the window. So I was taken and tried at Marylebone Police Court and sent to Feltham Industrial School. I had not been there a month before I planned with another boy to guy (run away), and so we did, but was stopped at Brentford and took back to the school, for which we got twelve strokes with the birch. I thought when I first went there that I knew a great deal about thieving, but I found there was some there that knew more, and I used to pal in with those that knew the most. One day, while talking with a boy, he told me he was going home in a day or so. He said his friends was going to claim him out because he was more than sixteen years old. When my friends came to see me I told them that they could claim me out,

Des *sorgues*, je *pionçais* dans *les pioles* de mes *fanandels*, quelquefois sous un hangar où il y avait un *rif* qui *riffodait jorne* et *sorgue*. Cependant, j'avais échappé aux *pinces* de la *riflette*, mais un *reluis* j'ai été *pomaqué* pour avoir *rincé* une *bagnole* de *lartonnier* et *enflacqué* pendant vingt et un *reluis*. *Lago* j'ai eu pour *amarre* un autre qui venait de Shoreditch et je lui ai promis un rendez-vous pour quand nous serions *défouraillés;* alors nous sommes devenus *amarres d'attaques* et nous avons laissé les autres *zigues* à Clapton.

Enfin, un jour nous nous trouvions à St. John's Wood et j'étais à *soulever de la blanquette*. Pendant que je mettais *la pogne dessus*, je *coquai le taf* à un *greffier* qui fit dégringoler un tas de *morfiantes* en sautant par la *vanterne*. De cette façon, je fus *pomaqué*, mis en *gerbement* au *carré des gerbes* de Marylebone et envoyé au pénitencier de Feltham. Y avait pas une *marque* que j'y étais que je me préparai avec un autre à *faire la cavale*. Après avoir *décarré*, nous fûmes *engraillés* à Brentford et *renflacqués* au pénitencier où l'on nous donna douze coups de la verge. Je croyais, quand j'y avais été *enfouraillé* tout d'abord, que j'étais un *pègre* bien *affranchi*, mais je *conobrai* là des *camerluches* qui en *conobraient* plus que *mézigue* et j'avais pour *amarres* ceux qui étaient les plus *mariolles*. Un *reluis* en *jaspinant* avec un *gosselin*, il me *jacte* que dans un *luisant* ou deux il allait *rappliquer à la niche*. Il me *bonnit* que ses parents allaient le réclamer

and with a good many fair promises that I would lead a new life if they did so. They got me out of the school. When I got home I found a great change in my father, who had taken to drink, and he did not take so much notice of what I done as he used. I went on all straight the first few moons at costering. One day there was a "fête" at Clapton, and I was coming home with my kipsy (basket); I had just sold all my goods out. I just stopped to pipe (see) what was going on, when a reeler came up to me and rapped (said), "Now, ——, you had better go away, or else I shall give you a drag (three months in prison)." So I said "all right;" but he rapped, "It is not all right; I don't want any sauce from you or else I shall set about (beat) you myself." So I said, "What for? I have done nothing; do you want to get it up for me?" Then he began to push me about, so I said I would not go at all if he put his dukes (hands) on me. Then he rammed my nut (head) against the wall and shook the very life out of me. This got a scuff (crowd) round us, and the people ask him what he was knocking me about for, so he said, "This is young —— just come home from a schooling (a term in a reformatory)." So he did not touch me again; so I went home, turned into kip (bed) and could not get up for two or three days, because he had given me such a shaking, him being a great powerful man, and me only a little fellow. I still went on all straight until things

parcequ'il avait plus de seize *bris-ques*. Quand mes parents sont venus me voir je leur *bonnis* qu'ils pouvaient me faire *défourailler*, et leur ayant fait de belles promesses de *rengracier* s'ils y consentaient ils m'ont fait *défourailler*. Quand j'ai *aboulé* à la *kasbah*, j'ai trouvé du changement chez mon *dab* qui s'était mis à *se poivrer*, et il n'a pas fait autant d'attention que *d'habitongue* à mes *flanches*. *Rangé des voitures* pendant les premières *marques* comme marchand des quatre saisons. Un *reluis* il y avait une fête à Clapton et je *rappliquais* avec mon panier. Je venais de *laver* toute ma *camelote* et de m'arrêter pour *rechasser* ce qui se passait quand un *roussin aboule* à moi et me *bonnit*, "Allons, dé-campe d'ici, ou je te *mets à l'ombre* pour trois *marques*." Je lui *bonnis* "c'est bien;" mais il me *jacte*, "C'est pas tout ça, tâche de filer doux, autrement je te *passe à tra-vers tocquardement*." Que je lui *bonnis*, "Pourquoi? Je n'ai rien fait; c'est une querelle d'allemand que vous me cherchez là." Alors il se met à me *refiler des poussées* et je lui dis que je ne le suivrais pas s'il me *harponnait*. Alors il me *sonne* la *tronche* contre le mur et me secoue *tocquardement*. Le *trèpe* s'assemble autour de *nouzailles* et les *gonces* lui *demandent* pourquoi il me bouscule. Alors, qu'il dit, "C'est le jeune —— qui vient de sortir du pénitencier." Puis, il me laisse tran-quille, de sorte que j'ai *rappliqué* à la *niche*, et je me suis mis au *pucier* où je suis resté deux ou trois *reluis*,

got very dear at the market. I had been down three or four days running, and could not buy anything to earn a deaner (shilling) out of. So one morning I found I did not have more than a caser (five shillings) for stock-pieces (stock-money). So I thought to myself, "What shall I do?" I said, "I know what I will do. I will go to London Bridge rattler (railway) and take a deaner ride and go a wedge-hunting (stealing plate)." So I took a ducat (railway ticket) for Sutton in Surrey, and went a wedge-hunting. I had not been at Sutton very long before I piped a slavey (servant) come out of a chat (house), so when she had got a little way up the double (turning), I pratted (went) in the house. When inside I could not see any wedge lying about the kitchen, so I screwed my nut in the washhouse and I piped three or four pair of daisy roots (boots). So I claimed (stole) them, and took off the lid of my kipsy and put them inside, put a cloth over them, and then put the lid on again, put the kipsy on my back as though it was empty, and guyed to the rattler and took a brief (ticket) to London Bridge, and took the daisies to a Sheney (Jew) down the gaff, and done (sold) them for thirty blow (shillings).

The next day I took the rattler to Forest Hill, and touched for (suc-

car il m'avait *harponné tocquarde-ment*, lui qui était un grand *balouf* et moi un pauvre petit *gosselin*. Tout a marché *chouettement* pendant quelque temps mais la *camelote* est devenue très chère au marché. Depuis trois ou quatre *reluis* je n'avais pas le moyen *d'abloquer* de quoi *affurer* un shilling. Alors un *reluis* je me suis aperçu que je n'avais pas plus de cinq shillings comme fonds de commerce et je me suis demandé: quel *truc* est-ce que je vais *maquiller?* Je me *bonnis*, je connais bien mon *flanche*. *J'acquigerai le roulant vif* de London Bridge pour un shilling et je tâcherai *de mettre la pogne* sur de la *blan-quette*. Alors je prends une *brème* pour Sutton en Surrey et je me mets en chasse pour la *blanquette*. Y avait pas longtemps que j'étais à Sutton quand j'*allume* une *cambrousière* qui *décarrait* d'une *piole*. Dès qu'elle a tourné le coin de la rue, j'*embarde* dans la *piole*. Une fois dedans je n'ai pas *re-mouché* de *blanquette* dans la cuisine, et, passant ma *sorbonne* dans l'arrière-cuisine, j'ai *mouchaillé* trois ou quatre paires de *ripatons*. J'ai *mis la pogne* dessus, et ôtant le couvercle de mon panier, je les y ai *plaqués* avec une pièce d'étoffe par dessus et j'ai remis le couvercle, puis j'ai *plaqué* mon panier sur mon *andosse* comme s'il était vide, et je me suis *cavalé* jusqu'au *roulant vif ; acquigé* un billet pour London Bridge, porté les *ripatons* à un *youtre* près du *beu-glant* et *fourgué* pour trente shillings.

Le lendemain j'ai *acquigé* le *rou-lant vif* jusqu'à Forest Hill, et j'ai

ceeded in getting) some wedge and a kipsy full of clobber (clothes). You may be sure this gave me a little pluck, so I kept on at the old game, only with this difference, that I got more pieces for the wedge. I got three and a sprat (3*s.* 6*d.*) an ounce. But afterwards I got 3*s.* 9*d.*, and then four blow. I used to get a good many pieces about this time, so I used to clobber myself up and go to the concert. But though I used to go to these places I never used to drink any beer for some time afterwards. It was while using one of those places I first met a sparring bloke (pugilist), who taught me how to spar and showed me the way to put my dukes up. But after a time I gave him best (left him) because he used to want to bite my ear (borrow) too often. It was while I was with him that I got in company with some of the widest (cleverest) people in London. They used to use at (frequent) a pub in Shoreditch. The following people used to go in there —toy-getters (watch-stealers), magsmen (confidence-trick men), men at the mace (sham loan offices), broadsmen (card-sharpers), peter-claimers (box-stealers), busters and screwsmen (burglars), snide-pitchers (utterers of false coin), men at the duff (passing false jewellery), welshers (turf-swindlers), and skittle-sharps. Being with this nice mob (gang) you may be sure what I learned. I went out at the game three or four times a week, and used to touch almost every time. I went on like this for very near a stretch (year) without

mis la pogne sur de la *blanquette* et un panier plein de *fringues.* Bien sûr, cela m'a donné un peu de courage, alors j'ai continué le même *flanche* avec cette différence seulement, que j'ai *affuré* plus d'*auber* pour la *blanquette.* On m'en a *foncé* trois shillings sixpence l'once. Mais après j'en ai eu trois shillings neuf pence, et puis quatre shillings. J'*affurais* pas mal de *galtos* à cette époque, de sorte que je me *peaussais chouettement* pour aller au *beuglant.* Mais si j'allais à ces sortes d'endroits, je ne *pictais* jamais de *moussante.* C'est à ce moment et dans un de ces endroits que j'ai fait la connaissance d'un lutteur qui m'a appris la boxe et à me servir de mes *louches.* Mais peu après, je l'ai *lâché* parcequ'il me *coquait* trop souvent *des coups de pied dans les jambes.* C'est en sa compagnie que j'ai fait la connaissance de quelques-uns des *pègres* les plus *mariolles* de Londres. Ils fréquentaient un *cabermon* de Shoreditch. Ceux qui y allaient étaient des *grinchisseurs de bogues,* des *américains,* des *guinals à la manque,* des *grecs,* des *valtreusiers,* des *grinchisseurs au fric-frac,* des passeurs de *galette à la manque,* des voleurs *à la broquille,* des bookmakers *à la manque,* et des *grinches* joueurs de quilles. Etant avec cette *gironde gance,* vous pouvez imaginer ce que j'ai appris. J'allais *turbiner* trois ou quatre fois par *quart de marque,* et je réussissais presque toujours. J'ai continué ainsi pendant près d'une *brisque* sans être *enfilé.* Une *nogue* que j'étais avec les *fanandes,* j'ai été

being smugged (apprehended). One night I was with the mob, I got canon (drunk), this being the first time. After this, when I used to go to concert-rooms, I used to drink beer. It was at one of these places down Whitechapel I palled in with a trip and stayed with her until I got smugged. One day I was at Blackheath, I got very near canon, and when I went into a place I claimed two wedge spoons, and was just going up the dancers, a slavey piped the spoons sticking out of my skyrocket (pocket), so I got smugged. While at the station they asked me what my monarch (name) was. A reeler came to the cell and cross-kidded (questioned) me, but I was too wide for him. I was tried at Greenwich; they ask the reeler if I was known, and he said no. So I was sent to Maidstone Stir (prison) for two moon. When I came out, the trip I had been living with had sold the home and guyed; that did not trouble me much. The only thing that spurred (annoyed) me was me being such a flat to buy the home. The mob got me up a break (collection), and I got between five or six foont (sovereigns), so I did not go out at the game for about a moon.

The first day that I went out I went to Slough and touched for a wedge kipsy with 120 ounces of wedge in it, for which I got nineteen quid (sovereigns). Then I carried on a nice game. I used to get canon every night. I done things now what I should have been ashamed to do before I took to that accursed

poivre pour la première fois. Et après ça, quand j'ai été au *beuglant*, j'ai *pitanché* de la *moussante*. C'est à un de ces endroits dans Whitechapel que je me suis *collé* avec une *largue*, et je suis resté avec elle jusqu'à ce que j'ai été *enfouraillé*. Un *reluis*, j'étais à Blackheath, je me suis presque *poivrotté*, et en*bardant* dans une *piole*, j'ai *grinchi* deux *poches* de *plâtre*. Je grimpais le *lève-pieds*, quand une *cambrousière* a *remouché* les cuillers qui sortaient de ma *profonde*, c'est comme cela que j'ai été *pomaqué*. A la *motte*, on m'a demandé mon *centre*. Un *rousse* est venu à la *botte* et m'a fait la *jactance*, mais j'ai été trop *mariolle* pour *entraver*. J'ai été mis en *sapement* à Greenwich ; on a demandé au *rousse* s'il me *conobrait* et il a répondu *nibergue*. Alors on m'a envoyé à la *motte* de Maidstone pour deux *marques*. Quand j'ai été *défouraillé*, la *largue* avec qui je vivais avait tout *lavé* et s'était fait la *débinette*, mais cela m'était égal. La seule chose qui m'a ennuyé, c'est que j'avais été assez *sinve* pour *abloquer* le *fourbi*. La *gance* m'a fait une *manche* et j'ai eu de cinq à six *sigues*, de sorte que je n'ai pas *rappliqué* au *turbin* pour près d'une *marque*.

Le premier *reluis* de ma *guérison* je suis allé à Slough et j'ai *soulevé* un panier, qui contenait 120 onces de *blanquette*, pour lequel j'ai reçu dix-neuf livres sterling. Alors j'étais bien *à la marre*. J'étais *pion* toutes les *sorgues*. J'ai *maquillé* des *flanches* alors que j'aurais eu honte de faire si je ne m'étais pas mis

e

drink. It was now that I got acquainted with the use of twirls (skeleton-keys).

A little time after this I fell (was taken up) again at St. Mary Cray for being found at the back of a house, and got two moon at Bromley Petty Sessions as a rogue and vagabond ; and I was sent to Maidstone, this being the second time within a stretch. When I fell this time I had between four and five quid found on me, but they gave it me back, so I was landed (was all right) this time without them getting me up a lead (a collection).

I did not fall again for a stretch. This time I got two moon for assaulting the reelers when canon. For this I went to the Steel (Bastile—Coldbath Fields Prison), having a new suit of clobber on me and about fifty blow in my brigh (pocket). When I came out I went at the same old game.

One day I went to Croydon and touched for a red toy (gold watch) and red tackle (gold chain) with a large locket. So I took the rattler home at once. When I got into Shoreditch I met one or two of the mob, who said, "Hallo, been out to-day? Did you touch?" So I said, "Usher" (yes). So I took them in, and we all got canon. When I went to the fence he bested (cheated) me because I was drunk, and only gave me £8 10s. for the lot. So the next day I went to him, and asked him if he was not going to grease my duke (put money into my hand). So he said, "No."

à *pitancher gourdement.* C'est alors que j'ai appris le *truc* des *caroubles.*

Peu après j'ai été *emballé* de nouveau à St. Mary Cray pour avoir été *pigé* derrière une *piole* et j'ai été *gerbé* à deux *marques* au *juste* de Bromley comme *ferlampier* et *purotin,* puis j'ai été envoyé à Maidstone pour la seconde fois dans la *brisque.* Quand j'ai été *emballé,* j'avais de quatre à cinq *sigues* sur mon *gniasse,* mais on me les a rendus, de sorte que j'ai pu cette fois me passer de la *manche.*

Je n'ai pas été *emballé* pendant une *brisque.* Cette fois, j'ai été *sapé* à deux *marques* pour avoir *refilé une voie* aux *rousses* pendant que j'étais *pion.* On m'a envoyé, pour ce *flanche,* à la Steel. J'avais des *fringues d'altèque* et environ cinquante shillings dans ma *fouillouse.* Quand j'ai *décarré* j'ai *rappliqué au truc.*

Un *reluis,* je suis allé à Croydon et j'ai *fait* un *bogue de jonc* et une *bride de jonc* avec un gros médaillon. Puis j'ai *acquigé* dare-dare le *roulant vif.* Quand j'ai *aboulé* à Shoreditch, je suis *tombé en frime* avec deux *pègres* de la *gance* qui m'ont *bonni,* "Eh bien, tu as *turbiné* ce *luisant,* as-tu *fait* quelque chose?" Alors que je *jacte,* "*Gy.*" Puis je les ai emmenés et nous nous sommes tous *piqué le blaire.* Quand je suis allé chez le *fourgat* il m'a *refait* parceque j'étais *poivre* et m'a *aboulé* seulement £8 10s. pour le tout. Alors le lendemain, je suis allé à lui et lui ai demandé s'il n'allait pas me *foncer du*

Then he said, "I will give you another half-a-quid;" and said, "Do anybody, but mind they don't do you." So I thought to myself, "All right, my lad; you will find me as good as my master," and left him.

Some time after that affair with the fence, one of the mob said to me, "I have got a place cut and dried; will you come and do it?" So I said, "Yes; what tools will you want?" And he said, "We shall want some twirls and the stick (crowbar), and bring a neddie (life preserver) with you." And he said, "Now don't stick me up (disappoint); meet me at six to-night." At six I was in the meet (trysting-place), and while waiting for my pal I had my daisies cleaned, and I piped the fence that bested me go along with his old woman (wife) and his two kids (children), so I thought of his own words, "Do anybody, but mind they don't do you." He was going to the Surrey Theatre, so when my pal came up I told him all about it. So we went and screwed (broke into) his place, and got thirty-two quid, and a toy and tackle which he had bought on the crook. We did not go and do the other place after that. About two moon after this the same fence fell for buying two finns (£5 notes), for which he got a stretch and a half. A little while after this I fell at Isleworth for being found in a conservatory adjoining a parlour, and got remanded at the Tench (House of Detention)

michon. Il répond, "*Nibergue.*" Puis il ajoute, "Je vais te *foncer* un autre demi-*sigue*," et aussi, "*Mène en bateau* les *sinves*, mais ne te laisse pas *mener en bateau*." Je me suis dit, "*Chouette*, ma *vieille branche;* tu me trouveras aussi *mariolle* que mon maître," et je l'ai quitté.

Quelque temps après ce *flanche* avec le *fourgat* une des *poisses* de la *gance* me *bonnit*, "J'ai un *poupard nourri*, veux-tu en être?" Que je lui *bonnis*, "*Gy*, de quelles *alènes* as-tu besoin?" Il me *jacte*, "Il nous faut des *rossignols* et le *sucre de pomme;* tu apporteras un *tourne-clef*." Il me *bonnit*, "Ne me *lâche* pas au bon moment, nous nous rencontrerons à six *plombes* cette *nogue*." Six *plombes crossaient* quand j'ai *aboulé* au rendez-vous, et en attendant mon *fanande* je faisais cirer mes *ripatons*, quand j'ai *mouchaillé* le *fourgue* qui m'avait *refait* qui se balladait avec sa *fesse* et ses deux *mômes*. Alors j'ai pensé à ce qu'il m'avait *bonni*, "*Mène* les *sinves* en bateau mais ne laisse pas *gourer tézigue*." Il allait à la *misloque* de Surrey, alors, quand mon *poteau aboule*, je lui *dégueularde* tout le *flanche*. Puis nous *filons le luctrème*, nous *enquillons* dans la *piole* et nous *mettons la pogne sur* trente-deux *sigues*, sur un *bogue* et une *bride* que le *fourgue* avait *abloqués à la manque*. Nous ne sommes pas allés aux autres endroits après cela. Deux *marques* après, ce même *fourgue* a été *poissé* pour avoir *abloqué* deux *fafiots* de cinq livres sterling, et *sapé* à une *longe* et six *marques*. Peu de temps

for nine days, but neither Snuffy (Reeves, the identifier) nor Mac (Macintyre) knew me, so I got a drag, and was sent to the Steel. While I was in there, I see the fence who we done, and he held his duke at me as much as to say, "I would give you something, if I could ;" but I only laughed at him. I was out about seven moon, when one night a pal of mine was half drunk, and said something to a copper (policeman) which he did not like ; so he hit my pal, and I hit him in return. So we both set about him. He pulled out his staff, and hit me on the nut, and cut it open. Then two or three more coppers came up, and we got smugged, and got a sixer (six months) each. So I see the fence again in Stir.

On the Boxing-day after I came out I got stabbed in the chest by a pal of mine who had done a school-ing. We was out with one another all the day getting drunk, so he took a liberty with me, and I landed him one on the conk (nose) ; so we had a fight, and he put the chive (knive) into me. This made me sober, so I asked him what made him such a coward. He said, "I meant to kill you ; let me kiss my wife and child, and then smug me." But I did not do that. This made me a little thoughtful of the sort of life I was carrying on. I thought, "What

après j'ai été *emballé* à Isleworth pour avoir été *pigé* dans une serre voisine d'un parloir et remis à la Tench pour neuf *reluis*, mais ni Snuffy ni Mac ne me *conobraient*, de sorte que j'ai été *sapé* à trois *marques* et *malade* à la *motte*. Pendant que j'y étais, j'ai vu le *fourgue* que nous avions *refait*, et il a tendu la *pince* de mon côté comme pour *bonnir*, "Je te *refilerais une purge* si je pouvais," mais cela m'a fait *rigoler*. J'étais *guéri* depuis environ sept *marques* quand une *sorgue*, un de mes *fanandes*, qui était *poivre*, *jacte* quelque chose à un *roussin* qui ne l'ayant pas à la *bonne*, l'a *sonné* et moi j'ai *sonné* le *roussin* à mon tour. Tous deux alors nous lui avons *tra-vaillé le cadavre*. Il a tiré son bâton, m'a *sonné* le *citron* et me l'a fendu. Alors deux ou trois *roussins* sont arrivés, nous ont *emballés* et nous avons été *gerbés* à six *marques*. De sorte que j'ai revu le *fourgue* au *château*.

Au Boxing-day après ma *guéri-son*, un de mes *fanandes* m'a *refilé* un coup de *bince* dans le *hari-cot*. Il avait été déjà *enfouraillé* au *collège*. Nous nous étions *balladés* tout le *luisant* en nous *poivrottant*, de sorte que m'ayant manqué de re-spect, je lui ai *collé une châtaigne* sur le *morviau*. Nous nous sommes *em-poignés* et il a joué du *surin*. Cela m'a dégrisé et je lui ai demandé pourquoi il s'était montré aussi lâche. Il me *bonnit*, "Je voulais t'*estourbir*. Laisse-moi aller *sucer la pomme* à ma *largue* et mon *môme* et fais-moi *emballer*." Mais je n'ai pas voulu.

if I should have been killed then!" But this, like other things, soon passed away.

After the place got well where I was chived, me and another screwed a place at Stoke Newington, and we got some squeeze (silk) dresses, and two sealskin jackets, and some other things. We tied them in a bundle, and got on a tram. It appears they knew my pal, and some reelers got up too. So when I piped them pipe the bundle, I put my dukes on the rails of the tram and dropped off, and guyed down a double before you could say Jack Robinson. It was a good job I did, or else I should have got lagged (sent to penal servitude), and my pal too, because I had the James (crowbar) and screws (skeleton keys) on me. My pal got a stretch and a half. A day or two after this I met the fence who I done; so he said to me, "We have met at last." So I said, "Well, what of that?" So he said, "What did you want to do me for?" So I said, "You must remember you done me; and when I spoke to you about it you said, ' Do anybody; mind they don't do you.'" That shut him up.

One day I went to Lewisham and touched for a lot of wedge. I tore up my madam (handkerchief) and tied the wedge in small packets and put them into my pockets. At Bishopsgate Street I left my kipsy at a barber's shop, where I always

Cela m'a fait réfléchir un peu au genre de vie que je menais et je me dis, "J'aurais bien pu être *refroidi.*" Mais bientôt je n'y pensai plus.

Une fois guéri du coup de *bince,* nous avons *refilé le luctrème* d'une *piole* à Stoke Newington, et nous avons *grinchi* des robes de *lyonnaise* et deux jaquettes de peau de phoque et d'autre *camelote.* Nous en avons fait un *pacsin* et nous avons pris le tram. On *conobrait* mon *fanande,* paraît-il, et des *rousses* y montent avec *nouzailles.* Quand je vois qu'ils *remouchent* le *pacsin,* je mets mes *agrafes* sur le *pieu* d'appui du tram, je saute, je *fais patatrot* au coin de la rue et je cours encore. C'est *bate* pour moi d'avoir agi ainsi autrement j'aurais été *gerbé à bachasse* et mon *fanande* aussi parceque j'avais le *Jacques* et les *caroubles* sur *mézigue.* Mon *fanande* a été *sapé* à une *longe* et demie. Un *reluis* ou deux après, je me *casse le mufle* sur le *fourgat* que j'avais *refait,* et il me *jacte,* "Te voilà enfin!" Je lui réponds, "Eh bien, et puis après?" "Pourquoi m'as-tu *refait?*" dit-il. Et je lui réponds, "Rappelle-toi que tu as *refait mon gniasse,* et quand je t'en ai *jacté* tu m'as *répondu,* ' *Mène en bateau* qui tu voudras, mais ne te laisse pas *enfoncer.*'" Et cela a coupé la *chique* à *sézigue.*

Un jour je vais à Lewisham et je *grinchis* un lot de *blanquette.* Je déchire mon *blavin,* je fais des petits *pacsins* de la *blanquette* et je les *plaque* dans mes *profondes.* A Bishopsgate St. je dépose mon panier dans la *boutogue* d'un *merlan* où je le laissais

left it when not in use. I was going through Shoreditch, when a reeler from Hackney, who knew me well, came up and said, "I am going to run the rule over (search) you." You could have knocked me down with a feather, me knowing what I had about me. Then he said, "It's only my joke; are you going to treat me?" So I said "Yes," and began to be very saucy, saying to him, "What catch would it be if you was to turn me over?" So I took him into a pub which had a back way out, and called for a pint of stout, and told the reeler to wait a minute. He did not know that there was an entrance at the back; so I guyed up to Hoxton to the mob and told them all about it. Then I went and done the wedge for five-and-twenty quid.

One or two days after this I met the reeler at Hackney, and he said, "What made you guy?" So I said that I did not want my pals to see me with him. So he said it was all right. Some of the mob knew him and had greased his duke.

What I am about to relate now took place within the last four or five moon before I fell for this stretch and a half. One day I went to Surbiton. I see a reeler giving me a roasting (watching me), so I began to count my pieces for a jolly (pretence), but he still followed me, so at last I rang a bell, and waited till the slavey came, and the reeler waited till I came out, and then said, "What are you hawking of?" So

toujours quand je ne m'en servais pas. Je traversais Shoreditch, quand un *rousse* de Hackney, qui me *conobrait* bien, *aboule* et *jacte,* "Je vais te *rapioter.*" J'avais la *frousse* en pensant à ce que j'avais sur mon *gniasse.* Alors il me *bonnit,* "C'est une *batterie douce ;* est-ce que tu ne vas pas me *rincer les crochets ?* " Je lui *jacte,* " *Gy,*" et je me mets à *blaguer* avec lui, lui disant, "Quelle bonne prise, si vous me fouilliez ?" Je l'emmène alors dans un *cabermon* qui avait une sortie de derrière, je demande une pinte de stout, et je dis au *rousse* d'attendre une *broquille.* Il ne *conobrait* pas la *lourde* de derrière ; alors *je me la tire* jusqu'à Hoxton et j'apprends aux *fanàndes* ce qui s'était passé. Puis je *fourgue* la *blanquette* pour vingt-cinq livres.

Un ou deux *reluis* après, je *tombe en frime* avec la *riflette* à Hackney, et il me *jacte,* "Pourquoi t'es-tu *débiné ?*" Et je lui réponds que je ne voulais pas que mes *fanandes* me *remouchent* en sa compagnie. Quelques *pègres* de la *gance* le *conobraient* et lui avaient *foncé* du *michon.*

Ce que je vais raconter maintenant a eu lieu dans le courant des quatre ou cinq *marques* avant mon *sapement* à une *longe* et demie. Un *reluis* je vais à Surbiton. Je *remouche* une *riflette* qui me *poireautait.* Je fais la *frime* de compter mon *carle,* mais il me *prend en filature.* A la fin je tire une *retentissante,* et j'attends que la *larbine aboule,* le *rousse* attend que je *décarre* et me *jacte,* "Qu'est-ce que vous vendez

I said, "I am not hawking anything; I am buying bottles." So he said, "I thought you were hawking without a licence." As soon as he got round a double, I guyed away to Malden and touched for two wedge teapots, and took the rattler to Waterloo.

One day I took the rattler from Broad Street to Acton. I did not touch there, but worked my way to Shepherd's Bush; but when I got there I found it so hot (dangerous), because there had been so many tykes (dogs) poisoned, that there was a reeler at almost every double, and bills posted up about it. So I went to the Uxbridge Road Station, and while I was waiting for the rattler I took a religious tract, and on it was written, "What shall it profit a man if he gain the whole world and lose his own soul?" So I thought to myself, What good has the money done me what I have had? So instead of getting out at Brondesbury, I rode on to Broad Street, and paid the difference, and went home, and did not go out for about a week.

The Sunday following when I went to Uxbridge Road, I went down a lane called Mount Pleasant, at Clapton; it was about six o'clock. Down at the bottom of the lane you could get a fine view of Walthamstow; so while I was leaning against the rails I felt very miserable. I was thinking about when I was at Feltham. I thought I had threw away the only chance I had of doing

donc?" Et je réponds, "Je ne vends rien; j'achète des bouteilles." Il me dit alors, "Je croyais que vous faisiez le commerce sans patente." Aussitôt qu'il a tourné le coin, je vais à Malden et je *fais* deux théières de *plâtre*, puis j'*acquige le roulant* pour Waterloo.

Un jour j'*acquige le roulant* de Broad Street à Acton. *Lago*, je ne *fais* rien, et je continue ma route jusqu'à Shepherd's Bush; mais quand j'y *dévale* je trouve qu'il y avait tant de *pet* à cause de tous les *tambours* qu'on avait empoisonnés, qu'on avait mis une *riflette* presque à chaque coin de rue et des *babilles* partout. Alors je vais à la station du *roulant* de Uxbridge Road, et pendant que je *poireautais* pour le *roulant* je prends une brochure religieuse et il y avait *capi* dessus, "A quoi bon acquérir le monde entier si l'on doit perdre son âme?" Et je me *jacte*, A quoi m'a servi le *carme* que j'ai *affuré?* Et alors au lieu de descendre à Brondesbury, je continue jusqu'à Broad Street et j'*aboule* la différence. Je *rapplique* à la *caginotte* d'où je ne *décarre* pas d'un *quart de marque.*

Le dimanche d'après, en allant à Uxbridge Road, je dégringole une ruelle appellée Mount Pleasant, à Clapton; il était à peu près six *plombes.* Au fond de la ruelle on avait une vue magnifique de Walthamstow; donc pendant que je m'appuyais contre la palissade j'avais *des papillons noirs dans la sorbonne.* Je pensais au temps où j'étais à Feltham. Je voyais que j'avais perdu

better ; and as I stood thinking, the bells of St. Matthew's Church began to play a hymn-tune I had heard at Feltham. This brought tears to my eyes : this was the first time in my life that I thought what a wretch I was. I was going home very down-cast, when I met some pals, who said, "Why, what is the matter? you look miserable." So I said, "I don't feel very well." So they said, "Are you coming to have some-thing to drink ?—that will liven you up." So I went in with them, and began to drink very hard to drown my thoughts.

Monday morning I felt just the same as I always did ; I felt ready for the old game again. So I went to Hoxton, and some of the mob said to me, "Why, where have you been the last week or so—we thought you had fell?" So I told them I had been ill.

I went out the next day to Maiden-head, and touched for some wedge and a poge (purse), with over five quid in it.

A little while after this I went with two pals to the Palace at Mus-well Hill; the races were on. So when we got there, there was some reelers there what knew me, and my pals said, "You had better get away from here; if we touch you will take your whack (share) just the same." So I went and laid down on the grass. While laying there I piped a reeler whom I knew ; he had a nark (a

la seule occasion que j'avais de *rengracier* et étant là à réfléchir, les *retentissantes* de la *rampante* de Saint-Matthew se mirent à jouer un hymne que j'avais entendu à Feltham. Ceci me fit *baver des clignots :* pour la première fois de ma vie je *jacte* à *mézigue,* Quel misér-able tu es ! Je *rappliquais à la niche,* en *paumant mes plumes,* quand je *tombe en frime* de deux *fanandes* qui *bonnissent,* "Eh bien, qu'est-ce qu'il y a ; tu as une *sale bobinette ?*" Alors je *jacte,* "Je suis *tocquard.*" "Alors viens avec nous te *rincer la dalle,* ça te ragaillardira." Je suis allé avec eux, et j'ai commencé à *picter d'at-taque* pour noyer le chagrin.

Le lundi matin d'après, je me suis senti comme d'*habitongue* et prêt à *rappliquer* au *turbin.* Je suis allé à Hoxton, et quelques-uns de la *gance* m'ont *fait la jactance,* "Eh bien, où as-tu été pendant tous ces *reluis—* nous pensions que tu t'étais fait *em-baller ?*" Je leur réponds que j'avais été *tocquard.*

Le lendemain je suis allé à Maiden-head. J'ai *fait* de la *blanquette* et une *filoche* qui contenait plus de cinq *sigues.*

Peu après, je suis allé avec deux *fanandels* à Muswell Hill où il y avait des courses. Quand *nouzailles* y avons *dévalé,* il y avait des *roussins* qui me *conobraient* et mes *fanandes* me *jactent,* "Tu ferais mieux de te *cavaler;* si nous *rinçons,* tu auras ton *fade* tout de même." Alors j'allai me *plaquer* sur l'herbe. Pendant que j'y étais, je *remouche* un *rousse* que je *conobrais.* Il était accompagné d'une

policeman's spy) with him. So I went and looked about for my two pals and told them to look out for S. and his nark. About an hour after this they came to me and woke me up, and they said, "Come on, we have had a lucky touch for a half century in pap" (£50 in paper, *i.e.* notes). I thought they was only kidding (deceiving) at first, so they said, "Let us guy from here, and you will see if we are kidding to you." When we got into the rattler they showed me the pap; yes, there it was, fifty quids in double finns (£10 notes). We did them for £9 10*s*. each to a fence.

I took the rattler one day to Reigate and worked my way to Red Hill. So I went into a place and see some clobber hanging up, so I thought to myself, I will have it and take the rattler home at once; it will pay all expense. So while I was looking about I piped a little peter (parcel). When I took it up it had an address on it, and the address was to the vicarage; so I came out and asked a boy who lived there, and he said "Yes," but to make sure of it I went back again. This time I looked to the clobber more closely, and I see it was the same as clergymen wear, so I left it where it was. I always made it a rule never to rob a clergyman's house if I knew one to live there. I could have robbed several in my time, but I would not. So I took the rattler to Croydon and touched for some wedge, and come home. I used to go to Henley most every year when the rowing matches

riflette. Je cherche alors mes deux *fanandes* et leur dis, "*Acresto*, attention à S. et à sa *riflette !*" Une *plombe* après, environ, ils *aboulent* vers *mézigue*, m'éveillent, et me *jactent*, "*Aboule*, nous avons *barboté schpille*, nous avons *acquigé* cinquante livres en *faffes.*" Je croyais qu'ils me *collaient des vannes* mais ils me *jactent*, "*Dévalons d'icigo* et tu verras si nous te *gourrons*." Quand nous nous sommes *plaqués* dans le *roulant vif* ils m'ont montré les *faffes ; gy*, il y avait bien cinquante *sigues* en *faffes* de dix livres. Nous les avons *lavés* pour £9 10*s*. à un *fourgue*.

Je prends un *jorne* le *roulant* pour Reigate et je *trimarde* jusqu'à Red Hill. Puis j'*embarde* en une *piole* et je *remouche* des *harnais* suspendus. Je me *jacte*, je vais les *pégrer* et *acquiger* aussitôt le *roulant;* cela couvrira toutes mes dépenses. Alors en *gaffinant* par ci par là je *remouche* un petit *pacsin*. Je *mets la pogne dessus* et je *reluque* une adresse. Celle du curé. Alors je *décarre* et je demande à un *gosse* si ce n'est pas un *ratichon* qui demeure *lago ?* "*gy*," qu'il dit. Mais pour qu'il n'y ait pas d'erreur, je retourne. Cette fois, je *gaffine* de plus près le *harnais*, je vois que c'était celui d'un prêtre, et alors je l'ai laissé où il était. J'ai toujours eu soin de ne jamais *barboter une cambriolle* de prêtre quand je savais que c'en était une. J'aurais pu en *barboter* mais je n'ai pas voulu. Alors j'ai pris le *roulant vif* pour Croydon, j'ai *effarouché* de la *blanquette* et *rappliqué* à la *kasbah*. J'allais à Henley

was on which used to represent Oxford and Cambridge, only it used to be boys instead of men. The day the Prince of Wales arrived at Portsmouth when he came home from India, me and two pals took the rattler from Waterloo at about half-past six in the morning. When we got to Portsmouth we found it was very hot, there was on every corner of a street bills stuck up, "Beware of pickpockets, male and female," and on the tramcars as well. So one of my pals said, "There is a reeler over there who knows me, we had better split out" (separate). Me and the other one went by ourselves ; he was very tricky (clever) at getting a poge or a toy, but he would not touch toys because we was afraid of being turned over (searched). We done very well at poges ; we found after we knocked off we had between sixty or seventy quid to cut up (share), but our other pal had fell, and was kept at the station until the last rattler went to London, and then they sent him home by it. One day after this I asked a screwsman if he would lend me some screws, because I had a place cut and dried. But he said, "If I lend you them I shall want to stand in" (have a share) ; but I said, "I can't stand you at that ; I will grease your duke, if you like." But he said, "That would not do ;" so I said, "We will work together then ;" and he said, "Yes." So we went and done the place for fifty - five quid. So I worked with him until I fell for this stretch and a half.

presque chaque *berge* pendant les régattes qui étaient comme celles entre Oxford et Cambridge, seulement c'était des *gosses* au lieu de *gonces*. Le *reluis* où le *linspré* de Galles a *dévalé* à Portsmouth quand il a *renquillé* des Indes, *mézigue* et deux *fanandes*, nous avons *acquigé* le *roulant vif* vers six *plombes* et trente *broquilles* au *matois*. Quand nous avons *dévalé* à Portsmouth nous avons trouvé qu'il faisait très chaud ; il y avait à chaque coin de rue des *babilles*, "Prenez garde aux filous, mâles et femelles," et aussi sur les *trains de vache*. De sorte qu'un de mes *fanandes jacte*, "Il y a un *roussin labago* qui *conobre mon gniasse*, et il vaut mieux nous séparer." *Mézigue* et l'autre nous nous *débinons* de notre côté ; il n'était pas très *mariolle* pour *faire* une *filoche* ou un *bogue*, mais il ne voulait pas *grinchir* de *bogues* parce-qu'il avait le *taf* d'être *rapioté*. Nous avons eu de la *bate* pour les *morningues ;* nous avons trouvé, après avoir *turbiné*, que nous avions de soixante à soixante-dix *sigues* à *fader*, mais notre autre *fanande* avait été *pigé* et gardé au *bloc* jusqu'au dernier *roulant vif* pour Londres, puis renvoyé chez lui par ce *roulant*. Un *reluis* après ce *flanche*, je demande à un *caroubleur* s'il voulait me prêter des *caroubles* parceque j'avais un *poupard nourri*. Mais il *bonnit*, "Si je les prête, je veux mon *fade*." Que je réponds, "Ça fait *nib dans mes blots*, mais je te *carmerai* tout de même, si tu l'*as à la bonne*." Mais qu'il *bonnit*, "Ça fait *nib dans mes blots* aussi." Alors je *jacte*, "Nous *turbinerons*

He was very tricky at making twirls, and used to supply them all with tools. Me and the screwsman went to Gravesend and I found a dead 'un (uninhabited house), and we both went and turned it over and got things out of it which fetched us forty-three quid. We went one day to Erith; I went in a place, and when I opened the door there was a great tyke (dog), laying in front of the door, so I pulled out a piece of pudding (liver prepared to silence dogs) and threw it to him, but he did not move. So I threw a piece more, and it did not take any notice; so I got close up to it, and found it was a dead dog, being stuffed, so I done the place for some wedge and three overcoats; one I put on, and the other two in my kipsy. We went to Harpenden Races to see if we could find some dead 'uns; we went on the course. While we was there we saw a scuff, it was a flat that had been welshed, so my pal said, "Pipe his spark prop" (diamond pin). So my pal said, "Front me (cover me), and I will do him for it." So he pulled out his madam and done him for it. After we left the course, we found a dead 'un and got a peter (cashbox) with very near a century of quids in it. Then I carried on a nice game, what with the trips and the drink I very near went balmy (mad). It is no use of me telling you every place I done, or else you will think I am telling you the same things over again.

ensemble," et il me *rentasse* "*gy.*" Alors nous avons *rincé* la *piole* et *acquigé* cinquante-cinq *sigues.* J'ai *turbiné* ensuite avec lui puis j'ai été *pigé* et *sapé* à ces dix-huit *marques.* Il était très *mariolle* pour *maquiller* les *caroubles* et il fournissait des *alènes* à toute la *gance. Mézigue* et le *caroubleur* nous sommes allés à Gravesend où nous avons trouvé une *piole* vide. Nous avons *embardé* dedans et l'avons *rincée* ce qui nous a *affuré* quarante-trois *sigues.* Nous sommes allés un *reluis* à Erith. J'ai *enquillé* dans une *piole,* et quand j'ai *débâclé* la *lourde* il y avait un gros *tambour* couché devant, de sorte que j'ai tiré de ma *profonde* un morceau de *bidoche* et je la lui ai *balancée,* mais il n'a pas bougé. Je lui en ai jeté un autre morceau mais il est resté tranquille. Alors je m'approche et je vois que c'était un *cab* empaillé. J'ai *rincé* la *piole* pour la *blanquette* et trois *temples,* j'en ai *peaussé* un et *plaqué* les deux autres dans mon panier. Nous sommes allés ensuite aux courses de Harpenden pour voir si nous pouvions trouver des *pioles* sans *longsué;* nous allons sur la piste. Pendant que nous y sommes, nous *remouchons* une *tigne,* c'était un *gonsse* qui venait d'être *refait,* alors mon *fanande* me *jacte,* "*Gaffine* son épingle. Couvremoi, et je vais la lui *faire.*" Alors il *tire* son *blavin* et la lui *poisse.* Après avoir quitté la piste, nous trouvons une *piole* vide et nous *faisons* un *enfant* qui contenait une centaine de *sigues.* A partir de ce jour je me suis mis à *la rigolade* et à force

I will now tell you what happened the day before I fell for this stretch and a half. Me and the screwsman went to Charlton. From there we worked our way to Blackheath. I went in a place and touched for some wedge which we done for three pounds ten. I went home and wrung myself (changed clothes), and met some of the mob and got very near drunk. Next morning I got up about seven, and went home to change my clobber and put on the old clobber to work with the kipsy. When I got home my mother asked me if I was not a going to stop to have some breakfast? So I said, "No, I was in a hurry." I had promised to meet the screwsman and did not want to stick him up. We went to Willesden and found a dead 'un, so I came out and asked my pal to lend me the James and some twirls, and I went and turned it over. I could not find any wedge. I found a poge with nineteen shillings in it. I turned everything over, but could not find anything worth having, so I came out and gave the tools to my pal and told him. So he said, "Wasn't there any clobber?" So I said, "Yes, there's a cartload." So he said, "Go and get a kipsy full of it, and we will guy home." So I went back, and as I was going down the garden, the gardener it appears had been

d'aller avec les *chamègues* et de *pitan-cher*, je suis presque devenu *louffoque*. Il est inutile de vous raconter toutes les *pioles* que j'ai *rincées*, ce serait toujours la même histoire.

Je vous raconterai maintenant ce qui est arrivé juste la veille du *reluis* où j'ai été *enfouraillé* pour dix-huit *marques*. *Mézigue* et le *caroubleur* nous allons à Charlton. De *lago* nous *trimardons* jusqu'à Blackheath. J'*enquille* en une *piole* et j'*effarouche* de la *blanquette* que nous *fourguons* pour trois livres dix. Je *rapplique à la niche* et je change de *fringues*, je rencontre quelques *fanandes* de la *gance* et je me *poivrotte* presque. Le lendemain matin je me lève vers sept *plombes* pour changer de *fringues* et je me *peausse* du vieux *harnais* pour aller *turbiner* avec le panier. Quand je *rapplique à la niche* ma *dabuche* me *jacte* de rester pour la *refaite* du *matois*. Je *bonnis*, "Non, j'*ai à me patiner*." J'avais promis de rencontrer le *grinchisseur au fric-frac* et je ne voulais pas *flancher*. Nous sommes allés à Willesden et j'ai trouvé une *piole* sans personne, de sorte que j'en suis *décarré* et j'ai demandé à mon *fanandel* de me prêter le *Jacques* et des *caroubles*, j'ai *renquillé* et j'ai cherché la *camelote*. Je n'ai pas trouvé de *blanquette*. J'ai trouvé une *filoche* avec dix-neuf shillings. J'ai tout retourné mais je n'ai trouvé rien de *schpille* de sorte que j'ai *décarré*. J'ai *refilé* les *alènes* à mon *fanandel* et je lui ai dit le *flanche*. Alors, qu'il *jacte*, "N'y avait-il pas de *fringues?*" Et je lui réponds, "*Gy*, il y en a une char-

put there to watch the house, so he said, "What do you want here?" So I said, "Where do you speak to the servants?" So he said, "There is not anyone at home, they are all out." So he said, "What do you want with them?" So I said, "Do you know if they have any bottles to sell, because the servant told me to call another day?" So he said, "I do not know, you had better call another time." So I said, "All right, and good day to him." I had hardly got outside when he came rushing out like a man balmy, and said to me, "You must come back with me." So I said, "All right. What is the matter?" So when we got to the door he said, "How did you open this door?" So I said, "My good fellow, you are mad! how could I open it?" So he said, "It was not open half-an-hour ago because I tried it." So I said, "Is that any reason why I should have opened it?" So he said, "At any rate you will have to come to the station with me."

The station was not a stone's throw from the place, so he caught hold of me, so I gave a twist round and brought the kipsy in his face, and gave him a push and guyed. He followed, giving me hot beef (calling "Stop thief"). My pal came along, and I said to him,

retée." Alors, qu'il dit, "*Acquiges*-en plein un panier et *débinons*-nous." Je retourne, et comme je *dévalais* le long du *jaffier*, l'arroseur de ver-*douze* qui paraît-il, avait *été plaqué logo* pour faire le *gaffe*, me *bonnit*, "Qu'est-ce que tu *maquilles icigo ?*" Je réponds, "Où peut-on parler aux *larbins ?*" Et il dit, "Il n'y a personne à la maison, ils sont tous sortis. Que leur voulez-vous?" et je lui réponds, "Savez-vous s'ils ont des bouteilles à vendre, parceque la servante m'a dit de revenir?" "Je ne sais pas, revenez un autre jour." "C'est bien," que je lui dis; "je vous souhaite le bonjour." J'avais à peine *décarré* qu'il *aboule* comme un *louffoque* et me *jacte*, "Vous allez revenir avec moi." Je lui dis, "C'est bien, mon brave; qu'est-ce qu'il y a?" Et quand nous *aboulons juxte* la *lourde* il *jacte*, "Comment avez-vous fait pour ouvrir cette porte?" "Mon brave homme," lui dis-je, "vous êtes fou, comment aurais-je fait?" Alors il *jacte*, "Elle n'était pas ouverte il y a une demi-heure, car je l'ai essayée pour voir." Alors je *bonnis*, "Est-ce une raison pour que je l'aie ouverte?" Et il *jacte*, "Dans tous les cas, vous allez m'accompagner au poste de police."

Le *bloc* était à deux pas, alors il me met la *louche* au *colas* et je pirouette en lui *refilant* un coup de panier sur le *citron ;* puis je lui *refile une pousse* et je *fais patatrot*. Il me suit en *gueulant à la chienlit.* Mon *fanande* me suivait et je lui *bonnis*, "Défends-moi contre ce *pante*, il

"Make this man leave me alone, he is knocking me about," and I put a half-James (half-sovereign) in his hand, and said, "Guy." As I was running round a corner there was a reeler talking to a postman, and I rushed by him, and a little while after the gardener came up and told him all about it. So he set after me and the postman too, all the three giving me hot beef. This set other people after me, and I got run out. So I got run in, and was tried at Marylebone and re-manded for a week, and then fullied (fully committed for trial), and got this stretch and a half. Marylebone is the court I got my schooling from.—*From Macmillan's Magazine, October,* 1879.

me *passe à travers ;*" je *refile* à son *gniasse* un demi-souverain dans sa *louche* et je lui *dis,* " *Crompe ! crompe !*" Comme je tournais le coin, il y avait un *flique* qui *jactait* avec un facteur, je le dépasse en *faisant la paire,* et peu après l'*arroseur de verdouze aboule* et lui *débine le truc.* Alors, il me *cavale* avec le facteur, tous les trois *gueulant à la chienlit.* De cette façon, d'autres *pantes* se mettent à me *refiler* et je suis *pigé.* On *m'emballe,* on me *met sur la planche au pain* à Marylebone et on me remet à huitaine, alors *gerbé* à une *longe* et six *marques.* Maryle-bone est le *carré* où j'ai été *gerbé* au pénitencier.

NINETEENTH CENTURY.

'ARRY AT A POLITICAL PICNIC (1884).

Extract from Punch.

DEAR CHARLIE,

'OW are yer, my ribstone?[1] Seems scrumptious[2] to
    write the old name.
I 'ave quite lost the run[3] of you lately. Bin playing
    some dark little game?
I'm keepin' mine hup as per usual, fust in the pick
    of the fun,
For wherever there's larks on the tappy[4] there's
    'Arry as sure as a gun.

The latest new lay's[5] Demonstrations. You've heard on 'em, Charlie, no
    doubt,
For they're at 'em all over the shop. I 'ave 'ad a rare bustle about.
All my Saturday arfs are devoted to Politics. Fancy, old chump,[6]
Me doing the sawdusty reglar,[7] and follering swells on the stump!

But, bless yer, my bloater,[8] it isn't all chin-music,[9] votes, and "'Ear!
    'ear!"
Or they wouldn't catch me on the ready, or nail me[10] for ninepence. No
    fear!
Percessions I've got a bit tired of, hoof-padding,[11] and scrouging's dry rot,[12]
But Political Picnics mean sugar to them as is fly to wot's wot.[13]

Went to one on 'em yesterday, Charlie; a reglar old up and down lark.
The Pallis free gratis, mixed up with a old country fair in a park,
And Rosherville Gardens chucked in,[14] with a dash of the Bean Feast
    will do,
To give you some little idear of our day with Sir Jinks Bottleblue.

1 Ribstone, *old fellow.*
2 Scrumptious, *good.*
3 Lost the run, *lost sight.*
4 On the tappy, *i.e. on the tapis.*
5 Lay, *dodge.*
6 Old chump, *old fellow.*
7 Sawdusty reglar, *regular nonsense.*
8 My bloater, *my dear fellow.*

9 Chin-music, *talking.*
10 Nail me, *have me.*
11 Hoof-padding, *walking.*
12 Scrouging's dry rot, *squeezing in a crowd is tiresome.*
13 Fly to wot's wot, *knowing.*
14 Chucked in, *into the bargain.*

Make much of us, Charlie? Lor bless you, we might ha' bin blooming
    Chinese
A-doing the rounds at the 'Ealthries. 'Twas regular go as you please.
Lawn-tennis, quoits, cricket, and dancing for them as must be on the shove,
But I preferred pecking[1] and prowling, and spotting the mugs[2] making
    love.

Don't ketch me a-slinging my legs about arter a beast of a ball
At ninety degrees in the shade or so, Charlie, old chap, not at all.
Athletics ain't 'ardly my form, and a cutaway coat and tight bags[3]
Are the spechies of togs[4] for yours truly, and lick your loose flannels to
    rags.

So I let them as liked do a swelter;[5] I sorntered about on the snap.[6]
Rum game this yer Politics, Charlie, seems arf talkee-talkee and trap.
Jest fancy old Bottleblue letting " the multitood " picnic and lark,
And make Battersea Park of his pleasure-grounds, Bathelmy Fair of his
    park !

" To show his true love for the People ! " sez one vote-of-thanking tall-
    talker,
And wosn't it rude of a bloke[7] as wos munching a bun to cry " Walker?"
I'm Tory right down to my boots, at a price, and I bellered " 'Ear ! 'ear ! "
But they don't cop[8] yours truly with chaff none the more, my dear Charlie,
    no fear !

Old Bottleblue tipped me his flipper,[9] and 'oped I'd refreshed, and all that.
" Wy rather," sez I, " wot do you think ? " at which he stared into his 'at,
And went a bit red in the gills.[10] Must ha' thought me a muggins,[11] old
    man,
To ask sech a question of 'Arry—as though grubbing short was his plan.

I went the rounds proper, I tell yer ; 'twas like the free run of a Bar,
And Politics want lots o' wetting.[12] Don't ketch me perched up on a car,
Or 'olding a flag-pole no more. No, percessions, dear boy, ain't my fad,[13]
But Political Picnics with fireworks, and plenty of swiz[14] ain't 'arf bad.

---

[1] Pecking, *eating.*
[2] Mugs, *young fellows.*
[3] Bags, *trousers.*
[4] Togs, *clothes.*
[5] Do a swelter, *to sweat.*
[6] On the snap, *eating and drinking.*
[7] Bloke, *fellow.*
[8] Cop, *catch.*

[9] Tipped me his flipper, *gave me his hand.*
[10] Gills, *cheeks.*
[11] Muggins, *greenhorn.*
[12] Wetting, *drinking.*
[13] My fad, *my fancy.*
[14] Swiz, *drinking.*

The palaver was sawdust[1] and treacle.   Old Bottleblue buzzed[2] for a bit,
And a sniffy young Wiscount in barnacles landed[3] wot 'e thought a 'it ;
Said old Gladstone was like Simpson's weapon, a bit of a hass and all jor,
When a noisy young Rad in a wideawake wanted to give him wot for !

"'Yah ! boo ! Turn 'im hout !" sings yours truly, a-thinkin' the fun was
    at 'and,
But, bless yer ! 'twas only a sputter.[4] I can't say the meeting looked grand.
Five thousand they reckoned us, Charlie, but if so I guess the odd three
Were a-spooning about in the halleys, or lappin' up buns and Bohea.

The band and the 'opping wos prime though, and 'Arry in course wos all
    there.
I 'ad several turns with a snappy young party with stror-coloured 'air.
Her name she hinformed me wos Polly, and wen, in my 'appiest style,
I sez, "Polly is nicer than Politics !" didn't she colour and smile ?

We got back jest in time for the Fireworks, a proper flare-up, and no kid,[5]
Which finished that day's Demonstration, an' must 'ave cost many a quid.[6]
Wot fireworks and park-feeds *do* Demonstrate, Charlie, I'm blest if I see,
And I'm blowed if I care a brass button, so long as I get a cheap spree.

The patter's[7] all bow-wow, of course, but it goes with the buns and the beer.
If it pleases the Big-wigs to spout, wy it don't cost hus nothink to cheer.
Though they ain't got the 'ang[8] of it, Charlie, the toffs[9] ain't,—no go and
    no spice !
Wy, I'd back Barney Crump at our Sing-song to lick 'em two times out o'
    twice !

Still I'm all for the Lords and their lot, Charlie, Rads are my 'orror, you
    know.
Change R into C and you've got 'em, and 'Arry 'ates anythink low.
So if Demonstrations means skylarks and lotion as much as you'll carry,
These "busts of spontanyous opinion" may reckon all round upon
                                'ARRY.

[1] Sawdust, *nonsense.*
[2] Buzzed, *talked.*
[3] In barnacles landed, *in spectacles said.*
[4] Sputter, *small affair.*
[5] And no kid, *and no joke.*

[6] Quid, *sovereign.*
[7] Patter, *talking.*
[8] Ain't got the 'ang of it, *are not the stuff for it.*
[9] Toffs, *swells.*

Nineteenth Century.

LE POCHARD ET LES SAINTS.

(*Le Cri du Peuple*, 30 Dec., 1886.)

IENS, tiens, v'là les tours Notre-Dame !
Qu'é' qu'és ont à m'barrer l'chemin ?
Malgré c'que va penser ma femme,
Ma foi, tant pis, j'rentrerai d'main.
Arrêter l'mond', c'est des sal's niches !
R'luquez-moi [1] donc tous ces nabots !
Parbleu ! c'est les saints, dans leurs niches !
Sortez donc d'vos boît's, hé ! cabots ! [2]

C'lui-là qu'a l es clefs, c'est saint Pierre,
L'fameux portier du Paradis.
J'y offrirais bien d'prendre un verre,
Mais voilà, j'ai p'us un radis, [3]
Il est endormi, l'vieux concierge :
J'ai beau crier : "Cordon ! s'vous plaît ! "
I'rest' là, planté comme un cierge !
Sors donc d'ta loge, eh ! sal' pip'let ! [4]

Et c't aut', là-bas, qu'est en extase . . .
J'ai beau le r'luquer, j'le r'mets pas.
Tiens, tiens, tiens, qu'é' qu'c'est donc que c'vase ?
J'te r'connais ; c'est toi qu'es Thomas.
Et c'troisième, on dirait qu'i' sacre,
Tell'ment il prend un air grognon.
J'parie un litr' que c'est saint Fiacre . . .
Sors donc d'ton siège, eh ! Collignon ! [5]

---

[1] R'luquez-moi, *do look at.*
[2] Cabots, *dogs.*
[3] Un radis, *a sou.*
[4] Pipelet, *doorkeeper.*

[5] Collignon, *an insulting term ; the name of a coachman who was executed for murder.*

Et c't' autr' qu'ébouriff' sa tignasse,
Qu'est coiffé comme un' bott' de foin ?
Pour sûr, ça doit êtr' saint Ignace,
L'patron du perruquier du coin.
Et c'cinquième, à la min' pleurarde,
Qu'est planté là comme un badaud . . .
C'est saint Médard ! Tiens ! i'me r'garde !
Sors donc d'ta turne,[1] eh ! porteur d'eau !

Tiens ! qu'est-c'que c'est donc que c'gros moine
Qui rigol'[2] sous son capuchon ? . . .
J'suis bêt' ; c'est l'fameux saint Antoine ;
Je le r'connais à son cochon !
Et c'vieux mendigo[3] qui s'délabre ?
Pour sûr, il ignor' l'emploi d'l'eau !
Ça doit êtr' ce pouilleux d'saint Labre.
Va donc prendre un bain, eh ! salop !

JULES JOUY.

NINETEENTH CENTURY.

FROM "LE CRI DU PEUPLE,"
30 DEC., 1886.

ONC—entr' nous—t'aurais aussi bien fait d'point dé-
cocher c'te pichenette d'joli professeur à un flanche[4]
qu' t'as pas encore complèt'ment découvert.

Et, si Trubl' condescend à peser avec toi la balance des œuvres d'l'année qu'est sur l'point d'tourner
d'l'œil,[5] tout en faisant mon pif[6] quant à l'*Abbesse
de Jouarre* et sans nier l'talent de Paul Bourget et
d'M. Anatole France (les trois seuls qu' trouvent
grâce d'vant ta férule), permets-moi d't'dire qu'y en a ou qu'y en aura
d'autres.

---

1 Turne, *house, room.*
2 Rigole, *laughs.*
3 Mendigo, *beggar.*

4 Flanche, *affair, dodge.*
5 Tourner de l'œil, *to expire.*
6 Faisant mon pif, *being disappointed.*

Sans m'arrêter à l'*Œuvre* qu' tu traites sous la jambe et à l'apparition d'l'admirable *Journal des Goncourt*, dont tu n'ouvres pas l'bec (j'sais, ça n'est pas encore édité en bouquin, mais ça a paru justement, 26, rue Drouot, dans l'propre canard[1] qu' tu fécondes), y en a-t-y pas quéq's autres et d'tapés,[2] dont t'aurais pu jaspiner[3] sans t'décrocher la mâchoire?   Quand ça s'rait qu' l'*Insurgé* du patron, c'te fière épopée, qu' l'ami Bourget donnait un jour comme l'plus chouette[4] "livre sur la politique, qui ait été écrit depuis la *Chartreuse de Parme*, de Stendhal."   Tu vois, myope universitaire, tu vois?

Et au théâtre donc?—Mais ça nous mènerait trop loin.—Enfin, j'te répète qu' t'as tort d'enterrer l'naturalisme qui fait des p'tits tous les jours.   Y a d'la jeunesse qui vient derrière.   Tiens, c'te année, v'là qu'on m'annonce jusqu'à du naturalisme en pantalon garance; plus des forbans, hein? des troupes régulières maintenant,—en uniforme ! ! !

Ils sont trois, presque une escouade, qui vont regarder ce que les Ramollot[5] ont d'pas beau dans leur gros ventre; y en a deux qui vont sortir de la citadelle Charpentier: Henry Fèvre, d'abord, un qui s'est déjà battu pour le naturalisme, et dont le camarade de combat, le pauvre Desprez est resté sur le champ de bataille; celui-là apporte un roman militaire qu'est bâti : *Au port d'arme*, et un autre, Abel Hermant, un aux pommes[6] dont j'sais plus l'titre ; et encore l'zig[7] Lucien Descaves, qui va déculotter quelques vieilles culottes d'peau[8] dans ses *Culs Rouges*.   Hein? un titre qu'a d'la couleur tout d'même : Voile-toi la figure, bon universitaire.

TRUBLOT.

[1] Canard, *newspaper.*
[2] Tapés, *first-rate.*
[3] Jaspiner, *to talk.*
[4] Chouette, *excellent.*
[5] Ramollot, *stupid old officer.*

[6] Aux pommes, *excellent.*
[7] Zig, *jolly fellow.*
[8] Culottes de peau, *narrow-minded soldiers.*

**ABADIE, abadis,** *f.* (thieves'), *crowd,* "**push**." According to Michel this word is derived from the Italian abbadia, *abbey.*

Abajoues, *f. pl.* (popular), *face,* "chops." Properly *chaps.*

Abalobé (popular), *astounded, abashed,* or "flabbergasted."

Abasourdir (thieves'), *to kill.* Properly *to astound.*

Abatis, abattis, *m. pl.* (popular), *hands and feet.* Proper sense, *giblets.* Avoir les — canailles, *to have coarse, plebeian hands and feet,* or "beetle crushers and mutton fists." Numérote tes —, *I'll break every bone in your body.*

Abat-jour, *m.* (popular), *peak of a cap;* — des quinquets, *eyelid.*

Abat-reluit (thieves'), *shade for the eyes.*

Abattage, *m.* (popular), *much work done; work quickly done; severe scolding* or "bully-ragging;" *action of throwing down one's cards* at baccarat when eight or nine are scored. Vente à l'—, *sale of wares spread out on the pavement.*

Abattoir, *m.* (thieves'), *cell at the prison of La Roquette occupied by prisoners under sentence of death;* corresponds to the Newgate "salt-box." It has also the meaning of *gaming-house* or "punting-shop." Properly a *slaughter-house.*

Abattre (familiar), en —, *to do much work,* or to "sweat."

Abbaye, *f.* (thieves'), *kiln in which thieves and vagrants seek a refuge at night;* — ruffante, *warm kiln;* — de Monte-à-regret, *the scaffold.*

Mon père a épousé la veuve, moi je me retire à l'Abbaye de Monte-à-regret.
VICTOR HUGO, *Le dernier Jour d'un Condamné.*

(Popular) — de Saint - Pierre, *the scaffold,* a play on the words "cinq-pierres," the guillotine being erected on five flagstones in front of La Roquette; — des s'offre à tous, *house of ill-fame,* or "nanny-shop."

Abbesse, *f.* (popular), *mistress of a house of ill-fame,* "bawd."

Abcès, *m.* (popular), *the possessor of a bloated face.*

B

Abélardiser, *to mutilate a man as Chanoine Fulbert mutilated Abélard, the lover of his daughter Héloïse.* The operation is termed by horse-trainers "adding one to the list;" *to castrate.*

Abéquer (popular), *to feed.* Literally *to give a billful.*

Abéqueuse, *f.* (popular), *wet nurse; landlady of an hotel.*

Abloquer, abloquir (thieves'), *to buy; to acquire.*

Abonné (familiar), être — au guignon, *to experience a run of ill-luck.* Literally *to be a subscriber to ill-luck.*

Aborgner (popular), s'—, *to scrutinize.* Literally *to make oneself blind of one eye by closing or "cocking"* it.

Aboté (popular), *clumsily adjusted or fitted,* "wobbly."

Aboulage, acré, *m.* (popular), *plenty.*

Aboulée (popular), *in childbed,* "in the straw."

Aboulement, *m.* (popular), *accouchement.*

Abouler (popular), *to be in childbed,* "to be in the straw;" *to give, to hand over,* to "dub."

Pègres et barbots aboulez des pépettes . . .
Aboulez tous des ronds ou des liquettes
Des vieux grimpants, bricheton ou arlequins.
    Le Cri du Peuple, Feb., 1886.

To come, "to crop up."

Et si tézig tient à sa boule,
Fonce ta largue, et qu'elle aboule
Sans limace nous cambrouser.
    RICHEPIN, *La Chanson des Gueux.*

Abour, *m.* (thieves'), *sieve.*

Aboyeur (popular), *crier or salesman at public or private sales; man employed at the doors of puff-*ing shops or theatrical booths to entice people in, "barker;" *man who is constantly clamouring in words or writing against public men; man in a prison whose function it is to call prisoners.*

Abracadabrant, *adj.* (familiar), *marvellous,* or "stunning." From Abracadabra, a magic word used as a spell in the Middle Ages.

Abraqué, *adj.* (sailors'), *tied; spliced.*

Abreuvoir, *m.* (popular), *drinking-shop,* or "lush - crib ;" — à mouches, *bleeding wound.*

Abruti, *m., a plodding student at the Ecole Polytechnique,* termed a "swat" at the R. M. Academy; *stolid and stupid man ;* — de Chaillot, *blockhead,* or "cabbagehead." Chaillot, in the suburbs of Paris, has repeatedly been made the butt for various uncomplimentary hits.

Abrutir (familiar), s'—, *to plod at any kind of work.* Literally *to make oneself silly.*

Abs, abbreviation of *absinthe.*

Absinthage, *m.* (familiar), *the drinking or mixing of absinthe.*

Absinthe, *f.* (familiar), faire son —, *to mix absinthe with water.* Absinthe à la hussarde *is prepared by slowly pouring in the water;* "l'amazone" *is mixed in like manner, but with an adjunction of gum;* "la panachée" *is absinthe with a dash of gum or anisette;* "la purée" *is prepared by quickly pouring in the water.* Faire son — en parlant, *to spit when talking.* Heure de l'—, *the hour when that beverage is discussed in the cafés, generally from four to six p.m.* Avaler son —, see **Avaler.**

Absinthé, *adj.* (familiar), *intoxicated on absinthe.*

Absinther (familiar), s'—, *to drink absinthe ; to be a confirmed tippler of absinthe.*

Absintheur, *m.* (familiar), *a drinker of absinthe ; one who makes it a practice of getting drunk on absinthe.*

Absinthier, or **absintheur,** *m., retailer of absinthe.*

Absinthisme, *m.* (familiar), *state of body and mind resulting from excessive drinking of absinthe.*

Absorber (familiar), *to eat and drink a great deal,* to "guzzle."

Absorption, *f., annual ceremony at the Ecole Polytechnique, at the close of which the seniors, or "anciens," are entertained by the newly-joined,* termed "melons" ("snookers" *at the Royal Military Academy).*

Acabit, *m.* (popular), *the person ; the body ; health ; temper.* Etre de bon —, *to enjoy sound health.* Un étrange —, *an odd humour,* or "strange kidney."

Acacias, *m.,* faire ses —, *to walk or drive, according to the custom of fashionable Parisians, in the "Allée des Acacias" from the Porte-Maillot to La Concorde.*

Acalifourchonner (popular), s'—, *to get astride anything.*

Accaparer (familiar), quelqu'un —, *to monopolize a person.*

Accent (thieves'), *signal given by spitting.*

Accentuer (popular), ses gestes —, *to give a box on the ear ;* in other terms, "to warm the wax of one's ear ;" *to give a blow,* or "bang."

Accessoires, *m. pl.* (theatrical), *stage properties,* or "props." As a qualificative it is used disparagingly, thus, Viande d'—, vin d'—, *are meat and wine of bad quality.*

Accoerer (thieves'), *to arrange.*

Accolade (popular), *smart box on the ear,* "buckhorse."

Accommoder (familiar), quelqu'un à la sauce piquante, *to beat severely,* "to double up ;" *to make one smart under irony or reproaches.* Might be rendered by, *to sit upon one with a vengeance ;* — au beurre noir, *to beat black and blue.*

Accordéon, *m.* (popular), *opera-hat.*

Accoufler (popular), s'—, *to squat.* From the word couffles, *cotton bales,* which may be conveniently used as seats.

Accroche-cœurs (familiar). Properly *small curl twisted on the temple,* or "kiss-curl." Cads apply that name to short, crooked whiskers.

Accrocher (popular), un paletot, *to tell a falsehood,* or "swack up ;" — un soldat, *to confine a soldier to barracks,* "to roost." S'—, *to come to blows,* "to come to loggerheads." (Familiar) Accrocher, *to pawn,* "to pop, to lumber, to blue."

Etes-vous entré quelquefois dans un de ces nombreux bureaux de prêt qu'on désigne aussi sous le nom de ma tante ? Non. Tant mieux pour vous. Cela prouve que vous n'avez jamais eu besoin d'y accrocher vos bibelots et que votre montre n'a jamais retardé de cinquante francs.— FRÉBAULT, *La Vie de Paris.*

Accrouer. See **Accoufler.**

A Chaillot ! (popular), *an energetic invitation to make oneself scarce ; an expression of strong disapproval coupled with a desire to see one turned out of doors.*

Achar (popular), d'—, abbreviation of acharnement, *with steadiness of purpose, in an unrelenting manner.*

Acheter (popular), quelqu'un —, *to turn one into ridicule, to make a fool of one.*

Achetoir, *m.,* **achetoires,** *f. pl.* (popular), *money,* " loaver."

Acœurer (popular), *to do anything with a will, to* " wire in."

Acoquiner (popular), s'—, used disparagingly, *to keep company, to live with one.*

Acré (thieves'), *strong,* " spry," *violent; silence!* " mum's the word !" *be careful!* "shoe leather !"

Acrée, acrie, *m.* (thieves'), *mistrust ;*— donc ! *hold your tongue !* " mum your dubber !" *be cautious.* From acrimonie.

Acteur - guitare (theatrical and journalistic), *actor who has only one string to his bow ; actor who elicits applause in lachrymose scenes only.*

Actionnaire, *m.* (literary), *credulous man easily deceived.* Proper sense, *shareholder.*

Adjectiver (popular), *to abuse,* to " slang."

Adjoint (thieves'), *executioner's assistant.*

Adjudant, *m.* (military), tremper un —, *to dip a piece of bread in the first, and consequently the more savoury broth yielded by the "pot au feu," a practice indulged in by cooks.*

Adjuger (gamesters'), une banque à un opérateur, *to cheat, to* "bite," *at cards.*

Adroit, *adj.* (popular), du coude, *fond of the bottle, or skilful in* " crooking the elbow."

Aff, affe, *f.* (popular), eau d'—, *brandy, or* " French cream." See **Tord-boyaux.**

La v'la l'enflée, c'est de l'eau d'affe (eau-de-vie), elle est toute mouchique celle-là.—VIDOCQ.

Affaire, *f.* (thieves'), *projected crime; projected theft or swindle,* "plant;" — juteuse, *profitable transaction;* — mûre, *preconcerted crime or theft about to be committed.* (Familiar) Avoir son —, *to have received a* "settler;" *to be completely drunk,* or " hoodman;" *to have received a mortal wound,* in other words, "*to have one's goose cooked.*" (Popular) Avoir une — cachée sous la peau, *to be pregnant,* or "lumpy." Faire l'— à quelqu'un, *to kill,* "to do for one."

Affaler (popular), s'—, *to fall,* "to come a cropper."

T'es rien poivre, tu ne tiens plus sur tes fumerons .... tu vas t'affaler.—RICHEPIN, *Le Pavé.*

Affe. See **Aff.**

Affistoler (familiar), *to arrange, to dress.* Mal affistolé, *badly done, badly dressed.*

Affluer (thieves'), *to deceive,* to "cram ;" *to cheat,* to "stick ;" *to swindle,* to "fox." From à flouer.

Affourcher (sailors'), sur ses ancres, *to retire from the service.* Properly *to moor a ship each way.*

Affranchi (thieves'), *convict who has* "done his time ;" *one who has ceased to be honest ; one who has been induced to be an accomplice in a crime.*

Affranchir (gamesters'), *to save a certain card at the cost of another; to initiate one into the tactics of card-sharpers ;* (thieves') *to corrupt ; to teach one dishonest practices ;* — un sinve avec de l'auber, *to corrupt a man by dint of money;* — un sinve pour grinchir, *to put an honest man up to thieving.*

Affres, *f. pl.* (popular), *upbraiding,* "blowing up." Proper sense, *agonies.*

Affur, affure, *m.* (thieves), *proceeds, profits.* Avoir de l'—, *to have money.*

> Quand je vois mon affure
> Je suis toujours paré,
> Du plus grand cœur du monde
> Je vais à la profonde
> Pour vous donner du frais.
> VIDOCQ.

Affurage, *m.* (thieves'), *proceeds of theft,* "regulars," or "swag."

Affurer, affûter (thieves'), *to deceive ; to make profits ; to procure ;* — de l'auber, *to make money.*

En goupinant comme ça on n'affure pas d'auber.—VIDOCQ.

Affût (thieves' and popular), être d'—, *to be able, cunning,* or "a downy cove ;" *to be wide awake,* or "to be one who knows what's o'clock." A l'—, *on the watch.*

Affûter (thieves'), *to deceive, to snatch,* "to click ;" *to whip up,* "to nip ;" *to make unlawful profits ;* — ses pincettes, *to walk,* to "pad the hoof ;" *to run,* to "leg it." Proper sense, *to sharpen.* S'— le sifflet, *to drink,* to "whet one's whistle."

Agaceur (sporting), *one who sets a thing going,* "buttoner."

Aganter (popular), *to take, to catch,* "to grab ;" — une claque, *to receive a box on the ear,* "to get one's ear's wax warmed."

Agate, *f.* (thieves'), *crockery.*

Agater (popular), *to be thrashed,* "tanned ;" *to be caught,* "nabbed."

Agenouillée, *f.* (journalists'), *prostitute whose spécialité is best described by the appellation itself.*

Agobille (thieves'), *implements,* "jilts."

Agonir (popular), *to abuse vehemently,* to "bully-rag," or "to haul over the coals."

Agout, *m.* (thieves'), *drinking-water.*

Agrafe, *f.* (popular), *hand,* "picker," "dooks," or "dukes."

Agrafer (thieves' and cads'), *to seize,* to "grab ;" *to arrest,* "to pull up," or "to smug."

Agrément, *m.* (theatrical), avoir de l'—, *to obtain applause.* (Popular) Se pousser de l'—, *to amuse oneself.*

Agripper (popular), *to seize secretly, to steal quickly,* to "nip." S'—, *to come to blows,* "to slip into one another."

Aguicher (popular), *to allure, decoy,* "to button ;" *to quicken, to excite.*

Il fallait lui faire comprendre qu'elle aguiche la soif du petit, en l'empêchant de boire.—RICHEPIN, *La Glu.*

Aguigner (popular), *to teaze,* "to badger."

Ahuri, *m.* (popular), de Chaillot, *block-head,* "cabbage-head." See **Abruti.**

Aide-cargot, *canteen servant.*

Aides. See **Aller.**

Aïe-aïe, *m.* (popular), *omnibus.*

Aiguille, *f.* (military), à tricoter les côtes, *sword,* "toasting-fork ;" (thieves') *key,* or "screw ;" *card made to protrude from a pack for cheating,* "old gentleman."

Aiguiller (card-sharpers'), la brème, *to make a mark or notch on a card.*

Aile, *f.*, **aileron,** *m.* (popular), *arm,* or "bender."

Aille, iergue, orgue, uche, *suffixes used to disguise any word.*

Aille (familiar), fallait pas qu'y —, *it is all his own fault, he has nobody to thank for it but himself.*

Aimant, *m.* (popular), faire de l'—, *to make a fussy show of affected friendliness through interested motives.*

Aimer (popular), à crédit, *to enjoy the gratuitous good graces of a kept woman.* Aimer comme ses petits boyaux, *to doat on one,* "to love like the apple of one's eye."

Air, *m.* (popular), se donner de l'—, se pousser de l'—, jouer la fille de l'—, *to run away,* to "cut and run." See **Patatrot.**

Airs, *m. pl.* (popular), être à plusieurs —, *to be a hypocrite, double-faced person,* "mawworm."

A la balade (popular), chanteurs —, *itinerant singers,* "chaunters."

A la barque, *street cry of mussel costermongers.*

A la bonne (popular), prendre quelquechose —, *to take anything good-humouredly.* Avoir —, *to love, to like.*

Je peste contre le quart d'œil de mon quartier qui ne m'a pas à la bonne.—Vidocq.

A la carre (thieves'), dégringoler —, *to steal from shops; kind of theft committed principally by women who pretend to be shopping;* "shoplifting."

A la clef (familiar), *an expletive.* Trop de zèle —, *too much zeal by half.* From a musical term. The expression is used sometimes with no particular meaning, thus, Il y aura du champagne —, is equivalent to, Il y aura du champagne.

A la corde (popular), logement —, *low lodging-house, where the lodgers sleep with their heads on a rope, which is let down early in the morning.* In some of these the lodgers leave all their clothes with the keeper, to ensure against their being stolen.

A la coule (popular), être —, *to be conversant with.*

S'il avait été au courant, à la coule, il aurait su que le premier truc du camelot, c'est de s'établir au cœur même de la foule.—Richepin.

Etre —, *to be happy; at one's ease; comfortable.* Je n'étais pas —, *I felt very uncomfortable.*

A la flan, à la rencontre, or **à la dure** (thieves'), fabriquer un gas —, *to attack and rob a person at night,* "to jump a cove."

A la grive! (thieves' and cads'), *take care!* "shoe leather !" Cribler —, *to call out "police!"* to "give hot beef."

> Par contretemps ma largue,
>
> Pour gonfler ses valades,
> Encasque dans un rade,
> Sert des sigues à foison ;
> On la crible à la grive,
> Je m'la donne et m'esquive,
> Elle est pommée maron.
>   *Mémoires de Vidocq.*

A la manque (thieves'), fafiots, or fafelards —, *forged bank notes,* "queer soft." Avoir du pognon, or de la galette —, *to be penniless.* Etre —, *not to be trustworthy; to betray.*

Pas un de nous ne sera pour le dab à la manque.—Balzac.

A la papa (popular), *quietly, slowly.*

A la petite bonne femme (popular), glisser —, *to slide squatting on one's heels.*

Alarmiste (thieves'), *watch-dog,* "tyke."

A-la-six-quatre-deux (popular), *in disorder,* "all at sixes and sevens ;" *anyhow,* "helter-skelter."

A la sonde (cads'), être —, *to be cunning, wide awake,* "fly."

Va, la môm', truque et n'fais pas four.
Sois rien mariolle et à la sonde !
       Richepin, *Chanson des Gueux.*

A la tienne Etienne! (popular), *your health !*

A la va-te-faire-fiche, *anyhow.*

Un béret nature, campé par une main paysanne, à la va-te-faire-fiche, sans arrière-pensée de pittoresque.—Richepin, *Le Pavé.*

Alènes, *f. pl.* (thieves'), *tools, implements,* "jilts." Properly *shoemakers' awls.*

Alentoir, *m.,* for alentour (thieves'), *neighbourhood, vicinity.*

A l'esbrouffe (thieves'), faire un coup — sur un pantre, *to steal a pocket-book from a person who has been seen to enter a bank, or other financial establishment.* The thief watches his opportunity in the neighbourhood of such establishments, and when operating keeps his hand concealed under an overcoat which he bears on his arm.

Aligner (freemasons'), *to lay the cloth.* S'—, in soldiers' language, *to fight a duel with swords.* The expression is used also by civilians.

Alinéaliste, *m.* (literary), *writer who is fond of short paragraphs.*

Allemand, *m.* (popular), peigne d'—, *the four fingers.*

Aller (familiar), à Bougival, in literary men's parlance, *is to write a newspaper article of no interest for the general public;* — à la cour des aides *is said of a married woman who has one or more lovers;* — au pot, *to pick up dominoes from those which remain after the proper number has been distributed to the players;* — au safran, *to spend freely one's capital,* an allusion to the colour of gold; — en Belgique *is said of a cashier who bolts with the cash-box, or of a financier who makes off with the money of his clients;* — se faire fiche, *to go to the deuce;* — se faire foutre *has the same meaning, but refers to a rather more forcible invitation yet;* — se faire lanlaire, *to go to the deuce.* Allez vous faire fiche, or foutre! *go to the deuce,* or "you be hanged!" Je lui ai dit d'— se faire lanlaire, *I sent him about his business.* Aller son petit bonhomme de chemin, *to do anything without any hurry, without heeding interruptions or hindrances.* On avait beau lui crier d'arrêter, il allait toujours son petit bonhomme de chemin. (Familiar and popular) Y aller, *to begin anything.* Allons-y! *let us begin! let us open the ball! now for business.* Y aller de quelque chose, *to contribute; to pay; to furnish.* Y — de son argent, *to pay,* "to stump up." Y — d'une, de deux, *to pay for one or two bottles of liquor.* Y — de sa larme, *to shed a tear, to show emotion.* Y — gaiment, *to do anything willingly, briskly.* Allons y gaiment! *let us look alive!* (Popular) Aller à la chasse avec un fusil de toile, *to go a begging,* "to cadge." An allusion to a beggar's canvas wallet. Compare this with the origin of the word "to beg," which is derived from "bag;" — à l'arche, *to fetch money;* — à niort, *to deny,* a play on the words "Niort," name of a town, and "nier," to deny; — à ses affaires, *to ease oneself,* "to go to Mrs. Jones';" — au persil *is said of street-walkers who ply their trade.* This expression may have its origin in the practice sometimes followed by this class of women of carrying a small basket as if going to the fruiterer's; — au trot *is said of a prostitute walking the street in grand attire,* or "full fig;" — au vice, *to make one's resort of places where immorality is rife;* — voir défiler les dragons, *to go without dinner.* The English have the expressions, "to dine out," used by the lower classes, and "to dine with Duke Humphrey," by the middle and upper. According to the *Slang*

Dictionary the reason of the latter saying is as follows : " Some visitors were inspecting the abbey where the remains of Humphrey, Duke of Gloucester, lie, and one of them was unfortunately shut in, and remained there *solus* while his companions were feasting at a neighbouring hostelry. He was afterwards said to have dined with Duke Humphrey, and the saying eventually passed into a proverb." Aller aux pruneaux *is said of the victim of a practical joke played in hospitals at the expense of a new patient, who, being sent at the conclusion of a meal to request another patient to furnish him with the customary dessert, gets bolstered for his pains;* — où le roi va à pied, *to go to the latrines,* or "chapel of ease ;" (printers') — en galilée, or — en germanie (a play on the words "Je remanie," I overrun), *to do some overrunning in a piece of composition ;* (soldiers') — à l'astic, *to clean one's equipment ;* (sporting) — pour l'argent, *to back one's own horse ;* (musicians') — au carreau, *to seek an engagement.* An allusion to "la Rue du Petit - Carreau," a meeting-place for musicians of the lowest class, and musical conductors. (Thieves') Aller à comberge, *to go to confession with a priest ;* — à la retape, *to waylay in order to murder ;* — chez Fualdès, *to share the booty,* "to nap the regulars." Fualdès was a rich banker, who was murdered in circumstances of peculiar atrocity.

Allez donc (familiar), et —, *a kind of flourish at the end of a sentence to emphasize an assertion.* Allez donc vous laver (popular), *be off,* go to "pot ;" — vous asscoir, "shut up !"

Alliances, *f. pl.* (thieves'), *hand-cuffs,* "bracelets." Properly *wedding-rings.*

Allonger (familiar), *to pay,* to "fork out ;" — les radis, *to pay,* "to shell out ;" (military) — la ficelle or la courroie, *to make an addition to a penalty.* S'—, *to fall,* to "come down a cropper."

Allume, *m., confederate who makes sham bids at auctions,* a "button."

Allumé (thieves'), *stared at.*

> Sur la placarde de Vergne
> Il nous faudrait gambiller,
> Allumés de toutes ces largues
> Et du trèpe rassemblé.
> *Mémoires de Vidocq.*

Allumer (thieves'), *to look,* "to stag," *to see,* or "to pipe ;" *to keep a sharp look-out, to watch,* "to nark."

Si le Squelette avait eu tantôt une largue comme moi pour allumer, il n'aurait pas été mouché le surin dans l'avaloir du grinche.—E. SUE, *Mystères de Paris.*

Allumer le miston, *to scan one's features ;* — ses clairs, *to look attentively,* "to stag ;" (prostitutes') — son pétrole, son gaz, *to get highly excited.* (Theatrical) Allumer, *to awake interest or enthusiasm among an audience ;* (popular) *to allure purchasers at fair stalls, or the public at theatrical booths or* "gaffs" *by glowing accounts.* In coachmens' parlance, *to whip,* "to flush." (Familiar) S'—, *to be slightly intoxicated,* "fresh ;" *excited by women's allurements ; brought to the proper pitch of interest by card-sharpers or salesmen.*

Un autre compère gagne encore un coup de dix francs cette fois. La galerie s'allume de plus en plus.—RICHEPIN, *Le Pavé.*

Allumette, *f.* (popular), avoir son —, *to be tipsy,* "screwed." The successive stages of this degree of intoxication are expressed by the qualifying terms, "ronde," "de marchand de vin," "de campagne."

Allumettes, *f. pl.* (popular), *arms,* "benders."

Allumeur, *m., confederate at auction rooms* (see **Allume**) ; *thief who gets workmen into a state of intoxication on pay day, after which they are seen home, and robbed of their earnings by his confederates, the "meneuses" and "travailleurs," or "bug hunters ;" gambling cheat who plays as if he were one of the general public, and who otherwise sets a game going,* a "buttoner," or "decoy-duck."

Allumeurs, *m. pl.* (military), *de gaz, lancers.* An allusion to their weapon, which has some resemblance with a lamp-lighter's rod.

Allumeuse, *f., woman who seeks to entice passers-by into patronizing a house of ill fame.*

Almanach, *m.* (popular), *des vingt-cinq mille adresses, girl or woman of dissolute character,* "public ledger." See **Gadoue.**

Alpaga, alpag, *m.* (popular), *coat,* "tog," or "Benjamin."

Alpague (popular), *clothing,* "toggery," *coat,* "Benjamin."

Alphonse (familiar), *man who protects prostitutes, ill-treats them often, and lives off their earnings,* "pensioner." These worthies go also by the names of "dos, barbeau, chevalier de la guiche, marlou," &c. See **Poisson.**

Alphonsisme (familiar), *the calling of an Alphonse.*

Alpion (gamesters'), *man who cheats at cards, one who "bites."*

Altèque (thieves'), *manly,* "spry," *handsome, excellent,* "nobby." From altus.

Amadou, *m.,* **amadoue,** *f.* (thieves' and tramps'), *substance with which vagabonds rub their faces to give themselves a sickly, wretched appearance.*

Les cagous emmènent avec sezières leurs apprentis pour leur apprendre à exercer l'argot. Premièrement, leur enseignent à acquiger de l'amadoue de plusieurs sortes, l'une avec de l'herbe qu'on nomme éclaire, pour servir aux francs-mijoux.—*Le Jargon de l'Argot.*

(Popular) *man with an inflammable heart.*

Amadouage, *m.* (thieves'), *marriage,* "buckling."

Amadouer, s'— (thieves' and tramps'), *to paint or otherwise make up one's face with a view to deceiving people.*

Amandes, *f. pl.* (popular), *de pain d'épice, black teeth, few and far between.*

Amant (prostitutes'), *de carton, lover of no importance, a poor lover in both senses ;* — *de cœur, one who enjoys a kept woman's affections gratis, one who is loved for "love," not money.*

Amar, amarre, *m.* (thieves'), *friend,* "pal," or "Ben cull ;" — *d'attaque, staunch friend.*

Amar-loer (Breton cant), *rope which has served to hang one.*

Amarrer (thieves'), *to act in such a manner as to deceive, to lay a "plant."* Properly *to moor.*

Amateur (in literary men's parlance), *writer who does not exact payment for his productions ;* (in officers' slang) *a civilian ; an officer who gives himself little trouble in his profession, who takes it easy ;* (familiar) *man who makes a living by playing at cards with people unable to leave their homes.*

Amazone, *f.* (thieves'), *female card-sharper.*

Ambassadeur, *m.* (popular), *shoemaker,* "snob;" (in gay girls' slang) *a bully.* See **Poisson**.

Ambes, *f. pl.* (thieves'), *legs,* "gambs."

Ambier (thieves'), *to flee,* "to pike." See **Patatrot**.
Et mezière de happer le taillis et ambier le plus gourdement possible.—*Jargon de l'Argot.* (*I got off, and ran away as fast as possible.*)

Ambrellin (Breton cant), *son.*

Ambulante, *f.* (thieves'), *female who is at once a hawker, a thief, and a prostitute.*

Amendier, *m.* (theatrical), fleuri, *stage manager,* "daddy." A play on the word amende, *a fine,* the connection being obvious.

Amener (popular), s'—, *to come, to go to.* Le voilà qui s'amène, *here he comes.*

Américain (thieves'), *confederate of a thief, who goes by the name of Jardinier.* The pair induce a simpleton to dig at the foot of a tree for a buried treasure, when they rob him of his money; *a swindler who pretends he has just returned from America;* (familiar) *a drink, something between grog and punch.* Faire l'œil —, *to scrutinize with searching glance.* Oeil —, *eye with purposely amorous,* "killing," *expression;* also *a very sharp eye.*

Américaine, vol à l' (see **Charriage**).

Ami (thieves'), *expert thief,* "gonnof;" — de collège, *prison chum.*

Amicablement (popular), *in a friendly manner, affectionately.*

Aminche, aminchemar, amincheminee, *m.* (thieves'), *friend,* "ben cull;" — d'aff, *accomplice,* "stallsman."

Amis, *m. pl.* (popular), comme cochons, "thick" *friends.*

Amiteux, *adj.* (popular), *friendly, amiable, gentle.*

Amocher (popular), *to bruise, to ill-treat,* to "manhandle." S'— la gueule, *to maul one another's face,* to "mug" one another.

Amorcé, *adj.* (popular), *furnished, garnished.*
V'la qu'est richement amorcé, j'en suis moi-même ébaubi.—RICHEPIN.

Amoureux (popular), *hunchback,* or "lord;" — de carême, *a timid lover.* Literally a "Lent lover." (Printers') Papier —, *paper that blots.*

Ampafle, *m.* (thieves'), *cloth.*

Amphi, *m.* (students'), abbreviation of amphithéâtre, *lecture room.*

Amphibie (typographers'), *typographer who is at the same time a printer and reader,* "donkey."

Amprefan (Breton cant), *a low, insulting expression.*

Amusatif, *adj.* (popular), *amusing, funny.*

Amuser (popular), s'— à la moutarde, *to neglect one's duty or work for trifles, tomfooleries.*

An, *m.* (thieves'), *litre, measure for wine.*

Anarcho, *m.*, *anarchist.*

Anastasie, *f.*, *literary and theatrical official censorship.*

Anchois, *m.* (popular), yeux bordés d'—, *eyes with inflamed eyelids.*

Anchtibler (thieves'), *to apprehend,* to "nab," or "to smug."

Ancien, ancienne (peasants'), *father, mother.* "Ancien" at the military schools *is a student who has been through the two years' course.* In the army, *a soldier who has served one term of service at least.*

Andalouserie, *f.*, *semi-heroic senti-mental song with Spain and things of Spain for themes.*

Andosse, *m.* (thieves'), *the back.*

Alors le rupin en colère, jura que s'il attrapait jamais des trucheurs dans son pipet qu'il leur ficherait cent coups de sabre sur l'andosse.—*Jargon de l'Argot.*

Andouille, *f.* (popular), *a man devoid of energy,* a *"muff."* Properly *chitterlings.* Faire l'—, *to play the fool.* Grand dépen-deur d'andouilles, *one who prefers good cheer to work.*

Viennent aussi des bat-la-flemme, des sans-douilles,
Fainéants, suce-pots, grands dépendeurs d'andouilles,
Qui dans tous les cabarets ont tué leur je dois,
Et qui ne font jamais œuvre de leurs dix doigts.
RICHEPIN, *La Mer.*

(Cod-fishers') Andouille, *wind blowing to sea-ward.*

Angauche, or **angluce,** *f.* (thieves'), *goose.* Tortiller de l'—, *to eat goose.*

Ange-gardien, *m.* (popular), *man whose calling is to see drunkards home ; muslin inside a chemisette.*

Anglais, *m.* (familiar), *creditor,* "dun ;" *man who keeps a mis-tress ; a carefully made up dummy parcel in shops.* Il a de l'—, *is said of a horse which shows blood.* Anglais à prunes, voyageurs à prunes, *prudent travellers, who, being aware of the long price asked for fruit at restaurants, are satisfied with a few plums ;* (cabmens') — de carton, *an expression of con-tempt applied to a stingy "fare."*

Anglaise, *f.* (mountebanks'), *the share of each partner in the busi-ness ; the expenses of each guest at a meal.* (Popular) Danser à l'—, *a practice followed by girls who pretend to go to the ball of the opera, and stop at a restaurant where*

they await clients. Faire une —, *to pay one's share in the reckoning ; also a favourite game of loafers.* One of the players tosses all the pence of the party ; those which turn up heads, or tails as the case may be, are his ; another player adjudges to himself the tails, and so on with the rest. Filer, or pisser à l'—, *to give the slip, to take* "French leave."

Angluce, or **angauche,** *f.* (thieves'), *goose.*

Angoulême, *f.* (thieves'), *the mouth,* "muns." From "engouler," *to swallow.* Se caresser l'—, *to eat and drink, to take* "grub and bub." See **Mastiquer.**

Anguille, *f.* (thieves'), *belt.* Pro-perly *eel ;* (familiar) — de buisson, *snake.*

Anis, *m.* (popular), de l'— ! *ex-clamation expressive of refusal,* may be rendered by "you be hanged !" See **Nèfles.**

Anisette, *f.* (popular), de barbillon, *water,* or "Adam's ale."

Anjez (Breton cant), *father.*

Ann doouzeg abostol (Breton cant), *twelve o'clock.* Literally *the twelve apostles.*

Annoncier, *m.* (printers'), *com-positor of advertisements ;* also *man who belongs to an advertising firm.*

Annuaire, *m.* (military), passer l'— sous le bras, *to be promoted according to seniority.*

Anonchali (popular), *discouraged, cast down,* "down in the mouth."

Anquilleuse, *f.* (thieves'), *female thief who conceals stolen property between her legs.* From " quilles," a slang term for legs.

Anse, *f.* (popular), *arm,* "bender." Faire le panier à deux anses, *to* *walk with a woman on each arm, to play the* "sandwich."

Antif, *m.,* **antiffe**, *f.* (thieves'), *act of walking.* Battre l'—, *to walk,* to "pad the hoof;" *to deceive,* "to kid;" *to dissemble; to spy,* to "nark."

Antiffer (thieves'), *to enter, to walk in ; to walk,* "to pad the hoof."

Antiffle (thieves'), *church.* Battre l'—, *to be a hypocrite,* "mawworm."

Antiffler (thieves'), *to be married in church,* "to be buckled."

Antilles, *f. pl.* (thieves'), *testicles.*

Antipather (popular), *to abominate.*

Antique, *student of the Ecole Polytechnique who has completed the regular course of studies.*

Antonne, entonne, *f.* (thieves'), *church.*

> Au matin quand nous nous levons,
> J'aime la croûte de parfond.
> Dans les entonnes trimardons,
> Ou aux creux de ces ratichons.
> *Chanson de l'Argot.*

Antroler, entroller (thieves'), *to carry away,* "to chuff."

> Un de ces luisans, un marcandier alla demander la thune à un pipet, et le rupin ne lui ficha que floutière : il mouchailla des ornies de baile qui morfiaient du grenu en la cour ; alors il ficha de son sabre sur la tronche à une, il l'abasourdit la met dans son gueulard et l'entrolle.—*Le Jargon de l'Argot.*

Apascliner (thieves'), s'—, *to get used to, acclimatized.*

A perpète (thieves'), *for life.* Gerbé à —, *to be sentenced to penal servitude for life, to be a* "lifer."

Apic (thieves'), *garlic ; eye,* "daylight," "glazier," *or* "ogle."

Aplatir (familiar), quelqu'un, *to thrash soundly,* "to lick ;" *to reduce one's arguments to nought,* "to nonplus." Properly *to flatten.*

Aplatisseur, *m.* (familiar), de pièces de six liards —, *one who is over particular ; one who attaches undue importance to trifles.*

Aplomb, *m.* (popular), être d'—, *to be strong, sound,* "game." Reluquer d'—, *to look straight in the face.*

Aplomber (thieves'), *to abash a person by one's coolness.*

Aponiché (popular), *seated.*

Apoplexie, *f.* (popular), de templier, *a fit of apoplexy brought on by excessive drinking.* From the saying, Boire comme un templier.

Apothicaire, *m.* (popular), sans sucre, *workman with but few tools ; tradesman with an insufficient stock in trade.*

Apôtres (thieves'), *fingers,* or "forks."

Appeler (theatrical), azor, *to hiss,* or "to goose." Literally *to whistle a dog.* Azor, a common name for a dog.

Appuyer (theatrical), *to let scenes down.*

Aquarium, *an assembly of prostitutes' bullies,* or "ponces." From their being denominated maquereaux, *mackerels.*

Aquicher (thieves'), *to decoy, allure.*

Aquiger, quiger (thieves' and cads'), *to steal,* "to lift ;" *to wound ; to beat,* "to wallop ;" *to make,* or "to fake ;" — les brèmes, *to mark cards for cheating,* or to "stock broads." It means also *to take, to procure, to find.*

> Dévalons donc dans cette piole
> Où nous aquigerons riole,
> Et sans débrider nos pouchons.
> RICHEPIN, *La Chanson des Gueux.*

Aquilin (popular), faire son —, *to pout*, or "*to hang one's latch-pan;*" *to turn up one's nose.*

Arabe, *m.* (popular), *savage, unrelenting fellow*, or "*tartar.*"

Araignée, *f.* (popular), *bicycle with a large fly-wheel;* — de bastringue, *female habituée of low dancing halls;* — de comptoir, *counter jumper*, or "*knight of the yard;*" — de trottoir, *dealer at a stall, or in the open air.* Avoir une — dans le plafond, *to be cracked, to have* "*a bee in one's bonnet.*" See **Avoir**.

Arbalète, *f.* (thieves'), *neck-cross;* — d'antonne, de chique, de priante, *church-cross.*

Arbi, arbico, *m.* (army), *Arab.*

Arbif, *m.* (thieves'), *violent man.*

Arcasien, arcasineur, *m.* (thieves'), *thief who employs the arcat* (which see); *a beggar who calls on people; cunning man.*

Arcat, *m.* (thieves'), monter un —, *to write a letter from prison to a person asking for an advance in cash on a supposed buried treasure which, later on, is to be pointed out to the donor.* From arcane, *mystery, hidden thing.*

Arcavot, *m.* (Jew traders'), *falsehood.*

Arche, *f.* (popular), aller à l'—, *to fetch money.* Fendre l'—, *to weary,* "*to bore.*"

Archicube, *m., student who has completed his three years' course of study at the Ecole Normale*, an institution where professors are trained for university professorships, and which holds the first rank among special schools in France.

Archipointu, *m.* (thieves'), *an archbishop.*

Archisuppôt de l'argot (old cant), *learned thief, arch-thief,* "*gonnof.*"

Les archisuppôts de l'argot sont les plus savants, les plus habiles marpeaux de toutime l'argot, qui sont des écoliers débauchés, et quelques ratichons, de ces coureurs qui enseignent le jargon à rouscailler bigorne. —*Le Jargon de l'Argot.*

Architecte de l'Univers (freemasons'), *the Deity.*

Arçon (thieves'), *sign of recognition made by passing the thumb down the right cheek and spitting at the same time.*

Si c'étaient des amis de Pantin, je pourrais me faire reconnaître mais des pantres nouvellement affranchis (des paysans qui font leurs premières armes), j'aurais beau faire l'arçon.—VIDOCQ.

Arçonner (thieves'), *to make one speak out; to speak*, or "*to patter.*"

Arcpincer, arquepincer (thieves' and popular), *to take*, or "*to collar;*" *to seize*, or "*to grab;*" — l'omnibus, *to catch the 'bus.* Veuillez — mon anse, *pray take my arm.*

J'ai promis de reconobrer tous les grinchisseurs et de les faire arquepincer.—VIDOCQ.

Ardent, *m.* (thieves'), *candle*, or "*glim.*" Fauche-ardents, *snuffers.*

Ardents, *m. pl.* (thieves'), *eyes*, or "*glaziers.*" See **Quinquets**.

Ardoise, *f.* (popular), *head*, or "*tibby;*" *hat*, or "*tile.*" Avoir l'—, *to have credit*, or "*jawbone.*" An allusion to the slate used for drawing up the reckoning.

Arga, *m.* (thieves'), *share of booty*, or "*snaps.*"

Arganeau, *m.* (thieves'), *a link connecting two convicts' irons.*

Argot, *m.* (thieves'), *animal; fool*, or "*go along;*" *thieves' brotherhood*, or "*family men.*"

Argoté (thieves'), *one who lays claim to being witty.*

Argotier, *m.* (thieves'), *one of the brotherhood of thieves,* or "family man."

Argousin, *m* (popular), *foreman,* or "boss."

Arguche, *m.* (thieves'), *cant,* or "flash;" *a fool, dunce,* or "go-along."

Arguemine, *f.* (thieves'), *hand,* or "famm."

Aricoteur, *m.* (thieves'), *executioner.*

Aristo, *m.* for *aristocrat* (popular), *a man in comfortable circumstances.*

Aristocrate, *m.,* *an appellation given by prisoners to one of their number whose means allow him to obtain victuals from the canteen.*

Arlequin (popular), *broken victuals of every description mixed up and retailed to poor people.* The word has passed into the language.

> Autrefois chez Paul Niquet
> Fumait un vaste baquet
>   Sur la devanture.
> Pour un ou deux sous, je crois,
> On y plongeait les deux doigts
>   Deux, à l'aventure.
> Les mets les plus différents
> Etaient là, mêlés, errants,
>   Sans couleur, sans forme,
> Et l'on pêchait sans fouiller,
> Aussi bien un vieux soulier
>   Qu'une truffe énorme.
>   RICHEPIN, *La Chanson des*
>   *Gueux.*

Arme, *f.* (military), passer l'— à gauche, *to die,* "to lose the number of one's mess." See **Pipe**.

Armée roulante, *f.* (thieves'), formerly *gang of convicts chained together which used to make its way by road to the hulks.*

Armoire, *f.* (popular), à glace, *the four of any card ; head ;* (military) — à poils, *soldiers' knapsack,* or "scran bag." An allusion to the hairy skin that covers or covered soldiers' knapsacks.

Arnac, *m.* (thieves'), à l'—, *with premeditation.*

Arnache, *f.* (popular), *deceit ; treachery.* Etre à l'—, *to be cunning, wide-awake,* a "deep one ;" *to deceive, and not allow oneself to be deceived.*

Arnacq, **arnache**, *m.* (thieves'), *detective, informer,* "nark."

Arnaud, *m.* (popular), avoir son —, être —, *to be in a bad humour,* to be "nasty."

Arnauder (popular), *to grumble.*

Arnelle (thieves'), *the town of Rouen.* From La Renelle, a small river.

Arnellerie, *f.* (thieves'), *rouennerie, printed cotton.*

Arnif, *m.* (thieves'), *policeman or detective.* Also denominated "bec de gaz, bourrique, cierge, flique, laune, peste, vache." In English cant or slang "crusher, pig, copper, cossack, nark."

Arpagar, *m.* (thieves'), *the town of Arpagon, near Paris.*

Arpette, *m.* (popular), *apprentice.*

Arpion, *m.* (thieves' and popular), *foot,* "trotter ;" *toe.*

> Moi, d'marcher ça n'me fout pas l'trac.
> J'ai l'arpion plus dur que des clous.
>   RICHEPIN, *Chanson des Gueux.*

Arpions. *m. pl.* (thieves' and popular), *toes.*

Arquepincer. See **Arcpincer.**

Arquer (popular), s'—, *to be bent down through age.*

Arracher (thieves'), du chiendent, *to be on the look-out for a victim* (chiendent, *dogs' grass*) ; (popular) — son copeau, *to work,* "to grind" (copeau, *shaving*).

Arrangemaner (thieves'), *to cheat,* or "to stick."

Arranger (swindlers'), les pantres, *to cheat the public by means of the three-card trick or other swindling dodges.*

Arrangeur, *m.* (gamesters'), *one who sets a game going,* or "buttonner."

Arrêter (familiar), les frais, *to put a stop to any proceedings.* (Les frais, *the fee for a game of billiards.*)

Arrière-train, *m.* (familiar), *the behind,* or "tochas." See **Vasistas.**

Arriver premier (sporting), *to be the winner.* Used figuratively to denote superiority of any kind over others. Arriver bon premier, "to beat hollow."

Arrondir (popular), se faire — le globe, *to become pregnant,* or "lumpy."

On s'a fait arrondir el'globe,
On a sa p'tit' butte, à c'qué vois . . . .
Eh ! ben, ça prouv' qu'on n'est pas d'bois.
    GILL, *La Muse à Bibi.*

Arrondissement, *m.* (popular), chef-lieu d'—, *woman in an advanced stage of pregnancy,* "lumpy," *or with a* "white swelling."

Arrosage, *m.* (popular), *action of drinking,* of "having something damp."

Arroser (gamesters'), *to stake repeatedly on the same card ; to make repeated sacrifices in money ;* (military) — ses galons, *treating one's comrades on being made a non-commissioned officer,* "paying for one's footing ;" (familiar) — un créancier, *to settle small portion of debt.*

Arroseur, *m.* (thieves'), de verdouze, *gardener,* or "master of the mint." Verdouze, for verdure.

Arrosoir, *m.* (thieves'), coup d'—, *a glass of wine ; a watering-pot.*

Arsenal, *m.* (thieves'), *arsenic.*

Arsonner (thieves'), *to overhaul pockets,* to "frisk," or "to rule over."

Arsouille, *m.* (familiar), *a man foul in language, a low cad,* a "rank outsider." The expression has passed into the language. Milor l'—, *a rich man with eccentric, low tastes.* The appellation was first given to Lord Seymour.

Arsouiller (popular), synonymous of engueuler, to "jaw," to "slang."

Arthur, *m.*, *a would-be lady-killer ;* also synonymous of **Amant de cœur,** which see.

Arthurine, *f.* (popular), *a girl of indifferent character, a* "Poll."

Artichaut, *m.* (popular), cœur d'—, *fickle-hearted.*

     . . . . Cœur d'artichaut,
C'est mon genre : un' feuille pour tout l'monde,
Au jour d'aujourd'hui, j'gobe la blonde ;
Après-d'main, c'est la brun', qu'i m'faut.
        GILL.

Artiche, *m.* (thieves'), retirer l'—, *to pick the pockets of a drunkard.*

Article, *m.* (familiar), faire l'—, *to puff up,* "to crack up." (Printers') Payer son — quatre, *to pay for one's footing.* An allusion to some item of a code of regulations. (Popular) Porté sur l'—, *one of an amatory disposition.*

Articlier, *m.*, *one whose spécialité is writing newspaper articles.*

Artie, artif, artiffe, lartie, larton, *m.* (thieves'), *bread ;* — de Meulan, *white bread ;* —du gros Guillaume, *brown bread ;* — de guinaut, *mouldy bread.*

Ecoutez marques et mions,
J'aime la croûte de parfond,
J'aime l'artie, j'aime la crie,
J'aime la croûte de parfond.
    Chanson de l'Argot.

Artilleur (popular), *drunkard ; one skilful in working the* "canon," *or glass of wine at wine-shops ;*

— à genoux, or de la pièce humide, *a military hospital orderly ;* — à l'aiguille, *tailor ;* — de la pièce humide, *a fireman ;* also, *one who is voiding urine,* or "lagging."

Artis, *m.* (thieves'), langage de l'—, *cant,* or "flash."

Artiste, *m.* (popular), *veterinary surgeon,* "vet ;" *spendthrift leading a careless life ; sweeper ; comrade,* or "pal."

Arton. See Artie.

Artoupan, *m.* (thieves'), *guard or warder at a penal servitude depôt,* or "bloke."

Art royal (freemasons'), *freemasonry.*

As, *m.* (popular), être à l'—, *to be short of cash,* "hard up ;" *at a restaurant or café, to be at table, or in private room No.* 1. Un — de carreau, *soldier's knapsack,* thus called from its shape ; *a town adjutant,* an allusion to the red facings of his uniform. (Thieves') As de carreau, *the ribbon of the Legion of Honour, which is red.* (Familiar) Fichu comme l'— de pique, *with a clumsily built form, badly dressed.* As de pique meant formerly a man of no consequence, of no intellectual worth.

Asinver (thieves'), *to make stupid.*

Asperge montée, *f.* (popular), *very tall, lanky person;* "sky-scraper," or "lamp-post."

Asphalte, *m.* (familiar), polir l'—, *to lounge on the Boulevards.*

Asphyxié, *adj.* (popular), *dead-drunk,* or "sewed-up."

Asphyxier (popular), *to drink ;* — le perroquet, *to drink a glass of absinthe,* green, like a parrot ; — un pierrot, *to drink a glass of white wine.* Pierrot, a pantomimic character, with face painted white, and costume to match.

Aspic, *m.* (popular), *a slanderer,* an allusion to "aspic," *a viper ;* (thieves') *a miser,* or "hunks."

Aspiquerie, *f.* (popular), *calumny.*

Asseoir (popular), s'—, *to fall.* Envoyer quelqu'un s'—, *to throw one down, to silence, get rid of one.* Allez vous —, *shut up, go to* "pot" (an allusion to the customary intimation of the judge to a witness whose examination is concluded). S'— sur le bouchon, *to sit on mother earth.* S'— sur quelqu'un, *to silence one, to shut him up.* S'— sur quelquechose, *to attach but slight importance to a thing.*

Assesseur (gamesters'), *player.*

Asseyez-vous dessus et qu' ça finisse ! (familiar), *silence him ! sit upon him !*

Assiette, *f.* (popular), avoir l'— au beurre, *to be lucky, fortunate in life.*

Assis, *m.* (literary), *clerks,* or "quill drivers."

Oh ! c'est alors qu'il faut plaindre . . . les malheureux qu'un travail sédentaire courbe sur un bureau . . . . c'est alors qu'il convient de se lamenter sur le sort des assis. —RICHEPIN, *Le Pavé.*

Assister (thieves'), *to bring victuals to a prisoner from outside.*

Associée, *f.* (printers'), mon —, *my wife, my* "old woman."

Assommoir, *m.* (familiar), *name of a wine-shop at Belleville, and which is now common to all low drinking-shops.* From as-sommer, *to knock over the head.*

Astec, *m.* (familiar), *stunted and weakly person,* or "barber's cat ;" (literary) *a weak, despicable adversary.* An allusion to the Mexican dwarfs.

Astic, *m.* (thieves'), *steel, sword,* or "poker" (from the German stich) ; (soldiers') *a mixture of pipe-clay for the furbishing of the brass fixtures of equipment.* Aller à l'—, *to clean one's equipment.*

Asticot, *m.* (popular), *vermicelli ; mistress of a bully or thief,* "mollisher ;" — de cercueil, *glass of beer* (a play on the words "ver" and "bière," asticot being a *fleshworm*).

Astiquage or **astique,** *m.* (military), *cleaning the equipments.*

Astiquer (popular), *to beat,* or "to towel ;" *to tease.* Literally *to clean, to furbish.* S'—, *to have angry words, as a prelude to a set to ; to fight.* Literally *to make oneself neat,* or "smug."

As-tu fini, or **as-tu fini tes manières !** *words implying that a person's endeavours to convince or to deceive another have failed.* The expression corresponds in some degree to "Walker !" "No go !" "What next ?"

A table (thieves'), se mettre —, or, casser du sucre, *to confess a crime.*

Atelier (freemasons'), *place of meeting.*

Atigé, *adj.* (thieves' and popular), *ill,* or "laid up ;" *stricken, ruined,* or "cracked up."

Atiger (thieves' and popular), *to wound, to strike,* "to clump."

Atômes crochus, *m. pl.* (familiar), *mysterious elements of mutual sympathy.*

Atouser (convicts'), *to encourage, to urge,* "to kid on."

Atout, *m.* (thieves' and popular), *courage,* or "wool ;" *self-possession ; a blow,* or "wipe ;" *stomach ; money,* or "rhino ;" *ability.* Proper meaning *trumps.* Avoir de l'—, *to have pluck,* or "spunk ;" *to have a strong arm.*

Tu m'as donné la bonne mesure, tu es un cadet qui a de l'atout.—E. Sue. (*You gave me a good thrashing, you are a strong chap.*)

Le plus d'—, *a kind of swindling game played at low cafés.*

Atout ! (popular), *exclamation to denote that a blow has taken effect.*

Attache, *f., love tie.*

Attacher (thieves'), un bidon, *to inform against one,* "to blow the gaff."

Attaches, *f. pl.* (thieves'), *buckles ;* — brillantes, *diamond buckles ;* — de gratousse, *lace shirt-frill ;* — de cés, *breeches buckles.*

> J'ai fait suer un chêne,
> Son auberg j'ai enganté.
> Son auberg et sa toquante,
> Et ses attach's de cés.
> V. Hugo, *Le Dernier Jour d'un Condamné.*

Attaque, d'—, *resolutely, smartly.* Un homme d'—, *a resolute man, one who is game.* Etre d'—, *to show energy, resolution.* Y aller d'—, *to set about anything with a will, smartly, as if one meant business.* (Popular) D'attaque, *violent, severe.*

> V'lan ! v'là l'vent qui m'fiche eun'claque.
> Fait vraiment un froid d'attaque.
> Richepin.

Attelage, *m.* (cavalry), un bon —, *a couple of good friends.*

Attendrir (familiar), s'—, *to have reached that stage of intoxication when one is "maudlin."*

Attiger. See Atiger.

Attignoles, *f. pl.* (popular), *tripe à la mode de Caen* (tripe stewed with herbs and seasoning).

> N'importe où nous nous empâtons,
> D'arlequins, d'briffe et d'rogatons,
> Que qu'fois d'saucisse et d'attignoles.
> Richepin.

Attrapage, *m.* (familiar and popular), *severe scolding, sharp criticism, quarrel, fight,* "mill ;"

C

(military) — du premier numéro, *serious duel.*

Attrape (popular), à te rappeler, *mind you remember!*

Attraper (popular), *to scold,* "to jaw;" — l'oignon, *to receive a blow intended for another; to have to pay for others' reckoning.* S'—, *to abuse, to* "slang" *one another.* Se faire —, *to get scolded, abused,* "blown up." Attraper le haricot, or la fève, *to have to pay for others.* An allusion to one who finds a bean in his share of the cake at the "fête des rois," or Twelfth-night, and who, being proclaimed king, has to treat the other guests. (Journalists') Attraper, *to sharply criticise or run down a person or literary production;* (theatrical) *to hiss,* or "goose;" (actors') — le lustre, *to open wide one's mouth; to make a fruitless attempt to give emission to a note.*

Attrape-science, *m., printer's apprentice,* or "devil."

Attrapeur, *m.* (literary), *a sharp or scurrilous critic.*

Attrimer (thieves'), *to take,* to "nibble;" *to seize,* to "grab."

Attriquer (thieves'), *to buy; to buy stolen clothes.*

Attriqueur, *m.,* **attriqueuse**, *f.* (thieves'), *receiver of stolen clothes,* "fence."

Auber, *m., a sum of money,* "pile." A play on the word "haubert," *coat of mail, an assemblage of* "mailles," *meaning* "meshes" or "small change." Compare the expression, Sans sou ni maille.

Aumône, *f.* (thieves'), voler à l'—, *stealing from a jeweller, who is requested to exhibit small trinkets, some of which, being purloined, are transmitted to the hand of a con-* federate outside who pretends to ask for alms.

Aumônier, *m.* (thieves'), *a thief who operates as described above.*

Au prix où est le beurre (familiar), *at the present rate of prices of things in general.*

Aure, or **haure** (thieves'), le grand —, *God.*

Aüs, *m.* (shopmen's), *perplexed purchaser who leaves without buying anything.*

Austo, *m.* (soldiers'), *guard-room, cells,* "Irish theatre," "mill," or "jigger."

Autan, *m.* (thieves'), *loft, attics* (old word hautain, *high*).

Autel (freemasons'), *table at which the master sits;* (popular) — de besoin, *prostitute,* or "bed-fagot;" — de plume, *bed,* "doss."

Auteur, *m.* (familiar), *father or mother,* "governor," or "mater;" — beurrier, *unsuccessful author whose works are sold as wrapping-paper for tradesmen.*

Autor (familiar and popular), jouer d'—, *to play cards without proposing.* Travailler d'— et d'achar, *to work with energy.*

Autor, d'— (thieves'), *in a peremptory manner; deliberately.*

Dis donc, fourline, la première fois que nous trouverons la Pégriotte, faut l'emmener d'autor.—EUGÈNE SUE.

Autre, *adj.* (popular), cet — chien, *that chap.* Etre l'—, *to be duped,* or "bamboozled;" *to be the lover; the mistress.* L'— côté, *appellation given by Paris students to that part of the city situated on the right bank of the river.* Femme de l'— côte, *woman residing in that part of Paris.*

Auvergnat, *m.* (popular), avaler l'—, *to take communion.*

Auverpin, *m.* (popular), *native of Auvergne.* Appellation given to commissionnaires, charcoal-dealers, water-carriers, &c., who generally hail from Auvergne.

Et là seulement vous trouverez les bals-musette, les vrais, tenus par des Auverpins à la fois mastroquets et charbonniers, hantés par des Auverpins aussi, porteurs d'eau, commissionnaires, frotteurs, cochers. — RICHEPIN, *Le Pavé.*

Auverpinches, *m. pl.* (popular), *clumsy shoes usually worn by Auvergnats.*

Aux (popular), petits oignons, *in first-rate style, excellently.* Etre — petits oiseaux, *to be comfortable, snug.*

Auxiliaire (prisoners'), *prisoner acting as servant,* or "fag."

Avalé (popular), avoir — le pépin, *to be pregnant,* or "lumpy." An allusion to the apple. Avoir — une chaise percée, *to have an offensive breath.* Avoir — un sabre, *to be stiff,* "to have swallowed a poker." Avoir — le bon Dieu en culotte de velours, *to have swallowed some excellent food or drink.*

Et toujours le patron doit terminer sa lampée par un hum engageant et satisfait comme s'il avait avalé le bon Dieu en culotte de velours.—RICHEPIN, *Le Pavé.*

Avaler (thieves'), le luron, *to receive the Host at communion.* (Popular) Avaler sa cuiller ; sa fourchette ; sa gaffe ; sa langue ; ses baguettes ; *to die.* In other words, "to lay down one's knife and fork ;" "to kick the bucket ;" "to croak ;" "to stick one's spoon in the wall," &c. ; — son poussin, *to be dismissed,* "to get the sack ;" —son absinthe, *to put a good face on some disagreeable matter.* (Familiar) Avoir l'air de vouloir tout —, *to look as though one were*

going to do mighty things ; to look savage and threatening.

Avale-tout-cru, *m.* (popular), *braggart,* or "swashbuckler ;" (thieves') *thief who conceals jewels in his mouth.*

Avaloir, *m.* (popular and thieves'), *throat,* "peck alley," or "gutter lane."

Avantages, *m. pl.,* avant-cœur, *m.,* avant-main, *f.,* avant-postes, *m. pl.,* avant-scènes, *f. pl.* (popular and familiar), *bosoms,* "Charlies," "dairies," or "bubbies."

Avantageux, *adj.* (popular), *convenient, roomy.* Des souliers —, *easy shoes.*

Avant-courrier, *m.* (thieves'), *auger.*

Avaro, *m.* (popular), *damage.* From avarie.

Avergot, *m.* (thieves'), *egg.*

Avertineux, *adj.* (popular), *of a suspicious, gruff disposition ; of a forbidding aspect.*

Avocat bêcheur, *m.* (printers'), *backbiter ;* (thieves') *public prosecutor.*

Avoine, *f.* (military), *brandy.* (Popular) Avoir encore l'—, *to have still one's maidenhead.* (Coachmens') Donner l'—, *to whip ; to thrash,* or "flush."

Avoir (popular), à la bonne, *to like, to love,* "to be sweet upon ;" — campo, *to have leave to go out ;* — celui, for avoir l'honneur de ; — dans le nez, *to have a strong dislike for a person or thing ;* (familiar) — dans le ventre, ce que quelqu'un a dans le ventre, *what stuff one is made of ;* (popular) — de ce qui sonne, *to be well off ;* in other words, *to have plenty of beans, ballast, rhino, the needful, blunt, bustle, dust, coal, oof, stumpy, brass, tin ;* — de la chance au bâtonnet, *to be unlucky.* Le jeu de bâtonnet is the game of nap the cat ; — de la glu aux mains, *to steal,* " to nibble ;" — de la ligne, *to have a nice figure ;* — de l'anis dans une écope : tu auras —, *don't you wish you may get it ;* — de l'as de Carreau dans le dos, *to be humpbacked ;* — des as dans son jeu, *to have an advantage, to be lucky, to have* " cocum ;" — des mots avec quelqu'un, *to fall out with one, to have a tiff with one ;* — des mots avec la justice, *to be prosecuted ;* — des mots avec les sergots, *to have some disagreement with the police ;* — des œufs sur le plat, *to have black eyes,* "to have one's eyes in mourning;" — des petits pois à écosser ensemble, *to have a bone to pick with one ;* — des planches, *to be an experienced actor ;* — du beurre sur la tête, *to have some misdeed on one's conscience ;* — du chien, *to possess dash,* "go ;" — du chien dans le ventre, *to have pluck, endurance,* or "stay ;" — du pain sur la planche, *to have a competency ;* — du poil au cul, *to possess courage,* or "hackle," *energy;* — du plomb dans l'aile, *to be wounded ;* — du sable dans les yeux, *to feel sleepy ;* — du toupet, *to have audacity, cool impudence ;* — fumé dans une pipe neuve, *to be tipsy,* or "obfuscated ;" — la flemme, *to be afraid ; to feel lazy,* or "Mondayish ;" — l'arche, *to have credit,* or "jawbone ;" — l'assiette au beurre, *to be fortunate in life ;* — la cuisse gaie *is said of a female of lax morals ;* — le pot de chambre dans la commode, *to have an offensive breath ;* — le caillou déplumé, le coco déplumé, *to be*

bald, *to have* " a bladder of lard ;" — le casque, *to fancy a man ;* — le compas dans l'œil, *to possess a sharp eye,* with respect to judging of distance or quantity ; — le front dans le cou, *to be bald,* or "stag-faced ;" — le nez creux, *to be clever at foreseeing, guessing ;* — le pouce long, *to be skilful, to be a* "dab" *at something ;* — le trac, *to be afraid,* "funky ;" — les calots pochés, *to have black eyes ;* — les côtes en long, *to be lazy,* a " bummer ;" — l'estomac dans les talons, dans les mollets, *to be ravenous, very* "peckish ;" — l'étrenne, *to be the first to do, or be done to, to have the* "wipe of ;" — le sac, *to be wealthy,* or "well ballasted ;" — mal au bréchet, *to have the stomach-ache,* or "botts ;" — mal aux cheveux, *to have a headache caused from overnight potations ;* — mangé de l'oseille, *to be sour-tempered, peevish,* or "crusty ;" — sa côtelette, in theatrical language, *to obtain great applause ;* (popular) — sa pointe, *to be slightly tipsy,* " fresh ;" — son caillou, *to be on the verge of intoxication,* or "muddled ;" — son coke, *to die ;* — son cran, *to be angry,* "to have one's monkey up ;" — son pain cuit. Properly *to have an income, to be provided for.* The expression is old.

Vente, gresle, gelle, j'ai mon pain cuit.
VILLON.

(Also) *to be sentenced to death ;* — son sac de quelqu'un, *to be tired of one ;* — un coup de marteau, *to be cracked,* "queer ;" — un fédéré dans la casemate, or un polichinelle dans le tiroir, *to be pregnant,* or "lumpy ;" — un poil dans la main, *to feel lazy ;* — un pot de chambre sous le nez, *to have an offensive breath ;* — un rat dans la trompe, *to feel irritated, provoked, exasperated,* "badgered;" — une chambre à louer, *to be eccentric, even to insanity;* "to have apartments to let;" *to be minus one tooth;* — une crampe au pylore, *to be blessed with a good appetite,* or "twist;" — une table d'hôte dans l'estomac, *to have an extraordinary appetite;* — vu le loup *is said of a girl who has lost her maidenhead.* En — la farce, *to be able to procure a thing.* Pour deux sous on en a la farce, *a penny will get it for you.* En — sa claque, *to have eaten or drunk to excess, to have had a "tightener."* (Familiar) Avoir une belle presse, *to be lauded by the press.*

Avoir (popular and familiar), la boule détraquée; le coco fêlé; le trognon détraqué; un asticot dans la noisette; un bœuf gras dans le char; un cancrelat dans la boule; un hanneton dans le réservoir; un hanneton dans le plafond; un moustique dans la boîte au sel; un voyageur dans l'omnibus; une araignée dans le plafond; une écrevisse dans la tourte; une écrevisse dans le vol-au-vent; une grenouille dans l'aquarium; une hirondelle dans le soliveau; une Marseillaise dans le kiosque; une punaise dans le soufflet; une sardine dans l'armoire à glace; une trichine dans le jambonneau; une sauterelle dans la guitare — Parisian expressions which may be rendered by *to be mad, or cracked, crazy, touched, to have rats in the upper storey, a bee in one's bonnet, a tile loose, to have apartments to let, to be wrong in the upper storey, to be off one's chump, &c., &c.*

Avoir, n'—, pas de toupet, *to show cool impudence;* (popular) — pas inventé le fil à couper le beurre *is said of a man of poor ability, not likely* "to set the Thames on fire;" — pas le cul dans une jupe, *to be manly,* or "spry;" — pas sa langue dans sa poche, *to have a ready tongue;* — rien du côté gauche, or sous le têton gauche, *to be heartless;* — rien dans le ventre, *to be devoid of ability, to be made of poor stuff;* — plus sa grille d'égoût, — plus sa pièce de dix ronds *is said of Sodomists;* — plus de chapelure sur le jambonneau, — plus de crin sur la brosse, — plus de fil sur la bobine, — plus de gazon sur le pré, — plus de mousse sur le caillou, or sur la plate-bande, — plus de paillasson à la porte, *to be bald,* or "to have a bladder of lard," "to be stag-faced," &c.; (thieves') — pas la trouille, le flubart, or le trac, *to have no fear.*

Azor, *m.* (popular), *dog;* (military) *knapsack*, or "scran-bag" (an allusion to the hairy covering of soldiers' knapsacks). Etre à cheval sur —, *to shoulder the knapsack.* Tenir — en laisse *is said of a discharged soldier who on leaving the barracks, with a view to showing that "Azor" is no longer his master, drags him ignominiously along the ground attached to a strap.* (Theatrical) Appeler, or siffler —, *to hiss,* or "to goose."

 **ABA,** *adj.* (popular), *dumb-founded, abashed,* "blue," or "fl a b bergasted."

Babillard *m.*(thieves'), *confessor; book; newspaper.* Griffonneur de —, *journalist.* It also means *a petition.*

Ma largue part pour Versailles,
Aux pieds d'sa Majesté,
Elle lui fonce un babillard
Pour m'faire détourailler.
    V. HUGO, *Dernier Jour d'un Condamné.*

Babillarde, *f.* (thieves'), *watch,* or "jerry," *letter,* "screeve," or "stiff."

Babillaudier, *m.* (thieves'), *bookseller.*

Babille, *f.* See **Babillarde.**

Babiller (thieves'), *to read.*

Babines, *f. pl.* (popular), *mouth,* "muzzle." S'en donner par les —, *to eat voraciously,* "to scorf." S'en lêcher les —, *to enjoy in imagination any kind of pleasure, past or in store.*

Babouine, *f.* (popular), *mouth,* "rattle-trap," "kisser," "dubber," or "maw." See **Plomb.**

Bac, for **baccarat** or **baccalauréat.**

Baccon, *m.*(thieves'), *pig,* or "sow's baby;" *pork,* or "sawney."

Bachasse, *f.* (thieves'), *hard labour; convict settlement.*

Bâche, *f.* (thieves' and cads'), *cap,* or "tile;" *stakes; bed,* or "doss." Se mettre dans la —, *to go to bed.* Bâche, properly a *cart tilt.*

Bachelière, *f., female associate of students at the Quartier Latin, the headquarters of the University of France.* Herein are situated the Sorbonne, Collège de France, Ecole de Médecine, Ecole de Droit, &c.

Bâcher, pagnotter, or **percher** (thieves' and popular). Se —, *to go to bed.*

Bachot, *m.* (students'), *baccalauréat, or examination for the degree of bachelor of arts or science conferred by the University of France.* Etre —, *to be a bachelor.* Faire son —, *to read for that examination.*

Bachotier, *m.* (students'), *tutor who prepares candidates for the baccalauréat,* "coach," or "crammer."

Bachotter (sharpers'), *to swindle at billiards.*

Bachotteur, *m.* (sharpers'), *confederate of blacklegs at a four game of billiards.* The "bachotteur" arranges the game, holds the stakes, &c., pretending meanwhile to be much interested in the victim, or " pigeon." His associates are "'l'emporteur," or "buttoner," whose functions consist in entering into conversation with the intended victim and enticing him into playing, and " la bête," who feigns to be a loser at the outset, so as to encourage the pigeon.

Bâcler, boucler (thieves'), *to shut, to arrest.* Bâclez la lourde ! *shut the door !* " dub the jigger." (Popular) Bâcler, *to put, to place.* Bâclez-vous là ! *place yourself there !*

Bacreuse, *f.* (popular), *pocket.* From creuse, *deep.*

Badaudière, *f.*, *the tribe of badauds, people whose interest is awakened by the most trifling events or things, and who stop to gape wonderingly at such events or things.*

Parmi tous les badauds de la grande badaudière parisienne, qui est le pays du monde où l'on en trouve le plus, parmi tous les flâneurs, gâcheurs de temps . . . bayeurs aux grues.—RICHEPIN, *Le Pavé.*

Badigeon, *m.* (popular), *painting of the face; paint for the face,* " slap." Se coller du —, *to paint one's face,* " to stick on slap."

Badigeonner, la femme au puits, *to lie,* " to cram." An allusion to Truth supposed to dwell in a well. Se —, *to paint one's face.*

Badigoinces, *f. pl.* (popular), *lips, mouth,* " maw." Jouer des —, or se caler les —, *to eat,* "to grub." S'en coller par les —, *to have a good fill,* " to stodge." See **Mastiquer.**

Badinguiste, badingâteux, badingouin, badingueusard, badingouinard, *terms of contempt applied to Bonapartists.* " Badinguet," nickname of Napoleon III., was the name of a mason who lent him his clothes, and whose character he assumed to effect his escape from Fort Ham, in which he was confined for conspiracy and rebellion against the government of King Louis Philippe.

Badouillard, *m.*, **badouillarde,** *f.* (popular), *male and female habitués of low fancy balls.*

Badouille, *f.* (popular), *henpecked husband,* or " stangey ;" *fool,* or " bounder."

Badouiller (popular), *to frequent low public balls; to wander about without a settled purpose,* " to scamander ;" *to have drinking revels,* " to go on the booze."

Badouillerie, *f.* (popular), *dissipated mode of living.*

Baffre, *f.* (popular), *a blow in the face with the fist,* a " bang in the mug."

Bafouiller, (popular), *to jabber ; to splutter ; to sputter.*

Bafouilleur, bafouilleux, *m.*, **bafouilleuse,** *f.*, *one who sputters.*

Bagniole, *f.* (popular), *carriage,* " trap," or " cask."

Bagnole, *f.* (popular), diminutive of bagne, *convict settlement, hulks ; wretched room or house,* or " crib ;" *costermonger's hand - barrow,* " trolly," or " shallow."

La maigre salade . . . que les bonnes femmes poussent devant elles dans leur bagnole à bras.—RICHEPIN, *Le Pavé.*

Bagou, bagoût, *m.* (familiar) (has passed into the language), *facility of speech* (used disparagingly). Quel — mes amis ! *well, he is the one to talk !* Avoir un fier —, *to have plenty of jaw.*

On se laissa bientôt aller à la joie ravivée sans cesse au bagoût du vieux, qui n'avait jamais été aussi bavard.—RICHEPIN, *La Glu.*

(Thieves') Bagou, *name*, "mon-niker," "monarch."

Bagoulard, *m.* (popular), *a very talkative man*, a " clack-box," or " mouth-all-mighty." C'est un fameux —, " He's the bloke to slam."

Bagouler (popular and thieves'), *to prattle*, to do the " Poll Parrot ; " *to give one's name*, or " dub one's monniker."

Bague, *f.* (thieves'), *name*, " mon-niker," "monarch.'"

Baguenaude (thieves' and cads'), *pocket*, " cly," " sky-rocket," or "brigh ; " — à sec, *empty pocket ;* — ronflante, *pocket full of money.* Faire la retourne des baguenaudes, *to rob drunkards who go to sleep on benches.*

. . . Une bande de filous, vauriens ayant travaillé les baguenaudes dans la foule.—RICHEPIN, *Le Pavé.*

Baguenots, *m. pl.* (popular), faire les —, *to pick pockets*, " to fake a cly."

Baguettes, *f. pl.* Properly *rods, or drum-sticks.* (Military) Avaler ses —, *to die.* (Familiar) Baguettes de tambour, *thin legs, spindle-shanks ; lank hair.*

Bahut, *m.* (popular), *furniture*, "marbles." Properly *large dresser, or press ;* (cadets') — spécial, *the military school of Saint-Cyr ;* (students') — paternel, *paternal house.* Bahut, *a crammer's establishment ; college, or boarding-school.*

Eux, les pauvres petits galériens, ils continuent à vivre entre les murs lépreux du bahut.—RICHEPIN, *Le Pavé.*

Bahuté (Saint-Cyr cadets'), ceci est —, *that is smart, soldier-like.* Une tenue bahutée, *smart dress or appearance.*

Bahuter (Saint-Cyr cadets'), *to create a disturbance*, " to kick up a row; " (schoolboys') *to go from one educational establishment to another.*

Bahuteur, *m.*, *one fond of a* "row; " *unruly scholar ; pupil who patronizes, willingly or not, different educational establishments.*

Baigne-dans-le-beurre (popular), *womens' bully, or* " pen-sioner." An allusion to " maque-reau," or mackerel, a common appellation for such creatures. They also go by the varied appellations of " dos, maq, mec, barbe, bar-beau, brochet, marlou, casquette à trois ponts, monsieur à roufla-quettes, poisson, chevalier de la guiche, benoît, visqueux, mangeur de blanc," &c. See **Poisson.**

Baigneuse, *f.* (thieves' and cads'), *head*, or " block," " canister," " nut." See **Tronche.**

Baignoire à bon Dieu, *f.* (cads'), *chalice.*

Bailler au tableau (theatrical), *to have an insignificant part in a new play.*

Baimbain (Breton cant), *potatoes.*

Bain de pied (familiar), *the over-flow into the saucer from a cup of coffee or glass of brandy ; third help of brandy after coffee, those preceding being* " la rincette " *and* " la surrincette."

Bain-Marie, *m.* (popular), *a per-son with a mild, namby-pamby disposition allied to a weakly con-stitution*, a " sappy " *fellow.*

Bain qui chauffe, *m.* (popular), *a rain cloud in hot weather.*

Baiser (popular), la camarde, *to die*, " to kick the bucket," " to snuff it ; " (gamesters') — le cul de la vieille, *not to score, to remain at* " love."

Baissier, *m.*, *man on 'Change who speculates for a fall in the funds*, "bear." See **Haussier.**

Baite, *f.* (thieves'), *house,* "crib."

Bajaf, *m.* (popular), *a stout, ple-thoric man.* Gros—, "forty guts."

Bajoter (popular), *to chatter,* "to gabble."

Bal, *m.* (military), *extra drill* (called a "hoxter" at the Royal Military Academy).

Baladage, balladage, *m.* (popular), chanteur au —, *street singer,* "street pitcher."

Balade, ballade, *f.* (popular and familiar), *walk, stroll, lounge,* "trolling." Canot de —, *plea-sure boat.* Faire une —, se payer une —, *to take a walk.* Chanteur à la —, *itinerant singer,* "chaun-ter." (Thieves') Balade, or ballade, *pocket;* also called "fouillouse, pro-fonde, valade," and by English rogues, "sky-rocket, cly, or brigh."

Balader (thieves'), *to choose; to seek.* (Popular) Se —, *to take a walk; to stroll;* "to mike;" *to make off; to run away,* "to cut one's lucky." See **Patatrot.**

Baladeur, *m.* (popular), *one who takes a walk.*

Baladeuse, *f.* (popular), *woman with no heart for work and who is fond of idly strolling about.*

Balai, *m.* (hawkers'), *police officer,* or *gendarme,* "crusher;" (mili-tary) — à plumes, *plumes of shako.* (Popular) Balai, *the last 'bus or tramcar at night.* Donner du — à quelqu'un, *to drive one away.*

Balancement, *m.* (clerks'), *dis-missal,* "the sack."

Balancer (popular), *to throw at a distance;* — quelqu'un, *to dismiss from one's employment,* "to give the sack;" *to get rid of one; to make fun of one; to hoax,* "to bamboozle;"* (thieves')— la rous-caillante, *to speak,* or "to rap;" — sa canne *is said of a vagrant who takes to thieving, of a convict who makes his escape, or of a ticket-of-leave man who breaks bounds;* — sa largue, *to get rid of one's mis-tress,* "to bury a Moll;" — ses alènes, *to turn honest; to forsake the burglar's implements for the murderer's knife;* — ses chasses, *to gaze about,* "to stag;" — son chiffon rouge, *to talk,* "to wag one's red rag;" — une lazagne, *to send a letter,* "screeve," or "stiff."

Balanceur, *m.* (thieves'), de braise, *money changer.* An allusion to the practice of weighing money.

Balancier, *m.* (popular), faire le —, *to wait for one.*

Balançoir, balançon, *m.* (thieves'), *window-bar.*

Balançoire, *f.* (familiar), *fib,* "flam;" *nonsense; stupid joke.* Envoyer à la —, *to get rid of one; to invite one to make himself scarce,* or *to send one to the deuce.*

Balançon, *m.* (thieves'), *iron ham-mer; window-bar.*

Balandrin, *m.* (popular), *parcel made up in canvas; a small ped-lar's pack.*

Balauder (tramps'), *to beg,* "to cadge."

Balayage, *m.* Properly *sweeping;* used figuratively *wholesale getting rid of.* On devrait faire un ba-layage dans cette administration, *there ought to be a wholesale dis-missal of officials.*

Balayer (theatrical), les planches, *to be the first to sing at a con-cert.*

Balayez-moi-ça, *m.* (popular), *woman's dress.* Literally *you just sweep that away.*

Balcon, *m.* (popular), il y a du monde, or il y a quelqu'un au —, *an allusion to well-developed breasts.*

Balconnier, *m.*, *orator who makes a practice of addressing the crowd from a balcony.*

Baleine, *f.* (popular), *disreputable woman,* "*bed-fagot.*" Rire comme une —, *to laugh in a silly manner with mouth wide open like a whale's.*

Baliverneur, *m.* (popular), *monger of* "*twaddle,*" *of tomfooleries, of* "*blarney.*"

Ballade, *f.* (popular), aller faire une — à la lune, *to ease oneself.*

Balle, *f.* (thieves'), *secret; affair; opportunity.* Ça fait ma —, *that just suits me.* Manquer sa —, *to miss one's opportunity.* Faire —, *to be fasting.* Faire la —, *to act according to instructions.* (Popular) Balle, *one-franc piece; face,* "*mug;*" *head,* "*block.*" Il a une bonne —, *he has a good-natured looking face, or a grotesque face.* Rond comme —, *is said of one who has eaten or drunk to excess; of one who is drunk, or* "*tight.*" Un blafard de cinq balles, *a five-franc piece.* (Familiar) Enfant de la —, *actor's child; actor; one who is of the same profession as his father.* (Prostitutes') Balle d'amour, *handsome face.* Rude —, *energetic countenance, with harsh features.* Balle de coton, *a blow with the fist,* a "*bang.*"

Ballerine, *f.* (swells'), *ballet dancer.*

Ballomanie, *f.*, *mania for ballooning.*

Ballon, *m.* (popular), *glass of beer; the behind,* or "*tochas.*" Enlever le — à quelqu'un, *to kick one in the hinder part of the body,* "*to toe one's bum,*" "*to root,*" or "*to land a kick.*" En —, *in prison,* "*in quod.*" Se donner du —, *to make a dress bulge out.* Se lâcher du —, *to make off rapidly,* "*to brush.*"

Ballonné, *adj.* (thieves'), *imprisoned,* "*in limbo.*"

Ballot, *m.* (tailors'), *stoppage of work.*

Balloter (tailors'), *to be out of work,* "*out of collar;*" (thieves') *to throw.*

Bal-musette, *m.*, *dancing place for workpeople in the suburbs.*

Les bals-musette au plancher de bois qui sonne comme un tympanon sous les talons tambourinant la bourrée montagnarde . . . que la musette remplit de son chant agreste.—RICHEPIN, *Le Pavé.*

Balochard, balocheur, *m.* (popular), *one who idles about town carelessly and merrily.*

Aussi j'laisse l'chic et les chars,
Aux feignants et aux galupiers,
Et j'suis l'roi des Balochards,
Des Balochards qui va-t-à pieds.
RICHEPIN, *Gueux de Paris.*

Balocher, (popular), *to be an habitué of dancing halls; to bestir oneself; to fish in troubled waters; to have on hand any unlawful business; to move things; to hang them up; to idle about carelessly and merrily,* or "*to mike.*"

Balots, *m. pl.* (thieves'), *lips.* Se graisser les —, *to eat,* "*to grub.*"

Balouf (popular), *very strong,* "*spry.*"

Balthazar, *m.* (familiar), *a plentiful meal,* "*a tightener.*"

Baluchon, *m.* (popular), *parcel,* or "peter."

Bambino, bambochino, *m.* (popular), *term of endearment for a child.*

Bamboche, *adj.* (popular), être —, *to be tipsy,* or "to be screwed."

Banban, *m. and f.* (popular), *lame person,* "dot and go one;" *small stunted person,* "Jack Sprat."

Banc, *m.* (convicts'), *camp bed;* (Parisians') — de Terre-Neuve, *that part of the Boulevard between the Madeleine and Porte Saint-Denis.* Probably an allusion to the ladies of fishy character, termed "morues," or *codfish,* who cruise about that part of Paris, and a play on the word Terre-Neuve, *Newfoundland,* where the real article is fished in large quantities. (Military) Pied de —, *sergeant.* See **Pied.**

Bancal, *m.* (soldiers'), *cavalry sword.*

> Et, je me sens fier, ingambe,
> D'un plumet sur mon colbac,
> D'un bancal, et du flic-flac
> De ce machin sur ma jambe.
> A. DE CHATILLON.

Bande. Properly *cushion of billiard table.* Coller sous —, *to get one in a fix,* in a "hole."

Bande d'air, *f.* (theatrical), *frieze painted blue so as to represent the sky.*

Bande noire, *f., a gang of swindlers who procure goods on false pretences and sell them below their value,* "long firm."

La Bande Noire comprises four categories of swindlers working jointly: "le courtier à la mode," who, by means of false references, gets himself appointed as agent to important firms, generally wine merchants, jewellers, provision dealers. He calls on some small tradesmen on the verge of bankruptcy, denominated "petits faisans," or "frères de la côte," and offers them at a very low price merchandise which they are to dispose of, allowing him a share in the profits. The next step to be taken is to bribe a clerk of some private information office, who is thus induced to give a favourable answer to all inquiries regarding the solvency of the "petit faisan." The courtier à la mode also bribes with a like object the doorkeeper of his clients. At length the goods are delivered by the victimized firms; now steps in the "fusilleur" or "gros faisan," who obtains the merchandise at a price much below value—a cask of wine worth 170 francs, for instance, being transferred to him at less than half that sum—the sale often taking place at the railway goods station, especially when the "petit faisan" is an imaginary individual represented by a doorkeeper in confederacy with the gang.— *Translated from the "République Française" newspaper, February,* 1886.

Bander (popular), la caisse, *to abscond with the cash-box.* Properly *to tighten the drum;* — l'ergot, *to run away,* "to crush."

Bannette (popular), *apron.*

Bannière, *f.* (familiar), être en —, *to be in one's shirt, in one's* "flesh bag."

Banque, *f.* (popular), *falsehood, imposition,* "plant." (Hawkers') La —, *the puffing up of goods to allure purchasers; the confraternity of mountebanks.* (Showmens') Truc de —, *password which obtains admission to booths or raree-shows.*

(Printers') Banque, *pay.* La — a fouaillé *expresses that pay has been deferred.* Etre bloqué à la —, or faire — blèche, *to receive no pay.*

Banquet, *m.* (freemasons'), *dinner.*

Banquette, *f.* (popular), *chin.*

Banquezingue, *m.* (thieves'), *banker,* "rag-shop cove."

Banquiste (thieves'), *one who prepares a swindling operation.*

Baptême, *m.* (popular), *head,* "nut."

Baquet, *m.* (popular), *washerwoman;* — insolent, *same meaning* (an allusion to the impudence of Parisian washerwomen) ; — de science, *cobbler's tub.*

Barant, *m.* (thieves'), *gutter, brook.* From the Celtic baranton, *fountain.*

Baraque, *f.*, *disparaging epithet for a house or establishment;* (servants') *a house where masters are strict and particular;* a "shop ;" *newspaper of which the editor is strict with respect to the productions;* (schoolboys') *cupboard;* (soldiers') *a service stripe;* (sharpers') *a kind of swindling game of pool.*

Barbaque, or bidoche, *f.* (popular), *meat,* or "carnish."

Barbe, *f.* (students'), *private coaching.* (Popular) Avoir de la — *is said of anything old, stale.* (Theatrical) Faire sa —, *to make money.* (Familiar) Vieille —, *old-fashioned politician.* (Printers') Barbe, *intoxication, the different stages of the happy state being* "le coup de feu," "la barbe simple," "la barbe indigne." Prendre une —, *to get intoxicated,* or "screwed." (Popular) Barbe, *women's bully,* or "pensioner."

Barbe à poux, *m.*, *an insulting expression especially used by cabbies, means lousy beard.*

Barbeau, *m.* (popular), *prostitute's bully.* Properly *a barbel.* These gentry go also by the appellations of "dos, maquereau, Alphonse, maq, mec, monsieur à rouflaquettes, chevalier de la guiche, marlou, barbe, brochet, baignedans-le-beurre, visqueux, benoît, casquette à trois ponts, barbillon, poisson, mangeur de blanc, macquet, dos vert, chevalier du bidet, costel, dessous, chiqueur de blanc, macrottin, écaillé, fish, foulard rouge, cravate verte, barbot, gentilhomme sous-marin, goujon, lacromuche." Londoners call the creature "pensioner," with an obscene prefix, according to the *Slang Dictionary.* See Poisson.

Barbeaudier (thieves'), *doorkeeper; turnkey,* "dubsman," or "jigger dubber ;" — de castu, *hospital overseer.*

Barberot, *m.* (convicts'), *barber,* a "strap."

Barbet, *m.* (thieves'), *the devil,* "old scratch," or "ruffin."

Barbichon, *m.* (popular), *monk.* An allusion to the long beard generally sported by the fraternity.

Barbille, barbillon, *m.*, *girl's bully, young hand at the business.*

Barbillons, *m. pl.* (popular), de Beauce, *vegetables* (Beauce, formerly a province) ; — de Varenne, *turnips.*

Barbiste, *m.*, *pupil of the Ecole Sainte-Barbe.* This school has or had a great reputation.

Barbot, *m.* (popular), *duck; girl's bully,* "ponce." See Poisson.

(Thieves') Vol au —, *pocket-picking*, or "buz-faking." Faire le —, *to pick pockets*, "to buz," or "to fake a cly."

Barbotage, *m.*, *theft*, "push." From barboter, *to dabble.*

Barbote, *f.* (thieves'), *searching of prisoners on their arrival at the prison*, "turning over."

Barboter (thieves'), *to search on the person*, "to turn over;" *to steal*, "to clift;" *to purloin goods and sell them;* — les poches, *to pick pockets*, "to buz;" (familiar) — la caisse, *to appropriate the contents of a cashbox.*

Barboteur, *m.* (thieves'), de campagne, *night thief.*

Barbotier, *m.*, *searcher at prisons.*

Barbotin, *m.* (thieves'), *theft; proceeds of sale of stolen goods*, "swag."

> Après mon dernier barbotin,
> J'ai flasqué du poivre à la rousse.
> RICHEPIN.

Barbue, *f.* (thieves), *pen.*

Bar-de-tire, *m.* (thieves'), *hose.*

Baril de moutarde (cads'), *breech.* See **Vasistas.**

Barka (military), *enough* (from the Arabic).

Baron, *m.* (popular), de la crasse, *man ill at ease in garments which are not suited to his station in life, and which in consequence give him an awkward appearance.*

Barre, *f.* (thieves'), *needle;* (popular) compter à la —, *primitive mode of reckoning by making dashes on a slate.*

Barré, *adj.* (popular), *dull-witted*, "cabbage-head."

Barrer (popular), *to leave off work;* *to relinquish an undertaking; to scold.* Se —, *to make off*, "to mizzle;" *to conceal oneself.*

Barres, *f. pl.* (popular), *jaws.* Se rafraîchir les —, *to drink*, "to wet or whet one's whistle."

Barrique, *f.* (freemasons'), *decanter or bottle.*

Bas (popular), de buffet, *a person or thing of no consequence;* — de plafond, — du cul, *short person.* Vieux — de buffet, *old coquette.*

Basane, or **bazane,** *f.* (popular), *skin*, or "buff." Tanner la—, *to thrash*, "to tan." (Military) Tailler une —, *is to make a certain contemptuous gesture the nature of which may best be described as follows:—*

Un tel, quatre jours de salle de police, ordre du sous-officier X . . . a répondu à ce sous-officier en lui taillant une bazane; la main appliquée sur la braguette du pantalon, et lui faisant décrire une conversion à gauche, avec le pouce pour pivot.— *Quoted by* L. MERLIN, *La Langue Verte du Troupier.*

Bas-bleuisme, *m.* (literary), *mania for writing.* Used in reference to those of the fair sex.

Bascule, *f.* (popular), *guillotine.*

Basculer (popular), *to guillotine.*

Bas-off, *m.* (Polytechnic School), *under-officer.*

Basourdir (thieves'), *to knock down; to stun; to kill*, "to give one his gruel." See **Refroidir.**

Basse, *f.* (thieves'), *the earth.*

Bassin, *m.*, **bassinoire,** *f.* (familiar), *superlatively dull person, a bore.*

Bassinant, *adj.* (familiar), *dull, annoying, boring.*

Bassiner (familiar), *to annoy, to bore.*

Bassinoire, *f.*, *large watch*, "turnip." See **Bassin.**

Basta (popular), *enough ; no more.* From the Spanish.

Bastimage (thieves'), *work*, "graft."

Bastringue, *m.* (popular), *low dancing-hall ; noise, disturbance,* "rumpus ;" (prisoners') *a fine steel saw used by prisoners for cutting through iron bars.*

Bastringueuse, *f.* (popular), *female habituée of* bastringues, *or low dancing-saloons.*

Bataclan, *m.* (popular), *set of tools ;* (thieves') *house-breaking implements,* or "jilts."

J'ai déjà préparé tout mon bataclan, les fausses clefs sont essayées.—Vidocq, *Mémoires.*

Bataille, *f.* (military), chapeau en —, *cocked hat worn crosswise.* Chapeau en colonne, *the opposite of* "en bataille."

Bâtard, *m.* (popular), *heap of anything.*

Bate, *f.* (popular), être de la —, *to be happy, fortunate, to have* "cocum."

Bateau, *m.* (popular), mener en —, *to swindle, to deceive.* Monter un —, *to impose upon ; to attempt to deceive.*

Bateaux, *m. pl.* (popular), *shoes,* "carts ;" *large shoes ; shoes that let in water.*

Bateaux-mouches, *m. pl.* (popular), *large shoes.*

Batelée, *f.* (popular), *concourse of people.*

Bath, or **bate** (popular), *fine ; excellent ; tip-top ; very well.* The origin of the expression is as follows : — Towards 1848 some Bath note-paper of superior qua-

lity was hawked about in the streets of Paris and sold at a low price. Thus "papier bath" became synonymous of excellent paper. In a short time the qualifying term alone remained, and received a general application.

Un foulard tout neuf, ce qu'il y a de plus bath !—Richepin.

C'est rien —, *that is excellent,* "fizzing." C'est — aux pommes, *it is delightful.* (Thieves') Du —, *gold or silver.* Faire —, *to arrest.*

Batiau, *m.* (printers'), jour du —, *day on which the compositor makes out his account for the week.* Parler —, *to talk shop.*

Batif, *m.* (thieves'), **bative, batifonne,** *f.*, *new ; pretty,* or "dimber." La fée est bative, *the girl is pretty, she is a* "dimber mort."

Batimancho (Breton), *wooden shoes.*

Bâtiment (familiar), être du —, *to be of a certain profession.*

Bâtir (popular), sur le devant, *to have a large stomach ; to have something like a* "corporation" *growing upon one.*

Bâton, *m.* (thieves'), creux, *musket,* or "dag ;" — de cire, *leg ;* — de réglisse, *police officer,* "crusher," "copper," or "reeler ;" *priest,* or "devil dodger ;" (mountebanks') — de tremplin, *leg.* Properly tremplin, *a spring board ;* (familiar) — merdeux, *man whom it is not easy to deal with, who cannot be humoured ;* (thieves') — rompu, *ticket-of-leave convict who has broken bounds.* Termed also "canne, trique, tricard, fagot, cheval de retour."

Bâtons de chaise, *m. pl.* (popular), noce de —, *grand jollification,* "flare up," or "break down."

Batouse, batouze, *f.* (thieves'), *canvas;* — toute battante, *new canvas.*

Batousier, *m.* (thieves'), *weaver.*

Battage (popular), *lie,* " gag ;" *imposition ; joke; humbug ; damage to any article.*

Battant, *m.* (thieves'), *heart,* "panter ;" *stomach ; throat,* " red lane;" *tongue,* "jibb." Un bon —, *a nimble tongue.* Se pousser dans le —, *to drink,* "to lush." Faire trimer le —, *to eat.*

Battante, *f.* (popular), *bell,* or "ringer."

Battaqua, *m.* (popular), *slatternly woman, dowdy.*

Batterie, *f.* (popular), *action of lying, of deceiving,* "cram ;" *the teeth, throat, and tongue ;* — douce, *joke.* (Freemasons') Batterie, *applause.*

Batteur, *m.* (popular and thieves'), *liar, deceiver;* — d'antif, *thief who informs another of a likely* "job;" — de beurre, *stockbroker;* — de dig dig, *thief who feigns to be seized with an apoplectic fit in a shop so as to facilitate a confederate's operations by drawing the attention to himself ;* (popular) — de flemme, *idler.*

Battoir, *m.* (popular), *hand,* "flipper ;" *large hand,* "mutton fist."

Battre (thieves'), *to dissemble ; to deceive ; to make believe.*

Ne t'inquiète pas, je battrai si bien que je défie le plus malin de ne pas me croire emballé pour de bon.—VIDOCQ.

Battre à la Parisienne, *to cheat,* "to do ;" — à mort, *to deny ;* — comtois, *to play the simpleton ; to act in confederacy ;* — de l'œil, *to be dying ;* — entifle, *to be a confederate,* or "stallsman ;" — Job, *to dissemble ;* — l'antif, *to walk,* "to pad the hoof ;" *to play the spy,* "to nark ;" — morasse, *to call out "Stop thief!"* "to give hot beef ;" — en ruine, *to visit.*

Drilles ou narquois sont des soldats qui . . . battent en ruine les entiffes et tous les creux des vergnes.—*Le Jargon de l'Argot.*

(Popular) Battre la muraille, *to be so drunk as* " not to be able to see a hole in a ladder," *or not to be able* "to lie down without holding on;" — la semelle, *to play the vagrant ;* — le beurre, *to speculate on 'Change ; to be* " fast ;" *to dissemble ;* — le briquet, *to be knockkneed ;* — sa flème, or flemme, *to be idle, to be* "niggling ;" — son quart *is said of prostitutes who walk the streets.* Des yeux qui se battent en duel, *squinting eyes,* or "swivel-eyes." S'en battre l'œil, la paupière, or les fesses, *not to care a straw.* (Familiar) Battre son plein, *to be in all the bloom of beauty or talent,* "in full blast ;" (military) — la couverte, *to sleep ;* (sailors') — un quart, *to invent some plausible story ;* (printers') — le briquet, *to knock the type against the composing-stick when in the act of placing it in.*

Batture. See **Batterie.**

Bauce, bausse, *m.* (popular), *master, employer,* "boss ;" (thieves') *rich citizen,* "rag-splawger;" — fondu, *bankrupt employer,* "brosier."

Bauceresse, *f.* (popular), *female employer.*

Baucher (thieves'), se —, *to deride ; to make fun of.*

Baucoter (thieves'), *to teaze.*

Baude, *f.* (thieves'), *venereal disease.*

Baudrouillard, *m.* (thieves'), *fugitive.*

Baudrouiller (thieves'), *to decamp,* "to make beef." See **Patatrot.**

Baudrouiller, or **baudru,** *m.* (thieves'), *whip.*

Bauge, *f.* (thieves'), *box, chest,* or "peter;" *belly,* "tripes."

Baume, *m.* (popular), d'acier, *surgeons' and dentists' instruments;* — de porte-en-terre, *poison.*

Bausser (popular), *to work,* "to graft."

Bavard, *m.* (popular), *barrister, lawyer,* "green bag;" (military) *punishment leaf in a soldier's book.*

Bavarde, *f.* (thieves'), *mouth,* "muns," or "bone box."

Une main autour de son colas et l'autre dans sa bavarde pour lui arquepincer le chiffon rouge.—E. SUE.

Baver (popular), *to talk,* "to jaw;" — des clignots, *to weep,* "to nap a bib;" — sur quelqu'un, *to speak ill of one, to backbite.* Baver, also *to chat.* The expression is old.

Venez-y, varletz, chamberières,
Qui sçavez si bien les manières,
En disant mainte bonne bave.
VILLON, 15th century.

Baveux, *m.* (popular), *one who does not know what he is talking about.*

Bayafe, *m.* (thieves'), *pistol,* "barking iron," or "barker."

Bayafer (thieves'), *to shoot.*

Bazar, *m.* (military), *house of ill-fame,* "flash drum;" (servants') *house where the master is particular,* "crib;" (popular) *any house;* (prostitutes') *furniture,* "marbles;" (students') *college or school,* "shop."

Bazarder (popular), *to sell off anything, especially one's furniture; to barter;* (military) *to pillage a house; to wreck it.*

Bazenne, *f.* (thieves'), *tinder.*

Bé, *m.* (popular), *wicker-basket which rag-pickers sling to their shoulders.*

Béar, *adj.* (popular), laisser quelqu'un —, *to leave one in the lurch.*

Beau, *m.,* *old term for swell;* ex——, *superannuated swell.*

Beau blond (thieves'), *a poetical appellation for the sun.*

Beauce, *f.* (thieves'), plume de —, *straw,* or "strommel."

Beauce, *m.,* **beauceresse,** *f., second-hand clothes-dealers of the Quartier du Temple.*

Beauge, *m.* (thieves'), *belly,* "guts."

Beausse, *m.* (thieves'), *wealthy man,* "rag-splawger," *or one who is* "well-breeched."

Bébé, *m.* (popular), *stunted man; female dancer at fancy public balls in the dress of an infant; the dress itself; term of endearment.* Mon gros —! *darling! ducky!*

Bec, *m.* (popular), *mouth,* "maw;" — salé, *a thirsty mortal.* Claquer du —, *to be fasting,* "to be bandied." Rincer le — à quelqu'un, *to treat one to some drink.* Se rincer le —, *to wet one's whistle.* Tortiller du —, *to eat,* "to peck." Casser du —, *to have an offensive breath.* Avoir la rue du — mal pavée, *to have an irregular set of teeth.* Ourler son —, *to finish one's work.* (Sailors') Se calfater le —, *to eat or drink,* "to splice the mainbrace." (Thieves') Bec de gaz, bourrique, flique, cierge, arnif, peste, laune, vache, *police-officer or detective,* "pig," "crusher," "copper," "cossack," "nark," &c.

Bécane, *f.* (popular), *steam engine,* "puffing billy;" *small printing machine.*

Bécarre *is the latest title for Parisian dandies; and the term is* also used to replace the now well-worn expression "chic." The "bé-carre" must be grave and sedate after the English model, with short hair, high collar, small moustache and whiskers, but no beard. He must always look thirty years of age ; must neither dance nor affect the frivolity of a floral button-hole nor any jewellery ; must shake hands simply with ladies and gravely bend his head to gentlemen. "Bécarre—being translated—is 'natural' in a musical sense."—*Graphic, Jan. 2,* 1886. The French dandy goes also by the appellations of "coco-dès, petit crevé, pschutteux," &c. See **Gommeux.**

Bécasse, *f.* (popular), *female guy.*

Eh ! va donc, grande bécasse !

Becfigue de cordonnier, *m.* (popular), *goose.*

Bêchage, *m.* (familiar), *sharp criticism.*

Bêcher (familiar), *to criticize, to run down ;* (popular) *to beat,* "to bash." Se —, *to fight,* "to have a mill."

Bêcheur, *m.* (thieves'), *beggar,* "mumper ;" *juge d'instruction, a magistrate whose functions are to make out a case, and examine a prisoner before he is sent up for trial.* Avocat —, *public prosecutor.*

Bêcheuse, *f.* (thieves'), *female thief.*

Bécot, *m.* (popular), *mouth,* "kisser ;" *kiss,* "bus."

Bécoter (popular), *to kiss ; to fondle,* "to firkytoodle."

Becquant, *m.* (thieves'), *chicken,* "cackling cheat," or "beaker."

Becquetance, *f.* (popular), *food,* "grub."

Becqueter (popular), *to eat,* "to peck."

Dis-donc ! viens-tu becqueter ? Arrive clampin ! Je paie un canon de la bouteille. —ZOLA.

Bedon, *m.* (popular), *belly,* "tripes," or "the corporation."

Bédouin, *m.* (popular), *harsh man,* or "Tartar ;" *one of the card-sharper tribe.*

Beek (Breton), *wolf.* Gwelet an euz ar beek *is equivalent to* elle a vu le loup, *that is, she has lost her maidenhead.*

Beffeur, *m.,* **beffeuse,** *f.* (popular), *deceiver, one who* "puts on."

Bègue, *f.* (thieves'), *oats ;* also abbreviation of bézigue, a certain game of cards.

Béguin, *m.* (popular), *head,* "nut ;" *a fancy.* Avoir un — pour quelqu'un, "*to fancy someone,* "to cotton on to one."

Beigne, *f.* (popular), *cuff or blow,* "bang."

Bêlant, *m.* (thieves'), *sheep,* "wool-bird."

Belêt, *m.* (horse-dealers'), *sorry horse,* "screw."

Belette, *f.* (popular), *fifty-centime piece.*

Belge, *f.* (popular), *Belgian clay-pipe.*

Belgique (familiar), filer sur —, *to abscond with contents of cash-box, is said also of absconding fraudulent bankrupts, who generally put the Belgian frontier between the police and their own persons.*

Bêlier, *m.* (cads'), *cuckold.*

Bellander (tramps'), *to beg,* "to cadge."

Belle, *f.* (popular and familiar), attendre sa —, *to wait one's oppor-*

D

tunity. Jouer la —, *to play a third and decisive game.* La perdre —, *to lose a game which was considered as good as won ; to lose an opportunity.* (Thieves') Etre servi de —, *to be imprisoned through mistaken identity ; to be the victim of a false accusation.* (Popular) Belle à la chandelle, *f., ugly ;* — de nuit, *female habituée of balls and cafés ;* (familiar) — petite, *a young lady of the demi-monde,* a "pretty horse-breaker."

Bénard, *m.* (popular), *breeches,* "kicks," or "sit-upons."

Bénef, *m.,* for bénéfice, *profit.*

Bénévole, *m.* (popular), *young doctor in hospitals.*

Béni-coco (military), être de la tribu des —, *to be a fool.*

Béni-Mouffetard (popular), *dweller of the Quartier Mouffetard, the abode of rag-pickers.*

Bénir (popular), bas, *to kick one in the lower part of the back,* "to toe one's bum," "to root," or "to land a kick ;" (popular and thieves') — des pieds, *to be hanged,* "to cut caper-sauce," or "to be scragged."

Bénisseur, *m.* (familiar), *one who puts on a dignified and solemn air, as if about to give his blessing, and who delivers platitudes on virtue, &c. ; one who makes fine but empty promises ; political man who professes to believe, and seeks to make others believe, that everything is for the best.* An historical illustration of this is General Changarnier thus addressing the House on the very eve of the Coup d'Etat which was to throw most of its members into prison, "Représentants du peuple, délibérez en paix !"

Benoît, *m.* (popular), *woman's bully,* "ponce." See **Poisson.**

La vrai' vérité,
C'est qu' les Benoîts toujours lichent
Et s'graissent les balots.
Vive eul' bataillon d' la guiche,
C'est nous qu'est les dos.
RICHEPIN, *Chanson des Gueux.*

Benoîton, *m.,* **benoîtonne,** *f., people eccentric in their ways and style of dress.* From a play of Sardou's, *La Famille Benoîton.*

Benoîtonner, *to live and dress after the style of the Benoîtons* (which see).

Benoîtonnerie, *f., style and ways of the Benoîtons.*

Beq, *m.* (engravers'), *work.*

Béquet, *m.* (shoemakers'), *patch of leather sewn on a boot ;* (wood engravers') *small block ;* (printers') *a composition of a few lines ; paper prop placed under a forme.*

Béqueter (popular), *to eat,* "to peck," or "to grub."

Béquillard, *m.* (popular), *old man, old* "codger;" (thieves') *executioner.*

Béquillarde, *f.* (thieves'), *guillotine.*

Béquillé, *f.* (thieves'), *gallows,* "scrag." Properly *crutch.*

Béquillé, *m.* (thieves'), *hanged person, one who has* "cut caper sauce."

Béquiller (popular), *to hang ; to eat,* "to grub."

Béquilleur, *m.* (thieves'), *executioner ; man who eats.*

Berce. Cheval qui se —, *horse which rocks from side to side when trotting, which* "wobbles."

Berdouillard (popular), *man with a fat paunch,* "forty guts."

Berdouille, *f.* (popular), *belly,* "tripes."

T'as bouffé des haricots que t'as la ber-douille gonfle.—RICHEPIN, *Le Pavé.*

Berge, *f.,* or **longe** (thieves'), *year; one year's imprisonment,* "stretch."

Bergère, *f.* (popular), *sweetheart,* "poll;" *last card in a pack.*

Béribono, béricain (thieves'), *silly fellow easily deceived,* a "flat," a "go along."

Berlauder (popular), *to lounge about,* "to mike;" *to go the round of all the wine-shops in the neighbourhood.*

Berline de commerce, *f.* (thieves'), *tradesman's clerk.*

Berlu, *m.* (thieves'), *blind,* or "hoodman." From avoir la ber-lue, *to see double.*

Berlue, *f.* (thieves'), *blanket,* "woolly."

Bernard, *m.* (popular), aller voir —, or aller voir comment se porte madame —, *to ease oneself,* "to go to Mrs. Jones."

Bernards, *m. pl.* (popular), *posteriors,* "cheeks."

Berniquer (popular), *to go away with the intention of not returning.*

Berri, *m.* (popular), *rag-picker's basket.*

Berry, *m.* (Ecole Polytechnique), *fatigue tunic.*

Bertelo, *m.* (thieves'), *one-franc piece.*

Bertrand, *m.* (familiar), *a swindler who is swindled by his confederates, who acts as a cat's-paw of other rogues.*

Berzélius, *m.* (college), *watch.*

Besoin, *m.* (popular), autel de —, *house of ill-fame,* or "nanny-shop."

Besouille, *f.* (thieves'), *belt.* From bezzi, Italian, *small coin kept in a belt.*

Bessons, *m. pl.* (popular), *the breasts,* "dairies." Properly *twins.*

Bestiasse, *f.* (popular), *arrant fool; dullard,* "buffle-head."

Bête, *f. and adj.* (thieves'), *confederate in a swindle at billiards.* See **Bachotter.** (Popular) — à bon Dieu, *harmless person* (properly *lady-bird*) ; —à cornes, *fork; lithographic press;* — à deux fins, *walking-stick ;* — à pain, *a man; also a man who keeps a woman;* — comme ses pieds, *arrant fool;* — comme chou, *extremely stupid; very easy;* — épaulée, *girl who has lost her maidenhead* (this expression has passed into the language) ; — noire, *an object of dislike.* C'est ma — noire, *I can't bear the sight of him.*

Bêtises, *f. pl.* (popular), *questionable,* or "blue," *talk.* Faire des —, *to have connection, to* "pulverize" *the seventh commandment.*

Bettander (thieves'), *to beg,* "to mump," or "cadge."

Betterave, *f.* (popular), *drunkard's nose, a nose with* "grog blossoms," or a "copper nose," *such as is possessed by an* "admiral of the red."

Beuglant, *m.* (familiar), *low music hall; music hall.*

Beugler (popular), *to weep,* "to nap one's bib."

Beugne, *f.* (popular), *blow,* "clout," "bang," or "wipe."

Beurloquin, *m.* (popular), *proprietor of boot warehouse of a very inferior sort.*

Beurlot, *m.* (popular), *shoemaker in a small way.*

Beurre, *m.* (familiar), *coin,* "oof;" *more or less lawful gains.* Faire son —, *to make considerable profits.* Mettre du —dans ses épinards, *to add to one's means.* Y aller de son —, *to make a large outlay of money in some business.* C'est un —, *it is excellent,* "nobby." Avoir l'assiette au beurre. See **Avoir.** Au prix où est le —. See **Au.** Avoir du — sur la tête. See **Avoir.**

Beurre demi-sel, *m.* (popular), *girl or woman already tainted, in a fair way of becoming a prostitute.*

Beurrier, *m.* (thieves'), *banker,* "rag-shop cove."

Bézef (popular), *much.* From the Arabic.

Biard (thieves'), *side.* Probably from biais.

Bibard, *m.* (popular), *drunkard,* or "mop;" *debauchee,* or "sad dog."

Bibarder (popular), *to grow old.*

Bibarderie, *f.* (popular), *old age.*

Bibasse, birbasse, *adj. and subst., f.* (popular), *old ; old woman.*

Moi j'suis birbass', j'ai b'soin d'larton.
RICHEPIN, *Chanson des Gueux.*

Bibasserie. See **Bibarderie.**

Bibassier, *m.* (popular), *sulky grumbler ; over-particular man ; drunkard,* "bubber," or "lushington."

Bibelot (familiar), *any object ;* (soldiers') *belongings ; knapsack or portmanteau ;* (printers') *sundry small jobs.* Properly *any small articles of artistic workmanship ; knick-knacks.*

Bibeloter (popular), *to sell one's belongings, one's* "traps ;" — une affaire, *to do some piece of business.*

Se —, *to make oneself comfortable ; to do something to one's best advantage.*

Bibeloteur, *m.* (familiar), *amateur of knick-knacks ; one who collects knick-knacks.*

Bibelotier, *m., printers' man who works at sundry small jobs.*

Bibi, *m.* (popular), *term of endearment generally addressed to young boys ; woman's bonnet out of fashion.* C'est pour —, *that's for me, for* "number one." La Muse à —, *the title of a collection of poems by Gill,* literally *my own muse.* A —! (printers') *to Bedlam!* abbreviation of Bicêtre, *Paris depôt for lunatics.* (Thieves') Bibi, *skeleton key,* or "betty;" (military) *infantry soldier,* "mud-crusher," "wobbler," or "beetle-crusher."

Bibine, *f., the name given by rag-pickers to a wine-shop,* or "boozing-ken."

Biboire, *f.* (schoolboys'), *small leather or india-rubber cup.*

Bibon, *m.* (popular), *disreputable old man.*

Bicarré, *m.* (college), *fourth year pupil in the class for higher mathematics.*

Biceps, *m.* (familiar), avoir du —, *to be strong.* Tâter le —, *to try and insinuate oneself into a person's good graces,* "to suck up."

Bich, kornik, or **kubik** (Breton), *devil.*

Biche, *f.* (familiar), *term of endearment,* "ducky!"; *girl leading a gay life,* or "pretty horse-breaker."

Bicheganego (Breton), *potatoes.*

Bicher (popular), *to kiss.* (Rod-fishers') Ca biche, *there's a bite ;* and in popular language, *all right.*

Bicherie, *f.* (familiar), *the world of* " biches " or " cocottes."

C'est là où . . . on voit défiler avec un frou-frou de soie, la haute et la basse bi-cherie en quête d'une proie, *quærens quem devoret.*—FRÉBAULT, *La Vie à Paris.*

Bichette, *f.* (familiar), *term of endearment,* " ducky."

Bichon, *m.,* *term of endearment.* Mon — ! *darling.* (Popular) Un —, *a Sodomist.*

Bichonner (soldiers'), coco, *to groom one's horse.*

Bichons, *m. pl.* (popular), *shoes with bows.*

Bichot, *m.* (thieves'), *bishop.* Pro-bably from the English.

Bidache, *f.* See **Bidoche.**

Bidard, *m.* (popular), *lucky.*

Bidet, *m.* (convicts'), *string which is contrived so as to enable pri-soners to send a letter, and receive the answer by the same means.*

Bidoche, or **barbaque,** *f.* (popu-lar), *meat,* " bull ; " (military) *piece of meat.*

Bidon de zinc, *m.* (military), *block-head.* Properly *a can, flask.*

Bidonner (popular), *to drink freely,* " to swig ; " (sailors') — à la cambuse, *to drink at the canteen,* " to splice the mainbrace."

Bie (Breton cant), *beer ; water.*

Bien (popular), pansé, *intoxicated,* " screwed." Mon —, *my husband,* or " old man ; " *my wife,* or " old woman." Etre du dernier — avec, *to be on the most intimate terms with.* Etre —, *to be tipsy,* " screwed." Etre en train de — faire, *to be eating.* Un homme —, une femme —, *means a person of the middle class ; well-dressed people.*

Bienséant, *m.* (popular), *the be-hind,* or " tochas." See **Vasistas.**

Bier (thieves'), *to go.*

Ils entrent dans le creux, doublent de la batouze, des limes, de l'artie et puis douce-ment happent le taillis et bient attendre ceux qui se portaient sur le grand trimar. —*Le Jargon de l'Argot.*

Bière, *f.* (popular), *domino box.*

Biffe, *f.* (popular), *rag-pickers' trade.*

Biffer (popular), *to ply the rag-pickers' trade ; to eat greedily,* " to wolf."

Biffeton, *m.* (thieves'), *letter,* " screeve," or " stiff ; " (popular) *counter-mark at theatres.* Donner sur le —, *to read an indictment ; to give information as to the prisoner's character.*

Biffin, or **bifin,** *m.* (popular), *rag-picker,* or " bone-grubber ; " *a foot soldier,* or " wobbler," his knap-sack being assimilated to a rag-picker's basket.

Biffre, *m.* (popular), *food,* " grub." Passer à —, *to eat.* Passer à — à train express, *to bolt down one's food,* " to guzzle."

Bifteck, *m* (popular), à maquart, *filthy,* " chatty " *individual* (Ma-quart is the name of a knacker) ; — de chamareuse, *flat sausage* (chamareuse, *a working girl*) ; — de grisette, *flat sausage.* Faire du —, *to strike,* " to clump ; " *to ride a hard trotting horse, which sometimes makes one's breech raw.*

Bifteckifère, *adj., that which pro-cures one's living, one's* " bread and cheese."

Bifurqué. At the colleges of the University students may, after the course of " troisième," take up science and mathematics instead of continuing the classics. This is called bifurcation.

Bigard, *m.* (thieves'), *hole.*

Bigardé (thieves'), *pierced.*

Bige, bigeois, bigeot, *m.* (thieves'), *blockhead*, "go along ;" *dupe*, or "gull."

Bigorne, *m.* (thieves'), jaspiner or rouscailler —, *to talk cant*, "to patter flash."

Bigorneau, *m.* (popular), *police officer*, or "crusher ;" *marine*, or "jolly."

Bigorniau, *m.* (popular), *native of Auvergne.*

Bigornion, *m.* (popular), *falsehood*, "swack up."

Bigoter (thieves'), *to play the religious hypocrite.*

Bigoteur, *m.* (thieves'), *devout person.*

Bigotter, (popular), *to pray.*

Bigrement (familiar), a forcible expression, *extremely*, "awfully."

Bijou, *m.* (popular), *broken victuals*, or "manablins ;" (freemasons') *badge ;* — de loge, *badge worn on the left side ;* — de l'ordre, *emblem.*

Bijouter (thieves'), *to steal jewels.*

Bijouterie, *f.* (popular), *money advanced on wages*, "dead-horse."

Bijoutier, *m.*, **bijoutière,** *f.* (popular), *retailer of* "arlequins" (which see) ; bijoutier sur le genou, en cuir, *shoemaker*, or "snob."

Bilboquet, *m.* (popular), *person with a large head ; man who is made fun of ; a laughing-stock ; a litre bottle of wine.* Bilboquet, properly *cup and ball.* (Printers') *sundry small jobs.*

Billancer (thieves'), *to serve one's full term of imprisonment.*

Billancher (popular), *to pay*, "to fork out," "to shell out."

Billard, *m.* (popular), dévisser son, *to die*, or "to kick the bucket."

Bille, *f.* (thieves), *money*, or "pieces" (from billon) ; (po-

pular) *head*, "tibby," "block," "nut," "canister," "chump," "costard," "attic," &c. ; — à châtaigne, *grotesque head* (it is the practice in France to carve chestnuts into grotesque heads) ; — de billard, *bald pate*, "bladder of lard ;" — de bœuf, *chitterling.*

Billemon, billemont, *m.* (thieves'), *bank-note*, "soft," "rag," or "flimsy."

Billeoz (Breton), *money.*

Billeozi (Breton), *to pay.*

Biller (thieves'), *to pay*, "to dub."

Billet, *m.* (popular), direct pour Charenton, *absinthe taken neat.* Prendre un — de parterre, *to fall*, "to come a cropper." Je vous en fous or fiche mon —, *I assure you it is a fact*, "on my Davy," "'pon my sivvy," or "no flies."

Billez (Breton), *girl ; peasant woman.*

Bince, *m.* (thieves'), *knife*, "chive."

Malheur aux pantres de province,
Souvent lardé d'un coup de bince,
Le micheton nu se sauvait.
RICHEPIN, *Gueux de Paris.*

Binelle, *f.* (popular), *bankruptcy.*

Binellier, *m.* (popular), *bankrupt*, "brosier."

Binellophe, *f.* (popular), *fraudulent bankruptcy.*

Binette, *f.* (familiar), *face*, "phiz ;" — à la désastre, *gloomy face.* Prendre la — à quelqu'un, *to take one's portrait.* Quelle sale —, *what an ugly face! a regular* "knocker face." Une drôle de —, *queer face.*

Binômes, *chums working together at the Ecole Polytechnique.* It is customary for students to pair off for work.

Binwio (Breton), *male organs of generation.* Literally *tools.*

Bique, *f.* (popular), *old horse;* — et bouque, *hermaphrodite* (equivalent to "chèvre et bouc ").

Birbade, birbasse, birbe, birbette, birbon, *m. and adj.* (thieves' and popular), *old ; old man ; old woman.*

Birbassier. See **Bibassier.**

Birbe (popular), *old man, old* " codger ;" (thieves') — dab, *grandfather.*

Birbette, *m.* (popular), *a very old man.*

Biribi, *m.* (thieves'), *short crowbar used by housebreakers,* " James," " the stick," or " jemmy." Termed also "pince monseigneur, rigolo, l'enfant, Jacques, sucre de pomme, dauphin."

Birlibi, *m.* (thieves'), *game played by swindling gamblers with walnut shells and dice.*

Birmingham (familiar), rasoir de — (superlative of rasoir), *bore.*

Bisard, *m.* (thieves'), *bellows* (from bise, *wind*).

Biscaye (thieves'), *Bicêtre, a prison.*

Biscayen (thieves'), *madman, one who is* " balmy." (Bicêtre has a dépôt for lunatics.)

Bischoff, *m. drink prepared with white wine, lemon, and sugar.*

Biscope, or **viscope**, *f.* (cads'), *cap.*

La viscope en arrière et la trombine au vent,
L'œil marlou, il entra chez le zingue.
    RICHEPIN, *Gueux de Paris.*

Biser (familiar), *to kiss.*

Bismarck, couleur —, *brown colour;* — en colère, — malade, *are various shades of brown.*

Bismarcker (gamesters'), *to mark twice ; to appropriate by fair or foul means.* It is to be presumed

this is an allusion to Bismarck's alleged summary ways of getting possession of divers territories.

Bisquant, *adj.* (popular), *provoking, annoying.*

Bissard, *m.* (popular), *brown bread.*

Bistourné, *m.* (popular), *hunting horn.*

Bistro, bistrot, *m.* (popular), *landlord of wine-shop.*

Bitte et bosse (sailors'), *carousing exclamation.*

Laisse arriver ! voiles largues, et remplissez les boujarons, vous autres ! Tout à la noce ! Bitte et bosse !—RICHEPIN, *La Glu.*

Bitter cuirassé, *m.* (familiar), *mixture of bitters and curaçoa.*

Bitume, *m. foot-pavement.* Demoiselle du —, *street-walker.* Faire le —, *to walk the street.* Fouler, or polir le —, *to saunter on the boulevard.*

Bitumer *is said of women who walk the streets.*

Biture, *f.* (familiar), *excessive indulgence in food or drink,* " scorf."

Biturer (popular), se —, *to indulge in a* " biture " (which see).

Blackboulage, *m.* (familiar), *black-balling.*

Blackbouler (familiar), *to blackball.* The expression has now a wider range, and is used specially in reference to unreturned candidates to Parliament. Un blackboulé du suffrage universel, *an unreturned candidate.*

Blafard (cads'), *silver coin.*

Il avait vu sauter une pièce de cent sous,
Se cognant au trottoir dans un bruit de
    cymbales,
Un écu flambant neuf, un blafard de cinq
    balles.
    RICHEPIN, *Chanson des Gueux.*

Blafarde (cads'), *death.*

Blague, *f.* Literally *facility of speech, not of a very high order; talk; humbug; fib; chaff; joke.* Avoir de la —, *to have a ready tongue.* N'avoir que la —, *to be a facile utterer of empty words.* Avoir la — du métier, *to be an adept in showing off knowledge of things relating to one's profession.* Nous avons fait deux heures de —, *we talked together for two hours.* Pas de —! *none of your nonsense; let us be serious.* Pousser une —, *to cram up; to joke.* Sans —, *I am not joking.* Une bonne —, *a good joke; a good story.* Une mauvaise —, *a bad, ill-natured joke; bad trick.* Quelle —, *what humbug! what a story!* Ne faire que des blagues *is said of a literary man whose productions are of no importance.* (Popular) Blague sous l'aisselle! *no more humbugging! I am not joking!* — dans le coin! *joking apart; seriously.*

Blaguer (familiar), *to chat; to talk; to joke; not to be in earnest; to draw the long-bow; to quiz, to chaff, to humbug one,* "*to pull the leg;*" *to make a jaunty show of courage.* Tu blagues tout le temps, *you talk all the time.* Il avait l'air de blaguer mais il n'était pas à la noce, *he made a show of bravery, but was far from being comfortable.*

Blagues à tabac, *f.* (popular), *withered bosoms.*

Blagueur, blagueuse (familiar), *humbug; story-teller; one who rails at, scoffer.*

Blaichard (popular), *clerk,* or "*quill-driver.*"

Et les ouvriers en vidant à midi une bonne chopine, la trogne allumée, les regards souriants, se moquent des déjetés, des blaichards.—RICHEPIN, *Le Pavé.*

Blair, blaire, *m.* (popular), *nose,* "*boko,*" "*smeller,*" "*snorter,*"

or "*conk.*" Se piquer le —, *to get tipsy.* See **Se sculpter.**

Si les prop' à rien . . .
Ont l'droit de s'piquer l'blaire,
Moi qu'ai toujours à faire . . .
J'peux boire un coup d'bleu.
RICHEPIN, *Chanson des Gueux.*

Blaireau, *m.* (military), *recruit,* or "*Johnny raw;*" *a broom; foolish young man who aspires to literary honours and who squanders his money in the company of journalistic Bohemians.*

Blanc, *m.* (popular), *street-walker; white wine; white brandy; one-franc piece.* (Printers') Jeter du —, *to interline.* (Thieves') N'être pas —, *to have a misdeed on one's conscience; to be liable to be* "*wanted.*" (Military) Faire faire — à quelqu'un de sa bourse, *to draw freely on another's purse; to live at another's expense in a mean and paltry manner,* "*to spunge.*" (Familiar) Blanc, *one of the Legitimist party.* The appellation used to be given in 1851 to Monarchists or Bonapartists.

Enfin pour terminer l'histoire,
De mon bœuf blanc ne parlons plus.
Je veux le mener à la foire,
A qui le veut pour dix écus.
De quelque sot fait-il l'affaire,
Je le donne pour peu d'argent,
Car je sais qu'en France on préfère
Le rouge au blanc.
PIERRE BARRÈRE, 1851.

Blanchemont, *m.* (thieves'), pivois de —, *white wine.*

Blanches, *f. pl.* (printers'). The different varieties of type are: "blanches, grasses, maigres, allongées, noires, larges, ombrées, perlées, l'Anglaise, l'Américaine, la grosse Normande."

Blanchi, *adj.* (popular), mal —, *negro,* or "*darkey.*"

Blanchir (journalists'), *to make many breaks in one's manuscript, much fresh-a-lining.*

Blanchisseur, *m.* (popular), *barrister ;* (literary) *one who revises a manuscript, who gives it the proper literary form.*

Blanchisseuse de tuyaux de pipe (popular), *variety of prostitute.* See **Gadoue.**

Blanc-partout, *m.* (popular), *pastry-cook's boy.*

Plus généralement connu sous le nom de gâte-sauce, désigné aussi sous le nom de blanc-partout, le patronnet est ce petit bout d'homme que l'on rencontre environ tous les cinq cents pas.—RICHEPIN, *Le Pavé.*

Blancs, *m. pl.* (familiar), d'Eu, *partisans of the D'Orléans family ;* — d'Espagne, *Carlists.*

Blanc-vilain, *m.* (popular), *man whose functions consist in throwing poisoned meat to wandering dogs.*

Blanquette, *f.* (thieves'), *silver coin ; silver plate.*

Il tira de sa poche onze couverts d'argent et deux montres d'or qu'il posa sur le guéridon. 400 balles tout cela, ce n'est pas cher, les bogues d'Orient et la blanquette, allons aboule du carle.—VIDOCQ, *Mémoires.*

Blanquetter (thieves'), *to silver.*

Blanquettier (thieves'), *silverer.*

Blard, or **blavard,** *m.* (thieves'), *shawl.*

Blasé, e, *adj.* (thieves'), *swollen.* From the German blasen, *to blow.*

Blave, blavin, *m.* (thieves'), *handkerchief,* " muckinger " (from the old word blave, *blue*) ; *necktie,* "neckinger."

Blavin, *m.* (thieves'), *pocket-pistol,* "pops." An allusion to blavin, *pocket-handkerchief.*

Blaviniste, *m.* (thieves'), *pickpocket who devotes his attention to handkerchiefs,* "stook hauler."

Blé, blé battu, *m.* (popular), *money,* "loaver."

Blèche, *adj., middling ; bad ; ugly.* Faire banque —, *not to get any pay.* Faire —, *to make a* " bad " *at a game, such as the game of fives for instance.*

Bleu, *m.* (military), *recruit,* or "Johnny raw ;" *new-comer at the cavalry school of Saumur ;* (thieves') *cloak ; also name given to Republican soldiers by the Royalist rebels of Brittany in* 1793. After 1815 the Monarchists gave the appellation to Bonapartists. (Popular) Petit —, *red wine.* Avoir un coup d'—, *to be slightly tipsy,* "elevated." See **Pompette.**

Quand j'siffle un canon . . .
C'est pas pour faire l'pantre.
C'est qu' j'ai plus d'cœur au ventre . . .
Après un coup d'bleu.
RICHEPIN, *Chanson des Gueux.*

(Familiar) Bleu, *adj. astounding ; incredible ; hard to stomach.* En être — ; en bailler tout — ; en rester tout —, *to be stupefied, much annoyed or disappointed,* "to look blue ;" *to be suddenly in a great rage.* (Theatrical) Etre —, *to be utterly worthless.*

Bleue (familiar), elle est — celle-là ; en voilà une de — ; je la trouve —, *refers to anything incredible, disappointing, annoying, hard to stomach.* Une colère —, *violent rage.*

Blézimarder (theatrical), *to interrupt an actor.*

Bloc, *m., military cell, prison,* "mill," "Irish theatre," "jigger."

Blockaus, *m.* (military), *shako.*

Blond, *m.* (popular), beau —, *man who is neither fair nor handsome ;* (thieves') *the sun.*

Blonde, *f.* (popular), *bottle of white wine ; sweetheart,* or "jomer ;" *glass of ale at certain cafés,* "brune" *being the denomination for porter.*

Bloqué, *adj.* (printers'), être — à la banque, *to receive no pay.*

Bloquer (military), *to imprison, confine ;* (popular) *to sell, to forsake ;* (printers') *to replace temporarily one letter by another, to use a "*turned sort."

Bloquir (popular), *to sell.*

Blot, *m.* (popular and thieves'), *price; affair; concern in anything; share,* or "whack." Ça fait mon —, *that suits me.* Nib dans mes blots, *that is not my affair ; that does not suit me.*

L'turbin c'est bon pour qui qu'est mouche,
A moi, il fait nib dans mes blots.
　　　RICHEPIN, *Chanson des Gueux.*

Bloumard, *m.,* **bloume,** *f.* (popular), *hat,* "tile."

Blouse, *f.* (familiar), *the working classes.* Mettre quelqu'un dans la —, *to imprison, or cause one to fall into a snare.* Une blouse is properly *a billiard pocket.*

Blousier, *m.* (familiar), *cad,* "rank outsider."

Bobe, *m.* (thieves'), *watch,* "tattler." Faire le —, *to ease a drunkard of his watch,* "to claim a canon's red toy."

Bobêchon, *m.* (popular), *head,* "nut." Se monter le —, *to be enthusiastic.*

Bobelins, *m. pl.* (popular), *boots,* "hock-dockies," or "trotter-cases." See **Ripatons.**

Bobinasse, *f.* (popular), *head,* "block."

Bobine, *f.* (popular), *face,* "mug" (old word bobe, *grimace*). Une sale —, *ugly face.* Plus de fil sur la —. See **Avoir.** Se ficher de la — à quelqu'un, *to laugh at one.*

Un cocher passe, je l'appelle,
Et j'lui dis : dites donc l'ami ;
V'la deux francs, j'prends vot' berline
Conduisez-moi Parc Monceau.
Deux francs ! tu t'fiches d'ma bobine,
　Va donc, eh ! fourneau !
　　　　　Parisian Song.

Bobino. See **Bobe.**

Bobonne, for **bonne,** *nursery-maid ; servant girl,* or "slavey."

Bobosse, *f.* (popular), *humpback,* "lord."

Bobottier, *m.* (popular), *one who complains apropos of nothing.* From bobo, *a slight ailment.*

Boc, *m.* (popular), *house of ill-fame,* "nanny-shop."

Bocal, *m.* (popular), *lodgings,* "crib ;" *stomach,* "bread basket." Se coller quelque chose dans le —, *to eat.* Se rincer le —, *to drink,* "to wet one's whistle." (Thieves') Bocal, *pane, glass.*

Bocard, *m.* (popular), *café ; house of ill-fame,* "nanny-shop ;" — panné, *small coffee-shop.*

Bocari, *m.* (thieves'), *the town of Beaucaire.*

Boche, *m.* (popular), *rake,* "rip," "molrower," or "beard splitter." Tête de —, *German.*

Bock, *m.* (familiar), *glass of beer.*

Bocker (familiar), *to drink bocks.*

Bocotter, *to grumble ; to mutter.* Literally *to bleat like a* bocquotte, *goat.*

Bocque, bogue, *m.* (thieves'), *watch,* "tattler."

Bocson (thieves'), *house of ill-fame,* "flash drum," *lodgings,* "dossing-ken."

　　Montron ouvre ta lourde,
　　Si tu veux que j'aboule
　　Et piausse en ton bocson.
　　　　VIDOCQ, *Mémoires.*

Bœuf, *m.* (popular), *king of playing cards ; shoemaker's workman, or journeyman tailor, who does rough jobs.* Avoir son —, *to get angry,* "to nab the rust." Etre le —, *to work without profit.* Se mettre dans le —, *to be reduced in* *circumstances*, an allusion to bœuf bouilli, very plain fare. (Printers') Bœuf, *composition of a few lines done for an absentee.* Bœuf, *adj. extraordinary*, "stunning;" *enormous;* synonymous of "chic" at the Ecole Saint-Cyr ; (cads') *pleasant.*

Bœufier, *m.* (popular), *man of choleric disposition, one prone* "to nab his rust."

Boffete, *f.*, *box on the ear*, "buckhorse." From the old word buffet.

Bog, or **bogue,** *f.* (thieves'), *watch;* — en jonc, — d'orient, *gold watch*, "red 'un," or "red toy;" — en plâtre, *silver watch*, "white 'un."

> J'enflaque sa limace,
> Son bogue, ses frusques, ses passes.
>   VIDOCQ.

Boguiste (thieves'), *watch-maker.*

Boire (printers'), de l'encre *is said of one who on joining a party of boon companions finds all the liquor has been disposed of.* He will then probably exclaim,

> Est-ce que vous croyez que je vais boire de l'encre?—BOUTMY.

(Familiar) — dans la grande tasse, *to be drowned;* (actors') — du lait, *to obtain applause;* — une goutte, *to be hissed*, "to be goosed."

Bois, *m.* (cads'), pourri, *tinder;* (thieves') — tortu, *vine.* (Theatrical) Avoir du —, *to have friends distributed among the spectators, whose applause excites the enthusiasm of the audience.*

Bois au-dessus de l'œil jars (thieves'), *he understands cant.*

Boisseau, *m.* (popular), *shako; litre wine bottle.*

Boissonner (popular), *to drink heavily*, "to swill."

Boissonneur (popular), *assiduous frequenter of wine-shop*, a "lushington."

Boissonnier (popular), *one who drinks heavily*, a "lushington."

Boîte, *f.* (familiar and popular), *mean house, lodging-house, or restaurant; trading establishment managed in an unbusiness-like manner; one's employer's establishment; workshop; crammer's establishment; disorderly household; carriage*, or "trap ;" — à cornes, *hat or cap;* — à dominos, *coffin*, "cold meat box ;" — à gaz, *stomach;* — à surprises, *the head of a learned man;* — à violon, *coffin;* — au sel, *head*, "tibby ;" — aux cailloux, *prison*, "stone-jug ;" — d'échantillons, *latrine tub;* (thieves') — à Pandore, *box containing soft wax for taking imprints of keyholes;* (military) *guard-room*, "jigger ;" — aux réflexions, *cells.* Boulotter de la —, coucher à la —, *to get frequently locked up.* Grosse —, *prison.* (Printers') Boîte, *printer's shop, and more particularly one of the inferior sort.*

> "C'est une boîte," dit un vieux singe ; "il y a toujours mèche, mais hasard ! au bout de la quinzaine, banque blèche."

Faire sa —, *to distribute into one's case.* Pilleur de —, or fricoteur, *one who takes on the sly type from fellow compositor's case.*

Boiter (popular), des calots, *to squint, to be* "boss-eyed ;" (thieves') — des chasses, *to squint, to be* "squinny-eyed."

Boléro, *m.* (familiar), *a kind of lady's hat, Spanish fashion.*

Bolivar, *m.* (popular), *hat,* " tile."

Bombe, *f.* (popular), *wine measure, about half a litre ;* (military) — de vieux oint, *bladder of lard.* Gare la — ! *look out for squalls !*

Bombé, *m.* (popular), *hunchback,* "lord."

Bon, *man to be relied on in any circumstance ; one who is* "game ;" *man wanted by the police.* Etre le —, *to be arrested, or the right man.* Vous êtes — vous ! *you amuse me ! well, that's good !* (Printers') Bon, *proof which bears the author's intimation,* "bon à tirer," *for press.* Avoir du —, *to have some composition not entered in one's account, and reserved for the next.* (Familiar) Bon jeune homme, *candid young man,* in other terms *greenhorn ;* (popular) — pour cadet *is said of a dull paper, or of an unpleasant letter ;* — sang de bon sang, *mild oath elicited by astonishment or indignation.* (Popular and familiar) Être des bons, *to be all right, safe.* Nous arrivons à temps, nous sommes des bons. Le — endroit, *posteriors.* Donner un coup de pied juste au — endroit, *to kick one's behind,* to "hoof one's bum." Arriver — premier, *to surpass all rivals,* "to beat hollow."

Bonbon, *m.* (popular), *pimple.*

Bonbonnière, *f.* (popular), *latrine tub ;* — à filous, *omnibus.*

Bonde (thieves'), *central prison.*

Bon-Dieu (soldiers'), *sword.* (Popular) Il n'y a pas de —, *that is,* il n'y a pas de — qui puisse empêcher cela. (Convicts') *Short diary of fatigue parties at the hulks.*

Bondieusard, *m.* (familiar), *bigot ; dealer in articles used for worship in churches.*

Bondieusardisme, *f., bigotry.*

Bondieuserie, *f., article used for worship ; dealing in such articles.*

Bonhomme, *m.* (thieves'), *saint.* (Familiar and popular) Un —, *an individual,* a "party." Mon —, *my good fellow.* Petit — de chemin, see **Aller.**

Bonicard, *m.,* **bonicarde,** *f.* (thieves'), *old man, old woman.*

Boniface, *m.* (popular), *simpleminded man,* "flat," or "greenhorn."

Bonifacement (popular), *with simplicity.*

Boniment, *m.* (familiar), *puffing speech of quacks, of mountebanks, of shopmen, of street vendors, of three-card-trick sharpers, and generally clap-trap speech in recommendation or explanation of anything.* Richepin, in his *Pavé,* gives a good specimen of the "boniment" of a "maquilleur de brèmes," or three-card-trick sharper.

Accroupi, les doigts tripotant trois cartes au ras du sol, le pif en l'air, les yeux dansants, un voyou en chapeau melon glapit son boniment d'une voix à la fois traînante et volubile : . . . . C'est moi qui perds. Tant pire, mon p'tit père ! Rasé, le banquier ! Encore un tour, mon amour. V'là le cœur, cochon de bonheur ! C'est pour finir. Mon fond, qui se fond. Trèfle qui gagne. Carreau, c'est le bagne. Cœur, du beurre, pour le voyeur. Trèfle, c'est tabac ! Tabac pour papa. Qui qu'en veut ? Un peu, mon neveu ! La v'là. Le trèfle gagne ! Le cœur perd. Le carreau perd. Voyez la danse ! Ca recommence. Je le mets là. Il est ici, merci. Vous allez bien ? Moi aussi. Elle passe. Elle dépasse. C'est moi qui trépasse, hélas ! . . . Regardez bien ! C'est le coup de chien. Passé ! C'est assez ! Enfoncé ! Il y a vingt-cinq francs au jeu ! &c.

Bonique, *m.* (thieves'), *white-haired old man.*

Bonir (thieves'), *to talk ; to say,* "to patter ;" — au ratichon, *to confess to a priest.*

Le dardant riffaudait ses lombes,
Lubre il bonissait aux palombes,
Vous grublez comme un guichemard.
RICHEPIN, *Chanson des Gueux.*

Bonisseur, *m.*, *one who makes a* "boniment" (which see); (thieves') *barrister ; —* de la bate, *witness for the defence.*

Bonjour, *m.* (thieves'), voleur au —, bonjourier, or chevalier grimpant, *thief who, at an early hour, enters a house or hotel, walks into a room, and appropriates any suitable article.* If the person in bed wakes up, the rogue politely apologises for his pretended error. Other thieves of the same description commence operations at dinner-time. They enter a dining-room, and seize the silver plate laid out on the table. This is called "goupiner à la desserte."

Bon motif, *m.* (familar). Faire la cour à une fille pour le —, *to make love to a girl with honourable intentions.*

Bonne, *adj.* (familiar), *amusing, or the reverse.* Elle est bien —, *what a good joke ! what a joke !* Elle est —, celle-là ! *well, it is too bad ! what next ?* (Popular) Etre à la —, *to be loved.* Etre de la —, *to be lucky.* Avoir à la —, *to like.* Bonne fortanche, *female soothsayer ; —* grâce, *cloth used by tailors as wrappers.*

Bonnet, *m.*, *secret covenant among printers.*

Espèce de ligue offensive et défensive que forment quelques compositeurs employés depuis longtemps dans une maison et qui ont tous, pour ainsi dire la tête sous le même bonnet. Rien de moins fraternel que le bonnet. Il fait la pluie et le beau temps dans un atelier, distribue les mises en page et les travaux les plus avantageux à ceux qui en font partie.—E. BOUTMY, *Argot des Typographes.*

(Thieves')—carré, *judge,* or "cove with the jazey ;" — vert à perpète, *one sentenced to penal servitude for life,* or "lifer ;" (popular) — de coton, *lumbering, weak man,* or "sappy ;" *mean man,* or "scurf ;" — de nuit sans coiffe, *man of a melancholy disposition,* or "croaker ;" — d'évêque, *rump of a fowl,* or "parson's nose." (Familiar) Bonnet, *small box at theatres ; —* jaune, *twenty-franc coin ;* (military) — de police, *recruit,* or "Johnny raw."

Bonneteau, *m.*, jeu de —, *card-sharping game ; three-card trick.*

Bonneteur, *m.*, *card-sharper,* or "broadsman."

Bonnichon, *m.* (popular), *working girl's cap.*

Bono (popular), *good, middling.*

Bons, *m.* (military), la sonnerie des — de tabac, (ironical) *trumpet call for those confined to barracks.*

Bordé (cocottes'), être —, *to have renounced love,* "sua sponte," *or otherwise.*

Bordeaux (familiar), petit —, *one sou cigar.*

Bordée, *f.* (familiar and popular), *unlawful absence.* Tirer une —, *to absent oneself for some amusement of a questionable character ; to go* "on the booze."

La paie de grande quinzaine emplissait le trottoir d'une bousculade de gouapeurs tirant une bordée.—ZOLA.

Bordée de coups de poings, *rapid delivery of blows,* or "fibbing."

Bordel, *m.* (popular), *small faggot ; tools ; —* ambulant, *hackney coach.*

Bordelier (popular), *libertine,* "mol-rower," or "mutton-monger."

Borgne, *m.* (cads'), *breech,* or "blind cheek;" *ace of cards;* — de cœur, *ace of hearts,* "pig's eye."

Borgner (cads'), *to look.*

Borgniat (popular), *one-eyed man,* "boss-eyed."

Borne de vieux oint, *f.* (popular), *bladder of lard.*

Bos (Breton), *well; well done!*

Bosco, boscot, boscotte, *stunted man or woman; hunchback.*

Bosse, *f.* (familiar), *excessive eating and drinking; excess of any kind.* Se donner, se flanquer une —, *to get a good fill,* "a tightener." Se faire des bosses, *to amuse oneself amazingly.* Se donner, se flanquer une — de rire, *to split with laughter.* Rouler sa —, *to go along.* Tomber sur la —, *to attack,* to "pitch into."

Bosselard, *m.* (familiar), *silk hat,* "tile."

Bosser (popular), *to laugh; to amuse oneself.*

Bossmar, *m.* (thieves'), *hunchback,* "lord."

Bossoirs, *m. pl.* (sailors'), *bosoms.* Gabarit sans —, *thin breasts.*

Botte, *f.* (popular), de neuf jours, or en gaîté, *boot out at the sole.* Jours, literally *days, chinks.* Du jus de —, *kicks.* (Sailors') Jus de — premier brin, *rum of the first quality.*

Botter (popular), *to suit.* Ça me botte, *that just suits me, just the thing for me.* Botter, *to kick one's breech,* or "to toe one's bum," "to root," or "to land a kick."

Bottier (popular), *one who is fond of kicking.*

Bouant, *m.* (cads'), *pig,* or "angel." From boue, *mud.*

Boubane, *f.* (thieves'), *wig,* "periwinkle."

Boubouar (Breton), *ox; cattle in general.*

Boubouerien (Breton), *threshing machine.*

Boubouille (popular), *bad cookery.*

Bouc, *m.* (popular), *husband whose wife is unfaithful to him,* a "cuckold." Properly *he-goat;* (familiar) *beard on chin,* "goatee."

Boucan, *m.,* *great uproar,* "shindy."

J'ai ma troupe, je distribue les rôles, j'organise la claque. . . . J'établis la contrepartie pour les interruptions et le boucan. —Macé.

(Popular) Donner un — à quelqu'un, *to give a blow or* "clout" *to one.*

Boucanade, *f.* (thieves'), *bribing* or "greasing" *a witness.* Coquer la —, *to bribe.* Literally *to treat to drink.* In Spain wine is inclosed in goatskins, hence the expression.

Boucaner (popular), *to make a great uproar; to stink.*

Boucaneur, *m.* (popular), *one fond of women, who goes* "molrowing," *or a* "mutton-monger."

Boucanière, *f.* (popular), *woman too fond of men.*

Boucard, *m.* (thieves'), *shop,* "chovey."

Boucardier, *m.* (thieves'), *thief who breaks into shops.*

Bouche-l'œil, *m.* (prostitutes'), *a five, ten, or twenty-franc piece.*

Boucher (thieves'), *surgeon,* "nimgimmer;" (familiar) — un trou, *to pay part of debt;* (popular) — la lumière, *to give a kick in the* *breech,* "to hoof one's bum," or "to land a kick." Lumière, properly *touch-hole.*

Bouche-trou, *m.* The best scholars in all University colleges are allowed to compete at a yearly examination called "grand concours." The "bouche-trou" is one who acts as a substitute for anyone who for some reason or other finds himself prevented from competing. (Literary) *Literary production used as a makeshift;* (theatrical) *actor whose functions are to act as a substitute in a case of emergency.*

Bouchon, *m.* (thieves'), *purse,* "skin," or "poge;" (popular) *a younger brother; bottle of wine with a waxed cork; quality, kind,* "kidney." Etre d'un bon —, *to be an amusing, good-humoured fellow,* or a "brick." S'asseoir sur le —, *to sit on the bare ground.*

Bouclage, *m.* (thieves'), *handcuffs,* or "bracelets;" *bonds; imprisonment.*

Bouclé (thieves'), *imprisoned,* or "slowed."

Boucler (thieves'), *to shut,* "to dub;" *to imprison.* Bouclez la lourde ! *shut the door!*

Boucle zoze, *m.* (thieves'), *brown bread.*

Bouder (literally *to be sulky) is said of a player who does not call for fresh dominoes when he has the option of doing so;* (popular) — à l'ouvrage, *to be lazy;* — au feu, *to show fear;* — aux dominos, *to be minus several teeth.*

Boudin, *m.* (thieves'), *bolt; stomach.*

Boudiné, *m.* (familiar), *swell,* or "masher." At the time the expression came into use, dandies sported tight or horsey-looking clothes, which imparted to the wearer some vague resemblance with a boudin, or *large sausage.* For list of synonymous expressions, see **Gommeux.**

Boudins, *m. pl.* (popular), *fat fingers and hands.*

Boueux, *m.* (popular), *scavenger.*

Bouffard, *m.* (popular), *smoker.*

Bouffarde, *f.* (popular), *pipe,* or "cutty."

Bouffarder (popular), *to smoke,* to "blow a cloud."

Bouffardière, *f.* (popular), *an estaminet, that is, a café where smoking is allowed; chimney.*

Bouffe, *f.* (popular), *box on the ear,* "buckhorse."

Bouffe-la-Balle, *m.,* gormandizer, or "stodger;" *man with a fat, puffed-up, dumpling face.*

Bouffer (military), la botte, *to be bamboozled by a woman,* in what circumstances it is needless to say. (Popular) Bouffer, *to eat.* Se — le nez, *to fight.*

Bouffeter (popular), *to chat.*

Bouffeur, *m.* (popular), de blanc, *prostitute's bully,* "pensioner;" — de kilomètres, *a nickname for the* "Chasseurs de Vincennes," *a picked body of rifles who do duty as skirmishers and scouts, and who are noted for their agility.*

Bouffiasse, *m.* (popular), *man with fat, puffed-up cheeks.*

Bougie, *f.* (popular), *walking-stick; a blind man's stick;* — grasse, *candle.*

Bougre, *m.* (popular), *stalwart and plucky man, one who is* "spry;" — à poils, *dauntless, resolute man.* Bon —, *a good fellow,* a "brick." Mauvais —, *man of a snarling, evil-minded disposition.* The word is used often with a disparaging sense, Bougre de cochon, *you dirty pig;* — de serin, *you ass.* Littré derives the word bougre from Bulgarus, *Bulgarian.* The heretic Albigeois, who shared the religious ideas of some of the Bulgarians, received the name of "bougres."

Bougrement (popular), *extremely.* C'est — difficile, *it is awfully hard.*

Boui, *m.* (popular), *house of ill-fame,* "nanny-shop."

Bouiboui, bouisbouis, *m. puppet; small theatre; low music-hall; gambling place.*

Bouif, *m.* (popular), *conceited* "priggish" *person; bad workman.*

Bouillabaisse (popular), *confused medley of things, people, or ideas.* Properly *a Provençal dish made up of all kinds of fish boiled together, with spicy seasoning, garlic, &c.*

Bouillante, *f.* (soldiers'), *soup.*

Bouillie, *f.* (popular), pour les chats, *unsuccessful undertaking.* Faire de la — pour les chats, *to do any useless thing.*

Bouillon, *m.* (familiar and popular), *rain; unsold numbers of a book or newspaper; financial or business losses;* — aveugle, *thin broth;* —de canard, *water;* — de veau, *mild literature;* — d'onze heures, *poison; drowning;* — gras, *sulphuric acid* (an allusion to a case of vitriol-throwing by a woman named Gras); — pointu, *bayonet thrust; clyster;* — qui chauffe, *rain-cloud.* Boire le —, *to die.* (Fishermens') Bouillon de harengs, *shoal of herrings.*

Bouillonner (popular), *to suffer pecuniary losses consequent on the* *failure of an undertaking; to have a bad sale; to eat at a bouillon restaurant.*

Bouillonneuse, *f., female who prepares bouillon at restaurants.*

Bouillote, *f.* (popular), vieille —, *old fool,* "doddering old sheep's head."

Bouis, *m.* (thieves'), *whip.*

Bouiser, *to whip,* "to flush."

Boulage, *m.* (popular), *refusal; snub.*

Boulange, *f.,* for boulangerie.

Boulanger, *m.* (thieves'), *charcoal dealer; the devil,* "old scratch," or "Ruffin." Le — qui met les damnés au four, *the devil.* Remercier son —, *to die.*

Boulangers, *m. pl.* (military), *formerly military convicts* (an allusion to their light-coloured vestments).

Boule, *f.* (popular), *head,* "block." Avoir la — détraquée, à l'envers, *to be crazy,* "wrong in the upper storey." Boule de jardin, *bald pate,* "bladder of lard;" — de Siam, *grotesque head;* — de singe, *ugly face.* Bonne —, *queer face,* "rum phiz." Perdre la —, *to lose one's head.* Boule de neige, *negro;* — rouge, *gay girl of the Quartier de la Boule Rouge, Faubourg Montmartre.* Yeux en — de loto, *goggle eyes.* (Military) Boule de son, *loaf, bread.* (Thieves') Boule, *a fair; prison loaf;* — de son étamé, *white bread;* — jaune, *pumpkin.*

Bouleau, *m.* See Bûcherie.

Boule-Miche, *m.,* abbreviation of *Boulevard Saint-Michel.*

Boulendos, *m.* (boule en dos), (popular), *humpback,* or "lord."

Bouler (popular), *to thrash,* "to whop;" *to beat at a game, to deceive, to take in.* Envoyer —, *to send to the deuce* (old word *bouler, to roll along*).

Boulet, *m.* (popular), *bore ;* — à côtes, à queue, *melon ;* — jaune, *pumpkin.*

Boulette, *f.* (popular), de poivrot, *bunch of grapes* (poivrot, slang term for *drunkard*).

Bouleur, *m.,* **bouleuse,** *f.* (theatrical), *actor or actress who takes the part of absentees in the performance.*

Bouleux, *m.* (popular), *skittle player.*

Boulevarder, *to be a frequenter of the Boulevards.*

Boulevardier, *m.,* *one who frequents the Boulevards ; journalist who is a frequenter of the Boulevard cafés.* Esprit —, *kind of wit peculiar to the Boulevardiers.*

Boulevardière, *f.* (familiar), *prostitute of a better class who walks the Boulevards.*

Depuis cinq heures du soir la Boulevardière va du grand Hôtel à Brébant avec la régularité implacable d'un balancier de pendule.—PAUL MAHALIN.

Boulin, *m.* (thieves'), *hole.* Caler des boulins aux lourdes, *to bore holes in the doors.*

Bouline, *f.* (swindlers'), *collection of money,* "break," or "lead."

Bouliner (thieves'), *to bore holes in a wall or shutters ; to steal by means of the above process.*

Boulinguer (thieves'), *to tear ;* (vagrants') *to lead.*

Boulinoire, *f.* (thieves'), *wimble.*

Bouloire, *f.* (popular), *bowling-green.*

Boulon, *m.* (thieves'), vol au —, *theft by means of a rod and hook passed through a hole in the shutters.*

Boulonnaise (popular), *girl of indifferent character who walks the Bois de Boulogne.*

Boulots, *m.* (popular), *round shaped beans.*

Boulotter (thieves'), *to assist a comrade ;* (popular) *to be in good health ; to be prosperous ; to eat,* "to grub ;" — de la galette, *to spend money.*

Et tout le monde se disperse, vivement, excepté les trois compères et le môme, qui rentrent d'un pas tranquille dans Paris, pour y fricoter l'argent des imbéciles, y boulotter la galette des sinves.—RICHEPIN, *Le Pavé.*

Eh ! bien, ma vieille branche ! comment va la place d'armes ? Merci, ça boulotte. *Well, old cock, how are you ? Thanks, I am all right.*

Boum ! *a high-sounding, ringing word bawled out in a grave key by café waiters in order to emphasize their call for coffee to the attendant whose special duty it is to pour it out.* Versez à l'as ! Boum ! This peculiar call was brought into fashion by a waiter of the Café de la Rotonde at the Palais Royal, whose stentorian voice made the fortune of the establishment.

Bouquet, *m.* (cads'), *gift, present.*

Bouquine, *f.,* *beard grown on the chin,* or "goatee."

Bourbe, *f.* (popular), *the hospital of* "*la Maternité.*"

Bourbon (popular), *nose,* "boko." From nez à la Bourbon, the members of that dynasty being distinguished by prominent thick noses verging on the aquiline.

E

Bourdon, *m.* (thieves'), *prostitute,* "bunter;" (printers') *words left out by mistake in composing.*

Bourdonniste, *m.* (printers'), *one in the habit of making* bourdons (which see).

Bourgeois, *m.* (thieves'), for bourg, *a large village.* Literally *man of the middle class.* The peasants give this appellation to the towns-people; a coachman to his "fare;" workmen and servants to their employer; workpeople to the master of a house; soldiers to civilians; artists and literary men use it contemptuously to denote a man with matter-of-fact, unartistic tastes, also a man outside their profession; the anarchists apply the epithet to one who does not share their views. (Popular) Mon —, *my husband*, "my old man." Eh! dites donc, —, *I say, governor.* (Officers') Se mettre en —, *to dress in plain clothes, in* "mufti." (Familiar) C'est bien —, *it is vulgar, devoid of taste.*

Bourgeoisade, *f., anything, whether it be deed or thought, which savours of the bourgeois' ways; a vulgar platitude.* The bourgeois, in the disparaging sense of the term of course, is a man of a singularly matter-of-fact, selfish disposition, and one incapable of being moved by higher motives than those of personal interest. His doings, his mode of life, all his surroundings bear the stamp of an unrefined idiosyncrasy. Though a staunch Conservative at heart, he is fond of indulging in a timid, mild opposition to Government, yet he even goes so far sometimes as to send to Parliament men whose views are at variance with his own, merely to give himself the pleasure of "teaching a lesson" to the "powers that be." A man of Voltairian tendencies, yet he allows his wife and daughters to approach the perilous secrecy and the allurements of the confessional. When he happens to be a Republican, he rants furiously about equality, yet he protests that it is a shocking state of affairs which permits of his only son and spoilt child being made to serve in the ranks by the side of the workman or clod-hopper. By no means a fire-eater, he is withal a bloodthirsty mortal and a loud-tongued Chauvinist, but as he has the greatest respect for the integrity of his person, and entertains a perfect horror of blows, he likes to see others carry out for him his pugnacious aspirations in a practical way.

Bourgeoise, *f.* (popular), *the mistress of a house or establishment.* Ma —, *my wife*, "my old woman."

Bourgeron, *m.* (popular), *small glass of brandy;* (soldiers') *a civilian.* Properly *a kind of short smock-frock.*

Bourguignon (popular), *the sun.*

Bourlingue, *m.* (popular)), *dismissal,* "the sack."

Bourlinguer, *to dismiss; to get on with difficulty in life.* From a naval term.

Bourlingueur, *m.* (popular), *master,* "boss;" *foreman.*

Bourrasque, *f.* (thieves'), *raid by the police.*

Bourreau des crânes, *m.* (military), *bully, fire-eater.*

Bourre-boyaux, *m.* (popular), *eating-house,* "grubbing crib."

Bourre-coquins, *m. pl.* (popular), *beans.* Beans form the staple food of convicts.

Bourre-de-soie, *f.* (cads'), *kept girl,* "poll."

Bourrée, *f.* (popular), *hustling,* "hunch."

Bourrer (familiar), en — une, *to smoke a pipe,* "to blow a cloud."

Bourreur, *m.* (thieves'), de pègres, *penal code ;* (printers') — de lignes, *compositor of the body part of a composition,* a task generally entrusted to unskilled compositors, unable to deal with more intricate work.

Bourriche, *f.* (popular), *blockhead,* "cabbage - head." Properly *hamper.*

Bourrichon, *m.* (popular), *head.* See **Tronche.** Se monter, or se charpenter le —, *to entertain strong illusions, to be too sanguine.*

Bourricot (popular), c'est —, *that comes to the same thing ; it is all the same to me.*

Bourrier, *m.* (popular), *dirt, dung.*

Bourrique, *f.* (popular), tourner en —, *to become stupid, or crazy.* Faire tourner quelqu'un en —, *to make one crazy by dint of badgering or angering.* Cet enfant est toujours à me tourmenter, il me fera tourner en —, *this naughty child will drive me mad.* (Thieves') Bourrique, *informer,* "nark ;" also *police officer.*

Bourrique à Robespierre (popular), comme la —, corresponds to the simile *like blazes.* Saoul comme la —, *awfully drunk.*

Bourser (popular), se —, *to go to bed, to get into the* "doss."

Boursicoter (familiar), *to speculate in a small way on the stocks.*

Boursicoteur, *f.,* **boursicotier,** *m.* (familiar), *speculator in a small way.*

Boursicotiérisme, *m.* (familiar), *occupation of those who speculate on 'Change.*

Boursillonner (popular), *to* "club" *for expenses by each contributing a small sum.*

Bouscaille, *f.* (thieves'), *mud.*

Bouscailleur, *street-sweeper, scavenger.*

Bouse, *f.* (popular), de vache, *spinach.*

Bousiller (popular), *to work rapidly but carelessly and clumsily.*

Bousilleur (popular), *careless, clumsy workman.*

Bousilleuse (popular), *woman who is careless of her belongings, who is the reverse of thrifty.*

Bousin, *m.* (popular), *uproar, disturbance, row,* "shindy ;" *drinking-shop,* "lush-crib ;" *house of ill-fame,* "flash drum."

Bousineur (popular), *an adept at creating a disturbance.*

Bousingot, *m.* (popular), *wineshop,* "lush-crib ;" *term of contempt applied to Republicans in* 1848.

Boussole, *f.* (familiar), *head, brains.* Perdre la —, *to lose one's head,* "to be at sea ;" *to become mad.* (Popular) Boussole de refroidi, or de singe, *a Dutch cheese.*

Boustifaille, *f.* (familiar), *provisions, food,* "grub."

Boustifailler, *to eat plentifully.*

Bout, *m.* (tailors'), flanquer son —, *to dismiss from one's employment.* (Military) Bout de cigare, *short man ;* (popular) — de cul, *short person,* or "forty foot ;" — d'homme, de femme, *undersized person,* or "hop o' my thumb;" — coupé, *kind of cheap cigar with a clipped end.*

Boutanche, *f.* (thieves'), *shop,* "chovey." Courtaud de —, *shopman,* a "knight of the yard."

Bouteille, *f.* (popular), *nose,* "boko." Avoir un coup de —, *to be tipsy.* C'est la — à l'encre *is said of any mysterious, incomprehensible affair.* (Printers') Une — à encre, *a printing establishment, thus called on account of the difficulty of drawing up accurate accounts of authors' corrections.*

Bouterne, *f.* (popular), *glazed case containing jewels exhibited as prizes for the winners at a game of dice.* The game is played at fairs with eight dice, loaded of course.

Bouternier, *m.,* **bouternière,** *f.,* *proprietor of a* bouterne (which see).

Boutique, *f.,* *used disparagingly to denote one's employer's office; newspaper offices; disorderly house of business; clique.* Esprit de —, *synonymous of esprit de corps, but used disparagingly.* Etre de la —, *to be one of, to belong to a political clique or administration of any description.* Montrer toute sa —, *is said of a girl or woman who accidentally or otherwise exposes her person.* Parler —, *to talk shop.*

Boutiquer (popular), *to do anything with reluctance; to do it badly.*

Boutiquier, *m.* (familiar), *narrow-minded or mean man.* Literally *shopkeeper.*

Boutogue, *f.* (thieves'), *shop,* or "chovey."

Bouton, *m.* (thieves'), *master key;* (popular) *twenty-franc piece;* — de guêtre, *five-franc gold-piece;* — de pieu, *bug,* or "German duck."

Boutonner (familiar), *to touch with the foil; to annoy, to bore.*

Bouture, *f.* (popular), de putain, low, insulting epithet, which may be rendered by the equally low one, *son of a bitch.* Bouture, *slip of a plant.*

Boxon, *m.* (popular), *brothel,* or "nanny-shop."

Boyau, *m.* (popular), rouge, *hard drinker,* or "rare lapper."

Boye, *m.* (thieves'), *warder,* or "bloke;" *convict who performs the functions of executioner at the convict settlements of Cayenne or New Caledonia.*

Brac, *m.* (thieves'), *name,* "monniker," or "monarch."

Braconner (gamesters'), *to cheat,* or "to bite." Properly *to poach.*

Brader (popular), *to sell articles dirt cheap.*

Braillande, braillarde, *f.* (thieves'), *drawers.* From the old word braies, *breeches.*

Braillard, *m.* (popular), *street singer,* or "street pitcher." According to the *Slang Dictionary,* the latter term applies to negro minstrels, ballad-singers, long-song men, men "working a board" on which has been painted various exciting scenes in some terrible drama, &c.

Braise, *f.* (popular), *money,* "loaver." See **Quibus.**

J'ai pas d'braise pour me fend' d'un litre, Pas même d'un meulé cass' à cinq.
RICHEPIN.

Braiser (popular), *to pay,* "to dub."

Braiseur (popular), *man who is very free with his money.*

Brancard (popular), *superannuated gay woman.*

Brancards, *m. pl.* (popular), *hands,* or "flappers;" *legs,* or "pins;" — de laine, *weak or lame legs.*

Un poseur qui veut me la faire à la redresse, que ces deux flûtes repêchées par vous dans la lance du puits n'avaient jamais porté une femme, je me connais en brancards de dames, c'est pas ça du tout.— MACÉ, *Mon Premier Crime.*

Branche, *f.* (popular), *friend,* "mate." Ma vieille —, *old fellow!* "old cock!" (Familiar) Avoir de la —, *to have elegance,* "dash."

Brancher (thieves' and cads'), *to lodge,* "to perch," or "roost."

Brandillante, brandilleuse, *f.* (thieves'), *bell,* or "ringer."

Branlante, *f.* (popular), *watch,* or "ticker."

Branlantes, *f. pl.* (popular), *old men's teeth.*

Branque, *m.* (thieves'), *donkey,* "moke."

Bras, brasse, *adj.* (thieves'), *large.* From brasse, *a fathom.*

Braser (thieves'), des faffes, *to forge documents,* to "screeve fakements;" *to forge bank-notes,* or to "fake queer-soft."

Brasset, *m.* (thieves'), *big, stout man.*

Brave, *m.* (popular), *shoemaker,* or "snob."

Bréchet, *m.* (popular), *stomach.*

Brèchetelles, *f.*, *a kind of German cakes eaten at beershops.*

Breda-street, *the quarter of Notre-Dame-de-Lorette patronized by women of the demi-monde* (the Paris Pimlico, or St. John's Wood).

Bredoche, *f.* (popular), *centime.*

Bredouille, *f.* (popular), chevalier de la —, *one who goes out shooting* on Sundays *in the purlieus of Paris.* From revenir bredouille, *to return with an empty bag.*

Breloque, *f.* (popular), *a clock.* Properly *watch trinket.*

Brème, *m. and f.* (popular), *vendor of countermarks at the door of theatres.* Une —, *f.* (thieves'), *playing card,* "flat," or "broad" (brème is a flat fish, *the bream*). Une — de pacquelins, *geographical map.* Maquiller les brèmes, *to handle cards, to play at cards,* "to fake broads;" *to mark cards in certain ways, to construct them on a cheating principle,* "to stock briefs." Maquilleur de brèmes, *card-sharper,* or "broadsman," *generally one whose spécialité is the three-card trick.*

Le perdant, blème, crispe ses poings. Les compères s'approchent du maquilleur de brèmes (tripoteur de cartes), qui s'est relevé, avec un éclair mauvais dans ses yeux ternes . . . il se recule et siffle. A ce signal arrive un gosse, en courant, qui crie d'une voix aiguë : Pet ! v'la la rousse ! Décanillons !—RICHEPIN, *Le Pavé.*

(Prostitutes') Une brème, *card delivered by the police to registered prostitutes.* Fille en —, *registered prostitute.*

Brêmeur, *m.* (thieves'), *card player,* "broad faker."

Brêmier, *m.* (thieves'), *manufacturer of playing cards.*

Brésilien, *m.* (popular), *wealthy, generous man,* "rag-splawger."

Bricabracologie, *art of dealing in or collecting bric-à-brac or knickknacks.*

Bricard, *m.* (popular), *staircase.*

Bricheton, *m.* (popular), *bread;* — d'attaque, *four-pound loaf.*

Bricole, *f.* (popular), *small, odd jobs that only procure scanty pro-*

fits. Properly *a shoulder-strap used by costermongers to draw their barrows.*

Bricoler (popular), *to make an effort ; to give a good pull ; to do anything in a hurried and clumsy manner ; to carry on some affair in a not over straightforward way.*

Bricoleur, *m.* (popular), *man who will undertake any kind of work, any sundry jobs.*

Bricul, briculé, *m.* (thieves'), *police inspector.*

Bridaukil (thieves'), *gold watch chain,* "redge slang," or "red tackle."

Bride, *f.* (thieves'), *watch chain,* "slang ;" *convict's chain.* (Popular) Vieille —, *worthless, discarded object ; term of contempt for individuals.*

Bridé (thieves'), *shackled.*

Brider (thieves'), *to shut,* "to dub ;" *to fasten on a fetter,* or "wife."

Brif (Breton), *bread.*

Briffe, *f.* (popular), *food,* "belly timber ;" *bread,* "tommy." Passer à —, *to eat,* "to grub."

> N'importe où nous nous empatons
> D'arlequins, d'briffe et d'rogatons.
> RICHEPIN, *Chanson des Gueux.*

Briffer (popular), *to eat,* "to grub."

Brigadier, *m.* (popular), *baker's foreman.*

Brigand, *m.* (popular), *term of friendliness.* Vieux —, *you old scamp!*

Brigant, brigeant, *m.* (thieves'), *hair,* or "strommel."

Brigante or **bringeante,** *f.* (thieves'), *wig,* or "periwinkle."

Brigeants or **bringeants,** *m. pl.* (thieves'), *hair,* "thatch." Termed also "tifs, douilles, douillards."

Brigeton, bricheton (popular), *bread,* "tommy."

Brig-fourre, *m.* (military), *brigadier fourrier.*

Brignolet, *m.* (popular), *bread,* "tommy."

Briller (thieves'), *to light.*

Brimade, *f.* (military), *euphemism for bullying ; practical and often cruel jokes perpetrated at the military school of Saint-Cyr at the expense of the newly-joined,* termed "melons" ("snookers" at the R. M. Academy), such as tossing one in a blanket, together with boots, spurs, and brushes, or trying him by a mock courtmartial for some supposed offence. An illustration with a vengeance of such practical joking occurred some years ago at an English garrison town. Some young officers packed up a colleague's traps, without leaving in the rooms a particle of property, nailed the boxes to the floor, and laid a he-goat in the bed. On the victim's arrival they left him no time to give vent to his indignant feelings, for they cast him into a fisherman's net and dragged him downstairs, with the result that the unfortunate officer barely escaped with his life.

Brimer, *to indulge in* brimades (which see).

Brinde, *f.* (popular), *tall, lanky woman ; landlord of a wine shop.*

Brindezingue, *m.* (thieves'), *tin case of very small diameter containing implements, such as a fine steel saw or a watch-spring, which they secrete in a peculiar manner.* Says Delvau:—

Comment arrivent-ils à soustraire cet instrument de délivrance aux investigations les plus minutieuses des geôliers ? C'est ce qu'il faut demander à M. le docteur Ambroise Tardieu qui a fait une étude spéciale des maladies de la gaine naturelle de cet étui.

(Mountebanks') Etre en —, *to be ruined, a bankrupt*, "cracked up," or "gone to smash."

Brindezingues, *m. pl.* (popular), être dans les —, *to be intoxicated.* From an old word brinde, *toast.*

Bringue, *m.* (popular), *bread,* or "soft tommy." Mettre en —, *to smash up.*

Brio, *m.* (familiar). Properly a *musical term.* Figuratively, Parler, écrire avec —, *to speak or write with spirit, in dashing style.*

Brioches, *f. pl.* (popular). Literally *gross mistake.* Figuratively, Faire des —, *to lead a disorderly life.*

Briolet, *m.* (popular), *thin, sour wine,* that is, "vin de Brie."

Briquemann, briquemon, *m.* (military), *cavalry sword.*

Briquemon, *m.* (thieves'), *tinder box.*

Brisac, *m.* (popular), *careless child who tears his clothes.*

Brisacque, *m.* (popular), *noise; noisy man.*

Brisant, *m.* (thieves'), *the wind.*

Briscard or **brisque,** *m.* (military), *old soldier with long-service stripes.*

Brise, *f.* (sailors'), à faire plier le pouce, *violent gale;* — à grenouille, *west wind.*

Briser (printers'), *to cease working.* (Popular) Se la —, *to go away,* "to mizzle." See **Patatrot.**

Briseur, *m.* The "briseurs" (gens qui se la brisent), according to Vidocq, are natives of Auvergne who pass themselves off for tradesmen. They at first gain the confidence of manufacturers or wholesale dealers by paying in cash for a few insignificant orders, and swindle them afterwards on larger ones. The goods, denominated "brisées," are then sold much under value, and the unlawful proceeds are invested in Auvergne.

Brisque, *f.* (thieves'), *year,* or "stretch."

Brisques, *f. pl.* (gamblers'), *the ace and figures in a pack of cards.* When a player possesses all these in his game he is said to have "la triomphe ;" (military) *stripes.*

Brisure, *f.* (thieves'), *swindle,* or "plant ;" (printers') *temporary cessation of work.* Grande —, *total stoppage of work.*

Au Rappel, la pige dure six heures avec une brisure d'une demi-heure à dix heures. — BOUTMY.

Brobèche, *m.* (popular), *centime.*

Brobuante, *f.* (thieves'), *ring,* "fawney."

Broc, *m.* (thieves'), *farthing,* or "fadge."

Brocante, *m.* (popular), *old shoe.*

Brocanter (familiar), *to be pottering about.*

Broche, *f.* (tradespeoples'), *note of hand,* or "stiff."

Broches, *f. pl.* (popular), *teeth,* or "head rails."

Brochet, *m.* (popular), *pit of the stomach,* for bréchet ; *women's bully,* or "ponce."

Brocheton, *m.* (popular), *young bully.*

Brochure, *f.* (theatrical), *printed play.*

Brodage, *m.* (thieves'), *writing.*

Brodancher (thieves'), *to write ; to embroider.* Tirants brodanchés, *embroidered stockings.*

Brodancheur, *m.* (thieves'), *writer;* — en cage, *scribe who for a consideration will undertake to do an illiterate person's correspondence* (termed écrivain public);—à la plaque, aux macarons, or à la cymbale, *notary public* (an allusion to the escutcheon placed over a notary's door).

Brodé, *m.* (thieves'), *melon.*

Broder (thieves'), *to write;* — sur les prêts *is said of a gamester who, having lent a colleague a small sum of money, claims a larger amount than is due to him.*

Broderie, *f.* (thieves'), *writing.*

Pas de broderie, par exemple, tu connais le proverbe, les écrits sont des mâles, et les paroles sont des femelles.—VIDOCQ, *Mémoires.*

Brodeur, *m.* (thieves'), *writer;* also *a gamester who claims a larger sum than is due to him.*

Broque, *m.* (thieves'), *farthing.* Il n'y a ni ronds, ni herplis, ni broque en ma felouse. *I haven't got a sou, or a farthing, in my pocket.*

Broquillage, *m.* (thieves'), *theft which consists in substituting paste diamonds for the genuine article which a jeweller displays for the supposed purchaser's inspection.*

Broquille, *f.* (theatrical), *nothing.* Used in the expression, Ne pas dire une —, *not to know a single word of one's part;* (thieves') *a ring,* or "fawney;" *a minute.*

Broquilleur, *m.,* **broquilleuse,** *f.* (thieves'), *thief who robs jewellers by substituting paste diamonds for the genuine which are shown to him as to a bonâ-fide purchaser.*

Brosse, *f.* (popular), *no; nothing;* — pour lui ! *he shan't have any !*

Brosser (familiar), se — le ventre, *to go without food, and, in a figurative sense, to be compelled to do without something.*

Brosseur, *m.* (artists'), *one who paints numerous pictures of very large dimensions.* Rubens was a "brosseur;" (military) *flatterer, one who "sucks up."*

Brouce, *f.* (popular), *thrashing,* "whopping."

Brouf, *m.* (codfishers'), *wind blowing from the main.*

Brouillard, *m.* (popular), chasser le —, *to have a morning drop of spirits,* "dewdrop." Être dans le —, *to be "fuddled," or tipsy.* Faire du —, *to smoke,* "to blow a cloud."

Brouille, *f.,* *series of pettifogging contrivances which a lawyer brings into play to squeeze as much profit as he can out of a law affair.*

Brouillé, *adj.* (familiar), avec la monnaie, *penniless,* "hard up;" — avec sa blanchisseuse, *with linen not altogether of a snow-white appearance;* — avec l'orthographe, *a bad speller.*

Broussailles, *f. pl.* (popular), être dans les —, *to be tipsy,* "obfuscated." See **Pompette.**

Brouta, *m.* (Saint-Cyr school), *speech.* From the name of a professor who was a good elocutionist.

Broute, *f.* (popular), *bread,* "tommy."

Brouter (popular), *to eat,* "to grub." The expression is used by Villon, and is scarcely slang.

Item, à Jean Raguyer, je donne . . .
Tous les jours une talemouze (*cake*),
Pour brouter et fourrer sa mouse.

Brouteur sombre, *m.* (popular), *desponding, melancholy man,* "croaker."

Broyeur de noir en chambre (familiar), *literary man who writes on melancholy themes.*

Bruant (Breton), *cock ; egg.*

Bruantez (Breton), *hen.*

Bruge, *m.* (thieves'), *locksmith.*

Brugerie, *f.*, *locksmith's shop.*

Brûlage, *m.* (familiar), *the act of being ruined,* "going to smash."

Brûlant, *m.* (thieves'), *fire ; hearth.*

Brûlé, *m. and adj.* (popular), *failure of an undertaking ;* (familiar) Il doit de l'argent partout il est —, *dans le pays, he owes money to everybody, his credit is gone.* C'est un article —, *an article which will no longer sell.* L'épicier est —, *the grocer refuses any more credit.* Un politicien —, *a politician whose influence is gone.* Un auteur —, *an author who has spent himself, no longer in vogue.* Une fille brûlée, *a girl who in spite of assiduous attendance at balls, &c., has failed to obtain a husband.* Une affaire brûlée, *an unsuccessful undertaking, or spoilt by bad management.* Un acteur —, *an actor who for some reason or other can no longer find favour with the public.*

Brûlée, *f.* (popular), *severe thrashing ; defeat ; hurried and unlawful auction for contracts.*

Brûler (theatrical), à la rampe *is said of an actor who performs as if he were alone, and without regard to the common success of the play, or his colleagues ;* — du sucre, *to obtain applause.* (Popular) Brûler, abbreviation of brûler la cervelle, *to blow one's brains out.* Fais le mort ou je te brûle, *don't budge, or I blow your brains out.* En — une, *to smoke,* "to blow a cloud." (Thieves') Brûler le pégriot, *to obliterate all traces of a theft or crime.* Ne — rien, *to suspect nothing.*

Brûleur, *m.* (theatrical), de planches, *spirited actor.*

Brusquer (gamesters'), la marque, *to mark more points than have been scored, when playing cards.*

Brutal, *m.* (familiar), *cannon.*

Brutifier (popular), *to make one stupid by dint of upbraiding or badgering him.*

Brution, *m.* (students'), *cadet of the* "Prytanée Militaire de la Flèche," *a Government school for the sons of officers.*

Brutium, *m.*, "*Prytanée Militaire de la Flèche.*" From Brutus, probably on account of the strict discipline in that establishment.

Brutus, *m.* (thieves'), *Brittany.*

Bruyances, *f. pl.* (familiar), *great puffing up in newspapers or otherwise.*

Bu, *adj.* (popular), *in liquor,* "tight." See **Pompette**.

Eh ben ! oui, j'suis bu. Et puis, quoi?
Qué qu'vous m'voulez, messieurs d'la
    rousse ?
Est-c'que vous n'aimez pas comme moi
A vous rincer la gargarousse ?
    RICHEPIN, *La Chanson des Gueux.*

Bûche, *f.* Literally *log ;* (tailors') *article of clothing.* Coller sa — au grêle, *to remit a piece of work to the master.* Temps de —, *work-time.* (Popular) Bûche, *lucifer match ;* (thieves') — flambante, or plombante, *lucifer match.*

Bûcher (familiar), *to work hard,* "to sweat ;" *to belabour,* "to lick." (Popular) Se —, *to fight,* "to slip into one another."

Bûcherie, *f.* (popular), *fight,* "mill."

Bûcheur, *m.* (familiar), *one who works hard*, "*a swat.*"

Buen-retiro, *m.* (familiar), *private place of retirement;* (ironically) *latrines*, or "West Central."

Buffet, *m.* (popular), avoir le — garni, *to have had a hearty meal;* — vide, *to be fasting, to have nothing in the* "locker." Bas de —, see **Bas**. Remouleur de —, *organ-grinder.*

Buif, *m.* (military), *shoemaker.*

Bull-Park, *m.* (students'), *Bullier's dancing-rooms*, situated near the Luxembourg, patronized by the students of the Quartier Latin, but invaded, as most places of a similar description now are, by the protectors of gay girls.

Buquer (thieves'), *to commit a robbery at a shop under pretence of asking for change.*

Bureau arabe, *m.* (soldiers' in Algeria), *absinthe mixed with* "orgeat," *a kind of liquor made with almonds.*

Burettes, *f. pl.* (thieves' and popular), *pistols*, "barking irons." Literally *phials.*

Burlin, burlingue, *m.* (popular), *office; desk.* For bureau.

Busard, *m.*, **buse**, *f.*, **buson**, *m.* (familiar and popular), *dull, slow, thick-witted man*, "a bounder."

Bustingue (thieves'), *lodging house*, "dossing ken."

Bute, butte, or **bute à regret**, *f.* (thieves'), *guillotine.* Monter à la —, *to be guillotined.*

Buté, *adj.* (thieves'), *guillotined; murdered.* See **Fauché**.

Ils l'ont buté à coups de vingt-deux.— E. SUE. (*They killed him by stabbing him.*)

Buter (thieves'), *to kill; to guillotine; to execute.*

On va le buter, il est depuis deux mois gerbé à la passe.—BALZAC. (*He is going to be executed, he was sentenced to death two months ago.*)

Buteur (thieves'), *murderer; executioner.* See **Taule**.

Butin, *m.* (soldiers'), *equipment.*

Butre (thieves'), *dish.*

Buvailler (popular), *to drink little or slowly.*

Buvailleur or **buvaillon**, *m.* (popular), *a man who cannot stand drink.*

Buveur d'encre, *m.* (soldiers'), *any military man connected with the administration; clerk*, or "quill-driver."

 *m.* (popular), être un C, *to be an arrant fool.* Euphemism for a coarse word of three letters with which the walls are often adorned ; — comme la lune, *extremely stupid.*

Ça (popular), être —, *to be the right sort.* C'est un peu —, *that's excellent,* "fizzing." Avoir de —, *to be wealthy.* (Familiar) Ça manque de panache, *it lacks finish or dash.*

Cab, *m.* (abbreviation of cabotin), *contemptuous expression applied to actors ; third-rate actor,* or "surf."

Cab, cabou (thieves' and popular), *dog,* "tyke." Le — jaspine, *the dog barks.*

Cabande, *f.* (cads'), *candle,* or "glim."

Cabas, *m.* (popular), *old hat.* Une mère —, *rapacious old woman.* Properly, cabas, *a woman's bag.*

Cabasser (popular), *to chatter, to gabble ; to delude,* or "bamboozle ;" *to steal,* "to prig."

Cabasseur, *m.* (popular), *scandalmonger ; thief,* "prig." See **Grinche.**

Cabe, *m., third year student at the Ecole Normale,* a higher training school for professors, and one which holds the first rank among Colleges of the University of France.

Cabermon, *m.* (thieves'), *wineshop,* "lush-crib."

Cabestan, *m.* (thieves'), *police inspector ; police officer,* "crusher," "pig," "copper," or "reeler."

Cabillot, *m.* (sailors'), *soldier,* "lobster."

Câble, *m.* (fishermens'), à rimouque, *tow-line.*

Souque ! attrape à carguer ! Pare à
l'amarre ! Et souque !
C'est le coup des haleurs et du câble à
rimouque.
La oula ouli oula oula tchalez !
Hardi ! les haleurs, oh ! les haleurs, halez !
RICHEPIN, *La Mer.*

Cabo, *m.* (popular), *dog,* or "buffer." Le — du commissaire, *the police magistrate's secretary.* See **Chien.** (Military) Elève —, *one who is getting qualified for the duties of a corporal.*

Cabochon, *m.* (popular), *blow,* "prop," or "bang."

Cabonte, or **camoufle,** *f.* (military), *candle.*

Cabot, *m.* (familiar), *third-rate actor,* or "surf ;" *term of contempt applied to an actor.* Abbreviation of cabotin.

Cabotinage, *m.* (familiar), *life of hardships which most actors have to live before they acquire any reputation.*

Cabotine (familiar), *bad actress; strolling actress, or one who belongs to a troupe of* "barn stormers."

Cabotiner (familiar), *to be a strolling actor ; to mix with* cabotins; *to fall into their way of living,* which is not exactly a "proper" one.

Caboulot, *m.* (familiar), *small café where customers are waited upon by girls ; small café where the* spécialité *is the retailing of cherry brandy, absinthe, and sweet liquors ; best sort of wine-shop.*

Cabriolet, *m.*, *short rope or strap with a double loop affixed, made fast to a criminal's wrists, the extremity being held by a police officer ; small box for labels; woman's bonnet.*

Cabrion, *m.* (artists'), *painter without talent,* or "dauber ;" *practical joker.* In the *Mystères de Paris* of Eugène Sue, Cabrion, a painter, nearly drives the doorkeeper Pipelet mad by his practical jokes.

Cachalot, *m.* (sailors'), *old sailor, old* "tar." Properly *spermaceti whale.*

Cache-folie, *m.* (popular), *drawers; false hair.*

Cachemar, cachemince, *m.* (thieves'), *cell,* "clinch." From cachot, *black hole.*

Cachemire, *m.* (popular), *clout; —* d'osier, *rag-picker's wicker basket.*

Voici les biffins qui passent, le crochet au poing et les pauvres lanternes sont recueillies dans le cachemire d'osier.—RICHEPIN, *Le Pavé.*

Cache-misère (familiar), *coat buttoned up to the chin to conceal the absence of linen.*

Cachemitte, *f.* (thieves'), *cell,* "clinch."

Cachemuche. See **Cachemar.**

Cacher (popular), *to eat,* "to grub."

Cachet, *m.* (thieves' and cads'), de la République, *the mark of one's heel on a person's face,* a kind of farewell indulged in by night ruffians, especially when the victim's pockets do not yield a satisfactory harvest. (Familiar) Le —, *the fashion,* "quite the thing."

Et ce n'est pas lui qui porterait des gants vert-pomme si le cachet était de les porter sang de bœuf. — P. MAHALIN, *Mesdames de Cœur Volant.*

Cacique, *m.*, *head scholar in a division at the Ecole Normale.*

Cadavre, *m.* (familiar and popular), *body ; a secret misdeed,* "a skeleton in the locker ;" *tangible proof of anything.* Grand —, *tall man.* Se mettre quelquechose dans le —, *to eat.* See **Mastiquer.**

Cadenne, *f.* (thieves'), *chain fastened round the neck.* La grande — *was formerly the name given to the gang of convicts which went from Paris to the hulks at Toulon.*

Cadet, *m.* (thieves'), *crowbar,* or "Jemmy." Termed also "l'enfant, Jacques, sucre de pommes, biribi, rigolo ;" (popular) *breech.* Baiser —, *to be guilty of contemptible mean actions ; to be a lickspittle.* Baise — ! *you be hanged!* Bon pour — *is said of any worthless object or unpleasant letter.*

Cadichon, *m.* (thieves'), *watch,* "Jerry," or "red toy."

Cador (thieves'), *dog,* "tyke ;" — du commissaire, *secretary to the* "commissaire de police," *a kind of police magistrate.*

Cadouille, *f.* (sailors'), *rattan.*

Effarés de ne pas recevoir de coups de cadouille, ils s'éloignent à reculons, et leurs prosternations ne s'arrêtent plus.—BONNE-TAIN, *Au Tonkin.*

Cadran, *m.* (popular), **breech**, or "**bum** ; " — *lunaire, same meaning.* See **Vasistas.**

Cadratin, *m.* (printers'), *top hat*, or "stove pipe;" (police) *staff of detectives* ; (journalists') *apocryphal letter.*

Cafard, *m.* (military), *officer who makes himself unpleasant ; a busybody.*

Cafarde, *f.* (thieves'), *moon*, "parish lantern ; " *cup.*

Cafarder (popular), *to be a hypocrite,* a "mawworm."

Café, *m.* C'est un peu fort de —, *it is really too bad, coming it too strong.* Prendre son —, *to laugh at.*

Cafetière, *f.* (thieves' and cads'), *head*, "canister." See **Tronche.**

Cafiot, *m., weak coffee.*

Cafouillade(boatmens'), *bad rowing.*

Cafouilleux, *m.* (popular), espèce de —! *blockhead!* "bally bounder!"

Cage, *f.* (popular), *workshop with glass roof; prison,* or "stone jug;" — à chapons, *monastery* ; — à jacasses, *nunnery* ; — à poulets, *dirty, narrow room,* "a hole ; " (printers') *workshop.*

Cageton, *m.* (thieves'), *may-bug.*

Cagne, *f.* (popular), *wretched horse,* or "screw ; " *worthless dog ; lazy person ; police officer,* or "bobby."

Cagnotte, *f.* (familiar), *money-box in which is deposited each player's contribution to the expenses of a game.* Faire une —, *to deposit in a money-box the winnings of players which are to be invested to the common advantage of the whole party.*

Cagou, *m.* (thieves'), *rogue who operates single-handed ; expert thief,* or "gonnof," *who takes charge of the education of the uninitiated after the manner of the old Jew Fagin* (see *Oliver Twist*) ; *a tutor such as is to be met with in a* "buz napper's academy," *or training school for thieves; in olden times a lieutenant of the* "grand Coëre," *or king of rogues.* The kingdom of the "grand Coëre" was divided into as many districts as there were "provinces" or counties in France, each superintended by a "cagou." Says *Le Jargon de l'Argot :—*

Le cagou du pasquelin d'Anjou résolut de se venger de lui et de lui jouer quelque tour chenâtre.

Cahua, *m.* (French soldiers' in Algeria), *coffee.* Pousse —, *brandy.*

Caillasse, *f.* (popular), *stones.*

Caillé (thieves'), *fish.*

Caillou, *m.* (popular), *grotesque face ; head,* or "block ; " *nose,* or "boko ; " — déplumé, *bald head,* or "bladder of lard." N'avoir plus de mousse sur le —, *to be bald,* "to be stag-faced."

Cailloux, *m. pl.* (popular), *petits* —, *diamonds.*

Caïman, *m.* (Ecole Normale school), *usher.*

Caisse, *f.* (popular), d'épargne, *mouth,* or "rattle-trap ; " (familiar) — des reptiles, *fund for the bribing of journalists* ; — noire, *secret funds at the disposal of the Home Secretary and Prefect of Police.* Battre la —, *to puff up.* Sauver la —, *to appropriate or abscond with the contents of the cash-box.*

Caisson, *m.* (familiar), *head*, "nut." Se faire sauter le —, *to blow one's brains out.*

Calabre, *m.* (thieves'), *scurf.*

Calain, *m.* (thieves'), *vine-dresser.*

Calancher (vagrants'), *to die,* "*to croak.*" See **Pipe.**

Calande (thieves'), *walk, lounge.*

Calandriner (popular), *le sable, to live a wretched, poverty-stricken life.*

Cale, *f.* (sailors'), *se lester la —, to eat and drink.* See **Mastiquer.**

Calé, calée, *adj.*, properly *propped up ;* (popular) *well off,* "with plenty of the needful."

Calebasse, *f.* (popular), *head,* or "cocoa-nut." Grande —, *tall, thin, badly attired woman.* Vendre la —, *to reveal a secret.*

Calebasses, *f.* (popular), *large soft breasts.* Literally *gourds.*

Calège, *f.* (thieves'), *kept woman.*

Calence, *f.* (popular), *dearth of work.*

Caler (popular), *to do ; to do nothing ; to be out of work,* or "out of collar ;" *to strike work ;* — l'école, *to play the truant.* Se —, *to eat.* Se — les amygdales, *to eat,* "to grub." (Thieves') Caler des boulins aux lourdes, *to bore holes in doors.*

Caleter (popular), *to decamp,* "to hook it." See **Patatrot.**

Caleur (popular), *lazy workman,* or "shicer ;" *man out of work ; butler ; waiter* (from the German *kellner*).

Calfater (sailors'), *se — le bec, to eat.* Literally *to caulk.*

Caliborgne. See **Calorgne.**

Calicot, *m.* (familiar), *draper's assistant,* or "counter jumper."

Calicote, *sweetheart,* or "flame," of a "knight of the yard."

Californien (popular), *rich,* "worth a lot of tin." See **Monacos.**

Câlin, *m., small tin fountain which the retailers of coco carry on their backs.* Coco is a cooling draught made of liquorice, lemon, and water.

Calino, *m.* (familiar), *ninny ; one capable of the most enormous* "bulls."

Calinotade, *f.*, *sayings of a* calino (which see).

Calinttes, *f.* (popular), *breeches,* or "hams," or "sit-upons."

Callot, *m.* (thieves'), *scurvy.*

Callots, *m. pl.* (old cant), *variety of tramps.*

Les callots sont ceux qui sont teigneux véritables ou contrefaits ; les uns et les autres truchent tant aux entiffes que dans les vergnes.—*Le Jargon de l'Argot.*

Calme et inodore (familiar), être —, *to assume a decorous appearance.* Soyez —, *behave yourself with decorum ; do not be flurried.*

Calombe. See **Cabande.**

Caloquet, *m.* (thieves'), *hat ; crown.* See **Tubard.**

Calorgne, *adj.* (popular), *one-eyed,* "boss-eyed," or "seven-sided."

Calot, *m.* (thieves'), *thimble ; walnut shell ; eye.* Properly *large marble.* Boiter des calots, *to squint.* Reluquer des calots, *to gaze,* "to stag."

J'ai un chouett' moure
La bouch' plus p'tit' que les calots.
RICHEPIN.

Calot, *clothier's shopman,* or "counter-jumper ;" *over-particular, troublesome customer.*

Calotin, *m.* (familiar), *priest ; one of the Clerical party.*

Calotte, *f.* (familiar), *clergy*. Le régiment de la —, *the company of the Jesuits.*

Calottée, *f.* (rodfishers'), *worm-box.*

Calvigne, or **clavigne**, *f.* (thieves'), *vine.*

Calvin, or **clavin**, *m.* (thieves'), *grapes.*

Calypso, *f.* (popular), faire sa —, *to show off, to pose.*

Cam, *f.* (thieves'), lampagne de —, *country*, or " drum."

Camarade, *m.* (popular), de pionce, *bed-fellow ;* (military) *regimental hair-dresser.* (Familiar) Bon petit — *is said ironically of a colleague who does one an ill turn, or slanders one.*

Camarde, *f.* (thieves'), *death.* Baiser la —, *to die.* See **Pipe**.

Camarder (thieves'), *to die.*

Camarluche, *m.* (popular), *comrade*, " mate."

Camaro, *m.* (popular), *comrade*, or " mate."

Camboler (popular), *to fall down.*

Cambouis, *m.* (military), *army service corps.* Properly *cart grease.*

Cambriau, cambrieux, *m.* (popular), *hat*, or " tile." See **Tubard**.

Cambriole, *f.* (thieves'), *room*, or " crib ; " *shop*, or " swag.

Gy, Marpaux, gy nous remouchons
Tes rouillardes et la criole
Qui parfume ta cambriole.
RICHEPIN.

Cambriole de milord, *sumptuous apartment.* Rincer une —, *to plunder a room or shop.*

Cambrioleur, *m.* (thieves'), *thief who operates in apartments ;* — à la flan, *thief of that description who operates at random, or on* " spec."

Cambriot, *m.* (popular), *hat*, " tile." See **Tubard**.

Cambroniser, euphemism for emmerder (which see).

Cambronne ! euphemism for a low but energetic expression of refusal or contempt, which is said to have been the response of General Cambronne at Waterloo when called upon to surrender (see *Les Misérables*, by V. Hugo). Sterne says, in his *Sentimental Journey*, that " the French have three words which express all that can be desired—' diable !' ' peste !' " The third he has not mentioned, but it seems pretty certain it must be the one spoken of above.

Cambrouse, *f.* (popular), *a tawdrily-dressed servant girl ; a semi-professional street-walker*, " dolly mop;" (thieves') *country, suburbs.*

Cambrouser (servants'), *to get engaged as a maid-servant.*

Cambrousien, *m.* (thieves'), *peasant*, or " joskin."

Cambrousier, *m.* (thieves'), *country thief.*

Cambroux, *m.* (thieves'), *servant ; waiter.*

Cambuse, *f.* (popular), *house*, or " crib ; " *sailors' canteen ; wineshop.*

Camélia, *m.*, *kept woman* (*La Dame aux Camélias*, by A. Dumas fils).

Camelot, *m.* (popular), *tradesman ; thief ; hawker of any articles.*

Le camelot, c'est le Parisien pur sang ... c'est lui qui vend les questions, les jouets nouveaux, les drapeaux aux jours de fête, les immortelles aux jours de deuil, les verres noircis aux jours d'éclipse ... des cartes transparentes sur le Boulevard et des images pieuses sur la place du Panthéon. —RICHEPIN, *Le Pavé.*

Camelote, *f.* (popular), *prostitute of the lowest class,* or "draggle-tail;" (thieves') — grinchie, *stolen property.* Etre pris la — en pogne, or en pied, *to be caught,* "*flagrante delicto,*" *with the stolen property in one's possession.* Laver la —, *to sell stolen property.* Prendre la — en pogne, *to steal from a person's hand.*

Cameloter (popular), *to sell; to cheapen; to beg; to tramp.*

Camerluche or **camarluche,** *m.* (popular), *comrade,* or "mate."

Camionner (popular), *to conduct; to lead about.*

Camisard, *m.* (military), *soldier of the "Bataillon d'Afrique,"* a corps composed of liberated military convicts, who, after having undergone their sentence, are not sent back to their respective regiments. They are incorporated in the Bataillon d'Afrique, a regiment doing duty in Algeria or in the colonies, where they complete their term of service; — en bordée, *same meaning.*

Camisole, *f.* (popular), *waistcoat,* or "benjy."

Camoufle, *f.* (thieves'), *description of one's personal appearance; dress; light or candle,* "glim." La — s'estourbe, *the light is going out.*

Camouflement, *m.* (thieves'), *disguise.*

Camoufler (thieves'), *to learn; to adulterate.* Se —, *to disguise oneself.*

Je me camoufle en pélican,
J'ai du pellard à la tignasse.
Vive la lampagne du cam !
RICHEPIN.

Camouflet, *m.* (thieves'), *candle-stick.*

Camp, *m.* (popular), ficher le —, *to decamp.* Lever le —, *to strike work.* Piquer une romance au —, *to sleep.*

Campagne, *f.* (prostitutes'), aller à la —, *to be imprisoned in Saint-Lazare, a dépôt for prostitutes found by the police without a registration card, or sent there for sanitary motives.* (Thieves') Barboteur de —, *night thief.* Garçons de —, or escarpes, *highwaymen or house-breakers who pretend to be pedlars.*

Campe, *f.* (cads'), *flight; camping.*

Camper (cads'), *to flee,* "to brush."

Camperoux. See **Cambroux.**

Camphre, *m.* (popular), *brandy.*

Camphrier, *m.* (popular), *retailer of spirits; one who habitually gets drunk on spirits.*

Campi (cads'), *expletive.* Tant pis — ! *so much the worse!*

Camplouse, *f.* (thieves'), *country.*

Camuse, *f.* (thieves'), *carp; death; flat-nosed.*

Can, *m.* (popular), abbreviation of canon, *glass of wine.* Prendre un — sur le comp, *to have a glass of wine at the bar.*

Canage, *m.* (popular), *death-throes.*

Canaillade, *f.* (popular), *offence against the law.*

J'ai fait beaucoup de folies dans ma jeunesse; mais au cours d'une existence accidentée et décousue, je n'ai pas à me reprocher une seule canaillade.—MACÉ.

Canaillon, *m.* (popular), vieux —, *old curmudgeon.*

Canard, *m.* (familiar), *newspaper; clarionet;* (tramcar drivers') *horse.* (Popular) Bouillon de —, *water.* (Thieves') Canard sans plumes, *bull's pizzle,* or *rattan used for convicts.*

Canarder (popular), *to take in,* "to bamboozle;" *to quiz,* "to carry on."

Canardier, *m.* (popular), *journalist; vendor of newspapers;* (journalists') *one who concocts* "*canards,*" *or false news;* (printers') *newspaper compositor.*

Canarie, *m.* (popular), *simpleton,* or "*flat.*"

Canasson, *m.* (popular), *horse,* or "*gee;*" *old-fashioned woman's bonnet.* Vieux —! *old fellow!* "old cock!"

Cancre, *m.* (fishermens'), *jus de —, landsman,* or "*land-lubber.*" Cancre, properly *poor devil.*

Cancrelat, *m.* (popular), *avoir un — dans la boule, to be crazy.* For other kindred expressions, see **Avoir.** Cancrelat, properly *kakerlac,* or *American cockroach.*

Cane, *f.* (thieves'), *death.*

Canelle, *f.* (thieves'), *the town of Caen.*

Caner (thieves'), *la pégrenne, to starve.* Caner, properly *to shirk danger.*

Caneson. See **Canasson.**

Caneton, *m.* (familiar), *insignificant newspaper.* Termed also "feuille de chou."

Caneur, *m.* (popular), *poltroon,* or "cow babe."

Caniche, *m.* (popular), *general term for a dog.* Properly *poodle.* Termed also "cabgie, cabot." It also has the signification of *spectacles,* an allusion to the dog, generally a poodle, which acts as the blind man's guide. (Thieves') Caniche, *a bale provided with handles,* compared to a poodle's ears.

Canne, *f.* (police and thieves'), *surveillance exercised by the police on the movements of liberated convicts.* Also *a liberated convict who has a certain town assigned him as a place of residence, and which he is not at liberty to leave.* Casser sa —, *to break bounds.* Une vieille —, or une —, *an old offender.* (Literary) Canne, *dismissal, the* "*sack.*" Offrir une —, *to dismiss from one's employment,* "to give the sack."

Canon, *m.* (popular), *glass of wine drunk at the bar of a wine-shop.* Grand —, *the fifth of a litre of wine,* and petit —, *half that quantity.* Viens prendre un — su' l' zinc, mon vieux zig, *I say, old fellow, come and have a glass at the bar.* Se bourrer le —, *to eat to excess,* "to scorf."

Canonner (popular), *to drink wine at a wine-shop; to be an habitual tippler.*

Canonneur, *m.* (popular), *tippler, a wine bibber.*

Canonnier, *m.* (military), de la pièce humide, *hospital orderly.*

Canonnière, *f.* (popular), *the behind,* or "*tochas.*" See **Vasistas.** Charger la —, *to eat,* "to grub." Gargousses de la —, *vegetables.*

Cant, *m.* (familiar), *show of false virtue.* From the English word.

Cantaloup, *m.* (popular), *fool,* "bounder," or "cull." Properly *a kind of melon.*

Canter, *m.* (sporting), *canter.* From the English.

Cantique, *m.* (freemasons'), *bacchanalian song.*

Canton, *m.* (thieves'), *prison,* or "stir." For synonyms see **Motte.** Comte de —, *jailer,* "dubsman," or "jigger-dubber."

Cantonade, *f.* (literary), écrire à la —, *to write productions which are*

F

not read by the public. From a theatrical expression, Parler à la —, *to speak to an invisible person behind the scenes.*

Cantonnier, *m.* (thieves'), *prisoner, one in* "quod."

Canulant, *adj.* (familiar), *tedious, tiresome,* "boring." From ca-nule, *a clyster-pipe.*

Canularium, *m.* (Ecole Normale), *ordeal which new pupils have to go through, such as passing a mock examination.*

Canule, *f.* (popular), *tedious man, bore.* Canule, properly speaking, is *a clyster-pipe.*

Canuler (popular), *to annoy, to bore.*

Canuleur. See **Canule.**

Caoutchouc, *m.* (popular), *clown.* Properly *india-rubber.*

Cap, *m.* (thieves'), *chief warder at the hulks.* (Familiar) Doubler le —, *to go a roundabout way in order to avoid meeting a creditor, or passing before his door.* Doubler le — des tempêtes, *to clear safely the* 1st *or* 15th *of the month, when certain payments are due.* Doubler le — du terme, *to be able to pay one's rent when due.* Doubler un —, *to be able to pay a note of hand when it falls due.*

Capahut, *f.* (thieves'), voler à la —, *to murder an accomplice so as to get possession of his share of the booty.*

Capahuter. See **Capahut.**

Cape, *f.* (thieves'), *handwriting.*

Capet, *m.* (popular), *hat,* or "tile." See **Tubard.**

Capine, *f.* (thieves'), *inkstand.*

Capir (thieves'), *to write,* or "to screeve."

Capiston, *m.* (military), *captain;* — bêcheur, *an officer who acts as public prosecutor at courts-martial.* Termed also "capitaine bêcheur."

Capitaine (thieves'), *stock-jobber; financier;* (military) — bêcheur, see **Capiston;** — de la soupe, *an officer who has never been under fire.*

Capitainer (thieves'), *to be a stock-jobber.*

Capital, *m.* (popular), *maidenhead.* Villon, fifteenth century, terms it "ceinture."

Capitole, *m.* (schoolboys'), formerly *the black hole.*

Capitonnée, *adj.* (popular), *is said of a stout woman.*

Capitonner (popular), se —, *to grow stout.*

Capitulard, *m.* (familiar and popular), *term of contempt applied during the war of* 1870 *to those who were in favour of surrender.*

Caporal, *m.*, *tobacco of French manufacture.*

Caporalisme, *m.* (familiar), *pipe-clayism.*

Capou, *m.* (popular), *a scribe who writes letters for illiterate persons in return for a fee.*

Capoul (familiar), bandeaux à la —, or des Capouls, *hair brushed low on forehead, fringe,* or "toffs." From the name of a celebrated tenor who some twenty years ago was a great favourite of the public, especially of the feminine portion of it.

Caprice, *m.*, *appellation given by ladies of the demi-monde to their lovers;* — sérieux, *one who keeps a girl.*

Capsule, *f.* (popular), *hat with narrow rim; infantry shako.* See **Tubard.**

Captif, *m.* (popular), abbreviation of ballon captif. Enlever le —, *to kick one in the hind quarters,* "to root."

Capucin, *m.* (sportsmen's), *hare.*

Capucine, *f.* (familiar and popular), jusqu'à la troisième —, *completely,* "awfully." Etre paf jusqu'à la troisième —, *to be quite drunk,* or "ploughed." See **Pompette.** S'ennuyer—, &c., *to feel* "awfully" *dull.*

Caquer (popular), *to ease oneself.* See **Mouscailler.**

Carabine, *f.* (popular), *sweetheart of a "carabin,"* or *medical student;* (military) *whip.*

Çarabiné, *adj.* (popular), *excessive, violent.* Un mal de tête —, *a violent headache.* Une plaisanterie carabinée, *a spicy joke.*

Carabiner (military), les côtes, *to thrash.* See **Voie.**

Carabinier, *m.* (popular), de la Faculté, *chemist.*

Carafe, *f.* (cads'), *throat,* or "gutter lane;" *mouth,* or "mug." Fouetter de la —, *to have an offensive breath.*

Carambolage, *m.* (popular), *collision; general set-to; coition,* or "chivalry." Properly *cannoning at billiards.*

Caramboler (popular), *to come into collision; to strike two persons at one blow; to have connection with a woman.* The old poet Villon termed this "chevaulcher," or "faire le bas mestier," and Rabelais called it, "faire la bête à deux dos." The English slang describes the act, more elegantly, as one of "chivalry," or as one in which the seventh commandment is "pulverized."

Carant, *m.* (thieves'), *board; square piece of wood.*

Carante, *f.* (thieves'), *table.*

Carapata, *m.* (popular), *pedestrian; bargee;* (cavalry) *recruit,* or "Johnny raw."

Carapater (popular), *to run,* "to brush." Se —, *to run away,* or "to slope." Literally, courir à pattes. See **Patatrot.**

Caravane, *f.* (popular), *travelling show,* or "slang." Des caravanes, *love adventures.* Termed also "cavalcades."

Carbeluche, *m.* (thieves'), galicé, *silk hat.*

Carcagno, or **carcagne,** *m.* (thieves'), *usurer.*

Carcagnotter (thieves'), *to be a usurer.*

Carcan, *m.* (popular), *worthless horse,* or "screw;" *opprobrious epithet; gaunt woman;* — à crinoline, *street-walker.* See **Gadoue.**

Carcasse, *f.* (thieves'), états de —, *loins.* Carcasse, in popular language, *body,* or "bacon." Je vais te désosser la —, *I'll break every bone in your body.*

Carcassier, *m.* (theatrical), *clever playwright.*

Carder (popular), *to claw one's face.* Properly *to card.*

Cardinale, *f.* (thieves'), *moon,* or "parish lantern."

Cardinales, *f. pl.* (popular), *menses.*

Cardinaliser (familiar), se — la figure, *to blush, or to get flushed through drinking.*

Care, *f.* (thieves'), *place of concealment.* Vol à la —, see **Careur.**

Carême, *m.* (popular), amoureux de —, *timid or platonic lover.* Literally *a Lenten lover,* one who is afraid of touching flesh.

Carer (thieves'), *to conceal; to steal.* See **Careur.** Se —, *to seek shelter.*

Careur, or **voleur à la care,** *m.* (thieves'), *thief who robs a money-changer under pretence of offering old coins for sale,* " pincher."

Carfouiller (popular), *to thrust deeply.*

Il délibéra . . . pour savoir s'il lui carfouillerait le cœur avec son épée ou s'il se bornerait à lui crever les yeux.—FIGARO.

Carge (thieves'), *pack.*

Cargot, *m.* (military), *canteen man.*

Carguer (sailors'), ses voiles, *to retire from the service.* Properly *to reef sails.*

Caribener, or **carer,** *to steal* "à la care." See **Careur.**

Caristade, *f.* (printers'), *relief in money ; charity.*

Carle, *m.* (thieves'), *money,* " lour," or " pieces."

Carline, *f.* (thieves'), *death.*

Carme, *m.* (popular), *large flat loaf ;* (thieves') *money,* " pieces." See **Quibus.** On lui a grinchi tout le — de son morlingue, *the contents of his purse have been stolen.* Carme à l'estorgue, or à l'estoque, *base coin,* or " sheen."

Carmer (thieves'), *to pay,* " to dub."

Carnaval, *m.* (popular), *ridiculously dressed person,* " guy."

Carne, *f.* (popular), *worthless horse,* or " screw ; " *opprobrious epithet applied to a woman, strumpet ; woman of disreputable character,* " bed-fagot," or " shake." Etre —, *to be lazy.*

Carottage, *m.* (popular), *chouse.*

Carotte, *f.* (military), *medical inspection ;* — d'épaisseur, *great chouse.* (Familiar) Tirer une — de longueur, *to concoct a far-fetched story for the purpose of obtaining something from one, as money, leave of absence, &c.* (Theatrical)

Avoir une — dans le plomb, *to sing out of tune, or with a cracked voice ;* (popular) *to have an offensive breath.* Avoir ses carottes cuites, *to be dead.* (Thieves') Tirer la —, *to elicit secrets from one,* " to pump " *one.*

Il s'agit de te faire arrêter pour être conduit au dépôt où tu tireras la carotte à un grinche que nous allons emballer ce soir.—VIDOCQ.

Carotter (familiar), l'existence, *to live a wretched, poverty-stricken life ;* — à la Bourse, *to speculate in a small way at the Stock Exchange ;* (military) — le service, *to shirk one's military duties.*

Caroublage, *m.* (thieves'), *picking of a lock.*

Carouble, *f.* (thieves'), *skeleton key,* " betty," or " twirl."

Caroubleur, *m.* (thieves'), *thief who uses a picklock,* or " screwsman ; " — à la flan, *thief of this description who operates at haphazard ;* — au fric-frac, *housebreaker,* " pannyman," " buster," or " cracksman."

Carquois, *m.* (popular), d'osier, *ragpicker's basket.*

Carre, *f.* (thieves'), du paquelin, *the Banque de France.* Mettre à la —, *to conceal.*

Carré, *m.* (students'), *second-year student in higher mathematics ;* (thieves') *room, or lodgings,* " diggings ; " — des petites gerbes, *police court ;* — du rebectage, *court of cassation,* a tribunal which revises cases already tried, and which has power to quash a judgment.

Carreau, *m.* (popular), de vitre, *monocular eyeglass.* Aller au —, see **Aller.** (Thieves' and cads') Carreau, *eye,* or " glazier ; " — brouillé, *squinting eye,* or " boss-eye ; " — à la manque, *blind eye.* Affranchir le —, *to open one's eye.*

Carreaux brouillés, *m. pl.* (popular), *house of ill-fame,* or "nanny-shop." Such establishments which are under the surveillance of the police authorities have white-washed window-panes and a number of vast dimensions over the street entrance.

Carrée, *f.* (popular), *room,* "crib."

Carrefour, *m.* (popular), des écrasés, *a crossing of the Faubourg Montmartre,* a dangerous one on account of the great traffic.

Carrer (popular and thieves'), se —, *to conceal oneself; to run away,* "to brush;" — de la débine, *to improve one's circumstances.*

Carreur, *m.* (thieves'), *receiver of stolen goods,* "fence." Termed also "fourgue."

Cartaude, *f.* (thieves'), *printer's shop.*

Cartaudé (thieves'), *printed.*

Cartauder (thieves'), *to print.*

Cartaudier (thieves'), *printer.*

Carte, *f.* (popular), *femme en —, street-walker whose name is down in the books of the police as a registered prostitute.* Revoir la —, *to vomit,* or "to cascade," "to cast up accounts," "to shoot the cat." (Cardsharpers') Maquiller la —, *to handle cards; to tamper with cards,* or "to stock broads."

Carton, *m.* (gamesters'), *playing-card,* or "broad." Manier, tripoter, graisser, travailler, patiner le —, *to play cards.* Maquiller le —, *to handle cards, to tamper with cards,* or "to stock broads."

Cartonnements, *m. pl.* (literary), *manuscripts consigned to oblivion.*

Cartonner (gamesters'), *to play cards.*

Cartonneur, *m.,* *one fond of cards.*

Cartonnier, *m.* (popular), *clumsy worker; card-player.*

Cartouche, *f.* (military), avaler sa —, *to die,* "to lose the number of one's mess." Déchirer la —, *to eat.* See **Mastiquer.**

Cartouchière à portées, *f., pack of prepared cards which swindlers keep secreted under their waistcoat,* "books of briefs."

Caruche, *f.* (thieves'), *prison,* or "stir." Comte de la —, *jailer,* or "dubsman." See **Motte.**

Carvel, *m.* (thieves'), *boat.* From the Italian caravella.

Cas, *m.* (popular), montrer son —, *to make an indecent exhibition of one's person.*

Casaquin, *m.* (popular), *human body,* or "apple cart." Avoir quelque-chose dans le —, *to be uneasy; ill at ease in body or mind.* Tomber, sauter sur le — à quelqu'un, *to give one a beating,* "to give one Jessie." Grimper, tanner, travailler le —, *to belabour,* "to tan." See **Voie.**

Cascader (familiar), *interpolating by an actor of matter not in the play; to lead a fast life.*

Cascades, *f. pl.* (theatrical), *fanciful improvisations;* (familiar) *eccentric proceedings; jokes.* Faire des —, *to live a fast life.*

Cascadeur (theatrical), *actor who interpolates in his part;* (familiar) *man with no earnestness of purpose, and who consequently cannot be trusted; fast man.*

Cascadeuse, *f.* (familiar), *fast girl or woman.*

Cascaret, *m.* (thieves'), *two-franc coin.*

Case, carrée, or **piole,** *f.* (thieves'), *room ; lodgings,* "diggings," or "hangs out ;" (popular) *house ; any kind of lodgings,* "crib." Le patron de la —, *the head of any establishment, the landlord, the occupier of a house or apartment.* (Familiar) N'avoir pas de case judiciaire à son dossier *is said of one who has never been convicted of any offence against the law.* The "dossier" is a record of a man's social standing, containing details concerning his age, profession, morality, &c. Every Parisian, high and low, has his "dossier" at the Préfecture de Police.

Casimir, *m.* (popular), *waistcoat,* "benjy."

Casin, *m.* (familiar), *pool at billiards.*

Casinette, *f.* (popular), *habituée of the Casino Cadet,* a place somewhat similar to the former Argyle Rooms.

Casoar, *m.,* *plume of shako,* in the slang of the students of the Saint-Cyr military school, the French Sandhurst.

Casque, *m.* (popular), *hat,* "tile." See **Tubard.** Casque à auvent, *cap with a peak ; — à mèche, cotton nightcap.* Avoir du —, *to have a spirited, persuasive delivery ; to speak with a quack's coolness and facility.* An allusion to Mangin, a celebrated quack in warrior's attire, with a large helmet and plumes. This man, who was always attended by an assistant who went by the name of Vert-de-gris, made a fortune by selling pencils. Avoir le —, *to have a headache caused by potations ; to have a fancy for a man.* Avoir son —, *to be completely tipsy.* See **Pompette.**

Casquer (popular), *to pay,* or "to fork out ;" *to fall blindly into a snare ; to mistake.*

Casquette, *f.* (familiar and popular), *money lost at some game at a café.* Une — à trois ponts, *a prostitute's bully,* or "ponce," thus termed on account of the tall silk cap sported by that worthy. See **Poisson.** Etre —, *to be intoxicated.* See **Pompette.** (Familiar) Etre —, *to have vulgar manners, to be a boor,* "roly-poly."

Casqueur, *m.* (theatrical), *spectator who is not on the free list.*

Cassant, *m.* (thieves'), *walnut tree ;* (sailors') *biscuit.*

Cassantes, *f. pl.* (thieves'), *teeth,* or "head-rails ;" *nuts ; walnuts.*

Casse, *f.* (popular), *chippings of pastry sold cheap.* Je t'en —, *that's not for you.*

Casse-gueule, *m.* (popular), *suburban dancing-hall ; strong spirits,* or "kill devil."

Cassement, *m.* (thieves'), de porte, *housebreaking,* "cracking a crib."

Casser, (thieves'), *to eat,* "to grub ;" — du sucre, or se mettre à table, *to confess ;* — du sucre, or — du sucre à la rousse, *to peach,* "to blow the gaff ;" — la hane, *to steal a purse,* "to buz a skin ;" — sa canne, *to sleep,* or "to doss ;" *to be very ill ; as a ticket - of - leave man, to break bounds ; to die ;* — sa ficelle, *to escape from the convict settlement ;* (popular) — un mot, *to talk ;* — du bec, *to have an offensive breath ;* — du grain, *to do nothing of what is required ;* — du sucre sur la tête de quelqu'un, *to talk ill of one in his absence, to backbite ;* — la croustille, *to eat,* "to grub ;" — la gueule à une négresse, *to drink a bottle of wine ;* — la gueule à un enfant de chœur, *to drink a bottle of wine* (red-capped like a chorister); — la marmite, *to quarrel with one's bread and cheese ;* — le cou à un chat, *to eat a rabbit stew ;* — le cou à une négresse, *to discuss a bottle of wine ;* — sa pipe, son câble, son crachoir, or son fouet, *to die,* "to kick the bucket," "to croak." See **Pipe**. Casser son œuf, *to have a miscarriage ;* — son pif, *to sleep,* "to have a dose of balmy ;" — son lacet, *to break off one's connection with a mistress,* "to bury a moll ;" — une roue de derrière, *to spend part of a five-franc piece.* Se la —, *to get away, to move off,* "to hook it." See **Patatrot**. N'avoir pas cassé la patte à coco, *to be dull-witted,* or "soft." (Familiar) A tout —, *tremendous ; awful.* Une noce à tout —, *a rare jollification,* "a flare-up," or "break-down." Un potin à tout —, *a tremendous row,* or "shindy."

Casserolage, *m.* (thieves'), *informing against an accomplice.*

Casserole, *f.* (thieves'), *informer,* or "buz-man ;" *spy,* or "nark ;" *police officer,* or "copper." See **Pot-à-tabac**. Casserole, *prostitute,* or "bunter." See **Gadoue**. Coup de —, *denunciation,* or "busting." Passer à —, *to be informed against.* (Popular) Casserole, *name given to the Hôpital du Midi.* Passer à —, see **Passer**.

Casseur, *m.* (thieves'), de portes, *housebreaker,* "buster," or "screwsman ;" — de sucre à quatre sous, *military convict of the Algerian* "*compagnies de discipline,*" *chiefly employed at stone-breaking.* The "compagnies de discipline," or punishment companies, consist of all the riff-raff of the army.

Cassine, *f.* (popular), *properly small country-house ; house where the master is strict ; workshop in which the work is severe.*

Cassolette, *f.* (popular), *chamber utensil,* or "jerry ;" *scavenger's cart ; mouth,* or "gob." Plomber de la —, *to have an offensive breath.*

Cassure, *f.* (theatrical), jouer une —, *to perform in the character of a very old man.*

Castagnettes, *f. pl.* (military), *blows with the fist.*

Caste, *f.* (old cant), de charrue, *one-fourth of a crown.*

Castor, or **castorin**, *naval officer who shirks going out to sea, or one in the army who is averse to leaving the garrison.*

Castorin, *m.* (popular), *hat-maker.*

Castoriser *is said of an officer who shirks sea duty, or who likes to make a long stay in some pleasant garrison town.*

Castroz, *m.* (popular), *capon.*

Castu, *m.* (thieves'), *hospital.* Barbeaudier de —, *hospital director.*

Castue, *m.* (thieves'), *prison,* or "stir." See **Motte**. Comte de —, *jailer,* or "jigger-dubber."

Cataplasme, *m.* (popular), au gras, *spinach ;* — de Venise, *blow,* "clout."

Cataplasmier, *m.* (popular), *hospital attendant.*

Catapulteux, catapulteuse, *adj.* (popular), *beautiful ; marvellous.* Une femme —, *a magnificent woman,* a "blooming tart."

Catiniser (popular), se —, *to be in a fair way of becoming a street-walker.*

Cauchemardant (popular), *tiresome, annoying,* "boring."

Cauchemarder (popular), *to annoy, to bore.* Se —, *to fret.*

Cause, *f.* (familiar), grasse, *case in a court of justice offering piquant details.*

Causotter (familiar), *to chat familiarly in a small circle.*

Cavalcade, *f.* (popular), *love intrigue.* Avoir vu des cavalcades *is said of a woman who has had many lovers.*

Cavale, *f.* (popular), *flight.* Se payer une —, *to run away,* or " to crush." See **Patatrot.** (Thieves') Tortiller une —, *to form a plan for escaping from prison.*

Cavaler (thieves' and cads'), quelqu'un, *to annoy one, to* " rile" *him.* Se —, *to make off,* "to guy." For list of synonyms see **Patatrot.** Se — au rebectage, *to pray for a new trial in the* "*Cour de Cassation.*" This court may quash a judgment for the slightest flaw in the procedure, such as, for instance, the fact of a witness not lifting his right hand when taking the oath. Se — cher au rebectage, *to pray for a commutation of a sentence.*

Cavalerie, *f.* (popular), grosse —, *man who works in the sewers, a* "rake-kennel." An allusion to his high boots.

Cavé, *m.* (popular), *dupe,* or "gull;" *cat's-paw.*

Cavée, *f.* (thieves'), *church.*

Cayenne, *m.* (popular), *suburban cemetery; suburban factory; workshop at a distance from Paris.* Gibier de —, *scamp, jail-bird.*

Cayenne-les-eaux, *m.* (thieves'), *the Cayenne dépôt for transported convicts.*

Cé, *m.* (thieves'), *silver.* Attaches de —, *silver buckles.* Bogue de —, *silver watch,* " white 'un." Tout de —, *very well.*

Cela me gêne (theatrical), *words used by actors to denote anything which interferes with the impression they seek to produce by certain tirades or by-play.*

Celui (popular), avoir — de ..., stands for avoir l'honneur de ..., *to have the honour to ... .*

Censure, *f.* (thieves'), passer la —, *to repeat a crime.*

Centiballe, *m.* (popular), *centime.* Balle, *a franc.*

Central, *m.* (familiar), *pupil of the* " *Ecole Centrale,*" a public engineering school; *telegraph office of the* " *Place de la Bourse.*"

Centre, *m.* (thieves'), *name,* "monarch or monniker." Also *a meeting-place for malefactors.* Un — à l'estorgue, *a false name,* or "alias." Un — d'altèque, *a real name.* Coquer son —, *to give one's name.* (Familiar) Le — de gravité, *the behind,* or "seat of honour." See **Vasistas.** Perdre son —, *to be tipsy,* "fuddled."

Centré, *adj.* (popular), *is said of one who has failed in business,* "gone to smash."

Centrier, or **centripète,** *m.* (military), *foot soldier,* " beetle-crusher or wobbler ;" (familiar) *member of the* " *Centre*" *party* (*Conservative*) *of the House, under Louis Philippe.* The House is now divided into "extrême gauche" (rabid radicals) ; "gauche"(advanced republicans); " centre-gauchers " (conservative republicans); " centre " (wavering members) ; " centre droit " (moderate conservatives) ; " droite " (monarchists and clericals) ; " extrême droite " (rabid monarchists and ultramontane clericals).

Centriot, *m.* (thieves'), *nickname.*

Cercle, *m.* (thieves'), *silver coin.* (Familiar) Pincer or rattraper au demi —, *to come upon one unawares, to catch,* "to nab" *him.* From an expression used in fencing.

Cercueil, *m.* (students'), *glass of beer.* A dismal play on the word "bière," which has both significations of *beer and coffin.*

Cerf, *m.* (popular), *injured husband, or cuckold.* Se déguiser en —, *to decamp ; to run away ; to be off in a* "*jiffy.*" See **Patatrot.**

Cerf-volant, *m.* (thieves'), *female thief who strips children at play in the public gardens or parks.* A play on the words "cerf-volant," *kite,* and "voler," *to steal.*

Cerise, *f. pl.* (popular), *mason of the suburbs.*

Cerises, *f.* (military), monter en marchand de —, *to ride badly, with toes and elbows out, and all of a heap, like a man with a basket on his arm.*

Cerisier, *m.* (popular), *sorry horse.* An allusion to the name given to small horses which used to carry cherries to market.

Cerneau, *m.* (literary), *young girl.* Properly *fresh walnut.*

Certificats, *m. pl.* (military), de bêtise, *long-service stripes.*

C'est (printers'), à cause des mouches, *sneering reply.*

Eh ! dis donc, compagnon, pourquoi n'es-tu pas venu à la boîte ce matin ? L'autre répond par ce coq-à-l'âne : C'est à cause des mouches.—BOUTMY.

Cet (popular), aut' chien, *that feller !*

Chabannais, *m.* (popular), *noise ; row ; thrashing.* Ficher un —, *to thrash,* "to wallop." See **Voie.**

Chabrol, *m.* (popular), *mixture of broth and wine.*

Chacal, *m.* (military), *Zouave.*

Chaffourer (popular), se —, *to claw one another.*

Chafrioler (popular), se — à quelque chose, *to find pleasure in something.*

Chahut, *m.* (familiar and popular), *eccentric dance, not in favour in respectable society, and in which the dancers' toes are as often on a level with the faces of their partners as on the ground ; uproar,* "shindy," *general quarrel.* Faire du —, *to make a noise, a disturbance.*

Chahuter (familiar and popular), *to dance the* chahut (which see) ; *to upset ; to shake ; to rock about.* Nous avons été rudement chahutés, *we were dreadfully jolted.* Ne chahute donc pas comme ça, *keep still, don't fidget so.*

Chahuteur, *m.* (popular), *noisy, restless fellow ; one who dances the* chahut (which see).

Chahuteuse, *f.* (popular), *habituée of low dancing-saloons.* Also *a girl leading a noisy, fast life.*

Chaillot (popular), à —! *go to the deuce!* à — les gêneurs ! *to the deuce with bores!* Ahuri de —, *blockhead.* Envoyer à —, *to get rid of one ; to send one to the deuce.*

Chaîne, *f.* (popular), d'oignons, *ten of cards.*

Chaîniste, *m.* (popular), *maker of gold chains.*

Chair, *f.* (cads'), dure ! *hit him hard! smash him!* That is, Fais lui la chair dure ! (Popular) Marchand de — humaine, *keeper of a brothel.*

Chaises, *f. pl.* (popular), manquer de — dans la salle à manger, *to be minus several teeth.* Noce de

bâtons de —, *grand jollification,*
or "flare-up."

Chaleur ! (popular), *exclamation
expressive of contempt, disbelief,
disappointment, mock admiration,
&c.*

Chaloupe, *f.* (popular), *woman
with dress bulging out.* (Students')
La — *orageuse, a furious sort of
cancan.* The cancan is an eccentric dance, and one of rather questionable character. See **Chahut.**

Chalouper (students'), *to dance the
above.*

Chamailler (popular), des dents, *to
eat.*

Chambard, *m.* (Ecole Polytechnique), *act of smashing the furniture and destroying the effects of
the newly-joined students.*

Chambardement, *m.* (sailors'),
overthrow ; destruction.

Chambarder (sailors'), *to hustle ;
to smash.* At the Ecole Polytechnique, *to smash, or create a disturbance.*

Chamberlan, *m.* (popular), *workman who works at home.*

Chambert, *m.* (thieves'), *one who
talks too much ; one who lets the
cat out of the bag.*

Chamberter (thieves'), *to talk in
an indiscreet manner.*

Chambre, *f.* (thieves'), de sûreté,
the prison of La Conciergerie. La
— des pairs, *that part of the dépôt
reserved for convicts sentenced to
penal servitude for life.*

Chambrer (swindlers'), *to lose ; to
steal ; to* "claim." See **Grinchir.**

Chambrillon, *m., small servant ;
young* "slavey."

Chameau, *m.* (popular), *cunning
man who imposes on his friends ;*

girl of lax morals ; prostitute ; —
à deux bosses, *prostitute.* Ce —
de . . ., *insulting expression applied
to either sex.*

Coupeau apprit de la patronne que Nana
était débauchée par une autre ouvrière, ce
petit chameau de Léonie, qui venait de
lâcher les fleurs pour faire la noce.—ZOLA,
L'Assommoir.

Chameliers, *m. pl.* (military), *name
formerly given to the old "guides."*

Champ, *m.* (familiar), *champagne,*
"fiz," or "boy ;" (popular) —
d'oignons, *cemetery ; —* de navets,
*cemetery where executed criminals
are interred.*

Champoreau, *m.* (military), *beverage concocted with coffee, milk, and
some alcoholic liquor, but more
generally a mixture of coffee and
spirits.* From the name of the inventor.

Le douro, je le gardais précieusement,
ayant grand soin de ne pas l'entamer.
J'eusse préféré jeûner un long mois de
champoreau et d'absinthe. — HECTOR
FRANCE, *Sous le Burnous.*

Chançard, *m.* (familiar), *lucky
man.*

Chancellerie, *f.* (popular), mettre
en —, *to put one in Chancery.*

Chancre, *m.* (popular), *man with a
large appetite,* a "grand paunch."

Chand, chande (popular), abbreviation of marchand.

Chandelier, *m.* (popular), *nose,*
"boko," "snorter," or "smeller."
For synonyms see **Morviau.**

Chandelle, *f.* (military), *infantry
musket ; sentry.* Etre conduit
entre quatre chandelles, *to be
marched off to the guard-room by
four men and a corporal.* La —
brûle, *it is time to go home.* Faire
fondre une —, *to drink a bottle of
wine.* Glisser en —, *to slide with
both feet close together.*

Mon galopin file comme une flèche.
Quelle aisance ! quelle grâce même ! Tan-

tôt les pieds joints, en chandelle ; tantôt accroupi, faisant la petite bonne femme.— RICHEPIN, *Le Pavé.*

Changer (popular), son poisson d'eau, or ses olives d'eau, *to void urine,* "to pump ship." See **Lascailler.**

Changeur, *m.* (thieves'), *clothier who provides thieves with a disguise ; rogue who appropriates a new overcoat from the lobby of a house or club, and leaves his old one in exchange.* Also *thief who steals plate.*

Chanoine, *m.,* **chanoinesse,** *f.* (thieves'), *person in good circumstances, one worth robbing ; — de* Monte-à-regret, *one sentenced to death ; old offender.*

Chantage, *m.* (familiar), *extorting money by threats of disclosures concerning a guilty action real or supposed,* "jobbery."

Chanter (familiar), *to pay money under threat of being exposed.* Faire — quelqu'un, *to extort money from one under threat of exposure ; to extort* "socket money." (Popular) Faire — une gamme, *to thrash one,* "to lead a dance." See **Voie.**

Chanteur, *m.* (thieves'), *juge d'instruction, a magistrate who investigates a case before trial ;* (familiar) *man who seeks to extort money by threatening people with exposure.* There are different kinds of chanteurs. Vidocq terms "chanteurs" the journalists who prey on actors fearful of their criticism ; those who demand enormous prices for letters containing family secrets ; the writers of biographical notices who offer them at so much a line ; those who entice people into immoral places and who exact hush-money. The celebrated murderer Lacenaire was one of this class. Chanteur de la Chapelle Sixtine, *eunuch.* Maître —, *skilful* chanteur (which see).

Chantier, *m.* (popular), *embarrassment,* "fix."

Chaparder (military), *to loot ; to steal,* "to prig."

Chapelle, *f.* (familiar), *clique.* Termed also "petite chapelle ;" (popular) *wine-shop,* or "lushcrib." Faire —, *is said of a woman who lifts her dress to warm her limbs by the fire.* Fêter des chapelles, *to go the round of several wine-shops, with what result it is needless to say.*

Chapelure, *f.* (popular), n'avoir plus de — sur le jambonneau, *to be bald,* "to have a bladder of lard." See **Avoir.**

Chapi, *m.* (popular), *hat,* or "tile." See **Tubard.**

Chapiteau, *m.* (popular), *head,* or "block." See **Tronche.**

Chapon, *m.* (popular), *monk.* Cage à chapons, *monastery.* Des chapons de Limousin, *chestnuts.*

Chapska, *m.* (popular), *hat,* or "tile." See **Tubard.**

Char, *m.* (familiar), numéroté, *cab.*

Charcuter (popular), *to amputate.*

Charcutier (popular), *clumsy workman ; surgeon,* "sawbones."

Chardonneret, *m.* (thieves'), *gendarme.* An allusion to his red, white, and yellow uniform. Properly *a goldfinch.*

Charenton, *m.* (popular), *absinthe.* The dépôt for lunatics being at Charenton, the allusion is obvious.

Chargé, *adj.* (popular), *tipsy,* "tight." See **Pompette.** (Coachmen's) Etre —, *to have a* "fare."

Charger (coachmen's), *to take up a "fare;"* (prostitutes') *to find a client;* (cavalry) — en ville, *to go to town.*

Charier (thieves'), *to try to get information,* "to cross-kid."

Charieur (thieves'), *he who seeks to worm out some information.*

Charlemagne, *m.* (military), *sabre-bayonet.*

Charlot, *m.* (popular and thieves'), *the executioner.* His official title is "Monsieur de Paris." Soubrettes de —, *the executioner's assistants,* literally *his lady's maids.* An allusion to "la toilette," or cropping the convict's hair and cutting off his shirt collar a few minutes before the execution. (Thieves') Charlot, *thief;* — bon drille, *a good-natured thief.* See **Grinche.**

Charmant, *adj.* (thieves'), *scabby.*

Charmante, *f.* (thieves'), *itch.*

Charmer (popular), les puces, *to get drunk.* See **Sculpter.**

Charogneux, *adj.* (familiar), roman —, *filthy novel.*

Charon, charron, *m.* (thieves'). See **Charrieur.**

Charpenter (playwrights'), *to write the scheme of a play.*

Charpentier, *m.* (playwrights'), *he who writes the scheme of a play.*

Charretée, *f.* (popular), en avoir une —, *to be quite drunk, to be* "slewed." See **Pompette.**

Charriage, *m.* (thieves'), *swindle;* — à l'Américaine *is a kind of confidence trick swindle.* It requires two confederates, one called "leveur" or "jardinier," whose functions are to exercise his allurements upon the intended victim without awakening his suspicions. When the latter is fairly hooked, the pair meet—by chance of course —with "l'Américain," a confederate who passes himself off for a native of America, and who offers to exchange a large sum of gold for a smaller amount of money. The pigeon gleefully accepts the proffered gift, and discovers later on that the alleged gold coins are nothing but base metal. This kind of swindle goes also by the names of "vol à l'Américaine," "vol au change." Charriage à la mécanique, or vol au père François, takes place thus : a robber throws a handkerchief round a person's neck, and holds him fast half-strangled on his own back while a confederate rifles the victim's pockets. Charriage au coffret : the thief, termed "Américain," leaves in charge of a barmaid a small box filled to all appearance with gold coin ; he returns in the course of the day, but suddenly finding that he has lost the key of the box, he asks for a loan of money and disappears, leaving the box as security. It goes without saying that the alleged gold coins are nothing more than brand-new farthings. Charriage au pot, another kind of the confidence trick dodge. One confederate forms an acquaintance with a passer-by, and both meet with the other confederate styled "l'Américain," who offers to take them to a house of ill-fame and defray all expenses, but who, being fearful of getting robbed, deposits his money in a jug or other receptacle. On the way he suddenly alters his mind, and sends the victim for the sum, not without having exacted bail-money from him as a guarantee of his return, after which both scamps make off with the fool's money. Swindlers of this description are termed "magsmen" in the English slang.

Charrier (thieves'), *to swindle one out of his money by misleading statements.* See **Charriage.**

Charrieur, *m.* (thieves'), *thief who employs the mode termed* charriage (which see) ; *confederate who provides cardsharpers with pigeons ;* — de ville, *a robber who first makes his victims insensible by drugs, and then plunders them,* a "drummer ; " — cambrousier, *itinerant quack ; clumsy thief.*

Chartreuse, *f.* (popular), de vidangeur, *small measure of wine.*

Chartron, *m.* (theatrical), faire le —, *is said of actors who place themselves in a row in front of the footlights.*

Chason, *m.* (thieves'), *ring,* "fawney."

Chasse, *f.* (popular), aller à la — au barbillon, *to go a-fishing.* Foutre une —, *to scold vehemently,* "to haul over the coals."

Châsse, *f.* (thieves'), *eye,* "glazier." Balancer, boiter des châsses, *to be one-eyed,* "boss-eyed ; " *to squint.* Se foutre l'apôtre dans la —, *to be mistaken.*

Chasse-brouillard (popular), *a drop of spirits ; a dram to keep the damp out,* a "dewdrop."

Chasse-coquin, *m.* (popular), *gendarme ; beadle,* "bumble ; " *bad wine.*

Chasselas, *m.* (popular), *wine.*

Chassemar, *m.* (popular), for chasseur.

Chasse-marée, *m.* (military), *chasseurs d'Afrique, a body of light cavalry.*

Chasse-noble, *m.* (thieves'), *gendarme.*

Chasser (popular), au plat, *to be a parasite,* a "quiller ; " — des reluits, *to weep,* "to nap a bib ; " — le brouillard, *to have a morning dram of spirits,* or a "dewdrop ; " — les mouches, *to be dying.* See **Pipe.** (Thieves' and cads') Chasser, *to flee,* "to guy." See **Patatrot.**

<small>Gn'a du pet, interrompt un second voyou qui survient, v'là un sergot qui s'amène . . . chassons !—RICHEPIN.</small>

Châsses, *f. pl.* (popular), d'occase, *squinting eyes,* or "squinny eyes." D'occase, *secondhand.*

Chassis, *m.* (popular), *eyes,* or "peepers." Fermer les —, *to sleep.*

Chassue, *f.* (thieves'), *needle.* Chas, *eye of a needle.*

Chassure, *f.* (thieves'), *wine.*

Chasublard, *m.* (popular), *priest,* or "devil dodger."

Chat, *m.* (thieves'), *turnkey,* "dubsman ; " (popular) *slater.* Avoir un — dans la gouttière, *to be hoarse.*

Châtaigne, *f.* (popular), *box on the ear,* or "buck-horse."

Chataud, chataude (popular), *greedy.*

Château, *m.* (familiar), abbreviation of **Châteaubriand** (which see). (Popular) Château branlant, *person or thing always in motion.* (Thieves') Château, *prison ;* — de l'ombre, *convict settlement.*

Châteaubriand, *m.* (familiar), *fillet of beef rolled up in a couple of rump steaks, and then grilled on a brisk fire,* thus called after the name of the celebrated author ; — aux pommes, *the above with fried potatoes.*

Château-Campêche (familiar and popular), *derisive appellation for* *bad wine, of which the ruby colour is often due to an adjunction of logwood.*

Chaton, *m.* (popular), *nice fellow ; Sodomist.*

Chatouillage au roupillon, *m.* (thieves'). See **Vol au poivrier.**

Chatouiller (theatrical), le public, *to indulge in drolleries calculated to excite mirth among an audience;* (familiar) — les côtes, *to thrash,* "*to lick.*"

Chatouilleur (familiar), *man on 'Change who by divers contrivances entices the public into buying shares,* a "buttoner ; " (thieves') *a thief who tickles a person's sides as if in play, and meanwhile picks his pockets.*

Chatte, *f.* (popular), *five-franc piece.*

Chaud, *adj. and m.* (popular), *cunning ; greedy ; wide awake,* or "*fly ;*" *high-priced.* Il l'a —, *he is wide awake about his own interests.* Etre —, *to look with watchful eye.* (Familiar) Un —, *an enthusiast ; energetic man.* Il fera —, *never,* "*when the devil is blind.*" Quand vous me reverrez il fera —, *you will never see me again.* Etre — de la pince, *to be fond of women, to be a* "*beard-splitter.*" (Artists') Faire —, *to employ very warm tints after the style of Rembrandt and all other colourists.* (Popular and thieves') Chaud ! *quick ! on !*

Chaud, chaud ! pour le mangeur, il faut le désosser.—E. Sue.

Chaudron, *m.* (familiar), *bad piano.* Taper sur le —, *to play on the piano.*

Chaudronner (popular), *to buy secondhand articles and sell them as new.*

Chaudronnier, *m.* (popular), *secondhand - clothes man ;* (mili-

tary) *cuirassier,* an allusion to his breastplate.

Chaufaillon (popular), *stoker.*

Chauffe-la-couche (familiar), *man who loves well his comfort ; henpecked husband,* or "*stangey.*"

Chauffer (popular), le four, *to drink heavily,* "*to guzzle.*" See **Rincer.** (Familiar) Chauffer un artiste, une pièce, *to applaud so as to excite the enthusiasm of an audience ;* — une affaire, *to push briskly an undertaking ;* — une place, *to be canvassing for a post.* Ça va chauffer, *there will be a hot fight.* Chauffer des enchères, *to encourage bidding at an auction.*

Chauffeur, *m.* (popular), *man who instills life into conversation or in a company ; formerly, under the Directoire, one of a gang of brigands who extorted money from people by burning the feet of the victims.*

Chaumir (thieves'), *to lose.*

Chaussette (thieves'), *ring fastened as a distinctive badge to the leg of a convict who has been chained up for any length of time to another convict, a punishment termed* "*double chaîne.*"

Chaussettes, *f. pl.* (military), *gloves ;* — russes, *wrapper for the feet made of pieces of cloth ;* (popular) — de deux paroisses, *odd socks.*

Chausson, *m.* (popular), *old prostitute.* Putain comme —, *regular whore.* (Ballet girls') Faire son —, *to put on and arrange one's pumps.*

"Laissez-moi donc, je suis en retard. J'ai encore mon mastic et mon chausson à faire." Autrement, pour ceux qui ne sont pas de la boutique, "il me reste encore à m'habiller, à me chausser et à me faire ma tête."—MAHALIN.

Chaussonner (popular), *to kick.*

Chauviniste, *m.*, synonymous of " chauvin," *one with narrow-minded, exaggerated sentiments of patriotism*, a " Jingo."

Chef, *m.* (military), abbreviation of maréchal-des-logis chef, *quarter-master-sergeant in the cavalry.* (Popular) Chef de cuisine, *foreman in a brewery ;* (thieves') — d'attaque, *head of a gang.*

Chelinguer (popular), *to stink.* Termed also " plomber, trouilloter, casser, danser, repousser, fouetter, vézouiller, véziner."

Cheminée, *f.* (popular), *hat,* " chimney pot."

Chemise, *f.* (popular), être dans la — de quelqu'un, *to be constantly with one, to be* " thick as hops " *with one.* (Thieves') Chemise de conseiller, *stolen linen.*

Chemises, *f. pl.* (popular), compter ses —, *to vomit,* or " to cascade." An allusion to the bending posture of a man who is troubled with the ailment.

Chenâtre, *adj.* (thieves'), *good, excellent,* " nobby."

Ils ont de quoi faire un chenâtre banquet avec des rouillardes pleines de pivois et du plus chenâtre qu'on puisse trouver.—*Le Jargon de l'Argot.*

Chêne, *m.* (thieves'), *man,* or " cove;" — affranchi, *thief,* or " flash cove." For synonyms see **Grinche.** Faire suer un —, *to kill a man,* " to give a cove his gruel."

Chenillon, *m.* (popular), *ugly girl.*

Chenique, or **chnic,** *m.* (popular), *brandy,* " French cream."

Cheniqueur, *m.* (popular), *drinker of brandy.*

Chenoc, *adj.* (thieves'), *bad ; good-for-nothing old fellow.*

Chenu, *adj.* (thieves'), *excellent,* " nobby." Properly *old, whitened by age ;* — pivois, *excellent wine ;* —reluit, *good morning;* — sorgue, *good night.*

> Je lui jaspine en bigorne,
> Qu'as-tu donc à morfiller ?
> J'ai du chenu pivois sans lance,
> Et du larton savonné.
> VIDOCQ.

Chenument (popular), *very well ; very good.*

Cher (thieves'), se cavaler —, *to decamp quickly, to* " guy." See **Patatrot.**

Chérance, *f.* (thieves'), être en —, *to be intoxicated,* or " canon."

Cherche (popular), *nothing,* or " love." Etre dix à —, *to be ten to love at billiards.*

Chercher (popular), la gueulée, *to be a parasite,* a " quiller." (Familiar and popular) Chercher des poux à la tête de quelqu'un, *to find fault with one on futile pretexts ; to try and fasten on a quarrel.*

Chérez ! (thieves'), *courage ! cheer up ! never say die !* Villon, 15th century, has " chère lye," *a joyous countenance.*

Chetard, *m.* (thieves'), *prison,* or " stir." See **Motte.**

Chétif, *m.* (popular), *mason's boy.*

Cheulard, *m.* (popular), *gormandizer,* " grand-paunch."

Cheval, *m.* (popular and thieves'), de retour, *old offender ; returned or escaped convict sent back to the convict settlement.* Termed also " trique, canne."

Me voilà donc cheval de retour, on me remet à Toulon, cette fois avec les bonnets verts.—V. HUGO.

(Military) Cheval de l'adjudant, *camp bed of cell;* (familiar) — qui la connaît dans les coins, *a clever horse.* Literally *skilful at turning the corners.* (Popular) Faire son — de corbillard, *to put on a jaunty look; to give oneself conceited airs; to bluster,* or, as the Americans say, "to be on the tall grass."

Chevalier, *m.* (popular), de la courte lance, *hospital assistant;* — de la grippe, *thief,* or "prig." See **Grinche.** Chevalier de la manchette, *Sodomist;* — de la pédale, *one who works a card-printing machine;* — de l'aune, *shopman,* or "knight of the yard;" — de salon, de tapis vert, *gamester;* — du bidet, *women's bully,* or "pensioner." See **Poisson.** Chevalier du crochet, *rag-picker,* or "bonegrubber;" — du lansquenet, *gambling cheat who has recourse to the card-sharping trick denominated "le pont"* (which see); — du lustre, "*claqueur,*" that is, *one who is paid for applauding at theatres;* — du printemps, or de l'ordre du printemps, *silly fellow who flowers his button-hole to make it appear that he has the decoration of the "Légion d'Honneur;"* — grimpant, see **Voleur au bonjour.**

Chevau-léger, *m.* (familiar), *ultra-Conservative of the Legitimist and Clerical party.* The chevau-légers were formerly a corps of household cavalry.

Chevaux, *m. pl.* (popular), à doubles semelles, *legs.* Compare the English expression, "to ride Shank's mare, or pony."

Chevelu, *adj.* (familiar), art —, littérateur —, poète —, *art, literary man, poet of the "école romantique,"* of which the chief in literature was Victor Hugo.

Cheveu, *m.* (familiar), *difficulty; trouble; hindrance; hitch.* Voilà le —, *ay, there's the rub.* J'ai un —, *I have some trouble on my mind, reason for uneasiness.* Il y a un — dans son bonheur, *there is some trouble that mars his happiness.* (Popular) Avoir un — pour un homme, *to fancy a man.* (Theatrical) Cheveu, *unintentional jumbling of words by transposition of syllables.* This kind of mistake when intentional Rabelais termed "équivoquer."

En l'aultre deux ou trois miroirs ardents dont il faisait enrager aulcunes fois les hommes et les femmes et leur faisait perdre contenance à l'ecclise. Car il disait qu'il n'y avait qu'une antistrophe entre femme folle à la messe et femme molle à la fesse.—RABELAIS, *Pantagruel.*

See also *Œuvres de Rabelais* (Garnier's edition), *Pantagruel,* page 159.

Cheveux, *m.* (familiar and popular), avoir mal aux —, *to have a headache caused by overnight potations.* Faire des — gris à quelqu'un, *to trouble one, to give anxiety to one.* Se faire des — blancs, *to fret; to feel annoyed at being made to wait a long time.* Trouver des — à tout, *to find fault with everything.* (Military) Passer la main dans les —, *to cut one's hair.*

Chevillard, *m.* (popular), *butcher in a small way.*

Chevilles, *f.* (popular), *fried potatoes.* Termed "greasers" at the R. M. Academy.

Chévinette, *f.* (popular), *darling.*

Chèvre, *f.* (popular), gober sa —, *to get angry, to bristle up,* "to lose one's shirt," "to get one's monkey up."

Chevron, *m.* (thieves'), *fresh offence against the law.* Properly *military stripe.*

Chevronné, *m.* (thieves'), *old offender, an old* "jail-bird."

Chevrotin, *adj.* (popular), *irritable,* "cranky," "touchy."

Chiade, *f.* (schoolboys'), *hustling, pushing.*

Chialler (thieves'), *to squall; to weep.*

> Bon, tu chial'! ah! c'est pas palas.—RICHEPIN.

Chiarder (schoolboys'), *to work,* "to sweat."

Chiasse, *f.* (popular), avoir la —, *to suffer from diarrhœa,* or "jerry-go-nimble."

Chibis, *m.* (thieves'), faire —, *to escape from prison; to decamp,* "to guy." See **Patatrot.**

> J'ai fait chibis. J'avais la frousse
> Des préfectanciers de Pantin.
> A Pantin, mince de potin !
> On y connaît ma gargarousse.
> RICHEPIN, *Chanson des Gueux.*

Chic, *m.* (English slang), "tzing tzing," or "slap up." The word has almost ceased to be slang, but we thought it would not be out of place in a work of this kind. (Familiar) Chic, *finish; elegance; dash; spirit.* Une femme qui a du —, *a stylish woman or dress.* Cet acteur joue avec —, *this actor plays in a spirited manner.* Ça manque de —, *it wants dash, is commonplace.* Pourri de —, *most elegant,* "nobby." Chic, *knack; originality; manner.* Il a le —, *he has the knack.* Il a un — tout particulier, *he has a manner quite his own.* Il a le — militaire, *he has a soldier-like appearance.* Peindre de —, faire de —, écrire de —, *to paint or write with imaginative power, but without much regard for accuracy.*

> Vous croyez peut-être que j'invente, que je brode d'imagination et que je fais de chic cette seconde vie.—RICHEPIN.

Chic, chique, *adj., excellent,* "fizzing;" *dashing, stylish.* Un pékin —, *well-dressed, rich man.* Un homme —, *a man of fashion, a well-dressed one, a well-to-do man.* Un — homme, *a good, excellent man.*

Chican, *m.* (thieves'), *hammer.*

Chicandard. See **Chicard.**

Chicander (popular), *to dance the "Chicard step."* See **Chicard.**

Chicane, *f.* (thieves'), grinchir à la —, *stealing the purse or watch of a person while standing in front of him, but with the back turned towards him*—a feat which requires no ordinary dexterity.

Chicard, *m.* (popular), *buffoon character of the carnival, in fashion from* 1830 *to* 1850. The first who impersonated it was a leather-seller, who invented a new eccentric step, considered to be exceedingly "chic;" hence probably his nickname of Chicard. His "get-up" consisted of a helmet with high plume, jackboots, a flannel frock, and large cavalry gloves. Pas —, *step invented by M. Chicard.*

Chicard, chicancardo, chicandard, *adj., superlative of* "chic," "tip-top," "out and out," "slap up," "tzing tzing."

Chicarder, *to dance the Chicard step.* See **Chicard.**

Chic et contre, *warning which mountebanks address to one another.*

Chiche ! (popular), *an exclamation expressive of defiance.*

Chickstrac, *m.* (military), *refuse, dung, excrement.* Corvée de —, *fatigue duty for sweeping away the refuse, and especially for emptying cesspools.*

Chicmann, *m.* (popular), *tailor.* A great many tailors in Paris bear Germanic names ; hence the termination of the word.

G

Chicorée, *f.* (popular), c'est fort de —, *it is really too bad!* Ficher de la —, *to reprimand,* "to give a wigging." Faire sa —, *is said of a person with affected or* "high-falutin" *airs.* Ne fais donc pas ta —, *don't give yourself such airs,* "come off the tall grass," as the Americans have it.

Chié, *adj.* (popular), tout —, "as like as two peas."

Chie-dans-l'eau, *m.* (military), *sailor.*

Chien, *m. and adj.* (popular), noyé, *sugar soaked in coffee.* (Journalists') Un — perdu, *short newspaper paragraph.* (Schoolboys') Un — de cour, *school usher,* or "bum brusher." (Military) Un —de compagnie, *a sergeant major.* Un — de régiment, *adjutant.* (Familiar and popular) Le — du commissaire, *police magistrate's secretary.* The commissaire is a police functionary and petty magistrate. He examines privately cases brought before him, sends prisoners for trial, or dismisses them at once, settles then and there disputes between coachmen and their fares, sometimes between husbands and wives, makes perquisitions. He possesses to a certain extent discretionary powers. Avoir du —, *to possess dash,* go, "gameness." Il faut avoir du — dans le ventre pour résister, *one must have wonderful staying powers to resist.* Avoir un — pour un homme, *to be infatuated with a man.* Faire le —, *is said of a servant who follows with a basket in the wake of her mistress going to market.* Rester en — de faience, *to remain immovable, like a block.* Se regarder en — de faience, *to look at one another without uttering a word.* Piquer un —, *to take a nap.* Dormir en — de fusil, *to sleep with the body doubled up.* Une coiffure à la —, *mode of wearing the hair loose on the forehead.* (Military) Un officier —, *a martinet.*

Chiendent, *m.,* arracher le —. See **Arracher.**

Chier (popular), *coarse word;* — dans la vanette, *to be too free and easy;* — de petites crottes, *to earn little money; to live in poverty;* — des carottes, *to be costive;* — des chasses, *to weep,* "to nap a bib;" — du poivre, *to fail in keeping one's promise; to abscond; to vanish when one's services or help are most needed;* — sur l'œil, *to laugh at one;* — sur, *to show great contempt for; to abandon.* Ne pas — de grosses crottes, *to have had a bad dinner, or no dinner at all.* Vous me faites —, *you bore me.* Un gueuleton à — partout, *a grand feast.* Une mine à — dessus, *a repulsive countenance.* (Printers') Chier dans le cassetin aux apostrophes, *to cease to be a printer.*

Chieur, *m.* (popular), d'encre, *clerk,* or "quill-driver."

Chiffarde, *f.* (thieves'), *summons; pipe.*

Chiffe (popular), *rag-picking;* tongue, "red rag."

Chifferlinde, *f.* (popular), boire une —, *to drink a dram of spirits.*

Chifferton (popular), *rag-picker,* "bone-grubber," or "tot-picker."

Chiffon, *m.* (popular), *handkerchief,* "snottinger;" — rouge, *tongue,* "red rag." Balancer le — rouge, *to talk,* "to wag the red rag."

Chiffonnage, *m.* (popular), *plunder of a rag-picker.*

Chiffonnier, *m.* (thieves'), *pickpocket who devotes his attention to handkerchiefs,* "stook-hauler;"

man of disorderly habits. (Literary) Chiffonnier de la double colline, *bad poet.*

Chiffornion, *m.* (popular), *silk handkerchief, or silk "wipe."*

Chiffortin, *m.* (popular), *rag-picker,* "bone-grubber," or "tot-picker."

Chignard, *m.* (popular), *inveterate grumbler,* "rusty guts."

Chigner (popular), *to weep,* "to nap a bib."

Chimique, *f.* (popular), *lucifer match.*

Chinage. See **Chine.** Vol au —, *selling plated trinkets for the genuine article.*

Chincilla (popular), *grey,* or "pepper and salt" *hair.*

Chine. Aller à la —, *to ply the trade of* chineur (which see).

Chiner (military), *to slander one ; to ridicule one ;* (popular) *to work ; to go in quest of good bargains ; to buy furniture at sales and resell it ; to follow the pursuit of an old clothes man ; to hawk ; to go about the country buying heads of hair from peasant girls.*

Chineur, or **margoulin,** *m.* (thieves'), *one who goes about the country buying heads of hair of peasant girls.* (Military) Chineur, *slanderer ;* (popular) *rabbit-skin man ; marine store dealer ; worker ; hawker of cheap stuffs or silk handkerchiefs.*

En argot, chineur signifie travailleur, et vient du verbe chiner. . . . Mais ce mot se spécialise pour désigner particulièrement une race de travailleurs *sui generis.* . . . Elle campe en deux tribus à Paris. L'une habite le pâté de maisons qui se hérisse entre la place Maubert et le petit bras de la Seine, et notamment rue des Anglais. L'autre niche en haut de Ménilmontant, et a donné autrefois son nom à la rue de la Chine. . . .
Les chineurs sont, d'ailleurs, des colons et non des Parisiens de naissance. Chaque génération vient ici chercher fortune, et s'en retourne ensuite au pays.—RICHEPIN, *Le Pavé.*

Chinois, *m.* (popular), *an individual,* a "bloke," a "cove ;" *proprietor of coffee-house ;* (familiar) *term of friendship ;* (military) *term of contempt applied to civilians,* hence probably the expression "pékin," *civilian.*

Chinoiserie, *f.* (familiar), *quaint joke ; intricate and quaint procedure or contrivance.*

Chipe, *f.* (popular), *prigging.* From chiper, *to purloin.*

Chipette, *f.* (popular), *trifle ; nothing ; Lesbian woman, that is, one with unnatural passions.*

Chipie, *f.* (familiar). Literally *girl or woman with a testy temper,* a "brim." Faire sa —, *to put on an air of supreme disdain or disgust.*

Chipoteuse, *f.* (popular), *capricious woman.*

Chiquandar. See **Chicard.**

Chique. See **Chic.**

Chique, *f.* Properly *quid of tobacco.* (Popular) Avoir sa —, *to be in a bad humour,* "to be crusty," or "cranky." Avoir une —, *to be drunk,* or "screwed." See **Pompette.** Ça te coupe la —, *that's disappointing for you, that* "cuts you up." Coller sa —, *to bend one's head.* Couper la — à quinze pas, *to stink.* Poser sa —, *to die ;* *to be still.* Pose ta — et fais le mort ! *be still ! shut up ! hold your row !* (Thieves') Chique, *church.*

Chiqué (artists'), *smartly executed.* Also *said of artistic work done quickly without previously studying nature.* (Popular) Bien —, *well dressed.*

Chiquement, *with* chic (which see).

Chiquer (familiar), *to do anything in a superior manner ; to do artistic work with more brilliancy than accuracy ;* (popular) *to thrash,* "to wallop," see **Voie** ; *to eat,* "to grub," see **Mastiquer**. Se —, *to fight,* "to drop into one another."

Chiquer contre or **battre à niort** (thieves'), *to deny one's guilt.*

Chiqueur, *m.* (popular), *glutton,* "stodger ;" (artists') *an artist who paints with smartness, or one who draws or paints without studying nature.*

Chirurgien, *m.* (popular), en vieux, *cobbler.*

Chnic. See **Chenique**.

Chocaillon, *m.* (popular), *female rag-picker ; female drunkard,* or "lushington."

Chocnoso, chocnosof, chocnosogue, koscnoff, *excellent, remarkable, brilliant,* "crushing," "nobby," "tip-top," "fizzing."

Chocotte, *f.* (rag-pickers'), *marrow bone ;* (thieves') *tooth.*

Choléra, *m.* (popular), *zinc or zinc-worker ; bad meat.*

Cholet, *m.* (popular), *white bread of superior quality.*

Cholette, *f.* (thieves'), *half a litre.* Double —, *a litre.*

Choper (popular), *to steal,* "to prig." See **Grinchir**. Old word *choper, to touch anything, to make it fall.* Se laisser —, *to allow oneself to be caught, to be* "nabbed."

Chopin, *m.* (thieves'), *theft ; stolen object ; blow.* Faire un —, *to commit a theft.*

Chose, *adj.* (familiar and popular), *ill at ease ; sad ; embarrassed.* Il prit un air —, *he looked sad or embarrassed.* Je me sens tout —, *I feel ill at ease ; queer.*

Chou ! (thieves' and cads'), *a warning cry to intimate that the police or people are coming up.* Termed also " Acresto !"

Choucarde, *f.* (military), *wheelbarrow.*

Chouchouter (familiar), *to fondle,* "to firkytoodle ;" *to spoil one.* From chouchou, *darling.*

Chou colossal (familiar), *a scheme for swindling the public by fabulous accounts of future profits.*

Choucroute, *f.* (popular), tête or mangeur de —, *a German.*

Choucrouter (popular), *to eat sauerkraut ; to speak German.*

Choucrouteur, choucroutmann, *m.,* *German.*

Chouette, chouettard, chouettaud, *adj., good ; fine ; perfect,* "chummy," "real jam," "true marmalade." C'est rien —, *that's first-class !* Quel — temps, *what splendid weather !* Un — régiment, *a crack regiment.* (Disparagingly) Nous sommes —, *we are in a fine pickle.*

Chouette, *f.* and *adj.* (thieves'), être —, *to be caught.* Faire une —, *to play at billiards against two other players.*

Chouettement (popular), *finely ; perfectly.*

Chouez (Breton), *house ;* — doue, *church.*

Choufflic (popular), *bad workman.* In the German schuflick, *cobbler.*

Chouffliquer (popular), *to work in a clumsy manner.*

Chouffliqueur, *m.* (popular), *bad workman ;* (military) *shoemaker,* "snob."

Choufretez (Breton), *lucifer matches.*

Chouia (military), *gently.* From the Arabic.

Chouil (Breton), *work ; insect.*

Chouila (Breton cant), *to work ; to beget many children.*

Chouista (Breton), *to work with a will.*

Choumaque (popular), *shoemaker.* From the German.

Chourin, for **surin** (thieves'), *knife,* " chive."

Si j'ai pas l'rond, mon surin bouge.
Moi, c'est dans le sang qu' j'aurais truqué.
Mais quand on fait suer, pomaqué !
Mieux vaut bouffer du blanc qu' du rouge.
RICHEPIN, *Chanson des Gueux.*

Chouriner, for **suriner** (thieves'), *to knife,* " to chive."

Chourineur, *m.,* for **surineur** (thieves'), *one who uses the knife ; knacker.* " Le Chourineur " is one of the characters of Eugène Sue's *Mystères de Paris.*

C'housa (Breton), *to eat.*

C'housach (Breton), *food.*

Chrétien, *adj.* (popular), *mixed with water,* " baptized."

Chrétien, *m.* (popular), viande de —, *human flesh.*

Chrysalide, *f.* (popular), *old coquette.*

Chtibes, *f. pl.* (popular), *boots,* " hock-dockies."

Chybre, *m.* (popular), *penis ;* (artists') *member of the Institut de France.*

Chyle, *m.* (familiar), se refaire le —, *to have a good meal,* a " tightener."

Cibiche, *f.* (popular), *cigarette.*

Cible, *f.* (popular), à coups de pieds, *breech.* See **Vasistas.**

Ciboule, *f.* (popular), *head,* or " block." See **Tronche.**

Cidre, *m.* (familiar), élégant, *champagne,* " fiz," or " boy."

Ciel, *m.* (fishermens'), le — plumant ses poules, *clouds.*

Les nuages, c'était le ciel plumant ses poules,
Et la foudre en éclats, Michel cassant ses œufs.
Il appelait le vent du sud cornemuseux,
Celui du nord cornard, de l'ouest brise à grenouille,
Celui de suroit l'brouf, celui de terre andouille.
RICHEPIN, *La Mer.*

Cierge, *m.* (thieves'), *police officer,* or " reeler." For synonyms see **Pot-à-tabac.**

Cig, *m.,* **cigale,** or **sigue,** *f.* (thieves'), *gold coin,* or " yellow boy."

Cigale, *f.* (popular), *female street singer.* Properly *grasshopper ;* also *cigar.*

Cigogne, *f.* (thieves'), *the* " *Préfecture de Police* " *in Paris ; the Palais de Justice ; court of justice.* Le dab de la —, *the public prosecutor ; the prefect of police.*

Je monte à la cigogne.
On me gerbe à la grotte,
Au tap, et pour douze ans.
VIDOCQ.

Cigue, *f.* (thieves'), abbreviation of cigale, *twenty-franc piece.*

Cimaise (painters'), faire sa — sur quelqu'un, *to show up one's own good qualities, whether real or imaginary, at the expense of another's failings,* in other words, *to preach for one's own chapel.*

Ciment, *m.* (freemasons'), *mustard.*

Cingler (thieves'), se — le blair, *to get drunk,* or " canon."

Cinq-à-sept, *m.,* *a kind of tea party from five o'clock to seven in the fashionable world.*

Cinq-centimadas, *m.* (ironical), *one-sou cigar.*

Cintième, *m.* (popular), *high cap generally worn by women's bullies,* or " pensioners."

Cintrer (popular), *to hold ;* (thieves') — en pogne, *to seize hold of ; to apprehend,* or "to smug." See **Piper.**

Cipal, *m.* (popular), abbreviation of garde-municipal. The "garde municipale" is a picked body of old soldiers who furnish guards and perform police functions at theatres, official ceremonies, police courts, &c. It consists of infantry and cavalry, and is in the pay of the Paris municipal authorities, most of the men having been non-commissioned officers in the army.

Cirage (popular), *praise,* "soft sawder," "butter."

Cire, *f.,* voleur à la —, *rogue who steals a silver fork or spoon at a restaurant, and makes it adhere under the table by means of a piece of soft wax.* When charged with the theft, he puts on an air of injured innocence, and asks to be searched ; then leaves with ample apologies from the master of the restaurant. Soon after a confederate enters, taking his friend's former seat at the table, and pocketing the booty.

Ciré, *m.* (popular), *negro.* From cirer, *to black shoes.* Termed also " boîte à cirage, bamboula, boule de neige, bille de pot au feu."

Cirer (popular), *to praise ; to flatter,* "to butter."

Cireux, *m.* (popular), *one with inflamed eyelids.*

Ciseaux, *m. pl.* (literary), travailler à coups de —, *to compile.*

Cité, *f.* (popular), d'amour, *gay girl,* "bed-fagot."

Je l'ai traitée comme elle le méritait. Je l'ai appeléefeignante, cité d'amour, chenille, machine à plaisir.—MACÉ.

Citron, *m.* (theatrical), *squeaky note ;* (thieves' and cads') *the head,* "nut," or "chump." Termed also "tronche, sorbonne, poire, cafetière, trognon, citrouille."

Citrouille, *f.,* citrouillard, *m.* (military), *dragoon ;* (thieves') *head,* "nut," or "tibby."

Civade, *f.* (thieves'), *oats.*

Civard, *m.* (popular), *pasture.*

Cive, *f.* (popular), *grass.*

Clairs, *m. pl.* (thieves'), *eyes,* or "glaziers." See **Mirettes.**

Clairté, *f.* (popular), *light ; beauty.*

Clamart, *m.* (popular), *cemetery for executed convicts.*

Clampiner (popular), *to idle about ; to lounge about lazily,* "to mike."

Clapoter (popular), *to eat,* "to grub." See **Mastiquer.**

Claqué, *m. and adj.* (popular), *dead, dead man.* La boîte aux claqués, *the Morgue, or Paris dead-house.* Le jardin des claqués, *the cemetery.*

Claquebosse, *m.* (popular), *house of ill-fame,* or "nanny-shop."

Claquedents, *m.* (popular), *house of ill-fame,* "nanny-shop ;" *gaming-house,* or "punting-shop ;" *low eating house.*

Claquefaim, *m.* (popular), *starving man.*

Claquepatins, *m.* (popular), *miserable slipshod person.*

Venez à moi, claquepatins,
Loqueteux, joueurs de musette,
Clampins, loupeurs, voyous, catins.
RICHEPIN.

The early French poet Villon uses the word "cliquepatin" with the same signification.

Claquer (familiar), *to die,* "to croak ;" *to eat ; to sell ;* — ses

meubles, *to sell one's furniture ;
— du bec, to be very hungry
without any means of satisfying
one's craving for food.*

Claques, *f. pl.* (familiar and popular), une figure à —, *face with an
impudent expression that invites
punishment.*

Clarinette, *f.* (military), de cinq
pieds, *musket, formerly* " Brown
Bess."

Classe, *f.* (popular), un — dirigeant, *said ironically of one of the
upper classes.*

Clavin, *m.* (thieves'), *nail ; grapes.*

Clavine, *f.* (thieves'), *vine.*

Claviner (thieves'), *to nail ; to
gather grapes.*

Clavineur, *m.* (thieves'), *vine-dresser.*

Clavinier, *m.* (thieves'), *nail-maker.*

Clef, *f.* (familiar), à la —. See **A
la.** Perdre sa —, *to suffer from
colic,* or " botts." (Military) La
— du champ de manœuvre, *imaginary object which recruits are requested by practical jokers to go
and ask of the sergeant.*

Cliabeau, *m.,* expression used by
the prisoners of Saint-Lazare,
doctor.

Cliche, *f.* (popular), *diarrhœa,* or
" jerry-go-nimble."

Cliché, *m.* (familiar), *commonplace
sentence ready made ; commonplace metaphor ; well-worn platitude.* (Printers') Tirer son —, *to be
always repeating the same thing.*

Client, *m.* (thieves'), *victim, or intended victim.*

Cligner (military), des œillets, *to
squint, to be* " boss-eyed."

Clignots, *m. pl.* (popular), *eyes,*
" peepers." Baver des —, *to
weep,* " to nap a bib." See
Mirettes.

Clipet, *m.* (thieves'), *voice.*

Clique, *f.* (popular), *scamp,* or
" bad egg ; " *diarrhœa,* or " jerry-go-nimble." (Military) La —, *the
squad of drummers and buglers.*

Exempts de service, ils exercent généralement une profession quelconque (barbier, tailleur, ajusteur de guêtres, etc.) qui
leur rapporte quelques bénéfices. Ayant
ainsi plus de temps et plus d'argent à dépenser que leurs camarades, ils ont une
réputation, assez bien justifiée d'ailleurs,
de bambocheurs ; de là, ce nom de clique
qu'on leur donne.—*La Langue Verte du
Troupier.*

Cliquettes, *f. pl.* (popular), *ears,*
or " wattles."

Clodoche, *m.* (familiar), *description of professional comic dancer
with extraordinarily supple legs,
such as the Girards brothers, of
Alhambra celebrity.*

Cloporte, *m.* (familiar), *door-keeper.*
Properly *wooalouse.* A pun on
the words clôt porte.

Clou, *m.* (military), *guard-room ;
cells,* " jigger ; " *bayonet.* Coller
au —, *to imprison,* " to roost."
(Popular) Clou, *bad workman ;
pawnshop.* Mettre au —, *to pawn,
to put* " in lug." Clou de girofle,
decayed black tooth. (Theatrical
and literary) Le — d'une pièce,
d'un roman, *the chief point of
interest in a play or novel,* literally *a nail on which the whole
fabric hangs.*

Clouer (popular), *to imprison,* " to
run in ; " *to pawn,* " to blue, to
spout, to lumber."

Clous, *m. pl.* (popular), *tools.*
(Printers') Petits --, *type.* Lever
les petits —, *to compose.* (Military) Clous, *foot-soldiers,* or " mud-crushers."

Coaguler (familiar), se —, *to get drunk.* See **Sculpter.**

Côbier, *m.,* *heap of salt in salt-marshes.*

Cocanges, *f. pl.* (thieves'), *walnut-shells.* Jeu de —, *game of swindlers at fairs.*

Cocangeur, *m.* (thieves'), *swindler.* See **Cocanges.**

Cocantin, *m.* (popular), *business agent acting as a medium between a debtor and a creditor.*

Cocarde, *f.* (popular), *head.* Avoir sa —, *to be tipsy.* Taper sur la —, *is said of wine which gets into the head.*

> Ma joie et surtout l'petit bleu
> Ça m'a tapé sur la cocarde !
> *Parisian Song.*

Cocarder (popular), se —, *to get tipsy.* See **Sculpter.**

> Tout se passait très gentiment, on était gai, il ne fallait pas maintenant se cocarder cochonnement, si l'on voulait respecter les dames.—ZOLA, *L'Assommoir.*

Cocardier, *m.* (military), *military man passionately fond of his profession.*

Cocasserie, *f.* (familiar), *strange or grotesque saying, writing, or deed.*

Coche, *f.* (popular), *fat, red-faced woman.*

Cochon, *m.* (popular), de bonheur ! (ironical) *no luck !* Ça n'est pas trop —, *that's not so bad.* C'est pas — du tout, *that's very nice.* Mon pauvre —, je ne te dis que ça ! *my poor fellow, you are in for it !* Etre —, *to be lewd.* Se conduire comme un —, *to behave in a mean, despicable way.* Soigner son —, *is said of one who lives too well.* Un costume —, *a suggestive dress.*

Cochonne, *f.* (popular), *lewd girl.* (Ironically) Elle n'est pas jolie, mais elle est si cochonne !

Cochonnement, *adv.* (popular), *in a disgusting manner.*

Cochonnerie, *f.* (popular), *any article of food having pork for a basis.*

Cochonneries, *f. pl.* (popular), *indecent talk or actions.*

Coco, *m.* (military), *horse.* La botte à —, *trumpet call for stables;* (literally) La botte de foin à coco. (Popular) Coco, *brandy; head.* See **Tronche.** Avoir le — déplumé, *to be bald, or to have a* "*bladder of lard.*" For synonymous expressions, see **Avoir.** Avoir le — fêlé, *to be cracked,* "*to be a little bit balmy in one's crumpet.*" For synonyms see **Avoir.** Colle-toi ça dans le —, or passe-toi ça par le —, *eat that or drink that.* Dévisser le —, *to strangle.* Monter le —, *to excite.* Se monter le —, *to get excited; to be too sanguine.* Il a graissé la patte à —, *is said of a man who has bungled over some affair.* (Familiar) Coco épileptique, *champagne wine,* "*fiz,*" or "*boy.*"

Cocodète, *f.* (familiar), *stylish woman always dressed according to the latest fashion,* a "*dasher.*"

Cocons, *m. pl.,* stands for co-conscrits, *first-term students at the École Polytechnique.*

Cocotte, *f.* (popular), *term of endearment to horses.* Allons, hue—! *pull up, my beauty !* (Familiar and popular) Cocotte, *a more than fast girl or woman,* a "*pretty horse-breaker,*" see **Gadoue;** (theatrical) *addition made by singers to an original theme.*

Cocotterie, *f.* (familiar), *the world of the cocottes.* See **Cocotte.**

Cocovieilles, *f. pl., name given by fashionable young ladies of the aristocracy to their old-fashioned elders, who return the compliment by dubbing them* "cocosottes."

Cocufieur, *m.* (popular), *one who cuckoos, that is, one who lays himself open to being called to account by an injured husband as the co-respondent in the divorce court.*

Coenne, or **couenne,** *f.* (thieves'), de lard, *brush.* (Familiar and popular) Couenne, *stupid man, dunce.*

Coëre, *m.* (thieves'), le grand —, *formerly the king of rogues.*

Cœur, *m.* (popular), jeter du — sur le carreau, *to vomit.* A pun on the words "hearts" and "diamonds" of cards on the one hand, avoir mal au —, *to feel sick,* and "carreau," *flooring,* on the other. Valet de —, *lover.*

Cœur d'artichaut, *m.* (popular), *man or woman with an inflammable heart.*

Paillasson, quoi ! cœur d'artichaut,
C'est mon genre ; un' feuille pour tout l'monde,
Au jour d'aujourd'hui j'gobe la blonde ;
Après d'main, c'est la brun' qu'i m'faut.
       GILL, *La Muse à Bibi.*

Coffier (thieves'), abbreviation of escoffier, *to kill,* "to cook one's gruel."

Coffin, *m., peculiar kind of desk at the Ecole Polytechnique.* From the inventor's name, General Coffinières.

Cognac, *m.* (thieves'), *gendarme or police officer,* "crusher," "copper," or "reeler." See **Pot-à-tabac.**

Cognade, *f.,* or **cogne** (thieves'), *gendarmerie.*

Cognard, *m.,* or **cogne,** *gendarme and gendarmerie ; police officer,* "copper."

Cogne, *m. and f.* (thieves'), la —, *the police.* Un —, *a police officer,* or "reeler." See **Pot-à-tabac.** Also *brandy.* Un noir de trois ronds sans —, *a three-halfpenny cup of coffee without brandy.*

Coiffer (popular), *to slap ; to deceive one's husband.* Se — de quelqu'un, *to take a fancy to one.*

Coin, *m.* (popular), c'est un — sans i, *he is a fool.*

Coire (thieves'), *farm ; chief.*

Je rencontrai des camarades qui avaient aussi fait leur temps ou cassé leur ficelle. Leur coire me proposa d'être des leurs, on faisait la grande soulasse sur le trimar.— V. HUGO.

Col, *m.* (familiar), cassé, *dandy,* or "masher." Se pousser du —, *to assume an air of self-importance or conceit,* "to look gumptious ;" *to praise oneself up.* An allusion to the motion of one's hand under the chin when about to make an important statement.

Colas, colabre, or **colin,** *m.* (thieves'), *neck,* or "scrag." Faire suer le —, *to strangle.* Rafraîchir le —, *to guillotine.* Rafraîchir means *to trim* in the expression, "Rafraîchir les cheveux."

Colback, *m.* (military), *raw recruit,* or "Johnny raw." An allusion to his unkempt hair, similar to a busby or bearskin cap.

Colin. See **Colas.**

Collabo, *m.* (literary), abbreviation of collaborateur.

Collage, *m.* (familiar), *living as husband and wife in an unmarried state.*

L'une après l'autre—en camarade—
C'est rupin, mais l' collage, bon Dieu !
Toujours la mêm' chauffeus' de pieu !
M'en parlez pas ! Ça m'rend malade.
       GILL, *La Muse à Bibi.*

Un — d'argent, *the action of a woman who lives with a man as his wife from mercenary motives.*

C'était selon la manie de ce corrupteur de mineures, le sceau avec lequel il cimentait ce que Madame Cornette appelait, en terme du métier, ses collages d'argent !
Mémoires de Monsieur Claude.

Collant, *m.* (familiar), *is said of one not easily got rid of ;* (military) *drawers.*

Collarde, *m.* (thieves'), *prisoner, one " doing time."*

Colle, *f.* (students'), *weekly or other periodical oral examinations to prepare for a final examination, or to make up the marks which pass one at the end of the year.*

Collège, *m.* (thieves'), *prison,* or "*stir.*" See **Motte**. Un ami de —, *a prison chum.* Les collèges de Pantin, *the Paris prisons.*

Collégien, *m.* (thieves'), *prisoner.*

Coller (students'), *to stop one's leave ; to orally examine at periodical examinations.* Se faire —, *to get plucked or "ploughed" at an examination.* (Popular) Coller, *to place ; to put ; to give ; to throw ;* — au bloc, *to imprison,* "to run in ;" — des châtaignes, *to thrash,* "to wallop." See **Voie**. Se — dans le pieu, *to go to bed.* Se — une biture, *to get drunk,* or "screwed." See **Sculpter**. Colle-toi là, *place yourself there.* Colle-toi ça dans le fusil, *eat or drink that.* Colle-toi ça dans la coloquinte, *bear that in mind.* (Military) Coller au bloc, *to send to the guard-room.* Collez-moi ce clampin-là au bloc, *take that lazy bones to the guard-room.* (Familiar and popular) Se —, *to live as man and wife, to live "a tally."* Se faire —, *to be nonplussed.* S'en — par le bec, *to eat to excess,* "to scorf." S'en — pour, *to go to the*

expense of. Je m'en suis collé pour dix francs, *I spent ten francs over it.*

Colletiner (thieves'), *to collar, to apprehend,* "to smug." See **Piper**.

Colleur, *m.* (students'), *professor whose functions are to orally examine at certain periods students at private or public establishments ; man who gets quickly intimate or "thick" with one, who "cottons on to one."*

Collier, or **coulant**, *m.* (thieves'), *cravat,* or "neckinger."

Collignon, *m.* (popular), *cabby.* An allusion to a coachman of that name who murdered his fare. The cry, "Ohé, Collignon !" is about the worst insult one can offer a Paris coachman, and he is not slow to resent it.

Colombe, *f.* (players'), *queen of cards.*

Colombé, *adj.* (thieves'), *known.*

Colon, *m.* (soldiers'), *colonel.* Petit —, *lieutenant-colonel.*

Colonne, *f.* (military), chapeau en —, see **Bataille**. (Popular) N'avoir pas chié la —, *to be devoid of any talent, not to be able to set the Thames on fire.* Démolir la —, *to void urine,* "to lag."

Coloquinte, *f.* (popular and thieves'), *head.* Avoir une araignée dans la —, *to be cracked,* or "to have a bee in one's bonnet." Charlot va jouer à la boule avec ta —, *Jack Ketch will play skittles with your canister.*

Coltiger (thieves'), *to arrest ; to seize,* to "smug."

C'est dans la rue du Mail
Où j'ai été coltigé
Par trois coquins de railles.
V. HUGO, *Le Dernier Jour d'un Condamné.*

Coltin, *m.* (popular), *strength.* Properly *shoulder-strap.*

Coltiner (popular), *to ply the trade of a porter ; to draw a hand-cart by means of a shoulder-strap.*

Coltineur, *m.* (popular), *man who draws a hand-cart with a shoulder-strap.*

Coltineuse (popular), *female who does rough work.*

Comberge, combergeante, *f.* (thieves'), *confession.*

Comberger (thieves'), *to reckon up; to confess.*

Combergo (thieves'), *confessional.*

Comblance, *f.* (thieves'), par —, *into the bargain.*

> J'ai fait par comblance
> Gironde larguecapé.
> VIDOCQ.

Comble, combre, combriau, combrieu, *m.* (thieves'), *hat,* "tile." See **Tubard.**

Combrie, *f.* (thieves'), *one-franc piece.*

Combrier, *m.* (thieves'), *hat-maker.*

Combrieu. See **Comble.**

Combrousier, *m.* (thieves'), *peasant,* or "clod."

Combustible, *m.* (popular), du —! *exclamation used to urge one on, On! go it!*

Come, *m.* (thieves'), *formerly a guard on board the galleys.*

Comédie, *f.* (popular), envoyer à la —, *to dismiss a workman for want of work to give him.* Être à la —, *to be out of work,* "out of collar."

Comestaux, *m. pl.* (popular), for comestibles, *articles of food,* "toke."

Comète, *f.* (popular), *vagrant, tramp.* Filer la —, or la sorgue, *to sleep in the open air,* or "to skipper it."

Comiques, *m. pl.* (theatrical), jouer les — habillés, *to represent a comic character in modern costume.*

Commander (thieves'), à cuire, *to send to the scaffold.*

Commandite, *f.* (printers'), *association of workmen who join together for the performance of any work.*

Comme if (popular), ironical for comme il faut, *genteel.* T'as rien l'air —! *What a swell you look, oh crikey!*

Commissaire, *m.* (popular), *pint or pitcher of wine.* An allusion to the black robe which police magistrates wore formerly. Le cabot du —, *the police magistrate's secretary.* See **Chien.**

Commode, *f.* (thieves'), *chimney.* (Popular) Une — à deux ressorts, *a vehicle,* or "trap."

Communard, or **communeux,** *m.,* *one of the insurgents of* 1871.

Communiqué, *m.* (familiar), *official communication to newspapers.*

Comp. See **Can.**

Compas, *m.* (popular), ouvrir le —, *to walk.* Allonger le —, *to walk briskly.* Fermer le —, *to stop walking.*

Complet, *adj.* (popular), être —, *to be quite drunk,* or "slewed." (Familiar) Etre —, *to be perfectly ridiculous.*

Comprendre (thieves'), la —, *to steal,* "to claim." See **Grinchir.**

Compte (popular), avoir son —, *to be tipsy*, or "*screwed* ;" *to die*, "*to snuff it.*" Son — est bon, *he is in for it.*

Compter (musicians'), des payses, *to sleep ;* (popular) — ses chemises, *to vomit*, "*to cast up accounts.*"

Comte, *m.* (thieves'), de caruche, or de canton, *jailor*, or "*jigger dubber ;*" — de castu, *hospital superintendent ;* — de gigot-fin, *one who likes to live well.*

Comtois, *adj.* (thieves'), battre —, *to dissemble ; to play the fool.*

Con, *m.* (familiar and popular), obscene word ; *man devoid of any ability ; arrant fool ;* — comme la lune, *extremely stupid*, "*a snide bally bounder.*"

Condé, *m.* (thieves'), *mayor ;* demi —, *alderman ;* grand —, *prefect ;* — franc, *corrupt, or bribed magistrate.*

Condice, *f.* (thieves'), *cage in which convicts are confined on their passage to the convict settlements.*

Condition, *f.* (thieves'), *house,* "*diggings,*" or "*hangs out.*" Faire une —, *to break into a house,* "*to crack a crib.*" Filer une —, *to watch a house in view of an intended burglary.* (Popular) Acheter une —, *to lead a new mode of life, to turn over a new leaf.*

Conduite, *f.* (popular), faire la —, *to drive away and thrash.* Faire la — de Grenoble, *to put one out of doors.*

Cone, *f.* (thieves'), *death.*

Confirmer (popular), *to box one's ears*, "*to warm the wax of one's ears.*"

Confiture, *f.* (popular), *excrement.*

Confiturier, *m.* (popular), *scavenger*, "*rake-kennel.*"

Confortable, *m.* (popular), *glass of beer.*

Confrère, *m.* (popular), de la lune, *injured husband.*

Coni, *adj.* (thieves'), *dead.*

Coniller (popular), *to seek to escape.* Conil, *rabbit.*

Conir (thieves'), *to conceal ; to kill ;* "*to cook one's gruel.*" See **Refroidir.**

Connais (popular), je la —, *no news for me ; do you see any green in my eye ? you don't take an old bird with chaff.*

Connaissance, *f.* (popular), ma —, *my mistress, or sweetheart, my* "*young woman.*"

Connaître (popular), le journal, *to be well informed ; to know beforehand the menu of a dinner ;* — le numéro, *to possess experience ;* — le numéro de quelqu'un, *to be acquainted with one's secrets, one's habits.* La — dans les coins, *to be knowing, to know what's o'clock.* An allusion to a horse clever at turning the corners in the riding school.

Regardez-le partir, le gavroche qui la connaît dans les coins.—RICHEPIN.

Connasse, *f.* (prostitutes'), *honest woman.* Literally *stupid woman.*

Connerie, *f.* (popular), *foolish action or thing.*

Conobler (thieves'), *to recognize.*

Conobrer (thieves'), *to know.*

Conscience, *f.* (printers'), homme de —, *typographer paid by the day or by the hour.*

Conscrar, conscrit, *m.*, *first-term student at the "Ecole Normale," a higher training-school for university professors.*

Conservatoire, *m.* (popular), *pawnshop.* Elève du — de la Villette, *wretched singer.* La Villette is the reverse of a fashionable quarter.

Conserves, *f.* (theatrical), *old plays.* Also *fragments of human flesh which have been thrown into the sewers or river by murderers, and which, when found, are taken to the "Morgue," or Paris dead-house.*

Je viens de préparer pour lui les conserves (les morceaux de chair humaine), l'os de l'égout Jacob et la cuisse des Saints-Pères (l'os retrouvé dans l'égout de la Rue Jacob et la cuisse repêchée au pont des Saints-Pères). — MACÉ, *Mon Premier Crime.*

Consigne, *f.* (military), à gros grains, *imprisonment in the cells.*

Consolation, *f.* (popular), *brandy; swindling game played by card-sharpers, by means of a green cloth chalked into small numbered spaces, and dice.*

Console, *f.* (thieves'), *game played by card-sharpers or "broadsmen" at races and fairs.*

Consoler (popular), son café, *to add brandy to one's coffee.*

Conter (military). Conte cela au perruquier des Zouaves, *I do not believe you,* "tell that to the Marines." Le perruquier des Zouaves is an imaginary individual.

Contre, *m.* (popular), *playing for drink at a café.*

Contre-allumeur, *m.* (thieves'), *spy employed by thieves to baffle the police spies.*

Contrebasse, *f.* (popular), *breech.* Sauter sur la —, *to kick one's behind,* "to toe one's bum," "to root," or "to land a kick."

Contre-coup, *m.* (popular), de la boîte, *foreman,* or "boss."

Contreficher (popular), s'en —, *to care not a straw, not a* "hang."

Contre-marque, *f.* (popular), du Père-Lachaise, *St. Helena medal.* Those who wear the medal are old, and le Père-Lachaise is a cemetery in Paris.

Contrôle, *m.* (thieves'), *formerly the mark on the shoulder of convicts who had been branded.*

Contrôler (popular), *to kick one in the face.*

Convalescence, *f.* (thieves'), *surveillance of the police on the movements of ticket-of-leave men.*

Cop, *f.* (printers'), for "copie," *manuscript.*

Copaille, *f.* (cads'), *Sodomist.* Termed also "tante, coquine."

Cope, *f.* (popular), *overcharge for an article; action of* "shaving a customer." The *Slang Dictionary* says that in England, when the master sees an opportunity of doing this, he strokes his chin as a signal to his assistant who is serving the customer.

Copeau, *m.* (popular), *artisan in woodwork* (properly copeaux, *shavings*) ; *spittle,* or "gob." Arracher son —. See Arracher. Lever son —, *to talk,* "to jaw."

Copeaux, *m. pl.* (thieves'), *housebreaking,* "screwing or cracking a crib." An allusion to the splinters resulting from breaking a door.

Copie, *f.* (printers'), de chapelle, *copy of a work given as a present to the typographers.* (Figuratively) Faire de la —, *to backbite.* Pisser de la —, *to be a prolific writer.* Pisseur de —, *a prolific writer ; one who writes lengthy, diffuse newspaper articles.*

Coquage, *m.* (thieves'), *informing against one,* or "blowing the gaff."

Coquard, *m.* (thieves'), *eye,* or "glazier." S'en tamponner le —, *not to care a fig.* See **Mirette.**

Coquardeau, *m.* (popular), *henpecked husband,* or "stangey;" *man easily duped,* or "gulpy."

Coquer (thieves'), *to watch one's movements; to inform against one,* "to blow the gaff."

Quand on en aura refroidi quatre ou cinq dans les préaux les autres tourneront leur langue deux fois avant de coquer la pègre.—E. Sue.

Also *to give; to put;* — la camoufle, *to hand the candle,* "to dub the glim;" — la loffitude, *to give absolution;* — le poivre, *to poison,* "hocus;" — le taf, *to frighten;* — le rifle, *to set fire to.*

Coqueur, *m.* (thieves'), *informer who warns the police of intended thefts.* He may be at liberty or in prison ; in the latter case he goes by the appellation of "coqueur mouton" or "musicien." The "mouton" variety is an inmate of a prison and informs against his fellow-prisoners ; the "musicien" betrays his accomplices. Coqueur de bille, *man who furnishes funds.*

Coqueuse, *female variety of the* "coqueur."

Coquillard (popular), *eye.* S'en tamponner le —, *not to care a straw,* "not to care a hang."

Coquillards, *m. pl.* (tramps'), *tramps who in olden times pretended to be pilgrims.*

Coquillards sont les pélerins de Saint-Jacques, la plus grande partie sont véritables et en viennent ; mais il y en a aussi qui truchent sur le coquillard.—*Le Jargon de l'Argot.*

Coquillon, *m.* (popular), *louse; pilgrim.*

Coquin, *m.* (thieves'), *informer,* "nark," or "nose."

Coquine, *f.* (cads'), *Sodomist.*

Corbeau, *m.* (popular), *lay brother of* "la doctrine chrétienne," *usually styled* "frères ignorantins." The brotherhood had formerly charge of the ragged schools, and were conspicuous by their gross ignorance ; *priest,* or "devil dodger ;" *undertaker's man.*

Corbeille, *f.* (familiar), *enclosure or ring at the Bourse where official stockbrokers transact business.*

Corbillard, *m.* (popular), à deux roues, *dismal man,* or "croaker;" — à nœuds, *dirty and dissolute woman,* or "draggle-tail ;" — des loucherbem, *cart which collects tainted meat at butcher's stalls.* Loucherbem is equivalent to bou-cher.

Voici passer au galop le corbillard des loucherbem, l'immonde voiture qui vient ramasser dans les boucheries la viande gâtée.—Richepin, *Le Pavé.*

Corbuche, *f.* (thieves'), *ulcer;* — lophe, *false ulcer.*

Corde, *f.* (literary), avoir la —, *to find true expression for accurately describing sentiments or passions.* (Popular) Dormir à la —, *is said of poor people who sleep in certain lodgings with their heads on an outstretched rope as a pillow.* The rope being let down in the morning is a signal for the lodgers to depart.

Corder (popular), *to agree, to get on* "swimmingly" *together.*

Cordon, *m.* (popular), s'il vous plaît ! or donnez-vous la peine d'entrer ! *large knot worn in the rear of ladies' dresses.*

Cordonnier, *m.* (popular), bec-figue de —, *goose.*

Cornage, *m.* (thieves'), *bad smell.*

Cornant, *m.,* **cornante,** *f.* (thieves' and tramps'), *ox and cow,* or "mooer."

Cornard, *m.* (students'), faire —, *to hold a council in a corner.*

Corne, *f.* (popular), *stomach.*

Cornemuseux, *m.* (codfishers'), *the south wind.*

Corner (thieves'), *to breathe heavily; to stink.* La crie corne, *the meat smells.*

Cornet, *m.* (popular), *throat,* "gutter-lane." Colle-toi ça dans l'—, *swallow that!* N'avoir rien dans le —, *to be fasting,* "to be bandied," "to cry cupboard." Cornet d'épices, *Capuchin.*

Il se voulut convertir; il bia trouver un chenâtre cornet d'épice, et rouscailla à sézière qu'il voulait quitter la religion prétendue pour attrimer la catholique.—*Le Jargon de l'Argot.*

Corniche, *f.* (popular), *hat,* or "tile," see **Tubard**; (students') *the military school of Saint-Cyr.*

Cornicherie, *f.* (popular), *nonsense; foolish action.*

Cornichon, *m.* (students'), *candidate preparing for the Ecole Militaire de Saint-Cyr.* Literally *greenhorn.*

Cornière, *f.* (thieves'), *cow-shed.*

Cornificetur, *m.* (popular), *injured husband.*

Corps de pompe, *m.,* *staff of the Saint-Cyr school, and that of the school of cavalry of Saumur.* Saint-Cyr is the French Sandhurst. Saumur is a training-school where the best riders and most vicious horses in the French army are sent.

Correcteur, *m.* (thieves'), *prisoner who plays the spy,* or "nark."

Correspondance, *f.* (popular), *a snack taken at a wine-shop while waiting for an omnibus* "correspondance."

Corridor, *m.* (familiar), *throat.* Se rincer le —, *to drink,* "to wet one's whistle." See **Rincer.**

Corser (familiar), *to impart body to wine by the adjunction of spirits or another kind of wine.* L'affaire se corse, *matters are getting complicated, looking serious.*

Corserie, *f.* (familiar), *a set of Corsican detectives in the service of Napoleon III.* According to Monsieur Claude, formerly head of the detective force under the Empire, the chief members of this secret bodyguard were Alessandri and Griscelli. Claude mentions in his memoirs the murder of a detective who had formed a plot for the assassination of Napoleon in a mysterious house at Auteuil, where the emperor met his mistresses, and to which he often used to repair disguised as a lacquey, and riding behind his own carriage. Griscelli stabbed his fellow-detective in the back on mere suspicion, and found on the body of the dead man papers which gave evidence of the plot. In reference to the mysterious house, Monsieur Claude says :—

L'empereur s'enflamma si bien pour cette nouvelle Ninon que l'impératrice en prit ombrage. La duchesse alors . . . . loua ma petite maison d'Auteuil que le général Fleury avait choisie pour servir de rendez-vous clandestin aux amours de son maître. —*Mémoires de Monsieur Claude.*

Corset, *m.* (popular), pas de —! *sweet sixteen!*

Corvée, *f.* (prostitutes'), aller à la —, *to walk the street,* une — being literally *an arduous, disagreeable work.*

Corvette, *f.* (thieves'), *a kind of low, rascally Alexis.*

Formosum pastor Corydon ardebat Alexin, Delicias domini. . . . .

Cosaque, *m.* (familiar), *stove.*

Cosser (thieves'), *to take; —* la hane, *to take a purse,* "to buz a skin."

Costel, *m.* (popular), *prostitute's bully,* "*ponce.*" See **Poisson.**

Costume, *m.* (theatrical), faire un *—, to applaud an actor directly he makes his appearance on the stage.*

Cote, *f.* (lawyers'), *stolen goods or money;* (sporting) *the betting.* Frère de la *—, stockbroker's clerk.* Cote, *quotations.* La — G., *purloining of articles of small value by notaries' clerks when making an inventory.* Literally, la cote j'ai.

Côte, *f.* (thieves'), de bœuf, *sword.* Frère de la *—,* see **Bande noire.** (Familiar) Etre à la *—, to be in needy circumstances, hard up.* (Sailors') Vieux frère la *—, old chum, mate.*

Côté, *m.* (theatrical), cour, *right-hand side scenes; —* jardin, *left-hand side scenes.* (Familiar) Côté des caissiers, *the station of the* "Chemin de fer du Nord," *at which absconding cashiers sometimes take train.*

Côtelard, *m.* (popular), *melon.*

Côtelette, *f.* (popular), de menuisier, de perruquier, or de vache, *piece of Brie cheese.* (Theatrical) Avoir sa *—, to obtain applause.* Emporteur à la *—,* see **Emporteur.**

Côte-nature, *f.* (familiar), for côte-lette au naturel, *grilled chop.*

Coterie, *f.* (popular), *chum.* Eh ! dis donc, la *— ! I say, old chum !* Coterie, *association of workmen; company.* Vous savez, la p'tite *—, you know, chums !*

Côtes, *f. pl.* (popular), avoir les *—* en long, *to be lazy, to be a* "bummer." Literally *to have the ribs* lengthwise, *which would make one lazy at turning about.* Travailler les côtes à quelqu'un, *to thrash one, to give one a* "hiding." See **Voie.**

Côtier, *m.* (popular), *extra horse harnessed to an omnibus when going up hill; also his driver.*

Côtière, *f.* (gambling cheats'), *a pocket wherein spare cards are secreted.*

Aussi se promit-il de faire agir avec plus d'adresse, plus d'acharnement, les rois, les atouts et les as qu'il tenait en réserve dans sa côtière.—*Mémoires de Monsieur Claude.*

Cotillon, *m.* (popular), crotté, *prostitute,* "draggle-tail."

Il était coureur . . . . il adorait le cotillon, et c'est pour moi un cotillon crotté qui a causé sa perte.—MACÉ, *Mon Premier Crime.*

Faire danser le *—, to thrash one's wife.*

Coton, *m.* (popular), *bread or food* (allusion to the cotton-wick of lamp); *quarrel; street-fight; difficulty.* Il y aura du *—, there will be a fight; there will be much difficulty.* Le courant est rapide, il y aura du *—, the stream is swift, we shall have to pull with a will.*

Cotret, *m.* (popular), jus de *—, thrashing with a stick,* or "larruping;" might be rendered by "stirrup oil." Des cotrets, *legs.* (Thieves') Çotret, *convict at the hulks; returned transport,* or "lag."

Cotte, *f.* (popular), *blue canvas working trousers.*

Cou, *m.* (popular), avoir le front dans le *—, to be bald, or to have* "a bladder of lard." See **Avoir.**

Couac, *m.* (popular), *priest,* or "devil-dodger."

Couche (popular), à quelle heure qu'on te —? *a hint to one to make himself scarce.*

Coucher (popular), à la corde, *to sleep in certain low lodging-houses with the head resting on a rope stretched across the room* ; — dans le lit aux pois verts, *to sleep in the fields.* Se — bredouille, *to go to bed without any supper.* Se — en chapon, *to go to bed with a full belly.*

Coucou, *m.* (popular), *watch.*

Coude, *m.* (popular), lâcher le —, *to leave one, generally when requested to do so.* Lâche moi le —, *be off, leave me alone.* Prendre sa permission sous son —, *to do without permission.*

Couenne, *f.* (popular), *skin,* or "*buff* ;" *fool,* or "*bounder* ;" — de lard, *brush.* Gratter, racler, or ratisser la —, *to shave.* Gratter la — à quelqu'un, *to flatter one, to give him "soft sawder;" to thrash one.* Est-il —! *what an ass!*

Couennes, *f. pl.* (popular), *flabby cheeks.*

Couillé, *m.* (popular), *fool, blockhead,* "*cabbage-head.*"

Couilles, *f. pl.* (popular), avoir des — au cul, *to be energetic, manly,* "*to have spunk.*"

Couillon, *m.* (popular), *poltroon ; foolish with the sense of abashed, crestfallen.* Il resta tout —, *he looked foolish.* The word is used also in a friendly or jocular manner.

Couillonnade, *f.* (popular), *ridiculous affair ; nonsense.*

Couillonner (popular), *to show cowardice ; to shirk danger.*

Couillonnerie, *f.* (popular), *cowardice ; nonsensical affair ; take in.*

Couiner (popular), *to whimper ; to hesitate.*

Coulage, *m.,* **coule,** *f.* (familiar), *waste ; small purloining by servants, clerks, &c.*

Coulant, *m.* (thieves'), *milk.*

Coulante, *f.* (thieves'), *lettuce.* (Cads') La —, *the river Seine.*

Coule, *f.* (popular), être à la —, *to have mastered the routine of some business, to be acquainted with all the ins and outs ; to be comfortable ; to be clever at evading difficulties ; to be insinuating ; to connive at.* Mettre quelqu'un à la —, *to instruct one in, to make one master of the routine of some business.*

Couler (popular), en —, *to lie,* "*to cram one up.*" La — douce, *to live comfortably.* Se la — douce, *to take it easy.*

Couleur, *f.* (popular), *lie ; box on the ear,* or "*buck-horse.*" Monter la —, *to deceive,* "*to bamboozle.*" Etre à la —, *to do things well.*

Couleuvre, *f.* (popular), *pregnant* or "*lumpy*" *woman.*

Coulisse, *f.* (familiar), *the set of coulissiers.* See this word.

Coulissier, *m.* (familiar), *unofficial jobber at the Bourse or Stock Exchange.* As an adjective it has the meaning of *connected with the back scenes,* as in the phrase, Des intrigues coulissières, *back-scene intrigues.*

Couloir, *m.* (popular), *mouth,* or "*rattle-trap ;*" *throat,* or "*peck alley.*"

Coup, *m.* (popular), *secret process ; knack ; dodge.* Il a le —, *he has the knack, he is a dab at.* Il a un —, *he has a process of his own.* Un — d'arrosoir, *a drink.* Se flanquer un — d'arrosoir, *to get tipsy,* or "*screwed.*" Un — de

H

bouteille, *intoxication.* Avoir son — de bouteille, *to be intoxicated,* "to be boozy." See **Pompette.** Coup de chancellerie, *action of getting a man's head* "into chancery," that is, to get an opponent's head firmly under one's arm, where it can be pommelled with immense power, and without any possibility of immediate extrication. Un — de chien, *a tussle ; difficulty.* Un — d'encensoir, *a blow on the nose.* Un — de feu, *a slight intoxication.* Un — de feu de société, *complete intoxication.* Un — de figure, *hearty meal,* or "tightener." Un — de fourchette, *digging two fingers into an opponent's eyes.* Un — de gaz, *a glass of wine.* Un — de gilquin, *a slap.* Un — de pied de jument or de Vénus, *a venereal disease.* Un — de Raguse, *action of leaving one in the lurch ;* an allusion to Marshal Marmont, Duc de Raguse, who betrayed Napoleon. Un — de tampon, *a blow,* or "bang;" *hard shove* (tampon, *buffer*). Un — de temps, *an accident ; hitch.* Un — de torchon, *a fight ; revolution.* Le — du lapin, *finishing blow or crowning misfortune, the straw that breaks the camel's back ; treacherous way of gripping in a fight.*

Coup féroce que se donnent de temps en temps les ouvriers dans leurs battures. Il consiste à saisir son adversaire, d'une main par les testicules, de l'autre par la gorge, et à tirer dans les deux sens : celui qui est saisi et tiré ainsi n'a pas même le temps de recommander son âme à Dieu.—DELVAU.

Coup du médecin, *glass of wine drunk after one has taken soup.* Un — dur, *unpleasantness, unforeseen impediment.* Attraper un — de sirop, *to get tipsy.* Avoir son — de chasselas, de feu, de picton, or du soleil, *to be half drunk,* "elevated." See **Pompette.** Avoir son — de rifle, *to be tipsy,* "screwed." Donner le — de pouce, *to give short weight ; to strangle.* Faire le —, or monter le — à quelqu'un, *to deceive, to take in,* "to bamboozle" *one.* Se donner un — de tampon, or de torchon, *to fight.* Se monter le —, *to be too sanguine, to form illusions.* Valoir le —, *to be worth the trouble of doing or robbing.* Voir le —, *to foresee an event ; to see the dodge.* Le — de, *action of doing anything.* Le — du canot, *going out rowing.* Coup de bleu, *draught of wine.* Avoir son — de bleu, *to be intoxicated,* or "screwed." Pomper un — de bleu, *to drink.*

> Faut ben du charbon . . .
> Pour chauffer la machine,
> Au va-nu-pieds qui chine . . .
> Faut son p'tit coup d'bleu.
> RICHEPIN, *Chanson des Gueux.*

(Thieves') Coup à l'esbrouffe sur un pantre. See **Faire.** Un — d'acré, *extreme unction.* Le — d'Anatole, or du père François. See **Charriage à la mécanique.** Un — de bas, *treacherous blow.* Le — de bonnet, *the three-card trick dodge.* Coup de cachet, *stabbing, then drawing the knife to and fro in the wound.* Un — de casserole, *informing against one,* "blowing the gaff." Le — de manche, *calling at people's houses in order to beg.* Un — de radin, *purloining the contents of a shop-till, generally a wine-shop,* "lob-sneaking." Un — de roulotte, *robbery of luggage or other property from vehicles.* Un — de vague, *a robbery ; action of robbing at random without any certainty as to the profits to be gained thereby.* (Military) Coup de manchette, *certain dexterous cut of the sword on the wrist which puts one hors de combat.* (Familiar) Un — de pied, *borrowing money,* or "breaking shins." English thieves call it

"biting the ear." Un — de pistolet, *some noisy or scandalous proceeding calculated to attract attention.* Le — de fion, *finishing touch.* Se donner un — de fion, *to get oneself tidy, ship-shape.*

C'est là qu'on se donne le coup de fion. On ressangle les chevaux, on arrange les paquetages et les turbans, on époussette ses bottes, on retrousse ses moustaches et on drape majestueusement les plis de son burnous.—H. FRANCE, *L'Homme qui tue.*

(Servants') Le — du tablier, *giving notice.*

Coupaillon, *m.* (tailors'), *unskilful cutter.*

Coup de traversin, *m.* (popular), se foutre un —, *to sleep.*

Trois heures qui sonn'nt. Faut que j'rapplique,
S'rait pas trop tôt que j'pionce un brin ;
C'que j'vas m'fout'un coup d'traversin !
Bonsoir.
        GILL, *La Muse à Bibi.*

Coup de trottinet, *m.* (thieves' and cads'), *kick.* Filer un — dans l'oignon, *to kick one's behind,* or "to toe one's bum," "to root," or "to land a kick."

Coupe, *f.* (thieves'), *poverty.* (Popular) Tirer sa —, *to swim.*

Coupé, *adj.* (printers'), *to be without money.*

Coupe-ficelle, *m.* (military), *artillery artificer.*

Coupe-file, *m.,* *card delivered to functionaries, which enables them to cross a procession in a crowd.*

Coupe-lard, *m.* (popular), *knife.*

Couper (popular), *to fall into a snare ; to accept as correct an assertion which is not so ; to believe the statement of more or less likely facts ;* — dans le pont, *or* — dans le ceinturon, *to swallow a fib, to fall into a snare.*

Vidocq dit comme ça qu'il vient du pré,

qu'il voudrait trouver des amis pour goupiner. Les autres coupent dans le pont (donnent dans le panneau).—VIDOCQ.

Couper la chique, *to disappoint ; to abash ;* — la gueule à quinze pas, *to stink ;* — la musette, *or le* sifflet, *to cut the throat ;* — le trottoir, *to place one in the necessity of leaving the pavement by walking as if there were no one in the way, or when walking behind a person to get suddenly in front of him ;* (military) — l'alfa, *or la verte, to drink absinthe.* Ne pas y —, *not to escape ; not to avoid ; to disbelieve.* Vous n'y couperez pas, *you will not escape punishment.* Je n'y coupe pas, *I don't take that in.* (Coachmens') Couper sa mèche, *to die.* See **Pipe.** (Gambling cheats') Couper dans le pont, *to cut a pack of cards prepared in such a manner as to turn up the card required by sharpers.* The cards are bent in a peculiar way, and in such a manner that the hand of the player who cuts must naturally follow the bend, and separate the pack at the desired point. This cheating trick is used in England as well as France, and is termed in English slang the "bridge."

Coupe-sifflet, *m.* (thieves'), *knife,* "chive." Termed also "lingre, vingt-deux, surin."

Courant, *m.* (thieves'), *dodge.* Connaître le —, *to be up to a dodge.*

Courasson, *m.* (familiar), *one whose bump of amativeness is well developed,* in other terms, *one too fond of the fair sex.* Vieux —, *old debauchee, old "rip."*

Courbe, *f.* (thieves'), *shoulder ;* — de marne, *shoulder of mutton.*

Les marquises des cagous ont soin d'allumer le riffe et faire riffoder la criolle ; les uns fichent une courbe de morne, d'autres un morceau de cornant, d'autres une échine de baccon, les autres des ornies et des ornichons.—*Le Jargon de l'Argot.*

Coureur, *m.* (thieves'), d'aveugles, *a wretch who robs blind men of the half-pence given them by charitable people.*

Courir (popular), quelqu'un, *to bore one.* Se la —, *to run, to run away,* "to slope." For synonyms see **Patatrot.**

Courrier, *m.* (thieves'), de la préfecture, *prison van,* or "black Maria."

Court-à-pattes, *m.* (military), *foot artilleryman.*

Courtaud, *m.* (thieves'), *shopman,* or "counter jumper."

Court-bouillon, *m.* (thieves'), le grand —, *the sea,* "briny," or "herring pond."

Courte, *f.* (popular), *penis.* Se travailler de la —, *to give oneself up to practices of onanism.*

Courtier, *m.* (thieves'), à la mode. See **Bande noire.** (Familiar) Courtier marron, *kind of unofficial stockjobber, an outsider,* or "kerbstone broker."

Cousin, *m.* (thieves'), *cardsharper,* or "broadsman;" — de Moïse, *husband of a dissolute woman.*

Cousine, *f.* (popular), *Sodomist;* — de vendange, *dissolute girl fond of the wine-shop.*

Cousse, *f.* (thieves'), de castu, *hospital attendant.*

Couteau, *m.* (military), grand —, *cavalry sword.*

Coûter (popular), cela coûte une peur et une envie de courir, *nothing.*

Couturasse, *f.* (popular), *sempstress; pock-marked or* "cribbage-faced" *woman.*

Couvent, *m.* (popular), laïque, *brothel,* or "nanny-shop."

Le 49 est un lupanar. Ce couvent laïque est connu dans le Quartier Latin sous la dénomination de : La Botte de Paille.— MACÉ, *Mon Premier Crime.*

Couvercle, *m.* (popular), **hat,** or "tile." See **Tubard.**

Couvert, *m.* (thieves'), *silver fork and spoon from which the initials have been obliterated, or which have been* "christened."

Couverte, *f.* (military), battre la —, *to sleep.* Faire passer à la —, *to toss one in a blanket.*

Couverture, *f.* (theatrical), *noise made purposely at a theatre to prevent the public from noticing something wrong in the delivery of actors.*

Nous appelons couverture le bruit que nous faisons dans la salle pour couvrir un impair, un pataquès, une faute de français. —P. MAHALIN.

Couvrante, *f.* (popular), *cap,* or "tile." See **Tubard.**

Couvre-amour, *m.* (military), *shako.*

Couvreur, *m.* (freemasons'), *doorkeeper.*

Couvrir (freemasons'), le temple, *to shut the door.*

Couyon. See **Couillon.**

Couyonnade, *f.* See **Couillonnade.**

Couyonnerie, *f.* See **Couillonnerie.**

Crabosser (popular), *to crush in a hat.*

Crac. See **Cric.**

Cracher (popular), *to speak out;* — des pièces de dix sous, *to be dry, thirsty;* — dans le sac, *to be guillotined, to die;* — ses doublures, *to be consumptive.* Ne pas — sur quelquechose, *not to object to a thing, to value it,* "not to sneeze at." (Musicians') Cracher son embouchure, *to die.* See **Pipe.**

Crachoir, *m.* (popular and thieves'), *mouth,* or "bone-box." See **Plomb.** Jouer du —, *to speak,* "to rap," "to patter."

Crampe, *f.* (popular), tirer sa —, *to flee,* "to crush." See **Patatrot.** Tirer sa —, *to have connection with a woman,* "to screw, to dille, to ride, to pulverize the seventh commandment," &c. Tirer sa — avec la veuve, *to be guillotined.*

Cramper (popular), se —, *to run away.* See **Patatrot.**

Crampon, *m.* (familiar), *bore; one not easily got rid of.*

Cramponne (popular), toi Gugusse ! (ironical) *prepare to be astounded.*

Cramponner (familiar), *to force one's company on a person ; to bore.*

Cramser (popular), *to die.*

Cran, *m.* (popular), avoir son —, *to be angry.* Faire un —, *to make a note of something ;* an allusion to the custom which bakers have of reckoning the number of loaves furnished by cutting notches in a piece of wood. Lâcher d'un —, *to leave one suddenly.*

Crâne, *adj.* (popular), *fine.*

Crânement (popular), *superlatively.* Je suis — content, *I am superlatively happy.*

Crâner (popular), *to be impudent, threatening.* Si tu crânes, je te ramasse, *none of your cheek, else I'll give you a thrashing.*

Crapaud, *m.* (thieves'), *padlock ;* (military) *diminutive man; purse in which soldiers store up their savings ;* — serpenteux, *spiral rocket.* (Popular) Crapaud, *child,* "kid."

Ben, moi, c't'existence-là m'assomme !
J'voudrais posséder un chapeau.
L'est vraiment temps d'dev'nir un homme.
J'en ai plein l'dos d'être un crapaud.
　　Richepin, *Chanson des Gueux.*

Crapoussin, *m.* (popular), *small man ; child,* or "kid."

Crapulos, crapulados, *m.* (familiar and popular), *one-sou cigar.*

Craquelin, *m.* (popular), *liar.* From craque, *fib.*

Crasse, *f.* (familiar), *mean or stingy action.* Baron de la —, see **Baron.**

Cravache, *f.* (sporting), être à la —, *to be at a whip's distance.*

Cravate, *f.* (popular), de chanvre, *noose,* or "hempen cravat ;" — de couleur, *rainbow ;* — verte, *women's bully,* "ponce." See **Poisson.**

Crayon, *m.*, *stockbroker's clerk.*

Créateur, *m.* (thieves'), *painter.*

Créature, *f.* (familiar), *strumpet.*

Crèche, *f.* (cads'), faire une tournée à la —, or à la chapelle, *is said of a meeting of Sodomists.*

Credo, *m.* (thieves'), *the gallows.*

Crêpage, *m.* (popular), *a fight ; a tussle.* Un — de chignons, *tussle between two females,* in which they seize one another by the hair and freely use their nails.

Crêper (popular), le chignon, or le toupet, *to thrash,* "to wallop." See **Voie.** Se — le chignon, le toupet, *to have a set to.*

Crépin, *m.* (popular), *shoemaker,* or "snob."

Crépine, *f.* (thieves'), *purse,* "skin," or "poge."

Crès (thieves'), *quickly.*

Crespinière (thieves'), *much.*

Creuse, *f.* (popular), *throat,* "gutter lane."

Creux, *m.* (thieves'), *house ; lodgings,* "diggings," "ken," or "crib." (Popular) Bon —, *good voice.* Fichu —, *weak voice.*

Crevaison, *f.* (popular), *death.*
Faire sa —, *to die.* Crever, *to
die,* is said of animals. See
Pipe.

Crevant, *adj.* (swells'), *boring to
death ; very amusing.*

Que si vous les interrogez sur le bal de
la nuit, ils vous répondront invariablement,
C'était crevant, parole d'honneur.—MA-
HALIN.

Crevard (popular), *stillborn child.*

Crevé (popular), *dead.* (Familiar)
Petit —, *swell,* or " masher."
See **Gommeux.**

Crève-faim, *m.* (military), *man
who volunteers as a soldier.*

Crever (popular), *to dismiss from
one's employment ; to wound ; to
kill ;* — la sorbonne, *to break
one's head.*

Mais c'qu'est triste, hélas !
C'est qu' pour crever à coups d'botte
Des gens pas palas,
On vous envoie en péniche
A Cayenne-les-eaux.
RICHEPIN, *Chanson des Gueux.*

Crever la pièce de dix sous *is
said of the practices of Sodomists ;*
— la paillasse, *to kill.*

Verger, il creva la paillasse
A Monseigneur l'Archevêque de Paris.

The above quotation is from a
" complainte" on the murder of
the Archbishop of Paris, Monseigneur Sibour, in the church
Sainte-Geneviève, by a priest
named Verger. A complainte is
a kind of carol, or dirge, which
has for a theme the account of a
murder or execution. (Familiar)
Crever l'œil au diable, *to succeed in
spite of envious people.* Tu t'en
ferais —, *expressive of ironical
refusal.* It may be translated by,
" don't you wish you may get
it ? " Se —, *to eat to excess,* " to
scorf."

Crever à (printers'), *to stop composing at such and such a line.*

Crevette, *f.* (popular), *prostitute,*
" mot."

Criblage, criblement, *m.*
(thieves'), *outcry, uproar.*

Cribler (thieves'), *to cry out ;* — à
la grive, *to give a warning call ; to
call out* " shoe-leather ! " *to call out*
" *police ! thieves !* " " to give hot
beef."

On la crible à la grive,
Je m' la donne et m'esquive,
Elle est pommée maron.
VIDOCQ.

Cribleur, *m.* (thieves'), de frusques,
clothier ; — de lance, *water-
carrier ;* — de malades, *man
whose functions are to call prisoners
to a room where they may speak
to visitors ;* — de verdouze, *a
fruiterer.*

Cric, or **cricque,** *m.* (popular),
brandy, called " French cream "
in English slang. Faire —, *to run
away,* " to guy." See **Patatrot.**

Cric ! (military), *call given by a
soldier about to spin a yarn to an
auditory, who reply by a* " crac ! "
thus showing they are still awake.
After the preliminary cric ! crac !
has been bawled out, the auditory
repeat all together as an introduction to the yarn : Cuiller à pot !
Sous-pieds de guêtres ! Pour l'enfant à naître ! On pendra la cré-
maillère ! Chez la meilleure canti-
nière ! &c., &c.

Cric-croc ! (thieves'), *your health !*

Crie, or **crigne,** *f.* (thieves'), *meat,*
" carnish."

Crin, *m.* (familiar), être comme un
—, *to be irritable or irritated, to
be* " cranky," or " chumpish."

Crinoline, *f.* (players'), *queen of
cards.*

Criolle, *f.* (thieves'), *meat,* " carnish." Morfiler de la —, *to eat
meat.*

Criollier, *m.* (thieves'), *butcher.*

Crique, *m. and f.* (popular), *brandy; an ejaculation.* Je veux bien que la — me croque si je bois une goutte en plus de quatre litres par jour ! *may I be jiggered if I drink more than four litres a day!*

Criquer (popular), se —, *to run away,* "to slope." See **Patatrot.**

Cris, *m. pl.* (popular), de merluche, *frightful howling; loud complaints.*

Cristalliser (students'), *to idle about in a sunny place.*

Croc, abbreviation of escroc, *swindler.*

Croche, *f.* (thieves'), *hand,* "famble," or "daddle."

Crocher (thieves'), *to ring; to pick a lock,* "to screw." (Popular) Se —, *to fight.*

Crocodile, *m.* (familiar), *creditor,* or "dun;" *usurer; foreign student at the military school of Saint-Cyr.*

Crocque, *m.* (popular), *sou.*

Crocs, *m. pl.* (popular), *teeth,* "grinders."

Croire (familiar), que c'est arrivé, *to believe too implicitly that a thing exists; to have too good an opinion of oneself.*

Croisant, *m.* (popular), *waistcoat,* or "benjy."

Croissant, *m.* (popular), loger rue du —, *to be an injured husband.* An allusion to the horns.

Croix, *f.* (popular), *six-franc piece.* An allusion to the cross which certain coins formerly bore. According to Eugène Sue the old clothes men in the Temple used the following denominations for coins : pistoles, ten francs ; croix, six francs ; la demi-croix, three francs ; le point, one franc ; le demi-point, half-a-franc ; le rond, half-penny. Croix de Dieu, *alphabet,* on account of the cross at the beginning.

Crôme, or **croume,** *m.* (thieves' and tramps'), *credit,* "jawbone," or "day."

Cromper (thieves'), *to save; to run away,* "to guy." See **Patatrot.** Cromper sa sorbonne, *to save one's head.*

Crompir, *potato.* From the German grundbirne.

Crône, *f.* (thieves'), *wooden platter.*

Crônée, *f.* (thieves'), *platter full.*

Croquaillon, *m.* (popular), *bad sketch.*

Croque. See **Crique.**

Croquemitaines, *m. pl.* (military), *soldiers who are sent to the punishment companies in Africa for having wilfully maimed themselves in order to escape military service.*

Croqueneau, *m.* (popular), *new shoe;* — verneau, *patent leather shoe.*

Croquet (popular), *irritable man.*

Crosse, *f.* (thieves'), *receiver of stolen goods,* or "fence;" *public prosecutor.*

Crosser (thieves'), *to receive stolen goods; to strike the hour.*

Quand douze plombes crossent,
Les pègres s'en retournent,
Au tapis de Montron.
VIDOCQ.

Crosseur, *m.* (thieves'), *bell-ringer.*

Crossin. See **Crosse.**

Crotal, *m.,* *student of the Ecole Polytechnique holding the rank of sergeant.*

Crottard, *m.* (popular), *foot pavement.*

Crotte d'Ermite, *f.* (thieves'), *baked pear.*

Crottin, *m.* (military), sergent de —, *non-commissioned officer at the cavalry school of Saumur.* Thus termed because he is often in the stables.

Croumier (horse-dealers'), *broker or agent of questionable honesty, or one who is "wanted" by the police.*

Croupionner (popular), *to twist one's loins about so as to cause one's dress to bulge out.*

Croupir (popular), dans le battant *is said of undigested food, which inconveniences one.*

Croustille (popular), casser un brin de —, *to have a snack.*

Croustiller (popular), *to eat,* "to grub." See **Mastiquer**.

Croûte, *f.* (popular), s'embêter comme une — de pain derrière une malle, *to feel desperately dull.*

Croûteum, *m.* (familiar), *collection of* "croûtes," *or worthless pictures.*

Croûton, *m.* (artists'), *painter devoid of any talent.*

Croûtonner (artists'), *to paint worthless pictures, daubs.*

Croyez (popular), ça et buvez de l'eau, *expression used to deride credulous people.* Literally *believe that and drink water.*

Cru (artists'), faire —, see **Faire**.

Crucifier (familiar), *to grant one the decoration of the Legion of Honour.* The expression is meant to be jocular.

Crucifix, or **crucifix à ressort**, *m.* (thieves'), *pistol,* "barking iron."

Cube, *m., student of the third year in higher mathematics* (mathematiques spéciales); (familiar) *a regular idiot.*

Cucurbitacé, *m.* (familiar), *a dunce, a "bounder."*

Cueillir (popular), le persil *is said of a prostitute walking the streets.*

Cuiller, *f.* (popular), *hand,* or "daddle."

Cuir, *m.* (popular), de brouette, *wood.* Escarpin en — de brouette, *wooden shoe.* Gants en — de poule, *ladies' gloves made of fine skin.* Tanner le —, *to thrash,* "to tan one's hide."

Cuirassé, *m.* (popular), *urinals.*

Cuirasser (popular), *to make* "cuirs," that is, in conversation carrying on the wrong letter, or one which does not form part of a word, to the next word, as, for instance, Donnez moi z'en, je vais t'y m'amuser.

Cuirassier, *m.* (popular), *one who frequently indulges in "cuirs."* See **Cuirasser**.

Cuire (popular), se faire —, *to be arrested.* See **Piper**.

Cuisine, *f.* (thieves'), *the Préfecture de Police;* (literary) — de journal, *all that concerns the details and routine arrangement of the matter for a newspaper.* (Popular) Faire sa — à l'alcool, *to indulge often in brandy drinking.*

Cuisiner (literary), *to do, to concoct some inferior literary or artistic work.*

Cuisinier, *m.* (thieves'), *spy,* or "nark;" *detective; barrister;* (literary) *newspaper secretary.*

Cuisse, *f.* (familiar), avoir la — gaie *is said of a woman who is too fond of men.*

Cuit, *adj.* (thieves'), *sentenced, condemned,* or "booked;" *done for.*

Cuite, *f.* (popular), *intoxication.*
Sc flanquci une ——, *to get so tight,*
or "screwed."

Cul, *m.* (popular), *stupid fellow,* or
"bounder;" — d'âne, *blockhead;*
— de plomb, *slow man,* or "bummer;" *clerk,* or "quill-driver;"
*woman who awaits clients at a
café;* — goudronné, *sailor,* or
"tar;" — levé, *game of écarté at
which two players are in league to
swindle the third;* — rouge, *soldier with red pants,* or "cherry
bum;" — terreux, *peasant, clod-
hopper.* Montrer son ——, *to become a bankrupt,* or "brosier."

Culasses, *f. pl.* (military), *revue
des* — mobiles, *monthly medical
inspection.* Culasse, properly *the
breech of a gun.*

Culbutant, *m.,* or **culbute,** *f.*
(thieves'), *breeches,* or "hams."
Termed also "fusil à deux coups,
grimpants." Esbigner le chopin
dans sa culbute, *to conceal stolen
property in one's breeches.*

Culbute, *f.* (thieves'), *breeches.*
(Popular) La ——, *the circus.*

Culerée, *f.* (printers'), *composing
stick which is filled up.*

Culotte, *m.* (popular and familiar),
*money losses at cards; excess of
anything, especially of drink.*
Grosse ——, *regular drunkard.*
Donner dans la — rouge *is said
of a woman who is too fond of
soldiers' attentions, of one who has
an attack of* "scarlet fever." Se
flanquer une ——, *to sustain a loss
at a game of cards, to get intoxicated.* (Students') Empoigner
une ——, *to lose at a game, and to
have in consequence to stand all*

round. (Artists') Faire ——, *exaggeration of* **Faire chaud** (which
see).

Culotté, *adj.* (popular), *hardened;
soiled; seedy; red, &c.* Etre ——,
to have a seedy appearance. Un
nez ——, *a red nose.*

Culotter (popular), se ——, *to get
tipsy; to have a worn-out, seedy
appearance.* Se — de la tête aux
pieds, *to get completely tipsy.*

Cumulard, *m.* (familiar), *official
who holds several posts at the same
time.*

Cupidon, *m.* (thieves'), *rag-picker,*
or "bone-grubber." An ironical
allusion to his hook and basket.

Cure-dents (familiar), venir en ——,
*to come to an evening party with-
out having been invited to the
dinner that precedes it.* Termed
also "venir en pastilles de Vichy."

Curette, *f.* (military), *cavalry sword.*
Manier la ——, *to do sword exercise.*

Curieux, *m.* (thieves'), *magistrate,*
"beak," or "queer cuffin." Also
juge d'instruction, a magistrate
who investigates cases before they
are sent up for trial. Grand ——,
chief judge of the assize court.

Cyclope, *m.* (popular), *behind,* or
"blind cheek."

Cylindre, *m.* (popular), *top hat,* or
"stove-pipe;" see **Tubard;**
body, or "apple cart." Tu t'en
ferais péter le ——, *is expressive of
ironical refusal;* "don't you wish
you may get it."

Cymbale, *f.* (thieves'), *moon,* or
"parish lantern;" (popular)
*escutcheon placed over the door of
the house of a notary.*

A (popular),
mon —, *my
father*, "my
daddy." Ma
—, *my mo-
ther*, " my
mammy."

Dab, dabe,
m. (thieves'),
father, or "dade," or "dadi;"
master; God. Le — de la cigogne,
*the procureur general, or public
prosecutor.* Grand —, *king.*

Ma largue part pour Versailles . . .
Pour m'faire défourailler.
Mais grand dab qui se fâche,
Dit par mon caloquet,
J'li ferai danser une danse
Où i n'y a pas d'plancher.
V. HUGO.

Dabe, *m.* (popular), d'argent, *speculum.* Cramper avec le — d'argent, *to ply the speculum.*

Dabérage, *m.* (popular), *talking,*
"jawing."

Dabérer (popular), *to talk,* " to
jaw."

Dabesse, *f.* (thieves'), *mother;
queen.*

Dabicule, *m.* (thieves'), *the master's
son.*

Dabot, dabmuche, *m.* (thieves'),
*the prefect of police, or head of the
Paris police; a drudge.*

Dabucal, *adj.* (thieves'), *royal.*

Dabuche, *f.* (thieves'), *mother;
grandmother,* or " mami;" *nurse.*

Dabuchette, *f.* (thieves'), *young
mother; mother-in-law.*

Dabuchon, *m.* (popular), *father,*
" daddy."

Dabuge, *f.* (thieves'), *lady,* "burerk."

Dache, *m.* (thieves'), *devil,* "ruffin,"
or "black spy;" (military) *hair-
dresser to the Zouaves, a mythical
individual.* Allez donc raconter
cela à —, *tell that to the marines.*

Dada, *m.* (military), aller à —, *to
perform the act of coition,* or " chivalry." The old poet Villon
termed this "chevaulcher."

Dail, *m.* (thieves'), je n'entrave que
le —, *I do not understand.*

Daim, *m.* (popular), *swell,* or
"gorger," see **Gommeux;** *fool,*
or "bounder;" *gullible fellow,*
"gulpy;" — huppé, *rich man,
one with plenty of* " tin."

Dale, dalle, *f.* (thieves'), *money,*
"quids," or "pieces," see **Quibus;**
five-franc piece; (popular) *throat,*
or " red lane;" — du cou, *mouth,*
" rattle-trap." Se rincer, or s'arroser la —, *to drink,* " to have
something damp." See **Rincer.**

J'ai du sable à l'amygdale.
Ohé ! ho ! buvons un coup,
Une, deux, trois, longtemps, beaucoup !
Il faut s'arroser la dalle
   Du cou.
RICHEPIN, *Gueux de Paris.*

Dalzar, *m.* (popular), *breeches,* "kicks," "sit-upons," or "kicksies."

Dame, *f.* (popular), blanche, *bottle of white wine;* — du lac, *woman of indifferent character who frequents the purlieus of the Grand Lac at the Bois de Boulogne.*

Damer (popular), une fille, *to seduce a girl, to make a woman of her.*

Danaïdes, *f.* (thieves'), faire jouer les —, *to thrash a girl.*

Dandiller (thieves'), *to ring; to chink.* Le carme dandille dans sa fouillouse, *the money chinks in his pocket.*

Dandinage, *m.,* dandinette, *f.* (popular), *thrashing,* "hiding."

Dandine, *f.* (popular), *blow,* "wipe," "clout," "dig," "bang," or "cant." Encaisser des dandines, *to receive blows.*

Dandiner (popular), *to thrash,* "to lick." See **Voie.**

Dandinette. See **Dandinage.**

Dankier (Breton), *prostitute.*

Danse, *f.* (familiar), du panier, *unlawful profits on purchases.* Flanquer une — à quelqu'un, *to thrash or "lick" one.* See **Voie.**

Danser (popular), *to lose money; to pay,* "to shell out." Ill'a dansée de vingt balles, *he had to pay twenty francs.* Danser devant le buffet, *to be fasting,* "to cry cupboard ;" — tout seul, *to have an offensive breath.* Faire — quelqu'un, *to make one stand treat ; to make one pay,* or "fork out ;" *to thrash,* "to wallop." See **Voie.** La —, *to be thrashed ; to be dismissed from one's employment,* "to get the sack."

Danseur, *m.* (popular), *turkey cock.*

Dardant, *m.* (thieves'), *love.*

Luysard estampillait six plombes,
Mezigo roulait le trimard,
Et, jusqu'au fond du coquemart,
Le dardant riffaudait ses lombes.
    RICHEPIN, *Gueux de Paris.*

Dardelle, *f.* (urchins'), *penny* (gros sou).

Dariole, *f.* (popular), *slap or blow in the face,* "clout," "bang," or "wipe." Properly *a kind of pastry.*

Darioleur, *m.* (popular), *inferior sort of pastrycook.*

Daron, *m.* (thieves'), *father,* "dade," or "dadi ;" *gentleman,* "nib cove ;" — de la raille, or de la rousse, *prefect of police, head of the Paris police.*

Daronne, *f.* (thieves'), *mother ;* — du dardant, *Venus ;* — du grand Aure, *holy Virgin ;* — du mec des mecs, *mother of God.*

Dattes, *f. pl.* (popular), des —! *contemptuous expression of refusal ;* might be rendered by "you be hanged !" See **Nèfles.**

Elle se r'tourne, lui dit : des dattes !
Tu peux t'fouiller vieux pruneau !
Tu n'tiens plus sur tes deux pattes.
Va donc, eh ! fourneau !
    Parisian Song.

Daube, *f.* (popular), *cook,* or "dripping."

Daubeur, *m.* (popular), *blacksmith.*

Dauche (popular), mon —, *my father ;* ma —, *my mother ;* "my old man, my old woman."

Dauffe, *f.,* dauffin, dauphin, *m.* (thieves'), *short crowbar.* Termed also " l'enfant, Jacques, biribi, sucre de pommes, rigolo," and in the language of English housebreakers, that is, the "busters and screwsmen," "the stick, James, Jemmy."

Dauphin, *m.* (popular), *girl's bully*, "ponce," see **Poisson**; (thieves') *short crowbar used by housebreakers*, "jemmy."

David, *m.* (popular), *silk cap*. From the maker's name.

Davone, *f.* (thieves'), *plum*.

De (familiar), se pousser du —, *to place the word " de " before one's name to make it appear a nobleman's.*

Dé, *m.* (popular), or — à boire, *drinking glass*. Dé ! *yes.* Properly *thimble*.

Débacle, *f.* (thieves'), *accouchement*. Properly *breaking up, collapse*.

Débacler (thieves' and popular), *to open ; to force open ;* — la lourde, *open the door.*

Débacleuse, *f.* (thieves' and popular), *midwife.* Termed also " tâte-minette, Madame Tire-monde."

Débagouler (popular), *to speak*, "to jaw."

Débalinchard, *m.* (popular), *one who saunters lazily about.*

Déballage, *m.* (popular), *undress; getting out of bed ; dirty linen.* Etre floué or volé au —, *to be grievously disappointed with a woman's figure when she divests herself of her garments.* Gagner au —, *to appear to better advantage when undressed.*

Déballer (popular), *to strip.* Se —, *to undress oneself.*

Débanquer (gamesters'), *to ruin the gaming bank.*

Débarbouiller (popular), à la potasse, *to strike one in the face*, " to give one a bang in the mug ;" *to clear up some matter.*

Débardeur, *m.*, **débardeuse**, *f.* (familiar), *dancers at fancy balls dressed as a* débardeur *or lumper.*

Débarquer (popular), se —, *to give up; to relinquish anything already undertaken*, to " cave in."

Débaucher (popular), *to dismiss.* Etre débauché, *to get the sack.* The reverse of embaucher, *to engage.*

Débecqueter (popular), *to vomit*, " to cast up accounts," " to shoot the cat."

Débectant (popular), *annoying ; tiresome ; dirty ; disgusting.*

Débinage, *m.* (familiar), *slandering ; running down.* From débiner, *to talk ill, to depreciate.*

Débiner (popular), *to depreciate ;* — le truc, *to disclose a secret ; to explode a dodge, or fraud.*

Parbleu ! je n'ignore pas ce que peuvent dire les blagueurs pour débiner le truc de ces fausses paysannes.—RICHEPIN, *Le Pavé.*

Se — des fumerons, *to run away*, " to leg it." Se —, *to abuse one another*, " to slang one another;" *to run away*, " to brush," see **Patatrot** ; *to grow weak.*

Débineur, *m.*, **débineuse**, *f.* (popular), *one who talks ill of people ; one who depreciates people or things.*

Déblayer (theatrical), *to curtail portions of a part; to hurry through a performance.*

A l'Opéra, ce soir . . . . on déblaye à bras raccourci : vous savez que déblayer signifie écourter.—P. MAHALIN.

Débloquer (military), *to cancel an order of arrest.*

Débonder (popular), *to ease oneself; to go to* " West Central," *or to the* " crapping ken." See **Mouscailler.**

Déborder (popular), *to vomit*, " to cast up accounts," or " to shoot the cat."

Déboucler (thieves'), *to open ; to set a prisoner at liberty.*

Déboucleur, *m.* (thieves'), de lourdes, *a housebreaker,* " buster," or " screwsman."

Débouler (popular), *to be brought to childbed,* " to be in the straw ; " *to arrive,* or " to crop up."

Déboulonné (popular), être —, *to be dull-witted,* or *to be a* " deadalive."

Déboulonner (popular), la colonne à quelqu'un, *to thrash one soundly,* " to knock one into a cocked hat." See **Voie.**

Débourré (horse-dealers'), cheval —, *horse which suddenly loses its fleshy appearance artificially imparted by rascally horse-dealers.*

Débourrer (popular), *to educate one,* " to put one up to ; " — sa pipe, *to ease oneself,* or " to go to the chapel of ease." See **Mouscailler.** Se —, *to become knowing,* " up to a dodge or two," or a " leary bloke."

Débouscailler (popular), *to black one's boots.*

Débouscailleur (popular), *shoeblack.*

Débrider (thieves'), *to open ;* — les chasses, *to open one's eyes ;* (popular) — la margoulette, *to eat,* " to grub." See **Mastiquer.**

Débridoir, *m.* (thieves'), *key ; skeleton key,* " screw," or " twirl."

Débrouillard, *m.* (popular), *one who has a mind fertile in resource, in contrivances to get on in the world,* or *to extricate himself out of difficulties,* a " rum mizzler." Also used as an adjective. Literally *one who gets out of the fog.*

Débrouiller (theatrical), un rôle, *to make oneself thoroughly acquainted with the nature of one's part before learning it, to realize fully the character one has to impersonate.*

Décadener (thieves'), *to unchain.*

Décalitre, *m.* (popular), *top hat,* "stove-pipe." See **Tubard.**

Décampiller (popular), *to decamp,* " to bunk."

Décanailler (popular), se —, *to rise from a state of abjection and poverty.*

Décanillage, *m.* (popular), *departure ; moving one's furniture ;* — à la manque, *moving after midsummer term.*

En juillet le déménagement est une fête. Mais en octobre, n, i, ni, c'est fini de rire : le déménagement est funèbre et s'appelle le décanillage à la manque.—RICHEPIN, *Le Pavé.*

Décarcassé, *adj.* (theatrical), *is said of a bad play.*

Décarcasser (popular), quelqu'un, *to thrash one soundly,* " to knock one into a cocked hat." See **Voie.** Se —, *to give oneself much trouble ; to move about actively, fussily.* Décarcasse-toi donc, rossard ! *look alive, you lazy bones !* Se — le boisseau, *to torture one's brains ; to fret grievously.*

Décarrade, *f.* (thieves'), *general scampering off ; departure.*

Décarre, *f.* (thieves'), *release from prison.*

Décarrement, *m.* (thieves' and popular), *escape.*

Décarrer (thieves'), *to leave prison ; to run away,* " to guy." See **Patatrot.**

On les emmène tous et pendant ce temps-là le gueusard décarre avec son camarade. —VIDOCQ.

Also *to come out.*

Nous allons nous cacher dans l'allée en face, nous verrons décarrer les messières.— E. Sue.

Décarrer à la bate, *to escape;* — cher, *to be released after having done one's "time;"* — de belle, *to be released without trial;* — de la geôle, *to be released on the strength of an order of discharge.*

Décartonner (popular), se —, *to grow old; to grow weak.*

Décati, *adj.* (popular), *no longer young or handsome; seedy, faded.* Elle a l'air bien —, *she has a faded, worn appearance.*

Décatir (popular), se —, *to get faded, worn, seedy.*

Décavage, *m.* (familiar), *circumstances of a gamester who has lost all his money, or who has "blewed" it.* From décavé, *ruined gamester.*

Décembraillard, *m., opprobrious epithet applied to Bonapartists.* An allusion to the coup d'état of the 2nd December, 1851, when Louis Napoléon Bonaparte, then President of the Republic, threw into prison dissentient members of parliament and generals who refused to join in the conspiracy, shelled the boulevards, shot down hundreds of harmless loungers, and transported or exiled 50,000 republicans or monarchists.

Décembrisade, *f., an act similar to the coup d'état of 2nd December,* 1851. See **Décembraillard.**

Déchanter (popular), *to recover from an error; to be crestfallen after one's illusions have been dispelled; to come down a peg or two.*

Déchard, *m.* (popular), *needy; man who is "hard up."*

Dèche, *f.* (popular), *neediness.* Etre en —, *to be "hard up" for cash; "to be at low tide."*

Décheux, *m.* (popular), *needy man, "quisby."*

Déchirée, *f.* (popular), elle n'est pas trop —, *is said of a woman who is yet attractive in spite of years.*

Déchirer (military), de la toile, *to perform platoon firing;* — la cartouche, *to eat.* See **Mastiquer.** (Popular) Déchirer son faux-col, son habit, son tablier, *to die.* (Ironical) Ne pas se —, *to have a good opinion of oneself and to show it.*

Déclaquer (popular), *to open one's heart; to make a clean breast of.*

Déclouer (popular), *to redeem objects from pawn, to get objects "out of lug."*

Décognoir, *m.* (popular), *nose, "boko," or "smeller."* See **Morviau.**

Décoller (popular), *to leave a place; to leave one's employment;* — son billard, *to die.* See **Pipe.** Se —, *to fail; to grow old, rickety; to die, "to kick the bucket."*

Décompte, *m.* (military), *mortal wound.* Recevoir son —, *to die;* see **Pipe;** "*to lose the number of one's mess.*"

Décors, *m. pl.* (freemasons'), *ornaments, insignia.*

Découcheur (military), *soldier who is in the habit of stopping away without leave.*

Découdre (familiar), en —, *to fight either in a duel or with the natural weapons.*

Découvrir (popular), la peau de quelqu'un, *to make one say things which he would rather have left unsaid;* "*to pump one;*" "*to worm*" *secrets out of one.*

Décramponner (familiar), se —, *to get rid of a troublesome person.*

Pourquoi ai-je quitté Paris? Pour me décramponner tout à fait de cet imbécile qui, panné, décavé, commençait à me porter la guigne.—RICHEPIN, *La Glu.*

Décrasser (popular), quelqu'un, *to corrupt one*, "to put one up to snuff;" (prostitutes') — un homme, *to clean a man out of his money*, and in thieves' language, *to rob a man.* See **Grinchir.**

Décravater (popular), ses propos, *to use language of an objectionable character*, or "blue talk."

Décrocher (popular), *to take articles out of pawn*, or "out of lug;" (military) *to shoot down*; (thieves') *to steal handkerchiefs*, "to haul stooks;" (popular) — un enfant, *to bring about a miscarriage*; (familiar) — la timbale, *to be fortunate*, or, as the Americans term it, "to get the cake," or "to yank the bun." An allusion to the practice of hanging a silver cup as a prize at the top of a greasy pole.

Décrochez-moi-ça (popular), *woman's bonnet; old clothes dealer; shop were secondhand clothes, or* "hand-me-downs," *are sold.*

Décrotter (popular), un gigot, *to leave nothing of a leg of mutton but the bare bone.*

Déculotté, *m.* (popular), *bankrupt*, "brosier."

Dedans (familiar), fourrer or mettre quelqu'un —, *to lock one up; to impose upon one*, "to bamboozle." Se mettre —, *to make a mistake; to get tipsy.* (Popular) Voir en —, *to be tipsy*, applicable especially to those who hold soliloquies when in their cups. See **Pompette.**

Dédèle, *f.* (popular), *mistress*, "moll."

Dédire (thieves'), se — cher, *to be at death's door.* Properly *to repent one's crimes.*

Dédurailler (thieves'), *to remove prisoners' irons.*

Défalquer (popular), *to ease oneself; to go to the* "crapping ken." See **Mouscailler.**

Défarguer (thieves'), *to grow pale; to be acquitted.*

Défargueur (thieves'), *witness for the defence.*

Défendre (popular), sa queue, *to defend oneself.*

Déffardeur, *m.* (popular), *thief*, "cross cove." See **Grinche.** From de and fardeau, literally *one who eases you of your burden.*

Défiger (popular), *to warm.* From de and figer, *to coagulate.*

Défiler (popular), aller voir — les dragons, *to go without a dinner.* See **Aller.** (Military) Défiler la parade, *to die*, "to lose the number of one's mess." See **Pipe.** (Popular) Se —, *to run away*, "to leg it." See **Patatrot.**

Défleurir (thieves'), la picouse, *to steal linen hung out to dry*, "to smug snowy."

Déformer (popular), *to break; to put out of gear.* Je lui ai déformé une quille, *I broke one of his legs.*

Défouque. See **Desfoux.**

Défourailler (thieves'), *to run*, "to pad the hoof," or "to guy;" see **Patatrot**; *to fall; to be released from jail.*

Défrimousser (popular), synonymous of dévisager, *to peer into one's face.*

Défrusquer, défrusquiner (popular), *to strip one of his clothes.* Se —, *to undress.*

Dégauchir (thieves'), *to steal,* "to nim," "to claim." See **Grinchir.**

Dégazonner (familiar), se —, *to become bald.* Il a· le coco tout dégazonné, *he is quite bald.* See **Avoir.**

Dégel, *m.* (popular), *death.*

Dégelé (popular), *corpse,* "cold meat."

Dégelée, *f.* (popular), *thrashing,* "walloping."

Dégeler (popular), se —, *to die,* "to kick the bucket;" see **Pipe;** *to become knowing.* (Fencing) Dégeler son jeu, *to put spirit into one's play.*

Déglinguer (popular), *to damage.*

Dégobillade, *f.* (popular), *vomit; very bad liquor,* "swizzle."

Dégommade (popular), *old age; decrepit state.*

Dégommage, *m.* (popular), *dismissal,* "the sack;" *ruin.*

Dégommer (popular), quelqu'un, *to excel over one.* Literally *to dismiss one from a situation; to kill.* Se —, *to grow old, faded.*

Dégorger (popular), *to pay,* "to fork out;" — sa sangsue, *to have connection with a woman; to perform an act of* "chivalry."

Dégottage, *m.* (popular), *action of surpassing one; of finding or discovering something.*

Dégotter (military), *to kill;* (popular) *to surpass one; to find; to discover.*

Tiens ! quoi donc que j'dégott' dans l'noir,
Qu'est à g'noux, là-bas su' l'trottoir ?
Eh ! ben, là-bas, eh ! la gonzesse.
GILL, *La Muse à Bibi.*

Dégouler (popular), *to take away; to fall,* "to come a cropper."

Dégoulinage (popular), *inferior drink,* "swizzle."

Dégouliner (popular), *to drip;* — ce qu'on a sur le cœur, *to unbosom.*

Dégourdi, *m.* (popular), ironical, *clumsy fellow,* "stick in the mud." Properly it has the opposite meaning.

Dégoûtation, *f.* (popular), *expression of disgust.* Une — d'homme, *a disgusting fellow.* The expression is a favourite one of the streetwalking tribe.

Dégoûté, *adj.* (popular), ironical. N'être pas —, *is said of one who expresses a desire of obtaining something considered by others to be too good for him; also of one who picks out for himself the most dainty bits.*

Dégraisser (popular), *to steal,* "to prig," see **Grinchir;** — quelqu'un, *to fleece one.* Se —, *to grow thin.*

Dégrimoner (popular), se —, *to bestir oneself; to struggle; to wriggle.*

Dégringiller (popular), *to come out.* Dégringillons de la carrée, *let us leave the room.*

Dégringolade, *f.* (thieves'), *theft in a shop;* — à la flûte, *robbery committed by a street-walker.*

Dégringoler (thieves'), *to steal,* "to nim;" — à la carre, *to steal property from shops.* This kind of robbery is practised principally by women, and the thief is called a "bouncer."

Dégrossir (freemasons'), *to carve.*

Dégrouper (popular), se —, *to separate.*

Dégueularder (thieves'), *to talk, to say,* "*to rap.*" Ne dégueularde pas sur sa fiole, *say nothing about him.*

Dégueulas, dégueulatif(popular), *annoying ; disgusting.*

J'conobre l'truc ; 'l est dégueulas. — RICHEPIN. (*I know the trade ; it is disgusting.*)

Dégueulatoire, *adj.* (popular), *disgusting ; repulsive.*

Dégueulbite, dégueulboche, *adj.* (popular), *disgusting.*

Dégueuler (popular), *to sing,* or "*to lip.*"

Dégueulis, *m.* (popular), *vomit.*

Déguis, *m.* (thieves'), *disguise.*

Déguiser (popular), se — en cerf, *to make off,* "*to brush,*" or "*to leg it.*" See **Patatrot.**

Déjeté, *adj.* (popular), *weakly ; ugly.* N'être pas trop —, *to be still handsome.*

Déjeûner, *m. and verb* (popular), de perroquet, *biscuit dipped in wine ;* (military) — à la fourchette, *to fight a duel.*

Déjoséphier (popular), *to educate,* not in the better sense of the word; "*to put one up to snuff.*" An allusion to Madame Potiphar's attempts on Joseph's virtue.

De la bourrache ! (popular), *expressive of refusal ;* might be rendered by "*no go !*" "*you be blowed.*" See **Nèfles.**

Délass. Com. (popular), *theatre of the Délassements Comiques.*

Délicat et blond (popular), *is said ironically of a dandy or* "*Jemmy Jessamy ;*" also *of an effeminate fellow who cannot bear pain or discomfort.*

Délicoquentieusement (theatrical), *marvellously.*

Délige, *f.* (popular), for diligence, *public coach.*

Démancher (popular), se —, *to bestir oneself ; to give oneself much trouble.*

Démaquiller (thieves'), *to undo.*

Démarger (thieves'), *to go away ; to make off,* "*to crush,*" "*to guy.*" See **Patatrot.**

Démarquer (literary), *to pirate others' productions, or to alter one's own so as to pass them off as original.*

Démarqueur, *m.* (literary), de linge, *literary pirate.*

Déménager (popular), *to become mad,* or "*balmy ;*" *to die,* "*to kick the bucket ;*" — à la cloche de bois, de zinc, or à la sonnette de bois, *to move one's furniture secretly, the street door bell having been muffled so as to give no more sound than a wooden one,* "*to shoot the moon ;*" — à la ficelle, *to remove one's furniture through a window by means of a rope ;* — par la cheminée, *to burn one's furniture on receiving notice to quit, so as to cheat the landlord.*

Demi-aune, *f.* (popular), *arm,* "*bender.*" Tendre la —, *to beg.*

Demi-cachemire, *f.* (familiar), *kept woman in a good position, but who has not yet reached the top of the ladder.*

Demi-castor, *f., woman of the demi-monde, a* "*pretty horsebreaker,*" or "*tartlet.*" See **Gadoue.**

Demi-cercle, pincer au —. See **Cercle.**

Demi-lune (popular), *rump,* "*cheek.*"

Demi-mondaine, *f.* (familiar), *woman of the demi-monde.* See **Gadoue.**

I

Demi-monde, *m.* (familiar), *the world of the higher class of kept women, of* "pretty horsebreakers."

Demi-sel, demi-poil, demi-vertu, *f.* (popular), *girl who has lost her maidenhead, her* "ceincture," as Villon termed it.

Demi-stroc, *m.* (thieves'), *half a* "setier," *that is, one-fourth of a litre.*

Démoc-soc, *m.* (familiar), *socialist.* An abbreviation for démocrate-socialiste.

Demoiselle, *f.* (popular), *a certain measure for wine, half a* "monsieur;" *bottle of wine.*

Demoiselles, *f.* (familiar), ces —, *euphemism for gay ladies ;* — du bitume, du Pont Neuf, *streetwalkers.*

Démolir (literary), *to criticise with harshness, to run down literary productions ;* (popular) *to thrash soundly,* "to knock into a cocked hat," see **Voie ;** *to kill.*

Démolisseur, *m.* (literary), *sharp and violent critic.*

Démorfilage (card-sharpers'), *setting right again cards which have been marked.*

Démorfiler, *action of doing* démorfilage (which see) ; also *to have one's wounds cured.*

Démorganer (thieves'), *to give in to one's arguments.*

Démurger (thieves'), *to leave a place ; to be set at liberty.*

Denaille, *m.* (thieves'), Saint —, *Saint-Denis, an arrondissement of Paris.*

Dénicheur, *m.* (popular), de fauvettes, *one fond of women,* "mutton-monger."

Dent, *f.* (popular), avoir de la —, *to have preserved one's good looks ;*

to be still young. Mal de dents, love. N'avoir plus mal aux dents, *to be dead.*

Dentelle, *f.* (thieves'), *bank notes,* "rags, flimsies, screenes, or long-tailed ones."

Déparler (popular), *to cease talking; to talk nonsense.*

Département, *m.* (popular), du bas rein, *breech.* See **Vasistas.** A play on the word Rhin.

Dépendeur, *m.* (popular), d'andouilles. See **Andouilles.**

Dépenser (popular), sa salive, *to talk,* or "to jaw away."

Dépiauter, dépioter (popular), *to skin.* Se —, *to break one's skin ; to undress,* "to peel."

Déplanquer (thieves'), *to remove stolen property out of hiding-place ;* — son faux centre, *to be convicted under an alias.*

Déplumer (popular), se —, *to get bald.* Avoir le coco déplumé, *to be bald,* "to have a bladder of lard," or "to be stag-faced." See **N'avoir plus.**

Déponer (popular), *to ease oneself,* "to go to the chapel of ease." See **Mouscailler.**

Déporter (popular), *to discharge from a situation,* "to give the sack."

Dépôt, *m.* (popular), dépôt de la Préfecture de Police, caisse des dépôts et consignations, *place of ease,* or "crapping ken."

Dépotoir, *m.* (thieves'), *confessional ;* (popular) *chamber pot,* or "jerry;" *strong box,* or "peter;" *house of ill-fame,* or "nanny-shop."

Dépuceleur, *m.* (popular), de nourrices, or de femmes enceintes, *ridiculous Lovelace.*

Député, *m.* (theatrical), *free ticket.*

De quoi (popular), *wealth; what next? what do you mean?*

Dérager (popular), *to get pacified.* Generally used in the negative. Il n'a pas encore déragé, *he is yet in a rage.*

Déraillé, *m.* (familiar), *one who has lost caste.*

Dérailler (familiar), *to talk nonsense, cock-and-bull-story fashion.*

Déralinguer (sailors'), *to die.* Properly *to detach from the bolt rope.* See **Pipe**.

Dérondiner (popular), *to pay,* "to shell out." Se —, *to spend or give away one's money.* Ronds, *halfpence.*

Dérouler (thieves'), se —, *to spend a certain time, not specified, in prison,* "to do time."

Derrière, *m.* (popular), roue de —, *five-franc piece.* Se lever le — le premier, *to get up in a bad humour.* Used as a preposition. (Printers') Derrière le poèle chez Cosson, *words used to evade replying to an inquiry.*

Désargenté, *adj.* (thieves'), *hard-up for money.*

Quand on est désargenté on se la brosse et l'on ne va pas se taper un souper à l'œil. —Vidocq.

Désargoté, *adj.* (thieves'), être —, *to be shrewd, to be a* "file," *to be* "fly," *or a* "leary bloke."

Désargoter (thieves'), *to employ cunning.*

Désarrer (thieves'), *to flee, to* "guy," *or* "to make beef." See **Patatrot**.

Désatiller (thieves'), *to castrate.* Horse-trainers term the operation "adding one to the list."

D'esbrouffe, or **d'esbrouf** (thieves'), *by force.* Pesciller —, *to take by force.* Estourbir —, *to knock over the head.*

Un grand messière franc . . .
Le filant sur l'estrade
D'esbrouf je l'estourbis.
　　　　　　　Vidocq.

Descendre (popular), quelqu'un, *to shoot one,* "to pot;" *to throw down;* — le crayon sur la colonne, *to thrash*, see **Voie**; — la garde, *to die*, see **Pipe**. (Theatrical) Descendre, *to approach the footlights.* (Sporting) Un cheval qui descend, *horse against which the odds are decreasing.*

Désenbonnetdecotonner, *to give elegance to.* "De," and "en bonnet de coton," *a nightcap.*

Désenflaquer (popular), se —, *to amuse oneself.* (Thieves') Se —, *to get out of prison; to get out of trouble.*

Désenfrusquiner (popular), se —, *to undress.*

Désentiflage, *m.* (thieves'), *separation; divorce.*

Désentifler (thieves'), *to separate; to divorce.*

Desfouque. See **Desfoux**.

Desfoux, *f.* (popular), *silk cap sported by women's bullies.* From the maker's name.

Desgenais, *a character of a comedy by Th. Barrière.* Faire son — en chambre, *to play the moralist.*

Desgrieux, *associate of prostitutes and swindlers.* A character from *Manon Lescaut*, by l'Abbé Prévost.

Déshabillage, *m.* (literary), *ill-natured criticism.*

Si l'on veut passer un joli quart d'heure on n'a qu'à faire jaser un peintre connu sur un autre peintre également connu. Quel déshabillage ! mes amis.

Déshabiller (popular), *to thrash,* "to wallop." See **Voie.**

Désoler (thieves'), *to throw.*

Désosse, *f.* (popular), *distress.* Jouer la —, *to be ruined,* "cracked up," "gone to smash."

Désossé, *m.* (popular), *very thin man ; ruined man,* "brosier."

Désosser (popular), quelqu'un, *to pommel one.* See **Voie.**

Dessalée, *f.* (popular), *prostitute,* or "bed-fagot." See **Gadoue.**

Dessaler(thieves'), *to drown.* (Popular) Se —, *to drink a morning glass of white wine ; to drink,* "to moisten one's chaffer."

Dessous, *m.* (theatrical), tomber dans le troisième, or trente-sixième —, *the expression is used to denote that a play has been a complete fiasco.* (Familiar) Tomber dans le troisième —, *to fall into utter discredit.* (Thieves') Dessous, *man loved for* "love," *not for money ; a bully.*

Dessus, *m.* (thieves'), *man who keeps a woman,* the dessous being the said woman's lover.

Destuc (thieves'), être d'—, *to be partners in a robbery ; to be in a* "push." "I'm in this push," is the notice given by an English thief to another that he means to "stand in."

Détaché, *adj.* (sporting), cheval —, *horse which keeps the lead.*

Détacher (thieves'), le bouchon, *to steal a watch,* "to nick a jerry," "to twist a thimble," or "to get a red toy."

Détaffler (thieves'), *to grow bold.* De and taf, *fear.*

Détailler (theatrical), le couplet, *to sing with appropriate expression the different parts of a song ; —* un rôle, *to bring out all the best points of a part.*

Détaroquer (thieves'), *to obliterate the marking of linen.*

Déteindre (popular), *to die,* "to kick the bucket," or "to snuff it." See **Pipe.**

Dételer (familiar), *to renounce the pleasures of love.*

Détoce, or **détosse,** *f.* (thieves'), *ill-luck ; poverty.*

Détourne, *f.* (thieves'), vol à la —, *robbery in a shop, or from the shop-window, generally committed by two confederates, the one engrossing the shopkeeper's attention while the other takes possession of the property.*

Détourneur, *m.,* **détourneuse,** *f.,* *thief who operates after the manner described under the heading of* "**Vol à la détourne**" (which see).

Détraquer (popular), se — le trognon, *to become crazy, to become* "balmy."

Dette (thieves'), payer une —, *to be in prison, in* "quod."

Deuil, *m.* (popular), demi —, *coffee without brandy.* Grand —, *with brandy.* (Familiar) Il y a du —, *things are going on badly.* Porter le — de sa blanchisseuse, *to have dirty linen.*

Deux (popular), les — sœurs, *the breech,* or "cheeks." See **Vasistas.** (Thieves') Partir pour les —, *to set out for the convict settlement,* "to lump the lighter."

Dévalidé, *adj.* (familiar), synonymous of invalidé, *unreturned candidate for parliament.*

Devant, *m.* (popular), de gilet, *woman's breasts,* "Charlies."

Déveinard, *m.* (popular), *unlucky.*

Un de ces ouvriers déveinards, un de ces inventeurs en chambre, qui ont compté sur le coup de fortune du nouvel an.—RICHE-PIN, *Le Pavé.*

Déveine, *f.* (popular), *constant ill-luck.*

Dévidage, *m.* (thieves'), *long speech, or yarn; walk in prison yard;* — à l'estorgue, *lie,* "gag;" *accusation.* Faire des dévidages, *to make revelations.*

Dévider (thieves'), *to talk,* "to patter;" — à l'estorgue, *to lie;* — le jars, *to speak the cant of thieves,* "to patter flash;" — une retentissante, *to break a bell;* (popular) — son peloton, *to talk a great deal; to make a confession.*

Dévideur, *m.,* **dévideuse,** *f.* (thieves'), *chatterer,* "clack-box."

Dévierger (popular), *to seduce a maiden.*

Dévirer (thieves' and cads'), *to turn round.*

Dévisser (popular), le coco, *to strangle;* — le trognon à quelqu'un, *to wring a person's neck.* Se —, *to go away.* Se — la pétronille, *to break one's head.*

Dévisseur, *m.* (popular), *slanderer, backbiter.*

Devoir (gay girls'), une dette, *to have promised a rendez-vous.*

Dévoyé, *adj.* (thieves'), *acquitted.*

Diable, *m.* (thieves'), *instigator in the employ of the police.*

Diamant, *m.* (theatrical), *voice of a fine quality,* "like a bell;" (popular) *paving stone.*

Dibolata, dibuni (Breton cant), *to fight, to thrash.*

Dictionnaire Verdier, *m.* (printers'), *imaginary dictionary of which the name is shouted loud whenever one speaks or spells incorrectly.*

Dieu (popular), le — terme, *rent day.* Il n'y a pas de bon —, see **Bon.**

Difficulté, *f.* (sporting), être en —, *is said of a horse which can just keep the start obtained at the cost of the greatest efforts.*

Difoara (Breton cant), *to pay.*

Dig-dig, or **digue-digue,** *m.* (thieves'), *epileptic fit.* Batteur de —, *vagabond who pretends to be seized with a fit.*

Digonneur, *m.* (popular), *ill-tempered man, a* "shirty" *one.*

Dijonnier (popular), *mustard-pot.* The best mustard is manufactured at Dijon.

Diligence, *f.* (popular), de Rome, *tongue,* or "velvet."

Dimanche (popular), or — après la grand' messe, *never, at Doomsday, or when the devil is blind.*

Dindonner (popular), *to deceive; to impose upon,* "to bamboozle." From dindon, *a dupe, a fool.*

Dindornier, *m.* (thieves'), *hospital attendant.*

Dîner (popular), en ville, *to dine off a small roll in the street.* A philosophical way of putting it.

Dinguer (theatrical), *to be out of the perpendicular;* (popular) *to walk, to lounge.* Envoyer —, *to send to the deuce.*

Discussion, *f.* (popular), avoir une — avec le pavé, *to fall flat,* "to come a cropper."

Disque, *m.* (popular), *breech,* or "tochas," see **Vasistas;** also *coin.*

Distingué, *m.* (popular), *glass of beer.*

Dix-huit (popular), *shoe made up of different parts of old ones.* A play on the words " deux fois neuf," *twice new,* or *eighteen.*

Dixième, *m.* (military), *passer au — régiment, to die.* See **Pipe.** A play on the word " décimer," *to kill one in ten.*

Doche, *f.* (thieves'), *mother.* Boîte à —, *coffin.*

Doigt, *m.* (familiar), *se fourrer le — dans l'œil,* or *le — dans l'œil jusqu'au coude, to be grossly mistaken.* Etre de la société du — dans l'œil, *to be one of those who form ambitious hopes not likely to be realized.* Name given after the Commune of 1871 to a group of Communists in exile who had separated from the rest, and had divided among themselves all the future official posts of their future government ; a case of selling chickens, &c., with a vengeance.

Domange (popular), marmite à —, *waggon which carries away the contents of cesspools.* Marmiton de —, *scavenger employed at emptying the cesspools.* Travailler pour M. —, *to eat.* See **Mastiquer.** M. Domange is the name of a contractor who has, or had, charge of the cleaning of all Paris cesspools.

Dome, *m.* (thieves'), Saint —, or saindomme, *tobacco,* or " fogus."

Dominer (theatrical), *is said of an actor standing behind another who is nearer to the footlights.* It must be said, in explanation, that the stage-floor has an incline from the back to the front of the stage.

Domino-culotte, *m., the last domino in a player's hand.*

Dominos, *m. pl.* (thieves'), jeu de —, *teeth.* Avoir le jeu complet de —, *to possess one's set of teeth complete.* Jouer des —, *to eat.* See **Mastiquer.**

Comme tu joues des dominos (des dents), à te voir, on croirait que tu morfiles (mords) dans de la crignole (viande).—Vidocq.

Donne, *f.* (gambling cheats'), la —, *the act of skilfully shuffling a pack so as to leave underneath certain cards which the cheat reserves for himself.*

Donner (thieves'), *to look ; to see,* " to pipe ;" *to peach,* or " to blow the gaff ; " — à la Bourbonnaise, *to scowl at one ;* — du chasse à la rousse, *to be on the look-out,* " to nark," or " to nose ;" — du flan, or de la galette, *to play fairly ;* — sur le buffeton, *to read an indictment ;* — un pont à faucher, *to lay a trap ; to prepare a snare for one ; to deceive one,* " to kid ;" — une affaire, *to give the information required for the perpetration of a robbery.* (Popular) Donner de la salade, *to give one something more than a good shaking,* see **Voie ;** — du cambouis à quelqu'un, *to make fun of one ; to play a trick ;* — du dix-huit, see **Donner cinq et quatre ;** — du vague, *to seek for one's living ;* — la savate, *to give a box on the ear,* or " buck-horse ;" — son bout, or son bout de ficelle, *to dismiss ; to give the* " sack ;" (ironical) — des noms d'oiseaux, *to be very loving ;* — cinq et quatre, *to slap one with the palm, then with the back of the hand ;* — un coup de poing dont on ne voit que la fumée, *to give a terrific blow in the face,* " a thumper." La —, *to sing,* " to' lip." Se — de l'air, *to go out.* Se la —, *to be off ; to run away,* " to slope," see **Patatrot ;** also *to fight,* " to pitch into one another." (Familiar) Donner la migraine à une tête de bois, *to be an insufferable bore ;* — son dernier bon à tirer, *to die ;* — de la grosse caisse, *to puff up a book or trade article ;* — du balai, *to dismiss ;* (Saint-Cyr cadets') — du vent, *to bully.*

Donneur, *m.*, de bonjour. See **Bonjour**. (Thieves') Donneur d'affaires, *malefactor of an inventive genius who suggests to others plans of robberies or "plants."*

Donnez-la ! (thieves'), *look out !* "shoe leather !" Synonymous of "chou !" "acresto !" "du pet !"

Dorancher (thieves'), *to gild.*

Dormir (popular), en chien de fusil, *to double oneself up, when sleeping, into the shape of an S ;* — en gendarme, *to sleep with one eye open ; to sleep a "fox's sleep."*

Dorna (Breton), *to get drunk.*

Dorner (Breton), *drunkard.*

Dort dans l'auge, *m.* (popular), *lazy individual,* "lazy bones," or "bummer."

Dort-en-chiant (popular), *extremely lazy man, with no energy whatever, with no heart for work,* "a bummer."

Dos, *m.* (general), *woman's bully,* "Sunday man ;" — d'azur, vert, *same meaning.* For synonymous terms see **Poisson**. Scier le — à quelqu'un, *to importune ;* "to bore" *one.*

Dose, *f.* (popular), *unpleasant thing.*

Dossière, *f.* (thieves'), *prostitute,* "bunter," see **Gadoue ;** — de satte, *arm-chair.*

Douanier, *m.* (popular), *glass of absinthe.* An allusion to the uni-

form of custom-house officers, which, like absinthe, is green. Termed also "un perroquet."

Doublage, doublé, *m.* (popular), *robbery.*

Double, *m.* (military), *sergeant-major ;* (popular) — six, *negro.* Also *the two upper front teeth.* (Thieves') Gras —, *sheet lead,* or "flap." Termed also "saucisson."

Doubler (thieves'), *to steal,* "to claim," or "to nick ;" (familiar) — un cap, *to avoid passing before a creditor's door ; to be able to settle a debt or pay a bill when it falls due ;* — le cap du terme, *to be able to pay one's rent when it becomes due, to be able to clear the dreaded reef of rent day.*

Doubleur, doubleux, *m.*, **doubleuse**, *f.* (thieves'), *thief,* "prig," see **Grinche ;** — de sorgue, *night thief.*

Doublin, *m.* (thieves'), *ten-centime piece.*

Doublure, *f.* (theatrical), *actor who at a moment's notice is able to take the part of another ;* (popular) — de la pièce, *breasts,* "Charlies."

Douce, *f.* (thieves'), *silk or satin stuff,* "squeeze." (Popular) A la —, *gently ; pretty well.* Comment qu'ça va aujourd'hui ? mais, à la —, *how are you to-day ? pretty bobbish.* La couler, or la passer à la —, *to live an easy life, devoid of cares.*

Doucette, *f.* (thieves'), *a file.* An endearing term for that very useful implement.

Douceur, *f.* (thieves'), faire en —, *to rob from the person without any violence, with suavity, so to speak.* Le mettre en —, *to extort property by dint of wheedling.*

Douillard, *m.* (thieves' and popular), *wealthy man*, "rag-splawger," "rhinoceral," *one* "well-ballasted."

Douillards, *m.* (thieves' and popular), *hair*.

Viv' la gaîté ! J'ai pas d'chaussettes ;
Mes rigadins font des risettes ;
Mes tas d'douillards m'servent d'chapeau.
    RICHEPIN, *Chanson des Gueux.*

Douille, *f.* (thieves' and popular), *money*, "pieces." See **Quibus.** Aboule la —, "dub the pieces."

Douiller (thieves'), *to pay*, "to dub ; " — du carme, *to give money*, "to dub pieces."

Douilles, *f.* (thieves'), *hair*, or "thatch ; " — savonnées, *white hair*. Termed also "tifs, douillards, plumes."

Douillet, *m.*, **douillette**, *f.* (thieves'), *hair*, "thatch ; " *mane*.

Douillure, *f.* (thieves'), *head of hair*.

Douleur, *f.* (popular), avaler or étrangler la —, *to drink a glass of brandy*, the great comforter it would appear.

Douloureuse, *f.* (popular), *reckoning at an eating-house*. The term is expressive of one's sorrow when comes the dreaded " quart d'heure de Rabelais."

Dousse, *f.* (thieves'), *fever*.

Doussin, *m.* (thieves'), *lead*, "bluey."

Doussiner (thieves'), *to line with lead*.

Doux, *m.* (popular), du —, *some sweet liquor such as Chartreuse, Curaçao.*

Dovergn (Breton), *horse*.

Dragée, *f.* (military), *bullet*, "plum." Dragée, properly *sweetmeat.* Gober une —, *to receive a bullet.*

Dragons. See **Aller voir défiler.**

Drague, *f. and m.* (popular), une —, *table, implements or plant of a conjuror, of a mountebank.* (Thieves') Un —, *surgeon*, "nim gimmer."

Dragueur, *m.* (popular), *quack*, " crocus ; " *conjurer ; mountebank.*

Drap (popular), manger du —, *to play at billiards, to play* " spoof."

Drapeau, *m.* (freemasons'), *serviette.* Grand —, *table-cloth.*

Drapeaux, *m.* (popular), *swaddling clothes.*

Dregneu, parler en —, *is to combine this word with other words.* " Je suis pris," becomes " Je dregue suidriguis pridriguis."

Drille, or **dringue**, *f.* (popular), *diarrhœa*, " jerry-go-nimble ; " (thieves') *five-franc piece.*

Drive (sailors'), être en —, *to be out on a spree*, or " on the booze."

Drogue, *f.* (popular), *article of bad quality*, " Brummagem article." Mauvaise —, *ill-natured man or woman.* Petite —, *wicked girl ; disreputable girl*, " strumpet."

Droguer (popular), *to wait a long time ;* (thieves') *to ask for.* The term seems to imply that asking for is a tedious process, and that it is preferable to help oneself.

Droguerie, *f.* (thieves'), *a request.* That is, an unpleasant task.

Drogueur, *m.* (thieves'), de la haute, *expert thief or swindler*, " gonnof."

Droguiste, *m.* (thieves'), *swindler ; sharper*, " shark." Termed also, in English slang, " hawk," in opposition to the " pigeon " or victim. See **Grinche.**

Droitier, *m.* (familiar), *member of the right, or monarchist party in parliament.* See **Centrier**.

Dromadaire, *m.* (popular), *prostitute,* or "*mot.*" Formerly *a veteran of the Egypt campaign.*

Drouillasse, *f.* (popular), *diarrhœa,* "jerry-go-nimble."

Duc, *m.* (familiar), *large carriage which holds two people inside, and has room for two servants in front and two behind;* —de guiche, *turnkey,* "dubsman;" — de la panne, *needy man;* — d'en face (ironical), *an allusion to an insignificant man who is seeking to make a show of undue importance or to give himself grand airs.*

Duce, *m.* (thieves'), *secret signal agreed upon among sharpers.*

Duchêne (popular), passer à —, *to get a tooth extracted.* An allusion to the name of a famous dentist.

Duel, *m.* (popular), des yeux qui se battent en —, *squinting eyes,* or "swivel eyes."

Du gas, *m.* (sailors'), *my lad.*

> Va bien. On t'emplira, du gas,
> Répond le capitaine.
> J'y fournirai, t'y fourniras
> Moi l'huile à ta lanterne,
> Toi l'huil' de bras.
> RICHEPIN, *La Mer.*

Dumanet (familiar), *appellation given to a private soldier, answers to the English* "Thomas Atkins." Dumanet is the name of one of the characters of a play.

Dun, parler en —, *art of disguising words by means of the syllable* "dun." The letter *n* is substituted for the first letter of the word when it is a consonant, added when a vowel. The last syllable is followed by *du*, which acts as a prefix to the first. Thus "maison" becomes "naisondumai," "Paris" becomes "Narisdupa."

Dunik (Breton), *mass.*

Dunon, parler en —, *process similar to the one called* "parler en dun" (which see).

Dur, *adj. and m.* (popular), à la détente, or à la desserre, *stingy, close-fisted; man who is slow in paying his debts.* Du —, *spirits.* (Printers') Etre dans son —, *to be working hard.*

Duraille, *f.* (thieves'), *stone; precious stone,* "spark."

Dure, *f.* (thieves'), *stone; the central prison;* — à briquemon, à rifle, *flint.* Voler quelqu'un à la —, *to rob a man with violence,* "to jump a cove."

Durême, *m.* (thieves'), *cheese.*

Durillon, *m.* (popular), *hump.*

Durin, *m.* (thieves'), *iron.*

Duriner (thieves'), *to tip with iron.*

Dusse. See **Duce**.

Du vent (popular), or de la mousse, de l'anis, des dattes, des navets, des nèfles, du flan, *derisive expressions of refusal;* might be rendered by, "you be blowed," "don't you wish you may get it," "you'll get it in a hurry," &c.

Dynamitard, *m.* (familiar), *dynamiter,* one who aims at regenerating society by the free use of dynamite.

**AU**, *f.* (popular), de moule, *a mixture of a little absinthe and a great deal of water.* Marchand d'— chaude, or d'— de javelle, *landlord of a wine-shop.*

Eau d'af, eau d'affe, *f.* (popular and thieves'), *brandy*, or "French cream."

Eau-fortier, *m.* (artists'), *an etcher.*

Eaux, *f. pl.* (popular), être dans les — grasses, *to hold a high official position.* Les — sont basses, *funds are low, funds are at* "low tide."

Ebasir (thieves'), *to knock down ; to murder,* "to cook one's goose."

Ebattre (thieves'), s'— dans la tigne, *to try and pick pockets in a crowd,* "to fake a cly in the push."

Ebéno, *m.* (popular), for ébéniste, *French polisher.*

Ecafouiller (popular), *to squash.*

Ecaillé, *m.* (popular), *prostitute's bully,* or "Sunday man." See **Poisson.**

Ecarbouiller (popular), s'—, *to run away,* "to bunk."

Ecart, *m.* (gambling cheats'), *sleight of hand trick by which the cheat conceals an ace under his wrist to use when convenient.*

Ecarter (familiar), du fusil, or de la dragée, *to spit involuntarily when talking.*

Echalas, *m.* (popular), jus d'—, *wine.* (Thieves') Echalas d'omnicroche, *coachman of an omnibus.*

Echalas, *m. pl.* (popular), *thin legs,* "spindle-shanks."

Echappé, *m.* (popular), de Charenton, *crazy fellow* (Charenton is the Paris dépôt for lunatics) ; — d'Hérode, *unsophisticated man,* or "greenhorn."

Echarpiller (popular), se faire —, *to get a terrible thrashing,* "to get knocked into a cocked hat." See **Voie.**

Echasses, *f. pl.* (popular), *thin legs,* "spindle-shanks."

Echassier, *m.* (popular), *tall man with thin, long legs,* or "spindle-shanks."

Echaudé (popular), être —, *to be overcharged ; to be fleeced,* "to be shaved."

Echauder (popular), *to charge more for an article than the real price,* "to shave a customer." Properly *to scald.* According to the *Slang Dictionary* (Chatto and Windus, 1885), when a London tradesman sees an opportunity of doing this, he strokes his chin as a signal to the assistant who is serving the customer.

Echelle, *f.* (popular), monter à l'—, *to ascend the scaffold.* Faire monter quelqu'un à l'—, *to get one into a rage by teazing or badgering him,* "to rile one."

Echiner (familiar), *to criticise sharply, to run down.* Properly *to thrash to within an inch of one's life.*

Echineur, *m.* (familiar), *sharp critic.*

Echo, *m.* (popular), *an encore at a place of entertainment.*

Echoppe, *f.* (popular), *workshop.*

Echos, *m. pl.* (journalists'), *reports on topics of the day.*

Echoter, *to write* "échos." See that word.

Echotier, *m.* (familiar), *writer of* "échos." See that word.

Indépendamment de la loge de Fauchery, il y a celle de la rédaction, de la direction et de l'administration, une baignoire pour son soiriste, une autre pour son échotier, quatre fauteuils pour ses reporters.—P. MAHALIN.

Eclairage, *m.* (general), *money laid down on a gaming table as stakes.*

Eclairer (general), *to pay,* "to dub ;" *to exhibit money ;* (gamesters') — le tapis, le velours, *to stake ;* (prostitutes') *to look about in quest of a client.*

Eclaireur, *m.* (gamesters'), *confederate of card-sharpers.*

Eclaireurs, *m. pl.* (popular), *large protruding breasts.* Properly *scouts.*

Ecluser (popular), *to void urine,* "to lag."

Ecluses, *f. pl.* (popular), lâcher les —, *to weep,* "to nap a bib ;" *to void urine,* "to lag."

Ecole préparatoire (thieves'), *prison,* "jug." A kind of compulsory "Buz-napper's Academy," or school in which young thieves are trained.

Ecopage, *m.* (popular), *blow,* "prop," "bang," or "wipe ;" *collision ; scolding,* "bully-ragging ;" *the art of calling on one just at dinner time, so as to get an invitation.*

Ecoper (popular), *to drink.* See **Rincer.** Properly *to bale a boat.* Ecoper, *to receive a thrashing,* "to get a walloping."

Ecopeur, *m.* (popular), *artful man who manages to get some small advantages out of people without appearing to ask for them.*

Ecornage, *m.* (thieves'), vol à l'—, *mode of robbery which consists in cutting out a small portion of a pane in a shop-window, and drawing out articles through the aperture by means of a rod provided with a hook at one of its extremities.*

Ecorné, *m.* (thieves'), *prisoner under examination,* or "cross kid ;" *prisoner charged with an offence,* "in trouble."

Ecorner (popular), *to slander ; to abuse,* "to bully rag ;" (thieves') *to break into ;* — une boutanche, un boucard, *to break into a shop,* "to crack a swag."

J'aimerais mieux faire suer le chêne sur le grand trimar, que d'écorner les boucards. —VIDOCQ.

Ecorneur, *m.* (thieves'), *public prosecutor.*

Ecornifler (thieves'), à la passe, *to shoot down.*

Ecossais (popular), en —, *without breeches.*

Ecosseur, *m.,* *secretary; one whose functions are to peruse letters.* Properly *sheller.* The Préfecture de Police employs twelve "écosseurs," whose duty it is to open the daily masses of correspondence conveying real or supposed clues to crimes committed. (*Globe Newspaper,* 1886.)

Ecoute, *f. and verb* (thieves'), *ear,* "wattle," or "hearing cheat." (Popular) Je t'—, je vous —, *just so! I should think so!*

Ecoute s'il pleut! (popular), *be quiet! hold your "row!"*

Ecoutilles, *f. pl.* (sailors'), *ears.* Ouvrir ses —, *to listen.* Properly *hatchway.*

Y es-tu, ma petite pouliotte, y es-tu? As-tu bien ouvert tes écoutilles? Te rappelles-tu tout ça et encore ça?—RICHEPIN, *La Glu.*

Ecrache, *f.* (thieves'), *passport;* — tarte, or à l'estorgue, *forged passport.*

Ecracher (thieves'), *to exhibit one's passport.*

Ecrasement, *m.* (thieves'), *crowd,* "push," or "scuff."

Ecraser (popular), un grain, *to have a glass of wine at a wine-shop;* — une bouteille, *to drink a bottle of wine.*

Je viens voir à présent si n'y aurait pas moyen d'écraser un grain pendant qu'i sont tous en train de folichonner.—TRUBLOT.

Ecrevisse, *f.* (popular), de boulanger, *hypocrite.* Avoir une — dans la tourte, or dans le vol-au-vent, *to be crazy,* "to have apart-ments to let." (Cavalry) Ecrevisse de rempart, *foot soldier,* or "beetle-crusher." (Theatrical) Quatorzième —, *female supernumerary.*

Ecrire (popular), à un juif, *to ease oneself,* "to go to the crapping ken." See **Mouscailler.**

Ecrivasser (literary), *to write in a desultory manner.*

Ecuelle, *f.* (popular), *plate.*

Ecume, *f.* (thieves'), de terre, *tin.* Properly *foam.*

Ecumoire, *f.* (familiar), *pockmarked face,* "cribbage face." Properly *skimmer.*

Ecurer (popular), son chaudron, *to go to confession.* Literally *to scour one's stewpan.*

Ecureuil, *m.* (popular), *man or boy whose functions consist in propelling the wheels of engineers or turners.*

Edredon, *m.* (popular), de trois pieds, *truss of straw.* (Prostitutes') Faire l'—, *to find a rich foreigner for a client.*

Vous me demanderez peut-être ce que signifie, faire l'édredon. . . . L'eider est un oiseau exotique au duvet précieux. . . . Avec ce duvet on se fabrique des couches chaudes et moelleuses. . . . Les étrangers de distinction, qu'ils viennent du Nord ou du Midi, sont, eux aussi, des oiseaux dont les plumes laissées entre des mains adroites et caressantes n'ont pas moins de valeur que le duvet de l'eider.—P. MAHALIN.

Ef, *m.* (prostitutes'), abbreviation of *effet.* Faire de l'—, *to show oneself to advantage.*

Effacer (popular), *to eat or drink,* see **Mastiquer;** — un plat, *to polish off the contents of a dish;* — une bouteille, *to drink off a bottle of liquor.*

Effaroucher (thieves'), *to steal,* "to ease," or "to claim." See **Grinchir.**

Effet (theatrical), *by-play, or those parts of a play which are intended to produce an impression on the audience.* Avoir un —, *to have to say or do something which will make an impression on the spectators.* Couper un —, *to spoil a fellow-actor's "effet" by distracting the attention of the public from him to oneself.*

Effets, *m. pl.* (familiar), faire des — de biceps, *to show off one's strength.* Faire des — de poche, *to make a show of possessing much money; to pay.* Faire des — de manchette, *to exhibit one's cuffs in an affected manner by a movement of the arm.*

Effondrer (popular), quelqu'un, *to beat one to a jelly,* "to knock one into a cocked hat." See **Voie.**

Egailler (gamesters'), les cartes, *to spread cards out.*

Egard, *m.* (thieves'), faire l'—, *to keep the proceeds of a theft to oneself.*

Egayer (theatrical), *to hiss,* "to give the big bird;" — l'ours, *to hiss a play.* Se faire —, *to get hissed,* "to get the big bird."

Eglisier, *m.* (popular), *bigot,* or "prayer monger."

Egnaffer (popular), *to astound.*

Egnolant (popular), *astounding.*

Egnoler (popular), *to astound.*

Egoût, *m.* (popular), prima donna d'—, *female singer at low music-halls,* or "penny gaffs."

Egraffigner (popular), *to scratch.*

Egrailler (popular), *to take.*

Egratignée. See **Déchirée.**

Egrené, *m.* (journalists'), *a kind of newspaper fag.*

Egrugeoir, *m.* (thieves'), *pulpit,* "hum-box."

Egruger (thieves'), *to plunder, to rifle.*

Egyptien, *m.* (theatrical), *bad actor, inferior sort of* "cackling cove."

Elbeuf, *m.* (familiar), *coat,* "tog."

Electeur, *m.* (commercial travellers'), *client.*

Eléments, *m. pl.* (card-sharpers'), *money,* or "pieces." See **Quibus.**

Elève, *m.* (thieves' and cads'), du Château, *prisoner; old offender.*

Elève-martyr, *m.* (cavalry), *one who is training to be a corporal,* and who in consequence has to go through a very painful ordeal, considering that French non-commissioned officers have the iron hand without the velvet glove.

Elixir, *m.* (popular), de hussard, *brandy.* See **Tord-boyaux.**

Eltrisa (Breton), *to seek for one's livelihood.*

Eltriz (Breton), *bread.*

Emanciper (familiar), s'—, *to take undue familiarities with women,* "to fiddle."

Emballer (thieves' and popular), *to apprehend,* "to smug." See **Piper.** S'—, *to get excited.* Properly *is said of a horse that runs away.*

Emballes, *f. pl.* (prostitutes'), *fussy, showing off.* Faire des —, *to make a fuss.*

Emballeur (thieves'), *police-officer,* "copper," or "reeler." See **Pot-à-tabac.** Properly *packer.* Emballeur de refroidis, *undertaker's man.*

Embaluchonner (popular), *to make up a parcel; to wrap up.*

Embander (thieves'), *to take by force.*

Embarder (popular), *to wander from one's subject ; to prevaricate ; to make a mistake ; to enter.* J'ai embardé dans la carrée, *I entered the room.*

Embarras, *m.* (thieves'), *bed sheet.* (Popular) Mettre une fille dans l'—, *to seduce a girl, with the natural consequences.*

Embaumé, *m.* (popular), vieil —, *old fool ; old curmudgeon,* "doddering old sheep's head."

Emberlificoteur, *m.* (popular), *artful man, or an expert at wheedling,* " sly blade."

Embistrouiller (popular), *to embarrass ; to perplex,* "to flummux."

Emblème, *m.* (thieves'), *deceit ; falsehood,* or "gag."

Emblémer (thieves'), *to deceive,* " to stick."

Emblèmes, *m. pl.* (popular), des —, *expression of disbelief ;* might be rendered by "all my eye !" See **Nèfles**.

Emboîter (theatrical), *to abuse.*

Embosser (sailors'), s'—, *to place oneself.* Properly *to bring the broadside to bear.*

Emboucaner (popular), *to stink.* Termed also "casser, plomber, chelinguer, trouilloter." S'—, *to feel dull, out of sorts,* "to have the blue devils."

Embrouillarder (popular), s'—, *is said of a person in that state of incipient intoxication that if he took more drink the effects would become evident.* See **Sculpter**.

Embroussaillés, *adj.* (familiar), cheveux —, *matted hair.*

Embusqué, *adj.* (military), *soldier who by reason of certain functions is excused from military duties.*

Eméché, *adj.* (familiar), *slightly intoxicated,* or "elevated." See **Pompette**.

Emécher (familiar), s'—, *to be in a fair way of getting tipsy.* See **Sculpter**.

Emérillonner (popular), s'—, *to become quite cheerful,* or "cock a hoop," *through repeated potations.*

Emigré, *m.* (popular), de Gomorrhe, *Sodomist.*

Emmailloter (thieves'), *to dupe,* "to best ; " — un môme, *to prepare a theft or other crime.* Synonymous of "engraisser un poupart."

Emmailloteur, *m.* (popular), *tailor,* " snip," "steel-bar driver," "cabbage contractor."

Emmanché, *m.* (popular), *slow, clumsy fellow,* "stick in the mud."

Emmargouillis, *m.* (popular), *obscene talk,* or " blue talk."

Emmastoquer (popular), s'—, *to live well ; to eat to excess,* "to stodge."

Emmerdement, *m.* (familiar and popular), *a coarse word ; great annoyance ; trouble.*

Emmerder (general), *a coarse word ; to annoy ; to bore.* Also *extremely forcible expression of contempt.* Properly *to cover with excrement.* The English have the word "to immerd," *to cover with dung.*

J'emmerde la cour, je respecte messieurs les jurés.—V. Hugo.

Emmieller, emmoutarder (popular), *euphemism for* **Emmerder** (which see).

Emmilliarder (popular), s'—, or s'emmillionner, *to become prodigiously rich.*

Emos, *f.* (popular), abbreviation of émotion.

Emouver (popular), s'—, *to shift noisily about ; to hurry*, or "*to look alive.*"

Empaffer (popular), *to intoxicate.* From paf, *drunk.* See **Sculpter.**

Empaffes, *f. pl.* (thieves'), *bed-clothes.*

Empaillé, *m.* (popular), *clumsy man ; slow man, lacking energy,* "*stick in the mud.*"

Empaler (popular), *to deceive one by false representations,* "*to bamboozle.*"

Empaouter (popular), *to annoy; to bore,* "*to spur.*"

Empaumé, *adj.* (popular), c'est —, *it's done.*

Empaumer (popular and thieves'), *to apprehend,* "*to smug.*" See **Piper.**

Empave, *f.* (thieves'), *crossway.*

Empêcheur (familiar), de danser en rond, *dismal man, who plays the dog in the manger,* "*mar-joy.*"

Empereur, *m.* (popular), *worn-out old shoe.*

Empiergeonner (popular), s'—, *to get entangled.*

> Margot dans sa cotte et ses bas
> S'empiergeonna là-bas, là-bas.
> RICHEPIN, *Chanson des Gueux.*

Empiffrage, *m.*, **empiffrerie**, *f.* (popular), *gluttony,* "*stodging.*"

Empilage, *m.*, or **empil** (popular), *cheating.*

Empiler (popular), *to cheat at a game.*

Empioler (thieves'), *to lock up,* "*to give the clinch.*"

Emplanquer (thieves'), *to come up ; to turn up,* "*to crop up.*"

Emplâtre, *m.* (card-sharpers'), de Thapsia, *shirt front and collar.* (Popular) Faire un —, *to arrange one's cards ready for playing.* (Thieves') Emplâtre, *wax imprint taken for housebreaking purposes.*

Emplâtrer (popular), *to thrash,* "*to wallop.*" Si tu crânes, je vais t'emplâtrer, *none of your cheek, else I'll give you a beating.* See **Voie.** S'—, *to encumber oneself.*

Employé, *adj.* (military), dans les eaux grasses, *clerk of the victualling department,* "*mucker.*"

Emplûcher (thieves'), *to pillage.*

Empoignade, *f.* (popular), *dispute,* "*row.*"

Empoigner (literary), *to criticise vigorously ;* (theatrical) *to hiss,* "*to give the big bird.*"

Empoisonneur, *m.* (popular), *the landlord of wine-shop.* Termed also "*mastroquet, troquet, bistrot.*"

Empoivrer (popular), s'—, *to get drunk,* "*to get screwed.*" See **Sculpter.**

Emporter (thieves'), *to swindle,* "*to stick ;*" (popular) — le chat, *to meddle with what does not concern one, and to get abused or thrashed for one's pains.* To act as Monsieur Robert in Molière's *Le Médecin malgré Lui,* when he upbraids Sganarelle for beating his spouse, and in return gets thrashed by both husband and wife.

Emporteur, *m.*, *swindler who gets into conversation with a stranger, gains his confidence, and takes him to a café where two confederates,* "*le bachotteur*" *and* "*la bête,*" *await him* (see **Bachotteur**); — à la côtelette, *card-sharper who operates at restaurants.*

Emposeur, *m.* (thieves'), *Sodomist.*

Empoté, *m.* (familiar), *slow, clumsy man,* "stick in the mud."

Empousteur, *m.* (thieves'), *swindler who sells spurious goods to tradesmen under false pretences.*

Emprunter (popular), un pain sur la fournée, *to beget a child before marriage;* — un qui vaut dix, *to conceal one's baldness by brushing the hair forward.*

Emu, *adj.* (popular), *slightly intoxicated,* "elevated." See **Pompette.**

En (popular), avoir plein ses bottes, *to be tired, sick of a person or thing.*

Enbohémer (familiar), s'—, *to get into low society.*

Enbonnetdecotonner, s'—, *to become commonplace in manner or way of thinking.*

Encaisser (popular), un soufflet, *to receive a smack in the face,* or "buck-horse."

Encarrade, *f.* (thieves'), *entrance.* Lourde d'—, *street door.*

Encarrer (thieves'), *to enter,* "to prat."

Encasquer (thieves'), *to enter,* or "to prat."

> Pour gonfler ses valades
> Encasque dans un rade,
> Sert des sigues à foison.
>   VIDOCQ.

Enceintrer (popular), *to make a woman big with child.* Abbreviation of enceinturer, an expression used in the eighteenth century.

Enchetiber (thieves'), *to apprehend,* "to smug." See **Piper.**

Encible (thieves'), *together.* For ensemble.

Encloué, *m.* (popular), *Sodomist; man without any energy.* A term expressive of utter contempt, and an euphemism for a very coarse word. The literal English rendering may be heard from the mouths of English workmen at least a dozen times in a lapse of as many minutes. The French expression might be rendered in less offensive language by "a snide bally bounder."

> Qu'est-ce qu'il a à m'emmoutarder cet encloué de singe ? cria Bec-Salé.—ZOLA, *L'Assommoir.*

Enclouer (popular), *to take some article to the pawnshop,* "to put in lug," " to blue," or "to lumber."

Encoliflucheter (popular), s'—, *to feel out of sorts; to have the* "blue devils."

Encre, *f.* (familiar), buveur d'—, *clerk,* or "quill-driver."

Encrotter (popular), *to bury.* Crotte, *mud, muck.*

Endécher (popular), *to get one into debt.* S'—, *to run into debt.*

Endormage, *m.* (thieves'), vol à l'—, *robbing a person who has been made unconscious by means of a narcotic.* The rogue who has recourse to this mode of despoiling his victim is termed in English slang "a drummer."

Endormeur, *m.,* *thief.* See **Endormage.**

Endormi, *m.* (popular), *judge,* or "beak."

Endormir (thieves'), *to kill,* "to give one his gruel," "to cook his goose." See **Refroidir.**

Endos, *m.* (popular), *the back.*

Endosse, or **andosse,** *f.* (thieves'), *shoulder ; back.* Raboter l'—, *to beat black and blue.* See **Voie.** Tapis d'—, *shawl.*

Endroguer (thieves'), *is said of a rogue who goes about seeking for a "job,"* quærens quem devoret.

Enfant, *m.* (thieves'), *short crowbar used by housebreakers.* Termed also "Jacques, sucre de pomme, rigolo, biribi, dauphin ; " and by English rogues, "the stick, James, jemmy ;" *strong box,* or "peter ;" — de la matte, *one of the confraternity of thieves,* or "familyman." (Popular) Un — de chœur, *sugar loaf.* Un — de giberne, *soldier's child.* Un — de trente-six pères, *a prostitute's offspring.* (Familiar) Un — de la balle, *an actor's child, or one who follows the same calling as his father.*

Enfifré, *m.* (popular), *Sodomist , slow man,* or "slow coach."

Enfigneur, *m.* (popular and thieves'), *Sodomist.* See **Gousse.**

Enfilage, *m.* (thieves'), *arrest.*

Enfiler (popular), *to take red-handed; to have connection with a woman ;* — des briques, *to be fasting ; to be* "bandied ;" — des perles. See **Perles.** Se faire —, *to be caught in the act of stealing.*

Enflammés, *m. pl.* (military), *soldiers under arrest whose fondness for the fair sex has caused them to delay their attendance at barracks more than is consistent with their military duties, and has brought them into trouble.*

Enflaneller (popular), s'—, *to take a grog,* "a nightcap."

Enflaquer (thieves'), *to seize; to apprehend,* "to smug." See **Piper.** J'ai enflaqué le bogue et le morningue du pante, *I laid hands on the "cove's" watch and purse.*
J'ai manqué d'être enflaqué sur le boulevard du Temple.—VIDOCQ.

S'—, *to be ruining oneself.*

Enflée, *f.* (thieves'), *bladder ; skin which contains brandy or wine.*

Enfler (popular), *to drink,* "to lush." See **Rincer.**

Enfoncé, *adj.* (familiar), *ruined ; outwitted,* "done brown."

Enfoncer (familar), *to outwit one,* "to do one."

Enfonceur, *m.* (familiar), *a business man or financier who makes dupes ; harsh critic ;* (thieves') *swindler,* or "shark ;" — de flancheurs de gadin, *rogue who robs of their halfpence players at the game called* "bouchon" (*played with a cork and halfpence*). He treads on one of the coins, which, by a skilful motion of the foot, remains in the interstices of his worn-out shoe. The "business" is, of course, not a very profitable one.

Enfourailler (thieves'), *to apprehend,* "to smug ;" *to imprison,* "to give the clinch." See **Piper.**

Enfourner (popular), *to imprison,* "to give the clinch." See **Piper.**

Enfrimer (thieves'), *to peer into one's face.*

Engagé, *adj.* (gamblers'), être —, *to have lost heavily at some game.*

Engager (sporting), *to enter a horse for a race.*

Engamé, *adj.* (thieves'), *enraged ; rabid.*

Enganter (thieves'), *to seize ; to steal,* "to nick." En être enganté, *to be in love with.*

> J'ai fait par comblance
> Gironde larguecapé, . . .
> Un jour à la Courtille,
> J'm'en étais enganté.
> VIDOCQ.

K

Engerber (thieves'), *to apprehend,* "to smug." From gerbe, *a sheaf of corn.* See **Piper.**

Engluer (thieves'), la chevêche, *to arrest a gang of rogues.*

Engourdi, *m.* (thieves'), *corpse,* or "cold meat."

Engrailler (thieves'), *to catch, to seize ; —* l'ornie, *to catch a fowl, generally by means of a baited hook.*

Je sais bien aquiger les luques, engrailler l'ornie.—*Le Jargon de l'Argot.* (*I know how to prepare pictures, to catch a fowl.*)

Engrainer (popular), *to arrive,* "to crop up."

Engraisser (thieves'), un poupart, *to make preparations for a theft or murder.* Literally *to fatten a child.*

Engrouiller (popular), s'—, *to stick fast ; to be inert, without energy.*

Engueulade, engueulage, synonymous of **Engueulement.**

Engueulement (popular), *abuse in any but choice language.* Also *insults by an abusive and scurrilous journalist who runs down public or literary men in expressions strongly savouring of the gutter.* Fair specimens of this coarse kind of pen warfare may be found daily in at least one notorious Radical print, which would be thought very tame by its habitual readers if it had not a ready stock of abuse at its disposal, the most ordinary being voleur, bandit, maquereau, scélérat, porc, traître, vendu, ventru, ventripotent, jouisseur, idiot, crétin, gâteux, &c., &c.

Enguirlander (popular), *to circumvent.*

Enlevé, *adj.* (familiar), *spirited.* Un article —, un discours —, *spirited article or speech.*

Enlever (theatrical), *to play with spirit ;* (general) — le ballon à quelqu'un, *to kick one,* "to root," or "to land a kick." (Thieves') S'—, *to be famished.*

Enleveur (theatrical), *actor who plays in dashing, spirited style.*

Enluminer (popular), s'—, *to be in the first stage of intoxication, or* "elevated." See **Sculpter.**

Enluminure, *f.* (popular), *state of slight intoxication.* See **Pompette.**

Ennuyer (popular), s'—, *to be on the point of death.*

Enplaque, *f.* (thieves'), *police,* "the reelers."

Enquiller (thieves'), *to conceal ; —* une thune de camelotte, *to secrete a piece of cloth under one's dress, or between one's thighs.* Also *to enter,* "to prat."

J'enquille dans sa cambriole
Espérant de l'entifler.
VIDOCQ.

Enquilleuse, *f., female thief who conceals stolen property under her apron or between her legs.* From quille, *leg.*

Enquiquiner (popular), *to annoy,* "to spur." Is also expressive of scornful feelings. Je vous enquiquine ! *a hang for you !* S'—, *to feel dull.*

Enrayer (popular), *to renounce love and its pleasures.*

Enrhumer (popular), *to annoy one, to bore one,* "to spur." Termed also " courir quelqu'un."

Enrosser (horse-dealers'), *to conceal the faults of a horse.* (Popular) S'—, *to get lazy,* or "Mondayish."

Ensecréter (showmens'), *to make a puppet ready for the show by dressing it up, &c.*

Enseigne de cimetière, *f.* (thieves'), *priest,* or "devil dodger."

Ensemble, *m.* (artists'), un modèle qui pose l'—, *a model who sits for the whole figure, that is, who poses nude.*

Entablement, *m.* (popular), *shoulders.*

Entailler (thieves'), *to kill one,* "to give one his gruel." See **Refroidir.**

Entame, *f.* (popular), à toi l'— ! *you make the first move !*

Entamer (thieves'), *to make one speak ; to worm out one's secrets.* Si le roué veut entamer tézigue, nib du truc, *if the magistrate tries to pump you, hold your tongue.*

Entauler (thieves'), *to enter,* "to prat."

Entendre (popular), de corne, *to mistake a word for another.* N'— que du vent, *not to be able to make head or tail of what one hears.*

Enterrement, *m.* (popular), *a piece of meat placed in a lump of bread, or an apology for a sandwich ;* (familiar) — de première classe, *grand, but dull ceremony.* Is said also of the total failure of a literary or dramatic production.

Enterver, or **entraver** (thieves'), *to listen ; to hear ; to understand.* Que de baux la muraille enterve ! *take care, the walls have ears !*

Le rupin sortant dehors vit cet écrit, il le lut, mais il n'entervait que floutière ; il demanda au ratichon de son village ce que cela voulait dire mais il n'entervait pas mieux que sezière.—*Le Jargon de l'Argot.*

Entières, *f. pl.* (thieves'), *lentils.*

Entiffer (popular), *to enter ;* (thieves') *to wheedle ; to adorn.*

Ah ! si j'en défouraille,
Ma largue j'entiferai.
J'li f'rai porter fontange,
Et souliers galuchés.
V. HUGO.

Entiffle, *f.* See **Antiffle.**

Entiffler (thieves'), *to wheedle ; to walk,* or "to pad the hoof ;" *to steal,* "to nick," or "to claim." See **Grinchir.**

Entonne, *f.* (thieves'), *church.* Termed also "chique."

Entonnoir, *m.* (popular), *throat,* or "peck-alley ;" — à patte, *drinking glass ;* — de zinc, *a throat which is proof against the strongest spirits.*

Entortillé, *adj.* (popular), *clumsy, awkward, gawky.*

Entravage, *m.* (thieves'), *hearing ; understanding,* "twigging."

Entraver (thieves' and cads'), *to understand,* "to twig." J'entrave pas dans tes vannes, *I don't take that nonsense in, I am not to be humbugged,* "do you see any green in my eye ?" J'entrave pas ton flanche, *I can't understand what you are at.*

En traverse, *f.* (thieves'), *at the hulks.*

Entrecôte, *f.* (popular), de brodeuse, *piece of Brie cheese.* (Thieves') Entrecôte, *sword.*

Entrée, *f.* (popular), de Portugal, *ridiculous rider ;* — des artistes, *anus.*

Entrefilet, *m.* (journalists'), *short newspaper paragraph.*

Entrelardé, *m.* (popular), *a man who is neither fat nor thin.*

Entrer (popular), aux quinze-vingts, *to fall asleep.* Les Quinze-vingts is a government hospital for the blind ; — dans la confrérie

de Saint-Pris, *to get married*, or
"spliced ;" — dans l'infanterie, *to
be pregnant ;* — en tempête, *to fly
into a passion*, "to lose one's
shirt."

Entripaillé, *adj.* (popular), *stout,
with a "corporation" in front.*

Entripailler (popular), s'—, *to
grow stout.*

Entroler, entroller (thieves'), *to
carry away.*

Il mouchailla des ornies de balle qui
morfilaient du grenu en la cour ; alors il
ficha de son sabre sur la tronche à une, il
l'abasourdit, la met dans son gueulard et
l'entrolle.—*Le Jargon de l'Argot.* (*He
saw some turkey cocks which were pecking
at some corn in the yard ; he then cut one
over the head with his sword, killed it,
put it in his wallet, and carried it off.*)

Envelopper (artists'), *to draw the
sketch of a painting.*

Envoyé, *adj.* (familiar), bien —, *a
good hit ! well said !*

Envoyer (general), à la balançoire,
à loustaud, à l'ours, dinguer, à
Chaillot, *to send to the deuce*, see
Chaillot ; — en paradis, *to kill,*
"to give one his gruel ;" — quelqu'un aux pelotes, *to send one to the
deuce.* (Thieves') Envoyer quelqu'un à Niort, *to say no to one, to
refuse ;* —en parade, *to kill.* (Popular and thieves') Se l'—, *to eat,*
"to grub." See **Mastiquer.**

Epais, *m.* (players'), *five and six
of dominoes.*

Epargner (thieves'), n'— le poitou,
to be careful.

N'épargnons le poitou,
Poissons avec adresse,
Messières et gonzesses,
Sans faire de regoût.
VIDOCQ.

Fpatage, *m.* (popular). See
Epatement.

Epatamment (popular), *wonderfully*, "stunningly."

Epatant, épatarouflant, *adj.*
(general), *wonderful ; wondrous,*
"stunning," "crushing."

Epate, *f.* (general), faire de l'—,
to show off.

Epatement, *m.* (general), *astonishment.*

Epater, épataroufler (general),
quelqu'un, *to astound one, to make
him wonder at something or other.*

Epateur, *m.*, **épateuse**, *f.* (general), *one who shows off ; one who
tries to astound people by showing
off.*

Epaule, *f.* (general), changer son
fusil d'—, *to alter one's opinion ;
to change one's mind.*

Epée, *f.* (popular), de Savoyard,
fisticuffs.

Epicé, *adj.* (general), *at an exaggerated price.* C'est diablement
—, *it is a long price.*

Epicemar, *m.* (familiar), *grocer.*

Epicéphale, *m.* (students'), *hat.*
See **Tubard.**

Epicer (popular), *to scoff at ; to deride.*

Epicerie, *f.* (artists'), *the world of
Philistines*, "non digni intrare."

Epice-vinette, *m.* (thieves'),
grocer.

Epicier, *m.* (familiar), *man devoid
of any artistic taste ; mean, vulgar
man ;* termed also "commerçant;"
(students') *one who does not take
up classics at college.*

Epiler (popular), se faire — la
pêche, *to get shaved.*

Epinards (artists'), plat d'—,
*painting where tones of crude
green predominate.* (Popular)
Aller aux —, *to receive money
from a prostitute.*

Epingle, *f.* (popular), avoir une —
à son col, *to have a glass of wine
waiting ready poured out for one
at a neighbouring wine-shop, and
paid for by a friend.*

Epiploon, *m.* (students'), *necktie.*

Epitonner (thieves'), s'—, *to grieve.*

Epointer (popular), son forêt, *to
die,* "to kick the bucket," or
"to snuff it." See **Casser sa
pipe.**

Eponge, *f.* (general), *paramour;
drunkard,* or "lushington ;" — à
sottises, *gullible man,* "gulpin ;"
— d'or, *attorney,* or "green bag."
An allusion to the long bills of
lawyers.

Epouffer (thieves'), *to pounce on
one.*

Epouse, *f.* (familiar), édition belge,
mistress, or "tartlet."

Epouser (thieves'), la camarde, *to
die,* "to croak ;" — la fourcandière, or la fauconnière, *to throw
away stolen property when pursued ;* — la veuve, *to be hanged.*

Eprouvé, *m.* (thieves'), *well-behaved convict who, after having
"done half his time," is recommended for a ticket-of-leave.*

Equerre, *f.* (popular), fendre son —,
to run away, "to make tracks."
See **Patatrot.**

Erailler (thieves'), *to kill one,* "to
cook his goose." See **Refroidir.**

Ereintement, *m.* (familiar), *sharp,
unfriendly criticism.*

Ereinter (familiar), *to run down a
literary work or a literary man ;
to hiss an actor,* "to give the big
bird."

Ereinteur, *m.* (familiar), *scurrilous
or sharp critic.*

Eréné (popular), *exhausted, spent,
done up,* "gruelled."

Ergot, *m.* (popular), se fendre l'—,
to run away, "to make tracks."
See **Patatrot.**

Erlequin (Breton), *frying-pan for
frying pancakes.*

Ernest, *m.* (journalists'), *official
communication from official quarters to the press.*

Erreur, *f.* Y a pas d'— ! *a Parisian
expression used in support of an
assertion.*

Y a pas d'erreur, va ; j'suis un homme,
Un chouett', un zig, un rigolo.
GILL.

Ervoanik plouilio (Breton), *death.*

Es, *m.* (popular), for escroc,
swindler, or "shark."

Esballonner (popular), *to slip away,*
"to mizzle." See **Patatrot.**

Esbigner (popular), s'—, *to slip
away,* "to mizzle." See **Patatrot.**

Esblinder (popular), *to astound.*

Esbloquant, *adj.* (popular), *astounding.*

Esbloquer (popular), *to astound.*
S'—, *to feel astonished.* Ne vous
esbloquez donc pas comme ça, *do
not be so astonished, keep cool.*

Esbrouf (thieves'), d'—, *all at
once ; violently ; by surprise.*

D'esbrouf je l'estourbis.—VIDOCQ. (*I
suddenly knocked him over the head.*)

Esbroufe, esbrouffe, coup à l'—.
See **A l'esbrouffe.**

Esbrouffeur, *m.* (thieves'), *thief
who practises the kind of theft
called* "**Vol à l'esbrouffe**"(which
see).

Esbrouffeuse, *f.,* *flash girl who
makes much fuss.*

Escaff, *m.* (popular), *kick in the breech*.

Escaffer (popular), *to give a kick in the breech*, " to root," or " to land a kick."

Escanne, *f.* (thieves'), à l'—, *away! and the devil take the hindmost*.

Escanner (thieves'), *to run away*, or " to make beef." See Patatrot.

Escarcher (thieves'), *to look on*, " to pipe."

Escare, *f.* (thieves'), *impediment; obstacle; disappointment*.

Escarer (thieves'), *to prevent*.

Escareur (thieves'), *one who prevents*.

Escargot, *m.* (popular), *slow, dull man*, or " stick in the mud;" *vagrant*; — de trottoir, *police officer*, or " crusher." See Pot-à-tabac. (Military) Escargot, *man with his tent when campaigning*.

Escarpe, *m.* (thieves'), *thief and murderer;* — zézigue, *suicide*.

Escarper (thieves'), *to kill*. See Refroidir. Escarper un zigue à la capahut, *to kill a thief in order to rob him of his booty*.

Escarpin, *m.* (popular), de Limousin, or en cuir de brouette, *wooden shoe;* — renifleur, *leaky shoe*.

Escarpiner (popular), s'—, *to escape nimbly; to give the slip*.

Escarpolette, *f.* (theatrical), *practical joke; an addition made to a part*.

Escaver (thieves'). See Escarer.

Esclot, *m.* (popular), *wooden shoe*.

Escouade, *f.* (military), envoyer chercher le parapluie de l'—, *to get rid of a person whose presence is not desired by sending him on a fool's errand*.

Escoutes, or écoutes, *f. pl.* (thieves'), *ears*, or " hearing cheats."

Escrime, *m.* (military), *clerk*, " quill-driver."

Esganacer (thieves'), *to laugh*.

Esgard, or égard, *m.* (thieves'), faire l'—, *to rob an accomplice of his share of the plunder*. The author of this kind of robbery goes among his English brethren by the name of " Poll thief."

Esgour, *adj.* (thieves'), *lost*.

Esgourde, esgouverne, esgourne, *f.* (thieves'), *ear*, or " hearing cheat." Débrider l'—, *to listen*.

Espagnol, *m.* (popular), *louse*.

Espalier, *m.* (theatrical), *a number of female supernumeraries drawn up in line*.

Espèce, *f.* (familiar), *woman of questionable character*.

Esprit, *m.* (familiar), des braves, *brandy*.

Esque, *m.* See Esgard.

Esquinte, *m.* (thieves'), *abyss*. Vol à l'—, *burglary*, "panny," "screwing," or "busting."

Esquintement, *m.* (general), *excessive fatigue;* (thieves') *burglary*, or "busting."

Esquinter (familiar), *to damage; to fatigue;* (popular) *to thrash;* see Voie; (thieves') *to kill;* see Refroidir; *to break*. La caroube s'est esquintée dans la serrante, *the key has been broken in the lock*. (Familiar) S'—, or s'— le tempérament, *to tire oneself out*.

Esquinteur(thieves'), *housebreaker,* "panny-man," "screwsman," or "buster."

Essayer (theatrical), le tremplin, *to act in an unimportant play, which is given as a preliminary to a more important one ; to be the first to sing at a concert.* (Soldiers') Envoyer — une chemise de sapin, *to kill.*

Essence, *f.* (general), de parapluie, *water.*

Esses (popular), faire des —, *to reel about.*

Essuyer (familiar), les plâtres, *to kiss the face of a female whose cheeks are painted.*

Essuyeuse, *f.* (familiar), de plâtres, *street-walker.* See Gadoue.

Estable, *f.* (thieves'), *fowl,* "beaker."

Estaffier, *m.* (familiar), *police officer ;* (thieves') *cat.*

Estaffin (popular), *cat.*

Estaffion, *m.* (popular), *blow on the head,* "bang on the nut ; " (thieves')*cat,* "long-tailed beggar."

Estafiler (military), la frimousse, *to cut one's face with a sword.*

Estafon, *m.* (thieves'), *capon.*

Estampiller (thieves'), *to mark ; to show* (in reference to the hour). Luysard estampillait six plombes, *it was six o'clock by the sun.*

Estaphe, *f.* (popular), *slap.*

Estaphle, *f.* (thieves'), *fowl,* "beaker," or "cackling cheat."

Estime (familiar), succès d'—, *a doubtful success.*

Estio, estoc, *m.* (thieves'), *intellect, wit.* Il a de l'—, *he is clever,* or "wide."

Estomac, *m.* (general), *courage, pluck,* "wool."

Estomaqué, *adj.* (popular), *astounded,* "flabbergasted."

Estorgue, estoque, *f.* (thieves'), *falsehood.* Chasses à l'—, *squinting eyes.*

Estourbir (thieves'), *to stun ; to kill.*

Estourbisseur, *m.* (popular), de clous de girofle, *dentist.*

Estrade, *f.* (thieves'), *boulevard.*

> Le filant sur l'estrade
> D'esbrouf je l'estourbis.
> VIDOCQ.

Estrangouillade, *f.* (popular), *the act of strangling or garrotting a man.*

Estrangouiller (popular), *to strangle ;* — un litre, *to drink a litre of wine.*

Estropier (popular), *to eat,* "to grub." Properly *to maim.*

Estuque, *m.* (thieves'), *share of booty,* or "regulars."

Estuquer (popular), *to thrash,* "to wallop."

Etagère, *f.* (general), *female assistant at restaurants who has the charge of the fruit, &c. ; bosom.*

Etal, *m.* (popular), *bosom.*

Etalage, *m.* (general), vol à l'—, *shoplifting.*

Etaler (familiar), sa marchandise, *to wear a very low dress, thus showing what ought to remain covered.*

Etamé, *adj.* (thieves'), *old offender.* Boule de son —, *white bread.*

Etanche, *f.* (popular), avoir le goulot en —, *to be thirsty, or dry.*

Eteignoir, *m.* (general), *large nose, or large* "conk ; " *dull per-*

son. Ordre de l'—, *the order of Jesuits.* (Thieves') Eteignoir, *préfecture de police, palais de justice, or law courts.*

Eteindre (popular), son gaz, *to die,* " to snuff it."

Eternuer (popular), sur une négresse, *to drink a bottle of wine;* (thieves') — dans le sac, or dans le son, *to be guillotined.*

Pauvre petit Théodore . . . il est bien gentil. C'est dommage d'éternuer dans le son à son âge.—BALZAC.

Etier, *m.,* *a kind of trench dug by the salt-marsh workers.*

Et le pouce, et mèche (popular), *and the rest!* Cette dame a quarante ans. Oui, et le pouce ! *This lady is forty years of age. Yes, and the rest!*

Etoffes, *f. pl.* (thieves'), *money,* "pieces."

Etouffage, *m.* (thieves'), *theft,* or " push; " (popular), *concealment of money on one's person; stealing part of the stakes by a player or looker-on.*

Etouffe, *m.* (thieves'), *clandestine gaming-house.*

Etouffer (popular), *to secrete money about one's person;* — un enfant de chœur, une négresse, *to drink a bottle of wine;* — un perroquet, *to drink a glass of absinthe.*

Etouffoir, *m.* See **Etouffe.**

Etourdir (popular), *to solicit; to entreat.* Properly *to make giddy.*

Etourdissement, *m.* (popular), *soliciting a service.*

Etourdisseur, *m.* (popular), *one who solicits, who asks for a service.*

Etrangère, *f.* (familiar), piquer l'—, *to allow one's thoughts to wan-* der *from a subject,* "to be wool gathering." Noble —, *silver five-franc piece.*

Etrangler (familiar), un perroquet, *to drink a glass of absinthe;* — une dette, *to pay off a debt.*

Etre (gay girls'), à la campagne, *to be confined at the prison of Saint-Lazare* (a prison for women, mostly street-walkers). (Popular) Etre à la cascade, *to be joyous;* —à l'enterrement, *to feel dull;* — à la manque, *to deceive; to betray;* — à la paille, *to be half dead;* — à l'ombre, *to be dead; to be in prison;* — à pot et à feu avec quelqu'un, *to be on intimate terms with one;* — argenté, *to have funds;* — au sac, *to have plenty of money;* — bien, *to be tipsy,* or " to be hoodman; " — bref, *to be short of cash;* — complet, see **Complet;** — crotté, *to be penniless;* (familiar and popular) — dans le troisième dessous, see **Dessous;** — dans les papiers de quelqu'un, *to be in one's confidence;* — dans les vignes, or dans la vigne du Seigneur, *to be drunk;* — dans ses petits souliers, *to be ill at ease;* — de la bonne, *to be lucky;* — de la fête, *to be happy, lucky;* — de la haute, *to belong to the aristocracy; to be a swell;* — de la paroisse de la nigauderie, *to be simple-minded;* — de la paroisse de Saint-Jean le Rond, *to be drunk,* or " screwed; " — de la procession, *to belong to a trade or profession;* — de l'F, see **F;** — démâté, *to be old;* — dessous, *to be drunk;* — du bâtiment, *to belong to a profession mentioned;* — d'un bon suif, *to be ridiculous or badly dressed, to be a* " guy; " — du 14ᵉ bénédictins, *to be a fool;* — en train, *to be getting tipsy,* see **Sculpter;** — exproprié, *to die,* see **Casser sa pipe;** — fort au batonnet, see **Batonnet;** — le bœuf, see **Bœuf;** — paf, *to be drunk,* see **Pompette;** — près de ses pièces, *to be hard up for cash ;* (sailors') — pris dans la balancine, *to be in a fix, in a* "hole;" — vent dessus or vent dedans, *to be drunk,* see **Pompette;** (thieves') — sur la planche, *to be had up before the magistrate ;* — bien portant, *to be at large ;* — dans la purée, — fauché, — molle, *to be penniless ;* (bullies') — sur le sable, *to be without means of existence, that is, without a mistress.* (Familiar) En —, *to be a spy or detective ; to be a Sodomist.*

Etrenner (general), *to receive a thrashing,* "to get a drubbing." See **Voie.**

Etriers, *m. pl.* (cavalry), avoir les — trop courts *is said of a man with bandy legs.*

Etrillage, *m.* (popular), *loss of money.*

Etriller (general), *to fleece,* "to shave."

Etroite, *f.* (popular), faire l'—, *to be affected,* or "high falutin ;" *to play the prude.*

Etron de mouche, *m.* (thieves'), *wax,* conveniently used for taking the impress of keyholes.

Etrusque, *adj.* (familiar), *old-fashioned.*

Et ta sœur (popular), *expression of refusal, disbelief, or a contemptuous reply to insulting words.*

Une fille s'était empoignée avec son amant, à la porte d'un bastringue, l'appelant sale mufe et cochon malade, tandis que l'amant répétait, "et ta sœur?" sans trouver autre chose.—ZOLA.

Etudiant de la grève, *m.* (popular), *mason.*

Etudiante, *f.* (familiar), *student's mistress, his* "tartlet."

Etui, *m.* (popular), *skin,* or "buff;" — à lorgnette, *coffin.* (Soldiers') Etuis de mains courantes, *boots.*

Evanouir (popular), s'—, *to make off,* or "to bunk ;" *to die.* See **Pipe.**

Evanouissement, *m.* (popular), *flight.*

Evaporer (popular), *to steal adroitly.* S'—, *to vanish,* "to mizzle."

Eventail à bourrique, *m.* (popular), *stick,* or "toco."

Eventrer une négresse (popular), *to drink a bottle of wine.*

Evêque de campagne, *m.* (popular), *a hanged person.* From the expression, Bénir des pieds, *to be hanged,* and properly *to bless with one's feet.*

Ever goad he vugale (Breton), *drunkard.* Literally *drinker of his children's blood.*

Exbalancer (thieves'), *to send one away ; to dismiss him.*

Excellent bon, *m.* (familiar), *young dandy.*

Exécuter (familiar), s'—, *to comply with a request ; to fulfil one's promise ; to pay unwillingly rather than otherwise.*

Exhiber (cads'), *to look at,* "to pipe." Nib de flanche, on t'exhibe, *stop your game, they are looking at you.* Exhiber son prussien, *to run away.*

Exhumé, *m.* (familiar), *swell,* "masher." See **Gommeux.**

Expert, *m.* (freemasons'), *a masonic dignity called* "officier de loge."

Expliquer (military and popular), s'—, *to fight a duel ; to fight.*

> Sauf el' bandeau
> Qu'a s'coll' chaqu' fois su' l'coin d'la hure,
> Après qu' nous nous somm's expliqués,
> C'est pas qu' j'aim' y taper dans l'nez ;
> J'haï ça ; c'est cont' ma nature.
>   GILL, *La Muse à Bibi.*

Extra, *m.* (popular), *good dinner ; guest at a military mess.*

Extrait, *m.* (popular), de garni, *dirty servant ; slattern.*

Extravagant, *m.* (popular), *glass of beer of unusual size,* "galopin" being the appellation for a small one. The latter term is quite recent as used with the above signification. According to the *Dict. Comique* it meant formerly *a small measure for wine :—*

> Galopin, c'est une petite mesure de vin, ce qu'on appelle à Paris un demi-setier.— LE ROUX.

 ETRE de l'— (popular), that is, être fichu, flambé, foutu, fricassé, frit, fumé, *to be lost, ruined, or done for,* "cracked up," "gone to smash," "to have run a mucker."

Fabricant, *m.* (popular), de culbutes, or de fourreaux, *tailor,* "snip," or "cabbage contractor, steel-bar driver, goose·persuader," &c. Je me suis carmé d'une bath pelure chez le — de culbutes, *I have bought a fine coat at the tailor's.*

Fabrication, *f.* (thieves'), passer à la —, or être fabriqué, *to be apprehended,* "to be smugged," "to fall." Faire passer à la —, *to apprehend.* See **Piper.**

Fabriquer (thieves'), *to apprehend,* "to smug." See **Piper.** Fabriquer, *to steal,* "to claim," see **Grinchir** ; — un gas à la flan, à la rencontre, or à la dure, *to rob from the person with violence,* "to jump," or "to ramp ;" — un poivrot, *to rob a drunkard.* A rogue who thus takes advantage of a "lushington's" helplessness is termed "poivrier," or "bughunter."

Façade, *f.* (popular), *head,* or "nut ;" *face,* or "mug." Démolir la — à quelqu'un, *to thrash one soundly,* "to knock one into a cocked hat." See **Voie.** (Cocottes') Se faire la —, *to paint one's face,* in other words, "to stick slap" *on one's face.*

Face, *f.* (popular and thieves'), *a sou.*

Je ne donnerais pas une face de ta sorbonne si l'on tenait l'argent.—BALZAC.

Face du Grand Turc, *the behind.* See **Vasistas.**

Face ! *an exclamation used when a smash of glass or crockery is heard,* the word being the French rendering for the exclamation "heads !" at pitch and toss. Avoir des faces, *to have money,* or the "oof-bird."

Facile à la détente (popular), *is said of one who readily settles a debt, or opens the strings of his purse.*

Factionnaire, *m.* (popular), *lump of excrement,* or "quaker." Poser un —, *to ease oneself,* "to bury a quaker." See **Mouscailler.** Relever un —, *to slip out of a workshop in order to go and drink a glass of wine kept ready by a comrade at a neighbouring wine-shop.* Factionnaire, properly *a sentry.*

Facturier, *m.* (theatrical), *one whose spécialité is to produce songs termed* "couplets de facture," *for the stage or music halls.*

Fadage, *m.* (thieves'), *the act of sharing the plunder,* or "cutting it up."

Fadard, *adj. and m.* (popular), *dandy,* or "gorger." For synonyms see **Gommeux.**

Fade, *m.* (popular), *a fop or empty swell,* a "dundreary;" *one's share in the reckoning,* or "shot;" *a workman's wages.* Toucher son —, *to receive one's wages.* (Thieves') Fade, *a rogue's share in the proceeds of a robbery,* or "whack;" *money,* or "pieces."

Puisque je ne l'ai plus, elle, pas plus que je n'ai du fade, Charlot peut aiguiser son couperet, je ne regrette plus ma tête.— *Mémoires de Monsieur Claude.*

Fadé, *adj.* (popular), *drunk,* or "screwed." See **Pompette.** Etre bien —, *to be quite drunk,* or "scammered;" *to have received a good share; to be well treated by fate.* Is used also ironically or sorrowfully: Me voilà bien —! *a bad job for me! Here I am in a fine plight!* (Thieves') Etre —, *to have received one's share of ill-gotten gains; to have had one's* "whack."

Fader (thieves'), *to divide the booty among the participators in a robbery,* "to nap the regulars," or "to cut up."

Fadeurs, *f. pl.* (popular), des —! *nonsense!* "all my eye!" Concerning this English rendering the supplementary *English Glossary* says: "All my eye, *nonsense, untrue.* Sometimes 'All my eye and Betty Martin.' The explanation that it was the beginning of a prayer, 'O mihi beate Martine,' will not hold water. Dr. Butler, when headmaster of Shrewsbury, ... told his boys that it arose from a gipsy woman in Shrewsbury named Betty Martin giving a black eye to a constable, who was chaffed by the boys accordingly. The expression must have been common in 1837, as Dickens gives one of the Brick Lane Temperance testimonials as from 'Betty Martin, widow, one child, and one eye.'—*Pickwick,* ch. xxxiii."

Fafelard, *m.* (thieves'), *passport; bank note,* or "soft;" — à la manque, *forged note,* or "queer soft;" — d'emballage, *warrant of arrest.*

Faffe, *m.* (thieves'), *paper;* — à roulotter, *cigarette paper; bank note,* or "soft."

Fafiot, *m.* (popular and thieves'), *document,* or "fakement;" *shoe,* or "trotter case." See **Ripaton.** Fafiot, *bank note,* or "soft."

Fafiot! n'entendez-vous pas le bruissement du papier de soie?—BALZAC.

Fafiot garaté, *bank note,* or "soft." An allusion to the signature of the cashier M. Garat, which notes of the Banque de France formerly bore.

On invente les billets de banque, le bagne les appelle des fafiots garatés, du nom de Garat, le caissier qui les signe.—BALZAC.

Un — en bas âge, *a one hundred franc note.* Un — femelle, *a five hundred franc note.* Un — lof, *a false begging petition; forged certificate,* or *false passport,* "fakement." Un — mâle, *a one thousand franc note.*

Le billet de mille francs est un fafiot mâle, le billet de cinq cents francs un fafiot femelle.—BALZAC.

Un — sec, *a genuine certificate or passport.* Fabriquer des fafiots, or du fafelard à la manque, *to forge bank notes,* "to fake queer soft."

Fafioteur, *m.* (thieves'), *paper manufacturer or merchant; banker,* "rag-shop boss;" *writer;* (popular) *cobbler,* or "snob."

Faflard. See **Fafelard.**

Fagaut (thieves'), the word faut disguised. Il ne — dégueularder sur sa fiole, *we must say nothing about him.*

Fagot, cotteret, or **falourde,** *m.* (thieves'), *convict,* probably from his being tied up like a bundle of sticks. Un — à perte de vue, *one sentenced to penal servitude for life,* or "lifer." Un — affranchi, *a liberated convict,* or "lag." Un —en campe, *an escaped felon.* (Familiar) Un —, *a candidate for the Ecole des Eaux et Forêts, a government training school for surveyors of State forests and canals.*

Fagotin, *m.* (popular), *vagrant, tramp,* "abraham-man," or "piky."

Faiblard, *m.* (popular), *sickly looking, weak person.* Called in English slang "barber's cat," a term used in connection with an expression too coarse to print, according to the *Slang Dictionary.*

Faignant, *m.* (popular), *coward.* A corruption of fainéant, *idle fellow.*

Failli chien, *m.* (sailors'), *scamp.* Un — de terrien, *a lubberly landsman.*

Le bateau va comme en rivière une gabarre,
Sans personne au compas, et le mousse à la barre,
Il faudrait n'être qu'un failli chien de terrien,
Pour geindre en ce moment et se plaindre de rien.
RICHEPIN, *La Mer.*

Faîne, *f.* (popular), *a sou.*

Fainin, *m.* (popular), *a centime.*

Faire (general), *to steal,* "to prig." See **Grinchir.**

Non qu'ils déboursent rien pour entrer, car ils font
Leur contre-marque aux gens qui sortent. . . .
RICHEPIN, *La Chanson des Gueux.*

Faire son nez, *to look crestfallen, to look* "glum;" — son beurre, *to benefit by; to make profits.*

Il m'a assuré que le général de Carpentras avait plus de quatre millions de rente. Je gagne bien de l'argent, moi, mais je ferais bien mon beurre avec ça.—E. MONTEIL.

(Thieves') **Faire banque,** *to kill,* see **Refroidir;** — un poivrot, *to pick the pockets or steal the clothes of a drunken man,* "bug-hunting;" — des yeux de hareng, *to put a man's eyes out;* —flotter un pante, *to drown one;* — du ragoût or regoût, *to talk about another's actions, and thus to awaken the suspicions of the police.*

Ne fais pas du ragoût sur ton dab ! (n'éveille pas les soupçons sur ton maître !) dit tout bas Jacques Collin.—BALZAC.

Faire la balle élastique, *to go with an empty belly,* "to be bandied." Literally *to be as light as an india-rubber ball;* — la console, or consolation, *one of a series of card-sharping games, termed as follows,* "arranger les pantres," or "bonneteau," "un coup de bonnet," or "parfaite," "flambotté aux rotins," or "anglaise;" — la bride, *to steal watch-guards,* "to buz slangs;" — la fuite, la jat jat, la paire, le patatrot, faire cric, faire vite, *to run away,* "to make beef, or to guy." See **Patatrot.** Faire la grande soulasse sur le trimar, *to murder on the highway;* — la grèce, or plumer le pantre, *to entice a traveller from a railway station into a café, where he is robbed of his money at a swindling game of cards;* — la retourne des baguenaudes, *to pick* the pockets of a helpless man, "to fake a cly ;" — la souris, *to rob stealthily,* "to nip ;" — la tire, *to pick pockets, generally by means of a pair of scissors delicately inserted, or a double-bladed penknife,* "to fake a cly ;" — la tire à la chicane, explained by quotation :—

Ils font la tire à la chicane, en tournant le dos à celui qu'ils dépouillent.—DU CAMP.

Faire la tortue, *to go without any food ;* — le barbot dans une cambriolle, *to steal property from a room,* "to do a crib ;" — le bobe, *to steal watches,* "toy getting ;" — l'égard, *to retain for oneself the proceeds of a robbery ;* — le gaf, *to watch,* "to nark, to give a roasting, to nose, to lay, or to dick ;" — le lézard, *to decamp,* "to guy," see **Patatrot ;** — le morlingue, *to steal a purse,* "to buz a skin or poge ;" — le mouchoir, *to steal pocket-handkerchiefs,* called "stook hauling, fogle hunting, or drawing the wipe ;" — le pantre, *to play the fool ;* — le rendème or rendémi, *to swindle a tradesman by picking up again from his counter a gold coin tendered for payment, and making off with both coin and change ;* — nonne *is said of accomplices,* or "jollies," *who form a small crowd so as to facilitate a thief's operations ;* — la balle à quelqu'un, *to carry out one's instructions.*

Fais sa balle ! (suis ses instructions), dit Fil-de-Soie.—BALZAC, *La Dernière Incarnation de Vautrin.*

Faire son temps, *to undergo a full term of imprisonment ;* — sauter la coupe, *to place, by dexterous manipulation, the cut card on the top, instead of at the bottom of the pack,* termed by English cardsharpers "slipping ;" — suer un chêne, *to kill a man,* "to cook his goose." See **Refroidir.** Faire

sur l'orgue, *to inform against,* "to blow the gaff ;" — un coup à l'esbrouffe, *to pick a person's pockets while hustling him,* "to flimp ;" — un coup d'étal, *to steal property from a shop.* A shoplifter is termed in English cant "buttock and file ;" — un coup de fourchette, *to pick a pocket by delicately inserting two fingers only ;* — coup de roulotte, *to steal property from a vehicle ;* — un rancart, *to procure information ;* — une maison entière, *to break into a house and to massacre all the inmates ;* (artists') — chaud, *to use warm tints in a painting, after the style of Rembrandt and other colourists ;* — culotte, — rôti, *comparative and superlative of* faire chaud ; — cru, *to use crude tints in a picture,* for instance, to use blue or red without any adjunction of another colour ; — cuire sa toile, *to employ very warm tints in the painting of a picture ;* — transparent, *to paint in clair obscur, or "chiaro oscuro ;"* — lanterne, *to exaggerate the "chiaro oscuro ;"* — grenouillard or croustillant, *to paint in masterly, bold, dashing style, with* "brio." The expression is used also in reference to the statuary art. The works of the painter Delacroix and those of the sculptor Préault are executed in that style ; — sa cimaise sur quelqu'un. See **Cimaise.** Faire un pétard, *to paint a sensational picture for the Salon.* The *Salomé* of H. Regnault, his masterpiece, may be termed a "pétard ;" — des crêpes, *to have a grand jollification,* or "flare up ;" (freemasons') — feu, *to drink ;* (theatrical) — feu, *to lay peculiar stress on words ;* (mountebanks') — la manche, *to make a collection of money among the public,* or "nobbing ;" (popular) — à la redresse, *to set one right, to correct one ;* — danser un homme sur une pelle à feu *is said of a woman who freely spends a man's money ;* (familiar and popular) — brûler Moscou, *to mix a large bowl of punch ;* — cabriolet, *to drag oneself along on one's behind ;* — cascader, see **Cascader ;** — de cent sous quatre francs, *to squander one's money ;* — de la musique, *to make audible remarks about a game which is proceeding ;* — de la poussière, *to make a great fuss, to show off ;* — de l'épate, *to show off.*

Ces jeunes troupiers font de l'épate, des embarras si vous aimez mieux.—J. No-RIAC.

Faire du lard, *to sleep ; to stay in bed late in the morning ;* — du suif, *to make unlawful profits, such as those procured by trade assistants who cheat their employers ;* — faire à quelqu'un blanc de sa bourse, *to draw freely on another's purse, to live at his expense,* "to sponge" *on him ;* — flanelle, *to visit a brothel with platonic intentions ;* — godard, *to be starving ;* — la place pour les pavés à ressort, *to pretend to be looking for employment with a secret hope of not finding any ;* — la retape, or le trottoir, *to be a street-walker ;* — l'écureuil, *to give oneself much trouble to little purpose ;* — le plongeon, *to confess when on the point of death ; to be ruined,* "to be smashed up ;" — mal, *to excite contemptuous pity.* Tiens, tu me fais mal ! *well, I pity you ! I am sorry for you !* Faire passer le goût du pain, *to kill,* "to give one his gruel ;" — patrouille, *to go on night revels with a number of boon companions,* "to be on the tiles."

Quatre jours en patrouille, pour dire en folies bachiques.—*Cabarets de Paris.*

Faire peau neuve, *to get new clothes ;* — petite chapelle *is said of a woman who tucks up her clothes ;* — pieds neufs, *to be in childbed,* or "in the straw ;" — pleurer son aveugle, *to void urine,* "to pump ship." See **Lascailler.** Faire saluer le polichinelle, *to be more successful than others.* An allusion to certain games at fairs, when a successful shy brings out a puppet-head like a Jack-in-the-box ; — sa Lucie, or sa Sophie, *to play the prude, to give oneself conceited or disdainful airs ;* — sa merde, or sa poire, *to have self-satisfied, conceited airs ; to take up an arrogant position ; assuming an air of superiority ; to be on the* "high jinks ;" — sa tata *is said of a talkative person, or of one who assumes an air of importance ; of a girl, for example, who plays the little woman ;* — ses petits paquets, *to be dying ;* — son Cambronne, *an euphemism for a coarse expression,* "faire sa merde" (which see) ; — son lézard, *to be dozing during the daytime,* like a lizard basking in the sun ; — un bœuf, *to guillotine ; to give cards ;* — suer, *to annoy ; to disgust.*

Ainsi, leur politique extérieure, vrai ! ça fait suer depuis quelque temps.—ZOLA, *L'Assommoir.*

Faire un tassement, or un trou, *to drink spirits in the course of a meal for the purpose of getting up a fresh appetite,* synonymous of "faire le trou du Normand ;" — une femme, *to succeed in finding a woman willing to give her favours ;* — son fendant, *to bluster ; to swagger ; to look big.* Ne fais donc pas ton fendant, "come off the tall grass !" (an Americanism). Faire une entrée de ballet, *to enter a room without bowing to the company.* En — son

beurre, *to put to good use, to good profit.*

Et, si ton monsieur est bien nippé, demande-lui un vieux paletot, j'en ferai mon beurre.—Zola, *L'Assommoir.*

La — à quelqu'un, *to deceive,* "to bamboozle" *one.* Faut pas m'la faire! may be rendered by "I don't take that in;" "no go;" "not for Joe;" "do you see any green in my eye?" "Walker!"

Vas-tu t' taire, vas tu t' taire,
Celle-là faudrait pas m'la faire,
As-tu fini tes façons?
Celle-là nous la connaissons!
Parisian Song.

La — à, *to seek to impose upon by an affected show of some feigned sentiment.* La — à la pose, *to show off; to pose.*

J' pense malgré moi à la gueule dégoûtée que f'rait un décadent, ou un pessimiste au milieu de ce méli-mêlo. . . . Y nous la f'rait diantrement à la pose.—Trublot, *Cri du Peuple,* Sept., 1886.

La — à la raideur, *to put on a distant manner, to look* "uppish." La — à l'oseille, *to treat one in an off-hand manner; to annoy one,* or "to huff;" *to play a scurvy trick; to exaggerate,* "to come it too strong." According to Delvau, the origin of the expression is the following:—A certain restaurant keeper used to serve up to her clients a mess of eggs and sorrel, in which the sorrel was out of all proportion to the quantity of eggs. One day one of the guests exclaimed in disgust, "Ah! cette fois, tu nous la fais trop à l'oseille!" (Popular) Se — caramboler *is said of a woman who gives her favours.*

Elle sentit très bien, malgré son avachissement, que la culbute de sa petite, en train de se faire caramboler, l'enfonçait davantage . . . oui, ce chameau dénaturé lui emportait le dernier morceau de son honnêteté.—Zola, *L'Assommoir.*

Se — relicher, *to get kissed.*

Ah! bien! qu'elle se laissât surprendre à se faire relicher dehors, elle était sûre de son affaire. . . . Dès qu'elle rentrait, . . . il la regardait bien en face, pour deviner si elle ne rapportait pas une souris sur l'œil, un de ces petits baisers.—Zola, *L'Assommoir.*

S'en — éclater le péritoine, or péter la sous-ventrière, *to eat or drink to excess,* "to scorf." Tu t'en ferais péter la sous-ventrière, or tu t'en ferais mourir, *expressive of ironical refusal; don't you wish you may get it?* or, as the Americans have it, "Yes, in a horn." Se — baiser, or choper, *to get abused; to be apprehended.* See **Piper.** Se — la débinette, *to run away,* "to guy," "to slope." See **Patatrot.** La — belle, *to be happy; to lead a happy life.* Faire des petits pains, du plat, or du boniment, *to eulogize; to try and persuade one into complying with one's wishes;* (military) — suisse, *to drink all by oneself at a café or wine-shop.* The cavalry maintain that infantry soldiers alone are capable of so hideous an offence; (printers') — banque blèche, *to get no pay;* (Sodomists') — de la dentelle, the explanation is furnished by the following quotation:—

Tantôt se plaçant dans une foule, . . . ils provoquent les assistants derrière eux en faisant de la dentelle, c'est à dire en agitant les doigts croisés derrière leur dos, ou ceux qui sont devant à l'aide de la poussette, en leur faisant sentir un corps dur, le plus souvent un long bouchon qu'ils ont disposé dans leur pantalon, de manière à simuler ce qu'on devine et à exciter ainsi les sens de ceux qu'ils jugent capables de céder à leur appel.—Tardieu, *Étude Médico-légale sur les Attentats aux Mœurs.*

(Card-sharpers') Faire le Saint-Jean, *to cough and spit as a signal to confederates.*

L'invitation acceptée, l'amorceur fait le Saint-Jean, c'est-à-dire qu'atteint d'une toux subite, il se détourne pour expectorer bruyamment. A ce signal deux complices

se hâtent de se rendre à l'endroit convenu d'avance.—Pierre Delcourt, *Paris Voleur.*

Faire le saut de coupe, *by dexterous manipulation to place the cut card on the top, instead of at the bottom of the pack,* "to slip" *a card ;* — la carte large, *to insert a card somewhat larger than the rest, and easily recognizable for sharpers' eyes,* this card being called by English sharpers "old gentleman;" — le pont, *cheating trick at cards, by which any particular card is cut by previously curving it by the pressure of the hand,* "bridge;" — le filage, *to substitute a card for another,* "to slip" *it ;* — la carte à l'œil, *to prepare a card in such a manner that it shall be easily recognized by the sharper.* English card-sharpers arrange cards into "concaves and convexes" and "longs and shorts," and term a card almost imperceptibly longer than the rest of the pack "old gentleman;" (thieves' and cads') — la jactance, *to talk ; to question,* or "cross kid ;" — la bourrique, *to inform against,* "to blow the gaff." Le curieux lui a fait la jactance, il a entravé et fait la bourrique, *the judge examined him ; he allowed himself to be outwitted, and peached.* Faire le saut, *to leave without paying for one's reckoning.* Se — enfiler, *to be apprehended,* or "smugged." See Piper. Se — enturer, *to be robbed, swindled ; to lose one's money at a game,* or "to blew it." La — à l'anguille, *to strike one with an eelskin or handkerchief filled with sand.*

Ah ! gredins, dit-il, vous me l'avez faite à l'anguille.... L'anguille ... est cette arme terrible des rôdeurs de barrière qui ne fournit aucune pièce de conviction, une fois qu'on s'en est servi. Elle consiste dans un mouchoir qu'on roule après l'avoir rempli de terre. En tenant cette sorte de fronde par un bout, tout le poids de la terre va à l'autre extrémité et forme une masse redoutable. — A. Laurin, *Le Million de l'Ouvrière.*

Rabelais has the expression "donner l'anguillade," with the signification of *to strike.* (Military schools') Faire une brimade, or brimer, *to ill-treat, to bully,* termed "to brock" at Winchester School.

Fais (popular), j'y —, *I am willing ; I consent.*

Faisan, *m.* See Bande noire.

Faisander (popular), se —, of persons, *to grow old, to become rickety ;* of things, *to be decayed, worn out,* "seedy."

Faisanderie, *f.,* or bande noire, *swindling gang composed of the* "frères de la côte, or de la flotte," *denominated respectively* "grands faisans," "petits faisans," "fusilleurs." See Bande noire.

Faiseur d'œil, *m.* (popular), *Lovelace.*

Faiseuse d'anges, *f.* (familiar), *woman who makes a living by baby-farming, or one who procures a miscarriage by unlawful practices.*

Faitré, *adj.* (thieves'), *lost ; safe for a conviction,* "booked," or "hobbled."

Falot, *m.* (military), *military cap.*

Falourde, *f.* (thieves'), *a returned transport,* a "lag ;" (players') *double six of dominoes ;* (popular) — engourdie, *corpse,* "cold meat."

Falzar, *m.* (popular), *trousers,* "kicks, sit-upons, hams, or trucks." Sans — autour des guibolles, *without any trousers, or with trousers in tatters.*

Familières, *f. pl., female prisoners employed as assistants at the prison*

L

of Saint-Lazare, and who, in consequence, are allowed more freedom than their fellow-convicts.

Fanal, *m.* (popular), *throat,* "gutter lane." S'éclairer le —, *to drink,* or "to wet one's whistle." See **Rincer.** Colle-toi ça dans l'—, *eat or drink that.* Altérer le —, *to make one thirsty.*

Ceux-ci insinuent que cette opération a pour but d'altérer le fanal et de pousser simplement à la consommation.—P. MAHALIN.

Fanande, *m.* (thieves'), abbreviation of fanandel, *m.,* *comrade,* or "pal."

> V'là les fanand's qui radinent,
> Ohé! tas d' pochetés.
> > J. RICHEPIN.

Fanandel, *m.* (thieves'), *comrade, friend,* "pal."

Ce mot fanandel veut dire à la fois: frères, amis, camarades. Tous les voleurs, les forçats, les prisonniers sont fanandels. —BALZAC.

Faner (popular). Mon verre se fane, *my glass is empty.* (Thieves') Fourche à —, *horseman.*

Fanfare, *f.* (popular), sale truc pour la —! exclamation of disgust, *a bad look-out for us!*

Fanfe, *f.* See **Fauve.**

Fanfouiner (thieves'), *to take snuff.*

Fanfouineur, *m.,* **fanfouineuse,** *f.* (thieves'), *person who is in the habit of taking snuff.*

Fantabosse, or **fantasboche,** *m.* (military), *infantry soldier,* "beetle-crusher," or "grabby."

Fantasia, *f.* (familiar), *noisy proceeding more brilliant than useful.* An allusion to the fantasia of Arab horsemen. Donner dans la —, *to be fond of noisily showing off.* (Popular) Une —, *a whim,* or "fad."

Fantassin, *m.* (military), *bolster.*

Faoen (Breton), *riddle.*

Faraud, *m.* (thieves'), *gentleman,* "nib cove."

Faraude, *f.* (thieves'), *lady,* or "burerk."

Faraudec, faraudette, *f.* (thieves'), *young girl,* or "lunan."

Farce, *f.* (general), en avoir la —, *to be able to procure.* Pour deux sous on en a la —, *an expenditure of one penny will procure it for you.* Une — de fumiste, *a practical joke.*

Veut-on savoir d'où vient l'origine de cette locution: une farce de fumiste? Elle provient de la manière d'opérer d'une bande de voleurs fumistes de profession, . . . ils montaient dans les cheminées pour dévaliser les appartements déserts et en faire sortir les objets les plus précieux par les toits.—*Mémoires de Monsieur Claude.*

Farceur, *m.* (artists), *human skeleton serving as a model at the Ecole des Beaux Arts, or the Paris Art School,* thus called on account of its being put to use for practical joking at the expense of newcomers.

Farcher (thieves'), for faucher dans le pont, *to fall into a trap; to allow oneself to be duped,* or "bested."

Fard, *m.* (popular), *falsehood,* or "swack up." Sans —, *without humbug,* "all square." Avoir un coup de —, *to be slightly intoxicated,* or "elevated." See **Pompette.** (Familiar and popular) Piquer un —, *to redden, to blush.* Fard, properly *rouge.* Termed "to blow" at Winchester School.

Fardach (Breton), *worthless people.*

Farder (popular), se —, *to get tipsy,* "to get screwed." For synonyms see **Sculpter.**

Fare, *f.,* *heap of salt in salt-marshes.*

Farfadet, *m.* (popular and thieves'), *horse,* or "prad."

Far-far, farre (popular and thieves'), *quickly, in a* "brace of shakes."

Farfouiller (popular), le — dans le tympan, *to whisper in one's ear.*

Fargue, *m.* (thieves'), *load.*

Farguement, *m.* (thieves'), *loading; deposition of a witness for the prosecution.*

Farguer (thieves'), *to load.*

Si vous êtes fargués de marchandises grinchies (si vous êtes chargés de marchandises volées).—VIDOCQ.

Farguer à la dure, *to pounce upon a person and rob him,* "to jump" *him.* Il fagaut farguer à la dure le gonsarès pour lui dégringolarer son bobinarès, *we must attack the fellow to ease him of his watch.*

Fargueur, *m.* (thieves'), *man who loads; witness for the prosecution.*

Faridole, *f.* (prostitutes'), *female companion.*

Faridon, *f.* (popular), *poverty.* Etre à la —, *to be penniless,* or a "quisby."

Farineux, *adj.* (popular), *excellent, first class,* "tip top, out and out, clipping, slap up, real jam, true marmalade, nap."

Farnandel, for **Fanandel** (which see).

Farrago, *m.* (literary), *manuscript with many alterations and corrections.*

Fassolette, *f.* (thieves'), *handkerchief,* "stook," or "madam."

Fatigue, *f.* (thieves'), *certain amount of labour which convicts have to do at the penal servitude settlement.*

Faubert, *m.* (marines'), *epaulet.* Properly *a mop.*

Faubourg, *m.* (popular), le — souffrant, *the Faubourg Saint Marceau,* one of the poorer districts of Paris. Détruire le — à quelqu'un, *to give one a kick in the breech,* "to root," "to hoof one's bum," or "to land a kick."

Fauchants, faucheux, *m. pl.* (thieves'), *scissors.*

Fauché, *adj.* (thieves'), être —, être dans la purée, or être molle, *to be penniless,* or a "quisby." Etre —, *to be guillotined.* The synonyms are : "être raccourci, être buté, mettre la tête à la fenêtre, éternuer dans le son, or dans le sac, épouser la veuve, jouer à la main chaude, embrasser Charlot, moufionner son mufle dans le son, tirer sa crampe avec la veuve, passer sa bille au glaive, aller à l'Abbaye de Monte-à-regret, passer à la voyante, être mécanisé, être glaivé."

Fauche - ardent, *m.* (thieves'), *snuffers.*

Faucher (popular), le persil, *to be a street-walker.* (Thieves') Faucher, *to deceive,* "to best;" *to steal,* "to claim." For synonyms see **Grinchir.** Faucher, *to guillotine.* See **Fauché.**

Aussitôt les forçats, les ex-galériens, examinent cette mécanique . . . ils l'appellent tout à coup l'Abbaye de Monte-à-Regret ! Ils étudient l'angle décrit par le couperet d'acier et trouvent pour en peindre l'action, le verbe faucher !—BALZAC, *La Dernière Incarnation de Vautrin.*

Faucher dans le pont, *to fall into a trap;* — le colas, *to cut one's throat;* — le grand pré, *to be undergoing a term of penal servitude at a convict settlement.* The convicts formerly were made to work on galleys, the long oar they plied being compared to a scythe and the sea to a large meadow. Lesage, in his *Gil Blas,* terms this "émoucher la mer avec un éventail de vingt pieds." A more recent expression describes it as "écrire ses mémoires avec une plume de quinze pieds."

Fauchettes, *f. pl.* (popular and thieves'), *scissors.*

Faucheur, *m.* (thieves'), *thief who steals watch - chains,* "slang or tackle buzzer ;" *executioner.* Properly *reaper.* Rabelais called him "Rouart," or *he who breaks on the wheel ;* (journalists') *dandy.* From his peculiar gait.

Faucheux, *m.* (thieves'), *scissors ;* (popular) *man with long thin legs,* or "daddy long-legs." Properly *a field spider.*

Fauchon, *m.* (popular), *sword,* "toasting-fork." Un — de satou, *a wooden sword.*

Fauchure, *f.* (thieves'), *a cut inflicted by some sharp instrument or weapon.*

Fauconnier, *m.* (thieves'), *confederate of the proprietor of a gaming-house.*

Faussante, *f.* (thieves'), *false name, alias.*

Fausse-couche, *f.* (popular), *man without any energy, a* "sappy" *fellow.* Properly *a miscarriage.*

Fausse-manche, *f., fatigue jacket worn by the students of the military school of Saint-Cyr.*

Fauve, *f.* (thieves'), *snuff-box,* or "sneezer."

Fauvette, *f.* (thieves'), à tête noire, *gendarme.*

Faux-col, *m.* (familiar), *head of a glass of beer.* Garçon, trop d'faux-col à la clef ! *Waiter, too much head by half !*

Fédéré, *m.* (popular), avoir un — dans la casemate, or un polichinelle dans le tiroir, *to be pregnant,* or "lumpy."

Fée, *f.* (popular and thieves'), *love ; young girl,* or "titter." La — n'est pas loffe, *the girl is no fool.* Gaffine la —, *look at the girl,* "nark the titter."

Féesant, *m.* (thieves'), *lover.* From fée, *love.*

Féesante, *f.* (thieves'), *sweetheart,* or "moll."

Fêlé, *adj.* (popular), avoir le coco —, *to be crazy, to be* "a bit balmy in one's crumpet."

Fêler (popular), se —, *to become crazy.*

Felouse, or fenouse, *f.* (thieves'), *meadow.*

Felouse, felouze, or **fouillouse,** *f.* (thieves'), *pocket,* or "cly ;" — à jeun, *empty pocket.*

Il demanda à sezière s'il n'avait pas quelques luques de son babillard ; il répondit qu'oui, et mit la louche en sa felouze et en tira une, et la ficha au cornet d'épices pour la mouchailler.—*Le Jargon de l'Argot.* (*He asked him whether he had any pictures from his book. He said yes, and put his hand in his pocket, drew one out, and gave it to the friar to look at.*)

Femme, *f.* (familiar), de Breda, *gay girl.* The Quartier Breda is the Paris Pimlico; (popular) — au petit pot, *rag-picker's consort ;* — de terrain, *low prostitute,* or "draggle-tail." See **Gadoue.** (Thieves' and cads') Femme de cavoisi, *dressy prostitute who frequents the Boulevard cafés ;* (military) — de l'adjudant, *lock-up,* "jigger," or "Irish theatre ;" — de régiment, *big drum ;* (familiar) — pur faubourg, *is said of a lady with highly polished manner,* or *ironically of one whose manners are anything but aristocratic.*

Fenasse, *f.* (popular), *man without energy, a lazy man.* Old word *fen, hay.*

Fendante, *f.* (thieves'), *door,* "jigger." Termed also "lourde."

Fendart, *m.* (popular), *braggart, swaggerer,* or "swashbuckler." Termed formerly "avaleur de charrettes ferrées." *Faire son* —, *to brag, to swagger, to look big, to bluster,* "to bulldoze" (American). *Ne fais donc pas ton* —, "come off the tall grass," as the Americans say.

Fendre (thieves'), *l'ergot, to run away.* Literally *to split the spur.* The toes being pressed to the ground in the act are naturally parted. For synonyms, French and English, see **Patatrot.** (Card-sharpers') *Fendre le cul à une carte, to notch a card for cheating purposes;* (military) — *l'oreille, to place on the retired list.* An allusion to the practice of splitting the ears of cavalry horses no longer fit for service and put up for auction, termed "cast" horses. (Popular) *Fendre l'arche à quelqu'un, to bore one to death.* Literally *to split one's head.* (General) *Se* —, *to give oneself or others an unusual treat. Je me fends d'une bouteille, I treat myself to (or I stand treat for) a bottle of wine.*

Zut ! je me fends d'un supplément ! . . . Victor, une troisième confiture !—ZOLA, *Au Bonheur des Dames.*

Se — *à s'écorcher, to be very generous with one's money.*

Fenêtre, *f.* (popular), *boucher une* — *à quelqu'un, to give one a black eye,* "to put one's eyes in half-mourning." *Faire la* —, *is said of a prostitute who lies in wait at a window, and who by sundry alluring signs seeks to entice passers-by into entering the house. Mettre la tête à la* —, *to be guillotined.* An allusion to the passing the head through the lunette or circular aperture of the guillotine.

Fenêtrière, *f.* (popular), *prostitute who lies in wait at a window, whence she invites passers-by to enter.*

Fenouse, or **felouse,** *f.* (thieves'), *meadow.*

Féodec, *adj.* (thieves'), *unjust.*

Fer à repasser, *m.* (popular), *shoe,* or "trotter-case." See **Ripaton.**

Fer-blanc, *m.* (familiar), *de* —, *worthless.* Des rognures de —, *inferior theatrical company.* Un écrivain de —, *author without any ability,* "penny-a-liner."

Ferblanterie, *f.* (familiar), *decorations.*

Ferblantier, *m.* (naval), *official.*

Ferlampier, or **ferlandier,** *m.* (thieves'), *bandit; sharper,* or "hawk;" *thief,* or "prig;" *lazy humbug; rogue,* or "bad egg." *Ferlampié* formerly had the signification of *dunce.*

Ferlingante, *f.* (thieves'), *crockery.*

Ferloques, *f. pl.* (popular), *rags.*

Fermer (popular), *maillard, to sleep,* "to doss." An allusion to M. Maillard, the inventor of iron-plate shutters ; — *son compas, to stop walking;* — *son parapluie, to die.* See **Pipe.** *Fermer son plomb, son égout,* or *sa boîte, to hold one's tongue. Ferme ta boîte,* "shut up !" "hold your jaw !" A synonymous but more polite expression, "Tace is Latin for a candle," is used by Fielding.

"Tace, madam," answered Murphy, "is Latin for a candle ; I commend your prudence."—FIELDING, *Amelia.*

Féroce, *m. and adj.* (familiar), être — sur l'article, *to be strict.* Pas —, *made of poor stuff.* Un —, *one devoted to his duty.*

Ferré, *adj.* (thieves'), être —, *to be locked up,* or "*put away.*"

Ferrer le goujon (popular), *to make one swallow the bait.*

Fertange, or **fertille,** *f.* (thieves'), *straw.*

Tu es un rude mion ; le même pantinois n'est pas maquillé de fertille lansquinée.— V. HUGO, *Les Misérables.* (*You are a stunner ; a child of Paris is not made of wet straw.*)

Fertillante, *f.* (thieves'), *feather ; pen ; tail.*

Fertille, *f.* (thieves'), *face,* or "*mug ;*" *straw,* or "*strommel.*"

Fertilliers, *m. pl.* (thieves'), *wheat.*

Fesse, *f.* (popular), *woman,* "*laced mutton.*" Ma —, *my better half.* Magasin de fesses, *brothel,* or "*nanny-shop.*" (Bullies') Fesse, *paramour,* "*moll.*" Ma — turbine, *my girl is at work.*

Fesser (popular), *to do a thing quickly ;* — le champagne, *to partake freely of champagne,* "*to swig sham or boy.*" Rabelais has the expression, "*fouetter un verre,*" *to toss off the contents of a glass to the last drop.*

Fouette-moi ce verre galentement.—RABELAIS, *Gargantua.*

Feston (popular), faire du —, pincer un —, *to reel about ; to make zigzags under the influence of drink.*

Festonnage, *m.* (popular), *reeling about under the influence of drink.*

Festonner des guibolles (popular), *to reel about while in a state of intoxication.*

Fête, *f.* (popular), de boudin, *Christmas.* (Popular and thieves')

Etre de la —, *to be lucky,* "to have cocum ;" *to have means,* or *to be* "well ballasted."

Moi je suis toujours de la fête, j'ai toujours bogue et bon radin.—VIDOCQ.

Fétiche, *m.* (gamesters'), *marker, or any object which temporarily represents the sum of money which has been staked at some game.*

Feu, *m.* (theatrical), faire —, *to lay particular stress on words ;* (freemasons') *to drink.* (Military) Ne pas s'embêter or s'embrouiller dans les feux de file, *to be independent ; not to stick at trifles.* (Familiar) Allumer les feux, *to set a game going.*

Il est tout et il n'est rien dans ce cercle pschutt. Sa mission est d'allumer les feux, d'où son nom bien connu : l'allumeur.—A. SIRVEN.

Feuille, *f.* (popular), de chou, *ear,* or "wattle." Une — de platane, *a bad cigar,* or "cabbage leaf." (Saumur school of cavalry) Une —, *a prostitute.* (Familiar) Une — de chou, *newspaper of no importance ; a worthless bond, not marketable.* Voir la — à l'envers, *to have carnal intercourse, is said of a girl who gives her favours.* See **Caramboler.** (Military) Feuilles de chou, *gaiters.*

Feuillet, *m.* (roughs'), *leaf of cigarette paper.* Aboule-moi un — et une brouettée d'allumettes, *give me some cigarette paper and a match.*

Feuilletée, *adj.* (familiar), properly *flaky.* Semelle —, *worn-out sole.* Termed also "pompe aspirante."

Parfois aussi elle n'a que des bottines suspectes, à semelles feuilletées qui sourient à l'asphalte avec une gaieté intempestive. —THÉOPHILE GAUTIER.

Fève, *f.,* attraper la —. See **Attraper.**

Fiacre, *m.* (popular), remiser son —, *to become sedate, well-behaved.*

Fiat, *m.* (thieves'), *trust ; confidence.*

Il y a aujourd'hui tant de railles et de cuisiniers, qu'il n'y a plus de fiat du tout.—Vidocq.

Ficard, *m.* (thieves' and cads'), *police officer*, "crusher," "pig," "copper," "reeler," or "bulky." See **Pot-à-tabac.**

Ficeler (familiar and popular), *to do ; to dress.* Bien ficelé, *carefully done ; well dressed.*

Voilà maman Vauquer belle comme un astre, ficelée comme une carotte.—Balzac, *Le Père Goriot.*

Ficelle, *f.* (familiar and popular), *dodge.* Etre —, *to be tricky, a* "dodger."

Cadet Roussel a trois garçons :
L'un est voleur, l'autre est fripon ;
Le troisième est un peu ficelle.
Cadet Roussel (an old song).

(Thieves' and police) Ficelle, *chain or strap.* (Police) Pousser de la —, *to watch a thief ; to give him a* "roasting." (Sporting) Un cheval —, *a horse of very slender build.*

Ficellier, *m.* (popular), *a tricky person who lives by his wits,* "an artful dodger."

Fichaise, *f.* (general), *a worthless thing,* "not worth a curse."

Fichant, *adj.* (popular), *annoying ; tiresome ; disappointing.*

Fichard, *m.* (popular), va t'en au — ! *go to the deuce !*

Fiche (familiar), va te faire — ! *go to the deuce !* Expressive also of disappointment. Je croyais réussir, mais va te faire fiche ! *I thought I should succeed, but no such thing.*

Du pain de son ! des sous de cuivre !
C'est pour nous vivre,
Mais va-t'-fair' fiche !
On nous prend pour des merlifiches.
Richepin.

Je t'en — ! *nonsense ! nothing of the kind !* Il croit réussir je t'en — ! Vous croyez qu'il a tenu sa promesse ? Je t'en — ! Fiche-moi le camp et plus vite que ça, *be off in double quick time,* "sling your hook."

Ficher (thieves'), *to yawn ;* — la colle, *to tell plausible falsehoods ;* — la colle gourdement, *to be an artful beggar ;* (popular) — la misère par quartiers, *to live in poverty ;* — la paresse, *to be idle.*

Je fiche la paresse, je me dorlote.—Zola.

Se — un coup de tampon, *to fight.* Se — de la fiole, or de la bobine de quelqu'un, *to laugh at one ; to seek to make a fool of him.* (Military) Se — un coup de latte, *to fight a duel with cavalry swords.*

Fichtrement (general), *very ; awfully.*

Fichu, *adj.* (general), *put ; given.* Il l'a — à la porte, *he turned him out of doors ; he has given him the* "sack." Fichu comme l'as de pique, comme un paquet de linge sale, *badly dressed ; clumsily built.* Fichu, *capable.* Il est — de ne pas venir, *he is quite capable of not coming at all.*

Fichumacer (popular), for ficher, *to do.* Qu'est-ce que tu fichumaces ? *what are you up to ?*

Fidibus, *m.* (familiar), *pipe-light ; spill.* Lorédan Larchey says :—

Une communication de M. Fey assigne à ce mot une origine allemande. Dans les universités de ce pays, les admonestations officielles commencent par les mots : *fidibus* (pour *fidelibus) discipulis universitatis*, &c. Les délinquants qui allument par forfanterie leurs pipes avec le papier de l'admonestation, lui ont donné pour nom le premier mot de sa première ligne.—*Dict. Hist. d'Argot.*

Fiérot, *m.* (popular), *stuck-up,* "uppish."

Fièvre, *f.* (thieves'), accès de — cérébrale, *accusation on the capital charge ; sentence of death.* Redoublement de —, *aggravating circumstances or new charge made against a prisoner who is already on his trial.*

La Cigogne a la digestion difficile, surtout en fait de redoublement de fièvre (révélation d'un nouveau fait à charge.—BALZAC.

Fiferlin, *m.* (popular), *soldier,* "swaddy," or "wobbler." From fifre, *fife.*

Fifi, *m. and f.* popular), un —, *a scavenger employed at emptying cesspools,* a "gold finder;" *scavenger's cask in which the contents of cesspools are carried away.* Une —, *a thin, skinny girl.*

Les plantureuses et les fifis, les grands carcans et les bassets . . . les rosières comme aussi les enragées qu'ont donné des arrhes à son promis.—TRUBLOT, *Le Cri du Peuple,* Sept., 1886.

Fifi-lolo, *m.* (popular), *one who plays the fool.*

Fifloche, *m.* (popular), *one more skilful than the rest, who leads the quadrille at a dancing hall.*

Fiflot, *m.* (military), *infantry soldier,* "beetle-crusher," "grabby."

Figariste, *m.* (familiar). Properly *a contributor to the Figaro newspaper,* and figuratively *term of contempt applied to unscrupulous journalists.*

Fignard, *m.,* **figne,** *f.* (popular), *the breech,* or "one-eyed cheek." See **Vasistas.**

Fignolade, *f.* (theatrical), *prolonged trilling.*

Fignole, *f. adj.* (thieves'), *pretty,* "dimber."

Alors aboula du sabri,
Moure au brisant comme un cabri,
Une fignole gosseline.
RICHEPIN.

Figuration, *f.* (theatrical), *staff of supernumeraries,* or "sups."

Figure, *f.* (popular), *the breech,* see **Vasistas;** *sheep's head.* Ma —, *myself,* "No. 1."

Figurer (thieves'), *to be in irons.*

Fil, *m.* (thieves'), de soie, *thief,* "prig." See **Grinche.** (Popular) Avoir le —, or connaître le —, *to know what one is about,* "to be up to a dodge or two." N'avoir pas inventé le — à couper le beurre *is said of one who is not particularly bright, who is* "no conjurer." N'avoir plus de — sur la bobine, *to be bald,* or "stag-faced." Prendre un —, *to have a dram of spirits, a drop of* "something damp," or a "drain." Un verre de —, *a glass of brandy.* Une langue qui a le —, *a sharp tongue.*

Filage, *m.* (card-sharpers'), *handling cards in such a manner that trumps will turn up ; juggling away a card as in the three-card trick,* "slipping ;" (thieves') *tracking one.*

Filasse, *f.* (popular), *mattress, bed,* "doss ;" *a piece of roast beef.* Se fourrer dans la —, *to go to bed, to get into the* "kip."

Filature, *f.* (thieves'), *following stealthily a person.* Faire la —, or lâcher de la — à quelqu'un, *to follow a person stealthily, to track one,* "to nose." Prendre en — un voleur, *to follow and watch a thief.* (Familiar) Filature de poivrots, *spirit-shop patronized by confirmed drunkards.*

Filendèche, *m.* (thieves'), *one of the vagabond tribe.*

Lorsque j'occupais mon poste de commissaire de police dans ce dangereux quartier, les habitants sans patente des carrières d'Amérique formaient quatre catégories distinctes : les Hirondelles, les Romanichels, les Filendèches et les Enfants de la loupe. —*Mémoires de Monsieur Claude.*

Fil-en-double, *m.* (popular), *wine.*

Fil-en-trois, fil-en-quatre, fil-en-six, *m.* (popular), *spirits.*

Allons . . . un petit verre de fil en quatre, histoire de se velouter et de se rebomber le torse.—TH. GAUTIER.

Filer (thieves'), *to steal.* See **Grin-chir.** Filer la comète, or la sorgue, *to sleep in the open air ;* — le luctrème, *to open a door by means of a picklock,* "*to screw ;*" — une pelure, *to steal a coat ;* — un sinve, *to dog a man,* "*to nose ;*" — une condition, *to watch a house and get acquainted with the ins and outs in view of a burglary.*

La condition était filée d'avance.
Le rigolo eut bientôt cassé tout !
Du gai plaisir, ils avaient l'espérance,
Quand on est pègre on peut passer partout.

From a song composed by Clément, a burglar (quoted by Pierre Delcourt, *Paris Voleur,* 1886). This poet of the "family men" was indiscreet enough, some days after the burglary described, to sing his production at a wine-shop frequented by thieves, and, unfortunately, by detectives also, with the result that he was sent over the water and given leisure time to commune with the Muses. (Sailors' and popular) Filer son nœud, or son câble, *to go away ; to run away,* "*to cut the cable and run before the wind.*" See **Patatrot.** Filer un nœud, *to spin a yarn.* File ton nœud, *go on with your story or your discourse,* "*pay away.*" With regard to the latter expression the *Slang Dictionary* says :—

Pay-away . . . from the nautical phrase pay-away, meaning to allow a rope to run out of a vessel. When the hearer considers the story quite long enough, he, carrying out the same metaphor, exclaims, "hold on !"

(General) Filer quelqu'un, *to follow one stealthily so as to watch his movements ;* (popular) — la mousse, *to ease oneself.* See **Mouscailler.** Filer le Plato, *to love in a platonic manner ;* — une poussée, *to hustle,* "*to ramp ;*" — des coups de tronche, *to butt at one's adversary with the head ;* — une ratisse, *to thrash,* "*to tan.*" See **Voie.** (Theatrical) Filer une scène, *to skilfully bring a scene to its climax ;* (card-sharpers') — la carte, *to dexterously substitute a card for another, to* "*slip*" *a card.*

Une fois le saut de coupe fait, le grec a le soin d'y glisser une carte large, point de repère marquant l'endroit où il doit faire sauter la coupe au mieux de ses intérêts. . . . Il file la carte, c'est à dire il change une carte pour une autre.—*Mémoires de Monsieur Claude.*

Filet de vinaigre, *m.* (theatrical), *shrill voice, one that sets the teeth on edge.*

Fileur, *m.* (police), *man who dogs one, a* "*nose ;*" (card-sharpers') *one who dexterously substitutes a card for another, who* "*slips*" *a card ;* (thieves') *confederate of the* floueurs *and* emporteurs (*which see*), *who levies a percentage on the proceeds of a card-sharping swindle ; person who follows thieves and extorts money from them by threats of disclosures ; detective ;* (familiar) — de Plato, *platonic lover.*

Fillaudier, *m.* (popular), *one who is fond of the fair sex,* "*mol-rower.*"

Fille, *f.* (familiar and popular), de maison, or — de tourneur, *prostitute in a brothel ; harlot ;* — en carte, *street-walker whose name is in the police books as a registered prostitute.* See **Gadoue.** Grande —, *bottle of wine.* (Familiar) Fille de marbre, *a cold-hearted* *courtesan ;* — de plâtre, *harlot,* "mot." For list of over 140 synonyms see **Gadoue.**

Fillette, *f.* (popular), *half a bottle of wine.*

Filoche, *f.* (thieves'), *purse,* "skin,'" or "poge." Avoir sa — à jeun, *to be penniless,* "hard up."

Filou, *adj.* (popular), *wily,* "up to a dodge or two."

Filsange, *f.* (thieves'), *floss silk.*

Fin, *f.* (thieves'), de la soupe, *guillotine.* See **Voyante.** (Familiar) Faire une —, *to get married,* "spliced," or "hitched" (Americanism).

Fine, *f. and adj.* (popular), *excrement,* or "quaker," abbreviation of "fine moutarde;" (familiar) abbreviation of "fine champagne," *best quality of brandy.* (Thieves') Etre en — pégrène, *to be in great danger ; to be in an* "awful fix."

La raille (la police) est là. . . . Je joue la mislocq (la comédie) pour un fanandel en fine pégrène (un camarade à toute extrémité).—BALZAC.

Finette, *f.* (card-sharpers'), *a pocket wherein are secreted certain cards.*

Il a sous son habit, au dos de son pantalon, une poche dite finette, dans laquelle il place les cartes non biseautées qu'il doit substituer aux siennes.—*Mémoires de Monsieur Claude.*

Fiole, *f.* (familiar), *bottle of wine ;* (popular) *head,* or "tibby;" *face,* or "mug." J'ai soupé de ta —, *I have had enough of you ; I will have nothing more to do with you.* Se ficher de la — à quelqu'un, *to laugh at one.*

On y connaît ma gargarousse,
Ma fiole, mon pif qui retrousse,
Mes calots de mec au gratin.
RICHEPIN.

Pour la — à quelqu'un, *for one.*

Songez qu' ça s'ra l'plus beau jour d'la carrière d'Trutru, toujours sur la brèche, qui s'donne tant d'mal pour vos fioles.—TRUBLOT, *Le Cri du Peuple,* 1886.

Sur la — à quelqu'un, *about one, concerning one.* Il fagaut ne pas dégueularder sur leur —, *we must say nothing about them.*

Fioler (familiar and popular), *to drink ;* — le rogome, *to drink brandy.* (Thieves') Fioler, *to stare at one.*

Fioleur, *m.* (familiar and popular), *one who is too fond of the bottle,* "a lushington."

Fion, coup de —. See **Coup.** (Cads' and thieves') Dire —, *to apologize, to beg one's pardon.*

Fionner (familiar and popular), *to play the dandy.*

Fionneur, *m.* (familiar and popular), *one who plays the dandy.*

Fiquer (thieves'), *to strike ; to stab,* "to chive."

Fiques, *f. pl.* (thieves'), *clothes,* or "clobber."

Fiscal, *adj.* (familiar), *elegant.*

Fish, *m.* (familiar), *women's bully,* or "ponce," generally called "maquereau," *mackerel.* For list of synonyms see **Poisson.**

Fissure, *f.* (popular), avoir une —, *to be slightly crazy,* "to be a little bit balmy in one's crumpet."

Fiston, *m.* (popular), *term of endearment.* Mon—, *my son, sonny.* Mon vieux —, *old fellow.*

Flac, *m.* (thieves'), *sack ;* — d'al, *money-bag ; bed,* or "kip."

Flache, *f.* (popular). See **Flanche.**

Flacons, *m.* (popular), *shoes,* "trotter cases." See **Ripatons.** Déboucher ses —, *to take off one's shoes.*

Flacul, *m.* (thieves'), *bed*, or "kip ; " *money-bag.*

Le vioque a des flaculs pleins de bille ; s'il va à Niort, il faut lui riffauder les pa-turons.—VIDOCQ. *(The old man has bag-fuls of money; if he denies it, we'll burn his feet.)*

Flafla, *m.* (familiar and popular), *great showing off.* Faire du —, *to show off ; to flaunt.*

Flageolet, *m.* (obsolete), *penis*, "John Thomas, or Dick."

Flageolets, *m.* (popular), *legs*, "pegs." Termed also "fume-rons, guibes, guibolles."

Flambant, *m. and adj.* (military), *artillery man*, "son of a gun ; " (familiar and popular) *magnifi-cent*, "slap up, clipping, nap."

Flambard, *m.* (thieves'), *dagger.* Formerly termed "cheery;" (fa-miliar and popular) *one who has dash ; one who shows off.*

Tas d'flambards, tas d'chicards,
Les canotiers de la Seine,
Sont partout, bien reçus,
Et partout font du chahut.
Parisian Song.

Flambarde, *f.* (popular), *pipe.* Termed "dudeen" by the Irish ; (thieves') *candle*, or "glim."

Flambe, *f.* (thieves'), *sword*, or "poker." Petite —, *knife*, or "chive." From Flamberge, name given by Renaud de Montauban (one of the four sons of Aymon who revolted against Charle-magne, and who have been made, together with their one charger Bayard, the heroes of chivalry legends), to his sword, and now used in the expression, Mettre flamberge au vent, *to draw.*

Flamber (mountebanks'), *to per-form ;* (familiar and popular) *to make a show ; to shine.*

Ils voulaient flamber avec l'argent volé, ils achetaient des défroques d'hasard.—E. SUE.

Flambert, *m.* (thieves'), *dagger.* Termed "cheery" in the old Eng-lish cant.

Flambotter aux rottins (card-sharpers'), *kind of swindling game at cards.*

Flamsick, flamsique, *m.* (thieves'), *Flemish.*

Flan, *m.* (thieves'), c'est du —, *it is excellent.* Au —, *it is true.* A la —, *at random*, at "happy go lucky." (Popular) Du — ! *an ejaculation expressive of re-fusal.* See **Nèfles.**

Flanchard, flancheur, *m.* (thieves'), *cunning player ; one who hesi-tates, who backs out.*

Flanche, *m.* (thieves'), *game of cards ; theft ; plant.* Grande—, *roulette or trente et un.* Un — mûr, *preconcerted robbery or crime for the perpetration of which the time has come.* (Popular) Flanche, *dodge ; contrivance ; affair ; job.* Il connaît le —, *he knows the dodge.* Foutu — ! *a bad job !* C'est — ! *it is all right.*

Toujours des injustices ; mais attendons ; c'est point fini c'flanche là.—TRUBLOT, *Le Cri du Peuple,* March, 1886.

(Thieves' and cads') Je n'entrave pas ton—, *I don't understand your game*, "I do not twig," or, as the Americans say, "I don't catch on." Nib du —, on t'exhibe ! *stop your game, they are looking at you !* Si tu es enfilé et si le curieux veut t'entamer, n'entrave pas et nib de tous les flanches, *if you are caught and the magistrate tries to pump you, do not fall into the snare, and keep all the "jobs" dark.*

Flancher (thieves'), *to play cards ;* (popular) *to laugh at ; to back out ; to hesitate ; to dilly-dally,* "to make danger" (sixteenth century).

Flanchet, *m.* (thieves'), *share; participation in a theft.* Foutu —, *bad job.*

> C'est un foutu flanchet.
> Douze longes de tirade,
> Pour une rigolade.
> VIDOCQ.

Flancheur, *m.* (thieves'), *an informer,* a "nark;" *one who backs out; a player;* (popular) — de gadin, *one who takes part in a game played with a cork, topped by a pile of halfpence, which the players try to knock off by aiming at it with a penny.* (Popular and thieves') Enfonceur de — de gadin, *poor wretch who makes a scanty living by robbing of their halfpence the players at the game described above.* He places his foot on the scattered coins, and works it about in such a manner that they find a receptacle in the interstices of his tattered soles.

Flâne, *f.* (popular), *laziness.*

Flanelle, *f.* (prostitutes'), *one who does not pay.* (General) Faire —, *to visit a house of ill-fame with platonic intentions.*

Flanocher (popular), *to be lazy; to saunter lazily about,* "to shool."

Flanquage, *m.* (popular), à la porte, *dismissal,* "the sack."

Flanque. See **Flanche.**

Flanquer une tatouille (general), *to thrash,* "to wallop." See **Voie.**

Flaquadin, *m.* (popular), *poltroon,* or "cow's babe."

Flaque, *f.* (cads' and thieves'), *lady's reticule; lump of excrement,* or "quaker."

Flaquer (popular), *to tell a falsehood; to ease oneself,* "to bury a quaker." See **Mouscailler.**

> V'là vot' fille que j' vous ramène,
> Elle est dans un chouet' état,
> Depuis la barrière du Maine
> Elle n'a fait qu'flaquer dans ses bas.
> *Parisian Song.*

Flaquet, *m.* (thieves'), *fob.* Avoir de la dalle au —, *to have well-filled pockets.*

Flaquot, *m.* (thieves'), *cash-box,* or "peter."

Flasquer (thieves'), *to ease oneself.* See **Mouscailler.** Flasquer du poivre à quelqu'un, *to avoid one; to fly from one.* J'ai flasqué du poivre à la rousse, *I fled from the police.*

Flatar, *m.* (thieves'), *four-wheeler,* or "growler."

Flaupée, flopée, *f.* (popular), *mass of anything; crowd.* Une — de, *much,* or "neddy."

Flauper (popular), *to thrash,* "to wallop." See **Voie.**

Flèche, rottin, or **pélot,** *m.* (thieves' and cads'), *five-centime coin,* or *sou.*

Flémard, *m.* (general), *lazy or "Mondayish" individual; poltroon,* or "cow's babe."

Flème, or **flemme** (general), *fear; laziness.* Lorédan Larchey says : "Flemme est une forme ancienne de notre *flegme.* Ce n'est pas douteux quand on voit dire en Berri *flème* pour manque d'énergie ; en Normandie et en Suisse *fleume;* en provençal et en italien, *flemma.* Sans compter le Trésor de Brunetto Latini qui dit dès le xiiie siècle : '*Flemme est froide et moiste.*'" Avoir la —, *to be afraid.*

> Ça fiche joliment la flème de penser qu'il faut remonter là-haut . . . et jouer !—E. MONTEIL.

Avoir la —, *to be disinclined for work.*

> Aujourd'hui, c'est pas qu'j'ai la flemme.
> Je jure mes grands dieux non qu'j'ai point

c'maudit poil dans la main qu'on m'accuse d'temps en temps d'avoir.—TRUBLOT, *Le Cri du Peuple*, Sept., 1886.

Battre sa —, *to be idling*, or "shooling."

Fleur, *f.* (popular), de macadam, *street-walker.* See Gadoue. Fleur de mai, de mari, *virginity.* (Card-sharpers') Verre en fleurs, *a swindling dodge at cards.* See Verre.

Le coup de cartes par lequel ces messieurs se concilient la fortune, est ce qu'on appelle le verre en fleurs.—VIDOCQ.

Fleurant, *m.* (thieves'), *nosegay ;* (popular) *the behind.* See Va-sistas.

Flibocheuse, *f.* (popular), *fast or* "gay" *girl,* "shoful pullet."

Flic-flac, or fric-frac (thieves'), faire le —, *to pick a lock,* "to screw," "to strike a jigger."

Fligadier, *m.* (thieves'), *sou.*

Flingot, *m.* (general), *butcher's steel ; musket.* Termed formerly "baston à feu."

Flingue, *f.* (naval), *musket.*

Flippe, *f.* (popular), *bad company.*

Fliquadard, *m.* (popular), *police officer,* "bobby," or "blue-bottle." Concerning the latter expression the *Slang Dictionary* says :—"This well-known slang term for a London constable is used by Shakespeare. In Part II. of *King Henry IV.*, act v., scene 4, Doll Tearsheet calls the beadle who is dragging her in, a 'thin man in a censer, a blue-bottle rogue.' This may at first seem singular, but the reason is obvious. The beadles of Bride-well, whose duty it was to whip the women prisoners, were clad in blue." For synonyms of fliqua-dard see Pot-à-tabac.

Flique, *m.* (popular), *commis-saire de police, or petty police magistrate ; police officer,* or "bobby." For synonyms see Pot-à-tabac.

Flopée. See Flaupée.

Floquot, *m.* (thieves'), *drawer.*

Flottant, *m.* (thieves'), *fish ;* (popu-lar) *ball patronized by women's bullies.* Literally *a company of* "poissons," *or bullies.*

Flottard, *m.* (students'), *student preparing for the naval school.*

Flotte, *f.* (students'), *monthly al-lowance.* A boy's weekly allow-ance is termed "allow" at Harrow School. (Popular) Etre de la —, *to be one of a company.* Des flottes, *many ; much,* "neddy." (Thieves') La —, *a gang of swin-dlers and murderers which existed towards* 1825.

La Flotte était composée de membres fa-meux ... ces membres de la haute pègre travaillaient par bandes séparées : Tava-coli l'Italien était un tireur de première force (voleur de poche). ... Cancan, Requin et Pisse-Vinaigre étaient des assassins, des surineurs d'élite. ... Lacenaire fréquen-tait la Flotte sans jamais dire son véritable nom qu'il gardait, en public.—*Mémoires de Monsieur Claude.*

Vendre la —, *to inform against accomplices,* "to turn snitch."

Flotter (popular), *to bathe.* Termed at the R. M. Academy "to tosh ;" *to swim.* (Popular and thieves') Faire —, *to drown.*

Nous l'avons fait flotter après lui avoir grinchi la négresse qu'elle portait sous le bras.—E. SUE.

Flotteur, *m.* (popular), *swimmer.*

Flou (thieves'), abbreviation of floutière, *nothing.* J'ai fait le —, *I found nothing to steal.*

Flouant, *m.* (thieves'), *game* (flouer, *to swindle*). Grand —, *high play.*

Flouchipe, *m.* (popular), *swindler,* or "shark." From flouer and chiper, *to swindle and to prig.*

Floue, *f.* (thieves'), *crowd,* "push or scuff." The anagram of foule, *crowd,* or else from flouer, *to swindle,* through an association of ideas.

Floué, *adj.* (general), *swindled, taken in,* "sold," "done brown."

Alors, en deux mots, il leur raconte la scène, le traité brûlé, l'affaire flambée . . . — Ah ! la drogue . . . je suis flouée . . . dit Séphora.—A. DAUDET.

Flouer, *f.* (general), *to cheat,* "to do," "to bilk ;" (thieves') *to play cards,* playing being, with thieves, synonymous of cheating.

S'il y avait des brèmes on pourrait flouer. —VIDOCQ.

Flouerie, *f.* (general), *swindle,* "take in," or "bilk."

La flouerie est au vol ce que la course est à la marche : c'est le progrès, le perfectionnement scientifique.—PHILIPON.

Floueur, *m.* (thieves'), *card-sharper who entices country folks or strangers into a café where, aided by confederates, he robs them at a swindling game of cards.*

Floume, *f.* (thieves'), *woman,* "muslin," or "hay bag."

Floutière (thieves'), *nothing.*

C'est qu'un de ces luisans, un marcandier alla demander la thune à un pipet et le rupin ne lui ficha que floutière.—*Le Jargon de l'Argot.* (*One day a mendicant went to ask for alms at a mansion, and the master gave him nothing.*)

Flu (Breton), *thrashing.*

Flubart, *m.* (thieves'), *fear,* "funk." N'avoir pas le —, *to be fearless.*

Flume, *adj. and m.* (popular), être —, *to be phlegmatic ; slow.*

Flûte, *f.* (familiar and popular), *bottle of wine ; glass of beer ; syringe.* Flûte ! *go to the deuce !*

Ah ! flûte !—Ah ! tu vois bien que je t'embête !—Pourquoi? Tu m'as dit "flûte !" —Oui, flûte ! zut ! tout ce que tu voudras ; mais fiche-moi la paix.—E. MONTEIL, *Cornebois.*

Joueur de —, *hospital assistant.* An allusion to his functions concerning the administering of clysters. (Military) Flûte, *cannon.* Termed also "brutal," sifflet."

Flûtencul, *m.* (popular), *an apothecary,* or "clyster pipe." Spelt formerly flutencu. The *Dictionnaire Comique* has the following :—

Peste soit du courteau de boutique et du flutencu.—*Pièces Comiques.*

Flûter (familiar and popular), *to drink.* See **Rincer.** Flûter, *to give a clyster.* The *Dictionnaire Comique* (1635) has the phrase, Se faire — au derrière, "façon de parler burlesque, pour dire, se faire donner un lavement." Envoyer —, *to send to the deuce.* C'est comme si vous flûtiez, *it is no use talking.*

Flûtes, *f. pl.* (popular), *legs,* or "pegs." Termed also flûtes à café.

Fort des flûtes et de la pince, Il était respecté, Navet.
RICHEPIN.

Astiquer ses —, *to dance,* "to shake a leg." Jouer des —, *to run,* "to cut." Se tirer les —, *to run away,* "to hop the twig." See **Patatrot.**

Flûtiste, *m.* (popular), *hospital attendant.*

Flux, *m.* (popular), avoir le —, *to be afraid.* Literally *to be suffering from diarrhœa.*

Fluxion, *f.* (popular), avoir une —, *to be afraid,* "to be funky."

Fœtus, *m., first year student at the military school of surgery.*

Fogner (popular), *to ease oneself, to go to the* "crapping ken." See **Mouscailler.**

Foie, *m.* (popular), avoir du —, *to be courageous, plucky, to have* "hackle." Avoir les foies blancs, *to be a coward,* a "cow's babe."

Foin, *m.* (popular), faire du —, *to make a noise,* "to kick up a row;" *to bustle about; to dance.*

Foire, *f.* (popular and thieves'), acheter à la — d'empoigne, *to steal,* "to claim." See **Grinchir.** Foire, *fair,* and empoigner, *to seize.*

Foiron, *m.* (popular), *behind.* From foire, *diarrhœa.* See **Vasistas.**

Foncé, *adj.* (popular), *well off,* "well ballasted." See **Monacos.**

Foncer (familiar and popular), à l'appointement, *to furnish funds* (*Dictionnaire Comique*). (Thieves') Foncer, *to give,* "to dub."

> Et si tezig tient à sa boule,
> Fonce ta largue et qu'elle aboule,
> Sans limace nous cambrouser.
> RICHEPIN.

Villon (fifteenth century) uses the word with the signification of *to give money :—*

> M. Servons marchans pour la pitance,
> Pour *fructus ventris,* pour la pance.
> B. On y gaigneroit ses despens.
> M. Et de foncer? B. Bonne asseurance,
> Petite foy, large conscience;
> Tu n'y scez riens et y aprens.
> *Dialogue de Messieurs de Malepaye et de Baillevent.*

(Popular) Se —, *to be getting drunk,* or "muddled." See **Sculpter.**

Fond (popular), d'estomac, *thick soup.* (General) Etre à — de cale, *to be penniless,* "hard up." Literally *to be down in the hold.*

Fondant, *m.* (popular and thieves'), *butter,* or "cow's grease."

Fondante, *f.* (popular and thieves'), *slice of bread and butter.*

Fondre (popular), *to grow thin;* — la cloche, *to settle some piece of business.* (Theatrical) Faire — la trappe, *to lower a trap door.*

Fondrière, *f.* (thieves'), *pocket,* "cly," "sky-rocket," or "brigh." Termed also "profonde, fouillouse, fouille, four banal, baguenaude."

Fonfe, *f.* (thieves'), *snuff-box,* or "sneezer."

Fontaine, *f.* (popular), n'avoir plus de cresson sur la —, *to be bald; to have* "a bladder of lard."

Fonts de baptême, *m.* (popular), se mettre sur les —, *to be involved in business from which one would like to back out.*

Forage, *m.* (thieves'), vol au —, *robbery from a shop.* A piece of the shutter being cut out, a rod with hook affixed is passed through the aperture, and the property abstracted.

Foresque, *m.* (thieves'), *tradesman at a fair.*

Foret, *m.* (popular), épointer son —, *to die,* "to kick the bucket." Foret, properly *drill, borer.* With respect to the English slang expression, the *Slang Dictionary* says the real signification of this phrase is to commit suicide by hanging, from a method planned and carried out by an ostler at an inn on the Great North Road. Standing on a bucket, he tied himself up to a beam in the stable; he then kicked the bucket away from under his feet, and in a few seconds was dead. The natives of the West Indies have converted the expression into "kickeraboo." (Thieves') Foret de Mont-rubin, *sewer.*

Forêt-noire, *f.* (thieves'), *a church, a temple.* Termed also "entonne, rampante."

Forfante, *f.* (thieves'), *bragging, big talk.* An abbreviation of forfanterie.

Forgerie, *f.* (popular), *falsehood,* or "cram."

Fort, *adj.* (popular), en mie, *fat,* "crummy;" (familiar) — en thème, *clever student.* The expression is sometimes applied ironically to a man who is clever at nothing else than book-work. C'est — de café, *it is hard to believe, it is* "coming it too strong."

C'est un pauvre manchot qui s'est approché de la vierge. . . . Et elle a éternué ? Non, c'est le bras du manchot qui a poussé —elle est fort de café, celle-là !—E. MONTEIL.

Fortanche, *f.* (thieves'), *fortune.*

Fortifes, *f. pl.* (popular), *fortifications round Paris.* A favourite resort for workmen who go for an outing, and a place which vagabonds patronize at night.

J' couch' que'qu'fois dans les fortifes ;
Mais on s'enrhum' du cerveau.
L'lend'main, on fait l'chat qui r'niffe,
Et l'blair coul'comme un nez d'veau.
         RICHEPIN.

Fortification, *f.* (popular), *cushion of a billiard table.* Etre protégé par les fortifications, *to have one's ball under the cushion.*

Fortin, *m.* (thieves'), *pepper.* From fort, *strong.*

Fortinière, *f.* (thieves'), *pepper-box.*

Fosse aux lions, *f.* (familiar), *box at the opera occupied by men of fashion.*

Fossile, *m.* (literary), *a disrespectful epithet for the learned members of the Académie Française.*

Fou, *adj.* (popular and thieves'), abbreviation of foutu, *lost, done for.*

Fouailler (familiar and popular), *to miss one's effect ; to be lacking in energy ; to back out ; to fail in business,* "to go to smash."

Fouailleur, *m.* (popular), *milksop,* a "sappy" *fellow ; a libertine,* or "rip."

Fouataison, *f.* (thieves'), *stick ;* — lingrée, *sword-stick ;* — mastarée, *loaded stick.*

Foucade, *f.* (popular), *sudden thought or action ; whim,* or "fad." Travailler par foucades, *to work by fits and starts.*

Fouchtra (familiar), *native of Auvergne, generally a coal retailer or water carrier.* From their favourite oath.

Fouette-cul, *m.* (popular), *schoolmaster,* or "bum brusher."

Fouetter (popular), *to emit a bad smell ;* — de la carafe, *to have an offensive breath.*

Tout cela se fond dans une buée de pestilence . . . et, comme on dit dans ce monde-là, ça remue, ça danse, ça fouette, ça trouillotte, ça chelipotte, en un mot ça pue ferme.—RICHEPIN, *Le Pavé.*

Fouetteux de chats, *m.* (popular), *a poor simpleton with no heart for work,* "a sap or sapscull."

Foufière, *f.* (thieves'), *watch,* "tatler, toy, or thimble."

Fouille, *f.* (popular and thieves'), *pocket,* "sky-rocket, cly."

Fouille-au-tas, *m.* (popular), *rag-picker,* or "tot finder."

Fouille-merde, *m.* (popular), *scavenger employed in emptying cesspools,* "gold finder ;" *also a very inquisitive man.*

Fouiller (familiar and popular), pouvoir se —, *to be compelled to do without ; to be certain of not getting.* Also expressive of ironical refusal. Si vous croyez qu'il va vous prêter cette somme, vous pouvez vous —, *if you reckon on his lending you that sum, you will have to do without it.* Tu peux te —, *you shall not have it ; you be hanged!*

Madame, daignerez-vous accepter mon bras?—Tu peux te fouiller, Calicot!—P. Mahalin.

Fouilles, *f. pl.* (popular), des — ! *is expressive of refusal;* may be rendered by the American "yes, in a horn." For synonyms see **Nèfles.**

Fouillouse, *f.* (thieves'), *pocket,* or "cly." The word is old. Rabelais has "Plus d'aubert n'estoit en fouillouse."

Fouinard, *m.* (popular), *cunning, sly man; a tricky* "dodger;" *coward,* or "cow's babe." Termed in old French tapineux.

Fouiner (popular), *to play the spy, or Paul Pry; to escape,* "to mizzle."

Foulage, *m.* (popular), *a great deal of work,* much "graft or elbow grease."

Foulard rouge, *m.* (popular), *woman's bully,* "pensioner." For synonymous expressions see **Poisson.**

Fouler (familiar), se la —, *to work hard.* Ne pas se — le poignet, *to take it easy.*

Du tonnerre si l'on me repince à l'enclume ! voilà cinq jours que je me la foule, je puis bien le balancer . . . s'il me fiche un abatage, je l'envoie à Chaillot.—Zola, *L'Assommoir.*

Foultitude, *f.* (popular), *many, much,* "neddy" (Irish).

Four, *m.* (familiar), *failure.* Faire —, *to be unsuccessful.* Un — complet, *a dead failure.* (Theatrical) Four, *the upper part of the house in a theatre.* An allusion to the heated atmosphere, like

that of an oven ; (popular) *throat,* or "gutter lane." Chauffer le —, *to eat or drink.* (Thieves') Un — banal, *an omnibus,* or "chariot ;" *a pocket,* or "cly."

Fourailler (thieves'), *to sell; to barter,* "to fence."

Fouraillis, *m.* (thieves'), *house of a receiver of stolen property, of a* "fence."

Fourbi, *m.* (thieves'), *the proceeds of stolen property;* (popular and military) *more or less unlawful profits on provisions and stores, or other goods; dodge; routine of the details of some trade or profession.*

Puis il faisait sa tournée, . . . rétablissait d'un coup de poing ou d'une secousse la symétrie d'un pied de lit, en vieux soldat sorti des rangs et qui connaît le fourbi du métier.—G. Courteline.

Connaître le —, *to be wide-awake,* "to know what's o'clock." Du —, *goods and chattels,* or "traps," termed "swag" in Australia; *furniture, movables,* or "marbles."

Voilà ce que c'est d'avoir tant de fourbi, dit un ouvrier . . . lui aussi, il a déménagé . . . emportant toute sa smala dans une charrette à bras.—Richepin, *Le Pavé.*

(Popular) Fourbi, *occupation.* A ce — là on ne s'enrichit pas, *one does not get rich at that occupation, at that game.*

Fourcandière, *f.* (thieves'), épouser la —, *to get rid of stolen property by casting it away when pursued.*

Fourche à faner, *f.* (thieves'), *horseman.*

Fourchette, *f.* (military), *bayonet.* Travailler à la —, *to fight with cold steel.* (Popular) Marquer à la —, *is said of a tradesman who draws up an incorrect account, to his own advantage, of course.* (Thieves') Vol à la —, *dexterous way of picking a pocket with two fingers only.*

M

Fourchettes, *f. pl.* (popular), *fingers,* "dooks;" *legs,* "pins;" — d'Adam, *fingers.* Jouer des —, *to run away,* "to hop the twig." See **Patatrot.**

Fourchu, *m.* (thieves'), *ox,* or "mooer."

Fourgat, or **fourgasse,** *m.* (thieves'), *receiver of stolen goods,* or "fence."

Le père Vestiaire était ce qu'on appelle dans l'argot des voleurs un fourgat (recéleur).—*Mémoires de Monsieur Claude.*

Fourgatte, *f.* (thieves'), *female receiver of stolen goods,* "fence."

Viens avec moi chez ma fourgatte, je suis sûr qu'elle nous prêtera quatre ou cinq tunes de cinq balles (pièces de cinq francs). —Vidocq.

Fourgature, *f.* (thieves'), *stock of stolen property for sale.*

Fourgonnier, *m.* (thieves'), *canteen man at the transport settlement.*

Fourgue, *m.* See **Fourgat.**

Fourguer (thieves'), *to sell,* or "to do;" *to sell or buy stolen property,* "to fence."

Elle ne fourgue que de la blanquette, des bogues et des broquilles (elle n'achète que de l'argenterie, des montres et des bijoux).—Vidocq.

Fourgueroles, *f. pl.* (thieves'), *stolen property,* "swag." Laver les —, or la camelotte, *to sell stolen property.*

Fourgueur, *m.* (thieves' and cads'), *seller, hawker;* — de flanches, *man who goes about offering for sale prohibited articles, such as certain indecent cards called* "cartes transparentes," *or contraband lucifer matches, the right of manufacture and sale of which is a monopoly granted by government to a single company.*

Fourline, fourlineur, *m.* (thieves'), *thief,* "prig." For synonyms see **Grinche.**

Fourliner (thieves'), *to steal,* "to nick;" *to pick pockets,* "to buz a cly."

Fourlineur, *m.* (thieves'), *pickpocket,* or "buz-faker."

Fourloure, *m.* (thieves'), *sick man.*

Fourlourer (thieves'), *to murder.* See **Refroidir.**

Fourloureur, *m.* (thieves'), *murderer.*

Fourmillante, *f.* (thieves'), *crowd,* "push," or "scuff."

Fourmiller (thieves'), *to move about in a crowd for the purpose of picking pockets.* Termed by English thieves "cross-fanning."

Fourmillon, *m.* (thieves'), *market;* — à gayets, *horse fair;* — au beurre, *Stock Exchange.* Literally *money market.*

Fourneau, *m.* (popular), *fool,* or "bounder;" *vagabond who sleeps in the open air; term of contempt.* Va donc eh ! —! *go along, you* "bally bounder."

J'lui dis : de t'voir j'suis aise,
Mais les feux d'l'amour ; nisco.
Quoi, m'dit-ell' : t'as mêm' plus d'braise !
Va donc, vieux fourneau !
Music-hall Song.

Fournier, *m.* (popular), *waiter whose functions are to pour out coffee for the customers.*

Fournil, *m.* (popular and thieves'), *bed,* "doss," or "bug walk."

Fournion, *m.* (popular), *insect.*

Fournir Martin (popular), *to wear furs.* Martin is the French equivalent for Bruin.

Fourobe, *f.* (thieves'), *overhauling of convict's clothes,* "ruling over."

Fourobé (thieves'), *one who has been searched,* or "turned over."

Fourober (thieves'), *to search on one's person,* "to frisk," or "to rule over."

Fourquer. See **Fourguer**.

Fourreau, *m.* (familiar), *lady's dress which fits tightly and shows the figure;* (popular and thieves') *trousers,* "hams, sit-upons, or kicks." Je me suis carmé d'un bate —, *I have bought for myself a fine pair of trousers.*

Fourrée, *adj.* (thieves'), pièce —, *coin which has been gouged out.*

Fourrer (familiar and popular), se — le doigt dans l'œil, *to be mistaken; to labour under a delusion.*

A la fin c'est vexant, car je vois clair, ils ont l'air de me croire mal élevée ... ah ! bien ! mon petit, en voilà qui se fourrent le doigt dans l'œil.—Zola, *Nana.*

Se — le doigt dans l'œil jusqu'au coude, *superlative of above.* S'en — dans le gilet, *to drink heavily,* "to swill."

Fourrier de la loupe, *m.* (popular), *lazy fellow,* or "bummer;" *loafer; roysterer,* "merry pin."

Fourrures, *f. pl.* (familiar), see **Pays ;** (fishermens') *plug used for stopping up holes in a boat.*

Foutaise, *f.* (popular), *worthless thing,* or "not worth a curse ;" *nonsense,* or "fiddle faddle ;" *humbug.* Tout ça c'est d'la —, *that's all nonsense,* "rot."

Fouterie, *f.* (popular), *nonsense,* "rot." C'est de la — de peau, *that's sheer nonsense.*

Foutimacer, foutimasser (popular), *to do worthless work; to talk nonsense.*

Foutimacier, foutimacière (popular), *unskilled workman or workwoman ; silly person,* or "bounder."

Foutimasseur. See **Foutimacier.**

Foutoir (familiar and popular), *house of ill-fame,* "academy ;" *disreputable house ;* — ambulant, *cab.*

Foutre (general), a coarse expression which has many significations, *to give; to do; to have connection with a woman, &c. ;* — du tabac, *to thrash.* See **Voie.** Foutre dedans, *to impose upon ; to imprison.*

Et qu'à la fin, le chef voulait m'fout' dedans, en disant que je commençais à l'embêter.—G. COURTELINE.

Foutre le camp, *to be off ; to decamp,* "to hook it."

Chargez-vous ça sur les épaules et foutez le camp, qu'on ne vous voie plus.—G. COURTELINE.

Foutre, *to put ; to send.*

Pa'c'que j'aime le vin,
Nom d'un chien !
Va-t-on pas m'fout' au bagne.
RICHEPIN.

Foutre la paix, *to leave one alone.*

Vous refusez formellement, c'est bien entendu ?—Formellement ! Foutez-nous la paix.—G. COURTELINE.

Foutre un coup de pied dans les jambes, *to borrow money,* "to break shins ;" — une pile, *to thrash,* "to wallop." See **Voie.** Foutre la misère, *to live in poverty.*

Il ajoutait ... que, sacrédié ! la gamine était, aussi, trop jolie pour foutre la misère à son âge.—Zola, *L'Assommoir.*

En — son billet, *to assure one of the certainty of a fact.* Je t'en fous mon billet or mon petit turlututu, *I give you my word 'tis a fact,* "my Davy" on it. Ne pas — un radis, *not to give a penny.* N en pas — un clou, un coup, or une secousse, *to be superlatively idle.*

Ces bougres-là sont épatants, ils n'en foutraient pas une secousse si on avait le malheur de les laisser faire.—G. COURTELINE.

Se — de quelque chose, *not to care a straw,* "a hang," *for.* Se — de quelqu'un, *not to care a straw for one ; to laugh at one ; to make game of one.*

Hein ? Bosc n'est pas là ? Est-ce qu'il se fout de moi, à la fin !—ZOLA, *Nana.*

Se — du peuple, du public, *to disregard, to set at defiance people's opinion ; to make game of people.* Se — par terre, *to fall.* Se — mal, *to dress badly.* Se — une partie de billard sur le torse, *to play billiards,* or "spoof." Se — un coup de tampon, *to fight.* S'en — comme de Colin Tampon, *not to care a straw.* Se — une bosse, *to do anything, or indulge in anything to excess.* (Military) Foutre au clou, *to imprison,* "to roost."

Comme ça on nous fout au clou ?—C'est probable, dit le brigadier.—G. COURTELINE.

Foutre ! *an ejaculation of anger, astonishment, or used as an expletive.*

Ah ! ça, foutre ! parlerez-vous ? Etesvous une brute, oui ou non ?—G. COURTELINE.

Foutreau, *m.* (popular), *row,* or "shindy ;" *fight.*

Oh ! il va y avoir du foutreau, le commandant s'est frotté les mains.—BALZAC.

Foutriquet, *m.* (familiar and popular), expressive of contempt : *diminutive man ; despicable adversary.* The appellation was applied as a nickname to M. Thiers by the insurgents of 1871.

Foutro, *m.* (military), *a game played in military hospitals.* A handkerchief twisted into hard knots, and termed M. Lefoutro, is laid on a table, and taken up now and then to be used as an instrument of punishment ; any offence against M. Lefoutro being at once dealt with by an application of his representative to the outstretched palm of the culprit.

Halte au jeu ! par l'ordre du roi, je déconsigne M. Lefoutro. . . . Votre main, coupable. L'interpellé tendit la main dans laquelle Lagrappe lança à tour de bras trois énormes coups de foutro, accompagnés de ces paroles sacramentelles : faute faite, faute à payer, rien à réclamer, réclamezvous ? . . . Oui, monsieur, je réclame. Eh bien, . . . c'est parceque vous avez levé les yeux. . . . C'était une impolitesse à l'égard de M. Lefoutro, et M. Lefoutro ne veut pas que vous lui manquiez de respect.— G. COURTELINE, *Les Gaietés de l'Escadron.*

Foutu, *adj.* (general), *put ; made ; bad ; wretched ; unpleasant ; ruined ; lost,* &c.

La police ! dit-elle toute blanche. Ah ! nom d'un chien ! pas de chance ! . . . nous sommes foutues !—ZOLA, *Nana.*

Foutu, *given.*

Qu'est-ce qui m'a foutu un brigadier comme ça ! Vous n'avez pas de honte . . . de laisser votre peloton dans un état pareil. —G. COURTELINE.

Il s'est — à rire, *he began to laugh.* On lui a — son paquet, *he got reprimanded ; dismissed from his employment,* or "got the sack." Un homme mal — or — comme quatre sous, *a badly dressed or clumsily built man.* Un travail mal —, *clumsy work.* C'est un homme —, *he is a ruined man,* "on his beam ends." Il est —, *it is all up with him,* "done for." Un — cheval, *a sorry nag,* a "screw." Un — temps, *wretched weather.* Une foutue affaire, *a wretched business.* Une foutue canaille, *a scamp.* (Thieves') C'est un — flanchet, *it is a bad job, an unlucky event.*

Fouyou (theatrical), *urchin ;* (familiar) — ! *you cad!* "rank outsider."

Fracassé, *adj.* (thieves'), *dressed in a coat.* From un frac, *a frockcoat, dress coat.*

Fracasser (popular), quelqu'un, *to abuse one,* "to slang one ; " *to ill-use one,* " to man-handle." Literally *to smash.*

Fraction, *f.* (thieves'), *burglary,* or "busting."

J'ai pris du poignon tant que j'ai pu, c'est vrai ! Jamais je n'ai commis de fraction !—*Mémoires de Monsieur Claude.*

Fracturer (popular), se la —, *to run away,* "to hop the twig." See **Patatrot.**

Fraîche, *f.* (thieves'), *cellar.*

Frais, *adj. and m.* (familiar and popular), ironical, *good ; fine.* Vous voilà —, *here you are in a sorry plight, in a fix, in a* "hole." C'est là l'ouvrage ? il est — ! *Is that the work ? a fine piece of work !* Arrêter les —, *to stop doing a thing.* From an expression used at billiard rooms, to stop the expenses for the use of the table. Mettre quelqu'un au —, *to imprison.* Literally *to put in a cool place.*

Fralin, *m.,* **fraline,** *f.* (thieves'), *brother ; sister ; chum,* "Ben cull."

Franc, *adj. and m.* (thieves'), *accomplice,* or " stallsman ; " *low ; frequented by thieves ; faithful.*

C'est Jean-Louis, un bon enfant; sois tranquille, il est franc.—VIDOCQ.

Un — de maison, *receiver of stolen property,* or " fence ; " *landlord of a thieves' lodging-house,* or " flash ken." Un — mijou, or mitou, *a vagabond suffering, or pretending to suffer, from some ailment, and who makes capital of such ailment.* Messière —, *bourgeois or citizen.*

En faisant nos gambades,
Un grand messière franc
Voulant faire parade
Serre un bogue d'orient.
VIDOCQ.

(Military) C'est —, *well and good; that's all right.*

Franc-carreau, *m.* (prisoners'), *punishment which consists in being compelled to sleep on the bare floor of the cell.*

Francfiler (familiar and popular), *was said of those who left Paris during the war, and sought a place of safety in foreign countries.*

Il n'avait pas voulu francfiler pendant le siège.—E. MONTEIL, *Cornebois.*

Franc-fileur, *m.* (familiar), *opprobrious epithet applied to those who left France during the war.*

Franchir (thieves'), *to kiss.*

Francillon, *m.,* **francillonne,** *f.* (thieves'), *Frenchman ; Frenchwoman ; friendly.* Le barbaudier de castu est-il francillon ? *Is the hospital director friendly ?*

Franc-mitou, *m.* (thieves'). See **Franc.**

Franco (cads' and thieves'), c'est —, *it is all right ; all safe.* Gaffine lago, c'est —, y a pas de trèpe, *look there, it is all safe, there's nobody.*

François (thieves'), la faire au père —, *to rob a man by securing a strap round his neck, and lifting him half-strangled on one's shoulders, while an accomplice rifles his pockets.*

Frangin, *m.* (popular and thieves'), *brother ; term of friendship ;* — dab, *uncle.* Mon vieux —, *old fellow !* " old ribstone ! "

Frangine, *f.* (thieves' and popular), *sister ;* — dabuche, *aunt.*

On la connaît, la vache qui nous a fait traire ! C'est la vierge de Saint-Lazare, la frangine du meg !... Il est trop à la coule, le frangin ! C'est au tour de la frangine maintenant à avoir son atout.—*Mémoires de Monsieur Claude.*

Frangir (thieves'), *to break.*

Franguettier, *m.* (thieves'), *card-sharper,* or " broadsman."

Fraonval (Breton), *to escape.*

Frapouille. See **Fripouille.**

Frappart, *m.* (thieves'), père —, *a hammer.*

Frappe, *f.* (popular), *a worthless fellow ; a scamp.*

Une frappe de Beauvais qui voudrait plumer tous les rupins.—*Cri du Peuple,* Mars, 1886.

Frappe - devant, *m.* (popular), *sledge-hammer.*

Fraternellados, or **inséparables,** *m. pl.* (popular), *cigars sold at two for three sous.*

Fraudeur, *m.* (thieves'), *butcher.*

Frayau (popular), il fait —, *it is cold.*

Fredaines, *f. pl.* (thieves'), *stolen property.*

Si tu veux marcher en éclaireur et venir avec nous jusque dans la rue Saint-Sébastien, où nous allons déposer ces fredaines, tu auras ton fade.—VIDOCQ.

Frégate, *f.* (popular), *Sodomist.*

Frelampier. See **Ferlampier.**

Frémillante. See **Fourmillante.**

Frémion, *m.* (thieves'), *violin.*

Frère (familiar), et ami, *demagogue;* (thieves') — de la côte, see **Bande noire ;** — de la manicle, *convict.* (Military) Gros —, *cuirassier.* (Sailors') Vieux — la côte, *old chum.*

Je suis ton vieux frère la côte, moi, et je t'aime, voyons, bon sang !—RICHEPIN, *La Glu.*

(Roughs') Les frères qui aggrichent, *the detectives.* Les frères qui en grattent, *rope dancers.* Les frères qui en mouillent, *acrobats;* "en mouiller" having the signification of performing some extraordinary feat which causes one to sweat.

Frérot de la cagne, *m.* (thieves'), *fellow-thief,* or " family man."

Freschteak, *m.* (military), *piece of meat ; stew.*

Eh ! eh ! on se nourrit bien ici ; . . . d'où avez-vous tiré ce freschteak ? où diable a-t-il trouvé à chaparder de la viande, ce rossard là ?—HECTOR FRANCE, *Sous le Burnous.*

Fressure, *f.* (popular), *heart,* or "panter." Properly *pluck or fry.*

Frétillante, *f.* (thieves'), *pen ; tail ; dance.*

Frétille, fertillante, fertille, *f.* (thieves'), *straw,* or " strommel."

Frétiller (thieves'), *to dance.*

Fretin, *m.* See **Fortin.**

Friauche, *m.* (thieves'), *thief, prig,* or "crossman," see **Grinche ;** *convict under a death-sentence who appeals.*

Fricasse (popular), on t'en —, *expressive of ironical refusal,* or, as the Americans say, " Yes, in a horn ! " See **Nèfles.**

Fricassée, *f.* (popular), *thrashing,* "wallopping." See **Voie.**

Fricasser ses meubles (popular), *to sell one's furniture.*

Fricasseur, *m.* (popular), *spendthrift ; libertine,* or " rip."

Fric-frac, *m.* (thieves'), *breaking open,* or " busting." Faire —, *to break into,* " to bust."

Frichti, *m.* (popular), *stew with potatoes.*

Fricot, *m.* (popular), s'endormir sur le —, *to relax one's exertions ; to allow an undertaking to flag.*

Fricoter (military), *to shirk one's military duties.*

Fricoteur (military), *marauder ; one who shirks duty, who only cares about good living.*

Frigousse, *f.* (popular), *food,* or
" prog ; " *stew.*

C'était trop réussi, ça prouvait où conduisait l'amour de la frigousse. Au rencart
les gourmandes !—ZOLA, *L'Assommoir.*

Frigousser (popular), *to cook.*

Frileux, *m.* (popular), *poltroon,*
" cow-babe."

Je suis un ferlampier qui n'est pas frileux.
—E. SUE.

Frimage, *m.* (thieves'), *appearing
before the magistrate, or in presence
of a prosecutor, for identification.*

Frime, *f.* (thieves'), *face,* or "mug."

Avec un' frim' comm' j'en ai une,
Un mariol sait trouver d'la thune.
RICHEPIN, *La Chanson des Gueux.*

Molière uses the word with the
signification of *grimace :*—

Pourquoi toutes ces frimes-là ? — *Le
Médecin malgré Lui.*

Frime à la manque, *ugly face ;
face à a one-eyed person,* termed
" a seven-sided animal," as, says
the *Slang Dictionary,* he has an
inside, outside, left side, right
side, foreside, backside, and blind
side. Tomber en —, *to meet face
to face.* (Popular) Une —, *falsehood ; trick.*

Quelque frime pour se faire donner du
sucre ! ah ! il allait se renseigner, et si elle
mentait !—ZOLA, *L'Assommoir.*

Frimer (thieves'), *to peer into one's
face.* Faire —, *to place a prisoner
in presence of a prosecutor for purpose of identification.* (Popular)
Frimer, *to make a good appearance ;
to look well ; to pretend.* Cet habit
frime bien, *this coat looks well.*
Ils friment de s'en aller, *they pretend to go away.*

Frimousse, *f.* (thieves'), *figure
card.* (Popular) C'est pour ma
—, *that's for me.* Literally *physiognomy.*

Frimousser (card-sharpers'), *to
swindle by contriving to turn up
the figure cards.*

Frimousseur (card-sharpers'), *card-
sharper,* " broadsman."

Fringue, *f.* (thieves'), *article of
clothing,* " clobber." (Popular)
Les fringues, *players at a game
called* " l'ours." These stand upright in a knot at the centre of a
circle, face to face, with heads
bent and arms passed over one
another's shoulders so as to steady
themselves. The business of other
players outside the circle is to
jump on the backs of those in the
knot without being caught by one
called " le chien " or " l'ours,"
who keeps running about in the
circle.

Fringuer (thieves'), se —, *to dress
oneself,* " to rig oneself out in
clobber."

Fripe, *f.* (popular), *food,* " prog."
From the old word fripper, *to eat ;
cooking of food ; expense ; share in
the reckoning,* or " shot ;" —
sauce, cook, or " dripping." Faire
la —, *to cook.*

Fripier, *m.* (popular and thieves'),
cook, or " dripping ;" *master of
an eating-house, of a* "carnish
ken."

Fripouille, *f.* (familiar), *rogue ;
scamp.* From fripe, *rag.* Tout
ce monde là c'est de la —, *these
people are a bad lot.*

Friques, *f. pl.* (thieves'), *rags.*

Friquet, *m.* (thieves'), *spy in the
employ of the police,* " nark," or
" nose."

Frire un rigolo (thieves'), *to pick
the pockets of a person while em-
bracing him, under a pretence of
mistaken identity.*

Frischti, *m.* (military), *dainty food; stew.*

Frisé, *m.* (popular), *Jew,* "sheney," or "mouchey." Termed also "youtre, pied-plat, guinal."

Frisque, *m.* (popular), *cold.*

Le frisque du matin, qui ravigote le sang, qui cingle la vie.—RICHEPIN, *Le Pavé.*

Frissante, *f. adj.* (sailors'), *with gentle ripples.*

La mé n'est pas toujours rêche comme une étrille.
Vois, elle est douce, un peu frissante, mais pas plus.
RICHEPIN, *La Mer.*

Frites, *f. pl.* (popular), for pommes de terre frites, *fried potatoes.* Termed "greasers" at the R. M. Academy.

Friturer (popular), *to cook.*

Frivoliste, *m.* (literary), *light writer; contributor, for instance, to a journal of fashion.*

Froisseux, *adj.* (popular), *traitor,* "cat - in - the - pan;" *slanderer.* From froisser, *to hurt one's feelings.*

Frollant, *m.* (thieves'), *slanderer; traitor, one who* "turns snitch."

Froller (thieves'), sur la balle, *to slander one.* From the old word frôler, *to thrash, to injure.*

Fromgibe, *m.* (popular), *cheese.*

Front, *m.* (popular), avoir le — dans le cou, *to be bald, to be* "stag-faced."

Froteska, *f.* (popular), *thrashing,* "tanning," or "hiding." See **Voie.**

Frotin, *m.* (popular), *billiards,* or "spoof." Coup de —, *game of billiards.* Flancher au —, *to play billiards.*

Frotte, *f.* (popular), *itch.*

Frottée, *f.* (familiar and popular), *thrashing,* or "licking." See **Voie.**

Cinq ou six matelots de l'Albatros furent attaqués par une dizaine de marins du Mary-Ann et reçurent une des plus vénérables frottées dont on eût ouï parler sur la côte du Pacifique.—J. CLARETIE.

Frotter (gamesters'), se — au bonheur de quelqu'un. The expression is explained by the following quotation :—

Le joueur est superstitieux, il croit au fétiche. Un bossu gagne-t-il, on voit des pontes acharnés se grouper autour de lui pour lui toucher sa bosse et se frotter à son bonheur. A Vichy, les joueurs sont munis de pattes de lapin pour toucher délicatement le dos des heureux du tapis vert.— *Mémoires de Monsieur Claude.*

Froufrou, *m.* (thieves'), *master-key.*

Frousse, *f.* (popular and thieves'), *diarrhœa; fear.*

J'ai fait chibis. J'avais la frousse
Des préfectanciers de Pantin.
RICHEPIN.

Fructidoriser (familiar), *to suppress one's political adversaries by violent means, such as transportation wholesale.* An allusion to the 18th Fructidor or 4th September, 1797.

Fruges, *f. pl.* (popular), *more or less lawful profits on sales by shopmen.* English railway ticket-clerks give the name of "fluff" to profits accruing from short change given by them.

Frusque, *f.* (popular), *coat,* "Benjamin."

Frusques, *f. pl.* (general), *clothing,* "toggery," or "clobber;" — boulinées, *clothes in tatters.*

On allait . . . choisir ses frusques chez Milon, qui avait des costumes moins brillants.—E. MONTEIL.

Frusquiner (popular), se —, *to dress,* "to rig" *oneself out.*

Frusquineur, *m.* (popular), *tailor*, "snip, steel-bar driver, cabbage contractor, or button catcher."

Frusquins, *m. pl.* (popular), *clothes*, or "toggery."

Fuir (popular), laisser — son tonneau, *to die.* For synonyms see **Pipe.**

Fumé, *adj.* (familiar and popular), *to be in an awful fix, past praying for,* "a gone coon." With regard to the English slang equivalent, the *Slang Dictionary* says: "This expression is said to have originated in the first American War with a spy who dressed himself in a racoon skin, and ensconced himself in a tree. An English soldier, taking him for a veritable coon, levelled his piece at him, upon which he exclaimed, 'Don't shoot, I'll come down of myself; I know I'm a gone coon.' The Yankees say the Britisher was so 'flummuxed' that he flung down his musket and 'made tracks' for home." The phrase is pretty general in England. (There is one difficulty about this story—how big was the man who dressed himself in a racoon skin?)

Fumer (popular), *to snore*, "to drive one's pigs to market;" — sans pipe et sans tabac, *to be* "riled;" *to fume.* Avoir fumé dans une pipe neuve, *to feel unwell in consequence of prolonged potations.*

Fumerie, *f.* (popular), *smoking*, "blowing a cloud."

Fumeron, *m.* (popular), *hypocrite*, "mawworm."

Fumerons, *m. pl.* (popular), *legs*, "pegs."

Fumiste, *m.* (familiar), *practical joker; humbug.* Farce de —, *practical joke.* For quotation see **Farce.** (Polytechnic School) Être en —, *to be in civilian's clothes*, "in mufti."

Fuseaux, *m. pl.* (popular), *legs*, or "pins." Jouer des —, *to run*, "to leg it." See **Patatrot.**

Il juge qu'il est temps de jouer des fuseaux, mais au moment où il se dispose à gagner plus au pied qu'à la toise . . . le garçon le saisit à la gorge.—VIDOCQ.

Fusée, *f.* (popular), lâcher une —, *to be sick*, "to shoot the cat."

Fuser (popular), *to ease oneself.* See **Mouscailler.**

Fusil, *m.* (popular), *stomach ;* — à deux coups, *trousers ;* — de toile, *wallet.* Aller à la chasse avec un — de toile, *to beg.* Colle-toi ça dans le —, *eat or drink that ; put that in your* "bread-basket." Ecarter du —, *to spit involuntarily when talking.* Se rincer, se gargariser le —, *to drink*, "to swig." See **Rincer.** Changer son — d'épaule, *to change one's political opinions, to turn one's coat.* Repousser du —, *to have an offensive breath.*

Fusiller (military), *to spend money.* Literally faire partir ses balles, the last word having the double signification of *bullets, francs ;* — ses invités, *to give one's guests a bad dinner ;* — le pavé, *to use one's fingers as a pocket-handkerchief ;* — le plancher, *to set off at a run ;* — son pèse, *to spend one's money ;* (thieves') — le fade, *to give one's share of booty ; to make one* "stand in."

Fusilleur, *m.* See **Bande noire.**

Futaille, *f.* (thieves'), vieille —, *old woman.*

 **GABARI,** *m.* (popular), passer au —, *to lose a game.*

Gabarit, *m.* (sailors'), *body; breast;* — sans bossoirs, *breast with thin bosoms.*

J'aime pas bien son gabarit sans bossoirs. Elle a plutôt l'air d'un moussaillon que d'autre chose.— RICHEPIN, *La Glu.*

Gâcher (popular), serré, *to work hard,* "*to sweat;*" — du gros, *to ease oneself.*

Gadin, *m.* (popular), *cork; shabby hat.* Flancher au —, *to play a gambling sort of game with a cork and coins.* Some halfpence being placed on the cork, the players aim in turns with a coin. A favourite game of Paris cads.

Gadouard, *m.* (popular), *scavenger,* a "rake-kennel." From gadoue, *street refuse or mud.*

Gadoue, *f.* (familiar and popular), *prostitute.* Properly *street mud or refuse.* The slang terms for the different varieties of prostitutes are, in familiar and popular language: "cocotte, demi-mondaine, horizontale, verticale, agenouillée, déhanchée, impure, petite dame, lorette, camélia, boulevardière, pêche à quinze sous, belle petite, soupeuse, grue, lolo, biche, vieille garde (*old prostitute*), fille de trottoir, gueuse, maquillée, ningle, pélican, pailletée, laqueuse, chameau, membre de la caravane, demi-castor, passe-lacet, demoiselle du Pont-Neuf, matelas ambulant, boulonnaise (*one who plies her trade in the Bois de Boulogne*), crevette, trumeau, traîneuse, fenêtrière, trychine, cul crotté, omnibus, carcan à crinoline, pieuvre, pigeon voyageur, piqueuse de trains, marcheuse, morue, fleur de macadam, vache à lait, camelote, roulante, raccrocheuse, génisse, almanach des trente-six mille adresses, chausson, hirondelle de goguenot, moelonneuse, mal peignée, persilleuse, lard, blanchisseuse en chemises, planche à boudin, galvaudeuse, poule, mouquette, poupée, fille de tourneur, fille de maison or à numéro, boutonnière en pantalons, fille en carte or en brème, lésébombe, baleine, traînée, demoiselle du bitume, vessie, boule rouge (*one who walks the Faubourg Montmartre*), voirie, rivette, fille à parties, terrière, terreuse, femme de terrain, rempardeuse, grenier à coups de sabre, saucisse, peau, peau de chien, vésuvienne, autel de besoin, cité d'amour, mangeuse de viande crue, dessalée, punaise, polisseuse de mâts de cocagne en chambre, pompe funèbre, polisseuse de tuyaux de pipe, pontonnière, pont d'Avignon, veau, vache, blanc, feuille, lanterne, magneuse, lipète, chamègue, bourdon, pierreuse, marneuse, paillasse de corps de garde, paillasse à troufion, rouleuse, dossière, fille de barrière, roulure, andre (old word), Jeanneton, taupe, limace, waggon, retapeuse, sommier de caserne, femme de cavoisi, prat, sauterelle, tapeuse de tal, magnée, torchon." The bullies of unfortunates call them "marmite, fesse, ouvrière, Louis, ponife, galupe, laisée." Thieves give them the appellations of "lutainpem, môme, ponante, calège, panuche, asticot, bourre de soie, panturne, rutière, ronfle, goipeuse, casserole, magnuce, larguèpe, larque, menesse, louille." In the English slang they are termed: "anonyma, pretty horse-breaker, demi-rep, tartlet, mot, common Jack, bunter, trollop, bed-fagot, shake, poll, dolly-mop, blowen, bulker, gay woman, unfortunate, barrack-hack, dress lodger, bawdy basket, mauks, and quædam" (obsolete), &c.

Gaffe, *m. and f.* (thieves'), *sentry; thief on the watch*, or "crow;" *prison warder*, or "bloke."

Les gaffes (gardiens) ont la vie dure. Ils tiennent sur leurs pattes comme des chats . . . si je l'ai manqué, je ne me suis pas manqué, moi, je suis sûr d'aller à la butte. —*Mémoires de Monsieur Claude.*

Gaffe à gail, *mounted police;* — de sorgue, *nightwatchman;* — des machabées, *cemetery watchman.* Etre en —, faire —, *to be on the watch*, "to dick."

Riboulet et moi, nous étions restés en gaffe afin de donner l'éveil en cas d'alerte. —Vidocq.

Grivier de —, *soldier of the watch.* (Popular) Gaffe, *f., joke; deceit; tongue*, or "red rag." Avaler sa —, *to die*, "to snuff it." See **Pipe**. Coup de —, *loud talking*, "jawing." Monter une —, *to*

play a trick; to deceive, "to bamboozle," "to pull the leg." (Familiar) Faire une —, *to take an inconsiderate step; to make an awkward mistake*, "to put one's foot in it."

Gaffer (thieves'), *to watch*, "to dick;" *to look*, "to pipe;" — la mirette, *to keep a sharp look-out.* Gaffe les péniches du gonse, *look at that man's shoes.* Gaffer, *to cause to stand; to stop.*

Il fallait faire gaffer un roulant pour y planquer les paccins (il fallait faire stationner un fiacre pour y placer les paquets).—Vidocq.

Gaffeur, *m.* (thieves'), *man on the watch.*

Gaffier, *m.* (thieves'), *pickpocket who operates at markets; warder in a prison or convict settlement*, a "bloke."

Gaffiner (thieves' and cads'), *to look at*, "to pipe." Gaffine lago, la riflette t'exhibe, *look there, the policeman is watching you*, or, in other words, "pipe there, the bulky is dicking."

Gafiler (thieves'), *to listen attentively.*

Gaga, *m.* (familiar), *man who, through a life of debauchery, has become almost an imbecile.*

Gagnie, *f.* (popular), *buxom lady.*

Gahisto, *m.* (thieves'), *the devil*, "ruffin," or "darble." From the Basque giztoa, *bad, wicked*, according to V. Hugo.

Gai, *adj.* (popular), être —, *to be slightly tipsy*, or "elevated." See **Pompette.** Avoir la cuisse gaie *is said of a woman of lax morality who is lavish of her favours.*

Gail, galier, *m.* (thieves'), *horse*, "prad." Vol au —, *horse stealing*, or "prad napping."

Gaillard à trois brins, *m.* (sailors'), *able sailor ; old tar.*

J'ai travaillé, mangé, gagné mon pain
   parmi
Des gaillards à trois brins qui me traitaient
   en mousse.
           RICHEPIN, *La Mer.*

Gaillon (popular and thieves'), *horse,* " prad, nag, or tit."

Gailloterie, *f.* (popular), *stable.*

Gaimar (popular), *gaily ; willingly.* Allons y —, *let us look alive ; with a will !*

Galapiat, galapian, galopiau, *m.* (popular), *lazy fellow,* or " bummer ; " *street boy.*

Quelle rigolade pour les gamins ! Et l'un de ces galapiats qui a peut-être servi chez des saltimbanques, chipe un clairon et souffle dedans un air de foire.—RICHE-PIN, *Le Pavé.*

Galbe, *m.* (familiar), *elegance, dash.* Etre truffé de —, *to be extremely elegant, dashing,* or " tsing tsing." Galbe, literally *elegance in the curve of vases, pillars.*

Galbeux, *adj.* (familiar), *elegant, dashing,* " tsing tsing."

Galerie, *f.* (familiar), faire —, *to be one of a number of lookers-on.* Parler pour la —, *to address to a person words meant in reality for the ears of others, or for the public.*

Galette, *f.* (popular), *money,* " tin." For synonyms see **Quibus.** Boulotter de la —, *to spend money.* (Military school of Saint-Cyr) Promenade —, *general marching out.* Sortie —, *general holiday.*

Galeux, *m.* (popular), *the master,* or " boss." Properly *one who has the itch.*

Galfâtre, *m.* (popular), *idiot ; greedy fellow.*

Certes il n'aimait pas les corbeaux, ça lui crevait le cœur de porter ses six francs à ces galfâtres-là qui n'en avaient pas besoin pour se tenir le gosier frais.—ZOLA, *L'Assommoir.*

Galier, *m.* (thieves'), *horse,* or " prad."

Galière, *f.* (thieves'), *mare.*

Galifard, *m.* (popular), *shoemaker,* or " snob ; " *errand boy ;* (thieves') *one who is not yet an adept in the art of thieving.*

Galifarde, *f.* (popular), *shop-girl.*

Galimard, *m.* (artists'), se touche ! *The expression is used in reference to a brother artist who extols his own self or own productions.* For the following explanation I am indebted to Mr. G. D., a French artist well known to the English public :—" Galimard se touche, phrase que vous avez lue probablement dans tous les Rambuteau de Paris, a pris origine dans notre atelier Cogniet. Galimard, un artiste de quelque talent, mais qui se croyait un génie, trouvant qu'on ne s'occupait pas assez de lui, écrivit sur le salon des articles fort bien faits mais par trop sévères pour les confrères. Il avait mis au bas un pseudonyme quelconque. Arrivé au tour de sa fameuse Léda, il ne tarissait pas d'éloges sur cette peinture vraiment médiocre. Bertall, que je connaissais fort bien, découvrit le pot aux roses. Galimard était son propre panégyriste ! J'arrive à l'atelier et je dis : ' Galimard se fait jouir lui-même, c'est lui l'auteur des articles en question.' De là, le fameux 'Galimard se touche' expression maintenant consacrée lorsqu'un artiste parle trop de lui-même. Il faut ajouter que les mots furent écrits dans tous les Rambuteau du Quartier du Temple puis, non seulement à Paris, mais par toute la France. L'empereur acheta la Léda après une tentative criminelle de la part d'un malfaiteur et sur la toile et sur Galimard. On fit une enquête et l'on découvrit que le malfaiteur n'était autre que . . . Galimard. L'affaire en resta là. La Léda fut placée au Musée du Luxembourg, après cicatrisation des coups de poignard, bien entendu."

Galiote, *f.* (thieves'), *conspiracy of card-sharpers to swindle a player.*

Galipoter (sailors'), *to smear.*

Galli-bâton, *m.* (popular), *general fight ; great row,* or "*shindy.*"

Galli-trac, *m.* (popular), *poltroon,* "*cow's babe.*"

Galoche, *f.* (thieves'), *chin ;* (popular) *a game played with a cork and halfpence.*

Galons, *m. pl.* (military), d'imbécile, *long-service stripes.* Arroser ses —, *to treat one's comrades on being made a non-commissioned officer ; to pay for one's footing.*

Galopante, *f.* (popular), *diarrhœa,* or "*jerry-go-nimble.*"

Galopé, *adj.* (popular), *done hurriedly, carelessly.*

Galoper (popular), *to annoy ; to make unwell.* Ça me galope sur le système, *or* sur le haricot, *it troubles me ; it makes me ill ;* — une femme, *to make hot love to a woman.*

Galopin, *m.* (familiar), *small glass of beer at cafés.* Had formerly the signification of *small measure of wine.*

Galoubet, *m.* (theatrical), *voice.* Avoir du —, *to possess a good voice.* Donner du —, *to sing.*

En scène, les fées ! Attaquons vivement le chœur d'entrée. Du galoubet et de l'ensemble !—P. MAHALIN.

Galouser (thieves'), *to sing,* "*to lip.*"

Galtos, *m.* (sailors'), *dish.* Passer à —, *to eat.* (Popular) Galtos, *money,* or "*pieces.*" See **Quibus.**

Galtron, *m.* (thieves'), *foal.*

Galuche, *f.* (thieves'), *braid ; lace.*

Galuché, *adj.* (thieves'), *braided ; laced.* Combriot —, *laced hat.*

Galuchet, *m.* (popular), *the knave at cards.*

Galupe, *f.* (thieves' and popular), *street-walker,* "*bunter.*" See **Gadoue.**

Les galup's qu'a des ducatons
Nous rincent la dent, nous les battons.
RICHEPIN.

Galupier, *m.* (popular), *man who keeps a "galupe."* See this word.

Galure, galurin (popular), *hat,* or "*tile.*" See **Tubard.**

Galvaudage, *m.* (popular), *squandering of one's money ; pilfering.*

Galvauder (popular), *to squander one's money.* Se —, *to lead a disorderly life.*

Galvaudeuse, *f.* (popular), *lazy, disorderly woman ; street-walker.* See **Gadoue.**

Galvaudeux, *m.* (popular), *lazy vagabond,* or "*raff ;*" *disorderly fellow ; bad workman.*

Gambettes, *f. pl.* (popular), *legs.* From the old word gambe, *leg.* Jouer des —, *to run.* See **Patatrot.**

Gambier, *f.* (popular), *cutty pipe.* From the name of the manufacturer.

Gambillard, *m.* (popular), *active, restless man.*

Gambiller (popular), *to dance,* "*to shake a leg.*" Is used by Molière with the signification of *to agitate the legs :*—

Oui de le voir gambiller les jambes en haut devant tout le monde.—*Monsieur de Pourceaugnac.*

Gambilles, *f. pl.* (popular), *legs,* or "*pins.*"

Gambilleur, *m.* (familiar), *political quack;* (thieves') *dancer;* — de tourtouse, *rope-dancer.*

Gambilleuse, *f.* (popular), *girl who makes it a practice of attending dancing halls.*

Gambriade, *f.* (thieves'), *dance.*

Game, *f.* (thieves'), *hydrophobia.*

Gamelad (Breton cant), *porringer.*

Gameler (thieves'), *to inform against one,* "to blow the gaff."

Gamelle, *f.* (sailors'), aux amours, *mistress.* (Popular and thieves') Attacher une —, *to decamp, to run away.* See **Patatrot**.

Gamme, *f.* (popular), *thrashing,* or "walloping." Faire chanter une —, or monter une —, *to thrash,* "to lead a dance." See **Voie**. The expression is used by Scarron :—

> Avec Dame Junon sa femme,
> Qui souvent lui chante la game.

Ganache, *f.* (theatrical), jouer les père —, *to perform in the character of a foolish old fellow.* Properly ganache, *an old fool,* "a doddering old sheep's head."

Gance, *f.* (thieves'), *a gang,* or "mob." The *Slang Dictionary* says "mob" signifies *a thief's immediate companions,* as "our own mob."

Gandille, *f.* (thieves'), *sword,* or "poker;" *dagger,* or "cheery;" *knife,* or "chive."

Gandin, *m.* (familiar), *dandy,* or "masher." Literally a frequenter of the "Boulevard de Gand," now Boulevard des Italiens. For list of synonymous expressions see **Gommeux**. (Second-hand clothes-men's) Gandin, *fine words to attract purchasers.* Monter un —, *to entice a purchaser in; to get a customer.* (Thieves') Gandin,

a "job" *in preparation, or quite prepared;* — d'altèque, *the insignia of any order.* Hisser un —, *to deceive,* "to kid," or "to best." See **Jobarder**.

Gandinerie, *f.*, **gandinisme**, *m.* (familiar), *the world of* gandins, or "swelldom."

Gandouse, *j.* (popular), *mud, dirt.*

Gannaliser (familiar), *to embalm.* From Gannal, name of a practitioner. The expression is little used.

Gant, *m.* (popular), moule de —, *box on the ear.* Properly *mould for a glove.*

Ganter (cocottes'), 5½, *to be close-fisted;* — 8½, *to be open-handed.*

Gantière, *f.* (familiar), *disreputable establishment where the female assistants make a show of selling gloves or perfumery, but where they retail anything but those articles.*

Gants de pied, *m. pl.* (military), *wooden shoes.*

Garçon, *m.* (popular), à deux mains, *slaughterer;* — de bidoche, *butcher boy.* (Thieves') Garçon, *thief,* "prig. Un brave —, *an expert thief.* Un — de campagne, or de cambrouse, *highwayman.* Termed formerly in the English cant "bridle-cull."

La cognade à gayet servait le trèpe pour laisser abouler une roulotte farguée d'un ratichon, de Charlot et de son larbin, et d'un garçon de cambrouse.—VIDOCQ. (*The horse-police were keeping back the crowd in order to open a passage for a cart which contained a priest, the executioner, his assistant, and a highwayman.*)

Gardanne, *f.* (familiar), *odd piece of silk.*

Garde, *m. and f.* (popular), national, *lot of bacon rind.* Gardes nationaux, *beans.* (Familiar) Descendre la —, *to die,* "to kick the

bucket." See **Pipe**. Vieille —, *superannuated cocotte*, or "played out tart."

Il pouvait citer tel et tel, des noms, des gentilshommes de sang plus bleu que le sien, aujourd'hui collés légitimement et très satisfaits, et pas reniés du tout, avec de vraies roulures, avec des vieilles-gardes ! —RICHEPIN, *La Glu.*

Garde-manger, *m.* (popular), *the behind.* See **Vasistas**.

Garde-proye (thieves'), *wardrobe.*

Garder (familiar), se — à carreau, *to take precautions in view of future mishaps.*

Gardien, *m.* (popular and thieves'), ange —, *man who undertakes to see drunkards home ; rogue who offers to see a drunkard home, robs, and sometimes murders him.*

Garé, *adj.* (popular), des voitures *is said of a steady, prudent man, or of one who has renounced a disreputable way of living.*

Gare-l'eau, *m.* (thieves'), *chamberpot*, or "jerry."

Gargagoitche, *f.* (thieves' and cads'), *face*, or "mug."

Gargariser (familiar and popular), se —, *to drink*, "to wet one's whistle." For synonyms see **Rincer**. The expression is old.

Donnez ordre que buvons, je vous prie ; et faictes tant que nous ayons de l'eau fraische pour me gargariser le palat.—RABELAIS, *Pantagruel.*

Se — le rossignolet, *to drink*, "to have a quencher."

Gargarisme, *m.* (popular), *a drink*, a "drain," or "quencher." (Familiar) Faire des gargarismes, *to trill when singing.*

Gargarousse, *f.* (popular and thieves'), *throat*, or "gutterlane;" *face*, or "mug." (Sailors') Se suiver la —, *to eat ; to drink*, or "to splice the mainbrace."

Gargoine, *f.* (popular and thieves'), *throat*, formerly "gargamelle ;" *mouth*, or "potato-trap." Termed formerly "potato-jaw," according to a speech of the Duke of Clarence's to Mrs. Schwellenberg :—

"Hold you your potato-jaw, my dear," cried the Duke, patting her.—*Supplementary English Glossary.*

Se rincer la —, *to drink*, "to smile, to see a man" (American).

Gargot, *m.* (familiar and popular), *restaurant ; cheap eating-house.* Some of the restaurants in Paris have two departments, the cheap one on the ground floor, and a more respectable one higher up.

Gargouenne. See **Gargoine**.

Gargouillade, *f.* (popular), *rumbling noise in the stomach.*

Gargouille, gargouine, gargue, *f.* (popular), *face ; mouth.* For list of synonyms see **Plomb**.

Gargousse, *f.* (sailors'), avec le cœur en —, *with sinking heart.*

> Un' brise à fair' plier l'pouce,
> Rigi, rigo, riguingo,
> Avec le cœur en gargousse,
> Rigi, rigo, riguingo,
> Ah ! riguinguette.
> J. RICHEPIN, *La Mer.*

Gargousses de la canonnière (popular), *turnips, cabbages, or beans.*

Garibaldi, *m.* (familiar), *red frock ; sort of hat.* (Thieves') Coup de —, *blow given by butting at one's stomach.*

Garnaffe, *f.* (thieves'), *farm.*

Garnaffier, *m.* (thieves'), *farmer*, or "joskin."

Garnir (popular), se — le bocal, *to eat*, "to grub." See **Mastiquer**.

Garnison, *f.* (popular), *lice*, "greybacked uns."

Garno, *m.* (popular), *lodging-house,* " dossing crib."

Gas, *m.* (familiar and popular), for gars, *boy ; fellow.* Grand —, *tall chap.* Mauvais —, *ill-tempered fellow.* (Roughs') Gas de la grinche, *thief.* Faut pas frayer avec ça, c'est un — de la grinche, *you must not keep company with the fellow, he is a thief.* Un — qui flanche, *a hawker.* (Thieves') Fabriquer un — à la flan, à la rencontre, or à la dure, *to attack a man at night and rob him,* "to jump a cove."

Gaspard, *m.* (popular), *cunning fellow,* or "sharp file ;" *rat ; cat,* or "long-tailed beggar." Concerning this expression there is a tale that runs thus : A boy, during his first very short voyage to sea, had become so entirely a seaman, that on his return he had forgotten the name for a cat, and pointing to Puss, asked his mother " what she called that 'ere long-tailed beggar ? " Accordingly, sailors, when they hear a freshwater tar discoursing too largely on nautical matters, are very apt to say, " but how, mate, about that 'ere long-tailed beggar ? "

Gâteau, *m.* (popular), feuilleté, *shoe out at the sole.* (Thieves') Avoir du —, *to get one's share of booty,* "to stand in."

Gâte-pâte, *m.* (popular), *redoubtable wrestler.*

Gâter (popular), de l'eau, *to void urine,* "to lag." Se — la taille, *to become pregnant,* or "lumpy."

Gâteuse, *f.* (familiar), *long garment worn over clothes to protect them from the dust.*

Gâtisme, *m.* (familiar), *stupidity.* Le — littéraire, *decaying state of literature.*

Gaucher, gauchier, *m.* (familiar), member of the Left whether in the Assemblée Nationale or Senate.

Gaudille, or **gandille,** *f.* (thieves'), *sword,* or " poker."

Gaudineur, *m.* (popular), *house decorator.* Probably from gaudir, *to be merry,* house decorators having the reputation of being light-hearted.

Gaudissard, *m.* (familiar), *commercial traveller,* from the name of a character of Balzac's ; *practical joker ; jovial man.*

Gaudrioler (familiar), equivalent to " dire des gaudrioles," *to make jests of a slightly licentious character.*

Gaudrioleur, *m.* (familiar), *one fond of* gaudrioler (which see).

Gaufres, *f. pl.* (popular), faire des —, *is said of pock-marked persons who kiss one another.* Moule à —, *pock-marked face,* or "cribbage-faced."

Gaule, *f.* (popular), d'omnicroche, *omnibus conductor.* Une gaule, properly *a pole.* (Thieves') Gaules de schtard, *bars of a cell window.*

Gaulé, *m.* (popular), *cider.*

Gaux, *m.* (thieves'), *lice,* " greybacked uns ;" — picantis, *lice in clothing.* Basourdir les —, *to kill lice.*

Gave, *adj. and f.* (popular and thieves'), *drunken man,* "lushington ;" *stomach.*

> Va encore à l'cave,
> Du cidre il faut
> Plein la gave,
> Du cidre il faut
> Plein l'gaviot.
>   RICHEPIN.

Etre —, *to be intoxicated.* See **Pompette.**

Gavé, *m.* (thieves'), *drunkard.* Faire les gavés, *to rob drunkards ;*

to go "bug-hunting." (Popular)
Gavé, *term of contempt applied to rich people.* From gaver, *to glut.*

Y a des gens qui va en sapins,
En omnibus et en tramways,
Tous ces gonc's-là, c'est des clampins,
Des richards, des muf's, des gavés.
RICHEPIN.

Gaveau, *m.* (thieves'), tortiller le —, *to kill one by strangulation.*

Gaviolé. See **Gavé.**

Gaviot, *m.* (popular), *throat; mouth.* See **Plomb.** Figuratively *stomach.*

Mais quoi ! ces ventrus sur leurs pieds
N'peuvent plus supporter leur gaviot.
RICHEPIN.

Gavot. See **Gavé.**

Gavroche, *m.* (familiar), *Paris street boy.* Faire le —, *to talk or act as an impudent boy.*

Gay, *adj.* (thieves'), *ugly; queer,* or "rum."

Gaye. See **Galiote.**

Gayet, *m.* (thieves'), *horse,* or "prad." Termed also "gail." La cognade à —, *mounted police.* Des gayets, *rogues who prowl about the suburbs just outside the gates of Paris.*

C'étaient des rôdeurs de barrière . . . c'étaient des gayets.—*Mémoires de Monsieur Claude.*

Gaz, *m.* (popular), allumer son —, *to look attentively,* "to stag." Eteindre son —, *to sleep,* "to doss;" *to die,* "to snuff it." See **Pipe.** Prendre un coup de —, *to have a dram of spirits.*

Gazette, *f.* (familiar), lire la —, *to eat nothing.*

Gazier, *m.* (popular), *humbug.*

Gazon, *m.* (popular), *wig,* or "periwinkle;" *hair,* or "thatch." N'avoir plus de — sur la plate-bande, or sur le pré, *to be bald.* See **Avoir.** Se ratisser le —, *to comb one's hair.*

Gazonner (popular), se faire — la plate-bande, *to provide oneself with a wig.*

Gazouiller (popular), *to speak; to sing; to stink.*

Oh ! la la ! ça gazouille, dit Clémence en se bouchant le nez.—ZOLA.

Géant, *m.* (thieves'), montagne de —, *gallows,* "scrag," "nobbing cheat," or the obsolete expression "government sign-post."

Geindre, *m.* (popular), *journeyman baker.* Properly *to groan heavily.*

Gendarme, *m.* (popular), *red herring; mixture of white wine, gum, and water; one-sou cigar; pressing iron.*

Général, *m.* (popular), le — macadam, *the street,* or "drag."

Gêneur, *m.* (familiar), *bore.*

Génisse, *f.,* *woman of bad character.* See **Gadoue.**

Géniteur, *m.* (popular), *father.*

Genou, *m.* (familiar), *bald pate.*

Genre, *m.* (familiar), grand —, *pink of fashion.* C'est tout à fait grand —, *it is quite "the" thing.* Se donner du —, *to assume fashionable ways or manners in speech or dress; to look affected, to have "highfalutin airs."*

Genreux, *adj. and m.* (familiar), *elegant; fashionable,* "dasher," "tsing tsing;" *one who gives himself airs.*

Gens, *m. pl.* (popular), être de la société des — de lettres, *to belong to a tribe of swindlers who extort money by threatening letters,* "socketers."

N

Gentilhomme sous-marin, *m.* (popular), *prostitute's bully,* "ponce." For synonyms see **Poisson.**

Georget, *m.* (popular), *waistcoat,* "benjy."

Les rupines et marquises leur fichent, les unes un georget, les autres une lime ou haut-de-tire, qu'ils entrolent au barbaudier de castu, ou à d'autres qui les veulent ablo-quir.—*Le Jargon de l'Argot.* (*The ladies and wives give them, some a waistcoat, others a shirt, or a pair of breeches, which they take to the hospital overseer, or to others who are willing to buy them.*)

Gerbable, *m.* (thieves'), *prisoner who is sure to be convicted, who is* "booked."

Gerbe, *m.* (thieves'), *trial,* or "patter;" *sentence.* Planque de —, *assize court.* Le carré des petites gerbes, *the police court.*

Gerbé, *adj.* (thieves'), *sentenced,* or "booked."

On dit qu'il vient du bagne où il était gerbé à 24 longes (condamné à 24 ans).—VIDOCQ.

Etre — à viocque, *to be sentenced to penal servitude for life,* or "settled."

Gerbement, *m.* (thieves'), *trial;* called also "sapement."

La conversation roulait sur les camarades qui étaient au pré, sur ceux qui étaient en gerbement (jugement).—VIDOCQ.

Gerber (thieves'), *to sentence.*

Te voilà pris par la Cigogne, avec cinq vols qualifiés, trois assassinats, dont le plus récent concerne deux riches bourgeois ... tu seras gerbé à la passe.—BALZAC.

Gerberie, *f.* (thieves'), *court of justice.*

Gerbier, *m.* (thieves'), *judge,* or "beak;" *barrister,* or "mouth-piece." Mec des gerbiers, *execu-tioner.*

Gerbierres, *f. pl.* (thieves'), *skele-ton keys,* or "screws."

Gerce, *f.* (thieves'), *wife,* or "mol-lisher;" *mattress;* (popular) *wo-man with unnatural passions.* Un qui s'est fait poisser la —, *a Sodomist.*

Germanie, *f.,* aller en —. See **Aller.**

Germiny, *m.* (familiar and popu-lar), *Sodomist.* From the name of a nobleman who a few years ago was tried for an unnatural offence.

Germinyser (familiar and popular), se faire —, *to be a Sodomist.*

Gernafle, *f.* (thieves'), *farm.*

Gernaflier, *m.* (thieves'), *farmer,* or "joskin."

Gérontocracie, *f.* (familiar), *nar-row-mindedness.*

Gésier, *m.* (popular), *throat.* Se laver le —, *to drink.*

Gesseur, *m.* (popular), *fussy man; eccentric man,* a "rum un'."

Gesseuse, *f.* (popular), *prude; female who gives herself airs.*

Gestes. See **Accentuer.**

Get, geti, *m.* (thieves'), *reed, cane.*

G—g, *m.* (popular), avoir du —, *to have good sense,* "to know what's o'clock," "to be up to a trick or two."

Gi, or **gy** (thieves'), *yes,* or "usher."

Gibasses, *f. pl.* (popular), *large skinny breasts.*

Gibelotte de gouttière, *f.* (popu-lar), *cat stew.*

Giberne, *f.* (popular), *the behind.* See **Vasistas.**

Gibier, *m.* (popular), à commis-saire, *woman of disorderly or drunken habits;* — de Cayenne, *incorrigible thief,* or "gallows' bird."

Giboyer, *m.* (literary), *journalist of the worst sort.* From a play by Émile Augier.

Gibus, *m.* (familar), *hat,* or "stove pipe." See **Tubard**.

Gigolette, *f.* (popular), *girl of the lower orders who leads a more than fast life, and is an assiduous frequenter of low dancing-halls.*

> Si tu veux être ma gigolette,
> Moi, je serai ton gigolo.
> *Parisian Song.*

Gigolo, *m.* (popular), *fast young man of the lower orders, a kind of* "'Arry," *the associate of a gigo-*lette (which see).

Gigot, *m.* (popular), *large thick hand,* "mutton fist."

Gigue et jon! *bacchanalian excla-mation of sailors.*

> Largue l'écoute ! Bitte et bosse !
> Largue l'écoute ! Gigue et jon !
> Largue l'écoute ! on s'y fout des bosses,
> Chez la mère Barbe-en-jonc.
> RICHEPIN, *La Mer.*

Gilboque, *m.* (thieves' and cads'), *billiards.* Termed "spoof" in the English slang.

Gilet, *m.* (popular), s'emplir le —, *to eat or drink.* Avoir le — doublé de flanelle *is said of one who has comforted himself with a plate of thick, hot soup.* The English use the term "flannel" or "hot flannel" for a comfort-ing drink of a hot mixture of gin and beer with nutmeg, sugar, &c. According to the *Slang Dictionary* there is an anecdote told of Goldsmith helping to drink a quart of "flannel" in a night-house, in company with George Parker, Ned Shuter, and a de-mure, grave-looking gentleman, who continually introduced the words "crap," "stretch," "scrag," and "swing." Upon the Doctor asking who this strange person might be, and being told his pro-fession, he rushed from the place in a frenzy, exclaiming, "Good God ! and have I been sitting all this while with a hangman?" Un — à la mode, *opulent breasts.* (Familiar) Un—en cœur, *a dandy,* or "masher."

> Amantha, que Corbois avait complète-ment perdue de vue, était aux Bouffes et faisait la joie des gilets en cœur.—E. MONTEIL.

Gille, *m.* (popular), faire —, *to run away,* "to slope," "bolt." See **Patatrot**. The expression is old.

> Jupin leur fit prendre le saut,
> Et contraignit de faire gille,
> Le grand Typhon jusqu'en Sicile.
> SCARRON.

Faire — déloge (obsolete), *to de-camp.*

Gilmont, *m.* (thieves'), *waistcoat,* or "benjy."

Gilquin, *m.* (popular), coup de —, *blow with the fist,* a "bang," or "biff" (Americanism).

Gimbler (sailors'), *to moan.* Le vent gimble, *the wind moans, roars.*

> Bon ! qu'il gimble tant qu'il voudra dans les agrès !
> Nous en avons troussé bien d'autres au plus près.
> Ce n'est pas encore lui qui verra notre quille.
> Souffle, souffle, mon vieux ! souffle à goule écarquille !
> RICHEPIN, *La Mer.*

Gin (thieves'), à son —, *see! behold!* This expression has been repro-duced in the spelling of my infor-mant, an associate of thieves.

Gingin, *m.* (popular), *good sense ; behind.* See **Vasistas**.

Ginginer (popular), *to make one's dress bulge out ; to ogle ; to flirt.*

Ginglard, ginglet, or **ginguet**, *m.* (popular), *thin sour wine.*

Girafe, *f.* (popular), grande —, petite —, *spiral flights of steps, in* *the Seine swimming baths, with a lower and upper landing serving as diving platforms.*

Girofle, *adj.* (thieves'), *pretty,* "dimber." Largue —, *pretty girl,* or "dimbermort."

Giroflerie, *f.* (thieves'), *amiability.*

Girofleter (popular), *to smack one's face,* "to warm the wax of one's ear." Synonymous of "donner du sucre de giroflée."

Girole (thieves'), expression of assent : *so be it,* "usher."

Il y a deux menées de ronds en ma henne et deux ornies en mon gueulard, que j'ai égraillées sur le trimar ; bions les faire riffoder, veux-tu ?—Girole, et béni soit le grand havre qui m'a fait rencontrer si chenâtre occasion.—*Le Jargon de l'Argot.* (*There are two dozen halfpence in my purse and two hens in my wallet, which I have caught on the road; we will cook them, if you like ?—Certainly, and blessed be the Almighty who made me fall in with such a piece of good luck.*)

Gironde, *adj. and f.* (thieves'), *gentle ; pretty,* "dimber ;" *pretty woman or girl,* "dimbermort." Also *a girl of bad character, a* "bunter."

Girondin, *m.* (thieves'), *simple-minded fellow,* "flat," or "jay." Le — a donné, "the jay has been flapped."

Girondine, *f.* (thieves'), *handsome young girl,* or "dimbermort."

Gîte, *m.* (popular), dans le —, *something of the best.* An allusion to gîte à la noix, *savoury morsel of beef.*

Gitre (thieves'), *I have.*

Gitre mouchaillé le babillard.—*Le Jargon de l'Argot.* (*I have looked at the book.*)

Giverner (popular), *to prowl about at night.*

Giverneur, *m.* (popular), *one who prowls at night ;* (thieves') — de refroidis, *one who drives a hearse.*

Glace, *f. and m.* (familiar and popular), passer devant la —, *to enjoy gratis the favours of a prostitute at a brothel ; to pay for the reckoning at a café.* An allusion to the large looking-glass behind the counter. (Popular) Un —, *glass of wine.* Sucer un —, *to drink a glass of wine.*

Glacé, *adj.* (popular and thieves'), pendu, *street lamps used till they were superseded by the present gas lamps.* A few are still to be seen in some lanes of old Paris. ,

Les pendus glacés, ce sont ces gros réverbères à quatre faces de vitre verte carrées comme des glaces . . . ce sont ces réverbères abolis qui pendent au bout d'une corde accrochée à un bras de potence.—RICHEPIN, *Le Pavé.*

Glacière pendue, *f.* (thieves'). See **Glacé**.

Glacis, *m.* (popular), se passer un —, *to drink,* "to take something damp," or "to moisten one's chaffer." See **Rincer**.

Gladiateur, *m.* (military), *shoe.* An ironical allusion to the fleetness of the celebrated racer Gladiateur.

Glaire, *f.* (popular), pousser sa —, *to talk,* "to jaw." As-tu fini de pousser ta —, *don't talk so much,* which may be rendered by the Americanism, "don't shoot off your mouth."

Glaive, *m.* (freemasons'), *carving-knife ;* (thieves') *guillotine.* Passer sa bille au —, *to be guillotined.* See **Fauché**.

Glaiver (thieves'), *to guillotine.*

Glao (Breton cant), *rain.*

Glaou (Breton cant), *firebrands.*

Glas, *m.* (popular), *dull man with a dismal sort of conversation,* "croaker."

Glaviot, *m.* (popular), *expectoration,* or "gob."

Glavioter (popular), *to expectorate.*

Glavioteur, *m.* (popular), *man who expectorates.*

Glier, glinet, *m.* (thieves'), *devil,* "ruffin." From sanglier, *a wild boar.* Le — t'entrolle en son pasclin, *the devil take you to his abode!*

Glissant, *m.* (thieves'), *soap.*

Glisser (popular), *to die,* "to stick one's spoon in the wall," "to kick the bucket," or "to snuff it." See **Pipe.**

Globe, *m.* (popular), *head,* or "nut," see **Tronche**; *stomach.* S'être fait arrondir le —, *to have become pregnant,* or "lumpy."

Glouglouter (popular), *to drink,* "to wet one's whistle." See **Rincer.**

Glousser (popular), *to talk,* "to jaw."

Gluant, *m.* (cads' and thieves'), *penis; baby,* "kinchin."

Paraît que j'suis dab'! ça m'esbloque.
Un p'tit salé, à moi l'salaud!
Ma rouchi' doit batt' la berloque.
Un gluant, ça n'f'rait pas mon blot.
RICHEPIN.

Gluau, *m.* (popular), *expectoration.* (Thieves') Poser un —, *to arrest,* "to smug." See **Piper.** Gluau, properly *a twig smeared over with bird-lime.*

Glutouse, *f.* (thieves'), *face,* or "mug."

Gnac, *m.* (popular), *quarrel.*

Gnaffé, *adj.* (popular), *clumsily done.*

Gnafle, *f.* (popular), *bad throw.* Après — raffle, *constant ill-luck.*

Gniaff, *m.* (familiar), *bad workman; writer or journalist of the worst description;* (shoemakers') *working shoemaker.*

Gniaffer (popular), *to work clumsily.*

Gniasse (cads' and thieves'), mon —, *I, myself,* "No. 1." Ton —, *thou, thee.* Son —, *he, him; I, myself.* Un —, *a fellow,* a "cove." Un bon —, *a good fellow,* a "brick."

Gniff, *adj.* (popular), ce vin est —, *that wine is clear.*

Gniol, gniole, gnolle, *adj.* (popular), *silly; dull-witted.* Es-tu assez —! *how silly,* or *what a* "flat" *you are!*

On voulait nous mettre à la manque pour lui (nous le faire livrer), nous ne sommes pas des gnioles!—BALZAC.

Gnognotte, *f.* (familiar and popular). The expression has passed into the language; *thing of little worth,* "no great scratch."

Ce farceur de Mes-Bottes, vers la fin de l'été, avait eu le truc d'épouser pour de vrai une dame, très décatie déjà, mais qui possédait de beaux restes; oh! une dame de la rue des Martyrs, pas de la gnognotte de barrière.—ZOLA, *L'Assommoir.*

Gnol-Chy (popular), abbreviation of Batignolles-Clichy.

Gnole, *f.* (popular), *slap,* "clout," "wipe;" or, as the Americans have it, "biff." Abbreviation of torgnole.

Gnon, *m.* (popular), *blow,* "clout," "bang," or "wipe;" *bruise,* or "mouse."

Gnouf-gnouf, *m.* (theatrical), *monthly dinner of the actors of the Palais Royal Theatre.* When ceremonious, the members are called, "Gnouf-gnoufs d'Allemagne;" when bacchanalian, "Gnouf-gnoufs de Pologne."

Go, parler en —, *is to use that syllable to disguise words.*

Gobage, *m.* (popular), *love.*

Gobante, *f.* (popular), *attractive woman.* From gober, *to like.*

Gobbe, gobelot, *m.* (thieves'), *chalice.*

Gobelet, *m.* (thieves'), être sous le —, *to be in prison,* or "put away."

Gobelin, *m.* (thieves'), *thimble.*

Gobelot. See **Gobbe.**

Gobe-mouches, *m.* (thieves'), *spy,* "nark," or "nose."

Gobe-prune, *m.* (thieves'), *tailor.* Termed also pique-poux, and in the English slang a "cabbage contractor," "steel-bar driver," "button catcher."

Gober (familiar and popular), *to like ; to love ; to please.* Je te gobe, *you please me ; I like you.* Gober la chèvre, or — son bœuf, *to get angry,* "to get one's monkey up," "to lose one's shirt," "to get into a scot." Termed "to be in a swot" at Shrewsbury School. Se —, *to have a high opinion of oneself ; to love oneself too much.*

Non, non, pas de cabotins. Le vieux Bosc était toujours gris ; Prullières se gobait trop.—ZOLA, *Nana.*

La —, *to be the victim ; to have to pay for others ; to be ruined ; to believe a false assertion.* Synonymous, in the latter sense, of the old expression, "gober le morceau."

Mais je ne suis pas homme à gober le morceau.—MOLIÈRE, *Ecole des Femmes.*

Cent pas loin, le camelot a recommencé son truc, après avoir ri, avec son copain, des pantes qui la gobent !—RICHE-PIN. (*A hundred steps further the sharper again tries his dodge, after laughing with his chum at the flats who take it in.*)

Si nous échouons, c'est moi qui la gobe, *if we fail, I shall be made responsible.*

Gobeson, *m.* (thieves'), *drinking-glass,* or "flicker ;" *cup ; chalice.*

Gobet, *m.* (popular), *piece of beef,* "a bit o' bull." Had formerly the signification of *dainty bit.*

Laisse-moi faire, nous en mangerons de bons gobets ensemble. — HAUTEROCHE, *Crispin Médecin.*

Gobet, *disorderly workman.* Mauvais —, *scamp,* or "bad egg."

Gobette, *f.* (thieves'), *drinking-glass,* or "flicker." Payer la —, *to stand treat.*

Gobeur, *m.* (familiar), *credulous man,* "flat."

Gobichonnade, *f.* (familiar and popular), *gormandizing.*

Gobichonner (familiar and popular), se —. *to regale oneself.*

Il se sentit capable des plus grandes lâchetés pour continuer à gobichonner.— BALZAC.

Gobichonneur, *m.,* **gobichonneuse,** *f.* (familiar and popular), *gormandizer,* "grand paunch."

Gobilleur, *m.* (thieves'), *juge d'instruction, a magistrate who instructs cases, and privately examines prisoners before trial.*

Gobseck, *m.* (familiar), *miser,* "skinflint," or "hunks." One of the characters of Balzac's *Comédie Humaine.*

Godaille, *f.* (popular), *amusement ; indulgence in eating and drinking.*

On doit travailler, ça ne fait pas un doute : seulement quand on se trouve avec des amis, la politesse passe avant tout. Un désir de godaille les avait peu à peu chatouillés et engourdis tous les quatre.— ZOLA, *L'Assommoir.*

Godan, *m.* (popular), *falsehood.* Connaître le —, *to be wide-awake, not easily duped,* "to know what's o'clock." Monter un — à quelqu'un, *to seek to deceive one,* or "best" one.

Godancer (popular), *to allow oneself to be duped,* "to be done brown."

Godard, *m.* (popular), *a husband who has just become a father.*

Goddam, or **goddem,** *m.* (popular), *Englishman.*

(Entraînant l'Anglais.) Maintenant, allons jouer des bibelots ... voilà un goddam qui va y aller d'autant.—P. MAHALIN.

Godet, *m.* (popular), *drinking glass.* A common expression among the lower orders, and a very old one.

Godiche, *adj.* (familiar and popular), *simple-minded, foolish.*

Que tu es donc godiche, Toinon, de venir tous les matins comme ça.—GAVARNI.

Godiller (popular), *to be merry ; to be carnally excited.*

Godilleur, *m.* (popular), *man who is fond of the fair sex,* a "molrower," or "beard-splitter."

Godillot, *m.* (popular), *military shoe.* From the name of the maker ; (military) *recruit,* or "Johnny raw."

Godiveau rance, *m.* (popular), *stingy man.*

Tu peux penser si je le traite de godiveau rance chaque fois qu'il me refuse un petit cadeau.—E. MONTEIL.

Goffeur, *m.* (thieves'), *locksmith.* From the Celtic goff, *a smith.*

Gogaille, *f.* (popular), *banquet.*

Gogo, *m.* (familiar), *simple-minded man who invests his capital in swindling concerns,* "gull ; " *man easily fleeced.*

Quand les allumeurs de l'Hôtel des Ventes eurent jugé le gogo en complet entraînement, il y eut un arrêt momentané parmi les enchères intéressées.—A. SIRVEN.

(Popular) Gogo, *greenhorn,* "flat." The term, with this signification, is hardly slang. Villon uses it in his *Ballade de Villon et de la Grosse Margot* (15th century).

Riant, m'assiet le poing sur mon sommet, Gogo me dit, et me fiert le jambot.

Gogotte, *adj.* (popular), *spiritless ; weak ; bad.* From gogo. Avoir la vue —, *to have a weak sight.* A corruption of cocotte, *disease of the eyes.*

Goguenau, gogueno, goguenot, *m.* (military), *tin can holding one litre, used by soldiers to make coffee or soup ;* also *howitzer ;* (military and popular) *privy.* Passer la jambe à Thomas —, *to empty the privy tub.* Hirondelle de —, *low street-walker,* or "draggle-tail." See Gadoue.

Goguette, *f.* (popular), *vocal society ; wine-shop.* Etre en —, *to be merrily inclined ; to be enjoying oneself, the bottle being the chief factor in the source of enjoyment.*

Goguetter (popular), *to make merry.* From the old word goguette, *amusement.*

Goguettier, *m.* (popular), *member of a vocal society.*

Goinfre, *m.* (thieves'), *precentor.* An allusion to his opening his mouth like that of a glutton.

Goiper (thieves'), *to prowl at night for evil purposes,* "quærens quem devoret."

Goipeur, *m.* (thieves'), *night thief.*

Goipeuse, *f.* (thieves'), *prostitute who prowls about the country.* See Gadoue.

Goîtreux, *m.* (familiar), *silly fellow; man devoid of all intellectual power.* Synonymous of crétin.

Goje (Breton cant), *well ; yes.*

Golgother (familiar), *to give oneself the airs of a martyr.* The allusion is obvious.

Gomberger (thieves'), *to reckon.*

Gombeux, *adj.* (popular), *nasty.*

Gomme, *f.* (familiar), *fashion ; elegance,* "swelldom." La haute

—, the "pink" *of fashion.* Etre
de la —, *to be a dandy, a*
"masher." See **Gommeux.**
The term formerly signified ex-
cellence, and was used specially
in reference to wine.

> Mais non pas d'un pareil trésor,
> Que cette souveraine gomme.
> *Parnasse des Muses.*

Gommeuse, *f.* (familiar), *showily
dressed girl or woman,* a
"dasher."

Gommeux, *adj. and m.* (familiar),
pretty ; dandy.

> C'était elle qui, pour la première fois,
> recevant un de ses amants astiqué des
> pieds à la tête, empesé, ciré, frotté, tiré,
> semblant, en deux mots, trempé dans de la
> gomme arabique en dissolution, avait dit
> de lui : un gommeux ! Le petit-crevé avait
> un successeur.—E. MONTEIL, *Cornebois.*

The different appellations corresponding to various periods are
as follows :—Under Louis XIV.,
"mouchar, muguet, petit-maître,
talon-rouge." After the revolution
of 1793, "muscadin." Under the
government of the Directoire from
'95 to '99, "incroyable, merveilleux." Then from the Restoration
come in succession, "mirliflor,
élégant, dandy, lion, fashionable,
and gandin." Under the Third
Empire, "cocodès, crevé, petit-
crevé, col-cassé." From 1870 to
the present day, "gommeux, luisant, poisseux, boudiné, pschutteux, exhumé, gratiné, faucheur,
and finally bécarre." The English
have the terms "swell, gorger,
masher," and the old expression
"flasher," mentioned in the following quotation from the *English Supplementary Glossary :*—

> They are reckoned the flashers of the
> place, yet everybody laughs at them for
> their airs, affectations, and tonish graces
> and impertinences.—MADAME D'ARBLAY,
> *Diary.*

The *Spectator* termed a dandy a
"Jack-pudding," and Goldsmith
calls him a "macaroni," "The
Italians," he says, "are extremely
fond of a dish they call macaroni,
. . . and as they consider this
as the *summum bonum* of all good
eating, so they figuratively call
everything they think elegant and
uncommon macaroni. Our young
travellers, who generally catch the
follies of the countries they visit,
judged that the title of *macaroni*
was very applicable to a *clever
fellow ;* and accordingly, to dis-
tinguish themselves as such, they
instituted a club under this denomination, the members of which
were supposed to be the standards
of *taste.* The infection at St.
James's was soon caught in the
City, and we have now macaronies
of every denomination, from the
Colonel of the Train'd-Bands
down to the printer's devil or
errand-boy. They indeed make
a most ridiculous figure, with hats
of an inch in the brim, that do
not cover, but lie upon the head ;
with about two pounds of fictitious
hair, formed into what is called a
club, hanging down their shoulders, as white as a baker's sack ;
the end of the skirt of their coat
reaching not down to the first
button of their breeches. . . .
Such a figure, essenced and per-
fumed, with a bunch of lace sticking out under *its* chin, puzzles the
common passenger to determine
the *thing's* sex ; and many have
said, *by your leave, madam,* without intending to give offence."

The Americans give the name
of "dude" to one who apes the
manners of swells. It may be
this word originated from a com-
parison between the tight and
light-coloured trousers sported by
swells, and the stem of a pipe
termed "dudeen" by the Irish.

Compare the French expression "boudiné," literally *sausage-like*, for a swell in tight clothing.

Gomorrhe, *m.* (familiar), un émigré de —, *Sodomist*. See **Gosselin**.

Gonce, gonse, gonze, *m.* (thieves'), *man*, or "cove."

Goncesse, gonzesse, *f.* (thieves'), *woman*, "hay-bag, cooler, or shakester."

Goncier, or **gonce,** *m.* (thieves'), *man*, or "cove."

Gondolé, *adj.* (thieves' and popular), avoir l'air —, *to look ill*. Un homme —, *high-shouldered man*.

Gonfle-bougres, *m.* (thieves'), *beans*, the staple food of prisoners.

Gonfler. See **Ballon.** (Popular) Se —, *to be elated*.

Mon vieux, c'que tu peux t'gonfler d'gagner des coupes Renaissance ! — *Le Cri du Peuple*, 17 Août, 1886.

Se — le jabot, *to look conceited*.

Tu es un bon artiste, c'est vrai, mais, vrai aussi, tu te gonfles trop le jabot.—E. MONTEIL.

Gonsalé, *m.* (thieves'), *man*, or "cove." Si le — fait de l'harmonarés, il faut le balancarguer dans la vassarés, *if the man is not quiet, we'll throw him into the water*.

Gonsarès, *m.* (thieves'), *man*. A form of gonse.

Gonse, *m.* (thieves' and popular), *man*, or cove ; " — à écailles, *women's bully*, "ponce." See **Poisson**.

Gonsier, or **gadouille,** *m.* (popular), *an individual*, "cove."

Gonsse, *m.* (police and thieves'), *fool*.

Vous êtes un gonsse, monsieur, murmura le chef à l'agent porteur du bijou, qu'il lui arracha aussitôt.—*Mémoires de Monsieur Claude*.

Gonzesse. See **Goncesse**.

Gorge, *f.* (thieves'), *case*.

Gorgniat, *m.* (popular), *dirty man*, a "chatty" *fellow*.

Gose, *m.* (popular), *throat*, or "red-lane." Abbreviation of gosier.

Gosse, *m.* and *f.* (general), *child*, "kid." Ah ! l'affreux gosse ! pialle-t'y ! Asseyez - vous dessus ! et qu' ça finisse ! *The horrible child ! how he does squall ! Sit upon him, and let there be an end of it.* This seemingly uncharitable wish is often expressed in thought, if not in speech, in France, where many children are petted and spoilt into insufferable tyrants.

Arrive l'enfant de la maison qui pleure. Au lieu de lui dire : Ah ! le joli enfant, même quand il pleure, on croirait entendre la voix de la Patti. . . . Maintenant ce n'est plus ça, l'on dit : Ah ! l'affreux gosse ! Pialles-t'y ! . . . en v'là un qui crie ! . . . pour sûr il a avalé la pratique à Thérésa ! —*Les Locutions Vicieuses*.

Gosselin, *m.* (popular), *young man*, "covey." Être en —, *to be a Sodomist*. Synonymous of the expression, "en être," concerning which Lorédan Larchey says :—"Ménage, dans ses *Origines*, dit Tallemant des Réaux, avait commencé sa dissertation sur le mot *bougre* par ces mots : *Bougre : Je suis de l'avis*, &c.— Ah ! lui dit Bautru en se moquant, vous *en êtes* donc aussi et vous l'imprimez. Tenez ! il y a bien moulé : *Bougre je suis*." Comme Bautru, et dans le même sens, on dit encore : *Il en est*.

Sur ce terrain honteux, les synonymes pullulent ; ils prouvent la persistance d'un vice qui semble éprouver, dans les deux sexes, le besoin de se cacher à chaque instant derrière un nom nouveau. Nous rappelons ici pour mémoire, et sans les expliquer ailleurs, les mots : pédé, bique et bouc, coquine, pédéro, tante, tapette, corvette, frégate, Jésus, persilleuse, honteuse, rivette, emproseur, &c.

Gosseline, *f.* (popular and thieves'), *young maiden.* Fignole —, *pretty lass.*

Gossemar, *m.* (popular), *child,* or "kid." A form of gosse.

Gossier, *m.* See **Gonce.**

Got, *m.,* for gau (thieves'), *louse,* or "gold-backed un."

Goteur, *m.* (popular), *whore-monger,* "mutton-monger, molrower, beard-splitter, or rip."

Gouache, *f.* (popular), *face, physiognomy,* or "mug." See **Tronche.**

Goualante, gouasante, *f.* (thieves'), *song ; street hawker.* Les goualantes avec leurs bagnioles, *the hawkers with their hand-barrows.*

Goualer (thieves'), *to sing,* "to "lip ;" — à la chienlit, *to cry out thieves !* "to give hot beef."

Goualeur, *m.,* **goualeuse,** *f.* (thieves'), *singer,* "chanter."

Dis donc, la goualeuse, est-ce que tu ne vas pas nous goualer une de tes goualantes ?—E. Sue, *Les Mystères de Paris.*

Gouape, *f.* (popular), *laziness ; drunken and disorderly state ; one who leads a lazy or dissolute life ; a reprobate ; thief,* or "prig." See **Grinche.**

Gouaper (popular), *to lead a disorderly life ; to prowl about lazily,* "to mike ;" *to tramp.*

Gouapeur, gouêpeur (general), *lazy man ; vagabond ; debauchee.*

Sans paffes, sans lime, plein de crotte,
Aussi rupin qu'un plongeur,
Un soir un gouêpeur en ribote
Tombe en frime avec un voleur.
VIDOCQ.

Gouapeur, *ironical appellation given by lazy prisoners to those who work.*

Gouapeuse, *f.* (general), *dissolute woman fond of good cheer.*

Gouêper (popular), *to lead the life of a* gouapeur (which see) ; *also to lead a vagrant life.*

J'ai comme un brouillard de souvenir d'avoir gouêpé dans mon enfance avec un vieux chiffonnier qui m'assommait de coups de croc.—E. Sue.

Gouêpeur. See **Gouapeur.**

Gouffier (obsolete), *to eat.*

Gougnottage, *m.* (popular), *unnatural intercourse between women.*

Gougnotte, *f.* (popular), *woman who indulges in* "gougnottage" (which see).

Gougnotter. See **Gougnottage.**

Gouille, *f.* (popular), envoyer à la —, *to summarily get rid of a bore ; to send a bore to the deuce.*

Gouillon, *m.* (popular), *street boy,* or *street arab.*

Goujon, *m.* (general), *dupe,* or "gull ;" *girl's bully,* or "Sunday man." For synonyms see **Poisson.** Un — d'hôpital, *a leech.* Avaler le —, *to die,* "to snuff it." See **Pipe.** Ferrer le —, *to cause one to fall into a trap, to make one swallow the bait.* Lâcher son —, *to vomit,* "to cascade," "to shoot the cat," or "to cast up accounts."

Goujonner (popular), *to deceive,* "to best," "to do."

Goule, *f.* (popular), *throat*, or "gutter lane;" *mouth*, or "rattle-trap." Old form of gueule used in the expression, now obsolete, Faire péter la goule, *to speak*.

Goulot, *m.* (popular), *mouth*, or "rattle-trap;" *throat*, or "gutter lane." Jouer du —, *to drink heavily*, "to swill." Se rincer le —, *to drink*, "to wet one's whistle." See **Rincer.** Trouilloter du —, *to have an offensive breath*.

Goulu, *m.* (thieves'), *a stove; a well.* Properly *greedy, glutton*.

Goupinage, *m.* (thieves'), *work,* "graft;" *thieving,* "faking."

Goupine, *f.* (cads' and thieves'), *head,* or "nut," see **Tronche;** (popular) *quaint dress*.

Goupiné, *adj.* (popular), mal —, *badly dressed*.

Goupiner (thieves'), *to steal*, "to nick." See **Grinchir.**

> En roulant de vergne en vergne
> Pour apprendre à goupiner.
> VIDOCQ.

Goupiner les poivriers, *to rob drunkards ; —* à la desserte, *to steal plate from a dining-room in the following manner :—*

> D'autres bonjouriers ne se mettent en campagne qu'aux approches du dîner : ceux-là saisissent le moment où l'argenterie vient d'être posée sur la table. Ils entrent et en un clin d'œil ils la font disparaître.— VIDOCQ.

Goupiner, *to do*.

> La largue est fine . . . et que goupine-t-elle? Elle est établie . . . elle gère une maison.—BALZAC.

Goupineur à la desserte, *m.* (thieves'). See **Goupiner.**

Goupline, *f.* (thieves'), *pint*.

Gour, *m.* (thieves'), *jug ; —* de pivois, *jugful of wine*.

Gourd, *m.* (thieves'), *fraud; deceit ; swindling ;* (Breton cant) *good; well*.

Gourdago (Breton cant), *food*.

Gourde, *f.* (popular), *simpleton,* "flat."

Gourdé, *m.* (popular), *fool*, "flat," or "bounder."

Gourdement (popular and thieves'), *much*, or, as the Irish say, "neddy ;" *very*.

> Ils piaussent dans les pioles, morfient et pictent si gourdement, que toutime en bourdonne.—*Le Jargon de l'Argot*. (*They sleep in the taverns, eat and drink so much that everything resounds with it.*)

Gourer, or **gourrer** (popular and thieves'), *to deceive*, "to kid ;" *to swindle*, "to stick." The word is old.

> Pour gourrer les pauvres gens,
> Qui leur babil veulent croire.
> *Parnasse des Muses.*

Se —, *to be mistaken ; to assume a jaunty, self-satisfied air*.

> C'est la raison pourquoi qu' je m' goure,
> Mon gniasse est bath : j'ai un chouett' moure.
> RICHEPIN.

Goureur, *m.* (thieves'), *deceiver ; cheat*, or "cross-biter ;" — de la haute, *swell mobsmen*. Goureurs, *rogues who assume a disguise to deceive the public, and who sell inferior articles at exorbitant prices*. The sham sailor, with rings in his ears, who has just returned from a long cruise, and offers parrots or smuggled havannahs for sale, the false countryman, &c., are goureurs.

Goureuse, *f.* (thieves'), *female deceiver or cheat*.

Gourgandin, *m.* (familiar), *a man too fond of cocottes*. Vieux —, *old debauchee*, old "rip."

Gourgandinage, *m.* (popular), *disreputable way of living*.

Gourgandiner (popular), *to lead a dissolute life.* From gourgandine, *a girl or woman of lax morals.*

Gourganer (popular), *to be in prison, eating* "gourganes," *or beans.*

Gourgaud, *m.* (military), *recruit,* or "Johnny raw."

Gourgoussage, *m.* (popular), *grumbling.*

Gourgousser (popular), *to grumble.*

Gourgousseur, *m.* (popular), *grumbler,* or "crib biter."

Gourt (popular), à son —, *pleased.* The word is old, Villon uses it :—

> L'hostesse fut bien à son gourt,
> Car, quand vint à compter l'escot,
> Le seigneur ne dist oncques mot.

Gouspin, or **goussepain,** *m.* (popular), *malicious urchin.*

> Il en tira le corps d'un chat : "Tiens dit le gosse
> Au troquet, tiens, voici de quoi faire un lapin."
> Puis il prit son petit couteau de goussepain,
> Dépouilla le greffier, et lui fit sa toilette.
> RICHEPIN, *La Chanson des Gueux.*

Gouspiner (popular), *to wander lazily about,* "to mike." From gouspin, *a malicious urchin.*

Gousse, *f.* (theatrical), la —, *monthly banquet of the actors of the Vaudeville Theatre.* See **Gosselin.**

Gousser (popular), *to eat,* "to grub." See **Mastiquer.**

Gousset, *m.* (popular), *armpit.* Properly *fob.* Avoir le — percé, *to be penniless,* "to be a quisby." Repousser du —, *to emit a disagreeable odour of humanity.*

Goût, *m.* (popular), faire passer, or faire perdre à quelqu'un le — du pain, *to kill one,* "to cook one's goose."

Goutte, *f.* (popular), marchand de —, *retailer of spirits.* (Familiar and popular) Goutte militaire, *a certain disease termed in the English slang* "French gout," or "ladies' fever."

Gouttière, *f.* (familiar), lapin de —, *a cat,* "long-tailed beggar."

Gouvernement, *m.* (popular), mon —, *my wife,* "my old woman," or "my comfortable impudence."

Goye, *m.* (popular), *fool ; dupe.*

Graffagnade, *f.* (familiar), *bad painting.*

Graffigner (popular), *to take ; to seize,* "to nab ;" *to scratch.*

Graffin, *m.* (popular), *rag-picker,* "bone-grubber," or "tot-picker."

Graigaille, *f.* (popular), *bread,* "soft tommy, or bran."

Graillon, *m.* (familiar), *dirty slatternly woman.* That is, one who emits an odour of kitchen grease.

Graillonneuse, *f.* (popular), *woman who not being a washerwoman washes her linen at the public laundry.*

Grain, *m.* (familiar and popular), avoir un —, *to be slightly crazy,* "to be a little bit balmy in one's crumpet." Avoir un petit —, *to be slightly tipsy,* or "elevated." See **Pompette.** (Popular) Un —, *fifty-centime coin.* Formerly *a silver crown.* Léger de deux grains (obsolete), an expression applied formerly to eunuchs. Un catholique à gros — (obsolete), the signification is given by the quotation :—

> On appelle catholique à gros grain, un libertin, un homme peu dévot, qui ne va à l'église que par manière d'acquit. — LE ROUX, *Dict. Comique.*

Graine, *f.* (familiar and popular), de bagne, *thief's offspring* ; (familiar) — de chou colossal, *grand promises made with the object of swindling credulous persons* ; — giberne, *soldier's child* ; — d'épinards, *epaulets of field-officers.* Avoir la — d'épinards, *to be a field-officer.* De la — d'andouilles *is said of a number of small children in a group.*

Graissage, *m.*, or **graisse**, *f.* (popular), *money,* "dust." That which serves " to grease the palm." See **Quibus**.

Graisse, *f.* (popular and thieves'), *money,* or "pieces." See **Quibus**. (Thieves') Voler à la graisse (for grèce), *to cheat at a game.* Also *to obtain a loan of money on* "brummagem" *trinkets, or paste diamonds represented as genuine.*

Voler à la graisse : se faire prêter sur des lingots d'or et sur des diamants qui ne sont que du cuivre et du strass.—VIDOCQ.

Graisser (military), la marmite, *as a new-comer, to treat one's comrades,* " to pay for one's footing ;" (general) — la peau, *to thrash,* " to wallop." See **Voie**. Graisser le train de derrière, *to give a kick in the behind,* " to toe one's bum ;" — les bottes à quelqu'un, *to help one* ; — les épaules à quelqu'un (obsolete), *to thrash one.*

Graisser les épaules à quelqu'un, pour dire, le bâtonner. Ce qui a fait dire aussi de l'huile de cotret, c'est-à-dire, des coups de bâton.—LE ROUX, *Dict. Comique.*

Graisser les roues, *to drink,* " to have something damp." See **Rincer**. (Thieves') Graisser, or gressier, *to steal,* " to nick." See **Grinchir**.

Graisseur, *m.* (thieves'), *card-sharper,* or " magsman."

Grand (popular), arroseur, *God,* termed " Charley " by the Americans ; — bonnet, *bishop* ; — carcan, *tall, lanky girl.* Also an opprobrious epithet ; — courbouillon, sea, or " briny ;" — lumignon, sun ; — singe, *President of the Republic* ; (thieves') — coëre, *formerly the king of mendicants* ; — meudon, *spy* ; *detective,* "nark ;" — trimar, *highway,* "high toby ;" (military) — montant tropical, *riding breeches* ; (theatrical) — trottoir, *stock of classical plays.*

Grande, *adj. and f.* (popular), boutique, *préfecture de police* ; — bleue, *the sea,* " briny," or " herring pond ;" — fille, *bottle.* (Thieves') Grande, *pocket,* or " cly," " skyrocket," " brigh." Termed also " profonde, fouillouse, louche, gueularde."

Grand' largue, *adv.* (sailors'), *excellent* ; *incomparable.*

Grands, *adj.* (theatrical), jouer les — coquets, *to perform in the character of an accomplished, elegant man.* (Cavalry school of Saumur) Les — hommes, *the corridors in the school buildings.*

Granik (Breton cant), *hunger.*

Graoudgem, *m.* (thieves'), *pork butcher,* or " kiddier." Faire un — à la dure, *to steal sausages.*

Graphiqué, *adj.* (thieves'), *filthy,* or "chatty."

Grappin, *m.* (popular), *hand,* or " flipper." Mettre or poser le — sur quelqu'un, *to apprehend one, or* "to smug" *one.* See **Piper**.

Grappiner (popular), *to seize* ; *to apprehend,* or "to smug." See **Piper**.

Gras, *adj. and m.* (popular), il y a —, *there is plenty of money to be got.* Attraper un —, *to get a* *scolding*, or "wigging." (Thieves' and cads') Gras, *privy*.

Gras-double, or **saucisson,** *m.* (thieves'), *sheet lead*, or "moss." Ratisser du —, *to steal lead off the roofs*, termed by English thieves "flying the blue pigeon." Porter du — au moulin, *to take stolen lead to a receiver's*, or "fence."

Gras - doublier, *m.* (thieves'), *plumber*.

Grasse, *f.* (thieves'), *strong box*, or "peter." Thus called by rogues because it contains "la graisse," or *the cash*.

Gratin, *m.* (popular), *thrashing*. Refiler un —, *to box one's ears*. (Familiar) Gratin, *tip-top of fashion; swelldom*.

Le Paris extra-mondain . . . le gratin, quoi !—P. MAHALIN.

Gratiné, *m.* (familiar), *swell*, "masher." For synonymous expressions see **Gommeux**.

Gratis (popular), faire —, *to borrow*, "to bite one's ear," or "to break shins;" *to lend*. (Thieves') Etre — malade, *to be in prison, to be* "put away."

Graton, *m.* (popular), *razor*. From gratter, *to scratch*.

Gratouille, *f.* (popular), *itch*. From gratter, *to scratch, to itch*.

Gratouse, *f.* (thieves'), *lace*.

Gratousé, *adj.* (thieves'), *adorned with lace*.

Gratte, *f.* (popular), *itch ; unlawful profits of shopmen on the sale of goods*, something like the "fluff" or profits on short change by railway ticket-clerks ; *bonus allowed to shopmen ;* — couenne, *barber*, "strap ;" — pavé, *loiterer seeking for a living, one* "on the mouch."

Grattée, *f.* (popular), *blows*, "props."

Gratte-papier, *m.* (familiar and popular), *clerk*, or "quill-driver;" (military) *non-commissioned officer filling the functions of clerk*.

Gratter (popular), *to shave ; to thrash*, "to wallop." See **Voie**. Gratter, *to purloin portions of cloth given for the making of apparel ; to apprehend*. See **Piper**. Gratter le papier, *to write ; to be a clerk*, or "quill-driver ;" — la couenne, *to shave*. En —, *to perform on the dancing-rope*. Les frères qui en grattent, *rope-dancers*. Gratter les pavés, *to lead a life of poverty*.

Grattoir, graton, *m.* (popular), *razor*. Passer au —, *to get shaved*, or "scraped."

Graveur sur cuir, *m.* (popular), *shoemaker*, "snob."

Grèce, *f.* (familiar), *the tribe of card-sharpers*. Tomber dans la —, *to become a card-sharper*. Vol à la —, *card swindle*. (Thieves') Grèce, or soulasse, *swindler who offers one a high profit on the change of gold coins, for which he substitutes base coin when the bargain has been struck*. A variety of the confidence trick. Vidocq thus describes the mode of operating of these gentry. A confederate forms an acquaintance with a farmer or country tradesman on a visit to town. While the new pair of friends are promenading, they are accosted by another confederate, who pretends to be a foreigner, and who exhibits gold coin which he wishes to exchange for silver. Subsequently the three adjourn to a wine-shop, where the pigeon, being entrusted with one of the coins, is requested to have it tested at a changer's, when he finds it to be genuine. A bargain is soon struck, and, when the thieves have decamped, the victim finds that in exchange for sound silver coin he has received a case full of coppers or gunshot.

Grécer (thieves'), *to swindle at cards.* From "grec," *card-sharper.*

Grecquerie, *f.* (familiar), *tribe of card-sharpers.*

Gréer (naval), se —, *to dress oneself,* "to rig oneself out."

Greffer (popular), *to be hungry,* "to be bandied." Je greffe, or je déclare, *I am hungry.* (Thieves') Greffer, *to steal an object by skilfully whisking it up,* "to nip."

Greffier, *m.* (popular and thieves'), *cat,* or "long-tailed beggar." From griffe, *claw.*

C'est la dabuche Michelon
Qu'a pomaqué son greffier,
Qui jacte par la venterne
Qui le lui refilera,
Le dab Lustucru
Lui dit : "Dabuch' Mich'lon,
Allez ! votre greffier n'est pas pomaqué ;
Il est dans le roulon,
Qui fait la chasse aux tretons,
Avec un bagaffre de fertange
Et un fauchon de satou."

Popular song of *C'est la mère Michel qui a perdu son chat,* in thieves' cant, quoted by F. Michel.

Greffique, *f.* (roughs'), *the magistracy and lawyers.*

Grefier (Breton cant), *cat.*

Grêle, *m. and f.* (popular), *master,* or "boss ;" *master tailor.*

Ils ne nous exploiteront plus en maîtres, ces grêles.—MACÉ.

(Thieves') Grêle, *row or fight,* "shindy."

Il va y avoir de la grêle, c'est un raille. —E. SUE.

(Popular) Grêle, *pockmarks.* Ne pas s'être assuré contre la —, *to be pockmarked,* or "to be cribbage-faced."

Grêlesse, *f.* (popular), *mistress of an establishment.*

Grelot, *m.* (popular), *voice.*

C'est bien le son du grelot, si ce n'est pas la frimousse.—BALZAC.

Grelot, *tongue,* or "red rag." Il en a un —! *how he does jaw away.* Faire péter son —, *to talk,* "to wag the red rag." Mettre une sourdine à son —, *to keep silent,* "to be mum." Mets une sourdine à ton —, *don't talk so much,* "don't shoot off your mouth" (Americanism).

Grelu, or **grenu**, *m.* (thieves'), *corn.*

Greluchonner (popular), *to be a* "greluchon," *that is, the lover of a married woman, or of a girl kept by another ; or one who lives at the expense of a woman.* Voltaire has used the word greluchon with the first meaning.

Grenadier, *m.* (popular), *louse,* "grey," or "grey-backed un."

Grenafe, grenasse, *f.* (thieves'), *barn.*

Grenier, *m.* (popular), à coups de poing, *drunkard's wife;* — à coups de sabre, *soldier's woman ;* — à lentilles, *pockmarked face,* or "cribbage face ;" — à sel, *head,* "tibby," or "canister." See **Tronche.**

Grenoble. See **Conduite.**

Grenouillard, *m.* (popular), *one fond of the water for the inside or outside.* (Artists') Faire —, *to paint in a bold, dashing style,* after the manner of Delacroix.

Grenouille, *f.* (popular), *woman.* An insulting epithet ; (military) *cash-box.* (General) Emporter la —, *to abscond with the cash-box.* Manger la —, *to spend for one's own purposes the contents of* the cash-box, or funds entrusted to one's keeping. (Popular) Sirop de —, water, "Adam's ale."

Grenouiller (popular), *to drink water.* Had formerly the signification of *to frequent wine-shops.*

Grenouillère, *f.* (general), *swimming bath.* La Grenouillère is the name of a well-known swimming establishment on the bank of the Seine at Chatou, a place much patronized by "mashers" and more than fast ladies.

Grenu, or **grelu,** *m.* (thieves'), *corn.*

Grenuche, *f.* (thieves'), *oats.*

Grenue, grenuse, *f.* (thieves'), *flour.*

Grès, *m.* (thieves'), *horse,* or "prad." Termed also "gail."

Grésillonner (popular), *to ask for credit,* "tick," "jawbone," or "day."

Gressier (thieves'), *to steal,* "to nick." See **Grinchir.**

Grève, *f.* (thieves'), hirondelle de —, *gendarme.* Executions formerly took place at the Place de Grève in front of the Hôtel de Ville, hence the expression, Des anges de — (obsolete), *porters.*

Gréviste, *m.* (popular), *workman on strike.* From grève, *strike.*

Du reste, la bande de grévistes . . . ne viendrait plus à cette heure ; quelque obstacle avait dû l'arrêter, des gendarmes peut-être.—Zola, *Germinal.*

Grézillon, *m.* (popular), *pinch.*

Gribis, gripie, grippis, grippefleur (thieves'), *miller.*

Il y avait en un certain tourniquet un gribis qui ne fichait rien que floutière aux bons pauvres.—*Le Jargon de l'Argot.* (*There used to be in a certain mill a miller who never gave anything to the worthy poor.*)

Griblage, criblage, *m.* (thieves'), *shout, shouting ;* (popular) *complaint, grumbling.*

Grie, *m.,* **grielle,** *f. adj.* (thieves'), *cold.*

Griffard, griffon, *m.* (popular), *cat.* Griffe, *claw.*

Griffarde, *f.* (thieves'), *pen.*

Griffer (popular), *to seize,* "to collar ;" *to take ; to purloin,* "to prig."

Griffeton, *m.* (popular), *soldier,* or "wobbler." From grive, grivier, *a soldier.*

Griffleur, *m.* (thieves'), *chief warder in a prison,* "head bloke."

Griffon, *m.* (thieves'), *writer.*

Griffonnante, *f.* (thieves'), *pen.* Griffonner, *to write a scrawl.*

Griffonner (thieves'), *to swear.*

Griffonneur, *m.* (thieves'), *one who swears;* (popular) — de babillards, *journalist.*

Grifler (thieves'), *to take,* "to grab."

Grifon (Breton cant), *dog.*

Grignolet, *m.* (popular), *bread,* "soft tommy."

Grignon, *m.* (thieves'), *judge,* "beak." Probably from "grigner les dents," *to show one's teeth threateningly.*

Grillée, *adj.* (familiar), *absinthe ; absinthe with sugar.* The sugar is held over the glass on a small grating (grille), until gradually melted by the liquid poured over it.

Griller (popular), quelqu'un, *to lock up one,* "to run in ;" *to deceive one (conjugally).* En — une, *to smoke a pipe or cigarette.* En —

une sèche, *to smoke a cigarette.*
Griller une bouffarde, *to smoke a pipe.*

Au gardien de la paix . . . sa consigne lui défend de boire et de fumer. Ni boire un verre, ni griller une bouffarde ! Voilà la consigne.—*Mémoires de Monsieur Claude.*

Grilleuse de blanc, *f.* (popular), *ironer.* From griller, *to toast, to singe.*

Grimer (popular), *to arrest.* See **Piper.** Se —, *to get drunk,* or "screwed." Properly *to paint one's face.* For synonyms see **Sculpter.**

Grimoire, *m.* (thieves'), *penal code; —* mouchique, *judicial documents; act of indictment.*

Grimoirier, *m.* (thieves'), *clerk of arraigns.*

Grimpant, *adj. and m.* (thieves'), chevalier —, voleur au bonjour, donneur de bonjour, or bonjourier, *thief who enters a house, pretending to be mistaken when discovered, and steals any property worth taking.* (Popular) Des grimpants, *trousers,* "sit-upons, or kicks." (Popular and thieves') Les grimpants, *staircase; steps,* or "dancers." (Military) Grand — tropical, *riding breeches.*

Grimpe-chats, *m.* (popular), *roof.*

Grimper une femme (general), *to have connection with a woman,* "to pulverize the seventh commandment." Also "faire ça, enfiler, rouscailler, sauter, le mettre." Termed formerly "chevaulcher, faire la bête à deux dos, le petit tracas, le vous m'entendez bien, la folie, le déduit ; fourbir, rataconniculer, fourgonner, fretintailler, fringuer," &c.

Grinche, *m. and f.* (thieves'), la —, *dancing.* Un —, *a thief,* or "prig."

Nous étions dix à douze,
Tous grinches de renom ;
Nous attendions la sorgue,
Voulant poisser des bogues,
Pour faire du billon.
VIDOCQ.

Un — de cambrouse, *a highwayman.* In the old English cant, "bridle-cull." Other varieties of the tribe of malefactors go by the appellations of "grinchisseur, pègre, chevalier de la grippe, fourline, escarpe, poisse, limousineur, charron, truqueur, locandier, vanternier, cambrioleur, caroubleur, solitaire, compagnon, deffardeur, pogne, tireur, voleur à la tire, doubleur, fil de soie, mion de boule, grinchisseur de bogues, friauche, tirebogue, Américain, jardinier, ramastiqueur, enfant de minuit, philosophe, philibert, voleur au bonjour, bonjourier, philantrope, frère de la manicle, garçon de campagne, garçon de cambrouse, tiretaine, enfant de la matte, careur, chêne affranchi, droguiste, &c. ; the English brethren being denominated "prig, cracksman, crossman, sneaksman, moucher, hooker, flash cove, bug-hunter, cross-cove, buz-faker, stook-hauler, toy-getter, tooler, prop-nailer, area-sneak, palmer, dragsman, lob-sneak, bouncer, lully-prigger, thimble-twister, gun, conveyancer, dancer, pudding-snammer, beak-hunter, ziff, drummer, buttock-and-file, poll-thief, little snakesman, mill-ben, a cove on the cross, flashman, finder, gleaner, picker, tax-collector," and formerly "a good fellow, a bridle-cull" (highwayman).

Grincher (thieves'), *to rob.* See **Grinchir.**

Quand ils vont décarrer nous les empaumerons. Je grincherai le sinve. Il est avec une largue, il ne criblera pas.—E. SUE. (*We'll follow them when they come out. I'll rob the cove. He is with a woman, he will not cry out.*)

O

Grincheur, *m.* (thieves'), *young thief,* or "ziff."

Grinchie, *adj.* (thieves'), camelotte —, *stolen goods,* "swag."

Grinchir (thieves'), *to steal.* Rabelais in his *Pantagruel* says of Panurge :—" Toutesfois il avoit soixante et trois manières d'en trouver toujours à son besoing (*de l'argent*), dont la plus honorable et la plus commune estoit par façon de larrecin furtivement faict." One may judge from what follows, and by the numerous varieties of "larrecin furtivement faict" described under the head of "grinchissage," that the imitators of Panurge have not remained far behind in the art of filling their pockets at the expense of the public. Some of the many expressions to describe robbery pure and simple, or the different varieties, are :—"Mettre la pogne dessus, travailler, faire, décrasser, rincer, entiffler, retirer l'artiche, savonner, doubler, barbotter, graisser, dégauchir, dégraisser, effaroucher, évaporer, agripper, soulever, fourmiller, filer, acheter à la foire d'empoigne, pégrer, goupiner à la desserte, sauter, marner, cabasser, mettre de la paille dans ses souliers, faire le saut, secouer, gressier, faire le bobe, faire la bride, faire le morlingue, faire un poivrot, faire un coup d'étal, faire un coup de radin, rincer une cambriolle, faire la soulasse sur le grand trimar, ramastiquer, fourlourer, faire le mouchoir, faire un coup de roulotte, faire grippe-cheville," &c., &c. The English synonyms are as follows :—" To cop, to touch, to claim, to prig, to wolf, to snake, to pinch, to nibble, to clift, to collar, to nail, to grab, to jump, to nab, to hook, to nim, to fake, to crib, to ease, to convey, to buz, to be on the cross, to do the sneaking-budge, to nick, to fang," &c., &c.

Grinchissage, *m.* (thieves'), *thieving ; theft,* or "sneaking-budge." The latter expression is used by Fielding.

Wild looked upon borrowing to be as good a way of taking as any, and, as he called it, the genteelest kind of sneaking-budge.—FIELDING, *Jonathan Wild.*

Le — à domicile is practised by rogues known under the following denominations :—" Le bonjourier," see this word ; "le cambrioleur," *who operates in apartments ;* "le caroubleur," *who effects an entrance by means of skeleton keys ;* "le chevalier du pince - linge," *one who steals linen,* "snowgatherer ;" "le déménageur," *who takes possession of articles of furniture, descending the staircase backwards, so that on an emergency he may at once make a show of ascending, as if he were bringing in furniture ;* "le grinchisseur à la desserte," *thief who enters a dining-room just after dinner-time, and lays hands on the plate ;* "le gras - doublier," *who steals lead off the roofs, who* "flies the blue pigeon ;" "le matelassier," *a thief who pretends to repair and clean mattresses ;* "le vanternier," *who effects an entrance through a window,* "dancer ;" "le voleur à la location," *who pretends to be in quest of apartments to let ;* "le voleur au recensement," *who pretends to be an official employed in the census.* Le grinchissage à la ballade, or à la trimballade, *the thief makes some purchases, and finding he has not sufficient money, requests a clerk to accompany him home, entrusting the parcel to a pretended commissionnaire, a confederate. On the way the rogues suddenly vanish.*

Le — à la broquille *consists in sub-stituting sham jewellery for the genuine article when offered for inspection by the tradesman.* Le — à la carre. See **Carreur.** Le — à la cire, *purloining a silver fork or spoon at a restaurant by making it adhere under the table by means of a piece of soft wax. After this preliminary operation the rogue leaves the place, gene-rally after having been searched by the restaurant keeper ; then an accomplice enters, takes his con-federate's place at the table, and obtains possession of the property.* Le — à la détourne, *the thief secretes goods in a shop while a confederate distracts the attention of the shopkeeper.* The rogue who thus operates is termed in English cant a "palmer." The thief is sometimes a female who has in her arms an infant, whose swad-dling-clothes serve as a receptacle for the stolen property. Le —, or vol à la glu, *takes place in churches by means of a rod with birdlime at one end, plunged through the slit in the alms-box, termed* tronc ; *the coins adhering to the extremity of the rod are thus fished out.* Le —, or vol à l'Américaine, *confidence-trick rob-bery.* It is the old story of a traveller meeting with a country-man and managing to exchange the latter's well-filled purse for a bag of leaden coins. Those who practise it are termed "Améri-cains," or "magsmen."

Il est aussi vieux que le monde. Il a été raconté mille fois ! . . . Ce vol suranné réussit toujours ! il réussira tant qu'il y aura des simples, jusqu'à la consomma-tion des siècles.—*Mémoires de Monsieur Claude.*

Le — à la mélasse, *the rogue has a tall hat, with the inside of the crown besmeared with treacle, which he suddenly places on the head of the tradesman, pushing it far down over his eyes, and thus making him temporarily helpless* (Pierre Del-court, *Paris Voleur*). Le — à la quête, *stealing part of the proceeds of a collection in a church when the plate is being passed round.* Le —, or vol à la reconnaissance, *consists in picking the pockets of a passer-by while pretending to re-cognize him and greeting him as an old friend.* Le —, or vol à la tire, *according to Monsieur Claude, for-merly head of the detective depart-ment, this species of theft is the classical one in which the celebrated Cartouche, a kind of French Jack Sheppard, was an adept. It con-sists in picking waistcoat pockets by means of a pair of scissors or a double-bladed penknife.* Le —, or vol à l'épate, *is high-class swinding. It comprises* "le brodage," "le chantage," "le négoce," *and* "le vol au cautionnement." *The first of these consists in the setting-up of a financial establishment and open-ing an account for unwary mer-chants, who are made to sign bills in exchange for the swindlers' paper endorsed by them. When these bills become due they are re-turned dishonoured, so that the vic-timized merchants are responsible for the payment not only of their own notes of hand but those of the swindlers as well.* "Le chantage" *is extorting money by threat of ex-posure.* The proceeds are termed in the English slang "socket-money." For full explanation see **Chanteur.** "Le négoce" *is practised by English swindlers who represent themselves as being the agents of some well-known firm, and thus obtain goods from continental merchants in exchange for ficti-tious bills.* "Le vol au cautionne-ment," *the rogues set up a sham financial establishment and adver-*

*tise for a number of clerks to be em-
ployed by the firm on the condition
of leaving a deposit as a guarantee.
When a large staff of officials, or
rather pigeons, have been found, the
managers decamp with the deposit
fund.* Le —, or *vol à la roulotte*
or *roulante, the thief jumps on the
box of a vehicle temporarily left in
the street by its owner and drives
off at a gallop. Sometimes the
horse alone is disposed of, the vehicle
being left in some out-of-the-way
place.* The " roulottiers " *also
steal hawkers' hand-barrows,* or
"shallows." One of these rogues,
when apprehended, confessed to
having stolen thirty-three hand-
barrows, fifty-three vans or carts,
and as many horses. Sometimes
the "roulottier" will rob property
from cabs or carriages by climbing
up behind and cutting the straps
that secure the luggage on the
roof. His English representative
is termed a "dragsman," according to Mr. James Greenwood.
See *The Seven Curses of London,*
p. 87. Le —, or *vol à l'esbrouffe,
picking the pockets of a passer-by
while hustling him as if by accident,* termed "ramping." Le —,
or *vol à l'étourneau, when a thief
who has just stolen the contents of
a till is making his escape, an accomplice who is keeping watch outside scampers off in the opposite
direction, so as to baffle the puzzled
tradesman, whose hesitation allows
of the rogues gaining ground.* Le
—, or *vol à l'opium, robbery from
a person who has been drugged.
The scoundrels who practise it are
generally Jewish money-lenders
of the lowest class, who attract
their victims to their abode under
pretence of advancing money.*
A robber who first makes his victim insensible by drugs is termed
in the English cant a "drummer."

Le — au boulon, *stealing from a
shop by means of a rod or wire
passed through a hole in the shutter,*
"hooking." Le —, or *vol au
cerf-volant, is practised by women,
who strip little girls of their trinkets
or ease them of their money or
parcels. The little victims sometimes get their hair shorn off as
well.* Le —, or *vol au chatouillage, a couple of rogues pretend to
recognize a friend in a man easing
himself. They begin to tickle him
in the ribs as if in play, meanwhile rifling the pockets of the helpless victim.* Le —, or *vol au colis,
the thief leaves a parcel in some
coffee-house with the recommendation to the landlord not to give it
up except on payment of say twenty
francs. He then seeks a commissionnaire simple-minded enough to
be willing to fetch the parcel and to
pay the necessary sum, after which
the swindler returns to the place
and pockets the money left by the
pigeon.* Le —, or *vol au fric-frac,
housebreaking,* or " crib-crack-
ing." Le —, or *vol au gail or
gayet, horse-stealing,* or " prad-
napping." Le —, or *vol au grimpant, a young thief,* or "little
snakesman," *climbs on to the roof
of a house and throws a rope-ladder
to his accomplices below, who thus
effect an entrance. When detected
they pass themselves off for workmen engaged in some repairs.* Le
—, or *vol au parapluie, a shop-
lifter,* or " sneaksman," *drops the
stolen property in a half-open umbrella.* Le —, or *vol au poivrier,
consists in robbing drunkards
who have come to grief. Rogues
who practise it are in most cases
apprehended, detectives being in the
habit of impersonating drunkards
asleep on benches late at night.* Le
— au prix courant, or *en pleine
trèpe, picking pockets or scarf-pins*

in a crowd, " cross-fanning." Le —, or vol au radin, *the landlord of a wine-shop is requested to fetch a bottle of his best wine ; while he is busy in the cellar the trap which gives access to it is closed by the rogues, and the counter, or* "radin," *pushed on to it, thus imprisoning the victim, who clamours in vain while his till is being emptied. It also takes place in this way : the rogues pretend to quarrel, and one of them throws the other's cap into a shop, thus providing him with an excuse for entering the place and robbing the till, or* " pinching the bob or lob." Le —, or vol au raton, *a little boy, a* " raton," *or* " anguille " (termed " tool or little snakesman " in the English cant), *is employed in this kind of robbery, by burglars, to enter small apertures and to open doors for the others outside* (Pierre Delcourt, *Paris Voleur*). Le —, or vol au rigolo, *appropriating the contents of a cash-box opened by means of a skeleton key.*

Le Pince-Monseigneur perfectionné, se porte aujourd'hui dans un étui à cigares et dans un porte-monnaie . . . les voleurs au rigolo ouvrent aujourd'hui toutes les caisses.—*Mémoires de Monsieur Claude.*

Le —, or vol au suif, *variety of card-sharping swindle.*

Il s'opère par un grec qui rôde chez les marchands de vin, dans les cafés borgnes, pour dégotter, en bon suiffeur, une frimousse de pante ou de daim.—*Mémoires de Monsieur Claude.*

Le —, or vol au timbre, *a tobacconist is asked for a large number of stamps, which the thief carefully encloses in an envelope. Suddenly, when about to pay for them, he finds he has forgotten his purse, returns the envelope containing the stamps to the tradesman and leaves to fetch the necessary sum. Needless to say, the envelope is empty.* Le —, or vol au tiroir, *the thief*

enters a tobacconist's or spirit shop, and asks for a cigar or glass of spirits. When the tradesman opens his till to give change, snuff is thrown into his eyes, thus making him helpless. This class of thieves is termed in the English cant " sneeze-lurkers."

Grinchisseur, *m.* (thieves'), *thief,* or "prig," see **Grinche ;** — de bogues, *pickpocket who devotes his attention to watches,* a "toy-getter," or " tooler."

Gringue, *f.* (popular), *bread,* or "soft tommy ;" *food,* or "prog."

Gripie, *m.* (thieves'), *miller.* See **Gribis.**

Grippe, *f.* (thieves'), chevalier de la —, *thief,* or "prig." See **Grinche.**

Grippe-cheville (thieves'), faire —, *to steal,* " to claim." See **Grinchir.**

Grippe-fleur, gripie, grippis, *m.* (thieves'), *miller.* Termed "Grindoff" in English slang.

Grippe-Jésus, *m.* (thieves'), *gendarme.*

Parcequ'ils arrêtent les innocents et qu'ils n'ont pas même épargné Jésus.—NISARD.

Grippemini, *m.* (obsolete), *barrister,* or "mouthpiece ;" *lawyer,* " sublime rascal, or green bag ;" *extortioner.* From grippeminaud, *thief.*

Gripper (thieves'), *to apprehend,* "to smug." See **Piper.** Rabelais uses the term with the signification of *to seize :*—

Parmy eulx règne la sexte essence, moyennant laquelle ils grippent tout, dévorent tout et conchient tout.

Gripperie, *f.* (popular), *theft* (obsolete).

Grippis, gripie, grippe-fleur, *m.* (thieves'), *miller.*

Gris, *adj. and m.* (thieves'), *dear ; wind ;* (popular) — d'officier, *slight intoxication ;* — jusqu'à la troisième capucine, *completely drunk*, or "slewed." Capucine, *a musket band.*

Grisaille, *f.* (popular), *sister of mercy.* An allusion to the grey costume worn by sisters of mercy.

Grises, *f. pl.* (general), en faire voir de —, *to lead one a hard life.*

Grisette. See **Bifteck.**

Grisotter (popular), se —, *to get slightly drunk*, or "elevated." See **Sculpter.**

Grispin, *m.* (thieves'), *miller.*

Grive, *f.* (thieves'), *army; military patrol ; warder.* Cribler à la —, *to cry out thieves*, "to whiddle beef." Synonymous of "crier à la garde." Harnais de —, *uniform.* Tapis de —, *canteen.*

Grivier, *m.* (thieves'), *soldier*, "swaddy, lobster, or red herring." From "grivois," formerly *a soldier of foreign troops in the service of France.* The word "grivois" itself seems to be a corruption of "gruyers," used by Rabelais, and signifying Swiss soldiers, natives of Gruyères, serving in the French army. Grivier de gaffe, *sentry ;* — de narquois, *deserter.* Literally *a bantering soldier.*

Grivoise, *f.* (obsolete), *soldier's wench, garrison town prostitute.* Termed by the English military "barrack-hack."

Grivoise, c'est à dire coureuse, putain, débauchée, aventurière, dame suivante de l'armée ou gibier de corps-de-garde, une garce à soldats.—*Dictionnaire Comique.*

Grobis, *m.* (familiar), faire du —, *to look big* (obsolete).

Et en faisant du grobis leur donnait sa bénédiction.—RABELAIS.

Grog au bœuf, *m.* (popular), *broth.*

Grogne, *f.* (obsolete), faire la —, *to grumble, to have* "the tantrums."

Faire la grogne, pour faire la moue, prendre la chèvre, faire mauvais visage, bouder, gronder, être de mauvaise humeur, dédaigner.—*Dictionnaire Comique.*

Grognon, *m.* (thieves'), *one about to be executed.* Properly *one who grumbles*, and very naturally so, at the unpleasant prospect. The English equivalent is "gallows-ripe."

Groller (popular), *to growl, to grumble.* Properly *to croak.* From the word grolle, used by Rabelais with the signification of *crow.*

Gromiau, *m.* (popular), *child*, "kid." Termed also "gosse, loupiau."

Grondin, *m.* (thieves'), *pig*, "sow's baby," or "grunting cheat."

Gros, *adv. and adj.* (popular), coucher — (obsolete), *to utter some enormity.* Gâcher du —, *to ease oneself.* See **Mouscailler.** Gros cul, *prosperous rag-picker ;* — lot, *venereal disease ;* (familiar and popular) — bonnet, *influential man ; high official*, "big-wig ;" — numéro, *brothel*, or "nanny-shop." An establishment of that description has a number of large dimensions placed over the front door, and window panes whitewashed. (Thieves') Artie de — Guillaume, *brown bread.* The expression, "du gros Guillaume," was formerly used by the Parisians.

On appelle du gros Guillaume, du pain destiné, dans les maisons de campagne, pour la nourriture des valets de cour.—Du gros Guillaume, mot Parisien, pour dire du pain bis, du gros pain de ménage, tel que le mangent les paysans.—LE ROUX, *Dict. Comique.*

(Military) Gros bonnet, *officer of high rank*, "bloke ;" — frères,

— lolos, or — talons, *the cuiras-siers;* — légumes, *field-officers.* A play on the words "épaulettes à graines d'épinards," *the insignia of such officers.* The word gros, considered as the masculine of "grosse," synonymous of "enceinte," was formerly used with the signification of *impatient, longing,* alluding to the uncontrollable desires which are sometimes manifested by women in a state of pregnancy. Thus people would express their eagerness by such ridiculous phrases as, "Je suis gros de vous voir, de boire avec vous, de le connaître."

Grosse, *adj. f.* (popular), caisse, *the body,* or "apple cart;" — cavalerie, *staff of scavengers,* or "rake kennels," an allusion to their big boots; — culotte, *drunkard.* (Convicts') Grosse cavalerie, *scum of the hulks, desperate scoundrels;* and, in theatrical language, *supernumeraries of the ballet.* (Tramcar conductors') Aller voir les grosses têtes, *to drive the first morning car to Bineau,* this part of Paris being inhabited by substantial people.

Grossiot, *m.* (popular), *person of good standing,* a "swell."

Grotte, *f.* (thieves'), *the hulks.* Gerbé à la —, *sentenced to transportation,* or "lagged." Aller à la —, *to be transported,* "to lump the lighter."

Grouchy, *m.* (printers'), petit —, *one who is late; small job, the composition of which has been delayed.* An allusion to the alleged tardiness of General Grouchy at Waterloo.

Grouiller (sailors'), attrape à ne pas —, *mind you do not move.*

Attrape à ne pas grouiller, fit le vieux. . . . Tu perdrais ton souffle à lui courir après.—RICHEPIN, *La Glu.*

Grouillis-grouillot, *m.* (popular), *swarm, crowd,* or "scuff."

Grouin, *m.* (popular), *face,* or "mug." Properly *snout.* Se lécher le —, *to kiss one another.* Donner un coup de — (obsolete), *to kiss.*

Groule, groulasse, *f.* (popular), *female apprentice; small servant; young* "slavey," or "marchioness."

Groumer (popular), *to grumble.*

Grubler (thieves'), *to grumble; to growl.*

Vous grublez comme un guichemard.— RICHEPIN. (*You growl like a jailer.*)

Grue, *f.* (familiar), *more than fast girl; kept woman,* or "demi-rep;" *foolish, empty-headed girl or woman.*

Gruerie, *f.* (familiar), *stupidity.*

Grun (Breton cant), *chin.*

Gruyère, *m.* (popular), morceau de —, *pockmarked face,* or "cribbage face."

Guadeloupe, *f.* (popular), *mouth,* or "rattle-trap." Charger pour la —, *to eat.* See **Mastiquer.**

Guano, *m.* (popular), *excrement,* or "quaker." An allusion to the guano of South America.

Guédouze, or **guétouse,** *f.* (thieves'), *death.*

Gueldre, *f.* (fishermens'), *bait prepared with shrimps for the fishing of sardines.*

La sardine est jolie en arrivant à l'air . . .
Mais pour aller la prendre il faut avoir le nez
Bougrement plein de poils, et de poils goudronnés;
Car la gueldre et la rogue avec quoi l'on arrose
Les seines qu'on lui tend, ne fleurent point la rose.
Gueldre, lisez mortier de crevettes, pas frais.
RICHEPIN, *La Mer.*

Guelte, *f.* (shopmens'), *percentage allowed on sales.*

Guelter (shopmens'), *to make a percentage on sales ; to pay such percentage.*

Guénaud, *m.* (thieves'), *wizard.*

Guénaude, *f.* (thieves'), *witch.*

Guenette, *f.* (thieves'), *fear,* "funk."

Guenilles, *f. pl.* (familiar), trousser ses —, *to run away* (obsolete), "to give one's rags a shaking."

> Gentil ambassadeur de quilles,
> Croyez-moi, troussez vos guenilles.
> 　　　SCARRON, *Gigantomachie.*

Guenon, *f.* (popular), *mistress of an establishment, the master being* "le singe."

Guéri, *adj.* (thieves'), *set at liberty ; free ;* the prison being termed "hôpital," and imprisonment "maladie."

> Hélas ! il est malade à Canelle (il est arrêté à Caen) . . . il a une fièvre chaude (il est fortement compromis), et vous, il paraît que vous êtes guéri (libre)?—VIDOCQ.

Guérite, *f.* (popular), à calotins, *confessional.* Guérite is properly *a sentry-box.* Enfiler la — (obsolete), *to run away.*

Guêtré, *m.* (military), *trooper who, for some reason or other, has to make the day's journey on foot.*

Gueulard, *m.* (thieves'), *bag ; wallet.*

> Ils trollent ordinairement à leur côté un gueulard avec une rouillarde pour mettre le pivois.—*Le Jargon de l'Argot.* (*They generally carry by their side a wallet with a bottle to keep the wine in.*)

(Popular) Un —, *a stove.* Gueulard, properly *a gormandizer.*

Gueularde, *f.* (thieves'), *pocket,* "cly," "sky-rocket," or "brigh." Termed also "fouillouse, louche, profonde, or grande."

Gueulardise, *f.* (popular), *dainty food.*

Gueule, *f.* (popular), d'empeigne, *palate which, by dint of constant application to the bottle, has become proof against the strongest liquors ; loud voice ;* — de raie, *ugly phiz,* or "knocker face ;" — de tourte, *stupid-looking face.* Bonne —, *grotesque face.* Crever la — à quelqu'un, *to break one's head.*

> Je te vas crever la gueule.—ALPHONSE KARR.

Faire la —, *to make a wry face.* Faire sa —, *to give oneself disdainful airs ; to look disgusted.*

> Dis donc, Marie bon-bec, ne fais pas ta gueule.—ZOLA.

Avoir de la —, *to be loud-mouthed.* Il n'a que la —, *he is a humbug.* Se chiquer la —, *to maul one another's face.* (Military) Roulement de la —, *beating to dinner.* Se sculpter une — de bois, *to get drunk,* or "screwed." For synonyms see **Sculpter.**

Gueulée, *f.* (popular), *howling ; meal.* Chercher la —, *to be a parasite,* or "quiller."

Gueulées, *f. pl.* (popular), *objectionable talk,* or "blue talk."

Gueuler (popular), comme un âne, *to be loud-tongued ;* (thieves') — à la chienlit, *to cry out thieves ! or police !* "to whiddle beef."

Gueuleton, *m.* (familiar and popular), *a feast,* or "spread."

> Et les artistes se levèrent pour serrer la main d'un frère qui offrait un gueuleton général.—E. MONTEIL.

Gueuletonner (familiar and popular), *to feast.*

Gueuse, *f.* (popular), *mistress ; prostitute,* or "mot." See **Gadoue.** Courir la —, *to be a whoremonger,* or "molrower."

Gueux, *m.* (popular), *small pan full of charcoal used as a foot-warmer by market women, &c.*

Une vieille femme . . . est accroupie près d'un gueux sur les cendres duquel une cafetière ronronne.—P. MAHALIN.

Gueux-gueux (obsolete), *rascal ;* the expression being used in a friendly manner.

Guibe(popular), *leg;* — à la manque, *lame leg;* — de satou, *wooden leg.* Jouer des guibes, *to dance ; to run away,* "to slope." See **Patatrot.**

Guibole, or guibolle, *f.* (popular and thieves'), *leg,* "pin."

Mais comment ? Lui, si démoli, si mal gréé à c't'heure, avec sa guibole boiteuse, et ses bras rouillés, et toutes les avaries de sa coque en retraite, comment pourrait-il saborder ce gaillard-là, d'aplomb et trapu ? —RICHEPIN, *La Glu.*

Jouer des guiboles, *to run; to dance.*

Puis, le soir, on avait fichu un balthazar à tout casser, et jusqu'au jour on avait joué des guiboles.—ZOLA, *L'Assommoir.*

Guibon. See **Guibonne.**

Guibonne, *f.* (popular and thieves'), *leg ;* — carrée, *ham.*

Mes jamb's sont fait's comm' des trombones.
Oui, mais j'sais tirer—gar' là-dessous !—
La savate, avec mes guibonnes
Comm' cell's d'un canard eud' quinze sous.
RICHEPIN, *La Chanson des Gueux.*

Guiche, *m. and f.* (popular and thieves'), duc de —, *jailer,* or "jigger dubber." From guichetier, *jailer.* Mec de la —, *prostitute's bully,* or "Sunday man." Thus termed on account of his kiss-curls. For list of synonyms see **Poisson.** Des guiches, *kiss-curls.* Termed in the English slang, "aggerawators," or "Newgate knockers." Regarding the latter expression the *Slang Dictionary* says : "'Newgate knocker,' the term given to the lock of hair which costermongers and thieves usually twist back towards the ear. The shape is supposed to resemble the knocker on the prisoners' door at Newgate—a resemblance that carries a rather unpleasant suggestion to the wearer. Sometimes termed a 'cobbler's knot,' or 'cow-lick.'" Trifouiller les guiches, *to comb the hair.* (Familiar) Chevalier de la —, *prostitute's bully,* or "pensioner." For list of synonymous expressions see **Poisson.** Le bataillon de la —, *the world of bullies.*

Et si la p'tit' ponif'triche
Su' l'compt' des rouleaux,
Gare au bataillon d'la guiche !
C'est nous qu'est les dos.
RICHEPIN.

Un —, *a prostitute's bully.*

C'est . . . un guiche, c'est-à-dire un jeune homme aux mains blanches, à l'accroche-cœur, l'Adonis des nymphes des musettes, quand ce n'est pas une tante ! . . . La moitié des crimes qui se commettent à Paris est conçue par le cerveau des guiches, exécutée par les bras des chefs d'attaque et finie par des assommeurs.—*Les Mémoires de Monsieur Claude.*

Guichemar, guichemard, guichemince, guichemuche, *m.* (thieves' and popular), *jailer,* "jigger dubber." For guichetier.

Guide, *m.* (thieves'), *the prime-mover in a murder.*

C'est toujours le pégriot, le guide ou le toucheur qui devient à priori le chef d'attaque responsable d'une affaire criminelle. —*Mémoires de Monsieur Claude.*

Guignard, *m.* (popular), *ill luck.*

Guigne-à-gauche, *m.* (popular), *squinting man, or one with* "swivel eyes." From guigner, *to scan.*

Guignol, *m.* (popular), *small theatre.*

Guignolant, *adj.* (popular), *unlucky ; annoying.*

Guignonné, *adj.* (popular), être —, *to be unlucky at a game.*

Guillotine sèche, *f.* (familiar), *transportation.* To be transported is expressed in the language of English rogues by the term "lighting the lumper."

Guimbard, *m.* (thieves'), *the van that conveys prisoners to gaol.* Called by English rogues "Black Maria."

Guimbarde, *f.* (popular), *door; voice; head; carriage; good-for-nothing woman.* Properly *Jew's-harp.*

Oui, une femme devait savoir se retourner, mais la sienne avait toujours été une guimbarde, un tas. Ce serait sa faute, s'ils crevaient sur la paille.—ZOLA, *L'Assommoir.*

Couper la — à quelqu'un, *to cut one short.*

Guinal, *m.* (thieves'), *usurer; Jew,* "sheney, Ikey, or mouchey." Termed also "youtre, frisé, pied-plat." Le grand —, *Mont de Piété,* or *government pawnbroking establishment.* (Rag-picker's) Guinal, *wholesale rag-dealer.*

Guinaliser (thieves'), *to be a usurer; to pawn.*

Guinche, *f.* (popular), *low dancing saloon in the suburbs.*

Guincher (popular), *to dance.* Se —, *to dress oneself hurriedly and badly.*

Guincheur, *m.* (popular), *frequenter of dancing saloons called* "guinches."

Guindal, *m.* (popular), *glass.* Siffler le —, *to drink,* "to wet one's whistle," or "to moisten one's chaffer." See **Rincer.**

Guinguette, *f.* (popular), *fast girl; low restaurant.*

Ça doit s'manger, la levrette.
Si j'en pince une à huis clos . . .
J'la f'rai cuire à ma guinguette.
J't'en fich'rai, moi, des pal'tots !
　　　　DE CHATILLON, *Poésies.*

Guirlande, *f.* (thieves'), *chain which secures two convicts together.*

Le poids de la manille et de la chaîne est de douze livres à peu près.—LORÉDAN LARCHEY.

Guitare, *f.* (familiar and popular), *head,* or "nut ; " *monotonous saying; well-worn platitude.* Jouer de la —, *to be monotonous.* Avoir une sauterelle dans la —, *to be cracked,* "to have a tile loose," or "a bee in one's bonnet." For the list of synonymous expressions see **Avoir.**

Gwammel (Breton cant), *woman ; mother.*

Gwilloik (Breton cant), *wolf.*

Gy, or **jaspin** (thieves'), *yes,* or "usher."

Quoi, tu veux rentiffer? Gy?—RICHEPIN. (*What, you wish to go home? Yes?*)

**ABILLÉ de soie,** *m.* (popular), *an elegant term for a pig,* "sow's baby," or, in the words of Irish peasants, "the gintleman that pays the rint."

Habiller (popular), *quelqu'un de taffetas à 40 sous, to say ill-natured things of one, to* "backbite" *him.* S'— de sapin, *to die.* See **Pipe.** S'— en sauvage, *to strip oneself naked, to strip to the* "buff," *so as to be* "in one's birthday suit."

Habin, happin, hubin, *m.* (thieves'), *dog,* or "tyke ;" — ergamé, or engamé, *rabid dog.*

Ils trollent cette graisse dans leur gueulard, en une corne, et quand les hubins la sentent, ils ne leur disent rien, au contraire, ils font fête à ceux qui la trollent.—*Le Jargon de l'Argot.*

A dog is also called by thieves "tambour, alarmiste."

Habiner (thieves'), *to bite.*

Habit, *m.* (popular), noir, *gentleman,* or "swell." Etre — noir, *to be simple-minded, easily duped, to be a* "flat." (Thieves') Un — vert, *an official of the* "octroi," *or office at the gates of a town for the levying of dues on goods which are brought in from the outside.*

C'était de l'un de ces fossés, . . . que les contrebandiers, au nez et à la barbe des habits verts, faisaient descendre la nuit, dans les souterrains, leurs marchandises pour les porter en ville et les affranchir de l'octroi.—*Mémoires de Monsieur Claude.*

Habitants, *m. pl.* (popular), *lice,* "grey-backed un's."

Habitongue, *f.* (thieves'), *for habitude, habit.*

Hacher de la paille (popular), *to murder the French language.* The English have the corresponding expression, "to murder the Queen's English." Also *to talk in German.*

Haleine, *f.* (familiar), à la Domitien, cruelle, or homicide, *offensive breath.* According to the *Dict. Comique* it used to be said of a man troubled with that incommodity : Il serait bon trompette, parcequ'il a l'haleine forte. (Popular) Respirer l'— de quelqu'un, *to get at one's secrets,* "to pump" *one.*

Halènes, or alènes, *f. pl.* (thieves'), *thieves' implements,* or "jilts." Alène, properly *shoemaker's awl.*

Haler sur sa poche (sailors'), *to pay,* "to shell out." Haler, properly *to haul, to tow.*

Halle, *f.* (popular), aux croûtes, *stomach,* or "bread-basket." Also *baker's shop.* La — aux draps, *the bed,* "doss, or bugwalk," and formerly "cloth-market," an expression used by Swift in his *Polite Conversation:*—

Miss, your slave ; I hope your early rising will do you no harm ; I find you are but just out of the cloth-market.

(Journalists') La — au son, *the Paris Conservatoire de Musique, or national music and dramatic academy.* (Bullies') Un barbise de la — aux copeaux, *a bully whose paramour brings him in but scanty profits, whose "business" is slack.*

Hallebarde, *f.* (popular), *tall, badly dressed woman,* a "gawky guy."

Halot, *m.* (popular), *box on the ear,* "smack on the chops."

Haloter quelqu'un (thieves'), *to box one's ears,* "to smack one's chops ; " *to ply the bellows.*

Haloteur, *m.* (thieves'), *one who uses bellows ; one who blows.*

Halotin, *m.* (thieves'), *bellows.* From haleter, *to pant.*

Hancher (popular), se —, *to put on a jaunty look ; to take up an arrogant position,* to be "on the high jinks," or to "look big."

Handicaper (sporting), *to handicap.*

Handicapeur, *m.* (sporting), *one who has the arranging of handicaps.*

Hane, *f.* (thieves'), *purse,* "skin," or "poge." Termed also "henne, bouchon, morlingue, mornif." Casser la — à quelqu'un, *to steal someone's purse,* "to buz a skin."

Hanneton, *m.* (familiar), *monomania.* Avoir un — dans le plafond, *to be cracked,* or "to have a bee in one's bonnet." See **Avoir.** Saoul comme un —,

completely drunk, "as drunk as Davy's sow."

"Davy's sow." The origin of this expression, according to Davies' *Supplementary English Glossary,* is the following :— "David Lloyd, a Welshman, had a sow with six legs ; on one occasion he brought some friends and asked them whether they had ever seen a sow like that, not knowing that in his absence his drunken wife had turned out the animal, and gone to lie down in the sty. One of the party observed that it was the drunkest sow he had ever beheld." Other synonymous expressions are, "drunk as a drum, to be a wheelbarrow, sow-drunk, drunk as a fish, as a lord, as a piper, as a fiddler, as a rat."

Hannetonner (familiar), *to have a hobby verging on monomania.*

Happer le taillis (thieves'), *to flee,* "to guy." See **Patatrot.** Compare with the expression, now obsolete, gagner le taillis, which has the same signification.

Happons le taillis, on crie au vinaigre sur nouzailles.—*Le Jargon de l'Argot.* (*They are "whiddling beef," and we must "guy."*)

Happin. See **Habin.**

Happiner. See **Habiner.**

Harauder (popular), quelqu'un (obsolete), *to cry out after one ; to pursue one with insults.*

Hardi, *adj.* (popular), à la soupe *is said of one who is more ready to eat than to fight.* Hardi ! *courage ! with a will ! go it !*

Hareng, *m.* (thieves'), faire des yeux de — à quelqu'un, *to put out one's eyes.* (Printers') Harengs, *name given by printers to fellow-workers who do but little work.*

Hareng-Saur, *m.* (popular), *gendarme ; a member of the Société de Saint-Vincent de Paul, a religious association.* (Roughs') Piquer son pas de —, *to dance.*

Hariadan Barberousse (thieves'), *Jesus Christ.*

Il rigolait malgré le sanglier qui voulait lui faire becqueter Hariadan Barberousse. —Vidocq.

Haricander (popular), *to find fault with one about trifles.*

Haricot, *m.* (popular), *body.* Cavaler, or courir sur le —, *to annoy, to bore one,* "to spur" one. (Thieves') Un — vert, *a clumsy thief, or one* "not up to slum." Se laver les haricots, *to be transported,* or "lagged." (Familiar) Hôtel des haricots, *formerly the prison for undisciplined national guards,* the staple food for prisoners there being haricot beans.

Haricoteur, *m.* (thieves'), *executioner.* Termed "Rouart" in the sixteenth century, that is, *one who breaks criminals on the wheel.*

Harmonarès, *m.* (thieves'), *noise,* or "row." Si le gonsalès fait de l'harmonarès il faut le balancarguer dans la vassarès, *if the fellow makes any noise we'll pitch him into the water.*

Harmonie, *f.* (popular), faire de l'—, *to make a noise,* "to kick up a row."

Harnais, *m.* (thieves'), *cards that have been tampered with,* or "stocked broads;" *clothes,* or "clobber;" — de grive, *military uniform.* Laver les —, *to sell stolen clothes,* "to do clobber at a fence's."

Harpe, *f.* (general), jouer de la —, *to slily take liberties with a woman by stroking her dress,* as Tartuffe did when pretending to ascertain the softness of Elmire's dress. The expression is old; it is to be met with in the *Dict. Comique.*

Jouer de la harpe signifie jouer des mains auprès d'une femme, la patiner, lui toucher la nature, la farfouiller, la clitoriser, la chatouiller avec les doigts.—J. Le Roux, *Dictionnaire Comique.*

(Thieves') Harpe, *prison-grated window.* Jouer de la —, *to be in prison,* or "in quod." Pincer de la —, *to put oneself at a window.*

Harper (popular), *to catch,* "to nab;" *to seize,* "to grab."

Harpions, *m. pl.* (popular and thieves'), *feet,* or "dew-beaters;" *hands,* or "dukes." From the old word harpier, concerning which the *Dictionnaire Comique* says :—

Harpier. Pour voler ou friponner impunément, prendre ou enlever par force, comme les harpies.

Harponner (popular), *to seize,* "to grab;" — *tocquardement, to lay rough hands on; to give one a shaking.*

Hasard ! or **h !** (printers'), ironical exclamation meaning *that happens by chance, of course !*

Haüs, or **aüs,** *m.* (shopmens'), *appellation applied by shopmen to a person who, after much bargaining, leaves without purchasing anything.*

Hausse-col, *m.* (military), *cartridge-box.* The expression has become obsolete.

Haussier, *m.* (familiar), a "bull," that is, *one who agrees to purchase stock at a future day, at a stated price, but who simply speculates for a rise in public securities to render the transaction a profitable one.* Should stocks fall, the "bull" is then called upon to pay the difference. The "bear" is the opposite of the "bull," the former selling, the latter purchasing—the one operating for a *fall*, the other for a *rise*. They are respectively called "liebhaler" in Berlin, and "contremine" in Vienna.

Haussmannisation, *f.* See below.

Haussmanniser (familiar), *to pull down houses wholesale,* after the fashion of M. Haussmann, a Prefect of the Seine under the Third Empire, who laid low many of the old houses of Paris, and opened some broad passages in the city, especially that of the Boulevard Sébastopol.

Haut-de-tire, *m.* (thieves'), *breeches,* "hams, kicks, sit-upons."

Haute, *f. and adj.* (general), for haute société, *the higher class of any social stratum,* "pink."

Il y a lorette et lorette. Mademoiselle de Saint-Pharamond était de la haute.—P. FÉVAL.

La — bicherie, *higher class of cocottes, the world of* "demi-reps." Un escarpe de la —, *a swindler moving in good society.* La — pègre, *swell mob,* and, used ironically, *good society.* Un restaurant de la —, *a fashionable restaurant,* a "swell" *restaurant.*

Si nous ne soupons pas dans la haute, je ne sais guère où nous irons à cette heure-ci. —G. DE NERVAL.

Hautocher (thieves'), *to ascend ; to rise.*

Haut-temps, *m.* (thieves'), for autan, *loft.*

Havre, or **grand havre,** *m.* (thieves'), *God.* Le — garde mézière, *God protect me.*

Henriquinquiste, *m.* (familiar), *partisan of the Comte de Chambord, who, had he reigned, would have done so under the name of Henri Cinq.*

Heol ar blei (Breton cant), *moon.*

Herbe, *f.* (popular), à grimper (obsolete), *fine bosoms or shoulders;* — à la vache, *clubs of cards.*

Quinte mangeuse portant son point dans l'herbe à la vache.—ZOLA, *L'Assommoir.*

Herbe sainte, *absinthe,* probably a corruption of the word.

Herplis, *m.* (thieves'), *farthing.* Sans un herplis dans ma fouillouse, *without a farthing in my pocket.*

Herr, *m.* (general), *a man of importance, one of position or talent, a* "swell."

Herse, *f.* (theatrical), *lighting apparatus on the sides of the stage which illuminates those parts which receive no light from the chandelier.*

Herz, or **hers,** *m.* (thieves'), *master,* or "boss ;" *gentleman,* or "nibcove." From the German herr.

High-bichery, *f.* (familiar), *the world of fashionable cocottes.*

Quelque superbe créature de la highbichery qui traîne son domino à queue avec les airs souverains d'une marquise d'autrefois.—P. MAHALIN.

Hirondeau, *m.* (tailors'), *journeyman tailor who shifts from one employer to another.* An allusion to the swallow, a migratory bird.

Hirondelle, *f.* (familiar), *penny boat plying on the Seine;* (popular) *commercial traveller ; journeyman tailor from the country temporarily established in Paris ; hackney coachman ;* — d'hiver, *retailer of roasted chestnuts ;* — de pont, *vagrant who seeks a shelter at night under the arches of bridges;* — du bâtiment, *mason from the* *country who comes yearly to work in Paris.* (Thieves') Une —, *variety of vagabond.*

Les Hirondelles, les Romanichels hantaient, comme les taupes, l'intérieur de leurs souterrains insondables. Romanichels et Hirondelles venaient y dormir, souper et méditer leurs crimes.—*Mémoires de Monsieur Claude.*

Une — de potence, *a gendarme* (obsolete).

Hisser (popular), *to give a whistle call;* — un gandin. See **Gandin**.

Histoires, *f. pl.* (general), *menses.* Termed also "affaires, cardinales, anglais."

Homard, *m.* (popular), *doorkeeper, or servant in red livery.* (Military) *spahis.* The spahis, called also cavaliers rouges, are a crack corps of Arab cavalry commanded by French officers. There are now four regiments of spahis doing duty in Algeria or in Tonkin.

Homicide, *m.* See **Haleine**.

Homme, *m.* (familiar), *au sac, rich man, one who is* "well ballasted." Un — affiche, *a* "sandwich" *man,* that is, a man bearing a back-and-front advertising board. Avoir son jeune —, *to be drunk,* or "tight." See **Pompette**. (Thieves') Un — de lettres, *forger;* — de peine, *old offender,* "jail-bird." (Printers') Homme de bois, *workman who repairs wooden fixtures of formes in a printing shop.*

Homme de lettres, or **singe,** *m.* (printers'), *compositor.*

Le compositeur est un bipède auquel on donne la dénomination de "singe." . . . Pour vous éblouir il triture une "matière pleine" de mots équivoques : "commandite, bordereau, banque, impositions" et cela avec la gravité d'une "Minerve." Fier du rang qu'il occupe dans l'imprimerie, ce chevalier du "composteur" s'intitule

"homme de lettres," mais c'est un "faux titre" qu'il a pris dans sa "galée," car de tous les ouvrages auxquels il a mis des "signatures" et qu'il prétend avoir "composés," il lui serait difficile de "justifier" une ligne, &c. &c.—*Déclaration d'amour d'un imprimeur typographe à une jeune brocheuse,* 1886.

Hommelette, *m.* (popular), *man devoid of energy,* "sappy."

Honnête, *m.* (thieves'), *the spring.*

Honteuse, *f.,* être en —. See **Gousse**.

Hôpital, *m.* (thieves'), *prison,* or "stir." See **Motte**. A thief in prison is said to be "malade," and when liberated he is, of course, "guéri." (Popular) Goujon d'—, *leech.*

Horizontale, *f.* (familiar), *prostitute,* or "mot;" — de grande marque, *fashionable cocotte,* or "pretty horse-breaker." For list of over one hundred and thirty synonyms, see **Gadoue**.

Horloger, *m.* (popular), avoir sa montre chez l'—, *to have one's watch at the pawnbroker's,* "in lug," or "up the spout."

Horreurs, *f. pl.* (popular), *broad talk,* or "blue talk." Dire des —, *to talk* "smut." Faire des —, *to take liberties with women,* "to fiddle," or "to slewther," as the Irish have it.

Hosto, or **austo** (soldiers' and thieves'), *prison,* or "stir," see **Motte ;** (popular) *house,* or "crib."

Hôtel, *m.* (popular), de la modestie, *poor lodgings ;* — des haricots, *prison,* or "jug." See **Motte**. Coucher à l'— de la belle étoile, *to sleep in the open air, on mother Earth,* or "to skipper it."

Hotteriau, hotteriot, *m.* (popular), *rag-picker,* or "tot-picker." From hotte, *wicker basket.*

Houblon, *m.* (popular), *tea.*

Houpe dentelée, *f.* (freemasons'), *ties of brotherhood.*

Housette, *f.* (thieves'), *boot*, or " daisy root." Traîne - cul - les housettes, *a tatterdemalion.*

Houssine, *f.* (thieves'), Jean de l'—, *stick ; bludgeon.*

Houste à la paille! (thieves'), *out with him !*

Hubin, *m.* (thieves'), *dog*, or "tyke."

Après, ils leur enseignent à aquiger certaines graisses pour empêcher que les hubins les groudent.—*Le Jargon de l'Argot.*

Hubins, *m. pl.* (old cant), *tramps who pretend to have been bitten by rabid dogs or wolves.*

Les hubins triment ordinairement avec une luque comme ils bient à Saint-Hubert. —*Le Jargon de l'Argot.*

Saint Hubert was credited with the power of miraculously curing hydrophobia. There is still a church in Belgium, not far from Arlon, consecrated to Saint Hubert, to whose shrine rabid people (in more than one sense) repair to be cured.

Hugolâtre, *m.* (familiar), *fanatical admirer of the works of V. Hugo.*

Hugrement (thieves'), *much*, or " neddy " (Irish).

Huile, *f.* (general), *wine ; suspicion ;* — *blonde*, *beer ;* — de bras, de poignet, *physical strength ; work,* or " elbow grease ; " — de cotret, *blows administered with a stick ;* might be rendered by " stirrup oil." The *Dict. Comique* has : " Huile de cotret, pour coups de bâton, bastonnade."

Qu'ils vinssent vous frotter les épaules de l'huile de cotret.—*Don Quichotte.*

Huile de mains, *money*, or " oil of

palm." For synonyms see **Quibus**. Pomper les huiles, *to drink wine to excess*, or " to swill."

Huit (theatrical), battre un —, *to cut a caper.* (Familiar) Un — ressorts, *a handsome, well - appointed two-horse carriage.* (Military) Flanquer — et sept, *to give a man a fortnight's arrest.*

Y m'a flanqué huit-et-sept à cause que j'avais égaré le bouchon de mon mousqueton.—G. COURTELINE.

Huîtres, *f. pl.* (popular), de gueux, *snails ;* (thieves') — de Varennes, *beans.*

Huîtrifier (familiar), s'—, *to become commonplace and dull of intellect.* From huître, figuratively *a fool.*

Humecter (popular), s'— les amygdales, la dalle du cou, or le pavillon, *to drink*, " to wet one's whistle." For synonyms see **Rincer**.

Huppé, *adj.* (popular), daim —, *rich person, one who is* " well ballasted."

Hure, *f.* (popular), *head*, or " tibby." Properly *wild boar's head.* See **Tronche**.

Huré, *adj.* (thieves'), *rich*, or " rag splawger."

Hurf, urf, *adj.* (general), c'est —, *that's excellent*, " tip-top, cheery, slap-up, first-chop, lummy, nap, jam, true marmalade, tsing-tsing." Le monde —, *world of fashion.*

Hurlubier, *m.* (thieves'), *idiot*, or " go along ;" *madman*, or " balmy cove ; " *tramp*, or " pikey."

Vous que le chaud soleil a teints, Hurlubiers dont les peaux bisettes, Ressemblent à l'or des gratins.
RICHEPIN.

Hussard, *m.* (popular), à quatre roues, *soldier of the train or army service corps.* Élixir de —, *brandy.* (Popular and thieves') Hussard de la guillotine, *gendarme on duty at executions.*

Il est venu pour sauver Madeleine . . . mais comment? . . . les hussards de la guillotine sont là.—BALZAC.

Hussard de la veuve, *gendarme on duty at executions.*

Oui, c'est pour aujourd'hui, les hussards de la veuve (autre nom, nom terrible de la mécanique) sont commandés.—BALZAC.

Hust-must (thieves'), *thank you very much.*

 **I**ANN al Lorans (Breton cant), *name for a fool.*

Icicaille, icigo, (thieves'), *here*. Gaffine —, *look here*.

Idée, *f*. (general), *a drop, or a* "suspicion," *of any liquid*. Termed also un soupçon, une larme, un scrupule. Avoir des idées, *to feel amorous*, "naughty, or randy." That particular signification of the latter expression seems to have originated in an association of ideas, the word "randi" having the meaning of *woman* in Hindostani.

Ienna (Breton cant), *to dupe*.

Ienner, *m*. (Breton cant), *deceiver*.

Ierchem (roughs'), *a coarse word disguised, to ease oneself*, "to bog." For synonyms see **Mouscailler.**

Iergue, parler en —, *to use the word as a suffix to other words*.

Igo (thieves'), *here*. La chamègue est —, *the woman is here*.

Il (popular), y a de l'empile, or de l'empilage, *there is some trickery,* *unfair play, cheating;* — y a de l'empile, la peau alors ! je me débine, *they are cheating, to the deuce then ! I'll go;* — y a des arêtes dans ce corps - là, *an euphemism to denote that a man makes his living off a prostitute's earnings*, alluding to the epithet "poisson" applied to such creatures; — a plu sur sa mercerie *is said of a woman with thin skinny breasts;* — est midi, *be cautious; it's of no use;* — tombera une roue de votre voiture *is said of a person in too high spirits, to express an opinion that his mirth will soon receive a damper;* — n'y a pas de Bon Dieu means *nothing will prevent me, or prevent it*. Il pleut ! *a warning to fellow-workers that the master or a stranger is making his appearance*, "nix !" (Theatrical) Il pleut ! *is used to denote that a play is a failure, that it is being hissed down, or* "damned."

Illico, *m*. (popular), *grog prepared on the sly by patients in hospitals;* (general) *immediately*.

Imbécile, *m*. (popular), à deux roues, *bicyclist*. (Military) Galons d'—, *long service or seniority stripes*.

Imbiber (popular), s'— le jabot, *to drink*, "to wet one's whistle." See **Rincer.**

Immobilité, *f.* (painters'), mercenaire de l'—, *model who makes a living by sitting to painters.*

Impair, *m.* (familiar), faire un —, *to make a blunder,* "to put one's foot in it." (Thieves') Impair ! *look out !* —, acré nous v'la noblés, *look out, be on your guard, we are recognised.*

Impératrice, *f.*, for impériale, *top of bus.*

Impère (popular), abbreviation of impériale, *or top of bus.*

Impériale, *f.* (general), *tuft of hair on the chin.* Formerly termed "royale." The word has passed into the language.

Importance (general), d' —, *strongly, vigorously.* J' te vas le moucher d'—, *I'll let him know a piece of my mind; I'll snub him.*

Impôt, *m.* (thieves'), *autumn.*

Impressionisme, *m.* (familiar), *school of artists who paint nature according to the personal impression they receive.* Some carry the process too far, perhaps, for if their retina conveys to them an impression that a horse, for instance, is indigo or ultramarine, they will reproduce the image in Oxford or Cambridge blue on the canvas. Needless to say, the result is sometimes startling.

Impressioniste, *m.*, *painter of the school called* impressionisme (which see).

Impure, *f.* (familiar), *kept woman,* or "demi-rep." For the long list of synonyms see **Gadoue.**

Incommode, *m.* (thieves'), *lantern, lamp-post.* Properly *inconvenient,* thieves being lovers of darkness.

Incommodé, *adj.* (thieves'), être —, *to be taken red-handed, to be* "nabbed" *in the act.*

Inconobré, *m. and adj.* (thieves'), *stranger; unknown.*

Incroyable, *m.* (familiar), *dandy under the Directoire at the end of the last century.* The appellation was given to swells of that period on account of their favourite expression, "C'est incroyable !" pronounced c'est incoyable, according to their custom of leaving out the r, or giving it the sound of w. For synonyms see **Gommeux.**

Index (popular), travailler à l'—, *to work at reduced wages.*

Indicateur, *m.* (general), *spy in the pay of the police,* "nark." Generally a street hawker, sometimes a thief.

Il y a deux genres d'indicateurs : les indicateurs sur place, tels que les marchands de chaînes de sûreté et les marchands d'aiguilles, bimbelotiers d'occasion, faux aveugles, etc., et les indicateurs errants : marchands de balais, faux infirmes, musiciens ambulants : . . . Il y avait, sous l'empire, des indicateurs jusque dans le haut commerce parisien.—*Mémoires de Monsieur Claude.*

Indicatrice, *f.* (familiar), *female spy in the employ of the police.*

Indigent, *m.* (bus conductors'), *outside passenger on a bus.* Thus termed on account of the outside fare being half that inside. Indigent, properly *pauper.*

Inexpressibles, *m. pl.* (familiar), from the English, *trousers.*

Infanterie, *f.* (popular), entrer dans l'—, *to become pregnant,* or "lumpy." Compare with the English expression "infantry," a nursery term for *children.*

Infect, *adj.* (general), *utterly bad.* The expression is applied to anything. Ce cigare est —, *that cigar is rank.* Ce livre est —, *that book is worthless.* Un — individu, *a contemptible individual.*

Infectados, *m.* (familiar), *cheap cigar*, " cabbage leaf."

Inférieur, *adj.* (popular), cela m'est —, *that is all the same to me.*

Infirme, *m.* (popular), *stupid fellow*, or " bounder."

Inglichmann, *m.* (popular), *Englishman.*

Ingrat, *m.* (thieves'), *clumsy thief.*

Ingurgiter son bilan (popular), *to die*, or " to snuff it." See **Pipe.**

Inodore, *adj.* (familiar), soyez calme et —, *be cool; don't get excited; be calm; be decorous*, or, as the Americans say, " pull your jacket down."

Inouisme, *m.* (familiar), ruisselant d'—, *extraordinarily fine, good, dashing*, " slap up, or tzing tzing."

Inséparables, *m. pl.* (familiar), *cigars sold at fifteen centimes a couple.*

Insinuant, *m.* (thieves'), *apothecary; one who performs, or used to perform, the* " clysterium donare " *of Molière.*

Insinuante, *f.* (thieves'), *syringe.*

Insinuation, *f.* (thieves'), *clyster.*

Insolpé, *m. and adj.* (thieves'), *insolent*, "cheeky."

Inspecteur des pavés, *m.* (popular), *workman out of work*, or " out of collar."

Institutrice, *f.* (popular), *female who keeps a brothel; the mistress of an* " academy."

Instruit, *adj.* (thieves'), être —, *to be a skilful thief*, a " gonnof."

Insurgé de Romilly, *m.* (popular), *lump of excrement*, or " quaker."

Interloquer (soldiers'), *to talk.* Je vais aller en — avec le marchi-chef, *I will talk about it to the quartermaster sergeant.*

Interver, entraver (thieves'), *to understand.* Je n'entrave que le dail, *I do not understand, I don't* " twig." Interver dans les vannes, *to allow oneself to be* " stuffed up," *to be* " bamboozled."

Intime, *m.* (theatrical), *man who is paid to applaud at a theatre.* Termed also " romain."

Intransigeant, *m.* (familiar), *politician of extreme opinions who will not sacrifice an iota of his programme.* The reverse of opportuniste.

Inutile, *m.* (thieves'), *notary public.*

Invalo, *m.* (popular), for invalide, *pensioner of the* " Hôtel des Invalides," *a home for old or disabled soldiers.*

Invite, *f.* (popular), faire une — à l'as *is said of a woman who makes advances to a man.*

Inviteuse, *f.* (general), *waitress at certain cafés termed* " caboulots." Her duties, besides serving the customers, consist in getting herself treated by them to any amount of liquor; but, to prevent accidents, the drinks intended for the inviteuse are generally water or some mild alcoholic mixture. The inviteuse often plies also another trade—that of a semi-prostitute.

Iot fetis (Breton cant), *porridge of buckwheat flour.*

Ioulc'h (Breton cant), *giddy girl.*

Ioulc'ha (Breton cant), *to play the giddy girl.*

Ipéca, *m.* (military), le père —, *the regimental surgeon.*

Irlande, *f.* (thieves'), envoyer en —, *to send anything from prison.*

Irréconciliable, *m.* (familiar), *member of the opposition under Napoleon III.*

Isgourde, *f.* (popular), *ear,* "wattle," or " lug."

Isolage, *m.* (thieves'), *abandonment; leaving in the lurch.*

Isoler (thieves'), *to abandon, to leave in the lurch.*

Isoloir, *m.* (familiar), se mettre sur l'—, *to forsake one's friends; to play a solo.*

Italian (Breton cant), *rum.*

Italique, *f.* (popular), avoir les jambes en —, *to be bandy-legged.* Pincer son —, *to reel about.*

Itou, *adv.* (popular), *also.* Moi —, *I too.*

Itrer (thieves'), *to have.*

J'itre mouchaillé le babillard,—*Le Jargon de l'Argot.* (*I have looked at the book.*)

Ivoires, *f.* (popular), *teeth,* "ivories." Faire un effet d'—, *to show one's teeth,* "to flash one's ivories."

Izabel (Breton cant), *brandy.*

**ABOT**, *m.* (popular), *stomach*, or "bread basket." Meant formerly *heart, breast*.

> L'amour qui dans mon cœur chante ville gaignée,
> Excite en mon jabot exhalaison ignée.
> SCARRON.

Faire son —, *to eat*, "to yaffle," or "to grub." See **Mastiquer**. S'arroser, s'imbiber le —, *to drink*, "to wet one's whistle." See **Rincer**. Chouette —, *fine breasts*, or "blooming Charlies."

Jacque, *m.* (thieves'), *a sou*.

Jacqueline, *f.* (popular), *fast girl; concubine*, or "moll;" (soldiers') *cavalry sword*.

Jacques, *m.* (thieves'), *crowbar*. Termed also "biribi, rigolo, l'enfant, sucre de pomme," and by English housebreakers, "Jemmy, James, the stick." (Military) Faire le —, *to manœuvre*.

Jactance, *f.* (thieves' and cads'), *speech, talking*, "jaw." Properly *silly conceit*. Caleter la —, *to stop talking*, "to put a clapper to one's jaw." Quelle sale — il a ! *how he does talk !* Faire la —, *to talk*, "to jaw ;" *to question*, or "cross-kid." Le curieux lui a fait la — et il a entravé, *the judge examined him and he allowed himself to be outwitted*.

Jacter (popular and thieves'), *to speak*, "to rap ;" *to cry out ; to slander*. Meant formerly *to boast*. Il faut igo avoir le loubion en poigne pour leur —, *here, we must always speak to them hat in hand*.

Jacteur, *m.* (popular), *speaker*.

Jaffe, *f.* (popular), *box on the ear*, or "buckhorse." Refiler une —, *to box one's ears*, "to smack one's chops." Jaffe, *soup*. Termed "clo" at Winchester School. (Thieves') Jaffes, *cheeks*, or "chops."

Jaffier, *m.* (thieves'), *garden*, or "smelling cheat."

Jaffin, *m.* (thieves'), *gardener*. Termed in English slang "master of the mint."

Jaffle, or **jaffe**, *f.* (thieves'), *soup*.

Jalo, *m.* (thieves'), *tinker*.

Jaluzot, *m.* (general), *umbrella*, or "rain napper, mush, or gingham." From the name of the proprietor of the "Printemps," who, being a wealthy man, said to his shopmen that he had not the means to buy an umbrella. So goes an idiotic song :—

> Il n'a pas de Jaluzot,
> Ça va bien quand il fait beau,
> Mais quand il tombe de l'eau,
> Il est trempé jusqu'aux os.

Jambe, *f.* (popular), de vin, *intoxication.* S'en aller sur une —, *to drink only a glass or a bottle of wine.* (Thieves') Jambe en l'air (obsolete), *the gallows,* " scrag, nobbing - cheat, or government signpost." (Familiar and popular) Lever la —, *to dance the can-can,* see **Chahut ;** *is said also of a girl who leads a fast, disreputable sort of life.* Faire — de vin had formerly the signification of *to drink heavily,* " to swill."

Dès ce matin, messieurs, j'ai fait jambe de vin.—LA RAPINIÈRE.

Jambes de coq, *thin legs,* "spindle-shanks." Jambes de coton, *weak legs.* Jambes en manche de veste, *bandy legs.* (Military) Sortir sur les jambes d'un autre, *to be confined to barracks or to the guard-room.*

Jambinet, *m.* (railway porters'), *coffee with brandy.*

Jambon, *m.* (popular), *violin.* (Military) Faire un —, *to break one's musket,* a crime sometimes punished by incorporation in the compagnies de discipline in Africa.

Jambonneau, *m.* (popular), ne plus avoir de chapelure sur le —, *to be bald.* For synonymous terms see **Avoir.**

Jambot, *m.* (obsolete), *penis.* The term is used by Villon.

Jappe, *f.* (popular), *prattling,* "jaw." Tais ta —, *hold your* "jaw," "put a clapper to your mug," or "don't shoot off your mouth" (American).

Japper (popular), *to scream, to squall.*

Jardin, *m.* (popular), faire du —, *to quiz,* " to carry on."

Jardinage, *m.* (popular), *running down, slandering.*

Jardiner (thieves' and cads'), *to slander ; to run down ; to quiz.*

> Les gonciers qui nous jardinent,
> I' s'ront vraiment j'tés.
> RICHEPIN.

Jardiner quelqu'un, *to make one talk so as to elicit his secrets from him,* to "pump" one.

Jardineur, *m.* (popular and thieves'), *man who seeks to discover a secret ; inquisitive man,* a kind of " Paul Pry."

Jardinier, *m.* (thieves'), see **Jardineur ;** *a thief who operates in the manner described at the word* " charriage."

Jargolle, or **jergole,** *f.* (thieves'), *Normandy.*

Jargollier, *m.* (thieves'), *a native of Normandy.*

Jargouiller (thieves'), *to talk incoherently.*

Jarguer (thieves'). See **Jars.**

Jarnaffe, *f.* (thieves'), *garter.*

Jarretière, *f.* (thieves'), *watch chain,* or " slang."

Jars, *m.* (thieves'), *cant,* or "flash." Dévider, jaspiner le—, or jarguer, *to talk cant,* "to patter flash." Entraver or enterver le —, *to understand cant.* The language of thieves is also termed " thieves' Latin," as appears from the following quotation :—

"Go away," I heard her say, "there's a dear man," and then something about a "queer cuffin," that's a justice in these canters' thieves' Latin.—KINGSLEY, *Westward Ho.*

Entendre le — had formerly the signification of *to be cunning.*

Jarvillage, *m.* (thieves'), *conversation ; dirt.* An illustrious Englishman, whose name I forget, gave once the definition of dirt as "matter in the wrong place."

Jarviller (thieves'), *to converse,* "to rap ;" *to dirty.*

Jasante, *f.* (thieves'), *prayer.*

Jaser (thieves'), *to pray.*

Jaspin, or **gy** (thieves'), *yes,* or "usher."

Y a-t-il un castu dans cette vergne ? Jaspin.—*Le Jargon de l'Argot.* (*Is there an hospital in this country ? Yes.*)

The word has also the meaning of *chat, language,* "jaw."

J'ai bien que'qu' part un camerluche
Qu'est dab dans la magistrat'muche.
Son jaspin esbloque les badauds.
RICHEPIN.

Jaspinement, *m.* (thieves'), *barking of a dog.*

Jaspiner (thieves'), *to talk, to speak,* "to rap, to patter." Termed also "débagouler, dévider, gazouiller, jacter, jardiner, baver, tenir le crachoir ;" — bigorne, *to talk in slang,* "to patter flash." Le cabe jaspine, *the dog barks.* Jaspiner de l'orgue, *to inform against,* "to blow the gaff."

Jaspineur, *m.* (thieves'), *talker; orator.*

Jaune, *m.* (thieves'), *summer;* (popular) *brandy.* See **Tord-boyaux.** Jaune, *gold,* or "redge." Aimer avec un — d'œuf *is said of a woman who deceives her husband or lover.* An allusion to the alleged favourite colour of cuckolds.

Jaunet, jauniau, or **sigue,** *m.,* *gold coin,* "canary, yellow-boy, goldfinch, yellow-hammer, quid, shiner, gingle-boy."

Jaunier, *m.* (popular), *retailer of spirits.* An allusion to the colour of brandy.

Javanais (familiar), *kind of jargon formed by disguising words by means of the letters of the syllable* "av " *properly interpolated ; thus* "je l'ai vu jeudi," *becomes* " javé lavai vavu javeudavi."

Argot de Breda où la syllabe av, jetée dans chaque syllabe, hache pour les profanes le son et le sens des mots, idiome hiéroglyphique du monde des filles qui lui permet de se parler à l'oreille—tout haut.—DE GONCOURT.

Javard, *m.* (thieves'), *hemp ;* (popular) *tattle-box.*

Javoter (popular), *to prattle.*

Javotte, *f.* (popular), *tattle-box.*

Jean, *m.* (popular), de la suie, *sweep ;* — guêtré, *peasant,* or "clod ;" — houssine, *stick,* or "toco." (Thieves') Un — de la vigne, *a crucifix.*

Jean-bête, *m.* (general), *blockhead,* "cabbage-head."

Jean-fesse, or **Jean-foutre** (general), *scamp.*

Jeanjean, *m.* (familiar and popular), *simpleton.*

La blanchisseuse était allée retrouver son ancien époux aussitôt que ce jeanjean de Coupeau avait ronflé.—ZOLA, *L'Assommoir.*

(Soldiers') Jeanjean, *recruit,* "Johnny raw."

Jeanneton, *f.* (popular), *servant wench at an inn ; girl of doubtful morals,* a "dolly mop."

Jem'enfoutisme, *m.* (familiar), *the philosophy of utter indifference.*

Aussi, lui n'était-il ni orléaniste, ni républicain, ni bonapartiste, il affichait le "jem'enfoutisme " qui mettait tout le monde d'accord.—J. SERMET.

Jérôme, *m.* (popular), *stick,* or "toco."

Jérusalem (thieves'), lettre de —, *letter written from prison to make* *a request of money.* The Préfecture de police, and consequently the lock-up, was formerly in the Rue de Jérusalem.

Jésuite, *m.* (thieves'), *turkey-cock.* This species of *gallinacea* was introduced into France by the Jesuit missionaries. Termed by English vagabonds " cobble colter." Engrailler un —, *to steal a turkey,* "to be a Turkey merchant."

Jésus, *m.* (thieves'), *innocent man,* thieves considering themselves as much-injured individuals. Grippe-Jésus, *gendarme.* (Popular) Petit —, or à quatre sous, *newly-born infant.* (Sodomists') Un —, *a Sodomist in confederacy with a rogue termed " chanteur," whose spécialité is to extort money from rich people with unnatural passions.*

Le persillard qui, une fois d'accord avec le chanteur pour duper son douillard, devient alors son compère, c'est-à-dire son Jésus ! Tel est dénommé aujourd'hui le persillard exploiteur.— *Mémoires de Monsieur Claude.*

Jet, *m.* (thieves'), *musket,* or " dag."

Jetar, *m.* (military), *prison,* " Irish theatre, or mill."

J'ai ordre du sous-officier de semaine de te faire fourrer au jetar sitôt rentré.—G. COURTELINE.

Jeté, *adj.* (popular), bien —, or bien gratté, *well done, well made, handsome.* Etre —, *to be sent to the deuce.*

Jeter (thieves' and cads'), *to send roughly away; to send to the deuce ;* — avec perte et fracas, *to bundle one out of doors forcibly ;* — un coup, *to look,* "to pipe." Jettes-en un coup sur le pante, *just look at that* " cove." Jeter de la grille, *to summons, to request in the name of the law ;* — une mandole, *to give one a box*

on the ear, "to smack one's chops." (Printers') Jeter, *to assure.* Je vous le jette, *I assure you it's a fact,* " my Davy on it."

Jeter du cœur sur carreau (general), or — son lest, *to vomit,* " to cast up accounts, to shoot the cat, or to spew." Literally *to throw hearts on diamonds, or to throw one's heart (which has here the meaning of stomach) on the floor.*

Jeton, *m.* (popular), *coin.*

Jeu de dominos, *m.* (popular and thieves'), *set of teeth.* Montrer son —, *to show one's teeth,* "to flash " one's " ivories."

Jeune France (literary), *name given to young men of the " Ecole romantique " in 1830—the " Byronian " school.*

Ils ont fait de moi un Jeune France accompli . . . j'ai une raie dans les cheveux à la Raphaël . . . j'appelle bourgeois ceux qui ont un col de chemise.—TH. GAUTIER.

Jeune homme, *m.* (familiar and popular), *measure of wine of the capacity of four litres.* Avoir son —, *to be drunk,* "screwed." For synonyms see **Pompette.**

Tiens ta langue, tu as ton jeune homme, roupille dans ton coin.—E. MONTEIL.

Suivez-moi —, *ribbons worn in the rear of ladies' dresses,* or "follow me, lads."

Jinglard. See **Ginglard.**

Jiroble, *adj.* (thieves'), for girofle, *pretty.*

Job, *m. and adj.* (popular), *silly fellow,* or "flat." Monter le —, *to deceive,* "to bamboozle." Se monter le —, *to entertain groundless hopes.* Job is an abbreviation of jobard.

Jobarder (general), *to deceive, to dupe, to fool one,* " to bamboozle." The equivalents for *to deceive* are in the different varieties of jargon : " mener en bateau, monter un bateau, donner un pont à faucher, promener quelqu'un, compter des mistoufles, gourrer, affluer, rouster, affûter, bouler, amarrer, battre l'antif, emblêmer, mettre dedans, empaumer, enfoncer, allumer, hisser un gandin, entortiller, faire voir le tour, la faire à l'oseille, refaire, refaire au même, faire la barbe, faire la queue, flancher, pigeonner, juiffer," &c. ; and in the English slang or cant, "to stick, to bilk, to do, to best, to do brown, to bounce, to take in, to kid, to gammon," &c.

Jobelin, *m.* (old word), jargon —, *cant.*

> Sergens à pied et à cheval,
> Venez-y d'amont et d'aval,
> Les hoirs du deffunct Pathelin,
> Qui scavez jargon jobelin.
> VILLON, *Les Répeues franches de François Villon et de ses compagnons,* 15th century.

Joberie, *f.* (popular), *nonsense,* "tomfoolery."

Jobisme, *m.* (popular), *poverty.*

Desroches a roulé comme nous sur les fumiers du Jobisme.—BALZAC.

Compare with the English expression, "as poor as Job's turkey;" "as thin and as badly fed,' says the *Slang Dictionary*, "as that ill-conditioned and imaginary bird."

Jocko, *m.* (familiar), pain —, *loaf of an elongated shape.*

Jocko, pain long à la mode depuis 1824, année où le singe Jocko était à la mode.—L. LARCHEY, *Dict. Hist. d'Argot.*

Jocrissiade, *f.* (familiar), *stupid action.* Jocrisse, *simpleton.*

Jojo, *adj. and m.* (popular), *pretty ; simpleton.* Faire son —, *to play the fool.*

Jonc, *m.* (thieves'), *gold,* or "redge." Etre sur les joncs, *to be in prison,* "in quod." Un bobe, or un bobinot de —, *a gold watch,* a "red toy."

Joncher (thieves'), *to gild.*

Joncherie, *f.* (popular), *deceit, swindle.* The word is old.

> Adonc le Penancier vit bien
> Qu'il y eut quelque tromperie ;
> Quand il entendit le moyen,
> Il congneut bien la joncherie.
> *Poésies attribuées à Villon,* 15th century.

Joncheur, *m.* (thieves'), *gilder.*

Jonquille, *adj.* (popular), mari —, *injured husband.* An allusion to the alleged favourite colour of cuckolds.

Jorne, *m.* (thieves'), *day* (Italian giorno). Refaite de —, *breakfast.*

Jose, *m.* (popular), *bank-note.* From papier Joseph, *tracing paper.*

Joseph, *m.* (familiar), *over-virtuous man.* Faire le or son —, *to give oneself virtuous airs.* An allusion to the story of Madame Potiphar and Joseph.

Je me disais aussi : voilà un gaillard qui fait le Joseph. Il doit y avoir une raison.—A. DUMAS FILS.

Joséphine, *f.* (thieves'), *skeleton key,* or "betty."

Tel grinche s'arrêtera à faire le barbot dans une cambriolle (à voler dans une chambre). S'il a oublié sa joséphine (fausse clef), jamais il ne se servira de la joséphine d'un autre de peur d'attraper des punaises, c'est-à-dire de manquer son coup ou d'avoir affaire à un mouchard.—*Mémoires de Monsieur Claude.*

(Popular) Faire sa —, *is said of a woman who puts on virtuous airs, indignantly tossing her head, or blushingly casting down her eyes, &c.*

Jouasser (familiar), *to play badly at a game or on an instrument.*

Jouasson (familiar), *poor player.*

Jouer (popular), à la ronfle, or de l'orgue, *to snore,* "to drive one's pigs to market;" — des guibolles, *to run away,* "to leg it;" see **Patatrot** ; — du cœur, *to vomit,* "to shoot the cat;" (familiar and popular) — de la harpe, *to stroke a woman's dress as Tartuffe with Elmire, or otherwise to take certain liberties with her.* See **Harpe.** Jouer des mandibules, *to eat,* "to grub;" see **Mastiquer;** — du Napoléon, *to be generous with one's money,* "to come down handsome;" an allusion to napoléon, *a twenty-franc coin;* — du fifre, *to go without food;* — du piano *is said of a horse which has a disunited trot, or of a man who is knock-kneed;* — du pouce, *to give money,* "to fork out;" *to spend freely one's money.* The expression is old; Villon uses it in his dialogue of *Messieurs de Mallepaye et de Baillevent,* 15th century :—

M. Sang bieu, la mousse
M'a trop cousté. B. Et pourquoy? M. Pource.
B. Hay! hay! tout est mal compassé.
M. Comment? B. On ne joue plus du poulce.

Jouer comme un fiacre, *to play badly;* — la fille de l'air, *to run away,* "to slope." See **Patatrot.** (Theatrical) Jouer à l'avant-scène, *to stand close to the footlights when acting;* — devant les banquettes, *to perform before an empty house;* (thieves') — à la main chaude, *to be guillotined.* Literally *to play hot cockles.* See **Fauché.** Jouer de la harpe, *to be in prison,* or "in quod;" — du linve, or du vingt-deux, *to knife,* or "to chive;" — du violon, *to file iron bars or irons.*

Joujouter (popular), *to play; to frolic.*

Jour de la Saint Jean Baptiste, *m.* (thieves'), *execution day,* or "wry-neck day."

Journée gourd (Breton cant), *good day's profits.*

Journoyer (popular), *to do nothing at all.*

Jouste, or **juste** (thieves'), *near.* From the old word jouxte, Latin juxta. Je trimardais jouste la lourde, *I was passing close to the door.*

Joyeuse, *f.* (thieves'), *sword,* or "poker."

Joyeux, *m. pl.* (military), *men of the "bataillon d'Afrique,"* a corps recruited with military convicts, who on being liberated serve the remainder of their term of service in this corps.

Jubile, *f.* (glove-makers'), *pieces of glove skins, the perquisites of glove-makers.*

Jubile, peau économisée par l'ouvrier gantier sur celles qu'on lui a confiées pour tailler une douzaine de paires de gants.— L. LARCHEY, *Dict. Hist. d'Argot.*

Judas, *m.* (popular), barbe de —, *red beard.* Bran de —, *speckles.* Le point de —, *thirteen.*

Judasser (popular), *to betray; to act as a* "cat in the pan," or, in thieves' cant, "to turn snitch."

Judasserie, *f.* (popular), *treacherous show of friendship.*

Judée, *f.* (thieves'), la petite —, *Préfecture de police, headquarters of the police,* situated formerly in the Rue de Jérusalem; hence the expression.

Jugé, *m.* (prisoners'), *young offender who has been sentenced to be confined in a house of correction.*

Juge de paix, *m.* (thieves'), *stick; a kind of roulette at wine-shops;* (gamblers') *pack of cards,* or "book of broads."

Jugeotte, *f.* (popular), *intellect.*

Jugulant, *adj.* (popular), *annoying.*

Juguler (popular), *to strangle; to bore; to cry out.* Scrongnieugneu! que j' jugulais! *darn it, I cried!*

Jules, *m.* (popular), *chamber pot,* or

"jerry." Aller chez —, *to ease one-self ; to go to the* "West Central." See **Mouscailler.** The *Slang Dictionary* says : "West Central, a water-closet, the initials being the same as those of the London postal district. It is said that for this reason very delicate people refuse to obey Rowland Hill's in-structions in this particular. An old maid who lived in this district was particularly shocked at having W.C. marked on all her letters, and informed the letter-carrier that she could not think of submitting to such an indecent fashion. On being informed that the letters would not be forwarded without the obnoxious initials, she re-marked that she would have them left at the post-office. ' Then, marm,' said the fellow, with a grin, 'they will put P.O. on them, which will be more ondacenter than the t'other.' " (Military) Prendre, pincer, or tirer les oreilles à —, *to carry away the privy tub.* Passer la jambe à —, *to empty the aforesaid tub.* Travailler pour —, *to eat.* See **Mastiquer.** Des jules, *socks.*

Jumelles, *f. pl.* (thieves'), *breech,* or "one-eyed cheek."

Juponnier, *m.* (familiar and popu-lar), *one who is fond of the petti-coat,* a "molrower."

Jus, *m.* (familiar and popular), *wine ; —* de bâton, *thrashing with a stick ; —* d'échalas, *wine.* Termed formerly jus d'octobre. Jus de réglisse, *negro.* Termed also "bamboula, boîte à cirage, boule de neige, bille de pot au feu, mal blanchi." Jus de chapeau or roupie de singe, *bad, weak coffee.* Avoir du —, *to possess elegance, dash.* Avoir du — de navet dans les veines, *to be devoid of energy.* (Popular) Jus, *profits in business ; —* de bras, *strength ; physical effort.* Hardi ! du — de bras, *now, with a will, my lads !*

> Encore un tour au treuil ! Hardi ! Du jus de bras !
> V'là le fer du chalut qui sort son nez au ras.
> Encore un tour ! Il va saillir hors de la tasse.
>
> RICHEPIN, *La Mer.*

Se coller un coup de —, *to get drunk,* or "screwed." See **Pom-pette.** (Sailors') Jus de cancre, *landsman,* or "land-lubber." Du — de botte premier brin, *rum of the best quality.*

Jusqu'à la gauche (military), *to a great extent ; for a long time.*

> Vous serez consigné jusqu'à la gauche . . . c'était son mot ce "jusqu'à la gauche," une expression de caserne . . . qui ne sig-nifiait pas grand chose . . . mais personni-fiait l'éternité.—G. COURTELINE.

Jusqu'à plus soif (popular), *to excess.*

Juste, *f.* (thieves'), *the assizes.*

Juste-milieu, *m.* (familiar), *the be-hind.* See **Vasistas.**

Juter de l'œil (popular), *to weep,* "to nap a bib."

> Spèce de tourte, n'jute donc pas d' l'œil d'une façon aussi incongrue.—G. FRISON, *Aventures du Colonel Ronchonot.*

Juteux, *m.,* **juteuse,** *f.* (dandies'), *elegant ; dashing,* "tzing tzing." (Familiar) Affaire juteuse, *profit-able transaction,* a "fat job."

Juxte. See **Jouste.**

Jy. See **Gy.**

**EBIR,** *m.* (military), *commander of a corps.* From the Arab. Also *c o l o n e l,* otherwise "colon."

Kif-kif (popular), c'est —, *it is all the same.*

> Expression qui vient des Arabes, importée assurément dans l'atelier par quelque Zéphir ou quelque Zouave typographe. Dans le patois algérien, kif-kif signifie, semblable à.—BOUTMY.

C'est — bourico or bourriquo, *it is all the same; it comes to the same thing.*

> Que tu dises comme moi ou qu' tu dises pas comme moi ça fait jus' kif-kif bourriquo.—G. COURTELINE.

According to Boutmy, kif-kif bourico signifies in Algerian patois *similar to an ass.*

Kil, *m.* (roughs'), *litre of wine.* Va donc voir dans ta fouille s'il ne te reste pas quelques ronds pour payer un —, *just feel in your pocket to see whether you haven't got a few coppers to treat us to a litre of wine.* Je me suis traversé d'un —, *I have drunk a litre of wine.*

Kilo, *m.* (popular), *litre of wine; false chignon; lump of excrement,* or "quaker." Traverser un —, *to drink a litre of wine.* Déposer un —, *to ease oneself by evacuation,* "to bury a quaker."

Klebjer (popular), *to eat.* See **Mastiquer.**

Kolback, *m.* (popular), *small glass of brandy.* Also *a large glass of wine.* Properly *busby.*

Koxnoff, *adj.* (popular), *excellent,* "first class, cheesy."

Krak, *m.* (familiar), *general collapse of financial firms in Austria some years ago which affected, and whose consequences still affect, the commercial world.*

> Déjà sur ce trône minable,
> Louis deux tombé dans le lac,
> Comme un locataire insolvable
> Etait mort, victime du Krak.
> GRINGOIRE.

Krapser, or **crapser** (popular), *to kill; to die.*

Kroumir, *m.* (popular), *rough fellow; dirty or* "chatty" *fellow.*

A, *m*. (familiar), donner le —, *to give the tone.*

Labadens (theatrical), *old schoolfellow.*

Depuis le vaudeville amusant de Labiche (l'affaire de la Rue de Lourcine) qui a mis ce terme à la mode, il a pris, avec le procès Bazaine, une valeur historique. Quand Régnier voulut en effet être mis en la présence du maréchal, il se fit annoncer ainsi : "Dites que c'est un vieux Labadens."—Lorédan Larchey.

Labago (thieves'), *is equivalent to* là-bas, *yonder.* Gaffine —, la riflette t'exhibe, *look yonder, the spy has his eye on you.*

Là-bas (prostitutes'), *the Saint-Lazare prison, a place of confinement for prostitutes who offend against the law, or are detected plying their trade without due authorization of the police;* (thieves') *the convict settlement in New Caledonia or at Cayenne.*

Laboratoire, *m.* (eating-house keepers'), *the kitchen,* a place where food is often prepared by truly chemical processes ; hence the appellation.

L'absinthe ne vaut rien après dîner (printers'), *words used ruefully by a typo to express his bitter disappointment at finding, on returning from dinner, that he has corrections of his own to attend to.*

Dans cette locution, on joue sur "l'absinthe," considérée comme breuvage et comme plante. La plante possède une saveur "amère." Avec quelle "amertume" le compagnon restauré, bien dispos, se voit obligé de se "coller" sur le marbre pour faire un travail non payé, au moment où il se proposait de pomper avec acharnement. Déjà, comme Perrette, il avait escompté cet après-dîner productif.—Boutmy.

Lac, *m.* (thieves'), être dans le —, *to be very* "hard up ;" *to be in a fix or in trouble, in a* "hole." Mettre dans le —, *to deceive, to make one fall into a trap.* (Gamesters') Mettre dans le —, *to lose all one's money, to have* "blewed" *it.*

Au cercle, où la conversation vient de rouler sur la mort tragique du roi de Bavière, un ponte perd un louis au baccarat, en tirant à cinq :—allons, dit-il d'un air résigné, encore un louis dans le lac !—*Le Voltaire,* Juin, 1886.

(Popular) Faire une descente au —, *an act described some time ago by an English lawyer as* "French vice."

Lacets, *m. pl.* (thieves'), *handcuffs,* or "bracelets." Marchand or solliceur de —, *gendarme.*

Lâchage, *m.* (popular), *the act of forsaking one.*

Lâche, *m.* (popular), Saint —, *lazy workman; one who likes to lounge about, who is* "Monday-ish." Réciter la prière de Saint —, *to sleep,* or "to doss."

Lâcher (popular), les écluses, son écureuil, or une naïade, *to void urine,* or "to pump ship." Termed also "changer ses olives d'eau, lascailler, écluser, faire le petit, changer son poisson d'eau, faire pleurer son aveugle, lancer, quimper la lance, gâter de l'eau, arroser les pissenlits;" — une pastille, *to break wind;* (familiar and popular) — d'un cran, *to leave one; to rid him of one's presence;* — la perche, *to die;* — les écluses, *to weep, to blubber,* "to nap a bib;" — le coude, *to leave one alone.*

Lâchez-nous donc le coude avec votre politique! cria le zingueur. Lisez les assassinats, c'est plus rigolo.—ZOLA, *L'Assommoir.*

Lâcher le paquet, *to disclose.*

Et Madame Lerat, effrayée, répétant qu'elle n'était même plus tranquille pour elle, lâcha tout le paquet à son frère.— ZOLA, *L'Assommoir.*

Lâcher la mousseline, *to snow.*

Le ciel restait d'une vilaine couleur de plomb, et la neige, amassée là-haut, coiffait le quartier d'une calotte de glace. . . . Gervaise levait le nez en priant le bon Dieu de ne pas lâcher sa mousseline tout de suite. —ZOLA, *L'Assommoir.*

Lâcher une femme, *to break off one's connection with a mistress,* "to bury a moll;" — un cran, *to undo a button or two after dinner.* Se — d'une somme, *to spend reluctantly a sum of money.* (Theatrical) Lâcher la rampe, *to die,* see **Pipe**; (thieves') — un pain, *to give a blow,* or "wipe."

La coulante, *f.* (popular), *the river Seine.*

Lacromuche, *m.* (popular), *women's bully,* or "Sunday man."

For synonymous expressions see **Poisson.**

Lafarger (popular), *to poison.* An allusion to the celebrated Lafarge poisoning case.

Laffe, *f.* (thieves'), *soup.*

Lagad-ijen (Breton cant), *five-franc piece.*

Lago (thieves'), *there.* Gaffine — le pante se fait la débinette, *look there, the "cove" is running away.*

Lagout, *m.* (thieves'), *water* ("agout" with the article).

Laigre, *f.* (thieves'), *fair; market.* Michel says this word is no other than the adjective "alaigre," of which the initial letter has disappeared.

Laine, *f.* (tailors'), *work,* "graft." Avoir de la —, *to have some work to do.* (Thieves') Tirer la —, *was formerly the term for stealing cloaks from the person;* hence the old expression tire-laine, *thief who stole cloaks.*

Lainé, *m.* (thieves'), *sheep,* or "wool-bird."

Laisée, *f.* (thieves' and roughs'), *prostitute,* or "bunter." See **Gadoue.**

Laisser (familiar and popular), aller le chat au fromage (obsolete), *is said of a girl who allows herself to be seduced, who loses her rose;* — tomber son pain dans la sauce (obsolete), *to manage matters so as to get profit out of some transaction;* — ses bottes quelque part, *to die.* The expression is found in Le Roux's *Dict. Comique.* Laisser fuir son tonneau, *to die,* "to kick the bucket." See **Pipe.** Laisser pisser le mérinos, *to wait for one's oppor-*

tunity. Synonymous of Laisser pisser le mouton, a proverbial saying.

Lait, *m.* (thieves'), à broder, *ink.* (Theatrical) Boire du —, *to be applauded.*

A peine le couplet est-il chanté, au milieu des applaudissements payés, que Biétry ... salue ... tous les applaudisseurs ... il n'est pas le seul, ce soir-là, à boire du lait, comme on dit en style de théâtre.— *Mémoires de Monsieur Claude.*

Laïus (familiar), *speech, or discourse.* Piquer un —, *to make a speech.* The English *Slang Dictionary* gives "patter," a speech or discourse, a pompous street oration, a judge's summing up, a trial. Ancient word for muttering. Probably from the Latin Paternoster, or Lord's Prayer. This was said before the Reformation in a "low voice" by the priest, until he came to "and lead us not into temptation," to which the choir responded, "but deliver us from evil." In the Reformed Prayer Book this was altered, and the Lord's Prayer directed to be said "with a loud voice." Dr. Pusey takes this view of the derivation in his *Letter to the Bishop of London.* Scott uses the word twice, in *Ivanhoe* and *The Bride of Lammermoor.*

Lambiasse, *f.* (popular), *rags.*

Lame, *f.* (military), vieille — ! *old chum !*

Lamine (thieves'), *Le Mans,* a town.

Lampagne du cam, *f.* (thieves'), *country,* or "drum." It is the word "campagne" itself disguised in the following way. The first consonant is replaced by the letter l, and the word is followed by its first syllable preceded by "du" (Richepin). English thieves and gipsies have a similar mode of distorting words, termed gibberish; called also pedler's French, St. Giles's Greek, and the Flash tongue. Gibberish means a kind of disguised language formed by inserting any consonant between each syllable of an English word, in which case it is called the gibberish of the letter inserted ; if F, it is the F gibberish ; if G, the G gibberish ; as in the sentence, How do you do ? Howg dog youg dog ?

Lampe, *f.* (freemasons'), *drinking-glass ;* (familiar) — amoureuse (obsolete), *woman's privy parts.* Termed in modern English slang "Fanny."

Lampie, *f.* (thieves'), *meal.* From lamper, *to gulp down.*

Lampion, *m.* (thieves'), *hat ; bottle ;* — rouge, *police officer,* "copper, or reeler." For synonymous expressions see **Pot-à-tabac.**

Lampions, *m. pl.* (thieves'), *eyes,* or "glaziers," see **Mirettes ;** — fumeux, *inflamed eyes.* Des — ! Des — ! *a call expressive of the impatience of a crowd, or rough elements of an audience, and made more forcible by stamping of feet.*

Lance, *f.* (popular and thieves'), *water,* or "Adam's ale ;" *rain,* or "parney." Il tombe de la —, *it rains.* Lance, *broom; shoemakers' awl.* Chevalier de la courte —, or de Saint-Crépin, *shoemaker,* or "snob." Du chenu pivois sans —, *good wine without water.* Lance had formerly the signification of *penis,* termed in the English slang "John Thomas, or Dick."

Lancé, *m. and adj.* (popular), *agile play of dancers' legs at dancing halls.* (Familiar) Lancé, *slightly intoxicated,* or "elevated." See **Pompette.**

Lancequiner (popular), *to rain ; to weep ; to void urine.*

Lancer (thieves'), *to void urine.* See **Lâcher.** (Popular) Lancer son prospectus, *to ogle.*

Lanceur, *m.* (familiar), bon —, *bookseller who is clever at making known to the public a new publication,* "un étouffeur" *being the reverse.* (Police) Lanceur allumeur, *a politician, generally a journalist, in the employ of the police of the Third Empire.* His functions consisted in exciting people to rebellion either by inflammatory speeches at public meetings or by violent articles.

On appelle allumeurs, en termes de police, les agents provocateurs chargés de se mêler aux sociétés secrètes, aux manifestations populaires. . . . Les allumeurs furent créés sous l'empire ; ils devinrent, sous la direction de M. Lagrange, la fleur du panier de la préfecture. Ce fonctionnaire fut lui-même . . . avec un nommé P. le metteur en œuvre du complot de l'Opéra-Comique . . . qui aboutit à cinquante-sept arrestations . . . et finit par mettre sur la défensive tous les républicains.—*Mémoires de Monsieur Claude.*

Lanceuse, *f.* (familiar), *superannuated cocotte who acts as the chaperone of a younger one.*

Lancier, *m.* (thieves' and cads'), *individual,* or "cove."

Que'qu' j'y foutrai dans la trompette,
A c' lancier-là, s'il vient vivant ?
RICHEPIN.

Lancier du préfet, *street-sweeper in the employ of the municipal authorities.*

Lanciers, *m. pl.* (popular), oui, les — ! *nonsense !* "tell that to the marines !" "how's your brother Job ?" or "do you see any green in my eye ?"

Landau à baleines, *m.* (popular), *umbrella,* "mush, or rain-napper."

Landernau, *m.* (familiar), *name of a small town in Brittany.* Il y aura du bruit dans —, *is said of an insignificant event which will set going the tongues of people who have nothing else to do.* The expression has passed into the language.

Landier, *m. and adj.* (thieves'), *official of the octroi.* The "octroi" is the office established at the gates of a town for the collection of a tax due for the introduction of certain articles of food or drink. (Thieves') Landier, *white.*

Landière, *f.* (old cant), *stall at a fair.*

On sait que le Landit était une foire célèbre qui se tenait à Saint-Denis.—MICHEL.

Landreux, *adj.* (popular), *invalid.*

Langouste, *f.* (popular), *simpleton, greenhorn,* "flat."

Langue, *f.* (familiar), verte, *slang of gamesters.* Also *slang.* The expression is Delvau's. (Popular) Avaler sa —, *to die,* "to kick the bucket." See **Pipe.** Prendre sa — des dimanches, *to use choice language.* (Familiar and popular) Une — fourrée, *lingua duplex, id est quum basiis lingua linguæ promiscetur* (RIGAUD).

Languineur, *m.* (popular), *man whose functions are to examine the tongues of pigs at the slaughterhouse to ascertain that they are not diseased.*

Lansquailler (thieves'). See **Lascailler.**

Lansque (popular), abbreviation of lansquenet.

Lansquinage, *m.* (thieves'), *weeping.*

Lansquine, *f.* (thieves'), *rain,* or "parny."

Aussi j'suis gai quand la lansquine,
M'a trempé l'cuir, j'm'essuie l'échine
Dans l'vent qui passe et m'fait joli.
RICHEPIN.

Q

Lansquiner (thieves' and cads'), *to rain ;* — des chasses, *to weep,* "to nap a bib."

Lanteoz (Breton cant), *butter.*

Lanterne, *f.* (popular), *window,* "jump." Had formerly the signification of *woman's privy parts,* "Fanny" in the modern English slang. Radouber la —, *to talk, to tattle.* The expression is old. Avoir la —, or se taper sur la —, *to be hungry,* "to be bandied, or to cry cupboard." Vieille —, *old prostitute.* See **Gadoue.** (Popular) Lanternes de cabriolet, *large goggle eyes.*

Lantimèche, *m.* (popular), *lamp-lighter ; also a word equivalent to* "thingumbob." Il a filé avec — pour mener les poules pisser, *a derisive reply to one inquiring about the whereabouts of a person.*

Lanturlu, *m.* (popular), *madcap.*

Laou Pharaou (Breton cant), *body lice.*

Lapin, *m.* (popular), *apprentice.* Des lapins, *shoes,* or "trotter-cases." (Familiar and popular) Lapin, *a clever or sturdy fellow.*

Ah! tu es un lapin! . . . lui disaient tous ceux qu'il abordait, il paraît que tu viens de faire une fameuse découverte! on parle de toi pour la croix !—E. GABORIAU, *M. Lecoq.*

Etre en —, *to ride by the side of the coachman.* Un — de gouttière, *cat,* or "long-tailed beggar." Coller or poser un —, *to deceive, to take in,* "to bilk." It is likely the expression draws its origin from the practice of certain sportsmen who used to invite themselves to dinner at some friend's house in the country, and repaid their host by leaving a rabbit as a compensation. The *Slang Dictionary* says that when a person gets the worst of a bargain he is said "to have bought the rabbit," from an old story about a man selling a cat to a foreigner for a rabbit. With reference to deceiving prostitutes the act is described in the English slang as "doing a bilk."

Je vous demande pardon, mais le vocable est consacré. "Poser un lapin" fut long-temps une définition malséante, bannie des salons où l'on cause. Maintenant, elle est admise entre gens de bonne compagnie, et le lapin cesse, dans les mots, de braver l'honnêteté.—MAXIME BOUCHERON.

Lapin, *one who plays a part in certain immoral practices.* Termed a "lamb" at some English public schools. Un fameux, or rude —, *a strong fearless man, one who is* "spry ;" also *a man who begets many children.* Voler au —, or étouffer un —, *is said of a bus conductor who swindles his employers by pocketing part of the fares.* Mon vieux — ! *old fellow!* "old cock !" (Thieves') Lapin ferré, *mounted gendarme.* (Printers') Manger un —, *to attend a comrade's funeral.*

Cette locution vient sans doute de ce que, à l'issue de la cérémonie funèbre, les assistants se réunissaient autrefois dans quelque restaurant avoisinant le cimetière et, en guise de repas de funérailles, mangeaient un lapin plus ou moins authentique. —BOUTMY.

Concerning this expression, there is an anecdote of a typo who was lying in hospital at the point of death, and who informed his sorrowing friends that he would try and wait till the Friday morning, so that they might have all the Saturday and Sunday for the funeral feast.

Je tâcherai d'aller jusqu'à demain soir . . . parceque les amis auraient ainsi samedi et dimanche pour boulotter mon "lapin." Cela ne vaut-il pas le "plaudite !" de l'empereur Auguste, ou le "Baissez le rideau, la farce est jouée !" de notre vieux Rabelais ?—BOUTMY.

(Familiar and popular) C'est le — qui a commencé *is said ironi-*

cally in allusion to a difference or fight between a strong man and a weak one, when the latter is worsted and blamed into the bargain. A cartoon of the late artist Gill, on the occasion of the assassination of Victor Noir by Pierre Bonaparte in the last days of the Third Empire, depicted the two principal actors in that mysterious affair under the features of a fierce bulldog and a rabbit, with the saying, "C'est le lapin qui a commencé," for a text line.

Lapiner (general), *to cheat a prostitute by not paying her her dues.*

Laqueuse, *f.* (familiar and popular), *cocotte who walks in the vicinity of the lake at the Bois de Boulogne.* See **Gadoue.**

Larantqué, *m.* (popular and thieves'), *two-franc coin.*

Larbin, *m.* (general), *man-servant, footman,* "flunkey," or "bone-picker."

Le savoureux Lebeau . . . ancien valet de pied aux Tuileries, laissait voir le hideux larbin qu'il était, âpre au gain et à la curée.—A. DAUDET, *Les Rois en Exil.*

(Popular) Larbin savonné, *knave of cards.*

Larbine, *f.* (popular), *maid-servant,* "slavey."

Larbinerie, *f.* (familiar), *set of servants,* "flunkeydom," or "flunkeyism."

Larcottier, *m.* (old cant), *one who yields too often to the promptings of a well-developed bump of amativeness,* a "beard-splitter."

Lard, *m.* (popular), *disreputable woman ; mistress ; skin, or body.* Sauver son —, *to save one's* "bacon." Perdre son —, *to become thin.* Faire son —, *to put on a conceited look.* (General) Faire du —, *to lie in bed of a*

morning. (Thieves') Manger du —, *to inform against,* "to turn snitch."

Larda (Breton cant), *to beat.*

Lardé, *m.* (popular), un — aux pommes, *mess of potatoes and bacon.*

Lardée, *f.* (printers'), *composition full of italics and roman.*

Larder (obsolete), *to have connection with a woman,* "to dille, to screw."

Terme libre, qui signifie, faire le déduit, se divertir avec une femme.—LE ROUX, *Dict. Comique.*

Lardives, *f. pl.* (prostitutes'), *female companions of prostitutes.*

Après tout, mes lardives ne valent pas mieux que moi et leurs megs valent le pante que j'ai lâché parcequ'il m'embêtait. —*Mémoires de Monsieur Claude.*

Lardoire, *f.* (popular), *sword,* or "toasting fork."

Large, *adj. and m.* (popular), il est —, mais c'est des épaules *is said ironically of a close-fisted man.* Une femme —, better explained by the following quotation :—

Mot qui se dit d'une femme dont la nature est grande, qui a l'ouverture au bas du ventre fort dilatée, ce qu'on appelle proprement une conasse, et qu'on tient pour une marque que la personne n'est pas pucelle, et s'escrime souvent du derrière. — LE ROUX, *Dict. Comique.*

N'en pas mener —, *to be ill at ease ; crest-fallen.* Envoyer quelqu'un au —, *to send one to the deuce.*

Largonji, *m.* (thieves'), *cant, slang.* Properly the word jargon disguised by a process described under the heading **Lampagne** (which see).

Largue, *f.* (popular and thieves'), *woman,* "hay-bag, cooler, shakester, or laced mutton." Concerning the word Michel says : "Je crains bien qu'une pensée obscène

n'ait présidé à la création de ce mot : ce qui me le fait soupçonner, c'est que je lis, p. 298 du livre d'Antoine Oudin, 'Loger au large, d'une femme qui a grand . . . . or, large se prononçait largue à l'italienne et à l'espagnole dès le xive siècle.'"

Deux mots avaient suffi. Ces deux mots étaient : vos largues et votre aubert, vos femmes et votre argent, le résumé de toutes les affections vraies de l'homme.—BALZAC.

Largue, *mistress,* or "poll ;" — d'altèque, *handsome woman,* or "dimbermort ;" — en panne, *forsaken woman,* or a "moll that has been buried ;" — en vidange, *female in childbed,* or "in the straw." Balancer une —, *to forsake a mistress,* "to bury a moll." (Sailors') Grand' —, *excellent,* "out and out." C'est grand' — et vrai marin, *it is* "out and out," *and quite sailor-like.*

Larguepé, *f.* (thieves'), *prostitute, or thief's wife,* "mollisher." See **Gadoue.** According to Michel this word is formed of largue, *woman,* and putain, *whore.*

Larme du compositeur, *f.* (printers'), *comma.*

Larnac, arnac, or **arnache,** *m.* (thieves'), *police officer,* "copper," or "reeler." Rousse à l'—, *detective.* For synonymous expressions see **Vache.**

Larque, *f.* (roughs'), *woman,* or "cooler ;" *registered prostitute.* A corruption of largue. See **Gadoue.**

Larrons, *m. pl.* (printers'), *odd pieces of paper which adhere to sheets in the press, producing* "moines" *or blanks.*

Lartif, lartie, larton, *m.* (thieves'), *bread,* "pannum." Termed also "briffe, broute, pierre dure, artie,

arton, brignolet, bringue, boule de son, bricheton."

Lartille à plafond, *f.* (thieves'), *pastry.*

Lartin, *m.* (old cant), *beggar,* "maunderer."

Larton, *m.* (thieves'), *bread,* "pannum ;" — brutal, *black bread ;* — savonné, *white bread.*

Lartonnier, *m.* (thieves'), *baker.* From larton, *bread.* In the English popular lingo a "dough-puncher."

Lascailler (thieves'), *to void urine,* "to pump ship." For synonyms see **Lâcher.**

Lascar, *m.* (military), *bold, devil-may-care fellow.* Allons, mes lascars ! *now, boys !*

Alors il se frottait les mains, faisait des blagues, ricanait : Eh ! eh ! mes lascars, il y a du bon pour le " chose," ce soir !—G. COURTELINE.

The term is also used disparagingly with the signification of *bad soldiers.*

Là-dessus, en arrière, à droite, et à gauche . . . marche ! A vos écuries, tas de lascars.—G. COURTELINE.

(Thieves') Lascar, *fellow.*

Tous les lascars à l'atelier pouvaient turbiner à leur gré. Moi, je n'avais pas plus tôt le dos tourné à mon ouvrage pour grignoter mon lartif (pain) ou pour chiquer mon Saint-père (tabac), que le louchon était sur mon dos pour m'écoper.—*Mémoires de Monsieur Claude.*

Las de chier, *m.* (popular), *grand* —, *big skulking fellow without any energy.*

Laten (Breton slang), *tongue.*

Latenni (Breton slang), *to chatter.*

Latif, *m.* (thieves'), *white linen,* "lully," or "snowy."

Latin, *m.* (thieves'), *lingo, cant,* "flash, thieves' Latin." The word meant formerly *language.*

Latine, *f.* (students'), *student's mis-tress.* From "Quartier Latin," a part of Paris where students mostly dwell.

Latte, *f.* (military), *cavalry sword.* Se ficher un coup de —, *to fight a duel.*

Laumir (old cant), *to lose,* "to blew."

Laune, *m.* (thieves'), *police officer,* or "copper." For synonymous expressions see **Pot-à-tabac.**

Laure, *f.* (thieves'), *brothel,* "nanny-shop, or academy." Concerning the inmates of a clandestine esta-blishment of that description in London, Mr. James Greenwood says :—

They belong utterly and entirely to the devil in human shape who owns the den that the wretched harlot learns to call her "home." You would never dream of the deplorable depth of her destitution if you met her in her gay attire . . . she is abso-lutely poorer than the meanest beggar that ever whined for a crust. These women are known as "dress lodgers."—*The Seven Curses of London.*

Lavabe, *m.* (popular), *note of hand ; theatre ticket at reduced price given to people who in return agree to applaud at a given signal.*

Lavage, *m.,* or **lessive,** *f.* (gene-ral), *sale of one's property ;* also *sale of property at considerable loss.*

Barbet n'avait pas prévu ce lavage ; il croyait au talent de Lucien.—BALZAC.

Lavarès (thieves'), for laver, *to sell stolen property.* Nous irons à lavarès la camelote chez le four-gueur, *we will go and sell the pro-perty at the receiver's.*

Lavasse, *f.* (popular), *soup ;* — sénatoriale, *rich soup ;* — prési-dentielle, *very rich soup.*

Lavement, *m.* (popular), au verre pilé, *glass of rank brandy ;* (fami-liar and popular), *troublesome man or bore ;* (military) *adjutant.*

Laver (general), *to spend ; to sell.*

Vous avez pour quarante francs de loges et de billets à vendre, et pour soixante francs de livres à laver au journal. — BALZAC.

(Thieves') Laver la camelote, or les fourgueroles, *to sell stolen pro-perty,* "to do the swag ;" — son linge, *to give oneself up after sen-tence has been passed in contuma-ciam ;* — le linge dans la saignante, *to kill.*

Voici le pante que j'ai allumé devant le ferlampier (bandit) mis au poteau,—il faut laver son linge dans la saignante. Vite ; à vos surins, les autres ! Une fois qu'il sera refroidi, qu'on le porte à la cave.—*Mé-moires de Monsieur Claude.*

Se — les pieds, se — les pieds au dur, or au grand pré, *to be trans-ported,* "to be lagged," or "to light the lumper." (Popular) Se — les yeux, *to drink a glass of white wine in the morning.* Se — le tuyau, *to drink,* "to wet one's whistle." Va te — ! *go to the deuce,* go to "pot !" Mon linge est lavé ! *I am beaten, I own I have the worst of it.* (General) Laver, *to sell.*

Lavette, *f.* (popular), *tongue,* or "red rag."

Lavoir, *m.* (cads'), *confessional.* A place where one's conscience is made snow-white. (Familiar) Lavoir public, *newspaper.*

L'avoir encore (popular). Elle l'a encore, *she has yet her maiden-head, her rose has not yet been plucked.*

Lazagne, or **lazagen,** *f.* (thieves'), *letter,* "screeve, or stiff."

On appelle lasagna, en Italien, une espèce de mets de pâte, et l'on dit pro-verbialement "come le lasagne," comme les lasagnes, ni endroit ni envers, pour dire, on ne sait ce que c'est. On comprend que, ignorants comme ils le sont pour la plupart, les gueux aient appliqué cette expression aux lettres, qui, d'ailleurs, sont loin d'être toujours lisibles. Il y a aussi des livres appelés "di lasagne."—Michel.

Balancer une —, *to write a letter.*

Lazaro, *m.* (military), *prison,* "shop."

Il lui avait ouvert la porte du cachot . . . au fond il se moquait pas mal d'être flanqué au lazaro.—G. Courteline.

Lazo-ligot, *m.* (police), *strap with a noose.*

Et Col-de-zinc, à l'aspect si raide, avait l'agilité du Mexicain pour jeter le lazo-ligot, pour entourer d'un seul coup le corps et le poignet de son sujet de façon à ce que la main restât attachée à sa hanche.—*Mémoires de Monsieur Claude.*

Lazzi-lof, *m.* (thieves'), *venereal malady.* Termed "French gout," or "ladies' fever," in the English slang.

Lèche-curé, *m.* (popular), *bigot,* "prayer-monger."

Léchée, *f.* (artists'), *picture minutely painted.*

Légitime, *m. and f.* (familiar), *husband,* or "oboleklo;" *wife,* or "tart." Manger sa —, *to squander one's fortune.*

Légume, *m.* (military), gros —, *field officer,* or "bloke." An allusion to his epaulets, termed "graine d'épinards."

Légumiste, *m.* (familiar), *vegetarian.*

Lem, parler en —, *mode of disguising words* by prefixing the letter "l," and adding the syllable "em" preceded by the first letter of the word; thus "boucher" becomes "loucherbem." This mode was first used by butchers, and is now obsolete. See **Lampagne.**

Lenquetré, *m.* (thieves'), *thirty sous.* The word "trente" disguised.

Lentille, *f.* (thieves'), grosse —, *moon,* "parish lantern."

Léon, *m.* (thieves'), *the president of the assize court.*

Lermon, *m.* (thieves'), *tin.*

Lermonner (thieves'), *to tin.*

Lesbien, *m.* (literary), *Sodomist,* or "gentleman of the back door." Formerly termed lesbin, as appears from the following :—

Lesbin, pour dire un jeune homme ou garçon qui sert de sucube à un autre et qui souffre qu'on commette la sodomie sur lui. —Le Roux, *Dict. Comique.*

Lesbienne, *f.* (literary), *female who has unnatural intercourse with those of her own sex.*

Lescailler. See **Lascailler.**

Lésébombe, or lésée, *f.* (popular), *prostitute,* or "mot." For synonymous expressions see **Gadoue.**

Lessivage, *m.* (popular), *selling of property;* (thieves') *pleading.*

Lessivant, *m.* (thieves'), *counsel,* or "mouthpiece."

Lessive, *f.* (popular), de gascon, *doubtful cleanliness.* Faire la —, *to turn one's dirty shirt-collar or cuffs on the clean side.* (Literary) Faire sa —, *to sell books sent to one by authors.* (Thieves') Lessive, *speech for the defence.* The prisoner compares himself to dirty linen, to be washed snow-white by the counsel.

Lessiver (thieves'), *is said of a barrister who pleads in behalf of a prisoner.* Se faire —, *to be cleaned out at some game,* "to have blewed one's tin," or "to be a muck-snipe," or in sporting slang a "muggins."

Lessiveur, *m.* (thieves'), *counsel,* or "mouthpiece." Literally *one who washes.*

Letern (Breton cant), *eye.*

Letez (Breton cant), *countryman.*

Letezen (Breton cant), *pancake.*

Lettre, *f.* (thieves'), de Jérusalem, *letter written by a prisoner to someone outside the prison, to request that some money may be sent him;* — de couronne (obsolete), *cup.*

Levage, *m.* (popular), *swindle; successful gallantry.*

Levé, *adj.* (general), had formerly the signification of *to be tracked by a bailiff who has found one's whereabouts.*

Levée, *f.* (popular), *wholesale arrest of prostitutes.*

Lève-pieds, *m.* (thieves'), *ladder; steps,* or "*dancers.*" Embarder sur le —, *to go down the steps,* "to lop down the dancers."

Lever (printers'), la lettre, or les petits clous, *to compose;* (popular) — boutique, *to set up as a tradesman.*

Un Toulousain . . . jeune perruquier dévoré d'ambition, vint à Paris, et y leva boutique (je me sers de votre argot).— BALZAC.

Lever des chopins, *to find some profitable stroke of business;* — la jambe, *to dance the cancan;* — le bras, *to be dissatisfied;* — le pied, *to abscond;* (familiar and popular) — une femme, *to find a woman willing to accord her favours;* — quelquechose, *to steal something,* "to wolf;" (military) — les baluchons, *to go away;* (prostitutes') — un miché, *to find a client,* "to pick up a flat."

Leveur, *m.* (popular), *pickpocket,* "buzcove." See **Grinche.** Leveur de femmes, *a Don Giovanni in a small way,* or a "molrower." (Printers') Bon —, *skilled typographer.*

Un bon leveur est un ouvrier qui compose bien et vite.—BOUTMY.

Leveuse, *f.* (familiar and popular), *a flash girl.*

Levure, *f.* (popular), *flight.* Faire la —, *to run away,* "to skedaddle," "to mizzle."

Lexicon, or **lécheur,** *m.* (familiar and popular), *a pet dog which prostitutes keep for purposes which may be better guessed at than described.*

Lézard, *m.* (popular), *an untrustworthy friend; dog stealer.* Faire son —, *to doze in the daytime like a lizard basking in the sun.* (Thieves') Faire le —, *to take to flight,* "to make beef." See **Patatrot.** Un —, *a traitor,* a "snitcher."

Lézardes, *f. pl.* (printers'), *white spaces.*

Raies blanches produites dans la composition par la rencontre fortuite d'espaces placées les unes au-dessous des autres.— BOUTMY.

Lézine, *f.* (thieves'), *cheating at a game.*

Léziner (thieves'), *to cheat,* "to bite;" *to hesitate,* "to funk."

Libretailleur, *m.* (familiar), *a libretto writer of poor ability.*

Lice, *f.* (popular), *lecherous girl.* Literally *bitch.*

Lichade, *f.* (popular), *embrace.*

Lichance, *f.* (popular), *hearty meal,* "tightener." From licher, equivalent to lécher, *to lick.*

Liche, *f.* (popular), *excessive eating or drinking.* Etre en —, *to be* "on the booze."

Licher (familiar and popular), *to drink,* "to lush." See **Rincer.**

Il a liché tout' la bouteille,
Rien n'est sacré pour un sapeur.
Parisian Song.

Licheur, *m.* (familiar and popular), *gormandizer.* The term is very old.

Lichoter un rigolboche (popular), *to make a hearty meal,* or "tightener."

Lie de froment, *f.* (popular), *excrement,* or "quaker."

Liège, *m.* (thieves'), *gendarme.*

Lierchem (cads'), *to ease oneself.* An obscene word disguised. See **Lem.**

Lignante, *f.* (thieves'), *life.*

Ce mot . . . vient de la ligne, dite de vie, que les bohémiens consultaient sur la main de ceux auxquels ils disaient la bonne aventure.—MICHEL.

Lignard, *m.* (familiar and popular), *foot-soldier of the line; journalist;* (printers') *compositor who has to deal only with the body part of a composition;* (artists') *artist who devotes his attention more to the perfection of the outline than to that of colour;* (popular) *rodfisher.*

Ligne, *f.* (artists'), *avoir la —, to have a fine profile.* (Literary) Pêcher à la —, or *tirer à la —, is said of a journalist who seeks to make an article as lengthy as possible.* (Popular) Pêcher à la — d'argent *is said of an angler who catches fish by means of a money bait, at the fishmonger's.* (Printers') Ligne à voleur, *line containing only a syllable, or a very short word, which might have been composed into the preceding line.*

Les lignes à voleur sont faciles à reconnaître, et elles n'échappent guère à l'œil d'un correcteur exercé, qui les casse d'ordinaire impitoyablement.—BOUTMY.

Ligore, *f.* (thieves'), *assize court.*

Ligorniau, *m.* (popular), *hodman.*

Ligot. See **Ligotante.**

Ligotage, *m.* (police), *binding a prisoner's hands by means of a rope or strap.*

Ligotante, or **ligotte,** *f.* (thieves'), *rope, or strap; bonds;* — de rifle, or riflarde, *strait waistcoat.*

Ligoter (police and thieves'), *to bind a prisoner's hands by means of ropes or straps.*

Nul mieux que lui ne savait prendre un malfaiteur sans l'abîmer, ni lui mettre les poucettes sans douleur ou le ligoter sans effort.—*Mémoires de Monsieur Claude.*

Ligotte, *f.* (thieves'), *rope; string; strap.*

Lillange (thieves'), *town of Lille.*

Lillois, *m.* (thieves'), *thread.*

Limace, *f.* (popular), *low prostitute,* or "draggle-tail;" *soldier's wench,* or "barrack-hack," see **Gadoue;** (thieves') *shirt,* "flesh-bag, or commission." From the Romany "lima," according to Michel.

Limacier, *m.,* **limacière,** *f.,* (thieves'), *shirt-maker.* From limace, *a shirt.*

Limande, *f.* (popular), *man made of poor stuff; one who fawns.* From limande, *a kind of sole* (fish).

Lime, *f.* (thieves'), for limace, *shirt,* or "commission" in old English cant; — sourde, *sly, underhand man.* The expression is old, and is used by Rabelais:—

Mais, qui pis est, les outragearent grandement, les appellants trop-diteux, bresche-dents, plaisants rousseaulx, galliers, chien-licts, averlans, limes sourdes. — *Gargantua.*

Limer (familiar and popular), *refers to a protracted carnal act.* Literally *to file.*

Limogère, *f.* (thieves'), *chambermaid.*

Limonade, *f.* (popular), *water,* or "Adam's ale;" *the trade of a "limonadier," or proprietor of a small café.* Tomber, or se plaquer

dans la —, *to fall into the water ;
to be ruined,* or "gone a mucker."
(Thieves') Limonade, *flannel vest ;
—* de linspré, *champagne.*
"Linspré" is the word "prince"
disguised.

Limonadier de postérieurs, *m.*
(popular), *apothecary.* Formerly
apothecaries performed the " clysterium donare" of Molière's
Malade Imaginaire.

Limousin, or **limousinant,** *m.*
(popular), *mason.* It must be
mentioned that most of the Paris
masons hail from Limousin.

Limousine, *f.* (thieves'), *sheet lead
on roofs,* or "flap." Termed
also "saucisson, gras-double."

Limousineur, *m.* (thieves'), *thief
who steals sheet-lead roofing.* Called
also "voleur au gras-double," a
"bluey faker," or one who "flies
the blue pigeon." See **Grinche.**

Linge, *m.* (familiar and popular),
faire des effets de —, *to display
one's body linen with affectation.*
Un bock sans —, or sans faux-
col, *a glass of beer without any
head.* A request for such a thing
is often made in the Paris cafés,
where the microscopic "bocks"
or "choppes" are topped by
gigantic heads. Se payer un —
convenable, *to have a stylish mistress,* an "out-and-out tart."
(Popular) Un — à règles, *a dirty,
slatternly woman.* Resserrer son
—, *to die.* (Thieves') Avoir son
— lavé, *to be caught, apprehended,*
or "smugged."

Lingé, *adj.* (popular), être —, *to
have plenty of fine linen.*

Lingre, or **lingue,** *m.* (thieves'),
knife, or "chive." From Langres,
a manufacturing town. The synonyms are "linve, trente-deux,
vingt-deux, chourin or surin,
scion, coupe - sifflet, pliant."

Jouer du —, *to stab,* "to stick, or
to chive."

Lingrer, or **linguer** (thieves'), *to
stab,* "to stick, or to chive."

Lingriot, *m.* (thieves'), *penknife.*

Linguarde, *f.* (popular), *woman
with a soft tongue.*

Lingue, *m.* (thieves'), *knife,* or
"chive."

Linspré, *m.* (thieves'), *prince.* See
Limonade.

Linvé, *m.* (popular), loussem,
twenty sous. The words "vingt
sous" distorted. Un —, *a franc ;*
"un lenquetré" being *one franc
and fifty centimes, or thirty sous,*
and "un larantqué," *two francs, or
forty sous.* These expressions are
respectively the words un, trente,
quarante, disguised.

Lion, *m.* (familiar), *dandy of*
1840. Fosse aux lions, *box at the
opera occupied by men of fashion.*
For synonymous terms see **Gommeux.**

Lionnerie, *f.* (familiar), *fashionable world.*

Lipète, *f.* (popular), *prostitute,*
"mot," or "common Jack." See
Gadoue.

Lipette, *f.* (popular), *mason.*
Termed also ligorgniot.

Lipper (popular), *to visit several
wine-shops in succession.*

Liquette, or **limace,** *f.* (thieves'),
shirt, in old English cant "commission." Décarrer le centre d'une
—, *to obliterate the marking of a
shirt.*

Liqueur, *f.* (popular), cache-bon-
bon à —, *dandy's stick-up collar.*
A malevolent allusion to scrofula
abcesses on the neck.

Lire (familiar), aux astres, *to muse,* "to go wool-gathering;" (familiar and popular)—le journal, *to go without a dinner;* — le Moniteur, *to wait patiently.* (Printers') Lire, *to note proposed alterations in a proof;* — en première, *to correct the first proof;* — en seconde, or en bon, *to correct a second proof on which the author has written "for press."* (Thieves') Savoir —, *to have one's wits about one,* "to know what's o'clock."

Lisette, *f.* (thieves'), *long waist-coat; sword,* or "poker."

Lisserpem (roughs'), *to void urine.* The word "pisser" disguised by prefixing the letter "l," and adding the syllable "em" preceded by the first letter of the word.

Listard, *m.* (journalists'), *one in favour of "scrutin de liste," or mode of voting for the election wholesale of all the representatives in parliament of a "département."* For instance, the Paris electors have to vote for a list of over thirty members.

Lit, *m.* (popular), être sous le —, *to be mistaken.*

Lithographier (popular), se —, *to fall,* "to come a cropper."

Litrer, or **itrer** (thieves'), *to have.*

Litronner (popular), *to drink wine.* From litron, *a wine measure.*

Litronneur, *m.* (popular), *one who is too fond of the bottle.*

Littérature jaune (familiar), *the so-called Naturalist literature.*

Littératurier, *m.* (familiar), *a literary man after a fashion.*

Livraison, *f.* (popular), avoir une — de bois devant sa porte, *to have well-developed breasts, to be possessed of fine* "Charlies."

Livre, *m.* (popular), des quatre rois, *pack of cards,* "book of briefs," or "Devil's books;" — rouge, *police registration book in which the names of authorized prostitutes are inscribed.* Etre inscrite dans le — rouge, *to be a registered prostitute.* (Freemasons') Livre d'architecture, *ledger of a lodge.* (Sharpers') Livre, *one hundred francs.*

Loa vihan (Breton cant), *coffee.*

Locandier, *m.* (thieves'). Called also "voleur au bonjour," *thief who visits apartments in the morning, and who when caught pretends to have entered the wrong rooms by mistake.* See **Grinche.**

Loche, *f.* (popular), mou comme une —, *slow, phlegmatic,* "lazy-bones." (Thieves') Loche, *ear,* or "wattle." Properly *loach or groundling.*

Locher (thieves'), *to listen;* (popular) *to totter,* "to be groggy."

Locomotive, *f.* (popular), *great smoker.*

Lof, loff, loffard, loffe, *m.* (popular), *fool,* or "bounder." "Lof" is the anagram of "fol."

A lui le coq, . . . pour inventer des emblèmes . . . quand j'y pense, fallait-il que je fusse loff pour donner dans un godan pareil !—*Mémoires de Vidocq.*

Loffat, *m.* (popular), *apprentice.*

Loffiat, *m.* (popular), *blockhead,* or "cabbage-head."

Loffitude, *f.* (thieves'), *stupidity; nonsense.* Bonisseur de loffitudes, *nonsense-monger.* Solliceur de loffitudes, *journalist.*

Loge infernale, *f.* (theatrical), *box occupied by young men of fashion.*

Loger rue du Croissant (familiar and popular), *is said of an* *injured husband,* or "buckface." An allusion to the horns of the moon.

Logis du moutrot, *m.* (thieves'), *police court.*

Loir, *m.* (thieves'), *prison,* "stir, or Bastile." See **Motte.**

Lokard (Breton cant), *peasant.*

Loko (Breton cant), *brandy.*

Lolo, *m.* (thieves'), *chief,* or "dimber damber;" (popular) *cocotte,* or "mot." See **Gadoue.** Fifi —, *large iron cylinder in which the contents of cesspools are carried away by the scavengers.* (Military) Gros lolos, *cuirassiers.*

Lombard, *m.* (popular), *commissionnaire of the "Mont de Piété," or government pawning establishment.*

Loncegué, *m.* (thieves' and cads'), *man,* "cove;" *master of a house,* "boss." The word gonce disguised.

Lonceguem, *f.* (thieves' and cads'), *woman,* or "hay-bag;" *mistress of a house.*

Long, *m. and adj.* (popular), *simpleton, greenhorn.* Etes - vous logé et nourri? Oui, le — du mur. *Do you get board and lodging? Yes, at my own expense.* (Thieves') Long, *stupid; blockhead,* or "go along." Abbreviation of long à comprendre.

Longchamps, *m.,* *a long corridor of w.c.'s at the Ecole Polytechnique;* (popular) *a procession.*

Longe, *f.* (thieves'), *year,* or "stretch." Tirer une —, *to do one "stretch" in prison.*

Longé, *adj.* (popular), *old.*

Longin, or **Saint-Longin,** *m.* (popular), *sluggard.*

Longine, or **Sainte-Longine,** *f.* (popular), *sluggish woman.*

Longuette de trèfle, *f.* (thieves'), *roll of tobacco,* or "twist of fogus."

Lophe, *adj.* (thieves'), *false; counterfeit,* "flash." Un fafiot —, *a forged bank-note,* or "queer screen."

Lopin, *m.* (popular), *spittle,* or "gob."

Loque, *m.* (thieves'), parler en —, *mode of disguising words.* The word is preceded by the letter "l," and the syllable preceded by the first letter of the word is added. Thus "fou" becomes "loufoque."

Loques, *f. pl.* (thieves'), *pieces of copper.*

Lorcefé, *f.* (thieves'), *old prison of "La Force."* La — des largues, *the prison of Saint-Lazare, where prostitutes and unfaithful wives are confined.*

Eh bien! si je te la fourrais à la lorcefé des largues (Saint-Lazare) pour un an, le temps de ton gerbement.—BALZAC.

Lordant. See **Lourdier.**

Loret, *m.* (popular), *lover of a lorette.*

Lorette, *f.* (familiar), *more than fast girl,* or "mot," *named after the Quartier Notre Dame de Lorette, the Paris Pimlico.* See **Gadoue.**

Lorgne, or **lorgne-bé,** *m.* (thieves'), *one-eyed man.* In English slang "a seven-sided animal;" *the ace of cards,* or "pig's eye."

Lorgnette, *f.* (thieves'), *keyhole,* this natural receptacle for a key being considered by thieves as an aperture convenient only for making investigations from the outside of a door. Etui à —, *coffin,* or "cold-meat box." Eteindre ses deux lorgnettes, *to close one's eyes.*

Lorquet, *m.* (popular), *sou.*

Lot, *m.* (popular), *venereal disease.*

Lou, or **loup**, *m.* (popular), faire un —, *to spoil a piece of work.*

Louanek (Breton cant), *brandy.*

Louave, *m.* (thieves'), *drunkard.* Etre —, *to be drunk,* "to be canon." Faire un —, *to rob a drunkard.* Rogues who devote their energies to this kind of thieving are termed ' 'bug-hunters."

Loubac, *m.* (popular), *apprentice.*

Loubion, *m.* (thieves'), *bonnet or hat.* See **Tubard**.

Loubionnier, *m.* (thieves'), *hat or bonnet maker.*

Louche, *f.* (thieves'), *hand,* or "duke." La —, *the police,* or "reelers." La — le renifle, *the police are tracing him, he is getting a* "roasting."

Louchée, *f.* (thieves'), *spoonful.* From louche, *a soup ladle.*

Loucher (popular), de la bouche, *to have a constrained, insincere smile;* — de l'épaule, *to be a humpback,* or a "lord;" — de la jambe, *to be lame.* Faire — un homme, *to inspire a man with carnal desire.*

Loucherbem, *m.* (popular and thieves'), the word boucher disguised, see **Lem**; *butcher.* Corbillard des —, see **Corbillard**.

Louchon, *m.*, **louchonne**, *f.* (popular), *person who squints, one with* "swivel-eyes."

Louffer (popular and thieves'), *to foist,* "to fizzle." Si tu louffes encore sans dire fion je te passe à travers, *if you* "fizzle" *again without apologizing I'll thrash you.*

Louffiat, *m.* (popular), *low cad.* Termed in the English slang a "rank outsider."

Loufoque, *adj. and m.* (popular and thieves'), *mad,* or "cracked, balmy, or one off his chump." The word fou disguised by means of the syllable loque. See **Loque**.

> Si nos doch' étaient moins vieilles,
> On les ferait plaiser,
> Mais les pauv' loufoques balaient
> Les gras d'nos laisées.
> RICHEPIN.

Louille, *f.* (thieves'), *prostitute,* or "bunter." See **Gadoue**.

Louis, *f. and m.* (bullies'), une —, *a bully's mistress, a prostitute.* Abbreviation of Louis XV., women in brothels often powdering and dressing their hair Louis XV. fashion. See **Gadoue**.

> J'couch' que'qu'fois sous des voitures ;
> Mais on attrap' du cambouis.
> J'veux pas ch' linguer la peinture
> Quand j'suc' la pomme à ma Louis.
> RICHEPIN.

(Popular) Un — d'or, *lump of excrement,* or "quaker."

Louisette, *f.*, *old appellation of the guillotine.*

Louiza (Breton cant), *water.*

Loup, *m.* (popular), *mistake ; debt ; creditor,* or "dun ;" *misfit, or piece of work which has been spoilt ;* (printers') *lack of type ; debt ; creditor.* Faire un —, *is to buy on credit.*

> Le jour de la banque, le créancier ou "loup" vient quelquefois guetter son débiteur (nous allions dire sa proie) à la sortie de l'atelier pour réclamer ce qui lui est dû. Quand la réclamation a lieu à l'atelier, ce qui est devenu très rare, les compositeurs donnent à leur camarade et au créancier une "roulance" accompagnée des cris : au loup ! au loup !—BOUTMY.

Loupate, *m.* (popular), the word "pou" disguised, *a louse,* or "grey-backed 'un."

Loup-cervier, *m.* (familiar), *stock-jobber.*

Loupe, *f.*, *laziness,* "loafing." Camp de la —, *vagabonds' meet-*

ing-place. Chevalier de la —, *a lazy rambler or gad-about who goes about pleasure seeking.* (Thieves') Un enfant de la —, *a variety of the vagabond tribe.*

Les Enfants de la loupe et les Filendèches habitaient de préférence l'extérieur des carrières, leurs fours à briques ou à plâtre.—*Mémoires de Monsieur Claude.*

Louper (popular), *to idle about pleasure seeking.*

Loupeur (popular), *lazy workman,* or one who is "Mondayish."

Loupiat, *m.* (popular), *lazy,* or "Mondayish," *workman ;* vagrant, or "pikey."

Loupiau, or **loupiot**, *m.* (popular), *child,* or "kid."

Loupion, *m.* (popular), *hat,* "tile." See **Tubard**.

Lourde, or **lourdière**, *f.* (thieves'), *door,* "jigger." Bâcler la —, *to shut the door,* "to dub the jigger."

Lourdeau, *m.* (thieves'), *devil,* "ruffin," or "darble."

Lourdier, *m.* (popular), *door-keeper.*

Lousse, *f.* (thieves'), *country gendarme or corps of gendarmerie.*

Loussés, *m. pl.* (cads'), dix —, *fifty centimes.* The word sous disguised.

Loustaud, *m.* (thieves'), *prison,* or "stir." See **Motte**. Envoyer à —, *to send to the deuce,* "to pot."

Louter (popular). See **Faire un lou**.

Louveteau, *m.* (freemasons'), *son of a freemason.*

Louvetier, *m.* (printers'), *man in debt.*

Ce terme est pris en mauvaise part, car le typo auquel on l'applique est considéré comme faisant trop bon marché de sa dignité.—Boutmy.

Lubre, *adj.* (thieves'), *dismal.* Lubre comme un guichemard, *as dismal as a turnkey.*

Luc, *m.* (popular), messire —, *breech,* or "tochas." "Luc" is the anagram of "cul." See **Vasistas**.

Lucarne, *f.* (popular), *woman's bonnet.*

Autrefois on assimilait le capuchon des moines à une fenêtre, d'où le proverbe : défiez-vous des gens qui ne voient le jour que par une fenêtre de drap.—Michel.

Lucarne, *monocular eye-glass.* Crever sa —, *to break one's eye-glass.*

Lucques, *m. pl.* (thieves'), *documents.* Porte —, *pocket-book,* "dee," or "dummy."

Lucrèce, *f.* (popular), faire sa —, *to put on a virtuous look.*

Luctrème, *m.* (thieves'), *skeleton key,* "screw," "Jack in the box," or "twirl." Filer le —, *to open a door by means of a skeleton-key,* "to screw."

Lugna (Breton cant), *to look.*

Luire, *m.* (old cant), *brain.*

Luis, or **luisant**, *m.* (thieves'), *day.*

Je rouscaille tous les luisans au grand haure de l'oraison.—*Le Jargon de l'Argot.* (*I pray daily the great God of prayer.*)

Luisant, *m.*, see **Luis** ; (familiar) *dandy,* "masher."

Voici d'abord le pschutt, le vlan, les luisants, comme nous les nommons aujourd'hui.—P. Mahalin.

For synonymous terms see **Gommeux**.

Luisante, or **luisarde**, *f.* (thieves'), *moon,* or "parish lantern ;" *window,* or "jump."

Luisard, or **luysard,** *m.* (thieves'), *sun.* Luysard estampille six plombes, *it is six o'clock by the sun.*

Luisarde, *f.* (thieves'), *moon,* "parish lantern, or oliver."

Lumignon, *m.* (thieves'), le grand —, *sun.* Properly lumignon is *a lantern.*

Luminariste, *m.* (theatrical), *lamplighter.*

Luncher (familiar), *to have lunch.* From the English.

Lune, *f.* (thieves'), *one franc ;* — à douze quartiers, *the wheel on which criminals were broken.* (Familiar and popular) Lune, *the behind.* See **Vasistas.** Lune, *large full face.* Amant de la —, *man with amatory intentions who frequently goes out on nocturnal, but fruitless* "caterwauling" *expeditions.* Voir la —, *is said of a maiden who is made a woman.*

La petite a beau avoir de la dentelle, elle n'en verra pas moins la lune par le même trou que les autres.—ZOLA, *L'Assommoir.*

Luné, *adj.* (popular), bien —, *in a good humour, well disposed.*

Lunette, *f.* (popular), d'approche, *guillotine.* Passer en —, *to take in,* "to do;" *to harm.* Etre passé en —, *to fail in business.* Les lunettes, *posteriors,* or "cheeks." (Popular) Lunettes, *small fry.* Je vais à la chasse aux —, *I am going to fish for small fry.*

Luque, *f.* (thieves' and mendicants'), *certificate; false certificate, or false begging petition,* "fakement ;" *passport ; picture.* Je sais bien aquiger les luques, *I know well how to forge a certificate, or to make up pictures.*

Porte —, *pocket - book,* or "dummy." It seems probable that the term "une luque," *a picture,* is derived from Saint-Luc, who formed the subject of the pictures used formerly by mendicants to ingratiate themselves with monks and nuns, as mentioned by *Le Jargon de l'Argot.*

Luquet, *m.* (thieves' and mendicants'), *forged certificate, or false begging petition,* "fakement."

Luron, *m.* (thieves'), avaler le —, *to partake of communion.* The term was probably, in the origin, "le rond," corrupted into its present form (Michel).

Lusignante, *f.* (popular), *mistress,* or "moll."

Lusquin, *m.* (thieves'), *charcoal.*

Lusquines, *f. pl.* (thieves'), *ashes.*

Lustre, *m.* (thieves'), *judge,* or "beak." (Theatrical) Chevaliers du —, *men who are paid to applaud at a theatre.* Termed also "romains." The staff of romains is termed "claque."

Lustrer (thieves'), *to try a prisoner, to have him in for* "patter."

Lutainpem, *f.* (thieves' and cads'), *prostitute,* or "bunter." See **Gadoue.** The term is nothing more than the word "putain" distorted by means of the syllable "lem." See **Lem.**

Lycée, *m.* (thieves'), *prison,* "stir, or Bastile." For synonyms see **Motte.**

Lycéen, *m.* (thieves'), *prisoner.* Termed also "élève du château."

Lyonnaise, *f.* (popular), *silk,* "floss." Etre à la —, *to wear a silk dress.*

**ABIL-LARDE,** *f.* (popular), *girl leading a dissolute life, an habituée of the Bal Mabille.*

glacé des abreuvoirs. Là-dessus, assez causé : debout !...—Debout à trois heures du matin ? Ah ! macache.—G. COURTE-LINE.

Mabillien, *m.*, **Mabillienne,** *f.* (popular), *male and female habitués of the Bal Mabille,* a place much frequented by pleasure-seeking foreigners.

Macadam (familiar and popular), faire le —, *to walk to and fro on the pavement as a prostitute.* Fleur de —, *street-walker.* See **Gadoue.** Le général —, *the public.* (Popular) Macadam, *sweet white wine.*

Chez nous c'est sous le noir et bas plafond d'un bouge que les voyous blafards, couleur tête de veau, font la vendange. Ils ont pour vin doux et nouveau le liquide appelé macadam, une boue jaunâtre fade.— RICHEPIN, *Le Pavé.*

Maboul, *adj.* (general), *one "cracked," or one with "a screw loose."* From the Arab.

C'est' y que t'es maboul ? dit l'chef.— J'suis pas maboul, que je réponds.—G. COURTELINE.

Macaire, *m.* (familiar and popular), un Robert —, *a swindler, one of the* "swell mob." Robert Macaire is a character in a play called *L'Auberge des Adrets.*

Mac, *m.* (popular), abbreviation of "maquereau," *girl's bully,* or "Sunday man." For synonyms see **Poisson.** The term also applies to any man living at a woman's expense.

Macairisme, *m.* (familiar), *any act referring to swindling operations.*

Macaron, *m.* (popular), huissier, *kind of attorney ;* (thieves') *informer, one who "blows the gaff," a "snitcher."*

Maca, *f.* (popular), *mistress of a bawdy-house ; the Paris Morgue or dead-house.* From machabée, *a corpse.*

Cet homme qui criait si fort contre ceux que les gens de sa sorte nomment des macarons s'est un des premiers mis à table.— VIDOCQ. (*That very man who complained so much of those whom such people term traitors has been one of the first to inform.*)

Macache (military), *no ;* — bono, *no good.*

Allons, les deux rosses, debout !... .— Pourquoi donc faire faut-il qu'on se lève ? —Pour aller, reprit l'adjudant, casser la

Macaronnage, *m.* (thieves'), *informing against,* "blowing the gaff."

Macaronner (thieves'), *to inform against,* " to blow the gaff," or "to turn snitch." Se —, *to run away,* "to guy." See **Patatrot.**

Macchoux, *m.* (popular), *prostitute's bully,* or " Sunday man." See **Poisson.**

Macédoine, *f.* (engine drivers'), *fuel.*

Machabé, *adj.* (popular), *drunk.* J'ai trop picté, je suis à moitié —, *I have been drinking too much, I am half drunk.*

Machabée, *m.* (popular), *gay girls' bully,* or " ponce"; see **Poisson** ; *Jew,* " mouchey, Ikey, or sheney;" *body of a drowned person.*

Je ne vois d'autre origine à cette expression que la lecture du chap. xii. du deuxième livre des Machabées, qui a encore lieu aux messes des morts ; ou plutôt c'est de là que sera venue la danse macabre, dont l'argot a conservé le souvenir.—MI-CHEL.

Case des machabées, *cemetery.* Le clou des machabées, *the " Morgue,"* or *Paris dead-house.* Mannequin à machabées, *hearse.* (Thieves') Machabée, *traitor,* or "snitcher." Literally *a corpse,* the informer in a prison, when detected, being generally murdered by those he has betrayed by means of the punishment termed "accolade," which consists in crushing him against a wall.

Machaber (popular), *to die,* "to kick the bucket." See **Pipe.** Machaber quelqu'un, *to drown one.* Se —, *to drink.* Je me suis machabé d'un litre, *I have treated myself to a litre bottle of wine.*

Machicot, *m.* (popular), *bad, mean player,* or one who plays a "tin-pot game." In the *Contes d'Eutrapel,* a French officer at the siege of Chatillon is ridiculously spoken of as Captain Tin-pot—Capitaine du Pot d'Etain. Tin-pot as generally used means worthless.

Machin, *m.* (general), *expression used when one cannot recollect the name of a person,* " thingumbob, or what's name."

Machine, *f.* (literary, artists', theatrical), *production.*

Cela m'est bien égal ! Il n'est pas le seul à me dévisager. Je lui chanterai sa " machine" et il me laissera tranquille.—J. SERMET, *Une Cabotine.*

Grande —, *drama.* Molière uses the word to describe an important affair or undertaking :—

J'ai des ressors tout prêts pour diverses machines.—L'*Etourdi.*

(Popular) Machine à moulures, *breech,* or " bum," see **Vasistas** ; — à lisserpem, *urinal ;* lisserpem being the word pisser disguised.

Mâchoire, *f.* (familiar and popular), *blockhead.* (Literary) Vieille —, *dull, old-fashioned writer ; ignorant man.*

L'on arrivait par la filière d'épithètes qui suivent : ci-devant, faux toupet, aile de pigeon, perruque, étrusque, mâchoire, ganache, au dernier degré de décrépitude, à l'épithète la plus infamante, académicien et membre de l'Institut.—TH. GAUTIER.

MacMahon, *m.* (dragoons'), *head of a Medusa at top of helmet.*

MacMahonnat, *m.,* *period of Marshal MacMahon's sway as President of the Republic.* Everybody recollects the famous "J'y suis, j'y reste !" of the Marshal, and Gambetta's reply, " Il faut se soumettre ou se démettre."

Maçon, *m.* (popular), *four-pound loaf ;* (freemasons') — de pratique, *mason ;* — de théorie, *freemason ;* (familiar) *disparaging epithet applied to any clumsy worker.*

Macque, macquet. See **Mac.**

Macquecée. See **Maca.**

Macrotage, or **maquereautage**, *m.* (familiar and popular), *living at a woman's expense ;* used also figuratively to denote agency in some fishy business.

Macroter (familiar and popular), *to live at a woman's expense ;* — une affaire, *to be the agent in some fishy business.*

Macrotin, *m.* (familiar and popular), *one living at a woman's expense,* "*pensioner*" *with an unmentionable prefix, young bully, young* "ponce." See **Poisson**.

Maculature, *f.* (printers'), attraper une —, *to get drunk, to get* "tight." See **Sculpter**.

Madame (popular), Milord quépète, *lazy woman, who likes to lie in bed ;* — Tiremonde (expression used by Rabelais), or Tirepousse, *midwife ;* (shopmen's) — Canivet, *a female customer who cannot make up her mind, and leaves without purchasing anything, after having made the unfortunate shopman display all his goods.*

Madeleine, *f.* (card-sharpers'), faire suer la —, *to cheat*, or "bite," *with great difficulty.*

Madelen (Breton cant), *salt.*

Mademoiselle Manette, *f.* (popular), *portmanteau*, or "peter."

Madrice, *f.* (thieves'), *cunning.* Il a de la —, *he is cunning*, or "is fly to wot's wot."

Madrin, madrine, *adj.* (thieves'), *cunning*, "leary, or fly to wot's wot."

Madrouillage, *m.* (thieves'), *bungle.*

Ma fiole (thieves'), *me ; myself,* "my nibs." Est-ce que tu te fiches de —? *are you laughing at me ?*

Magasin, *m.* (military), *military school,* "shop" at the R. M. Academy ; (popular) — de blanc, or de fesses, *brothel.*

Magistrat'muche, *f.* (thieves'), *magistracy.* Un pant' de la —, *a magistrate*, a "beak." Termed "queer cuffin" in old cant.

Magnanière, *f.* (thieves'), de —, *in order that.* Il fagaut dévider la retentissante de — à ne pas faire de l'harmonarès, *we must break the bell so as not to make any noise.*

Magnée, *f.* (thieves'), *prostitute,* or "bunter." See **Gadoue**.

Magnes, *f. pl.* (popular), *affectation,* "high-falutin" *airs.* Faire des —, *to make ceremonies.* As-tu fini tes —? *none of your airs !* "stop bouncing !" *I don't take that in !* From manières.

Magnette, *f.* (thieves'), *name,* or "monarch ;" — blague, *false name.* Il fagaut la — blague de magnanière que tu ne sois paga, *you must take a false name lest you should be caught.*

Magneuse, magnuce, manieuse, *f.* (popular), *variety of prostitute.* For synonyms see **Gadoue**. Also *female who has unnatural intercourse with those of her own sex.* Jouer à la magni-magno in the eighteenth century alluded to acts which take place previous to carnal connection.

Maguer (popular), se —, *to hurry.*

Maigre, *m.* (thieves'), du —! *silence !* "mum your dubber." Also *take care what you say,* or "plant the whids."

En vain se démanche-t-il à faire le signe qui doit le sauver, du maigre ! du maigre ! crie-t-il à tue-tête.—Vidocq.

Maillard, *m.* (popular), fermer —, *to sleep,* "to have a dose of balmy." Fermeture —, *sleep,*

R

"balmy." Etre terrassé par —, *to be extremely sleepy.* In the above expressions an allusion is made to Maillard, the inventor of a peculiar kind of shutters.

Maillocher (bullies'), *is said of a bully who watches a prostitute to see she does not secrete any part of her earnings, which are the aforesaid* "pensioner's" *perquisites.*

Main, *f.* (thieves'), jouer à la — chaude, *to be guillotined.* An allusion to the posture of one playing hot cockles. See **Fauché.** (Popular) Acheter à la —, *to buy for cash.* (Familiar) Une — pleine pour un honnête homme, *a strong, fresh, comely country lass;* in fact, one whose possession cannot fail to engross the whole attention of a man.

Mains courantes, *f. pl.* (popular), *feet,* or "everlasting shoes;" *shoes,* or "trotter-cases." Se faire une paire de — à la mode, *to run swiftly.* See **Patatrot.**

Maison, *f.* (familiar and popular), à parties, *a gaming-house in appearance, but in reality a brothel.*

Un grand salon est ouvert à tous les amateurs ; on risque galamment quelques louis . . . et entre deux parties on passe à une autre variété d'exercice dans une chambre ad hoc. Quelques-unes de ces maisons, connues sous le nom de "maisons à parties," sont le suprême du genre.— Léo Taxil.

Maison de société, or à gros numéro, *brothel,* "flash-drum, academy, buttocking-shop, or nannyshop." Fille de —, *prostitute at a brothel.* Maîtresse de —, *mistress of a brothel.* Maison de passe, *house of accommodation.*

Un grand nombre de maisons de passe sont sous la coupe de la police. Ce sont des maisons tolérées par l'administration, à qui elles rendent de fréquents services en dénonçant les prostituées inscrites qui viennent s'y cacher.—Docteur Jeannel.

(Military) Maison de campagne, *cells,* "mill, or Irish theatre." Aller à la — de campagne, *to be imprisoned,* or "shopped."

Maître d'école, *m.* (horsebreakers'), *well-trained horse harnessed with a young horse which is being broken in.*

Maîtresse, *f.* (popular), de maison, *mistress of a brothel;* — de piano, *old or ugly woman who acts as a kind of factotum to cocottes.*

Major, *m.* (familiar), de table d'hôte, *elderly man with a military appearance, who acts as a protector to low gaming-house proprietors;* (Ecole Polytechnique) *first on the list;* — de queue, *last on the list.*

Mal (popular), blanchi, *negro,* "darky, or snowball." Un — à gauche, *a clumsy fellow.* Une — peignée, *a dissolute girl.* (Thieves') Mal sucré, *perjured witness.* (Military) Avoir — aux pieds, *to wear canvas gaiters.* (Familiar) Avoir — aux cheveux, *to have a headache caused by prolonged potations,* especially when one is "stale drunk," which generally occurs after the "jolly dog" has taken too many hairs of the other dog. (Theatrical) Avoir — au genou, *to be pregnant.*

Malade, *m. and adj.* (thieves'), *in prison,* "put away." When the prisoner leaves the "hôpital," or *prison,* he is pronounced "guéri," or *free;* (popular) — du pouce, *idle,* or "Mondayish ;" *stingy,* or "clunch fist." With a bad thumb, of course, it is difficult to "fork out, to down with the dust, to sport the rhino, to tip the brads, or even to stump the pewter."

Maladie, *f.* (familiar and popular), de neuf mois, *pregnancy,* or "white swelling." The allusion is obvious. (Popular) Maladie !

an ejaculation of disgust which may be rendered by "rot !" (Thieves') Maladie, *imprisonment*, the convict being an inmate of "l'hôpital," or *prison*.

Maladroits, *m. pl.* (cavalry), sonnerie des —, *trumpet call for infantry drill.*

Malaisée, *f.* (popular), faire danser la — à quelqu'un, *to thrash one*, "to lead one a dance." For synonyms see **Voie**.

Malandreux, *adj.* (popular), *ill*, "seedy, or hipped ;" *ill at ease.*

Malapatte, *m.* (popular), *clumsy man*, "cripple." Literally mal à la patte.

Malastiqué, *m.* (military), *dirty ; slovenly.*

Maldine, *f.* (popular), "*pension bourgeoise*," or *boarding house ; boarding school*. Literally a place where one does not get a good dinner.

Malfrat, *m.* (popular), *scamp*, "bad egg."

Malheur ! (popular), *an ejaculation of disgust*, "rot !" "hang it all !"

Malheur ! . . . Tiens, vous prenez du vent'e Ah ! bon, chaleur ! J'comprends l'tableau ! Gill.

Malingrer (thieves'), *to suffer*. From malingre, which formerly had the signification of *ill*, and now means *weakly*.

Malingreux, *adj.* (popular), *weak*. In olden times *a variety of mendicants*.

Malingreux sont ceux qui ont des maux ou plaies, dont la plupart ne sont qu'en apparence ; ils truchent sur l'entiffe.—*Le Jargon de l'Argot*.

Malle, *f.* (popular), faire sa —, *to die*, "to kick the bucket, to snuff it, to stick one's spoon in the wall."

See **Pipe**. (Military) Malle, *lock-up*, or "mill."

En voilà assez, faut en finir ; tout le peloton couchera à la malle ce soir.—G. Courteline.

Malouse, *f.* (thieves'), *box*, or "peter."

Mal pensants (clericals'), les journaux —, *anti-clerical newspapers*.

Les journaux "mal pensants" ne manquent jamais de relater ces esclandres. Aussi, pour que la quantité ne puisse en être connue, l'archevêque a autorisé les prêtres du diocèse à ne pas porter la tonsure.—Léo Taxil.

Mal-rasés, *m. pl.* (military), *sappers ;* thus called on account of their long beards.

Maltais, *m.* (popular), *low eating-house*, a "grub ken."

Maltaise, or **maltèse**, *f.* (old cant), *gold coin*. According to V. Hugo, the coin was used on board the convict galleys of Malta. Hence the expression.

Maltouse, or **maltouze**, *f.* (thieves'), *smuggling*. Pastiquer la —, *to smuggle*.

Maltousier, *m.* (thieves'), *smuggler*.

Malvas, *m.* (popular), *scamp*. From the Provençal.

Malzingue, *m.* (thieves'), *landlord of wine-shop ; wine-shop*.

Allons, venez casser un grain de raisin. —Nous entrâmes chez le malzingue le plus voisin.—Vidocq. (*Come and have a glass of wine.—We entered the first wine-shop we came to.*)

Man (Breton cant), *to kiss*.

Manche, *m. and f.* (popular), had formerly the signification of *penis*, "rolling-pin, or John Thomas."

En me tâtant le pouls au manche, Elle me prédisait la santé.
Cabinet Satirique.

Déposer ses bouts de—, *to die*, "to kick the bucket." For synonyms see **Pipe**. (Mountebanks') Faire la —, *to make a collection of money*, or "break." From la buona mancia of the Italians, says Michel, which has the signification of *a gratuity* allowed a workman or guide, and "present" asked by a prostitute. (Familiar and popular) Le —, *the master.* Jambes en manches de veste, *bandy legs.* (Thieves') Faire la —, *to beg.*

M'est avis que vous avez manqué le bon, l'autre sorgue. Quoi, le birbe qui avait l'air de faire la manche dans les garnaffes et les pipés.—Vidocq. (*My opinion is that you missed the right man the other night. Why, the old fellow who pretended to be begging in the farms and mansions.*)

Manchette, *f.* (military), coup de —, *a certain clever sword cut on the wrist.*

Une . . . deux . . . parez celui-là, c'est le coup de flanc. Ah ! ah ! pas assez malin. Voilà le coup de manchette ! Pif ! paf ! ça y est.—H. France, *L'Homme qui tue.*

Mancheur, *m.* (popular), *street tumbler ;* thus called on account of his living on the proceeds of "la manche," or collection.

Manchon, *m.* (popular), *large head of hair.* Avoir des vers dans son —, *to have bald patches on one's head.*

Mandarin, *m.* (literary), *imaginary person who serves as a butt for attacks.* Tuer le —, *to be guilty, by thought, of a bad action.* An allusion to the joke about a question as to one's willingness to kill a wealthy man at a distance by merely pressing a knob, and afterwards inheriting his money.

Mandibules, *f. pl.* (popular), jouer des —, *to eat,* "to grub." See **Mastiquer**.

Mandole, *f.* (popular), *smack in the face.* Jeter une —, *to give a smack in the face,* "to fetch a wipe in the mug," or, as the Americans have it, "to give a biff in the jaw."

Mandolet, *m.* (thieves'), *pistol,* "barking-iron, or pop."

Manego (Breton cant), *handcuffs,* or "darbies."

Manette, *f.* (popular), Mademoiselle —, *a portmanteau,* or "peter."

Mangeoire, *f.* (popular), *eating-house,* "grubbing-crib."

Manger (theatrical), du sucre, *to be applauded ;* (military) — le mot d'ordre, or la consigne, *to forget the watchword ;* (popular) — de la misère, or du bœuf, *to be in poverty, to be a "* quisby ;" — de la prison, *to be in prison, in* "quod ;" — du fromage, or du bœuf, *to go to a comrade's funeral.* An allusion to the repast, or "wake," as the Irish term it, after the funeral ; — de la merde, *to be in a state of abject poverty, entailing all kinds of humiliations ;* — du drap, or du mérinos, *to play billiards,* or "spoof ;" — le bon Dieu, *to partake of communion.*

Et c'est du propre d'aller manger le bon Dieu en guignant les hommes.—Zola.

Manger le pain hardi (obsolete), *to act as servant ;* — le poulet, *to share unlawful profits ;* — le pissenlit par la racine, *to be dead and buried ;* — du pain rouge, *to make one's living by murder and robbery ;* — la soupe avec un grand sabre, *to be the possessor of a very large mouth,* like a slit made by a sword-cut ; — le nez à quelqu'un, *to thrash one terribly,* "to knock one into a cocked hat." Je vais te — le nez, *a cannibal-like offer often made by a Paris rough to his adversary as a preliminary to a set-to.* Manger une soupe aux herbes, *to sleep in the fields.* Se — le nez, *to fight.* (Thieves') Manger, *to inform against,* "to blow the gaff," or "to turn snitch."

Je vois bien qu'il y a parmi nous une canaille qui a mangé; fais-moi conduire devant le quart d'œil, je mangerai aussi.—Vidocq.

Manger le morceau, *to inform against,* "to turn snitch."

Mais t'es avertie, ne mange pas le morceau, sinon gare à toi !—Vidocq.

Manger sur l'orgue, *to inform against,* "to blow the gaff." Orgue has here the signification of person, as in "mon orgue," *I, myself,* "son orgue," *he, himself;* — sur quelqu'un, *to inform against.*

Le coqueur libre est obligé de passer son existence dans les orgies les plus ignobles; en relations constantes avec les voleurs de profession, dont il est l'ami, il s'associe à leurs projets. Pour lui tout est bon : vol, escroquerie, incendie, assassinat même ! Qu'est-ce que cela lui fait? Pourvu qu'il puisse "manger" (dénoncer) sur quelqu'un et qu'il en tire un bénéfice.—*Mémoires de Canler.*

Manger sur son nière, *to inform against an accomplice,* "to turn snitch against a pal ;" — du collège, *to be in prison, to be* "put away;" (familiar and popular) — la grenouille, *to appropriate the contents of a cash-box or funds entrusted to one's care.*

Mangeur, *m.* (general), de blanc, *women's bully,* "ponce, pensioner, petticoat's pensioner, Sunday-man." See **Poisson** for synonyms.

Le paillasson était il y a trente ans le "mangeur de blanc ;" on le désignait en 1788 sous le nom "d'homme à qualité" et quelques années auparavant c'était un "greluchon."—Michel.

Mangeur de bon Dieu, *bigot,* "prayer-monger ;" — de choucroute, *German;*—de nez, *quarrelsome, savage man.* Paris roughs, before a set-to, generally inform their adversary of the necessity of disfiguring him by the savage words, "Il faut que je te mange le nez." Mangeur de frimes, *humbug, impostor;* — de pommes, *a native of Normandy, the great orchard of France;* — de prunes, *tailor,* or "snip." Termed also "pique-prunes, pique-poux." (Thieves') Mangeur, *informer;* — de galette, *informer in the pay of the police,* "nark ;" (convicts') — de fer, *convict;* (military) — d'avoine, *thief; thievish fellow.*

Mangeuse de viande crue, *f.* (popular), *prostitute.* For synonyms see **Gadoue.**

Manicle, *f.* (thieves'), frère de la —, *thief,* or "prig." See **Grinche.**

Manières, *f. pl.* (popular), as-tu fini tes —? *don't be so stuck-up; none of your airs! don't put it on so!* "come off the tall grass" (Americanism), or "stop bouncing."

Manival, *m.* (thieves'), *charcoal dealer.*

Manneau (thieves'), *I, me* (obsolete), now termed "mézigue, mézigo, mézière, mon gniasse."

Mannequin, *m.* (popular), *insignificant, contemptible man,* or "snot." The term may also be applied to a woman; — à refroidis, or de machabées, *hearse.*

Mannezingue, *m.* (popular), *landlord of wine-shop.* Termed also "mastroc, mastroquet."

Pas seulement une goutte de cric à mettre dans ma demi-tasse. La Martinet en a acheté, elle, pour quinze sous chez le mannezingue.—P. Mahalin.

Mannezingueur, *m.* (popular), *habitué of wine-shops.*

Manon, *f.* (popular), *mistress; sweetheart,* or "young woman."

Manquant-sorti, *m.* (popular), *one who cannot understand a joke.*

Manque, *f.* (popular and thieves'), *treachery.*

Gaffré était comme la plupart des agents de police, sauf la manque (perfidie), bon enfant, mais un peu licheur, c'est à dire gourmand comme une chouette. —Vidocq.

A la —, *to the left*, from the Italian *alla* manca; *damaged; ill; bad.* Etre à la —, *to betray; to leave one in the lurch; to be short of cash; to be absent.* Affaire à la —, *bad piece of business.* Gonse à la —, *man not to be relied upon, who will leave one in the lurch; traitor*, or "snitcher." Fafiots, or fafelard à la —, *forged bank-notes*, or "queer soft." (Popular) Un canotier à la —, *awkward rowing man.* Termed also "cafouilleux."

Ecumeurs de calicot!—Ohé! les canotiers à la manque!—Viens que je te fasse avaler ta gaffe!—E. Monteil.

Une balle à la —, *face of a one-eyed man.*

Manquer le train, *to lose one's opportunities in life, and consequently to be the reverse of prosperous.*

A débute par un beau livre; B à vingt-cinq ans, expose un beau tableau. . . . Les mille obstacles de la bohême leur barrent le chemin. . . Ils resteront intelligents, mais . . . ils ont manqué le train. —Tony Révillon.

Manquesse, *f.* (thieves'), *bad character given to a prisoner on trial.* Raffiler la —, *to give a bad character.*

Manuscrit belge, *m.* (printers'), *printed copy to be composed.* According to Eugène Boutmy the origin of the expression is to be found in the practice which existed formerly of entrusting Belgian compositors in Paris with printed copy only, and not manuscript, on account of their ignorance of the language.

Mappemonde, *f.* (popular), *bosoms,* "Charlies, or dairies." Termed also "avant-scènes, œufs sur le plat, avant-postes," &c.

Maqua, *f.* (familiar and popular), obsolete, *mistress of a brothel.*

Maquart, *m.* (popular), bidoche, or bifteck de —, *horseflesh.* From the name of a knacker.

Maque. See **Mac.**

Maquecée, *f.* (popular), *mistress of a brothel.* Called also "abbesse."

Maquereautage. See **Macrotage.**

Maquereautin. See **Macrotin.**

Maqui, *m.* (popular and thieves'), *paint for the face, or complexion powder,* "slap, or splash." Mettre du —, *to paint one's face.* (Card-sharpers') Mettre du —, *to prepare cards for cheating,* "to stock broads."

Maquignon, *m.* (popular), *kind of Jack of all trades, not honest ones.* Properly *horse-dealer;* — à bidoche, *woman's bully*, or "pensioner." See **Poisson.**

Maquignonnage, *m.* (familiar and popular), *cheating on the quality of goods; making a living on the earnings of prostitutes.*

Maquignonnage, pour maquerellage, métier des maquereaux et des maquerelles, qui font négoce de filles de débauche.—Cholières.

Maquignonnage, *swindling operation.* Properly *horse-dealing.*

Maquillage, *m.* (popular and thieves'), *work*, or "elbow-grease;" *the act of doing anything,* "faking;" (card-sharpers') *card playing; tampering with cards*, or "stocking of broads;" (familiar) *the act of painting one's face.*

Elles font une prodigieuse dépense de comestiques et de parfumeries. Presque

toutes se fardent les joues et les lèvres avec une naïveté grossière. Quelques-unes se noircissent les sourcils et le bord des paupières avec le charbon d'une allumette à demi-brûlée. C'est ce qu'on appelle le "maquillage."—Léo Taxil.

Maquillée, *f.* (familiar), *harlot,* or "mot." Literally *one with painted face.*

Maquiller (thieves'), *to do,* "to fake;" — des caroubles, *to manufacture false keys;* — les brèmes, *to tamper with cards,* "to stock broads;" *to play cards; to cheat at cards;* — le papelard, *to write,* "to screeve;" — son truc, *to prepare a dodge;* — un suage, *to make preparations for a murder.* From faire suer, *to murder;* — — une cambriole, *to strip a room,* "to do a crib." The word "maquiller" has as many different meanings as the corresponding term "to fake." (Popular) Maquiller, *to do; to manage; to work;* — le vitriol, *to adulterate brandy.*

Vieille drogue, tu as changé de litre ! . . . Tu sais, ce n'est pas avec moi qu'il faut maquiller ton vitriol.—Zola, *L'Assommoir.*

Maquilleur, *m.,* **maquilleuse,** *f.* (thieves'), *card-player; card-sharper,* or "broadsman."

Maraille, *f.* (thieves'), *people; world.*

Marant, *adj.* (popular), *laughable.* Etre —, *to be ridiculous.*

Marauder (coachmen's), *to take up fares when not allowed to do so by the regulations; refers also to a* "cabby" *who has no licence.*

Maraudeur, *m.* (familiar), "cabby" *who plies his trade without a licence.*

Marbre, *m.* (journalists'), *MS. about to be composed.*

Marcandier, *m.,* **marcandière,** *f.* (thieves'), *tradespeople;* also *a variety of the mendicant tribe,* "cadger."

Marcandiers sont ceux qui bient avec une grande hane à leur costé, avec un assez chenastre frusquin, et un rabas sur les courbes, feignant d'avoir trouvé des sabrieux sur le trimard qui leur ont osté leur michon toutime.—*Le Jargon de l'Argot.* (*Marcandiers are those who journey with a great purse by their side, with a pretty good coat, and a cloak on their shoulders, pretending they have met with robbers on the road who have stolen all their money.*)

Marcassin, *m.* (popular), *signboard painter's assistant.* Properly *a young wild boar.*

Marchand, *m.* (familiar), de soupe, *head of a boarding-school;* (popular) — de larton, *baker,* "crumb and crust man, master of the rolls, or crummy." Termed also "marchand de bricheton, or lartonnier;" — d'eau chaude, "limonadier," *or proprietor of a café;* — d'eau de javelle, *wine-shop landlord;* — de cerises, *clumsy horseman,* one who rides as if he had a basket on his arm; — de morts subites, *surgeon or quack,* "crocus;" — de sommeil, *lodging-house keeper,* "boss of a dossing crib;" — de patience, *man who, having secured a place in the long train of people waiting at the door of a theatre before the doors are opened, and known as* "la queue," *allows another to take it for a consideration.*

Si l'attente est longue . . . les places seront plus chères ; et comme je l'ai entendu dire un jour à l'un de ces curieux gagne-petit : V'la le monde qui s'agace, chouette ! Y aura gras pour les marchands de patience !—Richepin, *Le Pavé.*

(Thieves') Marchand de tirelaine, *night thief;* — de lacets, formerly *a gendarme.*

Le gendarme a différents noms en argot : quand il poursuit le voleur, c'est un marchand de lacets ; quand il l'escorte, c'est une hirondelle de la Grève ; quand il le mène à l'échafaud, c'est le hussard de la guillotine.—BALZAC.

Un — de babillards, *a book-seller, or an "et cetera."* (Military) Marchand de morts su-bites, *professional duellist,* a "fire-eater ;" — de puces, *official who has charge of the garrison bedding.* The allusion is obvious ; (convicts') — de cirage, *captain of a ship.*

Est-ce que le marchand de cirage (elles appelaient ainsi le commandant), nous faisait peur ?—HUMBERT, *Mon Bagne.*

(Journalists') Marchands de lignes, *authors who write for the sake of gain more than to acquire literary reputation.*

Je crois fermement que le jour où n'au-raient plus accès à l'Académie certains hommes éminents qui ne font point de livres, elle tomberait, de bonne heure, au niveau de cette corporation de "marchands de lignes" qu'on nomme la Société des Gens de lettres.—A. DUBRUJEAUD.

(Military) Un — de marrons, *officer who looks ill at ease in mufti.*

Marchande, f. (popular), aux gosses, *seller of toys ;* — de chair humaine, *mistress of a brothel.*

Marche, m. (military), à terre, *foot-soldier,* "wobbler, beetle-crusher, mud-crusher, or grabby ;" — de flanc, *repose ; sleep ;* — des zouaves, *soldiers who go to medical inspection are said to execute the aforesaid march ;* — oblique indi-viduelle, *the rallying of soldiers confined to barracks going up to roll call.*

Marché des pieds humides, m. (familiar), *la petite Bourse, or meeting of speculators after the Ex-change has been closed.* Takes place on the Boulevards.

Marchef, m. (military), abbrevia-tion of maréchal-des-logis chef, *quartermaster sergeant.*

Marcher (popular), dans les souliers d'un mort, *to inherit a man's pro-perty ;* — plan plan, *to walk slowly ;* — sur une affaire, *to make a mull of some business.* (Printers') Marcher, *to be of another's opinion.* Qu'en pensez-vous ? Je marche. *What do you think of it ? I am of your opinion.*

Marches, f. pl. (popular), du palais, *wrinkles on forehead.* Les — basses (obsolete), *woman's privy parts.*

Marcheuse, f. (theatrical), *walking female supernumerary in a ballet.*

La marcheuse est ou un rat d'une grande beauté que sa mère, fausse ou vraie, a vendue le jour où elle n'a pu devenir ni premier, ni second, ni troisième sujet de la danse.—BALZAC.

L'emploi des "marcheuses" n'existe pas dans le ballet, en Russie. Le personnel féminin est entièrement composé de sujets qui dansent ou miment, selon les exigences de la situation.—A. BIGUET, *Le Radical,* 18 Nov., 1886.

(Popular) Marcheuse, *variety of prostitute.* See **Gadoue.**

Leurs fonctions les plus ordinaires sont de rester à la porte, d'indiquer la maison, d'accompagner, de surveiller et de donner la main aux jeunes. On les désigne dans le public sous le nom de marcheuses.—LÉO TAXIL.

Marchis. See **Marchef.**

Mardi s'il fait chaud (popular), *never* (obsolete), *at Doomsday,* "when the devil is blind."

Mare, or **mariolle,** adj. (popular and thieves'), *clever, sharp, cun-ning,* "leary," *or one who is* "fly to wot's wot."

Marécageux, adj. (popular), œil —, *eye with languid expression, with a killing glance.*

Margauder (familiar), *to run down a person or thing.*

Margoulette, f. (popular), rincer la — à quelqu'un, *to treat one to* *drink.* Débrider la —, *to eat,* " to put one's nose in the manger." See **Mastiquer.** Déboîter la — à quelqu'un, *to damage one's countenance.* Mettre la — en compote, *superlative of above.*

Margoulin, *m.* (commercial travellers'), *retailer.*

Margoulinage (commercial travellers'), *retailing.*

Margouliner (commercial travellers'), *to retail.*

Margoulis, *m.* (popular), *scandal.*

Marguerites, *f. pl.* (popular), or — de cimetière, *white hairs in the beard.*

Marguillier de bourrache, *m.* (thieves'), *juryman.* This expression is connected with "fièvre chaude," or *accusation,* borage tea being given to patients in cases of fever.

Marguinchon, *f.* (popular), *dissolute girl,* a "regular bitch."

Mariage, *m.* (popular), à l'Anglaise, *marriage of a couple who, directly after the ceremony, separate and live apart;* — d'Afrique, or — à la détrempe, *cohabitation of a couple living as man and wife, of a pair who live* "tally." From " peindre à la détrempe," *to paint in distemper.* Compare the English expression, " wife in watercolours," or *mistress.*

Marianne, *f.* (popular), la —, *the Republic.* (Thieves') Marianne, *guillotine.* See **Voyante.**

Mariasse, *m.* (popular), *scamp,* " bad egg."

Marida, *f.* (cads' and thieves'), *married woman.*

Marie - je - m'embête (popular), faire sa —, *to make many cere-*monies ; *to allow oneself to be begged repeatedly.*

Marie-mange-mon-prêt, *f.* (military), *mistress.* Literally *Mary spends my pay.*

Marin, *m.* (popular), d'eau douce, *one who sports a river-boat;* — de la Vierge Marie, *river or canal bargee.*

Maringotte, *f.* (popular), *mountebank's show-waggon,* or " slang."

Mariol, mariolle, *adj. and m.* (popular and thieves'), *cunning,* " downy, or fly to wot's wot."

Mariolisme, *m.* (popular and thieves'), *cunning.*

Mariolle, *m. and adj.* (popular and thieves'), *cunning, knowing man, a deep or artful one,* " one who has been put up to the hour of day, who is fly to wot's wot." Termed also a "file," originally a term for a pickpocket, when *to file* was to cheat and to rob.

C'est d'nature, on a ça dans l'sang :
J'suis paillasson ! c'est pas d'ma faute,
Je m'fais pas plus marioll' qu'un aut'e :
Mon pèr' l'était ; l'Emp'reur autant !
      GILL, *La Muse à Bibi.*

Marionnette, *f.* (popular), *soldier,* or " grabby."

Mari Robin (Breton cant), *gendarmes.*

Marlou, *m. and adj.* (general), *prostitute's bully,* " ponce, or pensioner." See **Poisson.**

Les marlous qui soutiennent les filles en carte, les insoumises du trottoir et les femmes des maisons de bas étage, ne se contentent pas de rançonner ces malheureuses qu'ils appellent leur marmite, leur dabe ; ils détroussent sans cesse les passants et assassinent pour s'entretenir la main.—LÉO TAXIL.

Marlou, *cunning,* " downy."

La viscope en arrière et la trombine au vent
L'œil marlou, il entra chez le zingue.
      RICHEPIN.

(Thieves') Le — de Charlotte, *the executioner*, nicknamed Charlot.

Marloupatte, or marloupin, *m.* (popular), *prostitute's bully*, or "petticoat's pensioner."

> Ce marloupatte pâle et mince
> Se nommait simplement Navet ;
> Mais il vivait ainsi qu'un prince . . .
> Il aimait les femmes qu'on rince.
> > RICHEPIN.

Marloupin, *m.* (popular and thieves'), *prostitute's male associate,* "pensioner, petticoat's pensioner, Sunday man, prosser, or ponce." See **Poisson.**

> Quand on paie en monnai' d'singe
> Nous aut' marloupins,
> Les sal's michetons qu'a pas d'linge,
> On les pass' chez paings.
> > RICHEPIN.

Marlousier. See **Marloupin.**

Marmier, *m.* (thieves'), *shepherd.*

Marmite, *f.* (bullies'), *mistress of a bully.* Literally *flesh-pot.* The allusion is obvious, as the bully lives on the earnings of his associate.

> Un souteneur sans sa marmite (sa maîtresse) est un ouvrier sans travail, . . . pour lui tout est là: fortune, bonheur, amour, si ce n'est pas profaner ce dernier mot que de lui donner une acception quelconque à l'égard du souteneur.—*Mémoires de Canler.*

Marmite de terre, *prostitute who does not pay her bully ;* — **de cuivre,** *one who brings in a good income ;* — **de fer,** *one who only brings in a moderate one.* (Military) La — est en deuil, *the fare is scanty at present, that is, the flesh-pot is empty.*

Marmiton de Domange, *m.* (popular), *scavenger employed in emptying cesspools,* or "goldfinder." Domange was a great contractor in the employ of the city authorities.

Marmot, *m.* (thieves'), nourrir un —, *to make preparations for a robbery,* "to lay a plant." Literally *to feed, to nurse a child.*

Marmottier, *m.* (popular), *a native of Savoy.* Literally *one who goes about exhibiting a marmot.*

Marmouse, *f.* (thieves'), *beard.*

Marmouset, *m.* (thieves'), *flesh-pot.* Le — riffode, *the pot is boiling.*

Marmousin, *m.* (popular), *child,* or "kid."

Marmyon, *m.* (thieves'), *flesh-pot,* and figuratively *purse.*

Marne, *f.* (popular), faire la —, *is said of prostitutes who prowl about the river-side.*

Marner (popular), *to steal,* or "to nick." See **Grinchir.** Marner, *to work hard,* "to sweat."

Marneur, *m.* (popular), *strong, active labourer.*

Marneuse, *f.* (popular), *prostitute of the lowest class who plies her trade by the river-side.* See **Gadoue.**

Maron, or marron, *adj.* (thieves'), *caught in the act.*

> Non, il n'est pas possible, disait l'un ; pour prendre ainsi "marons" les voleurs, il faut qu'il s'entende avec eux.—VIDOCQ.

Maron, or **muron,** *salt.*

Maronner (thieves'), *to fail.* Une affaire maronnée, *fruitless attempt at robbery.*

> Il y a du renaud à l'affaire de la chique, elle est maronnée, le dabe est revenu.—VIDOCQ. (*There is some trouble about the job at the church, it has failed, father is returned.*)

Marot, *adj.* (popular), *cunning ;* "up to snuff, one who knows wot's wot, one who has been put up to the hour of day, one who knows what's o'clock, leary."

Marottier, *m.* (thieves'), *hawker,* or "barrow-man ;" *pedlar travelling about the country selling stuffs, neckerchiefs, &c., to country people.* Termed, in the English cant, a "dudder" or "dudsman." "In selling a waistcoat-piece," says the *Slang Dictionary,* "which cost him perhaps five shillings, for thirty shillings or two pounds, he would show great fear of the revenue officer, and beg the purchasing clodhopper to kneel down in a puddle of water, crook his arm, and swear that it might never become straight if he told an exciseman, or even his own wife. The term and practice are nearly obsolete. In Liverpool, however, and at the East-end of London, men dressed up as sailors, with pretended silk handkerchiefs and cigars, 'only just smuggled from the Indies,' are still to be plentifully found."

Marpaut, or **marpeau,** *m.* (old cant), *man ; master of a house* (obsolete).

> Pour n'offenser point le marpaut,
> Afin qu'il ne face deffaut
> De foncer à l'appointement.
> *Le Pasquil de la rencontre des Cocus.*

The word was formerly used by the Parisians with the signification of *fool, greenhorn, loafer.*

Marpaud. Mot de Paris, pour sot, niais, nigaut, badaud.—Le Roux, *Dict. Comique.*

Again, Cotgrave renders it as *an ill-favoured scrub, a little ugly, or swarthy wretch ; also a lickorous or saucy fellow ; one that catches at whatever dainties come in his way.* Michel makes the remark that morpion (*crab-louse,* a popular injurious term) must be derived from marpaut.

Marquant, *m.* (thieves'), *man ; master ; chief of a gang,* or "dim-ber damber ;" *women's bully,* or "Sunday man," see Poisson ; *drunkard,* or *one who gets* "canon."

Marque, *f.* (familiar), horizontale de grande —, *very fashionable cocotte.* Horizontale de petite —, *the ordinary sort of cocottes.*

Décidément je ne sais quelle ardeur guerrière a soufflé sur nos horizontales de grande marque et de petite marque, mais depuis un mois nous avons à enregistrer un nouveau combat singulier dont elles sont les héroïnes.—*Le Figaro,* Oct., 1886.

(Thieves') Marque, *girl,* or "titter ;" *woman,* "laced mutton, hay-bag, cooler, shakester ;" *prostitute,* or "bunter ;" *month,* or "moon." Il a été messiadien à six marques pour pégrasse, *he has been sentenced to six months' imprisonment for theft.* Six marques, *six months,* or "half a stretch." Une — de cé, *a thief's wife.* Termed, in old cant, "autem-mort ;" autem, *a church,* and mort, *woman.* Marque franche, or marquise, *a thief's female associate,* or "mollisher." Concerning this expression, Michel says :—

On trouve dans l'ancienne germania espagnole "marca, marquida et marquisa" avec le sens de "femme publique."—*Dict. d'Argot.*

Quart de —, *week.* Tirer six marques, *to be imprisoned for six months,* "to do half a stretch, or a sixer."

Marqué, *m. and adj.* (thieves'), *month,* "moon." From the Italian marchese. Concerning this word, Michel says :—

Il ne saurait être douteux que ce nom ne soit venu à cette division de l'année, de l'infirmité périodique qu'ont les "marques" ou femmes, "lors que la Lune, pour tenir sa diette et vaquer à ses purifications menstruelles, fait marquer les logis féminins par son fourrier, lequel pour escusson n'a que son impression rouge."—*Dict. d'Argot.*

(Popular) Etre —, *to have a black eye,* or "*mouse.*" (Printers') Marqué à la fesse, *tiresome, over-particular man.*

Marque-mal, *m.* (printers'), *one who receives the folios from the printing machine ;* (popular) *an ugly man, one with a "*knocker face.*"

Marquer (popular), à la fourchette *is said of a restaurant or coffee-house keeper who adds imaginary items to a bill ;* — le coup, *to clink glasses when drinking.* Bien —, *to show a good appearance,* marquer mal being the reverse. Ne plus —, *is said of a woman who is past her prime ;* that is, who no longer has her menses. (Thieves') Marquer, *to have the appearance of a man in good circumstances.*

Marquin, *m.* (thieves'), *hat or cap,* "*tile.*" See **Tubard.**

Marquis d'Argentcourt, *m.* (popular), or de la Bourse Plate, *needy and vain-glorious man.*

Marquise, *f.* (familiar), *kind of mulled white claret ;* (thieves') *wife,* or "*raclan.*"

> Nouzailles pairons notre proie,
> A ta marquise d'un baiser,
> A toi d'un coup d'arpion au proye.
> RICHEPIN.

Marraine, *f.* (thieves'), *female witness.*

Marre, *f.* (popular), *amusement.* Etre à la —, *to be joyously inclined ; to amuse oneself.* J'en ai pris une —, *I have enjoyed myself.*

Marrer (popular), se —, *to amuse oneself ; to be amused.* Pensez si je me marre ? Mince ! *Don't I get amused, just !*

Marron, or **maron,** *adj.* (popular), sculpté, *grotesque, ugly face,* or

"*knocker-head.*" Cocher —, "*cabby*" *without a licence.* Etre —, *to be taken in,* "*bamboozled.*" (Military) Marron, *report of an officer who goes the rounds ;* (printers') *clandestine print ;* also *compositor working on his own account at a printer's, who furnishes him with the necessary plant for a consideration.* (Thieves') Paumer or pommer —, *to catch in the act, red-handed.*

> On la crible à la grive,
> Je m'la donne et m'esquive,
> Élle est pommée marron.
> VIDOCQ.

(Thieves') Etre servi —, *to be caught in the act.*

Que je sois servie marron au premier messière que je grinchirai si je lui en ouvre simplement la bouche.—VIDOCQ.

Marronner, or maronner (thieves'), un grinchissage, *to make an unsuccessful attempt at a robbery through lack of skill or due precautions.* Maronner, *to suspect.*

Je maronne que la roulotte de Pantin trime dans le sabri.—V. HUGO, *Les Misérables.* (*I suspect that the Paris mail-coach is going through the wood.*)

Marseillaise, *f.* (popular), *short pipe,* or "*cutty,*" called "*dudeen*" by the Irish. Avoir une — dans le kiosque, *to be "*cracked.*" For synonyms see **Avoir.**

Enfin, pour sûr la politique lui aura tourné la tête ! Il a une Marseillaise dans le kiosque.—*Baumaine et Blondelet.*

Marsouin, *m.* (popular), *smuggler ;* (military) *marine,* or "*jolly.*" Literally *porpoise.*

Martin, *m.* (popular), fournir —, *to wear furs.* "*Martin*" is the equivalent of "*Bruin.*" Le mal Saint-Martin had formerly the signification of *intoxication.* An allusion to the sale of wine at fairs held on Saint Martin's day.

Martinet, *m.* (thieves'), *punishment irons used at the penal servitude settlements.* Properly *a cat-o'-nine tails.*

Martingalier, *m.* (gamblers'), *gamester who imagines he is master of an infallible process for winning.*

· C'est un martingalier. C'est un des abstracteurs de quintessence moderne, qui s'imaginent avoir trouvé la marche infaillible pour faire sauter les banques.—RICHEPIN.

Martyr, *m.* (military), *corporal.* Termed also " chien de l'escouade."

Mascotte, *f.*, *gambler's fetish.*

Masquer en alezan (horsedealers'), *to paint a horse so as to deceive purchasers.* Termed also " maquiller un gayet." Among other dishonest practices, horsedealers play improper tricks with an animal to make him look lively: they " fig " him, the " fig " being a piece of wet ginger placed under a horse's tail for the purpose of making him appear lively, and enhance his price.

Massage, *m.* (popular), *work,* " graft," or " elbow grease."

Masse, *f.* (military), avoir la — complète, *to possess a well-filled purse.* La — noire, *mysterious cash-box, supposed, by suspicious soldiers, to enclose the proceeds of unlawful profits made at the expense of the aforesaid by non-commissioned officers entrusted with the victualling or clothing department.* (Thieves' and cads') Masse, *work,* " graft," or " elbow grease."

Masser (popular and thieves'), *to work,* " to graft."

Tu sais, j'dis ça à ton copain,
Pa'c'que j'vois qu' c'est un gonc' qui boude,
Mais entre nous, mon vieux lapin,
J'ai jamais massé qu'à l'ver l'coude.
RICHEPIN.

Masseur, *m.* (popular), *active workman.*

Mastar au gras-double, *f.* (thieves'), faire la —, or la faire au mastar, *to steal lead off roofs,* "to fly the blue pigeon."

Mastaré, *adj.* (thieves'), *leaden.*

Mastaroufleur, *m.* (thieves'), *one who steals lead,* a "bluey cracker."

Mastic, *m.* (freemasons'), *bread or meat ;* (popular) *deceit.* Péter sur le —, *to forsake work.* (Thieves') Mastic, *man,* or "cove ;" (printers') *long, entangled speech ;* (theatrical) *painting and otherwise making-up one's face.* Faire son —, *to paint one's face,* "to stick slap on."

C'est l'ensemble de ces travaux de badigeon qui constitue le mastic. Un mastic consciencieux exige près d'une heure de peine.—P. MAHALIN.

Mastiquer (popular), *to cobble ;* (familiar and popular) *to eat,* "to grub," "to yam." It seems this latter term is connected with the word *yam,* the English name of the large edible tuber *Dioscorea,* a corruption of the name used in the West Indies at the time of the discovery, *iniama* or *inhame.* With regard to the expression the *Slang Dictionary* says :—" This word is used by the lowest class all over the world ; by the Wapping sailor, West Indian negro, or Chinese coolie. When the fort called the 'Dutch Folly,' near Canton, was in course of erection by the Hollanders, under the pretence of being intended for an hospital, the Chinese observed a box containing muskets among the alleged hospital stores. 'Hyaw !' exclaimed John Chinaman, 'how can sick man yam gun?' The Dutch were surprised and massacred the same night." The synonyms for the term *to eat,* in

the various kinds of French slang, are the following : "Tortiller du bec, becqueter, béquiller, chiquer, bouffer, boulotter, taper sur les vivres, pitancher, passer à la tortore, tortorer, se l'envoyer, casser la croustille, briffer, brouter, se caler, se calfater le bec, mettre de l'huile dans la lampe, se coller quelque chose dans le fanal, dans le fusil, or dans le tube, chamailler des dents, jouer des badigoinces, jouer des dominos, déchirer la cartouche, gobichonner, engouler, engueuler, friturer, gonfler, morfiaillier, cacher, se mettre quelque chose dans le cadavre, se lester la cale, se graisser les balots, se caresser l'Angoulême, friper, effacer, travailler pour M. Domange, clapoter, débrider la margoulette, croustiller, charger pour la Guadeloupe, travailler pour Jules, se faire le jabot, jouer des osanores."

Mastiqueur, *m.* (popular), *cobbler.*

Mastroc, mastro, or **mastroquet,** *m.* (popular), *landlord of wine-shop.* Termed also "bistrot, troquet, mannezingue, empoisonneur."

Tout récemment, j'étais à la Bourbe, allé voir
Une fille, de qui chez un mastroc, un soir,
J'avais fait connaissance.
GILL.

Mata, *m.* (printers'), abbreviation of matador, *swaggerer,* one who "bulldozes," as the Americans say.

Matador, *m.* (popular), faire son —, *to give oneself airs ; to swagger, to look "botty."* From the Spanish matador, *bull-killer.*

Matagot, *m.* (obsolete), *funny, eccentric individual who amuses people by his antics.* Rabelais used it with the signification of *monkey, monk :—*

Ci n'entrez pas, hypocrites, bigots,
Vieux matagots, mariteux, boursoflé.
Gargantua.

Matatane, *f.* (military), *guard-room ; cells,* "mill, jigger, or Irish theatre."

Matelas, *m.* (popular), ambulant, *street-walker,* or "bed-fagot." See **Gadoue.**

Matelasser (popular), se —, *is said of a woman who makes up for nature's niggardliness by padding her bodice.*

Matelot, *m.* (sailors'), *chum, mate.*

Matelote, *f.* (sailors'), trimer à la —, *to be a sailor.*

Et de Nantes jusqu'à Bordeaux,
Trime à la matelote,
N'ayant qu'un tricot sur le dos,
Et pour fond de culotte
Le drap d'sa peau.
RICHEPIN, *La Mer.*

Mateluche, *m.* (sailors'), *bad sailor.*

Matériaux, *m. pl.* (freemasons'), *food.*

Matérielle, *f.* (gamesters'), *one's bread and cheese.*

Et alors, quelques malheureux pontes . . . se sont livrés au terrible travail qui consiste à gagner avec des cartes le pain quotidien, ce que les joueurs appellent la matérielle.—BELOT, *La Bouche de Madame X.*

Maternelle, *f.* (students'), *mother,* "mater."

Mathurin, *m.* (sailors'), *sailor,* "salt, or Jack tar." Termed also "otter ;" *wooden man-o'-war.* Parler —, *to speak the slang of sailors.*

Je ne suis pas de ces vieux frères premier brin
Qui devant qu'être nés parlaient jà mathurin,
Au ventre de leur mère apprenant ce langage,
Roulant à son roulis, tanguant à son tangage.
RICHEPIN.

(Thieves') Les mathurins, *dice*, or "ivories." (Popular) Mathurins plats, *dominoes*.

Ces objets doivent leur nom d'argot à leur ressemblance avec le costume des Trinitaires, vulgairement appelés Mathurins, qui chez nous portaient une soutane de serge blanche, sur laquelle, quand ils sortaient, ils jetaient un manteau noir.—MICHEL.

Matignon, *m.* (thieves'), *messenger.*

Matois, or **matouas,** *m.* (thieves'), *morning.*

Le condé de Nanterre et un quart d'œil, suivis d'un trèpe de cuisiniers sont aboulés ce matois à la taule.—VIDOCQ. (*The mayor of Nanterre and a commissaire de police, followed by a body of police, came this morning to the house.*)

Matou, *m.* (popular), *man who is fond of the petticoat.* Bon —, *libertine,* "rattle-cap," or "mol-rower." Literally *a good tom-cat.*

Matraque, *m.* (soldiers' in Africa), *bludgeon.*

Nous avions brûlé le pays. Vous dire pourquoi, j'en serais bien en peine : une poule volée à un colon influent, un coup de matraque appliqué par un Bédouin ruiné sur la tête d'un Juif voleur . . . et pif, paf, boum, coups de fusils, obus.—HECTOR FRANCE, *Sous le Burnous.*

Matriculer (military), *to steal ;* said ironically, as "le numéro matricule," borne by a soldier's effects, is the only proof of ownership. Se faire —, *to get punished,* "to be shopped."

Mâts, *m. pl.* (thieves'), les deux —, *the guillotine.* See **Voyante.**

Matte, *f.* (thieves'), enfant de la —, *thief,* a "family-man." For synonyms see **Grinche.** Michel says matte is derived from the Italian mattia, *folly ;* so that "enfants de la matte" signifies literally *children of folly.*

Maturbes, *m. pl.* (thieves'), *dice,* or "ivories." Jouer des —, *to eat,* "to grub."

Maube, *f.* (popular), Place —, for *Place Maubert,* a low quarter of Paris.

Maugrée, *m.* (thieves'), *governor of a prison.* From maugréer, *to grumble.*

Mauricaud, *m.* (thieves'), *cash-box,* "peter."

Il faut tomber sur ce mauricaud, et selon moi ce n'est pas la chose du monde la plus facile.—VIDOCQ. (*We must find the cash-box, and in my opinion it is not the easiest thing in the world.*)

Mauvaise (general), elle est — ! *bad joke ! bad trick !* "sawdust and treacle !" *none of that !* "draw it mild ! "

Mauve, *f.* (popular), *umbrella of a reddish colour, a kind of* "ging-ham."

Mauviette, *f.* (popular), *ribbon of a decoration in the button-hole.*

Mayeux, *m.* (popular), *humpback,* or "lord." Name given to a caricatured individual, a hump-back, who appears in many of the coloured caricatures of 1830. Mayeux is a form of the old name Mahieu (Mathieu).

Mazagran, *m.* (general), *coffee served up in a glass at cafés, or mixture of coffee and water.*

Mazaro, or **lazaro,** *m.* (military), *cells,* "jigger, Irish theatre, or mill.

Maze, *f.* (thieves'), abbreviation of *Mazas, a central prison in Paris.* Tirer un congé à la —, *to serve a term of imprisonment in Mazas.*

Mazette, *f.* (military), *recruit,* or "Johnny raw ; " *man,* or " cove."

Mec, or **meg**, *m.* (thieves'), *master; chief,* "dimber damber."

Bravo, mec ! faisons lui son affaire et renquillons à la taule, je cane la pégrenne. —VIDOCQ. (*Bravo, chief, let us do for him, and let us return home, I am dying of hunger.*)

(Popular and thieves') Mec, *women's bully,* or "ponce." See **Poisson.** Un — à la redresse, *good, straightforward man.* Le — des mecs, *the Almighty.*

Voyons, daronne . . . il ne faut pas jeter à ses paturons le bien que le mec des mecs nous envoie.—VIDOCQ. (*Come, mother, we must not throw at our feet the good things which the Almighty sends us.*)

Mec à la colle forte, *desperate malefactor;* — à sonnettes, *rich man,* "rag-splawger;" — de la guiche, *women's bully,* or "ponce," see **Poisson ;** — des gerbiers, *executioner;* — de la rousse, *prefect of police;* (popular) — à la roue, *one who is conversant with the routine of a trade.*

Mécanicien, *m.* (popular), *executioner's assistant.*

Mécanique, *f.* (popular), *guillotine.* Charrier à la —, see **Charrier.**

Mécaniser (thieves'), *to guillotine;* (popular) *to annoy.*

Coupeau voulut le rattraper. Plus souvent qu'il se laissât mécaniser par un paletot.—ZOLA.

Méchant, *adj.* (familiar and popular), n'être pas —, *to be inferior, of little value,* "tame, no great scratch." Un livre pas —, *a* "tame" *book.* Une plaisanterie pas méchante, *a dull joke.* Un caloquet pas —, *a plain bonnet.*

Mèche (popular), il y a —, *it is possible.* Il n'y a pas —, *it is impossible.* This expression has passed into the language. Et — ! *and the rest!* Combien avez-vous payé, dix francs?—Et mèche ! *How much did you pay, twenty francs ?—Yes,*

and something over. (Thieves') Etre de —, *to go halves.*

On vous obéira. J'ai trop envie d'être de mèche.—VIDOCQ. (*You shall be obeyed. I have too great a desire to go halves.*)

Also *to be in confederacy.*

M'est avis que tu es de mèche avec les rupins pour nous emblêmer. — VIDOCQ. (*My opinion is that you are in confederacy with the swells to deceive us.*)

Six plombes et —, *half-past six.* (Printers') Mèche, *work.* Chercher —, *to seek for employment.*

Méchi, *m.* (thieves'), *misfortune.* From the old French "meschief," *mischief.*

Méchillon, *m.* (thieves'), *quarter of an hour.*

Mecq, *m.* (popular), *prostitute's bully.* See **Poisson.**

Mecque, *f.* (thieves'), *man,* or "cove ;" *victim.*

Médaillard, *m.* (artists'), *artist who has obtained a medal at the Exhibition.*

Médaille, *f.* (popular), *silver fivefranc coin;* also called — de Saint-Hubert ; — d'or, *twentyfranc piece;* — en chocolat, *the Saint-Helena medal.* Called also "médaille de commissionnaire," or "contre-marque du Père-Lachaise."

Médaillon, *m.* (popular), *breech,* see **Vasistas ;** — de flac, *cul-desac,* or *blind alley.*

Médecin, *m.* (thieves'), *counsel,* or "mouth-piece." It is natural that thieves should follow the advice of a doctor when on the point of entering the "hôpital," or *prison,* where they will stay as "malades," or *prisoners,* and whence they will come out "guéris," or *free.*

Médecine, *f.* (thieves'), *defence by a counsel ; advice.* Une — flambante, *a piece of good advice.*

Collez-moi cinquante balles et je vous coque une médecine flambante.—VIDOCQ. (*Tip me fifty francs, and I'll give you a piece of good advice.*)

(Popular) Médecine, *dull, tiresome person.*

Méfiant, *m.* (military), *foot soldier,* " beetle-crusher, or grabby."

Meg, *m.* (thieves'), *chief.* Le — des megs, *God.*

Il y a un mot qui reparaît dans toutes les langues du continent avec une sorte de puissance et d'autorité mystérieuse. C'est le mot *magnus;* l'Ecosse en fait son *mac* qui désigne le chef du clan . . . l'argot en fait le *meck* et plus tard le *meg,* c'est à dire Dieu.—V. HUGO, *Les Misérables.*

Mégard, *m.* (thieves'), *head of a gang of thieves,* or " dimber damber."

Mégo, *m.* (popular), *balance in favour of credit.*

Mégot, *m.* (popular), *end of cigarette.*

Près des théâtres, dans les gares,
Entre les arpions des sergots,
C'est moi que j'cueille les bouts d'cigares,
Les culots d'pipe et les mégots.
                    RICHEPIN.

Mégottier, *m.* (popular), *one whose trade is to collect cigar or cigarette ends,* a "hard up."

Mélasse, *f.* (popular), tomber dans la —, *to be in great trouble,* or "hobble ; " *to be ruined,* or "to go a mucker."

Mélasson, *m.* (popular), *clumsy, awkward man,* "a cripple ; " *dunce,* or "flat."

Mêlé, *m.* (popular), *mixture of anisette, cassis, or absinthe, with brandy.*

Melet, *m.,* **melette,** *f.,* *adj.,* (thieves'), *small.*

Mélo, *m.* (familiar and popular), abbreviation of mélodrame.

Le bon gros mélo a fait son temps.— *Paris Journal.*

Melon, *m.* (cadets' of the military school of Saint-Cyr), *a first-term student.* Called " snooker " at the R. M. Academy, and "John" at the R. M. College of Sandhurst. (General) Un —, *a dunce,* or "flat." Termed "thick" at Winchester School.

Membre de la caravane, *m.* (popular), *prostitute,* or "mot." See **Gadoue.** Euphemism for " chameau."

Membrer (military), *to drill ; to work.*

Poussant éternellement devant eux une brouette qu'ils avaient soin de laisser éternellement vide, s'arrêtant pour contempler . . . les camarades qui membraient.—G. COURTELINE.

Ménage à la colle, *m.* (familiar), *cohabitation of an unmarried couple,* the lady being termed " wife in water-colours."

Mendiant, *m.* (familiar), à la carte, *a begging impostor who pretends to have been sent by a person whose visiting card he exhibits ;* — à la lettre, *begging-letter impostor ;* — au tabac, *beggar who pretends to pick up cigar ends.*

Mendigot, mendigo, or **mendigoteur** (popular), *a variety of the brotherhood of beggars that visits country houses and collects at the same time information for burglars;* a "putter up." La faire au mendigo, *to pretend to be begging.*

Mendigoter (popular), *to beg.*

Menée, *f.* (thieves'), *dozen.* Une — d'ornichons, *a dozen chickens.*

Mener (military), pisser quelqu'un, *to compel one to fight a duel.* (Popular) On ne le mène pas

s

pisser, *he has a will of his own, one can't do as one likes with him.* N'en pas — large, *to be ill at ease, or crestfallen,* "glum."

Puis une fois la fumée dissipée, on verra une vingtaine d'assistants sur l'flanc, foudrayés du coup en n'en m'nant pas large.—TRUBLOT, *Cri du Peuple.*

(Thieves') Mener en bateau, *to deceive,* "to stick."

Ces patriarches, pères et fils de voleurs, ne restent pas moins fidèles à leur abominable lignée. Ils n'instruisent la préfecture que pour la mener en bateau.—*Mémoires de Monsieur Claude.*

Mener en bateau un pante pour le refaire, *to deceive a man in order to rob him,* "to bamboozle a jay and flap him."

Menesse, *f.* (thieves' and cads'), *prostitute,* or "bunter," see **Gadoue**; *mistress,* or "doxy."

Menêtre, *f.* (thieves'), *soup.*

Meneuse, *f.* (popular), *woman who entices a passer-by to some back alley, where he is robbed, and sometimes murdered, by accomplices.* Also *woman whose calling is to take charge of babies, and take them to some country place, where they are left to the care of a wet nurse.*

Mengin, or **Mangin,** *m.* (familiar), *political or literary charlatan.* From the name of a celebrated quack, a familiar figure of cross-ways and squares in Paris under the Third Empire. He was attired in showy costume of the Middle Ages, and sported a glistening helmet topped by enormous plumes. He sold pencils, drew people's caricatures at a moment's notice, and was attended by an assistant known under the name of Vert-de-gris.

Ménilmonte, or **Ménilmuche** (popular), *Ménilmontant, formerly one of the suburbs of Paris.* Ac-

cording to Zola, the word is curiously used in connection with the so-called sign of the cross of drunkards :—

Coupeau se leva pour faire le signe de croix des pochards. Sur la tête il prononça Montpernasse, à l'épaule droite Ménilmonte, à l'épaule gauche la Courtille, au milieu du ventre Bagnolet, et dans le creux de l'estomac trois fois Lapin sauté.—*L'Assommoir.*

Menouille, *f.* (popular), *money, or change.*

Menteuse, *f.* (thieves'), *tongue,* or "prating cheat." Termed also "le chiffon rouge, la battante, la diligence de Rome, rouscaillante."

Menu. See **Connaître.**

Menuisier. See **Cotelette.**

Menuisière, *f.* (popular), *long coat.*

Méquard, or **mégard,** *m.* (thieves'), *head of a gang,* or "dimber damber." From mec, *master, chief.*

Méquer (thieves'), *to command.* From meq, meg, *chief, head of gang,* or "dimber damber."

Mercadet, *m.* (familiar), *man who sets on foot bubble companies, swindling agencies, and other fishy concerns.* A character of Balzac.

Mercandier, *m.* (popular), *butcher who retails only meat of inferior quality.*

Mercanti, *m., name given by the army in Africa to traders, generally thievish Jews.*

Cependant les mercantis, débitants d'absinthe empoisonnée et de vins frelatés, escrocs, banqueroutiers, repris de justice, marchands de tout acabit. — HECTOR FRANCE, *Sous le Burnous.*

Merdaillon, *m.* (popular), *contemptible man,* or "snot."

Merde, *f.* (thieves'), de pie, *fiftycentime piece.* (Popular) Faire sa —, *to give oneself airs, to look* "botty." Des écrase —, *fashionable boots, as now worn, with large low heels.* Termed also "bottines à la mouget."

Merdeux, *m.* (popular), *scavenger employed to empty cesspools,* "goldfinder;" *despicable mean fellow,* "snot."

Mère, *f.* (popular), abbesse, *mistress of a brothel;* — de petite fille, *bottle of wine;* — d'occase, *procuress who plays the part of a young prostitute's mother, or a beggar who goes about with hired children;* — aux anges, *woman who gives shelter to forsaken children, and hires them out to mendicants;* (thieves') — au bleu, *guillotine.* See **Voyante.** (Corporations') Mère, *innkeeper, where* "compagnons," *or skilled artisans of a corporation, hold their meetings.* The compagnons used to individually visit all the towns of France, working at each place, and the long journey was termed "tour de France."

Mérinos, *m.* (popular), *man with an offensive breath.* Manger du —, *to play billiards*, or "spoof."

Merlander (popular), *to dress the hair.* From merlan, popular expression for *hairdresser.*

Merlifiche, *m.* (thieves'), *mountebank, showman.* Probably from "merlificque," used by Villon with the signification of *marvellous.*

Merlin, *m.* (popular), *leg*, "pin." Un coup de passif dans le —, *a kick on the shin.*

Merlou. See **Marlou.**

Merlousier, **merlousière**, *adj.* (thieves'), *cunning.* La dabuche est merlousière, *the lady is cunning.*

Merluche, *f.* (popular), pousser des cris de —, *to squall; to scold vehemently.*

Merriflauté, *adj.* (thieves'), *warmly clad.*

Méruché, *f.*, **méruchon**, *m.* (thieves'), *stove, frying-pan.*

Méruchée, *f.* (thieves'), *stoveful.*

Merveilleux, *m.* (familiar), *dandy* of 1833. See **Gommeux.**

A l'avant-scène se prélassait un jeune merveilleux agitant avec nonchalance un binocle d'or émaillé.—TH. GAUTIER.

The *Slang Dictionary* includes the word "dandy" among slang expressions. It says: "Dandy, *a fop, or fashionable nondescript.* This word, in the sense of a fop, is of modern origin. Egan says it was first used in 1820, and Bee in 1816. Johnson does not mention it, although it is to be found in all late dictionaries. Dandies wore stays, studied a feminine style, and tried to undo their manhood by all manner of affectations which were not actually immoral. Lord Petersham headed them. At the present day dandies of this stamp have almost entirely disappeared, but the new school of muscular Christians is not altogether faultless. The feminine of dandy was dandizette, but the term only lived for a short season."

Mésigo, **mézière**, **mézigue**, (thieves'), *I, me,* "dis child," as the negroes say; — roulait le trimard, *I was tramping along the road.*

Messe, *f.* (popular), être à la —, *to be late.* Nous avons été à la — de cinq minutes, *we were five minutes late.* (Thieves') La — du diable, *examination of a prisoner by a magistrate, or trial,* an ordeal the unpleasant nature of which is eloquently expressed by the words. Termed by English rogues "cross kidment."

Messiadien, *adj. and m.* (thieves'), *convicted, sentenced,* "booked." The epithet is applied to one who has been compelled to attend "la messe du diable," with unpleasant consequences to himself. Il est — à six bergarès plombes, *he is in for six years' prison,* "put away" for "six stretches ;" — pour pégrasse, *convicted for stealing,* "in for a vamp." Il fagaut ta magnette blague de maniagnère que tu n'es paga les pindesse dans le dintesse pour pégrasse, autrement tu es messiadien et tu laveragas tes pieds d'agnet dans le grand pré, which signifies, in the thieves' jargon of the day, *You must take an alias, so that you may escape the clutches of the police ; if not, you will be convicted and transported.*

Messier, or **messière**, *m.* (thieves'), *man ; inhabitant.* A form of mézière, *a fool.* Les messiers de cambrouse, *the country folk,* or "clods."

Messière, *m.* (thieves'), *man ; victim ;* — de la haute, *well-to-do man,* "nib cove, or gentry cove ;" — franc, *citizen ; individual,* or "cove."

Messire Luc, *m.* (familiar), *breech,* or "Nancy." See **Vasistas**.

Mesure, *f.* (popular), prendre la — des côtes, *to thrash,* "to wollop."

Méthode Chevé, *f.* (familiar and popular), *playing billiards in an out-of-the-way fashion—with two cues, for instance, or by pushing the balls with the hand.*

Métier, *m.* (artists'), *skill in execution ; clever touch.* Avoir un — d'enfer, *to paint with great manual skill.*

Mètre, *m.* (familiar and popular), chevalier du —, *shopman,* "counter-jumper, or knight of the yard."

Metteux, *m.* (printers'), *metteur en pages, or maker-up.*

Mettre (general), au clou, *to pawn,* "to put in lug," or "to pop up the spout." An allusion to the spout up which the brokers send the ticketed articles until such time as they shall be redeemed. The spout runs from the ground-floor to the wareroom at the top of the house. English thieves term pawning one's clothes, "to sweat one's duds." Le —, is explained by the following :—

Mot libre, pour chevaucher, faire le déduit, se divertir avec une femme. Ce mot est équivoque et malicieux, car une personne laisse-t-elle tomber son busque ou son gant ? On dit, Mademoiselle, voulez-vous que je vous le mette ?—LE ROUX, *Dict. Comique.*

Termed, in the language of the Paris roughs, "mettre en prison." Mets ça dans ta poche et ton mouchoir par dessus, *said of a blow or repartee, and equivalent to, take that and think over it, or digest it, or let it be a warning to you,* "put that in your pipe and smoke it." Mettre à l'ombre, or dedans, *to imprison,* "to give the clinch." See **Piper**. Mettre à l'ombre signifies also *to kill,* "to cook one's goose ;"— du pain dans le sac de quelqu'un, *to beat one, or to kill him ;* —dans le mille, *to be successful, to have a piece of good luck,* or "regular crow ;" *to hit the right nail on the head.*

D'abord, en passant, faut y' régler son affaire à mon aminche eul' zig Gramont d' l'Intransigeant, qu'a mis dans l'mille en disant qu' eul' Théâtre de Paris sera naturaliste ou qu'i ne sera pas.—TRUBLOT, *Cri du Peuple.*

Mettre quelqu'un dedans, *to deceive, to cheat one, to outwit,* " to take a rise out of a person."

A metaphor from fly-fishing, the silly fish rising to be caught by an artificial fly. —*Slang Dictionary.*

Le — à quelqu'un, *to deceive one,* "to bamboozle" *one.*

Du reste, c'est un flanche, vous voulez me le mettre . . . je la connais.—V. HUGO.

(Popular) Mettre la tête à la fenêtre, *to be guillotined.* See **Fauché.** Mettre une pousse, *to strike, to thrash,* "to wallop ;" — à pied, *to dismiss from one's employment temporarily or permanently ;* — quelqu'un dans la pommade, *to beat one at a game ;* — en bringue, *to smash ;* — des gants sur ses salsifis, *to put gloves on ;* — la table pour les asticots, *to become food for the worms.* See **Pipe.** Mettre sous presse, *to pawn, to put* "in lug." Se — sur les fonts de baptême, *to get involved in some difficulty, to be in a fix, in a* "hole." (Theatrical) Se — en rang d'oignons *is said of actors who place themselves in a line in front of the foot-lights.* Formerly mettre en rang d'oignons meant *to admit one into a company on an equal standing with the others.* (Thieves') Mettre en dedans, *to break open a door,* "to strike a jigger ;" — la pogne dessus, *to steal,* "to nim." From the old English nim, *to take,* says the *Slang Dictionary.* Motherwell, the Scotch poet, thought the old word nim (*to snatch or pick up*) was derived from nam, nam, the tiny words or cries of an infant when eating anything which pleases its little palate. A negro proverb has the word :—

Buckra man nam crab,
Crab nam buckra man.

Or, in the buckra man's language,

White man eat (for steal) the crab,
And then crab eat the white man.

Shakespeare evidently had the word nim in his head when he portrayed Nym. Mettre une gamelle, *to escape from prison.* Se — à table, *to inform against one,* "to blow the gaff," "to nick." See **Grinchir.**

En v'là un malheur si la daronne et les frangines allaient se mettre à table.—VIDOCQ. (*That's a misfortune if the mother and the sisters inform.*)

(Popular and thieves') Se — en bombe, *to escape from prison.*

Mon magistrat, . . . nous nous sommes tirés pour faire la noce. Nous sommes en bombe ! Nous n'avons plus de braise et nous venons nous rendre.—*Un Flâneur.*

Mettre sur la planche au pain, *to put a prisoner on his trial,* "in for patter ;" (military) — le chien au cran de repos, *to sleep ;* — le moine, *to fasten a cord to a sleeping man's big toe, and to teaze him by occasionally jerking it ;* — les tripes au soleil, *to kill.*

A force d'entendre des phrases comme celles-ci : crever la paillasse, mettre les tripes au soleil, taillader les côtes, brûler les gueules, ouvrir la panse, je m'y étais habitué et j'avais fini par les trouver toutes naturelles.—H. FRANCE, *L'Homme qui Tue.*

(Bullies') Mettre un chamègue à l'alignement, *to send a woman out to walk the streets as a prostitute.*

Meuble, *m.* (popular), *sorry-looking person.*

Meubler (familiar), *to pad.*

Meudon, *m.* (thieves'), grand —, *police, the* "reelers."

Meulan. See **Artie.**

Meulard, *m.* (thieves'), *calf.* In old English cant "lowing cheat."

Meules de moulin, *f. pl.* (popular), *teeth,* or "grinders."

Meunier, *m.* (thieves'), *receiver,* or "fence." Porter au moulin *is to take stolen property to the receiver,* "to fence the swag."

Meurt-de-faim, *m.* (popular), *penny loaf.*

Mézière,*adj.,pron.,and m.*(thieves'), *simple-minded, gullible.* Etre —, *to be a* "cull or flat." The word, says Michel, derives its origin from the confidence-trick swindle, when one of the confederates who acts the part of a foreigner, and who pretends to speak bad French, addresses the pigeon as "mézière" instead of "monsieur."

Moi vouloir te faire de la peine ! plutôt être gerbé à vioque (jugé à vie); faut être bien mézière (nigaud) pour le supposer.—VIDOCQ.

Mézière, *I, me, myself.* Le havre protège —, *God protect me.* Un —, *a* "flat," *name given by thieves to their victims.*

Depuis que nous nous sommes remis à escarper les mézières, il ne nous en est pas tombé sous la poigne un aussi chouette que celui-ci.—VIDOCQ. (*Since we began again to kill the flats, we haven't had in our claws a single one as rich as that one.*)

Mézigue, mézigo (thieves'), *I, myself.*

Auquel cas, c' serait pas long ; mézigue sait c' qu'y lui rest'rait à faire.—TRUBLOT, *Le Cri du Peuple.*

Mib, or **mibre,** *m.* (street boys'), *thing in which one excels ; triumph.* C'est mon —, *that's just what I am a dab at.* C'est ton —, *you'll never do that ; that beat's you hollow.*

Michaud, *m.* (thieves'), *head,* or "tibby, nob, or knowledge box." Faire son —, *to sleep,* "to doss."

Miche, *f.* (popular and thieves'), *lace,* or "driz." An allusion to the holes in a loaf of white bread.

Miche, or — de profonde, *money.* The term in this case exactly corresponds to the English "loaver."

Miché, *m.* (general), *client of a prostitute.* Literally *one who has* "michon," *or money, who* "forks out."

Les filles isolées, soit en carte, soit insoumises . . . ont, par contre, le désagrément d'éprouver souvent certains déboires. Le client n'est pas toujours un "miché" consciencieux.—LÉO TAXIL.

Faire un —, *to find a client,* or "flat." Un — de carton, *client who does not pay well, or who does not pay at all.* Un — sérieux, *one who pays.*

Les femmes appellent "michés sérieux" les clients qui "montent" et "flanelles" ceux qui se contentent de "peloter" et de payer un petit verre.—LÉO TAXIL.

Concerning the language of such women Léo Taxil says :—"On a prétendu que toutes les prostituées de Paris avaient un argot ou un jargon qui leur était particulier . . . ceci n'est pas exact . . . nous avons vu qu'elles désignent le client sous le nom de 'miché,' le visiteur qui ne monte pas sous celui de 'flanelle.' Pour elles, les inspecteurs des mœurs sont des 'rails,' un commissaire de police un 'flique,' une jolie fille une 'gironde' ou une 'chouette,' une fille laide un 'roubiou,' etc. Ce sont là des expressions qui font partie du langage des souteneurs qui, eux, possèdent un véritable argot ; elles en retiennent quelques mots et les mêlent à leur conversation. Quant aux prostituées qui s'entendent avec les voleurs et qui n'ont recours au libertinage que pour cacher leur réelle industrie, il n'est pas étonnant qu'elles aient adopté le jargon de leurs suppôts ; mais on ne peut pas dire que ce langage soit celui des prostituées." (Popular) Miché, *fool.* From Michel. It is to be remarked, after Montaigne, that many names of men have been taken to signify the word fool; such are Grand Colas, Jean-Jean, and formerly Gautier, Blaise. (Photographers') Miché, *client.* (Familiar and popular) Un vieux —, *an old beau.*

> Tel, au printemps, un vieux miché
> Parade en galante toilette.
> GILL.

Michel, *m.* (fishermen's), cassant ses œufs, *thunder.* (Military) Ca fait la rue —, *it's the same for everybody.*

> Eh bien, si j'y coupe pas, v'là tout, j'coucherai à la boîte comme les camarades, et ça fera la rue Michel.—G. COURTELINE.

Michelet, *m.* (popular), faire le —, *to feel about in a crowd of women,* not exactly with righteous intentions.

Michet, miché, or **micheton,** *m.* (popular), *client of a prostitute.*

> Elles tournent la tête et jetant sur ce type,
> Par dessus leur épaule, un regard curieux,
> Songent : oh ! si c'était un miché sérieux !
> GILL.

Michon, *m.* (thieves'), *money* which procures a miche, or a *loaf,* "loaver." See **Quibus.**

> C'est ce qui me fait ambier hors de cette vergne ; car si je n'eusse eu du michon je fusse côni de faim.—*Le Jargon de l'Argot.*

> Foncer du —, *to give money,* "to grease the palm."

Midi ! (popular), *too late !* Il est —, *a warning to one to be on his guard ; I don't take that in !* "not for Joe !" Il est — sonné, *it's not for you ; it is impossible.*

> Faut pas te figurer comme ça qu' t'as l'droit de t'coller un bouc . . . quand tu seras de la classe, comme me v'là, ça s'pourra ; mais jusque-là c'est midi sonné. —G. COURTELINE.

Mie, *f.* (popular), de pain, *louse,* or "grey-backed 'un ;" (printers') *thing of little value,* or "not worth a curse." Compositeur — de pain, *an unskilled compositor,* or clumsy "donkey."

Miel ! (popular), *euphemism for a coarser word,* "go to pot !" "you be hanged !" C'est un —, *is expressive of satisfaction, or is used ironically.* Of a good thing they say : "C'est un miel !" On entering a close, stuffy place : "C'est un miel !" Of a desperate street fight : "C'est un miel !" "a rare spree !" "what a lark !" (DELVAU).

Miellé ! *adj.* (popular), du sort, *happy ; fortunate in life.*

> Il n'était pas plus miellé du sort, il n'avait pas la vie plus en belle.—RICHEPIN, *La Glu.*

Mignard, *m.* (popular), *term of endearment ; child,* or "kid."

Mignon, *m.* (thieves'), *mistress,* or "mollisher."

> J'avais bonheur, argent, amour tranquille, les jours se suive mais ne se ressemble pas. Mon mignon connaissait l'anglais, l'allemand, très bien le français, l'auvergna et l'argot.—*From a thief's letter, quoted by L. Larchey.*

(Popular and thieves') Mignon de port (obsolete), *porter.* Mignon had formerly the signification of *foolish, ignorant.*

Mignoter (popular), *to fondle,* "to forkytoodle."

Mikel, *m.* (mountebanks'), *dupe,* or "gulpin."

Milieu, *m.* (popular), *breech,* or "Nancy."

Millards, *m. pl.* (old cant), *in olden times a variety of the cadger tribe.*

> Millards sont ceux qui trollent sur leur andosse de gros gueulards ; ils truchent plus aux champs qu'aux vergnes, et sont haïs des autres argotiers, parce qu'ils morfient ce qu'ils ont tout seuls.—*Le Jargon de l'Argot.* (The "millards" are those who carry a large bag on their back ; they beg in the country in preference to the towns, and are hated by their brethren because they eat all alone what they get.)

Mille, *m.* and *f.* (familiar), mettre dans le —, *to meet with a piece of good luck,* or "regular crow ;" *to* *be successful.* One often sees at fairs a kind of machine for testing physical strength. A pad is struck with the fist, and a needle marks the extent of the effort, "le mille" being the maximum. (Thieves') Mille, *woman,* or "burrick" (obsolete).

Mille-langues, *m.* (popular), *talkative person ; tatler.*

Mille-pertuis, *m.* (thieves'), *watering pot* (obsolete).

Millerie, *f.* (thieves'), *lottery.* Thus termed on account of the thousands which every holder of a ticket hopes will be his.

Millet, millot, *m.* (popular), 1,000 *franc bank-note.* From mille.

Milliardaire, *m.* (familiar), *very rich man, one who rolls on gold.*

C'est de cette époque que date aujourd'hui sa fortune car il est aujourd'hui milliardaire.—A. SIRVEN.

Millour, *m.* (thieves'), *rich man,* "rag splawger" (obsolete). From the English *my lord.*

Milord, *m.* (familiar and popular), *rich man ; —* l'Arsouille, *nickname of Lord Seymour.* See **Arsouille.**

Les Folies-Belleville . . . où Milord l'Arsouille engueulait les malins, cassait la vaisselle et boxait les garçons.—P. MAHALIN.

Mince, *m. and adv.* (thieves'), *notepaper ; bank-note,* or "soft." (Popular) The word has many significations : it means, *of course ; certainly ; much.*

> Dois-tu comme Walder,
> Et comme la muscade,
> Te donner mince d'air
> Après ton escapade ?
> RAMINAGROBIS.

Mince ! *no ; certainly not.* It is sometimes expressive of disappointment or contempt. Tu n'as plus d'argent ? ah ! — alors, *you*

have no money? hang it all then ! Il a — la barbe, *he is completely drunk.* Pensez si je me marre, ah ! — ! *don't I get amused, just !* Aux plus rupins il disait —, *even to the strongest he said, "you be hanged!"* Mince de potin! *a fine row !* — de crampon ! *an awful bore !* — que j'en ai de l'argent ! *haven't I money? of course I have!* Ah ! — alors ! *to the deuce, then !* Mince de chic, *glass of beer.* The ejaculation mince ! in some cases may find an equivalent in the English word rather ! an exclamation strongly affirmative. It is also used as an euphemism for an obscene word.

> Et moi sauciss', j'su quand j'turbine.
> Mais, bon sang ! la danse s'débine
> Dans l'coulant d'air qui boit ma sueur.
> Eux aut's, c'est pompé par leur linge.
> Minc' qu'ils doiv' emboucanner l'singe.
> Vrai, c'est pas l'linge qui fait l'bonheur.
> RICHEPIN.

Mine, *f.* (popular), à poivre, *low brandy shop.*

Lui était un bon, un chouette, un d'attaque. Ah ! zut ! le singe pouvait se fouiller, il ne retournait pas à la boîte, il avait la flemme. Et il proposait aux deux camarades d'aller au *Petit bonhomme qui tousse,* une mine à poivre de la barrière Saint-Denis, où l'on buvait du chien tout pur.—ZOLA, *L'Assommoir.*

Une — à chier dessus, *ugly face,* "knocker face."

Qu'est-ce qu'il vient nous em . . . ieller, celui-là, avec sa mine à chier dessus.—RIGAUD.

Minerve, *f.* (printers'), *small printing machine worked with the foot.*

Minerviste, *m.* (printers'), *one who works the* Minerve (which see).

Mineur, *m.* (thieves'), *Manceau, or native of Le Mans.*

Minik (Breton cant), *small.*

Ministre (military), *sumpter mule ;* (peasants') *ass,* "moke," or *mule.*

Minois, *m.* (thieves'), *nose*, or " conk " (obsolete).

Minotaure, *m.* (familiar), *deceived husband*, " stag face." The expression is Balzac's.

Je serais le dernier de M. Paul de Kock ; minotaure, comme dit M. de Balzac.—TH. GAUTIER.

Minotauriser quelqu'un(familiar), *to seduce one's wife.* An allusion to the horns of the Minotaur.

Quand une femme est ·inconséquente, le mari, serait, selon moi, minotaurisé.—BALZAC.

Minson (Breton cant), *bad ; badly.*

Minsoner (Breton cant), *mean.*

Mintzingue, *m.* (popular), *landlord of wine-shop.*

Mais sapristi, jugez d'mon embargo,
Depuis ce temps elle est toujours pompette,
Et chez l'mintzingue ell' croque le magot.
 Almanach Chantant, 1869.

Minuit, *m.*(thieves'), *negro*. Termed also, in different kinds of slang, " Bamboula, boule de neige, boîte à cirage, bille de pot-au-feu, mal blanchi," and in the English slang, "snowball, Sambo, bit o' ebony, blacky." Enfant de — meant formerly *thief.* Enfants de la messe de minuit, says Cotgrave, " *quiresters of midnights masse ; night-walking rakehells, or such as haunt these nightly rites, not for any devotion, but only to rob, abuse, or play the knaves with others.*"

Minzingue, or **minzingo,** *m.* (popular), *landlord of tavern.* Termed also manzinguin, mindzingue.

La philosophie, vil mindzingue, quand ça ne servirait qu'à trouver ton vin bon.— GRÉVIN.

Mion, *m.* (thieves'), *child*, or "kid ;" — de gonesse, *stripling ;* — de boule, *thief,* "prig." See **Grinche.**

Mipe, *m.* (thieves'), faire un — à quelqu'un, *to outdrink one.*

Miradou, *m.* (thieves'), *mirror.*

Mirancu, *m.* (obsolete), *apothecary.*

Respect au capitaine Mirancu ! Qu'il aille se coucher ailleurs, car s'il s'avisoit de jouer de la seringue, nous n'avons pas de canesons pour l'en empêcher.—*L'Apothicaire empoisonné,* 1671.

Mirancu, a play on the words mire en cul, which may be better explained in Béralde's words, in Molière's *Le Malade Imaginaire :*—

Allez, monsieur ; on voit bien que vous n'avez pas accoutumé de parler à des visages.

Mirecourt, *m.* (thieves'), *violin.* The town of Mirecourt is celebrated for its manufactures of stringed instruments. Rigaud says that it is thus termed from a play on the words mire court, *look on from a short distance*, the head of the performer being bent over the instrument, thus bringing his eyes close to it.

Mire-laid, *m.* (popular), *mirror.* An expression which cannot be gratifying to those too fond of admiring their own countenances in the glass.

Mirettes, *f. pl.* (popular and thieves'), *eyes*, " peepers, ogles, top-lights, or day-lights." Fielding uses the latter slang term :—

Good woman ! I do not use to be so treated. If the lady says such another word to me, damn me, I will darken her day-lights.—FIELDING, *Amelia.*

In gipsy cant eyes are termed " glaziers."

Toure out with your glaziers, I swear by the ruffin,
That we are assaulted by a queer cuffin.
 BROOME, *A Jovial Crew.*

Which means *look out with all your eyes, I swear by the devil a magistrate is coming.* Mirettes en caoutchouc, or en caouche, *tele-scope ;* — glacées, or en glacis, *spectacles,* or "gig-lamps." Sans —, *blind,* or "hoodman."

Mireur, *m.* (popular), *one who looks on intently ; spy.*

Quand ils auront fini de se ballader, tous ces mireurs !—RIGAUD.

Also *person employed in the immense underground store cellars of the Halles to inspect provisions by candle-light.*

Deux cents becs de gaz éclairent ces caves gigantesques, où l'on rencontre diverses industries spéciales. . . . Les "mireurs," qui passent à la chandelle une délicate révision des sujets. Les "préparateurs de fromages" qui font "jaunir" le chester, "pleurer" le gruyère, "couler" le brie ou "piquer" le roquefort.—*E. Frébault.*

Mirliflor, *m.* (familiar), *dandy of 1820.* For synonyms see **Gommeux.** The term has now passed into the language with the signification of *silly, conceited dandy or fop.*

Mirliton, *m.* (popular), *nose,* or "smeller." For synonyms see **Morviau.** Also *voice.* Avoir le — bouché, *to have a bad cold in the head.* Le —, *the penis.* Rabelais termed it "Maistre Jehan Chouart":—

"Tenez" (monstrant sa longue braguette), "voici maistre Jehan Chouart qui demande logis." Et après la vouloit accoller.—*Pantagruel.*

Also "Maistre Jehan Jeudi":—

Or, dist-il, ce me seroit bien tout un d'avoir bras et jambes coupés, en condition que nous feissions vous et moi un transon de chère lie, jouants des mannequins à basses marches : car (monstrant sa longue braguette), voici maistre Jehan Jeudi, qui vous sonneroit une antiquaille, dont vous sentiriez jusques à la mouelle des os.—*Pantagruel.*

Jouer du —, *to talk,* "to jaw." Also *to make a sacrifice to Venus.*

C'soir là ma ménagère
Trouvant que j'rentrais tard,

J'lui dis : Ecout' ma chère,
J'apport' pour le moutard
Un joli p'tit mirlitir,
Un charmant p'tit mirliton.
Là-d'sus, se mettant à rir',
Ma femm', qui change de ton,
Veut jouer du mirlitir',
Veut jouer du mirliton,
Veut jouer du mir, du li, du ton,
Du mirliton !
Le Mirliton. Song.

Rabelais termed this "frotter son lard" :—

O dieux et déesses célestes, que heureux sera celui à qui ferez celle grâce de cesteci accoller, de la baiser et de frotter son lard avecques elle !—*Pantagruel.*

The act is also described as "faire la bête à deux dos." The expression is old.

Vous n'y allez pas par compas !
Et que dyable faites-vous ?
Vous faictes la beste à deux dous !
Farce du Badin qui se loue.

Mot ! mot ! paix ! paix ! là je les os.
Hon !. . . ils font la beste à deux dos !
Farce d'un Gentilhomme.

Says M. Génin :—

"Voltaire a mis une affectation maligne à reproduire le passage où Shakspeare emploie cette expression ; il y revient chaque fois qu'il s'agit du théâtre anglais et de ceux qui l'admirent . . . assurément la métaphore manque de noblesse tragique et de délicatesse . . . ce n'est pas de cela que je dispute. Mais on eût bien étonné Voltaire qui lui eût appris que cette scandaleuse expression, Shakspeare l'avait empruntée à la langue française elle-même, à notre vieux théâtre français ! et le fait ne saurait être douteux."

The passage incriminated by Voltaire runs thus :—

Iago. I am one, sir, that comes to tell you your daughter and the Moor are now making the beast with two backs.—*Othello.*

Mirobolamment (familiar and popular), *marvellously,* "stunningly."

Mirobolant, *adj.* (familiar and popular), *excellent,* "slap-up or scrumptious;" *marvellous,* "crushing."

Je me sens d'une incapacité mirobolante.
—BALZAC.

Miroir à putains, *m.* (popular), synonymous of bellâtre, *a handsome but vulgar man,* one likely to find favour with the frail sisterhood. Fielding thus expatiates on the readiness of women to look with more favour on a handsome face than on an intellectual one :—

How we must lament that disposition in these lovely creatures which leads them to prefer in their favour those individuals of the other sex who do not seem intended by nature as so great a masterpiece ! . . . If this be true, how melancholy must be the consideration that any single beau, especially if he have but half a yard of ribbon in his hat, shall weigh heavier in the scale of female affection than twenty Sir Isaac Newtons !—*Mr. Jonathan Wild the Great.*

Mirquin, *m.* (thieves'), *woman's cap.*

Mirzales, *f. pl.* (thieves'), *earrings.*

Mise, *f.* (prostitutes'), faire sa —, *to pay a prostitute her fee,* or "present." (Popular) Mise à pied, *temporary or permanent dismissal from one's employment, the* "sack."

Mise-bas, *f.* (popular), *strike of work ;* (servants') *cast-off clothes which servants consider as their perquisites.*

Miser (gamesters'), *to stake.*

Et si je gagne ce soir cinq à six mille francs au lansquenet, qu'est-ce que soixante-dix mille francs de perte pour avoir de quoi miser ?—BALZAC.

Misérable, *m.* (popular), *one half-penny glass of spirits,* "un monsieur" being one that will cost four sous, and "un poisson" five sous.

Misloque, or **mislocq,** *f.* (thieves'), *theatre ; play.* Flancher, or jouer la —, *to act.*

Ah ! ce que je veux faire, je veux jouer la mislocq.—VIDOCQ.

Misloquier, *m.,* **misloquière,** *f.* (thieves'), *actor,* "cackling cove," or "mug faker," and *actress.*

Mississipi, *m.* (popular), au —, *very far away.*

Mistenflûte, *f.* (popular), *thingumbob.*

Mistiche (thieves'), un —, *half a "setier," or small measure of wine.* Une —, *half an hour.*

Mistick, *m.* (thieves'), *foreign thief.*

Mistigris, or **misti,** *m.* (popular), *knave of clubs ; apprentice to a house decorator.*

Miston (thieves'). See **Allumer.** (Popular) Mon —, *my boy,* "my bloater."

Mistouf, or **mistouffle,** *f.* (popular), *practical joke ; scurvy trick.* Faire une — à quelqu'un, *to pain, to annoy one.*

Vous lui aurez fait quelque mistouf, vous l'aurez menacée de quelque punition, et alors—A. CIM, *Institution de Demoiselles.*

Coup de —, *scurvy trick brewing.* Faire des mistouffles, *to teaze,* "to spur," *to annoy one.* (Thieves') Mistouffle à la saignante, *trap laid for the purpose of murdering one.*

Voilà trop longtemps . . . que le vieux me la fait au porte-monnaie. Il me faut son sac. Mais . . . pas de mistouffle à la saignante, je n'aime pas ça. Du barbotage tant qu'on voudra.—*Mémoires de Monsieur Claude.*

Mistron, *m.* (popular), *a game of cards called* "trente et un."

Mistronneur, *m.* (popular), *amateur of* "mistron" (which see).

Mitaine, *f.* (thieves'), grinchisseuse à la —, *female thief who causes some property, lace generally, to fall from a shop counter, and by certain motions of her foot conveys it to her shoe, where it remains secreted.*

Mitard, *m.* (police), *unruly prisoner confined in a punishment cell.*

Mite-au-logis, *f.* (popular), *disease of the eyes.* A play on the words mite and mythologie.

Miteux, *adj.* (familiar and popular), *is said of one poorly clad, of a wretched-looking person.*

Quand nous arrivâmes à la posada, on ne voulut pas nous recevoir, l'aubergiste nous trouvant, comme disait La Martinière mon compagnon de route, trop "miteux."
—HECTOR FRANCE, *A travers l'Espagne.*

Mitraille, *f.* (general), *pence, coppers.* The expression is old. This term seems to be derived from the word "mite," copper coin worth four "oboles," used in Flanders.

Mitrailleuse, *f.* (popular), étouffer une —, *to drink a glass of wine.* Synonymous of "boire un canon."

Mitre, *f.* (thieves'), *prison,* or "stir." See **Motte.** Meant formerly *itch,* the word being derived from the name of a certain ointment termed "mithridate."

Mobilier, *m.* (thieves'), *teeth,* or "ivories." Literally *furniture.*

Moblot, *m.* (familiar), *used for Mobile in* 1870. "La garde mobile" at the beginning of the war formed the reserve corps.

Mocassin, *m.* (popular), *shoe.* See **Ripaton.**

Moc-aux-beaux (thieves'), *quarter of La Place Maubert.*

Moche, or **mouche,** *adj.* (popular and thieves'), *bad.*

Mode, *f.* (swindlers'), concierge à la —, *a doorkeeper who is an accomplice of a gang of swindlers* termed **Bande noire** (which see).

La "bande noire" était—et est encore, car le dixième à peine des membres sont arrêtés—une formidable association, ayant pour spécialité d'exploiter le commerce des vins de Paris, de la Bourgogne et du Bordelais. . . . Pour chaque affaire, le courtier recevait dix francs. Le concierge, désigné sous le nom bizarre de concierge à la mode, n'était pas moins bien rétribué. Il touchait dix francs également.—*Le Voltaire,* 6 Août, 1886.

Modèle, *m.* (familiar), *grandfather or grandmother.*

Moderne, *m.* (familiar), *young man of the "period,"* in opposition to antique, *old-fashioned.*

Modillon, *f.* (modistes'), *a second year apprentice at a modiste's.*

Modiste, *m.* (literary), formerly *a journalist who sought more to pander to the tastes of the day than to acquire any literary reputation.*

Moelleux, *m.* (popular), *cotton,* which is soft.

Moelonneuse, *f.* (popular), *prostitute who frequents builders' yards.* See **Gadoue.**

Moignons, *m. pl.* (popular), *thick clumsy ankles.* The *Slang Dictionary* says a girl with thick ankles is called a "Mullingar heifer" by the Irish. A story goes that a traveller passing through Mullingar was so struck with this local peculiarity in the women, that he determined to accost the next one he met. "May I ask," said he, "if you wear hay in your shoes?" "Faith, an' I do," said the girl, "and what then?" "Because," said the traveller, "that accounts for the calves of your legs coming down to feed on it."

Moine, *m.* (familiar), *earthen jar filled with hot water, which does duty for a warming pan;* (printers') *spot on a forme which has not been touched by the roller, and which in consequence forms a blank on the printed leaf.* Termed "friar" by English printers. (Popular) Mettre le —, *to fasten a string to a sleeping man's big toe.* By jerking the string now and then the sleeper's slumbers are disturbed and great amusement afforded to the authors of the contrivance. This sort of practical joking seems to be in favour in barrack-rooms. Donner, or bailler le —, was synonymous of mettre le —, and, used as a proverbial expression, meant *to bear ill luck.*

Moine-lai, *m.* (popular), *old military pensioner who has become an imbecile.*

Moinette, *f.* (thieves'), *nun*, moine being a *monk.*

Moïse, *m.* (familiar and popular), *man deceived by his wife.* The term is old, for, says Le Roux, "Moïse, mot satirique, qui signifie cocu, homme à qui on a planté des cornes."

Moitié, *f.* (popular), tu n'es pas la — d'une bête, *you are no fool.*

Oui, t'es pas la moitié d'une bête. Là-dessus aboule tes quatre ronds.—G. Cour-teline.

Molanche, *f.* (thieves'), *wool.* From mol, *soft.*

Molard, *m.* (familiar and popular), *expectoration*, or "gob."

Molarder (familiar and popular), *to expectorate.*

Molière, *m.* (theatrical), *scenery which may be used for the performance of any play of Molière.*

Molle, *adj.* (popular and thieves'), être —, *to be penniless,* alluding to an empty pocket, which is flabby ; "to be hard up."

Mollet, *m.* (popular). M. Charles Nisard, in his *Parisianismes Populaires,* says of the word, "Gras de la partie postérieure de la jambe" (the proper meaning), and he adds, "Partie molle de diverses autres choses."

Vous ne cachez pas tous vos mollets dans vos bas : c'est comme la barque d'Anières,

ça n'sart plus qu'à passer l'iau.—*Le Dé-jeuner de la Rapée.*

Following the adage, "Le latin dans les mots brave l'honnêteté," M. Nisard gives the following explanation of the above :—"Hæc sunt verba cujusdam petulantis mulierculæ ad quemdam jam senescentem virum, convalescentem e morbo, et carnale opus adhuc penes se esse male jactantem. In eo enim Thrasone mulieroso pars ista corporis quam proprie vocant 'Mollet,' non solum in tibialibus ejus inclusa erat, sed et in bracis, ubi, mutata ex toto forma, nil valebat nisi, scaphæ Asnieriæ instar, 'à passer l'eau,' id est, ad meiendum. Sed, animadvertas, oro, sensum locutionis 'passer l'eau' æquivocum ; hic enim unda transitur, illic eadem transit."

Mollusque, *m.* (familiar), *narrow-minded man ; routine-loving man;* huître being a common term for a *fool.*

Momaque, *m.* (thieves'), *child,* or "kid."

Momard, or **momignard,** *m.* (popular); *child,* or "kid."

Môme, *m. and f.* (popular and thieves'), *child,* or "kid."

Ces mômes corrompus, ces avortons flétris, Cette écume d'égoût c'est la levure immonde,
De ce grand pain vivant qui s'appelle Paris, Et qui sert de brioche au monde.
RICHEPIN.

Môme noir, *student at a priest's seminary.* Thus termed on account of their clerical attire. Called also by thieves, "Canneur du mec des mecs," *afraid of God.* Une —, *young woman,* "titter."

Va, la môme, et n'fais pas four.
RICHEPIN.

Une —, or **mômeresse,** *mistress,* "blowen." C'est ma —, elle est ronflante ce soir, *It is my girl, she*

has money to-night. Un — d'altèque, *handsome young man.*
Taper un —, *to commit a theft ;
to commit infanticide.*

Car elle est en prison pour un môme
qu'elle a tapé.—*From a thief's letter,
quoted by L. Larchey.*

Madame Tire-mômes, *midwife.*
Termed in the seventeenth century, "madame du guichet, or
portière du petit guichet." (Convicts') Môme bastaud, *convict who
is a Sodomist, a kind of male
prostitute.*

Mômeuse, *f.* See **Mômière.**

Momicharde, *f.* (popular), *little
girl.*

Envoie les petites . . . qu'elles aboulent,
les momichardes !—LOUISE MICHEL.

Mômière, *f.* (thieves'), *midwife.*
Termed also "Madame Tire-
mômes, Madame Tire-monde, or
tâte-minette."

Momignard, *m.* (popular and
thieves'), *child,* or "kid ;" *baby ;
—* d'altèque, *a fine child.*

Frangine d'altèque, je mets l'arguemine
à la barbue, pour te bonnir que ma largue
aboule de mômir un momignard d'altèque.
—VIDOCQ. (*My good sister, I take the
pen to say that my wife has just given
birth to a fine child.*)

Momignardage à l'anglaise, *m.*
(popular), *miscarriage.*

Momignarde, *f.* (popular and
thieves'), *little girl ; young girl,*
"titter."

Mes momignardes . . . allons, c'est dit,
on rebâtira le sinve. Il faut espérer que la
daronne du grand Aure nous protégera.—
VIDOCQ. (*My little girls . . . come, it's
settled, the fool shall be killed. Let us
hope the Holy Virgin will protect us.*)

Mômir (popular and thieves'), *to be
delivered of a child,* "to be in the
straw." The *Slang Dictionary*
says : "Married ladies are said to
be in the straw at their accouchement." The phrase is a coarse
metaphor, and has reference to

farmyard animals in a similar
condition. It may have originally
been suggested to the inquiring
mind by the Nativity. Mômir
pour l'aff, *to have a miscarriage.*
Termed also "casser son œuf,
décarrer de crac."

Monacos, *m. pl.* (familiar and
popular), *money.* See **Quibus.**

Je vais te prouver à toi et à ta grue, . . .
que je suis encore bonne pour gagner des
monacos. Et allez-y !—HECTOR FRANCE,
Marie Queue-de-Vache.

Avoir des —, *to be wealthy.*
Termed also "être foncé, être
sacquard, or douillard ; avoir le
sac, de l'os, des sous, du foin
dans ses bottes, de quoi, des
pépettes, or de la thune ; être californien." The English synonyms
being "to be worth a plum, to be
well ballasted, to be a rag-
splawger, to have lots of tin, to
have feathered one's nest, to be
warm, to be comfortable."
Abouler les —, *to pay,* "to fork
out, to shell out, to down with
the dust, to post the pony, to
stump the pewter, to tip the
brads."

Monant, *m.,***monante,** *f.*(thieves'),
friend.

Monarque, *m.* (popular), *five-franc
piece.* Termed also "roue de
derrière," the nearly corresponding coin, a crown piece, being
called in English slang a "hind
coach wheel." (Prostitutes') Monarque, *money.* Faire son —, *to
have found clients.*

Monde, *m.* (popular), renversé,
guillotine. See **Voyante.** Il y a
du — au balcon *is said of a
woman with large breasts, of one
with opulent* "Charlies." (Familiar) Demi —, *world of cocottes,
kept women.*

Dans ce qu'on appelle le demi-monde il
y a nombre de filles en carte, véritables

chevaliers d'industrie de la jeunesse et de l'amour qui, bien en règle avec la préfecture, mènent joyeuse vie pendant quinze ans et éludent constamment la police correctionnelle.—Léo Taxil.

(Showmen's) Du —, *public who enter the show.* There may be a large concourse of people outside, but no "monde."

Monfier (thieves'), *to kiss.*

Mongniasse (popular and thieves'), *me,* "my nibs."

Mon linge est lavé (popular), *I give in,* "I throw up the sponge."

Monnaie, *f.* (popular), plus que ça de —! *what luck!*

Mon œil! (popular), *expressive of refusal or disbelief,* "don't you wish you may get it?" or "do you see any green in my eye?" See **Nèfles.**

Monôme, *m.* (students'), *yearly procession in single file through certain streets of Paris of candidates to the government schools.*

Monorgue (thieves'), *I, myself.*

Monseigneur, *m.* (thieves'), or pince —, *short crowbar with which housebreakers force open doors or safes.* Termed "Jemmy, James, or the stick."

Ils font sauter gâches et serrures . . . avec une espèce de pied de biche en fer qu'ils appellent cadet, monseigneur, ou plume.—Canler.

Monseigneuriser (thieves'), *to force open a door,* "to strike a jigger."

Monsieur, *m.* (artists'), le —, *the principal figure in a picture.* (Popular) Un —, *a twopenny glass of brandy; a five-sous glass of wine from the bottle at a wine retailer's;* — Vautour, or Père Vautour, *the landlord;* also *an usurer.*

Vous accorder un nouveau délai pour le capital? . . . mais depuis trois ans . . . vous n'avez pas seulement pu rattraper les intérêts.—Ah! père Vautour, ça court si vite vos intérêts!—Gavarni.

Monsieur à tubard, *a well-dressed man, one who sports a silk hat;* — bambou, *a stick,* a gentleman whose services are sometimes put in requisition by drunken workmen as an irresistible argument to meet the remonstrances of an unfortunate better half, as in the case of Martine and Sganarelle in Molière's *Le Médecin malgré lui;* — Lebon, *a good sort of man, that is, one who readily treats others to drink;* — de Pétesec, *stuck-up man, with dry, sharp manner;* — hardi, *the wind;* — Raidillon, or Pointu, *proud, stuck-up man;* (thieves') — de l'Affure, *one who wins money at a game honestly or not;* — de la Paume, *he who loses;* (theatrical) — Dufour est dans la salle, *expression used by an actor to warn another that he is not acting up to the mark and that he will get himself hissed,* or "get the big bird." (Familiar and popular) Un —, à rouflaquettes, *prostitute's bully,* or "pensioner." For list of synonyms see **Poisson.** Monsieur de Paris, *the executioner.* Formerly each large town had its own executioner: Monsieur de Rouen, Monsieur de Lyon, &c. Concerning the office Balzac says:—

Les Sanson, bourreaux à Rouen pendant deux siècles, avant d'être revêtus de la première charge du royaume, exécutaient de père en fils les arrêts de la justice depuis le treizième siècle. Il est peu de familles qui puissent offrir l'exemple d'un office ou d'une noblesse conservée de père en fils pendant six siècles.

Monsieur personne, *a nobody.* (Brothels') Monsieur, *husband of the mistress of a brothel.*

Monsieur, avec son épaisse barbiche aux poils tors et gris.—E. de Goncourt, *La Fille Elisa.*

(Cads') Monsieur le carreau dans l'œil, *derisive epithet applied to a man with an eye-glass ;* — bas-du-cul, *man with short legs.*

Monstre, *m., any words which a musician temporarily adapts to a musical production composed by him.*

Monstrico, *m.* (familiar), *ugly person, one with a* " knocker face."

Montage de coup, *m.* (popular), *the act of seeking to deceive by misleading statements.*

> Mon vieux, entre nous,
> Je n'coup' pas du tout
> Dans c'montage de coup ;
> Faut pas m'monter l'coup.
> AUG. HARDY.

Montagnard, *m.* (popular), *additional horse put on to an omnibus going up hill.*

Montagne du géant, *f.* (obsolete), *gallows,* " scrag, nobbing cheat, or government signpost."

Montant, *m. and adj.* (thieves'), *breeches,* "trucks, hams, sit-upons, or kicks." (Military) Grand — tropical, *riding breeches ;* petit —, *drawers.* (Familiar) Montant, *term which is used to denote anything which excites lust.*

Montante, *f.* (thieves'), *ladder.* Literally *a thing to climb up.*

Monte-à-regret (thieves'), abbaye de —, *the guillotine.* Formerly *the gallows.* This name was given the scaffold because criminals were attended there by one or more priests, and on account of the natural repugnance of a man for this mode of being put out of his misery. Michel records the fact, that at Sens, one of the streets leading to the market-place, where executions took place, still bore, a few years ago, the name of Monte-à-regret. Chanoine de —, *one sentenced to death.* Termed also "grognon," or *grumbler.* Monter à l'abbaye de —, *to be guillotined,* meant formerly *to be hanged,* to suffer the extreme penalty of the law on "wry-neck day," when the criminal before being compelled to put on the "hempen cravat," would perhaps utter for the edification of the crowd his "tops, or croaks," that is, his last dying speech. It is curious to note how people of all nations have always striven to disguise the idea of death by the rope by means of some picturesque or grimly comical circumlocution. The popular language is rich in metaphors to describe the act. In the thirteenth century people would express hanging by the term "mettre à la bise ;" in the fifteenth and sixteenth centuries an executed criminal was spoken of as "vendangeant à l'eschelle, avoir collet rouge, croître d'un demi-pied, faire la longue lettre, tomber du haut mal," and later on : "Servir de bouchon, faire le saut, faire un saut sur rien, donner un soufflet à une potence, donner le moine par le cou, approcher du ciel à reculons, danser un branle en l'air, avoir la chanterelle au cou, faire le guet à Montfaucon, faire le guet au clair de la lune à la cour des monnoyes." Also, "monter à la jambe en l'air." Then a hanged man was "un évêque des champs" (on account of executions taking place in the open country) "qui bénit des pieds," and hanging itself, "une danse où il n'y a pas de plancher," which corresponds to the expression, "to dance upon nothing." The poor wretch was also said to be "branché," a summary proceeding performed on the nearest tree, and he was made to "tirer la langue d'un demi-pied." The poet François Villon being in the prison of the Châtelet in 1457, under sentence of death for a robbery supposed to have been committed at Rueil by himself and some companions, several of whom were hanged, but whose fate he luckily did not share, thus alludes with grim humour to his probable execution :—

Je suis François, dont ce me poise,
Né de Paris emprès Ponthoise,
Or, d'une corde d'une toise,
Saura mon col que mon cul poise.

When Jonathan Wild the Great is about to expiate his numerous crimes, and his career is soon to be terminated at Tyburn, Fielding makes him say: "D—n me, it is only a dance without music; . . . a man can die but once. . . . Zounds! Who's afraid?" Master Charley Bates, in common with his "pals," called hanging "scragging" :—

"He'll come to be scragged, won't he?"
"I don't know what that means," replied Oliver. "Something in this way, old feller," said Charley. As he said it, Master Bates caught up an end of his neckerchief, and holding it erect in the air, dropped his head on his shoulder, and jerked a curious sound through his teeth; thereby intimating, by a lively pantomimic representation, that "scragging" and hanging were one and the same thing.—DICKENS, *Oliver Twist.*

The expression is also to be met with in Lord Lytton's *Paul Clifford* :—

"Blow me tight, but that cove is a queer one! and if he does not come to be scragged," says I, "it vill only be because he'll turn a rusty, and scrag one of his pals!"

Again, the same author puts in the mouth of his hero, Paul Clifford, the accomplished robber, the "Captain Crank," or chief of a gang of highwaymen, a poetical simile, "to leap from a leafless tree":—

Oh! there never was life like the Robber's
—so
Jolly, and bold, and free;
And its end—why, a cheer from the crowd below
And a leap from a leafless tree!

Penny-a-liners nowadays describe the executed felon as "taking a leap into eternity;" facetious people say that he dies in a "horse's nightcap," *i.e.*, a halter, and the vulgar simply declare that he is "stretched." The dangerous classes, to express that one is being operated upon by Jack Ketch, use the term "to be scragged," already mentioned, or "to be topped;" and "may I be topped!" is an ejaculation often heard from the mouths of London roughs. Formerly, when the place for execution was at Tyburn, near the N.E. corner of Hyde Park, at the angle formed by the Edgware Road and the top of Oxford Street, the criminal brought here was said to put on the "Tyburn tippet," *i.e.*, Jack Ketch's rope. The Latins used to describe one hanged as making the letter I with his body, or the long letter. In Plautus old Staphyla says: "The best thing for me to do, is with the help of a halter, to make with my body the long letter." Modern Italians say of a man about to be executed, that he is sent to Picardy, "mandato in Picardia." They also use other circumlocutions, "andare a Longone," "andare a Fuligno," "dar de' calci al vento," "ballar in campo azurro." Again, the Italian "truccante" (*thief*), in his "lingue furbesche" (*cant of thieves*), says of a criminal who ascends the scaffold, the "sperlunga, or fati-

T

cosa" (*gallows*), with the "margherita, or signora" (*rope*) adjusted on his "guindo" (*neck*) by the "cataron" (*executioner*), that he may be considered as "aver la fune al guindo." The Spanish "azor" (*thief*, in *Germania*, or Spanish cant), under sentence of a "tristeza" (*sentence of death*), when about to be executed left the "angustia" (*prison*) to go to the gallows, or "balanza," which is now a thing of the past, having been superseded by the hideous "garote." The German "broschem-blatter" (*thief*, in "rothwelsch," or German cant), when sentenced to death was doomed to the "dolm," or "nelle," on which he was ushered out of this world by the "caffler" (*German Jack Ketch*).

Monter (popular), d'un cran, *to obtain an appointment superior to that one possesses already; to be promoted;* — à l'arbre, or à l'échelle, *to be fooled.* Alluding to a bear at the Zoological Gardens being induced to climb the pole by the prospect of some dainty bit which is not thrown to him after all. Also *to get angry*, "to get one's monkey up;" — en graine, *to grow old.* Literally *to run to seed;* — des couleurs, le Job, or un schtosse, *to deceive one by false representations*, "to bamboozle;" — une gamme, *to scold*, "to bully-rag;" — un coup, *to find a pretext; to lay a trap for one.*

C'est des daims huppés qui veulent monter un coup à un ennemi.—E. SUE.

Monter le coup, or un battage, *to deceive one by misleading statements.* Ça ne prend pas, tu ne me monteras pas le coup, "No go," *I am aware of your practices and* "twig" *your manœuvre*, or

"don't come the old soldier over me." Faire — à l'échelle, *to make one angry*, "to make one lose his shirt." Se — le bourrichon, or le baluchon, *to fly into a passion about some alleged injustice.* Also *to be too sanguine, to form illusions about one's abilities, or about the success of some project.*

Oh ! je ne me monte pas le bourrichon, je sais que je ne ferai pas de vieux os.— ZOLA, *L'Assommoir.*

Se — le coup, se — le verre en fleurs, *to form illusions.* Essayer de — un bateau à quelqu'un, *to seek to deceive one*, "to come the old soldier" *over one.* (Thieves') Monter un arcat, *to swindle*, "to bite;" — un gandin, *to deceive*, "to stick, or to best;" — un chopin, *to make all necessary preparations for a robbery*, "to lay a plant;" — à la butte, *to be guillotined.*

Un jour, j'ai pris mon surin pour le refroidir. Après tout, mon rêve c'est de monter à la butte.—*Mémoires de Monsieur Claude.*

Monter sur la table, *to make a clean breast of it; to inform against one*, "to blow the gaff." It also means *to tell a secret*, "to split."

While his man being caught in some fact
(The particular crime I've forgotten),
When he came to be hanged for the act,
Split, and told the whole story to Cotton.
Ingoldsby Legends.

(Theatrical) Monter une partie, *to get together a small number of actors to give out of Paris one or two performances;* (military) — en ballon, *practical joke at the expense of a new-comer.* During the night, to both ends of the bed of the victim are fixed two running nooses, the ropes being attached high up on a partition by the side of the bed. At a given signal the ropes being pulled, the occupant of the bed finds himself lifted in the air, with his couch upside down occasionally.

Monteur, *m.* (theatrical), de partie, *an actor whose spécialité is to get together a few brother actors for the purpose of performing out of town ;* (popular) —de coups, or de godans, *swindler ; one who is fond of hoaxing people ; one who imposes on others,* "humbug." Concerning the latter term the *Slang Dictionary* says : "A very expressive but slang word, synonymous at one time with hum and haw. Lexicographers for a long time objected to the adoption of this term. Richardson uses it frequently to express the meaning of other words, but, strange to say, omits it in the alphabetical arrangement as unworthy of recognition ! In the first edition of this work, 1785 was given as the earliest date at which the word could be found in a printed book. Since then 'humbug' has been traced half a century further back, on the title-page of a singular old jest-book, ' *The Universal Jester*, or a pocket companion for the Wits : being a choice collection of merry conceits, facetious drolleries, &c., clenchers, closers, closures, bon-mots, and humbugs, by Ferdinando Killigrew.' London, about 1735-40. The notorious orator Henley was known to the mob as Orator Humbug. The fact may be learned from an illustration in that exceedingly curious little collection of caricatures published in 1757, many of which were sketched by Lord Bolingbroke, Horace Walpole filling in the names and explanations. Haliwell describes humbug as 'a person who hums,' and cites Dean Milles's MS., which was written about 1760. In the last century the game now known as double-dummy was termed humbug. Lookup, a notorious gambler, was struck down by apoplexy when playing at this game. On the circumstance being reported to Foote, the wit said, ' Ah, I always thought he would be humbugged out of the world at last !' It has been stated that the word is a corruption of Hamburg, from which town so many false bulletins and reports came during the war in the last century. ' Oh, that is Hamburg (or Humbug),' was the answer to any fresh piece of news which smacked of improbability. Grose mentions it in his *Dictionary*, 1785 ; and in a little printed squib, published in 1808, entitled *Bath Characters*, by T. Goosequill, humbug is thus mentioned in a comical couplet on the title-page :—

> Wee Thre Bath Deities bee
> Humbug, Follie, and Varietee.

Gradually from this time the word began to assume a place in periodical literature, and in novels written by not over-precise authors. In the preface to a flat, and most likely unprofitable poem, entitled *The Reign of Humbug, a Satire*, 8vo, 1836, the author thus apologizes for the use of the word : ' I have used the term *humbug* to designate this principle (wretched sophistry of life generally), considering that it is now adopted into our language as much as the words dunce, jockey, cheat, swindler, &c., which were formerly only colloquial terms.' A correspondent, who in a number of *Adversaria* ingeniously traced bombast to the inflated Doctor Paracelsus Bombast, considers that humbug may, in like manner, be derived from Homberg, the distinguished chemist of the Court of the Duke of Orleans, who, according to the following passage from Bishop Berkeley's *Siris*, was an ardent and successful seeker after the philosopher's stone :—

Of this there cannot be a better proof than the experiment of Monsieur Homberg, who made gold of mercury by introducing light into its pores, but at such trouble and expense that, I suppose, nobody will try the experiment for profit. By this injunction of light and mercury, both bodies became finer, and produced a third different to either, to wit, real gold. For the truth of which fact I refer to the memoirs of the French Academy of Sciences.—BERKELEY, *Works.*"

The Supplementary English Glossary gives the word "humbugs" as the North-country term for certain lumps of toffy, well flavoured with peppermint. (Roughs') Monter à cheval, *to be suffering from a tumour in the groin, a consequence of venereal disease, and termed* poulain, *foal*, hence the jeu de mots ; (wine retailers') — sur le tonneau, *to add water to a cask of wine*, "to christen" *it*. Adding too much water to an alcoholic liquor is termed by lovers of the "tipple" in its pure state, "to drown the miller."

Monteur de coups, *m.* (popular), *story-teller ; cheat.*

Monteuse de coups, *f.* (popular), *deceitful woman ; one who "bamboozles" her lover or lovers.*

Montparno (thieves'), *Montparnasse.* See **Ménilmonte.**

J'ai flasqué du poivre à la rousse,
Elle ira de turne en garno,
De Ménilmuche à Montparno,
Sans pouvoir remoucher mon gniasse.
RICHEPIN.

Montrer (theatrical), la couture de ses bas, *to break off a stage engagement by the simple process of leaving the theatre ;* (familiar and popular) — toute sa boutique, *to expose one's person.*

Ah ! non . . . remettez votre camisole. Vous savez, je n'aime pas les indécences. Pendant que vous y êtes, montrez toute votre boutique.—ZOLA.

Montre-tout, *m.* (popular), *short jacket.* Termed also "ne te gêne pas dans le parc." (Prostitutes') Aller à —, *to go to the medical examination, a periodical and compulsory one, for registered prostitutes, those who shirk it being sent to the prison of Saint-Lazare.*

Monu, *m.* (cads'), *one-sou cigar.*

Monument, *m.* (popular), *tall hat,* or "stove-pipe."

Monzu, or **mouzu**, *m.* (old cant), *woman's breasts.* Termed, in other varieties of jargon, "avant-postes, avant-scènes, œufs sur le plat, oranges sur l'étagère," and in the English slang, "dairies, bubbies, or Charlies."

Morasse, *f.* (printers'), *proof taken before the forme is finally arranged ; — final proof of a newspaper article.* Also *workman who remains to correct such a proof, or the time employed in the work.* (Thieves') Morasse, *uneasiness ; remorse.* Battre —, *to make a hue and cry*, "to romboyle," in old cant, or "to whiddle beef."

Morassier, *m.* (printers'), *one who prints off the last proof of a newspaper article.*

Morbaque, *m.* (popular), *disagreeable child.* See **Morbec.**

Morbec, *m.* (popular), *a variety of vermin which clings tenaciously to certain parts of the human body.*

Morceau, *m.* (freemasons'), d'architecture, *speech ;* (popular) — de gruyère, *pockmarked face,* "cribbage-face ;" — de salé, *fat woman.* Un —, *a slatternly girl.*

(Thieves') Manger le —, *to peach,* "to blow the gaff."

> Le morceau tu ne mangeras
> De crainte de tomber au plan.
> VIDOCQ.

(Literary) Morceau de pâte ferme, *heavy, dull production.* (Artists') Faire le —, *to paint details skilfully.* (Military) Le beau temps tombe par morceaux, *it rains.*

Mord (familiar and popular), ça ne — pas, *it's no use; no go.*

Mordante, *f.* (thieves'), *file; saw.* The allusion is obvious.

Mordre (popular), se faire —, *to be reprimanded,* "to get a wigging;" *to get thrashed,* or "wolloped."

Moresque, *f.* (thieves'), *danger.*

Morfe, *f.* (thieves'), *meal; victuals,* or "toke."

> Veux-tu venir prendre de la morfe et piausser avec mézière en une des pioles que tu m'as rouscaillée?—*Le Jargon de l'Argot.*

Morfiante, *f.* (thieves'), *plate.*

Morfigner, morfiler (thieves'), *to do; to eat.* From the old word morfier. Rabelais uses the word morfialler with the signification of *to eat, to gorge oneself.*

> La, la, la, c'est morfiallé cela.—RABELAIS, *Gargantua.*

Morfiler, or **morfiller** (thieves'), *to eat,* "to yam."

> Un vieux fagot qui s'était fait raille pour morfiller.—VIDOCQ. (*An old convict who had turned spy to get a living.*)

Termed also morfier. Compare with morfire, or morfizzare, *to eat,* in the lingue furbesche, or Italian cant. Se — le dardant, *to fret.* Dardant, *heart.*

Morgane, *f.* (old cant), *salt.*

> C'est des oranges, si tu demandais du sel ... de la morgane! mon fils, ça coûte pas cher.—VIDOCQ. (*Here are some potatoes; just you ask for salt, my boy; it's cheap enough.*)

Morganer (roughs' and thieves'), *to bite.* Morgane le gonse et chair dure! *Bite the cove! pitch into him!*

Moricaud, *m.* (thieves'), *coal; wine-dealer's wooden pitcher.*

Mori-larve, *f.* (thieves'), *sunburnt face.*

Morlingue, *m.* (thieves'), *money; purse,* "skin." Faire le —, *to steal a purse,* "to fake a skin."

Mornante, *f.* (thieves'), *sheepfold.* From morne, *sheep.*

Morne, *f. and adj.* (thieves'), *sheep,* or "wool-bird." Termed "bleating cheat" by English vagabonds. Courbe de —, *shoulder of mutton.* Morne, *stupid; stupid man,* "go along."

Mornée, *f.* (thieves'), *mouthful.*

Mornier, morneux, or **marmier,** *m.* (thieves'), *shepherd.*

Morniffer (popular), *to slap one's face,* "to fetch a bang," or "to give a biff," as the Americans have it. Termed *to give a* "clo," at Winchester School.

Mornifle, *f.* (thieves'), *money,* or "blunt."

> When the slow coach paused, and the gemmen storm'd,
> I bore the brunt—
> And the only sound which my grave lips form'd
> Was "blunt"—still "blunt!"
> LORD LYTTON, *Paul Clifford.*

Mornifle tarte, *spurious coin,* or "queer bit." Refiler de la — tarte, *to pass off bad coin; to be a* "snide pitcher, or smasher." Properly mornifle has the signification of *cuff on the face.*

Mornifleur tarte, *m.* (thieves'), *coiner,* or "queer-bit faker."

Morningue, or **morlingue,** *m.* (thieves'), *money,* or "pieces;" *purse.* Faire le —, *to pick a* *pocket.* In the old English cant "to fang" *a pocket.*

O shame o' justice ! Wild is hang'd,
For thatten he a pocket fang'd,
While safe old Hubert, and his gang,
Doth pocket of the nation fang.
FIELDING, *J. Wild.*

Termed in modern English cant "to fake a cly," a pickpocket being called, according to Lord Lytton, a "buzz gloak" :—

The "eminent hand" ended with—"He who surreptitiously accumulates bustle, is, in fact, nothing better than a buzz gloak.—*Paul Clifford.*

Porte —, *purse,* "skin, or poge."

Mornos, *m.* (thieves'), *mouth,* "bone-box, or muns." Probably from morne, *mutton,* the mouth's most important function being to receive food.

Morpion, *m.* (popular), *strong expression of contempt ; despicable man,* or "snot." Literally *crab-louse.* Also *a bore,* one who clings to you as the vermin alluded to.

Morpionner (popular), *is said of a bore that you cannot get rid of.*

Morse (Breton cant), *barley bread.*

Mort, *f. and adj.* (popular), marchand de — subite, *physician,* "pill."

C'est bien sûr le médecin en chef . . . tous les marchands de mort subite vous ont de ces regards-là.—ZOLA.

Lampe à —, *confirmed drunkard whose thirst cannot be slaked.* (Familiar and popular) Un corps —, *an empty bottle.* The English say, when a bottle has been emptied, " Take away this bottle ; it has 'Moll Thompson's' mark on it," that is, it is M. T. An empty bottle is also termed a "marine, or marine recruit." "This expression having once been used in the presence of an officer of Marines," says the *Slang Dictionary,* "he was at first inclined to take it as an insult, until someone adroitly appeased his wrath by remarking that no offence could be meant, as all that it could possibly imply was : one who had done his duty, and was ready to do it again." (Popular) Eau de —, *brandy.* See **Tord-boyaux.** (Thieves') Etre —, *to be sentenced,* "booked." Hirondelle de la —, *gendarme on duty at executions.* (Military school of Saint-Cyr) Se faire porter élève-mort *is to get placed on the sick list.* (Gamesters') Mort, *stakes which have been increased by a cheat, who slily lays additional money the moment the game is in his favour.*

Morte paye sur mer, *f.* (thieves'), *the hulks* (obsolete).

Morue, *f.* (popular), *dirty, disgusting woman.*

Vous voyez, Françoise, ce panier de fraises qu'on vous fait trois francs ; j'en offre un franc, moi, et la marchande m'appelle . . . Oui, madame, elle vous appelle . . . morue !—GAVARNI.

Also *prostitute.* See **Gadoue.** Grande — dessalée, *expression of the utmost contempt applied to a woman.* Pedlars formerly termed "morue," *manuscripts,* for the printing of which they formed an association, "clubbed" together.

Morviau, *m.* (popular), *nose.* Termed also "pif, bourbon, piton, pivase, bouteille, caillou, trompe, truffe, tubercule, trompette, nazareth ;" and, in English slang, "conk, boko, nob, snorter, handle, post-horn, and smeller." Lécher le —, *to kiss.* The expression is old.

Lécher le morveau, manière de parler ironique, qui signifie caresser une femme, la courtiser, la servir, faire l'amour. Dit

de même que lécher le grouin, baiser, être assidu et attaché à une personne.—LE ROUX, *Dict. Comique.*

The term "snorter" of the English jargon has the corresponding equivalent "soffiante" in Italian cant.

Morviot, *m.* (popular), *secretion from the mucous membrane of the nose,* "snot."

Dans les veines d'ces estropiés,
Au lieu d'sang il coul' du morviot.
Ils ont des guiboll's comm' leur stick,
Trop d'bidoche autour des boyaux,
Et l'arpion plus mou qu' du mastic.
RICHEPIN.

Morviot, *term of contempt,* not quite so forcible as the English expression "snot," which has the signification of *contemptible individual.* Petit —, *little scamp.*

Moscou, *m.* (military), faire brûler —, *to mix a vast bowl of punch.* Alluding to the burning down of Moscow by the Russians themselves in 1812.

Mossieu à tubard, *m.* (popular), *well-dressed man,* a "swell cove." Tubard is a *silk hat.*

Mot, *m.* (popular), casser un —, *to have a chat,* or "chin music."

Motte, *f.* (general), *pudenda mulierum.* Termed also "chat," and formerly by the poets "le verger de Cypris." Le Roux, concerning the expression, says :—

La motte de la nature d'une femme, c'est proprement le petit bois touffu qui garnit le penil d'une femme.—*Dict. Comique.*

Formerly the false hair for those parts was termed in English "merkin." (Thieves') Motte, *central prison, or house of correction.* Dégringoler de la —, *to come from such a place of confinement.* The synonyms of prison in different varieties of slang are : "castue, caruche, hôpital, mitre,

chetard or jetard, collège, grosse boîte, l'ours, le violon, le bloc, boîte aux cailloux, tuneçon, austo, mazaro, lycée, château, lazaro." In the English lingo : "stir, clinch, bastile, steel, sturrabin, jigger, Irish theatre, stone-jug, mill," the last-named being an abbreviation of treadmill, and signifying by analogy *prison.* The word is mentioned by Dickens :—

"Was you never on the mill?" "What mill," inquired Oliver. "What mill? why the mill,—the mill as takes up so little room that it'll work inside a stone-jug.—*Oliver Twist.*

In Yorkshire a prison goes by the appellation of "Toll-shop," as shown by this verse of a song popular at fairs in the East Riding :—

But if ivver he get out agean,
And can but raise a frind,
Oh! the divel may tak' toll-shop,
At Beverley town end!

This "toll-shop" is but a variation of the Scottish "tolbooth." The general term "quod" to denote a prison originates from the universities. Quod is really a shortening of quadrangle ; so to be quodded is to be within four walls (*Slang Dict.*).

Motus dans l'entrepont! (sailors'), *silence!* "put a clapper to your mug," or "mum's the word."

Mou, *m.* (popular), avoir le — enflé, *to be pregnant,* or "lumpy."

Mouchailler (popular and thieves'), *to scan,* "to stag ;" *to look at,* "to pipe ;" *to see.*

J'itre mouchaillé le babillard . . . je n'y itre mouchaillé floutière de vain.—*Le Jargon de l'Argot.*

Mouchard, *m.* (popular), *portrait hung in a room ;* (popular and thieves') — à becs, *lamp-post,* the inconvenient luminary being compared to a spy. Mouchard, pro-

perly *spy*, one who goes busily about like a fly. It formerly had the signification of *dandy*.

A la fin du xvii⁰ siècle, on donnait encore ce nom aux petits-maîtres qui fréquentaient les Tuileries pour voir autant que pour être vus: C'est sur ce fameux théâtre des Tuileries, dit un écrivain de l'époque, qu'une beauté naissante fait sa première entrée au monde. Bientôt les "mouchars" de la grande allée sont en campagne au bruit d'un visage nouveau; chacun court en repaître ses yeux.— MICHEL.

Moucharde, *f.* (thieves'), *moon*, "parish lantern, or Oliver."

Mais déjà la patrarque,
Au clair de la moucharde,
Nous reluque de loin.
VIDOCQ.

La — se débine, *the moon disappears*, "Oliver is sleepy."

Mouche, *f.*, *adj.*, *and verb* (general), *police, or police officer; detective.* Compare with the "mücke," or spy, of German cant; (thieves') *muslin;* (students') — à miel, *candidate to the Ecole Centrale des Arts et Manufactures, a great engineering school.* Alluding to the bee embroidered in gold on their caps. (Popular) Mouche, *bad*, or "snide;" *ugly; stupid.* C'est bon pour qui qu'est —, *it is only fit for* "flats." Mouche, *weak.*

Il a reparu, l'ami soleil. Bravo! encore bien débile, bien pâlot, bien "mouche," dirait Gavroche.—RICHEPIN.

Non, c'est q' j' me —, *ironical negative expression meant to be strongly affirmative.* Synonymous of "non, c'est q' je tousse!" Vous n'avez rien fait? Non, c'est q' j' me —, *you did nothing? oh! didn't I, just!*

Moucher (popular), le quinquet, *to kill*, "to do" *for one; to strike, to give a* "wipe."

Allons, mouche-lui le quinquet, ça l'esbrouffera.—TH. GAUTIER.

Moucher la chandelle, *to give oneself up to solitary practices; to act according to the principles of Malthus with a view of not begetting children.* For further explanation the reader may be referred to a work entitled *The Fruits of Philosophy;* — sa chandelle, *to die,* "to snuff it." For synonyms see **Pipe.** Se — dans ses doigts (obsolete), *to be clever, resolute.* Se faire — le quinquet, *to get one's head punched.* (Gamesters') Se —, *is said of attendants who, while pretending to make use of their handkerchiefs, purloin a coin or two from the gaming-table.* It is said of such an attendant, who on the sly abstracts a gold piece from the stakes laid out on the table, il s'est "mouché" d'un louis.

Moucheron, *m.* (popular), *waiter at a wine-shop; child,* or "kid."

Mouches, *f. pl.* (popular), d'hiver, *snow-flakes.* Tuer les —, *to emit a bad smell,* capable of killing even flies. Termed also tuer les — à quinze pas. (Theatrical) Envoyer des coups de pied aux —, *to lead a disorderly life.*

Mouchettes, *f. pl.* (popular), *pocket-handkerchief,* "snottinger, or wipe." Termed "madam, or stook," by English thieves. Des —! *equivalent to* du flan! des navets! des nèfles, &c., forcible expression of refusal; may be rendered by "Don't you wish you may get it!" or, as the Americans say, "Yes, in a horn."

Moucheur de chandelles, *m.* (popular). See **Moucher.**

Mouchique, *adj.* (popular and thieves'), *base, worthless, bad,* "snide."

C'était un' tonn' pas mouchique,
C'était un girond tonneau,
L'anderlique, l'anderlique,
L'anderliqu' de Landerneau !
GILL.

The English cant has the old word "queer," signifying base, roguish, or worthless—the opposite of "rum," which signified good and genuine. "Queer, in all probability," says the *Slang Dictionary*, "is immediately derived from the cant language. It has been mooted that it came into use from a 'quære' (?) being set before a man's name; but it is more than probable that it was brought into this country by the gipsies from Germany, where *quer* signifies *cross*, or *crooked*." (Thieves') Etre — à sa section, or à la sec, *to be noted as a bad character at the police office of one's district*. The word "mouchique," says Michel, is derived from "mujik," *a Russian peasant*, which must have become familiar in 1815 to the inhabitants of the parts of the country invaded by the Russians.

Mouchoir, *m.* (popular), d'Adam, *the fingers*, used by some people as a natural handkerchief, "forks;" — de bœuf, *meadow*. Termed thus on account of oxen having their noses in the grass when grazing;— de poche, *pistol*, or "pops." (Familiar and popular) Faire le —, *to steal pocket-hand-kerchiefs*, "to draw a wipe." Coup de — (obsolete), *a box on the ear*, a "wipe in the chaps."

Voyez le train qu'a m' fait pour un coup de mouchoir que j'lui ai donné.—POM-PIGNY, 1783.

(Theatrical) Faire le —, *to pirate another author's productions*.

Mouchouar-godel (Breton cant), *pistol*.

Moudre (popular), or — un air, *to ply a street organ*.

Mouf (popular), abbreviation of *Mouffetard*, the name of a street almost wholly tenanted by rag-pickers, and situate in one of the lowest quarters of Paris. Quartier — mouf, *the Quartier Mouffetard*. La tribu des Beni Mouf-mouf, *inhabitants of the Quartier Mouffetard*. Champagne —, or Champagne Mouffetard, *a liquid manufactured by rag-pickers with rotten oranges picked out of the refuse at the Halles*. The fruit, after being washed, is thrown into a cask of water and allowed to ferment for a few days, after which some brown sugar being added, the liquid is bottled up, and does duty as champagne. It is the Cliquot of poor people.

Moufflanté, *adj.* (popular), *comfortably, warmly clad*.

Moufflet, *m.* (popular), *child*, or "kid;" *urchin; apprentice*.

Moufion, *m.* (popular), *pocket-handkerchief*, "snottinger, or wipe."

Moufionner (popular), *to blow one's nose*. (Thieves') Se — dans le son, *to be guillotined*. Literally *to blow one's nose in the bran*. An allusion to an executed convict's head, which falls into a basket full of sawdust. Termed also "éternuer dans le son, or le sac." See **Fauché**.

Mouget, *m.* (roughs'), *a swell*, or "gorger." Des péniches à la —, *fashionable boots, as now worn, with pointed toes and large square heels*.

Mouillante, *f.* (thieves'), *cod ;* (popular) *soup*.

Mouillé, *adj.* (popular), être —, *to be drunk*, or "tight." See **Pom-**

pette. Etre —, *to be known in one's real character.* Alluding to cloths which are soaked in water to ascertain their quality. (Thieves') Etre —, *to be well known to the police.*

Mouiller (popular), se —, *to drink,* " to have something damp," or as the Americans have it, " to smile, to see the man." The term is old.

> Mouillez-vous pour seicher, ou seichez pour mouiller.—RABELAIS.

Also *to get slightly intoxicated,* or "elevated." (Theatrical) Mouiller à, or dans, *to receive a royalty for a play produced on the stage.* Se —, *to take pains in one's acting.* (Thieves') Se — les pieds, *to be transported,* " to lump the lighter, or to be lagged." (Roughs') En —, *to perform some extraordinary feat with great expenditure of physical strength.* Les frères qui en mouillent, *acrobats.* (Military) Mouiller, *to be punished.*

Mouise, *f.* (thieves'), *soup.*

> Vous qui n'avez probablement dans le bauge que la mouise de Tunebée Bicêtre vous devez canner la pégrenne.—VIDOCQ.

Moukala, *m.* (military), *rifle.* From the Arab.

Moukère, or **moucaire,** *f.* (popular), *ugly woman ; girl of indifferent character ;* (military) *mistress.* Ma —, *my young* " 'ooman." Avoir sa —, *to have won the good graces of a fair one,* generally a cook in the case of an infantry soldier, the cavalry having the monopoly of housemaids or ladies' maids, and sappers showing a great penchant for nursery-maids.

Moulard, *m.* (popular), superlative of moule, *dunce,* or " flat."

Moule, *m. and f.* (popular), une —, *face,* or "mug." Also *a dunce, simpleton,* or "muff."

> Foutez-moi la paix ! Vous êtes une couenne et une moule !—G. COURTELINE.

Le — à blagues, *mouth,* or "chaffer." Literally *the humbug-box.* Un — à boutons, *a twenty-franc piece.* Un — à claques, *face with impertinent expression which invites punishment.* Termed also — à croquignoles. Un — à gaufres, or à pastilles, *a face pitted with small-pox marks,* "crumpet-face, or cribbage - face." Un moule à gaufres is properly *a waffle-iron.* Un — à poupée (obsolete), *a clumsily-built, awkward man.*

> Ah ! ah ! ah ! C'grand benêt ! a-t-il un air jaune . . . dis donc eh ! c'moule à poupée, qu' veux-tu faire de cette pique ?—*Riche-en-gueule.*

Un — à merde, *behind,* "Nancy." For synonyms see **Vasistas.** Also *a foul-mouthed person.* Un — de gant, *box on the ear,* or "bang in the gills." Un — de bonnet, *head,* or "canister." Un — de pipe à Gambier, *grotesque face,* or "knocker face." Un --- à melon, *humpback,* or "lord." (Military) Envoyer chercher le — aux guillemets, *to send a recruit on a fool's errand,* to send him to ask the sergeant-major for *the mould for inverted commas,* the joke being varied by requesting him to fetch the key of the drill-ground. Corresponds somewhat to sending a greenhorn for pigeon's milk, or a pennyworth of stirrup-oil.

Mouler (familiar and popular), un sénateur, *to ease oneself by evacuation,* "to bury a quaker;" (artists') — une Vénus, *same meaning.* Artists term "gazonner," *the act of easing oneself in the fields.* See **Mouscailler.**

Moulin, *m.* (popular), de la halle (obsolete), *the pillory.*

Mais pour qu'à l'avenir tu fass' mieux ton devoir,
Fais réguiser ta langu' sur la pierre infernale,
Et puis j'te f'rons tourner au moulin de la halle.
Amusemens à la Grecque, 1764.

Moulin, *hairdresser's shop ;* — à café, *mitrailleuse.* Thus termed on account of the revolving handle used in firing it off, like that of a coffee-mill. Also *street organ ;* — à merde, *slanderer ;* — à vent, *the behind.* See **Vasistas.** Concerning the expression Le Roux says :—

Moulin à vent, pour cul, derrière. Moulin à vent, parcequ'on donne l'essor à ses vents par cette ouverture-là.—*Dict. Comique.*

(Thieves') **Moulin,** *receiver's,* or "fence's," *house.* Termed also "maison du meunier." Porter du gras-double au —, *to steal lead and take it to a receiver of stolen property,* "to do bluey at the fence." (Police) Passer au — à café, *to transport a prostitute to the colonies.*

Moulinage, *m.* (popular), *prattling,* "clack."

Mouliner (popular), *to talk nonsense ; to prattle.* A term specially used in reference to the fair sex, and an allusion to the rapid, regular, and monotonous motion of a mill, or to the noise produced by the paddles of a water-mill, a "tattle-box" being termed moulin à paroles.

Mouloir, *m.* (thieves'), *mouth,* "bone-box, or muns ;" *teeth,* "ivories, or grinders."

Moulure, *f.* (popular), *lump of excrement,* or "quaker." Machine à moulures, *breech,* or "Nancy." See **Vasistas.**

Mouniche, *f.* (thieves'), *woman's privities,* "merkin," according to the *Slang Dictionary.*

Mounin, *m.* (thieves'), *child,* or "kid ;" *apprentice.*

Mounine, *f.* (thieves'), *little girl.*

Mouquette, *f.* (popular), *cocotte,* or "poll." See **Gadoue.**

Assez ! Taisez vos becs ! . . . à la porte les mouquettes !—P. MAHALIN.

Moure, *f.* (thieves'), *pretty face,* "dimber mug."

Mourir (popular), tu t'en ferais — ! *is expressive of refusal.* Literally *if I gave you what you want you would die for joy.* See **Nèfles.**

Mouron, *m.* (popular), ne plus avoir de — sur la cage, *to be bald,* or *to sport* "a bladder of lard." For synonymous expressions see **Avoir.**

Mouscaille, *f.* (thieves'), *excrement,* or, as the Irish say, "quaker."

Mouscailler (thieves'), *to ease oneself by evacuation.* The synonyms are "mousser, enterrer son colonel, aller faire une ballade à la lune, mouler un sénateur, mouler une Vénus, gazonner, aller au numéro cent, déponer, fogner, flaquer, écrire à un Juif, déposer une pêche, poser un pépin, un factionnaire, or une sentinelle ; envoyer une dépêche à Bismark, flasquer, touser, faire corps neuf, déposer une médaille de papier volant, or des Pays-Bas (obsolete), faire des cordes, mettre une lettre à la poste, faire le grand, faire une commission, débourrer sa pipe, défalquer, tarter, faire une moulure, aller quelque part, aller à ses affaires, aller où le roi va à pied, filer, aller chez Jules, ierchem, aller où le roi n'envoie personne, flaquader, fuser, gâcher du gros, galipoter, pousser son rond, filer le cable de proue, faire un pruneau, aller au buen-retiro, aller voir Bernard, faire ronfler le bourrelet, la chaise percée, or la chaire percée." In the English slang, "to go to the West Central, to go to Mrs. Jones, or to the crapping-ken, to the bog-house, to the chapel of ease, to Sir Harry; to crap, to go to the crapping-case, to the coffee-shop, to the crapping castle," and, as the Irish term it, "to bury a quaker."

Mouscailleur, *m.* (popular), *scavenger employed in emptying cesspools*, or " gold-finder."

Mousquetaire gris, *m.* (popular), *louse*, or " grey-backed 'un."

Moussaillon, *m.* (sailors'), *a ship-boy*, or "powder-monkey." From mousse, *ship-boy*.

Moussante, *f.* (popular and thieves'), *beer*, or " gatter." Un pot de —, a "shant of gatter." A curious slang street melody, known in Seven Dials as *Bet the Coaley's Daughter*, mentions the word " gatter":—

> But when I strove my flame to tell,
> Says she, " Come, stow that patter,
> If you're a cove wot likes a gal,
> Vy don't you stand some gatter?"
> In course I instantly complied,
> Two brimming quarts of porter,
> With sev'ral goes of gin beside,
> Drain'd Bet the Coaley's daughter.

Moussante mouchique, *bad, flat beer*, " swipes, or belly vengeance."

Moussard, *m.* (thieves'), *chestnut tree*.

Mousse, *f.* (popular and thieves'), *excrement; wine*. The word is old. Villon, a poet of the fifteenth century, uses it with the latter signification. For quotation see

Jouer du pouce. (Popular) De la —! *nonsense!* "all my eye," or "all my eye and Betty Martin." Is also expressive of ironical refusal; "yes, in a horn," as the Americans say.

Moussecailloux, *m.* (popular), *infantry soldier*, "wobbler, or beetle-crusher."

Mousseline, *f.* (thieves'), *white bread*, or " pannum," alluding to a similarity of colour. Also *prisoner's fetters*, " darbies."

Mousser (popular), *to ease oneself by evacuation*. See **Mouscailler**. Also *to be wroth*, "to have one's monkey up." Faire — quelqu'un, *to make one angry by* "riling" him.

Mousserie, *f.* (thieves'), *privy*, " crapping-ken."

Mousseux, *adj.* (literary), *hyperbolic*.

Moussue, *f.* (thieves'), *chestnut.*

Moustachu, *m.* (familiar), *man with moustache.*

Moustique, *m.* (popular), avoir un — dans la boîte au sel, *to be* "cracked," "to have a slate off." For synonymous expressions see **Avoir**.

Mout, *adj.* (popular), *pretty, handsome.*

Moutarde, *f.* (popular), *excrement*. Baril à —, *the behind*. For synonyms see **Vasistas**. The expression is old.

> En le lançant, il dit : prends garde,
> Je vise au baril de moutarde.
> *La Suite du Virgile travesti.*

Moutardier, *m.* (popular), *breech*, or " tochas." See **Vasistas**.

> Et en face! Je n'ai pas besoin de renifler ton moutardier.—Zola.

Mouton, *m.* (popular), *mattress,* or "mot cart;" (general) *prisoner who is set to watch a fellow-prisoner, and, by winning his confidence, seeks to extract information from him,* a "*nark.*"

Comme tu seras au violon avant lui, il ne se doutera pas que tu es un mouton.—VIDOCQ.

Deux sortes de coqueurs sont à la dévotion de la police : les coqueurs libres, et les coqueurs détenus autrement dit moutons.—*Mémoires de Canler.*

Moutonnaille, *f.* (popular), *crowd.* Sheep will form a crowd.

Moutonner (thieves' and police), *to play the spy on fellow-prisoners.*

Celui qui est mouton court risque d'être assassiné par les compagnons . . . aussi la police parvient-elle rarement à décider les voleurs à moutonner leurs camarades.—CANLER.

Moutrot, *m.* (thieves'), *Prefect of police.* Le logis du —, *the Préfecture de Police.*

Mouvante, *f.* (thieves'), *porridge.*

Mouvement, *m.* (swindlers'), concierge dans le —, *doorkeeper in league with a gang of swindlers,* for a description of which see **Bande noire.**

Mouzu, *m.* (thieves'), *woman's breasts,* "Charlies, or dairies."

Muche, *adj. and m.* (prostitutes'), *polite, timid young man ;* (popular) *excellent, perfect,* "bully, or ripping."

Muette, *f.* (Saint-Cyr School), *drill exercise in which cadets purposely do not make their muskets ring.* This is done to annoy any unpopular instructor. (Thieves') Muette, *conscience.* Avoir une puce à la —, *to feel a pang of remorse.*

Mufe, or **muffle,** *m. and adj.* (thieves'), *mason ;* (familiar and popular) *mean fellow ; mean.*

Son pâtissier s'était montré assez mufe pour menacer de la vendre, lorsqu'elle l'avait quitté.—ZOLA, *Nana.*

Mufe, *scamp, cad,* "bally bounder."

Elles restaient gaies, jetant simplement un "sale mufe !" derrière le dos des maladroits dont le talon leur arrachait un volant.—ZOLA, *Nana.*

Muffée, *f.* (popular), en avoir une vraie —, *to be completely intoxicated.* See **Pompette.**

Muffeton, muffleton, *m.* (popular), *young scamp ; mason's apprentice.*

Muffleman (popular), *mean fellow.*

Mufflerie, *f.* (popular), *contemptible action ; behaviour like a cad's.*

Mufle, *m.* (thieves'), se casser le —, *to meet with.* Termed also "tomber en frime."

Tel escarpe ou assassin ne commettra pas un crime un vendredi, ou s'il s'est cassé le mufle devant un ratichon (prêtre).—*Mémoires de Monsieur Claude.*

Mufrerie, *f.* (popular), *disparaging epithet ;* — de sort ! *curse my luck !*

Muitar, *f.* (thieves'), être dans la —, *to be in prison,* or "in quod."

Mulet, *m.* (military), *marine artillery man ;* (printers') *compositor,* or "donkey." "In the days before steam machinery was invented, the men who worked at press," says the *Slang Dictionary,* "the pressmen, were so dirty and drunken a body that they earned the name of pigs. In revenge, and for no reason that can be discovered, they christened the compositors 'donkeys.'" (Thieves') Mulet, *devil.*

Les meusniers, aussi ont une mesme façon de parler que les cousturiers, appelant leur asne le grand Diable, et leur sac, Raison. Et rapportant leur farine à ceux ausquels elle appartient, si on leur demande s'ils en ont point prins plus qu'il ne leur en faut, respondent : Le grand Diable m'emporte, si j'en ay prins que par raison. Mais pour tout cela ils disent qu'ils ne desrobent rien, car on leur donne.—TABOUROT.

Muraille (familiar and popular), battre la —, *to be drunk and to reel about, now in the gutter, now against the wall.*

Murer (popular), je te vas — ! *I'll knock you down, or I'll double you up !* See **Voie.**

Muron, *m.* (thieves'), *salt.*

Muronner (thieves'), *to salt.*

Muronnière, *f.* (thieves'), *salt-cellar.*

Musardine, *f.* (familiar), *name given some forty years ago to a more than fast girl, or to a girl of indifferent character,* termed sometimes by English "mashers," a "blooming tartlet." The synonyms corresponding to various epochs are :—Under the Restoration "femme aimable," a term of little significance. In Louis Philippe's time, "lorette," on account of the frail ones mostly dwelling in the Quartier Notre Dame de Lorette. Under the Third Empire "chignon doré" (it was then the fashion, as it still is, for such women to dye their hair a bright gold or auburn tint), or "cocodette," the feminine of "cocodès," *young dandy.* Now-a-days frequenters of the Boulevards use the term "boudinée," "boudiné, bécarre, or pschutteux," being the latest appellations for the Parisian "masher." The term "musardine" must first have been applied to fast girls frequenting the Bals Musard, attended at the time by all the "dashing" elements of Paris. "In English polite society, a fast young lady," says the *Slang Dictionary,* "is one who affects mannish habits, or makes herself conspicuous by some unfeminine accomplishment, talks slang, drives about in London, smokes cigarettes, is knowing in dogs and horses, &c. An amusing anecdote is told of a fast young lady, the daughter of a right reverend prelate, who was an adept in horseflesh. Being desirous of ascertaining the opinion of a candidate for ordination, who had the look of a bird of the same feather, as to the merits of some cattle brought to her father's palace for her to select from, she was assured by him they were utterly unfit for a lady's use. With a knowing look at the horses' points, she gave her decision in these choice words, ' Well, I agree with you ; they are a rum lot, as the devil said of the ten commandments.' Charles Dickens once said that ' fast,' when applied to a young man, was only another word for loose, as he understood the term ; and a fast girl has been defined as a woman who has lost her respect for men, and for whom men have lost their respect."

Musée, *m.* (popular), le — des claqués, *the Morgue, or Paris deadhouse.*

Muselé, *m.* (popular), *dunce,* or "flat ; " *good-for-nothing man.* Alluding to a muzzled dog who cannot use his teeth.

Musette, *f.* (popular), *voice.* Couper la — à quelqu'un, *to silence one,* "to clap a stopper on one's mug ; " *to cut one's throat.*

Musicien, *m.* (thieves'), *dictionary; variety of informer,* or "snitcher ; " (familiar) — par intimidation, *a street melodist who obtains money from people desirous of getting rid of him.*

J'y ai retrouvé aussi le "musicien par intimidation," l'homme à la clarinette, qui s'arrête devant les cafés du boulevard en faisant mine de porter à ses lèvres le bec de son instrument. Les consommateurs épouvantés se hâtent de lui jeter quelque monnaie afin d'éviter l'harmonie.—ELIE FRÉBAULT, *La Vie de Paris.*

It, however, occurs occasionally that people annoyed by the har- monists of the street have their revenge whilst getting rid of them without having to pay toll, as in the case of the "musicien par intimidation." One day a French artist in London, who every day was almost driven mad by the performances of a band of green- coated German musicians, hit upon the following singular stra- tagem. Placing himself at the window, and facing his tormen- tors, he applied a lemon to his lips. The effect was instantaneous, as through an association of ideas the mouths of the musicians began to water to such an extent that, un- able to proceed with their sym- phony, they surrendered the battle- field to the triumphant artist. (Popular) Des musiciens, *beans,* alluding to the wind they gene- rate in the bowels. (Printers') Des musiciens, *large number of corrections made on the margin of pages ; unskilled compositors who are unable to proceed with their work.*

Musique, *f.* (popular), *second-hand articles ; odd pieces of cloth sewn together ; kind of penny loaf.* Termed also " flûte." Also *what remains in a glass ;* (thieves') *in- forming ; informers.*

La deuxième classe, que les voleurs dé- signent sous le nom de musique, est com- posée de tous les malfaiteurs qui, après leur arrestation, se mettent à table (dé- noncent).—CANLER.

Passer à la —, *to be placed in the presence of informers for identi- fication ;* (card-sharpers') *swind- ling at cards.*

Musiquer (card-sharpers'), *to mark a card with the nail.*

Musser (popular), *to smell.*

Mutilés, *m. pl.* (military), *soldiers of the punishment companies in Africa, who are sent there as a penalty for purposely maiming themselves in order to escape mili- tary service.*

Mylord, *m.* (popular), *hackney coach,* "growler."

**AGEANT,**
or na-
geoir, *m.*
(thieves'),
fish.

Nageoires,
f. pl. (popu-
lar), *large
whiskers in
the shape of fins ; arms,* or
"benders ;" *hands,* or "fins."
Un monsieur à —, *a prostitute's
bully,* or "pensioner." For list
of synonyms see **Poisson.**

Naguet, *m.* (thieves'), *purse,* or
"skin."

Naïade, *f.* (popular). See **Lâcher.**

Naïf, *m.* (printers'), *employer,* or
"boss." The expression is scarcely
used nowadays.

Le vieux pressier resta seul dans l'imprimerie dont le maître, autrement dit le
"naïf," venait de mourir.—BALZAC.

Narquois, or **drille,** *m.* (old cant),
formerly *a thievish or vagrant old
soldier.*

Drilles ou narquois sont des soldats qui
truchent la flamme sous le bras, et battent
en ruine les entiffes et tous les creux des
vergnes . . . ils ont fait banqueroute au
grand coëre et ne veulent pas être ses sujets
ni le reconnaître.—*Le Jargon de l'Argot.*

Parler — formerly had the signification of *to talk the jargon of
vagabonds.* This variety of vagabonds has much contributed to
the formation of the lingo.

Nase, *m.* (popular), *nose,* or
"snorter." For synonyms see
Morviau.

Nasée, *f.* (popular), *pinch of snuff.*
Literally *a noseful.*

Naser quelqu'un (popular), is
equivalent to "avoir quelqu'un
dans le nez," *to have a strong dislike for one, to abominate one.*

Naturalisme, *m.* (familiar), *method of the Naturalistic School.*

Notre République va avoir son expression littéraire. Cette expression, selon moi,
sera forcément le naturalisme, j'entends la
méthode expérimentale et analytique.—
ZOLA.

Rigaud's definition of "naturalisme" is worth recording. He
says of it : "Nouvelle couche
de littérateurs qui sont en train
de fonder le musée Dupuytren de
la syphilis morale, en s'attachant
à faire ressortir dans leurs œuvres
les côtés monstrueux et ignobles
de la nature humaine."

Naturaliste, *adj. and m.* (familiar),
which depicts life from nature.

Pour qu' eul' théâtre soit vraiment naturaliste, camaro, faut qui soit humain.
—TRUBLOT, *Cri du Peuple.*

Un —, *a writer of the Naturalistic
School,* one who in most cases has
a natural penchant for filth.

Nature, *f.* (familiar), comme c'est
— ! *how human-like !* Un bifteck
—, *a steak with no accompaniment
in the shape of vegetables.* (Popular) Nature, *woman's privities.*

Vous allez voir ensuite la belle Anarchiste qui possède deux natures.—Gros Claude, *Gil Blas.*

Navarin, *m.* (thieves'), *turnip;* (familiar) *a kind of Irish stew;* (popular) *scraps of meat from butchers' stalls retailed at a low price to poor people.*

Navet, *m.* (familiar), *hypocrite with bland polished manners,* a kind of Mr. Pecksniff; *fool, dunce,* or "*flat.*" Le champ de navets, *the cemetery.*

Je ne sais pas seulement à quel endroit du champ de navets on a enterré le pauvre vieux, j'étais au dépôt.—Louise Michel.

(Familiar and popular) Avoir du jus de — dans les veines, *to be lacking in energy, to be a "sappy."* Des navets! *an ejaculation of refusal.*

Ohé! les gendarmes, ohé! des navets!—H. Monnier.

Also *is expressive of incredulity, impossibility.* See **Nèfles.**

Il faut avoir fait trois ans de Conservatoire pour savoir parler ... alors on sait donner aux mots leur valeur; mais sans cela! ...—Des navets!—E. Monteil.

(Artists') Navets, *rounded arms or legs showing no muscle.*

Navette, *f.* (thieves'), *pedlar.*

Nazaret, *m.* (popular), *nose,* "boko." See **Morviau.**

Naze, *m.* (popular and thieves'), *nose,* "smeller, or smelling-cheat." For synonyms see **Morviau.**

Nazi, *m.* (popular and thieves'), *venereal disease,* "Venus' curse."

Naziboter (popular), *to speak through the nose.* J'ai le mirliton bouché, ça me fait —, *I have a cold in the head, that makes me speak through my nose.*

Nazicot, *m.* (popular), *small nose.* See **Morviau.**

Nazonnant, *m.* (popular), *big nose,* "conk." See **Morviau.**

Nèfles, *f. pl.* (familiar and popular), des —! *an expression of refusal, or ejaculation of incredulity.*

Il paraît que cette vierge est bonne, bonne!—à quoi?—A tout. Elle fait des miracles superbes.—Des nèfles!—Monteil.

Kindred expressions are: "Des navets! De l'anis! Tu auras de l'anis dans une écope! Du flan! Tu t'en ferais mourir! Tu t'en ferais péter la sous-ventrière! Mon œil! Flûte! Zut! Et ta sœur? Des plis! La peau! Peau de nœud! De la mousse! Du vent! Des emblèmes! Des vannes! Des fouilles! On t'en fricasse!" which might be rendered by, "Walker! All my eye! You be blowed! You be hanged! Not for Joe! How's your brother Job? Don't you wish you may get it?" &c., and by the Americanism, "Yes, in a horn."

Neg, *m.* (popular), au petit croche, *rag-dealer.* Neg, for négociant; — en viande chaude, *prostitute's bully,* or "pensioner." For the list of synonyms see **Poisson.**

Négociante, *f.* (familiar), *woman who keeps a small shop, and who pretends to sell gentlemen's gloves or perfumery.* When the purchaser tenders a twenty-franc piece for payment, "Do you require change?" the lady asks with an inviting smile, the required change being generally returned "en nature."

Négresse, *f.* (popular), *bottle of red wine.*

Allons, la mère, du piccolo! et deux négresses à la fois, s'il vous plaît.—Ch. Dubois de Gennes.

Une — morte, *an empty bottle,* one which has "M. T." on it, *i.e.,* "Moll Thompson's mark." Termed also "marine."

Le tas de négresses mortes grandissait. Un cimetière de bouteilles.—Zola.

U

Etouffer, éreinter une —, or éternuer sur une —, *to drink a bottle of red wine,* "to crack" *it.* Négresse, *flea.*

Qu'il s'ra content le vieux propriétaire,
Quand il viendra pour toucher son loyer,
D'voir en entrant tout' la paill' par terre
Et les négress's à ses jamb's sautiller.
Parisian Song.

Négresse, *parcel made up in oilskin ;* (sailors') *belt.*

Négriot, *m.* (thieves'), *strong box,* "peter ;" *casket.*

Vous avez entendu ma femme et mes deux momignardes (filles) vous bonnir (dire) que le négriot (coffret) était gras et qu'il plombait (pesait beaucoup).—VIDOCQ.

Neige, *f.* (familiar and popular), boule de —, *negro.* Termed also "bamboula, boîte à cirage, bille de pot-au-feu, mal blanchi," and in the English cant or slang, "bit o' ebony, snowball, lily-white, darky, black cuss."

Nénets, or nénais, *m. pl.* (familiar), *woman's breasts,* "Charlies, dairies, or bubbies." Termed also "avant-postes, avant-scènes, nichons, deux œufs sur le plat ;" (popular) — de veuve, *feeding bottle.*

Nep, *m.* (thieves'), *rascally Jew dealing in counterfeit diamonds, sham jewellery, or who seeks to sell at a high price the cross of an order studded with glass pearls or paste diamonds.*

Ne-te-gêne-pas-dans-le-parc, *m.* (familiar and popular), *short jacket.* Termed also "saute-en-barque, pet-en-l'air, montretout."

Net, *adj.* (popular), un atelier —, *a workshop tabooed by workmen, who forbid any of their fellows to accept work there.*

Nettoyage, *m.* (popular), *loss of all one's money at a game,* or "mucking-out ;" *selling of property ; robbing of property.*

Nettoyé, *adj.* (familiar and popular), *given up for dead,* "done for," or, as the Americans say, a "gone coon ;" *dead,* "settled," *robbed.* Etre —, *to have lost all one's money at some game,* "to have blewed it, or to be a muck-snipe." Also *to be exhausted, done up,* or "gruelled." La monnaie est nettoyée, *the money is gone, spent.*

De la jolie fripouille, les ouvriers ! Toujours en noce. Se fichant de l'ouvrage, vous lâchant au beau milieu d'une commande, reparaissant quand leur monnaie est nettoyée.—ZOLA.

Nettoyer (familiar and popular), *to sell ; to rob ; to clean out at some game,* "to muck out ;" *to kill,* "to do" *for one.* Se faire —, *to be killed.* (Thieves') Nettoyer un bocart, *to break into a house and strip it of all its valuables,* "to do a crib," *or to do a* "ken-crack-lay." Nettoyer, *to apprehend,* "to smug."

Nez, *m.* (familiar and popular), *disappointed look.*

Plus de parts de gâteaux ! Il fallait voir le nez de Boche.—ZOLA.

Prendre dans le —, *to reprimand,* "to give a wigging." Un — en pied de marmite, *short nose with a thick end.* Un — où il pleut dedans, *turned-up nose,* or "pug nose." Nez passé à l'encaustique, *nose which shows a partiality for potations on its owner's part,* or "copper nose." Avoir le — sale, *to be drunk,* or "tight." See **Pompette.** Avoir quelqu'un dans le —, *to entertain feelings of dislike towards one.* Faire son —, *to make a wry face, to look* "glum."

On se mouilla encore d'une tournée générale ; puis on alla à la *Puce qui renifle,* un petit bousingot où il y avait un billard. Le chapelier fit un instant son nez, parce que c'était une maison pas très propre. Le schnick y valait un franc le litre.—Zola, *L'Assommoir.*

Avoir le — creux, *to be cunning,* "to be fly to wot's wot;" *to possess perspicacity.*

Oh! elle avait le nez creux, elle savait déjà comment cela devait tourner.—Zola.

Mettre son — dans le bleu, or se piquer le —, *to get drunk.* See **Pompette.**

Lui se piquait le nez proprement, sans qu'on s'en aperçût. . . . Le zingueur au contraire, devenait dégoûtant, ne pouvait plus boire sans se mettre dans un état ignoble.—Zola, *L'Assommoir.*

Nez de pompettes formerly meant *drunkard's nose,* like that of an "Admiral of the Red," with "grog blossoms."

Nez-de-chien, *m.* (popular), *mixture of beer and brandy.* Avoir le —, *to be drunk.* See **Pompette.**

Niais, *m.* (thieves'), *thief who repents, or who has qualms of conscience.*

Nias, *m.* (thieves'), *me,* "my nibs;" in Italian cant, "monarco, or mia madre." C'est pas pour mon —, *that's not for me.*

Nib, nibergue, niberte (thieves' and cads'), *no; not;* — de braise, *no money.* Ça fait — dans mes blots, *that does not suit me, that's not my game;* — du flanche! *leave off!* "stow faking!" Nib du flanche, le gonse t'exhibe, *leave off, the man is looking at you.* In other terms, "stow it, the gorger's leary." Nib de tous les flanches! S'ils te font la jactance, n'entrave pas dans leurs vannes, ne norgue pas. *Keep dark about all our jobs; if they try to pump you, don't allow yourself to be taken in, do not confess.* Nib au truc, or — du truc, *hold your tongue about any job,* "keep dark."

Nibé (thieves'), *hold your tongue,* "mum your dubber;" *enough.*

Niber (thieves'), *to see,* "to pipe;" *to look,* "to dick." Nibe la gonzesse, *look at the girl,* or "nark the titter." Le rousse te nibe, *the policeman is looking at you,* "the bulky is dicking."

Nibergue (thieves'), *nothing,* "nix."

Est-ce que tu coupes dans les rêves, toi? Quoiqu' ça peut faire des rêves? nibergue! (rien).—Vidocq.

Niberte (thieves'), *nothing,* "nix."

J'avais balancé le bogue que j'avais fourliné et je ne litrais que niberte en valades. —Vidocq. (*I had thrown away the watch which I had stolen, and I had nothing in my pockets.*)

Nicdouille, *m.* (popular), *dunce,* "dunderhead."

Niche, *f.* (roughs'), *house; home.* Rappliquer à la —, *to go home.*

Quand qu' all' rappliqu' à la niche,
Et qu' nous sommes poivrots,
Gare au bataillon d'la guiche,
C'est nous qu'est les dos.
Richepin, *Chanson des Gueux.*

A c'te — ! *go home!*

Nichons, *m. pl.* (familiar), *bosoms,* or "Charlies."

Nana ne fourrait plus de boules de papier dans son corsage. Des nichons lui étaient venus.—Zola.

Nid, *m.* (popular), à poussière, *the navel.* Un pante sans — à poussière, *Adam.* According to a quotation in Mr. O. Davies' *Supplementary English Glossary,* the navel being only of use to attract the aliment *in utero materno,* and Adam having no mother, he had no use of a navel, and therefore it is not to be conceived he had any. Un — à punaises, *a room in a lodging-house,* where the bed is generally a mere "bug-walk."

Un — de noirs, *priests' semi-nary*, alluding to their black vestments.

Nière, or **niert**, *m.* (thieves'), *individual*, "cove, bloke, or cull." The Americans say "cuss."

C'est le moment il n'y a pas un niert dans la trime.—VIDOCQ. (*It's just the time when there's nobody on the road.*)

Nière, *accomplice*, or "stallsman." Manger son —, *to inform against an accomplice*, "to turn rusty and split," or "to turn snitch." Cromper son —, *to save one's accomplice*. Un — à la manque, *accomplice not to be trusted*. Un bon —, *a good fellow*, or "ben cove." Mon —, *I, me*, "my nibs." Termed also mon — bobéchon. Un —, *a clumsy fellow*.

Nif, or **nib** (thieves'), *nothing*, "nix;" *no*. Termed "ack" at Christ's Hospital or Blue Coat School.

Nifer (thieves'), *to cease*, "to stash, to stow, or to cheese."

Nigaudinos, *m.* (popular), *simple-minded fellow*, or "flat."

Nikol (Breton cant), *meat*.

Ningle, *f.* (literary), *gay girl*, "mot." See **Gadoue**.

Niolle, or **gniole**, *m. and adj.* (popular and thieves'), *dunce*, or "flat;" *foolish*.

Vous comprenez que je n'étais pas si niolle (bête) de donner mon centre (nom) pour me faire nettoyer par vos rousses (arrêter par vos agents).—CANLER.

Niolle, *old hat*.

Niolleur, *m.* (popular), *dealer in old hats*.

Niort, *m.* (thieves'), *name of a town*. Aller, or battre à —, *to deny one's guilt*. A play on the above name, and nier, *to deny*.

Niorte, *f.* (thieves'), *flesh*, or "carnish."

Nippe-mal, *m.* (popular), *badly-dressed man*.

Nique, *f.* (thieves'), être — de mèche, *to have no share in some evil deed*.

Elle est nique de mèche (sans aucune complicité), répondit l'amant de la Biffe.—BALZAC.

Niquedoule, *m.* (thieves'), *dunce*, or "go-along."

Ah ! ah ! dit l'Frisé, te v'là morte ! Et l'grand niqu'doul' s'mit à pleurer.
RICHEPIN.

Nisco, or **nix** (popular), *nothing*, "nix;" *no such thing*.

Et moi ! je m'en irais bredouille ? Nisco ! ma biche.—P. MAHALIN.

Nisco braisicoto, *no money*, *no* "tin."

Nisette, *f.* (thieves'), *olive*.

Niveau, *m.* (popular), ne pas trouver son —, *to be drunk*, or "snuffy." See **Pompette**.

Nivet, *m.* (old cant), *hemp*.

Nivette, *f.* (old cant), *hemp-field*.

Nix. See **Nisco**.

Noble étrangère, *f.* (literary), *five-franc piece*.

Nobrer, or **nobler** (thieves'), *to recognize*. Nous sommes noblés et filés, *we are recognized and followed*.

Noc, *m.* (popular), *blockhead*, "cabbage-head."

Noce, *f.* (popular), de bâtons de chaise, *grand jollification*, or "flare up." Also *a fight between a married couple*. Faire la —, *to lead a gay life ; to hold revels*.

Nocer. See **Faire la noce**; (popular) — en Père Peinard, *to indulge in solitary revels*.

Nocerie, *f.* (popular), *revels,* "boozing."

Noceur, *m.* (popular), *one who leads a gay life, a sort of* "jolly dog."

Noceuse, *f.* (popular), *woman of questionable character who shows a partiality for good cheer.*

Nocher (popular), *to ring.* Noche la retentissante, *ring the bell,* or "jerk the tinkler."

Noctambule, *m.* (familiar), *one fond of roving about on the Boulevards at night.*

Noctambuler (familiar), *to sit up, or rove about at night,* "to be on the tiles."

Noctambulisme, *m.* (familiar), *roving about at night.*

Nœud, *m.* (popular), *penis.* Mon — ! *an ejaculation of contempt or refusal.* Filer son —, *to go away,* "to slope;" *to run away,* "to cut the cable and run before the wind," in the language of English sailors. See **Patatrot.** Peau de —, see **Peau.**

Nogue, *f.* (roughs'), *night,* or "darkmans."

Noir, *m. and adj.* (popular), *coffee;* — de peau de nègre, *miserable man, an assistant of rag-pickers.* Du —, *lead,* or "bluey." Un — de trois ronds sans cogne, *a threehalfpenny cup of coffee without brandy.* Pierre noire, *slate.* Un petit père —, *a tankard of wine.* (Familiar) Le cabinet —, *an office in which the letters of persons suspected of being hostile to the government were opened previous to their being forwarded by the post office.*

Le cabinet noir, supprimé en 1830, fut rétabli par le ministre des affaires étrangères, le général Sébastiani. . . . Le cabinet noir n'existait plus de nom sous l'Empire ; il existait de fait aux Tuileries.—*Mémoires de Monsieur Claude.*

La chambre noire, *a councilchamber where Napoléon III. received his agents and formed secret plans.*

Ce fut dans ce cabinet secret que furent résolus la mort de Kelch et l'enlèvement secret des premiers fomentateurs du complot de l'Opéra-Comique.—*Mémoires de Monsieur Claude.*

Bande noire, *a gang of swindlers.* See **Bande.** The *Écho de Paris,* August, 1886, mentions a gang of this description which formed a vast association and victimized wine merchants in all parts of the country :—

Les associés se divisaient en quatre catégories : 1° "Les Faisans ;" 2° "Les Courtiers à la mode ;" 3° "Les Concierges dans le mouvement ;" 4° "Les Fusilleurs." Les "Courtiers à la mode" étaient des individus qui avaient réussi à se faire agréer comme représentants par des maisons de gros. Les "Faisans," par l'intermédiaire des "courtiers," et avec la complaisance des "concierges dans le mouvement," se faisaient faire des envois de pièces de vins soit en gare, soit à domicile. Les "Fusilleurs" achetaient ces pièces de vin à vil prix et les revendaient aussi cher que possible.

(Saint-Cyr School) Une noire fontaine, *an inkstand.*

Noisette, *f.* (popular), avoir un asticot dans la —, *to be* "cracked." For synonyms see **Avoir.**

Noix, *f.* (popular), escailleux de — (obsolete), *slow man,* "slow-coach."

Et Dieu, quelz escailleux de noix,
Qui venez cy de tous cottez,
Ou, par la foy que je vous doys,
D'une grosse pelle de boys
Vos trouz de cul seront sellez.
Farce nouvelle.

Une coquille de —, *a very small glass.* (Military) Gauler des —, *to fence badly.* An allusion to a man knocking down walnuts from a tree with a rod.

A ce compte-là on ne doit pas faire de grands progrès en escrime ?—Eh ! justement . . . on a beau être cavalier et avoir toujours le bancal au côté . . . on barbotte . . . on gaule des noix. — DUBOIS DE GENNES.

Nom, *m.* (theatrical), *actor of note,* " star."

Bourgoin prenait des élèves du Conservatoire pour accompagner son "nom," quelquefois aussi des cabotins de province. —E. MONTEIL.

(Popular) Un — de Dieu, *disparaging epithet,* the equivalent being, in English slang, "bally fellow."

L'homme de chambre, au café ! Dort-t'y assez ce nom de Dieu-là !—G. COURTELINE.

Nombril (card-players'), de religieuse, *the ace of cards,* or "pig's eye." (Thieves') Nombril, *noon.*

Nonnant, *m.,* **nonnante,** *f.* (thieves'), *friend.*

Nonne, *f.* (thieves'), *abettor of a pickpocket.* The accomplices press round the victim during the thief's operations. The proceeds of the robbery pass at once into the hands of one of the "nonnes," called "coqueur," or "bob," in English cant. Faire —, *to form a small crowd in the street so as to attract idlers, and thus to facilitate a pickpocket's operations.* Those who thus aid a confederate are termed "jollies" in the English slang.

Nonneur, *m.* (thieves'), *accomplice.* Termed by English thieves "stallsman, or Philiper." The "Philiper" stands by and looks out for the police while the others commit a robbery, and calls out "Philip !" when anyone approaches. According to Vidocq, there is a variety of "nonneurs" who are merely in the service of other thieves. Their functions are to watch, to hustle the intended victim, and to make off with the valuables handed to them by their principal. The "nonneur" is not always rewarded by a share in the proceeds of the robbery ; he generally receives wages for the day proportionate to the profits obtained in the "business." Manger sur ses nonneurs, *to inform against one's accomplices,* "to blow the gaff, or to turn snitch."

Le quart d'œil lui jabotte
Mange sur tes nonneurs,
Lui tire une carotte,
Lui montant la couleur.
VIDOCQ, *Mémoires.*

Norguer (thieves' and cads'), *to own to a crime ; to confess.* Si le curieux te fait la jactance n'entrave pas, ne norgue pas, *If the judge examines you, do not fall into the snare, do not confess.*

Nosigues, or **nousailles** (thieves'), *we, ourselves.*

Notaire, *m.* (popular), *bar of drinking-shop ; landlord of drinking-shop,* "boss of lushing-crib ;" *tradesman who allows credit.*

Note, *f.* (dandies'), être dans la —, *to be well up in events of the day ; to be a man of the* "period."

Noter (Breton cadgers'), *night.*

Notre, *m.* (thieves'), *accomplice,* or "stallsman ;" "one of our mob."

Nouet (Breton cant), *dead drunk.*

Noueur, *m.* (thieves'), *accomplice,* or "stallsman."

Noujon, *m.* (thieves'), *fish.*

Noune, or **nonne,** *m.* (thieves'), *accomplice who follows in the wake of a pickpocket and receives the stolen property,* "bob."

Nourrice, *f.* (thieves'), *female who purchases stolen property,* or "fence." (Familiar and popular) Et les mois de — (ironical), *and the rest.* Cette dame a trente ans. Et les mois de nourrice ! *This lady is thirty years old. And the rest!* Un dépuceleur de nourrices, *a simpleton,* a "duffer ;" *a silly Lovelace.*

Nourrir (thieves'), une affaire, *to preconcert a scheme for a theft or murder.*

Nourrir une affaire, c'est l'avoir en perspective, en attendant le moment propice pour l'exécution.—VIDOCQ.

Nourrir un poupard, or un poupon, *synonymous of* "nourrir une affaire."

Chacun donnait dix-huit ans à ce garçon qui devait avoir nourri ce poupon (comploté, préparé ce crime) pendant un mois.—BALZAC.

Nourrisseur, *m.* (popular), *eating-house keeper,* or "boss of a grubbing-crib;" (thieves') *thief who a long time beforehand makes every preparation with the view of committing a robbery or crime.*

Les nourrisseurs préméditent leurs coups de longue main, et ne se hasardent pas à cueillir la poire avant qu'elle ne soit mûre.—VIDOCQ.

Nourrisseur, *housebreaker who devotes his attentions to houses or apartments whose tenants are away on a journey,* such houses being termed "dead 'uns" by English "busters."

Nousailles, or **nouzailles** (thieves'), *we, ourselves.*

Je crois que nous avons été donnés par le chêne qui s'est esgaré de chez nouzailles avec mes frusquins.—VIDOCQ. (*I think we have been informed against by the man who ran away from our place with my clothes.*)

Nouveau jeu, *m.* (literary), *new model; new fashion.*

Nouveauté, *f.* (prostitutes'), faire sa —, *is to take to a fresh* "beat."

Nouvelle, *f. and adj.* (familiar), à la main, *short newspaper paragraph containing some more or less witty aphorism or joke,* "tit-bit;" — couche, *the* "coming" *people.* La —, *the penal settlement of New Caledonia.* Passer à la —, *to be transported,* "to lump the lighter,"

or "to serve Her Majesty for nothing." (Military) Faire une descente sur de nouvelles côtes, *a jeu de mots which has reference to the searching by imprisoned soldiers on the person of a comrade whose first visit it is to the cell, in order to get possession of any money he may have secreted about him.*

Il me semble que ça sent la chair fraîche par ici.—Moi de même ; et il m'est avis que nous allons avoir à faire une "descente sur de nouvelles côtes."—CHARLES DUBOIS DE GENNES, *Le Troupier tel qu'il est à cheval.*

Novembre 33, *m.* (military), *officer or non-commissioned officer who strictly adheres to military regulations;* also *a stew which contains all kinds of condiments.*

Noyau, *m.* (military), *recruit,* "Johnny raw." In the slang of the workshop or prison, *a new-comer.* (Popular) Avoir des noyaux, *to have money,* or "tin."

Nozigue (thieves'), *us.*

T'as donc taffe de nozigue ?—VIDOCQ. (*Are you then afraid of us ?*)

Nuit, *f.* (journalists'), bourgeois de —, *police officers, or detectives, in plain clothes.*

Mon ami d'Hervilly appelle ces sergents de ville déguisés des "bourgeois de nuit ;" l'expression est juste et comique.—FRANCIS ENNE.

Numéro, *m.* (familiar and popular), onze, *legs,* or "Shanks's mare." Prendre la voiture, or le train onze, *to walk;* termed facetiously "pedibus cum jambis." Etre d'un bon —, *to be grotesque or dull.* Gros —, *brothel,* "flash drum, academy, or nanny-shop." Thus called on account of the number of large dimensions placed over the front door of such establishments ; recognizable also by their whitewashed window-panes. Le — cent, *the W.C.,* or "Mrs. Jones." A play on the word sent.

Numéro sept, *rag-picker's hook.*
Je connais ton — (threateningly),
I know who you are! This latter
ejaculation seems to be an awful
threat in the mouths of English
cads. Je retiens ton — (threateningly), *I'll not forget you!* Un
—, *a prostitute in a brothel.* Une
fille à —, *same meaning.*

Il y a trois classes de prostituées : 1° les
filles à numéro ou filles de bordel ; 2° les
filles en carte ou filles isolées ; 3° les filles
insoumises ou filles clandestines. — Léo
Taxil.

(Cocottes') Le — un, *he who keeps
a girl.*

Ça l'amant d'Amanda ! . . . Oui ! Ah !
mais, tu sais, chéri, c'est pas son numéro
un.—Grévin.

Numéroté, *adj.* (familiar), char —,
cab, "shoful, rattler, or growler."

Et sautant dans un char numéroté vous
vous feriez conduire chez elle.—P. Mahalin.

Numérote tes os (popular), *get
ready for a good thrashing*, or *I'll
break every bone in your body*, words
generally uttered previous to a set
to. Varied also by the amiable
invitation, "Viens que je te mange
le nez!"

La rigolade tournait aux querelles et
aux coups. Un grand diable dépenaillé
gueulait : "Je vas te démolir, numérote
tes os !"—Zola.

Nymphe, *f.* (familiar and popular),
girl of indifferent character; — de
Guinée, *negress, a female* "bit o'
ebony;" — verte, *absinthe*, the
beverage being green.

N'y pas couper (military), *to be
confined in the guard-room or cells,
"to be roosted."* Literally *to be
prevented from shirking one's
duties, or deceiving one's superiors.*

Ah ! tu es garde de nuit, fit-il ; eh bien,
attends, mon vieux, tu n'vas pas y couper !
— Quoi, y couper ? hurla le malheureux.
Mais l'autre écumait de colère. Il beu-
glait :—. . . ah ! tu veux faire le paillasse,
mon salaud ; ah ! tu veux empêcher les
autres de dormir ! Laisse faire, va, je vas
l'dire au major, et tu n'y couperas pas de
tes quinze jours de boîte !—G. Courteline.

Also *to be prevented from taking
advantage of others, of* "taking a
rise out of them." Vous n'y
couperez pas, *I'll stop your* "little
game."

Ah ! hurla-t-il alors, vous faites de l'esprit ! Eh bien, mon petit ami, allez vous
rhabiller, je vous fiche mon billet que vous
n'y couperez pas. Je ne saisis pas, sur le
moment, toute l'importance de cette parole
et le sens de l'expression "n'y pas couper"
ne laissa pas que de m'échapper un peu. Je
compris quelques mois plus tard, en apprenant que le brave jeune homme m'avait re-
commandé à l'avance, par une petite lettre
bien sentie, à l'adjudant de mon escadron.
—G. Courteline.

**N'y pas couper de cinq ans de
biribi,** *not to escape five years' service in the* "Compagnies de discipline," *or punishment companies
in Africa.*

Vous avez beau être de la classe, allez,
vous n'y couperez pas de cinq ans de biribi.
—G. Courteline.

 **BÉLIS-ÇAL,** or **obélisqual,** *adj.* (familiar), *very good; splendid; wonderful, marvellous,* "crushing."

Splendide, aveuglant, obélisqual ! Un ban pour la néophyte. Hip, hip, hip, hurrah !—P. Mahalin.

The popular English slang equivalent is "stunning." Says the *Slang Dictionary:* "Costermongers call anything extra good, 'stunning !' sometimes amplified to 'stunning Joe Banks !' when the expression is supposed to be in its most intense form. Joe Banks was a noted character in the last generation. He was the proprietor of a public-house in Dyott Street, Seven Dials, and afterwards, on the demolition of the Rookery, of another in Cranbourne Alley. His houses became well known from their being the resort of the worst characters, while at the same time the strictest decorum was always maintained in them. Joe Banks also acquired a remarkable notoriety by acting as a medium betwixt thieves and their victims. Upon the proper payment to Joe, a watch or a snuff-box would at any time be restored to its lawful owner—'no questions in any case being asked.' The most daring depredators in London placed the fullest confidence in Joe; and it is believed (although the *Biographie Universelle* is quiet upon this point) that he never, in any instance, 'sold' them. He was of the middle height, stout and strongly made, and was always noted for a showy pin and a remarkably 'stunning' necktie. It was this peculiarity in the costume of Mr. Banks, coupled with those true and tried qualities of a friend for which he was famous, that led his customers to proclaim him as 'Stunning Joe Banks !'"

Observasse, *f.* (popular), *remark.* For observation.

Obusier, *m.* (military), *the behind.* Properly *a howitzer.* See **Vasistas.**

Occase, *f.* (general), abbreviation of *occasion.*

En ce bas monde, il ne faut jamais perdre une occase de s'amuser.—E. Monteil.

Mère d'—, *pretended mother.* (Popular) Œil d'—, *glass eye.* (Thieves') Chasse d'—, *glass eye.*

Occasion, *f.* (thieves'), *candle-stick.*

Occir (familiar), used jocularly, *to kill,* "to put one out of his misery."

Occuper (thieves'), s'— de politique, *to extort money from persons by threats of disclosures.*

Les hommes qui se livrent au genre d'escroquerie dit chantage et qui dans leur argot, prétendent s'occuper de politique . . . spéculent sur les habitudes vicieuses de certains individus, pour les attirer, par l'appât de leurs passions secrètes, dans des pièges où ils rançonnent sans peine leur honteuse faiblesse.—TARDIEU, *Etude Médico-légale sur les attentats aux mœurs.*

Oches, or **loches,** *f. pl.* (popular), *ears,* "wattles, or lugs."

Ocréas, *m. pl.* (Saint-Cyr cadets'), *shoes.*

Oculaire astronomique, *m.* (billiard players'), *two balls touching one another,* or "kissing."

Odeur de gousset, *f.* (obsolete), *money.*

Ça fait d'bons lurons qui ont l'odeur du gousset chenument forte. Falloit les gruger d'la bonne faiseuse.—*Amusemens à la Grecque,* 1764.

Œil, *m.* (familiar and popular), *américain, sharp eye.*

Tu vois clair, ma vieille !—Oh ! on a de l'œil.—L'œil américain ! Quand on a fait la campagne d'Afrique !—E. MONTEIL.

Taper dans l'—, *to take one's fancy.* Œil bordé d'anchois, *inflamed eye ;* — de bœuf, *five-franc piece ;* — de verre, *eye-glass ;* — d'occase. See **Occase.** Œil en dedans *is used to express the dull, lack-lustre expression of a drunkard's eye.*

Pris d'absinthe—selon sa louable habitude—Hurluret présidait la cérémonie en sa qualité de capitaine commandant, les poignets enfouis dans les poches, l'œil en dedans.—G. COURTELINE.

Œil en tirelire, *eye with amorous expression ;* — marécageux, *eye with killing expression ;* — qui dit zut, or merde, à l'autre, *squinting eye,* "swivel-eye." A l'—, *gratis.*

L'abbé R. . . . qui s'y connaît, traite un peu les enfants comme sa protégée Annette ; il les exploite ; ils travaillent "à l'œil" pour un salaire au moins insignifiant et pour une becquetée de fayots, accompagnés d'hosties de temps en temps.—FRANCIS ENNE, *Le Radical.*

Avoir l'—, *to have credit,* "tick, jawbone, or day." Faire l'—, *to allow credit.* Crever un — à quelqu'un, *to refuse one credit, to refuse him* "ready gilt tick ;" *to give one a kick behind,* "to toe one's bum," or "to land a kick." L'— est crevé, *no more credit.* The following announcement is sometimes to be read on shop windows : "Crédit est mort ; les mauvais débiteurs lui ont crevé l'œil," which might be rendered by "touch pot, touch penny."

"We know the custom of such houses," continues he, "'tis touch pot, touch penny."—GRAVES, *Spiritual Quixote.*

Ouvrir l'— de 20 francs, de 30 francs, &c., *to give credit for* 20 *francs, &c.* Avoir de l'—, or du chien, *to have elegance, to be* "tsing-tsing." Faire de l'— à une femme, *to court a woman.* Mon — ! *is expressive of refusal ;* may be rendered by "don't you wish you may get it !" or the Americanism, "yes, in a horn." See **Nèfles.** Avoir de l'—, du cheveu, et de la dent *is said of a woman who has preserved her good looks.* Se mettre le doigt dans l'—, *to be mistaken.* S'en battre l'—, *not to care a straw,* a "hang." Un tape à l'—, *a one-eyed man,* or a "seven-sided animal," as "he has an inside, outside, left side, right side, foreside, backside, and blind side." Taper dans l'— à quelqu'un, *to please one, to suit one.* Taper de l'—, *to sleep,* "to have a dose of balmy." Tortiller, or tourner de l'—, *to die*, "to kick the bucket." Avoir un — au beurre noir, *to have a black eye, or eyes in* "half-mourning."

Mais il aperçut Bibi-la-Grillade, qui lisait également l'affiche. Bibi avait un œil au beurre noir, quelque coup de poing attrapé la veille.—ZOLA, *L'Assommoir.*

Des yeux au beurre noir, *black eyes,* "in mourning." The possessor of these is said in pugilistic slang to have his "peepers painted," or to have his "glaziers darkened."

Œillets, *m. pl.* (popular), *eyes,* "top lights, or peepers." Cligner des —, *to wink.*

Œuf, *m.* (popular), *head,* or "nut." Casser son —, *to have a miscarriage.* Un — sur le plat, *twenty-five francs* (*a silver five-franc piece and a twenty-franc gold coin*). Des œufs sur le plat, *black eyes,* or "eyes in mourning." Also *small breasts.*

N'allez pas m'dire qu'une femme qui n'a qu'deux œufs sur le plat posés sur la place d'armes, peut avoir une fluxion vraisemblable à une personne avantagée comme la commandante ? — CHARLES LEROY, *Le Colonel Ramollot.*

Officier, *m.* (popular), *working confectioner; assistant waiter at a café ;* (gamesters') — de tango, or de topo, *cheat,* "tame cheater, or hawk." A play on the words "carte topographique;" (thieves') — de la manicle, *swindler;* (military) — de guérite, *a private soldier ;* — payeur, *comrade who treats the company to drink.*

Officieux, *m.* (familiar), *man-servant.*

Ogre, *m.* (popular), *wholesale rag-dealer.* Formerly *one who kept an office for providing substitutes for those who, having drawn a bad number at the conscription, had to serve in the army; usurer ;*

(thieves') *receiver of stolen property,* or "fence ; *landlord of a wine-shop frequented by thieves,* or "boss of cross-crib ;" (printers') *compositor who works by the day.*

Ogresse, *f.* (thieves'), *proprietress of a wine-shop frequented by thieves,* or "cross-crib ;" *proprietress of a brothel.*

Oie, *f.* (familiar), la petite — (obsolete), *preliminary caresses,* better explained by quotation.

Ce sont les petites faveurs qu'accordent les femmes à leurs amants, comme petits baisers tendres, attouchements et autres badineries, qui conduisent insensiblement plus loin. La petite oie, c'est proprement les préludes de l'amour.—LE ROUX, *Dict. Comique.*

Oignes, *m. pl.* (popular), aux petits —, *excellently, in first-rate style.* For aux petits oignons.

Oignon, *m.* (popular), *money,* or "blunt." For synonyms see **Quibus.** It has been said that the term "blunt" is from the French "blond," sandy or golden colour, and that a parallel may be found in brown or browns, the slang for halfpence. This etymology, it has been said again, may be correct, as it is borne out by the analogy of similar expressions ; blanquillo, for instance, is a word used in Morocco and southern Spain for a small Moorish coin. The "asper" (ασπρὸν) of Constantinople is called by the Turks akcheh, *i.e.,* little white. It seems to me more probable, however, that the word is derived from blanc, an old French coin, or from the nature of the coin itself, which has a blunt circular edge. Arranger aux petits oignons, *to scold vehemently,* "to bully-rag." Chaîne d'oignons, *ten of cards.* Champ d'oignons, see **Champ.** Il y a de l'—, *there is much groaning* *and gnashing of teeth.* An allusion to the tears brought to the eyes by the proximity of onions. Peler des oignons, *to scold,* " to give a wigging." (Familiar and popular) Faire quelque chose aux petits oignons, *to do something excellently, in first-rate style.*

Vous savez, elle est cocasse votre chanson, et vous l'avez détaillée . . . aux petits oignons !—E. MONTEIL.

Un —, *a large watch,* "turnip."

Oiseau, *m.* (popular), faire l'—, *to play the fool.* Aux oiseaux, *very fine, or very good, excellent, perfect,* " out-and-out, first-class."

Ca m' paroît bien tapé, "aux oiseaux," mamzelle. Fourrez un peu la main sous l'empeigne pour voir tout l'fini d'l'ouvrage. —SAINT-FIRMIN, *Le Galant Savetier.*

The origin of this expression comes, no doubt, from certain bindings in fashion in the eighteenth century, which bore birds in the corners. People would say then, une reliure aux oiseaux. Se donner des noms d'—, *is said ironically of gushing lovers who give one another fond appellations.* Oiseau de cage, *prisoner,* " canary ;" — fatal, *crow.* The expression reminds one of Virgil's—

Sæpe sinistra cava prædixit ab ilice cornix,

and of La Fontaine's—

Un corbeau
Tout à l'heure annonçait malheur à quelque oiseau.

Olive de savetier, *f.* (popular), *turnip.* See **Changer.**

Ombre, *f.* (general), *prison,* or " quod."

Elle sera condamnée dans le gerbement de la Pouraille, et grâciée pour révélation après un an d'ombre !—BALZAC.

A l'—, *in prison, in* " quod." Mettre quelqu'un à l'—, *to kill one,* "to do for one." See **Refroidir.**

Omelette, *f.* (military), *practical joke which consists in turning topsy-turvy the bed of a sleeping soldier ;* — du sac, *similar operation performed on the contents of a knapsack.*

Omettre (thieves'), l'—, *to kill him.*

Omnibus, *m.* (popular), *overflow of liquids on the counter of a wine-shop collected in a tank and retailed at a low price ; glass holding a demi-setier of wine.* On some wine-shops in the suburbs may yet be seen the inscription : " Ici on prend l'omnibus." Un —, *a prostitute,* or " mot." Literally *one who may be ridden by all.* For synonyms see **Gadoue.** Omnibus, *extra waiter at a restaurant or café;* also *one who loafs about the streets of Paris without any visible means of livelihood.*

Omnibus, batteur de pavé, c'est-à-dire des gens que l'on rencontre sur tous les points de Paris comme les véhicules dont ils portent le nom, mais qui diffèrent de ceux-ci en ce qu'ils n'ont ni couleur, ni enseigne, ni lanterne pour indiquer où ils vont et d'où ils viennent.—PAUL MAHALIN.

Attendre l'—, *to wait for one's glass to be filled ;* (thieves') — de coni, *hearse ;* — à pègres, *prison van,* or " black Maria."

Omnibusard, *m.* (popular), *beggar who plies his trade in omnibuses.* He pretends not to have sufficient money wherewith to pay his fare, and by a pitiful tale awakens the compassion of the passengers.

Omnicochemar à la colle, *m.* (thieves'), *bus driver.* Thus called because he seems stuck to his box.

Omnicroche, *f.* (thieves'), *omnibus,* " chariot." Faire l'—, *to pick pockets in an omnibus,* an operation which goes among English thieves by the name of " chariot-

buzzing." Gaule d'—, *bus driver.*
Termed also échalas d'—.

On (thieves'), à sa gin, *here is ;* —
à lavarès, *drunken man.* On à
sa gin on à lavarès, *here is a
drunken man.* I have given the
expression in my informant's own
spelling. (Popular) On pave !
*words which mean that a certain
street is to be avoided for fear of
meeting a creditor.*

Exclamation pittoresque qui exprime
l'effroi d'un débiteur amené par hasard à
passer dans une rue où se trouve un "loup."
Le "typo" débiteur fait alors un circuit
plus ou moins long pour éviter la rue où
l' "on pave."—BOUTMY.

(Familiar and popular) On dirait
du veau, *ironical ejaculation of
eulogy.*

> Ici-bas, chacun sur terre
> Cherche à faire du nouveau ;
> Soit un engin pour la guerre,
> Soit à distiller de l'eau.
> Ce que j'veux faire est pratique :
> Changer : "On dirait du veau"
> Par cette phrase plus énergique :
> Va donc, eh ! fourneau !
> A. QUEYRIAUX.

Onchets, *m. pl.* (military), partie
d'—, *a duel.* Onchets, properly
spellicans.

C'est-à-dire que tu es dans l'intention
d'entamer une seconde partie d'onchets,
conséquemment.—C. DUBOIS DE GENNES.

Oncle, *m.* (popular), *usurer.*

Ce mot symbolise l'usure, comme dans
la langue populaire ma tante signifie le prêt
sur gage.—BALZAC.

Mon — du prêt, *pawnbroker's,* or
"lug-shop." (Thieves') Oncle,
jailer, or "jigger-dubber."

Onclesse, *f.* (thieves'), *jailer's
wife.*

Ondoyeuse, *f,* (thieves'), *wash-
hand basin.*

Ongle, *m.* (popular), croche, *miser,*
or "hunks." Avoir les ongles
croches, *to be deceitful, not over-
scrupulous.*

Onguent, *m.* (old cant), *money,* or
"palm grease." See **Quibus.**

Onze (familiar), du — gendarme,
extra large size for gloves.

Ses vastes mains aux doigts écartés,
chaussées de gants presque blancs, dont la
pointure ne devait point être inférieure à
ce que l'on appelle familièrement du "onze
gendarme."—*Le Mot d'Ordre.*

Op', *m.* (boulevards'), for Opéra.

Le premier bal de l'Op', ou, pour mieux
parler, le premier bal masqué de l'Opéra,
est le commencement de l'ère des plaisirs.—
MIRLITON, *Gil Blas.*

Opérateur, *m.* (thieves'), *executioner.*

Opérer (thieves'), *to guillotine.* See
Fauché.

Opineur hésitant, *m.* (popular),
juryman.

Opiumiste, *m.* (familiar), *one who
smokes opium.*

Oranger, *m.* (popular), *woman's
breasts,* "Charlies, dairies, or
bubbies." Termed also "œufs
sur la place d'armes, avant-postes,
avant-scènes, nénais."

Oranges, *f. pl.* (popular), à cochons,
potatoes, "spuds, or bog oranges."

La pomme de terre est aussitôt saluée
par l'argot d'orange à cochons.—BALZAC.

Potatoes are also termed "mur-
phies," probably from the Irish
national liking for them. They are
sometimes called "Donovans."
At the R. M. Academy fried
potatoes go by the name of
"greasers." Des — sur l'étagère,
woman's breasts, "Charlies, bubbies, or dairies."

Les sœurs Souris, dont l'aînée avait été
surnommée la Reine des Amazones, eu égard
à certaine opération chirurgicale qui lui
avait enlevé "une des oranges de son
étagère."—P. MAHALIN.

Orbite, *m.* (popular), se calfeutrer
l'—, *to close one's eyes.*

Ordinaire, *m.* (familiar and popular), *soup and boiled beef at a small restaurant.* Les ordinaires, *menses.*

Ordonnance, *f.* (military), papier qui n'est pas d'—, *bank-notes.* D'ordonnance, properly *regulation.* The French soldier's pay does not, as a rule, enable him to have bank-notes in his possession ; hence the allusion.

Ordonne (popular), Madame J'—, *is said of a woman who likes to order people about, of an imperious person.*

> Quand s'lève Madame J'ordonne,
> Demand' son chocolat.
> Dépêchez-vous, la bonne,
> Surtout n'en buvez pas.
> RÉMY, *Victoire la Cuisinière.*

Ordre, *m.* (military), copier l'—, *to do fatigue duty.* Military wags when detailed for fatigue duty will sometimes say, pointing to their brooms, that they are going to copy the order. (Familiar) Ordre moralien, *ironical appellation applied to the Conservative party by their opponents in* 1879.

Or-dur, *m.* (familiar and popular), *gold-plated brass.* A play on the words or, *gold,* and ordure, *filth.*

Ordures, *f. pl.* (journalists'), boîte aux —, *special column in certain newspapers, reserved, of course, for quotations from hostile contemporaries.* (Popular) Boîte aux —, *the breech.* See **Vasistas.**

Oreillard, *m.* (popular), *ass,* or " moke."

Oreille à l'enfant, *f.* (familiar), avoir fait une —, *is said of a man who has done all that is necessary, in co-operation with others, to be able to think that a child's paternity may be traced to him.*

Orfèvre, *m.* (familiar and popular), *facetiously used for* Morphée. Etre dans les bras de l'—, *to be asleep,* or " in Murphy's arms."

Organe, *f.* (thieves'), *hunger.*

Orgue, *m.* (popular), jouer de l'—, *to snore,* " to drive one's pigs to market." (Thieves') Orgue, *man,* or " cove." Manger sur l'—, or jaspiner de l'—, *to peach, to inform,* " to blow the gaff, to turn snitch." Mon —, ton —, son —, &c., *I, thou, he, myself,* &c. Parler en —, or en iergue, en aille, en muche, *to disguise words by the use of these words as suffixes.* " Vouziergue trouvaille bonorgue ce gigotmuche ? " *Do you think this leg of mutton good ?* A question put to a jailer by the celebrated rogue Cartouche—a French Jack Sheppard and Dick Turpin put together—with a view to ascertain whether his preferred bribe was deemed sufficient.

Orient, *m.* (thieves'), *gold,* or " redge." Une bogue d'—, *a gold watch,* or " red 'un."

> Rebouise donc ce niert, ses maltaises et son pèze sont en salade dans la valade de son croisant ; pécille l'orient avec ta fourchette.—CANLER. (*Look at that man ; his gold coin and change are loose in his waistcoat pocket ; take out the gold with your fingers.*)

Orléanerie, *f.* (journalists'), *series of disparaging anecdotes or facts concerning the Orléans family, and published under the above head in Radical papers.*

Orléans, *m.* (thieves'), *vinegar.* An allusion to the vinegar manufactories at Orleans.

Ornichon, *m.* (thieves'), *chicken,* " cackling cheat."

Ornie, *f.* (thieves' and beggars'), *hen,* " margery prater ;" — de balle, *turkey-hen,* or " cobble colter." Engrailler l'—, *to catch* *a fowl*, generally by angling with a hook and line, the bait being a worm or snail. Termed "snaggling" in the English cant. Engrailler l'— de balle, *to steal turkeys, to be a* "Turkey merchant."

Ornière, *f.* (thieves'), *hen-house,* "cackler's ken."

Ornion, *m.* (thieves'), *capon.*

Orphelin, *m.* (popular), *cigar end ;* — de muraille, *lump of excrement,* "quaker." (Thieves') Orphelin, *goldsmith.* Des orphelins, *gang of thieves,* "mob."

Orpheline de Lacenaire (journalists'), *prostitute of the Boulevard.*

Orphie, *m.* (thieves'), *bird.*

Os (familiar and popular), *money,* "oof, or stumpy." See **Quibus**. With regard to the English slang expression, Mr. T. Lewis O. Davies, in his *Supplementary English Glossary,* says : "Stumpy, *money, that which is paid down on the nail or stump.*"

Reduced to despair, they ransomed themselves by the payment of sixpence a head, or, to adopt his own figurative expression in all its native beauty : "till they was reg'larly done over, and forked out the stumpy."—*Sketches by Boz.*

Called also " pécune," which corresponds to the Eton boys' term "pec" for money, from pecunia. Avoir de l'—, *to have money, to have the* "oof-bird." (Popular) Os à moelle, *a repulsive term for nose,* " conk, smeller, snorter, boko." See **Morviau**. Faire juter l'— à moelle, *to use one's fingers as a handkerchief.* Casser les — de la tête, *to kiss one heartily.*

Osanores, *m. pl.* (thieves'), *teeth,* or "grinders." Jouer des —, *to eat,* "to grub." See **Mastiquer**.

Oseille, *f.* (popular), *money,* "stumpy, or oof." See **Quibus**.

Avoir mangé de l'—, *to be in a bad humour, to be* "snaggy." (Thieves') La faire à l'—, *to do a good* "job." See **Faire**. (Theatrical) Scènes de l'—, *scenes in which the female supernumeraries make their appearance in very suggestive attire.*

Osselets, *m. pl.* (thieves'), *teeth,* " ivories," or " bones."

Ostant (Breton cant), *individual ; master of a house.*

Ostrogoth, *m.* (general), *dunce.* Also *rude, rough fellow.*

Otage, *m.* (popular), *priest,* or " devil-scolder, sky-pilot, snub-devil, cushion-smiter." An allusion to the priests shot during the insurrection of 1871.

Otolondrer (thieves'), *to annoy, to bore,* "to spur."

Otolondreur, *m.* (thieves'), *tiresome man.*

Otro (Breton cant), *pig.*

Ouater (painters'), *to paint outlines with too much vagueness, without vigour.* Properly *to pad.*

Oui (printers'), en plume ! *fiddle-faddle !* (popular) — les lanciers ! *nonsense !* "rot."

Ouistiti, *m.,* envoyer un —, *to break off one's connection with a mistress,* or, as the English slang has it, "to bury a moll."

Lorsqu'une liaison commence à le fatiguer, il envoie un de ses ouistitis P. P. C. Une façon à lui de faire la grimace à ce qu'il n'aime plus. . . . Au grand club on ne dit plus lâcher une maîtresse, mais lui envoyer son ouistiti.—A. DAUDET.

Ourler. See **Beq**.

Ours, *m.* (theatrical), *play which a manager produces on the stage only when he has nothing else at his disposal ; a literary production or article which has been refused* *by every editor.* Marchand, or meneur d'—, *playwright or literary man whose spécialité is to produce "ours," which he offers to every manager or editor.* (Printers') Ours, *idle talk.* Poser un —, *to bore one by idle talk.*

Se dit d'un compagnon, peu disposé au travail, qui vient en déranger un autre sans que celui-ci puisse s'en débarrasser.—BOUTMY.

Ours, *pressman,* or "pig."

Le mouvement de va-et-vient qui ressemble assez à celui de l'ours en cage, par lequel les pressiers se portent de l'encrier à la presse, leur a valu sans doute ce sobriquet.—BALZAC.

(Familiar and popular) Ours, *prison ; guard-room, or cells,* "Irish theatre, or mill." Flanquer à l'—, *to imprison,* "to put in limbo." The latter term, according to the *Slang Dictionary,* comes from limbus, or limbus patrum, a mediæval theological term for purgatory. The Catholic Church teaches that "limbo" was that part of hell where holy people who died before the Redemption were kept. Envoyer à l'—, *to send to the deuce.* A l'—! *to the deuce!*

Assez! assez! à l'ours!—Mes enfants je vous rappelle au calme.—E. MONTEIL, *Cornebois.*

(Popular) Ours, *goose.*

Ourserie, *f.* (popular), *living the life of a bear.*

Oursin, *m.* (thieves'), *young thief,* or "ziff."

Ous' (popular), qu'est mon fusil ? *is expressive of feigned anger at some silly assertion or bad joke;* — que tu demeures? *is expressive of a mock show of interest ;* — que vous allez sans parapluie, *you are a simpleton,* "how's your brother Job?"

Outil, *m.* (prostitutes'), de besoin, *good-for-nothing bully.* (Thieves') Des outils, *housebreaking implements,* "jilts, or twirls."

Outrancier, *m., name given in* 1870 *to those who wished to continue the war.*

Ouvrage, *m.* (popular), *excrement,* or "quaker ;" (thieves') *robbery,* "push, or sneaking budge." See **Grinchissage.**

Ouvrier, *m.* (thieves'), *thief,* or "prig." See **Grinche.**

Il me dit qu'il venait de travailler en cambrouze avec des ouvriers qui venaient de tomber malades.—VIDOCQ. (*He told me he had done some job in the country with thieves who had just been convicted.*)

Ouvrière, *f.* (bullies'), *prostitute ; mistress of a bully.*

Ouvrir. See **Compas.** (Familiar) Ouvrir son robinet, *to begin talking.*

Oh ! bien ! si Linois ouvre son robinet ! . . . On va en entendre de salées.—E. MONTEIL.

Ouvrir l'œil et le bon, *to watch carefully ; to seek to avoid being deceived.*

Ovale, *m.* (thieves'), *oil.* De l'— et de l'acite, *oil and vinegar.*

 **(popular),** faire le —, *to look displeased.*

Pacant, *m.* (thieves'), *peasant,* or "clod;" *clumsy fellow; intruder.*

Mais ce pacant-là va tout gâter.—BALZAC, *Pierre Grassou.*

Paccin, or **pacmon,** *m.* (thieves'), *parcel,* or "peter." From paquet, *parcel.*

Pacquelin, *m.* (thieves'), *country.*

Un suage est à maquiller la sorgue dans la tolle du ratichon du pacquelin.—VIDOCQ. (*A murder and robbery will take place at night in the country priest's house.*)

Brème de —, *map.* Le — du raboin, *the infernal regions.*

Pacquelinage, *m.* (thieves'), *journey.*

Pacqueliner (thieves'), *to travel.*

Pacquelineur, *m.* (thieves'), *traveller.*

Pacsin, paccin, or **pacmon,** *m.* (thieves'), *parcel,* or "peter."

Paf, *adj.* (popular), *drunk,* or "tight." See **Pompette.**

Vous avez été joliment paf hier.—BALZAC.

Paff, *m.* (thieves'), *brandy,* or "bingo," in old English cant.

Quelques voleurs qui, dans un accès de cette bonhomie que produisent deux ou trois coups de "paff" versés à propos, se laisseraient "tirer la carotte" sur leurs affaires passées.—VIDOCQ.

Paffe, *f.* (popular), donner une —, *to thrash,* "to wallop." See **Voie.** Paffe, *shoe,* "trotter-case."

Paffer, or **empaffer** (popular), se —, *to get drunk,* "to get tight." See **Sculpter.**

Pagaie, *f.* (military), mettre en —, literally *en pas gaie, to play on recruits a practical joke, which consists in arranging their beds in such a way that everything will come to the ground directly they get into them.*

Page, *f.* and *m.* (printers'), blanche, *good workman.* Etre — blanche en tout, *to be a good workman and good comrade; to be innocent.*

En cette affaire vous n'êtes pas page blanche.—BOUTMY.

(Popular) Page d'Alphand, *scavenger in the employ of the city of Paris,* M. Alphand being the chief engineer of the Board of Works of that town.

Pagne, *m.* (popular and thieves'), *bed,* "doss, bug-walk, or kip;" (thieves') *provisions brought by friends to a prisoner.*

J'ai un bon cœur; tu l'as vu lorsque je lui portais le "pagne à la Lorcefé" (provision à la Force).—VIDOCQ.

X

Pagnoten (Breton cant), *shrew; girl of indifferent character.*

Pagnoter (popular), *to go to bed;* — avec une grognasse, *to sleep with a woman.*

Pagnotte, *adj.* (popular), *cowardly* (obsolete).

Pagoure (thieves'), *to take; to steal.* Ils l'ont fargué à la dure pour pagoure son bobinarès, *they attacked him in order to steal his watch.*

Paies (popular), c'est tout ce que tu — ? *have you nothing more interesting to say? or, what next?*

Prenez garde, mon fils ! la pente du vice est glissante ; tel qui commence par une peccadille peut finir sur l'échafaud !—C'est tout ce que tu paies ?—RANDON.

Paillasse, *f.* (popular), *body*, or "*apple - cart.*" Termed also "paillasse aux légumes." Crever la — à quelqu'un, *to kill one,* "*to do for one.*"

En voilà assez avec "au chose," il faut lui crever la paillasse ; qui est-ce qui en est ?—G. COURTELINE.

Manger sa —, *to say one's prayers by one's bedside,* "*to chop the whines.*" Bourrer la —, *to eat,* "*to peck.*" Paillasse, *low prostitute,* or "*draggle-tail.*"

Du temps qu'elle faisait la noce,
Jamais on n'aurait pu rencontrer,— c'est certain—
Paillasse plus cynique et plus rude catin.
GILL.

Paillasse à soldats, or de corps de garde, *soldier's wench,* or "*barrack-hack.*" Termed also — à troufion. (Prostitutes') Brûler —, *to make off without paying a prostitute,* termed, in the English slang, "*to do a bilk.*"

Le client n'est pas toujours un miché consciencieux. Quelquefois elles ont affaire à de mauvais plaisants qui ne se font aucun scrupule de ne pas les payer ; en argot de prostitution on appelle cela "brûler paillasse."—LÉO TAXIL.

(Military) Traîne —, *a fourrier, or non-commissioned officer who has charge of the bedding and furniture department.*

Paillasson, *m.* (theatrical), *short play acted before a more important one is performed.*

Le spectacle commença par une petite pièce, le lever de rideau habituel que l'on a, depuis, appelé en argot de coulisses le "paillasson," parcequ'on la joue pendant que les retardataires arrivent.—A. SIRVEN, *La Chasse aux Vierges.*

(Popular) N'avoir plus de — à la porte, *to be bald,* "*to have a bladder of lard.*" For synonyms see **Avoir.**

Eh ! ben ! en v'là un vieux gâteux ! avec son crâne à l'encaustique. S'il avait des cheveux, il serait encore assez réussi. Mais il n'a plus de fil sur la bobine, plus de zin sur la brosse, plus de gazon sur le pré, il a l'caillou déplumé, quoi? Enfin, n'y a plus de paillasson à la porte.—BAUMAINE ET BLONDELET.

Paillasson, *prostitute's lover.* See **Poisson.** Un —, *one who is too fond of the petticoat,* a "*molrower,* or mutton-monger.*"

Paillasson, quoi ! Cœur d'artichaut.

. . . .
A c'fourbis-là, mon vieux garçon,
—Qu'vous m'direz,—on n'fait pas fortune,
Faut un' marmite,—et n'en faut qu'une ;
Y a pas d'fix' pour un paillasson.
GILL, *La Muse à Bibi.*

Paille, *f.* (thieves'), *lace,* or "*driz.*" (Popular) C'est une —! *only a trifle!* The expression is ironical, and is meant to convey just the opposite. Ne plus avoir de — sur le tabouret, *to be bald.* (Military) Paille de fer, *bayonet,* "*cold steel;*" *sword.* Avoir la — au cul, *to be declared physically unfit for military service.* (Card-sharpers') Paille, *swindle at cards, which consists in bending a certain card at the place where it is required to cut the pack.* Couper dans la —, *to cut a pack thus pre-*

pared. Synonymous of "couper dans le pont."

Pailler (gambling cheats'), *to arrange cards, when shuffling them, for cheating,* "to stock broads."

Pailletée, *f.* (popular), *gay girl of the Boulevards.* For list of synonyms see **Gadoue.**

Paillot, *m.* (popular), *door-mat.* Plaquer la tournante sous le —, *to conceal the key under the door-mat.*

Pain, *m.* (popular), *blow;* — à cacheter, *consecrated wafer.* Also *the moon.* Tortorer le — à cacheter, *to partake of communion.* Du — ! *ironical expression of refusal.* Prête-moi dix francs. Dix francs? et du —? *Lend me ten francs? Ten francs? what next?* Manger du — rouge, *to live on the proceeds of thefts.* (Military) Pain à trente-six sous, *soldier's biscuit.* Ton —, son —, a reply which is equivalent to *nothing of the kind, not at all.* Le brigadier a dit qu'il te ficherait au Mazarot. Il y foutra son —. *The corporal said he would send you to the cells. He will do nothing of the kind.*

Paing, *m.* (popular), *blow,* "bang, clout, wipe,"or, as the Americans say, "biff." Passer chez —, *to thrash,* "to wallop." See **Voie.**

Paire, *f.* (popular), de cymbales, *ten francs.* (Thieves') Se faire la —, *to run away,* "to guy." Se faire une — de mains courantes, *to run away,* "to guy." For synonyms see **Patatrot.** (Military) Une — d'étuis de mains courantes, *a pair of boots.*

Pairs, *m. pl.* La chambre des —, *was formerly, at the hulks, the part assigned to convicts for life.*

Paix-là, *m.* (popular), *usher in a court of justice.* I find in Larchey's

Dictionnaire d'Argot the following anecdote :—

Le parasite Montmaur fut un jour persiflé dans une maison. Dès qu'il parut sur le seuil, un des convives se mit à crier guerre ! guerre ! C'était un avocat dont le père avait été huissier. Montmaur n'eut garde de l'oublier en lui répondant : " Combien vous dégénérez, monsieur, car votre père n'a jamais dit que paix ! paix ! "

Palabre, *f.* (popular), *tiresome discourse.*

Paladier, *m.* (thieves'), *meadow.*

Palais, *m.* (thieves'), le courrier du —, *the prison van.* Called " Black Maria " at Newgate. Termed also " panier à salade."

Palas, *adj.* (thieves'), *handsome, pretty, nice,* "dimber."

Pâle, *m.* (domino players'), *the white at dominoes.*

Paleron, *m.* (thieves'), *foot,* "dew-beater."

Palet, *m.* (popular), un —, une thune, or une roue de derrière, *a five-franc piece.*

Paletot, *m.* (popular), *coffin,* "cold meat box." (Familiar) Un — court, *a dandy or* "masher" *of the year* 1882. See **Gommeux.**

Palette, *f.* (popular and thieves'), *guitar ; tooth,* or "ivory ;" *hand,* "duke."

Le diable m'enlève si je me sauve ! Les palettes et les paturons ligotés (les mains et les pieds attachés).—VIDOCQ.

Palichon, *m.* (domino players'), *double blank.*

Pallas, *m.* (popular and thieves'), *puffing speech of mountebanks.*

Ah! c'était le bon temps du "boniment," de l' "invite," du "pallas" :—Prenez, prenez, prenez vos billets.—*Journal Amusant.*

Faire —, *to make a great fuss.* Concerning this term Michel says :—" Terme des camelots et des saltimbanques, emprunté à l'ancienne germania espagnole ou 'hacer pala' se disait quand un voleur se plaçait devant la personne qu'il s'agissait de voler, dans le but d'occuper ses yeux." (Printers') Pallas, *emphatic speech.* Faire —, *to make a great fuss apropos of nothing.* Concerning the expression Boutmy says :— "C'est sans doute par une réminiscence classique qu'on a emprunté ironiquement, pour désigner ce genre de discours, l'un des noms de la sage Minerve, déesse de l'éloquence."

Combien qui y en a, des pègres de la haute qui après avoir roulé sur l'or et l'argent et avoir fait pallas sont allés mourir là-bas.—VIDOCQ.

Pallasser (printers'), *to talk in an emphatic manner.* Probably for parlasser.

Pallasseur, *m.* (printers'), *one who makes diffuse incoherent speeches while seeking to be emphatic.*

Palmé, *m. and adj.* (popular), *stupid, foolish fellow,* a "flat." Literally *one with webbed feet like a goose's.*

Palmipède. See **Palmé.**

Palot, pallot, *m.* (thieves'), *countryman,* "clod." From paille.

Palote, *f.* (thieves'), *peasant woman; moon,* "parish lantern, or Oliver."

Palper (popular), de la galette, *to receive money.* Se —, *to have to do without.*

Je dirai tout ce que tu voudras ; seul'-ment, tu sais, tu peux t' palper, c'est comme des dattes pour être reçu au rapport.—G. COURTELINE.

Palpitant, *m.* (thieves), *the heart,* or "panter."

Va, nous l'avons échappé belle, j'en ai encore le palpitant (cœur) qui bat la générale ; pose ta main là-dessus, sens-tu comme il fait tic-tac ?—VIDOCQ.

Pâmeur, *m.* (thieves'), *fish.* A fish gasps like one swooning.

Pampeluche, Pantin, Pantruche, *m.* (thieves'), *Paris.*

Pampez (Breton cant), *rustic.*

Pampine, *f.* (thieves'), *ugly face,* "knocker-face ;" *sister of mercy.* Pampine (obsolete), *thick-lipped, coarse mouth.*

Et toi, où qu't'iras, vilaine pampine, figure à chien, tête de singe, matelas d'invalide ?—*Riche-en-gueule.*

Pâmure, *f.* (popular), *smart box on the ear,* or "buck-horse."

Pana, *m.* (popular), vieux —, *old miser, old* "hunks."

Panache, *m.* (familiar), avoir du —, *to be elegant, dashing,* "to be tsing-tsing." (Popular) Avoir le —, *to be drunk,* or "screwed." See **Pompette.** Faire —, *to take a flying leap over one's horse's head,* an unwilling one, of course.

Panade, *f. and adj.* (popular), *ugly person ; without energy,* "sappy."

Panailleux, *m.* (popular), *poor starving wretch,* or "quisby."

Panais, *m.* (popular), être en —, *to be in one's shirt, in one's* "flesh bag."

Panama, *m.* (printers'), *gross error,* "mull."

Bévue énorme, dans la composition, l'imposition ou le tirage, et qui nécessite un carton ou un nouveau tirage.—BOUTMY.

(Popular) Panama, *dandy,* or "gorger." For synonyms see **Gommeux.**

Panaris, *m.* (popular), *mother-in-law.* An allusion to the irritating pain caused by a white swelling on the finger.

Panas, *m. pl.* (popular), *dandy,* or "gorger," see **Gommeux;** *rags ; glass splinters and other refuse.* Un —, *poor man out of work, out of* "collar."

Pancarte, *f.* (military), se faire aligner sur la —, *to get punished.*

Pandore, *m.* (familiar and popular), *gendarme.* From a song by Nadaud.

Pané, *adj. and m.* (general), *needy, hard up,* one " in Queer street."

Tous des panés, mon cher ! Pas un n'a coupé dans le pont. Me mènes-tu boulotter au Bouillon Duval?—P. MAHALIN.

Panier à salade, *m.* (popular and thieves'), *prison van,* or " Black Maria."

Puis il se détira et se secoua violemment pour rendre l'élasticité à ses membres engourdis par l'exiguité du compartiment du " panier à salade."—GABORIAU.

Panier au pain, *stomach,* or " bread - basket." Avoir chié dans le — de quelqu'un jusqu'à l'anse, *to have behaved very ill to one.* (Saint Lazare prisoners') Recevoir le —, *to receive provisions brought from the outside.* (Popular) Panier aux crottes, *behind,* or " Nancy."

Pas de clarinette pour secouer le panier aux crottes des dames.—ZOLA.

Remuer le — aux crottes, *to dance,* " to shake a leg." Le — aux ordures, *bed,* "doss, or bug-walk." Panier à deux anses, *man walking with a woman on each arm.* (Journalists') Le — aux ordures, *that part of the paper reserved for quotations from hostile journals.* (Thieves') Le — à Charlot, *the executioner's basket, that which receives the body of the executed criminal.* Charlot is the nickname of the executioner.

A l'autre extrémité de la salle, un groupe de détraqués dévisagent une fille qui a été la maîtresse d'un guillotiné . . . ils aiment l'odeur du panier à Charlot. — LOUISE MICHEL.

Paniot. See **Revidage.**

Panioter. See **Pagnoter.**

Paniquer (thieves), *to be afraid,* or " funky." Se —, *to be on one's guard.* Synonymous of " taffer, avoir le taf, le trac, or la frousse."

Panne, *f.* (general), *poverty ; bad circumstances,* or " Queer street."

Quand il n'y a plus de son, les ânes se battent, n'est-ce pas ? Lantier flairait la panne ; ça l'exaspérait de sentir la maison déjà mangée.—ZOLA.

(Picture dealers') Panne, *inferior picture sold above value.*

Le brocanteur avait groupé un ramassis d'objets tarés, invendables . . . vous m'entendez, vieux . . . pas de carottes, pas de pannes . . . La dame s'y connait.—A. DAUDET, *Les Rois en Exil.*

(Theatrical) Panne, *unimportant part, consisting of a few lines, or part which does not show to advantage an actor's powers.*

Puis, cette saleté de Bordenave lui donnait encore une panne, un rôle de cinquante lignes.—ZOLA.

(Sailors') Laisser quelqu'un en —, *to forsake one in difficulties ; to leave one in the lurch.* Properly *to leave one lying to.*

Amen ! répondit le matelot, mais sans vouloir vous fâcher, la mère, m'est avis que les saints, les anges, et le bon Dieu nous laissent joliment en panne depuis quelque temps.—RICHEPIN, *La Glu.*

Panné, *adj. and m.* (general), *needy ; needy man ;* — comme la Hollande, *very needy, very " hard up."* Etre —, *to be in bad circumstances.*

J'suis un homme propre, moi, et électeur . . . et ouvrier . . . sans ouvrage depuis qu' ma sœur est à Lazare. (La dame lui donne dix sous.) Dix sous ! Va donc eh ! pannée ! (La dame lui dit zut !)—MIRLITON, *Gil Blas,* 1887.

Ça ne serait pas sans faute, car je suis "panné," dieu merci, ni peu ni trop.—VIDOCQ.

The English have the expression, " to be in Queer street."

I am very high in "Queer Street" just now, ma'am, having paid your little bills before I left town.—KINGSLEY, *Two Years Ago.*

Panner quelqu'un (popular), *to win one's money at some game,* "to blew one" *of his money.*

Panoteur, *m.* (popular), *poacher.*

Panoufle, *f.* (popular), *wig,* "periwinkle," Old word panufle, *list-shoe.*

Panser de la main (popular), *to thrash,* "to wallop." Panser, *to groom.*

Pantalon, *m,* (familiar and popular), donner dans le — rouge *is said of a girl who keeps company with a soldier, who has* "an attack of scarlet fever." In the slang of English officers, a girl fond of their company, and who is passed on from one officer to another, is termed "garrison-hack," an officer who is very attentive to such being called a "carpet tomcat." Une boutonnière en —, *a semi-prostitute; a sempstress who walks the street at night for purposes of prostitution.* See **Gadoue.**

Pantalonner une pipe (popular), *to colour a pipe.* From the expression, culotter une pipe.

Pantalzar, *m.* (popular), *trousers,* "sit-upons, hams, or kicks."

Pante, *m.* (popular and thieves'), *man,* "cove." From pantin, *dancing puppet.*

C'est lorsque la marmite n'a pas donné son fade au barbillon, ou quand un pante refuse de payer l'heureux moment qu'il doit à la dame de l'assommoir. Alors il y a une bûchade géngrale,—*Mémoires de Monsieur Claude.*

(Thieves') Dégringoler les pantes, *to rob fools,* that is, people, "to do a cove."

Jusqu'à la hardie gonzesse qui a dégringolé les pantes et vidé jusqu'au fond les finettes des ballonés.—LOUISE MICHEL. (*Up to the bold woman who has* "done the flats," *and emptied the pockets of rich people.*)

Faire le — au machabée, *to murder a man.*

Ah ! c'est . . . la celle qui est au grand pré ! Ça s'en donnait, des airs de la madame bienfaisante ! et ça faisait le pante au machabée pendant ce temps-là.—LOUISE MICHEL. (*Ah ! it's the woman who is at the convict settlement ! She gave herself the airs of a kind lady, and she all the while was murdering men.*)

Pante argoté, *stupid fool,* or "go along ;" — arnau, *man who is alive to the fact that he has been robbed, and who objects ;* — désargoté, *wary man, not easily deceived,* a "wide one, one who is up to the hour of day, or who is fly to wot's wot." Arranger le —, plumer le —, *to swindle a man of his money at cards.* Un — en robe, *a judge,* or "beak ;" *priest,* "devil-dodger, or snub-devil."

J'ai pensé, pour me tirer d'peines,
A m'fair' frèr' des écoles chrétiennes.
Ah ! ouiche ! Et l'taf des tribunaux ?
Puis, j' suis pas pour les pant' en robe,
Avoir l'air d'un mâl, v'là c' que j'gobe.
　　J'aim' mieux êt' dos.
　　RICHEPIN, *La Chanson des Gueux.*

Panthère, or **panthe,** *f.* (popular), faire sa —, or pousser sa —, *to walk up and down in a workshop ; to go from one wine-shop to another.*

Pantière, *f.* (thieves'), *mouth.* From pannetière, *bread-basket.* So it exactly corresponds to the English slang "bread-basket."

Pantin, or **Pantruche,** *m.* (popular), *Paris.* Properly *one of the suburbs of Paris.*

J'ai fait la connaissance d'une petite fille corse, que j'ai rencontrée en arrivant à Pantin (Paris).—BALZAC.

Pantinois, pantruchois, *m. and adj.* (popular), *Parisian.*

Pantouflards, *m. pl.* (familiar and popular), *name given during the siege of* 1871 *to Parisians serving in the* "Garde nationale sédentaire," *whose duties were to keep guard in the interior of the city.*

Pantoufle, *f.* (popular), et cetera . . . —! *words used jocularly on* *completing some arduous, tiresome task,* meaning *nothing more, and so on.* The expression is also used in lieu of an objectionable word forming a climax in sequence to an enumeration, and which, consequently, may easily be divined. In the phrase, C'est un sot, un âne bâté, " et cætera pantoufle," the quaint term acts as a substitute for an obscene word of three letters, which, in the mouth of a Frenchman, expresses the acme of his contempt for another's intellectual worth. The *Voltaire* newspaper says concerning the expression : " *Et cætera . . . pantoufle!* Que signifie cette expression, employée dans le langage populaire? Lorédan Larchey, répond le *Courrier de Vaugelas,* déclare cette locution peu traduisible et dit que le peuple s'en sert comme d'un temps d'arrêt dans une énumération qui menace de devenir malhonnête. Elle est même tout à fait intraduisible si l'on ne considère que le mot français en lui-même et sa signification vulgaire de chaussure de chambre. A ce point de vue étroit, il est impossible de saisir la corrélation existant entre cette pantoufle et un discours dont on veut taire la fin, ou plutôt qu'on n'achève pas parce que la conclusion est trop connue. Le français, qui souvent s'est taillé un vêtement dans la chlamyde des Grecs, n'a pas dédaigné non plus de s'introduire dans leurs pantoufles. Nous disons : *Et cætera pantoufle.* Les Grecs entendaient par là : *Et les autres choses, toutes de même sorte.* Nous sommes en France des traducteurs si serviles, nous avons serré le grec de si près que nous nous sommes confondus avec lui, nous avons traduit le mot grec par *pantoufle!*

Mais d'où nous est venue cette bizarre expression? Comment a-t-elle passé dans notre langue? M. Ch. Toubin pense qu'elle nous est vraisemblablement arrivée par Marseille. C'est possible, mais nous aimons mieux croire que les écoliers du moyen âge, élevés dans le jardin des racines grecques, ont été frappés de la consonnance de *pantoufle* avec l'expression grecque et l'ont adoptée en la francisant, à la façon plaisante des écoliers."

Pantouflé, *m.* (popular), *tailor's assistant.*

Pantre, *m.* (thieves'), *fool,* " flat." An appellation applied by thieves to their victims.

Eh oui, buvons ! qui payera ? ça sera les " pantres."—VIDOCQ.

Faire un coup à l'esbrouffe sur un —, see **Coup à l'esbrouffe.** Arranger les pantres, see **Arranger.**

Pantriot, *m.* (popular and thieves'), *employer,* or "boss;" *foolish young fellow.*

Pantriote, *f.* (popular and thieves'), *foolish girl.*

N'allez pas, dit la grosse boulotte, me vendre, pantriotes que vous êtes.—LOUISE MICHEL.

Pantrouillard, *m.* (popular and thieves'), *man,* the slang synonyms being "pante, gonce, chêne, type, pékin," and the English, "cove, chap, cull, article, codger, buffer."

Pantruche, (thieves'), *Paris.* Termed also " Pantin."

Panturne, *f.* (bullies'), *prostitute,* "doxie." From the Italian cant.

Les souteneurs, dans leur argot, disent : Gaupe, marmite, dabe, largue, ouvrière, guénippe, ponante, ponisse, panturne, panuche, bourre-de-soie.—LÉO TAXIL.

Panuche, *f.* (thieves'), *showily dressed woman,* or "burerk;" *prostitute who lives in a brothel,* a "dress-lodger." See **Gadoue.**

Papa, *m.* (popular), à la —, *in a quiet, sedate manner ; in negligent or slovenly style.*

Deux infectes petites salles éclairées par une demi-douzaine de quinquets, tenues à la papa.--RICHEPIN, *Le Pavé.*

Pape, *m.* (popular), *stupid fellow,* a "flat." (Students') Un —, *a glass of bitters.*

Au Quartier Latin, l'absinthe s'appelle une purée, l'eau-de-vie un pétrole, le bock un cercueil, le bitter un pape.—*Mémoires de Monsieur Claude.*

Papelard, *m.* (thieves') *paper.* Maquiller le —, *to write,* "to screeve."

Papier, *m.* (familiar), à chandelle, *insignificant newspaper ;* — à douleur, *dishonoured bill ;* —Joseph, or de soie, *bank-note,* "rag, screene, soft, or long-tailed one." Parler —, *to write,* "to screeve." Une médaille de — volant, or médaille des Pays-Bas (obsolete), *lump of excrement.*

Oh ! je vais te faire voir à qui tu parles, va, médaille de papier volant vis-à-vis de l'hôtel des Ursins.—*Les Raccoleurs,* 1756.

"In explanation of the above quotation, it must be mentioned that a piece of ground opposite the Hôtel des Ursins in the Cité (that is, in one of the two islands which formed the nucleus of old Paris), was frequented by people for whom *nécessité n'a pas de loi.*" Hence the allusion.

Papillon, *m.* (thieves'), *laundryman ;* — d'auberge, *table-linen ; plate.*

Bientôt à défaut de flamberges
Volent les papillons d'auberges ;
On s'accueille à grands coups de poing
Sur le nez et sur le grouin,
Les Porcherons.

Avoir des papillons noirs (or bleus) dans la sorbonne, *to be despondent, to have the* "blue devils."

Elle soutient que Pavie avait en effet des papillons noirs dans la sorbonne et qu'il n'était venu la trouver . . . que pour se périr.—*Mémoires de Monsieur Claude.*

Papillonner (thieves'), *to steal linen,* "to smug snowy."

Papillonneur, *m.* (thieves'), *a rogue who steals wet clothes hung on lines to dry,* "lully prigger," *or who rifles washerwomen's carts.*

Papillotes, *f. pl.* (familiar), *banknotes,* "flimsies, or long-tailed ones."

Papotage, *m.* (familiar), *chat.*

Papote, or **pocheté,** *m.* (popular), *fool,* or "softy."

Papoter (familiar), *to chat,* "to gabble."

Paquelin, *m.* (thieves'), for patelin, *flatterer.*

Paqueliner (thieves'), *to flatter.*

Paquemon, *m.* (thieves'), *parcel,* or "peter." Paquet, with suffix mon.

Paquet, *m.* (popular), *ridiculously dressed woman,* a "guy." Avoir son —, *to be drunk,* "to be primed." See **Pompette.** (Familiar and popular) Risquer le —, *to venture.* (Card-sharpers') Faire le —, *to cheat by arranging cards in a peculiar manner when shuffling them.*

Paquetier, *m.* (printers'), *compositor who has to deal only with the composition of lines, without titles, &c. ;* — d'honneur, *head* "paquetier."

Parabole, *f.* (thieves'), *paradise.*

Parade, *f.* (military), défiler la —, *to die,* "to lose the number of one's mess." See **Pipe.** (Printers') Parade, *any kind of joke, good or bad*, a " wheeze." (Popular) Bénédiction de —, *kick on the behind ;* alluding to kicks clowns give one another in a preliminary farcical performance outside a booth.

Paradouze, or part-à-douze, *m.* (military), *paradise.* A play on the word paradis.

Paralance, *m.* (popular), *umbrella,* " mush, or rain-napper." From parer, *to ward off*, and lance, *water.*

Parangonner (printers'), *to adjust properly type of different sizes in the composing stick.* Se —, *to steady oneself when one feels groggy.*

Paraphe, *f.* (popular), *slap, blow,* " wipe," or " bang." Détacher une —, or parapher, *to slap one's face,* " to fetch one a wipe in the mug."

Parapluie, *m.* (popular), essence de —, *water,* " Adam's ale." (Military) Envoyer chercher le — de l'escouade, *to send for the squad's umbrella.* A joke perpetrated at the expense of a recruit, or " Johnny raw," who gets crammed by the knowing ones, who make him believe that each squad possesses a gigantic umbrella, entrusted to the care of the latest joined recruits.

Parc, *m.* (thieves'), *theatre,* " gaff." (Popular) Ne-te-gêne-pas-dans-le —, *short jacket.*

Paré, *adj.* (thieves'), être —, *to be ready for execution.* The convict's hair is shorn close by the executioner a few minutes before he is led to the terrible engine. The operation is termed " la toilette du condamné." Hence the expression.

Pareil, *adj.* (thieves'), être —, *to act in concert.*

Parent, *m.* (thieves'), *parishioner.*

Parer (popular), la coque, *to escape some deserved punishment by taking to flight ; to get out of some scrape.* (Thieves') La — à quelqu'un, *to assist one*, that is, to ward off a blow from fortune. La rien — à un aminche, *to readily assist a friend.* (Cocottes') Parer sa côtelette, *to dress, to adorn oneself.*

On n'a pas besoin de tant d'étoffe, d'abord. Et puis ces demoiselles dégottent un boucher dans l'art de parer leurs côtelettes.— P. MAHALIN, *Mesdames de Cœur-volant.*

Parfait, *adj.* (popular), amour, or crème de cocu, *sweet liquor for ladies ;* — amour de chiffonnier, *coarse brandy.* Termed " bingo " in old English cant.

Parfond, *m.* (thieves'), *pie ; pastry,* " magpie."

J'aime la croûte de parfond,
Nos luques nous leur présentons,
Puis dans les boules et frémions,
J'aime la croûte de parfond.
Chanson de l'Argot.

Parfonde, or profonde, *f.* (thieves'), *pocket,* " cly, sky-rocket, or brigh ; " *cellar.*

C'est lui qui a rincé la profonde (cave) de la fille, dit Fil-de-soie à l'oreille du Biffon. On voulait nous coquer le taffe (faire peur) pour nos thunes de balles (nos pièces de cent sous).—BALZAC, *La dernière Incarnation de Vautrin.*

Parigot, *m.* (popular), *Parisian.*

Paris, *m.* (familiar), Monsieur de —, *official title of the executioner.* The office was held by the Samson family for a considerable time. See **Monsieur.**

Parisien, *m.* (military), *active, cheery, knowing soldier ;* (sailors') *awkward man,* " a lubber ; " (horse-dealers') *worthless horse which finds no purchaser,* "screw." Probably an allusion to Paris cabhorses, which are anything but high-mettled steeds. (Domino players') Parisien, *cheating at a game of dominoes.*

Parlement, or **parlementage** (popular), *language, discourse.*

> Un méchant bailli de malheur
> S'avisi de rendre eun' sentence . . .
> Mais si j'savions l'parlementage,
> Tous ces Messieurs qui ont l'honneur,
> Aurient réparé not' malheur,
> En empêchant tout' leux malice
> Par la bonté de leux justice.
> *Les Citrons de Javotte.*

Ouvrir le —, *to talk*, "to jaw."

Parler (popular), chrétien, *to speak intelligibly ;* (theatrical) — du puits, *to waste one's time in idle discourse ;* — sur quelqu'un, *to give the cue before a brother performer has concluded his tirade,* "to corpse" *him ;* (artists') — en bas-relief, *to mutter ;* (popular) — landsman, *to speak German ;* (military) — papier, *to write.*

Parloir des singes, *m.* (prisoners'), *room where prisoners are allowed to see their friends from behind a grating.*

Le meurtrier . . . dépassa la salle des gardiens, laissa à droite le "parloir des singes" et entra dans le greffe.—GABORIAU, *Monsieur Lecoq.*

Parlotter (familiar), *to chat.*

Parlotterie, *f.* (familiar), *chat.*

Parlotteur, *m.* (familiar), *chatterbox,* "clack-box."

Parmesard, *m.* (popular), *poor devil with threadbare clothes.* A play on the word "râpé," *rasped, threadbare*—râpé comme du Parmesan.

Paroissien, *m.* (familiar and popular), *individual.* Un drôle de —, *a queer fellow,* a "rum cove." (Popular) Paroissien de Saint-Pierre aux bœufs, *blockhead,* "cabbage-head."

Paron, *m.* (thieves'), *square,* pas rond.

Paroufle, *f.* (thieves'), *parish.*

Parquet, *m.* (familiar), le —, *is the company of official stockbrokers, who transact business round* "la corbeille," *or circular enclosure in the Stock Exchange.* "Les coulissiers" are the unofficial jobbers, and "courtiers marrons," the kerbstone brokers, many of whom are swindlers. The offices of the Procureur de la République, or public prosecutor, go also by the name of parquet.

Parrain, *m.* (thieves'), *witness.*

Des parrains aboulés dans le burlin du quart d'œil ont bonni qu'ils reconnobraient ma frime pour l'avoir allumée sur la placarde du fourmillon, au moment du grinchissage.—VIDOCQ. (*Some witnesses who came to the office of the "commissaire de police" said that they knew my face because they had seen it in the market-place when the theft took place.*)

Parrain, *barrister,* "mouthpiece ;" *deputy judge ;* — d'altèque, *witness for the defence ;* — bêcheur, *public prosecutor ;* — fargueur, *witness for the prosecution.* Faire suer un —, *to kill a witness.* Un — à la manque, *a false witness,* or "rapper."

It was his constant maxim that he was a pitiful fellow who would stick at a little rapping for his friend.—FIELDING, *J. Wild.*

Parrainage, *m.* (thieves'), *depositions.*

Part, *f.* (obsolete), *kindness.*

C'est-t'y parler ça? Monsieur, j'pense tout d'même que comme vous.—Ma commère, c'est un effet de . . . de votre part.—VADÉ.

Part-à-douze, *m.* (military), *paradise.*

Tas de "gourgauts," vocifère-t-il, ce sont eux qui sont cause de ça ! . . . ah ! nom d'une soupe à l'oignon ! Ils ne le porteront pas en "part-à-douze."—C. DUBOIS DE GENNES.

Partageuse, *f.* (familiar), *kept woman.*

Partageux, *m.* (peasants'), *re-publican.*

Parterre, *m.* (popular), prendre un billet de —, *to fall,* "to come a cropper." A pun : le parterre, *the pit in a theatre ;* par terre, *on the ground.*

Parti, *adj.* (familiar and popular), *drunk ; asleep.*

> Allons, les voilà partis, dit Vautrin en remuant la tête du père Goriot et celle d'Eugène.—BALZAC.

Parti pour la gloire, *drunk,* or "screwed." See **Pompette.**

Particulier, *m.* (military), *civilian;* (familiar) *individual,* " party."

> Vous protestez comme un beau diable, et, si l' particulier s'entête, vous allez sur lui, vous montrez qu' vous n'avez point froid aux yeux en lui disant : "Toi, j' te vas sortir !"—*Le Cri du Peuple,* Janvier, 1887.

Particulière, *f.* (general), *mistress.* Ma —, *my little girl,* my " lady-bird." The word had formerly the meaning of *prostitute.*

Partie, *f.* (popular), faire une — de traversin, *to sleep two in a bed,* "to read a curtain lecture." Fille à parties, *variety of prostitute.* See **Gadoue.**

> En général, pour être admis chez elles, il faut y être présenté par un habitué de leurs réunions ; elles donnent des dîners et des soirées.—LÉO TAXIL.

Partir (military), la paille au cul, *to be discharged after having been under arrest or in prison.* An allusion to the straw in the cells ; — du pied droit, *to act against regulations ;* (familiar and popular) — pour la gloire, *to get drunk,* or "screwed." See **Sculpter.**

Pas, *m.* (military), mettre au —, *to reprimand, to punish ;* (thieves') — si cher ! *do not speak so loud ! hold your tongue !* "mum your dubber!" (popular) — mal . . .

pour le canal *is said of an ugly woman.*

Pascailler (thieves'), *to supplant one.*

Pasclin, pasquelin, *m.* (thieves'), *country.* Le boulanger t'entrolle en son —, *may the devil take you to his abode.*

Passade, *f.* (printers'), *pecuniary aid allowed to workmen for whom work cannot be found ;* (familiar) *temporary intercourse with a woman.* Donner une —, *to place one's hands on a bather's shoulders and pass over him, meanwhile sending him below the surface.*

Passant, *m.* (thieves'), *shoe,* or "trotter-case."

Passante, *f.* (thieves'), *shuttle.* Pousser la —, *to weave.*

> Elle pousse la passante, là-bas à Aube-rive pour du temps, va ! Elle aura de la neige sur la hurse (tête) quand tu la re-verras.—LOUISE MICHEL.

Passe, *f.* (thieves'), *guillotine.* Etre gerbé à la —, *to be sentenced to death.* Ecornifler à la —, *to kill.* (Prostitutes') Faire une —, *to meet a man in a house of accom-modation.*

> En province . . . les maisons de la plus haute classe sont assez luxueuses sans at-teindre au faste sardanapalesque des lu-panars aristocratiques de la capitale: le prix de la passe y est de dix francs, cinq francs au minimum.—LÉO TAXIL.

(Familiar) Maison de —, *house of accommodation,* "flash drum."

Passé, *adj.* (popular) être — au bain de réglisse, *to belong to the negro race, to be a* "bit o' ebony." Negroes go by the appellations of "boîte à cirage, bamboula, bille de pot au feu, boule de neige."

Passe-cric, *m.* (thieves'), *passport.*

Passe-de-cambre, *f.* (thieves'), *slipper.*

Passe-lacet, *m.* (familiar), *gay girl,* "mot." For list of synonyms see **Gadoue.**

Passe-lance, *m.* (thieves'), *boat.* From passer, and lance, *water.*

Passe-passe, *m.* (card-sharpers'), *swindling trick at cards, which consists in passing a card over.* Joueur de —, *swindler.* Rabelais uses the term jouer de passe-passe with the signification of *to steal :—*

Qui desrobe, ravist et joue de passe-passe.—*Pantagruel.*

Passer (popular), au bleu, *to disappear ;* (military) — à la casserole, *the operation consists in placing a man suffering from a dangerous venereal disease in a vapour bath, and leaving him there till he becomes unconscious.* It is for him a case of " kill or cure ; " — au dixième, *to become mad ;* — des curettes, *to make a fool of one,* " to bamboozle."

Mon lapin, faut pas qu' çà te la coupe, mais j'suis trop ancien au peloton pour qu'on essaye de me passer des curettes.— G. COURTELINE.

Passer la jambe à Thomas, or à Jules, *to empty the privy tub.* (Familiar) Passer devant la glace, *to pay,* " to shell out." An allusion to the looking-glass behind the counter of cafés or restaurants, and before which one must stand while paying for the reckoning ; *to obtain gratis the favours of a prostitute at a brothel ;* — devant la mairie, *to get married without the assistance of the registrar, to live* " tally ; " — la main dans les cheveux, *to praise,* " to give soft sawder." Termed " genuine " at Winchester School ; (general) — l'arme à gauche, *to die,* " to kick the bucket." See **Pipe.** Termed, in the English military slang, " to lose the number of one's mess."

Un criminel que la débauche
Avait conduit à l'échafaud,
Au moment d'passer l'arme à gauche
Dit à l'oreille du bourreau :
Y a plus moyen d'rigoler,
Plus d'cascades, d'rigolades,
C'est inutil' d'essayer,
Y a plus moyen d'rigoler !
LÉON GARNIER.

Se — quelque chose sous le nez, *to drink,* " to liquor up." See **Rincer.** (Shopmen's) Passer debout, *to be punctual at the shop ;* (thieves') — à la plume, *to be ill-treated by a detective,* " to be set about by a nark ; " — à casserole, *to be informed against ;* — à la fabrication, *to be robbed ;* — à la sorgue, *to sleep,* " to doss ; " — chez paings, or au tabac, *to thrash ;* — par les piques, *to be in danger.* Se — de belle, *not to get one's share of booty,* or " regulars ; " *to find nothing to rob.* (Theatrical) Ne pas — la rampe *is said of an actor or play that find no great favour with the public.* (Familiar) Ne pas pouvoir, or ne plus pouvoir — sous la porte Saint-Denis *is said of an unfortunate man whose wife has one or more lovers.* (Roughs') Passer à travers, *to thrash, to be thrashed.* See **Voie.** Se — le chiffon, *to wash one's face.* (Police) Passer au tabac, *to compel a prisoner to obey by ill-treating him ;* — la censure, *to inspect prisoners so as to pick out old offenders ;* (convicts') — sur le banc, *to be flogged.*

Passé-singe, *m.* (popular and thieves'), *very cunning, knowing man, an old bird not to be caught by chaff.*

Pas d'ça Lisette, casquez d'abord. Je vous connais, vous êtes marlou mais je suis passé-singe.—VIDOCQ. (*None of your tricks ; pay first of all. I know you ; you are a cunning fellow, but I am an old bird, not to be caught by chaff.*)

Passes, *m. pl.* (thieves'), *shoes ;* — à la rousse, *elegant shoes.*

Passez-moi le fil (military), ironical expression which may be rendered by, *Well, what next I wonder !*

Passifleur, *m.* (popular and thieves'), *shoemaker,* or "*snob.*"

Passifs, *m. pl.* (printers' and thieves'), *shoes.*

> Et mes passifs, déjà veufs de semelle,
> M'ont aujourd'hui planté là tout à fait.
> *Chanson du Rouleur.*

Pastille, *f.* (familiar), venir en pastilles de Vichy, *to go to an evening party without having been invited to the dinner which precedes it.* Vichy salts facilitate digestion. (Popular) Pastille, *fifty-centime coin.* See **Moule.** Détacher une — dans son culbutant, *to ease oneself in a manner which may be better described by the Latin word* "*crepitare.*"

Pastiquer (thieves'), *to pass ;* — la maltouze, *to smuggle.* From passer.

Pastourelle, *f.* (military), *trumpet call for extra drill.*

Patagueule, *adj. and m.* (popular), *one who gives himself airs ; a conceited ass.* Etre —, *to show ridiculous affectation.*

> C'est lui qui trouvait ça patagueule, de jouer le drame devant le monde !... elle le prenait peut-être pour un dépuceleur de nourrices, à venir l'intimider avec ses histoires.—ZOLA.

Patarasses, *f. pl.* (thieves'), *small pads made of rags used by convicts to avoid the painful friction of their fetters.*

> Il me semble encore le voir sur le banc treize faire des patarasses (bourrelets pour garantir les jambes) pour les fagots (forçats).—VIDOCQ.

Patard, *m.* (popular), *a two-sous coin.* Termed patac by Rabelais.

Patatrot, *m.* (thieves'), faire le —, *to decamp, to run away.* The synonyms for various kinds of slang are : "Faire la fille de l'air, le lézard, le jat jat, la paire, cric, gilles ; jouer la fille de l'air, se déguiser en cerf, s'évanouir, se cramper, tirer sa crampe, se lâcher du ballon, se la couler, se donner de l'air, se pousser du Zeph, se sylphider, se la trotter, se la courir, se faire la débinette, jouer des fourchettes, se la donner, se la briser, ramasser un bidon, se la casser, se la tirer, tirer ses grinches, valser, se tirer les pincettes, se tirer des pieds, se tirer les baladoires, les pattes, les trimoires, or les flûtes ; jouer des guibes, or des quilles, se carapater, se barrer, baudrouiller, se cavaler, faire une cavale, jouer des paturons, happer le taillis, flasquer du poivre, décaniller, décarer, exhiber son prussien, démurger, désarrer, gagner les gigoteaux, se faire une paire de mains courantes à la mode, fendre l'ergot, filer son nœud, se défiler, s'écarbouiller, esballonner, filer son cable par le bout, faire chibis, déraper, fouiner, se la fracturer, jouer des gambettes, s'esbigner, ramoner ses tuyaux, foutre le camp, tirer le chausson, se vanner, ambier, chier du poivre, se débiner, caleter, attacher une gamelle, camper." In the English slang : "To skedaddle, to cut one's lucky, to sling one's hook, to make beef, to guy, to mizzle, to bolt, to cut and run, to slip one's cable, to step it, to leg it, to tip the double, to amputate one's mahogany, to make or to take tracks, to hook it, to absquatulate, to slope, to slip it, to paddle, to evaporate, to vamose, to speel, to tip your rags a gallop, to walk one's chalks, to pike, to hop the twig, to turn it up, to cut the cable and run before the wind."

Pâte, *m. and f.* (artists'), *quality of the layer of colour in oil paintings,*

(popular) *employer,* or "boss."
(Thieves') Une —, or patte, *a file.*
(Printers') Mettre en —, *to allow
a forme of composition to fall, the
letters getting mixed up ; to make
"pie."* (Literary) Pâte ferme, *an
article written throughout without
any blanks.* Se mettre en —, *to fall.*
Etre mis en —, *to receive a blow
or a wound in a fight.*

Pâté, *m.* (printers'), *type of different
kinds, which has got mixed up.*
Faire du —, *to distribute such
type.* Pâté de la veille, *meal provided for the compositors who are
about to do night work.* (Popular)
Pâté d'ermite, *walnut.*

Il ne faisoit chez soi plus grand festin que
de pastez d'hermite.—Qu'est-ce que cette
viande ?—Noix, amandes, noisettes.—*Le
Moyen de Parvenir.*

Pâtée, *f.* (popular), *thrashing,*
"walloping." See **Voie.**

Patente, *f.* (popular), *bully's cap.*

Patenté, *m.* (popular), *woman's
bully,* "pensioner." For synonyms see **Poisson.**

Paternel, *m.* (students'), *father,*
"governor."

Patinage, *m.* (popular), *liberties
taken with a woman,* "slewthering," as the Irish term it, or
"fiddling."

Patiner (popular), *to handle ; to
take liberties with a woman ; —* le
trottoir, *to walk the street as a
prostitute ; —* la dame de pique,
or le carton, *to play cards.* Se —,
to hurry ; to run away, "to
brush." See **Patatrot.** Se —
en double, *to hurry.*

Donnez-moi votre bagage tout en bloc,
que j'arrange tout ça en deux temps et cinq
mouvements ; il s'agit de se patiner en
double.—C. DUBOIS DE GENNES.

Pâtissier, *m.* (popular), sale —,
dirty man, "chatty ;" *an unscrupulous, heartless man.*

Patoche, *f.* (school-boys'), *cut on
the hand given by a schoolmaster
with a ruler ;* (popular) *hand,*
"daddle."

Retire tes patoches, colle-moi ça dans un
tiroir.—ZOLA.

Patouiller (popular), *to handle.*

Patraque, *f.* (thieves'), *patrol.*
(Military) Perdre la —, *to become
crazy.*

Au colon? C'est-y que tu perds la patraque ? Où c'est qu' t'as vu que les hommes
punis de cellule peuvent causer au colonel ?
—G. COURTELINE.

Patrarque, or **patraque,** *f.*
(thieves'), *police patrol.*

Mais déjà la patrarque,
Au clair de la moucharde
Nous reluque de loin.
VIDOCQ.

Patrie, *f.* (Bohemians'), *chest of
drawers.*

Patron, *m.* (military), *colonel.*
Termed also "colon."

Patron-minette, *m.* (popular),
dawn ; formerly *a gang of notorious rogues.*

Patrouille, *f.* (popular), être en —,
to have drinking revels, "to be
on the tiles."

Patte, *f.* (artists'), avoir de la —,
to have a skilful touch. Une —
d'enfer, *a dashing style.*

Je le transportai le plus fidèlement possible
sur ma toile . . . il me dit d'un ton rogue :
"Cela est plein de chic et de ficelles ; vous
avez une patte d'enfer."—TH. GAUTIER,
Les Jeune France.

(Popular) Un entonnoir à —, *a
wine-glass.* Fournir des pattes,
to go away, "to bunk." Se payer
une paire de pattes, or se tirer des
pattes, *to run away,* "to crush."
See **Patatrot.**

Un fichu tour que m'a fait un voyageur,
il s'est tiré des pattes pendant que ma
berline roulait.—*Mémoires de Monsieur
Claude.*

(Military) Pattes de crapaud,

epaulets. (Roughs') Ramasser les pattes à un gas, *to thrash one,* "to wallop" *one*. (Familiar and popular) Pattes de lapin, *short whiskers*. Termed also "hauts de côtelettes." Aller à —, *to go on foot*.

Patte-d'oie, *f.* (popular), *crossways*.

Patu, *m.* (popular), *flat cake*.

Pâturer (popular), *to eat,* "to grub." See **Mastiquer**.

Paturons, *m. pl.* (popular and thieves'), *feet,* "dew-beaters." Jouer des —, se tirer les —, *to run away,* "to brush, to guy." See **Patatrot**.

Paume, *f.* (popular), *loss; difficulty; fix*. Faire une —, *to fail*.

Paumer (thieves'), *to take,* "to collar;" *to apprehend,* "to smug." Etre paumé, *to be apprehended,* "to be smugged."

Tu n'as pas oublié c't escarpe qui après avoir voulu buter une largue sur le Pont au Change, se jeta à la lance pour échapper à la poursuite de l'abadis et que tu fis enquiller chez mézigue au moment où il allait être paumé.—Vidocq.

Paumer la sorbonne, *to become mad,* or "balmy." Se faire — marron, *to be caught in the act, red-handed*. Paumé marron, *caught in the act*.

Les voilà, comme dans la chanson de Manon, "tretous paumés marrons."—Vidocq.

(Thieves' and cads') Paumer, *to lose,* "to blew." T'es à l'affure? Non, j'ai paumé tout mon carme. *Have you made any profits? No, I have lost all my money*. Paumer son fade, *to spend one's money;* — l'atout, *to lose heart*.

Paupière, *f.* (popular), s'en battre la —, *not to care a straw, not to care a* "hang."

Pauses, *f. pl.* (musicians'), compter des —, *to take a nap*.

Pavé, *m.* (familiar), réclame, *overdone puff which misses the mark*. An allusion to the proverbial pavé de l'ours, or act of an ill-advised friend who, thinking to render a service, does an ill turn. (Familiar and popular) Des pavés, *creditors*.

De là on communiquait avec les caves et la cour, ce qui permettait à Tom d'entrer, de sortir, sans être vu, d'éviter les fâcheux et les créanciers, ce qu'en argot parisien on appelle les "pavés."—A. Daudet.

A man who has several creditors living in a street which he deems prudent to avoid, will say, "Il y a des barricades." (Popular) Faire la place pour les pavés à ressort, *to pretend to be looking for some work to do*. Inspecteur des pavés, *idle fellow who prefers sauntering about to working*. N'avoir plus de pavés dans la rue de la gueule, *to be toothless*. (Freemasons') Pavé mosaïque, *hall of meeting of freemasons*. For other expressions connected with the word see **Fusiller, Gratter**.

Pavée, *f.* (popular), rue —, *street where one may fall in with one's creditors, and which, in consequence, is to be avoided*. See **Paver**.

Paver (familiar). On pave ! *exclamation which is meant to denote that a certain street alluded to is to be avoided as being frequented by one's creditors*.

Pavillon, *m.* (popular), *madcap; throat*. S'humecter le —, *to drink,* "to wet, or whet one's whistle." See **Rincer**.

Pavillonner (thieves'), *to drink; to make merry*.

Ensuite on renquillera dans la taule à mézigue pour refaiter gourdement et chenument pavillonner.—Vidocq.

Pavois, *adj.* (popular), *intoxicated,* "screwed." See **Pompette.** Etre —, *to be intoxicated, or to talk nonsense, like one in his cups, like one* " cup shotten."

Pavoiser (sailors'), se —, *to dress oneself in Sunday clothes.* Etre pavoisé en noir, *to be in a towering rage, to look as black as thunder.*

Payer (popular), se — une culotte, *to get drunk, to go on the* "booze."

J' mets pas d'habit, mais sacrebleu ! Faudra que j' me paie un' culotte.
E. CARRÉ.

(Theatrical) Faire — la goutte, *to hiss,* "to goose." (Printers') Payer son article sept, *to pay for one's footing.* An allusion to some regulation of printers' by-laws. (Thieves') Faire —, *to get one convicted.*

Il complota de me faire payer (condamner).—VIDOCQ.

Payot, *m.* (thieves'), *convict employed as accountant at a penal settlement*—an office eagerly sought after.

Pays, *m.* (literary), Bréda, *the Quartier Bréda, one much patronized by cocottes—a kind of Paris Pimlico.* (Popular) Le — des marmottes, *mother earth.* S'en aller dans le — des marmottes, *to die,* "to kick the bucket." (Familiar) Le — des fourrures, *group of certain speculators on 'Change.*

Il (le Krach) a jeté l'alarme parmi les toquets de loutre et dans le Pays des fourrures. On appelle ainsi : d'un côté les femmes qui jouent, les timbalières, comme je les ai appelées ; de l'autre, des gens du monde qui se groupent, couverts de paletots fourrés d'astrakan ou de loutre, dans un coin de la Bourse.—J. CLARETIE.

Pays-Bas, *m. pl.* (popular), *the breech,* or " Nancy." Properly *the Netherlands.*

Payse, *f.* (military), *sweetheart.*

Pchutt, pschutt, gratin, vlan, *m.* (familiar), *the pink of fashion.*

Pchutteux, *m. and adj.* (familiar), *dashing,* " tsing tsing ; " *dandy,* or " masher." For synonymous expressions see **Gommeux.**

Peau, *f.* (popular), *woman of questionable character ; prostitute.*

Guy qui m' préfère une Christiane Andermatt ! . . . parc' qu'elle a du linge, et de l'éducation, et des principes. . . . A faute bien, parbleu ! comm' les autres, c'te peau-là, mais y lui faut des accessoires : eul' clair d'lune, des ruines.—*Le Cri du Peuple,* 14 Janvier, 1887.

Une — de chien, *same meaning.* For list of synonyms see **Gadoue.** Une — de bouc, *skinny breasts.* Une — de lapin, *a vendor of checks or countermarks at a theatre.* Faire la — de lapin, *to sell countermarks.* La — ! *no ! blow it all !* Faire ronfler la — d'âne, *to beat the drum.* Pour la —, *for nothing, gratis.* Traîner sa —, *to be idling, not knowing what to do,* "to loaf." (Sailors') Peau de bitte et balai de crin, *nothing, not a farthing !* (Soldiers') Peau de balle, de libi, or de nœud, *no, nothing ;* — d'zèbe, — d'balle et balai de crin, *nothing.*

Ici, les hommes ed' la classe, comme v'là moi, ont tout juste peau d'zèbe, peau d'balle et balai de crin !—G. COURTELINE.

Il est poli — d'nœud, *he is polite, oh, just !* (Printers') La peau, *nothing at all.*

De quoi ? on nous apprend la peau. Après le bourrage des lignes, basta. Si on fait quelquechose en sortant de là c'est pas la faute au type qui est censé nous faire l'école.—*Journal des Imprimeurs.*

Peaufiner (popular), *to impart finish to some piece of work.*

Peausser (thieves'), se —, *to dress oneself ; to disguise oneself.*

Bien, je vais me peausser en gendarme j'y serai ; je les entendrai, je réponds de tout.—BALZAC, *Vautrin.*

Peccavi, *m.* (thieves), *sin.*

Pêche, *f.* (popular), *head,* or "tibby," see **Tronche**; *countenance,* or "phiz." Déposer une —, *to ease oneself.* Se faire épiler la —, *to get oneself shaved at the barber's.* Une canne à —, *a lanky individual.* (Literary) Une —à quinze sous, *cocotte of the better sort,* a "pretty horse-breaker." The expression belongs to A. Dumas fils.

N'étaient-elles pas plus sympathiques, ces filles de Paris, que toutes ces drôlesses, pêches à quinze sous de Dumas fils.— MAXIME RUDE.

Pêcher (familiar), à la ligne. See **Ligne**. Pêcher une friture dans le Styx, *to be dead.* Aller — une friture dans le Styx, *to die.* See **Pipe**.

Pêcheur. See **Ligne**.

Péchon, *m.* (old cant), *young scamp; child,* or "kid."

Pécoreur, *m.* (thieves'), *card-sharper,* or "magsman;" *street thief,* or "gun." The latter is a diminutive of gonnuf, or gunnof. A "gun's" practice is known as "gunoving."

Pectoral, *m.* (familiar), s'humecter le —, *to drink,* "to have a drop of something damp, or to wet one's whistle." See **Rincer**.

Pécune, *f.* (popular), *money,* "needful," or loaver." See **Quibus**.

La lune au ras des flots étincelants
Casse en morceaux ses jolis écus blancs.
Bon sang ! que de pécune !
Si ton argent, folle, t'embarrassait
Pourquoi ne pas le mettre en mon gousset,
Ohé, la Lune ?
RICHEPIN, *La Mer.*

Pédé, or **pédéro,** *m.* (popular). From pédéraste, *Sodomist,* or "gentleman of the back door."

Pedzouille, *m.* (familiar and popular), *peasant,* "clod, or chaw-

bacon;" *fellow without any energy; coward.*

Pégale, or **pégole,** *f.* (popular), *pawnbroker's shop,* or "lug chovey."

Pégoce, *m.* (thieves'), *louse,* "gold-backed 'un."

Pégocier, *m.* (thieves'), *a lousy individual,* a "chatty" *fellow.*

Pégrage, or **pégrasse,** *m.*(thieves'), *theft,* "lay;" *thieving,* "prigging." See **Grinchissage**.

Pègre, *m. and f.* (thieves'), un —, *a thief,* or "prig." From the Italian pegro, *idle fellow.* See **Grinche**.

Montron drogue à sa largue,
Bonnis-moi donc, girofle,
Qui sont ces pègres-là ?
Des grinchisseurs de bogues,
Esquinteurs de boutogues,
Les conobres-tu pas ?
VIDOCQ.

Fielding uses the term "prig" for a thief :—

He said he was sorry to see any of his gang guilty of a breach of honour ; that without honour "priggerý" was at an end ; that if a "prig" had but honour he would overlook every vice in the world.—*Mr. Jonathan Wild the Great.*

Un — à marteau, *rogue who confines his attentions to property of small value.* La pègre, *the confraternity of thieves, swindlers, burglars, &c.,* or "family-men." La haute-pègre, *the swell-mob.* La basse-pègre, *low thieves.*

La Haute-Pègre comprend généralement tous les voleurs en habit noir . . . la haute-pègre s'affirme par une adresse incompa-rable ; la basse-pègre, par une férocité qui ne se retrouve que dans le pays des cannibales. —*Mémoires de Monsieur Claude.*

Un — de la haute, *one of the swell-mob.*

Il résultera la preuve que le susdit marquis est tout simplement un pègre de la haute.—VIDOCQ.

Pégrenne, *f.* (thieves'), *hunger.* "Pigritia," says V. Hugo, " est un mot terrible. Il engendre un monde, la pègre, lisez le vol, et un enfer, la pégrenne, lisez la faim. Ainsi la paresse est mère. Elle a un fils, le vol, et une fille, la faim." Caner la —, *to be starving,* "to be bandied."

Si queuquefois la fourgate et Rupin ne lui collaient pas quelques sigues dans l'arguemine, il serait forcé de caner la pégrenne.—VIDOCQ. (*Should the receiver and Rupin not put some money in his hand now and then he would starve.*)

Pégrenner (thieves'), *to have but scanty fare; to suffer from hunger.*

Pégrer (thieves'), *to arrest,* "to smug;" *to steal,* "to claim." See **Grincher.** Pégrer, *to be destitute, to be* "quisby." Je me suis fait — toute ma galette, *I have been* "done" *of all my* "tin." Je viens de — l'artiche à son gniasse, je me suis fait cric et la riflette a cavalé derrière moi pour me —, *I have just eased him of his money and the policeman ran after me to apprehend me.*

Pégriot, *m.,* (thieves'), *young thief,* "ziff."

Le pégriot débute dans cette triste carrière à l'âge de dix à douze ans : alors il vole aux étalages des épiciers, fruitiers ou autres.—CANLER.

Pégriot, *thief who steals only articles of small value.*

Le pégriot occupe les derniers degrés de l'échelle au sommet de laquelle sont placés les pègres de la haute.—*Mémoires de Canler.*

Brûler le —, *to obliterate all traces of a robbery or crime.*

Peigne, *m.* (thieves'), *key,* or "screw;" (popular)—d'allemand, *the fingers.* The expression is old. Rabelais uses it :—

Après se peignoit du peigne de Almaing, c'estoit des quatre doigts et le poulce.—*Gargantua.*

Peigne-cul, *m.* (popular), *coarse, rude fellow ; contemptible fellow.*

Peignée, *f.* (popular), se repasser, or se foutre une —, *to fight,* "to have a mill."

Peigner (popular), avoir d'autres chiens à —, *to have far more important things to do.*

Vous comprenez que j'ai d'autres chiens à peigner que de m'en aller chercher des lits dans un endroit où il n'y en a pas.—G. COURTELINE.

Se —, *to fight.*

Peintre, *m.* (military), *sweeper ;* the broom being assimilated to a brush, and termed "pinceau."

Peinturlure, *f.* (familiar), *worthless picture,* a "daub."

Peinturlurer (familiar), se —, *to paint one's face, to put* "slap" *on.*

Peinturlureur, *m.* (familiar), *artist devoid of any ability,* a "dauber."

Peinturomanie, *f.* (familiar), *mania for pictures.*

Pékin, peckin, or **péquin,** *m.* (military), *civilian.* Michel traces it to pequichinus, and Du Cange to piquechien, both meaning *low fellow;* but more probably it is meant for habitant de Pékin, or it originated from an allusion to the cloth called pékin, much worn under the First Empire by civilians.

Je suis fantassin,
Cet état j'l'aim' bien
Et j'fais autant d'béguins,
Que si j'étais peckin.
E. OUVRARD.

The expression is used also by civilians with the signification of *man,* "party." The term "party" is said to have arisen in the old English justice courts, where, to save "his worship" and the clerk of the court any trouble in exercising their memories with the names of the different plaintiffs, defendants, and witnesses, the word party was generally employed. (Familiar and popular) Pékin chic, *swell; generous or clever fellow.* S'habiller en —, *to dress in mufti.* (Popular) Bousculeur de —, *workman who hates middle-class people, and who seeks to annoy them*—a mason, for instance, who, going by a well-dressed person, brushes with his sackful of plaster against the person's coat, &c. (Saint-Cyr cadets') Pékin de bahut, *a cadet who has finished his studies.* The word "pékin" is synonymous of "chinois," a term of contempt.

Pélago, or **Pélague,** *f.* (thieves'), *the prison of Sainte-Pélagie,* where offenders against the press laws are confined.

> On l'a fourré dans la tirelire
> Avec les pègres d'Pélago.
> RICHEPIN.

Pélard, *m.* (thieves'), *hay.* From pelouse.

Pélarde, *f.* (thieves'), *scythe.*

Pélaud, pélo, or **pélot,** *m.* (popular), *sou.* Corruption of palet.

> Si tu fais ce coup-là, j'arrose de deux litr's de marc ! Ça y est, fais voir tes pélauds.—G. COURTELINE.

Pelé, *m.* (thieves'), *main road,* "high Toby."

Pélican, *m.* (thieves'), *peasant,* or "clod." (Popular) Se camoufler en —, *to assume the garb of a peasant.* (Popular and thieves') Un —, *a dressy prostitute of the Boulevards.*

Pelle (gay girls'), faire danser un homme sur la — à feu, *to make repeated calls on a man's purse.* (Popular) Recevoir la — au cul, *to be dismissed, to get* "the sack."

Pelletas, *m.* (popular), *poor devil.*

Pélo, *m.* (popular). See **Pélaud.**

Pelochon, or **polochon,** *m.* (popular), *bolster.* Se flanquer un coup de —, *to sleep,* "to doss." (Military) Mille pelochons ! *a mild oath,* "darn it."

Pelotage, *m.* (familiar), *flattery,* or "blarney;" *taking liberties with a woman,* or "fiddling." Il y a du —, *is said of a woman with fine, well-developed bosoms, and other charms to match.*

Peloter (familiar and popular), *to thrash; to flatter with a view to obtaining some advantage from one.*

> Il ne blaguait plus le sergent de ville en l'appelant Badingue, allait jusqu'à lui concéder que l'empereur était un bon garçon, peut-être. Il paraissait surtout estimer Virginie . . . c'était visible ; il les pelotait.—ZOLA.

Peloter une femme, *to take liberties with a woman,* "to fiddle," or, as the Irish term it, "to slewther ;" — la dame de pique, or le carton, *to play cards ;* (thieves') — le carme, *to gaze with loving and longing eyes at the gold and silver coins in a money-changer's window ;* (fencing) — quelqu'un, *to worst one at a fencing bout.*

Peloteur, *m.* (popular), *one who is soft-spoken, plausible,* "mealy-mouthed." Also *one fond of taking liberties with the fair sex, fond of* "fiddling," or, as the Irish have it, of "slewthering."

Peloton de chasse, *m.* (military), *extra drill.* Termed "hoxter" at the R. M. Academy.

> Ça vaut tout de même mieux qu'une heure de peloton de chasse.—G. COURTELINE.

Pelouet, *m.* (thieves'), *wolf.*

Pelure, *f.* (general), *coat,* or "benjamin." A parallel expression in furbesche is "scorza," *coat,* properly *bark.*

> Et, en un tour de main, vous auront forcé d'essayer un habillement complet, du galurin (chapeau), aux ripatons (souliers)

en passant par le culbutant, qui est le pantalon, et par la limace qui est la chemise. Puis après que vous leur aurez payé quinze francs une pelure (paletot), qu'elles vous faisaient cent cinquante.—P. Mahalin.

Pendante, *f.* (thieves'), *earring; watch guard,* or "slang."

Pendu, *m.* (Saint-Cyr cadets'), *instructor at the military school of Saint-Cyr;* (popular)—glacé, *street lamp of olden times.* (Drapers') Pendu, *piece of cloth stretched out and hung up.*

Les pièces de drap sont étalées dans de vastes couloirs et suspendues dans toute leur longueur. Ce sont ces pièces de drap que l'on nomme des pendus.—Macé, *Mon Premier Crime.*

Pendule, *f.* (popular), à plumes, *a cock,* or "rooster." Remonter sa —, *to thrash one's wife,* "to quilt one's tart." (Thieves') Faire le coup de la —, *to hold a man with his head down and shake him so that his money drops on the ground.* English thieves term this "hoisting," and hold it to be no robbery.

Péniches, *f. pl.* (popular), *shoes,* or "trotter-cases." See **Ripatons.**

Pénitence, *f.* (gamesters'), être en —, *to be unable to play through want of money.*

Etre en pénitence à Monte-Carlo, ne pas jouer. Elles sont en pénitence pour la journée, la semaine ou la fin du mois, parce-qu'elles ont perdu ce qu'elles avaient à jouer.—*Revue Politique et Littéraire.*

Pénitencier, *m.* (prisoners'), *one who has been sentenced to be imprisoned in a house of correction.*

Penne, *f.* (thieves'), *key,* or "screw," "plume" being a *false key.*

Pente, *f.* (thieves'), *pear.* Probably from pendre. (Popular) Avoir une —, *to be the worse for liquor,* or "screwed." For synonyms see **Pompette.**

Pépette, *f.* (popular), *fifty-centime coin.* Des pépettes, *money.*

Un retentissant succès à pépettes. — Trublot, *Le Cri du Peuple.*

Pépin, *m.* (familiar), *umbrella,* "gingham, or mush." (Popular) Avoir un — pour une femme, *to fancy a woman,* "to be mashed on, or to cotton on" *to a woman.* Déposer un —, *to ease oneself,* "to go to the chapel of ease." See **Mouscailler.** Avoir avalé un —, *to be pregnant,* "to have a white swelling."

Pépitier, *m.* (literary), *adventurer who seeks to make his fortune in business in the colonies.* From pépite, *nugget.*

Percer (familiar), en — d'un autre (d'un autre tonneau), *to relate another story.*

Perche, *f.* (popular), être à la —, *to starve.*

Perche à houblon, *f.* (military). Formerly, before the suppression of the regiments of lancers, *a lance.* Also *very tall, thin man,* "skyscraper, or lamp-post."

Percher (thieves' and popular), *to go to bed.* Termed also "pagnotter, bâcher."

Perdre (popular), le goût du pain, *to die,* "to snuff it." See **Pipe.** Faire — le goût du pain, *to kill.* See **Refroidir.** Perdre ses bas, *not to know what one is about through absence of mind or otherwise;* — son bâton, *to die,* see **Pipe.** Perdre sa clef, *to suffer from diarrhœa;* — un quart, *to attend a friend's funeral.*

Perdrix hollandaise, *f.* (sportsmen's), *pigeon.*

Père, *m.* (thieves' and popular), caillou, *wary man,* or "chick-a-leary bloke," *not to be entrapped by gamblers.* Petit — noir de quatre ans, *a wine tankard hold-*

ing four litres. (Thieves') Le — la reniflette, or le — des renifleurs, *the prefect or head of the police.* Petit — noir, *small wine tankard.*

Bravo ! s'écrièrent tous les bandits en empoignant les petits pères noirs. A la santé du birbe.—Vidocq.

Le — coupe-toujours, *the executioner.* (Artists') Père éternel à trois francs la séance, *a model who poses for holy subjects ;* (gay girls') — douillard, *he who keeps a girl, who has "*douille,*" or money.*

Père-Lachaise. See **Contremarque.**

Périr (popular), se —, *to commit suicide.*

J'avais l'intention de me périr soit avec du poison, soit en me jetant à l'eau.— Canler.

Péritoine, *m.* (popular) tu t'en ferais éclater le —, *expressive of refusal,* "don't you wish you may get it ?" or "yes, in a horn," as the Americans say. See **Nèfles.**

Péritorse, *m.* (students'), *coat, or overcoat.*

Perlot, *m.* (popular), *tobacco,* "baccy." From perle.

Perlotte, *f.* (tailors') *button-hole.*

Permanence, *f.* (gamesters'), *a series of numbers which turn up in succession at roulette or trente et quarante.*

Permission, *f.* (familiar), de dix heures, *a kind of lady's overcoat ; bludgeon ; sword - stick.* (Military) Avoir une — de vingt-quatre heures, *to be on guard duty.* La — trempe, *leave which is expected, but not much hoped for.* Se faire signer une —, *to hand one a leaf of cigarette paper, and to obtain from him in return the tobacco wherewith to roll a cigarette.*

Perpendiculaire, *f.* (thieves' and cads'), *watch-guard,* or "slang." Secouer la —, *to steal a watch-guard,* "to claim a slang."

Perpète, *f.* (thieves'), à —, *for life.* Etre gerbé à —, *to be sentenced to transportation for life, to be booked for a "*lifer.*"*

Perpignan, *m.* (coachmen's), *whip-handle.* It appears that the best whip-handles come from Perpignan.

Perroquet, *m.* (familiar), *glass of absinthe.* Asphyxier, étouffer, étrangler, plumer, or tortiller un —, *to drink absinthe.* Perroquet de savetier, *blackbird.* It is worthy of remark that blackbirds are great favourites with cobblers in all countries.

Perruche, *f.* (popular), *glass of absinthe.*

Perruque, *adj. and f.* (familiar), *old-fashioned.* (Popular) Faire en —, *to procure anything by fraud.* Used especially by workmen in reference to any of their own tools procured at the expense of the master.

Perruquemar, *m.* (popular), *hair-dresser.* From perruquier. Termed also "merlan."

Perruquier, *m.* (military). Dache, — des zouaves, *an imaginary character.* Allez donc raconter cela à Dache, *tell that to the marines.* (Popular) Perruquier de la crotte, *shoeblack.*

Persiennes, *f. pl.* (popular), *spectacles,* "barnacles, or gig-lamps."

Persigner (thieves'), *to break open ;* — une lourde, *to break open a door,* "to strike a jigger ;" — un client, *to cheat a man,* "to stick a cove."

Persil, *m.* (familiar and popular), *the world of cocottes who frequent places of entertainment.*

L'excentrique aventure d'un de ses membres, héros du "Persil" et de la "Gomme." —A. DAUDET.

Aller au —, cueillir le —, travailler dans le —, faire son —, *to walk the street as a prostitute, or to be seeking for clients in public places.*

La grande lorette qui a chevaux et voiture, et qui fait son persil autour du lac, au bois de Boulogne.—LÉO TAXIL.

Ces dames du —, *prostitutes in general.* Le jour du —, *day on which a public entertainment is patronized by cocottes.*

C'est le grand jour du Cirque, jour du persil et du gratin ; le jour des demoiselles qui se respectent et qui sont seules, du reste, à remplir cette fonction et des messieurs dont la boutonnière se fleurit d'un gardénia acheté un louis à la bouquetière du cercle. —P. MAHALIN, *Mesdames de Cœur-Volant.*

Persillard, *m.* (familiar and popular), *Sodomist who lounges about.*

Voici comment un douillard, celui qui cherche son persillard ou sa persilleuse, se reconnaît. . . . Le douillard porte une canne à bec recourbé. Il fait un léger attouchement de sa canne, ou de l'épaule gauche à l'épaule droite du persillard.—*Mémoires de Monsieur Claude.*

Persilleuse, *f. and adj.* (familiar and popular), *street-walker,* or "mot." See **Gadoue.**

La fille persilleuse attend son miché à la gare.—*Mémoires de Monsieur Claude.*

Also *a Sodomist.*

La persilleuse est toujours cravatée (cravaté, voulais-je dire) à la colin ; sa coiffure est une casquette dont la visière de cuir verni tombe sur les yeux et sert en quelque sorte de voile ; elle porte une redingote courte ou une veste boutonnée de manière à dessiner fortement la taille qui déjà est maintenue dans un corset.—LÉO TAXIL.

Personne, *f.* (familiar), la —, *my mistress,* my "little girl," or "tartlet." (Popular) Aller où le roi n'envoie —, *to go to the W. C.,* "to Mrs. Jones." See **Mouscailler.**

Perte, *f.* (thieves'), à — de vue, *for life.* Fagot à — de vue, *one sentenced to penal servitude for life,* or "lifer."

Pertuis, *m.* (popular), aux légumes, *the throat,* or "gutter-lane." Faire tour-mort et demi-clef sur le — aux légumes, *to throttle one.*

Pesciller, pesciguer (thieves'), *to seize, to lay hold of,* "to collar ;" — d'esbrouffe, *to take by force.*

Quel mal qu'il y aurait à lui pesciller d'esbrouffe tout ce qu'elle nous a esgaré, la vieille altriqueuse.—VIDOCQ. (*What harm would there be in taking away from her by force all that she has swindled us out of, the old receiver ?*)

Se —, *to get angry,* "to lose one's hair, to lose one's shirt."

Pèse, or **pèze,** *m.* (thieves'), *collection of money made among thieves at large for the benefit of one who is locked up in jail,* "break, or lead ;" *money,* or "pieces." See **Quibus.** Descendre, or fusiller son —, *to spend one's money.*

Pessigner (thieves'), *to raise.*

Es-tu sinve (simple !), tu seras roide gerbé à la passe (condamné à mort). Ainsi, tu n'as pas d'autre lourde à pessigner (porte à soulever) pour pouvoir rester sur tes paturons (pieds), morfiler, te dessaler et goupiner encore (manger, boire, et voler).— BALZAC.

Peste, *f.* (thieves' and cads'), *police officer,* or "reeler." See **Pot-à-tabac.**

Pet, *m.* (popular), à vingt ongles, *baby.* Abouler un — à vingt ongles, *to be in childbed,* "in the straw." Faire du —, *to kick up a row.* Faire le —, *to fail in business,* "to go to smash." Glorieux comme un —, *insuffer-*

ably conceited. Curieux comme un —, *extremely inquisitive.* Il y a du —! *things look dangerous ; there is a row.* Il n'y a pas de —, *there's nothing to be done there ; all is quiet,* "all serene." (Thieves') Il y a du —! *the police are on the look-out!* Pet! *a rogue's warning cry when he hears footsteps or the police,* "shoe-leather! Philip!" Termed also "chou!"

Pétage, *m.* (thieves'), *trial,* "patter."

Pétarade, *f.* (thieves'), la —, *the hospital of La Salpétrière.*

Pétard, *m.* (artists'), *sensational picture.* The *Salomé* of Henri Regnault, his masterpiece, belongs to that class of paintings. Rater son —, *is said of an artist whose success in producing a sensation at the Exhibition has fallen short of his expectations.* (Literary) Pétard, *sensational book which has a large sale.*

Pourquoi ce qui n'avait pas réussi jusqu'alors, a-t-il été, cette fois, un événement de librairie? ce qu'on appelle, en argot artistique, un pétard.—*Gazette des Tribunaux,* 1882.

Also *a sensational play.*

Si je fais du théâtre, ce sera pour être joué, et, tout en le faisant comme je comprends qu'il doit être,—l'image de la vie. Je ne casserai aucune vitre, ne lancerai aucun pétard.—ZOLA.

(Popular and thieves') Pétard, *the behind,* "Nancy." See **Vasistas.** Pétard, *sou.*

J'aimerais mieux encore turbiner d'achar du matois à la sorgue pour affurer cinquante pétards par luisant que de goupiner.—VIDOCQ. (*I had rather work hard from morning till night to get fifty sous a day than to steal.*)

(Popular) Pétard, *a box on the ear,* or "bang in the gills;" *disturbance, noise, quarrel, scandal.*

Faire du —, *to create a disturbance,* "to kick up a row."

J'sais ben c'que vous m'dit's : qu'il est tard,
Que j'baloche et que j'vagabonde.
Mais j'suis tranquill', j'fais pas d'pétard,
Et j'crois qu'la rue est à tout l'monde.
RICHEPIN.

Des pétards, *haricot beans.* Faire du —, *to make a fuss.*

Inutile de faire tant de pétard . . . l'homme de garde refuse de se lever, c'est très bien, j'en rendrai compte au major.—G. COURTELINE.

Pétarder (popular), *to create a sensation ; to cause scandal, or a disturbance,* "to kick up a row."

Pétardier, *m.* (popular), *one who causes scandal, or a disturbance.*

Pétée, *f.* (popular), se flanquer une fameuse —, *to have a regular* "booze." See **Sculpter.**

Pet-en-l'air, *m.* (popular), *short jacket.*

Contre l'habit léger et clair
La loutre a perdu la bataille.
Nous arborons le pet-en-l'air,
Et les femmes ne vont qu'en taille.
RICHEPIN.

Péter (thieves'), *to make a complaint to the magistrates ;* (popular) — dans la main à quelqu'un, *to be unduly familiar with one ; to fail in keeping one's promise ;* — dans le linge des autres, *to wear borrowed clothes ;* — dans la soie, *to wear a silk dress ;* — sur le mastic, *to forsake work ; to send one to the deuce.* Faire — la châtaigne, *to make a woman of a maiden.* Se faire — la panne, *to eat to excess,* "to scorf." S'en faire — la sous-ventrière. See **Faire.** (Sailors') Péter son lof, *to die.* See **Pipe.** (Military) Tu t'en ferais — le compotier, *ironical expression of refusal.*

Et pour porter mon sabre sous le bras, macache, c'est midi sonné; tu t'en ferais péter l'compotier.—G. COURTELINE.

Pète-sec, *m.* (popular), *strict employer, who never trifles, and is not to be trifled with.*

Péteur, *m.* (thieves'), *complainant; informer,* "nose."

Péteux, *m.* (popular), *breech,* or "Nancy." See **Vasistas**. (Thieves') Etre —, *to feel remorse.*

Petit, *adj.* (familiar and popular), bleu, *rough wine,* such as is retailed at the Paris wine-shops; (popular) — homme noir, *tankard of wine;* — noir, *coffee;* — père noir de quatre ans, *tankard of wine holding four litres;* — pot, *paramour.* Lingère à — crochet (obsolete), *female rag-picker.*

Ma mère voyant qu'elle ne f'roit rien dans le méquier d'actrice publique pour le chant voulut entrer dans l'commerce et s'mit lingère à p'tit crochet.—*Amusemens à la Grecque.*

Petit salé, *baby,* "squeaker." Termed also "gluant."

Avec mes ronds (sous) te voilà fadé (muni, qui a reçu sa part). Tu pourras te payer ton petit salé (enfant) de carton. Oui, répondit-il, merci. Mais tout de même j'aimerais mieux en piger un d'occase, à la foire d'empoigne. Ça serait plus mariolle (malin). Et avec la galette (argent) j'achèterais à la daronne des oranges et du trèfle à blaire (tabac à priser).— RICHEPIN, *Le Pavé.*

Petit chien, *lover, mistress.*

> Mon p'tit chien,
> Ça va bien.
> J't'ach'terai d'abord
> Un p'tit bonnet sans dentelle.
> *Album Lyrique.*

(Thieves') Du — monde, *lentils.* Un — faisan. See **Bande Noire**. Des petits pois, *pimento, allspice.* (Sodomists') Petit Jésus, *a young Sodomist, the abettor of another who obtains money from persons by threats of exposure.*

Le chanteur est un homme jeune encore . . . toutefois, seul, il ne peut "travailler;" il lui faut un compère, . . . puis un jeune et beau garçon qu'il appelle un "petit

Jésus," entièrement vendu à ses intérêts, ayant perdu tout sentiment d'honnêteté, de pudeur. . . . Celui-ci doit servir d'appeau. —LÉO TAXIL.

(Familiar) Bon — camarade *is said ironically of an ill-disposed malevolent colleague.* (Prostitutes') Petit Jésus, *lover or associate of a prostitute,* "Sunday - man." (Printers') Aligner les petits soldats de plomb, *to compose.*

Quand on sait bien aligner les petits soldats de plomb, on vous colle devant une casse, et vous bourrez à quart de pièces; un peu plus tard vous avez demi-pièces et ça vous mène à la fin de l'apprentissage.— *From a Paris printers' newspaper.*

(Tailors') Petits bœufs, *apprentices.*

Pourquoi des coupeurs, des culottiers, des giletiers . . . des pompiers, des tartares (apprentis) nommés aussi petits-bœufs.— MACÉ, *Mon Premier Crime.*

Petit - bocson, *m.* (popular), *church.* Termed also rampante.

Petit-crevé, *m.* (familiar), *dandy,* or "masher." For synonyms see **Gommeux**. A dandy in the seventeenth century went by the quaint appellation of "quand pour Philis." In explanation M. Génin, in his *Récréations Philologiques,* says that all the fops of the period thought themselves bound to be able to sing a certain ditty which was then all the rage and began by the words, "Quand pour Philis." Hence the expression. Tallemant des Réaux, in his *Historiettes,* says of a certain Turcan :—

> Turcan ne saurait vivre
> S'il ne fait le coquet ;
> A l'une il donne un livre
> Et à l'autre un bouquet.
> Il dit de belles choses,
> Ne parle que de roses,
> Que d'œillets et de lys :
> C'est un quand-pour-Philis.

Scarron also mentions the expression :—

A cette heure de tous costés,
Arrivent lui des beautés,
Qu'y n'y viennent qu'à la nuit sombre ;
A ceste heure quand-pour-Philis
Poudrez, frisez, luisans, polis,
Les appelans soleils à l'ombre,
Leur disent fleurettes sans nombre,
Sur leurs roses et sur leurs lys.

Petite, *adj.* (familiar), dame, an euphemism for "cocotte," or "pretty horse-breaker."

Il arrivera que les "petites dames," bien conseillées par les "petits messieurs," comprendront qu'elles ont infiniment plus d'avantages à nous poursuivre devant les juges—qu'à se faire suivre sur les boulevards.—*Echo de Paris*, Oct., 1886.

Petite main, *girl apprenticed to a fleuriste.*

Petit-hôtel, *m.* (thieves'), *police station.* Faire une pose au —, *to be locked up in jail,* "to be in quod."

Petit-que, *m.* (printers'), *semi-colon.*

Il est ainsi nommé parceque le signe (;) remplaçait autrefois le mot latin *que* dans les manuscrits et les premiers livres imprimés.—BOUTMY.

Petits, *adj.* (familiar), messieurs, *despicable young men who live at the expense of prostitutes*—in fact, "pensioners" with an obscene prefix. (Rag-pickers') Charger des — produits, *to work at rag-picking.*

Petmuche, *m.* (thieves' and cads'), *a signal that people are approaching,* "Philip ! or shoe-leather !" Acrémuche, il y a une retentissante ; y a du — voilà le lonsgué. *Look out, there's a bell; someone is coming; here's the master of the house.*

Pétoche, *f.* (popular), être en —, *to follow close in the rear, at one's heels.*

Pétouze, *f.* (old cant), pistole, *old coin.*

Pétra, *m.* (popular), *clumsy man, awkward lout.*

Pétrole, *m.* (popular), *brandy,* or "French cream."

Des bouges où se rassemble la racaille de l'égout, où les faces blèmes sont souvent tatouées de pochons noirs, où il coule parfois du sang dans les saladiers gluants de vin bleu, où les pierreuses viennent se donner du cœur à l'ouvrage en avalant un verre de pétrole qui leur flanque un coup de fer rouge dans l'estomac.—RICHEPIN, *Le Pavé.*

Allumer son —. See **Allumer**.

Pétroleur, *m.* (familiar), *opprobrious name given to the insurgents of* 1870.

Pétronille, *f.* (popular), dévisser la —, *to smash one's head.*

Pétrouskin, *m.* (popular), *idle fellow,* or "bummer;" *breech,* or "Nancy," see **Vasistas**; *peasant,* "clod."

Pétun, *m.* (obsolete), *tobacco; snuff.* From a Brazilian word.

Pétunière, *f.* (popular), *snuff-box,* "sneezer."

Petzouille, *m.* (popular), *the behind,* or "Nancy." See **Vasistas**.

Peuple, *m.* (popular), faire un —, *to be on the staff of supernumeraries at a theatre.* Se foutre du —, *to act as if one cared for nobody's opinion.* Est-ce que vous vous foutez du — ? *Do you mean to laugh at me?*

Peuplier, *m.* (popular), *large twist of tobacco.*

Pévouine, *f.* (sailors'), *little girl, a wee lassie.*

Pèze, *m.* (thieves'), *money,* or "pieces." See **Pèse**.

Je voudrais bien que tous les chouettes zigues qui m'ont fait affurer du pèze puissent en dire autant.—VIDOCQ. (*I wish all the jolly fellows who made me earn some money could say as much.*)

Phalanges, *f. pl.* (familiar), serrer les —, *to shake hands,* "to tip one's daddle."

Pharamineux, *adj.* (familiar), *astounding, marvellous,* "stunning."

Vous savez, Nana vient d'arriver . . . oh ! une entrée, mes enfants ! quelque chose de pharamineux !—ZOLA.

Phare, *m.* (printers'), *lamp.* Properly *lighthouse.*

Pharmacope, *m.* (popular), *apothecary,* "pill-driver."

Pharos, or **pharaut,** *m.* (old cant), *governor of a town.* Michel thinks the word comes from the Spanish faraute, *head man.*

Philantrope, *m.* (pedlars'), *thief,* "prig." For synonyms see **Grinche.**

Philibert, *m.* (thieves'), *thief,* "prig;" *swindler or sharper,* "shark." See **Grinche.**

Philippe, *m.* (popular), *silver or gold coin.* An allusion to the effigy of Louis Philippe.

On dit que tu as poissé nos philippes (filouté nos pièces d'or).—BALZAC.

Philippine, *f.* (familiar and popular). When a person cracks an almond for another, should there be a double kernel, he who cries out first, "Bonjour, Philippine !" can exact a present from the other. The word seems to be a corruption of the German vielliebchen.

Philistin, *m.* (artists'), *a man who belongs to a different set, an outsider, a bourgeois,* a "Philistine." The *Slang Dictionary* says : "Society is supposed to regard all outside its bounds as belonging to the Philistine world. Bohemians regard all cleanly, orderly people who conform to conventionality as Philistines;" (medical) *medical man who, not being on*

the staff *of an hospital, visits the establishment, generally prolonging his stay more than is pleasant or convenient for the members of the staff;* (tailors') *journeyman tailor.* In the English slang a Philistine is a policeman. The German students call all townspeople not of their body "Philister," as English ones say "cads." The departing student says, mournfully, in one of the *Burschenlieder*: "Muss selber nun Philister sein !" *i.e.* "I must now Philistine be !"

Philosophe, *m.* (popular), *poverty-stricken,* or "quisby;" *old or cheap shoe.*

Plus d'une ci-devant beauté, aujourd'hui réduite à l'humble caraco de drap, à la jupe de molleton et aux sabots, si elle ne préfère les "philosophes" (souliers à quinze, vingt et vingt-cinq sols).—VIDOCQ.

Philosophe, *rag-picker,* or "bone-grubber." Philosophes de neuf jours, *shoes out at the sole.* (Thieves') Un —, *one of the light-fingered gentry,* see **Grinche ;** *card-sharper who dispenses with the assistance of an accomplice.*

Philosophie, *f.* (popular), *poverty, neediness.*

Photographier (popular), allez vous faire —, *go to the deuce,* "go to pot."

Pi, parler en —, *to add* "pi" *to each syllable of a word.* Thus couteau becomes coupiteaupi.

Piaf, *m.* (thieves'), *pride ; boasting,* "bouncing."

Pianiste, *m.* (popular), *executioner's assistant.* He is the accompanyist to the executioner, the principal performer.

Piano, *m.* (horse-dealers'), jouer du —, *is said of a horse which has a disunited trot.* Maîtresse de —. See **Maîtresse.**

Pianoter (familiar), *to be a poor performer on the piano.*

On ne devait pas pianoter pendant la nuit.—BALZAC.

Piau, *m.* (printers'), *falsehood,* "cram." From la peau ! *nonsense !* (thieves') *bed.* Pincer le —, *to go to bed, to get into* "kip." See **Pieu.**

Piaulle, piole, or **piolle,** *f.* (thieves'), *house,* "crib, hangs-out, ken ;" *tavern.* Same origin as picter. La — a l'air rupin, *there's plenty to steal in that house.*

Piausser (thieves'), *to sleep,* "to doss." Se —, *to dress ; to go to bed, to get into* "kip."

Ils sont allés se piausser (se coucher) chez Bicêtre.—VIDOCQ.

(Printers') Piausser, *to lie ; to humbug.*

Piausseur, *m.* (printers'), *liar ; humbug.*

Picaillons, *m. pl.* (popular), *money,* "tin." See **Quibus.** Avoir des —, *to be well off,* or "well ballasted." Picaillons is probably a corruption of picarons, *Spanish coin.*

Picanti, *adj.* (thieves'), gau —, *louse,* "gold-backed 'un." See **Basourdir.**

Piccolet, or **picolo,** *m.* (popular), *thin wine.* From picton, which itself comes from the Greek πιεῖν, through picter.

Le suave fromage à la pie . . . et qu'ils mangeaient avec un chanteau de pain bis, avant de boire un gobelet de picolo, de ce vert petit reginglard qui leur piquait un cent d'épingles dans la gorge.—RICHEPIN, *Le Pavé.*

Piche, *m.* (popular), for pique, *spades of cards.*

Pichenet, *m.* (popular), *thin wine.* See **Picton.**

Le pichenet et le vitriol l'engraissaient positivement.—ZOLA.

Pickpocketer (familiar), *to pick pockets.*

Picorage, *m.* (thieves'), *highway robbery.*

Picoure, *f.* (thieves'), *hedge.* Déflotter, or défleurir la —, *to steal linen laid out on a hedge to dry,* "lully prigging." A thief who steals linen is termed "snow-gatherer." La — est fleurie, *there is linen on the hedge,* "snowy on the ruffman."

Picter (popular and thieves'), *to drink,* "to liquor up," or, as the Americans say, "to smile, or to see the man." From the Greek πιεῖν.

Laissez-le donc, nous le ferons picter à la refaite de sorgue.—VIDOCQ. (*Leave him alone, we'll make him drink at dinner.*)

Picter des canons, *to drink glasses of wine.*

Comme moi gagne de la pièce,
Tu pourras picter des canons.
Et sans aller trimer sans cesse,
Te lâcher le fin rigaudon.
Ne crains pas le pré que je brave,
Car de la bride je n'ai pas peur ;
Dans une tôle enquille en brave,
    Fais-toi voleur !

       VIDOCQ.

Allons — un kil, *let us go and drink a litre of wine.* Picter du pivois sans lance, *to drink wine without water.* Picter une rouillarde, *to drink a bottle of wine.* La — à la douce, *to sit over a bottle of wine.*

Picton, *m.* (popular and thieves'), *wine.* Termed also "picolo, nectar, ginglet, ginglard, pichenet, briolet, pivois, bleu, petit bleu, vinasse, blanc, huile,"&c. Picton sans lance, *wine without water*. Un coup de —, *a glass of wine*.

> Encore un coup d'picton,
> La mère Bernard, il n'est pas tard,
> Encore un coup d'picton
> Pour nous mettre à la raison.
> *Old Song.*

Pictonner (popular), *to drink heavily*, "to swill." See **Rincer**.

Pictonneur, *m.* (popular), *drunkard*, "lushington." See **Poivrot**.

Pièce, *f.* (military), de quatre, *syringe;* — grasse, *cook*, or "dripping;" — de sept, *stout man*, "forty guts;" (freemasons') —d'architecture, *speech;* (literary) — de bœuf, *gushing article on the topics of the day;* (theatrical) — de bœuf, *a play in which one obtains the most success;* — à tiroirs, *play with transformation scenes;* — d'été, *bad play;* (prostitutes') — . d'estomac, *lover*, "Sunday man." (Thieves') Vol à la — forcée. This kind of theft requires two confederates, one of whom tenders in payment of a purchase a marked coin. His friend then steps in, makes a purchase, and maintains he has paid for it with a coin of which he gives a description, and which of course is found in the till by the amazed tradesman. (Popular) Une — du pape, or suisse, *an ugly woman*. La — de dix sous, or de dix ronds, *the anus*. N'avoir plus sa — de dix ronds, *to be a Sodomist*. Cracher des pièces de dix sous, *to be parched, dry*.

Coupeau voyant le petit horloger cracher là-bas des pièces de dix sous, lui montra de loin une bouteille ; et, l'autre ayant accepté de la tête, il lui porta la bouteille et un verre.—Zola.

The English have the expression, "to spit sixpences," *to be thirsty*.

He had thought it a rather dry discourse; and beginning to spit sixpences (as his saying was), he gave hints to M. Wild-goose to stop at the first public-house they should come to — Graves, *Spiritual Quixote*.

Pied, *m.* (popular), à dormir debout, *large flat foot;* — de cochon, *pistol*, or "barking iron;" — de nez, *one sou;* — plat, *a Jew*, or "mouchey, Ikey, or sheney." Mettre à —, *to dismiss*, "to give the sack." En avoir son —, *to have had enough of it*. (Thieves') Pied de biche, *short crowbar*, or "jemmy." Termed also "Jacques, l'enfant, sucre de pomme, biribi." Le —, *the ground;* termed also "la dure;" *share*, or "whack." Mon —, ou je casse ! *my share, or I peach*, or "my whack, or I blow the gaff." (Military) Pied, or — bleu, *recruit*, or "Johnny raw."

Je t'en fiche ; y prend un air digne, toise l'infirmier du haut en bas, et te l'engueule comme un pied.—G. Courteline.

Pied de banc, *sergeant*. There are just as many sergeants in a company as there are feet to a bench.

Les sous-officiers sont l'âme de l'armée si les officiers en sont la tête . . . les soldats le savent et le disent bien, et se rendant compte de l'utilité de ces humbles subalternes, ils les appellent les pieds de banc. Enlevez un officier à la compagnie, nul ne s'apercevra du vide ; ôtez un sergent elle deviendra boiteuse. — Hector France, *L'Homme qui Tue*.

Pieds, *m. pl.* (popular), avoir mangé ses —, *to have an offensive breath*. Se tirer des —, *to go away, to run away*, "to hook it." See **Patatrot.** Où mets-tu tes pieds ? *what are you meddling about?* (Military) Avoir les — de châlit, *to be particular, careful*. Avoir les — nattés, *to feel a disinclination for going out, or not to be able to go out*. (Printers') Pieds de mouche, *notes in a book, generally printed in small type*. (Thieves') Avoir les — attachés dans le dos, *to be dogged by the police*, " to get a roasting." (Popular and thieves') Bénir des pieds, *to be hanged*, " to swing, to be scragged." Termed formerly " to fetch a Tyburn stretch," or " to preach at Tyburn Cross," alluding to the penitential speeches made on such occasions. In olden times a hanged person was termed in France " évêque des champs," alluding to the cap which was drawn over the face of the convict, and which represented the mitre, also to the convulsive movements of his legs. It was the custom to erect the gallows in the open country. Hence the expression, " évêque des champs qui donne la bénédiction avec les pieds."

Pier (thieves'), old word, *to drink.* In English slang, " to liquor up," and, as the Americans term the act, " to smile," or " to see the man." See **Rincer**.

Pierre, *f.* (popular), à affûter, *bread,* or " soft tommy ;" (freemasons') — brute, *bread ;* (thieves') — de touche, *confrontation of a male-factor with his victim or with wit-nesses.*

Pierreau, *m.* (military), *recruit,* or " Johnny raw." Also *soldier who has been for one year in the corps.*

Ils tranchaient les questions d'un mot, . . . considéraient du haut de leur impor-tance les brigadiers qu'ils qualifiaient de bleus et de pierreaux, comme s'ils fussent arrivés de la veille.—G. COURTELINE.

Pierreuse, *f.* (popular), *prostitute of the lowest class, who generally prowls near heaps of stones on the road, or in building yards,* " draggle-tail." See **Gadoue**. Concerning this class of prosti-tutes Léo Taxil says : " Il est une classe absolument ignoble, qui est la lie des filles en carte : les pierreuses. On donne ce nom à un genre particulier de femmes

qui ont vieilli dans l'exercice de la prostitution du plus bas étage . . . elles sortent la nuit . . . elles sta-tionnent auprès des chantiers ou à proximité des terrains vagues."

Pierrot, *m.* (popular), *glass of white wine.* Asphyxier un —, *to drink a glass of white wine.* Pierrot, properly, is a pantomimic cha-racter with face painted white and dressed in white attire. (Hair-dressers') Pierrot, *application of lather on the face ;* (military) *recruit,* or " Johnny raw." Termed also " bleu."

Les anciens commencèrent par faire la sourde oreille, supportèrent avec patience les quolibets et les piqûres d'aiguille jusqu'au jour ou un " pierrot," tout nou-vellement arrivé . . . reçut une paire de ca-lottes.—G. COURTELINE.

Also bad soldier who shirks his duty and incurs punishment.

De temps en temps, l'adjudant Flick, en cherchant ses deux " pierrots," constatait leur disparition. Les deux pierrots . . . s'étaient donné un peu d'air. Ces bordées duraient six journées, au bout desquelles ils revenaient fiers comme des paons, fri-sant la désertion de cinq minutes.—G. COURTELINE.

Piesto, *m.* (popular), *money,* " the needful, gilt, or loaver." See **Quibus**.

Piètre, *m.* (thieves'), *rogue who plays the lame man so as to excite the commiseration of the public.*

Pieu, *m.* (thieves'), *crossbar ;* — de la vanterne, *crossbar of a window ;* (popular and thieves') *bed.* From old word piautre, *straw mattress.* The synonyms are, " pucier, halle aux draps, dodo, panier, filasse, fournil ;" in the English slang, " lib, doss, kip," and, in old cant, " lybbege."

Les pant's sont couchés dans leurs pieux, Par conséquent je n'gên' personne. Laissez-moi donc ! j'suis un pauv' vieux. Où qu' vous m'emm'nez, messieurs d'la sonne ?
RICHEPIN.

Spelt also pieux.

> Dès que le réveil entendras
> Tes deux châssis épongeras ;
> La botte aux Cocos donneras,
> Et leur crottin enlèveras,
> A la chambre remonteras
> Faire ton pieux.
> *Les Litanies du Cavalier.*

Se coller dans le —, *to go to bed, to get into the* "kip." **Etre en route pour le —**, *to feel sleepy.* **Etre rivé au —**, *to be passionately attached to a woman.*

Pieuté, *adj.* (popular), **être —**, *to be in bed.*

> Il réfléchit, partagé entre l'inquiétude de coucher le soir à la boîte et le plaisir de rester "pieuté."—G. COURTELINE, *Les Gaietés de l'Escadron.*

Pieuvre, *f.* (familiar), *kept woman.* Properly *octopus.* See **Gadoue**.

Pieuvrisme, *m.* (familiar), *prostitution ; the world of prostitutes.*

Pif, or **pifre**, *m.* (familiar and popular), *nose,* " handle, conk, or snorter." See **Morviau**. The word "pifre" is used by Rabelais with the signification of *fife.* It is, therefore, not improbable that the nasal organ received the appellation on account of its being assimilated to that wind instrument, the more so as other parts of the body bear the names of musical instruments, as trompette, or musette, *face ;* sifflet, *throat ;* guitare, or guimbarde, *head ;* grosse caisse, *body ;* flûtes, *legs,* &c.

> Où que j'vas ? ça vous r'garde pas.
> J'vas où que j'veux, loin d'où que j'suis.
> C'est à côté, tout près d'là-bas.
> Mon pif marche d'vant, et je l'suis.
> RICHEPIN.

C'est pas pour ton —, *that's not for you.* (Thieves') **Etre dans le — comme grinche**, *to be noted as a swindler.* (Prostitutes') **Faire un — d'ocas**, *to find a client,* or "flat."

> J'ai fait que poiroter sous les lansquines en battant mon quart pour faire un pif d'ocas, qui me donne de quoi que mon marlou ne m'éreinte pas de coups.—LOUISE MICHEL.

Piffard, *m.* (popular), *the possessor of a nose remarkable on account of its large proportions or vermilion hue,* like that of a drunkard, an "Admiral of the Red," whose nasal organ bears "grog blossoms."

Piffe, *m.* (thieves'), *breech,* or "blind cheek." See **Vasistas**.

Piffer (popular), *to be discontented, or to look disappointed,* " down in the mouth." Synonymous of " faire son nez."

Pige, *f.* (thieves'), *year,* or "stretch;" *hour ; prison,* or "stir." See **Motte**. (Familiar) **Faire la —**, *to race.* (Printers') **Pige**, *a certain number of lines to be composed in an hour.* **Prendre sa —**, *to ascertain the length of a page or column.*

Pigeon, *m.* (card-sharpers'). **Elever des pigeons**, *to entice dupes into playing in order to fleece them of their money.* (General) **Pigeon**, *a gullible or soft person,* a "pigeon." The vagabonds and brigands of Spain also used the word in their "germania," or robber's language, "palomo," *ignorant, simple.* In the sporting world "sharps and flats" are often called "rooks and pigeons" respectively—sometimes "spiders and flies." When the "pigeon" has been done, he then is entitled to the appellation of "muggins." **Pigeon voyageur**, *a girl of indifferent character who travels up and down a line seeking for clients.* (Cocottes') **Avoir son —**, *to have found a client, to have a* "flat." (Theatrical) **Pigeon**, *part payment of a fee due to an author by the manager of a theatre.* (Familiar) **Aile de —**, *old-fashioned.* An allusion to the headdress preserved by émigrés on their return to France.

Pigeonner (familiar and popular), *to dupe,* or " to do."

Dans celle-là, ce n'est plus moi qui pige, c'est moi qui suis pigeonné.—*Mémoires de Monsieur Claude.*

Pigeonnier, *m.* (familiar), *the boudoir of a cocotte.*

Piger (general), *to detect ; to take,* " to collar ;" *to apprehend,* " to nab."

Eh ! la Gribouille, comment que t'as été pigée, dit une vagabonde à une autre.—Louise Michel.

Piger, *to understand,* " to twig," or, as the Americans say, " to catch on."

Moi aussi . . . mais piges-tu, pas de braise ; ceux qu'ont du poignon dans les finettes peuvent décaniller.—Louise Michel. (*Oh, I also . . . but do you understand, no money ; those who have money in their pockets can go.*)

Piger, *to race ; to compete.*

Et je vous jure bien que dans cette foule de fillettes de magasin qui descendent en capeline, . . . petites gueules fraîches toussotant à la brume, toujours talonnées de quelque galant, aucune n'aurait pu piger avec elle.—A. Daudet.

Piger, *to find.*

Tiens, v'là Casimir, c'est ta femme, cette colombe-là ? où as-tu pigé ce canasson-là, c'est bon pour le muséum, mon cher.—Baumaine et Blondelet, *Les Locutions Vicieuses.*

Piger la vignette, *to look attentively and with pleasure on some funny person or amusing scene,* " to take it in." Se faire —, *to allow oneself to be detected or apprehended; to allow oneself to be done,* or " bested." Piger, *to catch,* " to nab."

On grimp' pas su' les parapets !
Attends ! attends ! j'y vas . . . cré garce,
Pigé, j'te tiens ! Dit's donc, c'est farce
Tout d'même.
GILL.

Piget, or **pipet,** *m.* (thieves'), *castle.* The root of this word is pigeon, in the Low Latin pipio.

Pignard, *m.* (thieves'), *breech,* or " blind cheek." See **Vasistas.**

Pignocher (popular). Means properly *to pick one's food.* Se —, *to fight,* " to slip into one another;" (artists') *to put too much finish in a work.*

Pignouf, *m.* (general), *one who behaves like a cad; coarse fellow ; mean, paltry fellow.*

J'ai vu que tu avais par moments ennuyé les critiques. Tu sais, il ne faut pas faire attention à eux, c'est des tas de pignoufs.—E. Monteil.

(Shoemakers') Pignouf, *apprentice,* the master being denominated " pontife," and a workman " gniaf."

Pignoufle, *m.* (general), *cad.*

La faille rose braquant sa jumelle—" A qui en ont-ils ces pignoufles ?"—P. Mahalin.

Pigoche, *f., a game.* Some coins being placed inside a circumference traced out on the ground, are to be knocked out of it by aiming with another coin.

Nous arrachions tout, les boutons
Des portes et des pantalons
Pour la pigoche.
DE CHATILLON.

The word has passed into the language.

Pile ! (popular), *exclamation uttered when one sees a person falling, or hears a smash of crockery or other article.* Properly *tails !* at pitch and toss. Termed also d'autant ! a favourite ejaculation of waiters.

Piler (popular), du poivre, *to walk on the tips of one's toes on account of blistered feet; to wait; to slander.* Faire — du poivre à quelqu'un, *to throw one down repeatedly.* Piler le bitume *is said of a prostitute who walks the streets ;* (military) — du poivre, *to mark time ; to be on sentry duty ;*

to ride a hard trotting horse ; — du poivre à quelqu'un, *to forsake one ; to leave off keeping company with one.*

Ah ! pompon du diable ! il y a longtemps que j'avais envie de lui piler du poivre.— C. DUBOIS DE GENNES.

Piler le poivre, *to be on sentry duty.*

Pilier, *m.* (familiar), de cabaret, *drunkard,* or " mop." See **Poivrot.** (Thieves') Le —, *the master.* Un — de boutanche, *a shopman.* Un —, *the master of a brothel.* Un — de pacquelin, *a commercial traveller.*

Quel fichu temps ! le pilier de pacquelin ne viendra pas.—VIDOCQ.

Le — du creux, *the master of the house,* the " omee of the carsey." From uomo della casa in lingua franca.

Pille, *f.* (thieves'), *one thousand francs.*

Pillois vain, *m.* (thieves'), *village judge,* a kind of " beak, or queer cuffin."

Piloches, *f. pl.* (thieves'), *teeth,* " bones, or ivories." Termed also " chocottes." Montrer ses —, " to flash one's ivories."

Piloirs, *m. pl.* (thieves'), *fingers,* " forks, stealers, or pickers."

Pilon, *m.* (thieves'), *finger or thumb ;* (popular) *maimed beggar.*

Pimpeloter (popular), se —, *to eat and drink of the best, to take care of number one in that respect.*

Pimpions, *m. pl.* (thieves'), *coin,* " pieces." See **Quibus.**

Pinçants, *m. pl.* (old cant), *scissors.* Termed also " fauchants, fauchettes."

Pinçard, *m.* (cavalry), *horseman who possesses strong thighs, and*

has, *in consequence, a firm grip in the saddle.* From pince, *grip.*

Pince, *f.* (thieves'), *hand,* or "duke." (Horsemen's) Pince, *grip of the thighs.* (Popular) Chaud de la —, *fond of women, or one fond of his* "mutton."

Puis, comme c'était un chaud de la pince qui faisait des enfants à toutes les figurantes de l'Odéon.—E. MONTEIL.

(Card-sharpers') Pince, *a box constructed on cheating principles, and used by sharpers at the game called consolation, a game played with dice.*

Pinceau, *m.* (military), *broom.*

Allons . . . nous sommes de corvée de quartier, il va falloir aller jouer du pinceau avant un quart d'heure.—DUBOIS DE GENNES.

(Freemasons') Pinceau, *pen ;* (popular) *hand, or foot,* "daddle, or hoof." Détacher un coup de — dans la giberne, *to kick one's behind,* "to toe one's bum." Détacher un coup de — sur la frimousse, *to give a box on the ear,* " to give a bang in the mug, to fetch a wipe in the gills, or mug," or, as the Americans term it, " to give a biff in the jaw."

Pince-cul, *m.* (popular), *low dancing-hall patronized by prostitutes and roughs.* An allusion to the liberties which male dancers take with their partners.

Pince-dur, *m.* (military), *adjutant.* From pincer, *to nab.*

Pince-loque, *m.* (thieves'), *needle.*

Pincer (familiar and popular), le cancan, *to dance the* "cancan." A kind of choregraphy which requires great agility, the toes of the female performers being often on a level with the faces of their partners than on the floor. The cancan is in great favour at Bullier and kindred dancing-halls, its devotees being generally medical students and their female friends, the "étudiantes;" also "horizontales" and their protectors, or "poissons;" — au demi-cercle, *to catch unawares*, " to nab ; " — quelqu'un, *to catch one, to take one red-handed.* Se faire —, *to be detected ; to be caught, to get* "nabbed." Pincer un coup de sirop, *to be slightly the worse for liquor,* or slightly "elevated." See **Pompette.** En — pour une femme, *to be smitten with a fair one's charms,* "to be mashed on, sweet on, keen on, or to be spooney." (Thieves') Pincer, *to steal,* " to nick." For synonyms see **Grinchir.**

Cartouche.—Qu' avez-vous pincé ? Harpin.—Six pièces de toile et quatre de mousseline.—Le Grand, *Les Fourberies de Cartouche.*

Pincer de la guitare, or de la harpe, *to be locked up in jail, to be* " in quod." An allusion to the bars of the prison cell assimilated to the strings of a guitar.

Pince - sans - rire, *m.* (thieves'), *police officer,* "copper," or "reeler." See **Pot-à-tabac.**

Pincettes, *f. pl.* (popular), affûter, or se tirer les —, *to decamp in a hurry,* "to guy." See **Patatrot.**

Pinchard, *adj.* (literary), *vulgar, in bad taste,* "jimmy."

Pindarès (thieves'), *the gendarmes; city police, or rural police.* Pindarès ! *we wash our hands of it !* an exclamation uttered by malefactors after committing some crime.

Pinet, or **pino,** *m.* (thieves'), *farthing.* Termed in English cant, "fadge."

Pingouin, *m.* (popular), *fool,* or "flat ; " *good-for-nothing man.* (Mountebanks') Le —, *the public.*

Vois-tu le pingouin comme il s'allume ? . . . ça n'est rien, à la reprise je vas l'incendier.—E. Sue.

Pingouin maigre, *small audience ;* — gras, *large audience.*

Pingre, *adj.* (thieves'), *poor,* "quisby."

Pioche, *f.* (freemasons'), *fork ;* (popular) *work,* or "graft." Se mettre à la —, *to set oneself to work.* Tête de —, *blockhead,* "cabbage-head." (Thieves') Une —, *a pickpocket,* or "finger-smith."

Piocher (barristers'), les larmes, *to prepare a pathetic oration with a view to exciting the commiseration of the jury, and enlisting their sympathy in favour of the accused.* There is an old joke about a barrister who, having undertaken to defend a scoundrel accused of murdering his own father and mother, wound up his speech by beseeching the jury to be merciful unto his client, on the plea of his being a "poor orphan left alone and unprotected in this wicked world." The celebrated and truthful author of a recent diatribe on the manners and customs of the French, reproduces the story, presenting it to his readers as a striking but "genuine" specimen of the forensic eloquence in favour with John Bull's neighbours ! (Thieves') Piocher, *to carry on the business of a pickpocket,* " to be on the cross." See **Grinchir.**

Piole, or **piolle,** *f.* (thieves'), *house.* The synonyms are, "cambuse, cassine, boîte, niche, kasbah, barraque, creux, bahut, baite, case, taule, taudion," and, in the English slang, "diggings, ken, hangsout, chat, crib," &c. Piole, *lodging-house,* or "dossing-ken."

Veux-tu venir prendre de la morfe et piausser avec mézière en une des pioles que tu m'as rouscaillées ?—*Le Jargon de l'Argot. (Will you come eat and sleep*

Z

with me in one of the cribs which you were talking about ?)

Piole, *tavern*, or "lush-crib ;" — blindée, *fortress;* — à machabées, *cemetery;* — de lartonnier, *baker's shop*, or "mungarly casa." The English cant term is a corruption of the Lingua Franca phrase for an eating-house. Mangiare, *to eat*, in Italian.

Pioller (popular and thieves'), *to pay frequent visits to the wine-shop ; to get the worse for liquor, to get* "cut, or canon."

Piollier, *m.* (popular and thieves'), *landlord of a drinking-shop*, "the boss of a lush-crib."

Pion, *m. and adj.* (familiar), un —, *an usher at a school*, or "bum-brusher." Properly *a pawn;* (thieves') *louse*, "grey-back, or German duck." The *Slang Dictionary* says : "These pretty little things are called by many names, among others by those of 'grey-backs' and 'gold-backed 'uns,' which are popular among those who have most interest in the matter." Etre —, *to be drunk.* From an old word pier, *to drink.* Villon in his *Grand Testament*, fifteenth century, has the word with the signification of *toper, drunkard :—*

Brief, on n'eust sçeu en ce monde chercher
Meilleur pion, pour boire tost et tard.
Faictes entrer quand vous orrez trucher
L'ame du bon feu maistre Jehan Cotard.

Rabelais uses pion with the same signification :—

Ce feut ici que mirent à bas culs
Joyeusement quatre gaillards pions,
Pour banqueter à l'honneur de Bacchus,
Buvants à gré comme beaulx carpions.
Pantagruel, chap. xxvii.

Pionce, *f.*, or **pionçage**, *m.* (popular), *sleep*, or "balmy." Camarade de —, *bedfellow.*

Il avait couché dans un garno où l'on est deux par paillasse. Son camarade de

pionce était un gros père à mine rouge qui avait une tête comme un bonnet d'astrakan.—RICHEPIN, *Le Pavé.*

Pioncer (familiar and popular), *to sleep*, "to have a dose of balmy."

Quoi ? vrai ! vous allez m'ramasser ?
Ah ! c'est muf ! Mais quoi qu'on y gagne !
J'm'en vas vous empêcher d'pioncer
J'ronfle comme un' toupi' d'All'magne.
RICHEPIN, *La Chanson des Gueux.*

The synonyms are : "casser une canne, piquer un chien, piquer une romance, faire le lézard, faire son michaud, roupiller, se recueillir, compter des pauses, taper de l'œil, mettre le chien au cran de repos."

Pionceur, *m.* (familiar and popular), *man who sleeps.*

Pionne, *f.* (scholars'), *governess at a school.*

Piote, *f.* (cavalry), *insulting term applied by a cavalry man to a foot-soldier.*

Piou, or **pioupiou**, *m.* (familiar and popular), *infantry soldier, the French* "Tommy Atkins."

Pipe, *f.* (familiar and popular), *head, face.* Casser sa —, *to die.* The synonyms are : "dévisser, or décoller son billard, graisser ses bottes, avaler sa langue, sa gaffe, sa cuiller, or ses baguettes, cracher son âme, n'avoir plus mal aux dents, poser sa chique, claquer, saluer le public, recevoir son décompte, ingurgiter son bilan, cracher ses embouchures, déposer ses bouts de manche, déteindre, donner son dernier bon à tirer, lâcher la perche, éteindre son gaz, épointer son forêt, être exproprié, péter son lof, fumer ses terres, fermer son parapluie, perdre son bâton, descendre la garde, passer l'arme à gauche, défiler la parade, tourner de l'œil, perdre le goût du pain, lâcher la rampe, faire ses petits paquets, casser son cracholr, remercier son boulanger, canner, dévider à l'estorgue, baiser la camarde, camarder, fuir, casser son câble, son fouet; faire sa crevaison, déralinguer, virer de bord, déchirer son faux-col, dégeler, couper sa mèche, piquer sa plaque, mettre la table pour les asticots, aller manger les pissenlits par la racine, laisser fuir son tonneau, calancher, laisser ses bottes quelquepart, déchirer son habit, or son tablier, souffler sa veilleuse, pousser le boum du cygne, avoir son coke, rendre sa secousse," and, in the English slang, "to snuff it, to lay down one's knife and fork, to stick one's spoon in the wall, to kick the bucket, to give in, give up, to go to Davy Jones, to peg out, to hop the twig, to slip one's cable, to lose the number of one's mess, to turn one's toes up." The latter is to be met with in Reade's *Cloister and Hearth* :—

"Several arbalestriers turned their toes up, and I among them." "Killed, Denys? Come now!" "Dead as mutton."

Pipé, *adj.* (thieves'), être — sur le tas, *to be caught red-handed.*

Pipelet, *m.* (general), *doorkeeper.* A character in Eugène Sue's *Les Mystères de Paris.*

Je les ai vus causer ensemble,
Mes deux Pip'lets.
Et j'ai dit dans ma peau qui tremble,
Dieu ! qu'ils sont laids.
     J. DE BLAINVILLE, *Mes deux Pipelets.*

The Pipelet of Eugène Sue was the victim of a ferocious practical joker, a painter, Cabrion by name, who made his life a burden to him. The doorkeepers have retaliated by calling "un Cabrion" a lodger who does not pay his rent.

Je sais aussi qu'on me traite d'ivrogne,
Si du raisin je rapporte le fard,

Que Cabrion aperçoive ma trogne
Il s'écriera : le Pip'let est pochard !
Mais ce matin, j'ai vu Anastasie,
Qui du cognac savourait les roideurs ;
Je m'consol'rai dans les bras d'une amie.
Les m'lons sont verts, les chardons sont en
    fleurs.
     DUBOIS, *Rêves de Vieillesse ou
      le Départ de Pipelet.*

Pipelette, *f.* (general), *the wife of a concierge or doorkeeper.* Termed also Madame Pipelet. See **Pipelet.**

Vous n'connaissez pas ma concierge,
La nommée Madam' Benoiton,
Une grand' sèch' longu' comm' un cierge
Et sourd' comm' un bonnet d'coton.
Si malheureus'ment j'm'attarde,
C'est l'diable pour la réveiller.
Pendant deux heur's je mont' la garde,
D'vant la porte et j'ai beau crier :
Ous-qu'est ma pip', ous-qu'est ma pip',
    ous-qu'est ma pip'lette ?
     A. BEN et H. D'HERVILLE.

Piper (familiar and popular), *to smoke,* or "to blow a cloud."

Il me semble qu'on a pipé ici.—GAVARNI.

(Thieves') **Piper**, *to catch.*

Comprend-on après cela qu'un homme qui changeait si fréquemment de nom ... ait été se loger ... sous le nom de Mahossier qui lui avait servi à piper sa victime ?—CANLER.

Piper un pègre, *to apprehend a thief,* "to smug a prig." The different expressions signifying *to apprehend or to imprison* are: "poisser, grimer, coquer, enflacquer, enfourailler, mettre dedans, fourrer dedans, mettre à l'ombre, mettre au violon, boucler, grappiner, poser un gluau, empoigner, piger, emballer, gripper, empoiler, encoffrer, encager, accrocher, ramasser, souffler, faire tomber malade, agrafer, mettre le grappin dessus, enchetiber, enfourner, coltiger, colletiner, poser le grappin, faire passer à la fabrication, fabriquer," and, in the English slang, "to smug, to nab, to run in."

Pipet, *m.* (thieves'), *castle, mansion,* "chat, or hangings-out." See **Piget.**

Il arriva que je trimardais juste la lourde de ce pipet . . . une cambrouze du pipet me mouchaillait et en avertit le rupin.— *Le Jargon de l'Argot.* (*It happened that I was just going by the door of that mansion . . . a servant girl of the mansion perceived me and warned the master.*)

Pipo, or **pipot,** *m., the Ecole Polytechnique ; student at that school.* This establishment is the great training school for government civil engineers, who are chosen, after a two years' course, out of those who come first on the competitive list, and for officers of the engineers and artillery, the latter being sent for a three years' course to the "Ecole d'application" at Fontainebleau, with the rank of sub-lieutenant.

Piquage, *m.* (military), *de romance, sleep,* "balmy;" *snoring,* or "driving one's pigs to market."

Les autres cavaliers . . . continuaient, à poings fermés, le piquage de leur romance. —C. DUBOIS DE GENNES.

(Popular) Faire un —, *to steal wine by boring a hole in a cask which is being conveyed in a van to its destination.* Also *to abstract wine or spirits from a cask by the insertion of a tube,* or "sucking the monkey." The English expression has also the meaning of drinking generally, and originally, according to Marryat, to drink rum out of cocoa-nuts, the milk having been poured out and the liquor substituted.

Piquante, *f.* (thieves'), *pin.*

Piquantine, *f.* (thieves'), *flea.* Called sometimes " F sharp," bugs being the "B flats."

Piqué, *adj.* (popular), pas — des hannetons, *good,* or "bully;" *ex-*cellent, or " first-class, real jam, nap, ripping, clipping, slap-up."

Pique-chien, *m., doorkeeper at the Ecole Polytechnique.* See **Pipo.**

Pique-en-terre, *m.* (popular and thieves'), *fowl,* "cackling cheat, or margery prater."

Piquelard, *m.* (popular), *pork-butcher,* or "kiddier."

Pique-poux, *m.* (popular), *a tailor.* Termed also pique-prunes, or pique-puces. Called among English operatives a "steel-bar driver, cabbage - contractor, or goose-persuader;" by the world, a "ninth part of a man;" and by the "fast" man, a "sufferer." Termed also " snip," from "snipes," *a pair of scissors,* or from the snipping sound made by scissors in cutting up anything.

Piquer (students'), *to do;* — l'étrangère, *to be absent or distraught,* " to go moon-raking," or " wool-gathering;" — un laïus, *to make a speech ;* — une muette, *to remain silent,* "to be mum." J'ai piqué 17 à la colle, *I obtained* 17 *marks at the examination.* See **Colle.** Piquer le bâton d'encouragement, *to obtain* 1 *mark, the maximum being* 20 *;* — une sèche, *to get no marks at all,* or a " duck's egg ;" (familiar and popular) — un chien, *to sleep,* "to have a dose of balmy;" — un fard, or un soleil, *to blush;* — un renard, *to vomit,* "to shoot the cat, to cast up accounts, or to cascade." Rabelais termed the act " supergurgiter ;" — une victime, *to dive from a great height with arms uplifted and body perfectly rigid;* (sailors') — sa plaque, *to sleep ; to die.* See **Pipe.** (Artists') Piquer un cinabre, *to blush;* (popular) — dans le tas, *to choose.*

Nous v'là . . . nous sont point pressées : piquez donc vite dans eul' tas, au p'tit bonheur.—TRUBLOT.

Piquer une romance, *"to sleep,*" "to have a dose of balmy;" *to snore,* "to drive one's pigs to market."

Et puisqu'ils pioncent tous comme des marmottes. . . . À ton tour, mon bon de piquer une romance.—C. DUBOIS DE GENNES.

Se — le tasseau, *to get drunk,* or "tight." For synonyms see **Sculpter.** Piquer un chahut, *to dance the cancan.*

Revenant ensuite dans les environs de la Gare Saint-Lazare, dansant à Bullier, piquant un "chahut" à l'Elysée-Montmartre ou même à la Boule-Noire, aux heures de dèche.—DUBUT DE LAFOREST, *Le Gaga.*

Piquet, *m.* (popular), *prayer-book.* Also *juge de paix,* a kind of county court magistrate.

Piqueton, *m.* (popular), *thin wine.*

Et les verres se vidaient d'une lampée. . . . Il pleuvait du piqueton, quoi ? un piqueton qui avait d'abord un goût de vieux tonneau.—ZOLA.

Piqueuse de trains, *f.* (popular), *prostitute who prowls about railway stations.* See **Gadoue.**

Pissat, *m.* (popular), d'âne, *brandy,* or "French cream;" *beer;* — de vache, *sour or small beer,* "swipes."

Pisse-froid dans la canicule, *m.* (popular), *man of an extremely phlegmatic disposition, who on all occasions remains* "as cool as a cucumber." Also "pisse-verglas."

Pisse-huile, *m.* (schoolboys'), *lamplighter.*

Pissenlits, *m. pl.* (popular), arroser les —, *to void urine in the open air.* Manger les — par la racine, *to be dead and buried.*

Pisser (familiar and popular), à l'Anglaise, *to give the slip,* "to take French leave." From the act of a man who, wishing to get rid of another, pretends to go to the "lavatory," and disappears. Pisser au cul de quelqu'un, *to entertain feelings of utter contempt for one;* — contre le soleil, *to strive in vain, to make useless efforts;* — dans un violon, *to waste one's time in some fruitless attempt;* — des enfants, *to beget a large number of children;* — des yeux, *to weep,* "to nap a bib;" — sa côtelette, *to be in child-bed,* or "in the straw;" — sur quelqu'un, *to despise one.* Faire — des lames de rasoir en travers, *to annoy one terribly, to* "rile" *one,* or to "spur" *him.* Mener les poules —, *to leave off working under false pretences.* Une histoire à faire — un cheval de bois, *astounding story hard to swallow, story told by one who can* "spin a twister." (Literary) Pisser de la copie, *to be a facile writer, to write lengthy journalistic productions off-hand.*

Pisse-trois-gouttes, *m.* (popular), *one who frequently stops on the road in order to void urine, one who* "lags;" — dans quatre pots de chambre, *slow man who does little work.*

Pisseur de copie, *m.* (literary), *facile writer, one who writes lengthy journalistic productions off-hand.*

Pisseuse, *f.* (popular), *little girl, little chit.*

Pisse-verglas, *m.* (popular). See **Pisse-froid.**

Pissin de cheval, *m.* (popular), *bad beer,* "swipes, or belly-vengeance."

Pissote, *f.* (popular), *urinals.* Faire une —, *to void urine,* "to pump ship."

Pistache, *f.* (familiar), *mild stage of intoxication.* Pincer sa —, *to be slightly the worse for liquor,* "to be elevated."

Pistaon, *m.* (Breton cant), *money.*

Piste, *f.* (military), suivez la —, *go on talking, proceed.*

Pister (popular), *is said of hotel touts who follow and generally bore travellers;* (thieves') *to follow.* La riflette me pistait mais je me suis fait une paire de mains courantes à la mode, *the spy was following me, but I ran away.*

Elle la piste, elle arrive essouflée au Bureau des mœurs pour prévenir la police. —Dr. Jeannel.

Pisteur, *m.* (familiar), *an admirer of the fair sex, whose principal occupation is to follow women in the streets.* Rigaud makes the following remarks : "Il ne faut pas confondre le pisteur avec le suiveur. Le suiveur est un fantaisiste qui opère à l'aventure. Il emboîte le pas à toutes les femmes qui lui plaisent, ou, mieux, à toutes les jolies jambes. Parmi cent autres, il reconnaîtra un mollet qu'il aura déjà chassé. Il va, vient, s'arrête, tourne, retourne, marche devant, derrière, croise, coupe l'objet de sa poursuite, qu'il perd souvent au détour d'une rue. Plus méthodique, le pisteur surveille d'un trottoir à l'autre son gibier. Il suit à une distance respectueuse, pose devant les magasins, sous les fenêtres, se cache derrière une porte, retient le numéro de la maison, fait sentinelle et ne donne de la voix que lorsqu'il est sûr du succès. Le pisteur est, ou un tout jeune homme timide, plein d'illusions, ou un homme mûr, plein d'expérience. Le pisteur d'omnibus est un désœuvré qui suit les femmes en omnibus, leur fait du pied, du genou, du coude, risque un bout de conversation, et n'a d'autre sérieuse opération que celle de se faire voiturer de la Bastille à la Madeleine et vice versa. Cet amateur du beau sexe est ordinairement un quinquagénaire dont le ventre a, depuis longtemps, tourné au majestueux. Il offre à tout hasard aux ouvrières le classique mobilier en acajou ; les plus entreprenants vont jusqu'au palissandre. Les paroles s'envolent, et acajou et palissandre restent . . . chez le marchand de meubles. Peut-être est-ce un pisteur qui a trouvé le proverbe : promettre et tenir font deux."

Pistole, *f.* (popular). Grande —, *ten-franc piece.* Petite —, *fifty-centime coin.*

Pistolet, *m.* (obsolete), de manœuvres, *stone.*

Ils chassèrent le sergent et tous ceux qui étoient avec lui, à grands coups de pierres que ces palots nommoient des pistolets de manœuvres. — *L'Apothicaire empoisonné.*

(Familiar) Pistolet, *a pint bottle of champagne, a pint of* "boy, or fiz." Un drôle de —, *a queer* "fish." (Popular) Pistolet à la Saint-Dôme, *small hook used by cigar-end finders to whisk up bits of cigars or cigarettes.* Ous qu'est mon —? *expression of mock indignation.*

Faites donc attention, jeune homme. Vous allez chiffonner ma robe, c'est du 60 francs le mètre ça, mon petit! Que j'lui dis . . . soixante francs le mètre, ous qu'est mon pistolet? Je ne donnerais pas cent sous de l'enveloppe avec la poupée qu'est d'dans.— *Les Locutions Vicieuses.*

Pistolet, in the fifteenth century, *a dagger manufactured at Pistoie.*

Pistolier, *m.* (prisoners'), *prisoner who lives at the* "pistole," *a separate cell allowed to a prisoner for a consideration.*

Piston, *m.* (students'), *assistant to a lecturer on chemistry or physics ;* (popular) *man who is well recommended for a situation.* In the slang of naval cadets, *a busybody, a bore.*

Pistonner (familiar and popular), quelqu'un, *to give one who is seeking a post the support of one's influence ; to annoy,* "to rile ; " *to guide one.*

Ayant rencontré un portefaix qu'il connaissait, il s'est fait "pistonner" par lui, suivant son expression, à travers la ville.— *Le Voltaire,* Nov., 1886.

Pitaine-crayon, *m.* (Ecole Polytechnique), *orderly acting as servant at the drawing classes.*

Pitancher (popular), *to drink,* "to liquor up." Termed by the Americans, "to smile, to see the man ;" — de l'eau d'aff, *to drink brandy.*

Piton, *m.* (popular), *nose,* " handle, conk, boko, snorter, smeller." See **Morviau.**

J'ai l'piton camard en trompette.
Aussi soyez pa' étonnés
Si j'ai rien qu' du vent dans la tête :
C'est pa'c'que j'ai pas d'poils dans l'nez.
RICHEPIN.

Un — passé à l'encaustique, *red nose,* " copper nose," *or one with* " grog blossoms," *such as is sported by an* " Admiral of the Red."

Pître du comme, *m.* (thieves'), *commercial traveller.* Pître, properly *mountebank's fool,* or "Billy Barlow," and figuratively a *literary or political quack.*

Pitroux, pétouze, *m.* (thieves'), *gun,* or " dag ;" *pistol,* " barking iron," or " barker."

Pituiter (popular), *to slander ; to prattle, to gabble,* " to clack, or to jaw."

Pivase, *m.* (popular), *nose of large dimensions,* "conk." See **Morviau.**

Pivaste, *m.* (thieves'), *child,* " kid, or kinchin." Termed also " mion, loupiau, môme."

Pive, or **pivre,** *m.* (popular), *wine.* Marchand de —, *landlord of a wine-shop.* Rabelais called wine "purée septembrale," or " eau beniste de cave," as appears from the following :—

Maistre Janotus, tondu à la césarine, vestu de son liripipion à l'antique, et bien antidoté l'estomach de cotignac de four et eau beniste de cave, se transporta au logis de Gargantua.—*Gargantua.*

Pivert, *m.* (thieves'), *fine saw made out of a watch-spring,* used by prisoners to file through the bars of a cell-window. An allusion to the sharp beak of the woodpecker.

Pivoiner (popular), *to redden.* From pivoine, *peony.*

Pivois, pive, or **pie,** *m.* (thieves'), *wine.* Charles Nodier says : " Un certain vin se dit 'pivois' à cause de la ressemblance de son raisin avec la pive, nom patois du fruit appelé improprement pomme de pin ; " — à quatre nerfs, *small measure of wine costing four sous ;* — citron, *vinegar ;* — vermoisé, *red wine ;* — savonné, *white wine.*

Mais que ce soit le pétrole ou le pivois savonné, dans le godet ou dans l'entonnoir à patte, toujours les buveurs ont soin de dire : à la vôtre, patron !— RICHEPIN.

The synonyms are the following : "picton, tortu, reginglard, picolo, bleu, petit bleu, ginglet, briolet, huile, sirop, jus d'échalas."

Pivot, *m.* (thieves'), *pen.*

Frangin et frangine.—Je pésigue le pivot pour vous bonnir que mézigue vient d'être servi maron à la lègre de Canelle.—VI-DOCQ. (*Brother and sister.—I take the pen to tell you that I have just been caught in the act at the fair of Caen.*)

(Military) Envoyer chercher le — de conversion, *to send one on a fool's errand, something like sending one for* "*pigeon's milk.*" Envoyer chercher "la clef du champ de manœuvre, le moule à guillemets, or le parapluie de l'escouade," are kindred jokes perpetrated on unsophisticated recruits.

Pivoter (military), *to work; to drill; to be on duty.*

Tour à tour, c'était le brigadier de semaine qui pivotait, les bleus qui en fichaient un coup.—G. COURTELINE.

Placarde, *f.* (thieves'), *public square in a city, generally the one where executions take place.* Before 1830 the death sentence was carried out at the Place de Grève, later on at the Place St. Jacques, and nowadays criminals are executed in front of the prison of La Roquette; — au quart d'œil, *place of executions.* La — de vergne, *the town public place.*

Crompe, crompe, mercandière,
Car nous serions béquillés ;
Sur la placarde de vergne,
Il nous faudrait gambiller.
VIDOCQ.

Place d'armes, *f.* (popular), *stomach,* "bread-basket ;" *body,* "apple-cart."

Vous êtes invité à passer la soirée chez des bourgeois. . . . Vous entrez. . . . Au lieu de dire : bonjour, cher ami ; madame est bien ? Allons tant mieux ! enchanté de vous voir en bonne santé, l'on dit carrément ; bonjour, ma vieille branche, comment va la place d'armes ? Et le bourgeois pour se mettre à la mode, répond ; merci, mon vieux, ça boulotte, et ta sœur ?—*Les Locutions Vicieuses.*

Placeur de lapins, *m.* (familiar), *humbug who plays the moralist.*

Desgenais n'est, malgré ses malédictions à fracas, qu'un simple placeur de lapins.—L. CHAPRON, *Le Gaulois.*

It also means *man who lives at the expense of others and introduces his friends to women of the demi-monde.*

Plafond, *m.* (familiar and popular), *head, skull,* "nut." Avoir une araignée dans le —, *to be* "cracked," "to have a slate off." See **Avoir.**

·— Voilà encore un de nos jolis "toqués," disait l'un d'eux à demi-voix.
— Il a une belle "araignée dans le plafond," murmurait un autre.—P. AUDEBRAND.

Avoir des trychines dans le —, *same signification as above.* Se défoncer, or se faire sauter le —, *to blow one's brains out.* (Theatrical) Plafond d'air, *long strips of painted canvas stretched across the upper part of the stage to represent the sky.*

Plaider la ficelle (lawyers'), *is said of a counsel who has recourse when pleading to some transparent ruse, such as diverting the attention from the point at issue by treating of questions irrelevant to the case.*

Plamousse, *f.* (popular), *box on the ear,* "wipe in the gills."

Plan, *m.* (familiar and popular), *pawnbroker's establishment,* "lug chovey." Mettre au —, or en —, *to pawn,* "to put up the spout."

Le lendemain elle mit son châle "en plan" pour cinq francs.—LÉO TAXIL.

Etre en —, *to remain at a restaurant while a friend goes to fetch wherewith to defray the common expenses for a meal.* Laisser en —, *to abandon, to leave one in the lurch.* Laisser tout en —, *to leave or* "chuck up" *everything in hand.* (Popular) Il y a —, *it is possible.* (Military) Plan, *arrest.* Etre au —, *to be under arrest,* "to be roosted." (Thieves') Plan, *prison,* "stir." See **Motte.** Plan de couillé, *remand.* Etre mis au — de couillé, *to be imprisoned for another.* Etre mis au —, *to be imprisoned,* "to get the clinch."

Tomber au —, *to be apprehended,* or " smugged." See **Piper.** (Theatrical) Laisser en plan *is said of the claque, or paid applauders, when they do not applaud an actor.*

Vous ferez Madame B. (faire ici veut dire applaudir ou soigner) vous laisserez en plan Monsieur X. (cela signifie vous ne l'applaudirez pas).—BALZAC.

Planche, *f.* (familiar and popular), *woman the reverse of buxom, who is not* " built that way ; " (popular) — à boudin, *woman of indifferent character.* Faire la —, *to be a prostitute,* or " mot." Faire sa —, *to give oneself airs.* Sans —, *without any ceremonies, frankly.* (Freemasons') Planche à tracer, *table ; sheet of white paper ; letter.* (Thieves') Planche, *sword,* or "poker ; " — à grimaces, *altar ;* — à sapement, *police court ;* — au chiquage, or à lavement, *confessional ;* — au pain, *tribunal ; bench occupied by prisoners in the dock.* Etre mis sur la — au pain, *to be committed for trial,* " to be fullied."

On m'empoigne, on me met sur la planche au pain. J'ai une fièvre cérébrale.—VICTOR HUGO.

(Theatrical) Avoir des planches, *to be an experienced actor.* Brûler les planches, *to play with spirit.*

Ce n'était pas un mauvais acteur. Il avait de la chaleur, il brûlait même un peu les planches.—E. MONTEIL, *Cornebois.*

(Military) Une — à pain, *a tall lanky man.* (Tailors') Une —, a " goose." Avoir fait les planches, *to have worked as a journeyman tailor.*

Planché, *adj.* (thieves'), être —, *to be convicted,* " to be booked, or to be in for a vamp."

Plancher (military), *to be confined in the cells, or guard-room ;* (popu-

lar and thieves') *to be afraid ; to laugh at ; to joke.*

Tu planches, mon homme.—VIDOCQ. (*You are joking, my good fellow.*)

Plancherie, *f.* (popular and thieves'), *joke,* " wheeze," *or practical joke.*

Plancheur, *m.* (popular and thieves'), *joker ; practical joker.*

Planque, *f.* (thieves'), en —, *on the watch.*

J'allai en compagnie de H. au Passage du Cheval Rouge, et, le laissant en planque (en observation).—CANLER.

Planque, *place of concealment ; police station.* Le truc de la —, *the secret concerning a place of concealment.*

Par une chouette sorgue, la rousse est aboulée à la taule ... un macaron avait mangé le morceau sur nouzailles et bonni le truc de la planque ; tous les fanandels avaient été servis.—VIDOCQ. (*One fine night the police came to the house . . . a traitor had peached on us, and revealed the secret of the hiding place ; all the comrades had been apprehended.*)

Planque à corbeaux, *priest's seminary ;* — à larbins, *servants' registering office ;* — des gouâpeurs, *dépôt of the Préfecture de Police ;* — à plombes, *clock ;* — à sergots, *police station ;* — à suif, *gaming-house,* or " punting-shop ;" — à tortorer, *eating-house,* " grubbing-ken, or spinikin." Etre en —, *to be locked up,* or " put away." See **Piper.**

Planquer (popular), *to pawn,* " to put in lug ;" (thieves') *to imprison,* " to smug." See **Piper.** Planquer, *to conceal.*

A c'te plombe j'suis si bien planquée que je ne crains ni cognes, ni griviers, ni railles, ni quart d'œil, ni gerbiers.—VIDOCQ. (*I am now so well concealed that I fear no gendarmes, soldiers, detectives, police magistrate, or judges.*)

Planquer le marmot, *to conceal the*

booty, *to put away the* "swag."
It also means *to place, to put in.*
Planquer les paccins dans un roulant, *to put the parcels in a cab.*
(Printers') Planquer des sortes, *to
put by, for one's personal use, and
with much inconvenience to fellow-
compositors, some particular description of type required in large
quantities for a common piece of
composition.*

Plantation, *f.* (theatrical), *arrangement of scenic plant, such as furniture, &c.*

J'avais dit de poser là une chaise pour
figurer la porte. Tous les jours, il faut
recommencer la plantation.—ZOLA, *Nana.*

Planter (theatrical), *refers to the
effecting of all scenic arrange-
ments ;* — un acte, *to settle all the
scenic details of an act ;* — un
comparse, *to give directions to a
supernumerary as to his make-up,
position on the stage, movements,
&c. ;* (sailors') — le harpon, *to
express some idea, some proposal.*
(Popular) Planter, *to make a sacrifice to Venus ;* — son poireau, *to
be waiting for someone who is
not making his appearance ;* — le
drapeau, *to leave without paying
one's reckoning ; not to pay a debt ;*
(familiar) — un chou, *to deceive,*
"to bamboozle." See **Jobarder.**

Plantes, *f. pl.* (popular), *feet,*
"everlasting shoes."

Eh ! bien, vous êtes de la jolie fripouille,
cria-t-il, j'ai usé mes plantes pendant trois
heures sur la route, même qu'un gendarme
m'a demandé mes papiers. Ah ! non, vous
savez, blague dans le coin, je la trouve
raide.—ZOLA, *L'Assommoir. (Well, he
cried, you are nice un's, you are; here I
have been scraping the road with my everlasting shoes these three hours. None of
that you know, and no kid, you come it
rather too strong.)*

Plaque, *f.* (popular), avoir sa —
d'égout défoncée, *to be a Sodomist.*
(Military) Des plaques de garde-

champêtre, *an old sergeant's
stripes.*

Plaquer (popular), *to put, to leave,
to forsake ;* — sa viande sous
l'édredon, *to go to bed ;* — son
nière, *to forsake one's friend.* Se
—, *to fall flat ; to put oneself ; to
have one's wet clothes sticking to
one's body.* Se — dans la limonade, *to jump into the water.*

Vous comprenez la rigolade
Vous, la p'tit' mèr' ; vrai que' potin !
C'est donc marioll', c'est donc rupin
De s'plaquer dans la limonade?
Pourquoi ? Peut-êt' pour un salaud ;
Pour un prop' à rien, pour un pant'e,
Malheur !... Tiens, vous prenez du vent'e.
Ah ! bon, chaleur ! J'comprends l'tableau !
                                    GILL.

Plastronneur, *m.* (popular), *swell,*
"gorger." From the stiff plas-
tron, or shirt-front, sported by
dandies when in "full fig." See
Gommeux.

Plat, *m.* (popular), deux œufs sur
le —, or deux œufs, *small breasts.*

C'ment ça ! c'que vous m'f... là, cap'-
taine ! n'allez pas m'dire qu'une femme qui
n'a qu'deux œufs posés sur la place d'armes,
peut avoir une fluxion vraisemblable à une
personne avantagée comme la commandante ?—CH. LEROY, *Ramollot.*

Plat d'épinards, *painting,* or
"daub." (Popular) Faire du —,
*to create a disturbance; to make
a noise,* "to kick up a row."
Prendre un — d'affiches, *to have
no breakfast in consequence of absence of means to pay for it.*
Literally *to walk about with an
empty stomach, reading the bills
posted up, to while away the time.*
Plats à barbe, *ears,* "wattles,
lugs, hearing cheats."

Le nez s'appelle un "piton ;" la bouche,
un "four ;" l'oreille un "plat à barbe ;"
les dents des "dominos," et les yeux des
"quinquets."—*Les Locutions Vicieuses.*

(Restaurants') Plat du jour, *dish
which is got ready specially for the
day, and which consequently is*

generally the most palatable in the bill of fare.

Ce que le restaurateur appelle dans son argot un plat du jour, c'est-à-dire un plat humain, possible, semblable à la nourriture que les hommes mariés trouvent chez eux.—TH. DE BANVILLE, *La Cuisinière Poétique.*

(Military) Plat, *gorget formerly worn by officers.*

Platane, *m.* (familiar), feuille de —, *rank cigar,* "cabbage-leaf."

Plateau, *m.* (freemasons'), *a dish.*

Plato. See **Filer.**

Plâtre, *m.* See **Essuyer.** (Printers') Plâtre, for emplâtre, *bad compositor.* (Thieves') Plâtre, *silver,* or "redge." Je viens de dégringolarer un bobinot en plâtre, *I have just stolen a silver watch.* Etre au —, *to have money.*

Platue, *f.* (thieves'), *a kind of flat cake.*

Playant, *m.* (obsolete), for pliant. Marchand de playants, *one who gives himself up to practices of onanism.*

Plein, *m. and adj.* (popular), avoir son —, *to be intoxicated,* "to be primed;"—comme un œuf, comme un sac, *drunk,* "drunk as Davy's sow." See **Pompette.** Gros — de soupe, *a stout, clumsy man.*

Pleine, *adj.* (popular), lune, breech, or "Nancy." See **Vasistas.** (Familiar) Faire une — eau, *to dive into a river or the sea from a boat, and swim about in deep water.*

Plette, *f.* (thieves'), *skin,* "buff."

Pleurant, *m.* (thieves'), *onion.* From pleurer, *to weep.* The allusion is obvious. Du cabot avec des pleurants, *a mess of dogfish and onions.*

Pleurer (popular), en filou, *to pretend to weep, crocodile fashion.* Faire — son aveugle, *to void urine,* "to pump ship."

Pleut (popular), il —! *ejaculation of refusal; silence! be careful!* The expression is used by printers as a warning to be silent when the master or a stranger enters the workshop.

Pleuvoir (thieves'), des châsses, *to weep,* "to nap a bib." Termed also "baver des clignots." (Military) Pleuvoir, *to void urine.*

Pli, *m.* (familiar), avoir un — dans sa rose, *to have something that mars one's joy or disturbs one's happiness.*

La Martinière avait un "pli dans sa rose" comme il le disait lui-même.—H. FRANCE, *A Travers l'Espagne.*

Pliant, *m.* (thieves'), *knife,* or "chive." Termed also "vingt-deux, surin, or lingre." Jouer du —, *to knife,* "to chive."

Plier (popular), ses chemises, *to die,* "to snuff it." See **Pipe.** Plier son éventail, *to make signals to men in the orchestra stalls.*

Plis, *m. pl.* (popular), des —, *derisive expression of refusal;* might be rendered by, *Don't you wish you may get it?* or by the Americanism, "Yes, in a horn!" See **Nèfles.**

Plomb, *m.* (restaurants'), *entremets.* Probably from plum pudding; (popular) *venereal disease.* Laver la tête avec du —, *to shoot one.* Manger du —, *to be shot.* Le —, *the throat,* or "red lane;" *the mouth.* Termed also "l'avaloir, le bécot, la bavarde, la gargoine, la boîte, l'égout, la babouine, la cassolette, l'entonnoir, la gaffe, le mouloir, le gaviot." In the

English slang, "mug, potato-trap, rattler, kisser, maw-dubber, rattle-trap, potato-jaw, muns, bone-box." Ferme ton —, *hold your tongue*, "put a clapper to your mug, mum your dubber, or hold your jaw."

— D'où sort-elle donc celle-là ? Elle ferait bien mieux de clouer son bec.
— Celle-là... celle-là vaut bien Madame de la Queue-Rousse. Ferme ton plomb toi-même. — H. FRANCE, *Le Péché de Sœur Cunégonde.*

Jeter dans le —, *to swallow.*

Qui qu'a soif? qui qui veut boire à la fraîche ?
Sur mon dos au soleil ma glace fond.
De crier, ça me fait la gorge rèche.
J'ai le plomb tout en plomb. Buvons mon fond !
RICHEPIN, *La Chanson des Gueux.*

Plombe, *f.* (thieves'), *hour.* Six plombes se décrochent, *it is six o'clock.* Luysard estampillait six plombes, *it was six o'clock by the sun.* Douze plombes crossent, *it is twelve o'clock.*

Voilà six plombes et une mèche qui crossent... tu pionces encore.—Je crois bien, nous avons voulu maquiller à la sorgue chez un orphelin, mais le pantre était chaud ; j'ai vu le moment où il faudrait jouer du vingt-deux et alors il y aurait eu du raisinet.—VIDOCQ. (*It is half-past six ... sleeping yet ?—I should think so ; we wanted to do a night job at a goldsmith's, but the cove was wide-awake. I was very near doing for him with my knife.*)

Plomber (popular and thieves'), *to emit a bad smell.*

Birbe camard,
Comme un ord champignon tu plombes.
RICHEPIN.

Plomber de la gargoine, *to have an offensive breath.* Plomber, *to strike the hour.* La guimbarde ne plombe pas, *the clock does not strike the hour.* Etre plombé, *to be drunk*, or "lumpy," see **Pompette** ; *to suffer from a venereal disease*, from "French gout, ladies' fever," or worse.

Plombes, *f. pl.* (thieves'), *money*, "pieces." See **Quibus.**

De vieux marmiteux de la haute lui ont offert de l'épouser. Mais ils n'avaient que le titre (elle veut, dit-elle, le titre avec les plombes).—LOUISE MICHEL.

Plonger (thieves'), les pognes dans la profonde, or fabriquer un poivrot, *to pick the pockets of a drunken man who has come to grief on a bench.*

Plongeur, *m.* (thieves'), *poverty-stricken man*, or "quisby;" *tatter-demalion ;* (popular) *scullery man at a café or restaurant.*

Plotte, *f.* (thieves'), *purse*, "skin, or poge." Termed, in old English cant, "bounge." Faire une —, "to fake a skin."

Plouse, *f.* (thieves'), *straw*, "strommel."

Ployant, or **ployé**, *m.* (thieves'), *pocket-book*, "dee," or "dummy."

J'étais avec lui à la dînée au tapis, lorsque les cognes sont venus lui demander ses escraches et j'ai remarqué que son ployant était plein de tailbins d'altèque.—VIDOCQ. (*I was with him at dinner in the inn when the gendarmes came to ask him for his passport, and I noticed that his pocket-book was full of bank-notes.*)

Pluc, *m.* (thieves'), *booty*, "regulars," or "swag."

Plumade, *f.* (obsolete), *straw mattress.*

Plumard, *m.* (popular), *bed*, "doss," or "bug-walk." Termed also "panier, pagne, pucier."

Plumarder (military), se —, *to go to bed.*

Plume, *f.* (thieves'), *false key ; a short crowbar which generally takes to pieces for the convenience of housebreakers.* Termed also, "Jacques, sucre de pommes, l'enfant, biribi, rigolo." Denominated by English housebreakers, "the stick, Jemmy, or James." Passer à la —, *to be ill-treated by the police.* Plume de Beauce (obsolete), *straw,* or "strommel."

Quand on couche sur la plume de la Beauce (la paille), des rideaux, c'est du luxe.—VIDOCQ.

Piausser sur la — de Beauce, *to sleep in the straw.* (Popular) Plumes, *hair,* or "thatch." Termed also "tifs, douilles, douillards." Se faire des plumes, or paumer ses plumes, *to feel dull, to have the "*blues." (Familiar) Ecrire ses mémoires avec une — de quinze pieds *was said formerly of galley slaves.* An allusion to the long oar which such convicts had to ply on board the old galleys. (Military) Plume! *an ejaculation to denote that the soldier referred to will spend the night at the guard-room or in prison.* An ironical allusion to the expression "coucher dans la plume," *to sleep in a feather-bed,* and to the hard planks which are to form the culprit's couch. (Journalists') Gen de —, *literary man.* The term is used disparagingly.

C'est comme ça! continue le gen de plume. X... a osé m'envoyer son ouvrage en vers... oh! la! la! quelle guitare!—LOUISE MICHEL.

Plumeau, *m.* (popular), va donc vieux — ! *get along, you old fool,* or "doddering old sheep's head."

Plumepatte, *m.,* synonymous of **Dache** (which see).

Plumer (thieves'), le pantre, or faire la grèce, *is said of rogues who, having formed an acquaintance with travellers whom they fall in with in the vicinity of railway stations, take them to a neighbouring café and induce them to play at some swindling game, with the result that the pigeon's money changes hands.* (Popular) Plumer, *to sleep.* Se —, *to go to bed.*

Plumet, *m.* (familiar and popular), avoir son —, *to be drunk,* or "tight." Termed also "avoir son petit jeune homme, être paf, s'être piqué le nez." For other synonyms see **Pompette.** One day, in 1853, Alfred de Musset, who then had become a confirmed tippler of absinthe, called on M. Empis, the manager of the Théâtre Français, and asked one of the officials of the theatre to introduce him into his presence. The official entered the directorial office, says Philibert Audebrand, when the following dialogue took place :—

— Monsieur le directeur . . .
— Quoi ? qu'y a-t-il ?
— Eh bien, c'est M. Alfred de Musset.
— Mais, monsieur le directeur . . .
— Quoi donc ?
— C'est qu'il a son "petit jeune homme."
— Qu'est-ce que ça fait, Lachaume ? Faites entrer M. Alfred de Musset avec son petit jeune homme.

Le plus piquant de l'histoire, c'est que M. Empis ne savait pas ce que voulaient dire ces mots : "avoir son petit jeune homme."

The expression led to the following conversation between two savants :—

Un Grammairien. Eh bien, "avoir son petit jeune homme," qu'est-ce que ça veut dire ?
Un Philologue. C'est "avoir son plumet."
Le Grammairien. Bon ! me voilà bien avancé ! Qu'est-ce qu'avoir son plumet ?
Le Philologue. Monsieur, c'est "être paf."

Le Grammairien. De mieux en mieux. Qu'est-ce donc qu' " être paf " ?

Le Philologue. Selon le dictionnaire de la langue verte, le mot se dit de ceux qui " se piquent le nez."

Le Grammairien. Je ne comprends toujours pas.

Le Philologue. Eh bien, traduisez : ceux qui se saoulent.

Le Grammairien. Pour le coup, j'y suis !

Faux —, *wig,* "flash, or periwinkle."

Plumeuse, *f.* (popular), *woman who draws so largely on a man's purse as not to leave him a sou.*

Plus (popular), n'avoir — de fil sur la bobine, — de crin sur la brosse, — de gazon sur le pré, — de paillasson à la porte, *to be bald,* " to be stag-faced, to have a bladder of lard," &c. See **Avoir.** (Familiar and popular) Ne — pouvoir passer sous la Porte Saint-Denis. See **Passer.** Plus que ça de chic ! *how elegant !* — que ça de toupet ! *what* " cheek !" N'avoir — de mousse sur le caillou, *to be bald.* See **Avoir.**

Plus de mousse sur le caillou, quatre cheveux frisant à plat dans le cou, si bien qu'elle était toujours tentée de lui demander l'adresse du merlan qui lui faisait la raie.— ZOLA.

C'est — fort que de jouer au bouchon, *words meant to express the speaker's astonishment or indignation,* "it is coming it rather too strong."

Moi? exclama le fourrier stupéfait, j'aurai huit jours de salle de police? Eh ben, vrai, c'est plus fort que de jouer au bouchon ! — G. COURTELINE.

Plus souvent (familiar and popular), *certainly not ; never.*

C'est moi qui me chargerai de toi.— Plus souvent, va ! c'est encore toi qui sera

bien aise de revenir manger mon pain.—E. MONTEIL.

Pocharder (general), se —, *to get drunk,* "to get screwed." See **Sculpter.**

Pocharderie, *f.* (general), *drunkenness.*

Pochards. Signe de la croix des —. See **Ménilmuche.**

Poche, *adj. and subst.* (popular), être —, *to be drunk, to be* " screwed." See **Pompette.** (Thieves') Une —, *a spoon,* or " feeder." Termed by Rabelais " happesoupe."

Poche-œil, *m.* (popular), *blow in the eye.* Donner un —, *to give a black eye,* "to put one's eyes in half-mourning."

Pocher (printers'), better explained by quotation.

Prendre trop d'encre avec le rouleau et la mettre sur la forme sans l'avoir bien distribuée.—BOUTMY.

Poché, *m.* (popular), *dunce,* or " flat." Used sometimes as a friendly appellation.

Pochetée, *f.* (popular), en avoir une —, *to be dull-witted.*

Pochonner (popular), *to give one a couple of black eyes,* "to put one's eyes in mourning."

Poèle à châtaignes, *f.* (popular), *pock-marked face,* "cribbage-face."

Poétraillon, *m.* (familiar), *poet who writes lame verses.*

Pogne, *f.* (thieves'), *thief,* " prig," see **Grinche** ; *hand,* or " duke." Plonger les pognes dans la profonde, or dans la valade, *to pick a pocket,* "to fake a cly." See **Grinchir.**

Pogne-main (popular), à —, *heavily, roughly.*

Pognon, or **poignon**, *m.* (popular), *money*, or "*dimmock*." For synonyms see **Quibus**.

> Elle dit : je te régale,
> Et aussi tes compagnons,
> Je vas vous lester la cale,
> Mais gardez votre pognon.
> RICHEPIN, *La Mer.*

Poignard, *m.* (tailors'), *the act of touching up some article of clothing.*

Poigne, *f.* (popular), *hand*, "*daddle*." Donne-moi ta —, "*tip us your daddle*." Ergot de la —, *finger-nail*. Avoir de la —, *to be strong; energetic.*

Poignée, *f.* (popular), foutre une — de viande par la figure à quelqu'un, *to box one's ears*, "to warm the wax of one's ears."

Poignet, *m.* (familiar and popular), Madame Veuve —, *onanism.*

Poigneux, *adj.* (popular), *strong, vigorous*, "spry."

> De vieux pêcheurs venus à l'âge
> Où la poigne n'est plus poigneuse aux avirons ;
> Mais, tout de même, encor larges des palerons,
> Ayant toujours un peu de sève sous l'écorce,
> Râblés, et, s'il le faut, bons pour un coup de force.
> RICHEPIN, *La Mer.*

Poignon, *m.* (popular), *money*, "tin."

> Dis donc, l'enflé, si t'as du poignon, remuche-moi la môme. Elle est rien gironde. —RICHEPIN.

Poil, *m.* (popular), avoir un — dans la main, *to be lazy; to feel disinclined for work*, or "Mondayish."

> Gervaise s'amusa à suivre trois ouvriers, . . . qui se retournaient tous les dix pas . . . ah ! bien ! murmura-t-elle, en voilà trois qui ont un fameux poil dans la main.—ZOLA, *L'Assommoir.*

Avoir du — au cul, *to have courage,*

"spunk." Faire le —, *to surpass.* Flanquer un —, *to reprimand, to give a "wigging."* Tomber sur le —, *to thrash*, "to wallop." See **Voie**. Un bougre à poils, *a sturdy fellow, a "game" one.* (Sailors') Un cachalot bon —, *a good sailor.* Un terrien à trois poils, *a swell landsman.* (Picture dealers') Cuir et poils, *at a high price.*

> Il vend son Corot très cher, "cuir et poils," comme on dit dans ce joli commerce ; et c'est son droit ; car la valeur d'un objet d'art est facultative.—A. DAUDET.

(Familiar and popular) Prendre du — de la bête, *to take a "modest quencher" on the morning following a debauch*, "to take a hair of the dog." When a man has tried too many "hairs of the dog that bit him," he is said to be "stale drunk." If this state of things is too long continued, it is often called, "same old drunk," from a well-known nigger story. The nigger was cautioned by his master for being too often drunk within a given period, when the "cullud pusson" replied, "Same old drunk, massa, same old drunk." (Students') Le faste en —, *the garden of the Palace of Luxembourg*, by synonyms on the words luxe en bourre. Faire son petit ourson au faste en —, *to stroll in the Luxembourg garden.*

Poins (Breton cant), *theft.*

Poinsa (Breton cant), *to steal.*

Poinser (Breton cant), *thief.*

Point, *m.* (popular), *one franc* ; — de côté, *a nuisance.* Properly *a stitch in the side ; creditor*, or "dun ;" *police-officer whose functions are to watch prostitutes.* (Ecole Polytechnique) Point gamma, *yearly examination.* See

Pipo. Jusqu'au — M, *up to a certain point ; in a certain degree.* Le — Q, *breech.* Tangente au — Q, *sword.*

Pointe, *f.* (familiar), avoir sa —, *to be slightly in drink,* or "elevated." See **Pompette.**

Pointeau, *m.* (popular), *clerk who keeps a record of the working hours in manufactories.*

Pointer (popular), *to thrash,* "to give a walloping." See **Voie.**

Si ta Dédèle est gironde, faut la gober, si elle est rosse, faut la pointer ferme.— *Le Cri du Peuple,* Feb., 1886. (*If your little woman is a nice one you must love her, if she is a shrew you must thrash her well.*)

Pointu, *m.* (popular), or bouillon —, *clyster ; bishop.* (Military) Un — carré, *a slow fellow,* "stick in the mud."

Eh bien ! et les "bleus," ils ne descendent pas ? Ils n'ont donc pas entendu sonner le demi-appel, ces "pointus-carrés !" T'as de carapatas, va !—C. Dubois de Gennes.

Pointue, *f.* (thieves'), *the Préfecture de Police.* Ballonné à la —, *imprisoned in the lock-up of the Préfecture.*

Poire, *f.* (cads' and thieves'), *head,* or "tibby." See **Tronche.** Tambouriner la — à quelqu'un, *to slap one's face,* "to fetch one a wipe in the mug," or "to give a biff in the jaw" (Americanism). (Familiar and popular) Faire sa —, *to give oneself airs; to have an air of self-conceit, to look* "gumptious." Synonymous of "faire sa tête," and, in the elegant language of cads, "faire sa merde."

Poireau, *m.* (popular). Properly *leek.* Faire le —, *to be kept waiting at an appointed time or place,* "to cool, or to kick one's heels." Surtout ne me fais pas faire le —, *mind you don't* "stick me up."

Il est comme les poireaux, *he is ever young and* "spry." The expression is old.

Tu me reproches mon poil grisonnant et ne consydere point comment il est de la nature des pourreaux esquels nous voyons la teste blanche et la queue verte, droicte et vigoureuse.—Rabelais.

(Familiar and popular) Un —, *a rogue who extorts money from Sodomists under threats of disclosures.*

Par malheur le poireau, le chanteur, connaît aussi ce signe de reconnaissance. Si ces deux antiphysiques ont derrière eux cette araignée, toujours prête à tendre sa toile pour les surprendre c'en est fait du douillard.—*Mémoires de Monsieur Claude.*

Poireauter (popular), *to wait a long while at an appointed place,* "to cool, or to kick one's heels." Fielding uses the latter expression in his *Amelia :*—

In this parlour Amelia cooled her heels, as the phrase is, near a quarter of an hour.

Poirette, *f.* (thieves'), *face,* or "mug." Laver la —, *to kiss.*

Poirier, *m.* (dancing halls'), *a variety of pas seul included in the cancan,* a rather questionable sort of choregraphy.

L'orchestre joue et l'on répète le "canard qui barbote," la "tulipe orageuse," le "poirier" avec un ensemble parfait.—*Gil Blas,* Janvier, 1887.

Poiroté, *m.* (police and thieves'), *rogue who is being watched by the police.*

Poiroter (police and thieves'), *to watch,* "to give a roasting," or "to dick."

Pois, *f. pl.* (popular), coucher dans le lit aux — verts, *to sleep in the fields.*

Poison, *f.* (familiar and popular), *insulting epithet applied to a woman.*

Poisse, *f.* (popular and thieves'), *thief*, "prig." For synonyms see **Grinche.**

Voilà comment on devient grinche, l'homme pauvre devient gouêpeur, on l'envoie à la Lorcefé, il en sort poisse.—VI-DOCQ. (*That is how one takes to thieving; a poor man becomes a vagrant, he is sent to La Force, when he leaves he is a thief.*)

Une — à la détourne, *a shop-lifter*, or "sneaksman," termed formerly "buttock - and - file." "Robbing a shop by pairs is termed 'palming'—one thief bargaining with apparent intent to purchase," says the *Slang Dictionary*, "whilst the other watches his opportunity to steal. The following anecdote will give an idea of their *modus operandi*. A man once entered a 'ready-made' boot and shoe shop, and desired to be shown a pair of boots, his companion staying outside and amusing himself by looking in at the window. The one who required to be fresh shod was apparently of a humble and deferential turn, for he placed his hat on the floor directly he stepped into the shop. Boot after boot was tried on until at last a fit was obtained, when in rushed a man, snatched up the customer's hat left near the door, and ran down the street as fast as his legs could carry him. Away went the customer after his hat, and Crispin, standing at the door, clapped his hands, and shouted, 'Go it, you'll catch him?' little thinking that it was a concerted trick, and that neither his boots nor the customer would ever return." Detectives occasionally learn something from thieves, as appears from the stratagem resorted to by a French member of the *Sûreté* some time ago, who, himself a small man, and having a warrant for the arrest of an herculean and desperate scoundrel, proceeded as follows. He dogged his man, who pretended to hawk chains and watches, and, watching his opportunity, when the man had laid down his merchandise on the table of a wine-shop, he suddenly caught up one of the articles, and made off in the direction of the police station, followed thither by his quarry in hot pursuit, and crying out, "Stop thief!" Needless to say that the result was quite the reverse of that anticipated by the burly malefactor. (Dandies') La —, *the world of cads*, of "rank outsiders."

Poissé, *adj.* (thieves'), *stolen ; caught.* Au bout d'un an — avec une pesée de gigot que j'allais fourguer. *After one year nabbed with some leg of mutton which I was taking away to sell.*

Poisser (popular and thieves'), *to catch ; to steal*, "to cop, to clift, or to claim ;" — les philippes, or l'auber, *to steal money.* See **Grinchir.**

Il fait nuit, le ciel s'opaque.
Viens-tu ? J'vas poisser l'auber . . .
Au bagn' j'aurai eun' casaque !
C'est pas rigolo, l'hiver.
RICHEPIN.

Se —, *to get drunk.* See **Sculpter.** Se faire — la gerce, *to be a passive Sodomist*, or "tante."

Poisseur, *m.* (popular and thieves'), *thief*, or "prig." See **Grinche.**

Poisseuse, *f.* (familiar), *dressy, stylish woman*, a "blooming tart."

Poisseux, *m.* (familiar), *dandy*, or "masher." For list of synonyms see **Gommeux.**

Les petits jeunes gens, les poisseux, les boudinés . . . étaient à leur poste.—A. SIRVEN, *Au Pays des Roublards.*

Dandies used to apply the epithet to a cad, a "rank outsider."

A A

Poisson, *m.* (familiar and popular), *one who lives on the earnings of a prostitute, whom he terms " sa marmite," as providing him with his daily bread.*

Seulement . . . tout souteneur qui ne venge pas sa largue est considéré comme un fainéant. Il est condamné par la bande des poissons. — *Mémoires de Monsieur Claude.*

Bullies frequent all parts of Paris, but principally the outer Boulevards and Quartier Montmartre. Those of the lower sort are recognizable by their vigorous appearance, kiss-curls, tight light-coloured trousers, and tall silk cap. These degraded creatures, who are the bane of the outer quarters, readily turn murderers when "business" is slack. Léo Taxil says : " Every day the newspapers are full of the exploits of these wretches, who ply the knife as jugglers do their balls. The police are powerless against them." In a curious pamphlet, written in 1830, as a protest of the Paris bullies against a police order, forbidding prostitutes from plying their trade in public places, we have a marlou's portrait painted by himself :—

Un marlou, monsieur le Préfet, c'est un beau jeune homme, fort, solide, sachant tirer la savate, se mettant fort bien, dansant le chahut et le cancan avec élégance, aimable auprès des filles dévouées au culte de Vénus, les soutenant dans les dangers éminents (*sic*), sachant les faire respecter et les forcer à se conduire avec décence . . . vous voyez bien qu'un marlou est un être moral, utile à la société. — *Le beau Théodore Cancan.*

The synonyms of " poisson " are the following : "Alphonse, baigne-dans-le-beurre, barbise, barbe, barbillon, barbeau, marlou, benoît, brochet, dos, dos vert, casquette à trois ponts, chevalier du bidet, chevalier de la guiche, chiqueur de blanc, bouffeur de blanc, costel, cravate verte, guiche, dessous, écaillé, fish, foulard rouge, gentilhomme sous-marin, ambassadeur, gonce à écailles, goujon, lacromuche, retrousseur, dos d'azur, dauphin, macchoux, machabée, macque, macquet, macrottin, maq, maquereau, poisson frayeur, releveur de fumeuse, maquignon à bidoche, mangeur de blanc, tête de patère, marloupatte, marloupin, marlousier, marquant, mec, mec de la guiche, monsieur à nageoires, monsieur à rouflaquettes, nég en viande chaude, patenté, porte-nageoires, roi de la mer, rouflaquette, roule-en-cul, soixante-six, un qui va aux épinards, valet de cœur, visqueux, bibi, and formerly bras de fer." The English slang has " Sunday-man, petticoat pensioner, pensioner with an obscene prefix, ponce, prosser," &c. (Popular) Poisson, *large glass of brandy.*

Tous les matins, quand je m'lève,
J'ai l'cœur sens sus d'sous ;
J'l'envoi' chercher contr' la Grève
Un poisson d' quatr' sous.
Il rest' trois quarts d'heure en route,
Et puis en r'montant,
I'm'lich' la moitié d'ma goutte
Qué cochon d'enfant !
Popular Song.

Poitou, *m.* (thieves'), *the public.* Epargner le —, *to take one's precautions.* Poitou, or poiton, *no ; nothing.* As-tu vingt ronds ? Du poiton. *Have you a franc ? No.*

Poitrinaire, *f.* (popular), *woman with opulent breasts.* Properly *consumptive person.*

Poitrine, *f.* (military), d'acier, *cuirassier ;* — de velours, *officer of the engineers,* or " sapper." An allusion to the velvet front of his tunic. (Popular) Du casse —, *brandy.* Un casse —.

The celebrated physician Tardieu, in his *Etude Médico-Légale sur les Attentats aux Mœurs*, says : "Qui manu stupro dediti sunt, casse-poitrine appellantur."

Poitriner (players'), *to hold cards close to one so as to conceal one's game.*

Poivrade, *f.* (popular), *syphilis, or other kind of venereal disease,* one of which the English slang terms " French gout, or ladies' fever."

Poivre, *m. and adj.* (thieves'), *poison.* Flasquer du — à la rousse, *to keep out of the way of the police, to be in* "lavender." (Popular and thieves') Poivre, *brandy ; glass of brandy.*

De la bière, deux poivres ou un saladier ? —P. MAHALIN.

Se flanquer une culotte de —, *to get intoxicated on brandy.* Chier du —, *to abscond.* Une mine à —, *a shop where alcoholic liquors are retailed, a kind of low* "gin palace."

Comment, une bride de son espèce se permettait de mauvaises manières. . . . Tous les marchands de coco faisaient l'œil ! Il fallait venir dans les mines à poivre pour être insulté !—ZOLA.

Etre —, *to be drunk,* or "tight." See **Pompette.**

Dans la langue imagée qui a cours du côté de Montparnasse, on dit qu'un buveur est "poivre" quand il a laissé sa raison au fond des pots.—GABORIAU.

Canarder un —, *to rob a drunkard.*

Poivreau, or **poivrot,** *m.* (popular), *drunkard,* "lushington." From poivre, *rank brandy.* Boutmy says : "Un 'poivreau' que le culte de Bacchus a plongé dans la plus grande débine, se fit renvoyer de son atelier. Par pitié . . . ses camarades font entre eux une col-

lecte . . . notre poivreau revient une heure après complètement ivre.

"— Vous n'êtes pas honteux, de vous mettre dans un état pareil avec l'argent que l'on vous avait donné pour vous acheter un vête- ment ?

"— Eh bien ! répondit l'incor- rigible ivrogne, j'ai pris une 'culotte.'"

Poivrement, *m.* (thieves'), *pay- ment.*

Poivrer (general), *to overcharge,* or "to shave ;" *to give a venereal disease.*

Toi louve, toi guenon, qui m'as si bien poivré,
Que je ne crois jamais en être délivré.
ST. AMANT.

Poivreur, *m.* (thieves'), *one who pays ; one who* "shells out the shiners."

Poivrier, *m.* (popular and thieves'), *drunkard.* See **Poivrot.** Faire le —, barboter le —, *to rob a drunkard.*

A nous trois, nous avons barboté pas mal de poivriers.—*Le Petit Journal.*

Poivrier, *spirit shop ; thief who robs drunkards,* a "bug-hunter."

Poivrière, *f.* (popular), *woman suffering from a venereal disease.* Vol à la —, *robbing drunkards.*

Le pillage d'un étalage par le jeune Z. ; enfin le pillage "à la poivrière" d'un ivrogne, couché sur un banc. — GROS- CLAUDE, *Gil Blas.*

Poivrot, *m.* (general), *drunkard, or habitual drunkard,* "mop." To be on the "mop" is to be on the drink from day to day, to be per- petually "stale drunk." The synonyms of poivrot are "polo- nais, poivrier, pompier, éponge, mouillard, sac à vin," &c., and in the English slang, "lushington, bibber," and the old word "swill-pot," used by Urquhart in his translation of Rabelais :—

What doth that part of our army in the meantime which overthrows that unworthy swill-pot Grangousier?

Une filature à poivrots, *an establishment where spirits are retailed.* (Thieves') Fabriquer un —, cueillir un —, *to pick the pockets of a drunken man,* the thief being termed in the English slang a "bug-hunter."

Poivrotter (popular), se —, *to get drunk,* or "tight." For synonyms see **Sculpter.**

Police, *f.* (military), bonnet de —, *recruit,* or "Johnny raw."

Ah! mille milliards de trompettes à piston! S'être laissé tarauder ainsi par un bleu . . . par un blanc bec . . . un carapata . . . un bonnet de police ; un conscrit enfin !—Dubois de Gennes.

Police (prostitutes'), se mettre à la —, *to have one's name taken down in the police-books as a prostitute.* All such women have to fulfil that formality, failing which they are liable to be summarily locked up.

Polichinelle (popular), avaler le —, *to partake of communion.* Avoir un — dans le tiroir, *to be pregnant,* or "lumpy." Un —, *large glass of brandy.*

Si mon auguste épouse ne reçoit pas sa trempée ce soir, je veux que ce polichinelle-là me serve de poison.—Gavarni.

Agacer un — sur le zinc, *to have a glass of brandy at the bar.*

Polik (Breton cant), *cat ; attorney.*

Polir. See **Asphalte, Bitume.**

Polisseuse de mâts de cocagne en chambre, *f.* (popular), *a variety of the prostitute tribe, whose* spécialité *may more easily be guessed at than described.* In Latin fellatrix. See **Gadoue.**

Polisson, *m.* (vagrants'). Formerly *one of the tribe of rogues and mendicants, a miserably clad beggar.*

Polissons sont ceux qui ont des frusquins qui ne valent que floutière ; en hiver quand sigris bouesse, c'est lorsque leur état est plus chenastre.—*Le Jargon de l'Argot.* ("*Polissons*" *are those who possess clothes in rags ; in winter, when it is cold, then is their trade more profitable.*)

(Familiar) Polisson, *pad worn under the dress to make up for the lack of rotundity in a certain part of the body, bustle,* or "birdcage."

Dames et demoiselles quelconques, qui, pour suppléer au manque de rondeur de certaines parties, portent ce que Madame de Genlis appelle, tout crûment, un polisson, et que nous appelons une tournure.—Th. Gautier.

Polissonner (theatrical), *to hiss,* "to give the big bird."

L'auteur est un client, sa dernière pièce a été un peu polissonnée (sifflée). Il s'agit de lui donner une revanche pour celle-ci !—Balzac.

Politiculard, *m.* (journalists'), *a contemptuous term for a worthless politician.*

Y a pas . . . C'est un rude homme tout d'même, qu'eul' Bismarck qui vient d'gueuler comm' un tonnerre au Reichstag. . . . En v'là-z-un qui leur-z-y parle comm' y méritent, à c'troupeau d'politiculards allemands, presqu' aussi toc qu' les nôtres, au fond, j'm'imagine.—*Le Cri du Peuple,* 16 Janvier, 1887.

Polka, *f.* and *m.* (models'), *indecent photograph of nude figures.* (Popular) Faire danser la — à quelqu'un, *to thrash one,* "to wallop." See **Voie.** (Familiar) Polka, *silly young dandy, an indefatigable dancer.*

Les jolies femmes dédaignent les petits polkas.—*Figaro.*

Polkiste, *m.* (familiar), *in favour of the polka.*

Polochon, *m.* (popular), *bolster.* (Military) Mille polochons ! *a mild oath.*

Polonais, *m.* (popular), *drunken man,* see **Poivrot** ; *man employed to keep order in a brothel, and who is called upon to interfere when any disturbance takes place among the clientèle and ladies of the place.*

Quand la dame du lieu, à bout de prières, parle de faire descendre le Polonais, le tapage s'apaise comme par enchantement. —DELVAU.

Polonais, *a small pressing iron.*

Elle promenait doucement, dans le fond de la coiffe, le polonais, un petit fer arrondi des deux bouts.—ZOLA, *L'Assommoir.*

Pomaquer (thieves'), *to lose.* Votre greffier n'est pas pomaqué, *your cat is not lost.* Pomaquer, *to arrest,* " to smug." See **Piper.** Mon poteau s'est fait — par la rousse, *my comrade has allowed himself to be apprehended by the police, or my* "pal" *got* "smugged" *by the* " reelers." Pomaquer, *to take.*

Voilà ! En rangeant les cambrioles (petites boutiques) on a peut-être laissé se plaquer (tomber) un gluant (bébé) de carton, et je voudrais le pomaquer (prendre) pour ma daronne (mère).—RICHEPIN.

Pommade, *f.* (popular), *flattery,* " soft sawder." Jeter de la —, *to flatter,* " to butter up." Pommade, *ruin ; misfortune.* Tomber dans la —, *to be ruined,* " to be chawed up," or " smashed up."

Pommader (popular), quelqu'un, *to thrash one,* or " to anoint," see **Voie** ; *to flatter,* " to butter up." Se —, *to get drunk,* or " screwed." See **Sculpter.**

Pommadeur, *m.* (popular), *flatterer, one who gives* " soft sawder ; " *man who buys damaged furniture and sells it again after having filled up the cracks with putty.*

Pommadin, *m.* (popular), *assistant to a hair-dresser ; swell,* or " gorger." See **Gommeux.**

Pommard, *m.* (old cant), *cider.* From pomme, *apple.*

Pomme, *f.* (popular and thieves'), *head,* or " tibby ; " *face,* or " mug." See **Tronche.**

Allons, ho ! fais-moi voir ta pomme ;
Rapplique un peu sous l'bec ed'gaz,
J'te gob' ; faut profiter de l'occas'.
GILL.

(Popular) Pomme de rampe, *bald head,* " bladder of lard." Sucer la —, *to kiss.* Une — à vers, *Dutch cheese.* Une — de canne, *grotesque face,* or "knocker face." Avoir une — de canne fêlée, *to be deranged,* " to have a slate off," " to be balmy." See **Avoir.** Aux pommes, or bate aux pommes, *excellent, first-rate,* " slap up." Concerning the expression Rigaud says : " Deux consommateurs, un habitué et un étranger, demandent, dans un café, chacun un bifteck, le premier aux pommes, le second naturel, nature, dans l'argot des restaurateurs. Le garçon chargé des commandes vole vers les cuisines et s'écrie d'une voix retentissante, ' Deux biftecks, dont un aux pommes, soigné !' Le mot fit fortune. C'est depuis ce jour qu'on dit, Aux pommes, pour soigné." (Military) C'est comme des pommes, *it is useless.*

Pommé, *adj.* (familiar and popular), *excessive,* " awful." Bêtise pommée, *great stupidity.*

Pommer, or **paumer** (thieves' and cads'), *to apprehend,* " to nail," or " to smug."

Enfin que'qu'fois quand on m'pomme,
J'couch' au post'. C'est chouett', c'est
    chaud,
Et c'est là qu'on trouve, en somme,
Les gens les plus comme il faut.
      RICHEPIN, *La Chanson des Gueux.*

Paumer ses plumes, *to feel dull.*

Pommier, m. (popular), en fleurs, *breasts of a young maiden ;* — stérile, *skinny breasts.*

Pompage, m. (popular), *libations,* " lushing."

Pompe, f. (tailors'), *touching up of ill-fitting garments.* Petite —, grande —, respectively, *touching up of waistcoats and coats.* (Familiar and popular) Pompe funèbre, *a variety of prostitute.* In Latin fellatrix. (Military schools') Le corps de —, *the staff of instructors.* La —, *work.*

La pompe ! à ce grand mot votre intel-
    lect se tend
Et cherche à deviner. . . . La pompe, c'est
    l'étude,
La pompe, c'est la longue et funeste habi-
    tude
De puiser chaque jour chez messieurs les
    auteurs
Le suc et l'élixir de leurs doctes labeurs . . .
La pompe, c'est l'effroi du chasseur, du
    houzard,
Du spahi, du dragon, et, malgré sa cuirasse,
Du cuirassier.—Voilà la pompe.
      THEO-CRITT, *Nos Farces à Saumur.*

(Military) La — du part-à-douze, *imaginary pump in the paradise from which rain is supposed to spout.*

Parfait, s'écrie Cousinet, il me paraît que le père Eternel il a mis quatre hommes de renfort à la pompe du part-à-douze ! . . . Voilà ce qui peut s'appeler une averse de bonheur !—DUBOIS DE GENNES.

(Popular and thieves') Pompe, *shoe,* " trotter case, or daisy root." See **Ripaton.** Refiler un coup de — dans l'oignon, *to kick one in the behind,* " to root."

Pomper (popular), *to drink much,* " to guzzle," see **Rincer ;** *to work hard,* " to sweat ;" (shopmen's) — le gaz, *to be the victim of a practical joke, which consists in making a new-comer ply an imaginary gas-pump.* Pomper meant formerly *to make a sacrifice to Venus.* Le Roux gives the explanation in the following words : " Dans un sens équivoque et malicieux, pour faire le déduit."

Pompette, adj. (general), être —, *to be intoxicated.*

Ce serait moule de ne pas rigoler parfois. . . . On se sépara à trois heures, délicatement pompettes.—EMILE KAPP, *La Joie des Pauvres.*

Rabelais uses the word with the signification of " grog-blossoms." The terms graduating the scale of drunkenness, beginning with those which denote mild intoxication, are : " Avoir sa pointe, son allumette, sa pistache, un grain ; être bien, monté, en train, lancé, parti, poussé, en patrouille, éméché, ému, bamboche ; voir en dedans, être dessous, dans les brouillards, pavois, allumé, gai, dans un état voisin, mouillé, humecté, casquette, bu, bien pansé, pochard, poche, gavé, cinglé, plein, rond, complet, rond comme une balle, raide, raide comme la justice, paf, slasse, poivre, riche, chargé, dans la paroisse de Saint-Jean le Rond, dans les vignes du seigneur, vent dessus dessous, fier, dans les broussailles, dans les brindezingues ; avoir un coup de bouteille, de sirop, de soleil, de gaz, de feu, sa chique, un sabre, son paquet, son casque, une culotte, le nez sale, son plumet, son jeune homme, son caillou, sa cocarde, une barbe, son pompon, son poteau, son toquet, son sac, sa cuite, son affaire, son compte, son plein, sa pente, en avoir une vraie mufée ; être saoul comme un âne, comme un hanneton, comme une grive, comme un Polonais ; être pion, en avoir jusqu'à la troisième capucine, saoul comme trente mille hommes, être asphyxié." According to the *Slang Dictionary* the slang terms for mild intoxication are certainly very choice; they are, "beery, bemused, boozy, bosky, buffy, corned, foggy, fou, fresh, hazy, elevated, kisky, lushy, moony, muggy, muzzy, on, screwed, slewed, tight, and winey." A higher or more intense state of beastliness is represented by the expressions, "podgy, beargered, blued, cut, primed, lumpy, ploughed, muddled, obfuscated, swipey, three sheets in the wind, and top-heavy." But the climax of fuddlement is only obtained when the "disguised" individual "can't see a hole in a ladder," or when he is "all mops and brooms," or "off his nut," or "with his mainbrace well spliced," or with "the sun in his eyes," or when he has "lapped the gutter," and got the "gravel-rash," or is on the "ran-tan," or on the "ree-raw," or when "sewed up," and regularly "scammered,"—then, and not till then, is he entitled, in vulgar society, to the title of "lushington," or recommended to "put in the pin," *i.e.*, the linch-pin, to keep his legs steady. We may add to this long list the expression which is to be found in *A Supplementary English Glossary*, by T. Lewis O. Davies, "to hunt a tavern fox," or "to be foxed."

Else he had little leisure time to waste,
Or at the ale-house huff-cap ale to taste ;
Nor did he ever hunt a tavern fox.
J. TAYLOR, *Life of Old Parr*, 1635.

The same author gives "mucki-

bus," *tipsy*, to be found in Walpole's *Letters*.

Pompier, *m.* (popular), *drunken man, one who is* "screwed;" *drunkard,* or "lushington;" *a mixture of vermout and cassis ; pocket-handkerchief,* "snottinger;" — de nuit, *scavenger employed in emptying the cesspools,* "gold-finder." (Tailors') Pompier, *journeyman tailor whose functions are to touch up the ill-fitting parts of garments ;* (École Polytechnique) *musical rigmarole which the students sing on the occasion of certain holidays ;* (military) *soldier who is the reverse of smart ;* (literary) *productions written in a conventional, commonplace style ;* (students') *member of the Institut de France ; a student preparing for an examination.* (Artists') Faire son —, *consisted in painting a large picture representing some Roman or Greek hero in full armour, and armed with shield, lance, or sword.* For the following explanation I am indebted to Mr. G. D., a French artist well known to the English public :—

Du temps de David et plus tard on disait d'un artiste qui n'avait pas eu le prix de Rome : bah ! il fera son pompier, il réussira tout de même. Or, faire son pompier, c'était peindre un grand tableau représentant un Grec ou un Romain célèbre avec casque, bouclier et lance ; une ville en flammes dans le fond ; et si le nu,—car il n'y avait d'autre costume que l'armure,—si le nu dis-je, était bien, l'artiste obtenait un succès. Le pompier était acheté généralement par le gouvernement pour être placé dans un musée de province. Quand vous visiterez les musées de France, vous n'aurez pas de chance si vous ne trouvez pas au moins trois pompiers. Il paraît que les greniers du Louvre en possèdent des quantités qui y restent faute de place dans les musées.

Pompon, *m.* (popular), *head,* "nut," or "tibby." See **Tronche**. Dévisser le — à quelqu'un, *to break one's head.* Un vieux —, *an old* *fool*, "doddering old sheep's head." Avoir son —, *to be drunk*, or "screwed." See **Pompette.**

> J'avais mon pompon
> En r'venant de Suresnes ;
> Tout le long de la Seine,
> J'sentais qu' j'étais rond.
> *Parisian Song.*

(Military) Pompon, *drunkard.*

Ponant, *m.* (popular), *the behind.* See **Vasistas.**

Ponante, *f.* (thieves'), *prostitute of the lowest class*, "draggle-tail." The connection with "ponant" is obvious. See **Gadoue.**

Ponce, *f.* (thieves' and roughs'), refiler une —, *to thrash*, "to set about" *one.* See **Voie.**

Pondant, *m.* (schools'), *guardian of a school-boy whose parents live at a distance, who takes him out on holidays.*

Pondre (popular), *to work*, "to graft;" — sur ses œufs, *to keep on increasing one's wealth;* — un œuf, *to ease oneself*, "to go to the chapel of ease." See **Mouscailler.**

Poney, *m.* (sporting), *five hundred francs.* Double —, *carriage and pair of ponies.*

> Son petit air fripon et la crânerie avec laquelle elle conduit son double poney.— *Figaro*, Oct., 1886.

Poniffe, or **poniffle,** *f.* (thieves'), *prostitute*, "bunter." See **Gadoue.**

> Et si la p'tit' ponif'e triche
> Su' l'compt' des rouleaux,
> Gare au bataillon d'la guiche !
> C'est nous qu'est les dos.
> RICHEPIN, *La Chanson des Gueux.*

Ponifler (thieves'), *to make love to a woman.*

Pont, *m.* (popular), d'Avignon, *prostitute*, or "mot." See **Gadoue.** (Card-sharpers') Faire le — sec, *to slightly bend a card at the place*

at which it is desired the pack should be cut. (Familiar and popular) Couper dans le —, *to believe a falsehood; to fall into a snare.* (Thieves') Donner un — à faucher, *to prepare a snare for one.* (Officials') Faire le —, *is to keep away from one's office on a day preceded and followed by a holiday.* (Popular) Pont-levis de cul (obsolete), *breeches.*

> Chausses à la martingale ce qui est un pont-levis de cul.—RABELAIS.

(Roughs') Le — aux bergères, *the Halles, or Paris central market.* Aller au — aux bergères, *to go to that place for the purpose of meeting with a prostitute.*

Pontaniou, *m.* (sailors'), *prison.*

Ponter (gamesters'), *to stake;* — dur, *to play high;* — sec, *to stake large sums at intervals.* (Bohemians') Ponter, *to pay*, "to fork out."

Pontes pour l'af, *f. pl.* (thieves'), *a gathering of card-sharpers.*

Ponteur, *m.* (popular), *man who keeps a woman;* (familiar and popular) *gamester.*

Pontife, *m.* (popular), *shoemaker.* An allusion to the souliers à pont in fashion at the beginning of the seventeenth century. Souverain —, *master shoemaker.*

Ponton, *m.* (popular), d'amarrage, *hulks.* (Sailors') Devenir —, *to become old, worn out.*

> Jamais si longtemps qu'il vivra
> Si ponton qu'il devienne,
> Jamais ceux qui l'ont pris sous l'bras,
> Jamais le capitaine,
> Il n'oubliera !
> RICHEPIN, *La Mer.*

Pontonnière, *f.* (popular), *prostitute who plies her trade under the arches of bridges.*

> Les pontonnières fréquentent le dessous des ponts . . . toutes ces filles sont des

voleuses. Le macque qui joue ici un rôle plus actif que le barbillon ne quitte sa largue ni jour ni nuit.—Canler.

Popotte, *f.* (familiar), *table d'hôte.* Faire la —, *to cook.* Etre —, *is said of a very plain, homely woman.* (Military) Popotte, *military mess in a small way.*

L'unique cabaret de Hanoï le vit donc à l'heure de l'absinthe, mêlé aux uniformes, et il connut les réunions de table par "fractions de corps," les popottes où les officiers dévoraient joyeusement les vivres ferrugineux des boîtes de conserves.—P. Bonnetain, *L'Opium.*

Popotter. See **Popotte.**

Populo, *m.* (familiar), *populace,* or "mob." Swift informs us, in his *Art of Polite Conversation,* that "mob" was, in his time, the slang abbreviation of mobility, just as nob is of nobility at the present day.

It is perhaps this humour of speaking no more words than we need which has so miserably curtailed some of our words, that in familiar writing and conversation they often lose all but their first syllables, as in mob, red. pos. incog. and the like.—Addison's *Spectator.*

Burke called the populace "the great unwashed."

Porc-épic, *m.* (thieves'), *the Holy Sacrament.* An allusion to the metal beams which encircle the Host.

Portanche, *m.* (thieves'), *doorkeeper.*

Port d'armes, *m.* (military), laisser au —, *to leave the service before another ; to leave one waiting.*

Porte, *f.* (familiar and popular), ne plus pouvoir passer sous la — Saint-Denis, *to be an injured husband.* Alluding to the height of his horns. Un clos —, *a doorkeeper.* A play on the words clot porte and cloporte, *woodlouse.* It must be said that in

Paris the concierges are generally much detested by lodgers, and deservedly so.

Et quoique d'aucuns m'appell't clos porte
J'n'ai pas fait l'vœu d'passer pour sot.
Lamentations du Portier d'en face.

Porté, *adj.* (familiar and popular), sur l'article, *one with a well-developed bump of amativeness ;* (military schools') — sur la liste des élèves morts, *on the sick list.*

Porte - aumusse, *m.* (popular), *master shoemaker,* or "snob."

Porte-balle, *m.* (popular), *humpback,* or "lord."

Porte-bonheur, *m.* (familiar and popular), *pig.* Termed in English thieves' cant, "grunting cheat, or patricoe's kinchen." An allusion to certain trinkets which represent this animal and are said to bring luck to the wearer.

Porte-bottes, *m.* (military), *trooper,* in opposition to "guêtré," *foot-soldier.*

L'hiver c'est à l'écurie que le porte-bottes précède de beaucoup le réveil de ses bons voisins les guêtrés.—Dubois de Gennes.

Porte-chance, *m.* (popular), *lump of excrement,* or "quaker." Literally *luck-bearer.* Superstitious people in France believe that treading by chance on the abovementioned is an unfailing sign of a forthcoming moneyed windfall.

Porte-crème, *m.* (popular), *scavenger employed at emptying the cesspools,* "gold-finder."

Porte de prison, *f.* (popular), *ill-natured, snarling person ; one who is constantly* "nasty," or "grumble guts ;" one whose speeches jar on the ear as unpleasantly as the grating of a prison door.

Portefeuille, *m.* (familiar and popular), *bed,* "doss, bug-walk, kip." Se fourrer dans son —, *to go to bed, to get into* "kip." Mettre un lit en —, *to make an* "apple-pie" *bed.*

De classe en classe les soldats se transmettent un certain nombre de facéties . . . mettre le lit du bleu en portefeuille, de façon qu'il ne puisse entrer plus loin que les chevilles.—G. COURTELINE.

Portefeuilliste, *m.* (familiar), *minister of state.*

Porte-luque, *m.* (thieves'), *pocketbook,* "dummy, or dee."

Porte-maillot, *m.* (theatrical), *ballet dancer.* Literally *one who wears tights.*

Porte-manteau, *m.* (popular), épaules en —, *high and flat shoulders.*

Porte-mince, *m.* (thieves'), *pocketbook,* "dee, or dummy."

Porte-morningue, *m.* (thieves'), *purse,* "skin," or "poge." Termed also "porte-mornif."

Porte-nageoires, *m.* (familiar and popular), *man who lives on prostitutes' earnings,* "pensioner." For synonyms see **Poisson.**

Porte-pipe, *m.* (popular), *mouth,* "mug, rattle-trap, kisser, gob."

Porte-poigne, *m.* (popular), *glove.*

Porter (familiar and popular), en faire —, *to deceive conjugally.* For faire porter des cornes.

Avoir un gendre ! Ah ! c'est superbe !
Quand nous irons tous à Meudon
L'été prochain dîner su' l'herbe,
Ça s'ra lui qui port'ra l'melon.
Ma femm', qu'a d' l'esprit quand a'cause,
Craint qu' Véronique ait fait le vœu
D'y fair' porter . . . même autre chose !
        E. CARRÉ.

En —, *to be deceived conjugally.* Porter à la peau, *to inspire with carnal desires ;* — le deuil de sa blanchisseuse, *to have linen the reverse of snow-white.* Literally *to be in mourning for one's*

washerwoman ; —sa malle, *to be a humpback,* or "lord ;" (thieves') — gaffe, *to be on sentry duty.* Un grivier qui porte gaffe, *a soldier on sentry duty.* Porter du gras - double au moulin, *to sell stolen lead to a receiver,* or "fence."

Porte-trèfle, *m.* (popular), *trousers,* "kicks."

Porteur, *m.* (thieves'), de camoufle, *prostitute's bully,* "ponce." See **Poisson.** "Camoufle" is equivalent to chandelle, and "tenir la chandelle" *is to favour the intercourse of lovers.* (Popular) Avoir cassé la gueule à son — d'eau, *to have one's menses.*

Porteuse, *f.* (thieves') *hand,* "picker, famm, duke, or daddle."

Porte-veine. See **Porte-bonheur.**

Portez ! remettez ! (cavalry), *a mock command said when anyone has just uttered something foolish,* or *a* "bull."

Portier, *m.,* **portière,** *f.* (familiar and popular), *scandal-monger.* Alluding to the propensity of Paris doorkeepers for scandal.

Portion, *f.* (military), *prostitute,* or "barrack - hack." Demi —, *chum.*

— Mon bon camarade Cousinet, hé donc !
— Ah ! tu es la demi-portion du Merlan ?
C'est un bon zigue.—DUBOIS DE GENNES.

Portrait, *m.* (popular), *face,* "mug." Dégrader le — à quelqu'un, *to strike one in the face, to give one a* "facer," "to fetch one a bang in the mug," or "to give a biff in the jaw" (Americanism).

Portugal, *m.* (popular), une entrée de —, *said of a bad, awkward rider.*

Pose, *f.* (familiar and popular), la faire à la —, *to assume an air of*

superiority. Faut pas me la faire
à la —, "you mustn't come Shakespeare over me, you mustn't come
Rothschild over me," &c. (Popular) A moi la — ! *words used by a
man who has just received a blow, to
express his intention of returning
it with interest.* Literally, expression used by domino players,
my turn to play !

Poser (artists'), l'ensemble, *to
pose nude ;* (familiar and popular)
— un factionnaire, or un pépin,
to ease oneself, " to bury a quaker,"
see **Mouscailler;** — un lapin,
or lapiner, *to deceive, to take one
in.* More specially *to enjoy the
good graces of a cocotte and make
off without giving her a fee,* "to
do a bilk."

Si l'abbé Roussel a essayé de " poser un
lapin " et s'il laisse vraiment cette petite
noceuse sous une prévention de ce genre,
voilà qui m'indigne.—FRANCIS ENNE, *Le
Radical.*

For explanation see **Lapin.**
Faire — quelqu'un, *to make one
wait a long time ; to fool one,* "to
bamboozle." Poser pour le torse,
*to bear oneself so as to show off
one's figure ;* (popular) — sa
chique, *to hold one's tongue,* "to
be mum." Pose ta chique, "hold
your jaw, or stubble your whids."
Poser et marcher dedans, *to get
bewildered ; to betray oneself ;*
(thieves') — un gluau, *to lay a
trap, or make preparations for the
apprehension of a criminal,* of one
who is "wanted" by the police.
Gluau, *bird-lime.*

Poses, *f. pl.* (gamesters'), faire des
—, *to insert certain cards prepared
for cheating purposes in a pack.*

Poseur de lapins, *m.* (familiar and
popular), *artful fellow who fools
simple-minded folk.*

Le garçon.—Trente-sept francs soixante-
quinze, messieurs.

Deuxième provincial, bondissant. —
Trente-sept francs soixante-quinze ! Comment, nous n'avons que nos deux "as-
sinthes " et les deux bocks de ce monsieur !
Le garçon.—Oui, mais il y a l'addition
de ce monsieur qui a déjeûné avec une
dame . . . vous êtes du Midi, n'est-ce pas,
messieurs? . . . Eh bien, croyez-moi : à
Paris, mieux vaut encore parler tout seul
que de lier conversation avec un "poseur
de lapins."—PAUL MAHALIN.

The epithet is also applied to a
man who deceives a woman of
indifferent character by making
promises of money or presents,
one who does a " bilk."

Eva sonne sa femme de chambre qui
vient pendant qu'il murmure : châmante,
châmante !
— Tu peux le prendre, s'il te convient,
moi, je n'aime pas les poseurs de lapins.—
MATHURINE, *La Marotte.*

Poseuse, *f.* (theatrical), *female
singer whose business is to pose.*

Là, il put à son aise imposer son répertoire aux chanteurs, répertoire fort varié,
du reste, car pour les "poseuses" on fit
murmurer le rossignol et le papillon se poser
sur la rose à peine éclose.—J. SERMET.

Position, *f.* (thieves'), *trunk, portmanteau,* "peter." Thieves judge
of a man's standing by his
"traps."

Possédé, *m.* (thieves'), *brandy,*
"bingo," in old cant.

Posséder son embouchure (popular), *to have a natural talent
for speechifying,* "to have the
gift of the gab."

Poste, *m.* (sailors'), or — aux choux,
victualling boat.

Postérieurs, *m. pl.* (popular), limonadier des —, *apothecary,* one
who used to perform the "clysterium donare" of Molière.
Termed also "flûtencul," and
formerly "mirancu."

Postiche, *f.* (printers'), *dull story ;
humbug,* "regular flam, or gam-
mon ;" (thieves') *gathering of*

people in the street, enabling rogues to ease someone of his valuables, "scuff."

Postière, *f.* (popular), *female clerk employed at the post office.*

Postige, *f.* (mountebanks'), *preliminary performance of mountebanks.*

Postillon, *m.* (thieves'), *pellet used as a mode of communication between prisoners, or between a prisoner and outsiders.*

Un postillon est tout simplement une boulette de mie de pain pétrie entre les doigts et renfermant une lettre, un avis.—*Mémoires de Canler.*

Envoyer le —, *to correspond thus.* (Popular) Postillon d'eau chaude, *engine driver,* "puffing billy" *driver; hospital assistant whose functions consist in administering clysters to patients,* an operation described by Molière as "clysterium donare."

Postillonner (thieves'), *to correspond by means of the* "postillon" (which see); (familiar and popular) *to spit involuntarily when talking.*

Posture, *f.* (popular), en —, *apothecary,* or "pill-driver." Termed also "potard."

Pot, *m.* (thieves'), *cabriolet, a kind of gig.* Termed also "cuiller à pot, or potiron roulant."

Enlevez le gré, le pot et les frusquins du sinve qui s'est esgaré avec les miens.—VIDOCQ. (*Take away the horse, the gig, and the clothes of the fool who ran away with mine.*)

Pot, *crucible used by coiners.* (Popular) Fouille au —, *man who is fond of taking liberties with women.*

Il fallait le voir toujours en petoche autour d'elle. Un vrai fouille-au-pot, qui tâtait sa jupe par derrière, dans la foule, sans avoir l'air de rien.—ZOLA.

Potache, *m.* (students'), *pupil at a lycée, a government school.* Pro-bably a corruption of "potasse," from "potasser," a slang term used by students to signify *to work.* L. Larchey says the origin of the word may be found in "pot-à-chien," *college cap.*

Potager, *m.* (popular), *brothel,* "nanny-shop, flash-drum, or academy."

Pot-à-minium, *m.* (popular), *painter or house decorator.*

Pot-à-moineaux, *m.* (popular), *large hat,* "mushroom."

Potard, *m.* (popular), *apothecary,* "pill-driver, gallipot, or squirt."

C't Arthur de Bretagne, n'fut même pas l'premier ouvrage d' Claude Bernard puisque ... l'élève pharmacien avait fait représenter à Lyon une bluette pas méchante. ... Avec son manuscrit dans sa malle le jeune potard vint à Paris.—TRUBLOT, *Le Cri du Peuple.*

Potasser (students'), *to work.* Termed "to sap" at Winchester and many other schools. Also *to work hard,* "to mug."

Pot-à-tabac, *m.* (popular), *short and stout person,* "humpty dumpty;" *dull, insignificant man,* "very small potatoes;" (thieves') *policeman.* Termed also "rousse, roussin, bâton de réglisse, baladin, cagne, cogne, balai, serin, pousse, vache, arnif, peste, tronche à la manque, flaquadard, cabestan, raille (*detective officer*), railleux, sacre, grive, laune, flique, bec-de-gaz, estaffier, bourrique, pousse-cul, lampion rouge, escargot de trottoir, cierge, sergo;" in the English cant and slang, "crusher, worm, pig, bobby, blue-bottle, reeler, copper, Johnny Darby (corruption of gendarme), philip, philistine, peeler, raw lobster, slop;" and in ancient cant of beggars, "harmanbek.' Whence "beak," or *magistrate.*

Pot-au-feu, *m.* (popular), *behind,* see **Vasistas**; (coiners') *crucible in which coiners melt the metal used in their nefarious trade.* (Familiar) Etre —, *to be commonplace, plain.*

Ce n'est pas cet imbécile, qui m'aurait éclairée . . . il est d'ailleurs bien trop pot-au-feu.—BALZAC.

Pot au vin, *m.* (familiar and popular), obsolete, *the head.*

Si Dieu me sauve le moule du bonnet, c'est le pot au vin, disait ma mère-grand.—RABELAIS.

Pot-bouille, *f.* (familiar and popular), *kitchen and household duties in a small way.* The term has passed into the language.

Poteau, *m.* (thieves'), un —, *a friend,* or "ben cull;" *a top man, or prince among the canting crew.* Also *the chief rogue of the gang, or the completest cheat,* "dimber damber." Termed "upright man" in old English cant. Poteaux de bal, *prison chums,* "schoolmen." (Engine-drivers') Avoir son — kilométrique *is said of a man who is in a state of intoxication, but who can yet find his way.* Avoir son — télégraphique, *to be completely drunk,* or "slewed." See **Pompette.** According to M. Denis Poulot the different stages are "attraper une allumette ronde," "avoir son allumette de marchand de vin," "prendre son allumette de campagne," "avoir son poteau," and as above.

Potée, *f.* (popular), enfiler sa —, *to drink a litre measure of wine.*

Potence, *f.* (popular), *rascally person of either sex;* "bad egg," in the case of a man.

Potet, *m.* (popular), *whimsical man; old fool,* or "doddering old sheep's head."

Potin, *m.* (popular), *row, uproar.* Faire du —, *to make loud complaints.*

I s'retourne, i fait du potin . . .
Mais de la levrett' le larbin
Le trait' de p'tit' gouape et d'fripouille !
GILL.

Faire du —, *is said also of some event which causes great excitement.*

Avant-hier a été donné aux ambassadeurs un dîner de douze couverts qui certainement fera du potin dans le monde qui s'amuse.—*Figaro,* Oct., 1886.

(Familiar and popular) Potin, *scandalous report.* Synonymous of cancans. Concerning the latter expression Madame de Genlis quotes the following conversation between General Decaen, who was at the time aide-de-camp to his brother, and who had been arrested by the gendarmerie on his way to the camp :—

Comment vous nommez-vous? lui demanda le brigadier.
— Decaen.
— D'où êtes-vous ?
— De Caen.
— Qu' êtes-vous ?
— Aide de camp.
— De qui ?
— Du général Decaen.
— Où allez-vous ?
— Au camp.
— Oh ! oh ! dit le brigadier, qui n'aimait pas les calembourgs, il y a trop de cancans dans votre affaire ; vous allez passer la nuit au violon, sur un lit de camp.—*Mémoires.*

Potiner (familiar and popular), *to talk scandal.*

Potinier (familiar and popular), *scandal-monger.*

Potiron, *m.* (popular), *the behind;* (thieves') — roulant, *gig.*

Potot, or **poteau,** *m.* (convicts'), *friend,* or "pal;" *Sodomist.*

Potred ann taouen (Breton cant), *cod-fishers.*

Potred ann tok-tok (Breton cant), *slaters.*

Pou affamé, *m.* (popular), *greedy man, a worshipper of money.*

Poubelles, *f. pl.* (familiar), *kind of dust-bins which the inhabitants have to place at their doors every morning, in accordance with a recent regulation promulgated by M. Poubelle, Prefect of the Seine.*

Pouce, *m.* (popular), avoir le — rond, *to be dexterous, skilful.* Donner le coup de —, *to give short weight ; to strangle.* Et le — ! *and ever so many more !* (Artists') Avoir du —, *is said of a picture painted in bold, vigorous style.*

Poucette, *f.* (card-sharpers'), *act of adding to one's stakes laid on the table directly the game is favourable.* From pouce, the money being pushed with the thumb.

Pouchon, *m.* (thieves'), *purse,* " skin, or poge."

Poudre, *f.* (freemasons'), faible, *water ;* — forte, *wine ;* — fulminante, *brandy ;* — noire, *coffee.*

Pouffiace, or **pouffiasse,** *f.* (thieves'), *prostitute ; low prostitute,* " draggle-tail." See **Gadoue.**

Si j'ai pas l'rond, mon surin bouge.
Or, quand la pouffiace a truqué,
Chez moi son beurre est pomaqué.
Mieux vaut bouffer du blanc qu'du rouge.
RICHEPIN.

Pouffiasbourg, *m.* (popular), *nickname for Asnières,* a locality in the vicinity of Paris, where many ladies leading a gay life have their abode ; a kind of Parisian St. John's Wood, in that respect.

Poufiasser (popular), *is said of persons of either sex whose fondness for the opposite sex leads them into living a life of a questionable description.* A man in that case is said to " go molrowing."

Poufs, *m. pl.* (familiar), faire des —, *is said of a person who runs*

into debt knowing he will be unable to meet his liabilities, and then suddenly decamps.

Pouic (thieves'), *no ; nothing,* " nix."

Pouiffe, *f.* (thieves'), *money,* " dinarly," " pieces," see **Quibus ;** *woman of questionable character, or prostitute.* Termed by English rogues, " blowen, or bunter."

Pouilleux, *m.* (familiar), *poor devil,* or " quisby ;" *miser, skinflint,* " hunks." Properly *lousy man.*

Poulailler, *m.* (popular), *house of ill-fame,* or " nanny-shop." Properly *hen-house ; upper gallery in a theatre,* " up among the gods."

Poulain, *m.* (military), faire un —, *to fall from one's horse,* " to come a cropper."

Poulainte, *f.* (thieves'), *swindle on an exchange of goods.*

Poularde, *f.* (journalists'), *kept woman.*

Poule, *f.* (popular), laitée, *man devoid of energy,* " sappy," or " henpecked fellow ;" — d'eau, *washerwoman.* Termed also " baquet insolent." Des poules, *female inmates of a house of ill-fame,* " dress lodgers."

Poulet, *m.* (popular), manger le —, *to be in confederacy with a builder, so as to divide the proceeds of unlawful gains.* The expression is used by masons, carpenters, and others employed in house-building, in reference to architects and their accomplices. Poulet de carême, *red herring,* or " Yarmouth capon ;" *frog.* Frogs not being considered as flesh. Poulet d'hospice, *lean, hungry-looking fellow, one who looks like a half-drowned rat ;* — d'Inde, *fool, or* "flat ;" and in military slang, *horse,* or "gee."

Oui, répondit-il en ramassant son cheval . . . j'allais vous proposer un tour de promenade. Si cela vous sourit, en route ! J'ai dit à Saïd de seller votre poulet d'Inde. —Bonnetain, *L'Opium.*

Poulot, *m.* (popular), for poulailler, *the gallery in a theatre,* "up amongst the gods."

Poupard, *m.* (thieves'), *swindle, or crime,* "plant." Nourrir un —, *to make all necessary preparations in view of committing a robbery or murder.* Goury de —, *accomplice,* "stallsman."

Poupée, *f.* (popular), *paramour,* "moll ;" (thieves') *soldier ;* (sailors') *figure-head.* Etre entre poupe et poupée, *to be out at sea.*

Poupon, *m.* (popular), *tool-bag ;* (thieves') *any kind of crime,* "job."

Voici la balle ! Dans le poupon, Ruffard était en tiers avec moi et Godet.—Balzac.

Pour (cads' and thieves'), *perhaps ;* — chiquer, *nonsense, gammon !* (Familiar and popular) Ce n'est pas — enfiler des perles *is expressive of doubt as to the innocence of purpose or harmlessness of some action.*

Et veux-tu savoir ce qui t'embête, chéri ? . . . C'est que toi-même tu trompes ta femme. Hein ? tu ne découches pas pour enfiler des perles.—Zola.

(Popular) Pour la peau, *for nothing.*

Alors c'est pour la peau que j'ai tiré cinquante-neuf mois et quinze jours de service ?—G. Courteline.

(Printers') Aller chou — chou, *to imitate closely a printed copy when composing.* (Prostitutes') C'est — les bas, *gratuity to prostitutes in a brothel.* Alluding to their habit of using their stockings as a receptacle for the money they receive.

Pour-compte, *m.* (tailors'), *misfit.*

Pourlécher (popular), s'en — la face, *to be delighted with something,* the result being that one is in "full feather, or cock-a-hoop." Tu t'en pourlécheras la face, *that will give you great pleasure,* "that'll rejoice the cockles of your heart."

Pourri, *adj.* (familiar), *full ;* — de chic, *very elegant, dashing,* "tsing tsing."

Pousse, *f,* (thieves'), *police, gendarmerie.* (Popular) Ce qui se —, *money,* "loaver." See **Quibus.** (Roughs') Filer, or refiler une — à quelqu'un, *to hustle,* "to flimp ;" *to throw down.* Y veut m' coller un coup d' sorlot dans les accessoires ; je l'y file une pousse et j' te l'envoie dinguer sur le trime. *He tried to kick me in the privy parts ; I threw him down and sent him sprawling in the road.*

Poussé, *adj.* (thieves'), *drunk,* or "canon." See **Pompette.**

Pousse-au-vice, *f.* (popular), *Spanish fly.*

Pousse-bateau, *m.* (popular), *water.*

Pousse-café, *m.* (familiar), *a small glass of brandy or liqueur drunk after taking coffee,* le repousse-café being a second glass.

Pousse-cailloux, *m.* (popular), *infantry soldier,* "wobbler." In the slang of the cavalry, "mud-crusher, or beetle-crusher."

Pousse-cul, *m.* (familiar and popular), obsolete, "archer," *or soldier of the watch.*

Pousse-cul, pour archer, ou ce qu'on appelle vulgairement à Paris des sergens, ou des archers de l'écuelle, qui vont d'un côté et d'autre pour prendre les gueux.— Le Roux.

Nisard, in his interesting work,

De quelques Parisianismes populaires, says that the foot-soldiers of the watch were termed "pousse-culs," whereas the mounted police went by the name of "lapins ferrés," lapin being the general term for a soldier, as shown by a letter from a general of the army in Italy to Bonaparte, written in true Spartan-like spirit :—

Citoyen général en chef—Les lapins mangent du pain ; pas de pain, pas de lapins ; pas de lapins, pas de victoire : ainsi ouvre l'œil n, i, ni, c'est fini.

Pousse-cul (obsolete), *Lovelace*. It now has the signification of *police-officer.*

Poussée, *f.* (popular), *reprimand,* or "wigging ;" *urgent work.* Voilà une belle — de bateaux *is expressive of disappointment at finding that something which has been praised falls short of one's expectations.*

Pousse-moulin, *m.* (popular), *water,* "Adam's ale." Termed "lage" in old English cant. Evidently the old French word "aigue, aige," preceded by the article. "Lagout" in old French cant.

Pousser (popular), le boum du cygne, *to die,* "to kick the bucket." See **Pipe.** Pousser son rond, *to ease oneself by evacuation,* "to bury a quaker." See **Mouscailler.** Pousser un bateau, *to tell a falsehood,* or "flam ;" — son glaire, *to talk,* "to jaw." Se — de l'air, *to go away,* "to mizzle." S'en — dans le battant, le cornet, or le fusil, *to drink or eat heartily.* (Familiar and popular) Se — du col, *to feel proud of one's achievements.*

Quand j'la descendis de voiture
J'me dis en me poussant du col,
Vieux veinard, c'est pas d'la p'tit' bière,
J'vais r'cevoir dans mon entresol,
Je l'parierais, une rosière !
         E. DU BOIS.

(Roughs') Pousser son pas d'hareng saur, *to dance ;* (thieves') — la goualante, *to sing,* "to lip a chant." Se — un excellent, *to eat a dish of the ordinary prison fare.* (Police) Pousser de la ficelle, *to watch a thief,* "to give a roasting " Termed also "poiroter, prendre en filature." (Ecole Polytechnique) Pousser une blague, *to smoke,* "to blow a cloud." (Bakers') Pousser, *to rise,* is used in reference to the dough.

Poussier, *m.* (popular), *bed,* "doss ;" — de motte, *snuff.* (Thieves') Poussier, *gunpowder ; money,* or "pieces." See **Quibus.**

Poussière, *f.* (popular), faire de la —, *to make a great fuss or show.* (Thieves') Poussière, *spirits.* (Familiar) Couleur — des routes, *a kind of greyish brown.*

Elle était en toilette de voyage, la robe poussière des routes retroussée sur un jupon écarlate.—P. MAHALIN.

Poussin, *m.* (popular), avaler son —, *to be dismissed from one's employ,* "to get the sack."

Poussinière, *f.* (thieves'), *seminary.*

Poutrone, *f.* (popular), *prostitute.*

Pouvoir siffler (popular). Vous pouvez siffler, *you will have to do without it ; you will not get what you ask for.*

Prandion, *m.* (artists'), *hearty meal,* "tightener."

Prandionner (artists'), *to make a hearty meal.*

Prantarsac, *m.* (thieves'), *purse,* or "skin."

Prat, *m.* (popular), *girl of indifferent character,* "mot."

Pratique, *f.* (military), *worthless soldier ; unscrupulous soldier who*

is always seeking to shirk his duties, or to deceive others.

Du reste, il n'y a ici ni blanc-bec, ni cara-patas, ni moutard ; vous êtes deux pra-tiques qui, en voyant des conscrits vous êtes dit qu'il serait facile . . . de leur faire payer la consommation.—C. Dubois de Gennes.

Il ne faudrait pas cependant exagérer l'héroïsme des "pratiques." Si d'aucuns se battent bien, un plus grand nombre ne sont que des maraudeurs et des pillards.—Hector France, *L'Armée de John Bull.*

Praule, *m.* (thieves'), *central prison,* "stir, or steel."

Elles en avaient pour dix ans de praule (centrale) comme elles disaient et pourtant la môme (enfant) n'avait pas été estourbie (tuée).—Louise Michel.

Pré, *m.* (thieves'), *convict settle-ment.* Formerly *the galleys.* Termed also " pré des fagots," or " grand pré." Acresto, gaffine labago.—Tout est franco, y a pas d'trèpe. Quand le pante et la gonzesse décarreront de la cassine, nous les farguerons à la dure pour pagour leurs bobinarès, et leurs prantarsacs. Toi, tu babillonne-ras la largue. S'ils font du renaud et de l'harmonarès, nous les em-plâtrerons et chair dure ! Si tu veux nous les balancarguerons dans la vassarès ; et après, pin-darès. Ne manquons pas le coup, autrement nous irions laver nos pieds d'agnet dans le grand pré. Which signifies, in the jargon of modern malefactors, *Be careful, look yonder.—All right, there's nobody. When the man and woman leave the house, we'll attack them to ease them of their watch and purse. You gag the female. Should they resist and make a noise, we'll knock them over and smash them. If you wish it, we'll pitch them into the water, after which we wash our hands of the matter. Let us*

not make a mull of it, otherwise we can make sure of being trans-ported. Faucher au grand —, *to be a convict in a penal servitude settlement.* Le — salé, *the sea,* or " briny." Etre au — à vioque, *to be at the penal servitude settle-ment for life.*

Apprête-toi à retourner au pré à vioque. . . . Tu dois t'y attendre.—Balzac.

Le — au dab court toujours, *the prison of Mazas.* Le — est en taupé, *it is a bad job.*

Voyons, c'est pas la peine de remonter dans vote guimbarde, le pré est en taupé d'abord.—Louise Michel.

Préfectanche, *f.* (thieves'), *Pré-fecture de Police*, the headquarters of the Paris police.

Préfectancier, *m.* (thieves'), *police-officer,* "crusher," " copper," or " reeler."

Premier, *m.*, **première,** *f.* (shop-men's), *head assistant in a shop.*

Premiero (military), *firstly.*

Premiero : tu l'étrilleras,
Deuxo : tu le bouchonneras,
Et troisso : tu le brosseras.
De temps en temps tu jureras
Tourne carcan !
        Litanies du Cavalier.

Premier - Paris, *m.* (familiar), *leading article.*

Prendre (thieves'), un rat par la queue, *to steal a purse,* "to fake a poge ;" (gamesters') —la culotte, *to lose a large sum of money,* "to win the shiny rag ;" (theatrical) — au souffleur, *to perform throughout with the aid of the prompter ;* — des temps de Paris, *to add to the effect of a tirade by preliminary by-play.* Also *to bring in by-play when one has forgotten his part and wishes to*

B B

gain time ; (popular) — Jacques
Déloge pour son procureur, *to
run away, to escape, to abscond.*

Cette expression qui est encore usitée
avec ces autres " prendre de la poudre
d'escampette, lever le paturon, dire adieu
tout bas " avait déjà cours au xviie siècle,
où l'on disait surtout, en plaisantant,
" Faire Jacques desloges," pour s'enfuir.—
MICHEL.

Prendre de l'air, *to vanish,* "to
bunk," see **Patatrot ;** — son café
aux dépens de quelqu'un, *to laugh
at one, to quiz him ;* — un billet
de parterre, *to fall,* "to come a
cropper." A play on the words
billet de parterre, *pit-ticket,* and
par terre, *on the ground.* (Saint-
Cyr cadets') Prendre ses draps,
*to go to the guard-room under
arrest,* "to be roosted ;" (police)
— en filature, *to follow and watch
a thief, to give him a* "roasting."
Synonymous of " poiroter, pousser de la ficelle ;" (roughs') —
d'autor une femme, *to ravish a
woman ;* (printers') — une barbe,
to get drunk, or "tight."

La " barbe " a des degrés divers. " Le
coup de feu " est la " barbe " commençante.
Quand l'état d'ivresse est complet, la barbe
est simple ; elle est indigne quand le sujet
tombe sous la table, cas extrêmement rare.
Il est certains " poivreaux " qui commettent la grave imprudence de " promener
leur barbe " à l'atelier ; presque tous devien-
nent alors " pallasseurs," surtout ceux qui
sont taciturnes à l'état sec.—BOUTMY.

" Prendre une barbe " is " to
quad out" in the slang of English
printers. Prendre la mesure du
cul avec le pied (obsolete), *to
bring one's foot in violent contact
with another's posteriors.*

S'il me regarde de travers, je lui prends
la mesure de son cul avec mon pied, de
son mufle avec mon poing.—*Dialogue,*
1790.

(Military) Prendre le train d'onze
heures, *punishment inflicted on a
soldier by his comrades,* the culprit

being dragged about in his bed
by means of ropes attached.

Prends garde (popular), de t'enrhumer, *ironical words addressed
to one who is easing himself in the
open air ;* — de casser le verre de
ta montre, *recommendation shouted
out to one who has just fallen ;*
— de te décrocher la fressure,
*ironical words addressed to one
who is slow in his movements,*
" don't lose your hair."

Préparateur, *m.* (thieves'), *confederate of thieves who rob shops
by pairs.* Termed " palming ;"
one thief bargaining with apparent intent to purchase, whilst
the other watches his opportunity
to steal.

Ceux qui remplissent le rôle de préparateurs, disposent à l'avance et mettent à
part sur le comptoir les articles qu'ils dé-
sirent s'approprier : dès que tout est prêt
ils font un signal à leurs affidés qui sont à
l'extérieur.—VIDOCQ.

Préparer sa petite chapelle (military), *to pack up one's effects in the
knapsack.*

Préponderance à la culasse, *f.*
(military), *large breech.*

Presse, *f.* (brothels'), la dame est
sous —, *the lady is engaged.*
(Popular) Mettre sous —, *to pawn,*
" to put in lug."

Prêt, *m.* (cavalry), *soldiers' pay ;*
(prostitutes') *money allowed to a
bully by a prostitute out of her
earnings.*

Prêter (popular), cinq louis à
quelqu'un, *to give one a box on the
ear,* " to warm the wax of one's
ear ;" (thieves') — loche, *to listen.*
Loche, *ear,* " lug."

Prêtez loche, j'entrave cribler. Tiens,
c'est vrai, c'est le clipet d'un homme.—
VIDOCQ. (*Listen, I hear someone crying
out. Why, 'tis true, it's a man's voice.*)

Prêtre, *m.* (thieves'), *actor,* " cack-ling cove, or mug-faker."

Preu, *m.* (schools'), for premier, *first ;* (popular) *first floor.*

Tiens, v'là l'bijoutier du N°. 10 qui n's'embête pas lui : il vous a loué tout son preu ?—HENRI MONNIER, *L'Exécution.*

Prévence, *f.* (thieves' and cads'), *for* " *prévention,*" *or remand.*

Le monde s'amasse . . . et les sergos s'amènent. . . . Moi, qui avais voulu seule-ment retenir Fluxion-de-Poitrine on me ramasse comme lui. Total : huit jours de prévence pour chacun.—MACÉ, *Mon Pre-mier Crime.*

Prévôt (prisoners'), *head of a prison squad ; prison scout.*

Priat, *m.* (thieves'), *beads, rosary.*

Priaute, *f.* (thieves'), *church.* Termed also " rampante," and in old English cant, " autem."

On voit bien que vous venez de la priaute car vous bigotez.—VIDOCQ.

Prie-Dieu, *m.* (thieves'), *penal code.*

Prima dona. See **Egout.**

Prin, *m.* (schools'), *head of a school,* the " gaffer." Abbreviation of principal.

Prince, *m.* (popular), *one who suf-fers from the itch.* See **Princi-pauté.** Prince du sang, *mur-derer ; —* russe, *man who keeps a woman.*

Principauté, *f.* (popular), *the itch.* A play on principauté de Galles and gale, *itch.* Termed in Eng-lish slang, " Scotch fiddle." " To play the Scotch fiddle," says the *Slang Dictionary,* " is to work the index finger of the right hand like a fiddlestick between the index and middle fingers of the left. This provokes a Scotchman in the highest degree, as it implies that he has the itch. It is sup-posed that a continuous oatmeal diet is productive of cutaneous affection." In Scotland the ejacu-lation, " God bless the Duke of Argyle ! " is an insinuation made, when one shrugs his shoulders, of its being caused by parasites, or cutaneous affection. It is said to have been originally the thank-ful exclamation of the Glasgow folk at finding a certain row of iron posts, erected by his Grace in that city to mark the division of his property, very convenient to rub against. Some say the posts were put up purposely for the benefit of the good folk of Glas-gow, who were at the time suffer-ing from the " Scotch fiddle."

Prine, *wife of the* " prin " (which see).

Prison, *f.* (popular), être dans la — de Saint-Crépin, *to have tight boots on.* Saint-Crépin is the patron saint of shoemakers.

Probité, *f.* (thieves'), *kindness.*

Si je ne suis pas si gironde (gentille) j'ai un bon cœur ; tu l'as vu lorsque je lui por-tais le pagne à la Lorcefé (la provision à la Force) ; c'est là qu'il a pu juger si j'avais de la probité (bonté).—VIDOCQ.

Problème, *m.* (students'), *watch chain in the possession of the owner.* The problem is, how comes it that such an ornament is not at the pawnshop ?

Produisante, *f.* (thieves'), *the earth.*

Profonde, or **parfonde,** *f.* (thieves'), *cellar ; pocket,* "cly, sky-rocket, or brigh."

Il rôde autour des beaux cafés
Où boivent les gommeux, ineptement coiffés,
A la porte des grands hôtels, autour des gares,
Il ramasse des bouts, mordillés, de cigares,
Les met dans sa profonde.
        GILL, *La Muse à Bibi.*

Retirer l'artiche de la —, *to pick a pocket,* " to fake a cly."

Proie, *f.* (thieves'), *share,* or "whack;" *one's share in the reckoning.*

Prolo, *m.* (popular), for prolétaire, *working man.*

Prolonge, *f.* (Polytechnic School), *leave up till midnight.*

Promenade. See **Galette.**

Promener quelqu'un (popular), *to make a fool of one,* "*to bamboozle" one.*

Promoncerie, *f.,* or **promont,** *m.* (thieves'), *trial,* " patter."

Prompto (military), *quickly.*

> A peine tes yeux fermeras
> Demi-appel réentendras,
> Prompto, tu te relèveras.
> *Litanies du Cavalier.*

Pronier, *m.,* **pronière,** *f.* (thieves'), *father, mother.* Termed also "dab, dabuche."

Proprio, *m.* (popular), for propriétaire, *landlord.*

Prose, *m.,* or **prouas,** *m.* (popular), *the behind.* See **Vasistas.** Filer le prouas, *to ease oneself.* From filer le câble de proue.

Prote, *m.* (printers'), à manchettes, *principal foreman at printing works.*

> C'est le véritable prote; il ne travaille pas manuellement; son autorité est incontestée. Il représente le patron vis-à-vis des clients tout aussi bien que vis-à-vis des ouvriers.—Boutmy.

> Prote à tablier, *workman who does duty as a foreman;* — aux gosses, *senior apprentice.*

> Le prote à tablier est un ouvrier qui, en prenant les fonctions de prote, ne cesse pas pour cela de travailler manuellement. Le prote aux gosses est le plus grand des apprentis.—Boutmy.

Protenbarre, or **vingt-deux,** *m.* (printers'), *foreman.*

Prout, *m.* (popular), *wind.* Faire —, *to break wind.*

Proute, *f.* (thieves'), *complaint.*

Prouter (thieves'), *to complain;* (popular) *to call out, to holloa.*

Prouteur, *m.,* **prouteuse,** *f.* (thieves'), *one who grumbles, snarling person.*

Proye, *m.* (old cant), *the behind,* "one-eyed cheek." See **Prose.**

Prudhomme, *m.* (familiar), *canting individual, man who is in the habit of giving utterance to grandiloquent platitudes.* From the character of Monnier's Joseph Prudhomme. Monsieur Prudhomme, who has also been portrayed by the caricaturist Cham, is the type of the pompous, silly bourgeois. He is made to say on one occasion, "Ce sabre est le plus beau jour de ma vie," and on another, "Le char de l'état navigue sur un volcan."

Prudhommesque, *adj.* (familiar), *after the fashion of Monsieur Prudhomme* (which see).

Prune, *f.* (popular), or **pruneau,** *bullet, or shell;* — de Monsieur Bishop. Literally *a large violet-coloured plum.* Prunes, *testicles,* or "stones." Gober la —, *to receive a mortal wound.* Avoir sa —, *to be intoxicated,* or "lushy." Mangeur de prunes, *tailor,* "goose-persuader, or button-catcher."

Pruneau, *m.* (popular), *bullet; lump of excrement,* or "quaker." Recevoir un —, *to be shot.* Pruneau, *quid of tobacco.* Sucer un —, *to chew tobacco.* Les pruneaux, *the eyes,* or "peepers." Boucher ses pruneaux, *to sleep,* "to doss."

Prunot, *m.* (popular), *spirit and tobacco shop.*

Prusse, *f.* (familiar and popular), travailler pour le roi de —, *to work to no purpose, gratis.*

Prussien, *m.* (popular), *the behind.* Exhiber son —, *to take to one's heels, to show the white feather.* See **Patatrot.**

Pschutt, *adj. and m.* (familiar), un homme —, *a dandy,* or "masher." See **Gommeux.** Le —, *the height, or* "pink" *of fashion; swelldom.*

Dans le palais de cette fée. On y donne des soupers où l'extrême pschutt est seul admis.—A. SIRVEN.

Pschutteux, *m.* (familiar), *dandy,* or "masher." See **Gommeux.**

Un tas de pschutteux, gratin verdegrisé de races fainéantes, popotent dans les coins les plus chauds de l'établissement.—LOUISE MICHEL.

Puant, *m.* (thieves'), *capuchin;* (popular) *swell,* or "masher." See **Gommeux.** Literally *stinker.* An allusion to the strong perfumes which sometimes are wafted from a dandy's person.

Public, *m.* (officials'). Officials of an administration thus term any person who comes to the offices on business matters; (theatrical) — de bois, *ill-natured audience.*

Puce, *f.* (popular), à l'oreille, *creditor,* or "dun;" — travailleuse, *Lesbian woman, that is, one who has unnatural intercourse with those of her own sex.* Secouer les puces à quelqu'un, *to scold one,* "to haul one over the coals," "to bully-rag" *him, or to thrash him.* See **Voie.** Boîte à puces, *bed,* or "bug-walk," Charmer les puces, *to sleep.* (Thieves') Puce d'hôpital, *louse,* or "gold-backed 'un."

Puceau, *m.* (popular), *unsophisticated, soft fellow,* or "flat." Properly *one who has yet his virginity.*

Pucelage, *m.* (popular), avoir encore son —, *to be new at, not to be acquainted with the routine of some business; to have sold nothing.* Pucelage, *virginity.*

Pucier, *m.* (popular), *bed,* "bug-walk." From puce, *flea.*

Ma rouchi' doit batt' la berloque.
Un gluant, ça n'f'rait pas mon blot.

Et puis, quoi, Fifine a trop d'masse
Pour s'coller au pucier. Mais non!
Pendant qu'elle y f'rait la grimace,
Quoi donc que j'bouff'rais, nom de nom?
　　　　　　　　　　RICHEPIN.

Pudibard, *m.* (popular), *one who affects virtuous airs.*

Puff, *m.* (familiar), *bankruptcy.*

Il serait homme à décamper gratis. Ce serait un puff abominable.—BALZAC.

Also *noisy, impudent eulogy.*

Puffisme, *m.* (familiar), *puffing up, quackery.*

Il est écrit que le général ... passera par tous les échelons du puffisme ... le voilà qui fait crier sa biographie avec ses faits d'armes, ses blessures et son portrait pour 10 centimes.—*Le Figaro,* 14 Août, 1886.

Puffiste, *m.* (familiar), *literary, political, or other kind of quack.*

Puits, *m.* (theatrical), parler du —, *to waste one's time in talking of useless things.* (Thieves') Badigeonner la femme au —, *to tell fibs.* Alluding to Truth supposed to dwell in a well.

Puloch (Breton cant), *to fight; to work hard.*

Punaise, *f.* (general), *disagreeable woman; prostitute.* See **Gadoue.**

Une femme.—Au Bois! Boire du lait!
A la vacherie du Pré-Catelan!
Toutes les autres.—Oui, le Bois!
Un chiffonnier.—Les punaises, faut toujours que ça se fourre dans le bois.—P. MAHALIN.

Encore une — dans le beurre!

one more boulevard girl making her appearance on the stage! Une — de caserne, *soldier's wench.* (Popular) Avoir une — dans le soufflet, *to be crazy,* "to have a tile off." For synonyms see **Avoir.** (Thieves') Attraper des punaises, *to fail in one's undertaking, or to find that one is dealing with an informer.*

Punaisière, *f.* (popular), *suspicious café frequented by habitués of low dancing halls.*

Pur, *m.* (familiar), *dandy,* "masher."

Vous ignorez complètement que de ne pas mettre de pardessus constitue actuellement ce que nous appelons être pur, ou si vous aimez mieux le chic anglais.—*Événement,* 1882.

Purée, *f.* (thieves'), *cider;* (popular) — de Corinthe, *wine;* — de pois, *absinthe.* Faire de la — de marrons, *to strike one in the face so as to leave marks.* Tomber dans la —, or être molle, *to become poor,* or a "quisby." Je déclare la —, *I haven't a farthing, not a* "rap," (Familiar) La —. See **Absinthe.** Purée septembrale (obsolete), *wine.*

L'indisposition qui lui étoit advenue par trop humer de purée septembrale.—RABELAIS.

(Students') Une —, *a glass of absinthe,* a glass of beer being termed "un cercueil," a glass of bitters "un pape," and of brandy "un pétrole." (Prostitutes') Une —, *a man who does not show himself sufficiently generous.*

Pureuse, *f.* (prisoners') *female prisoner in the employ of the prison authorities.* Such prisoners enjoy some degree of liberty and certain privileges.

Purgation, *f.* (thieves'), *speech for the defence.*

Purge, *f.* (thieves'), refiler une —, *to thrash,* "to set about one." See **Voie.**

Purger la vaisselle (popular), *to make very thin sauce.*

Purotin, *m.* (popular and thieves'), *needy man; vagrant,* or "piky."

Pur-sang, *f.* (familiar), *handsome, elegant kept woman,* a "blooming tartlet."

Putain, *f.* (familiar), avoir la main —, *to shake hands with anybody.* Bouture de —, *child of unknown father.* Putain comme chausson *is said of an extremely immoral woman.*

Putasser (popular), *to be fond of prostitutes, to be a* "mutton-monger."

Putasserie, *f.* (familiar and popular), *acts of immorality on the part of a woman; the street-walking tribe.*

Putassier, *m.* (popular), *one fond of prostitutes,* "mutton-monger."

Putiner. See **Putasser.**

Putiphariser (familiar), *is said of a woman who seeks to win a young man's affections, and gives practical evidence thereof; to violate.*

 **UAI Jemmapes** (popular), avoir l'air —, *to look like a fool, like a* " flat."

Quailler, (obsolete), *to make a sacrifice to Venus.* Le Roux says, " Pour faire l'acte."

Quand, *m.* (printers'), payer son — est-ce (quand-est-ce que tu payes la bienvenue?), *to pay for one's footing.* (Popular) Quand les poules pisseront, *never,* "when the devil is blind."

Quantès (printers'), for quand-est-ce, *paying for one's footing.*

Lorsqu'un compositeur est nouvellement admis dans un atelier, on lui rappelle par cette interrogation qu'il doit payer son article 4; c'est pourquoi "Payer son quantès" est devenu synonyme de payer son article 4. Cette locution est usitée dans d'autres professions.—Boutmy.

Quarante-cinq, *m.* (familiar), *dunce; dirty scamp;* (popular) —! or — à quinze! *words uttered sometimes when a smash of crockery is heard.*

Quart, *m.* (popular and thieves'), d'œil, *commissaire de police,* or *petty magistrate.*

Et de là vient le nom de quart-d'œil que les voleurs leur ont donné dans leur argot puisqu'ils sont quatre par arrondissement. —Balzac.

Also *police officer,* or " crusher." (Popular) Battre son —, *to go backwards and forwards on the pavement for purposes of prostitution.* The women from brothels thus ply their trade for a quarter of an hour in turns before the establishment.

Et comme le disait sa digne maîtresse : lorsque je bats mon quart, mon macq boit ma recette au café.—*Mémoires de Monsieur Claude.*

(Thieves') Quart de marque, *week.* Battre un —, *to talk nonsense.* (Roughs') Avoir chié les trois quarts de sa merde, *to be old, worn out.*

Eh ! dis donc, ma vieille, comme t'es décati ! On dirait que t'as chié les trois quarts de ta merde !—Rigaud.

(Familiar) Quart d'agent de change, *partner of a stockbroker.* Le — de monde, *the world of cocottes one grade lower than the* " demi-monde." Quart d'auteur, *an author who cannot produce anything without collaboration.*

Quartier, *m.* (students'), *abbreviation of Quartier Latin,* where the seat of the University and its different faculties are established ; (rag-pickers') — gras, *a part of*

the town where rag-pickers reap a good harvest ; — maigre, *the reverse.* (Military) Chien du —, *adjutant.*

Trompette, sonne à l'adjudant . . . le trompette Villerval, à moitié ivre comme de coutume, tournait l'embouchure de son cuivre aux quatre points cardinaux :—
Au chien du quartier ! au chien du quartier !
Au chien du quartier ! au chien du quartier !
HECTOR FRANCE, *Sous le Burnous.*

Quasi-mort, *adj.* (prisoners'), être —, *to be confined in a cell without being allowed to see anybody.*

Quatorze, *m.* (popular), d'as, or de nombril, *piquet,* a kind of game of cards.

Quatorzième écrevisse, *f.* (theatrical), *female supernumerary.*

Quatre (military), comptez-vous —, *four of you get ready,* words used especially in reference to preparations for tossing one in a blanket.

Comptez-vous quatre, en couverte ! en couverte !—G. COURTELINE.

Quatre à six, *m.* (familiar), *afternoon reception in fashionable circles.*

Quatre-coins, *m.* (thieves'), *pockethandkerchief,* "stook, madam, wipe, or snottinger."

Quatre sous (familiar and popular), de —, *inferior,* "no great shakes, or not worth a curse."

En voilà des républicains de quatre sous, ces sacrés fainéants de la gauche ! Est-ce que le peuple les nomme pour baver dans leur eau sucrée !—ZOLA.

Quatre-vingt-dix, *m.* (booth salesmen's at fairs), *a lottery at a fair ; secret of a trade ; dodge.* Vendre le —, *to reveal the secret.*

Quatrième cantine, *f.* (cavalry), *the lock-up,* there being three canteens for cavalry regiments.

Quatuor, *m.* (domino players'). Rigaud says : " Quatre d'un jeu de dominos. Les joueurs mélomanes ne manquent pas de dire : quatuor de Beethoven."

Quelle, *f.* (thieves'), ça m' fiche une belle — à mézigue, *of no advantage to me; what's that to me ?*

Quelpoique (thieves'), *nothing,* or " nix ; " *never.* Literally quel poique, *how little.* Poique for pouic.

On peut enquiller par la venterne de la cambriolle de la larbine qui n'y pionce quelpoique, elle roupille dans le pieu du raze.—VIDOCQ. (*One may effect an entrance by the window of the servant's room, where she never sleeps ; she sleeps in the parson's bed.*)

Quelque part (familiar and popular), *in the behind.* Donner un coup de pied —, *to kick one in the seat of honour,* "to toe one's bum." Aller —, *to go to the privy,* or " Mrs. Jones." The secret memoirs of Bachaumont mention this term in the repartee of the financier La Popelinière, to a courtier who said disdainfully, " Il me semble, monsieur, vous avoir vu quelque part." À quoi le financier répondit, " En effet, monsieur, j'y vais quelquefois." Avoir quelqu'un, or quelque chose —, *to be superlatively bored by a person or thing.*

Quelqu'un, *m.* (familiar), faire son —, *to give oneself airs.*

Si madame fait un peu sa quelqu'une.—BALZAC.

Quem, *m.* (thieves'), faire son —, *to give oneself airs.*

Queniente (thieves'), *not ; not at all.* From the Italian.

Quenottier, *m.* (old cant), *dentist.*

Quépette (roughs'), *an expression referring to the hour.* Il est deux heures —, *it is two o'clock.* Il est midi —, *it is twelve o'clock.* Madame milord quépette, *a lazy woman who gets up late in the day,* a "lady-fender."

Quéquette, *f.* (general), *penis.*

Que t'es (printers'), *derisive exclamation uttered by printers to interrupt one who is making use of a word which gives them their cue for the joke.*

Riposte saugrenue que les compositeurs se renvoient à tour de rôle, quand l'un d'eux, en lisant ou en discourant, se sert d'un qualificatif prêtant au ridicule. Donnons un exemple pour nous faire mieux comprendre. Supposons que quelqu'un dans l'atelier lise cette phrase : " Sur la plage nous rencontrâmes un sauvage . . ." un plaisant interrompt et s'écrie : " Que t'es !"—BOUTMY.

Queue, *f.* (familiar and popular), faire une —, *to be unfaithful conjugally.* Also *to leave part of debt unpaid.* Faire la — à quelqu'un, *to deceive one,* "to bamboozle" *him, or to take a* "rise" *out of him.* Habit en — de pie, *dress coat.* Termed also "sifflet d'ébène."

Mon gendr' pour la cérémonie,
A voulu s'ach'ter un chapeau,
Lâcher l'habit noir à queue d'pie,
La cravat' blanche et les gants d'peau.
   E. CARRÉ, *J'ai mon Coup d'Feu.*

Habit en — de morue, *dress coat.*

Il donna un coup de poing dans son tuyau de poêle, jeta son habit à queue de morue et jura sur son âme qu'il ne le remettrait de sa vie.—TH. GAUTIER.

Une — de rat, *a snuff-box,* "sneezer."

Au dîner (c'que l'vin vous fait faire !
Voyez un peu si j'suis distrait !)
Mathieu m' demande la poivrière.
Au lieu d'y passer c'qu'i' voulait,
J'y tends ma queu' d'rat, qu'était pleine,

Aussi distrait qu' moi, v'là Mathieu
Qui met l'tabac dans sa Julienne !
   E. CARRÉ, *J'ai mon Coup d'Feu.*

Une — de renard, *vomit.* Piquer une — de renard, *to vomit,* "to cast up accounts, or shoot the cat." Des queues, *nonsensical phrases tailed on to one another and uttered rapidly without taking breath.* Çam'épatedemouchearti-chautshuredesanglierarchiecoré e-mifasolaugratintamarre, that is, ça m'épate, patte de mouche, mouchard, artichaut, chaussure, hure de sanglier, hiérarchie, chi-corée, ré mi fa sol, sole au gratin, tintamarre. (Thieves') Faire la queue, *to pick pockets in a crowd at the door of a theatre.* Couper une — de rat, *to steal a purse,* "to fake a poge, or to nip a boung." An allusion to the strings of purses. (Journalists') Queue, *newspaper which has the same matter as another with a different title.*

A Bruxelles, plus d'un journal quotidien compte de quatre à cinq "queues," c'est-à-dire qu'il transforme son titre en conservant la même matière de texte ou à peu près, et sert ainsi plusieurs catégories d'abonnés.— *Le Figaro.*

Queuiste, *m.* (popular), *man who secures a place in the crowd, or* "queue," *at the door of a theatre, and sells his chance to another.*

Et puis surtout il y a les queuistes de profession pour qui la place tenue est un gagne-pain . . . choisir dans la queue est encore une science difficile . . . les toutes premières places ne sont pas forcément les meilleures. Les plus courues sont celles où l'on peut s'appuyer, s'asseoir, les en-coignures, les pas de portes, les bornes. . . . N'est pas queuiste qui veut.—RICHEPIN, *Le Pavé.*

Qui a du onze corps-beau? (printers'), "qui a du onze" *is a call for certain type;* "corps-beau" *stands for* corbeau, crow ; *phrase used to warn one's fellow-*

workers that a priest has just entered the workshop.

Quibus, *m.* (familiar and popular), *money,* abbreviation of quibus fiunt omnia.

S'il vous vient des enfants, les voir, dès
　　leur jeune âge, . . .
Se corrompre au contact du quibus pa-
　　ternel,
Sachant bien que quand vous passerez
　　l'arme à gauche
Ils trouveront de quoi rigoler amplement.
　　　　　　　　　　GILL.

Termed also, in different kinds of slang: "De l'os, des monacos, du nerf, des pépettes, des ache-toires, de la galette, des picail-lons, de ce qui se pousse, de quoi, de l'oignon, de l'oseille, de la douille, des jaunets, des sous, de la graisse, du piesto, du galtos, du pognon, de l'artiche, du morningue, du foin, du plâtre, du poussier, des soldats, de la mornifle, de la sauvette, de l'huile, du beurre, de la braise, du bathe, du graissage, de la thune, de la miche de profonde, de l'oignon pèse, du sable, des pimpions, des mouscaillons, des rouscaillons, de l'affure, du métal, du zinc, du pèse, du pedzale, des noyaux, des plombes, des sonnettes, du quantum, du gras, de l'atout, de l'huile dé mains, des patards, de la vaisselle de poche, du carme, de la pécune, du pouiffe, des ronds, de la bille, du sine qua non, du sit nomen." An amusing remark of the journal *La France* may not be here out of place. "Though the word money," it says, "be the object of every-body's preoccupation, it is men-tioned as infrequently as possible. The banker says, mes 'fonds;' the young girl, ma 'dot,' and the young man, mes 'espérances;' the trooper, mon 'prêt;' the employé, mes 'appointements;'

the administrator, mes 'jetons de présence;' the female atten-dant at a theatre, mes 'petits bénéfices;' the lawyer, mes 'ho-noraires;' the editors of certain journals, ma 'subvention;' the actor or singer, mes 'feux;' the servant, mes 'gages;' the heir, mes 'legs;' the landlord, ma 'fortune;' the rough, mes 'pi-caillons;' the monk, ma 'pré-bende;' the Pope, mon 'denier de Saint-Pierre;' the prince, ma 'dotation.' Finally, from the 'liste civile' of our kings to the 'tirelire' of our children, synonyms are in every case sub-stituted for the proper terms." The English slang has the following: "Oof, stumpy, muck, ballast, brass, loaver, blunt, needful, rhino, bustle, gilt, dust, dim-mock, coal, feathers, brads, chink, quids, pieces, clinkers, stuff, dumps, chips, corks, dibbs, di-narly, gent, horse nails, huckster, mopusses, palm oil, posh, ready, Spanish, rowdy," &c. Abouler du —, or de la braise, *to pay,* "to shell out, to fork out, to down with the dust, to stump the pew-ter, to flap the dimmock, to tip the brads, to sport the rhino."

Quilles, *f. pl.* (familiar and popu-lar), *legs.*

La madame du pavillon qui met ses bas !
—Plus que ça de quilles.—GAVARNI.

The synonyms are, "flûtes, guibes, guibonnes, guibolles, trimoires, gambettes, échalas, ambes, train numéro onze, bâtons de cire, bâtons de tremplin," and, in the English slang, "gambs, pins, spindle-shanks, Shanks' mare, stumps, pegs, timbers, stems," &c. Jouer des —, *to bolt,* "to skedaddle." For syno-nyms see **Patatrot.** (Popular and thieves') Quilles d'échasse, *long-legged man,* "daddy long-legs."

J'te connais, toi, l'gros, et toi aussi, les quilles d'échasse.—LOUISE MICHEL.

Quimper (thieves'), *to fall;* — la lance, *to void urine.*

Quinquets, *m. pl.* (popular), *eyes.* Termed also "mirettes, reluits, calots, chas, or châsses, châssis, falots, lampions, apics, ardents;" in the English slang, "peepers, glaziers, ogles, daylights, top-lights." Allumer ses —, *to gaze about attentively,* "to stag." Eteindre les —, *to put out a person's eyes.* (Roughs') Remoucher un pante avec des quinquets comme des roues de derrière, *to look at a man with eyes like crown pieces,* "to pipe at a cove with glaziers like hind coach-wheels." Baisser les abat-jour de ses —, *to shut one's eyes; to go to sleep.*

Il est temps de baisser les abat-jour de nos quinquets. Bonsoir donc et bonne nuit.—DUBOIS DE GENNES.

Quinte, *f.* (popular), avoir — et quatorze, *to suffer from a venereal disease; to be unlucky,* "down on one's luck." J'en ai-t'y de la chance! En v'la une quinte et quatorze. *That's just my cursed ill-luck!* (Popular and military) Avoir —, quatorze, et le point, *to be suffering from a complicated venereal disease.*

Notre héros . . . ne le porta pas cependant en paradis. Une belle Italienne lui donna son compte. Quinte, quatorze et le point. Jeu complet. Il est mort à l'hôpital.—HECTOR FRANCE, *Le Roman du Curé.*

English sailors use the term, "to take one's coals in," to express that they have caught the venereal disease. "It means," says the *Slang Dictionary,* "that they have gotten that which will keep them hot for a good many months."

Quinte mangeuse *is the quinte majeure at the game of piquet.*

Quinze, *m.* (popular), vingts, *blind man.* Alluding to an inmate of the Government home for the blind, known under the name of Les Quinze-Vingts; — cents francs, *one-year volunteer in the army.* He has to pay the State a sum of 1,500 francs for his out-fit; — broquilles, *a quarter of an hour;* (familiar and popular) — ans et pas de corset! "sweet sixteen!" *is said of any female whose charms have still a youthful appearance.*

Oui, c'était ça! quinze ans, toutes ses dents et pas de corset!—ZOLA.

Quiqui, *m.* (rag-pickers'), *fowl; scraps of food of all kind,* "scran."

Quirtourne, *f.* (popular), *window.*

Au moment où j'avais fini d'allumer la quirtourne (d'allumer la lumière derrière le rideau de la fenêtre). Mes mirettes (mes yeux) l'avaient chauffé. Mais moi qui, pourtant, faisais le crottard (trottoir) pour pêcher un Philistin, je me défie du pante. Je ne l'ai pas plutôt attiré dans ma turne que je le fais sortir du pieu, prétextant que j'ai besoin, avant de batifoler avec le zig, de fader (partager) avec lui, sur le comptoir du mastro, un verre de verte. Nous redescendons et je lui rends sa bougie (argent). Chance! car j'évitais le butteur qui, quatre heures après, attirait chez la Blafarde (conduisait à la mort) ma faridole (compagne) avec son gosse. Ah! le gredin! . . . m'a-t-il fait baver des clignots (pleurer) depuis qu'il a suriné ma vieille Mage et son gosse! Que je serai heureuse le jour où je verrai son mufle moufionner dans le son (quand je verrai sa tête tomber dans le panier du bourreau).—*Mémoires de Monsieur Claude.*

Qui-va-là, *m.* (popular), donner le —, *to ask for one's passport.*

Qui-va-vite, *f.* (popular), *diarrhœa,* or "Jerry go nimble."

Quocqter (thieves'), *to deceive,* "to do."

Quoniam, *m.*, or **quoniam bonus** (obsolete). The signification is given by the quotation:—

Mot inventé, pour signifier à mots couverts la nature d'une femme, et est fort usité à Paris.—LE ROUX.

Quoquante, *f.* (thieves'), *cupboard.*

Quoquard, *m.* (thieves'), *tree.*

Quoqueret, or **ququeret,** *m.* (old cant), *curtain.*

Quoquille, *m.* (thieves'), *arrant fool,* "go along."

 **ABAT,** *m.* (popular and thieves'), *cloak,* "ryder, or topper."

Rabateux de sorgue, *m.* (old cant), *night thief.* Termed also "doubleur de sorgue." Michel says: "On donnait le nom de 'rabats' aux lutins et c'est ainsi que le chartreux Jacques de Clusa, ou Junterburck, qui a écrit un traité des Apparitions des âmes après la mort et de leurs retraites, remarque qu'ils sont appelés. Rabelais qui écrivait postérieurement au crédule chartreux, place dans la bibliothèque de Saint-Victor *la Mommerye des rabats et luitins.* De rabat est venu rabater, lutiner, que Nicot, Pontus de Tyard et Trippault dérivent de ραϐάττειν, dont les Grecs se sont servis pour dire se promener haut et bas, frapper, et faire du bruit. . . . En somme, il n'est pas douteux que 'rabateux' ne vienne de 'rabater,' et ne signifie étymologiquement rôdeur de nuit."

Rabatteur de pantes, *m.* (thieves'), *detective,* "cop." Termed also "baladin.' Literally *a beater,* man being the quarry.

Rabatteuse, *f.* (popular), *procuress; small omnibus which plies between Paris and the outlying districts.*

Rabattre (thieves'), *to return.*

C'est égal, t'as beau en coquer, tu rabattras au pré.--Vidocq. (*Never mind, in spite of all your informing, you will one day return to the hulks.*)

Rabiage, *m.* (thieves'), *income; profits.*

Rabiau, rabio, or **rabiot,** *m.* (military), *what remains of provisions or drink after all have had their share; profits on victuals or forage.* The word has the general signification of *remainder, overplus.*

— C'que c'est que c' paquet-là?
— Mon colonel, c'est . . . du sel.
— Du sel . . . tant qu' ça de sel ! c'que vous f . . . d'tant qu' ça d'sel ?
— Mon colonel, c'est que . . . c'est un peu de rabio.
— Rabio ! c'ment ça, rabio ? Pour lors vous avez volé tout c'sel-là aux hommes ! S'crongnieugnieu ! . . . allons f . . . moi tout ça dans la soupe !—Ch. Leroy, *Guibollard et Ramollot.*

Rabiot, *convalescent soldier; what remains of a term of service; term of service in the compagnies de discipline, or punishment companies,* termed "biribi."

Il acheva la journée dans des transes

indicibles, poursuivi de l'atroce pensée qu'il allait faire du rabiot, se voyant déjà à Biribi, en train de casser des cailloux sur les routes.—G. COURTELINE.

Rabiauter, or rabioter (military), *to eat or drink what others have left.*

Rabibochage, *m.* (familiar and popular), *reconciliation.*

Rabibocher (familiar), *to effect a reconciliation between people who have quarrelled.* Se —, *to forget one's differences, to become friends again.*

Les moindres bisbilles maintenant, finissaient par des attrapages, où l'on se jetait la débine de la maison à la tête ; et c'était le diable pour se rabibocher, avant d'aller pioncer chacun dans son dodo.—ZOLA, *L'Assommoir.*

Rabiot. See **Rabiau.**

Rabioter. See **Rabiauter.**

Raboin, *m.* (thieves'), *devil,* "ruffin, black spy, darble, old hairy."

En v'là un de bigoteur qui a le taffetas d'aller en glier où le Raboin le retournera pour le faire riffauder.—VIDOCQ.

Michel says : " Ce mot doit venir de l'espagnol 'rabo,' queue, le raboin est donc le personnage à la queue. Je ne serais pas étonné que le nom de rabbin, par lequel on désigne encore les docteurs juifs, ne fût l'origine de la croyance qui régnait parmi le peuple, au moyen âge, que les Israélites naissaient avec une queue." Termed also " rabouin."

Il lansquine à éteindre le riffe du rabouin. —VICTOR HUGO.

Compare the word with the Italian cant " rabuino," which has a like signification.

Raboter (popular), l'andosse, *to thrash one,* "to dust one's jacket." Se — le sifflet, *to drink a glass of strong brandy.* A metaphor which recalls the action of a plane on a piece of wood.

Raboteux. See **Rabateux.**

Rabouillère, *f.* (familiar), *wretched looking house,* a " hole."

Rabouler (popular and thieves'), *to return.* American thieves term this, " to hare it ; " — à la cassine, *to return home,* " to speel to the crib."

Raccord, *m.* (theatrical), *partial rehearsal of a play.*

Raccourcir (familiar and popular), *to guillotine.* The expression dates from 1793. We find the following synonyms in *Le Père Duchêne* of '93, edited by Hébert : " cracher dans le sac," an allusion to the head falling into the basket and the blood spouting up ; " mettre la tête à la fenêtre," shows the condemned one passing his head through the aperture; " jouer à la main-chaude," which alludes to his hands tied behind his back, la main-chaude being literally *hot cockles ;* " passer sous le rasoir national," which needs no explanation. After '93 Louis XVI. was called " Louis le raccourci."

Raccourcisseur, *m.* (popular), *the executioner.* Called also " Charlot." See **Monsieur de Paris.**

Rachevage, *m.* (popular), *depraved individual ; a foul-mouthed man.*

Racine de buis, *f.* (popular), *epithet applied to a humpback, to a* " lord." Also *long yellow tooth.*

Râcler (thieves'), *to breathe.* Tortille la vis au pante ; il râcle encore, *throttle him, he breathes still.* (Popular) Râcler du fromage, *to play the violin.*

Râclette, *f.* (popular), *chimney-sweep ;* (thieves') *spy,* "nose;" *detective,* " cop."

Râclure d'aubergine, *f.* (familiar), *the ribbon of the decoration* *of officier d'Académie,* which is violet.

Des hommes un peu plus âgés et portant à la boutonnière la "râclure d'aubergine" (le ruban d'officier d'Académie).—DIDIER, *Echo de Paris,* 1886.

Rade, radeau, *m.* (thieves'), *till,* or "lob ;" *shop,* "chovey." Encasquer dans un rade, *to enter a shop.*

Radicaille, or **radicanaille,** *f.* (familiar), *the Radical party.*

Radicaillon, *m.* (familiar), *contemptuous epithet applied to a Radical.*

Radicon, *m.* (thieves'), *priest,* "devil - dodger." Termed also "Bible-pounder, white choker."

Radin, *m.* (thieves'), *fob.* Friser le —, *to pick a fob.* Un — fleuri, *a well-filled pocket.* Un —, *a till,* or "lob." Faire un coup de —, *to steal the contents of a till.* Termed by English thieves, "lob sneaking," or "to draw a damper." Un —, *a cap,* or "tile." Vol au —, *robbery in a shop.* Two rogues pretend to quarrel, and one of them, as if in anger, throws the other's cap into a shop, thus providing his accomplice with a pretext for entering the place, and an excuse should he be detected. See **Vol au radin.**

Radiner (thieves'), *to return,* "to hare it ;" *to arrive,* "to tumble up." Rigaud says, "Radiner est sans doute une déformation du verbe rabziner qui, dans le patois picard, a la même signification."

Radis (familiar and popular), *money,* "tin." N'avoir pas un —, *to be penniless, to be* "dead broke." Ne pas foutre un —, *not to give a farthing.*

Qu'a pleur', qu'a rigol' ; c'est tout comme ; Sûr ! J'y foutrai pas un radis. "T'as qu'à turbiner, comme j'y dis, J'travaill' ben, moi qui suis un homme !" GILL, *La Muse à Bibi.*

Un — noir, *priest,* "white choker ;" *police officer,* or "crusher."

Radouber (popular), se —, or passer au grand radoub, *to eat,* "to yam."

Radurer (thieves'), *to whet.*

Radureur, *m.* (thieves'), *grinder.*

Rafale, *f.* (popular and thieves'), *poverty.* A poor man without a farthing is said to be "dead broke, or a willow."

Cela est assez étonnant, dit la brune, tous les "nierts" qui sont venus pioncer "icigo" étaient dans la "rafale ;" c'est un vrai guignon.—VIDOCQ.

Rafalé, *m. and adj.* (popular and thieves'), *poor,* "willow ;" *one with squalid clothes.* (Familiar) Un visage —, *face with worn features.*

Rafalement, *m.* (popular), *humiliation ; squalid poverty.*

Rafaler (popular), *to humiliate ; to make one wretched.* Se —, *to become poor or squalid.*

Raffe, *f.* (popular and thieves'), *booty, spoil,* "swag." "He cracked a case and fenced the swag," *he broke into a house and took the booty to a receiver's.*

Raffiler la manquesse (thieves'), *to give one a bad character.*

Raffiné, *m., name given to court gallants and to duellists under Charles IX.*

Un raffiné est un . . . homme qui se bat quand le manteau d'un autre touche le sien, quand on crache à quatre pieds de lui.— P. MÉRIMÉE, *Chronique du Règne de Charles IX.*

Raffurer (thieves'), *to recover ; to recoup.* From re and affurer, *to procure money.* From the Latin fur.

Raffut, *m.* (popular), *uproar ; row,* "shindy."

Rafiau, *m.* (popular), *servant at an hospital ; hospital attendant.*

Rafiot, *m.* (popular), *thing of small importance,* "no great shakes;" *adulterated article of inferior quality.* Termed "surat" in the English slang. This word affords a remarkable instance of the manner in which slang phrases are coined. In the report of an action for libel in the *Times,* some few years back, it was stated that since the American Civil War it has been not unusual for manufacturers to mix American cotton with Surat, and, the latter being an inferior article, the people in Lancashire have begun to apply the term "surat" to any article of inferior or adulterated quality.

Rafraîchir (military), se —, *to fight with swords.* From rafraîchir, *to trim,* the swords being the trimming instruments. (Popular) Se — les barbes, *to drink,* "to wet one's whistle." American thieves term this, "to sluice one's gob."

Rage de dents, *f.* (popular), *great hunger.*

Ragot, *m.* (thieves'), *quarter of a crown ;* (popular) *short fat person,* "humpty-dumpty." The famous Ragotin of Scarron's *Roman Comique* is short and fat. Faire du —, *to talk ill of one, to slander.*

Ragougnasse, *f.* (popular), *unsavoury stew.*

Ragoût, *m.* (painters'), *vigorous style of painting.*

Les mots dont ils se servaient pour apprécier le mérite de certains tableaux étaient vraiment bizarres. Quelle superbe chose ! . . . comme c'est tripoté ! comme c'est torché ! Quel ragoût !—Th. Gautier.

(Popular) Ragoût de poitrine, *breasts,* or "Charlies."

T'as encore une belle nature pour parler d'z'autres ! Est-ce parceque j'nons pas d'ragoût d'poitrine sus l'estoma ? J'ons

la place, plus blanche que la tienne, et j'n'y mettons pas d'chiffons comme toi.— *Amusemens à la Grecque.*

(Thieves') Ragoût, *suspicion.* Faire du —, *to awake suspicion.*

Ragoûter (thieves'), *to awake suspicion.*

Raguse. See **Coup.**

Raide, *adj. and m.* (popular), *drunk,* "tight." See **Pompette.** Raide comme balle, *with the utmost rapidity.* Filer — comme balle, *to disappear rapidly,* "like winkin'," or, as American thieves say, "to amputate like a go-away." "This panny's all on fire *(house is dangerous).* I must amputate like a go-away, or the frogs *(police)* will nail me." La trouver —, *to be dissatisfied or offended.* Je la trouve raide, *it is coming it rather too strong.* Raide comme la justice, *completely drunk,* or "drunk as a lord."

Ces noceurs-là étaient raides comme la justice et tendres comme des agneaux. Le vin leur sortait par les yeux.—Zola, *L'Assommoir.*

Du —, *brandy,* "French cream." Termed "bingo" in old English cant. Siffler un verre de —, *to have a dram,* "a drop o' summat' short, or a nail in one's coffin." The lower orders say to each other at the moment of lifting a glass of spirits to their lips, "Well, good luck ! here's another nail in my coffin." Other phrases are "shedding a tear, or wiping an eye."

Raideur, *f.* (popular), la faire à la —, *to give oneself dignified,* "noli me tangere" *airs.*

Raidir (popular), or — l'ergot, *to die,* "to snuff it." See **Pipe.** To express that one is dead English and American thieves say that he has been "put to bed with a shovel."

> Played out they lay, it will be said
> A hundred stretches (years) hence;
> With shovels they were put to bed
> A hundred stretches hence!
> *Thieves' Song.*

Raie. See **Gueule.**

Raille, *f. and m.* (thieves'), la —, *the police,* the "reelers." Etre —, *to be in the employ of the police,* a "nose."

> C'est vrai, mais vous ne m'avez pas dit que vous étiez raille (mouchard).—VI-DOCQ.

Un —, or railleux, *police officer,* or "copper;" *a detective, or police spy.*

> Ils parlaient aussi des railles (mouchards). A propos de railles, vous n'êtes pas sans avoir entendu parler d'un fameux coquin, qui s'est fait cuisinier (mouchard).—VI-DOCQ.

Victor Hugo says the word comes from the English "rascal," but Michel derives it with more reason from "raillon," a kind of javelin with which the archers or police were armed formerly.

> Ci gist et dort en ce sollier,
> Qu'Amour occist de son raillon,
> Ung pouvre petit escollier
> Jadis nommé François Villon.
> *Le Grand Testament de François Villon.*

Raisiné, *m.* (thieves'), *blood.* Properly *jam made of grapes.* Faire couler le —, *to shed blood.*

> Je suis sûr que tu es marqué. Qu'avons-nous fait? Avons-nous tué notre mère ou forcé la caisse à papa? Avons-nous fait suer le chêne et couler le raisiné?—TH. GAUTIER.

(Popular) Faire du —, *to bleed from one's nose.*

Raisins, *m. pl.* (popular), huile de —, *wine;* "red tape," in the jargon of American thieves.

> Auguste, un peintre en bâtiment,
> Qui travaillait en face,

> Entre, et nous dit comm' ça m'z'enfans
> J'ai l'gosier qui s'encrasse.
> Faut y mettr' de l'huil' de raisin.
> H. P. DENNEVILLE

Raisons, *f. pl.* (familiar and popular), avoir des — avec quelqu'un, *to have a quarrel with one.*

Râler (popular), *to deceive,* "to best;" *to cheapen.*

Râleur, *m.* (second-hand booksellers'), *person who handles the books without buying any,* and generally *one who bargains for a long time and buys nothing.* Also *liar.*

Râleuse, *f.* (shop-keepers'), *female who cheapens many articles and leaves without having made a purchase.* Also *liar.*

Rallie-papier, *m.* (familiar), *paper chase on horseback.*

Rama, parler en—, formerly *mode of using the word as a suffix to other words.* The invention of the Diorama had brought in the fashion of using the word rama as stated above. It was much in vogue in Balzac's time, and had been first used in the studios.

> "Eh bien, Monsieur Poiret," dit l'employé, "comment va cette petite santé-rama?"—BALZAC.

(Convicts') Mettre au —, *to place in irons.*

> Le soir, après la soupe, on nous mit au rama; nous étions étonnés. Ce n'était pas l'habitude de nous enchaîner sitôt.—HUM-BERT, *Mon Bagne.*

Ramamichage, *m.* (familiar), *reconciliation.*

Ramamicher (popular), *to bring about a reconciliation.*

Ramasser (military), de la boîte, *to be locked up.*

> J'ai mon truc à matriculer pour à c'soir; si c'est pas fait, j' ramasserai de la boîte.—G. COURTELINE.

Ramasser les fourreaux de bayonnette, *to come up after the battle has been fought;* (thieves' and roughs') — les pattes, or filer une ratisse à un gas, *to thrash one.* See **Voie.** Ramasser un bidon, *to make off,* "to make beef." See **Patatrot.** (Popular) Ramasser ses outils, *to die,* "to snuff it;" — quelqu'un, *to apprehend,* "to nail" one ; *to thrash one.* Se faire —, *to be locked up by the police, to be* "run in;" *to get a thrashing.*

Si le patron m'embête, je te le ramasse et je te l'asseois sur sa bourgeoise, tu sais, collés comme une paire de soles !—ZOLA, *L'Assommoir.*

Ramasse-toi (popular), *words addressed to a person who is talking incoherently.*

Ramastiquer (thieves'), *to pick up; to do the ring-dropping trick,* or "fawney rig." See **Ramastiqueur.**

Ramastiqueur, or **ramastiqué,** *variety of thief,* "money-dropper." The rogue scrapes up an acquaintance with a dupe by inquiring about a coin or article of sham jewellery which he pretends to have just picked up in the street, and offers for sale, or otherwise fleeces the pigeon. Many of these rogues are rascally Jews. This kind of swindle is varied by dropping a pocket-book, the accomplice being termed in this case "heeler." The heeler stoops behind the victim and strikes one of his heels as if by mistake, so as to draw his attention to the pocket-book. Also *beggar who picks up halfpence in courts thrown to him from windows.*

Les arcassineurs sont les mendiants à domicile. Les ramastiqueurs les mendiants de cours qui ramassent les sous. Les tendeurs de demi-aune, les mendiants des rues. —*Mémoires de Monsieur Claude.*

(Popular) Ramastiqueur d'orphelins, *poor wretch who goes about picking up cigar and cigarette ends,* a "hard up."

Rambiner (popular), *to patch up old shoes.*

Tout le monde sait que son père rambinait les croknaux.—*Le Tam-Tam.*

Rambuteau, *m.* (familiar and popular), *urinals on the boulevards.* From the name of a prefect of police who caused them to be set up.

Ramener (familiar), *to brush the hair forward to conceal one's baldness.* Il ramène, *he is getting bald.* Termed also "emprunter un qui vaut dix."

Rameneur, *m.* (gamesters'), *man of gentlemanly appearance, whose functions are to induce people to attend a gaming-house or gaming club.*

Un personnel de rameneurs qui, membres réguliers du cercle, gentlemen en apparence . . . ont pour mission de racoler . . . ceux qui bien nourris à la table d'hôte, seront une heure après dévorés à celle du baccara.—HECTOR MALOT, *Baccara.*

The American "picker-up" somewhat corresponds to the "rameneur." The picker-up takes his man to a gambling saloon, and leaves him there to be enticed into playing. The picker-up is always a gentleman in manners, dress, and appearance. He first sees the man's name on the hotel register and where he is from. Many of the servants of hotels are in the pay of pickers-up, and furnish them with information concerning guests. (Familiar) Rameneur, *old beau who seeks to conceal his baldness by brushing forward the scanty hair from the back of his head.*

Rameneuse, *f.* (popular), *girl who makes it a practice to wait for clients at the doors of cafés at closing time.*

Ramicher, or **ramamicher** (popular), *to bring about a reconciliation.* Se —, *to be friends again.*

Ramijoter (popular), *to effect a reconciliation.* Se —, *to make it up.*

Ils se sont ramijotés (réconciliés) ; et d'après des mots de leur conversation, je répondrais bien qu'il a couché avec Félicité. —Vidocq.

Ramollot, *m.* (familiar and popular), *stupid old soldier.* From a character delineated by Charles Leroy.

Ramonage, *m.* (popular), *muttering nonsense.*

Ramoner (popular), *to mutter, to mumble.* An allusion to the rumbling noise produced by sweeping a chimney. Se faire —, *to go to confession ; to take a purgative.* Also *to get thrashed or scolded.* Ramoner ses tuyaux, *to run away.* For synonyms see **Patatrot.**

Ramor, *m.* (Jewish tradespeople's), *fool,* "*flat.*"

Rampant, *m.* (popular), *priest,* or "*white choker ;*" *Jesuit ; steeple.* Probably from the old signification of ramper, *to climb, to ascend.*

Rampante, *f.* (popular), *church.*

Rampe, *f.* (familiar), princesse de la —, *actress.* Une pomme de —, *a bald head,* or "*bladder of lard.*" (Theatrical) Se brûler à la —, *to approach close to the footlights, and play as if no other actors were present.* Lâcher la —, *to die.* See **Pipe.**

Ramponner (popular), *to drink,* "*to lush ;*" *to get drunk,* or "*screwed.*"

Rancart, *m.* (familiar), *object of little value,* "*no great shakes.*" (Thieves') Faire un —, *to procure information.*

Rancké, *m.* (thieves'), *two-franc coin.*

Rangé des voitures, *adj.* (thieves'), *is said of one who has become honest.*

A vingt et un ans rangé des voitures.— *From a thief's letter.*

Ranger (popular), se — des voitures, *to become honest.* Is said also of a man who, after having sown his wild oats, leads a quiet life.

Rapapiotage, *m.* (popular), *reconciliation.*

Rapapioter (popular), *to effect a reconciliation.*

Rapapioteur, *m.* (popular), *one by whose kind efforts a reconciliation is effected.*

Rapatu, *m.* (thieves'), *body-louse.*

Râpe, *f.* (thieves'), *back.* Used more in reference to a humpback.

Râpé, *m. and adj.* (military), *officer without any private means ;* (popular) — comme la Hollande, *very poor,* "*quisby.*" An allusion to râper, *to rasp,* and Dutch cheese.

Râper (popular), *to sing,* "*to lip.*" Also *to sing in a monotonous fashion.*

Rapiat, *subst. and adj.* (familiar and popular), *stingy,* "*close-fisted,* or *near.*" Termed "brum" at Winchester School. Une —, *a miserly woman.*

C'est égal, t'es une jolie fille ; ça faisait mal de te voir chez cette mauvaise rapiat de bonapartiste de mère Lefèvre.—Hector France.

Un —, *a native of Auvergne.* The natives of each province of France are credited with some particular characteristics ; thus, as seen above, the Auvergnats are said to be thrifty, stingy, miserly ; the Normans thievish, fond of going to law ; the Picards are hot-headed, of an irate disposition; the Bretons have a reputation for being pig-headed ; the Gascons for possessing a mind fertile in resource, and for being great storytellers—also for bragging ; the Champenois is supposed to be stupid ; the Parisians are "artful dodgers ;" the Lorrains are, it is alleged, treacherous ; and the natives of Cambrai are all mad. Hence the proverbial sayings : avare comme un Auvergnat ; voleur comme un Normand ; entêté comme un Breton ; 99 moutons et un Champenois font cent bêtes, &c. Again, among soldiers "un Parisien" is synonymous of a soldier who seeks to shirk his duty ; sailors apply the epithet to a bad sailor, horsedealers to a "screw," &c., &c. Daniel Defoe thus depicts the characteristic vices of the different nations :—

Pride, the first peer, and president of hell,
To his share, Spain, the largest province
    fell. . . .
Lust chose the torrid zone of Italy,
Where blood ferments in rapes and so-
    domy. . . .
Drunkenness, the darling favourite of hell,
Chose Germany to rule. . . .
Ungovern'd passion settled first in France,
Where mankind lives in haste, and thrives
    by chance. . . .
By zeal the Irish, and the Russ by folly,
Fury the Dane, the Swede by melancholy ;
By stupid ignorance the Muscovite ;
The Chinese by a child of hell, called wit ;
Wealth makes the Persian too effeminate ;
And poverty the Tartar desperate. . . .
Rage rules the Portuguese, and fraud the
    Scotch ;
Revenge the Pole, and avarice the Dutch.
From this amphibious, ill-born mob began,
That vain ill-natured thing, an Englishman.
        The True-Born Englishman.

Rapiot, *m.* (popular), *patch on a coat or shoe ;* (thieves') *searching on the person,* "frisking, or ruling

over." Formerly the term referred to the searching of convicts about to be taken to the hulks. Le grand —, *was the general searching of convicts.*

Rapioter (popular), *to patch up ;* (thieves') *to search,* "to frisk."

Butons les rupins d'abord, nous refroidirons après la fourgate et nous rapioterons partout. Il y a gros dans la taule.—VIDOCQ.

Rapointi, *m.* (popular), *clumsy, awkward workman.*

Rappliquer (popular and thieves'), *to return,* "to hare it ;" — à la niche, or à la taule, *to return home.*

Tout est tranquille . . . la sorgue est noire, les largues ne sont pas rappliquées à la taule, la fourgate roupille dans son rade.—VIDOCQ. (*All* "serene" . . . *the night is dark, the women have not returned home, the receiver sleeps inside his counter.*)

Rasé, or **razi,** *m.* (thieves'), *priest.* He has a shaven crown.

Raser (familiar), *to annoy, to bore one ; to ruin one.*

Elle s'est essayée sur le sieur Hulot qu'elle a plumé net, oh ! plumé, ce qui s'appelle rasé.—BALZAC.

(Shopmen's) **Raser,** *to swindle a fellow shop-assistant out of his sale ;* (sailors') *to tell* "fibs ;" *to humbug.*

Rase-tapis, *m.* (familiar), *a horse that trots or gallops without lifting its feet much from the ground,* "daisy-cutter."

Raseur, *m.* (familiar), *a bore.*

Ce type est en même temps un "raseur de l'espèce spéciale dite "des déboutonneurs à histoires bien bonnes." Vous savez bien ces braves gens à qui vous ne pouvez pas adresser la parole sans qu'ils vous répondent par : "Je vais vous raconter une bien bonne histoire" et qui commencent immédiatement par vous arracher, un à un, les boutons de votre redingote.—*Gil Blas.*

(Shopmen's) **Raseur,** *one who swindles a fellow shop-assistant out of his sale.*

Rasibus, *m.* (popular), le père —, *the executioner.* A play on the word raser, *to shave.*

Et le coup de la bagnole au père Rasibus, quand il fouette les cadors au galop et que les cognes font un blaire.—RICHEPIN.

Rasoir, *m. and adj.* (familiar and popular), *bore ; boring.*

On commence à nous embêter avec les bleus. Tout le temps les bleus, ça devient rasoir à la fin ; on nous prend trop pour de bonnes têtes.—G. COURTELINE.

Rasoir de Birmingham, *superlative of bore.* (Popular) Rasoir ! *expression of contemptuous refusal ;* may be rendered by the Americanism, "yes, in a horn." Faire —, *to be penniless.* (Gamesters') Banque —, *gaming* "banque" *which has a run of luck, and in consequence leaves the players penniless.* Faire —, *to lose all one's money,* "to blew" it. Ça fait —, *nothing is left.*

Mangeux de tout ; excepté l'tien,
Car tu n'as rien ; ça fait rasoir.
Riche-en-gueule.

(Thieves') Rasoir à Roch, or — de la Cigogne, *guillotine.* M. Roch was formerly the executioner, and la Cigogne is the epithet applied to the Préfecture de Police. The knife of the guillotine was termed in '93, "rasoir national."

Raspail, *m.* (popular), *brandy,* "French cream," and "bingo" in old English cant. Termed also "troix-six, fil-en-quatre, dur, raide, chenique, rude, crik, eau d'aff, schnapps, camphre, sacré chien, goutte, casse-poitrine, jaune, tord-boyaux, consolation, riquiqui, eau de mort."

Rassembler (military), se faire —, *to get reprimanded or punished.*

Rastacouère, or **rastaquouère,** *foreign adventurer or swindler,* generally hailing from the sunny south, or from South America, who lives in high style, of course at somebody or other's expense.

La petite Raymonde D . . ., sa chère adorée, qu'on avait surnommée, je ne sais pourquoi, sa "chair à saucisses," l'a lâché comme un vulgaire rastaquouère, pour se mettre avec un jockey.—*Gil Blas.*

Rat, *m.* (thieves'), *young thief who is generally passed through a small aperture to open a door and let in the rest of the gang, or else conceals himself under the counter of a shop before the doors are closed,* "little snakesman, or tool."

He kept him small on purpose, and let him out by the job. But the father gets lagged.—CH. DICKENS, *Oliver Twist.*

Also *thief who exercises his skill at inns or wine-shops.* Courir le —, *to steal at night in lodgings, or at lodging-houses.* Rat, *thief who steals bread ;* — de prison, *barrister,* or "mouthpiece." Prendre des rats par la queue meant formerly *to steal purses,* when persons wore their purses at their girdles. A cutpurse was formerly called a "nypper." A man named Wotton, in 1585, kept in London an academy for the education of pickpockets. Cutting them was a branch of the light-fingered art. Instruction in the practice was given as follows : a purse and a pocket were separately suspended, attached to which, both around and above them, were small bells ; each contained counters, and he who could withdraw a counter without causing any of the bells to ring was adjudged to be a "nypper." The old English cant termed cutting a purse, "to nyp a bunge." Dickens, in *Oliver Twist,* shows Fagin educating the Dodger and Charley

Bates by impersonating an old gentleman walking about the streets, the two boys following him and seeking to pick his pockets. (Popular) Rat de cave, *excise officer, gauger ;* — d'égout, *scavenger.* (Ecole Polytechnique) Rat, *student who is late ;* — de pont, *student whose total of marks at the final examination does not entitle him to an appointment in the corps of government civil engineers of the Ponts et Chaussées ;* — de soupe, *one late for dinner.* From rater, *to miss.* (Familiar) Rat, or — d'opéra, *young ballet dancer between the ages of seven and fourteen.* (Sailors') Rat de quai, *man who looks out for odd jobs in harbours.*

> Le grand-père est un rat de quai,
> Le petit-fils mousse embarqué.
> La grand' mère, aux jours les meilleurs,
> Porte la hotte aux mareyeurs.
> RICHEPIN, *La Mer.*

Etre —, *to be stingy,* "close-fisted."

> Ce jeune rat—moins "rat" que son adversaire.—*Gil Blas.*

Rata, *m.* (general), *kind of stew.*

> Le rata diminutif de ratatouille . . . se compose de pommes de terre . . . avec assaisonnement d'un morceau de lard . . . en société d'une botte d'oignons.—DUBOIS DE GENNES.

> La mère Nassau lui vociféra une longue kyrielle d'injures dont une partie sans doute lui avait été adressée à elle-même le jour où elle fut surprise crachant dans le rata.—H. FRANCE, *La Pucelle de Tebessa.*

Rata, used in a figurative sense, signifies *a coarse, unmeaning article, or literary production.*

> Vous avez lu la lettre si digne de —? Xau, poli, comme un marbre, a dû faire un signe d'assentiment, mais il est trop occupé pour absorber ce rata soi-disant naturaliste.—*Gil Blas,* 1887.

Rataconniculer (obsolete), *to cobble.* Referred also to the carnal act.

Ratafia de grenouille, *m.* (popular), *water.* Called, in the English slang, "Adam's ale," and the old term "fish broth," as appears from the following :—

> The churlish frampold waves gave him his belly-full of fish-broth.—NASHE, *Lenten Stuff.*

Ratapiaule, *f.* (popular), *thrashing,* "walloping."

Ratapoil, *m.* (familiar), *epithet applied to old soldiers of the First Empire,* and generally *to Bonapartists.* Literally rat à poil.

Ratatouille, *f.* (familiar and popular), flanquer une —, *to thrash.* See **Voie.**

Rateau, *m.* (popular), *police officer.* (Military) Faire son —, *to remain some time with the corps, as a punishment, at the expiration of the twenty-eight days' yearly service as a réserviste.*

Ratiboisé, *adj.* (general), *done for ; ruined,* "gone to smash."

> J'ai fait faillite comme un vrai commerçant ; ratiboisé ma chère.—HUYSMANS.

Ratiboiser (general), *to take ; to steal,* "to prig." See **Grinchir.** Termed in South Africa, "to jump." An officer to whom a settler had lent a candlestick was recommended not to allow it to be "jumped," mysterious words which at first were to him quite unintelligible. In the English jargon, "to jump" a man is to rob him with violence.

Ratiche, *f.* (popular and thieves'), *church.* Blaireau de —, *holy water brush or sprinkler.*

Ratichon, *m.* (popular and thieves'), *priest,* "devil-dodger, snub-devil, parish bull, parish stallion, cushion-smiter, sky-pilot," and in old cant, "rat, patrico." Concerning

the latter word see **Sanglier.**
Serpillière de —, *priest's cassock.*

J'avais de plus beaux sentiments sous mes guenilles qu'il n'y en a sous une serpillière de ratichon.—V. Hugo.

Un — de cambrouse, *a village priest.*

J'ai moi-même une affaire avec deux amis de collège (prison) chez un particulier qui va tous les dimanches passer la journée chez un ratichon de cambrouse (curé de campagne).—Canler.

Un —, *a comb.*

Ratichonner (popular), *to comb one's hair.*

Ratichonnière, *f.* (popular and thieves'), *cloister, or any religious community.*

Ratier, *m.* (tailors'), *journeyman tailor who does night-work at home.*

Ration de la ramée, *f.* (thieves'), *prison food.*

Ratisse, *f.* (thieves' and roughs'), *refiler une* —, *to thrash.* See **Voie** for synonyms.

Ratissé, *adj.* (popular), *exhausted,* "gruelled."

R'tourner à pied, fallait pas y penser, j'étais ratissé et courbaturé d'm'être balladé dans la foire.—G. Frison, *Les Aventures du Colonel Ronchonot.*

Ratisser (popular), en — à quelqu'un, *to mock, to laugh at one.* Je t'en ratisse! *a fig for you!* Se faire — la couenne, *to get thrashed; to get oneself shaved.* (Familiar) Se faire —, *to lose all one's money at a game, to have* "blewed it."

Vous lui avez même emprunté cinq louis ... quand vous avez été ratissé au baccarat.—J'ai été ratissé?—Raiguisé si vous voulez.—P. Mahalin.

Ratisseuse de colabres, *f.* (thieves'), *guillotine.* Colabre is the cant for *neck.*

Raton, *m.* (thieves'), *very young thief,* "little snakesman," see **Rat**; (Breton cant) *priest.*

Rattrapage, *m.* (printers'), *piece of composition which forms the complement of another.*

Ravage, *m.* (popular), *sundry pieces of metal found in the gutters or on the banks of the river.*

Ravager (thieves'), *to steal linen from a lavoir public, or washerwoman's punt.*

Ravageur, *m.* (thieves'), *thief who exercises his industry on washerwomen's punts established on the banks of the Seine;* (popular) *man who drags the banks of the river, or the gutters, in the hope of finding lumps of metal or other articles, a kind of* "mudlark." Concerning the latter term, the *Slang Dictionary* says a mudlark is a man or woman who, with clothes tucked above the knee, grovels through the mud on the banks of the Thames, when the tide is low, for silver or pewter spoons, old bottles, pieces of iron, coal, or any article of the least value, deposited by the retiring tide, either from passing ships or the sewers.

Ravaudage, *m.* (popular), faire du —, *to make love to several girls at a time, so as not to remain* "in the cold."

Raverta, *m.* (Jewish tradesmen's), *servant.*

Ravescot, *m.* (obsolete), *venereal act.*

Ravignolé, *m.* (thieves'), *new offence.*

Ravine, *f.* (popular), *wound; scar.*

Raviné, *adj.* (familiar), *the worse for wear.* Des dents ravinées, *bad teeth.*

Rayon, *m.* (popular), sur l'œil, *black eye*, "mouse." (Thieves') Rayon de miel, *lace*, or "driz."

Raze, or **razi**, *m.* (thieves'), *priest, parson*, "devil-dodger;" — pour l'af, *actor*, "cackling cove, or faker."

Réac, *m.* (familiar and popular), *Conservative.*

C'était à la Salamandre ou au Sacré Bock que se tenaient les inspecteurs masqués de la Commune.... Vermorel y était traité de bourgeois, Rochefort, de réac.—*Mémoires de Monsieur Claude.*

Réaffurer (thieves'), *to win back.*

Rebâtir (thieves'), un pante, *to kill a man*, "to give one his gruel, to quash." Also "to hush." You know, if I wished to nose (*to peach*), I could have you twisted (*hanged*); not to mention anything about the cull (*man*) that was hushed for his reader (*pocket-book*).

Rébecca, *f.* (popular), *impudent girl with a saucy tongue*, a "sauce-box, or imperence."

Rebecquat, *m.* (thieves' and roughs'), *insolence; resistance.* Pas de — ou bien je t'encaisse, *don't show your teeth, else I'll give you a thrashing.*

Rebectage, *m.* (thieves'), *medicine; Cour de cassation.* Se cavaler au —, *to appeal for the quashing of a judgment.*

Rebecter (popular), se —, *to get reconciled.*

Rebecteur, *m.* (popular), *doctor*, "pill-box;" *surgeon*, "sawbones."

Rebéqueter (popular), *to repeat; to ruminate.*

Rebiffe, *f.* (thieves'), *revolt; revenge;* — au truc, *repeating an offence.* Faire de la —, *to oppose resistance.*

Rebiffer (popular and thieves'), *to begin again;* — au truc, *to return to one's old ways, to be at the "old game" again; to do anything again.*

"Tiens, mon petit, rebiffe au truc ; c'est moi qui verse." Elle rapporte un nouveau rafraîchissement d'absinthe au chanteur.—Louise Michel.

Rebomber (familiar), se — le torse, *to recover one's spent energy by taking refreshment.*

Rebondir (popular), *to turn out of doors, to expel.* Envoyer —, *to turn out, to send to the deuce.*

Rebonnetage, *m.* (popular), *reconciliation;* (thieves') *flattery*, "soft sawder."

Rebonneter (popular and thieves'), *to flatter.* The word bonneter was formerly used with nearly the same signification, and the English had a similar expression, "to bonnet," used by Shakespeare :—

He hath deserved worthily of his country ; and his ascent is not by such easy degrees as those who having been supple and courteous to the people, bonneted, without any further deed to heave them at all into their estimation and report.—*Coriolanus.*

Rebonneter pour l'af, *to give ironical praise.* Se —, *to console oneself.* Also *to be of better behaviour, to turn over a new leaf.*

Rebonneteur, *m.* (thieves'), *confessor.*

Si ce que dit le rebonneteur (confesseur) n'est pas de la blague, un jour nous nous retrouverons là-bas.—Vidocq.

Rebonnir (thieves'), *to say again.*

Reboucler (thieves'), *to re-imprison.*

Rebouis, *adj. and m.* (thieves'), *dead*, said of one who has been "put to bed with a shovel;"

corpse, "cold meat, or pig;" *shoe*, "trotter-case." English thieves call cleaning their boots "japanning their trotter-cases."

Rebouiser (thieves'), *to kill*, "to give one his gruel," see **Refroidir;** *to patch up a shoe.* Rabelais termed this "rataconniculer," and also uses the word with an obscene signification, as appears from the following:—

Et si personne les blasme de soi faire rataconniculer ainsi sus leur grosse, vu que les bestes sus leurs ventrées n'endurent jamais le masle masculant, elles respondront que ce sont bestes, mais elles sont femmes.—*Gargantua.*

Also *to notice, to gaze on.*

Faut pas blaguer, le treppe est batte ;
Dans c'taudion i's'trouve des rupins.
Si queuq's gonziers traînent la savate,
J'en ai r'bouisé qu'on d's escarpins.
Chanson de l'Assommoir.

Rebouiseur, *m.* (popular), *cobbler*, in old French "taconneur;" *old clothes man who repairs second-hand clothes before selling them.*

Rebours, *m.* (roughs'), *moving of one's furniture on the sly*, "shooting the moon."

Recaler (artists'), *to correct.* (Popular) Se —, *to recover one's strength*, and generally *to improve one's outward appearance.*

Dédèle s'r'cale les joues et Trutru r'prend des forces pour masser d'plus belle.—*Le Cri du Peuple.*

Also *to better one's position.*

Recarrelure, *f.* (popular), *meal.*

Recarrer (popular), se —, *to strut.*

Récent, *adj.* (popular), avoir l'air —, *to walk steadily though drunk.*

Recevoir (popular), la pelle au cul, *to be dismissed from one's employment*, "to get the sack;" (military) — son décompte, *to die*, "to lose the number of one's mess."

Rechâsser (popular), *to survey attentively*, "to stag;" *to see.* From châsse, *eye.*

Réchauffante, *f.* (thieves'), *wig*, "periwinkle;" (military) *great coat.*

Réchauffer (popular), *to annoy, to bore.*

Rèche, *m.* (popular), *a sou.*

Récidiviste, *m.* (familiar), *old offender.* According to a new law, repeating a certain specified offence makes one liable to be transported for life.

Reçoit-tout, *m.* (popular), *chamber-pot*, or "jerry."

Recollardé, *adj.* (thieves'), *caught again.*

Recoller (popular), *to be convalescent.* Se —, *to have a reconciliation with a woman, and cohabit with her again.*

Reconduire (theatrical), *to hiss*, "to goose, or to give the big bird;" (popular) — quelqu'un, or faire la conduite à quelqu'un, *to thrash one*, "to wollop." (Military) Se faire —, *to be compelled to retreat in hot haste.*

Reconnaissance, *f.* (printers'), *thin flat ruler of metal or wood used by printers.*

Reconnebler (thieves'), *to recognize.*

C'est bon, je vois bien que je suis reconneblé (reconnu) et qu'il n'y a pas moyen d'aller à Niort (de nier).—CANLER.

Reconobrer (thieves'), *to recognize.* Me reconobres-tu pas ? *Don't you know me again ?*

Il faut d'abord défrimousser ces gaillards-là de manière à ce qu'ils ne soient pas reconobrés.—VIDOCQ. (*We must at first disfigure these here fellows, so that they may not be known.*)

Recoquer (popular), se —, *to re-cover one's strength ; to dress one-self in new attire.* From coque, hull.

Recordé, *adj.* (thieves'), *killed,* "easy."

Recorder (thieves'), *to warn one of some impending danger ; to kill one,* "to quash, to hush." Se —, *to plot, to concert together.*

Recourir à l'émétique (thieves'), *to get forged bills discounted.*

Recuit, *adj.* (popular), *ruined again.*

Récurer (popular), la casserole, or se —, *to take a purgative.* Se faire —, *to be under treatment for syphilis.*

Redam, *m.* (thieves'), *pardon.* From rédemption.

Redin, *m.* (thieves'), *purse,* "skin." The word has the same significa-tion in the Italian jargon, and comes from retino, *small net.* Hence reticule, a *lady's bag,* cor-rupted into ridicule.

Redoublement, *m.* (thieves'), de fièvre, *fresh charge brought against a prisoner who is being tried for an offence ;* — de fièvre cérébrale, *fresh charge against a prisoner who is being tried for murder.*

Pour peu que des parrains ne viennent pas leur coquer un redoublement de fièvre cérébrale, ma largue et mes gosselines se tireront de ce mauvais pas.—Vidocq.

Redouiller (popular), *to push back ; to repel ; to ill-treat,* "to man-handle."

Redresse, *f.* (thieves'), être à la —, *to be cunning, knowing,* "downy."

I am . . . we all are, down to the dog. And he's the downiest one of the lot.—Ch. Dickens.

Mec à la —. See **Mec.** Cheva-lier de la —, *professional parasite, spunger,* "quiller."

Redresseur, *m.* (obsolete), *thief, pickpocket,* "fogle-hunter." In old English cant, "foyster."

Redresseuse, *f.* (obsolete), *prosti-tute and thief,* "mollisher."

Réduit, *m.* (thieves'), *purse,* "skin."

Réemballer (popular), *to imprison afresh.*

Refaire (familiar and popular), *to dupe,* "to do."

Z . . . un autre journaliste, après avoir longtemps bohémisé, carotté, refait tous ses camarades.—A. Sirven.

Refaire au même, *to pay back in the same coin, to give a Roland for an Oliver.* Se —, *to recoup one's losses at a game.* (Popular) Re-faire dans le dur, *to dupe,* "to bilk." Se — le torse, *to have refreshment.* (Thieves') Se — de sorgue, *to have supper.*

Refait, *adj.* (general), être —, *to be duped,* or "done."

La voiture remonte péniblement la chaus-sée. Le cocher, qu'on a pris le matin et qui a peur d'être refait, juronne entre ses dents.—P. Mahalin.

(Thieves') Etre — sans donjon, *to be apprehended again as a rogue and vagabond.*

Refaite, *f.* (thieves'), *meal ;* — du matois, *breakfast ;* — de jorne, *dinner ;* — de côni, *last sacra-ments of the church ;* —du séchoir, *meal after a funeral ;* — de sorgue, *supper.*

Je vous dis que lorsque j'ai quitté le tapis, il allait achever sa refaite de sorgue et qu'il venait de donner l'ordre de seller son gaye.—Vidocq.

Refaiter (thieves'), *to partake of a meal.*

Refaitier, *m.* (thieves'), *master of a victualling house,* "boss of a grubbing ken."

Reffoler (thieves'), *to steal by surprise.*

Refilé, *m.* (popular), aller au —, *to confess.* Ne pas aller au —, *to deny.*

Refiler (thieves'), *to restore ; to give,* "donnez."

> Au clair de la luisante,
> Mon ami Pierrot,
> Refile-moi ta griffonnante,
> Pour broder un mot.
> Ma camouche est chtourbe,
> Je n'ai plus de rif ;
> Déboucle-moi ta lourde
> Pour l'amour du Mec.
> *Au Clair de la Lune en Argot.*

Refiler, *to pass from one person to another,* "to sling ;" *to pass on to a confederate by throwing,* "to ding ;" — un pante, *to dog a man,* "to pipe ;" (popular) — des beignes, *to strike one on the face,* "to fetch one a wipe in the mug ;" — une ratisse, *to thrash,* "to wallop ;" — une poussée, *to hustle,* "to shove ;" — la pâtée, *to feed.* S'en — sous le tube, *to take a pinch of snuff.*

Refondante, *f.* (thieves'), *lucifer match,* "spunk."

Refouler (popular), *to refuse ; to hesitate ;* — au travail, *to leave off working ;* — à Bondy, *to rudely send one about his business.* It is to Bondy that the contents of cesspools are conveyed.

Réfractaire, *m.* (familiar), *more or less talented man who will not bend to the fashion or ideas of the day.*

Refroidi, *m.* and *adj.* (thieves'), *corpse,* "cold meat ;" *dead,* "easy."

Refroidir (thieves'), *to kill.*

> Les chiens bourrés de boulettes, étaient morts. J'ai refroidi les deux femmes.— BALZAC.

Refroidir à la capahut, *to kill an accomplice for the purpose of robbing him of his share of booty.* From the name of a celebrated bandit, the head of a large gang of murderers named "chauffeurs," who spread terror towards the year III. of the Republic, in the vicinity of Paris. The different modes of taking life are expressed thus : "chouriner, or suriner, estourbir, scionner, buter, basourdir, faire un machabée, faire flotter, crever la paillasse, laver son linge dans la saignante, dévisser le trognon, faire suer un chêne, or faire suer le chêne coupé, capahuter, décrocher, descendre, ébasir, endormir, couper le sifflet, watriniser, entailler, entonner, estrangouiller, tortiller la vis, tourlourer, terrer, cônir, expédier, faire, faire la grande soulasse, rebâtir, sauter à la capahut, sonner, lingrer, envoyer ad patres, démolir, moucher le quinquet, saigner, sabler, tortiller le gaviot, faire banque, érailler, escarper, suager, faire le pante au machabée;" in the English slang, "to settle his hash, to cook his goose, to give one his gruel, to quash, to hush."

Régaler (popular), ses amis, *to take a purgative ;* — son cochon, *to treat oneself to a good dinner, to have a* "tightener ;" — son suisse *is said of two playing for drink, who win an equal number of games ;* (thieves') — la veuve, *to set up the guillotine.*

Regargarde ! (thieves'), *look !* "nark !"

Régatte, *f.* (rag-pickers'), *meat.*

Regatter (rag-pickers'), *to eat,* "to grub."

Régiment, *m.* (popular), des boules de Siam, *Sodomists.* S'engager dans le — des cocus, *to marry,* "to get spliced." (Military) Le chien du —, *the adjutant.*

Reginglard, *m.* (popular), *thin, sour wine.*

Registre, *m.* (printers'), faire le —. *to pour out the contents of a bottle so that each has an equal share.*

Réglette, *f.* (printers'), arroser la —, *to pay for one's footing.*

Réglisse. See **Jus.**

Regon, *m.* (thieves'), *debt.*

Regonser (thieves'), *to dog,* "to pipe."

Regoût, *m.* (thieves'), *unpleasant-ness.*

Il faut espérer que l'ouvrage de la chique aura été maquillé sans regoût.—VIDOCQ.

Du —, *uneasiness ; remorse ; fear.* Faire du —, *to make reve-lations.*

Reguicher (thieves'), *to attack.*

V'là qu'on me tire par la jambe ; j'me cavale, mais y zétaient du monde, on me reguiche, je m'ai défendu et me v'là.—LOUISE MICHEL.

Réguisé, or **raiguisé,** *adj.* (popu-lar), être —, *to be thrashed ; swindled ; ruined,* or "smashed ;" *to be deceived,* or "done ;" *to be sentenced to death.*

Réguiser, or **raiguiser** (popular), *to thrash ; to ruin.*

Rejacter (thieves'), *to say again.*

Réjouissance, *f.* (familiar), *bones placed into the scale by butchers with the meat and charged as meat.*

Une femme qui a plus de — que de viande, *a bony, skinny woman.*

Relanceur de pleins, *m.* (thieves'), *variety of card-sharpers.*

Relevante, *f.* (thieves'), *mustard.*

Relève, *f.* (popular), être à la —, *to be in better circumstances.*

Relever (popular), la —, or relever le chandelier, *to live on a prosti-tute's earnings.* From the practice of placing the fees of such women under a candlestick.

Releveur, *m.* (popular), de fumeuse, *blackguard who lives on a prosti-tute's earnings,* "pensioner." See **Poisson.** (Thieves') Releveur de pésoche, *money collector.*

Relicher (popular), *to toss down a glass of wine or liquor ; to kiss.* Se —, or se — le morviau, *to kiss one another.*

Relié, *adj.* (popular), *dressed.* Etre élégamment —, *to sport fine clothes.*

Relingue, *m.* (thieves'), *old offender.*

Il y avait là des relingues (récidivistes), allant voir ce qui leur arriverait un jour ou l'autre.—LOUISE MICHEL.

Relinguer (thieves'), *to stab re-peatedly.*

Reliquer (thieves'), *to say.*

Qu'as-tu reliqué ?—Qu'il était venu seul.—LOUISE MICHEL.

Reluire dans le ventre (popular), *to make one's mouth water.*

Reluit, *m.* (thieves'), *day,* or "light-mans ;" *eye,* or "ogle." See **Chasser.**

Reluquer (popular and thieves'), *to gaze,* "to stag ;" *to look atten-tively,* "to dick." Le sergo nous reluque, *the policeman has his eye on us,* "the bulky is dicking."

Reluquer une affaire, *to contemplate a theft.*

Il y a deux ou trois affaires que je reluque, nous les ferons ensemble.—VIDOCQ.

Les jours où il lansquine, il y a un tas de pantes à reluquer les flûtes des gonzesses qui carguent leurs ballons. *When it is raining, there are a lot of fellows who look at the legs of the girls who tuck up their clothes.* The old French had relouquer and reluquer with the same signification. The Norman patois has "louquer," which reminds one of the English to look.

Reluqueur, *m.* (popular), *one who plays the spy,* a "nose."

Reluqueuse, *f.* (popular), *opera glass.*

Remaquiller (popular and thieves'), *to do again.*

Remballé, retoqué, or requillé (students'), être —, *to be disqualified at an examination,* "to be spun, or ploughed."

Rembarbe, or ranquessé, *m.* (thieves'), *rentier, that is, man of independent means.*

Rembourrer (familiar), se — le ventre, *to make a good meal,* "to have a tightener."

Rembrocable, *adj.* (thieves'), *perceptible, visible.*

Rembrocage de parrain, *m.* (thieves'), *act of bringing one into the presence of a witness.*

Rembrocant, *m.* (thieves'), *looking-glass.*

Rembroquer (thieves'), *to recognize.*

Rême, *m.* (thieves'), *one who scolds, who growls,* a "crib-biter."

Remède d'amour, *m.* (popular), *ugly face,* or "knocker-face."

Remercier son boulanger (familiar and popular), *to die,* "to kick the bucket." For synonyms see **Pipe.**

Beauvallet, d'une voix tonnante.—Le pauvre homme ! comment, il a "claqué?"
Arsène Houssaye.—Mon Dieu, oui, il a "dévissé son billard," comme on dit à la cour.
Mademoiselle Augustine Brohan.—Vous vous trompez, mon cher directeur. . . . A la cour de Napoléon III., on dit maintenant : il a "remercié son boulanger."—P. AUDEBRAND.

The above conversation, according to the author of *Petits Mémoires d'une Stalle d'Orchestre,* took place at the Théâtre Français, of which M. Arsène Houssaye was then the manager. To explain this invasion of the Parisian jargon in the house of Molière, it must be said, that it coincided with the publication of a decree by M. Achille Fould, then Secretary of State. Being aware that the idiom of the hulks and gutter was used to an alarming extent on the Parisian stage, his Excellency had declared that the Government, declining to be an accomplice of these literary misdemeanours, had prohibited the use of the degrading lexicology, and had ordered a "commission de censure" (whose functions are somewhat similar, in theatrical matters, to those of the Lord Chamberlain in England) to taboo any play offering such enormities. The injunction had been specially enforced with respect to the Théâtre Français as being the official guardian of the purity of the French language and the leading playhouse. But the offended comedians, in retaliation, began to affect making use of the "langue verte."

Remettez donc le couvercle (roughs'), *a polite invitation to one who has an offensive breath to cease talking.*

Remisage, *m.* (thieves'), *place kept by a receiver of stolen property, chiefly vehicles of every description.*

Dans les remisages . . . vont s'engouffrer tous les camions, voitures, carrioles volés, pendant que les chevaux s'en vont au marché, et que les victimes sont déjà au fond de l'eau !—*Mémoires de Monsieur Claude.*

Remiser (popular), le fiacre à quelqu'un, *to shut one up.*

Comme il a voulu faire du pétard, j'y ai salement remisé son fiacre.—G. COURTE-LINE.

Remiser son fiacre, *to hold one's tongue ; to die.* Se faire —, *to get sat upon.*

Remiseur, *m.* (thieves'), *a receiver of stolen property,* or "fence."

Remisier, *m.* (familiar), *tout at the Stock Exchange.*

Rémone, *f.* (popular), faire de la —, *to bluster.*

Rémonencq, *m.* (literary), *old clothes man ; marine store dealer.* A character of Balzac's *La Comédie Humaine.*

Remontée, *f.* (popular), *afternoon.*

Remonter (popular), sa pendule, *to occasionally chastise one's better half ;* — le tournebroche, *to remind one of the non-observation of some rule.*

Remorque, *f.* (boulevardiers'), se laisser aller à la —, *is said of a man who allows himself to be enticed into inviting a girl to dinner.*

Remouchage, *m.* (thieves'), *revenge.*

Remoucher (thieves'), *to revenge*

oneself ; to kill, "to hush ;" (popular and thieves') *to look,* "to ogle."

R'mouchez-moi un peu c'larbin
Sous sa fourrure ed'cosaque.
Comme i'pu' bon l'eau d'Lubin !
I's'gour' dans son col qui craque
Comme un' areng dans sa caque.
Oh ! la ! la ! c't'habillé d'vert !
Oui, mais moi, v'là que j'me plaque.
C'est pas rigolo, l'hiver.
RICHEPIN.

Remouche le pante, "ogle the cove." Remoucher, *to spy,* "to nose."

Tandis que je le remouchions à la Porte Saint-Denis, il est sorti par la barrière des Gobelins.—BIZET.

Remouchicoter (popular), *to go about in quest of a love adventure, or seeking to pick a quarrel with anyone.*

Rempardeuse, *f.* (popular), *prostitute who frequents the ramparts.*

Remplir le battant (popular), *to eat,* "to grub."

Remplumer (popular), se —, *to grow fat ; to grow rich, to become* "rhino fat."

Remporter une veste (popular), *to be unsuccessful.*

Remue-pouce, *m.* (thieves'), *money,* "dinarly."

Remuer (thieves'), la casserole, *to be in the police force,* a detective being termed "cuisinier." (Popular) Remuer, *to stink ;* — la commode, *to sing.*

En v'là un qui vous bassine, à remuer la commode ses dix heures par jour !—RI-GAUD.

Remueur de casseroles, *m.* (thieves'), *spy, informer,* "nark."

Ce nouveau copain-là ne me dit rien de bon ; je crois que nous brûlons et que nous avons affaire à un remueur de casseroles.—*Mémoires de Monsieur Claude.*

Renâché, *m.* (thieves'), *cheese,* "casey."

Renâclant, *m.* (thieves'), *nose,* "snorter." See **Morviau.**

Renâcle, *f.* (thieves'), *the police.*

Ils nous regardèrent effrontément ; ils dirent après avoir vidé deux verres de mêlé-cassis : attention, la renâcle (la police) est en chasse.—*Mémoires de Monsieur Claude.*

Renâcler (popular), *to scold ; to grumble ; to feel disinclined.*

De temps en temps, quand les clients renâclent, il vide lui-même sa coupe en levant les yeux au ciel avec tous les signes de la béatitude.—HECTOR FRANCE, *Les Va-nu-pieds de Londres.*

The word has passed into the language.

Renâcleur, *m.* (popular), *grumbler,* "crib-biter;" (thieves') *police officer,* or "reeler;" *detective,* "nark, or nose."

Et comme vous êtes des renâcleurs venus pour nous boucler, vous allez aussi éternuer avec la largue et ses jobards.—*Mémoires de Monsieur Claude.*

Renaissance, *f.* (popular), *shoddy.*

Renanisme, *m.* (literary), a newly-coined expression, better explained by quotation :—

M. Jules Lemaître assure quelque part que M. Renan "jouit le premier du renanisme" . . . et l'essence ou l'essentiel du "renanisme," n'est-ce pas d'aimer les idées avec la multitude de leurs "nuances" parcequ'elles font les civilisations, les religions, les œuvres du génie humain, le drame mystérieux de la vie, dont le dénouement, peut-être, échappera à toute critique ?—MARCEL FOUQUIER.

Renard, *m.* (popular), *apprentice ; mixture of broth and wine ; vomit.* Piquer un —, *to vomit,* "to shoot the cat." Queue de —, *vomited matter.* (Thieves') Renard, *spy at the hulks.* (Booksellers') Renard, *valuable work found by an amateur at a bookstall among worthless books.*

Renarder (popular), *to vomit,* "to shoot the cat." Termed formerly "chasser, or escorcher le regnard."

Et tous ces bonnes gens rendoyent là leurs gorges devant tout le monde, comme s'ilz eussent escorché le regnard.—RABE-LAIS.

Cotgrave translates this expression by "*to spue, cast, vomit (especially upon excessive drinking) ; either because in spuing one makes a noise like a fox that barks ; or (as in* escorcher) *because the flaying of so unsavory a beast will make any man spue.*"

Renaré, *m.* (popular), *crafty man,* "sly blade, or sharp file," *one who is* "fly to wot's wot."

Renaud, *m.* (thieves'), *trouble.*

La nuit dernière, j'ai rêvé de greffiers, c'est signe de renaud.—VIDOCQ. (*Last night I dreamed of cats, that's a sign of trouble.*)

Renaud, *reproach ; uproar ; row.* Faire du —, *to scold ; to cause a disturbance.*

C'est ça ! c'est pas bête ; il faut être sûr avant de faire du renaud (du tapage).—VIDOCQ.

Renauder (popular and thieves'), *to be in a bad humour, to be* "shirty ;" *to grumble.*

Ne renaude pas, viens avec nousiergue. Allons picter une rouillarde encible.—V. HUGO, *Les Misérables.* (*Do not be angry, come with us. Let us go and have a bottle of wine together.*)

Also *to be threatening, to show one's teeth.*

Ohé les aminches ! c'est bientôt qu'on va casser la g . . . à ces feignants de socialisses. C'qu'on leur z'y esquintera les abatis, ah, malheur ! . . . Et qu'ils n'renaudent pas, si y voulaient fourrer leurs pattes sales su l'manteau impérial, si y tâchaient d'embêter les abeilles, elles auraient bien vite fait d'y répondre : miel !—*Gil Blas,* 1887.

Renaudeur, *m.* (thieves'), *grumbler,* or "crib-biter."

Rencontre, *f.* (thieves'), faire à la —, *to butt one in the stomach.* Fabriquer un gas à la —, à la flan, or à la dure, *to attack and rob a man at night*, "to jump a cull."

Rende, rendème, rendémi, *m.* (thieves'), vol au —, *theft which consists in requesting a trades-man to give change for a coin laid on the counter and dexterously whisked up again together with the change.*

Rendève, *m.* (popular), *rendez-vous.*

Rendez-moi (thieves'), vol au —, or faire le rendème. See **Rende.**

Rendoublé, *adj.* (thieves'), *full; said of one who has eaten a hearty meal, who has had a "tightener."* Un roulant — de camelote, *a cab-ful of goods.*

Rendre (tailors'), sa bûche, *to give up a piece of work to the master tailor; to die;* (military) —sa canne au ministre, *to die;* (bohemians') — sa clef, *to die;* (popular) — son livret, *to die;* — son permis de chasse, *to die.* See **Pipe.** Rendre le tablier *is said of a ser-vant who gives notice;* — visite à M. Du Bois, *to ease oneself,* "to go to the chapel of ease;" — ses comptes, *to vomit,* "to cast up accounts."

Rêne, *f.* (familiar), prendre la cin-quième —, *to seize hold of the mane of one's mount to save oneself from a fall.*

Renfoncement, *m.* (popular), *blow with the fist,* "bang."

Renfrusquiner (popular), se —, *to dress oneself in a new suit of clothes.*

Reng, *m.* (thieves'), *hundred.*

Rengainer son compliment (popular), *is said of one who stops*

short when about to say or do some-thing.

Rengoler (roughs'), *to return, to re-enter;* — à la caginotte, *to go home.*

Rengrâcier (thieves'), *to repent and forsake evil ways.*

Je suis lasse de manger du collège (de la prison), je rengrâcie (je m'amende), veux-tu boire la goutte?—VIDOCQ.

Rengrâcier, *to cease.*

Rengrâciez alors, mauvais escarpes de grand trime, ma filoche vous passera de-vant le naze.—VIDOCQ.

Also *to hold one's tongue,* "to mum one's dubber."

Renifiant, *m.* (thieves'), *nose,* "snorter." See **Morviau.**

Renifiante, *f.* (popular), *boot out at the sole and down at the heel.*

Renifler (popular), *to hesitate; to refuse; to drink,* "to sluice one's gob;" — la poussière du ruisseau, *to fall into the gutter.* Bottines qui reniflent l'eau, *leaky boots.* La — mal, *to stink.* Renifler sur le gigot, *to hesitate;* (billiards') — sa bille, *to screw back.*

Reniflette, *f.* (thieves'), *police,* the "frogs." I must amputate like a go-away (decamp in hot haste), or the frogs will nail (ap-prehend) me, and if they do get their fams (hands) on me, I'll be in for a stretch of air and exercise (year's hard labour). Le père —, *the head of the police.*

Renifleur, *m.* (thieves'), *police officer,* "crusher." Le père des renifleurs, *the prefect of police.* Renifleur de camelotte à la flan, *rogue who steals articles from shop-windows.*

Renifleurs, *m. pl.* (obscene). The celebrated physician Tardieu, in his *Etude Médico-légale sur les Attentats à la Pudeur,* says :—

Renifleurs, qui in secretos locos, nimirum circa theatrorum posticos, convenientes quo complures feminæ ad micturiendum festinant, per nares urinali odore excitati, illico se invicem polluunt.

Reniquer (popular), *to be in a rage,* "to have one's monkey up."

Renquiller (thieves'), *to re-enter, to return home.*

Tu as donc oublié que le dabe qui est allé ballader sur la trime avec les fanandels ne renquillera pas cette sorgue.—VIDOCQ. (*Then you forget that father, who is on the road with the pals, will not return home to-night.*)

(Printers') Renquiller, *to grow stout ; to succeed ; to get rich.*

Renseignement, *m.* (boating men's), prendre un —, *to have a glass of wine or liquor,* "to smile, or to see the man," as the Americans say.

Rentier à la soupe, *m.* (popular), *workman.*

Rentiffer (thieves'), *to enter ; to return,* "to hare it."

Rentoiler (popular), se —, *to recover one's strength after having suffered from illness.*

Rentré dans ses bois, *adj.* (popular), être —, *to wear wooden shoes.*

Rentrer (popular), bredouille, *to return home quite drunk ;* — de la toile, *to take rest on account of old age.* Literally *to take sail in.* (Medical students') Rentrer ses pouces, *to die.* (Gamesters') Rentrer, *to lose.*

Un joueur qui perd, dit : je suis rentré ! S'il est après plusieurs parties, dans une déveine persistante, il dit : je suis engagé ! —*Mémoires de Monsieur Claude.*

Renversant, *adj.* (familiar), c'est —! *astounding! wonderful!* "stunning!"

Renverser (popular), *to vomit,* "to cast up accounts ;" — son casque, *to die ;* (familiar) — la marmite, *to discontinue giving dinners.*

Répandre (popular), se —, *to fall sprawling ; to die.*

Réparation de dessous le nez, *f.* (popular), *drinking and eating.*

Il y aurait un roman en plusieurs volumes à écrire sur ce bonhomme, qui a fait tous les métiers, et qui a, comme Panurge, trente-trois façons de gagner son argent, et soixante-six de le dépenser, sans compter la réparation de dessous le nez.—RICHEPIN, *Le Pavé.*

Repas de l'âne, *m.* (popular), faire le —, *to drink only at the conclusion of a meal.*

Repasse, *f.* (popular), *bad coffee.*

Repasser (popular), *to give ;* — la chemise de la bourgeoise, *to chastise one's better half.*

Oh ! ce n'est rien ! je repasse la chemise de ma femme.—HUYSMANS.

Repasser le cuir à quelqu'un, *to thrash,* or "*tan*" *one;* — une taloche à quelqu'un, *to give one a slap in the face,* "to fetch one a wipe in the mug."

Repaumer (popular), *to apprehend anew ; to take back.*

Repérir (popular), *to watch,* "to nark ;*" (thieves') *to find again.*

Repésigner (thieves'), *to re-catch, to re-apprehend.*

Répéter (popular), or aller à la répétition, *to make a double sacrifice to Venus.* (Theatrical) Répéter en robe de chambre, or dans ses bottes, *to practise repeating one's part only for the sake of learning the words, without attempting the stage effects.*

Repic, *m.* (thieves'), *beginning again, relapse.* Le — de relingue, *fresh offence.*

Le machabée était resté au bord de l'eau. C'est sur moi qu'on farfouille le repic de relingue.—LOUISE MICHEL.

D D

Repiger (popular), *to catch again.*

Repioler (thieves'), *to re-enter a house ; to go home,* "to speel to the crib."

Repiquer (popular), *to retake courage ; to get out of some scrape ; to go to sleep again ;* — *sur le rôti, to have another drink.*

Replâtrée, *f.* (popular), *woman with an outrageously painted face.*

Reporter, *verb and m.* (popular), son fusil à la mairie, *to be getting old.* An allusion to the limit of age for obligatory service in the old national guard. Reporter son ouvrage *is said of a doctor who attends at a patient's funeral.* (Familiar) Reporter à femmes, *one who reports on the doings of cocottes.*

Terminons cette variété . . . par ce grand diable de reporter à femmes, fournisseur breveté des feuilles pornographiques. . . . Les drôlesses friandes de scandale le tutoient et lui offrent à souper en échange de quelques lignes ou d'une biographie.—A. Sirven.

Reposante, *f.* (thieves'), *chain.* Il y a une — à la lourde, *there is a chain on the door.*

Reposoir, *m.* (popular), *lodging-house,* or "dossing-crib." Les reposoirs, *feet,* or "dew-beaters."

Les pieds s'appellent des "reposoirs ;" les mains, des "battoirs ;" la figure, une "binette ;" les bras, des "allumettes ;" la tête, une "trompette ;" les jambes, des "flûtes à café ;" et l'estomac, une "boîte à gaz."—*Les Locutions Vicieuses.*

(Thieves') Reposoir, *place tenanted by a receiver of stolen property.*

Le reposoir, tenu par le fourgat, est un lieu de recel pour le criminel qui ne travaille qu'en ville.—*Mémoires de Monsieur Claude.*

Also *a low eating-house, wine-shop,* or *lodging-house for prostitutes.*

Paris, en dépit de ses démolitions . . . renferme toujours des Tapis francs comme au temps d'Eugène Sue ; leurs noms seuls ont changé ; ce sont des Bibines, des Reposoirs, des Assommoirs dont le Château-Rouge, rue de la Calandre, possède en fait d'alphonses, d'escarpes ou de gonzesses, la fleur du panier.—*Mémoires de Monsieur Claude.*

Repoussant, *m.* (thieves'), *musket,* or "dag."

Repousser (popular), du goulot, du tiroir, or du corridor, *to have an offensive breath.*

Reprendre du poil de la bête (popular), *to continue the previous evening's debauch,* "to have a hair of the dog that bit you."

Reptile, *m.* (familiar), *journalist in the pay of the government.*

République. See **Cachet.**

Requiller. See **Retoquer.**

Requin, *m.* (thieves'), *custom-house officer ;* (popular) — de terre, *lawyer,* "land-shark, or puzzle-cove." The *Slang Dictionary* also gives the expression "sublime rascal" for a "limb of the law."

Requinquer (popular), se —, *to dress oneself in a new suit of clothes.*

Devine qui j'ai rencontré . . . la petite modiste . . . et requinquée . . . je ne te dis que ça.—P. Mahalin.

Réserve, *f.* (theatrical), *free tickets kept in reserve.*

C. est bon, . . . il doit avoir une réserve sur laquelle il consentira bien à me donner deux fauteuils.—*Echo de Paris.*

Réservoir, *m.* (popular), *réserviste,* or *soldier of the reserve.*

Résinon, *m.* (popular), *midnight meal.* Probably an allusion to torchlight.

Resolir (thieves'), *to resell.*

Respecter ses fleurs (popular), *to defend one's virginity against any attempt.*

Respirante, *f.* (thieves'), *mouth.* Bâcle ta —, *shut your mouth,* "button your bone-box."

Resserrer son linge (popular), *to die,* "to snuff it." For synonyms see **Pipe.**

Ressorts, *m. pl.* (popular), *woman's privities,* "Fanny." Une commode à —, *a carriage,* or "cask." (Thieves') Un crucifix à ressorts, *a dagger,* "chive."

Restaurant à l'envers, *m.* (popular), *privy,* "Mrs. Jones."

Rester (popular), en — baba, *to be astounded,* or "flabbergasted." Rester en figure, *to be at a loss for words.* (Prostitutes') Rester dans la salle d'attente à reconnaître ses vieux bagages, *to return home late at night without a client.*

Restituer en doublure (popular), *to die,* "to snuff it." For synonyms see **Pipe.**

Restitution, *f.* (obsolete), faire —, *to vomit,* "to cast up accounts."

Resucée, *f.* (popular), *thing which has already been said or heard.*

Résurrection, *f.* (popular and thieves'), la —, *the prison of Saint-Lazare, in which prostitutes and unfaithful wives are incarcerated.*

Retape, *f.* (general), *the act of a prostitute seeking clients.*

C'était la grande retape, le persil au clair soleil, le raccrochage des catins illustres.—ZOLA.

Aller à la —, or faire la —, *to walk the streets or public places for purposes of prostitution.* La — also refers to *the act of men who are the protectors of abandoned women, and procure clients for them in a manner described by the following:*—

Il faut, toutefois, classer à part une variété d'hommes entretenus qui se livrent à une industrie qu'on nomme la "retape" ... ils servent de chaperons. Tout chamarrés de cordons et de croix, ils sont presque toujours âgés. ... Leur prétendue maîtresse ou leur soi-disant nièce est censée tromper leur surveillance jalouse.—LÉO TAXIL.

(Thieves') Aller à la —, *to lie in ambush for the purpose of robbing or murdering wayfarers.*

Retapé, *adj.* (popular), *well-dressed.*

Retaper (popular), se faire — les dominos, *to have one's teeth looked to, and deficiencies made good.*

Retapeuse, *f.* (popular), *street-walker,* "mot."

Retenir (popular). Je te retiens pour la première contre-danse, *you may be sure of a thrashing directly I get a chance.*

Retentissante, *f.* (popular and thieves'), *bell,* "ringer, or tinkler." Acresto, il y a une —, dévide-la. *Look out, there's a bell, break the hammer.*

Retiration, *f.* (printers'), être en —, *to be getting old.*

Retirer (thieves'), l'artiche, or le morlingue, *to pick the pockets of a drunkard,* "to pinch an emperor of his blunt."

Retoquer (students'), *to disqualify one at an examination,* "to spin." Etre retoqué, *to fail to pass an examination,* "to be ploughed." About twenty years ago "pluck," the word then used, began to be superseded by "plough." It is said to have arisen from a man who could not supply the examiner with any quotation from Scripture, until at last he blurted out, "And the ploughers ploughed on my back, and made long furrows." "Etre retoqué" may also be rendered into English slang by "to be plucked." The supposed origin of "pluck" is that when, on degree day, the proctor, after having read the name of a candidate for a degree, walks down the hall and back, it is to give any creditor the opportunity of plucking his sleeve, and informing him of the candidate being in debt. Un retoqué du suffrage universel, *an unreturned candidate for parliament.*

Retour, *m.* (police and thieves'), cheval de —, *old offender who has been convicted afresh,* "jailbird."

Un vieux repris de justice, un "cheval de retour," comme on dit rue de Jérusalem, n'eût pas fait mieux.—GABORIAU.

Also *one who has been a convict at the penal servitude settlement.*

Ce n'est pas non plus le bouge sinistre de Paul Niquet, . . . dont ces mêmes tables et ce même comptoir voyaient les mouches de la bande à Vidocq, en quête d'un grinche ou d'un escarpe, trinquer avec les bifins . . . les chevaux de retour (forçats libérés). —P. MAHALIN.

(Popular) L'aller et le — et train rapide, *the act of slapping one's face right and left, or kicking one on the behind.*

Retourne, *f.* (gamesters'), *trumps.* Chevalier de la —, *card-sharper,* or "magsman."

Retourner (popular), sa veste, or son paletot, *to fail in business,* "to be smashed up;" *to die,* "to snuff it." S'en —, *to be getting old.* De quoi retourne-t-il? *What is the matter at issue?* (Roughs') Retourner quelqu'un, *to thrash one.* See **Voie.** (General) Retourner sa veste (the expression has passed into the language), *to become a turncoat,* or "rat." The *Slang Dictionary* says the late Sir Robert Peel was called the Rat, or the Tamworth

Rat-catcher, for altering his views on the Roman Catholic question. From rats deserting vessels about to sink. The term is often used amongst printers to denote one who works under price. Old cant for a clergyman.

Rétréci, *m.* (popular), *stingy man, one who is close-fisted.*

Retrousseur, *m.* (popular), *prostitute's bully,* "ponce." For the list of synonyms see **Poisson.**

Réussi, *adj.* (familiar), *well done; grotesque.*

Revendre (thieves'), *to reveal a secret,* "to blow the gaff."

Réverbère, *m.* (popular), *head,* or "tibby." See **Tronche.** Etre au —, *to be on the watch, on the look-out.*

Moi aussi je suis au réverbère et mes mirettes ne quitteront pas les siennes dès que le pante aura passé la lourde du train. —*Mémoires de Monsieur Claude.*

Revers, *m.* (card-sharpers'), faire un —, *to lose purposely so as to encourage a pigeon.*

Reversis, *m.* (popular), jouer au —, *formerly referred to the carnal act.*

Revidage, *m.* (dealers in second-hand articles), faire le —, *to share among themselves after a sale goods which they have bought at high prices to prevent others from purchasing them.* The share of each is called "paniot."

Revider, *to perform the* "revidage" (which see).

Revideurs, *m. pl., marine store-dealers who employ the mode called* "revidage" (which see).

Révision. See **Revidage.**

Revoir la carte (popular), *to vomit,* "to cast up accounts."

Révolution, *f.* (card-players'), *score of ninety-three points.* An allusion to the revolution of '93.

Cependant, Mes-Bottes, qui regardait son jeu, donnait un coup de poing triomphant sur la table. Il faisait quatre-vingt-treize. J'ai la Révolution, cria-t-il. — ZOLA.

Revolver à deux coups, *m.* (roughs'), *the penis.*

Revoyure, *f.* (military), jusqu'à la — ! *till we meet again!*

Voilà, les fantassins ! jusqu'à la revoyure ! et le chasseur poussa son cheval.—BONNE-TAIN, *L'Opium.*

Revue, *f.* (military), de ferrure *refers to the action of a horse which plunges and kicks out;* — de pistolets de poche, *a certain sanitary inspection concerning contagious diseases.*

Revueux, *m.* (journalists'), *a writer of "revues," or topical farces.*

Revure, *f.* (popular), à la — ! *goodbye! till we meet again!*

Ribler (obsolete), *to steal; to swindle; to steal at night.*

Item, je donne à frère Baulde,
Demourant à l'hostel des Carmes,
Portant chère hardie et baulde,
Une sallade et deux guysarmes,
Que de Tusca et ses gens d'armes
Ne luy riblent sa Caige-vert.
VILLON.

Ribleur, *m.* (obsolete), *pickpocket; night-thief.* From ribaldi, *rogues.*

A fillettes monstrans tetins,
Pour avoir plus largement hostes ;
A ribleurs meneurs de hutins,
A basteleurs traynans marmottes,
A fol et folles, sotz et sottes,
Qui s'en vont sifflant cinq et six,
A veufves et à mariottes,
Je crye à toutes gens merciz.
VILLON.

Riboui, *m.* (popular), *second-hand clothes dealer.*

Ribouit, *m.* (thieves'), *eye,* " ogle."

Ribouler des calots (popular and thieves'), *to stare,* " to stag."

Riche, *adj.* (popular), être —, *to be drunk,* or " tight." For synonyms see **Pompette.** Etre — en ivoire, *to have a good set of teeth.* Un homme — en peinture, *a man who passes himself off as a rich man.*

Richommer, or **richonner** (thieves'), *to laugh.*

Rideau, *m.* (popular), rouge, *wine-shop.* An allusion to the red curtains which formerly adorned the windows of such establishments. Rideaux de Perse, *torn curtains.* A play on the word percé, *pierced.* (Thieves') Rideau, *long blouse,* a kind of smockfrock worn by workmen and peasants.

Nous somm's dans c'goût-là toute eun' troupe,
Des lapins, droits comme des bâtons,
Avec un rideau sur la croupe,
Un grimpant et des ripatons.
RICHEPIN.

(Theatrical) Lever le —, *to be the first to appear on the stage at a music-hall or concert.*

Ses artistes sont les Sociétaires des cafés-concerts, car l'artiste qui "lève le rideau" touche déjà 300 francs par mois.— *Maître Jacques.*

Ridicule, *m.* (military), endosser le —, *to put on civilians' clothes.*

Rien, *m. and adv.* (thieves'), un —, *a police officer.* (Popular) Rien, *very, extremely.* C'est — chic, *it is first-class,* " real jam." Il est — paf, *he is extremely drunk.* C'est — folichon ! *how funny !* N'avoir — de déchiré, *to have yet one's maidenhead.*

Il fallait se presser joliment si l'on voulait la donner à un mari sans rien de déchiré.— ZOLA, *L'Assommoir.*

Rien-du-tout, *f.* (popular), *girl or woman of indifferent character.*

Une boutique bleue à cette rien-du-tout, comme si ce n'était pas fait pour casser les bras des honnêtes gens !—ZOLA.

Rif, or **riffle,** *m.* (thieves'), *fire.* From the Italian jargon ruffo. De —, *without hesitation.*

Riffaudant, *m.* (thieves'), *cigar.*

Riffaudante, *f.* (thieves'), *flame.*

Riffaudate, *m.* (thieves'), *conflagration.*

Riffauder (thieves'), *to warm ; to blow one's brains out.*

A bas les lingres, tas de ferlampiers, ou je vous riffaude.—Vidocq. (*Down with the knives, ruffians, else I'll blow your brains out.*)

Faire —, *to cook.* Se —, *to warm oneself.* Le marmouzet riffaude, *the pot is boiling.* Riffauder, *to burn.*

Ah ! pilier, que gître été affuré gourdement, car le cornet d'épice a riffaudé ma luque où étaient les armoiries de la vergne d'Amsterdam en Hollande ; j'y perds cinquante grains de rente.—*Le Jargon de l'Argot.*

Riffaudeur, *m.* (thieves'), *incendiary.* Les riffaudeurs, better known under the name of "chauffeurs," were brigands who, towards 1795, overran the country in large gangs, and spread terror among the rural population. They besmeared their faces with soot, or concealed them under a mask. They burned the feet of their victims in order to compel them to give up their hoardings. The government of the Directoire was powerless against these organized bands, and it was only under Bonaparte's consulate in 1803 that they were hunted down and captured by the military. Le — à perpète, *the devil,* or "Ruffin."

Riffer. See **Riffauder.**

Riflard, *m.* (familiar and popular), *umbrella,* "mush." From the name of a character in a play by Picard. (Thieves') Riflard, *rich man,* or "ragsplawger;" *fire.* (Masons') Compagnon du —, *mason's assistant.* Le riflard signifies *a shovel.* (Popular) Des riflards, *old leaky shoes.*

Riflardise, *f.* (popular), *stupidity.*

Riflart, *m.* (obsolete), *police officer.* From **Rifler** (which see).

Rifle, *m.* (thieves'), *fire.*

Nous serions mieux je crois devant un chouette rifle que dans ce sabri (bois) où il fait plus noir que dans la taule du raboin (la maison du diable).—Vidocq.

Coquer le —, *to set afire.* Ligotte de —, *strait-jacket.* See **Coup.**

Rifler (thieves'), *to burn ;* (popular) *to take ; to steal,* "to nick." Compare with the English *to rifle.* The word is used by Villon in his *Jargon Jobelin.* Rifler du gousset, *to emit a strong odour of humanity.*

Riflés, or **riffaudés,** *m. pl.* (old cant), *rogues who used to go soliciting alms under pretence of having been ruined through the destruction of their homes by fire.*

Riflés ou riffaudés, sont ceux qui triment avec un certificat qu'ils nomment leur bien : ces riflés toutimes menant avec sezailles leurs marquises et mions, feignant d'avoir eu de la peine à sauver leurs mions du rifle qui riflait leur creux.—*Le Jargon de l'Argot.*

Riflette, *f.* (roughs' and thieves'), *detective,* or "nose." Acresto, la riflette nous exhibe. *Look out, the detective is looking at us.*

Rifolard, *adj.* (popular), *amusing, funny.*

Rigade, rigadin, or **rigodon,** *m.* (popular), *shoe,* "trotter-case." See **Ripaton.**

He applied himself to a process which Mr. Dawkins designated as "japanning his trotter-cases."—Ch. Dickens.

Rigolade, *f.* (popular and thieves'), *amusement.*

Ma largue n'sera plus gironde,
Je serai vioc aussi ;
Faudra pour plaire au monde,
Clinquant, frusque, maquis,
Tout passe dans la tigne,
Et quoiqu'on en jaspine,
C'est un foutu flanchet.
Douze longes de tirade,
Pour une rigolade,
Pour un moment d'attrait.
VIDOCQ.

Etre à la —, *to be amusing one-self.* Coup de —, *lively song.* Enfilé à la —, *dissolute fellow.* Rigolage is used with the same signification in *Le Roman de la Rose*, by Guillaume de Lorris and Jehan de Meung.

Rigolbochade, *f.* (popular), *droll action; amusement,* "spree;" *much eating and drinking.*

Rigolboche, *adj.* (popular), *amusing ; funny.*

Parfait ! . . . Très rigolo ! . . . rigolboche ! répondait le petit sénateur.—DUBUT DE LAFOREST.

Une —, *female habituée of public dancing-halls.* From the name of a female who made herself celebrated at such places.

Ainsi jadis ont cavalé,
Le tas défunt des Rigolboches,
Au bras vainqueur de Bec-Salé,
Faisant leurs premières brioches.
GILL.

Un —, *a feast,* "a tightener."

On va trimbaler sa blonde, mon vieux ; nous irons lichoter un rigolboche à la Place Pinel.—HUYSMANS.

Rigolbocher (popular), *to have a feast, or drinking revels.*

Tu seras de nos tournées, et après la re-présentation, nous rigolbocherons. — E. MONTEIL.

Rigolbocheur, *adj. and m.* (popu-lar), *funny ; licentious.*

Les mots rigolbocheurs, épars
De tous côtés dans le langage,
Attrape-les pour ton usage,
Et crûment dévide le jars.
GILL.

Un —, *one fond of fun, of amuse-ment, of revelling.*

Rigole, *f.* (thieves'), *good cheer.*

Rigoler (familiar and popular), *to amuse oneself.* From rigouller.

Et là sus l'herbe drue dansarent au son des joyeux flageolets, et doulces corne-muses, tant baudement que c'estoit passe-temps céleste les voir ainsi soi rigouller.—RABELAIS, *Gargantua.*

Quant au gamin, c'était l'gavroche
Qui parcourt Paris en tous sens,
Et qui sans peur et sans reproche
Flan', rigole et blagu' les passants.
GILL.

Also *to laugh.*

J'peux m'parler tout ba' à l'oreille
Sans qu' personne entend' rien du tout.
Quand j'rigol', ma gueule est pareille
A cell' d'un four ou d'un égout.
RICHEPIN, *La Chanson des Gueux.*

Rigoler comme une tourte, *to laugh like a fool.*

Rigolette, *f.* (popular), *female habituée of low dancing saloons.*

Rigoleur, *m.* (popular), *one joyously disposed and fond of the bottle,* a "jolly dog."

Rigolo, *m. and adj.* (gamblers'), *a swindle,* explained by quota-tion :—

Il n'avait plus qu'à surveiller les mains de cet aimable banquier pour voir . . . s'il ne ferait pas passer de sa main droite dans sa main gauche une portée préparée à l'avance—un "cataplasme," si cette portée était épaisse ; un "rigolo" si elle était mince.—HECTOR MALOT, *Baccara.*

An allusion to the mustard plas-ters of Rigolo. (Popular) Rigolo, *amusing, funny.*

Moi j'emmène mes deux exotiques chez Coquet, au cimetière Montmartre. C'est rigolo en diable.—P. MAHALIN.

Rien n'est plus rigolo que les petites filles, A Paris. Observer leurs mines, c'est divin.

A dix, douze ans ce sont déjà de fort gen-tilles

Drôlesses, qui vous ont du vice comme à vingt
GILL.

Il est rien —! *he is so amusing!* Rigolo pain de seigle, or pain de sucre, *extremely amusing.*

Retour des choses d'ici-bas.—Rigolo pain de sucre, ça par exemple !—E. MONTEIL.

Rigolo, *short crowbar used by housebreakers.* Termed also "biribi, l'enfant, sucre de pommes, or Jacques," and, in the English slang, "James, Jemmy, the stick." Also *a revolver.* Acresto, rigolo ! *Be on your guard ! he's got a revolver.*

Rigouillard, *m.* (printers'), *funny, amusing fellow.*

Rigri, *m.* (popular), *over-particular man ; stingy man,* "hunks."

Riguinguette, *f.* (popular), *cigarette.* Griller une —, *to smoke a cigarette.*

Rince - crochets, *m.* (military), *extra ration of coffee.*

Rincée, *f.* (popular), *thrashing,* "walloping." See **Voie.**

Rincer (popular), *to thrash ; to worst one at a game ; —* la poche, *to ease one of his money.*

Dans les cours il y en a qui achèvent de se griser, de bons jeunes gens qu'elles lâchent après avoir rincé leurs poches.—P. MAHALIN.

Se — l'œil, *to look on with pleasure.* Se — l'avaloir, le bec, le bocal, la gargoine, la corne, la cornemuse, le cornet, la dalle, la dalle du cou, la dent, le fusil, le goulot, le gaviot, le sifflet, le tube, la trente-deuxième, la gargarousse, *to drink.* The synonyms to describe the act in various kinds of slang are : "se passer un glacis, s'arroser le jabot, s'affûter le sifflet, se gargariser le rossignolet, se laver le gésier, sabler, sucer, licher, se rafraîchir les barres, se suiver, pitancher, picter, siffler le guindal, graisser les roues, pier, fioler, écoper, enfler, se calfater le bec, se blinder, s'humecter l'amygdale or le pavillon, siffler, flûter, renifler, pomper, siroter, biturer, étouffer, asphyxier, se rafraîchir les barbes, s'arroser le lampas, se pousser dans le battant, pictonner, soiffer ;" and in the English slang : "to wet one's whistle, to have a gargle, a quencher, a drain, something damp, to moisten one's chaffer, to sluice one's gob, to swig, to guzzle, to tiff, to lush, to liquor up." The Americans to describe the act use the terms, "to see a man, to smile." Se faire rincer, *to lose all one's money at a game, to* "blew" *it.* Se faire — la dalle, *to get oneself treated to drink.* Rincer la dent, *to treat one to drink.*

C'est nous qu'est les ch'valiers d'la loupe.
. . . .

Les galup's qu'a des ducatons
Nous rinc'nt la dent. Nous les battons
Qu' les murs leur en rend'nt des torgnioles.
L'soir nous sommes soûls comm' des hann'-
tons
    Du cabochard aux trottignolles.
            RICHEPIN.

Rincette, *f.* (familiar), *brandy taken after coffee.*

Rinceur de cambriole, *m.* (thieves'), *housebreaker,* or "buster."

Le voleur à la tire, le rinceur de cambriole, ceux qui font la grande soulasse sur les trimards, mènent une vie charmante en comparaison.—TH. GAUTIER.

Rincleux, *m.* (popular), *miserly man,* "hunks."

Ringuer (sporting), *to be a bookmaker.* From the English word ring, used by French bookmakers to denote their place of meeting.

Ringueur, *m.* (sporting), *bookmaker.*

Riole, or **riolle**, *f.* (popular and thieves'), *river ; brook ;* (popular) *joy ; amusement.* Etre en —, *to be out* "on the spree."

Ouvriers en riolle, soldats en bordées, bourgeois en goguette et journalistes en cours d'observations.—P. Mahalin.

Etre un brin en —, *to be slightly tipsy,* "elevated."

Les braves gens semblaient être un brin en riole ;
Mais l'ouvrier est bon même quand il rigole.
Gill.

(Thieves') Aquiger —, *to find amusement.*

Ripa, or **ripeur**, *m.* (thieves'), *river-thief.*

Ripaton, or **ripatin**, *m.* (popular), *foot,* "crab, dew-beater, or ever-lasting shoe." Also *shoe.*

La pittoresque échoppe du savetier . . . où l'on voit, pêle-mêle entassés, le lourd ripaton du prolétaire, le rigadin éculé du voyou, la bottine claquée de la petite rentière.—Richepin, *Le Pavé.*

The synonyms are : "croqueneaux, bateaux, péniches, trottinets, trottins, cocos, pompes, bateaux-mouches, rigadins, escafignons, tartines, bichons, paffes, passants, paffiers, passes, bobelins, flacons, sorlots, passifs ;" and in the English slang : "trottercases, hock-dockies, grabbers, daisy-roots, crab-shells, bowles." Jouer des ripatons, *to run.* See **Patatrot.**

Ripatonner (popular), *to patch up old shoes.*

Riper (popular), *to have connection.*

Ripeur, *m.* (popular), *libertine,* "rip."

Ripioulement, *m.* (thieves'), *bedroom,* "dossing-crib."

Ripiouler (thieves'), *to sleep,* "to doss."

Ripopée, or **ripopette**, *f.* (popular), *worthless article ; mixture of wine left in glasses, or which flows on the counter of a wine-retailer.*

Dans la chambre de nos abbés,
L'on y boit, l'on y boit,
Du bon vin bien cacheté.
Mais nous autres,
Pauvres apôtres,
Pauvres moines, tripaillons de moines,
Ne buvons que d'la ripopée !
Song.

Riquiqui, *m.* (popular), *brandy of inferior quality,* see **Tordboyaux** ; *thing badly done, or of inferior quality.* Avoir l'air —, *is said of a woman attired in ridiculous style, who looks like a* "guy."

Rire (popular), comme une baleine, *to open, when laughing, a mouth like a whale's ;* — comme un cul, *to laugh with lips closed and cheeks puffed out ;* — comme une tourte, *to laugh like a fool.* Entendre — de l'argenterie, *to ring a bell.* Faire — les carafes, *to say such absurd things as to make the most sedate persons laugh.* (Theatrical) Rire du ventre, *to shake one's sides as if in the act of laughing.*

Risquer un verjus (popular), *to discuss a glass of wine or brandy at the bar of a wine-shop.*

Rivancher (thieves'), *to make a sacrifice to Venus.*

Et mezig parmi le grenu
Ayant rivanché la frâline,
Dit : Volants, vous goualez chenu.
Richepin.

Termed formerly "river."

Dans Paris la bonne ville
L'empereur est arrivé ;
Il y a eu mainte fille
Qui a eu le cul rivé.
Recueil de Farces, Moralités et Sermons joyeux, 1837.

Rive gauche, *f.* (students'), *a part of Paris, on the left bank of the*

Seine, wherein are situated the University higher colleges and schools, such as l'Ecole de Médecine, l'Ecole de Droit, la Sorbonne, le Collège de France, &c.

J'en viens de ce coin de Paris qu'on a appelé jadis le pays latin puis le quartier latin et ensuite le quartier des écoles et qui aujourd'hui s'intitule simplement la rive gauche.—DIDIER, *Echo de Paris,* 1886.

River. See **Pieu, Rivancher.**

Rivette, *f.* (popular and thieves'), *prostitute,* or "punk." See **Gadoue.** Also *name given by Sodomists to wretches whom they plunder under threats of disclosures.*

La rivette se récrie ; le faux agent persiste, s'emporte, jure . . . il finit par obtenir une somme d'argent.—LÉO TAXIL.

Riz-pain-sel, *m.* (military), *anyone connected with the commissariat,* a "mucker."

Les deux hommes tenaient conseil. T'as entendu ce qu'a dit le colonel ?—C'est pas un colonel, c'est un riz-pain-sel. Ça y fait rien. . . . Faut en finir avec nos deux particuliers. Nous allons leur brûler la gueule d'un coup de flingot.—BONNETAIN, *L'Opium.*

Robaux, or **roveaux,** *m. pl.* (old cant), *gendarmes.* Attrimer les —, *to run away from gendarmes, to show them sport.* The term seems a corruption of royaux.

Rober (thieves'), *to steal ; to steal a man's clothes.* This is the old form of *dérober,* which formerly signified *to disrobe,* and nowadays *to purloin.* Provençal raubar. Compare with the English *to rob.* See **Grinchir.**

Robignol, *adj.* (thieves'), *extremely amusing ; extremely good.*

Robinson, or **pépin,** *m.* (popular), *umbrella,* "mush."

Rochet, *m.* (thieves'), *bishop ; priest,* or "devil-dodger."

Rogne, *adj. and f.* (familiar and popular), être —, *to be in a rage,* "to be shirty." Avoir des rognes avec un gas, *to have a quarrel.* Flanquer la —, *to get one in a rage.* Properly rogne signifies *itch, mange,* and it stands to reason that anyone suffering from the ailment would naturally be in anything but a good humour.

Les hôtes de la posada, intimidés et méfiants, nous prenant pour des bandits, "avaient la frousse" selon l'expression pittoresque de L. M. qui, mourant de faim, comme d'habitude, déclara furieux que cette réception lui "flanquait la rogne," surtout lorsqu'il vit la vieille mégère, horrible compagnonne, faire signe à son mari de charger le tromblon.—HECTOR FRANCE, *A Travers l'Espagne.*

Avoir la —, *to be out of temper,* or "riled." A person is then said to have his "monkey up." An allusion to the evil spirit which was supposed to be always present with a man, but more probably to the unenviable state of mind of a man who should have such a malevolent animal firmly established on his shoulders, comparable only to the maddening sensation expressed by "avoir un rat dans la trompe," *i.e.,* "to be riled," *to be badgered.*

Rogner (thieves'), *to guillotine.* Literally *to pare off.* (Popular) Rogner, *to be in a rage.*

L'infirmier se fout à rogner, naturellement.—Comment, qu'y dit, vous osez dire ça.—G. COURTELINE.

Rogneur, *m.* (military), *fourrier,* or *non-commissioned officer employed in the victualling department.* Literally *one who gives short commons, paring off part of the provisions.*

Rognon, *m.* (popular), un sale —, *a lousy,* or "chatty" *person.* Applied especially to a low woman, (Familiar) Rognon, *face-*

tious term applied to a man with a big sword across his loins. Literally un rognon brochette, *broiled kidney.*

La lame, sans fourreau, attachée dans le dos par une double chaîne pouvant se croiser sur la poitrine. . . . Il entre et un spectateur l'assassine de ce mot : " Tiens, un rognon brochette ! "—A. GERMAIN, *Le Voltaire.*

Rognures, *f. pl.* (theatrical), *inferior actors.* See **Fer-blanc.**

Rogommier, *m.* (popular), *a brandy-bibber.*

Rogommiste, *m.* (popular), *retailer of brandy.*

Roi de la mer, *m.* (popular), *prostitute's bully,* " ponce." See **Poisson.**

Romagnol, or romagnon, *m.* (thieves'), *hidden treasure.*

Romain, *m.* (familiar), " *claqueur,*" *or man paid to applaud at a theatre.* An allusion to the practice of certain Roman emperors who had a kind of choir of official applauders.

Les Romains de Paris n'ont rien de commun avec les habitants de la ville aux sept collines. . . . Leur champ de bataille, c'est le parterre du théâtre . . . en un mot les romains sont ces mêmes hommes que l'on nommait vulgairement autrefois des claqueurs.—BALZAC.

Romaine, *f.* (popular), *scolding.* Also *a mixture of rum and orgeat.*

Romamitchel, romanitchel, or romanichel, *m.* (thieves'), *gipsy.* Romnichal in England, Spain, and Bohemia has the signification of *gipsy man,* and romne-chal, romaniche, is a *gipsy woman.* In England Romany is a gipsy, or the gipsy language—the speech of the Roma or Zincali Spanish gipsies, termed Gitanos. " Can you patter Romany ? " *i.e., Can you talk* " black," *or gipsy* "lingo." See **Filendèche.**

Romance. See **Camp.**

Rome, *f.* (thieves'), aller, or passer à —, *to be reprimanded.*

Romilly. See **Insurgé.**

Romture, or rousture, *f.* (thieves'), *man under police supervision.*

Ronchonner (popular), *to grumble; to mutter between one's teeth.*

Ronchonneur, *m.,* ronchonneuse, *f.* (popular), *grumbler.*

Elle m'en veut donc toujours la vieille ronchonneuse ?—ZOLA.

Rond, *m.* and *adj.* (popular), *a sou.* Termed also " rotin."

Deux ronds d'brich'ton dans l'estomac, C'est pas ça qui m'pès' sur les g'noux.
RICHEPIN.

Avoir le —, *to have money; to be well off,* or " well ballasted." Pousser son —, *to ease oneself by evacuation.* Rond, *drunk,* or " tight;" — comme balle, comme une bourrique, or comme une boule, *completely tipsy,* or " sewed up." See **Pompette.**

Au cidre ! au cidre ! il fait chaud.
Tant mieux si j'me soûle.
Au cidre ! au cidre ! il fait chaud.
J'sons plus rond qu'eun' boule.
Du cidre il faut
Dans la goule.
Du cidre il faut
Dans l'goulot.
RICHEPIN.

(Familiar) Un — de cuir, *employé ; clerk,* or " quill-driver."

Rondache, *f.* (thieves'), *ring,* "fawney."

Rondelets, *m. pl.* (obsolete), *small breasts.*

Rondement (obsolete), chier —, *not to hesitate, to act with resolution, without dilly-dallying.*

Pardienne, mamselle, vous l'avez déjà fait. A quoi bon tant tortiller. . . . Il faut chier rondement, et ne pas faire les choses en rechignant.—*Isabelle Double,* 1756.

Rondier, *m.* (thieves'), *watchman, or overseer at the hulks.* From faire une ronde, *to go one's rounds.*

Rondin, *m.* (popular), *lump of excrement,* or " quaker ; " (popular and thieves') *five-franc coin.*

— Et combien qu'ça coûte, ste bête ? — Un rondin, deux balles et dix Jacques. — N . . . de D . . . ! Sept livres dix sous !—Vidocq.

Rondin jaune, *gold coin,* " yellow boy ; " — jaune servi, *gold coin stolen and then stowed away.*

Ah ! s'il voulait cromper ma sorbonne (sauver ma tête), quelle viocque (vie) je ferais avec mon fade de carle (ma part de fortune), et mes rondins jaunes servis (et l'or que je viens de cacher).—Balzac, *La Dernière Incarnation de Vautrin.*

Rondine, *f.* (thieves'), *ring,* or " fawney ; " *walking-stick ; ball.*

Rondiner (thieves'), *to cudgel one ;* (popular) *to spend money.* From rond, *a sou ;* — des yeux, *to stare.*

Rondinet, *m.* (thieves'), *ring,* " fawney."

Rond-point-des bergères, *m.* (roughs'), *the Halles,* or *Paris market.*

Rondqué, *m.* (popular), *one sou.*

Ronflant, *adj.* (thieves'), *well-dressed.* Is also said of one who has a well-filled purse.

Ronfle, *f.* (popular), jouer à la —, *to sleep soundly and to snore.* (Thieves') Ronfle, *prostitute,* or " punk ; " *woman,* or " blowen ;" — à grippart, *same meaning.*

Ronfler (popular), faire — Thomas, *to ease oneself.* (Thieves') Une poche qui ronfle, *a well-filled pocket,* one " chockful of pieces."

A cette époque, quand un voleur avait fait un coup, quand la poche ronflait, toute sa bande se rendait au Lapin Blanc, boire, manger, faire la noce aux frais du meg.— *Mémoires de Monsieur Claude.*

Ronfler à cri, *to pretend to sleep.*

Ronge-pattes, *m.* (popular), *child,* or " squeaker."

Rongeur, *m.* (familiar), or ver rongeur, *cab taken by the hour.* Paris cabs generally go at a snail's pace, with consequent increase of fare.

Roquille, *f.* (popular), *one-fourth of a setier,* or *eighth part of a litre.*

Rosbif de rat d'égout ! *m.* (roughs'), *insulting epithet.* Might be rendered by " you skunk ! "

Hé ! dis donc, éclanche de bouledogue, rosbif de rat d'égout, tu vas te faire taper sur la réjouissance.—A. Scholl, *L'Esprit du Boulevard.*

Rose des vents, *f.* (popular), *breech,* or " Nancy." See **Vasistas.**

Rosière de Saint-Laze, *f.* (popular), for Saint-Lazare, *an inmate of the prison of Saint-Lazare,* which serves for prostitutes and unfaithful wives. Properly une "rosière," or rose queen, is a virtuous, well-behaved maiden. At Nanterre and other country places a maid is proclaimed rosière at a yearly ceremony in which the authorities play their part, the famous pompiers of the not less famous song being one of the most important factors in the pageant.

Rossaille, *f.* (horse-dealers'), *worthless horse,* " screw."

Rossard, *m.* (familiar and popular), *man with no heart for work,* a " bummer."

Trubl' est un rossard,
Toujours en retard,
D'mandez à Massard . . .
Trubl' est un flegmard
Qui se fait du lard !
Trublot, *Le Cri du Peuple.*

Rosse, *f.* (familiar and popular), *lazy fellow.* Etre —, *to be cantankerous, ill-natured.*

> Vanter la neig', c'te bêt' féroce !
> Nous somm's pas dans l'pays des ours !
> C'est gentil, j'dis pas ; mais c'est rosse ;
> Comm' la femm', ça fait patt' de v'lours.
> JULES JOUY, *La Neige.*

Une —, *a peevish, stubborn, or lazy woman.*

Rossignante, *f.* (old cant), *flute.*

Rossignol, *m.,* or **carouble,** *f.* (thieves'), *picklock,* or "*betty* ;" (familiar) *any inferior article left unsold.* The expression specially refers to books.

Rossignoler (thieves'), *to sing,* "*to lip.*"

Rossignoliser (familiar), *to sell articles without any value, or soiled articles.*

Rosto, *m.* (Ecole Polytechnique), *gas-lamp.* From the name of General Rostolan, who introduced the gas apparatus into the establishment.

Roter (popular), en —, *to be astounded.* Literally *to belch for astonishment.*

> En disant que . . . les soldats n'étaient pas de la charcuterie, qu'on traitait les chiens mieux que ça ; enfin, un boniment à ne pas s'y reconnaître. La sœur en rotait ! —G. COURTELINE.

En — le fond de son caleçon, *superlative of* "en roter," *to be* "*flabbergasted.*" Je montrais à des touristes Américains toutes les merveilles de la ville, ils en rotaient le fond de leur caleçon. *I showed some American tourists all the curiosities of the town ; they were utterly astounded.*

Rôti, *m.,* formerly *brand on convict's shoulder.*

Rotin, *m.* (popular), *sou.* Termed also "*flèche, pélot.*" (Cardsharpers') Flamboter aux rotins,

termed also "consolation anglaise," *variety of swindling card trick.*

Rôtisseuse, *f.* (popular), *roast chicken.* Exhibe la —, *look at the chicken.*

Rototo, *m.* (popular), coller du —, *to cudgel,* "*to larrup.*" Rototo ! *expression of contempt or refusal.*

Rouâtre, *m.* (thieves'), *bacon,* "*sawney.*" Jack speeled to the crib (went home) when he found Johnny Doyle had been pulling down sawney (bacon) for grub.

Roubignole, *f.* (card-sharpers'), *small ball made of cork and used at a swindling game.*

Roubignoleur, *m.* (card-sharpers'), *swindler who plays at* "*roubignole* " (which see).

Roublage, *m.* (thieves'), *deposition of a witness.*

Roublard, *adj. and m.* (thieves'), *ugly ; inferior,* "*rot* ;" "*quyer,*" in old English cant ; *police officer,* or "*reeler.*" Soufflé par les roublards et ballonné à la pointue, *taken by the police and imprisoned in the dépôt de la Préfecture.* Un —, *a cunning fellow,* "*an artful dodger.*"

> C'était un vieux roublard, un antique marlou.
> Jadis on l'avait vu, denté blanc comme un loup,
> Vivre pendant trente ans de marmite en marmite.
> Plus d'un des jeunes dos, et des plus verts, l'imite.
> RICHEPIN, *La Chanson des Gueux.*

(Prostitutes') Roublard, *rich man, one who possesses roubles,* "*rhino, fat.*"

Roublardise, *f.* (familiar and popular), *cunning ; trickery.*

> Les roublardises de la politique la laissaient froide.—HECTOR FRANCE, *La Pudique Albion.*

Roubler (thieves'), *to make a deposition ; —* à la manque, *to make a deposition against one, or a false one.* A false witness is called by English thieves "a rapper."

Roubleur, *m.* (thieves'), *witness.*

Rouchi, *m.* (familiar and popular), *man of repugnant manners or morals ; low cad,* "rank outsider."

Rouchie, *f.* (familiar and popular), *low, abandoned girl or woman,* "draggle-tail ;" *dirty, disgusting woman.*

Roue, *f.* (popular and thieves'), de derrière, thune, or palet, *silver five-franc piece.* Le messière a dégaîné une roue de derrière, *the gentleman has given a five-franc piece.* In the English slang a crown is termed a "hind coach-wheel," and half-a-crown a "fore coach-wheel."

Ils ouvraient des quinquets grands comme des roues de derrière en nous reluquant d'un air épaté.—RICHEPIN.

Roue de devant, *two-franc piece.*

Roué, *m.* (thieves'), *juge d'instruction ;* (card-sharpers') *swindler who handles the cards at the three-card game, his confederate being termed* "amorceur."

Rouen, *m.* (obsolete), aller à —, *to be ruined,* "to go a mucker." A play on the word ruiner. Envoyer à —, *to ruin.* Michel records the following expressions formed by a similar play on words : Aller à "Dourdan," *to be beaten* (old word dourder, *to beat*) ; aller à "Versailles," *to be upset* (from verser) ; aller en "Angoulême," *to eat* (from en and gueule) ; aller à "Niort," *to deny* (from nier, *to deny*) ; aller à "Patras," *to die* (from ad patres) ; aller à "Cachan," *to conceal oneself* (from cacher). To kill was expressed by envoyer à "Mortaigne." It used to be said of a person conjugally deceived, that he travelled in "Cornouaille," alluding to the horns. An ignorant man was said to have received his education at "Asnières" (âne). A threat of dismissal was made in the words "envoyer à l'abbaye de Vatan." A madman was a native of "Lunel," &c. (Theatrical) Aller à Rouen, *to be hissed,* "to get the big bird."

Rouffier, *m.* (thieves'), *soldier.* The old English cant had the word "ruffler" to designate beggars pretending to be old or maimed soldiers, and who robbed or even murdered people. From the Italian ruffare, *to seize.*

Rouffion, *m.* (shopmen's), *shop-boy at a haberdasher's.* "Rouffionne," *shop-girl.*

Rouffionner (popular), *to break wind ; —* sans dire fion, *to do so without apologizing.*

Rouffle, *f.* (thieves'), *blow,* "wipe." Also *a kick.*

Roufflée, *f.* (military), *a terrible thrashing,* after which one is "knocked into a cocked hat."

Rouflaquette, *f.* (familiar and popular), *lock of hair worn twisted from the temple back towards the ear,* "aggerewaters, or Newgate knockers."

Sous l'bord noir et gras d'ma casquette,
Avec mes doigts aux ongu' en deuil,
J'sais rien m'coller eun' rouflaquette
Tout l'long d'la temp', là, jusqu'à l'œil.
　　　　　RICHEPIN.

"When men," says the *Slang Dictionary,* "twist the hair on each side of their faces into ropes, they are sometimes called 'bellropes,' as being wherewith to *draw the belles.* Whether 'bell ropes' or 'bow-catchers,' it is singular they should form part of a prisoner's adornment." These ornaments in France are sported only by prostitutes' bullies, who on that account are termed "rou-flaquettes."

Rouge, *adj. and m.* (obsolete), *cunning,* "downy." The expression is used as a cant word by Villon, 15th century.

> Je vis là tant de mirlificques,
> Tant d'ameçons et tant d'afficques,
> Pour attraper les plus huppez.
> Les plus rouges y sont happez.
> *Poésies attribuées à Villon.*

So the proverb, "il est méchant comme un âne rouge," signifies *he is as vicious as a cunning donkey.* The expression "les plus rouges y sont pris," *the most cunning are deceived,* is to be found in Cotgrave. The Latins used the word ruber with the figurative signification of *cunning.* Faire tomber le —, *to have an offensive breath.* Faire —, *to have one's menses.* (Thieves'), Lampion —, *police officer,* or "reeler." See **Pot-à-tabac.** C'est — de boudin, *the thing goes wrong, matters look bad.* (Military) Les culs rouges, *the chasseurs and hussars, a corps of light cavalry with red pants.* Similarly, the English hussars are termed "cherry-bums."

Rougemont, *m.* (thieves'), pivois de —, *red wine,* "red fustian."

Rouget, *m.* (popular), *man with reddish hair.* Les rougets (obsolete), better explained by the following :—

> Pour les ordinaires des femmes, les mois, les menstrues, les découlements lunaires des femmes.—Le Roux.

(Thieves') Rouget, *copper.*

Rougiste, *m.* (literary), *one fond of Stendhal's style of writing.* An allusion to his famous work, *Le Rouge et le Noir.*

Rougoule. See **Rendez-moi.**

Rouillarde, or **rouille,** *f.* (thieves'), *bottle,* "bouncing cheat ;" *bottle of old wine.* From rouler.

Roulance, *f.* (printers'), *great noise made by stamping of feet or rattling of hammers when a brother compositor enters the workshop.* This ceremony is complimentary or the reverse, as the case may be.

Roulant, *m.* (popular), *pedlar who sells articles of clothing ;* (popular and thieves') *hackney-coach,* "growler ;" — vif, *railway train,* or "rattler ;" *pedlar.* Roulants, *peas.*

Roulante, *f.* (popular), *prostitute.* See **Gadoue.**

Rouleau, *m.* (thieves'), *coin.* See **Quibus.**

Roule-en-cul, *m.* (bullies'), *an insulting term.* Might be rendered by the word "pensioner" with an obscene prefix. See **Poisson.**

Roulement, *m.* (popular), *hard work.* Du — ! mes enfants ! *with a will, lads !* (Military) Roulement de gueule, *beating to dinner ;* (thieves') — de tambour, *barking of a dog.*

Rouler (familiar and popular), quelqu'un, *to thrash one,* "to wallop" him. See **Voie.** Also *to swindle,* "to stick, to bilk."

> Une grande compagnie d'assurance sur la vie vient d'être dupée d'une jolie façon. Il n'y a pas grand mal, du reste, les compagnies ne se faisant guère scrupule de rouler le client.—A. Sirven.

(Popular) Rouler dans la farine, *to play a trick, to deceive a sim-*

pleton, "to flap a jay." Rouler sa bosse, *to go along, to go away.*

C'est pas tant le gendarm' que je r'grette !
C'est pas ça ! Naviguons, ma brunette !
Roul' ta bosse, tout est payé.
RICHEPIN, *La Glu.*

Rouler sa viande dans le torchon, *to go to bed.* Comment vont les affaires ? Ça roule. *How is business ? Not bad.* (Roughs') Se rouler, *to amuse oneself ; to be much amused.* (Familiar) Rouler quelqu'un, *to worst one ; to beat another in argument or repartee.* Termed "to snork" at Shrewsbury School.

Rouletier, *m.* (thieves'), *a thief who robs cabs or carriages by climbing up behind and cutting the straps that secure the luggage on the roof,* "dragsman."

Des classes entières de voleurs étaient aux abois, de ce nombre était celle des rouletiers (qui dérobent les chargements sur les voitures).—VIDOCQ.

Rouleur, *m.* (popular), *swindler ; rag-picker,* or "tot-picker." The *Slang Dictionary* says, "tot" is a bone, but chiffonniers and cinder-hunters generally are called "tot-pickers" nowadays. Totting has also its votaries on the banks of the Thames, where all kinds of flotsam and jetsam are known as "tots." Un —, *a man whose functions are to act as a medium between workmen and masters who wish to engage them.*

Rouleuse, *f.* (familiar), *debauched woman.*

Les rangs de l'armée du charlatan apostolique se sont grossis de nombre de petites rouleuses sans emploi.—HECTOR FRANCE.

Roulier, or **rouletier,** *m.* (thieves'), *thief who steals property off vans,* "dragsman."

Les rouliers ou rouletiers s'attaquent aux camions des entrepreneurs de roulage.—CANLER.

Roulis, *m.* (sailors'), avoir du —, *to be drunk,* "to have one's mainbrace well spliced."

Roulon, *m.* (thieves'), *loft, attic.*

Roulotage, *m.* (thieves'), *theft of property from vehicles,* "heaving from a drag."

Roulotin, *m.* (thieves'), *driver of a van,* "rattling-cove."

Roulotte, *f.* (thieves'), *vehicle.*

Puis dans un' roulotte, on n'voit rien ;
Tout d'vant vous fil' comme un rébus.
Pour louper, faut louper en chien
L'chien n'mont' pas dans les omnibus.
RICHEPIN.

Roulotte à trèpe, *omnibus ;* — du grand trimar, *mail coach.* Faire un coup de —, or grinchir une — en salade, *to steal property from a vehicle.*

Roulottier, *m.* (general), *itinerant showman.*

Allez à la Place du Trône, quand la foire au pain d'épice est dans la fièvre des derniers préparatifs, avant le dimanche qui est la grande première des saltimbanques. Tous les roulottiers de France s'y donnent rendez-vous. Et parmi eux l'on a chance encore de trouver quelques Bohémiens.—RICHEPIN.

Roulottier, *rogue who devotes his attention to vans, carts, or any other kind of conveyance, stealing luggage, goods, or provisions,* "dragsman."

Une bande importante de roulottiers, voleurs qui ont pour spécialité de dérober sur les camions qui stationnent dans les rues . . . a été arrêtée hier.—*Le Radical,* Dec., 1886.

Roulure, *f.* (popular), *woman of the most abandoned description.*

Si bien que, la croyant en bois, il est allé ailleurs, avec des roulures qui l'ont régalé de toutes sortes d'horreurs.—ZOLA, *Nana.*

Also *despicable, degraded fellow.*

Si c'est possible, une femme honnête tromper son mari, et avec cette roulure de Fauchery !—ZOLA.

Roumard, *m.* (thieves'), *malicious fellow;* (popular) *rake,* or "beard-splitter."

Roupie, *f.* (popular), *bug,* or "heavy dragoon;" — *de singe, nothing; weak coffee; — de sansonnet, bad coffee.*

Le zingueur voulut verser le café lui-même. Il sentait joliment fort, ce n'était pas de la roupie de sansonnet.—ZOLA.

Roupiller (general), *to sleep,* "to doss." Chenue sorgue, roupille sans taf, *good night, sleep without fear.*

Tout est renversé, quoi !—Et du reste, voilà le bouquet, écoutez-moi ça, on ne dit plus : je t'aime ! on dit : j'te gobe. On ne dit plus : laisse-moi tranquille ! on dit : va t'asseoir ! On ne dit plus : tu m'ennuies ! on dit : tu m'la fais à l'oseille ! On ne boit plus, on liche. On ne mange plus, on béquille. On ne dort plus, on roupille ! On ne se promène plus, on se ballade ! Pour dire : je sors, on dit : je m'la casse !—*Les Locutions Vicieuses.*

Roupiller dans le grand, *to be dead.*

Roupillon, *m.* (thieves'), *man asleep.* Chatouiller un —, *to pick the pockets of a sleeping man.*

Roupiou, *m.* (medical students'), *a student who practises in hospitals without being on the regular staff, and who administers purgatives, prepares blisters, &c.*

Rouscaillante, *f.* (thieves'), *tongue,* "glib, or red rag." Stubble your red rag, *hold your tongue.* Balancer la rouscaillante, *to talk,* "to patter."

Rouscailler (popular), *to have connection.* Probably from rousse-caigne (rousse chienne, or *red bitch*), which formerly signified *prostitute.* (Thieves') Rouscailler, *to speak,* "to patter ;" — bigorne, *to talk the cant jargon,* "to patter flash." Rouscailler had the signification of *to mislead,* and bigorne

was an epithet applied to the police, so that "rouscailler bigorne" means literally *to mislead the police.*

Rouscailleur, *m.* (popular), *libertine,* or "mutton-monger ;" (thieves') *speaker.*

Rouscailleuse, *f.* (popular), *debauched woman.*

Rouspétance, *f.* (popular), *bad humour ; resistance.*

Voulez-vous me foutre la paix ! vous êtes une forte tête à ce que je vois ; vous voulez faire de la rouspétance.—G. COURTELINE.

(Prostitutes') Rouspétance, *a detective whose particular functions are to watch prostitutes.*

Rouspéter (popular), *to be in a bad humour ; to resist.*

Rouspettau, *m.* (thieves'), *noise.*

Rouspetter (popular), used in a disparaging manner, *to talk ; to reply.* Qu'est-ce que vous me rouspettez-là ? *What the deuce are you talking about?*

Rousse, *m. and f.* (popular and thieves'), la —, *the police, the* "reelers." Un —, *police officer,* or "crusher;" *detective,* or "nark." See **Pot-à-tabac.**

Va, c'est pas moi qui ferais jamais un trait à un ami ; si je suis rousse (mouchard), il me reste encore des sentiments.—VIDOCQ.

La — à l'arnac, *the detective force.* Red-haired people are supposed to be treacherous, hence the epithet "rousse"applied to the police. According to an old proverb,

Barbe rousse, noir de chevelure,
Est réputé faux de nature.

Scarron expressed the following wish :—

Que le Seigneur en récompense
Veuille augmenter votre finance . . .
Qu'il vous garde de gens qui pipent . . .
D'hommes roux ayant les yeux verds.

E E

Judas was red-haired, as everyone knows. Shakespeare makes the following allusion :—

Rosalind.—His hair is of the dissembling colour.
Celia.— Something browner than Judas's : marry, his kisses are Judas's own children.
                    As You Like It.

Un — à l'arnache, or harnache, *a detective.*

Un jour, avec ma largue, je venais d'bal-
    lader,
J'vois la rousse à l'arnach' qui voulait l'em-
    baller.
Je m'dis pas de bêtises, en vrai barbillon,
Pour garer ma marquis' j'ai décroché l'tam-
    pon.
        Mémoires de Monsieur Claude.

La —à la flan, *city police.* Flasquer du poivre à la —, *to keep out of the way of the police, to escape their clutches.*

Rousselette, *f.* (popular and thieves'), *spy,* or "*nark.*" Termed also une riflette, un baladin.

Roussi, *m.* (thieves'), *prisoner who acts as a spy on fellow-prisoners.*

Ton orgue tapissier aura été fait marron.
. . . Il faut être arcasien. C'est un galifard.
Il se sera laissé jouer l'harnache par un roussin, peut-être même par un roussi, qui lui aura battu comtois . . . je n'ai pas taf, je ne suis pas un taffeur, c'est colombé, mais il n'y a plus qu'à faire les lézards, ou autrement on nous la fera gambiller.—V. HUGO, *Les Misérables.* (*Your friend the innkeeper must have been taken in the attempt. One ought to be wide awake. He is a flat. He must have been bamboozled by a detective, perhaps even by a prison spy, who played the simpleton. I am not afraid, I am no coward, that's well known ; the only thing to be done now is to run away, else we are done for.*)

Roussin, *m.* (thieves'), *police officer,* "*crusher ;*" *detective.*

Entre eux, ils sont un peu frères, un peu
    cousins ;
Aussi dénichent-ils des gosses, des petites,
Qu'ils envoient mendier, en guettant les
    roussins,
Pour se payer deux ronds de frites.
        RICHEPIN, *Les Mômes.*

Roussiner (popular), *to call the attention of the police to one.*

Roustamponne, *f.* (thieves'), *police,* "*reelers,* or *frogs.*"

Rousti, *adj.* (popular and thieves'), *ruined,* "*smashed ;*" *apprehended,* "*nailed,* or *nabbed.*"

Roustir (popular and thieves'), *to cheat,* "*to stick ;*" *to rob one of all his valuables.*

A l'heure qu'il est l'entonne est roustie.
—VIDOCQ. (*And now the church is stripped of all its valuables.*)

Neuf plombes. La fête bat son plein . . . eul' joueur d'bonneteau m'a déjà rousti vingt ronds.—TRUBLOT, *Le Cri du Peuple,* Sept., 1886.

Roustisseur, *m.* (thieves'), *thief,* "*prig.*"

Roustisseuse, *f.* (popular), *woman of lax morals,* "*poll.*"

Roustissure, *f.* (theatrical), *insignificant part ;* (popular) *bad joke ; swindle ; worthless thing.*

Roustons, *m. pl.* (popular), *testiculæ.*

Rousture, *f.* (thieves'), *man under police surveillance.*

Route, *m.* (popular), mettre au —, *to rout ; to break ; to destroy.*

Vous avez beau dire . . . faut que tout ça soit foutu au route, qu'i n'en reste pu miette.—*Le Drapeau Rouge de la Mère Duchesne,* 1792.

Old word roupte, from the Low Latin rupta, signifying *rout.* The word is used by Villon :—

De maulx briguans puissent trouver tel
    route
Que tous leurs corps fussent mis par mor-
    ceux.
        Ballade Joyeuse des Taverniers.

Routière, *f.* (popular), *prostitute who plies her trade on the high road.* See **Gadoue.**

Roveau, or **robau,** *m.* (old cant), *mounted police.*

Ru, *m.* (thieves'), *brook* (old word).

Je vais dans le ru pêcher à la ligne.
Beaux poissons d'argent je vous ferai signe.
Voyez au soleil briller mon couteau,
   Oh ! oh !
  Avec mon couteau
  Je vous ferai signe
   Dans l'eau.
  RICHEPIN, *La Chanson des Gueux.*

Rub de rif, *m.* (thieves'), *railway train,* "*rattler.*"

Ruban de queue, *m.* (popular), *never-ending road.*

Rubis, *m.* (popular), sur pieu, *ready money ;* — cabochon (obsolete), *penis.*

  Deux perles orientales
  Et un rubis cabochon.
   Parnasse des Muses.

Rublin, *m.* (thieves'), *ribbon.*

Rude, *m.* (popular), *brandy.* See **Tord-boyaux.**

Rudement, *adv.* (familiar and popular), *awfully.*

Rue, *f.* (popular), au pain, *throat,* "*gutter lane ;*" — barrée, or où l'on pave, *street in which a creditor lives, and which is to be avoided ;* — du bec dépavée, *gap-toothed mouth, one with* "*snaggle teeth.*" (Rag-pickers') Aller voir Madame la —, *to go to work picking rags, &c., in the street.*

Ruelle, *f.* (popular), il ne tombera pas dans la —, *is said of a drunken man lying in the gutter, and who in consequence does not risk falling from the wall side of his bed.* In English slang he is said, when in that state, to "*lap the gutter.*"

Ruette, *f.* (popular), *mouth,* or "*kisser.*"

Ruf, *m.* (thieves'), *prison warder.*

Rufan, *m.* (Breton cant), *fire.* Italian cant ruffo.

Ruffante. See **Abbaye.**

Ruiné, *adj.* (horse-trainers'), un cheval — sur son devant, *a horse with bent knees, inclined* "*to say his prayers.*"

Ruisselant d'inouisme, *adj.* (familiar), *superlatively fine ; marvellous,* "*crushing.*"

Rumfort (familiar), voyage à la —, *is said of one who goes on a pretended journey, so as to escape the toll of new year's gratuities and gifts.*

Rup, or **rupin,** *adj. and m.* (popular), *excellent ; fine ; handsome.*

Su' le moment, ça vous a bonn' mine ;
C'est frais, c'est pimpant, c'est rupin ;
Que qu' temps après, la blanche hermine
S'transforme en vulgaire peau d'lapin.
  JULES JOUY, *La Neige.*

Avoir l'aspect —, *to look rich.*

Ils s'emparent des portières et les défendent contre les gens qui n'ont pas l'aspect rupin. Ils ne les laissent libres que pour les gens qui leur paraissent avoir de la douille.—*Mémoires de Monsieur Claude.*

C'est un —, *he is clever, understands thoroughly his business,* "*he is a regular tradesman.*" No better compliment, says the *Slang Dictionary,* can be passed on an individual, whether his profession be house-breaking, prize-fighting, or that of a handicraftsman, than the significant "He is a regular tradesman." Le — des rupins, *the best of the thing.*

Et puis, l'plus bath ! Le rupin des rupins,
C'est qu'on n'sait pus où nous parquer.
   Parole !
Ainsi dans l'doute on nous laisse là,
  Le Contentement du Récidiviste,
   à l'ancre.

(Thieves') Rupin, *rich,* "*well ballasted.*"

Les plus rupins, depuis qu'on a imprimé des dictionnaires d'argot, entravent bigorne comme nouzailles.—VIDOCQ.

Rupin, *gentleman,* or "*nib cove.*"

Ils s'enquièrent où demeurent quelques marpeaux pieux, rupins et marcandiers dé-

vots, qu'ils bient trouver en leur creux.—
Le Jargon de l'Argot.

The word rupin is derived from
the Gipsy rup, Hindustani rupa,
money. The synonyms are: "chic,
chicard, chicandard, chouette,
bath, bath aux pommes, chocnosof, enlevé, tapé, c'est ça, aux
pommes, aux petits oignons, numéro un, snoboye, superlifico,
schnuf, urf, sgoff;" and in the
English slang: "first-class, A one,
real jam, nap, crushing, tzing-
tzing, tip-top, ripping, cheesy."
In Breton cant rup has the meaning of *citizen or wealthy man.*

Rupine, *f.* (thieves'), *lady,* "burerk;" *well-dressed lady.*

Rupinskoff, *adj.* (popular), *excellent,* "out and out;" *rich.*

Rural, *m.*, *name given to the Conservative members of the Assemblée
Nationale in* 1871.

Rusquin, *m.* (old cant), *silver
crown,* or "hind coach-wheel."

Rusquiner (old cant), *to steal
money.*

Russes, *adj. and m.* (military),
bas, or chaussettes —, *strips of
linen wrapped round the feet at
the time when soldiers were not
provided with regulation socks.*

> De bas russes tu garniras
> Tes bottes où tu plongeras
> Les dix arpions de tes pieds plats.
>   Dubois de Gennes.

Des —, *short whiskers.* Termed
also "hauts de côtelette, or pattes
de lapin."

Rustau, *m.* (thieves'), *variety of receiver of stolen property,* "fence."

> Le remisage, tenu par le rustau, est le
> fourgat des voleurs ou assassins de grandes
> routes travaillant en province et opérant
> jusqu'à l'étranger.—*Mémoires de Mon-
> sieur Claude.*

Rustique, *m.* (thieves'), *clerk of the
court of justice.*

Rustu, *m.* (thieves'), *clerk's office
at the court of justice.*

**ABACHE,** *adj. and m.* (popular), *foolish; dunce,* or "d u n d e r-head." A corruption of "sabot," a disparaging epithet.

Sable, *m.* (thieves'), *sugar; stomach,* or "middle piece." Les sables, *the cells.* (Popular) Sable, *money.* An allusion to the colour of gold. (Freemasons') Sable blanc, *salt ;* — jaune, *pepper.*

Sabler (thieves'), *to kill one by striking him with an eel-skin bag filled with sand.*

Sablon, *m.* (popular), *moist-sugar.*

Saboche, *f.* (popular), *awkward person; bad workman.* A corruption of "sabot."

Sabocher (popular), *to do bad work.*

Sabord, *m.* (popular), jeter un coup de —, *to examine the accuracy of the work ; to control.*

Saborder (sailors'), *to thrash.* See **Voie.** Properly *to scuttle.*

Sabot, *m.* (popular), *nose,* or "boko;" *bad workman; carriage,* or "rumbler;" (popular and familiar) *bad billiard table; bad musical instrument; small boat;* (thieves') *ship.* Aller au —, *to get on board ship.* Termed in furbesche "traversare."

Saboter (popular), *to work carelessly.*

Saboteur, *m.* (popular), *slovenly workman.*

Sabouler (popular), *to work carelessly ; to scold; to thrash.* See **Voie.** Sabouler, *to clean boots,* "to japan trotter-cases."

Sabouleur, *m.* (popular), *shoeblack.*

Sabouleux, *m.* (old cant), *rogue who shams epilepsy.* Termed now-a-days "batteur de dig-dig." These impostors chew a piece of soap to make it appear that they are frothing at the mouth. Now, *soap* is sabo in the old Provençal, so that "sabouleux" literally means *soapy.*

Sabourin, *m.* (popular), *clumsy man; bad workman.*

Sabre, *m.* (old cant), *cudgel,* or "toko." Also *wood,* from the furbesche "sorbe," which has the same signification. (Popular) Avoir un —, *to be drunk,* or "screwed." Probably from the fact that a drunkard stumbles about as if he were impeded by a sword beating about his legs. See **Pompette**. Avoir un coup de — sur le ventre *is said of a woman who has a military man for her lover, who has* "an attack of scarlet fever." Un joli coup de —, *a large mouth*, like a slit made by a cut of a sword, a "sparrow mouth."

Sabrée, *f.* (old cant), *a yard measure.*

Sabrenas, *m.* (popular), *cobbler*, "snob." An allusion to a maker of wooden shoes, as "sabre" had the meaning of *wood*. Also *clumsy workman.*

Sabrenasser, or **sabrenauder**, *to work in a slovenly manner.*

Sabreneux, *m.* (popular), *good-for-nothing fellow.* Literally sale breneux.

Sabrer (shopmen's), *to measure cloth with a yard ;* (popular) *to do a thing hurriedly and badly.*

Sabre-tout, *m.* (general), *fire-eater.*

Sabreur, *m.* (popular), *slovenly workman.*

Sabri, *m.* (thieves'), *wood ; forest.* See **Sabre**.

Sabrieu, *m.* (thieves'), *rogue who steals wood.*

Sac, *m.* (thieves'), un —, or un millet, *one hundred francs.* (Familiar) N'avoir rien dans son —, *to be devoid of ability.* Donner le —, *to dismiss from one's employ*, "to give the sack." Un — à vin, *drunkard*, or "lushington." (Popular) Avoir le — plein, *to be drunk ; to be pregnant*, or "lumpy." Cracher, or éternuer dans le —, *to be guillotined.* See **Fauché**.

En avoir plein son —, *to be completely drunk*, or "obfuscated." Le — de pommes de terre, *protuberance of the muscles.*

Un tout jeune homme . . . frêle et charmant dans une veste de chasse, dont le coutil laissait apercevoir aux biceps le "sac de pommes de terre" du savetier.— E. DE GONCOURT, *La Fille Elisa.*

Sac à diables, *knowing, cunning person*, a "downy, or leary" one.

But stick to this while you can crawl,
To stand till you're obliged to fall,
And when you're wide awake to all,
You'll be a leary man.
　　　　　　The Leary Man.

Un — à os, *a thin, skinny person*, a "bag o' bones." Un — au lard, *a shirt*, or "flesh-bag." Un — à puces, *a dog*, or "buffer." En avoir plein son —, or son —, *to have enough of, to be disgusted with.*

J'en ai mon sac, moi, d'mon épouse ;
Mince d'crampon ; j'y trouv' des ch'veux,
C'est rien de l'dire. C'que j'me fais vieux !
Par là-d'sus madame est jalouse !
　　　　　　GILL.

(Military) Le — à malices, *a bag which contains a soldier's brushes, thread, needles, &c.* De mon —, *insulting expression, signifying worthless, good-for-nothing.*

S'pèce de canaille ! sale pâtissier de mon sac ! bougre d'escroc !— CHARLES LEROY.

Saccade, *f.* (obsolete), donner la —, *to sacrifice to Venus.*

Elle aura par Dieu la saccade, puisqu'il y a moines autour.—RABELAIS.

Sacdos, *m.* (popular), *thin, skinny person*, a "bag o' bones."

Sacdoser (popular), *to become thin.*

Sachets, *m. pl.* (popular), *stockings or socks.*

Sacqué, *adj.* (popular), être —, *to be well off, to be* "well ballasted."

Sacquer (popular), *to throw ; to dismiss one from one's employ,* "to give the sack."

Sacré-chien, *m.* (familiar and popular), *coarse brandy.*

Vous vous râperez le gosier avec du rhum et du rack, avec le troix-six et le sacré-chien dans toute sa pureté, tandis qu'ils se l'humecteront avec les onctueuses liqueurs des îles.—TH. GAUTIER.

Sacrer (thieves'), *to affirm.*

Sacristain, *m.* (obsolete), formerly *husband of an* "abbesse," *the mistress of a house of ill-fame,* "abbaye des s'offre à tous."

Sacristie, *f.* (popular), *privy,* "chapel of ease."

Saffre, *m.* (popular), *gormandizer,* "grand paunch." Saffre is an old French word to be found in *Le Roman de la Rose,* 13th and 14th centuries.

Safran, *m.* (popular), accommoder au —, *to be unfaithful to one's spouse.* Saffron is of the colour said to be the favourite one of injured husbands.

— Paraît que ce sera très gai chez Madame Brischkoff : rien que des femmes mariées !
— Un bal jaune, quoi !—*Journal Amusant.*

Saignante, *f.* (thieves'). See **Laver.**

Saignement de nez, *m.* (thieves'), *examination of a prisoner,* "cross-kidment."

Saigner (thieves'), faire — du nez, *to kill,* "to hush ;" *to cross-examine,* or "to cross-kid." (Popular) Faire — du nez, *to borrow money,* "to bite the ear," or "to break shins."

Saint-ciboire, *m.* (popular), *heart,* "panter."

Saint-Crépin, *m.* (popular), *shoemakers' tools.* The brothers Cré-

pin and Crépinien, after preaching the Gospel in Gaul in the third century, settled down at Soissons as shoemakers, and one of them is the patron of shoemakers. Etre dans la prison de —, *to have tight shoes on.* Saint-Crépin, or Saint-Frusquin, *savings ; property.*

Saint de carême, *m.* (popular), *hypocrite,* "mawworm."

Saint-Dôme, *m.* (popular), *tobacco.* From Saint-Domingue, where tobacco was grown in large quantities.

Sainte Chiette, *m.* (popular), *good-for-nothing fellow.*

Sainte-Espérance, *f.* (popular), *the eve of the pay-day.*

Sainte-Nitouche, or **Sainte-Sucrée,** *f.* (popular), *prude.* Faire sa —, *to play the prude.*

Sainte-Touche, *f.* (popular), *pay-day.*

Saint-Frusquin, *m.* (familiar and popular), *one's property ; effects.* Manger tout son —, *to spend all one's means.* An imaginary saint, from "frusques," *clothes ;* "rusca," in furbesche.

Saint-Hubert, *m.* (popular), médaille de —, *five-franc piece.* Alluding to the medal of the knightly order of Saint-Hubert, founded by a German duke in 1444.

Saint-Jean, *m.* (printers'), *effects.* Probably from the expression, être nu comme un petit Saint-Jean, the lack of effects being taken to mean the effects themselves. Also *printers' tools.* Prendre son —, *to leave the workshop for good.* (Popular) Faire son petit —, *to put on innocent airs ; to play the fool.* Saint-Jean le rond, *the behind ;* — Baptiste, *landlord of a wine-shop.* An allusion to the water he adds to his wine.

Saint-Jean-porte-latine, *m.* (printers'), *the fête-day of printers.*

Saint-Lâche, *m.* (popular), *patron of lazy people.*

Saint-Lambin, *m.* (popular), *slow man.*

Saint-Laz, *m.* (popular), abbreviation of Saint-Lazare, *a prison for unfaithful wives and prostitutes.* La confrérie de —, *the world of* "unfortunates." Bijou de —, *prostitute imprisoned in Saint-Lazare.*

Saint-Lichard, *m.* (popular), *gormandizer,* "grand paunch."

Saint-Longin, *m.* (popular). See **Longin.**

Saint-Lundi, *f.* (popular), fêter la —, *to get drunk.* See **Sculpter.**

Saint-Pansart, *m.* (popular), *man with a large paunch,* "forty guts."

Saint-Pris. See **Entrer.**

Saisissement, *m.* (thieves'), *straps which bind the arms and legs of a convict who is being led to the guillotine.*

Salade, *f.* (thieves'), *answer.* A play on the word raiponce (réponse), *a kind of salad called rampion ;* (popular) *whip.* Salade de Gascon (obsolete), *rope, string.* Salade de cotret, *cudgelling.*

Je me souvien qu'i me menère chez trois ou quatre capitaines qui leur dirent qu'ils leur ficheroient une salade de coteret.— *Dialogue sur les Affaires du Temps.*

Saladier, *m.* (popular), *bowl of sweetened wine,* which is mixed in a salad basin.

Salaire, *m.* (thieves'), *shoe,* "daisy root." Corruption of soulier.

Salbin, *m.* (thieves'), *oath.*

Salbiner (thieves'), *to take the oath.*

Salbrenaud (thieves'), *shoemaker, or cobbler,* "snob."

Sale, *adj.* (popular), coup, or — truc pour la fanfare, *a bad job for us, a sad look-out.* The expression is generally expressive of disappointment, or when any disagreeable affair occurs which there is no means of averting. "Here's the devil to pay, and no pitch hot," English sailors will say. Avoir une — jactance, "to be the one to jaw," or "to be the one to palaver." (Bullies') Un — gibier, *a prostitute who does not bring in much money.*

Salé, *m.* (printers'), *wages paid in advance,* or "dead horse." Morceau de —, *part payment of debt.* Demander du — à la banque, *to ask for an advance on wages.* Le grand —, *the sea,* or "briny."

Saler (popular), *to scold,* "to haul over the coals ;" — quelqu'un, *to charge too much, to make one* "pay through the nose," or "to shave" *him.* C'est un peu salé *is said of an extravagant bill.*

Salière, *f.* (popular), répandre la — dessus, *to charge too much,* "to shave." Montrer ses salières *is said of a woman with thin breasts who wears low dresses.* Elle a deux salières et cinq plats *is said of a woman with skinny breasts.* A play on the words "seins plats," *flat bosoms.*

Salin, *m.* (thieves'), *yellow.*

Salir, or **solir** (thieves'), *to sell.* A corruption of saler, *to charge too much.* (Popular) Se — le nez, *to get drunk.* See **Sculpter.**

Saliverne, or **salivergne** (old cant), *cup ; plate ; platter,* or "skew," in English beggars' and Scottish gipsies' lingo. Rabelais uses the ·word salverne with the signification of *cup.* When Pantagruel and Panurge pay a visit to "l'oracle de la Bouteille," they found :—

Le trophée d'un buveur bien mignonnement insculpé : sçavoir est . . . bourraches, bouteilles, fioles, ferrières, barils, barreaulx, bomides, pots . . . en aultre, cent formes de verre à pied . . . hanaps, breusses, jadeaulx, salvernes.—*Pantagruel.*

Salverne, from the Spanish salva. Saliverne nowadays signifies *salad.*

Salle, *f.* (theatrical), de papier, *a playhouse full of people with free tickets.* (Saumur school of cavalry) La — Cambronne, *the W.C.* Alluding to General Cambronne's more than energetic alleged reply at Waterloo when called upon to surrender. (Popular) Salle à manger, *mouth.* N'avoir plus de chaises dans sa — à manger, *to be toothless.* (Bullies') Salle de danse, *the behind.* Thus termed because they think it is the proper object on which to exercise one's feet.

Salonnier, *m.* (familiar), *art critic who reviews the art exhibition.*

Salopette, *f.* (popular), *pair of canvas trousers worn over another pair.*

Salopiat, or **salopiaud,** *m.* (popular), *dirty or mean fellow,* "snot." A diminutive of salope, which itself comes from the English sloppy.

Salsifis, *m.* (popular), *fingers,* "dooks, or dukes."

Saltimbe, *m.* (popular), abbreviation of saltimbanque, *mountebank.*

Saluer (theatrical), le public, *to die.* See **Pipe.**

Salutations à cul ouvert, *f. pl.* (popular), *much bowing and scraping of feet.*

Sanctus, *m.* (obsolete), *mark, seal.* A play on the words saint and seing.

Ils sont sortis ; le gendarme n'a plus été qu'un jean-f. . ., l'officier l'y a foutu son sanctus, que le manche de son épée l'y faisoit emplâtre.—*Journal de la Rapée.*

Sang, *m.* (popular and thieves'), de poisson, *oil.* See **Prince.** Se manger les sangs, *to fret.*

Sang-de-Versaillais, *adj.* (familiar), facetious term for *deep red.* An allusion to the epithet of Versaillais given to the supporters of the government during the insurrection of 1871. Journaliste —, *a journalist who is of rabid Republican opinions.*

Le bel Antony, journaliste Sang-de-Versaillais et orateur dynamitard.—A. Sirven.

Sanglé, *adj.* (popular), *short of cash,* with one's resources at "low tide."

Sangler (popular), se —, *to stint oneself.*

Sanglier, *m.* (thieves'), *priest,* or "devil-dodger." An allusion to his black robe, or from the words sans, *without,* and glier, *infernal regions.* The priest, or rather he who performed the marriage ceremony, was termed in old English cant, "patrico." Dekker says of the "patrico" that he performs the marriage ceremony under a tree, in a wood, or in the open fields. The bridegroom and bride place themselves on each side of a dead horse or other animal. The "patrico" then bids them live together until death do part them. Thereupon they shake hands, and all adjourn to a neighbouring tavern.

Sangsue, *f.* (popular), *kept woman who ruins her lover.* (Printers') Poser une —, *to correct a piece of composition for an absentee.*

Sangsurer (popular), *to draw largely on one's purse.* Se —, *to ruin oneself in favour of another.*

Sans (thieves'), condé, *without permission or passport.* Condé signified *mayor, authorities,* and the word was imported by Spanish quacks. Sans dab, *orphan.* The word "dab" has the signification of *father, chief, king.* In the sixteenth and seventeenth centuries "dabo" meant *master of a house,* and probably was derived from dam, damp (dominus), used by Rabelais with the signification of *lord.* The English slang has "dab," *expert,* which the *Slang Dictionary* believes comes from the Latin adeptus. It is more likely the origin is the French dab, dabo. Etre — canne *is said of a convict under the surveillance of the police who has broken bounds.*

Sans-beurre, *m.* (popular), *rag-picker,* or "tot-picker."

Sans-bout, *m.* (popular), *hoop.*

Sans-camelotte, *m.* (thieves'). Termed also solliceur de zif, *swindler who gets money advanced on imaginary goods supposed to be in his possession.*

Sans-chagrin, *m.* (thieves'), *thief,* "prig." See **Grinche**.

Sans-châsses, *m.* (thieves'), *blind man,* "groper, or puppy."

Sans-cœur, *m.* (popular), *usurer.*

Sans-culotte, *m.,* *name given to the Republicans of* 1793, either because they discarded the old-fashioned breeches for trousers, or as an allusion to the scanty dress of the Republican soldiers. The word has passed into the language.

Sans-dos, *m.* (popular), *stool.*

Sans-fade, *m.* (thieves'), être —, *to be penniless,* or "dead broke."

Sans-feuille, *f.* (thieves'), *gallows.* This expression corresponds to the "leafless tree" of Paul Clifford's song. Hanging was termed formerly, "être élevé sur une bûche de quinze pieds, épouser cette veuve qui est à la Grève, danser sous la corde, danser une cabriole en l'air sans toucher à terre, avoir le collet secoué, être tué de la lance d'un puits, regarder par une fenêtre de chanvre, jouer du haut-bois." For other synonyms see **Monte - à - regret**. American thieves use the expression "to twist," *i.e. to hang.*

Sans-le-sou, *m.* (popular), *needy man, one who is* "hard up."

Sans-loches, *adj.* (thieves'), être —, *to be deaf.*

Sans-mirettes, *adj. and m.* (thieves'), *blind ; blind man,* "groper, or puppy."

Sansonnet, *m.* (popular), *penis.* Properly *starling.*

Santache, *f.* (popular), *health.*

Santaille, *f.* (popular), *the prison of La Santé.*

Santarelle, *f.* (card-sharpers'), faire une —, *to give cards to one's partner in such a way as to be able to see them.*

Santu, *f.* (thieves'), *health.*

Saoul comme un âne (familiar and popular), "drunk as a lord;" a common saying, says the *Slang Dictionary*, probably referring to the facilities a man of fortune has for such a gratification. The phrase had its origin in the old hard-drinking days, when it was almost compulsory on a man of fashion to get drunk regularly after dinner.

Saoulle, *f.* (thieves'), *blackguard.*

Sap, *m.* (popular), *coffin,* "eternity box." From sapin, *fir wood.* Taper dans le —, *to be dead,* "to have been put to bed with a shovel."

Sapajou, *m.* (popular), vieux —, *old debauchee, old* "rip." One as lecherous as a monkey.

Sapement, *m.* (thieves'), or gerbement, *sentence.*

Saper (thieves'), *to sentence;* — au glaive, *to sentence to death.*

Sapeur, *m.* (thieves'), *judge,* or "beak;" (popular) *cigar partly smoked.*

Sapin, *m.* (familiar and popular), *hackney coach,* or "shoful."

Elle causait de l'intérieur de son landau, égayée, le trouvant cocasse, au milieu des embarras de voiture, quand "il s'engueulait avec les sapins."—ZOLA.

(Popular) Redingote de —, *coffin,* or "cold meat box." Sentir, or sonner le —, *to look dangerously ill.*

Elle avait un fichu rhume qui sonnait joliment le sapin.—ZOLA.

(Thieves') Sapin, *floor; garret;* — de muron, *garret where salt is stored away;* — des cornants (obsolete), *the earth; a field.* Compare with the modern expression "plancher des vaches."

Sapinière, *f.* (popular), *common grave for poor people.*

Saquet, *m.* (popular), *shaking.*

Sardine, *f.* (popular). Serrer les cinq sardines, *to shake hands.* Rabelais uses the verb fourcher with a like signification. (Military) Sardines, *stripes on the sleeves of a tunic.* Sardines blanches, *those worn by gendarmes.*

Deux gendarmes un beau dimanche,
Chevauchaient le long d'un sentier.
L'un avait la sardine blanche,
L'autre le jaune baudrier.
G. NADAUD, *Les Deux Gendarmes.*

Sardiné, *m.* (military), *non-commissioned officer.*

Sarrasin, *m.* (printers'), *workman who works at reduced wages, or refuses to join in strikes,* a "knobstick."

Sarrasinage, sarrasiner. See **Sarrasin.**

Satin, *f.* (popular), *girl who has unnatural intercourse with others of her own sex.* From a character in Zola's *Nana.*

Satonnade, *f.* (convicts'), *bastinado.* La — roule à balouf igo, *there is much giving of bastinado here.*

Satou, or **satte,** *m.* (thieves'), *wood; forest; stick; itinerant mountebank's plant.*

Satousier, *m.* (thieves'), *joiner.*

Satte. See **Satou.**

Sauce, *f.* (popular), *reprimand,* "wigging." Gare à la —! *look out for squalls!* Gober la —, *to be reprimanded or punished for others.* Il va tomber de la —, *it is going to rain.* Accommoder à la — piquante. See **Accommoder.** (Prostitutes') Sauce tomate, *menses.* Formerly donner la —, had the signification given as follows:—

Manière de parler libre, qui . . . signifie donner du mal vénérien.—LE ROUX.

Saucé, *adj.* (familiar), être —, *to be wet to the skin.*

Saucier, *m.* (restaurants'), *cook who has charge of the making of sauces in good restaurants.*

Saucisse, *f.* (popular), *prostitute,* or " mot ;" — plate, *thin prostitute ;* — municipale, *poisoned meat thrown to straying dogs.* Moi —, *I also.* For moi aussi.

Saucisson, *m.* (popular), à pattes, or de Bologne, *short and fat person,* "humpty dumpty." (Thieves') Saucisson, *lead,* or "bluey." Termed also "grasdouble."

Saut, *m.* (familiar), faire le —, explained by quotation :—

Obliger une femme à se rendre, la pousser à bout, profiter de sa faiblesse, en jouir.— LE ROUX.

Formerly faire le saut signified *to steal.*

Saute-dessus, *m.* (thieves'), se prendre au —, *to assume a threatening tone.*

Après avoir provoqué à la débauche celui qui a eu le malheur de les aborder, ils changent tout à coup de ton, le prennent, comme ils disent, au saute-dessus et se donnant pour des agents de l'autorité les menacent d'une arrestation.—TARDIEU, *Etude Médico-légale.*

Sauter (popular), *to stink ;* — à la perche, *to be unable to procure food ;* — sur le poil à quelqu'un, *to attack one.* (Thieves') Sauter, *to steal ; to conceal from one's accomplices the proceeds of a robbery ;* — à la capahut, *to murder an accomplice in order to rob him of his share of the booty.* (Familiar) Sauter le pas, *to become a bankrupt,* "to go to smash." Also *to die.* See **Pipe.** Sauter le pas, *to lose one's maidenhead,* "to have seen the elephant;" — une femme, *to have connection with a woman.* (Card-sharpers') Faire — la coupe, *to place the cut card on the top, by dexterous manipulation, instead of at the bottom of the pack,* "to slip" *a card.* (Cavalry) Sauter le basflanc, *to jump over the walls of the barracks for the purpose of spending the night in town.*

Sauterelle, *f.* (familiar), *prostitute ;* see **Gadoue ;** (thieves') *flea,* called sometimes " F sharp." (Shopmen's) Sauterelle, *woman who examines a number of articles without purchasing any.*

On appelle ainsi dans les magasins de nouveautés les femmes qui font plier et déplier vingt ballots sans acheter.—L. NOIR.

Exécuter une —, *to summarily get rid of such a troublesome person.*

Sauterie, *f.* (familiar), *dance,* or "hop."

Sauteron, or **sauterondolles** (thieves'), *banker ; changer.* Sauteron is only another name for thief.

Sauteur, *m.* (familiar), *man not to be relied on ; political turn-coat,* "rat." In military riding schools, *horse trained to buck jump, and ridden without a saddle or bridle.*

Sauteuse, *f.* (popular), *ballet-girl ; girl of indifferent character,* or "shake ;" *flea,* or " F sharp."

Sauvage. See **Habiller.**

Sauver la mise à quelqu'un (popular), *to help one out of a difficulty.*

Sauvette, *f.* (popular), *money,* or "oof." See **Quibus.** Sauvette, *wicker basket used by rag-pickers.*

Savate, *f.* (popular), *bad workman.* (Familiar and popular) Jouer comme une—, *to play badly.* (Military) Savate, *corporal punishment inflicted by soldiers on a comrade,* "cobbing ;" (sailors') — premier brin, *rum of the first quality.*

Et le tafia du coup de la fin, du jus de bottes, ne plus ne moins, de la savate premier brin ! Comme c'était bon, ohé, les frères, de se suiver ainsi l'estomac.—RICHEPIN.

Savater (popular), *to work carelessly.*

Savetier, *m.* (popular), *clumsy workman;* (familiar) *man who does anything carelessly, without taste.*

Savon, *m.* (familiar), *reprimand.* Donner un —, synonymous of laver la tête, *to reprimand, to scold,* "to haul over the coals."

Savonné, *adj.* (thieves'), *white.*

Je vais alors chercher deux doubles cholettes de picton, du larton savonné.—VIDOCQ.

Savonner (popular), *to reprimand,* "to haul over the coals;" *to chastise,* "to dust one's jacket," see **Voie ;** (thieves') *to steal,* "to claim ;" — une cambuse, *to strip a house,* "to do a crib."

Savoyard, *m.* (familiar), *rough, ill-mannered man,* a "sweep." Sweeps hailed formerly from Savoy.

Savoyarde, *f.* (thieves'), *portmanteau,* "peter, or rodger." Faire la —, *to steal a portmanteau,* "to heave a peter from a drag."

Scarabombe, *f.* (thieves'), *astonishment.*

Scarabomber (thieves'), *to astonish.*

Scène, *f.* (theatrical), être en —, *to give all one's attention to one's part during the performance.* (Familiar and popular) Avant-scènes. See **Avantages.**

Schabraque, *f.* (military), vieille —, *old prostitute.*

Schaffouse, *m.* (popular), *the behind.* A play on the town of that name, chute du Rhin, and chute du rein, *lower part of back.*

Schako, *m.* (popular), *head,* "nut."

Schelingophone, *m.* (popular), *the breech.* See **Vasistas.** Enlever le — à quelqu'un, *to kick one's behind,* "to hoof one's bum."

C'est moi, si eune dame m'parlait ainsi, que j'aurais vite fait d'i enlever le schelingophone.—GRÉVIN.

Schlague, *f.* (popular), *thrashing with a stick,* "larruping." From the German.

Schlaguer (popular), *to thrash,* "to larrup." See **Voie.**

Schloff, *m.* (popular), *sleep,* or "balmy." Faire —, *to sleep,* "to have a dose of the balmy."

Schloffer (popular), *to sleep,* "to have a dose of the balmy." From the German.

Schnaps, *m.* (popular), *brandy.* See **Tord-boyaux.**

Et surtout n'oubliez pas le café avec le schnaps.—MAHALIN.

Schness, *m.* (thieves'), *physiognomy.*

Schnick, *m.* (popular), *brandy,* "French cream." See **Tord-boyaux.**

Schniquer (popular), *to get drunk on brandy.*

Schniqueur (popular), *brandy-bibber.*

Schpile, *adj.* (popular), *good; excellent,* or "clipping ;" *fine.* Synonymous of "becnerf." Il n'est pas — à frayer, *he is not good company.*

Schpiler (popular), *to do good work.*

Schproum, *m.* (thieves'), faire du —, *to make a noise,* "to kick up a row."

Schtard, *m.* (thieves'), *prison,* "stir." See **Motte.** La — aux frusques, *a pawnbroker's shop.* La — des lascars, *the prison of La Roquette.*

Schtardier, *m.* (thieves'), *prisoner,* "canary."

Schtosse. See **Monter.**

Schtosser (thieves'), se —, *to get drunk,* or "canon." See **Sculpter.**

Sciant, *adj.* (familiar and popular), *tiresome, annoying.*

Scie, *f.* (familiar and popular), *annoyance ; tiresome person ; exasperating rigmarole.* Monter une — à quelqu'un, *to annoy one by the continual repetition of words or joke.* (Popular) Scie, *wife,* or "comfortable impudence." Porter sa —, *to walk with one's wife.*

Scier (familiar and popular), or — le dos, *to annoy,* "to bore."

Je m'en fiche pas mal de votre Alexandre ! Voilà trop longtemps que vous me sciez avec votre Alexandre ! J'en ai assez de votre Alexandre !—P. MAHALIN.

Scier du bois, *to play on a stringed instrument.*

Scieur de bois, *m.* (familiar), *violinist.*

Scion, *m.* (popular), *stick.* From scier ; (thieves') *knife,* "chive."

Scionner (popular), *to apply the stick to one's shoulders,* "to larrup," see **Voie ;** (thieves' and cads') *to knife.* Scionne ! morgane ! *stick him ! bite him !*

Scionneur, *m.* (thieves'), *murderer.* See **Sionneur.**

Scribouillage, *m.* (literary), *bad style of writing,* "penny-a-lining."

Scrutin, *m.* (familiar), assister au — de ballotage, *to be present while a lady is undressing herself.*

Sculpsit, *m.* (artists'), *sculptor.*

Sculpter (popular), se — une gueule de bois, *to get drunk,* or "screwed." The synonyms are: "s'allumer, se flanquer une culotte, se poivrotter, partir pour la gloire, se poisser, se schtosser, se schniquer, se pocharder, se tuiler, prendre une barbe, se piquer le nez, se cingler le blaire, s'empoivrer, s'empaffer, mettre son nez dans le bleu, se piquer le tasseau, se coller une biture, faire cracher ses soupapes, se cardinaliser, écraser un grain, se coaguler, se farder, se foncer, s'émérillonner, s'émêcher, s'enluminer," &c. For the English slang terms see **Pompette.**

Séance, *f.* (thieves' and roughs'), refiler une —, *to thrash.* See **Voie.**

Séant, *m.* (popular), *the breech,* "Nancy." See **Vasistas.**

Seau, *m.* (military), être dans le —, *to be gone to the privy.*

Sec, *m. and adj.* (players'), jouer en cinq —, *to play one game only in five points.* (Thieves') Etre —, *to be dead.* (Military) Il fait —, *we are thirsty.*

Sec-aux-os, *m.* (popular), *bony, skinny fellow.*

Ce grand dur-à-cuir, au cuir tanné, ce long sec-aux-os, tel qu'un pantin en bois des îles, avec son corps sans fin et noueux d'articulations.—RICHEPIN.

Sèche, *f.* (popular), *cigarette.* (Thieves') La —, *death.*

Séché, *adj.* (students'), être —, *to be disqualified at an examination,* "to be spun, or ploughed." (Popular) Etre —, *to become sober again.* (Military schools') Etre —, *to be punished.*

Séchée, *f.* (military schools'), *punishment ; arrest.*

Sécher (schoolboys'), le lycée, *to play truant ;* — un devoir, *not to* *do one's exercise ;* — un candidat, *to disqualify a candidate.* (Popular) Sécher, *to drink,* "*to lush.*" See **Rincer.** Sécher un litre, une absinthe, un bock, *to drink a litre of wine, a glass of absinthe, of beer.*

C'était un singulier coco ... il séchait des bocks à faire croire que son gosier était capable d'absorber le canal Saint-Martin.— *Mémoires de Monsieur Claude.*

Sécher la tata, *to bore one.*

Séchoir, *m.* (popular), *cemetery.*

Sécot, *m.* (popular), *thin boy or man.*

Secouer (popular), les bretelles à quelqu'un, *to give one a good shaking.* Secouer, or — les puces, *to scold,* "*to haul over the coals ;*" *to thrash.* See **Voie.** Secouer ses puces, *to dance ;* — la commode, *to grind the organ ;* (thieves') — l'artiche, *to steal a purse ;* — la perpendiculaire, *to steal a watch-chain,* "to claim a slang ;*" — un chandelier, *to rob with violence at night,* "*to jump.*"

Secousse, *f.* (popular), prendre sa —, *to die.* See **Pipe.** Un contre-coup de la —, *a foreman.* Termed thus on account of his generally coming in for the greater share of a reprimand. (Military) N'en pas foutre, or fiche une —, *to do nothing, to be idling.*

Eh ben, mon colon, faut croire que c'est l'monde ertourné, pisque c'est les hommes ed' la classe qui sont commandés de fourrage durant que les bleus n'en fichent pas une secousse.—G. COURTELINE.

Secretmuche, *m.* (popular), *secretary.*

Seigneur à musique, *m.* (thieves'), *murderer.* From saigner, *to bleed,* and alluding to the shrieks of the victim.

Seize, *m.* (popular), souliers —, *tight shoes.* A play on the words "treize et trois," that is, "très étroits."

Seize-mayeux, *m.* (familiar), *name given to the conspirators of 16th May, 1877, who, being at the head of the government of the Republic, were seeking to upset it.*

Pour les partisans du ministère du 16 mai, on a trouvé le nom de seize-mayeux. —*Gazette Anecdotique.*

Sellette à criminel, *f.* (obsolete), *prostitute, an associate of thieves.*

Je veux te procurer un habit de vestale
Pour une année au moins au Temple de la gale.
Selette à criminel, matelas ambulant.
Amusemens à la Grecque.

Semaine, *f.* (familiar), des quatre jeudis, *never,* "when the devil is blind." (Military) N'être pas de —, *to have nothing to do with some business.*

Semelle. See **Chevaux, Feuilletée.**

Semer quelqu'un (popular), *to get rid of one ; to knock one down.* Semer des miettes, *to vomit,* "to cast up accounts."

Séminaire, *m.* (old cant), *the hulks.*

Semper, *m.* (popular), *tobacco,* "fogus." For superfin, distorted into semperfinas, and finally semper.

Senaqui, *m.* (thieves'), *gold coin,* "yellow boy."

Sénat, *m.* (popular), *wine-shop frequented by a certain class of workmen.*

Depuis longtemps, les travailleurs appellent les marchands de vin où ils se réunissent par spécialité, des sénats.—*Le Sublime.*

Sénateur, *m.* (popular), *well-dressed man,* " gorger ;" *workman who frequents* " sénats " (which see) ; (butchers') *bull.*

Sens devant dimanche (popular), *upside down.*

Sentinelle, *f.* (popular), *lump of excrement,* or " quaker ;" (printers') *glass of wine awaiting one at the wine-shop.* Sentinelles, *badly-adjusted letters.*

Sentir (popular), le bouquin, *to emit a strong odour of humanity, to be a* " medlar." The expression reminds one of the " olet hircum " of Horace, and of Terence's " apage te a me, hircum oles." (General) Sentir le coude à gauche, *to feel certain of the support of friends.* Cela sent mauvais, *there's something wrong,* " I smell a rat."

S'entraîner à la barre (ballet dancers'), *mode of practising one's steps.*

Sept, *m.* (rag-pickers'), *hook used for picking up pieces of paper or rags.* (Sporting) Sept-à-neuf, *morning riding-suit.*

Quel joli sept-à-neuf cela ferait !—*Le Figaro.*

Ser, *m.* (thieves'), *signal.* Faire le —, *to be on the watch, on the* " nose."

Serge, or **sergot,** *m.* (popular), *police officer,* or " crusher." See **Pot-à-tabac.**

Voyez-vous, frangins, eh ! sergots,
Faut êt' bon pour l'espèce humaine.
D'vant l'pivois les homm's sont égaux.
D'ailleurs j'ai massé tout' la s'maine.
RICHEPIN.

Sergent, *m.* (military), de crottin, *non-commissioned officer at the Cavalry School of Saumur.* The allusion is obvious ; — d'hiver, *soldier of the first class.* An allusion to his woollen stripes, which

are supposed to keep him warm in winter. (Popular) Sergent de vieux, *nurse in hospitals.*

Sergo, or **sergot,** *m.* (popular), *police officer.* From sergent de ville. See **Pot-à-tabac.** Avoir des mots avec les sergots, *to be apprehended.* Literally *to quarrel with the police.*

Et apprit que Joséphine, ayant eu des " mots avec les sergots," pour une vilaine affaire, avait été faire une saison à Saint-Lazare.—GYP.

Sergolle, *f.* (thieves'), *belt.*

Série, *f.* (university), *the staff of examiners for the doctor's degree.*

Sérieux, *adj.* (cocottes'), homme —, *one who has means.*

Serin, *m.* (popular), *gendarme of the suburbs ;* (familiar) *foolish fellow, greenhorn.*

Seriner (familiar), quelque chose à quelqu'un, *to keep repeating something to one, so that he may get it into his head.* (Thieves') Seriner, *to divulge,* " to blow the gaff."

Serinette, *f.* (thieves'), *man who swindles one under threat of exposure ;* — à caractères, *newspaper.*

Qu'est-ce qu'il vient faire ici ce journaleux de malheur ? . . . Si nous le surinions ! . . . Comme cela il ne jaspinera plus de l'orgue dans sa serinette à caractères.—*Mémoires de Monsieur Claude.*

Serinette, *passive Sodomist.*

La tante est tantôt appelée tapette, tantôt serinette.—CANLER.

Seringue, *f.* (popular), *cracked voice.* Chanter comme une —, *to sing out of tune.* Seringue à rallonges, *telescope.*

C'est Vénus que je veux voir ou je te démolis, toi et ta seringue à rallonges.—RANDON.

(Familiar and popular) Seringue, *dull, tiresome person.*

Seringuinos, *m.* (familiar), *simple-minded fellow,* "flat."

Serpent, *m.* (Ecole Polytechnique), *one of the fifteen first on the list after the entrance examination;* (military) *leathern belt used as a purse;* — des reins, *same meaning.*

Que ze veux dire, mon ancien, que vous n'aurez pas la peine de tâter mes côtes pour voir si ma ceinture elle est rondement garnie de picaillons. Ze connais le truc! et z'ai déposé mon serpent des reins en lieu sûr avant de venir ici.—DUBOIS DE GENNES.

Serpentin, *m.* (thieves'), *convict's mattress.*

Serpettes, *f. pl.* (military), *short and bandy legs.*

Ces pauvres tourlourous! ça vous a six pouces de serpettes et le dos tout de suite.—RANDON.

Serpillière de ratichon, *f.* (thieves'), *priest's cassock.* The long surtout worn by some of the English clergy, says the *Slang Dictionary,* is termed M.B. (*i.e.* mark of the beast), a modern Puritan form of abuse, said to have been accidentally disclosed to a High Church customer by a tailor's orders to his foreman. Serpillière comes, through the old French sarpillière, *cloth, or cassock,* from the Low Latin serpeilleria, *woollen stuff.* Grocers' assistants give this name to their aprons.

Serrante, *f.* (thieves'), *lock;* (popular) *belt, sash.*

Il se dandine dans son large pantalon de velours à côtes, la taille sanglée par sa serrante écarlate.—RICHEPIN, *Le Pavé.*

Serré, *adj.* (familiar), *needy; close-fisted,* or "near." (Thieves') Etre —, *to be locked up.*

La plus cruelle injure qu'une fille puisse jeter au front déshonoré d'une autre fille, c'est de l'accuser d'infidélité envers un amant serré (mis en prison).—BALZAC.

Serrebois, *m.* (thieves'), *sergeant.*

Serrepogne, *m.* (popular), *hand-cuffs,* "darbies, or hand gyves."

Serrer (popular), *to imprison;* — la vis, *to strangle;* — le brancard, or la cuiller, *to shake hands;* — les fesses, *to be afraid,* or "funky;" — le nœud, *to marry,* to get "switched." Se — le gaviot, *to go without food.* (Thieves') Serrer la gargamelle, or le quiqui, *to strangle;* (familiar) — la pince, *to shake hands;* (military) — la croupière à quelqu'un, *to watch one narrowly; to become strict to one.*

Serrure, *f.* (popular), avoir la — brouillée, *to have an impediment in one's speech.* Avoir laissé la clef à la —, *to have failed in one's resolve of having no more children.* Avoir mis un cadenas à la —, *refers to the determination of a woman to live in a state of chastity.*

Sert, or **ser,** *m.* (thieves'), *signal.*

Servante, *f.* (theatrical), *lamp.*

Ce fut Massourier, qui connaissait les détours, qui prit la servante dans un coin derrière les décors, la vissa à la rampe et l'alluma.—E. MONTEIL.

Service, *m.* (theatrical), *free season ticket.*

Qu'est-ce que cela signifie? Voilà Fauchery, du Bartholo, qui me renvoie son service. Il n'entend pas avoir une loge de côté, quand le Druide a une loge de face.—MAHALIN.

(Roughs' and thieves') Le — du Château, *prison van,* or "Black Maria."

Serviette, *f.* (thieves'), *stick, cudgel,* "toko."

Servir (thieves'), marron, *to arrest in the act.* Probably from as-servir.

Le fait est, qu'avec son air effrayé et tremblant, il était bien capable de me faire servir marron (arrêter en flagrant délit).—CANLER.

F F

Servir, *to inform against one,* " to blow the gaff ;" *to steal,* "to nim ;" *to apprehend,* " to smug." See **Piper.** Servir le trèpe, *to keep back the crowd ;* — de belle, *to inform falsely against one.*

Maintenant il s'agit de servir de belle une largue (de dénoncer à faux une femme).
—BALZAC.

Sévère, *f.* (familiar), en voilà une —! *is said of incredible news.* It also means *that is really too bad,* " coming it too strong."

Sèvres, *m.* (popular), passer à —, *to receive nothing.* From sevrer, *to wean.*

Sézière, sézigue, or **sézingard** (thieves'), *he ; him ; she ; her.* Mézigo n'enterve pas mieux que sézière, *I do not understand better than he does.* Rouscaillez à sézière, *speak to him.*

Et les punit en la forme qui suit : premièrement on lui ôte toutime son frusquin, puis on urine dans une saliverne de sabri avec du pivois aigre, une poignée de marrons et un torchon de frétille, et on frotte à sézière tant son proye, qu'il ne démorfie d'un mois après.— *Le Jargon de l'Argot.*

Sgoff, *adj.* (popular), *first-rate.* See **Rup.**

Siamois, *adj.* (thieves'), les frères —, *the testicles.* An allusion to the Siamese twins.

Siante, *f.* (thieves'), *chair.* For séante.

Sibérie, *f.* (printers'), *back part of workshop, where apprentices work in the cold.*

Sibiche, sibigeoise, or **sibijoite,** *f.* (popular), *cigarette.*

Siècle, *m.* (familiar), fin de —, *dandy,* or " masher."

Un jeune " fin de siècle " est en train d'essayer un veston. Le vêtement est ajusti comme un maillot.
— Je voudrais, dit le jeune homme, que ça colle davantage.

— Très bien, dit le coupeur, on mettra à monsieur des pains à cacheter en guise de doublure.— *Le Voltaire.*

Sifernet (Breton cant), *drunk.*

Siffle, *f.* (thieves'), *throat,* or "red lane ;" *voice,* or " whistle."

Siffler (popular), *to spend money ;* — la linotte, *to wait in the street.* (General) Siffler au disque, *to wait for money ; to wait.* An allusion to a signal of engine-drivers.

Rien à faire de cette femme-là. . . . J'ai sifflé au disque assez longtemps. . . . Pas mèche. . . . La voie est barrée. . . . Pardieu, nous savons votre façon de siffler au disque, dit Christian, quand il eut compris cette expression passée de l'argot des mécaniciens dans celui de la haute gomme.—A. DAUDET.

Avoir tout sifflé, *to be ruined.* Tu peux —, *it is in vain, you'll not get it.* Siffler, *to drink.*

Elle-même quand elle sifflait son verre de rogomme sur le comptoir prenait des airs de drame, se jetait ça dans le plomb en souhaitant que ça la fît crever.—ZOLA, *L'Assommoir.*

Sifflet, *m.* (popular), *throat,* "gutter-lane, red-lane,* or *whistle.*" Termed also "avaloir, bec, bocal, corne, cornemuse, cornet, dalle, dent, fusil, gargoine, trente-deuxième." Raboter le —, *to burn one's throat.*

Hein ! ça rabote le sifflet ! avale d'une lampée.—ZOLA.

(Familiar and popular) Couper le — à quelqu'un, *to silence one ; to kill one.* Sifflet, or — d'ébène, *dress coat.* Termed " tails " at Harrow School.

Des jeunes gens dont le pardessus recouvre le sifflet d'ébène de cérémonie.—P. MAHALIN.

(Military) Sifflet, *gun.*

Siffran, or **six-francs,** *m.*(tailors'), *board used by tailors for pressing clothes.*

Il y avait en outre une planche en noyer, dite siffran, dont les tailleurs se servent pour repasser les coutures et presser les étoffes.—MACÉ.

Sigisbéisme, *m.* (familiar), *dancing attendance upon one.*

Comme l'a fort bien dit Henri Murger, lorsque cette sorte de sigisbéisme naît de la sympathie que l'on éprouve pour les œuvres d'un écrivain et de l'attachement que vous inspire sa personne, comme toute chose sincère, ce sentiment est très honorable même dans ce que peut avoir d'outré l'admiration caniche du "strapontiniste."— A. DUBRUJEAUD, *Echo de Paris.*

Sigle, sigue, sigolle, or **cig,** *f.* (thieves'), *twenty-franc coin.* Double —, *forty-franc coin.* Servir des sigues, *to steal gold coin.* A sovereign is termed in the English slang or cant, "canary, yellow boy, gingle boy, shiner, monarch, couter."

Signer (popular), se — des orteils, *to be hanged,* "to be scragged." See **Monte-à-regret.**

Sigris bouesse, or **bouzolle** (old cant), *it freezes; it is cold.* These words seem a compound of gris, cant term for *wind,* and boue, *mud.*

Sime, *m. and f.* (thieves'), un —, *a townsman.* La —, *townspeople.*

Passe devant et allume si tu remouches la sime ou la patraque.—VIDOCQ.

Simon, *m.* (popular), aller chez —, *to ease oneself.* See **Mouscailler.** (Scavengers') Simon, *a man whose cesspool is being emptied.*

Simonner (thieves'), *to swindle,* "to best."

Simonneur, *m.* (thieves'), *swindler,* or "mobsman."

Simpliste (journalists'), *one who is in favour of a reform in the spelling of words, who would have* *every word written as it is pronounced.*

Il y a longtemps que des "simplistes" ont préconisé l'orthographe phonétique.— *Le Voltaire,* 7 Janvier, 1887.

Here is a specimen of the mode recommended : Notre ortografe actuelle est absurde, tou le monde e d'accor la-dessu. Elle fé le désespoar des écolié, elle absorbe le melieur tan de leurs études, &c.

Sine qua non, *m.* (familiar), *money.* See **Quibus.**

Singe, *m.* (popular), *foreman; master,* or "boss;" *passenger on top of bus;* (printers') *compositor,* or "donkey." Also *master.* Un — botté, *a funny, amusing man.* (Thieves') Singe à rabat, *magistrate,* or "beak;" — de la rousse, *police officer,* or "reeler." See **Pot-à-tabac.**

Singeresse, *f.* (popular and thieves'), *mistress, or landlady.*

Sinqui (thieves'), *that.*

Sinve, *m.* (thieves'), *simple-minded man,* "flat." Faire le —, or sinvre, *to flinch.*

L'ami, m'a-t-il dit, tu n'as pas l'air brave. Ne va pas faire le sinve devant la carline. Vois-tu, il y a un mauvais moment à passer sur la placarde.—V. HUGO.

Sinverie, *f.* (thieves'), *foolery.*

Sionneur, *m.* (thieves'), *murderer.* See **Scionneur.**

Les sionneurs sont ceux qui, après minuit, vous attendent au coin d'une rue, vous abordent le poing sur la gorge en vous demandant . . . la bourse ou la vie.—*Mémoires de Monsieur Claude.*

Sirènes de la gare Saint-Lazare, *f. pl.* (thieves'), *gang of prostitutes who, in* 1875, *used to attract travellers to a cut-throat place where male accomplices stripped them of their valuables.*

Sirop, *m.* (popular), de l'aiguière, de baromètre, or de grenouille, *water*, "Adam's ale."

Cet animal de Mes-Bottes était allumé ; il avait bien déjà ses deux litres ; histoire seulement de ne pas se laisser embêter par tout ce sirop de grenouille que l'orage avait craché sur ses abattis.—Zola, *L'Assommoir.*

Siroter (popular), *to drink*, "to lush." See **Rincer.** Siroter le bonheur, *to be spending one's honeymoon.* (Hairdressers') Siroter, *to dress one's hair carefully.*

Siroteur, *m.* (popular), *drunkard*, or "lushington."

Sitrin, *adj.* (thieves'), *black.*

Sive, *f.* (thieves'), *hen*, "margery prater." From the Romany chi, chiveli.

Six, *m.* (popular), un — et trois font neuf, *a silly and cruel expression applied by low people to a lame man.* In the English slang, "dot and go one."

Six broque ! (thieves'), *go away.*

Six-clous, *m.* (popular), *roofer.*

Skasa (Breton cant), *to steal.*

Skaser (Breton cant), *cunning ; swindler ; thief.*

Skrap (Breton cant), *theft.*

Skrapa (Breton cant), *to steal.*

Skraper (Breton cant), *thief.*

Slasse, or **slaze**, *adj.* (roughs'), être —, *to be drunk*, or "screwed." See **Pompette.**

Slasser, or **slassiquer** (popular), *to get drunk*, or "screwed." See **Pompette.**

Smala, *f.* (familiar), *family ; household.* From the Arab.

Snoboye, *adj.* (familiar and popular), *good, excellent*, "tip-top, slap up, first-class." The synonyms are : "rup, chic, chicard, chicandard, chouette, bath, superlifico, chocnosof, enlevé, tapé, aux pommes, bath aux pommes, aux petits oignons, numéro un."

Soc, *m.* (familiar), for "démocsoc," *name given to Socialists.*

Société, *f.* (popular), la — du doigt dans le cul, *the Société de Saint-Vincent de Paul, a religious association chiefly composed of Jesuits.* An allusion to their duties as assistants at hospitals. See **Doigt.** (Theatrical) Société du faux-col, *agreement between comedians to help one another in order to get rid of bores.*

Sœur, *f.* (thieves'), de charité, *a variety of female thief.* Les sœurs blanches, *the teeth*, or "ivories."

Soie, *f.* (popular), faire l'asticot dans la —, *is said of a lazy woman who likes dress and pleasure.*

Fallait p't'ê'te pas l'embocquer à faire l'asticot dans la soie sans rien astiquer.—Louise Michel.

Aller comme des bas de — à un cochon *is said of apparel or anything else not suited to one's appearance or station in life.*

Le sifflet d'ébène, rien que ça d'chic ! ça te va comme des bas d'soie à un cochon.—Rigaud.

Soiffard, *m.* (familiar and popular), *one too fond of drink*, a "lushington."

Soiffer (familiar and popular), *to drink to excess*, "to swig."

Moi je trouve que c'est bon de soiffer ! Qu'est-ce qu'elle nous dévide de la mélancolie, celle-là ?—Louise Michel.

Soiffeur, *m.* (familiar), *bibber*, or "lushington."

Quant au copain que voilà, c'est un bon garçon ; mais soiffeur endiablé, par exemple. Il est déjà alcoolique.—MACÉ.

Soiffeuse, *f.* (familiar), *woman who is fond of drink.*

Une riche idée que j'ai eue d'envoyer la petite . . . à la place de cette soiffeuse d'Aphrodite qui est restée huit jours à déjeûner chez Coquet.—P. MAHALIN.

Soigné, *m.* (familiar), du —, *something of the best quality.*

Soignée, *f.* (popular), *sound thrashing.*

Soigner (theatrical), ses entrées, *to get oneself applauded by paid applauders when making one's appearance on the stage ;* (popular) — quelqu'un, *to thrash soundly,* "to knock one into a cocked hat." See **Voie.**

Soir, *m.* (familiar), un —, *an evening paper.*

Soireux, *m.* (journalists'), *dramatic critic.*

Et, l'grand jour, avec tout' la presse théâtrale, pontifes, d'mi pontifes et soireux, M. Boscher, directeur du Théâtre-Déjazet s'ra invité, parbleu !—*Le Cri du Peuple.*

Soiriste, *m.* (journalists'), *a journalist whose functions are to report on events of the evening.*

Soissonnais, *m.* (thieves'), *beans.* Termed also "musiciens."

Soixante-six, *m.* (popular), *prostitute's bully,* or "pensioner" with an obscene prefix. See **Poisson.**

Soldat, *m.* (popular), du pape, *bad soldier.* (Printers') Les petits soldats de plomb, *type.* Aligner les petits soldats de plomb, *to compose.* (Thieves') Des soldats, *money,* or "pieces." See

Quibus. Probably from the expression, "money is the sinews of war."

Money is a good soldier, sir, and will on. — SHAKESPEARE, *Merry Wives of Windsor.*

Solde, *m.* (familiar), cigare de —, *bad cigar.* Dîner de —, *bad dinner.*

Soleil, *m.* (familiar), avoir un coup de —, *to be the worse for liquor.* See **Pompette.** Piquer un coup de —, *to blush.* Recevoir un coup de —, *to be in love, to be* "mashed on, or sweet on."

Soliçage, *m.* (thieves'), *sale.*

Solicer, or **sollicer** (thieves'), *to sell,* or "to do ;" *to steal,* or "to claim ;" — sur le verbe, *to buy on credit,* "on tick."

Soliceur, or **sollisseur**, *m.* (thieves'), *tradesman ;* — à la gourre, *a swindler who sells to simple-minded persons worthless articles ;* — à la pogne, *pedlar ;* — de lacets, *gendarme ;* — de zif, *rogue who sells imaginary goods and exhibits genuine samples to entice the purchaser.*

Solir, or **salir** (thieves'), *to sell,* "to do." Le —, *the belly,* or "tripes." From a similarity of sound between vendre, *to sell,* and ventre, *belly.*

Solitaire, *m.* (thieves'), *one who operates single-handed.*

Les tireurs se divisent en deux classes : le solitaire et le compagnon. Le premier, son nom l'indique, opère toujours seul ; il constitue l'exception dans l'honorable confrérie des tireurs.—PIERRE DELCOURT.

(Theatrical) Solitaire, *man who only pays half-price on condition that he shall applaud.* Etre en —, *is said of members of the claque or staff of paid applauders who are distributed among the audience.*

Puis on envoie quelques romains en solitaire, c'est-à-dire qu'on permet à ceux-là de se placer seuls au milieu des payants.—BALZAC.

Soliveau, *m.* (popular), *head,* or "nut."

Sombre, *f.* (thieves'), *the Préfecture de Police.*

Sommier de caserne, *m.* (popular), *prostitute who prowls about barracks,* "barrack hack."

Somno, *m.* (popular), *sleep,* or "balmy."

Son, *m. and adj.* (thieves'), *gold,* or "red ;" — nière, or — gniasse, *me, him.*

Sonde, *f.* (popular and thieves'), *physician,* or "pill-box." Etre à la —, *to be cunning, wary,* "downy."

Sondeur, *m. and adj.* (popular), *official of the octroi,* thus termed from his long probe. Aller en —, *to act prudently.* Père —, *wily man,* "leary bloke." Aller en père —, *to seek adroitly for information.* (Thieves') *spy,* or "nark ;" *barrister,* or "mouthpiece." Les sondeurs, *the police,* or "reelers." (Familiar) Un —, *an amateur of the fair sex who at places of entertainment casts a lecherous glance on the charms of ladies with low dresses, and strives to see more than that which is exhibited,* one who would not say like Tartufe—

Cachez, cachez ce sein que je ne saurais voir.

Sonne, *f.* (thieves'), *the police,* "reelers."

Sonner (popular and thieves'), *to strike ; to kill a man by knocking his head on the pavement.*

Route d'Allemagne. L'endroit où des coquins . . . ont sonné l'an dernier un inspecteur de police, mort le lendemain de ses blessures.—P. MAHALIN.

Se la —, *to have a hearty meal.*

Sonnette, *f.* (popular), *silver coin,* or "gingle boy." That which rings, chinks.

J'accours à l'Opéra et les sonnet's en poche.—DÉSAUGIERS.

Des sonnettes, *money.* Scottish gipsies call money "sonnachie." The French slang has "graisse," *fat,* which reminds one of the proverbial expression, "graisser le marteau."

On avait beau heurter et m'ôter son chapeau,
On n'entrait point chez nous sans graisser le marteau
Point d'argent, point de suisse.
RACINE, *Les Plaideurs.*

Sonnette, *young Sodomist.* The quotation will explain the allusion :—

Le duc de Mantoue, qu'on appelait le Gobin, parcequ'il estoit fort bossu, voulant espouser la sœur de l'empereur Maximilian, il fut dict à elle qu'il estoit fort bossu. Elle respondit, dict-on : "non importa pur ché la campana habia qualche diffetto, ma ch'el sonaglio sia buono ;" voulant entendre le Cazzo mantuan.—BRANTOME.

Sonnettes,—the signification may be gathered from the following :—

Je ne voudrois pas être
La femme d'un châtré.
Ils ont le menton tout pelé
Et n'ont point de sonnettes.
Parnasse des Muses.

(Familiar) Une — de nuit, *silk tuft on a lady's hood.* (Prisoners') Une —, *woman employed on the staff of assistants at the prison of Saint-Lazare.* (Printers') Des sonnettes, *badly-adjusted type.*

Sophie, *f.* (popular), de carton, *girl of indifferent character.* Faire sa —, *to put on prudish, disdainful,* or "uppish" *airs.*

Sans doute, il trouvait Lantier un peu fiérot, l'accusait de faire sa Sophie devant

le vitriol, le blaguait parce qu'il savait lire
. . . mais à part ça, il le déclarait un bougre
à poils.—Zola, *L'Assommoir.*

Ne fais donc pas ta — ! *don't put
on such airs!* or, as the Americans
say, "come off the tall grass !"

Sorbonne, *f.* (thieves'), *head.* See
Tronche.

Je suis sûr de cromper sa Sorbonne des
griffes de la Cigogne.—Balzac.

The term must have been first
used by students of the University.

Sorbonner (thieves'), *to think.*

Sorgabon, *m.* (thieves'), *good night,*
"bene darkmans" in old English
cant. An inversion of bonne
sorgue.

Sorgue, or **sorne,** *f.* (thieves'),
night. From the Spanish cant
sorna.

Belle fichue vie que d'avoir continuelle-
ment le taf des griviers, des cognes, des
rousses et des gerbiers, que de n'pas savoir
le matois si on pioncera la sorgue dans
son pieu, que de n'pas pouvoir entendre
aquiger à sa lourde sans que l'palpitant
vous fasse tic-tac.—Vidocq.

Faire dévaler la — à quelqu'un,
to make one reveal à secret.

Emmener la Maugrabine, la faire dévaler
la sorgue des autres ! elle ne dit pas une
parole de vrai.—Louise Michel.

Se refaire de —, *to have supper.*

Si au lieu de pitancher de l'eau d'aff
nous allions nous refaire de sorgue chez
l'ogresse du Lapin Blanc ?—E. Sue.

Sorguer (thieves'), *to sleep,* "to
doss."

Content de sorguer sur la dure,
Va, de la bride je n'ai pas peur.
Ta destinée est trop peu sûre,
Fais-toi gouêpeur.
                    Vidocq.

Sorgueur, *m.* (thieves'), *night
thief.*

Les sorgueurs vont sollicer des gails à
la lune.—V. Hugo.

Sorlot, *m.* (thieves'), *shoe,* or
"daisy root." See **Ripaton.**

Sorne, *adj.* (thieves'), *black.*

Sort (popular), il me —, an abbreviation of a filthy expression,
I cannot bear the sight of him.

Sorte, *f.* (printers'), *fib ; nonsense,*
"gammon ;" *practical joke.*
Conter une —, *to tell a fib.* Faire
une —, *to play a practical joke.*

Sortie d'hôpital, *f.* (popular), *long
overcoat.*

Sortir (popular), les pieds devant,
to be buried. Avoir l'air de —
d'une boîte, *to be neatly dressed,
to be spruce.*

Sosie-mannequin, *m.* (military),
*bolster arranged so as to represent
a man in bed.*

Il était impossible en effet que son sosie-
mannequin ne fût pas pris pour lui.—
Dubois de Gennes.

Soubise. See **Enfant.**

Soubrette de Charlot, *f.* (popular),
executioner's assistant.

Souche, *f.* (popular), fumer une
—, *to be buried,* "to have been
put to bed with a shovel."

Soudardant, *adj.* (old cant), *said of
anything referring to soldiers.*

Soudrillard, *m.* (thieves'), *libertine,*
"rip."

Soufflant, *m.* (thieves'), *pistol,* or
"barking iron ;" (military) *bugler.*
Termed also "trompion."

L'appel aux trompettes vient éveiller les
échos . . . et un quart d'heure ne s'était pas
écoulé, que tous les soufflants firent résonner
en chœur la retentissante fanfare du réveil.
—Dubois de Gennes.

Soufflé, *adj.* (thieves'), *caught ;
apprehended by the police,*
"smugged." See **Piper.**

Souffler (popular), des pois, *to
snore,* "to drive one's pigs to

market ; " — sa chandelle, *to use one's fingers as a pocket-handker-chief;* — sa veilleuse, *to die,* "to snuff it ; " — ses clairs, *to sleep.* (Thieves') Souffler, *to apprehend.*

Si dans l'intervalle il était soufflé jamais la bande ne mangeait le morceau.—CLAUDE.

Souffler la camoufle, *to kill,* "to hush."

C'est pour elle que son chevalier a soufflé la camoufle d'une vieille rentière.—LOUISE MICHEL.

La donne souffle mal, *the police are suspicious.*

Soufflet, *m.* (popular), *head; breech.* Avoir donné un — à sa pelure, *to wear a coat that has been turned.* Vol au —, *consists in boxing a lady's ears while pretending to be an irate husband, and leaving her minus her purse.*

Souffleur, *m.* (popular), de boudin, *chubby-faced fellow;* — de poireau, *flute player.*

Soufrante, *f.* (thieves'), *lucifer match,* "spunk."

Souillot, *m.* (popular), *low debauchee.*

Soulager (familiar), *to steal,* "to ease."

Soulasse, *f.* (thieves'), *informer,* or "snitcher." Faire la grande — sur le trimar, *to practise high-way robbery and murder,* or "high Toby consarn." Also to be " on the snaffle-lay."

I thought by your look you had been a clever fellow, and upon the snaffling-lay at least, but I find you are some sneaking budge.—FIELDING, *Amelia.*

Soulever (familiar), *to steal.*

Souliers, *m. pl.* (familiar), à musique, *creaking shoes;* — seize, *tight shoes.* See **Seize.** Souliers se livrant à la boisson, *leaky shoes.*

Soulographe, *m.* (familiar), *confirmed drunkard.*

Soulographie, *f.* (familiar), *intoxication.*

Tiens, voilà dix francs. Si je les leur donne, Monsieur, ils feront de la soulographie et adieu votre typographie.—BALZAC.

Souloir, *m.* (thieves'), *drinking glass,* or "flicker ; " — des ratichons, *the altar.*

Soupape, *f.* (popular), serrer la —, *to strangle.* Faire cracher ses soupapes, *to get drunk.*

Soupe, *f.* (familiar and popular), marchand de —, *schoolmaster,* " bum brusher."

Style de marchand de soupe . . . une lettre de directeur d'institution. . . . " Je suis très mécontent d'Armand qui après avoir perdu sa grammaire, a trouvé le moyen d'égarer son arithmétique."—SI Armand a perdu sa grammaire, le directeur nous semble l'avoir légèrement oubliée.—ZADIG, *Le Voltaire.*

Marchande de —, *head of a ladies' school.*

Elle me bassine, la marchande de soupe ! Dis-lui donc de me flanquer la paix, hein, à cette vieille cramponne !—ALBERT CIM.

Une — au lait, *a man easily moved to anger.* Une — de perroquet, *bread soaked in wine.* (Popular) Faire manger la — au poireau, *to make one wait a long time.*

Soupente, *f.* (popular), *the belly or stomach,* "middle piece." Je t'vas défoncer la — à coups de sorlots, *I'll kick the life out of you.* Vieille — ! *old slut !*

Souper (popular), de la tronche à quelqu'un, *to be disgusted with one.* See **Fiole.** En —, *to be sick of it.*

Soupeser (popular), se faire —, *to be reprimanded,* "to get a wigging."

Soupe-tout-seul, *m.* (popular), *bearish fellow.*

Je les entendois dire entre elles, parlant de moy : c'est un ry-gris (rit-gris), un loup-garou, un soupe-tout-seul.— *Les Maistres d'Hostel aux Halles.*

Soupeuse, *f.* (familiar), *woman fond of " cabinets particuliers " at restaurants.*

Souquer (popular), *to scold, or to thrash.*

Sourde, *f.* (thieves'), *prison,* " stir."

Souricière, *f.* (prisoners'), *dépôt at the Préfecture de Police.*

La voiture, après avoir versé à la souricière son chargement de coquins.—GA-BORIAU.

(Police) *Souricière,* *trap laid by the police.*

L'on a établi une souricière au tapis du Bien Venu. Avez-vous envie d'aller vous fourrer dedans ?—VIDOCQ.

Souris, *f.* (popular), *a kiss on the eye.* Faire une —, *to give a kiss on the eye.*

Ah ! mon minet . . . je te ferais plutôt une souris.—VIDOCQ.

Faire la —, *to tickle with the finger tips.*

Sous (military), être en — verge, *to be second in command.*

Sous-maîtresse, *f.* (brothels'), *kind of female overseer employed at such establishments.*

Sous-merde, *f.* (popular), *man of utter insignificance ; utterly contemptible man,* " snot."

Sous-off, *m.* (military), *non-com-missioned officer.*

— J'étais simple sous-off.
— Sous-lieutenant ?
— Eh ! non, sous-off. Nous disons sous-off, nous autres, abréviation de sous-officier.—HECTOR FRANCE.

Sous-ouille, *m.* (popular), *shoe,* or " trotter-case."

Sous-pied, *m.* (military), *tough piece of meat.* Properly *foot-strap.* Sous-pied de dragon, *infantry soldier,* " mud-crusher."

Soussouille, *f.* (popular), *slatternly girl.* From souillon.

Sous-ventrière, *f.* (popular), *sash of a mayor,* his insignia of office. See **Faire.**

Soutados, *m.* (familiar), *one-sou cigar.*

Soute au pain, *f.* (popular), *stomach,* or " bread-basket."

Soutellas, *m.* (popular), *one-sou cigar.*

Soutenante, *f.* (thieves'), *stick,* or " toko."

Soutirer au caramel (popular), *to wheedle one out of his money.*

Soyeux, *m.* (shopmen's), *an assis-tant in the silk department,* the lady assistant being termed " so-yeuse."

Spade, *f.* (old cant), *sword,* or " poker." From spada.

Spec, *m.* (thieves'), *bacon,* or " sawney." From the German.

Spectre, *m.* (familiar), *old debt ;* (gamesters') — de banco, *ruined gamester who moves round the tables without playing.*

Stafer (thieves'), *to say,* " to rap."

Stick, *m.* (familiar), *small cane sported by dandies,* " swagger."

Ils brandissent d'un air vainqueur une cravache ou un stick minuscule suivant qu'ils sont dans la garde à cheval ou à pied.—HECTOR FRANCE.

Stores, *m. pl.* (popular), *eyes,* or " peepers." Baisser les —, *to close one's eyes.*

Stoubinen (Breton cant), *woman of indifferent character.*

Strapontin, *m.* (journalists'), *pad worn under the dress, bustle,* or "bird-cage."

Une vitrioleuse lâchée par son amant, alla tout tranquillement trouver son voisin l'épicier, lui demanda une petite fiole de la liqueur en question, la cacha avec soin, peut-être sous son "strapontin."—*Un Flâneur.*

(Journalists') En —, explained by quotation :—

Lié à un grand nom, leur petit nom vivra ; c'est ce que j'appelle aller à la postérité en strapontin, c'est-à-dire en lapin, par-dessus le marché, en compagnie d'un important qui se carre à la bonne place et paie la course : Corbinelli en strapontin avec la marquise de Sévigné ; Brouette en strapontin avec Boileau ; d'Argental et autres en strapontin avec Voltaire. Si la postérité, laissant passer Voltaire, prétend barrer le tourniquet à d'Argental et demande : " Quel est ce gentilhomme ? " Voltaire se retourne pour dire : " C'est quelqu'un de ma suite."—A. DUBRUJEAUD.

Stroc, *m.* (thieves'), *a "setier," small measure of wine.*

Stropiat, *m.* (thieves'), *lame beggar.*

Mes braves bons messieurs et dames,
Par Sainte-Marie-Notre-Dame,
Voyez le pauvre vieux stropiat.
Pater noster ! Ave Maria !
Ayez pitié.

RICHEPIN.

Stuc, *m.* (thieves'), *share of booty,* "regulars."

Style, *m.* (popular), *money.* See **Quibus.**

Stylé, *adj.* (popular), *well-dressed ; rich.*

Suage, *m.* (thieves'), *killing; murder.* From *suer, to sweat.* Faire suer has the signification of *to kill.*

Suageur, *m.* (thieves'), *murderer.*

Subir l'écart (gamesters'), *to lose.*

Un joueur n'avoue jamais qu'il perd, il a horreur du mot perdre, il subit seulement un écart.—*Mémoires de Monsieur Claude.*

Sublime, *m.* (popular), *lazy, good-for-nothing workman.*

Fils d'une poitrinaire et d'un sublime, il était à la fois phtisique et rachitique.—RICHEPIN.

Sublimer (students'), *to work hard, especially at night.* (Popular) Se —, *to become debased.*

Sublimeur, *m.* (students'), *hard-working student,* a "swot."

Sublimisme, *m.* (popular), *idleness ; degradation.*

Subtiliser (popular), *to steal,* "to ease." See **Grinchir.**

Suçage de pomme, *m.* (popular), *kissing.*

Succès. See **Estime.**

Succession, *f.* (familiar), côtelette à —, *a very inferior chop,* one which is indigestible enough to give one's heirs a chance.

Quand sous l'émail de leurs dents de crocodile, elles ont dévoré . . . le beefteack à la Borgia et la "côtelette de succession" des alchimistes à prix fixe du Palais-Royal. —P. MAHALIN.

Suce-larbin, *m.* (thieves'), *office for servants out of place.* Larbin is a "flunkey."

Sucer (popular), *to drink,* "to liquor up ; " — la fine côtelette, *to have a " déjeuner à la fourchette ;"* — le caillou, la pomme, or le trognon, *to kiss.* Se — les pouces, *to have nothing to eat.*

Elle mettrait la main sur la monnaie, elle achèterait les provisions. Une petite heure d'attente au plus elle avalerait bien encore ça, elle qui se suçait les pouces depuis la veille.—ZOLA.

Suceur, *m.* (theatrical), *parasite,* or "quiller ; " (popular) — de pomme, *one fond of kissing girls.*

Suçon, *m.* (familiar and popular), *stick of barley sugar ; small bruise* *produced by a kiss given in a peculiar way, by sucking the spot.*

Un soir elle reçut encore une danse parcequ'elle lui avait trouvé une tache noire au cou. La mâtine osait dire que ce n'était pas un suçon !—ZOLA.

Sucre, *m.* (popular), à cochon, *salt.* C'est un — ! *that's excellent,* "real jam." Sucre ! *euphemism for a coarse word,* may be rendered by "go to pot ;" — de giroflées, *cuffs.*

Et cependant, bien sûr une bonne roulée le remettrait au Nord. Ah ! c'est la vieille qui devrait se charger de ça, lui tricoter les joues, lui flanquer une double ration de sucre de giroflées.—RICHEPIN.

Allez vous faire sucre ! *go to the deuce !* (Military) Casser du — à deux sous le mètre cube, *to be in the punishment companies, breaking stones.* (Thieves') Sucre de pommes, *short crowbar,* "jemmy."

Sucrer (familiar), *to fondle, to spoil one.*

Sucrier, *m.* (familiar), *man suffering from diabetes.* Alluding to the quantity of sugar generated by the kidneys.

Malheureusement pour lui, il est diabétique au suprême degré. Ce n'est pas un homme, c'est un sucrier.—A. SIRVEN.

Suée, *f.* (popular), *reprimand,* or "wigging ;" *fear,* "funk ;" — de monde, *large crowd.*

Suer (general), ça m'fait —, *that* "riles" *me, disgusts me.*

Ça m'fait suer, quand j'ai l'onglée,
D'voir des chiens qu'ont un habit !
Quand, par les temps de gelée,
Moi j'n'ai rien, pas même un lit.
DE CHATILLON.

Faire — des lames de rasoir, *to bore.*

Oh ! assez, hein ? Tu nous fais suer des lames de rasoir en travers.—E. MONTEIL.

Faire — son argent, *to be a usurer,* or *to invest one's money at a high* percentage. Faire — les cordes, *to play on a stringed instrument.* Faire — le cuivre, *to play on a brass instrument.* (Theatrical) Faire — le lustre, *to play in such a wretched manner that even the claqueurs are disgusted.* (Thieves') Faire suer, *to kill.* See **Chêne.**

Sueur de cantonnier, *f.* (popular), *a thing of rare occurrence.* A cantonnier is a labourer employed in the repairing of roads, and is supposed to be extremely lazy.

Sufficit ! (popular), *enough ! I understand,* "I twig."

Suffisance, *f.* (popular), avoir sa —, *to have drunk as much liquor as one can imbibe.*

Suif, *m.* (popular), *money ; reprimand,* "wigging." Flanquer un —, *to give a* "wigging." Gober son —, *to be reprimanded.* (Sharpers') Suif, *concourse of card-sharpers.* (Boulevards) Un —, *a dinner for which one has not to pay.*

Il . . . était heureux de trouver au cercle un bon dîner qui ne lui coutât rien,—le "suif."—HECTOR MALOT.

Suiffard, *m.* and *adj.* (popular), *stylish man ; rich ; stylish.*

Etait-il assez suiffard, l'animal ! Un vrai propriétaire ; du linge blanc et des escarpins un peu chouettes !—ZOLA.

Suiffé, *adj.* and *f.* (popular), *fine ; well-dressed ; stylish.* Une femme suiffée, *a stylish woman.* Une —, *a thrashing.*

Suifferie, *f.* (popular), *gaming-house,* or "punting-shop." A play on the word grèce.

Suisse, *m.* (military), *guest.* See **Faire.**

Suissesse, *f.* (popular), *glass of absinthe and orgeat.* From absinthe suisse.

Suiver (sailors'), se — l'estomac, *to make a hearty meal.*

Suiveur, *m.* (familiar), *man who makes a practice of following women ;* (prostitutes') *man who follows a prostitute.*

La grisette dévoyée qui se fait suivre et conduit le suiveur dans un hôtel borgne.—Léo Taxil.

Suivez-moi jeune homme, *m.* (familiar), *ribbons hanging from a lady's cloak.*

Nous avons gardé nos suivez-moi jeune homme.—Grévin.

The English have a similar expression to designate curls hanging over a lady's shoulder, " follow-me-lads."

Sultan, *m.* (theatrical), *the public.*

Suna (Breton cant), *to be a parasite.*

Suner (Breton cant), *parasite.*

Superlificoquentieux, *adj.* (familiar), *marvellous,* " crushing."

Supin, *m.* (thieves'), *soldier.* Probably from soupe, the staple fare of the soldier.

Sur le gril (thieves'), être —, *to be awaiting judgment.*

Surbin, *m.* (thieves'), *overseer ; spy.*

Surbine, *f.* (thieves'), *watching,* or " roasting ;" *surveillance by the police of a ticket-of-leave man.*

Surbiner (thieves'), *to watch one,* " to give one a roasting."

Surclouer (popular), *to renew a loan at a pawnshop.*

Surfine, *f.* (thieves'), *a variety of female thief.*

Surgerbement, *m.* (thieves'), *fresh conviction in the Cour de Cassation.*

Surgerber (thieves'), *to convict on appeal.*

Surie, *f.* (old cant), *killing.* Literally *sweating.*

Surin, or **chourin,** *m.* (thieves'), *knife,* or "chive ;" — muet, *life-preserver,* " neddy." Scottish gipsies call a knife or bayonet a "chourie."

Suriner, or **chouriner** (thieves'), *to stab,* " to stick."

Les malfaiteurs lui prirent sa montre . . . si tu cries, nous te surinons.—*Le Radical,* 1887.

Surineur, or **chourineur,** *m.* (thieves'), *murderer.*

Surmouleur, *m.* (literary), *writer who imitates the defective features of another's style of writing.*

Surprenante, *f.* (gamesters'), *one of the modes employed in arranging cards for cheating purposes.*

Surrincette, *f.* (familiar and popular), *second help of brandy after coffee.*

Surse, *m.* (shopmen's), faire le —, *to be on the look-out for the master.* From **Sur-seize** (which see).

Sur-seize ! (shopmen's), *warning call when the master is approaching.*

Surtaille, *f.* (thieves'), *detective force.* From sûreté.

Sydonie (hairdressers'), *dummy.*

Sylphider (popular), se —, *to disappear,* " to mizzle."

Symbole, *m.* (popular), *head,* or " nut ;" *credit,* or "jawbone."

Symphoneries, *f. pl.* (popular), *nonsense,* or " rot." Lâcher des —, *to talk nonsense.*

Synagogue (popular), c'est —, *it comes to the same thing.*

Système, *m.* (popular), *the body.* Taper sur le —, *to annoy ; to exasperate,* "to rile." Se faire sauter le —, *to blow one's brains out.* Système ballon, *pregnancy ;* — Jardinière, *complete suit of clothes.* An allusion to La Belle Jardinière, a large outfitting firm ; — Pinaud, *silk hat.* From the name of a celebrated hat-maker. Rompre le —, *to irritate,* " to "rile." S'en faire péter le —, *to undertake a task to which one is not equal.* Tu t'en ferais péter le —, *is expressive of ironical refusal.* See **Nèfles.**

 **ABAC,** *m.* (students'), *old student;* (military) — à deux sous la brouette, *canteen tobacco;* (popular) — de démoc, *cigar ends chopped up.* Etre dans le —, *to be in trouble, in difficulties.* Foutre, or coller du —, *to thrash.* This was termed formerly, "coller une prune, une chasteloigne, une aumône de Bourgogne, un oignement de Bretagne, de la monnaie de l'empire."

Tabatière, *f.* (popular), *the behind.*

Tabernacle, *m.* (popular), *the behind.* Défoncer le —, *to kick one's behind.*

Table, *f.* (familiar), mettre les pieds sous la —, *to eat.* Faire le tour de la —, *to eat of every dish.*

Table d'hôte. See **Avoir.**

Tableau, *m.* (popular), je comprends le —, *I see what it is,* I "catch on," as the Americans say. Tableau ! *exclamation expressive of comical surprise or malicious joy at the sight of some laughable accident.*

> Tiens pig's-tu la lun' qui s'ballade ?
> Que'qu'a boit donc, c'te bourriqu'-là

Pour avoir la gueul' blanch' comme ça ?
Y a pas d'bon sens. Vrai, que' panade !
Si j'y payais un lit' ?—Tableau !
  Gill, *La Muse à Bibi.*

(Sportsmen's) Tableau, *the* "bag."

> Madame d'— qui est une sportswoman des plus intrépides portait un superbe costume de chasse, c'est elle qui a eu les honneurs de la journée en tuant 44 pièces. Le tableau était superbe, il portait 204 pièces. —*Le Figaro,* Oct., 1886.

Tableau-radis, *m.* (artists'), *picture returned unsold from the Arts Exhibition or from a picture-dealer's.*

Tableautin, *m.* (artists'), *worthless picture,* or "daub."

Tablier, *m.* (popular), blanc, *nurserymaid.* Le — lève *is said of a woman in a state of advanced pregnancy.* Faire lever le — à une femme, *to get a woman with child, to give her a* "white swelling."

Tabouret, *m.*, figure à — (obsolete), *one who was put in the pillory with an iron collar round his neck, or one likely to be put there.*

> Va donc, figure à tabouret,
> J't'irons voir en face le Palais ;
> C'est là qu't'auras l'air d'un butor,
> Monsieur l'négociant z'en chiens morts.
>   *Riche-en-gueule.*

Taf, or **taffe,** *m.* (popular and thieves'), *fear,* "funk."

Je n'ai pas coqué mon centre, de taffe du ravignolé, ainsi si vouzailles brodez à

mézigue il faut balancer la lazagne au centre de J. au castu de Canelle.—Vidocq.

Avoir le —, *to be afraid,* "to
come it."

— Que veux-tu, Zénobie? chacun a sa
misère. Le lièvre a le taf, le chien les
puces, le loup la faim . . . l'homme a la
soif—Et la femme a l'ivrogne !—Gavarni.

Coquer le —, *to frighten.* Etre
pris de —, *to be seized by fear.*

Seigneur ! qu'est-ce qu'il a donc, répétait Gervaise prise de taf.—Zola.

Michel is inclined to believe that
taf comes from a proverbial locution, "les fesses lui font taf taf,"
he is quaking with terror, or "le
cul lui fait tif taf." According to
L. Larchey the corresponding
verb "taffer" is derived from the
German taffein.

Taffer, *m.* (popular and thieves'),
to be afraid. See **Taf.**

Taffetas, *m.* (thieves'), *fear.* From
Taf (which see).

Le taffetas les fera dévider et tortiller la
planque où est le carle.—Vidocq.

Taffeur, *m.* (popular and thieves'),
poltroon.

Taffouilleux, *m.* (popular), explained by quotation :—

Chiffonnier de la Seine, écumant ses
bords, ramassant les épaves et volant au
besoin.—F. du Boisgobey.

Literally un qui fouille dans le tas.

Tafia, *m.* (popular), *coffee.* Properly *sweet rum.*

Tailbin d'altèque, *m.* (thieves'),
bank note, or "long-tailed one."

S'ils ne vous coquaient pas dix tailbins
d'altèque de mille balles, vous mangeriez
sur leur orgue.—Vidocq.

Tailbin is derived from the old
cant word talle, *tail.*

Tailler une bazane (popular), *to
make a certain contemptuous gesture.* See **Bazane.**

Et tandis que du revers de sa main il se
caressait le menton, de l'autre il se giffla la
cuisse, taillant une bazane gigantesque au
nez du colonel absent.—G. Courteline.

(Cavalry) Tailler une croupière,
to surpass; (schoolboys')—l'école,
to play truant.

Tais-toi mon cœur! (popular),
*an ejaculation expressive of mock
emotion.*

Tal, *m.* (popular), *the behind,* or
"tochas." Taper dans le —, *to
be a Sodomist.*

Talar (Breton cant), *meal.*

Talbin, *m.* (thieves'), *attorney;
note of hand;* — de la carre,
bank note, or "soft;" — d'encarrade, *theatre ticket.* Literally
entrance ticket. See **Tailbin.**

Talbine, *f.* (thieves'), *market.*

Talbiner (thieves'), *to summons.*

Talbinier, *m.* (thieves'), *dealer at
a market.*

Talentueux, *adj.* (familiar),
talented.

Taleri (Breton cant), *to eat.*

Talochon, *m.* (popular), *slight box
on the ear.*

Talon, *m.* (familiar), rouge, *aristocrat.* In the seventeenth century
courtiers wore red-heeled shoes.
Etre — rouge jocularly means *to
have aristocratic manners.* Avoir
les talons courts. Rigaud says :—

Se dit d'une femme que le moindre
souffle de l'amour renverse dans la position
horizontale.—*Dict. d'Argot.*

(Popular) Talon, *postscript.* Se
donner du — dans le cul (obsolete),
to strut.

Tout ça c'est bon pour s'aller donner du
talon dans le c . . à une parade, pour
s'quarrer avec d'belles épaulettes. — *Le
Drapeau Rouge de la Mère Duchesne.*

Faire tête du — (obsolete), *to flee.*

Tambouille, *f.* (popular), *very plain stew ; small kitchen.* Faire sa —, *to busy oneself with the cooking of food.*

Tambour, *m.* (cavalry), *élève brigadier fourrier, or one training to be a kind of quartermaster ;* (thieves') *dog,* or "tyke."

Il n'avait pas déjà si tort de croire au mec des mecs . . . nous n'avons pas été jetés sur la terre pour vivre comme des tambours.—Vidocq.

Roulement de —, *barking of a dog.* Formerly "tambour de nature" signified *woman's privities.* (Military) Foutre au clou comme un —, *to punish a soldier without the slightest compunction, in an off-hand manner.*

Tampon, *m.* (popular), s'allonger un coup de —, *to fight.*

On s'est allongé un coup de tampon, en sortant de chez la mère Baquet. Moi je n'aime pas les jeux de mains . . . vous savez, c'est avec le garçon de la mère Baquet qu'on a eu des raisons.—Zola, *L'Assommoir.*

Tamponne, *f.* (obsolete), faire la —, *to regale oneself.*

Tamponner (popular), *to knock one about.* Also *to annoy ;* — de l'œil, *to stare,* "to stag ;" — l'auriculaire, *to tell.*

Si j'allais trouver vos patrons dans leur boutique pour leur tamponner l'auriculaire de c'lui-ci : Ronchonot, col'nel, décoré, une fesse gelée au siège d'Sébastopol, massacré d'blessures, sans compter les chevaux tués sous lui.—G. Frison.

See **Coquillard.**

Tam-tam, *m.* (popular), *quarrel ; great noise.* Faire du —, "to kick up a row."

Tangente, *f.* The students of the Ecole Polytechnique thus term their swords.

Tannant, *adj.* (popular), *irksome, annoying.*

Etes-vous tannante avec vos idées d'enterrement, interrompit Madame Putois, qui n'aimait pas les conversations tristes.—Zola.

Tanner (popular), *to importune,* "to bore ;" — le cuir, or le casaquin, *to thrash,* "to hide." See **Voie.**

De même qu'à Barochon on lui avait infligé : huit jours de mazarot pour s'être fait tanner le cuir par un gars qu'il ne voulait pas nommer.—Dubois de Gennes.

Tante, *f.* (general), ma —, *the pawnshop,* or "my uncle."

Demander . . . à ce grand bohème qui connaissait tous les monts-de-piété parisiens, s'en était servi depuis vingt ans comme de réserves où il mettait l'hiver ses vêtements d'été, l'été ses vêtements d'hiver ! . . . s'il connaissait le clou ! s'il connaissait ma tante !—A. Daudet.

Termed also ma — Dumont, *i.e.* du Mont de Piété, *pawnshop.* Accrocher quelque chose chez sa —, *to pawn an article,* "to spout," to pop, to lumber, or to blue it." (Thieves') Une —, *an informer,* or "nose." (Familiar and popular) Une —, *a passive Sodomist.*

Dans la société ordinaire où ce penchant contre nature est en quelque sorte inné chez certains individus, ces antiphysiques s'appellent tantes ; chez les marins, corvettes ; dans l'armée, étendards. . . . Ces courtisanes, hommes-femmes, sont plus nombreuses qu'on ne le pense dans tous les rangs de la société. Elles forment une franc-maçonnerie qui part du sommet de l'échelle sociale pour se perdre jusque dans ses bas-fonds. — *Mémoires de Monsieur Claude.*

Taouanen (Breton cant), *beggar.*

Taouen (Breton cant), *lice.*

Tap, *m.* (thieves'), *mark with which thieves used to be branded.* The practice was discontinued in 1830. Faire la parade au — meant formerly *to be placed in the pillory.* Jardiner sur le — vert (tapis vert), *to play cards.*

Tapage, *m.* (popular). Rigaud says :—

Séduction exercée sur une femme. Est d'un degré plus relevé que le "levage," en ce sens que la femme "tapée" songe moins à ses interêts qu'au plaisir qu'elle aura.— *Dict. d'Argot.*

Tapage, *borrowing money,* "breaking shins."

Tapamort, *m.* (popular), *drummer.*

Tapance, *f.* (popular), *mistress or wife.* Literally *a thing made to be beaten.* Termed a "tart" in the English slang, as appears from the following :—

Two bally black eyes !
Oh ! what a surprise !
And that only for kissing another man's tart.
Two bally black eyes.
Music-hall Song.

La — du meg, *the employer's wife.*

Tapé, *adj.* (general), *good; excellent,* or "nap;" *well got up.*

Jupiter avait une bonne tête, Mars était tapé.—ZOLA.

(Popular) Tapé à l'as, or dans le nœud, "first-class, or ripping; " — aux pommes, *excellent; welldressed; handsome.*

Une particulière tapée aux pommes. Pas cocotte pour deux liards. Jamais je n'en ai vu une pareille venir dans la boîte à Monsieur.—P. MAHALIN.

Tape-cul, *m.* (cavalry), aller à —, *to ride without stirrups.*

Tape-dur, *m.* (thieves'), *locksmith.*

Tapée, *f.* (familiar), *a quantity,* a "lot."

Taper (familiar and popular), *to borrow money,* "to bite one's ear."

Il songea un instant à taper Théophile, mais il était déjà son débiteur de dix louis. —VAST RICOUARD, *Le Tripot.*

Du vin qui tape sur la boule, *wine that is heady.* Taper dans le tas, *to strike at random;* — sur le ventre à quelqu'un, *to be familiar or intimate with one;* — sur les vivres et sur la bitture, *to eat and drink much;* (popular) — dans le tas, *to act in a straightforward blunt manner.* Se — de quelquechose, *to do without or deprive oneself of something.* S'en —, *to drink to excess,* "to swill." (Roughs') Taper sur la réjouissance, *to thrash.* Réjouissance is bone added by butchers to meat retailed.

Tapette, *f.* (familiar and popular), *passive Sodomist; chatterbox.* Avoir une fière —, *to be a great talker.*

Tapeur, *m.* (familiar), *needy man who lives on small loans which he procures from acquaintances.*

Il va, il revient, il arpente le trottoir. Il a la guigne aujourd'hui . . . celui-ci couperait peut-être dans le pont ? mais quoi ! il a déjà casqué hier . . . il désespère, car il entend partir derrière lui, de toutes les tables, ce mot cruel : attention ! voilà le tapeur !—RICHEPIN.

Tapeuse de tal (popular), *prostitute.* See **Tal.**

Tapin, *m.* (popular), *drum; drummer.* Ficher un —, *to give a blow.* Ficher le — (obsolete), *to importune.*

Tapiquer (thieves'), *to inhabit.*

Tapis, *m.* (familiar), amuser le —, *to divert the company by pleasant conversation.* Cheval qui rase le —. See **Rase-tapis.** (Gamesters') Le — brûle ! *expression used to excite one into playing.* Jardiner sur le — vert, *to gamble.* Etre au —, *to have lost all one's money.* (Popular) Le — bleu, *the skies.* Tapis de pied, *courtier.* (Thieves') Tapis, *wine-shop; inn;* — de dégelés, *the Morgue, or Paris dead-house;* — d'endosse,

G G

shawl ; — de grives, *soldiers' canteen ;* — de malades, *prison canteen ;* — de refaite, *eating-house ;* — vert, *gaming-house,* or "*punting-shop ;*" *thieves' coffee-house ; meadow.*

Tapisserie, *f.* (familiar), faire —, *is said of ladies at a ball, who, being neglected for some reason or other by gentlemen devoid of gallantry, are compelled to sit and look on as mere spectators.* This unpleasantness is termed "doing the wall-flower." (Gamesters') Avoir de là —, *to have several figure-cards in one's game.*

Tapissier, *m.* (thieves'), *inn-keeper,* or *landlord of a wine-shop,* "boss of a lush-crib."

Nous ne voulons enquiller chez aucun tapissier.—VIDOCQ.

(Gamblers') Allumeur —, *confederate who entices others into playing, but who does not take an active part in the game.*

Celle qui vit du jeu et des joueurs, depuis les gros mangeurs. . . jusqu'aux rameneurs, aux dîneurs, aux allumeurs-tapissiers.—HECTOR MALOT.

Tapon, *m.* (popular), *heap of rags.* Mettre sa cravate en —, *to tie one's necktie in a slovenly manner.*

Tapoter (familiar), *to be an indifferent player on the piano.*

Tapoteur, *m.* (familiar), *indifferent pianist.*

Tapotoir, *m.* (cocottes'), *the piano.*

Taqueté (ballet dancers'), explained by quotation :—

C'est la vivacité, la rapidité, ce sont les petits temps sur les pointes.—CH. DE BOIGNE.

Taquiner (popular), le dandillon, *to ring,* "to jerk the tinkler ;" — les dents d'éléphant, *to play the piano.*

Tarauder (popular), *to make a disagreeable noise by shifting chairs about ; to thrash.* Se —, *to quarrel ; to fight.*

Tard-à-la-soupe, *m.* (popular), *guest who is late for dinner.*

Tariek (Breton cant), *tobacco ; tip of money.*

Taroque, *f.* (thieves'), *mark on linen.*

Taroquer (thieves'), *to mark linen.*

Tarre, *f.* (thieves'), vol à la —, *picking pocket-handkerchiefs,* or "stook-hauling."

Tartare, *m.* (tailors'), *apprentice.*

Tarte, tartelette, *adj.* (thieves'), *bad, spurious,* or "snide." The word snite is found in Urquhart's *Rabelais,* with the modern signification of "snot," or base fellow:—

Here enter not vile bigots, hypocrites, Externally devoted apes, base snites.

Or in Rabelais' words :—

Ci n'entrez pas hypocrites, bigots, Vieux matagots, mariteux boursoflé.

Tarte bourbonnaise (obsolete), *lump of excrement,* or "quaker."

Tarter, tartir (popular and thieves'), *to ease oneself by evacuation.* In furbesche "tartire" has the same signification, and also means *to ease one's conscience by confessing to a priest.* Ça m'fait —, *that bores me.*

J'couch' que'qu'fois sur un banc d'gare ; Mais l'ch'min d'fer à côté Fait tout l'temps du tintamarre. Les ronfleurs, ça m'fait tarter. RICHEPIN.

Tartine, *f.* (familiar), *dull, long speech,* or *writing.* (Popular) Des tartines, *shoes,* or *boots,* "trotter-cases."

Fais donc au moins cirer tes tartines. . . . C'qu'elles sont sales ! Ah ! j'avais pas pigé l'coup ! C'est pas des pieds, mon vieux, c'est des cercueils d'enfant ! C'est-il vrai que c'est là-dessus qu'on va bâtir la tour Eiffel ? Ah ! mince alors.—*Gil Blas,* 1887.

Tartiner (familiar), *to write articles.*

Tartinier, *m.* (familiar), *writer of newspaper articles.*

Tartouiller (popular), *to scribble.*

Tartouve, *f.* (thieves'), *handcuffs,* "bracelets."

> Ils m'ont mis la tartouve,
> Grand Meudon est aboulé,
> Dans mon trimin rencontre,
> Un pègre du quartier.
> V. Hugo, *Le Dernier Jour d'un Condamné.*

Tas, *m.* (popular), *person devoid of energy,* "sappy." Prendre sur le —, *to take one red-handed.* Synonymous of " prendre la main dans le sac." Repiquer au —, *to begin afresh.* (Bullies') Faire le —, or le turbin, *to walk the streets as a prostitute.* (Popular and thieves') Le — de pierres, *the prison,* or " stone jug."

Tous ceux qui rigolent encore à Pantin viennent d'être fourrés dans le tas de pierres.—Vidocq.

Tasse, *f.* (popular), *nose,* or "boko." See **Morviau.** (Familiar) La grande —, *the sea.* Called in the English slang, "briney," "herring-pond," or, in the language of sailors, "Davy's locker." See **Boire.** (Printers') Buvons une —, *let us have a glass of wine.*

Tasseau, *m.* (popular), *the nose.* See **Morviau.** Se sécher le —, *to sneeze.*

Tassée, *adj.* (theatrical). A play is said to be "tassée" when it is performed more rapidly in consequence of the actors knowing their parts better after a few performances.

Tata, *f.* See **Faire, Sécher.**

Tâte-minette, *f.* (popular), *midwife.* Literally *feel pussy.*

Tâte-poule, *m.* (popular), *simple-minded man,* a " duffer."

Tâteur, *m.* (popular), de femmes, *man fond of taking liberties with women.* (Thieves') Tâteur, *skeleton key,* or " betty."

Tâtez-y, *m.* (popular), *trinket worn on the bosom.*

Une bague de cornaline, une paire de manches avec une petite dentelle, un de ces cœurs en doublé, des "tâtez-y" que les filles se mettent entre les deux nénais.—Zola, *L'Assommoir.*

Tatouille, *f.* (popular), *sound thrashing.*

Tatouiller quelqu'un (popular), *to give a sound thrashing,* "to knock into a cocked hat."

Taude, *f.,* **taudion,** *m.* (popular), *small lodging-house, small* "crib." From taudis, *wretched, disorderly room.*

Taule, *m. and f.* (old cant), *executioner,* "Jack Ketch." The various modern or old synonyms are : "Charlot, le père Rasibus, béquillard, buteur, tolle, tollart, aricoteur, rouastre, Charlot casse-bras, marieux, lamboureur." (Thieves') Une —, *a house.*

Etienne Lardenois avait été gerbé à cinq longes de dur, pour un grinchissage au fric-frac dans une taule habitée.—Vidocq.

(Popular) La —, *the head,* "tibby."

> — A-t-il l'air féroce !
> — Il doit avoir tué bien du monde, O le gueux ! ô le scélérat !
> — C'te balle ! oh, c'te taule !—Th. Gautier.

Taupage, *m.* (cads' and thieves'), *selfishness.*

Taupe, *f.* (familiar), *girl of indifferent character ;* (military) — de rempart, *soldier of the engineers.*

Tauper (popular), *to work,* " to graft ; " — dessus, *to thrash.*

Taupier, *m.* (thieves'), *selfish fellow.*

Taupin, *m.* (students'), *student in the division of mathématiques spéciales, or higher mathematics.* Name given specially to those who prepare for the Ecole Polytechnique.

Aussi le jeune Anglais a-t-il le mépris du cul-de-plomb scientifique, du fort en thème, du "book-worm" comme il l'appelle, s'il n'est rembourré de muscles solides ; du taupin, si le taupin est un faiblard.—Hector France.

The "taupins" are divided into "taupin carré" and "taupin cube," respectively *second and third year student in the course of higher mathematics.* (Military) Taupin, *soldier or officer of the engineers.* From taupe, *a mole.*

Taupiner (thieves'), *to murder.*

Taupinière, *f.* (students'), *cramming establishment which prepares candidates for the army.*

Te Deum, *m.* (popular), faire chanter un — raboteux, *to thrash.*

Teigne, *f.* (popular), être —, *to have a bad temper.* Mauvaise —, *snarling, evilly-disposed person.*

Teinté, *adj.* (popular), être —, *to be in a fair way of being intoxicated, to be slightly* " elevated."

Teinturier, *m.* (popular), *wine retailer ;* (familiar) *literary man who revises another's writings.*

Télégraphe, *m.* (familiar), sous-marin, *signals made by lovers by pressure of the foot under a table.* (Gambling cheats') Faire le —, *to stand behind a player and by sundry signals to give information to an accomplice.*

Tempérament, *m.* (familiar), acheter à —, *to buy on the instalment system.*

Ce genre d'opération est très usité entre filles galantes et marchandes à la toilette. Ces dames qui ont le petit mot pour rire, appellent encore ce mode de payement " à tant par amant."—Rigaud.

Tempête. See **Cap.**

Temple, *m.* (freemasons'), *hall of meeting ;* (thieves') *cloak.* Second-hand clothes are mostly sold in the Quartier du Temple.

Temps, *m.* (popular), salé, *warm weather which makes one feel dry ;* — de demoiselle, *weather which is neither hot nor cold ;* (theatrical) — froid, *prolonged silence,* when, for instance, an actor's memory fails him. (Fencing) Voir le coup de —, *to see the feint.*

Tenante, *f.* (thieves'), *pint measure.*

Tendeur, *m.* (cads'), *man under the influence of a well-developed bump of amativeness,* "*homo salax.*" Vieux —, *old debauchee,* old " rip." (Popular) Tendeur de demi-aune, *beggar.*

Tend-la-main (popular), *beggar.*

Tendresse, *f.* (journalists'), *euphemism for prostitute.* Literally vendeuse de tendresses.

Tenir (familiar), la chandelle, *to favour, willingly or unwittingly, the loves of a couple ;* — la corde, *to surpass ; to excel.* En —, *to be in love with,* or "mashed on." Il en tient, *his wife deceives him.* (Popular) Se — à quarante sous avec son croque-mort, *to die hard.* (Theatrical) Cet auteur tient l'affiche, *this author's play has a long run.* (Thieves') Tenir quelqu'un sur les fonts, *to be a witness for the prosecution ;* (sailors') — bien sur ses ancres, *to enjoy good health.*

Ténor, *m.* (journalists'), *writer of leading articles.*

Tenue, *f.* (freemasons'), *meeting.* (Thieves') En petite — de dragon, *in one's shirt, in one's* "mish."

Terreau, *m.* (popular), *snuff.* Se flanquer du — par le tube, *to take snuff.*

Terre-neuve. See **Banc.**

Terrer (thieves'), *to murder; to guillotine.*

On va terrer (guillotiner) Théodore . . . oui Théodore Calvi morfile (mange) sa dernière bouchée.—BALZAC.

Terreur, *f.* (thieves'), *desperate scoundrel of herculean strength who lords it over his fellow-malefactors.*

Chaque quartier, aux portes de Paris, possède sa terreur. Le champs-clos des terreurs . . . se tient aux voisinages de la Roquette ou du Père Lachaise. . . . Là, celui qui a tombé son adversaire a le droit de lui retirer son titre de Terreur dès qu'il parvient à lui manger une partie du nez, à lui supprimer un œil ou la moitié de la mâchoire.—*Mémoires de Monsieur Claude.*

Terreuse, *f.* (popular), *prostitute who prowls about deserted spots.* See **Gadoue.**

Terrien, *m.* (sailors'), *landsman,* or "land-lubber;" (familiar) *peasant,* "clod-hopper."

Terrine, *f.,* être dans la — (obsolete), *to be drunk.*

Terrinière, *f.* (popular), *lowest sort of prostitute,* or "draggle-tail."

Tesson, *m.* (roughs'), *head,* or "tibby."

Têtard, *m.* (popular), *stubborn, or* "pig-headed" *man; long-headed man.*

Bien sorbonné (raisonné), mon homme, tu es toujours le roi des têtards (hommes de tête).—E. SUE.

Tétasses, *f. pl.* (popular), *large, pendulous breasts.* Termed by Voltaire, "grands pendards."

Tétassière, *f.* (popular), *woman with large, lank breasts.*

Tête, *f.* (familiar and popular), de buis, *bald head,* "bladder of lard;" — de canne, or de pipe, *ugly, grotesque head or face,* "knocker-face;" — de choucroûte, or carrée, *German.*

Une superbe paire de pantoufles de satin qu'il avait dénichée, je ne sais où, dans une chambre abandonnée par les "têtes carrées."—*Almanach Illustré de la Petite République Française,* 1887.

Une bonne —, *a simple-minded person, one easily imposed upon.*

Je suis trop bon, on me prend pour une bonne tête. Zut ! à partir de ce matin, je fous tout le monde dedans et voilà !—G. COURTELINE.

Faire sa —, *to give oneself airs.*

Y' a-t'y rien qui vous agace
Comme une levrette en pal'tot !
Quand y'a tant d'gens su' la place
Qui n'ont rien à s'mett' su' l'dos ?

J'ai l'horreur de ces p'tit's bêtes,
J'aim' pas leux museaux pointus ;
J'aim' pas ceux qui font leux têtes
Pass' qu'iz'ont des pardessus.
DE CHATILLON, *La Levrette en Paletot.*

Avoir une — qui dépasse les cheveux, *to be bald,* or "to have a bladder of lard." Avoir une bonne —, *to have a grotesque face.*

— Mon pauvre vieux, si je vous disais que vous avez une bonne tête !
— N'achève pas, ô ange ! tu me la mettrais à l'envers !—*Journal Amusant.*

(Military) Tête mobile, *instructor in musketry;* — à corvées, *blockhead;* (printers') — de clous, *worn-out type;* (theatrical) — à l'huile, *director of the staff of supernumeraries.* Faire sa —, or se faire une —, *refers to the* "make-up" *of one's countenance.* (Familiar) Tête de Turc, *person taken as a butt for ironical hits, jokes, or insults.* An allusion to the Turk's head used at fairs to be pummelled by persons desirous of testing their strength.

Je savais que dans les réunions publiques, mes collègues et moi étions la "tête de turc," sur laquelle s'exerçaient à plaisir et essayaient leurs forces les orateurs plébéiens de l'époque.—MACÉ.

Avoir une —, better explained by the following :—

Que diable appelez-vous "avoir ou n'avoir pas une tête?" ... Avoir une tête, c'est n'être pas guillotiné. Ne pas avoir une tête, c'est être guillotiné. Cette explication vous suffit-elle? Non? Eh bien! avoir une tête, c'est jouir de la plénitude de sa beauté. C'est avoir ... un aspect, un air, une physionomie qui ne soient pas ceux de tout le monde.—A. SCHOLL.

(Popular) Tête d'acajou, *negro*, or "bit o' ebony ;" — de boche, or de pioche, *very stupid man*, "dunderhead." See **Boche**. Tête de patère, *prostitute's bully*, or "ponce ;" — de veau lavée, *white face*, or "muffin-face."

Téter (popular), *to drink*, "to lush."

Téton, *m.* (popular), de satin blanc tout neuf, *virgin's breasts*. Tétons de Vénus, *well-shaped breasts*.

Comme elle portait une robe légère malgré décembre, on voyait sous son fichu pointer les tétons de Vénus que le froid raidissait. Et pas de flic-flac ... non, c'était planté solidement.—RICHEPIN, *Le Pavé*.

Tétonnière, *f.* (popular), *woman with well-developed breasts*, like Juno's.

Têtue, *f.* (thieves'), *pin*.

Tézière, or **tézigo** (thieves'), *thou, thee*.

Tézigue (thieves'), *thee, thou*.

Le dardant a coqué le rifle dans mon palpitant qui n'aquige plus que pour tézigue.—VIDOCQ.

Théâtre, *m.* (popular), le — rouge, *the guillotine*.

Thêta X., *m.*, *second year student at the Ecole Polytechnique*. See **Pipo.**

Thomain, *m.* (theatrical), *insignificant part.*

Thomas, *m.* (familiar and popular), *a facetious synonym for pot de chambre*. Thus termed in connection with the alleged inquisitive disposition of the apostle of that name. The English have the expression "looking-glass," which probably originated from a malicious pun not easy to explain in polite language. (Popular) La mère —, or la veuve —, *nightstool*. Avoir avalé —, *to have an offensive breath*. (Thieves') Pipe à —, *a variety of cheating game.*

Thunard, *m.* (thieves' and popular), *silver coin.*

Thune, or **tune**, *f.* (thieves'), *money; coin*. See **Tune**. Thune de camelotte, *spurious coin ;* — de cinq balles, *five-franc coin.*

Si tu veux qu'elle t'obéisse, montre-lui une thune de cinq balles (pièce de cinq francs) et prononce ce mot-ci : Tondif !—BALZAC.

Tibi, *m.* (familiar), *stud for the shirt collar.*

Tiche, *f.* (shopmen's), *profits.*

Ticquage, *m.* (card-sharpers'), *signal made to a confederate by moving cards up and down.*

Tierce, *f.* (thieves'), *gang ;* — de pègres, *gang of thieves*, "mob." Il y a de la —, *the police are in full force*. (Popular) Tierce à l'égout, *tierce of nine at the game of piquet.*

J'ai une tierce à l'égout et trois colombes ... les crinolines ne me quittent pas.—ZOLA.

Tiffes, or **tifs**, *m. pl.* (roughs' and thieves'), *hair*, or "thatch."

Tigne, *f.* (thieves'), *crowd.*

Tigner (thieves'), d'esbrouffe, *to pick pockets in a crowd.*

Tigre, *m.* (familiar), *small groom,* or " tiger ; " (theatrical) *young ballet dancer ;* (popular) — à cinq griffes, *five-franc coin.* (Military) Tigre, *urinals.*

Timbalière, *f.* (familiar), *woman who speculates on the Stock Exchange.*

Timbre-poste, *m.* (sportsmen's), *cartridge.*

Tinette, *f.* (popular), *mouth.* Chevalier de la —, *scavenger employed in emptying privies,* "gold-finder." Couvre ta —, *hold your tongue.* Plomber comme une —, *to stink.*

Ça me remettra un peu du sale mec qui vient de me r'faire, y plombe comme une tinette.—LOUISE MICHEL.

(Thieves') Tinette, *boot,* or " daisy-root."

Tinteur, *m.* (old cant), *Sodomist.*

Tintouiner (popular), se —, *to fret.*

Tipe, *m.* (sporting), *piece of information,* "tip."

Tique, *f.* (popular), saoul comme une —, *completely drunk,* " sewed up."

Tiquer, or **ticquer** (card-sharpers'), *to signal by moving the cards up and down.*

Tirades, *f. pl.* (thieves'), *convict's fetters,* " wife."

Tirage, *m.* (familiar), *difficulty.*

Tiraillon, *m.* (thieves'), explained by quotation :—

Vêtus très mesquinement . . . ils se bornent à fouiller les poches des habits et des paletots, et exploitent ordinairement les curieux qu'un événement fortuit rassemble dans les rues ou qui forment cercle autour des chanteurs ou des saltimbanques. — *Mémoires de Canler.*

Tirante, *f.* (thieves'), *garter ; bell-rope.*

Tirants, *m. pl.* (thieves'), *stockings.* In furbesche " tiranti." Tirants de filsangue, *floss-silk stockings ;* — radoucis, *silk stockings ;* — de trimilet, *thread stockings.*

Tire, *verb and f.* (military), jouer à — qui a peur, *duel in which the adversaries fire at will.*

Il faut que l'un de nous descende la garde . . . mais comme nous avons tous les deux la vie dure, et qu'avec nos sabres nous aurions de la peine à en finir, nous nous trouverons demain matin, hors du camp, avec nos deux pieds de cochon, et alors ma vieille, nous jouerons à " tire qui a peur. '—DUBOIS DE GENNES.

La —, *pocket-picking.*

Tire-au-flanc, *m.* (military), *one who shirks his duties.*

Le chef et moi, nous rappliquons à l'hôpital. Y avait là tous les tire-au-flanc de l'escadron.—G. COURTELINE.

Tire-bogue, *m.* (thieves'), *rogue whose spécialité is to steal watches,* a " toy-getter."

Tire-braise, *m.* (popular), *infantry soldier.*

Tire-fiacre, *m.* (popular), *tough meat,* like the flesh of a cab-horse.

Tire-gosse, or **tire-mômes,** *f.* (popular), *midwife.*

Tire-jus, *m.* (popular), *pocket-handkerchief,* or " muckinger."

Tire-juter (popular), se —, *to blow one's nose.*

Tire-liards, *m.* (popular), *miser,* " hunks."

Tirelire, *f.* (popular), *behind.* Rigaud says, " gagne-pain des filles de joie." Coller un atout dans la —, *to kick one's behind.* La —, *the head,* or "nut." See **Tronche.** Vieille —, *old fool,* " doddering old sheep's head." (Popular and thieves') La —, *the prison,* or " stir."

> On l'a fourré dans la tir'lire
> Avec les pègres d'Pélago.
> RICHEPIN.

Tire-moelle, or **tire-molard,** *m.* (popular), *pocket-handkerchief,* or " muckinger,"

Tire-môme, *f.* (popular), *midwife.*

Tire-point, *m.* (thieves'), buter au —, *to kill by stabbing in the back with a saw-file.*

Tire-poire, *m.* (popular), *photographer.* Poire is *the head.*

Tirer (familiar), à boulets rouges sur quelqu'un, *to sue one without mercy ;* — la corde, or la ficelle, *to be in bad circumstances ;* — la langue d'un pied, or d'une aune, *to be very thirsty,* " to be as dry as a lime-basket." Also *to be in great distress ;* — une dent, *to obtain a loan of money under false pretences.* See **Ligne.** (Popular) Tirer le chausson, *to run away,* In the English slang, " to pike it," as appears from quotation :—

> Joe quickly his sand had sold, sir,
> And Bess got a basket of rags ;
> Then up to St. Giles's they roll'd, sir ;
> To every bunter Bess brags.
> Then unto the gin-shop they pike it,
> And Bess was admitted, we hear ;
> For none of the crew dare but like it,
> As Joey, her kiddy, was there.
> *The Sand-Man's Wedding.*

Tirer une rapée, *to have connection with a woman.* Se la —, or se — les balladoires, *to run away.* See **Patatrot.** Se — d'épaisseur, *to extricate oneself from some difficulty.* En — une d'épaisseur. See **Carotte.** Tirer la dig-dig, *to pull the bell,* " to jerk the tinkler ;" (police) — la droite, or de la droite, *to have a peculiar limp of the right leg, caused by the weight of the fetters which a convict has worn*

when at the penal servitude settlement.

Ce n'est pas un sanglier, . . . c'est un cheval de retour. Vois comme il tire la droite ! Il est nécessaire d'expliquer ici . . . que chaque forçat est accouplé à un autre (toujours un vieux et un jeune ensemble) par une chaîne. Le poids de cette chaîne, rivée à un anneau au-dessus de la cheville, est tel, qu'il donne, au bout d'une année, un vice de marche éternel au forçat. . . . En termes de police, il tire la droite.— BALZAC.

(General) Tirer la carotte, *to take in,* " to bamboozle ;" — une carotte, *to obtain something from one under false pretences ; to deceive,* " to bilk."

Nul, d'ailleurs, n'entrait à la malle sans avoir passé par ses mains, Flick tenant à bien se convaincre qu'aucun de ses lascars ne lui tirait de carotte.—G. COURTELINE.

The Italians have the corresponding expression, " piantar carota," the origin being that, in a soft soil, an appropriate image of credulity, the carrot will thrive wonderfully. The wary Italian only plants the aforesaid vegetable, biding his time and watching his opportunity, whilst the impetuous Gaul at once plucks it by the roots. (Military) Tirer de la cellule, *to be confined in a military cell.*

Oui, c'est comme ça, je tire de la cellule avant que je me tire moi-même.—G. COURTELINE.

Tirer au cul, *to shirk one's duties.* An allusion to unfair thrusts not allowed in fencing.

Tu vas me foutre le camp au pansage, tout de suite, et tu coucheras à la boîte ce soir pour t'apprendre à tirer au cul. Ah ! carotier ! ah ! fricoteur !—G. COURTELINE.

Termed also Tirer au grenadier, — au renard, — aux flancs.

De tous les coins de l'infirmerie des cris de colère montaient : Y tire aux flancs, ce cochon-là.—G. COURTELINE.

Tirer au cul, *to deceive one's*

superiors by feigning sickness, &c.

Eh bien oui, hurla-t-il, c'est vrai ! C'est vrai que j'ai tiré au cul ... mais si j'ai pas la diarrhée, comme j'ai voulu le faire accroire, c'est pas faute que j'age tout fait pour l'attraper ; je vous en fiche mon billet ... j'm'ai flanqué douze paquets de bismuth dans l'estomac ; j'pouvais pourtant pas faire pluss !—G. COURTELINE.

Ca se tire, *things are progressing favourably.* La chose se tire, *the plan is being carried out, the thing is being done.*

Il faut lui crever la paillasse ; qui est-ce qui en est ? ... Il n'y eut pas une désertion ... ni parmi ceux de la classe, pour qui "ça se tirait."—G. COURTELINE.

(Thieves') Tirer la longe, *to limp ;* — sa crampe, *to escape from prison ;* — son plan, *to be in prison ;* — un congé à la Maz, *to be imprisoned in the prison of Mazas.*

Moi, j'ai besoin qu'ma Louis turbine,
Sans ça, j'tire encore un congé
A la Maz ! Gare à la surbine !
J'deviens grinch' quand j'ai pas mangé.
RICHEPIN.

Tirer une coupe sur le grand flanche, *to be transported,* "to lump the lighter."

Tiretaine, *m.* (thieves'), *country thief.*

Tire-t'arrière (sailors'), une dégelée de --, *an awful thrashing.*

Il se demandait s'il ne fallait point sauter sur le gas ... le ramener de force à la maison, sous une dégelée de tire-t'arrière. —RICHEPIN, *La Glu.*

Tireur, *m.* (thieves'), *pickpocket,* "cly-faker."

Tireuse de vinaigre, *f.* (obsolete), explained by quotation :—

Femme prostituée, coureuse, putain, garce, fille de joye, de mauvaise vie.—LE ROUX.

Tiroir, *m.* (card-sharpers'), *variety of swindling by abstracting one or more cards from the game ;* (popu-

lar) — de l'œil, *gains on odd pieces of material.*

Tirou, *m.* (thieves'), *by-road.*

Tisanier, *m.* (popular), *hospital attendant.*

Titi, *m.* (popular), *typographer ; fowl.* The word is used also as a name for a Paris street-boy.

Toc, *m. and adj.* (familiar and popular), *gold or silver plated metal.*

Ça? c'est une boucle d'oreille en imitation.... Ah ! de mon temps, les femmes qui fréquentaient le Café de Paris se respectaient trop pour porter du toc ! –P. MAHALIN.

Toc, *ridiculous.*

Il est joliment toc, va ! quand il la fait à la dignité et qu'il est en chemise.—E. MONTEIL.

Toc, *crazy ; inferior, deteriorated,* "pinchbeck." Une femme —, *an ugly woman.* Il est un peu —, *he is slightly crazy,* or a "little bit balmy in his crumpet." C'est—, *it is inferior,* or "jimmy." (Thieves') Le —, *the executioner at the convict settlement.* (Artists') Un tableau —, *a picture not painted in good style, not up to the mark.*

Tocandine, *f.* (popular), *kept woman.*

Tocard, *m. and adj.* (popular), *old beau ; ugly, bad, ill.* Diminutive of **Toc** (which see). C'est —, *it is not right.* Etre — pour le galtos, *to have but scanty means.* Also *to be stingy.*

Tocarde, *f.* (popular), *old coquette.*

Tocasse, *adj.* (thieves'), *wicked ; malicious.*

Tocasserie, *f.* (thieves'), *wickedness ; malice.*

Tocasson, *m.* (popular), *ugly woman.*

Tocquardement (popular), *badly; roughly.* Harponner —, *to lay rough hands on.*

Toc-toc, *adj.* (popular), *cracked.*

Togue, *adj.* (thieves'), *cunning.*

Toile, *f.* (popular), *d'emballage, shroud.* Les toiles se touchent, *expression which denotes that one has no money in his pocket.* (Tailors') Faire de la —, *not to have sufficient means to procure food.*

Toilette, *f.* (shoemakers'), *green canvas wrapper for boots;* (general) *cutting the hair of convicts previous to execution.* La chambre de —, *room at Mazas where that operation is performed.*

C'est au dépôt que se fait la toilette sur un escabeau, toujours le même depuis trente ans. . . . Dès que le condamné est sorti de sa cellule pour entrer dans cette chambre de toilette, il appartient au bourreau.—*Mémoires de Monsieur Claude.*

Toilier, *m.* (shopmen's), *an assistant in the linen department.*

Vous savez que les bobinards ont leur club maintenant. . . . Il parlait des vendeurs de la mercerie. . . . Est-ce qu'ils ont un piano comme les toiliers ?—ZOLA.

Toisé, *adj.* (familiar), il est —, *used disparagingly, we know his worth, or what he is capable of.*

Toiture, *f.* (popular), *hat,* "*tile.*"

Tok-tok (Breton cant), *hammer.*

Tolède (familiar), de — (jocular), *of the best quality.*

Tollard, *m.* (thieves'), *office ; executioner,* see **Taule** ; (convicts') *camp bed.*

Tomate, *f.* (popular), rester comme une —, *to be confused, to look foolish.*

Tombage, *m.* (gambling cheats'), *extortion of money by gambling* cheats *from their confrères, or loan made by a gamester and not likely to be repaid,* "*biting the ear.*"

Tombeau, *m.* (popular), *bed,* or "*doss.*"

Tomber (familiar), quelqu'un, *to nonplus one.* Si vous me tombez jamais sous la coupe (threateningly), *if ever I have any power over you.* (Popular) Tomber une femme, *to obtain a woman's favours;* — dans la mélasse, *to become poor, to be ruined ;* — dans la limonade, *to fall in the water ;* — dans le bœuf, *to become poor ;* — en figure, *to fall in with a person whom one would rather avoid ;* — pile, *to fall on one's back ;* — sur le dos et se casser le nez, *to be constantly unsuccessful ;* — sur le dos et se faire une bosse au ventre, *words used to denote that a girl has been seduced, with the natural consequences ;* — sur un coup de poing, *to receive a black eye, and to pretend that it is the result of a fall ;* — une bouteille, *to drink a bottle of wine ;* (thieves') — dans le malheur (euphemism), *to be transported,* "*to go over the water ;*" *to be apprehended ;* — en frime, *to meet with ;* — en litharge (léthargie), *to be in solitary confinement ;* — malade, *to be apprehended,* or "*smugged.*"

Tombeur, *m.* (popular), *redoubtable wrestler ; Lovelace ;* (theatrical) *bad actor ;* (familiar) *slanderous journalist.*

Tompin, *m.* (familiar), le genre —, *something between vulgarism and elegance.*

Tondeur, *m.* (popular), de nappes, *parasite,* or "*quiller ;*" — d'œufs, *over-particular man, one who sticks at trifles ; a pedantic person ; a miser,* or "*hunks.*"

Tonneau, *m.* (popular), être d'un bon —, *to be ridiculous.* Etre d'un fort —, *to be extremely stupid,* a "dunderhead." (Roughs') Tonneau diviseur, *cab.* Properly *privy tub.*

Tonnerre de poche, *m.* (obsolete), *wind.* In Latin, crepitus ventris.

Toper (military), *to seize ; to apprehend.*

Topiser (thieves'), *to recognize ; to stare at.*

Topo, *m.* (military), *topographic survey ; staff ; staff officer.*

Toquade, *f.* (familiar), *fancy for a girl or for a man ; whim.* Avoir une —, *to be "spooney."*

J'ai pour toi une toquade insensée depuis la première de Marion Delorme.—E. Monteil.

Toquadeuse, *f.* (familiar), *cocotte of a sentimental turn of mind, capable of loving a man "for love."*

Toquante, *f.* (popular and thieves'), *watch,* or "tatler."

Son auber j'ai enganté,
Son auber et sa toquante,
Et ses attach's de cé.
V. Hugo.

Toque, *f.* (thieves'), *watch,* or "tatler."

Toqué, *m. and adj.* (familiar), *eccentric man ; one who is cracked,* or "queer." Etre — de, *to be in love with,* "spooney on, mashed on, sweet on, or keen on."

Et moi qui étais toqué de Blanche. Oh ! mais toqué comme une enclume depuis que je lui avais vu jouer la machine à coudre dans la Revue.—P. Mahalin.

Toqué, from toquet, *cap.* Compare with the expressions, avoir la tête près du bonnet, and to have a bee in one's bonnet.

Toquemann, *m.* (cocottes'), *eccentric, extravagant man.*

Toquer (familiar), se —, *to fancy ; to fall, or to be in love,* "to be spooney, or gone on." (Popular) Toquer, *to ring.*

Toquet, *m.* (familiar), de loutre, *name given in* 1881 *to females who speculated on the Stock Exchange.* (Popular) Avoir son —, or en avoir dans le —, *to be drunk,* or "tight."

Torchecul, *m.* (popular), *disparaging epithet used in reference to a newspaper or document.*

Torcheculatif, *adj.* (familiar). Propos torcheculatifs, *dirty talk.* See Rabelais' *Gargantua,* chap. xiii. :—

Or poursui ce propos torcheculatif ; je t'en prie. Et par ma barbe, pour un bussart, tu auras soixante pipes.

Torchée, *f.* (popular), *blows ; set to.*

Torchenez, *m.* (popular), mettez un — à votre langue, *hold your tongue,* "put a clapper to your mug."

Torcher (popular), *to do something hurriedly and carelessly ;* — de la toile, *to do anything hurriedly ;* — les plats, *to have an appetite.* Se —, *to fight.* Se — le cul de quelquechose, *not to care a straw for a thing.* S'en — le nez, *to have to do without.* Se — la gueule, *to fight.* (Literary) Torcher, *to write a neat article.*

Torchette, *f.* (popular), net comme —, *very tidy.*

Torchon, *m.* (popular), *dirty prostitute ;* (familiar and popular) *slattern.* Le — brûle à la maison, *words used to denote that a domestic quarrel is taking place.* (Military) Se flanquer un coup de —, *to fight.*

Tord-boyaux, *m.* (familiar and popular), *brandy,* or *strong brandy,* "French cream," and in old cant, "bingo."

Le tord-boyaux est versé à la ronde dans les lourds godets de verre sale, et les nez enchifrenés le reniflent bruyamment, avant qu'on ne l'envoie détruire ce fameux ver qui a la vie si dure.—RICHEPIN.

Tordre (popular), le cou à une négresse, *to discuss a bottle of wine.* (Familiar and popular) Se —, *to laugh enough to split one's sides.*

Il disait comme un parfait gommeux: "Chic, très chic . . . c'est infect . . . on se tord" . . . mais il le disait moins vulgairement, grâce à son accent étranger qui relevait l'argot.—A. DAUDET, *Les Rois en Exil.*

Tordu, *m.* (gambling cheats'), "pigeon" *who has been robbed by card-sharpers.* Literally *pigeon whose neck has been twisted.*

Torniquet, *m.* (popular), *mill.*

Torpiaude, *f.* (peasants'), *woman of bad character.*

Torpille, *f.* (familiar), *woman of lax morals;* — d'occasion, *street-walker.*

Torse, *m.* (familiar), poser pour le —, *to show off one's figure.* (Popular) Torse, *stomach.* Se velouter le —, *to comfort oneself with a glass of wine or brandy.*

Torta (Breton cant), *to sleep; to kill.*

Tortillade, *f.* (thieves'), *food,* or "toke." The other English synonyms are: "mungarly, grub, prog, crug."

Tortillante, *f.* (thieves'), *vine.*

Tortillard, *m.* (popular), *lame man;* (thieves') *wire.*

Tortillé, *adj.* (popular), être —, *to be dead.*

Bah! . . . un petit verre de cric, ce n'est pas mauvais. Moi, ça me donne du chien. . . . Puis, vous savez, plus vite on est tortillé, plus c'est drôle.—ZOLA.

Tortiller (popular), *to limp; to eat; to hesitate.* Il n'y a pas à —, or à — des fesses, *there must be no hesitation.*

Tonnerre de scrongnieugnieu, murmure Ronchonot en se promenant d'un air grognon dans son cabinet ; n'y a pas à tortiller des fesses, c'est pour d'main matin à dix heures et demie.—G. FRISON.

Tortiller de l'œil, *to die.* See **Pipe.** (Thieves') Tortiller, *to confess; to inform against,* "to snitch;" — la vis, or le gaviau, *to strangle.*

Si vous me tortillez le gaviau, de la vie ni de vos jours, vous ne verrez Microscopique.—DE GENNES.

(Gamesters') Tortiller le carton, *to play cards.* (Sailors') Se — du boyau, *to vomit.*

Tortillette, *f.* (popular), *girl who wriggles when dancing or walking.*

Tortillon, *m.* (popular), *young girl; young servant maid,* or "slavey;" *the behind.* See **Vasistas.**

Tortorage, *m.* (thieves'), *food,* or "mungarly."

Tortore, *f.* (thieves'), *meal.* Passer à la —, se l'envoyer, or casser la croustille, *to eat.*

Tortorer (thieves'), *to eat,* "to grub." See **Mastiquer.** Tortorer le pain à cacheter, *to partake of the Lord's Supper.*

Tortouse, *f.* (thieves'), *rope.* Ligoter une —, *to tie a rope.*

Tortu, *m.* and *adj.* (thieves'), *wine.* Bois —, *vine.*

Tortue, *f.* (popular), *mistress; wife,* "tart." Faire la —, *to fast.*

J'aime mieux faire la tortue et avoir des philosophes aux arpions que d'être sans eau-d'aff dans l'avaloir et sans tréfoin dans ma chiffarde.—E. SUE.

Toto (Breton cant), *beadle.*

Touche, *f.* (familiar and popular), *appearance ; physiognomy.* Bonne —, *grotesque face or appearance.* Une sacrée —, *a wretched appearance.* Touches de piano, *teeth.*

Attention au mouvement . . . ne craignez pas de casser vos touches de piano sur les côtelettes des patates. — DUBOIS DE GENNES.

(Popular) Gare la —! *look out or you will get a thrashing.* La sainte —, *pay-day.*

On célébrait la sainte Touche, quoi ! une sainte bien aimable, qui doit tenir la caisse au paradis.—ZOLA.

Touché, *adj.* (familiar), c'est —, *it is well done.* Un article —, *article to the point.*

Toucher (theatrical), les frises, *to obtain a great success ;* (prostitutes' bullies') — son prêt, *to share a prostitute's earnings.*

Tous deux se ménagent des entrevues et des sorties où ils règlent leurs comptes. Un marlou appelle cela "toucher son prêt." —LÉO TAXIL.

Toucheur, *m.* (thieves'), *murderer ; the leading man in a gang of murderers.*

L'assommeur n'est . . . que l'aide du pégriot. Son chef d'attaque, c'est le toucheur. On qualifie de toucheur celui qui, après avoir donné le premier coup à la victime, est aussi le premier à faire sauter le tiroir et à toucher la monnaie . . . d'ordinaire le toucheur est un gamin de dixsept à dix-huit ans, aussi grêle, aussi chétif que son assommeur est d'aspect redoutable. —*Mémoires de Monsieur Claude.*

Touillaud, *m.* (popular), *sturdy fellow ; one fond of the fair sex,* or "*molrower.*"

Toul (Breton cant), *prison.*

Toulabre, or **Toulmuche,** *m.* (thieves'), *the town of Toulon.*

Toupet, *m.* (popular), *head ; impudence ; coolness.* Avoir un — bœuf, *to show cool impudence.*

Toupet de commissaire, *extraordinary impudence.* Se mettre, or se foutre quelquechose dans le —, *to get something into one's head ; to remember.*

Toupie, *f.* (popular), *head ; woman of very lax morality.* Avoir du vice dans la —, *to be cunning,* "up to a dodge or two."

Tour, *m.* (familiar), du bâton, *unlawful profits on some business transaction.* (Popular) Faire voir le —, *to deceive,* "to bamboozle." Connaître le —, *to be cunning, wide awake,* "to be up to a trick or two." (Military) Passer à son — de bête, *to be promoted according to seniority.*

Il passa capitaine à l'ancienneté, à son tour de bête, comme il disait en rechignant. —E. ABOUT.

(Thieves') Donner un — de cravate à quelqu'un, *to strangle one.* La —, or la — pointue, *the Préfecture de Police, or headquarters of the police.* Se donner un — de clef, *to rest oneself.*

Tourbe, *f.* (popular), être rien dans la —, *to be in great distress.*

Tourlourou, or **tourloure,** *m.* (general), *infantry soldier.*

Tourmente, *f.* (thieves'), *colic,* or "botts."

Tournant, *m.* (thieves'), *mill ; head.* Détacher une beigne sur le —, *to hit one on the head,* "to fetch one a wipe in the gills."

Tournante, *f.* (thieves'), *key,* or "screw."

Tourne-à-gauche, *m.* (popular), *man.* Alluding to a physical peculiarity.

Tourne-autour, *m.* (popular), *cooper.* The allusion is obvious.

Tourne-clef, *m.* (roughs'), *life-preserver,* or "neddy."

Tournée, *f.* (popular), offrir une —, *to treat all round to drink.* Payer une — à quelqu'un, *to thrash one.* Recevoir une —, *to get thrashed.* (Familiar) Faire une — pastorale, *to go with a number of friends to a house of ill-fame with platonic intentions.* (Thieves') Faire une — rouge, *to murder.*

Tourner (popular), l'œil, *to be sleepy ;* — de l'œil, *to die.*

> Deux étoiles. . . . L'une était brune et l'autre blonde. . . . Et toutes deusses avaient du talent. . . . Et toutes deusses ont tourné d'l'œil, avant l'âge.—*Le Cri du Peuple.*

(Thieves') Tourner la vis, *to strangle one.*

Tournevis, *m.* (roughs'), *infantry soldier.* Chapeau à —, *gendarme.*

Tourniquet, *m.* (sailors'), *surgeon,* "sawbones ;" (thieves') *mill.*

Tourte, *f.* (popular), *head,* or "tibby ;" *arrant fool.*

> J'vous dis qu'vous n'êtes qu'une tourte, tendez-vous c'que j'vous parle, s'pèce de moule !—CHARLES LEROY, *Le Colonel Ramollot.*

Avoir une écrevisse dans la —. See **Avoir.** Rire comme une —, *to grin like an idiot.*

Tourtouse, tortouse, or **tourtousine,** *f.* (thieves'), *rope.*

Tourtouser (thieves'), *to bind.*

Tourtousier, *m.* (thieves'), *ropemaker.*

Touser (thieves'), *to ease oneself.*

Tousse (popular), ce n'est pas cher ça, non ! c'est que je —, *that's not dear that, oh dear no !* C'est de l'argent ça comme je —, *that's no more silver than I am.*

Tousser (popular), dessus, *to reject with disdain.* Faire —, *to make one pay,* or "fork out."

Tout, *adj.* (familiar), le — Paris, *the select portion of the pleasure-seeking society of Paris.*

> Son profil narquois et fin . . . avait pris place désormais dans les médaillons du "tout Paris" entre la chevelure d'une actrice en vogue et la figure décomposée de ce prince en disgrâce.—A. DAUDET.

(Thieves') Tout de cé, *very well,* "bene."

Tout-à-l'œil, *m.* (popular), *member of parliament.* Literally *one who can procure everything gratis.*

Toutime, *adj.* (old cant), *all.*

> A été aussi ordonné que les argotiers toutime qui bieront demander la thune, soit aux lourdes ou dans les entiffes ne se départiront qu'ils n'aient été refusés neuf mois, sous peine d'être bouillis et plongés en lance jusqu'au proye.—*Le Jargon de l'Argot.*

Tout-potins des premières, *m.* (journalists'), *select set of play-going Parisians.*

Toxon, *m.* (obsolete), *ugly, grotesque-looking man.*

> Si tu n'tires pas tes guêtres d'ici, j'boxons, vilain toxon, soldat de Satan.—*Riche-en-Gueule.*

Trac, or **trak,** *m.* (general), *fear,* "funk."

> En vérité, sa voix devenait tout à fait agréable, maintenant que le "trac" disparaissait.—J. SERMET.

Flanquer le —, *to frighten.* Avoir le —, *to be afraid,* "funky."

> Cornebois répéta. Il avait un trak épatant. Il avait figuré, c'était facile ; mais parler en public . . . c'est une autre paire de manches.—E. MONTEIL.

Ficher le —, *to frighten.*

> Tout ça, c'est des histoires pour nous ficher le trac, à cause que nous ne sommes pas anciens à l'escadron.—G. COURTELINE.

Tracquer (general), *to be afraid,* or "funky." The word seems to be derived from traquer, *to track*. He who is tracked has reasons for being afraid, and both the cause and result are expressed by one and the same word.

> Quoi ! tu voudrais que je grinchisse
> Sans tracquer de tomber au plan ?
> J'doute qu'à grinchir ou s'enrichisse,
> J'aime mieux gouêper, c'est du flan.
> Viens donc remoucher nos domaines,
> De nos fours goûter la chaleur.
> Crois-moi, balance tes alènes :
> Fais-toi gouêpeur.
>
> VIDOCQ.

Spelt also "traker."

> Tâche de ne pas traker. . . . Ce serait d'un sot.—E. MONTEIL.

Tracqueur, *m.* (general), *poltroon.*

Tractis, *adj.* (thieves'), *tractable ; soft.* Tractis is an old French word.

> Qu'est devenu ce front poly,
> Ces cheveulx blonds, sourcils voultyz,
> Grand entr'œil, le regard joly,
> Dont prenoye les plus subtilz ;
> Ce beau nez droit, grand ne petiz ;
> Ces petites joinctes oreilles,
> Menton fourchu, cler vis traictis
> Et ces belles lèvres vermeilles.
>
> VILLON.

Train, *m.* (popular), *noise ; uproar.* Faire du —, "to kick up a row." Du —! *quick.* Donner un coup de pied dans le — à quelqu'un, *to kick one's behind*, "to land one a kick in his bum." Train des vaches, *tramcar*. Le — blanc, *a train which used to be chartered by Madame Blanc of Monaco for the use of ruined gamesters*. Le — jaune, *Saturday till Monday cheap train taken by husbands who go to see their wives at the seaside*. A malicious allusion to the alleged favourite colour of injured husbands. Un — de charcuterie, *train with third class carriages*. Un — direct pour Charenton, *a glass of absinthe*. Charenton is a Paris dépôt for lunatics, and many cases of delirium tremens are due to excessive drinking of absinthe. Un — direct coupé, *litre of wine poured out into a couple of glasses, a kind of* "split." Prends le —, *run away*, "hook it." Prendre le — d'onze heures, *to loiter, to stroll.* Manquer le —, *to be late, to lose a good opportunity.*

Traineau, *m.* (popular), faire —, *to drag oneself on one's behind.*

Traîne-cul-les-housettes, *m.* (familiar), *vagrant, tramp.*

Traînée, *f.* (familiar), *woman of indifferent character.*

> A son âge la petite Maria Blond avait un joli toupet. Avec ça que de pareilles histoires arrivaient à des traînées de son espèce !—ZOLA.

Traîne-guêtres, *m.* (popular), *lazy fellow who strolls about ; vagrant,* "pikey."

Traîne-paillasse, *m.* (military), "fourrier," *or commissariat non-commissioned officer, who in this instance has charge of the bedding.*

Traîner (popular), le cheval mort, or faire du chien, *to do work paid for in advance*, "to work the dead horse ;" — la savate quelque part, *to go for a walk ;* — ses guêtres, *to idle about.*

Traîneur de sabre, *m.* (familiar), *uncomplimentary epithet applied to a soldier.*

Traîneuse, *f.* (familiar and popular), *prostitute who prowls about railway stations.* See **Gadoue.**

Train-train, *m.* (general), aller son petit —, *to live a quiet, unobtrusive life, free from care.*

Trait, *m.* (familiar). Faire des traits, *to be guilty of conjugal unfaithfulness.* (Gay girls') Avoir un — pour un miché, *to have a tender feeling for a man.*

Trait-carré, *m.* (obsolete), *the absolution given by a priest to a repentant sinner by making the sign of the cross.*

Tralala, *m.* (popular), faire du —, *to make a great fuss, a great show.* Se mettre sur son grand —, *to dress oneself in grand attire, " in full fig."*

Tranchant, *m.* (thieves'), *paving stone.*

Tranche, *f.* (military), j'ai soupé de ta —, *I am tired of you.* Se payer une — de, *to treat oneself to.* Refers to anything, from a bottle of wine to a woman.

> C'qui m'fait rigoler, c's'rin de poète,
> Avec son bout d'alexandrin !
> Vanter la neige ! Faut-i' êtr' bête !
> Pourquoi pas Cartouche et Mandrin ?
>
> S'i' la gob', qu'i s'en paye un' tranche !
> Qu'i' crach' pas su' les gazons verts !
> Ça lui suffit pas qu'a soy' blanche !
> Faut encor' qu'i' la mette en vers !
>   J. Jouy, *La Neige.*

Tranche-ardent, *m.* (thieves'), *snuffers.*

Tranche-fromage, *m.* (military), *sword.*

Trancher de l'éléphant (obsolete), *to give oneself an air of importance.*

> Il estoit encore jeune enfant
> Qu'il tranchoit de son éléfant.
>   *Paraphrase sur le Bref de sa Sainteté envoyé à la Reyne Régente,* 1649.

Tranquille comme Baptiste (popular), *as cool as a cucumber.*

Transaill (Breton cant), *small change.*

Traquer, traqueur. See **Tracquer, tracqueur.**

Trav (thieves'), bonne à —, *a likely place for a robbery.*

Travail, *m.* (freemasons'), *eating;* (thieves') *stealing; cheating.*

(Popular) Le — du casaquin, *act of thrashing soundly.* (Prostitutes') Le —, *prostitution.*

Travailler (theatrical), le succès, *to be head of the staff of paid applauders at a theatre.* Se faire —, *to be hissed, " to get the big bird."* (Popular) Travailler pour Jules, or — pour Monsieur Domange, *to eat.* Alluding to the contractor for the emptying of privies ; — le cadavre, le casaquin, les côtes, *to thrash, "to wallop."* See **Voie.** Se — le trognon, *to torture one's brains.* (Prostitutes') Travailler, *to walk the streets.* The word has the general meaning of *to ply.*

> Quelles sont donc vos sources principales de renseignements ? Les chiffonniers, . . . nous nous abouchons avec les Diogènes qui travaillent cette rue et nous leur achetons tous les papiers trouvés devant la porte de la maison signalée.—A. Sirven.

(Thieves') Travailler, *to steal ; to murder ;* — à la tire, *to pick pockets ; to be a pickpocket,* or "buzfaker."

> — Que faites-vous maintenant ?
> — Je m'exerce à voler.
> — Diable ! répondis-je avec un mouvement involontaire et en portant la main sur ma poche.
> — Oh ! je ne travaille pas à la tire, soyez tranquille, je méprise les foulards . . . je vole en l'air.—Th. Gautier.

Travailler dans le rouge, *to murder.*

> Un meurtre ! travailler dans le rouge ! C'est grave !—P. Mahalin.

Travailler dans le bât (bâtiment), *to break into houses, "to crack cribs."*

Travailleur, *m.* (thieves'), *gambling cheat,* or "shark ;" *thief,* or "prig ;" (popular) — de nuit, *ragpicker.*

Travailleuse, *f.* (thieves'), *variety of Sodomist.*

> La troisième classe est entièrement formée d'individus appartenant à la grande famille

des ouvriers et ne vivant que du produit de leur travail. De là est venu le nom de "travailleuses."—LÉO TAXIL.

Travers (roughs'), passer quelqu'un à —, *to hustle, to thrash one,* "to wallop." See **Voie.** Si tu ne dis pas fion je vais te passer à —, *if you don't apologize, I'll thrash you.*

Traverse, *f.* (thieves), *penal servitude settlement.* From traversée, *passage across the sea.* Etre en — à perpète, *to be a convict for life, to be a* "lifer."

They know what a clever lad he is ; he'll be a lifer. They'll make the Artful nothing less than a lifer.—CH. DICKENS.

Aller en —, *to be transported,* "to lump the lighter," or "to go abroad."

The Artful Dodger going abroad for a common twopenny-halfpenny sneeze-box ! —CH. DICKENS.

The corresponding expression in furbesche is " andar a traverso."

Traverser un litre (popular), *to drink a litre bottle of wine.*

Traversin, *m.* (popular), *infantry soldier.* Alluding to the small size of the infantry. Se foutre un coup de —, *to sleep,* "to doss."

Travesti, *m.* (theatrical), *part of a male character played by a female.*

Traviole, *f.* (popular and thieves'), *cross-road ; ravine.* Avoir des travioles, *to be uneasy.* De — (de travers), *crosswise ; awry ; all wrong.*

> J'ons la chance d'traviole.
> V'là les mendigots, les indigents,
> Bon jour bon an, les bonn's gens,
> J'allons pas en carriole.
> RICHEPIN.

Trébuchet, *m.* (thieves'), *the guillotine.*

Trèfle, or **tref,** *m.* (popular and thieves'), *tobacco,* "fogus ;" (popular) *behind.* Vise au —, *apothe-* cary, or " squirt." (Familiar) Roi de —, *rival of a fast girl's lover,* termed " roi de cœur." (Military) Boucillon de —, *roll of tobacco,* "twist of fogus."

Tenez, mirez un peu, mes bons camarades . . . voici d'abord deux boucillons de trèfle qui ne seront pas mauvais à fumer ? —DUBOIS DE GENNES.

Tréflière, or **tréfouine,** *f.* (popular and thieves'), *tobacco pouch.*

Treizième, *adj.* (familiar), se marier au — arrondissement, *to live as man and wife though not married, to live* "tally." The expression has become obsolete, Paris being now divided into twenty arrondissements.

Tremblant, *m.* (popular), *bed,* "doss, or bug-walk."

Tremblante, *f.* (thieves'), *fever.*

Tremblement, *m.* (theatrical), *mixture of vermout, cassis, and brandy ;* (military) *fight.* (Popular) Et tout le —, *all complete ; a grand show.*

Et des chantres, et des enfants de chœur, et un commissaire en habit et l'épée au côté ; enfin, comme disait Fumeron, tout le tremblement.—HECTOR FRANCE.

Trembler (popular), faire — la volaille morte, *to utter stupendously foolish things.*

Trembleuse, *f.* (popular), *electric bell.*

Tremblotte, *f.* (popular), *fear.* Termed also " trouille, flubart, trac."

Trémousser (familiar), faire — le baluchon *is said of wine which gets into the head.*

Pour du vin, dit la petite Linois tout-à-coup, si celui-là ne vous fait pas trémousser le baluchon !—E. MONTEIL.

Trempage, *m.* (printers'), *intoxication.*

H H

Trempe, or **trempée,** *f.* (popular), *thrashing.*

Madame, si je ne me respectais pas, je vous ficherais une drôle de trempée !— GAVARNI.

Tremper (popular), une soupe à quelqu'un, *to thrash one.* See **Voie.** (Military) Tremper son pied dans l'encre, *to be confined to barracks,* " *to be roosted.* "

Trempette, *f.* (popular), *rain.*

Tremplin, *m.* (theatrical), *the stage.* (Prostitutes') Le —, *the particular street or boulevard where prostitutes ply their trade.*

Trente-et-un, *m.* (familiar), être sur son —, *to be dressed in one's best clothes.*

Vous n'êtes pas habitués à me voir comme ça sur mon trente-et-un, la pelure et le pantalon noirs avec un tuyau de poêle et des souliers vernis.—*From a Parisian song.*

From the game termed trente-et-un, that figure being the highest score.

Trente-six, *m.* (popular), le — du mois, *never,* " when the devil is blind."

Trente-sixième. See **Dessous.**

Treo-torret (Breton cant), *pastry.*

Trèpe, *m.* (thieves'), *crowd,* or " push." The word comes either from the Italian cant treppo, which has a like signification, or from the old French treper, *to press, to trample.* Roulotte à —, *omnibus,* or "chariot." S'ébattre dans le —, *to move about in a crowd.*

Trepeligour, *m.* (old cant), *vagabond.* From treper, *to trample,* and le gourd, *the high road.*

Trépignard, *m.* (thieves'), *thief who moves about in a crowd picking pockets.*

Trépignée, *f.* (popular), *thrashing.* Flanquer une — dans le gîte, *to thrash soundly.*

Trépigner (popular), *to give a sound thrashing.* See **Voie.**

Tresser des chaussons de lisière (familiar), *to be in prison.*

Treton, *m.* (old cant), *rat.* Deformation of trottant.

Triangle, *m.* (freemasons'), *hat ;* (artists') *mouth.* Clapoter du —, *to have an offensive breath.*

Tribu, *f.* (military), se mettre en —, *to start a mess.*

Tribunalier, *m.* (journalists'), *reporters at courts of justice.*

Un procès, dont les "tribunaliers" des journaux parisiens . . . n'ont pas soufflé mot.—*Gil Blas,* 1887.

Tric, *m.* (old cant), *meeting.* Faire le —, *to leave the workshop* " en masse" *to repair to the wine-shop.*

Tricher (familiar), *to act upon the suggestions of Malthus.*

Trichine, *f.* (popular), *gay girl.*

Trichiner (popular), *to eat pork.*

Tricorne, *m.* (popular), *gendarme.*

Tricoter (popular), des flûtes, *to run away ; to dance ;* — les côtes à quelqu'un, *to thrash one ;* — les joues, *to slap one's face.* (Military) Aiguille à — les côtes, *sword,* " cheese-knife."

Comment se fait-il que tu sois si ferré à glace sur les aiguilles à tricoter les côtes ?— DE GENNES.

Triffonnière, *f.* (popular), *tobacco pouch.*

Trifoin, *m.* (popular and thieves'), *tobacco,* " fogus."

Trifouiller (popular), *to search ; to fumble ;* — les guiches, *to comb.*

Trimancher (thieves'), *to walk along the road.*

Trimar, trimard, *m.* (thieves'), *road,* or "*Toby.*" Trimar, from *trimer, to run about on some unpleasant duty.* Aller au —, *to be a highwayman.* In English cant a highwayman was termed a "bridle-cull."

A booty of £10 looks as great in the eye of a "bridle-cull," and gives as much real happiness to his fancy, as that of many thousands to the statesman.—FIELDING, *Jonathan Wild.*

(Prostitutes') Faire son —, *to walk the street.* Synonymous of "faire le trottoir, faire son quart, aller au persil, aller au trot."

Trimardant, *m.* (thieves'), *wayfarer.*

Trimarde, *f.* (thieves'), *street,* or "*drag.*"

Trimarder, or **trimer** (thieves'), *to walk along the road or street.*

Il va passer tout à l'heure un pilier de paquelin qui trimarde à gaye.—VIDOCQ.

Trimardeur, *m.* (thieves'), *highwayman,* a "*High-Toby man.*"

Trimbaler (familiar and popular), quelqu'un, *to take a person about* ; — quelquechose, *to drag or carry a thing about ;* — son cadavre, *to take a walk ;* — son crampon, *to take one's wife or mistress for a walk.* Se —, *to walk about.* The corresponding expression for trimbaler in the Berry patois is triquebaler. Rabelais uses the term triquebalarideau with the signification of *fool,* that is, *one who will allow himself to be ordered about.*

Trimbaleur, *m.* (popular), *man not to be relied on, one who puts you off with excuses ;* — des cônis, or — de refroidis, *driver of a hearse.* Termed also — de machabées ; — de rouchies, or — de carne pour la sèche, *prostitute's bully,* "*Sun-day-man ;*" — d'indigents, *omnibus driver.* (Thieves') Trimbaleur, *coachman,* "*rattling-cove ;*" — de piliers de boutanche, *rogue who having purchased goods which he is to pay for at his residence, gets them taken away by a shopman, and on the way manages to obtain possession of the property.*

Trimballée, *f.* (popular), *a number, a quantity.*

Trime, *f.* (thieves'), *street,* or "*donbite ;*" *way ; road,* "*Toby.*"

Nous ne rencontrerons pas seulement un ferlampier sur la trime.—VIDOCQ.

En —, *let us go, away !*

Il y a gras (du butin), mes enfants ; allons, en trime, nous faderons (partagerons) au plus prochain tapis (auberge).—VIDOCQ.

Trimer (familiar and popular), *to work hard ; to be waiting.* Faire —, *to make people wait.* Faire — les mathurins, *to eat.* Literally *to make the teeth work.* (Thieves') Trimer, *to walk along the road ;* (commercial travellers') *to walk about in order to get orders.*

Trimilet, *m.* (thieves'), *thread.*

Trimoires, *f. pl.* (thieves'), *legs.*

Trinckman, *m.* (popular), *wine retailer.*

Tringle (popular), *nothing ; no ; naught.*

Tringlot, *m.* (military), *soldier of the army service corps.* From train and a suffix.

Trinquer (popular and thieves'), *to be compelled to pay for others, or to have to make good any damage for which one is held responsible ; to lose at a game.*

Le trèfle gagne. Trop petit, bibi, t'as mal maquillé ton outil. V'là celle qui perd. J'ai trinqué (perdu), c'est pas gai. V'là celle qui gagne. La v'là encore. Du carreau, c'est pour ton veau. Du cœur, c'est pour ta sœur. Et v'là la noire.—RICHEPIN.

Faire — quelqu'un, *to thrash one,* "to wallop."

Triomphe, *m.,* explained by quotation :—

Le triomphe est une vieille coutume de Saint-Cyr, qui consiste à promener sur une prolonge d'artillerie les vainqueurs du jour (lors de l'inspection), tandis que les élèves forment dans la cour une immense farandole et chantent le chœur légendaire de la galette.—*Figaro.*

Tripaillon de sort ! (popular), *ejaculation expressive of intense disappointment.*

Tripasse, *f.* (popular), *ugly and fat woman.*

Triper (popular), *to suckle an infant.*

Tripes, *f. pl.* (popular), *large, soft breasts.* Secouer les —à quelqu'un, *to thrash one.* See **Voie.** Porter son argent aux — (obsolete), *to employ one's money in the purchase of very cheap articles.* Used to be said by fishwives to customers who cheapened too much.

Tripière, *f.* (popular), *girl or woman with well-developed breasts.* Forte —, *one with enormous breasts.*

Tripoli, *m.* (popular), *rank brandy,* "French cream" and "bingo" in old English cant. Un coup de —, *a glass of brandy.*

Tripot, *m.* (popular and thieves'), *police officer; municipal guard.*

Tripoter (familiar), le carton, *to play cards.*

Un braconnier, qui n'a pas employé sa journée à tripoter le carton, sort d'un fourré avec son arme.—P. MAHALIN.

Comme les héroïnes de Molière n'ont d'esprit que l'éventail en main, d'Axel ne retrouvait un peu de vie qu'en tripotant le "carton."—A. DAUDET.

(Artists') Tripoter la couleur, *to*

paint. Tripoté, *painted in masterly style.*

Comme c'est tripoté ! . . . quel beurre ! Il est impossible d'être plus chaud et plus grouillant. — TH. GAUTIER *Les Jeune France.*

Triquage, *m.* (rag-pickers'), *sorting of rags.*

Triquart, *m.,* or **trique,** *f.* (thieves'), *liberated convict under the surveillance of the "haute police."* Similarly to ticket-of-leave convicts in England, a man under the surveillance of the police is obliged to report himself from time to time, and a place of residence is assigned to him which he cannot leave without permission.

Trique, *f.* (thieves'), *tooth,* or "ivory;" *cab,* or "cask;" *a convict returned from transportation before his time,* or "yoxter." Also *one under police supervision.* (Popular) Trique à larder, or — à picoter, *sword-stick.* Faire flamber la — à larder, *to use a sword-stick.* Trique, properly *cudgel,* termed "trucco" in the Italian cant.

Triquebille, *m.* (obsolete), *privy member.*

Triquer (popular), *to sort rags; to cudgel;* (thieves') *to be under police surveillance as a ticket-of-leave.*

Triquet, *m.* (thieves'), *police spy,* one who watches ticket-of-leave men, termed "triques."

Triqueur, *m.* (popular), *master rag-picker,* one who sorts rags.

Troez (Breton cant), *porridge.*

Trognade (schoolboys'), *dainties, such as sweets, fruit, cakes.*

Trogner (schoolboys'), *to eat dainties.*

Trogneur, *m.* (schoolboys'), *one who eats dainty things.*

Trognon, *m.* (popular), *head,* or "*nut.*"

Comment, Scrongnieugnieu, faut donc que j'vous l'répète cinquante fois, qu' c'est à cause des sales idées qu' vous m'avez foutues dans l'trognon, vous et Kelsalbecq, que d'puis huit jours j'suis dévasté d'un embêtement vraiment consécutif.—G. FRISON.

Dévisser le —, *to kill.* (Familiar and popular) Mon petit —, *my sweet little one, my little* "ducky." Other fond expressions are: "mon loup, mon chien, mon petit chou, mon chat, mon loulou, mon gros minet, ma petite chatte, ma bichette, ma minette, ma poule, ma poupoule, mon gros poulet, ma petite cocotte," and others quite as ridiculous. Our fathers used the endearing term, "mon petit bouchon," from bouchonner, *to fondle.*

Sganarelle (embrassant sa bouteille). Ah! petite friponne. Que je t'aime, mon petit bouchon.—MOLIÈRE, *Le Médecin malgré lui.*

Troisième. See **Dessous.**

Trois-mâts, *m.* (military), *veteran with three stripes.*

Trois-ponts, *m.* (familiar), *high silk cap.* Casquette à —, *prostitute's bully.* See **Poisson.**

Trôleur, *m.* (popular), *commissionnaire; vagrant,* "pikey;" *rabbit-skin man.*

Trôleuse, *f.* (popular), *streetwalker.* See **Gadoue.** From the verb trôler, *to go about,* derived from the German trollen. In English, to troll, hence trull.

Trombille, *f.* (thieves'), *beast.*

Trombine, *f.* (popular), *head,* or "tibby;" *physiognomy,* or "phiz." See **Tronche.** Trombine en dèche, *ugly face,*

"knocker-face." Une rude —, *a grotesque face.*

Tromblon, *m.* (familiar), *hat,* or "stove-pipe."

Tromboller (roughs'), *to love;* — les gonzesses, *to be fond of women.*

Trombone, *m.* (military), faire —, *to pretend to take money out of one's pocket to pay for the reckoning.* The movement to and fro of the hand is likened to the action of playing the trombone.

Trompe, *f.* (popular), *nose.*

Trompe-chasses, *m.* (thieves'), *picture.*

Trompe-la-mort, *m.* (familiar), *swell,* "masher."

Trompette, *f.* (popular), *face,* or "mug;" *mouth,* or "rattle-trap;" *nose,* or "conk;" *cigar.*

Trompeur, *m.* (obsolete), *melon.* Thus termed probably from its yellow colour, which is supposed to be that in favour with deceived husbands.

Trompion, *m.* (military), *bugler.*

Tronche, *f.* (thieves' and roughs'), *head,* or "tibby."

— J'espère bien qu'on lui coupera la tronche à celui-là.
— Je parie que je l'attrape à la sorbonne avec un trognon de chou.—TH. GAUTIER.

The slang synonyms are: "le baldaquin, le coco, la boule, la balle, la ciboule, la calebasse, la boussole, la pomme, la coloquinte, le caillou, la cafetière, le caisson, le tesson, la cocarde, la bobine, le citron, la poire, le grenier à sel, la boîte au sel, la boîte à sardines, la boîte à surprises, la tire-lire, la hure, la gouache, la noisette, le char, le réservoir, le chapiteau, le bourrichon, la goupine, la tourte, le trognon,

la guitare, la guimbarde, le soliveau, le bobéchon, la bobinasse, le kiosque, le vol-au-vent,
l'omnibus, la sorbonne, la ca-
boche, le ciboulot, l'ardoise, le
soufflet, le jambonneau, l'armoire
à glace, la baigneuse, le schako ; "
and in the English slang :
" knowledge-box, tibby, costard,
nut, chump, upper storey, crumpet,
and nab." Tronche à la manque,
police officer, or "reeler." See **Pot-
à-tabac.** The proper signification
of tronche is *billet of wood, piece of
wood which has been cut off the
trunk.*

Troncher (thieves'), *to kiss.* Termed
also "sucer la pomme."

Tronchiner (obsolete), used to
signify *to take a morning walk,*
a "constitutional." From the
name of a celebrated doctor of
the eighteenth century, by name
Tronchin, whom it was then the
fashion to consult. Tronchinade
had the meaning of *walk.*

Tronchinette, *f.* (roughs'), *young
girl's head or face.*

Trône, *m.* (popular), *night-stool.*
Etre sur le —, *to be at the W.C.*

Troploc, *m.* (popular), *employer,*
"boss."

Troquet, *m.* (popular), abbreviation of mastroquet, *landlord of
wine-shop.* Called also "bistrot,
empoisonneur, mannezingue."

Tout ce que je sais, c'est que je sortais
du troquet quand j'ai reçu mon atout par
trois zigs qui ont pu me déshabiller, après
avoir eu des nouvelles de mon biceps. S'ils
m'ont donné des châtaignes, je les ai bien
arrangés.—*Mémoires de Monsieur Claude.*

Trot, *m.* (prostitutes'), aller au —,
*to walk the street as a prostitute in
full* "fig." (Military) Au — ! a
favourite expression in the cavalry,
look sharp !

Allez mettre votre blouse, et au trot !
qu'est-ce qui m'a bâti un pierrot comme ça !
—G. COURTELINE.

Trotach (Breton cant), *soup.*

Trottant, *m.* (thieves'), *rat.*

Trottante, *f.* (thieves'), *mouse.*

Trotter (popular), se —, or se la
—, *to go away.*

Il m'a donné du poignon pour me trotter
toute seule à Paris. Je suis revenue, avec
le sac de l'homme sauvage, à la turne de
l'ogresse.—*Mémoires de Monsieur Claude.*

Trotte-sec, *m.* (cavalry), *foot-
soldier,* "mud-crusher."

Trotteuse, *f.* (popular), *railway
engine,* "puffing, or whistling
Billy."

Trottignole, *f.* (popular and
thieves'), *foot,* "crab ;" *shoe,*
"crab-shell." Du cabochard aux
trottignoles, *from head to foot.*

Trottin, *m.* (popular), *errand boy
or girl.*

Les trottins se feront des révérences
comme les marquises de l'ancien temps.—
Le Voltaire, Nov., 1886.

Trottins, *feet,* or "everlasting
shoes ;" *shoes,* or "trotter-cases."
Des trottins feuilletés, *worn-out,
leaky shoes.* (Thieves') Trottin,
horse, or "prad."

Trottinard, *m.* (popular), *child,*
"kid."

Trottinet, *m.* (popular), *lady's
shoe.*

Trottoir, *m.* (familiar), femme de
—, *prostitute,* or "common Jack."
Le grand —, *fashionable cocottes, high-class* "tarts" *of that
description.* Le petit —, *the
street-walking females,* or "unfortunates." (Theatrical) Le grand
—, *stock of classical plays.* Le
petit —, *class of lighter productions.*

Trou, *m.* (familiar), faire son —, *to get on in the world.* (Popular) Le — aux pommes de terre, *the mouth,* "potato-trap." Le — de balle, de bise, or du souffleur, *anus.* Avoir un — sous le nez, *to be a great bibber of wine.* Etre dans le —, *to be dead and buried,* "to have been put to bed with a shovel;" *to be in prison, in* "quod." Un — du cul, *an arrant fool,* "bally flat;" *a mean fellow,* or "skunk." On lui boucherait le — du cul avec un grain de sable—explained thus by Rigaud :—

Se dit en parlant de quelqu'un que la peur paralyse, parceque, alors, selon l'expression vulgaire, il "serre les fesses."—*Dict. d'Argot Moderne.*

Faire un — à la lune, *to fail in business, to be bankrupt.* It formerly signified *to disappear.* Literally to *vanish behind the moon.* (Thieves') Trou, *prison,* or "quod."

Vive le vin ! vive la bonne chère !
Vive la grinche ! vive les margotons !
Vive les cigs ! vive la bonne bière !
Amis, buvons à tous les vrais garçons !
Ce temps heureux a fini bien trop vite,
Car aujourd'hui nous v'là tous dans l'trou.
Song written by CLÉMENT, *a burglar.*

Troubade, or **troubadour,** *m.* (popular), *infantry soldier.*

Ta tournure guerrière,
Ta de rata, tata, ta de rata, ta taire,
Sait captiver la plus fière !
Et, pour le parfait amour,
En filant un doigt de cour,
Tu te montreras toujours
Plus fort que dix troubadours.
DUBOIS DE GENNES.

Trouée, *f.* (thieves'), *lace,* or "driz."

Troufignard, troufignon, *m.* (popular), *the behind; the anus.*

Troufion, *m.* (popular), *soldier.*

Trouillarde, *f.* (popular), *prostitute.* From the verb trôler, *to roam about.*

Trouille, *f.* (popular), *dirty servant; slut; dissipated-looking woman; trull;* (thieves') *fear.* Avoir la —, *to be afraid.* Synonymous of "avoir le taf, le trac, le flubart, la frousse."

Trouilloter (popular), *to stink.*

Troupe, *f.* (theatrical), d'argent, *second-rate company;* — de carton, *company composed of very inferior actors;* — de fer-blanc, *one numbering actors of ordinary ability.* Termed also "troupe d'été," the Paris season taking place in winter; — d'or, or d'hiver, *first-rate theatrical company.* In the language of journalists the expressions, "troupe de fer-blanc," "troupe d'or," are used to denote respectively *a middling or excellent staff of writers.*

Trousse, *f.* (thieves'), *anus.*

Troussequin, *m.* (popular), *the behind,* or "Nancy." See **Vasistas.**

Trouvé, *adj.* (artists' and journalists'), *new, original.*

Trouver (familiar), la — mauvaise, *to be highly dissatisfied.* Trouver des puces, *to have a quarrel, or to get a thrashing.* Se — mal sur, *to appropriate another's property.*

Troyen, *m.* (domino players'), *three of dominoes.*

Truc, *m.* (familiar and popular), *affair; mode; knack; dodge.* Avoir le —, *to have the knack, to have the secret.*

Est-ce que je ne connais pas toutes les couleurs? J'ai le truc de chaque commerce.—BALZAC.

Avoir le —, *to find a dodge.*

Ce farceur de Mes-Bottes avait eu le truc d'épouser une dame très décatie.—E. ZOLA.

Truc, *any kind of small trade in*

the streets. Avoir du —, *to be ingenious ; to possess a mind fertile in resource.* Le — vert, *billiards,* or "spoof." (Popular and thieves') Piger le —, *to discover the fraud, the dodge.* Le — de la morgane et de la lance, *christening.*

A la chique à six plombes et mèche pour que le ratichon maquille son truc de la morgane et de la lance.—VIDOCQ.

Le —, *thieving,* "lay." Le grand —, *murder.* Des trucs, *things, objects.* Donner le —, *to give the watchword.* Boulotter le —, *to reveal the watchword.* (Theatrical) Truc, *engine used to effect a transformation scene.* Pièce à trucs, *play with transformation scenes.* (Prostitutes') Faire le —, *to walk the streets.* (Military) Truc, *room.*

Nous arrivons dans une espèce de sale truc, grand à peu près comme v'là la chambre, seul'ment pas t'tafait aussi haut. —G. COURTELINE.

Also *military equipment.* Truc, from the Provençal tric, *deceit.* Then we have the old-fashioned word "triche," which corresponds to the English trick at cards. A thief in Italian lingo is termed "truccante." Literally *trickster.* In old French "truc" meant *blow,* and in the Italian jargon "trucco" is used to denominate a *stick,* from a correlation between the effect and the cause.

Trucage, *m.*, *selling new articles for antiquities.*

Trucageur, *m.*, *manufacturer of articles sold as genuine antiquities.*

Trucard, *m.* (popular), *artful dodger.*

Truche, *f.* (thieves' and tramps'), *begging,* "cadging."

Je suis ce fameux argotier,
Le grand Coesre de ces mions.

J'enterve truche et doubler
Dedans les boules et frémions.
　　　La Chanson des Argotiers.

La faire à la —, *to beg,* "to cadge."

Trucher (old cant), *to beg,* "to cadge ;" — sur l'entiffe, *to beg on the road.* From truc.

Trucheur, or **trucheux**, *m.* (old cant), *beggar,* or "cadger;" *tramp,* or "pikey."

Qui veut rouscailler,
D'un appelé du grand Coesre,
Dabusche des argotiers,
Et des trucheurs le grand maître,
Et aussi de tous ses vassaux.
Vive les enfans de la truche,
Vive les enfans de l'argot.
　　　La Chanson des Argotiers.

Trucsin, *m.* (thieves'), *house of ill-fame,* "flash-drum, nanny-shop, or Academy." In America certain establishments of this description are termed "panel-cribs." I find the following description in a book called the *Slang Dictionary of New York, London, and Paris* (the last-named town might have been left out) : Panel-crib, a place especially fitted up for the robbery of gentlemen, who are enticed thereto by women who make it their business to pick up strangers. Panel-cribs are sometimes called badger-cribs, shake-downs, and touch-cribs, and are variously fitted for the admission of those who are in the secret, but which defy the scrutiny of the uninitiated. Sometimes the casing of the door is made to swing on well-oiled hinges which are not discoverable in the room, while the door itself appears to be hung in the usual manner, and well secured by bolts and lock. At other times the entrance is effected by means of what appears to be an ordinary wardrobe, the back of which revolves like a turnstile on pivots. When the victim has got into bed with the woman, the thief enters, and picking his pocket-book out of his pocket, abstracts the money, and supplying its place with a small roll of paper, returns the book to its place. He then withdraws, and coming to the door raps and demands admission, calling the woman by the name of wife. The frightened victim dresses himself in a hurry, feels his pocket-book in its proper place, and escapes through another door, congratulating himself on his happy deliverance. The panel-thief who fits up a panel-crib tries always to pick up gentlemen that are on a visit to the city on business or pleasure, who are not likely to remain and prosecute the thieves.

Truelle, *f.* (freemasons'), *spoon.* Termed also "pelle."

Truffard, or **truffardin,** *m.* (popular), *soldier,* "swaddy." Truffard also means *happy, lucky.*

Truffe, *f.* (popular), *nose of considerable proportions,* or "conk;" *potato,* "spud;" — de savetier, *chestnut.* Aux truffes, *excellent,* "first-class, fizzing, out-and-out, nap." Il a un nez à chercher des truffes *is used to compare a man to a pig,* as a porcine assistant is necessary for the finding and rooting up of truffles.

Truffé, *adj. and m.* (familiar), *arrant,* or "captious" *fool;* — de chic, *superlatively elegant or stylish,* "tsing tsing."

Truffer (popular), *to deceive,* "to cram up."

Trufferie, *f.* (popular), *fib,* "cramming up."

Truffeur, *m.* (popular), *one who tells fibs, who* "throws the hatchet," or "draws the long-bow." The English slang expressions come from the wonderful stories which used to be told of the Norman archers, and more subsequently of Indians' skill with the tomahawk.

Truffier, *m.,* **truffière,** *f.* (popular), *fat person.* An allusion to a pig used for finding truffles, and which is called truffier in certain parts of France. It appears that peasants, in order to discover an animal with a fine nose, go to the fair with a bit of truffle in their shoe, and they know a good truffle-finder at once, as he never fails to sniff at their heels.

Trumeau, *m.* (popular), *woman of indifferent character.* See **Gadoue.** Vieux —! *old fool,* "doddering old sheep's head."

Truquage, *m.* (artists'), *putting the name of an old master to a modern picture.*

Truquer, *m.* (popular), *to live by one's wits;* (thieves') *to swindle,* "to bite;" *to give oneself up to prostitution;* — de la pogne, *to beg,* "to cadge." (Tradespeoples') Truquer, *to manufacture articles sold as genuine antiquities.*

Truqueur (popular), *one who lives by his wits; swindler, one of the* "swell-mob;" *card-sharper,* "rook;" *Sodomist,* "gentleman of the back door;" *seller of theatre checks; one who does sundry odd jobs, such as opening the doors of carriages, &c.,* "one who lives on the mooch," *or who sells small articles in the streets; pedlar.*

Je vous assure qu'il me répugne de verser le raisiné de ces deux truqueurs.—VIDOCQ.

Truqueur de cambrouse, *tramp,* or "pikey."

Les deux truqueurs de cambrouse nous entendront si on rebâtit le sinve.—VIDOCQ.

Truye, *f.*, fils de — (obsolete), *used to be said of a man who vanishes,* alluding to La Truye qui file, the signboard of a celebrated wine-shop of the seventeenth century.

Tual (Breton cant), *fox.*

Tuant, *adj.* (familiar), *dull in the superlative degree.*

Tubard, *m.* (popular), *silk hat.* Various kinds of covering for the head are termed : "capet, carbeluche, combre, combrieu, capsule, tuyau de poêle, tromblon, tube, tube à haute pression, casque, viscope, bolivar, couvre-amour, tuile, épicéphale; galurin, lampion, nid d'hirondelle, caloquet, cadratin, ardoise, marquin, bâche, décalitre, corniche, couvercle, couvrante, loupion, bosselard; " and in the English slang : "tile, chimney-pot, stove-pipe, goss." To complete this *chapitre des chapeaux,* which has nothing in common with the one said by Sganarelle to have been written by Aristotle, we may add that Fielding calls hats "principles," and in explanation of the term he says :—

As these persons wore different "principles," *i.e.* hats, frequent dissensions grew among them. There were particularly two parties, viz. those who wore hats fiercely cocked, and those who preferred the "nab" or trencher hat, with the brim flapping over their eyes. The former were called "cavaliers" and "tory rory ranter boys," &c. The latter went by the several names of "wags, roundheads, shakebags, oldnolls," and several others. Between these continual jars arose, insomuch that they grew in time to think there was something essential in their differences, and that their interests were incompatible with each other, whereas, in truth, the difference lay only in the fashion of their hats.—*Jonathan Wild.*

Tube, *m.* (familiar and popular), *silk hat,* "stove-pipe." See **Tubard.**

Et . . . le tube sur l'oreille . . . suivi

d'horizontales, de verticales, de déhanchées et d'agenouillées, on le verra s'en aller dans les rues.—*Le Voltaire.*

(Popular) Le —, *the throat,* "gutter-lane, or whistler;" *the nose,* or "smeller." See **Morviau.** Se coller quelquechose dans le —, *to eat,* "to grub." Se piquer le —, *to get drunk,* or "tight." Se flanquer du terreau dans le —, *to take snuff.* Un —, *a musket,* or "dag." Un — à haute pression, *silk hat.*

Tuber (popular), *to smoke.* Tubons en une, *let's* "blow a cloud."

Tubercule, *m.* (familiar), *big nose,* "conk."

Tué, *adj.* (familiar), *astounded, aghast,* "flabbergasted."

Tuer (thieves'), le ver, *to silence the calls of one's conscience,* a not unusual thing for thieves to do. (Popular) Tuer les mouches à quinze pas, *to have an offensive breath ;* — le colimaçon, *to have a morning glass of white wine ;* — le ver, *to have an early glass of spirits,* a "dew-drink."

Ensuite on tue le ver abondamment : vin blanc, mêlé-cassis, anisette de Bordeaux, d'aucunes grognardes, à la peau couleur de tan ne crachent pas sur une couple de perroquets, le demi-setier de casse-poitrine ou la chopine d'eau-de-vie de marc.—P. **Mahalin.**

Tuffre, *m.* (thieves'), *tobacco,* "fogus."

Tuile, *f.* (freemasons'), *plate ;* (familiar) *disagreeable and unforeseen event ;* (roughs') *hat,* or "tile."

Tuileau, *m.* (roughs'), *cap,* "tile."

I'm a gent, I'm a gent,
In the Regent-Street style,—
Examine my costume
And look at my tile.
Popular Song.

Tuiler (popular), *to measure, to judge of one's character or abilities; to survey one with suspicious eye.* Se —, *to reach the stage of intoxi-*

cation when the drunkard looks apoplectic, when he is as "drunk as Davy's sow."

Tulipe orageuse, *f.*, *a step of the cancan*, a pas seul danced in such places as Bullier or L'Elysée Montmartre by a young lady with skirts and the rest tucked up so as to disclose enough of her person to shock the sense of decorum of virtuous lookers-on, whose feelings must be further hurt by the energetic and suggestive gyratory motions of the performer's body. This pas is varied by the " présentez armes ! " when the lady handles her leg as a soldier does his musket on parade. Other choregraphic embellishments are, "le passage du guet, le coup du lapin, la chaloupe en détresse, le pas du hareng saur," &c.

Tune, or thune, *f.* (thieves'), *money*, or " pieces ; " *five-franc piece*.

> J'suis un grinche, un voleur, un escarpe ; je buterais le Père Éternel pour affurer une tune, mais . . . trahir des amis, jamais !—
> VIDOCQ.

La —, or tunebée (old cant), *the old prison of Bicêtre*. In the fifteenth century the king of mendicants was called Roi de Thune, or Tunis, as mentioned by V. Hugo in his description of La Cour des Miracles under Louis XI. (see *Notre Dame de Paris*), in imitation of the title of Roi d'Egypte, which the head of the gipsies bore at that time. It is natural that rogues should have given the appellation to the prison of Bicêtre, where so many of the members of the " canting crew " were given free lodgings, and which was thus considered as a natural place of meeting for the subjects of the King of Thune.

Tuneçon, *f.* (old cant), *prison*, or " stir."

Tuner (old cant), *to beg*, " to maunder." The latter term seems to be derived from mendier, *to beg*.

Tuneur, *m.* (old cant), *beggar*, " maunderer."

Tunnel, *m.* (medical students'), *the anus*.

Tunodi (Breton cant), *to talk cant*, " to patter flash."

Tunodo (Breton cant), *cant expressions ; —* minson, *falsehoods*.

Turbin, *m.* (popular), *annoyance*.

> Bon sang d'bon Dieu ! quel turbin !
> J'viens d'mett'mon pied dan' eun' flaque :
> C'est l'hasard qui m'offre un bain,
> V'lan ! v'la l'vent qui m'fiche eun' claque.
> RICHEPIN.

Turbin, *work*, " graft."

> Après six jours entiers d'turbin
> J'me sentais la gueule un peu sale.
> Vrai, j'avais besoin d'prend'un bain ;
> Seul'ment j'l'ai pris par l'amygdale.
> RICHEPIN.

(Thieves') Le —, *thieving*. (Prostitutes') Le —, *prostitution*. Aller au —, *to walk the streets as a streetwalker*.

Turbiner (popular), *to work*, to do " elbow grease."

> Plus joyeux encore l'ouvrier qui turbine en plein air, suspendu sur un échafaudage, plus près du bleu, éventé par les souffles de l'horizon.—RICHEPIN, *Le Pavé*.

> Turbiner une verte, *to drink a glass of absinthe*. (Thieves') Turbiner, *to thieve*.

Turbineur, *m.* (popular), *labourer*.

Turc, *m.* (thieves'), *a native of Touraine*. See **Tête, Face**.

Turcan, *m.* (thieves'), *the town of Tours*.

Turfiste (sporting), *turfist*.

Turin, *m.* (thieves'), *earthenware pot*.

Turlurette, *f.* (popular), *fast girl.*

Turlutaine, *f.* (popular), *caprice, whim.*

Turlutine, *f.* (military), *campaigning ration consisting of pounded biscuit, rice, and bacon.*

Turne, *f.* (familiar and popular), *ill-furnished, wretched room or lodgings.*

Turquie, *f.* (thieves'), *Touraine.*

Tutoyer (popular), une chose, *to take hold of a thing unceremoniously ; to purloin.*

Tutu, *m.* (familiar), *kind of short muslin drawers worn by ballet girls.* Termed also " cousu."

Son maillot tendu sans un pli, avant d'enfiler cette sorte de jupon-caleçon de mousseline, bouffant aux hanches, fermé au-dessus du genou et qui répond au joli petit nom harmonieux de tutu ou cousu.— A. SIRVEN.

Tuyau, *m.* (popular), *ear,* or " wattle ;" *throat,* or " red lane." Se jeter quelque chose dans le —, *to eat or drink.* Avoir le—bouché, *to have a cold in the head.* (Familiar and popular) Tuyau de poêle, *silk hat,* " stove-pipe."

Ni blouses, ni vestes, ni casquettes : redingotes, paletots, tuyaux de poêle.—A. SIRVEN.

(Military) Tuyau de poêle, *regulation boots.* (Popular) Les tuyaux, *legs,* " pins." Ramoner ses tuyaux, *to run away.* See **Patatrot.** (Sporting) Tuyau, " tip," that is, confidential information about a horse that is likely to win. Given in le tuyau de l'oreille.

Après mon opération, le cheval que j'ai pris devient subitement le tuyau.—*Le Gil Blas.*

Donner un —, *to give such information,* " to give the office."

Type, *m.* (familiar and popular), *individual,* " bloke, cove," or " cuss," as the Americans say.

Nous ne parlerons que pour mémoire du garçon de café qui, dédaignant aujourd'hui le pourboire, ne rend jamais exactement la monnaie, lorsqu'il a flairé un type à ne pas compter.—A. SIRVEN.

Type has also the signification of *odd fellow,* " queer fish." The term " type" was first used by cocottes as synonymous of *dupe,* or " flat," as appears from the following dialogue between two " soupeuses," frequenters of Brébant's restaurant.

— Avec qui as-tu passé ta soirée ?
— M'en parle pas : avec deux types qui m'ont embêtée à cent francs par tête.—P. AUDEBRAND, *Petits Mémoires d'une Stalle d'Orchestre.*

Typesse, *f.* (familiar and popular), *woman.*

Typo, *m.* (popular), *compositor.*

Typote, *f.* (popular), *female compositor.*

**LCÈRE,**
m. (popular), faire dégorger son —, *to make oneself vomit.*

Un (popular), cinq contre —, *expression which refers to practices of onanism.* Termed also "bataille des Jésuites." (Mountebanks') Un peu de courage à la poche, *words to encourage the generosity of the public, which may be rendered by* "tuppence more and up goes the donkey," a vulgar street phrase, says the *Slang Dictionary,* for extracting as much money as possible before performing any task. The phrase had its origin with a travelling showman, the finale of whose performance was the hoisting of a donkey on a pole or ladder. (Familiar) Un de plus *refers to an injured husband.*

Uonik (Breton cant), *the sun.*

Urf, *adj.* (popular), *excellent, first-class.* C'est rien —! *excellent,* "real jam." Le monde —, *fine people.*

Urge, *m.* The word is used by the ladies or "tartlets" of the Boulevards to qualify a man's financial status. The scale ranges from the humble "un urge," denoting a poor or very stingy man, to the superlative "dix urges." A stingy man is also said to wear gloves of the size 6½, whilst a generous one sports the 8½.

Urle, *f.* (thieves'), *the room where prisoners have interviews with visitors.*

Urne, *f.* (popular), *head,* or "tibby." Avoir un député dans l'—, *to be enceinte.*

Urpino, *adj.* (popular), *excellent,* "fizzing." For rupino, rupin.

Ursule, *f.* (familiar), *old maid.*

Usager (popular), *man with genteel manners.*

User (military), son matricule, *to serve in the army.* Le numéro matricule is *the soldier's number.* (Gamesters') User le tapis, *to play low ;* (familiar) — sa salive, *to argue uselessly.* Ne pas avoir usé ses culottes sur les bancs, *to be ignorant.* (Thieves') User la pierre ponce, *to be a convict at a penal servitude settlement.*

Usine, *f.* (popular), *place where one works.*

Usiner (popular), *to work,* "to graft."

Ustensile, *m.* (bullies'), *mistress.*

Ustensilier, *m.* (theatrical), *one who has charge of the minor articles of the plant.*

Ustoches, *m. pl.* (popular), *scissors.* Deformation of eustache, *knife.*

Ut ! (printers'), *your health !* First word of a sentence formerly used by printers when drinking together, "Ut tibi prosit meri potio !" The Germans use the expression, "prosit !"

Utilité, *f.* (theatrical), *useful actor, able to take any part.*

VACHARD, *m.* (popular), *man with no energy; lazy fellow,* "bummer."

Vache, *f.* (popular), *woman of indifferent character; —* à lait, *prostitute.* See Gadoue. Vache ! *an insulting epithet applied to either sex.*

Ce fut, pendant une minute, une clameur assourdissante. . . .
— Cochon !
— Salaud !
— Bougre de vache !—G. Courteline.

Etre —, faire la —, *to be lazy.* Prendre la — et le veau, *to marry a girl who is pregnant.* Le train des vaches, *the tramcar.* A play on the word tramway. (Thieves') La —, *the police,* "reelers." Une —, *police spy, or policeman.*

Elle avait été amenée là par deux horribles petits drôles, . . . Ils étaient en train de dresser la "gonzesse" avant de l'envoyer battre le trimar (le trottoir) lorsque les roussins, les vaches, survinrent.—Albert Cim, *Institution de Demoiselles.*

Mort aux vaches ! *is a motto often found tattooed on malefactors' bodies.*

Vacher, *m.* (thieves'), *police officer,* or "reeler."

Vacherie, *f.* (popular), *laziness; a place where drinks are served by women.*

Va - comme - je - te pousse, *f.* (popular), à la —, *at haphazard.*

Vacquerie, *f.* (thieves'), aller en —, *to sally forth on a thieving expedition.*

Vade, *f.* (thieves'), *crowd,* or "push." Termed also "tigne."

Va-de-la-gueule, *m.* (popular), *gormandizer,* or "grand paunch;" *orator.*

Va-de-la-lance, *m.* (popular), *boon companion, a sort of* "jolly dog."

Vadoux, *m.* (obsolete), *servant.*

Vadrouillard, vadrouilleur, *m.* (popular), *low fellow fond of holding revels with prostitutes.*

Vadrouillarde, vadrouille, vadrouilleuse, *f.* (familiar and popular), *low prostitute,* or "draggle-tail." Vadrouille, *low graceless fellow.*

Fais-toi connaître. Il faut
Que je saches où tu perches.
Je fais mille recherches,
O gibier d'échafaud.
Et je reviens bredouille ! . . .
Ainsi chantait T— or,
Mais l'horrible vadrouille
Ricana : cherche encor.
Raminagrobis.

Vadrouille is properly *a swab.*

Aller en —, or faire une —, *to go and amuse oneself with gay girls.* (Thieves' and roughs') En —, *wandering about,* "on the mooch."

Vadrouiller (popular), *to go with prostitutes, to be a* "mutton monger."

Vague, *m.* (thieves'), aller au —, *to go about seeking for a* "job," *quærens quem devoret.* Coup de —, *theft.* Pousser un coup de —, *to commit a robbery.*

Un certain soir étant dans la débine,
Un coup de vague il leur fallut pousser,
Car sans argent l'on fait bien triste mine.
Song written by CLÉMENT,
a burglar.

(Bullies') Envoyer une femme au —, *to send a woman out for purposes of prostitution.* (Popular) Du —! *an expression of refusal,* which may be rendered by the Americanism, "yes, in a horn." Se lâcher du —, lancer une gousse au —, *to send a woman out to walk the streets.*

Vaguer (prostitutes'), *to wander about.*

Vain, *adj.* (thieves'), *bad.*

Vaisseau du désert, *m.* (popular), euphemism for chameau, *prostitute.*

Vaisselle, *f.* (popular), de poche, *money,* "needful." (Military) Vaisselle, *decorations.* Mettre sa — à l'air, *to put on one's decorations.*

Valade, *f.* (thieves'), *pocket,* or "cly."

J'ai toujours de l'auber dans mes valades, bogue d'orient, cadenne, rondines et frusquins.—VIDOCQ.

From avaler, *to swallow up.* Sonder les valades, *to feel pockets in a crowd.*

Valet de cœur, *m.* (popular), *the lover of a prostitute,* or "Sunday-man." See **Poisson.**

Valoir (popular), ne pas — cher, *to have a disagreeable,* "nasty" *temper.* Valoir son pesant de moutarde, *not worth much ;* (thieves') — le coup de fusil, *to be worth robbing.*

Valser (popular), *to go away ; to run away,* "to hook it." Balzare in furbesche ; — du bec, *to have an offensive breath.*

Valtreuse, *f.* (thieves'), *portmanteau,* or "peter."

Valtreusier, *m.* (thieves'), *rogue who devotes his attentions to portmanteaus,* "dragsman."

Vandale, *f.* (thieves'), *empty pocket.*

Vannage, *m.* (gambling cheats'), faire un —, *to allow a* "pigeon" *to win the first game.* Termed also maquiller un —.

Vanné, *adj.* (familiar and popular), *exhausted,* "gruelled."

C'est vrai que je suis un peu vanné . . . dit Elysée en souriant, et il montait ses cinq étages, le dos rond, écrasé.—A. DAUDET.

Vanner (thieves'), *to run away,* "to speel." Alluding to the motions of the body and arms of a winnower, or from the old French word vanoyer, *to disappear.*

Vannes, *f. pl.* (popular), *falsehood; humbug,* "flam."

Am I dreaming? or what? Pinch me, Jesse ! I am quite awake, am I not? And the thing is no "flam?"—*The Globe,* Dec., 1886.

Des —! *ejaculation of disbelief,* "over, or over the shoulder." C'est des —! *that's all humbug,* "all my eye."

Vanneur, *m.* (thieves'), *one who runs away ; coward.*

Vanterne, or **venterne,** *f.* (thieves'), *window,* or "jump." From the Spanish ventana, or more probably from vent, *wind*, so that venterne literally signifies *which lets in the wind.* Ventosa in Spanish cant. Vanterne (for lanterne), *lantern ;* — sans loches, *dark lantern,* or " darky."

Vanternier, *m.*(thieves'), *robber who effects an entrance through a window,* " dancer, or garreter."

Vapeur, *f.* (popular), une demi —, *a glass of absinthe.*

Vaquerie, *f.* (old cant), bier en —, *to sally forth on a thieving expedition.*

Vase, *m. and f.* (familiar), étrusque, *chamber-pot,* or " jerry." Concerning this utensil Viscount Basterot, in his work *De Québec à Lima,* speaks of a curious custom of the Peruvians. He says : " On a su de tout temps que les Espagnols ne se font pas prier pour annoncer bruyamment qu'ils ont bien dîné ; témoin une certaine histoire du Maréchal Bassompierre. Mais il est une certaine habitude péruvienne dont vraiment je n'avais jamais entendu parler. Il est un peu embarrassant de la décrire, mais pourquoi la tairais-je ? Ne faut-il pas raconter, quels qu'ils soient, les usages et les mœurs ? Quel serait sans cela l'intérêt des voyages ? Le fait est qu'au Pérou, le pot de chambre est arrivé à la hauteur d'une institution nationale. On se mettrait plutôt en route sans malle que sans cet ustensile précieux. Les personnes riches les font faire en argent. Mais, hélas ! la vieille aristocratie est sur son déclin, et la faience domine aujourd'hui. Les dames surtout les étalent avec une complaisance infinie ; il est vrai qu'ils servent aussi quelquefois de meuble de toilette. On voit arriver une brillante senora ; elle tient quelque chose à la main : c'est sans doute un bouquet de fleurs, ou un mouchoir de dentelle ? Non, c'est son vase de nuit ! Encore si elles se dispensaient de s'en servir publiquement ! Mais elles pensent probablement, avec quelques cyniques, que les choses naturelles ne sont pas indécentes." (Popular and thieves') De la —, *rain,* or " parney." Il tombe de la —, or de la flotte, *it rains.*

Vaser (popular and thieves'), *to rain.* Termed also " lansquiner, tomber de la lance."

Vasinette, *f.* (popular), *bath.* Aller à la —, *to bathe.* Termed "to tosh" by the gentlemen cadets of the R. M. Academy.

Vasistas, *m.* (popular), *monocular eye-glass ; the behind.* The synonyms are : " le piffe, le médaillon, l'arrière-train, le trèfle, messire Luc, le moulin à vent, le ponant, la lune, le bienséant, le pétard, le ballon, le moutardier, le baril de moutarde, l'obusier, la tabatière, la tire-lire, la giberne, le proye, cadet, la figure, la canonnière, l'oignon, la machine à moulures, la rose des vents, le département du Bas-Rhin, le démoc, le schelingophone, le Prussien, le panier aux crottes, le visage de campagne or sans nez, le fignard, le pétrouskin, la face du Grand Turc, le tortillon, le fleurant, le pedzouille, le cadran, le foiron, le tal, le garde-manger, le naze, le soufflet, le prouas, la contrebasse, le cyclope, le schaffouse, le gingin."

Vassarès, *f.*, (thieves'), *water.*

Vas-y-t'assir, *m.* (roughs'), *chair.*

Vas-y-vas-y, *m.* (roughs'), *casement of a window.* Play on vasistas.

I I

Va te faire suer! (popular), *go to the deuce!*

Va-te-laver, *m.* (popular), *box on the ear, right and left.*

Et il regardait les gens, tout prêt à leur administrer un va-te-laver s'ils s'étaient permis la moindre rigolade.—ZOLA.

Va-t' faire-panser, *m.* (popular), *box on the ear; blow,* or *"wipe."*

Je lui ai flanqué un va-t' faire-panser sur l'œil.—RANDON.

Vaticanaille, *f.* (familiar), *clericals.*

Va-trop, *m.* (thieves' and roughs'), *servant; — de charretier, carter's man.*

Ah! ah! personn' ne sait c'qu'il fiche
Depuis qu'il roul' par les grands ch'mins.
Oh! oh! p't'êt' qu'il est merlifiche,
Va-trop d'chartier, ou tend-la-main.
           RICHEPIN.

Vaudevillière (literary), *actress of no ability who is engaged only on account of her personal attractions.*

Vautour, *m.* (popular), *hard-hearted landlord; gambling cheat,* or *"hawk."*

Veau, *m.* (popular), *young prostitute; — morné, drunken woman.* (Military) Veau, *knapsack,* or *"scran-bag."*

Vécu, *adj.* (artists' and literary), c'est —, *that is true to nature.*

Vedette, *f.* (theatrical), avoir son nom en —, or être en —, *to have one's name in large type on a play-bill.*

— Laissez-moi, répondait-elle, vous me déchirez.
— Tu seras en vedette.
— Vous êtes insupportable.
— En étoile !
— Assez !—J. SERMET.

Veilleurs de morts, *m. pl.* (brothels'), *young scamps who amuse themselves by causing an uproar in brothels and putting everything topsy-turvy.*

En argot de lupanar, on appelle "veilleurs de morts" les jeunes vauriens qui emploient leur soirée à mettre sens dessus dessous les maisons de tolérance. Ils sont la terreur des maquerelles, et les pertes qu'ils leur font subir sont les revers de la médaille du proxénétisme.—LÉO TAXIL.

Veilleuse, *f.* (thieves'), *stomach,* "middle piece;" — à sec, *empty stomach.* Une —, *a franc.* Demi —, *fifty centimes.* (Familiar) Souffler sa —, *to die,* "to kick the bucket, or to snuff it."

Veinard, *adj. and m.* (familiar and popular), *lucky; lucky fellow.*

J'suis connu d'Charonne à Plaisance
Sous le nom d'Chançard dit l'veinard . . .
V'là Chançard, un veinard
Qu'a d'la chance en abondance.
      A. JAMBON, *V'là Chançard.*

Veine, *f.* (familiar and popular), de cocu, *great luck.* Veine alors ! *what luck!*

Le colonel lui jeta un coup d'œil, rendit le salut et passa. Laigrepin, stupéfait, se dit—Veine alors ! Il est myope comme une chaufferette.—G. COURTELINE.

Vêler (popular), *to be in childbed,* "in the straw."

Vélin, *m.* (printers'), *wife.* Arrangemaner, or secouer son —, *to chastise one's better half.*

Vélo, *m.* (old cant), *postilion.*

Vélocipède, *m.* (popular), casser son —, *to die.* For synonyms see **Pipe.**

Ah! ben! en v'là un crevé, ça veut fumer, ça n'tient pas sur ses pattes, s'il ne dégèle pas cet hiver, s'il ne dévisse pas son billard au printemps, pour sûr à l'automne, il va casser son vélocipède. — BAUMAINE ET BLONDELET.

Velours, *m.* (gamesters'), *gaming-table.* Eclairer le —, *to lay one's stakes on the green cloth.* Jouer sur le —, *to stake one's winnings.* (Familiar) Faire un —, or cuir, *to put in a consonant at the end of a word and carry it on to the next,* *as :* Je suis venu z'à Paris. (Popular) Un —, *crepitus ventris.* Rigaud says : "Le velours se produit dans le monde avec une certaine timidité mélancolique et rappelle les sons filés de la flûte (ceci pour les gens qui aiment la précision). ' C'est un —, *that is excellent* (of drink). (Thieves') Un —, *robbing without violence.* Faire du —, *to play the good fellow ; to seek to wheedle one out of something.*

Velouter (familiar), se —, *to comfort oneself by a drink.*

Velu, *adj.* (students'), synonymous of chic, *excellent, first-rate,* "true marmalade."

Vendanger (old cant), *to ill-treat ; to execute ;* — à l'échelle, *to hang.*

Vendangeuse d'amour, *f.* (familiar), *gay girl.* The expression is Delvau's.

Vendre (thieves'), la calebasse, *to inform against,* "to blow the gaff, or to turn snitch."

Toujours est-il, reprit le recéleur, que c'est lui qui a vendu la calebasse, et que sans lui . . .—VIDOCQ.

(Popular) Vendre des guignes, *to squint,* "to have swivel eyes ;" (familiar and popular)— la mèche, *to reveal a secret.*

Vendu, *m.* (popular and journalists'), *epithet expressive of a vague accusation of extortion, but generally used with no particular meaning.*

Oui, je lui en prêterai, hurla Mes-Bottes. Tiens ! Bibi, jette-lui sa monnaie à travers la gueule, à ce vendu !—ZOLA, *L'Assommoir.*

Vénérable, *m.* (popular), *the behind.*

Vent, *m.* (popular), du —! *is expressive of derisive refusal,* "go to pot." (Hawkers') Vent du nord, *fan.* (Students') Donner du —, *to*

bully. (Sailors') Avoir du — dans les voiles, être — dessus, — dedans, *to be in a state of intoxication,* "to have one's mainbrace well spliced."

Vente. See **Abattage.**

Ventre, *m.* (popular), bénit, *beadle ; verger ; chorister.* An allusion to "pain bénit," supposed to be their staple food. C'est le — de ma mère, *I shall never return there, or I shall have nothing more to do with this.* Un — d'osier, *a drunkard,* or "lushington." (Familiar) Nous allons voir ce qu'il a dans le —, *we will see what stuff he is made of.* Se brosser le —, *to go without food.*

J'aime mon art . . . ma foi, dit un acteur, si je pouvais passer mes jours à me brosser le ventre, le théâtre . . .—E. MONTEIL.

Avoir du chien dans le —, *to have pluck, endurance ; to be made of good stuff.*

Je suis sûr que ce nez l'aidera à faire son chemin. Il joue ce soir. Jugez-le. Vous verrez qu'il a du chien dans le ventre.—P. AUDEBRAND.

Ventrée, *f.* (popular), *copious meal,* "buster." Se foutre une —, *to make a hearty meal,* or "tightener."

Vénus, *f.* (artists'), mouler une —, *to ease oneself by evacuation.*

Ver, *m.* (familiar), rongeur, *cab taken by the hour.* Tuer le —, *to have an early glass of spirits* "to keep the damp out."

Verbe, *m.* (thieves'), sur le —, *on credit.*

Verdet, *m.* (old cant), *wind.*

Verdouse, or **verdouze,** *f.* (thieves'), *apple ; meadow.* In the Italian cant verdume signifies *grass.* See **Arroseur, Cribleur.**

Verdousier, *m.* (thieves'), *apple-tree ; garden ; fruiterer.*

Verdousière, *f.* (thieves'), *frui-terer's wife.*

Verds, *m. pl.* (thieves'), formerly *name given to the Paris police.*

Oh ! c'est que nous avons eu la moresque (la peur) d'une fière force : je sais bien que quand je m'ai senti les verds au dos le treffe (cœur) me faisait trente et un.—*Mémoires de Vidocq.*

Véreux, *m.* (thieves'), *ticket-of-leave man.*

Vergne, *f.* (thieves'), *town.* La grande —, *Paris.* Une — de miséricorde, literally une ville de misère et corde, *a town where thieves have little chance of success.* Michel says vergne is literally *winter quarters,* from the Italian verno, *winter.* More probably, however, it comes from vergne, *alder plantation.* Every small town has a square planted out with trees, used as a promenade, or for the holding of fairs, &c., a meeting-place for pedlars (who have contributed so many expressions to the jargon). Thus aller à la vergne possibly signified *to go to the public square,* and, by an association of ideas, *to go to the town.* It is to be noted, on the other hand, that the Latin verna, vernaculus, respectively mean *slave born in the house of his master, native ;* so that the word vergne would be *a native house, collection of native houses*—hence *town.*

Vermeil, *m.* (thieves'), *blood,* " claret."

Vermicelles, *m. pl.* (popular), *hair,* " thatch."

Le Pierrot birbe, avec ses vermicelles autour du gniasse ! oh ! esbloquant, ça !— RICHEPIN.

(Thieves') Vermicelles, or ver-michels, *blood-vessels.*

Par le meg des fanandels, tu es sans raisiné dans les vermichels (sans sang dans les veines).—BALZAC

Vermillon, *m.* (thieves'), *an English-man,* supposed to invariably sport a red coat.

Verminard, **vermineux**, *m.* (students'), *contemptible man,* " skunk."

Vermine, *f.* (thieves'), *lawyer,* " land-shark."

Vermois, *m.* (thieves'), *blood,* " claret."

Vermoisé, *adj.* (thieves'), *of a red colour.*

Véronique, *f.* (rag-pickers'), *lantern.*

Verre, *m.* (popular), de montre, *the behind.* Casser le — de sa montre, *to fall on one's behind.* (Gambling cheats') Montrer le verre, more correctly le vert (tapis vert), en fleurs, *one of two confederates engaged in a game of cards shows such a good array of trumps that lookers-on are induced to stake.*

Verseuse, *f.* (familiar), *waitress at certain cafés.*

Versigo, *m.* (thieves'), *the town of Versailles.*

Vert, *m.* (popular), se mettre au —, *to play ; to gamble.* Montrer le — en fleur. See **Verre.** (Thieves') Il fait —, *it is cold.*

Verte, *adj.* (familiar), la —, *absinthe.* Garçon, une —, *waiter, a glass of absinthe.* L'heure de la —, *the time of day when absinthe is discussed in the cafés, generally from five o'clock to seven.*

Verticale, *f.* (familiar), *a variety of prostitute best described by the appellation itself.*

Verver (thieves'), *to weep,* " to nap a bib." A deformation of verser.

Verveux, *adj.* (journalists'), *possessing verve or spirit.*

Le plus verveux des journalistes—un Gascon devenu parisien.—*La Vie Populaire,* 1887.

Vervignoler (obsolete), *to have connection.*

Mais vervignolant, me faisait quelquefois de chaudes caresses.—*Parnasse des Muses.*

Vessard, *m.* (popular), *poltroon.*

Vesse, *f.* (popular), avoir la —, *to be afraid.* (Schoolboys') Vesse ! cave ! or " chucks ! "

Vesser du bec (popular), *to have an offensive breath.*

Vessie, *f.* (popular), *low prostitute.* See **Gadoue.**

Veste, *f.* (familiar), remporter une —, *to meet with complete failure.*

Vestiaire, *m.* (familiar), laisser sa langue au —, *to have lost one's tongue.*

Vestige, *m.* (thieves'), coquer le —, *to frighten ; to be afraid.* Des vestiges, or vestos, *haricot beans,* which generate wind in the bowels. From vesse, *wind.*

Vesto de la cuisine, *m.* (thieves'), *detective officer,* "cop." La cuisine, vesto, respectively *detective force, haricot bean.*

Vésuve, *m.* (familiar), faire son —, *to make a fuss ; to show off.*

Vésuver (popular), *to be very liberal with one's money.*

Vésuvienne, *f.* (familiar), *gay girl.* For synonyms see **Gadoue.**

Veuve, *f.* (thieves'), formerly *the gallows,* "scrag;" nowadays *the guillotine.* Crosser chez la —, tirer sa crampe avec la —, or épouser la —, *to be guillotined.* (Familiar) Veuves de colonel, *female adventurers who attend gaming-tables, passing themselves off as widows of military men.* Veuve d'un colonel mort . . . d'un coup de pied dans le cul, *woman who passes herself off as a colonel's widow.*

Veux-tu-cacher-ça, *m.* (familiar and popular), *short coat.*

Maintenant on ne dit plus les paletots d'hommes, on dit des veux-tu-cacher-ça.— BAUMAINE ET BLONDELET.

(Auctioneers') Veuve rentrée, *seller whose property has not been knocked down at an auction-room.* Etre logé chez la — j'en tenons (obsolete), *to be enceinte.*

Véziner (thieves'), *to stink.*

Je voudrais avoir un homme comme toi ! Il me dégoûte. . . . D'abord il vézine (il sent mauvais), puis il est marié ! Rien ne me dit qu'il ne me serrera pas un jour la vis pour sa largue.—*Mémoires de Monsieur Claude.*

Vezou, *f.* (popular), *prostitute.* See **Gadoue.**

Quant aux filles publiques, les hommes les désignent par un grand nombre d'appellations . . . les autres termes employés, avec le plus de grossièreté sont les suivants : toupie, bagasse, calèche, grenouille, tortue, volaille, rouscailleuse, couillère, vessie, vezou.—LÉO TAXIL.

Vezouiller (popular), *to stink.*

Viande, *f.* (popular), coller sa — dans le torchon, *to go to bed,* " to get into kip." Montrer sa —, *to wear a low dress.* Ramasse ta —, *pick yourself up.* Viande de Morgue, *insulting epithet applied to a person who imprudently imperils his limbs or life.* Morgue, *dead-house.* Basse —, or viande de seconde catégorie, *woman with flabby charms.*

Viauper (popular), *to lead a dissolute life,* or " to go molrowing ; " *to weep,* or " to nap a bib."

Vice, *m.* (popular), avoir du —, *to be cunning,* " to be fly."

La femme qui a un peu de vice, s'émancipe tôt ou tard de la tutelle d'une maîtresse

de maison et travaille pour son compte.—
E. DE GONCOURT.

Victoire, *f.* (rag-pickers'), *shirt,*
"flesh-bag."

Vidange, *f.* (thieves' and roughs'),
largue en —, *woman in childbed,*
"in the straw."

Vidée, *f.* (rag-pickers'), *basketful
of a rag-picker's findings.*

Vider (popular), le plancher, *to go
away,* "to slope;" — ses poches,
to play the piano. (Familiar) Etre
vidé, *to be spent in point of intellectual productions.* (Prostitutes')
Vider un homme, *to leave a man
penniless.*

Vie, *f.* (familiar), faire une — de
Polichinelle, *to make a great
noise; to lead a dissolute life.*

Viédaser (obsolete), *to work carelessly.*

Vieille, *adj.* (familiar), un verre de
—, *a glass of old brandy.* La —
garde, *the set of superannuated
cocottes,* of "played-out tarts."

Tout ce qu'on appelait déjà, il y a quinze
ans, la vieille-garde, a passé par le Moulin-
Rouge. C'étaient Esther Guimond, dont
un ministre de la guerre disait : "Elle est
de ma promotion."—MAHALIN.

(Familiar and popular) Ma —
branche, *old fellow, my hearty,*
"old chump, my ribstone, or my
bloater."

D'là-haut j'applaudis chaque acteur
Surtout si la pièce est bien franche.
J'cri' : chaud ! chaud ! vas-y, ma vieill'
branche.
BURANI ET BUGUET.

Vieille barbe, *old-fashioned politician who will not keep up with
the times.*

Invitez là tous ces fossiles
Remis à neuf et rempaillés.
Les vieilles barbes indociles,
Fourbus, cassés, crevés, rouillés.
Le Triboulet, 1880.

The term is applied specially to
the Republican politicians of 1848.

Vieux, *adj.* (familiar and popular),
se faire —, *to feel dull; to be
waiting for a long while.* Se faire
de — os, *to wait for a long while.*
Un — cabas, *a stingy old woman.*
(Popular) Vieux meuble, *old man;*
— comme Mathieu-salé, *very
old.* (Literary) Vieux jeu, *old-
fashioned;* (familiar) — tison, *old
"gallivant."* Un — de la vieille,
old veteran. (Military) C'est — !
I am not to be taken in, "tell that
to the marines."

Vieux plumeau, *m.* (popular), *old
fool,* "doddering old sheep's
head."

Ell' dit : Il ne sent pas bon !
— Pas bon ?. . . Espèc' de vieille cruche !
Dit la marchand'—Vieux plumeau !
T'en mang'rais plus que d'merluche !. . .
Va donc, eh ! fourneau !
A. QUEYRIAUX.

Vif-argent, *m.* (thieves'), *cash.*

Vignette, *f.* (printers'), *face.*

Vigousse, *f.* (popular), *energy,
strength.* For vigueur.

Villois, *m.* (thieves'), *village.* An
old French word from the Low
Latin villaticum.

Si j'venais d'faire un gerbement et que
j'en aye de la surbine on m'enverrait dans
un trou d'vergne ou dans un villois de la
Jargole.—VIDOCQ.

Vinaigre, *m.* (thieves'), *rum.*
(Familiar) Du vinaigre ! *faster!*
Expression used by children who
are rope-skipping.

Vinasse, *f.* (popular), *wine.*

Vingt-cinq (popular), à — francs
par tête, *superlatively.* Rigoler à
— francs par tête, *to amuse oneself enormously.*

Vingt-deux, *m.* (thieves'), *knife,*
or "chive."

Prends le vingt-deux en cas de malheur.
—VIDOCQ.

(Printers'). Le —, *the master or chief overseer.* Vingt-deux ! *is used to notify that the master is approaching.* A signal of the same description used by English schoolboys or workmen is "nix!"

Vingt-huit-jours, *m.* (popular), *soldier of the reserve.* Thus termed on account of his yearly twenty-eight days' service.

Viocque, *adj. and f.* (thieves') *old; life.* From the old word viouche, pronounced viouque.

Violon, *m.* (popular), boîte à —, *lock-up at a police station.*

> J'suis connu d'tous les sergents d'ville,
> J'connais tout's les boît's à violon,
> C'est chez eux qu' j'élis domicile,
> J'pourrais pas vivr' dans les salons !
> E. DU BOIS, *C'est Pitanchard.*

The word violon itself signifies *lock-up,* on account of the window-bars of a cell being compared to the strings of that instrument. The lingo terms, "jouer de la harpe," *to be in prison,* and "jouer du violon," *to file through the window-bars of a cell,* seem to bear out this explanation. Some philologists, however, think that the stocks being termed psaltérion, "mettre au psaltérion," *to put in the stocks,* became synonymous of *to imprison,* the expression being superseded in time by "mettre au violon" when that instrument itself superseded the psaltérion.

Violoné, *adj.* (thieves'), *poor.* A man who comes out of prison is generally "hard-up."

Virolets, *m.* (obsolete), explained by quotation :—

Pour les testicules, les génitoires, les marques de virilité d'un homme. — LE ROUX.

Vis, *f.* (familiar and popular), tortiller, or serrer la —, *to strangle.* See **Refroidir.**

Visage, *m.* (popular), à culotte, — cousu, *thin, spare man,* "a scarecrow ;" — de bois flotté, *haggard face ;* — de constipé, *sour countenance ;* — de campagne, or sans nez, *the behind ;* — à culotte, *ugly face.*

Viscope, *f.* (thieves' and roughs'), *cap,* "tile."

Vise - au - trèfle, *m.* (popular), *apothecary,* "squirt."

Visqueux, *m.* (popular), *most degraded variety of prostitutes' bullies.* See **Poisson.**

Visser (thieves'), *to abash by a stern glance.*

Visuel, *m.* (popular), s'en injecter, or s'en humecter le —, *to look attentively.*

Vitam (Breton cant), *brandy.*

Vitelotte, *f.* (popular), *red nose, one with* "grog blossoms."

Vitres, *f. pl.* (popular), *eyes,* or "glaziers."

Vitriers, *m. pl.* (military), *chasseurs à pied, or rifles.* Thus nicknamed, either from their high knapsack compared to an itinerant glazier's plant, or from the expression, casser les vitres, *to be reckless.* The appellation forms the theme of the following verse set to one of their bugle marches:—

> Encore un carreau d'cassé,
> V'là l'vitrier qui passe,
> Encore un carreau d'cassé,
> V'là l'vitrier passé.

(Popular) Les vitriers, *diamonds of cards.*

Tierce major dans les vitriers, vingt-trois ; trois bœufs, vingt-six ; trois larbins, vingt-neuf ; trois borgnes, quatre-vingt-douze.—ZOLA.

Vitrine, *f.* (popular), *opera glass ; spectacles,* or "barnacles." (Familiar) Etre dans la —, *to be well-dressed.*

Vitriol, *m.* (popular), *brandy.*

Vitrioler (general), *to throw oil of vitriol at one's face.*

Je la vitriolerais ! . . . je la tuerais plutôt, la vieille gredine, à coups de revolver.—D. DE LAFOREST.

Vitrioleuse, *f.* (general), *woman who out of revenge throws vitriol at her lover or rival.*

Les vitrioleuses font décidément fortune : les graves jurés les acquittent avec une complaisance singulière . . . place aux récidivistes du vitriol.—*Un Flâneur.*

Vitriolisateur, *m.* (journalists'), *imaginary instrument recommended for the use of those of the fair sex who throw oil of vitriol at their lovers.*

Cet instrument n'est autre que le vitriolisateur, qui, sur la table de toilette de ces dames, prendra place à côté du vaporisateur.—*Un Flâneur.*

Vlan, *adj. and m.* (familiar), *pink of fashion ; the world of dandies, or " swelldom."*

Voici, d'abord, les Trossuli, comme ils s'appelaient autrefois : le "pschutt," le "vlan," les "luisants," comme nous les nommons aujourd'hui. Oh ! ce n'est plus à des "Troyens" qu'ils ont l'ambition de ressembler.—P. DE MAHALIN.

Vlan, or **v'lan**, *elegant ; of the fashionable world.*

La pauvre Mathilde C. est dans la désolation. Elle croyait avoir mis la main sur un homme v'lan et voilà qu'elle découvre que c'est rien du tout.—*Gil Blas.*

Voie, *f.* (popular), foutre une — de bois à quelqu'un, *to thrash, to cudgel one.* Refiler une —, *to thrash.* The synonyms to describe the act in the various kinds of slang are : "donner une tournée, graisser les bottes, reconduire, faire la conduite, donner du tabac, passer chez paings, rouler, retourner, donner une roulée, une frottée, une froteska, de la salade ; faire valser,

déshabiller, faire danser sans violons, faire chanter un Te Deum raboteux, chiquer, refiler une purge, une séance, une ratisse, une pousse, estuquer, bûcher, démolir, mettre en compote, flauper, manger le nez, aplatir, astiquer, suifer, murer, donner une dandinette, caresser or tricoter les côtes, pointer, schlaguer, savonner, faire danser la malaisée, amocher, faire chanter une gamme, sabouler, saborder, donner une raclée, une danse, une torchée, une brûlée ; flanquer une tripotée, une cuite, une dégelée, une peignée, une brossée, une tatouille, une ratatouille, une trempe, une trempée, une rincée, une pile, une trépignée, une grattée, de l'huile de cotterets ; tremper une soupe, descendre le crayon sur la colonne, raboter l'andosse, balayer, dandiner, coller des châtaignes, accommoder au beurre noir, passer quelqu'un à travers, foutre du tabac, faire trinquer, tomber sur le casaquin, tamponner, tanner le cuir, travailler le cadavre, le casaquin ; ramasser les pattes, atiger, tomber sur le poil, trépigner, pommader, cogner, faire étrenner, secouer les tripes, les puces ; ratisser la couenne, panser de la main, donner une pâtée, repasser le bufle, emplâtrer, encaisser, flanquer une ratapiaule ;" and in the English slang : " to give a hiding, a walloping, to dust one's jacket, to set about, to tan, to walk into, to slip into, to quilt, to pay, to manhandle, to give one Jessie, to give one gas, to dowse," &c.

Voile, *m.* (freemasons'), *table-cloth.* Termed also " grand drapeau."

Voir (familiar), *to have one's menses ;* (popular) — en dedans, *to sleep, "*to doss." Also *to be* *drunk.* See **Pompette.** Voir la lune, *to lose one's maidenhead.* A girl whose "rose has thus been plucked" is said to have "vu le loup," or, in the English slang, "to have seen the elephant;" — à travers la verte, *to labour under a delusion caused by over-indulgence in absinthe drinking.* (Military) Ne pas — quelqu'un blanc, *to entertain fears concerning one's prospects or one's affairs.* (Thieves') Voir, *to apprehend,* "to smug."

Voirie, *f.* (popular), *disreputable woman; vagabond.*

Voite, *f.* (popular and thieves'), *vehicle,* "drag." Regarde donc ce pante qui s'fait trimballer dans une voite, *look at that* "cove" *who sports a carriage.*

Voiture à talons, *f.* (popular), *the legs,* or "Shanks's mare."

Vol, *m.* See **Américain, Bonjour, Grinchissage, Rendème.** (Thieves') Vol à l'endormage, *robbery by hocussing the victim.* The thief is called "drummer" in the English lingo.

Une certaine quantité de pavots et de pommes épineuses (datura stramonium) mise dans un litre d'eau . . . produit un narcotique très violent . . . l'endormeur en emporte toujours sur lui dans une petite fiole.—CANLER.

Vol à la bousculade, *robbery by hustling the victim;* — au poupon, *robbery from a shop by a woman with a baby in her arms;* — au radin. See **Grinchissage.** Vol sous-comptoir, *robbing a tradesman of articles taken away for another person to choose from.*

Volailler (familiar), *to make friends with the first comer;* (popular) *to keep company with disreputable women.*

Volaillon, *m.* (popular), *clumsy thief.*

Volant, *m.* (old cant), *cloak,* or "ryder."

Volante, *f.* (thieves'), *feather; pen.*

Volapuk, *m.* (familiar), *bustle,* or "back-staircase." Properly "volapuk," says the *Echo,* "is the artificial language, or gibberish, which an industrious German savant has been inventing by eclectic process from all languages of the world. It is intended by its ingenious author to undo the mischief caused by the confusion of tongues at Babel. But, judging by the published specimens of it, it is horribly cacophonous." A Volapuk grammar has already been published in Paris.

Vol-au-vent, *m.* (popular), *head.* See **Tronche, Avoir.** (Thieves') Vol-au-vent, *kind of robbery from the person described as follows :—*

L'opérateur choisit son sujet parmi les passants qui n'ont pas leur chapeau bien assujéti sur la tête. Il s'élance alors vers lui, le heurte, reçoit son couvre-chef entre les mains et le lui rend avec un gracieux sourire. Pendant que le monsieur se confond en remerciements, l'escroc lui fait son porte-monnaie avec une adresse exquise.—E. FRÉBAULT.

Voleur, *m.* (printers'), *scrap of paper which gets stuck to the composition in the press;* (military) — d'étiquettes, *quartermaster.* He is supposed to steal the card (which is placed over every soldier's bed, and bears his name, number, and other particulars) so as to be able to charge for a new one.

Tour à tour, c'était . . . le "voleur d'étiquettes" qui n'y couperait pas à cause que depuis un quart d'heure le trompette le sonnait au trot.—G. COURTELINE.

Volige, *f.* (popular), *thin person.*

Voltigeante, *f.* (popular), *mud.*

Voltigeur, *m.* (popular), *hodman.*

Vousaille, vouzaille, vouzigo, vozières, vozigue (thieves'), *you.*

Vous-n'avez-rien, *m.* (popular), *official of the octroi.*

Vousoyer (familiar), *to say "vous" to a person whom one is in the habit of addressing as "tu."*

Voyage, *m.* (mountebanks'), *tour through the whole of France.* (Popular) Faire un — au long cours, *to be transported.*

Voyager (ballet-dancers'), *to whirl rapidly up and down the stage.*

Voyageur, *m.* (hotel-keepers'), sec, *traveller who spends little in the hotel at which he puts up.* (Popular) Voyageurs à quinze francs le cent, *passengers on top of bus.*

Voyante, *f.* (thieves'), *the guillotine.* Termed also : "butte or bute, le monde renversé, Marianne, la veuve, la passe, la mère au bleu, la bute à regret, l'abbaye de Monte-à-regret, l'abbaye de Monte-à-rebours, la bascule, la béquillarde, les deux mâts."

C'est le docteur Louis, secrétaire du Collège des chirurgiens, qui fit, en 1792, le rapport pour l'adoption de la première guillotine. Elle fut établie par un nommé Tobias Schmitz, fabricant de pianos . . . c'était à tort que le nom du docteur Guillotin avait été donné à l'instrument de supplice.—G. Frison.

Voyeur, *m.* (brothels'), better explained by quotation :—

Je ne puis pourtant omettre une catégorie de sadistes assez étonnants ; ce sont ceux qu'on désigne sous le nom de "voyeurs." Ceux-ci cherchent une excitation dans les spectacles impudiques.—Léo Taxil.

Voyoucratados, *m.* (familiar), *one-sou cigar.* From voyou, *cad.*

Qu'y voulez-vous faire ? Il y aura toujours plus de fumeurs de voyoucratados à un sou que d'aristocratès à un franc.—Scapin, *Le Voltaire.*

Voyoucrate, *m.* (familiar), *a politician whose sympathies, real or pretended, are with the mob.*

Voyoucratie, *f.* (familiar), *mob government, mobocracy.*

Voyoutados, *m.* (familiar), *one-sou cigar.*

Voyoutisme, *m.* (familiar), *caddishness.*

Vrignole, *f.* (thieves'), *meat,* or "carnish."

Vrille, *f.* (bullies'), *Lesbian woman, that is, one with unnatural passions.*

**AGON,** or wagon à bestiaux, *m.*(popular), *dirty prostitute,* "draggle-tail." Wagon, *large glass of wine.*

Wallace, *m.* (popular), *water.*

Et comme il faut boire en mangeant,
Comme ils adorent boire à la fraîche, à la
    glace,
Comme ils ne veulent pas dépenser leur
    argent,
Ils s'ingurgitent du Wallace.
                  RICHEPIN.

Wallacer (popular), *to drink water at a fountain.* Everyone knows that Sir Richard Wallace has endowed Paris with numerous drinking fountains.

Water (Breton cant), *water.*

Wateri (Breton cant), *to rain ; to void urine.*

Waterloo, *m.* (roughs'), *the behind.*

Watriniser (popular), *to lynch.* An allusion to the murder of the engineer, M. Watrin, by the Decazeville miners in 1886.

Watteau, *m.* (familiar), en —, *elegantly dressed in gay colours, like china figures.* An allusion to the style of the figures in Watteau's paintings.

Christian en veston, la reine dans son amazone de voyage, Herbert et sa femme en Watteau des boulevards.—A. DAUDET.

Wiou (Breton cant), *no.*

 , *m.* (students'), un —, *a student at the Ecole Polytechnique.* Aller à l'X, *to go to that school.* (Familiar) L'—, *mathematics.* Termed the "swat" by gentlemen cadets of the Royal Military Academy. Un —, *a thorough mathematician, one who devotes himself entirely to the study of mathematics.* There is a story about a mathematician (some say he was no other than Arago) who used to work out problems wherever he found himself at the time they occurred to him. One day he was drawing figures with a piece of chalk on the back of a hackney coach when it began to move, but so wrapped up was he in his favourite occupation that he followed his extemporized blackboard at a walk at first, then at a run, but never stopped till he had found a solution of the problem. Un fort en —, *one well up in mathematics, but who knows little of other subjects.* Une tête à —, *one who has a good head for mathematics.* A pun on the formula $\theta\chi$, pronounced théta X.

 (military), a
du bon,
good news.

Eh ben, mon
vieux, y a du
bon ! les bleus
ne vont pas y
couper ! — G.
Courteline.

(Popular) Y
a pas mèche, *it is impossible.*

Mais y paraît qu'l'il' des Pins, y a pas
mèche.
Y a déjà quelqu'un c'est épatant.
L'gouvernement maronn' ! Moi j'suis con-
tent.
J'suis en bateau et j'ai lâché la dèche.
Gringoire, *Le Contentement du
Récidiviste, à l'ancre !*

Yeux, *m. pl.* (familiar), culottés,
*eyes surrounded with a dark
circle ;* — en trou de vrille, *small
eyes with stupid expression.*

Youte, or **youtre,** *m.* (popular),
Jew. From the German. Termed
also "frisé, pied plat, guinal,"
and, in the English slang, "ikey,
sheney, mouchey." Jardin des
youtres, *Jewish cemetery.*

Youtrerie, *f.* (popular), *gathering
of Jews ; avarice.*

You-you, *m.* (convicts'), *warder
at the penal servitude settlement.*

ÉPH, *m.* (popular), *wind.* Se pousser du —, *to run away.* See **Patatrot.**

Zéphir, *m.* (military), *soldier of the "bataillon d'Afrique,"* a corps serving in Africa only, composed of soldiers who have been in prison for a common law offence, and who have not completed their term of service. A pun on the words voler comme le zéphir.

> Dans la plaine tourbillonne
> La nuée aux burnous blancs ;
> A la tête de la colonne
> Allons rejoindre nos rangs.
> Déjà le soleil levant
> Nous jette un regard oblique !
> Pan ! du bataillon d'Afrique,
> Pan ! les zéphirs en avant.
> H. FRANCE, *Chanson du Bataillon d'Afrique.*

Zer (Breton cant), *apples.*

Zerasined-douar (Breton cant), *potatoes.*

Zif, *m.* See **Solliceur.**

Zig, zigue, zigorneau, or **zigard,** *m.* (popular), *a jolly fellow,* a "regular brick ;" *a friend.*

Polyte Chupin lui eût tendu la main comme à un ami . . . à un "zig."—GABORIAU.

Mince ! s'écria l'autre, j'me fais rien de belles journées depuis quelque temps. Vous êtes vraiment des zigues, les artisses !—J. RICHEPIN, *Braves Gens.*

Mon vieux —, *old "cock," old fellow,* "my bloater, my ribstone." Mes bons zigues, *my good fellows, old fellows.*

Mes bons zigues, dit le lutteur, inutile de crier ainsi comme la truie de David.—HECTOR FRANCE.

Bon—d'attaque, *a staunch friend.* Un — à la rebiffe, *old offender.* Quel — ! *a splendid chap ! a rare un' !*

Quel sacré zig, tout de même, ce Mes-Bottes. Est-ce qu'un jour il n'avait pas mangé douze œufs durs et bu douze verres de vin pendant que les douze coups de midi sonnaient.—ZOLA.

Un bon zig is synonymous of un bon bougre (whose origin is Bulgare), and concerning the expression M. Génin says : "Un fait d'argot des plus curieux, c'est le synonyme que donne aujourd'hui le peuple à un mot (bougre) qui commence apparemment à lui sembler trop grossier : 'c'est un bon zigue !' 'tu es un bon zigue !' Or il se trouve que les Zigues figurent à côté des Bulgares dans une chronique grecque, en vers politiques, des premières années du XIV⁰ siècle.—'Théodore Lascaris, dit l'auteur, approvisionna ses forteresses et prit à son service, moyennant salaire, des Turcs, des Cumans, des Lains, des Zigues et des Bulgares' (Buchon, *Chronique de Roumanie*). Comment peut-être venue, à des hommes du peuple, l'idée de cette maligne substitution des Zigues aux Bulgares? C'est un trait d'érudition très raffinée! Je ne vois d'autre explication sinon que ce mot et ce rapprochement s'étaient conservés au fond de la tradition populaire depuis la conquête de Constantinople et l'établissement des Français en Morée. Mais cette explication même donne beaucoup à réfléchir, et montre combien le langage du peuple mérite l'attention des philosophes."

Zinc, *m.* (popular), *money ; venereal ailment,* "Venus' curse ;" *elegance, dash ; wine-shop bar.* Tomber un —, *to have a glass of liquor at the bar.* (Theatrical) Avoir du —, or être zingué, *to possess a clear, sonorous voice ; to play in dashing style.*

Je joue le rôle d'un pigeon du Jockey-Club qui se croit aimé pour lui-même. . . . Il faut que j'y aie du zinc ce soir. Sans ça, les vieux de l'orchestre regretteraient trop Déjazet ; et ils appelleraient Azor.— P. AUDEBRAND.

Zingo, *m.* (wine retailers'), *a good fellow,* "a brick."

Zinguer (popular), *to drink at a bar.* Etre zingué, *to be well off,* "well ballasted."

Zingueur, *m.* (cocottes'), le —, *he who furnishes the funds, who keeps a woman.*

Je t'engage donc à raconter tout ce que tu me racontes là au zingueur ! Il te croira parcequ'il t'aime ! Et lui du moins est assez riche pour se permettre le luxe de la paternité.—*Mémoires de Monsieur Claude.*

Zinguot, *m., shed in the courtyard at the Ecole de Saint-Cyr.*

Zousill (Breton cant), *drink ; drunken man.*

Zousilla (Breton cant), *to get drunk.*

Zousilladen (Breton cant), *drink.*

Zousiller (Breton cant), *drunkard.*

Zousill hirr (Breton cant), *cider.*

Zousill-tan (Breton cant), *brandy.*

Zouzou, *m.* (familiar), *a Zouave.*

Zozotte, *f., appellation given by bullies to the money given them by prostitutes.*

Zut ! (familiar and popular), *exclamation expressive of refusal, careless defiance, &c.* Je te dis zut ! *you be hanged ! go to the deuce !* Ah ! zut alors ! *confound it, then ! I give it up,* "it's no go." Je dis zut au service, *I say good-bye to the service.*

Zut pour les aristos ! Coupeau envoyait le monde à la balançoire.—ZOLA.